Philippa Gregory is an established writer and broad-caster for radio and television. She holds a PhD in eighteenth-century literature from the University of Edinburgh. She has been widely praised for her historical novels, including *Virgin Earth* and *A Respectable Trade* (which she adapted for BBC Television), as well as her works of contemporary suspense. *The Other Boleyn Girl* won the Parker Romantic Novel of the Year Award in 2002. Philippa Gregory lives in the North of England with her family.

D1353643

PHILIPPA GREGORY

EARTHLY JOYS

VIRGIN EARTH

Grafton

Garden plan of Hatfield House reproduced by courtesy of
The Public Record Office; map of Virginia c. 1812: The Royal Geographical
Society; engraving by Theodor de Bry of a 'Virginia' Indian village
from Thomas Harriot's *A brief and true report*; view of a fish weir,
after Elliott, *Fox Hill: Its People and Places*, 1976.

HarperCollins*Publishers*
77-85 Fulham Palace Road
Hammersmith, London W6 8JB

This omnibus edition published in 2004
by HarperCollins*Publishers*

ISBN 0 00 771200 6

Set in Postscript Linotype Minion
with Medici Script display

Printed and bound in Great Britain by
Mackays of Chatham plc, Chatham, Kent

EARTHLY
JOYS

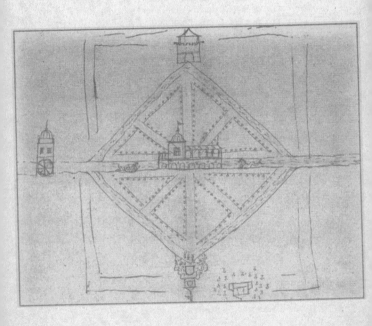

April 1603

The daffodils would be fit for a king. The delicate wild daffodils, their thousand heads bobbing and swaying with the wind, light-petalled, light-stemmed, moving like a field of unripe barley before a summer breeze, scattered across the grass, thicker around the trunks of trees as if they were dewponds of gold. They looked like wild flowers; but they were not. Tradescant had planned them, planted them, nourished them. He looked at them and smiled – as if he were greeting friends.

Sir Robert Cecil strolled up, his uneven tread instantly recognisable in the crunch of the gravel. John turned and pulled off his hat.

'They look well,' his lordship observed. 'Yellow as Spanish gold.'

John bowed. The two men were near each other in age – both in their thirties – but the courtier was bent under a humped back and his face was lined by a lifetime of caution at court, and with pain from his twisted body. He was a small man, little more than five feet tall – his enemies called him a dwarf behind his hunched back. In a beauty-conscious, fashion-mad court where appearance was everything and a man was judged by his looks and his performance on the hunting field or battlefield, Robert Cecil had started his life with an impossible disadvantage: crooked, tiny, and struggling with pain. Beside him the gardener Tradescant, brown-faced and strong-backed, looked ten years younger. He waited in silence for his master to speak. It was not his place to prolong the conversation.

'Any early vegetables?' his lordship asked. 'Asparagus? They say His Majesty loves asparagus.'

1

'It's too early, my lord. Even a king new-come to his kingdom cannot hunt deer and eat fruit in the same month. They each have their season. I cannot force peaches for him in spring.'

Sir Robert smiled. 'You disappoint me, Tradescant, I had thought you could make strawberries grow in mid-winter.'

'With a hothouse, my lord, and a couple of fires, some lanterns, and a lad to water and carry, perhaps I could give you Twelfth Night strawberries.' He thought for a moment. 'It's the light,' he said to himself. 'I think you would need sunlight to make them ripen. I don't know that candlelight or even lanterns would be enough.'

Cecil watched him with amusement. Tradescant never failed in the respect he owed his master, but he readily forgot everything but his plants. As now, he could fall silent thinking of a gardening problem, wholly neglecting his lord who stood before him.

A man more conscious of his dignity would have dismissed a servant for less. But Robert Cecil treasured it. Alone of every man in his train, Sir Robert trusted his gardener to tell him the truth. Everyone else told him what they thought he wanted to hear. It was one of the disadvantages of high office and excessive wealth. The only information which was worth having was that given without fear or favour; but all the information a spy-master could buy was worthless. Only John Tradescant, half his mind always on his garden, was too busy to lie.

'I doubt it would be worth your effort,' Sir Robert remarked. 'There are seasons for most endeavours.'

John suddenly grinned at him, hearing the parallel between his own work and his master's. 'And your season has come,' he said shrewdly. 'Your fruiting.'

They turned together and walked back to the great house, Tradescant a step behind the greatest man in the kingdom, respectfully attentive, but looking from side to side at every pace. There were things that wanted doing in the garden – but then there were always things that wanted doing in the garden. The avenue of pleached limes needed retying before their early summer growth thrust wands of twigs out of control, the kitchen garden needed digging over; and radishes, leeks, and onions should be sown into the warming spring soil. The great watercourses which were the wonder of Theobalds Palace needed weeding and cleaning; but he strolled as if he had all the time in the world, one step behind his master, waiting in silence, in case his master wanted to talk.

'I did right,' Sir Robert said half to himself, half to his gardener. 'The old queen was dying and she had no heir with as strong a claim as he. Not one fit to rule, that is. She would not hear his name, you had to whisper King James of Scotland if she were anywhere in any of her palaces. But all the reports I had of him were of a man who could hold two kingdoms, and perhaps even weld them together. And he had sons and a daughter – there'd be no more fretting over heirs. And he's a good Christian, no taint of Papistry. They breed strong Protestants in Scotland . . .'

He paused for a moment and gazed at his great palace set on the high terrace looking towards the River Thames. 'I don't complain,' he said fairly. 'I've been well repaid for my work. And there's more to come.' He smiled at his gardener. 'I'm to be Baron Cecil of Essenden.'

Tradescant beamed. 'I'm glad for you.'

Sir Robert nodded. 'A rich reward for a hard task . . .' He hesitated. 'Sometimes I felt disloyal. I wrote him letter after letter, teaching him the way of our country, preparing him to rule. And she never knew. She'd have had me beheaded if she had known! She'd have called it treason – towards the end she called it treason even to mention his name. But he had to be prepared . . .'

Sir Robert broke off, and John Tradescant watched him with silent sympathy. His master often strolled into the garden to find him. Sometimes they spoke of the grounds, the formal garden, the orchards, the park, of seasonal plantings, or new plans; sometimes Sir Robert spoke at length, indiscreetly, knowing that Tradescant could keep a secret, that he was a man without guile, with solid loyalty. Sir Robert had made Tradescant his own, as effectually as if the gardener had gone down on the loam and sworn an oath of fealty, on the day that he had trusted him with the garden of Theobalds Palace. It had been a massive task for a twenty-four-year-old but Sir Robert had taken the gamble that Tradescant could do it. He was a young man himself, desperate to inherit his father's position at court, desperate for older and more powerful men to recognise his merit and his skill. He took a risk with Tradescant and then the queen took a risk with him. Now, six years later, both of them had learned their craft – statesmanship and gardening – and Tradescant was Sir Robert's man through and through.

'She wanted him left ignorant,' Sir Robert said. 'She knew what would happen to her court if she named him as heir; they'd have all slipped away from her, slipped away up the Great North Road to Edinburgh, and she'd have died alone, knowing herself to be an old woman, an ugly old woman with no kin, no lovers, no friends. I owed it to her to keep them at her beck and call to the very end. But I owed it to him to teach him as best I could ... even at a distance. It was to be his kingdom, he had to learn how to govern it, and there was no-one but me to teach him.'

'And he knows now?' John asked, going to the very heart of it.

Sir Robert was alert. 'Why d'you ask? Is there gossip that he does not?'

John shook his head. 'I've heard none,' he said. 'But he's not a lad who has sprung up from nowhere. He must have his own way of doing things. He's a man grown; and he has his own kingdom. I was wondering if he would take your teaching, especially now that he will have his pick of advice. And it matters ...'

He broke off and his master waited for him to finish.

'When you have a lord or a king,' John went on, choosing his words with caution, 'you have to be sure that he knows what he's doing. Because he's going to be the one who decides what you do.' He stopped, bent and whisked out the little yellow head of a groundsel plant. 'Once you're his man, you're stuck with him,' he said frankly. 'He has to be a man of judgement, because if he gets it wrong then he is ruined; and you with him.'

Cecil waited in case there was more but John looked shyly down into his face. 'I beg your pardon,' he said. 'I did not mean to suggest that the king did not know what he has to do. I was thinking of us subjects.'

Sir Robert waved away the apology with one gesture of his long-fingered hand. They strolled together up the great avenue through the large formal knot garden towards the front terrace of the palace. It was done in the old style, and John had changed nothing here since his arrival as gardener. It had been laid out by Sir Robert's father in the bleak elegance of the period. Sharply defined geometric patterns of box hedging enclosed different coloured gravels and stones. The beauty of the garden was best seen if you looked down on it, from the house. Then you could see that it was as complex and lovely as a series of neat diagrams of cropped hedging and stone. John had a private ambition to change the garden after the new fashion – to break up the regular square and rectangular beds and make all the separate beds one long whole, like an embroidered hem or scarf – a twisting pattern that went on and on, serpentined in and about itself. When his master was less absorbed with statecraft John was going to suggest melding the beds one into another.

Once he had persuaded Sir Robert to follow the new fashion for the knot garden he had an ambition to go yet further. He longed to take out the gravel from the enclosed shapes and plant the patterns with herbs, flowers and shrubs. He wanted to see the whole disciplined shape softened and changing every day with foliage and flowers which would bloom and wilt, grow freshly green, and then pale. He had a belief, as yet unexpressed, almost unformed, that there was something dead and hard about a garden of stone paths edged with box enclosing beds of gravel. Tradescant had a picture in his mind's eye of plants spilling over the hedges, of the thick green of the box containing wildness, fertility, even colour. It was an image that drew on the hedgerow and roadside of the wild country of England and brought that richness into the garden and imposed order upon it.

'I miss her,' Sir Robert admitted.

John was recalled to his real duty – to be his master's man heart and soul, to love what he loved, to think what he thought, to follow him to death without question if need be. The image of the creamy tossing heads of gypsy lace and moon daisies encased by hawthorn hedging in its first haze of spring green vanished at once.

'She was a great queen,' John volunteered.

Sir Robert's face lightened. 'She was,' he said. 'Everything I learned about statecraft, I learned from her. There never was a more cunning player. And she named him at the very end. So she did her duty, in her own way.'

'You named him,' John said dryly. 'I heard that it was you that read the proclamation which named him as king while the others were still hopping between him and the other heirs like fleas between sleeping dogs.'

Cecil shot John his swift sly smile. 'I have some small influence,' he agreed. The two men reached the steps which led to the first terrace. Sir Robert leaned on John's sturdy shoulder and John braced himself to take the slight weight.

'He'll not go wrong while I have the guiding of him,' Sir Robert said thoughtfully. 'And neither I, nor you, will be the losers. It takes a good deal of skill to survive from one reign to the next, Tradescant.'

John smiled. 'Please God this king will see me out,' he said. 'I've seen a queen, the greatest queen that ever was; and now a new king. I don't expect to see more.'

They reached the terrace and Sir Robert dropped his hand from John's shoulder and shrugged. 'Oh! You're a young man still! You'll see King James and then his son Prince Henry on the throne! I don't doubt it!'

'Amen to their safe succession,' John Tradescant replied loyally. 'Whether I see it or not.'

'You're a faithful man,' Sir Robert remarked. 'D'you never have any doubts, Tradescant?'

John looked quickly at his master to see if he was jesting; but Sir Robert was serious.

'I made my choice of master when I came to you,' John said baldly. 'I promised then that you would have no more faithful servant than me. And I promise my loyalty to the queen, and now to her heir, twice every Sunday in church before God. I'm not a man who questions these things. I take my oath and that's the end of it for me.'

Sir Robert nodded, reassured as always by Tradescant's faith, as straight as an arrow to the target. 'It's the old way,' he said, half to himself. 'A chain of master and man leading to the very head of the kingdom. A chain from the lowest beggar to the highest lord and the king above him and God above him. Keeps the country tied up tight.'

'I like men in their places,' Tradescant agreed. 'It's like a garden. Things ordered in their right places, pruned into shape.'

'No wild disorder? No tumbling vines?' Sir Robert asked with a smile.

'That's not a garden, that's outside,' John said firmly. He looked down at the knot garden, the straight lines of the low clipped hedges, and behind them the sharply defined coloured stones, each part of the pattern in its right place, each shape building up the design which could not even be seen clearly by the workers on the ground who weeded the gravel. To understand the symmetry of the garden you had to be gentry – looking down from the windows of the house.

'My job is to make order for the master's pleasure,' Tradescant said.

Sir Robert touched his shoulder. 'Mine too.'

They walked together along the terrace to the next great flight of steps. 'All ready for His Majesty?' Sir Robert asked, knowing what the answer would be.

'All prepared.'

Tradescant waited to see if his master would speak more and then he bowed, and fell back, and watched Sir Robert limp onward, towards the grand house, to supervise the preparation for the visit of the Lord's Anointed, England's new, glorious king.

April 1603

They had news of the arrival long before the first outriders clattered in through the great gates. Half the country had turned out to see what sort of man the new king might be. The whole royal court moved with the king – the baggage trains behind his carriages carried everything from silver and gold cutlery to pictures for his walls. One hundred and fifty English noblemen had attached themselves at once to the new king, their hats banded with red and gold to demonstrate their loyalty. But travelling with him also was his own Scots court, drawn south by the promise of easy pickings from the fat English manors. Behind them came all the retainers – twenty for each lord – and behind them came their baggage and horses. It was a massive battalion of idlers on the move. In the centre of the whole train came the king, riding his big black hunter, and scarcely able to see the country he had come to claim as his own for the lords and gentry who milled about him.

Half of the commoners who had joined the progress as it moved along the dusty roads were turned back at the great palace gates by Sir Robert's retainers – a private army of his own – and the king rode down the great sweep of the tree-lined avenue to the house. When they reached the base court the followers broke away, looking for their own apartments and shouting for grooms to stable their horses. The king was greeted by Sir Robert's chief servant, the master of the house, who had a paper to read to welcome the king on coming to his kingdom, and then Sir Robert himself stepped forward, and knelt before him.

'You can get up,' the new king said gruffly, his accent extraordinary to those subjects who had only ever heard a monarch speak in the queen's ringing rounded tones.

Sir Robert rose, awkward on his lame leg, and led his king into the great hall of Theobalds. King James, prepared for English wealth and English style, nonetheless checked at the doorway and gasped. The walls and the ceilings were so massively carved with branches and flowers and leaves that the walls themselves looked like the boughs of a wood, and on the warm spring day even the wild birds were misled and came flying in and out of the huge open windows with their vast panes of expensive Venetian glass. It was a flight of fancy in stone, wood, and precious metals and jewels, an excess of folly and grandeur in one splendid hall as big as a couple of barns.

'This is magnificent. What jewels in those planets! What workmanship in the wood!'

Sir Robert smiled, as modest as he could be, and bowed slightly; but not even his courtier skills were able to conceal his pride of ownership.

'And this wall!' the king exclaimed.

It was the wall which showed the Cecil family connections. Other older members of court, other greater families might sneer at the Cecils who had come from a farm in Herefordshire only a few generations ago; but this wall was Sir Robert's answer. It was emblazoned with his family shield showing the motto *Prudens Qui Patiens* – a good choice for a family who had made their fortune in two generations by advising the monarch – and linked by swags and ropes of laurel and bay leaves to the coats of arms and branches of the family. The garlands showed the extent of the Cecil power and influence. This was a man who had a cousin or a niece in every noble bed in the land and, conversely, every noble family in the land had, at one time or another, sought the seal of Cecil approval. The rich swooping loops of carved and polished foliage which connected one shield to another were like a map of England's power from the fountainhead of the Cecil family, closest to the throne, to the most distant tributaries of petty northern lordships and baronetcies.

On the opposite wall was Cecil's great planetary clock, which showed the time of day in hours and minutes as it shone on Cecil's house. A great solid gold orb represented the sun, and then at one side was a moon hammered from pure silver, and the planets in their courses, all moving in their spheres. Each planet was made from silver or gold and encrusted with jewels, each kept perfect time, each demonstrated in its symmetry and beauty the natural order of the universe that put England at the centre of the universe and mirrored the arrangement of the opposite wall that put Cecil at the centre of England.

It was an extraordinary display even for a house of extraordinary displays.

The king looked from one wall to another, stunned by the richness. 'I've seen nothing like this in my life before,' he said.

'It was my father's great pride,' Sir Robert said. At once he could have bitten off his tongue rather than mention his father to this man. William Cecil had been the queen's adviser when she had hesitated over the death of her cousin, Queen Mary of Scotland. It was Cecil's father who had put the death warrant on the table and told the queen that, kin or no, monarch or no, innocent or no, the lady must die, that he could not guarantee Queen Elizabeth's safety with her dangerously attractive rival alive. It was William Cecil who had responsibility for Mary's death and now his son welcomed the dead queen's son into his house.

'I must show you the royal apartments.' Robert Cecil recovered rapidly. 'And if there is anything you lack you must tell me, Your Majesty.' He turned and waved to a man holding a heavy box. The man, whose cue should have come later, started forward and presented the jewel box on one knee.

The gleam from the diamonds completely obscured Cecil's small blunder. James beamed with desire. 'I shall lack nothing,' he declared. 'Show me the royal rooms.'

It seemed odd to Cecil, taking this stocky, none-too-clean man into the rooms which had belonged exclusively to the queen, and were always left empty when she was not there, filled only with the aura of royalty. When she was in residence, on her long and expensive visits, the place was scented with rose-water and orange blossom and the richest strewing herbs and pomanders. Even when she was absent there was a ghost of her perfume in the room which made any man coming into it pause in awe on the threshold. There was a tradition that her chair was placed in the centre of the room like a throne, and like a throne it was vested with her authority. Everyone, from serving maid to Cecil, bowed to it on entering the room and on leaving, such was the power of England's queen even in her absence.

It seemed odd, against the grain of all things, and wrong in itself that the heir she had never seen, whose name she had hated, should cross her threshold and exclaim with greedy pleasure at her carved and gilded wooden bed where he would now lie, the rich curtains around it and the hangings on the walls. 'This is a palace fit for a king indeed,' James said, his chin wet as if he were salivating at the sight.

Sir Robert bowed. 'I shall leave you to take your ease, Your Majesty.'

Already the room was losing that slight scent of orange blossom. The new king smelled of horses and of stale sweat. 'I shall dine at once,' he said.

Sir Robert bowed low and withdrew.

John had the final ordering of the vegetables to the kitchen, checking the great baskets as they went from the cold house in the kitchen garden into the back door of the vegetable kitchens and so he did not see the royal entourage arrive. The palace kitchens were in uproar. The meat cooks were sweating and as red as the great carcasses, and the pastry chefs were white with flour and nerves. The three huge kitchen fires were roaring and hot and the lads turning the spits were drunk with the small ale they were downing in great thirsty gulps. In the rooms where the meat was butchered for the spit the floor was wet with blood and the dogs of the two households were everywhere underfoot, lapping up blood and entrails.

The main kitchen was filled with servants running on one errand or another, and loud with shouted orders. John made sure that his barrows of winter greens and cabbage had gone to the right cook and made a hasty retreat.

'Oh, John!' one of the serving maids called after him and then blushed scarlet. 'I mean, Mr Tradescant!'

He turned at the sound of her voice.

'Will you be taking your dinner in the great hall?' she asked.

John hesitated. As Sir Robert's gardener he was undoubtedly one of his entourage, and could eat at the far end of the hall, watching the king dine in state. As one of the household staff he could eat in the second sitting for the servers and cooks, after the main dinner had been served. As Sir Robert Cecil's trusted envoy and the planner of his garden he could eat at a higher table, halfway up the hall: below the gentry of course, but well above the men at arms and the huntsmen. If Sir Robert wanted him nearby he might stand at his shoulder while his lord was served with his dinner.

'I'll not eat today,' he declared, avoiding the choice which brought with it so many complexities. Men would watch where he sat and guess at his influence and intimacy with his master. John had long-ago learned discretion from Sir Robert; he never flaunted his place. 'But I'll go into the gallery to watch the king at his vittles.'

'Shall I bring you a plate of the venison?' she asked. She stole a little glance at him from under her cap. She was a pretty girl, an orphan niece of one of the cooks. Tradescant recognised, with the weary familiarity of a man who has been confined to bachelorhood for too long, the stirring of a desire which must always be repressed.

'No,' he said regretfully. 'I'll come to the kitchen when the king is served.'

'We could share a plate, and some bread, and a flagon of ale?' she offered. 'When I've finished my work?'

John shook his head. The ale would be strong, and the meat would be good. There were a dozen places where a man and a maid might meet in the great house alone. And the gardens were John's own domain. Away from the formality of the knot gardens there were woodland walks and hidden places. There was the bathing house, all white marble and plashing water and luxury. There was a little mount with a summerhouse at the pinnacle, veiled with silk curtains. Every path led to an arbour planted with sweet-smelling flowers, around every corner there was a seat sheltered with trees and hidden from the paths. There were summer banqueting halls, there were the dozens of winter sheds where the tender plants were nursed. There was the orangery scented with citrus leaves, with a warm fire always burning. There were potting sheds, and tool stores. There were a thousand thousand places where John and the girl might go, if she were willing, and he were reckless.

The girl was only eighteen, in the prime of her beauty and her fertility. John was a cautious man. If he went with her and she took with child he would have to marry her, and he would lose forever his chance of a solid dowry and a hitch up the long small-runged ladder which his father had planned for him when he had betrothed him, two years ago, to the daughter of the vicar at Meopham in Kent. John had no intention of marrying before he had the money to support a wife, and no intention of breaking his solemn betrothal. Elizabeth Day would wait for him until her dowry and his savings would make their future secure. Not even John's wage as a gardener would be enough for a newly married couple to prosper in a country where land prices were rising and the price of bread was wholly dependent on fair weather; and if the wife proved fertile then they would be dragged down to poverty with a new baby every year. John had an utter determination to keep his place in the world and, if possible, to improve it.

'Catherine,' he said. 'You are too pretty for my peace of mind, I cannot go courting with you. And I dare not venture more . . .'

She hesitated. 'We might venture together . . .'

He shook his head. 'I have nothing but my wages, and you have no portion. We should do poorly, my little miss.'

Someone shouted for her from the kitchen table. She glanced behind her, chose to ignore them and stepped closer to him.

'You're paid a vast sum!' she protested. 'And Sir Robert trusts you. He gives you gold to buy his trees, and he is high in favour with the king. They say he is certain to take you to London to make his garden there . . .'

John hid his surprise. He had thought that she had been watching him and desiring him, as he, despite his caution, had been watching and wanting her. But this careful planning was not the voice of a besotted eighteen-year-old. 'Who says this?' he asked, carefully keeping his voice neutral. 'Your uncle?'

She nodded. 'He says you are set fair to be a great man, although you are only a gardener. He says that gardens are the fashion and that Mr Gerard and you are the very men. He says you could go as far as London. Perhaps even into the king's service!' She broke off, excited by the prospect.

John had disappointment like a sour taste in his mouth. 'I might.' He could not resist testing her liking for him. 'Or I might prefer to stay in the country and try my hand at breeding flowers and trees. Would you come with me, to a little cottage, if I become a gardener in a small way, and husband a little plot?'

Involuntarily she stepped back. 'Oh, no! I couldn't bear anything mean! But surely, Mr Tradescant, that is not your wish?'

John shook his head. 'I cannot say.' He felt himself fumbling for a dignified retreat, conscious of the desire in his face, the heat in his blood, and the contradictory, sobering awareness that she had seen him as an opportunity for her ambition, and never looked at him with desire at all. 'I could not promise to take you to London. I could not promise to take you anywhere. I could not promise wealth or success.'

She pouted her lower lip, like a child who has been disappointed. Tradescant put both his hands in the deep pockets of his coat so that he would not be able to put them around her yielding waist, and pull her to him for consolation and kisses.

'Then you may fetch your own dinner!' she cried shrilly and turned abruptly away from him. 'And I'll find a handsome young man to dine with. A Scots man with a place at court! There are many who would be glad to have me!'

'I don't doubt it,' John said. 'And I would too, but . . .' She did not wait to hear his excuses, she flounced around and was gone.

A serving man pushed past him with a huge platter of fine white bread, another ran behind with flagons of wine clutched four in each hand. John turned from the noise of the kitchen area and went towards the great hall.

The king was seated, drinking red wine at the enormous hearthside. He was already vastly, deeply drunk. He was still filthy from the day's hunting and the travel along the muddy roads and he had not washed. Indeed, they said that he never washed, but merely wiped his sore and blotchy hands gently on silk. The dirt beneath his fingernails had certainly been there since his triumphant arrival in England, and probably since childhood. Sitting beside him was a handsome young man dressed as richly as any prince but who was neither Prince Henry the older son and heir, nor Prince Charles the younger brother. As John waited at the back of the hall and watched, the king pulled the youth towards him and kissed him behind his ear, leaving a dribble of red wine along the pleats of his white ruff.

There was a roar of laughter at some joke and the king plunged his hand into the favourite's lap and squeezed his padded codpiece. The man snatched up the hand and kissed it. There was high ribald laughter, from women as well as men, sharing the joke. No-one paused for a moment at the sight of the King of England and Scotland with his dirty hand thrust into the lap of a man.

John watched them as if they were curiosities from another country. The women were painted white from their large horsehair wigs to their half-naked breasts, their eyebrows plucked and shaped so their eyes seemed unnaturally wide, their lips coloured pink. Their gowns were cut low and square over their bulging breasts and their waists were nipped in tight by embroidered and jewel-encrusted stomachers. The colours of the silks and satins and velvet gowns glowed in the candlelight as if they were luminous.

The king was sprawled in his seat with half a dozen intimates around him, most of them already drunk. Behind them all the court drank flagon after flagon of rich wine, and flirted, and schemed and caroused, some inarticulate with drink, some incomprehensible with their broad Scots accents. One or two, with an eye to the English scrutiny, spoke quietly to each other in Scots.

There was to be a masque later representing Wisdom meeting Justice, and some of the court were already in their masquing clothes. Justice was dead drunk, slumped over the table, and one of the handmaidens of Wisdom was at the back of the hall, backed up against the wall, with one of the Scots nobles investigating the layers of her petticoats.

John, conscious of the great disadvantage of watching this scene stone-cold sober, took a cup from a passing servant and downed a great gulp of the very best wine. He thought briefly of the old queen's court where there had been vanity and wealth indeed, but also the rigid discipline of the autocratic old woman who ruled that since she had denied herself pleasure, the rest of the court should be chaste. There had been parties everywhere she had gone, masques and balls and picnics, but all behaviour that fell under the scrutiny of that fierce gaze had been strictly constrained. John realised that the long carnival-like journey from Scotland to England must have been a revelation to the English courtiers and what he was seeing was the consequence of a rapid recognition that anything was now permitted.

The king emerged from a slobbering kiss. 'We must have more music!' he shouted.

In the gallery, the musicians who had been fighting to make themselves heard above the hubbub of the hall started another air.

'Dance!' the king exclaimed.

Half a dozen of the court formed two lines and started to dance, the king pulled the young man down to sit between his knees and caressed the dark ringlets of his hair. He bent down and kissed him full on the mouth. 'My lovely boy,' he said.

John felt the wine in his veins and in his head but feared that no wine would be strong enough to persuade him that this scene was joyful, or this king was gracious. Such thoughts were treason, and John was too loyal to think treason. He turned around and left the hall.

July 1604

'What do we have that is the most impressive?' Sir Robert came upon John in the scented garden, a square internal court where John had grown jasmine, honeysuckle, and roses against the walls to soften their grim greyness. John was balanced on the top of a ladder, pruning the honeysuckle which had just finished flowering.

John turned to look at his master and took in at once the new lines of strain on his face. The first year of the new king's reign had been no sinecure for his Secretary of State. Wealth and honour had been showered on Cecil and on his family and adherents; but wealth and honour had equally been poured on hundreds of others. The new king, born into a kingdom of bleak poverty, thought the coffers of England were bottomless. Only Cecil knew and appreciated that the wealth that Queen Elizabeth had hoarded so jealously was flowing out of the treasure room of the Tower quicker than he could hope to gather it back in.

'Impressive?' John asked. 'An impressive flower?' His expression of complete bewilderment made his master suddenly laugh aloud.

'God's blood, John, I have not laughed for weeks. With this damned envoy from Spain at my heels all the time and the king slipping away to hunt at every moment and them always asking me, what will the king think? and I without an answer! Impressive. Yes. What do we grow that is impressive?'

John considered for a moment. 'I never think of plants as impressive. D'you mean rare, my lord? Or beautiful?'

'Rare, strange, beautiful. It is for a gift. A gift which will make men stare. A gift which will make men wonder.'

John nodded, slid down the ladder like a boy, and turned from the garden at a brisk walk. At once he remembered who he was leading and slowed his pace.

'Don't humour me,' his lord snapped from a few paces behind. 'I can keep up.'

'I was slowing to think, my lord,' John said swiftly. 'My trouble is that the main flowering season is over now we are in midsummer. If you had wanted something very grand a couple of months ago I could have given you some priceless tulips, or the great rose daffodils which were better this year than any other. But now . . .'

'Nothing?' the earl demanded, scandalised. 'Acres of garden and nothing to show me?'

'Not nothing,' Tradescant protested, stung. 'I have some roses in their second bloom which are as good as anything in the kingdom.'

'Show me.'

Tradescant led the way to the mount. It was as high as two houses, and the lane which led the way to the top was broad enough for a pony and a carriage. At the summit was a banqueting hall with a little table and chairs. Sometimes it would amuse the three Cecil children to dine at the top of the hill and look down on all that they owned; but Robert Cecil only rarely came here. The climb was too steep for him and he did not like to be seen riding while his children walked.

The hedges of the lane which wound to the summit were planted with all the varieties of English roses that Tradescant could find in the neighbouring counties: cream, peach, pink, white. Every year he grafted and re-grafted new stock on to old stems to try to make a new colour, a new shape or a new scent.

'They tell me this is sweet,' he said, proffering a rose striped white and scarlet. 'A Rosamund rose, but with a perfume.'

His lord bent and sniffed. 'How can you breed for scent when you cannot smell them yourself?' he asked.

John shrugged. 'I ask people if they smell good or better than other roses. But it is hard to judge. They always tell me the scent in terms of another scent. And since I have never had a nose which could smell then it's no help to me. They say "lemony" as if I would know what a lemon smells like. They say "honey" and that is no help either, for I think of one as sour and one as sweet.'

Robert Cecil nodded. He was not the man to pity a disability. 'Well, it smells good to me,' he said. 'Could I have great boughs of it by August?'

John Tradescant hesitated. A less faithful servant would have said 'yes' and then disappointed his master at the final moment. A better courtier would have guided him away to something else. John simply shook his head. 'I thought you wanted it for today or tomorrow. I cannot give you roses in August, my lord. Nobody can.'

Cecil turned away and started to limp back to the house. 'Come with me,' he said shortly over his sloped shoulder. Tradescant fell in beside him and Cecil leaned on his arm. Tradescant took the burden of that light weight and felt himself soften with pity for the man who had all the responsibility for running three, no, four kingdoms with the new addition of Scotland, and yet none of the real power.

'It's for the Spanish,' Cecil told him in an undertone. 'This gift that I need. What do people in the country think of the peace with Spain?'

'They mistrust it, I think,' John said. 'We have been at war with Spain for so long, and avoided defeat so narrowly. It's impossible to think of them as friends the very next day.'

'I cannot let us stay at war in Europe. We will be ruined if we go on pouring men and gold into the United Provinces, into France. And Spain is no threat any more. I must have a peace.'

'As long as they don't come here,' John said hesitantly. 'No-one cares what happens in Europe, my lord. Ordinary people care only for their own homes, for their own county. Half the people here at Cheshunt or Waltham Cross care only that there are no Spaniards in Surrey.'

'No Jesuits,' Cecil said, naming the greatest fear.

John nodded. 'God preserve us. We none of us want to see burnings in the market place again.'

Cecil looked into the face of his gardener. 'You're a good man,' he said shortly. 'I learn more from you in a walk from my mount to my orangery than I do from a nation full of spies.'

The two men paused. The orangery at Theobalds was open at every doorway, the double white-painted doors allowing the warm summer sunshine to flood into the rooms. Tender saplings and whips of oranges, lemons, and vines were still kept inside – Tradescant was a notoriously cautious man. But the mature fruit trees were out in the fine weather, housed in great barrels with carrying loops at four points so they could adorn the three central courts of Theobalds in the summer, and bring a touch of the exotic to this most English of palaces. Long before the first hint of frost Tradescant would have them carried back into the orangery and the fires lit in the grates to keep them safe through the English winter.

'I suppose oranges are not impressive,' he said. 'Not to Spaniards who live in orange groves.'

Cecil was about to agree but he hesitated. 'How many oranges could we muster?'

John thought of the three mature trees, one placed at the centre of each court. 'Would you strip the trees of all their fruit?' he asked.

Cecil nodded.

John swallowed at the thought of the sacrifice. 'A barrel of fruit. By August, perhaps two barrels.'

Cecil slapped him on the shoulder. 'That's it!' he cried. 'The whole point is that we show them that they have nothing which we need. We give them great boughs of oranges and that shows them that anything they have, we can have too. That we are not the supplicants in this business but the men of power. That we have all of England and orange orchards too.'

'Boughs?' John asked, going to the central point. 'You don't mean to pick the fruit?'

Cecil shook his head. 'It is a gift for the king to give to the Spanish ambassador. It has to look wonderful. A barrel of oranges could have been bought on the quayside, but a great branch of a tree with the fruit on it – they will see that it has been fresh-cut by the quality of the leaves. It has to be boughs laden with fruit.'

John, thinking of the savage hacking of his beautiful trees, suppressed an exclamation of pain. 'Certainly, my lord,' he said.

Cecil, understanding at once, hugged Tradescant around the

shoulders and planted a hearty kiss on his cheek. 'John, I have had men lay down their lives for me with an easier heart. Forgive me, but I need a grand gesture for the king. And your oranges are the sacrificial lamb.'

John reluctantly chuckled. 'I'll wait till I hear then, my lord. And I'll cut the fruit and send it up to London as soon as you order.'

'Bring it yourself,' Cecil directed him. 'I want no mistake, and you of all men will guard it as if it were your firstborn son.'

August 1604

John's oranges were the centre of the feast to celebrate the peace. King James and Prince Henry held bibles and swore before the nobles and the Spanish ambassadors that the Treaty of London would install a solemn and lasting peace. In a glorious ceremony de Velasco toasted the king from an agate cup set with diamonds and rubies and then presented him with the cup. Queen Anne at his side had a crystal goblet and three diamond pendants.

Then King James nodded to Cecil, and Cecil turned to where Tradescant was behind him and John Tradescant walked forward bearing in his arms, almost too great a weight to carry, a great spreading bough of oranges, their leaves glossy and green with drops of water like pearls still rolling on the central vein, their fruit round, scented like oil of sunshine, blazing with colour, ripe and fleshy. The king touched the bough and at his gesture Tradescant laid it at the Spanish ambassador's feet as two of his lads laid another and then another in a heap of ripe wealth.

'Oranges, Your Majesty?' the man exclaimed.

James smiled and nodded. 'In case you were feeling homesick,' he said.

De Velasco threw a quick look back at his entourage. 'I had no idea that you could grow oranges in England,' he said enviously. 'I thought it was too cold here, too damp.'

Robert Cecil made a casual gesture. 'Oh, no,' he replied nonchalantly. 'We can grow anything we desire.'

A page came through the crowd, carrying a great pannier of fruit, and another followed him with a basket. In pride of place, nestling amid some aromatic southernwood leaves, was a large pale melon.

'Wait a minute,' said John. 'Let me see that.'

The page was in Lord Wootton's livery. 'Let me pass,' he said urgently. 'I am to present this to the king to give to the Spanish ambassador.'

'Where's it from?' John hissed.

'From Lord Wootton's garden at Canterbury,' the lad replied and pushed through.

'Lord Wootton's gardener can grow melons?' John asked. He turned to his neighbour, but no-one but John cared one way or the other. 'How does Lord Wootton grow melons at Canterbury?'

The question remained unanswered. In a nearby inn John sought out Lord Wootton's gardener, who merely laughed at him and said there was a trick to it but John would have to join Lord Wootton's service if he wanted to learn it.

'D'you plant them in the orangery?' John guessed. 'D'you have an earth bed inside?'

The man laughed. 'The great John Tradescant asking me for advice!' he mocked. 'Come to Canterbury, Mr Tradescant, and you shall learn my secrets.'

John shook his head. 'I'd rather serve the greatest lord in the greatest gardens in England,' he said loftily.

'Not the greatest for long,' the gardener warned him.

'Why? What d'you mean?'

The gardener drew a little closer. 'There are those who are saying that he has signed his own letter of resignation from service,' he said. 'Now that Spain is at peace with England, who can doubt that the lords who stayed with the true faith through all the troubles will come back to court? They'll find their places at court again.'

'Catholics at court?' John demanded. 'With a king like ours? He'd never bear it.'

The man shrugged. 'King James is not the old queen. He likes differences of opinion. He likes to dispute with them. Queen Anne herself takes the Mass. My own lord takes the Mass when he is abroad and avoids the English church whenever he can. And if he is high in the king's favour, giving him melons and the like, then the tide is turning. And stout old defenders of the faith like your lord may find their time has gone.'

John nodded, bought the man another ale, and left the tavern to find Cecil.

His master was in one of the courtyards at Whitehall, about to board his barge to take him upriver to Theobalds.

'Ah, John,' he said. 'Will you come home with me by water or travel back with the wagon?'

'I'll come with you, if I may, my lord,' John said.

'Get your bag then, for we leave at once, I want to catch the tide.'

John hurried to fetch his things and came back as the barge was preparing to cast off. The rowers stood at salute, their oars raised. The Cecil pennant flew at bow and stern. Robert Cecil was seated amidships, a canopy over his head and a rug at his side to ward off the evening chill. John leaped nimbly aboard and sat at the rear of the boat behind the golden chair.

The boatmaster cast off and the rowers started the regular beat, beat of their rowing, the oars splashing in the water and the boat pulling forward and then resting, pulling and then resting. It was a soporific, lulling movement, but John kept his eyes on his master.

He saw the head flecked with premature grey hair nod and then sink. The man was exhausted after months of painstaking negotiation and unending civility, mostly conducted in a foreign language. John drew a little closer and watched over his master's sleep as the sun went down before them and painted the sky gold and peach, and turned the river into a shining path which took them slowly and steadily back to their garden.

When the sky grew darker blue and the first stars came out, John reached for his lord and gathered the blanket around his crooked shoulders. The man, the greatest statesman in the land, probably the greatest in Europe, was as light as a girl. His head lolled to John's shoulder and rested there. John gathered his lord to him and guarded his rest as the boat went quietly on the inward-flowing tide all the way up the river.

Just before the Theobalds landing stage Cecil awoke. He smiled to find John's arms around him.

'A warm pillow you've been to me this evening,' he said pleasantly.

'I did not want to disturb you,' John replied. 'You looked weary.'

'Weary as a dog after a whipping,' Cecil yawned. 'But I can rest now for a few days. The Spanish are gone, the king will return to Royston for the hunting. We can prune our orange trees back into shape, eh John?'

'There's one thing, my lord,' John said cautiously. 'A thing that I heard and thought I should tell you.'

Cecil was instantly awake, as if he had never dozed at all. 'What thing?' he asked softly.

'It was Lord Wootton's man, he suggested that now there is peace with Spain the Roman Catholics will come back to court, that there will be new rivals for you at court, and in the king's favour. He knew that the queen has become a Roman Catholic. He knew she takes Mass. And he named his own lord as a man who worships in the old way when he can, when he is abroad, and avoids his own church when he can at home.'

Cecil nodded slowly. 'Anything else?'

John shook his head.

'Do they say I am in the pay of Spain? That I took a bribe to get the peace treaty through?'

John was deeply shocked. 'Good God, my lord! No!'

Cecil looked pleased. 'They don't know about that yet then.'

He glanced at John's astounded face and chuckled. 'Ah, John, my John, it is not treason to the king to take money from his enemies. It is treason to the king to take money from his enemies and then do their bidding. I do the one, I don't do the other. And I shall buy much land with the Spanish gold and pay off my debts in England. So the Spanish will pay hardworking English men and women.'

John looked scarcely comforted. Cecil squeezed his arm. 'You must learn from me,' he said. 'There is no principle; there is only practice. Look to your practice and let other men worry about principles.'

John nodded, hardly understanding.

'As to the return of the Catholic lords,' Cecil said thoughtfully, 'I don't fear them. If the Catholics will live at peace in England, under our laws, then I can be tolerant of some new faces in the king's council.'

'Are they sworn to obey the Pope?'

Cecil shrugged. 'I care nothing for what they think in private,' he said. 'It's what they do in public that concerns me. If they will leave good English men and women to follow their own consciences in peace and quiet, then they can worship in their own way.' He paused. 'It's the wild few I fear,' he said softly. 'The madmen who lack all judgement, who care nothing for agreements, who just want to act. They'd rather die in the faith than live in peace with their neighbours.'

The boat nudged the landing stage and the rowers snapped their oars upright. A dozen lanterns were lit on the wooden pier and burned either side of the broad leafy path to the house to light the lord homeward. 'If they attempt to disturb the peace of the land that I have struggled so hard to win – then they are dead men,' Cecil said gently.

October 1605

The peace Cecil worked for did not come at once. A year later in mid-autumn John saw one of the house servants picking his way down the damp terrace steps to where he was working in the knot garden. Cecil had finally agreed that he should take out the gravel and replace it with plants. John was bedding in some strong cotton lavender which he thought would catch the frost and turn feathery white and beautiful in the winter, and convince his master that a garden could be rich with plants as well as cleanly perfect in shapes made with stones.

'The earl wants you,' the servant said, emphasising the new title, reflecting the pleasure the whole household felt. 'The earl wants you in his private chamber.'

John straightened up, sensing trouble. 'I'll have to wash and change my clothes,' he said, gesturing to his muddy hands and his rough breeches.

'He said, at once.'

John went towards the house at a run, entered through the side door from the Royal Court, crossed the great hall, silent and warm in the afternoon quiet after the hubbub of the midday dinner, and then went through the small door behind the lord's throne which led to his private apartments.

A couple of pageboys and menservants were tidying the outer room, a couple of the lord's gentlemen gambling on cards at a small table. John went past them and tapped on the door. The sound of the Irish harp playing a lament abruptly stopped and a voice called: 'Come in!'

John opened the door a crack and sidled into the room. His lordship was, unusually, alone, seated at his desk with his harp on his knee. John was instantly wary.

'I came at once; but I'm dirty,' he said.

He wanted Robert Cecil to glance up, but the man's face was down, looking at the harp on his lap. John could not see him, nor read his expression.

'The man said it was urgent –'

The figure at the desk was still.

There was a silence.

'For God's sake, my lord, tell me you are well and that all is well with you!' John finally burst out.

At last Cecil looked up and his face, normally scored with pain, was alive with mischief. His eyes were sparkling, his mouth, under his neat moustache, was smiling.

'I have a game to play, John. If you will take a hand for me.'

The relief to see his lord happy was so great that John assented at once, without thinking. 'Of course.'

'Sit down.'

John pulled a little stool up to the dark wood desk and the two men went head to head, Robert Cecil speaking so softly that a man in the same room could not have heard them, let alone any of them waiting outside the door.

'I have a letter that I want delivered to Lord Monteagle,' he whispered. 'Delivered to him and none other.'

John nodded and leaned back. 'I can do that.'

Cecil reached across and pulled him closer again. 'It's more than a messenger boy I want,' he whispered. 'The contents of the letter are enough to hang Monteagle, and to hang the messenger. You must not be seen delivering it, you must not be seen with it. Your own life depends on you getting it to him with no man seeing you.'

John's eyes widened.

'Will you do it for me?'

There was a brief silence.

'Of course, my lord. I am your man.'

28

'Don't you want to know what's in the letter?'

Superstitiously, John shook his head.

Cecil, mightily amused at the sight of his gardener stunned into silence, broke down and laughed aloud. 'John, my John, what a poor conspirator you will make.'

John nodded. 'It is not my trade, my lord,' he said with simple dignity. 'You have others in your service better skilled. But if you want me to take a letter and deliver it unseen, then I will do that.' He paused for a moment. 'It will not undo Lord Monteagle? I would not be a Judas.'

Cecil shrugged his shoulders. 'The letter itself is nothing more than words on a page. It's not poison, it won't kill him. What he does with the letter is his own choice. His end will be determined by that choice.'

John felt himself to be swimming in deep and dark waters. 'I'll do what you wish,' he muttered, clinging only to his faith in his lord and his own vow of loyalty.

Cecil leaned back and tossed a small note across the table. It was addressed to Lord Monteagle, but the hand was not Robert Cecil's nor that of any of his secretaries.

'Get it to him tonight,' Robert Cecil said. 'Without fail. There's a boat waiting for you at the jetty. Make sure you are not seen. Not in the streets, not at his house, and not, *not*, with the letter. If you are captured, destroy it. If you are questioned, deny it.'

John nodded and rose to his feet.

'John –' his master called as he reached the door. John stopped and turned around. His lord sat behind his desk, his face, his whole stance alive with joy at plotting and trickery and the game of politics which he played so consummately well. 'I would trust no other man to do this for me,' Cecil said.

John met his master's bright gaze and knew the pleasure of being the favourite. He bowed and went out.

He went first to the knot garden and gathered up his tools. The plants which were not yet bedded in he took back to his nursery plots and heeled them into the earth. Not even an act of high treason could make John Tradescant forget his plants. He glanced around the walled nursery garden. There was no-one there. He rose to his feet and brushed the earth from his hands and then he went to the potting shed where he had left his winter cloak. He carried it over his arm, as if he were headed for the hall for a bite to eat, but turned instead towards the river.

There was a wherry boat waiting at the lord's private jetty but it was otherwise deserted.

'For London?' the man asked without much interest. 'In a hurry?'

'Yes,' John said shortly.

He stepped into the little boat and he thought the lurch it made at his weight was what caused the sudden pounding of his heart. He sat in the prow of the boat so the man might not have the chance to look in his face, and he wrapped himself warm in his cape and pulled down his hat over his face. He was sure that the sunlight along the river was pointing a rippling finger towards him so that every fisherman and riverside walker, pedlar and beggar took particular note of him as the boat went swiftly downstream.

The river flowed fast down to London, and the tide was on the ebb. They did the journey quicker than John had hoped and when the boat nudged against the Whitehall steps and John leaped ashore it was only dusk. He blamed his sense of sickness on the movement of the boat. He did not want to recognise his fear.

No-one paid any attention to the working man with his hat pulled down over his eyes and his cape up to his ears. There were hundreds, thousands of men like him, making their way across London for their suppers. John knew the way to Lord Monteagle's house and slipped from shadow to shadow, making little sound on the dirt and mud of the streets.

Lord Monteagle's house was lit by double burning torches in the sconces outside. The front door stood wide open and his men, hangers-on, friends, and beggars passed in and out without challenge. His lordship was dining at the top table at the head of the hall, there was a continual press of people all around him, friends of his household, servants, retainers and, towards the back of the hall, suppliants and common people who had come in for the amusement of watching the lord at his dinner. John hung back and surveyed the scene.

As he waited and watched, a man touched his shoulder and went to hurry past him. John recognised one of Lord Monteagle's servants, a man called Thomas, hurrying to dinner.

The note was in John's hand, the direction clear. 'A moment,' he said, and pressed it into the man's hand. 'For your master. For the love of Mary.'

He knew what a potent spell that name would weave. The man took it and glanced at him, but John was already turning away and diving into an alley out of sight. He took a moment and then peered cautiously out.

Thomas Ward had entered the big double doors and was making his way to the head of the table. John saw him lean to whisper in his master's ear and hand him the note. The job was done. John stepped out into the street again and strolled onward, careful not to hurry, resisting the temptation to run. He strolled as if he were a working man on his way to an inn, hungry for his supper. As he turned the corner and there was no shout of alarm, and no running footsteps behind him, he allowed his pace to quicken – as fast as a man who knows that he should be home by a certain time. One more corner and John allowed himself to run, a gentle jogging run, as a man might do when he was late for an appointment and hoping to make up for the delay. He kept a sharp watch out among the dirt and cobblestones so that he did not slip and fall, and he kept a brisk pace until he was ten, fifteen minutes away from Lord Monteagle's, out of breath, but safe.

He took his dinner at an inn by the river and then found he was too weary to face the journey back to Theobalds. He headed instead for his lord's house near Whitehall, where Tradescant might always command a bed. He shared an attic room with two other men, saying that he had been sent to the docks for some rarity promised by an East India trader but which had proved to be nothing.

When all the clocks in London struck eight, John went down to the great hall and found his master, as if by magic, also resident in London calmly seated to break his fast at the big chair at the head of the big table at the top of the hall. Robert Cecil raised an eyebrow at him, John returned the smallest nod, and master and man, at either end of the hall, fell on their bread and cheese and small ale and ate with relish.

Cecil summoned him with a crook of his long finger. 'I have a small task for you today and then you can go back to Theobalds,' he said.

John waited.

'There is a little room in Whitehall where some kindling is stored. I should like it damped down to prevent the danger of a fire.'

John frowned, his eyes on his master's impish face. 'My lord?'

'I've got a lad who will show you where to go,' Cecil continued smoothly. 'Take a couple of buckets and make sure the whole thing is soaked through. And come away without being observed, my John.'

'If there is a danger of fire I should clear it all out,' John offered. He had the sense of swimming in deep and dangerous water and knew that this was his master's preferred element.

'I'll clear it out when I know who laid the fire in the first place,' Cecil said, very low. 'Just damp it down for me now.'

'Then I'll get back to my garden,' Tradescant said.

Cecil grinned at the firmness of the statement. 'Then your job is finished here, go and plant something. My work is coming into its flowering time.'

It was only after 5 November that John learned that the whole Gunpowder Plot had been discovered by Lord Monteagle who had received a letter warning him not to go near Parliament. He had, quite rightly, taken the letter to Secretary Robert Cecil who, unable to understand its meaning, had laid the whole thing before the king. The king, quicker-witted than them all – how they praised him for the speed of his understanding! – had ordered the Houses of Parliament to be searched and found Guido Fawkes crouched amid kindling, and nearby, barrels of gunpowder. On the wave of anti-Catholic sentiment Cecil enforced laws to control Papists, and mopped up the remaining opposition to the English Protestant succession. The handful of desperate, dangerous families were identified as one confession led to another, and as the young men who had staked everything on a barrel of wet gunpowder were captured, tortured and executed. The one bungled plot forced everyone from the king to the poorest beggar to turn against the Catholics in a great wave of revulsion. The one dreadful threat – to the king, to his wife, to the two little princes – was such that no monarch in Europe, Catholic or Protestant, would ever plot again with English Catholics. The Spanish and French kings were monarchs before they were Catholics. And as monarchs they would never tolerate regicide.

Even more importantly for Cecil, the horror at the thought of what might have happened if Monteagle had not proved faithful, if the king had not proved astute, persuaded Parliament to grant the king some extraordinary revenue for the year and pushed back for another twelve months the impending financial crisis.

'Thank you, John,' Cecil said when he returned to Theobalds in early December. 'I won't forget.'

'I still don't understand,' John said.

Cecil grinned at him, his schoolboyish conspiratorial grin. 'Much better not to,' he replied engagingly.

May 1607

After the king's first successful visit to Theobalds it was as if he could not keep away. Every summer brought the court hungry as locusts out of London and into the country, to stay at Theobalds and then to move on in a constant circle of all the wealthy houses. The courtiers braced themselves for the unimaginable expense of entertaining the king, and sighed with relief when he moved on. He might shower the host with honours or with favours, or with some of the new farmed-out taxes, so that a favourite might grow rich collecting a newly invented duty from some struggling industry; or the king might merely smile and pass on. Whether he paid for his board in privileges or took it with nothing more than a word of thanks, his courtiers had to provide him with the best of food, the best of drink, the best hunting they could manage, and the best entertainment.

They had learned their skills with Queen Elizabeth; no-one could teach them anything about lavish hospitality, extravagant gifts, and outright sycophancy. But King James demanded all this and more. His favourites too must be honoured, and his days filled with un-ending sport, hunting hunting hunting, until gamekeepers were at a premium and no man dared cut down a tree in a forest which the king knew and loved. His evenings must be filled with a parade of pretty men and pretty women. No-one refused him. No-one even thought to refuse him. Anything the new king wanted he must have.

Even when he wanted Theobalds Palace itself.

'I shall have to give it to him.' Sir Robert had left his palace as he often did to find Tradescant. The gardener was directing the garden lads at the entrance to the maze. A team of boys was being supplied with blunt knives and sent into the maze on their hands and knees to root up weeds in the gravel. A team of older men would go with them with little hatchets and knives to trim the yew hedging; they had already been lectured with passion and energy by John as to the care they must take to keep the top of the hedge even, and on no account, on pain of instant dismissal, were they to cut an unruly bough in such a way that it might leave a hole which would make a peephole from one path to another and spoil the game.

John took one look at his master's dark expression, abandoned the pruning gang and came to him.

'My lord?'

'He wants it. My house, and the gardens too. He wants it, and he's promised me Hatfield House in return. I'll have to give it to him, I suppose. I can't refuse the king, can I?'

John gave a little gasp of horror at the thought of losing Theobalds Palace. 'The king wants this house? Our house?'

Robert Cecil gave an unhappy shrug, beckoned to Tradescant and leaned on his shoulder as they walked. 'Aye, I knew that you would feel it almost as much as me. I came to tell you before I told anyone else. I don't know how I can bear to lose it. Built for me by my own father – the little islands and the rivers, and the fountains, and the bathing house . . . all this to be given away in exchange for that drab little place at Hatfield! A hard taskmaster, the new king, don't you think, Tradescant?'

John paused. 'I don't doubt you will get a better price than you might have had from any other monarch,' he said cautiously.

The earl's cunning courtier face crinkled into laughter. 'Better than from the old queen, you mean? Good God! I should think so! There never was a woman like her for taking half your wealth and giving you nothing but a smile in return. King James has a freer hand for his favourites . . .' He broke off and turned back towards the house. 'With all the favourites,' he muttered. 'Especially if they're Scots. Especially if they're handsome young men.'

They walked side by side together, the earl leaning heavily on John's shoulder.

'Are you in pain?' John asked.

'I'm always in pain,' his master snapped. 'I don't think about it if I can help it.'

John felt a sympathetic twinge in his own knees at the thought of his master's twisted bones. 'Doesn't seem right,' he said with gruff sympathy. 'That with all the striving and worry you have to suffer pain as well.'

'I don't look for justice,' said England's foremost law maker. 'Not in this world.'

John nodded and kept his sympathy to himself. 'When do we have to leave?'

'When I have made Hatfield ready for us. You'll come with me, won't you, John? You'll leave our maze and the fountain court and the great garden for me?'

'Your Grace . . . of course . . .'

The earl heard at once the hesitation in his voice. 'The king would keep you on here if I told him you would stay and mind the gardens,' he said a little coldly. 'If you don't wish to come with me to Hatfield.'

John turned and looked down into his master's wretched face. 'Of course I come with you,' he said tenderly. 'Wherever you are sent. I would garden for you in Scotland, if I had to. I would garden for you in Virginia, if I had to. I am your man. Whether you rise or fall, I am your man.'

The earl turned and gripped John's arms above the elbows in a brief half-embrace. 'I know it,' he said gruffly. 'Forgive my ill humour. I am sick to my belly with the loss of my house.'

'And the garden.'

'Mmm.'

'I have spent my life on this garden,' John said thoughtfully. 'I learned my trade here. There's not a corner of it that I don't know. There's not a change that it makes from season to season that I cannot predict. And there are times, especially in early summer, like now, when I think it is perfect. That we have made it perfect here.'

'An Eden,' the earl agreed. 'An Eden before the Fall. Is that what gardeners do all the time, John? Try to make Eden again?'

'Gardeners and earls and kings too,' John said astutely. 'We all want to make paradise on earth. But a gardener can try afresh every spring.'

'Come and try at Hatfield,' the earl urged him. 'You shall be head gardener in a garden which shall be all your own, you will follow in no man's footsteps. You can make the garden at Hatfield, my John, not just maintain and amend, like here. You shall order the planting and buy the plants. You shall choose every one. And I will pay you more, and give you a cottage of your own. You need not live in hall.' He looked at his gardener. 'You could marry,' he suggested. 'Breed us little babes for Eden.'

John nodded. 'I will.'

'You are betrothed, aren't you?'

'I have been promised these past six years, but my father made me swear on his deathbed never to marry until I could support a wife and family. But if I can have a cottage at Hatfield, I will marry.'

The earl laughed shortly and slapped him on the back. 'From great men do great favours flow like the water in my fountains,' he said. 'King James wants Theobalds for a royal palace and so Tradescant can marry. Go and tie the knot, Tradescant! I will pay you forty pounds a year.'

He hesitated for a moment. 'But you should marry for love, you know,' he said. He swallowed down his grief, his continual grief for the wife he had married for love, who had taken him despite his hunched body and loved him for himself. He had given her two healthy children and one as crooked as himself, and it was the birth of that baby which had killed her. They had been together only eight years. 'To have a wife you can love is a precious thing, John. You're not gentry, or noble, you don't have to make dynasties and fortunes, you can marry where your heart takes you.'

John hesitated. 'I'm not gentry, my lord, but my heart cannot take me to a maid without a portion.' Irresistibly the thought of the kitchen maid from the first dinner for King James came into his head. 'My father left me with a debt to a man which is cleared by this betrothal to his daughter, and she is a steady woman with a good dowry. I have been waiting until I could earn enough for us to marry, until I had savings which might take us through difficult years, savings to buy a house and a little garden for her to tend. I have plans, my lord – oh, never to leave your service, but I have plans to take my fortune upwards.'

The earl nodded. 'Buy land,' he advised.

'To farm?'

'To sell.'

John blinked; it was unusual advice. Most men thought of buying land and keeping it, nothing was more secure than a small-holding.

The earl shook his head. 'The way to make money, my John, is to move fast, even recklessly. You see an opportunity, you take it quickly, you move before other men have seen it too. *Then* when they see it, you pass it on to them and they crow at having spotted their chance, when you have already skimmed the cream of the profit. And move fast,' he advised. 'When you see an opening, when a place comes open, when you see a chance, when a master dies, take what you're owed and move on.'

He glanced up into John's frowning face. 'Practice,' he reminded him. 'Not principles. When Walsingham died, who was the best man to take his place? Who had the correspondence at his fingertips, who knew almost as much as Walsingham himself?'

'You, my lord,' Tradescant stammered.

'And who had Walsingham's papers which told everything a man who wanted to be Secretary of State would need to know?'

John shrugged. 'I don't know, my lord. They were stolen, and the thief never found.'

'Me,' Cecil admitted cheerfully. 'The moment I knew he would not recover, I broke into his cabinet and took everything he had written and received over the previous two years. So when they were casting around for who could do the work there was no-one but me. No-one could read the papers and learn what needed doing, for the papers were missing. No-one could know Walsingham's mind, nor what he had agreed, because the papers were missing. Only one man in England of the dozen who had worked for Walsingham was ready to take his place. And that was me.'

'Theft?' John asked.

'That's principle,' Cecil said swiftly. 'I'm advising you to look to practice. Think what you want, my John, and make sure that you get it, for be very certain that no-one will give it to you.'

John could not help but glance up at the great palace of Theobalds, a place so grand that a king could envy it and insist on owning it, knowing that he could never build better.

'Aye,' said the earl, following his gaze. 'And if a more powerful man can do it, he will take it from you. He will be guided by practice and not principles too. Buy land and take risks is my advice. Steal if you need to and if you will not be detected. When your master dies – even if it is me – have your next place secure. And also – marry your woman with a dowry, she sounds the very one for a rising man like you. And bid her be careful with her housekeeping.'

John Tradescant rode down the Kentish lanes to his old village of Meopham, where he had been expected every day for the last six years. The hedges were white with hawthorn and may blossoms, the air warm and sweet-scented. The rich green pastureland of Kent glowed lush where cattle were knee-deep in water meadows. These were prosperous times and rich fields. John rode in a daze of pleasure, the lushness of the fields and the greening of the trees and the hedges acting on him as strong wine might turn another man's head. In the hedgerows were the white floss of gypsy lace and the little white stars of meadowsweet. Through gaps in the hedge where trees had been coppiced was a sea of blue where bluebells had sprung up to carpet the floor of the forest. Ahead of him the road was drifted with the tiny petals of the hawthorn flower like spring snow, and at every verge the lemon-yellow flowers of primroses were stuffed into roots and nooks like nosegays in a belt. When the road wound through meadowlands, John could see the light yellow of cowslips nodding as the breeze ran across the grasses; they put a veil of gold over the green as a woman might toss a shawl of gold net over a green silk gown.

The oak trees were clench-fisted with flowers, the small delicate catkins which looked like lumpy little buds at the end of the tough contorted branches. The silver birches shivered with new pale leaves amid the dancing catkins, and the beeches on the uplands were wet with spring leaves, vibrant with growth.

John was not deliberately plant-collecting but his awareness of every small budding orchid, every flowering nettle, every thick clump of violets in purple, white and even pale blue, was not something that he could ever ignore. By the time he had ridden into Kent his hat band and his pockets were stuffed with shoots and soft damp trailing roots, and he felt himself wealthier than his own lord because he had ridden for days through a treasure chest of colour and freshness and life, and come home with his pockets stuffed with booty.

Meopham High Street wound up the little hill to the grey-stoned church set like a cherry on the top of a bun. To the right of it was the small farmhouse of the Day family, built near the church where Elizabeth's father had been vicar. There were fat hens in the yard, and the pleasing smell of roasted hops which always hung around the storeyards and the little oast house.

Elizabeth Day came out of the front door. 'I thought I heard a horse,' she said. She was dressed in sober grey and white, and had a plain cap on her head. 'Mr Tradescant, you are very welcome.'

John dismounted and led his horse to a stall.

'William will take his tack off if you wish,' she offered calmly.

It was a loaded question. 'If I may, I'll stay the night,' John said. 'William can take his saddle and bridle and turn him out to graze.'

She looked away to hide her pleasure. 'I'll tell William,' she said simply. 'Will you take a glass of ale? Were the roads bad?'

She led the way into the house. The wainscoted parlour was dark and cool after the bright sunshine. She left him for a moment while she fetched a tankard from the brew house. John looked out of the tiny thickly leaded window at the orchard.

The pink and white blossoms of the apple trees were bobbing above the white and pink daisies starring the cropped grass of the orchard. The family had neither the time nor the inclination to make a good garden before the house, though Elizabeth had the care of the kitchen and herb garden in the walled area outside the back door. Six years ago, when John had visited and confirmed his engagement, he had planted a little square of lavender with a bush of rue at each corner in the area before the window; but this was a working farm and no-one had the time to plan or weed an elaborate knot garden. He saw that the rue had gone straggly as if remembrance itself was wearing thin; but the lavender was looking well.

The door behind him opened and George Lance, her stepfather, came in.

'Good to see you, Tradescant,' he said.

Elizabeth brought them two mugs of ale and went quietly out of the room.

'I'm come to ask for the marriage to take place,' John announced abruptly. 'I've delayed too long.'

'You've not delayed too long for her,' George said defensively. 'She's a virgin still.'

'Too long for me,' John said. 'I'm impatient to start a family. I've waited long enough.'

'Still working for Sir Robert?'

John nodded. 'He's an earl now.'

'Still in favour?'

John nodded again. 'Never better.'

'Have you seen the new king?' George demanded. 'Is he a great man? I had heard that he is a fine man – a huntsman and a man of God, an educated man and a father of fine children. Just what the kingdom needs!'

John thought for a moment of the slack-mouthed lecher and the parade of pretty men who had come to Theobalds Palace a dozen times, the loud tempestuous Scots followers and the wanton drunken lechery of the new court.

'He is all kingly virtues, thank God,' he said carefully. 'And now the earl is secure in his place, and I in mine. There's a chance that the earl will have a new house, and I will have the ordering of the garden. I will be paid more, and I will be head gardener in a new garden to make all my own. At last I can offer Elizabeth a proper home.'

'Your pay?' George asked directly.

'Forty pounds a year, and a cottage to live in.'

'Well, she's been ready and waiting for six years,' George said. 'And she'll have what her father promised. A dowry of a fifty pounds,' and her clothes and some household goods. She'll be glad to go, I don't doubt. She and her mother don't always agree.'

'They quarrel?'

'Oh, no! Nothing to disturb a man's quiet,' George replied hastily. 'She'll make an obedient wife, I don't doubt. But two grown women and only one kitchen to order . . .' He broke off. 'It's sometimes hard to keep the peace. Shall you call the banns at the church here?'

John nodded. 'And I'll take a cottage for us in the village. I shall be between Theobalds and my lord's new house for some time. Elizabeth will like to be near her family when I am away. I shall have to travel abroad to seek trees and plants, as soon as Hatfield is ready. I am to go to the Low Countries and buy their bulbs, I am to go to France and buy their trees. I am planning an orangery where the tender trees can be reared in winter.'

'Yes, yes. Well, Elizabeth will want to know all about it.'

John was reminded that his new kindred had little interest in gardening. 'And I shall be paid a good wage,' he repeated.

George hesitated for a moment, looking at his future son-in-law. 'By God, you're a cool fish, Tradescant,' he said critically. 'Or have you been banging the ladies of the court all this time and only now thought of Elizabeth?'

John found himself flushing. 'No. You misunderstand me. I have always been intending to come for Elizabeth. It was always agreed that when I had enough money to buy a house, and a little land, then we would marry; and not before. I was not able to offer her a house before now.'

'Didn't you think you might chance it?' George asked curiously.

'And you and your wife?' John demanded, stung. 'How much of a chance did you take?'

It was a shrewd blow. The whole of Kent knew that his wife had come to him with a farm and a handsome fortune from her husband, Elizabeth's father, and a widow's jointure from the husband before that. George nodded abruptly and went to the door.

'Elizabeth!' George shouted into the hall, and then turned back to John. 'Shall you want to be on your own with her?'

John found himself suddenly embarrassed. 'I think so . . . perhaps . . . or you could stay?'

'Speak for yourself, man,' George said. 'It'll hardly come as a surprise!'

They heard her quick footsteps coming across the wooden floor of the hall. George went to meet her.

'Never fear!' he whispered. 'He has come for you at last. He has a good wage, and his future is secured. He's to buy a cottage here, in the village. He'll tell you himself. But you're to be a wife, Elizabeth.'

The colour rushed into her face and then drained away again. She nodded gravely, and stood for a moment in thought, her eyes downcast. She was saying a silent prayer of thanksgiving. There had been times in the long years of waiting that she had thought he had broken faith with her, and would not come. Then her head went up and she went with her quick steady steps to the parlour.

John was at the window again, looking at the apple trees. When she came in he turned. For a moment he saw not the grave Elizabeth in her sober Puritan dress; but little Cathy the serving maid in her mob cap with her gown cut low over her plump breasts, and her inviting smile. Then he put his hands out to Elizabeth, drew her to him and kissed her gently on the forehead.

'I can marry you,' he said, as if it were the conclusion to a business arrangement which had been tediously delayed.

'Thank you,' she said coolly. She wanted to tell him that she had been waiting for this moment ever since her father had come to her and folded her in his arms and said quietly: 'I have got you the gardener, my dear. You will be John Tradescant's wife as soon as he has saved enough to marry.' She wanted to tell him that in the nightmare summer when her little sister and then her father sickened of plague and then died, she had prayed every night for John Tradescant to come for her, like a hero in a romance, to take her away from the fear of sickness and from the depths of mourning. She wanted to tell him that she had waited and waited, while her mother put off her grief and gleefully remarried. That she waited while the newlyweds kissed before their fireside. That she waited though she thought he might never come, and that, with her father dead and a hard-hearted mother who used her labour and never paid her, there would be no-one to hold John Tradescant to his binding promise to marry.

She waited, in the end, because she was in the habit of waiting, because there was no escape from waiting, because there was nothing else she could do. Elizabeth was twenty-seven years old, no longer a girl in her first looks. She had been waiting for John for six long years.

'I hope you are glad?' John retreated to his place at the window. 'Yes,' she said carefully from her place at the door.

Three weeks later they were married at the parish church. They walked up the narrow path to the church door hand in hand; John could not stop himself noticing the yew trees, which were extraordinarily fine. One was growing like a castle with pretty pinnacle towers, the branches of the other fell like layers of cloth in a deep green dress. Elizabeth saw the direction of his gaze and smiled and patted his arm.

Her stepfather George Lance and Gertrude her mother were witnesses. Elizabeth wore a new gown of white, instead of her usual grey, and John wore a new suit of brown with white and crimson slashings in the sleeve. The sunlight through the stained-glass windows dappled the tiles on the floor with splashes of additional colour. John stood tall and made his responses in a firm voice, and felt with pleasure Elizabeth's little hand resting lightly on his arm.

There were those waiting outside the flint-walled church to see the couple who complained that the bridegroom was dressed too fine for a working man. They murmured that he was getting above his station and that the slashings in his sleeve were made of silk as if he thought himself to be a gentleman. But then the wedding ale at the back door of the farmhouse was strong and sweet, and the grumblings gave way to a roar of ribald jokes by mid-afternoon.

Gertrude had laid on a grand wedding dinner with three different sorts of cooked meats and half a dozen puddings. John found himself beside the vicar, the Reverend John Hoare, at the dinner table and took his compliments and accepted a toast and then tried to make stilted conversation.

'You serve a great lord,' the vicar commented.

John warmed at once. 'None greater.'

The Reverend Hoare smiled at his loyalty. 'And he has put you in charge of the gardens of his new palace?'

John nodded. 'He has done me that honour.'

'Will you have to live at Hatfield? Or shall you keep a house at Meopham?'

'I shall keep the house here,' John said. 'But I shall be much with my lord. My wife knows that his service must come first. Anyone who has the honour to serve a great man knows that his lord comes before everything.'

The vicar assented. 'The master comes before the man.'

'I wonder if you can tell me one thing though, vicar?' John asked.

The vicar at once looked cautious. These were not the times for theological enquiry. Sensible men confined themselves to the catechism and the commandments and left questions to heretics and papists who would have to pay with their lives if they got their answer wrong. 'What thing?' he asked.

'It puzzles me that God should have made so many things the same, and yet just a little different,' Tradescant confided. 'So many things He has made which are the same; but differ only in shape or in colour. And I cannot understand why He should make the difference. Nor how Eden can have looked, crammed with such –' he sought the word for a moment '– such diversity.'

'Surely every rose is the same,' the vicar replied. 'It differs only in colour. And a daisy is a daisy wherever it grows.'

John shook his head. 'You wouldn't say that if you had looked as closely as I. To be sure they have their families, a rose is still a rose, but there are hundreds of different kinds of roses,' he explained. 'Every county has a different sport. They have different shapes of petals, they have different numbers of petals, they have different preferences as to light and shade. Some are scented, they tell me, and some are not. And sometimes I think I see them being made. Making themselves while I watch, almost.'

'What d'you mean?'

'When they throw a sport, when from one main stem you can see another grow different, and if you take the different one you can breed another from it – God didn't make that, surely? I made it.'

The vicar shook his head but John went on. 'And daisies are not the same wherever they grow. I have seen a Kent daisy different from a Sussex daisy and a French daisy which was bigger and tipped with pink. I don't know how many daisies there are. A man would have to travel the whole world over with his eyes on his boots all the way to be sure. Why should such a thing be? Why should God make hundreds of the same thing?'

The vicar glanced around for rescue but nobody was looking his way. 'God in His wisdom gave us a world filled with variety,' he began.

He was relieved to see that Tradescant was not arguing. This was not a man who was quarrelsome in his cups. This was a man urgently in quest of a truth. The vicar had an odd sense of a man in search of his destiny. Tradescant was concentrating, passionately concentrating, with a deep line engraved between his brows as he listened to the vicar's answer. 'It was God's great wisdom to give us many things of great beauty. We cannot question His choice to give us many things which are only a little different, one from another, if you tell me that is how they are.'

Slowly John shook his head. 'I don't mean to question my God,' he said humbly. 'Any more than I would question my lord. It just seems odd to me. And God did not make all things at once in Eden, and give them to us. I know that cannot be, though I read it in the Bible, because I see them changing from season to season.'

The vicar nodded, quick to move on. 'That is no more than a craftsman making a table, I suppose. It is using the skills which God has given you and the materials which He has provided to make something new.'

John hesitated. 'But if I made a new daisy, say, or a new tulip, and a man came along and saw it growing in a garden, he would think it was the work of God and praise Him. But he would be wrong. It would have been my work.'

'Yours and God's,' the vicar said smoothly. 'For God made the parent tulip from which you made one of another colour. Undoubtedly it is God's purpose to give us many things of beauty, many things which are rare and different and strange. And it is our duty to thank Him and praise Him for them.'

John nodded at the mention of duty. 'It would be a man's duty to gather the varieties?' he asked.

The vicar drank a little wedding ale. 'It could be,' he said judiciously. 'Why would a man want to collect varieties?'

'To the glory of God,' John said simply. 'If it is God's purpose that we should know His greatness by the many varieties of plants that are in the world now, and that can be made, then it is to the glory of God to make sure that men know of His abundancy.'

The vicar thought for a moment, fearful of heresy. 'Yes,' he said cautiously. 'It must be God's will that we know of His abundancy, to help us to praise Him.'

'So a man making a garden, a fine garden, is like a man making a church,' John said earnestly. 'Showing men the glory of God as a stonemason might carve the glory of God into his pillars and gargoyles.'

The vicar smiled. 'Is that what you want to do, Tradescant?' he asked, seeing his way at last to the heart of it. 'Being a gardener and digging up weeds is not enough for you – it has to be something more?'

For a moment John might have disclaimed the idea, but the strong wedding ale was working on him and his pride in his work was powerful. 'Yes,' he admitted. 'It is what I want to do. My Lord Cecil's gardens are to his glory, to be a setting to his fine house, to show the world that he is a great lord. But the gardens are also a glory to God. To show every visitor that God has made abundant life, life in such variety that a man could spend all his days finding it and collecting it and still not see it all.'

'You have your life's task then!' the vicar said lightly, hoping to end the conversation. But John did not smile in return.

'I have indeed,' he said seriously.

At the end of the dinner Gertrude rose from the table and the ladies followed her lead. The serving girls stayed behind with the poorer

47

neighbours and drank themselves into a satisfying stupor. Elizabeth completed the last of the tasks in her old family home and waited for John in his turn to leave the dinner. At dusk he came away from the hall and the trestle tables and found her sitting at the kitchen table with the other women, waiting for him. He took his bride by the hand and they went down the hill a little way to their new cottage followed by a shouting, singing train of family and villagers.

In the cottage the women went upstairs first, and Elizabeth's cousins and half-sisters helped her out of her new white dress and into a nightdress of fine lawn. They brushed her dark hair and combed it into a fat plait. They pinned her cap on her head, and sprayed her with a little water of roses behind each ear. Then they waited with her in the little low-ceilinged bedroom until the shouts and snatches of song from the stair told them that the bridegroom had been made ready too and was come to his bride.

The door burst open and John was half-flung into the room by the joyous enthusiasm of the wedding party. He turned on them at once and pushed them out over the threshold. The women around Elizabeth's bed made false little cries of alarm and excitement.

'We'll warm the bed! We'll kiss the bride!' the men shouted as John barred their way at the door.

'I'll warm your backsides!' he threatened and turned to the women. 'Ladies?'

They fluttered like hens in a coop around Elizabeth, straightening her cap and kissing her cheek, but she brushed them off and they pattered to the door, ducking under John's arm as he held the door firmly. More than one woman shot a quick look at the gardener and the strength of his outstretched arm and thought that Elizabeth had done better than she could possibly have hoped for. John closed the door and shot the bolt on them all. The rowdiest hammered on the door in reply. 'Let us in! We want to drink your healths! We want to see Elizabeth to bed!'

'Go away! We'll drink our own healths!' he shouted back. 'And I shall bed my own wife!' He turned, laughing, from the door but the smile died from his face.

Elizabeth had risen from her bed and was kneeling at the foot, her head in her hands, praying.

Someone hammered on the door again. 'What are you going to plant, Gardener John?' they shouted. 'What seeds do you have in your sacks?'

John swore under his breath at their bawdy humour, and wondered that Elizabeth could stay so still and so quiet.

'Go away!' he shouted again. 'Your sport is over! Go and get drunk and leave us in peace!'

With relief he heard the clatter of their feet going downstairs.

'We'll be back in the morning to see the sheets!' he heard a voice shout. 'We expect stains, glorious red and white stains!'

'Roses and lilies!' shouted one wit. 'Red roses and white lilies in John Tradescant's flower bed!' There was a great guffaw at this sally, and then the front door of the cottage banged, and they were in the streets.

'Dig deep, Gardener John!' came the shout from the darkness outside. 'Plant well!'

John waited until he could hear the staggering footsteps go up the lane to the village's only ale house. Still Elizabeth knelt at the foot of the bed, her eyes closed, her face serene.

Hesitantly John kneeled down beside her, closed his eyes and composed himself for prayer. He thought first of the king – not the man he saw and knew, but the man he thought of when he said the word 'king' – a being halfway between earth and heaven, the fount of law, the source of justice, the father to his people. A man like the Lord Jesus, sent from God, directly from God, for the guidance and good ruling of his people. A man whose touch could heal, who could perform miracles, whose mantle covered the nation. 'God save the king,' Tradescant whispered devoutly.

Then he thought of his master, another man half-touched with divinity, a step lower than the king but so high in power that he must be, surely, especially favoured by God, and was in any case John's lord, a role of unique potency. John thought of the word 'lord' and had a sense of the holiness of it – Lord Jesus, Lord Cecil, both lords. But Cecil with his special trust in John, Cecil with his engaging child-size body and his cunning wise mind, was easy for John to bless in his prayers. John's lord, John's great love. Then his mind slipped at once to the old royal palace of Hatfield. Cecil would build a new house there, undoubtedly it would be a great house, and he would want a beautiful garden set around it. Perhaps an avenue . . . John had never planted an avenue. He lost the thread of his prayers altogether at the thought of the work of planting an avenue, and his great desire to see a double row of fine trees, limes, he thought longingly. They must be limes, there was nothing like lime for an avenue. 'God give me the skill to do it,' John whispered. 'And grant me, in Your mercy, enough saplings.'

Elizabeth was very close, kneeling beside him, he could feel the warmth of her body, he could hear the soft rhythm of her indrawn and exhaled breath. 'God bless us both,' John thought. 'And let us live in friendship and kindliness together.'

He did not expect more than friendship from Elizabeth, friendship and a lifelong partnership of indissoluble shared interest. Unbidden, the picture of Catherine with her dark eyes and low-cut bodice rose behind his eyelids. A man newly wedded to a girl like Catherine would not spend his bridal night on his knees praying.

John opened his eyes and got into bed. Still Elizabeth kneeled at the bedside, her head bowed, her lips moving. In sudden irritation, John leaned over and blew out his bedside candle. Darkness invaded the room. In the darkness and the quietness he felt, rather than saw, Elizabeth rise from her knees, pull her nightdress over her head, lift the sheets and slip in beside him, naked.

For a moment he was stunned at the frank sensuality of the gesture. That a woman could arise from prayer and strip herself naked confounded his simple division of women into good or bad, saintly or sexual. But she was his newly married wife and she had a right to lie beside him. John's desire rose at the glimpse of the moonlit body and he was sorry he had no light for the candle that he had blown out in a moment of temper and left himself in the dark.

They lay side by side on their backs.

'Like effigies on a tomb,' John thought, awkwardly.

It was for him to make the first move, but anxiety locked him into place. After years of avoiding sin and living in mortal terror of sexual temptation which would lead to pregnancy and disgrace, John was unprepared for the free embrace of a willing partner.

His hand strayed towards her side of the bed and encountered the unmistakable solidity of her thigh. The skin was as smooth as the fruit of an apple, but yielding, like a ripe plum. Elizabeth said nothing. John stroked her thigh with the back of his hand like a man brushing the soft foliage of a scented plant. He rather feared she might be praying again.

Cautiously he moved his hand up her thigh to the round warm mound of her belly, the navel set in the flesh like a little duckpond in a hill. Up these new mysterious byways John's hand slowly went, one breast – and he heard her little indrawn breath as his hand moved across the soft rolling crest of her breast and took into its keeping the tender warm nipple which immediately hardened under his touch. He moved towards her, and heard that little gasp once more which was not quite alarm, and yet not quite welcoming. He raised himself up so that he was above her. In the moonlight he could see her face, her eyes resolutely shut, her mouth expressionless, as she had looked when she was praying. He bent his head and kissed her on the lips. She was warm and soft; but she lay completely still, as if she were asleep.

John stroked gently down her belly and beyond and found the downy softness of the hair between her legs. As he touched her she turned her head to one side, but still she did not open her eyes or stir. Gently he pressed his knee against her thigh and slowly, she opened her legs to him. Feeling like a king coming in to his kingdom, John moved across in the bed and lay between the legs of his wife, started to ease forward, started to know the power of his desire.

There was a sudden rush and a clatter of mud and stones against the window.

'God's wounds! What's that?' John exclaimed in alarm. 'Fire?'

In one swift sinuous movement Elizabeth was out of bed, her gown clutched to her heavy swinging breasts, peering out of the window into the darkness of the village street.

'Are you done, John?' came a jovial beery yell. 'Sowed your seeds, have you?'

'God's blood, I shall murder them!' John exclaimed, dashing his nightcap to the floor.

Slowly Elizabeth put her nightgown to one side and came back to bed beside him. At last she spoke to him, the first words she spoke in their bedroom, the first words she said naked before him: 'Never take the Lord's name in vain, husband. It is His own commandment. I want our house to walk in His ways.'

John flung himself back on the bed, deserted by desire, as soft as a gelding. 'I shall sleep,' he declared sulkily. 'And then I shall avoid offending you.' He humped all the bedclothes around him, turned his back on her and closed his eyes. 'You can pray again if you like,' he added spitefully.

Elizabeth, robbed of the blankets, lay in silence on the cool sheet, humiliatingly naked, her new nightgown spread across her breasts and belly. Only when she heard his breathing deepen and she was certain that he was asleep did she move close to his broad back and wind her arms around his sleeping body, pressing her cold nakedness against him. She wept a little before she finally fell asleep. But she did not wish her words unsaid.

June 1607

Next day, before Elizabeth had done more than stir the fire in the new grate and set the morning porridge on to heat, there was a knock on the door and a messenger from the earl.

'His Grace wants you in London,' the man said shortly.

Elizabeth glanced at her new husband, half-expecting him to refuse, but John was already seated in his chair at the fireside pulling on his riding boots.

The man doffed his hat to her but looked beyond her to John. 'At the docks,' he said. 'You're to meet him at Gravesend.'

Another swift bow and he was gone. Cecil's servants were not encouraged to linger and gossip. The common belief was that Cecil had ears everywhere and an indiscreet servant would not last long.

Elizabeth took John's travelling cloak from the press where she had laid it in lavender. She had thought then that it was worth protecting it against moths for months of storage.

'When will you be back?' she asked quietly.

'I can't say,' John replied briskly.

Elizabeth flinched at the coldness of his tone. 'Am I to join you at Hatfield?' she asked. 'Or come to Theobalds?'

He looked at her and saw the coat she was holding for him. 'I thank you,' he said courteously. 'I'll send you word. I don't know what is happening, I don't know what he wants me for. These are dangerous times for him. I must go at once.'

Elizabeth felt her village-based view of the world shudder under the weight of great events which would now impinge on her life. 'I didn't think these were dangerous times. How are they dangerous?'

He glanced at her quickly, as if her ignorance surprised him. 'All times are dangerous to men with great power,' he explained. 'My lord is the greatest in the land. Every day he faces one danger or another. If he sends for me I go without question and I make no plans other than his will.'

Elizabeth nodded. There was no arguing with a man's duty to follow his lord.

'I'll wait till I hear from you then,' she said.

John kissed her forehead in that passionless meaningless gesture which seemed to have started with their betrothal and hung over them still. Elizabeth curbed her impulse to turn up her face and kiss him on the lips. If he did not want to kiss her, if he did not want to lie with her, then it was not the part of a good wife to complain. She would have to wait. She would have to do her duty by him, as he did his by his lord.

'Thank you,' John said, as if she had obliged him in some little courtesy, and went out to saddle his horse, mounted the animal and rode him from the back of the cottage to the village street. Elizabeth was at the doorway, her head high; none of the village gossips would know that her husband was leaving her as virginal as she had been on her wedding day.

John doffed his hat to her, conscious also of the dozens of watching windows. He did not lean down to kiss her, nor did he offer one word of assurance or comfort. Seated high on his horse he looked down on the pale face of the wife he was leaving without bedding and knew himself to be behaving badly, with his duty as an excuse as well as an obligation. 'Farewell,' he said shortly, and turned his horse and rode briskly out at a trot. The knowledge of his unkindness to a woman who, wedding night or no, mother-naked or clothed, had said no more than she had every right to say, and who, before that accursed interruption, had laid warm and pleasant to his touch, galled him all the way along the lanes going north to Gravesend.

He met his master at the quayside, at the docks of the East India Company, the air rich with the smell of cinnamon and spices and loud with the curses of the dockers.

A merchant welcomed them on board his ship at the gangplank.

'Follow me,' he said and led them between the sailmakers and the rope chandlers to the captain's cabin. 'A glass of wine?' he offered.

The earl and his gardener nodded.

'I have some curious roots,' he said when they had a glass each. 'I bought them for their weight in gold because I knew that a man such as yourself, Your Grace, would pay much more for them.'

'And what are they?' the earl asked.

The merchant opened a wooden box. 'I have kept them dry and sweet, and hidden from the light as Mr Tradescant advised me.'

He held out a handful of woody twisted roots, brown, with a dusty earth still clinging to them. The earl took them gingerly and handed them to John.

'They are the roots of flowers of exceeding fineness,' the merchant said rapidly, his eyes on Cecil's impartial face. 'Roots of course, Your Grace, never look well. But in the hands of your gardener you could bring these on to flower in great profusion . . .'

'And what is the flower like?' John asked.

'Like a geranium,' the merchant said. 'And the leaves are sweet, like geranium leaves. But much finer, a quite extraordinary blossom.'

Cecil raised an eyebrow at John. John made a small shrug of his shoulders. They looked like the roots of a geranium but with neither leaf nor flower no-one could tell. They would have to be bought on trust. 'Anything else?' Cecil asked.

'These.' The merchant pulled a little hessian purse from the bottom of the box and opened it. Inside were fat green globes as large as a bantam's egg with hard little spines all over.

'A new chestnut,' the merchant promised. Gently he prised open one of the shells, and spilled, into John's cupped palm, a bold round handsome nut, dappled like a brown roan horse in light and dark brown, with a paler grey and brown circle at the top. John caressed the moist inside casing of the shell, turned the nut in the light to see the sheen on it. Bigger than a walnut, shinier than mahogany, it was a delightful nut, a great jewel of a nut, a brown warm pearl.

'Where did you get these?' John could not keep the quiver of excitement from his voice.

'Turkey,' the merchant said. 'And I saw the tree that gave this fruit.'

'Can you eat them?' Cecil asked.

The man hesitated for that single half-moment which reveals a lie. 'Surely,' he said. 'They are chestnuts, after all. And they are a powerful medicine. The man that sold them to me says they use them for curing broken-winded horses. They mend the lungs of horses, perhaps of men too.'

'Is the leaf the same as our chestnut?' John asked.

'Bigger,' the merchant replied. 'And spreading. And the trees are massive round trees, better-shaped than ours, like a great ball on a stick. And when they are in flower they are covered all over with huge white cones of flowers, as big as both your hands. White blossoms and the tongues of the flowers are speckled with pink.' He thought for a moment. The price would depend on his description. 'Like apple blossom,' he said at once. 'White and pink together like apple blossom, but in a great shape like a cone.'

John fought to keep the excitement from his voice. 'Great trees? What height?'

The man waved his hand. 'As big as a full-grown oak. Not tall like a fir but broad and tall, like a big oak tree.'

'And the wood?' Cecil interrupted, thinking of the nation's insatiable demand for timber for shipbuilding.

'Fine wood,' the merchant said quickly. Too quickly for truth, Cecil thought. 'Though I did not see it myself, they tell me the wood is very fine.'

'How many?' John asked, his eyes on the box, but he kept the chestnut in his hand. 'How many do you have?'

'Only half a dozen,' the merchant said seductively. 'Just six. And that's the only six in the whole of the kingdom, the only six outside Turkey. The only six in Christendom. For you to own, Your Grace; for you to grow, Mr Tradescant.'

'Anything else?' Cecil asked nonchalantly.

'These seeds,' the merchant said, and showed a little purse filled with hard black seeds. 'Of rare flowers.'

'What flowers?' John asked. The nut was warm and smooth and comforting in his hand. He thought he could almost feel the life enfolded inside it, like a new-laid egg.

'Rare beauties, like lilies,' the merchant said.

Tradescant looked doubtful. Lilies grew from corms, not little seeds. He suddenly doubted the merchant, and his fingers closed tightly. At least the beauty and promise of the nut could not lie.

'How much?' Cecil asked. 'For the roots, the seeds and the chestnuts?'

The merchant looked quickly from the gardener to the master, and read, correctly, the speechless desire in Tradescant's face. 'Fifty pounds.'

Cecil choked. 'For a handful of wood?'

The merchant smiled and nodded at Tradescant. Cecil followed his gaze and was forced to laugh. John was turning the chestnut over and over in his hand, unaware of the two men. He looked besotted.

'It is a treasure beyond price to a gardener,' the merchant said. 'A new tree. A completely new tree, which blooms like a rose and stands as broad as an oak.'

'Eight pounds now, and eight pounds if the tree grows,' the earl said gruffly. 'You may come to me next spring and if it has rooted I shall pay you the remainder. If it is a fine tree in five years with flowers like apple blossoms and broad as an oak I shall pay another eight then.'

'Perhaps nine,' the merchant said thoughtfully.

'No more than nine,' the earl said, and got to his feet. 'Nine now, and nine if it roots, and nine in five years if it is good.'

'I shall take these to Theobalds at once,' John said, emerging from his trance. He still had hold of the chestnut. The merchant put the roots and seeds back in the box and handed them to him.

'I thought you were newly wed?' Cecil commented.

'A wife can wait,' John said firmly. 'But I should like to see these well-planted and well-nursed. And the chestnut tree nuts should be in warm damp soil at once, unless –' He broke off and looked at the merchant. 'Is it cold there, in winter?'

The man shrugged. 'I have only been in the spring.'

Cecil laughed shortly and led the way down the gangplank to the quayside.

John followed him, and then called back up to the ship as the thought struck him. 'Do the leaves turn colour in autumn? Or does it keep fresh and green all the year round?'

'How should I know?' the merchant called back. 'I've never been there in autumn. Why does it matter to you? You'll see soon enough when it grows.'

'So that I know when to plant, of course!' John shouted irritably. 'If it grows all the year around then I can plant any time, best in the summer. But if it loses its leaves and its seeds in winter then it should be planted into cold ground!'

The merchant shrugged his shoulders and laughed. 'I will ask when I go back! And if they do not take then I will get you some more! At double the price next time!'

Cecil had walked away limping on the cobbles. Tradescant ran to catch up with him.

'You really must learn a little cunning, Tradescant,' Cecil complained. 'If you are to travel and to buy for me you must learn to barter and hide your desire. Your face is as open as a book of receipts.'

'I am sorry, my lord. But I couldn't be indifferent.'

'They will cheat you from Flushing to Dresden.'

'I will learn world-weariness,' John promised. 'I shall cultivate it. I shall be as weary as a Scotsman with a small bribe.'

Cecil laughed shortly. 'Do you come in my boat across the river? I'm going to Whitehall.'

John looked down the quayside to where the earl's boat was gently rocking, the oars upright in salute, the bright colours of the liveried boatman reflected in the clean water of the Thames.

'I'll take a horse to Theobalds,' he said. 'And get these planted up at once.'

'And then go back to your wife,' Cecil called up to the quayside as he went down the steps to his waiting boat. 'Take a few days to spend with her, Tradescant. You must dig your own garden too, you know.'

At Meopham, Elizabeth was waiting for John again.

'Married only a day and left already,' her mother said sharply. 'I hope you did not do something to give him a distaste for you, Elizabeth?'

Elizabeth smoothed a loose strand of hair under her cap. 'Of course not,' she said levelly. 'He was summoned by the earl himself, he could hardly send a message back and say he would not go!'

'And was the bedding properly done?' Gertrude asked in an undertone. 'You will not hold him to the marriage if he can argue that the work was not undertaken or carried through.'

'Of course. And he does not wish to withdraw from the marriage. He was summoned away to his lord. He sent me a message from London. I expect him back every day.'

'The sheets were hardly marked at all,' Gertrude pointed out.

Elizabeth flushed. She had resorted to strawberry jam on the bed linen. It was the tradition that the newlyweds' sheets be put to air over their windowsill so that the neighbours and the community might be assured that a marriage had been made and consummated and was now indissoluble. Not even people of the class of Elizabeth and John could escape public scrutiny.

'They were marked enough,' Elizabeth said.

'Oh, well!' Gertrude sat back in the hard chair and looked around the little parlour. 'He has left you comfortably, at least. As long as he provides for you I daresay you will not miss him, having been a spinster so long.'

'He will provide for me, and he will return to me,' Elizabeth replied calmly. 'He had to go to Theobalds with some new plants for the earl. But I expect his return any day.'

'You'd have done better to marry a farmer!' Gertrude gave a malicious little laugh. 'Better a little mud on your parlour floor than a husband who leaves you the very morning after you are wed.'

'Better to be married to a man high in the favour of the Earl Cecil himself than to be a woman who knows nothing beyond the hills of her home!' Elizabeth flared up.

'Do you mean me, you saucy miss!' Gertrude exclaimed, leaping to her feet. 'For I shall not be insulted by you. Your stepfather shall hear of it! And he will make you sorry for your impertinence! I shall send him down here after he's had his dinner and he will tell you what we think of impertinent spinsters, married a night and abandoned the next day! You'll be lucky if your husband ever comes home at all!

I shall see you at my back door wanting your own bed back, I don't doubt it!'

Elizabeth strode to the door and flung it open. 'I am not a miss, saucy or otherwise,' she declared. 'And my stepfather has no rights over me any more and neither do you. I do not have to listen to you, and I certainly don't have to obey him. My father would not have used me so!'

'Easy to say!' Gertrude retorted. 'Since he is not here to contradict you!'

'He would not contradict me,' Elizabeth rejoined. 'He was like me. The faithful kind: we love and stay loyal. We don't flit from one to another like a drunk bee.'

The reference to her mother's four marriages could not be borne. Gertrude flounced to the door. 'Well, I thank you, Mrs Tradescant!' she spat. 'I shall go home to my husband at my fireside, and enjoy company and good cheer. We will drink and be merry. And I shall sleep in a warm bed with the man who loves me! And I daresay you wish you could say the same!'

Elizabeth waited until Gertrude was on her way and then she flung the door shut with a crack which sounded down the length of the street to mark her defiance. But when she was quite sure that Gertrude was gone, and not returning for a final retort, she dropped to her knees on the hearthrug, put her face on the empty seat of the master chair and cried for John.

August 1607

He did not come until late in the summer, nor did he send for her to go to Theobalds. He did not send her so much as a note to tell her that he was delayed – absorbed in the work of replanting and maintaining the most beautiful garden in England. First it was the newly designed knot gardens which took his attention. The continuous twist of hedging was much harder to keep cut than the old straight lines, and inside the box hedges the lavender had flourished too strongly. Now it needed cutting back so that it did not thrust wands of navy blue out of their place; but at least Cecil agreed that the softness of their shape and the spiky azure flowers had added beauty to the geometric precision of the garden and that Tradescant should plant other shrubs inside the hedging.

Then the bathing pools in the marble temple turned green in the hot weather, and he had them drained and scrubbed with salt and rinsed clean and refilled. Then the kitchen gardens started fruiting, first strawberries, then raspberries, gooseberries, peaches, and apricots. It was not until the currants came into season that John took time from his work to borrow a horse and ride down the dusty lanes to his home in Kent.

He took two of the new chestnuts in his pocket, still shining from the polishing he continually gave them. Of the six in the merchant's box he had planted two in large pots and left them in a shady place in the garden, watering them gently every day from the dish placed underneath the pot to encourage their roots to grow down. Two he had kept in a net hung high out of the way of rats in his shed, planning that they should feel the heat of the summer on their glossy backs before he planted them in autumn, when the weeds died back and before the first frosts came, hoping to mimic the trees' natural time for growth. Two he carried in the safe darkness of his pocket, planning to plant them in spring in case they needed to be hidden from frost and to feel the warmth of a new season and the damp richness of the spring earth to make them flourish. He thought he should have left them in a stone box in the darkness and coldness of the floor of the marble bath house but he could not resist their smooth round shapes, tucked in his waistcoat. A dozen times a day his fingers found their way into the little pocket to caress them like a broody hen turning over two precious eggs.

He buttoned down the flaps with care when he mounted his horse.

'I shall stay some weeks with my wife,' he said to the gardener's lad who held the horse. 'You can send for me, if I am needed. Otherwise I shall come home at the end of September.' He did not notice he had called Theobalds 'home'. 'And have a care that you keep the gates shut,' he reminded the boy, 'and weed the grass every day. But do not touch the roses, I shall be back in time to see to them myself. You may take the heads off when they are finished flowering, and take the petals to the still room, but that is all.'

It was a two-day journey to Meopham. John enjoyed travelling through the Surrey countryside where the hayfields were showing green again after the rain, and where the wheat stooks stood high in the field. Horsemen cantered past him, covering him in blinding clouds of dust; he sometimes rode alongside great wagons and could hitch his horse behind, taking a seat with the driver for a rest from the saddle and a sup of the driver's ale. There were many people walking the roads: artisans on the tramp looking for work, harvesting gangs at the end of their season, apple-pickers making their way to Kent like John, gypsies, a travelling fair, a wandering preacher ready to set up at any crossroads and preach a gospel which needed neither church nor bishops, pedlars waddling beneath the weight of their packs, goose girls driving their flocks to the London markets, beggars, paupers, and sturdy vagrants forced away from parish to parish, bullocks being driven to Smithfield by swearing, anxious cattle drovers.

In the inn at night John ate at an 'ordinary', the daily dinner with a set price which humble travelling men preferred, but he paid extra to sleep alone. He did not want to appear before Elizabeth scratching with another man's fleas.

At the long dining table in the inn's front room the talk was of the new king, who could not agree with Parliament although he had been in the kingdom only four years. The men dining at table were mostly on the side of the king. He had the charm of novelty and the glamour of royalty. So what if Parliament complained of the Scots nobles who hung around the court, and so what if the king was extravagant? The king of England could afford a little luxury, surely to God! And besides, the man had a family to support, a brace of princes and princesses, how else should he live but well? One man at the table had suffered at the hands of the Court of Wards and claimed that no man's fortune was safe from a king who would take orphans into his keeping and farm out their fortunes among his friends, but he gained little sympathy. The complaint was an old one, and the king was new and novelty was a pleasure.

John kept his head down over his mutton and kept his own counsel. When someone shouted for a toast to His Majesty, John rose to his feet as swiftly as any man. He was not disposed to gossip about the painted women and painted boys of court, and besides, no man who had worked for Robert Cecil would ever voice a dangerous political opinion in a public place.

'I care nothing if we have no parliament!' a man exclaimed. 'What have they ever done for me? If King James, God bless him, can do without a parliament – why! then so can I!'

John thought of his master, who believed that a monarch could only rule by a combination of bluff and seduction to gain the consent of the people, and whose watchword was practice not principle, kept silent, touched the chestnuts in his waistcoat pocket for luck, took up his hat and went from the room to his solitary bed.

He arrived at Meopham at noon and nearly turned into the courtyard of the Days' family farmhouse, before he recalled that he should find Elizabeth in her new cottage – in their new cottage. He rode back down the mud track of the village street and then skirted around to the back of the little house where there was a lean-to shed and a patch of ground for his horse. He took off its saddle and bridle and turned the animal into the field. It raised its head and whinnied at the strangeness of the place and he saw Elizabeth's face at an upstairs window, looking out at the noise.

As he walked towards the little cottage's back gate he heard her running down the wooden stairs and then the back door burst open and she was racing towards him. As she suddenly recollected her dignity, she skidded to an abrupt halt. 'Oh! Mr Tradescant!' she said. 'I should have killed a chicken if I had known you were coming today.'

John stepped forward and took her hands and kissed her, formal as ever, on her forehead. 'I did not know what time I should arrive,' he said. 'The roads were better than I thought they would be.'

'Have you come from Theobalds?'

'I left the day before yesterday.'

'And is everything well?'

'It is.' He glanced down at her and saw that her usually pale face was rosy and smiling. 'You look very well . . . wife.'

She peeped up at him from under her severe white cap. 'I am well,' she said. 'And very happy to see you. The days are rather long here.'

'Why?' John asked. 'I should have thought you would have much to do in a house of your own at last?'

'Because I am used to running a farmhouse,' she said. 'With care for the still room, and the laundry, and the mending, and the feeding of the family and all the farm workers, and the health of the staff, the herb garden and the kitchen garden too! Here all I have to look after is two bedrooms and a kitchen and parlour. I have not enough to do.'

'Oh.' John was genuinely surprised. 'I had not thought.'

'But I have started on a garden,' she said shyly. 'I thought you might like it.'

She pointed to a level area of ground outside the back door. The ground was marked out with pegs and twines into a square shape containing the serpentine twists of a maze. 'I was going to make it with chalk stones and flints in patterns of black and white,' she said. 'I don't think anything tender will thrive because of the chickens.'

'You can't have chickens in a knot garden,' John said decidedly.

She chuckled and John looked down and saw with surprise that rosy happy face again. 'Well, we have to have chickens for their eggs and for your dinner,' she said. 'So you must think of a way that chickens can be kept out.'

John laughed. 'At Theobalds I am plagued with deer!' he said. 'It seems very hard that in my own garden I shall still have pests to come and spoil my plants.'

'Perhaps we could get another plot of land for the chickens,' she suggested. 'And fence this off so that you might grow whatever you wish.'

John glanced down at the overworked light brown soil and the nearby midden. 'It is hardly the ideal place,' he said.

At once he saw the colour and the happiness drain from her face. She looked weary. 'Not after Theobalds Palace, I suppose.'

'Elizabeth!' he exclaimed. 'I did not mean . . .'

She turned away from him and was leading the way into the cottage.

He stepped after her and was about to take her hand but some stupid shyness checked the movement. 'Elizabeth!' he said more gently.

She hesitated, but she did not turn. 'I was afraid you were never coming back,' she whispered. 'I was afraid that you had married me to fulfil the agreement, and to get my dowry, and that you would never come back to me at all.'

'Of course! Of course I would come back!' He was astounded at her. 'I married you in good faith! Of course I would come back!'

She dipped her head down and then pulled up her apron to rub at her eyes. Still she did not turn around to him. 'You did not write,' she said softly. 'And it has been two months.'

Now it was he who turned away. He looked away from the house, over the little plot where his horse grazed, and towards the hill where the square-towered church pointed up at the sky. 'I know,' he said shortly. 'I meant to . . .'

She raised her head but still she did not turn around. He thought they must look a pair of fools, back to back in their own yard instead of in each other's arms.

'Why did you not?' she asked softly.

He cleared his throat to hide his embarrassment. 'I cannot write very fair,' he said awkwardly. 'That is to say, I cannot write at all. I can read a bit, I can reckon very swiftly, but I cannot write. And anyway . . . I should not know what to say.'

She turned to him; but in his embarrassment, he did not see her. He was digging the heel of his riding boot into the corner of her little square of hen-scratched dust.

'What would you have said, if you had written?' she asked and her voice was very soft and tempting. It was a voice which a man would turn to and rest upon. John resisted the temptation to spin on his heel, snatch her up and bury his face in her neck.

'I would have said I was sorry,' he confessed gruffly. 'Sorry to have been ill-tempered on our wedding night, and sorry that I had to leave you that very morning. When I was angry with them for making a noise I had thought that we would have the next day in peace, and that anything troublesome could be mended then. I had thought to wake early in the morning and love you then. But then the message came and I went up to London and there was no way of telling you that I was sorry.'

Hesitantly she stepped forward and put a hand on his shoulder.

'I am sorry too,' she said simply. 'I thought these things were easier for men. I thought that you were doing just exactly what you wished. I thought that you had not bedded me because . . .' her voice became choked and she ended in a thin whisper '. . . because you have an aversion to me, and that you went back to Theobalds to avoid me.'

John spun around and snatched his wife to his heart. 'I do not!' He felt her whole frame convulse with a deep sob. 'I do not have an aversion!'

She was warm in his arms and her skin was soft. He kissed her face and her wet eyelids, and her smooth sweet neck and the dimples of her collarbone at the neck of her gown, and suddenly he felt desire sweep over him as easy and as natural as a spring rainstorm across a field of grass. He scooped her up and carried her into the house and kicked the door shut behind him, and he laid her down on the hearthrug before the little spinster's fire where she had sat, alone and lonely, for so many evenings, and loved her until it grew dark outside and only the firelight illuminated their enfolded bodies.

'I do *not* have an aversion to you,' he said.

At suppertime they rose from the floor, chilled and uncomfortable. 'I have some bread and cheese and a broth,' Elizabeth said.

'Whatever you have in the larder will do for me,' John replied. 'I'll fetch some wood for the fire.'

'I'll run up the road to my mother's house and borrow a jug of beefstock,' she said, pulling her grey gown on over her head. She turned her back to him and offered him the ties on her white apron. 'I'll only be a moment.'

'Give them my good wishes,' John said. 'I'll call up and see them tomorrow.'

'We could go up to the house for supper,' she suggested. 'They would be glad to see you tonight.'

'I have other plans for tonight,' John said with a meaning smile. Elizabeth felt herself warm through with the intensity of her blush. 'Oh.' She recovered herself. 'I'll get the beefstock then.'

John nodded and listened to her quick step down the brick path and out into the main street. He stacked the fireplace with a liberal supply of logs and then went out through the back yard to the little field to see to his horse. When he came back Elizabeth was stirring a pot hung on a chain from the spit, and there was bread and new cheese on the table and two jugs of small ale.

'I brought my book,' she said carefully. 'I thought you might like us to look at it, together.'

'What book?'

'My lesson book,' she said. 'My father taught me to read and write and I did my writing in this book. It has clean pages in it still. I thought, if you wished, I might teach you.'

For a moment John was going to rebuff her; the idea of a wife teaching her husband anything was contrary to the laws of nature and of God; but she looked very sweet and very young. Her hair was tumbled and her cap was slightly askew. Lying on his cape on the floor of the little cottage she had been tender and ready to be pleased, and at the end, openly passionate. He found he did not feel much like supporting the laws of God and nature; instead he found that he was rather disposed to oblige her. Besides, it would be good to know how to read and write.

'D'you know how to write in French?' he asked. 'And Latin words?'

'Yes,' she said. 'Do you want to learn French?'

'I can speak French, and a bit of Italian, and enough German to see that my lord is not cheated when I am buying plants for him from a sea captain. And I know some plant names in Latin. But I never learned to write any of it down.'

Her face was illuminated with her smile. 'I can teach you.'

'All right,' he said. 'But you must tell no-one.'

Her gaze was open and honest. 'Of course not. It shall be between the two of us, as everything else will be.'

That night they made love again in the warmth and comfort of the big bed. Elizabeth, free from her fear that he did not love her, and discovering a sensuality which she had not imagined, clung to him and wrapped her arms and legs around him and sobbed for pleasure. Then they wrapped their blankets around their shoulders and sat side by side on the bed and looked out at the deep blue of the night sky and the sharp whiteness of the thousands of stars.

The village was all quiet, not one light showed. The road away from the village, north to Gravesend and London, was empty and silent, ghostly in the starlight. An owl hooted, quartering the fields on silent wings. John reached for his waistcoat folded on the chest at the foot of the bed.

'I have something I should like to give you,' he said quietly. 'I think it is perhaps the most valuable thing I own. Perhaps you will think it foolish; but if you would like it, I should like to give it to you.'

His hand closed over one of the precious chestnuts. 'If you do not like it I will keep it, by your leave,' he said. 'It is not really mine to give away, it is entrusted to me.'

Elizabeth lay back on the pillow, her hair spread as brown and as glossy as his chestnut. 'What is it?' she asked, smiling. 'You sound like a child in the schoolyard.'

'It is precious to me . . .'

'Then it is precious to me too, whatever it may be,' she said.

He brought his clenched fist out of his waistcoat pocket and she put her hand out flat, waiting for him to open his fingers.

'There are only six of these in the country,' he said. 'Perhaps only six in the whole of Europe. I have five in my keeping and, if you like, you may have the sixth.'

He dropped the heavy nut like a round smooth marble into her hand.

'What is it?'

'It is a chestnut.'

'It is too big and too round!'

'A new chestnut. The man who sold it to me told me that it grows into a great tree, like our chestnut tree, but it flowers like a rose, the colour of apple blossom. And this great nut comes only one to a pod, not two nuts to a pod like ours, and the pod is not prickly like our chestnuts but waxy and green with a few sharp spines. He sold it to my lord for nine pounds down, and another eighteen pounds if it grows. And I shall give this one to you.'

Elizabeth turned the nut over in her hand. It nestled heavily in her palm, its brown glossy colour dark against her callused hand.

'Shall I plant it in the garden?'

John instantly flinched, thinking of the voracious chickens. 'Put it in a pot, somewhere that you can easily watch it,' he said. 'In soil with some muck well stirred in. Water it from the base of the pot with a little water every day. Perhaps it will grow for you.'

'Shall you not regret giving me this precious nut, if it fails for me?'

John closed her fingers around the nut. 'It is yours,' he said gently.

'Do with it as you will. Perhaps you will be lucky. Perhaps together, now that we are married, we shall be lucky together.'

John stayed a full month at Meopham with his wife, and when the time came for him to go back to Theobalds a number of innovations had been made. She had a pretty little miniature knot garden outside the back door, incongruously planted with leeks, beets, carrots and onions and fenced with rooted willow twigs woven into a dwarf living fence against the marauding chickens. He could both read and write a fair-enough script, the chestnut was in a pot on the windowsill showing a pale snout above the earth, and Elizabeth was expecting their child.

Summer 1608

'The boy should be called George, for his grandfather,' Gertrude remarked. She was seated in the best chair in Elizabeth's parlour. The wooden crib stood beside the open window, and John, leaning against the windowsill, was rocking it gently with his foot and looking down into the sleeping face of the baby. He was a dark-skinned child, with black hair as thick as John's own. When he was awake his eyes were a deep periwinkle blue. John kept his foot nudging the crib, repressing the desire to lift his son to his face and smell again his haunting smell of spilled milk and sweet buttercream skin.

'George David, for his grandfather and godfather,' Gertrude said. She glanced sideways at John. 'Unless you wish to call him Robert and see if the earl can be persuaded to take an interest in him?'

John gazed out into the garden. The little vegetable knot garden was doing well and this spring he had added another square beside it, planted with herbs for strewing, for medicines, and for cooking. There was now a withy hurdle penning Elizabeth's hens into the far end of the garden with wormwood planted around it to hide the fencing, to give them shade, and to prevent fowlpest.

'Or we might call him James in a compliment to His Majesty,' Gertrude went on. 'Though it will do him little good, I suppose. We could call him Henry Charles for the two princes. But they say Prince Charles is a sickly boy. D'you ever see him at Theobalds, John?'

She glanced up to John, who had leaned out of the window and was thoughtfully weighing a flowerpot in his hand. Poking from the moist earth was a whippy slim stem crowned with a little hand of green leaves.

'Oh! that eternal pot! Every day Elizabeth sighs over it as if it were worth its weight in gold! I told her! No twig in the world is worth that sort of attention! But I was asking you – John – d'you ever see Prince Charles at Theobalds? I heard he was sickly?'

'He's not strong,' John replied, putting the chestnut tree gently on the windowsill. 'They say he is much better since he came from Scotland. But I rarely see him. The king does not keep his family by him. When he comes hunting, he comes with only his most intimate circle.'

Gertrude leaned forward, avid for gossip. 'And are they as bad as everyone says? I've heard that the king adores the Duke of Rochester, that he loads him with pearls, that the duke rules the king and the king rules the kingdom!'

'I wouldn't know,' John said unhelpfully. 'I'm just the gardener.'

'But you must *see* them!'

John thought of the last visit of the king. He had come without his wife Anne, who now never travelled with him. She was completely replaced by his young men. John had seen him walking in the garden with his arm around the Duke of Rochester's waist. They had sat together in the arbour and the king had rested his head on the duke's shoulder, like a country girl mooning over a blacksmith. When they kissed, the court turned aside and pretended to be busy about its own concerns. No-one pried, no-one condemned. The young Duke of Rochester was the favourite of everyone who wanted to be the favourite of the king. A whole court was formed around his handsome lithe figure. A whole morality was lightly constructed around the king's love for him that permitted any sort of display, any sort of drunkenness.

At night the duke went openly to his bed in the king's room. The king was said to be afraid of assassination and it soothed him to sleep with a companion, but there were loud groans of pleasure from the inner chamber and the repetitive squeaking of the royal bed.

'They go out hunting, I weed the paths,' John said unhelpfully.

'I hear the queen misses him and pines for him, and has become a Papist for consolation . . .'

John shrugged.

'And what of the children, the royal princes and princesses?'

John looked deliberately vague. He was disinclined to gossip and in any case he had seen more than enough of the royal princes and princess. Princess Mary was only a baby and not yet at court but Prince Henry, the heir and the darling of the whole court, was an arrogant boy whose charm could be blown away in a moment's rage. His sister, Elizabeth, had all the Tudor temper and all the Tudor hastiness, and poor little Prince Charles, the second surplus heir, the rickety-legged runt of the litter, ran behind his stronger, older, more attractive siblings all the day, breathless with his weak chest, stammering with his tied tongue, longing for them to turn and pay him attention.

They never did. They were courted beloved spoiled children, the first children of four kingdoms, and they had no time for him. John would see them boating on the lake or riding across the park and never looking back as poor little Charles struggled to keep up.

'I scarcely see Their Highnesses,' he said.

'Oh, well!' Gertrude leaped to her feet in frustration. 'Tell Elizabeth I called in to wish her well. I'm surprised she is not downstairs by now. Tell her that I said she should stir herself. And tell her that the baby should be called George David.'

'No, I don't think so,' John said in the same quiet tone of voice.

'What?'

'I will not tell her any of that. And you shall not tell her either.'

'I beg your pardon?'

John smiled his easy smile. 'Elizabeth shall stay in bed until she is well again,' he said. 'We were lucky not to lose her. It was a hard birth for her, and she was hurt inside. She shall rest as long as she wants. And we won't be calling the child George or Robert or James or Charles or Henry or David. He'll be John, after my grandfather, and after my father, and me.'

Gertrude flounced towards the door. 'It's very dull!' she exclaimed. 'You should save your name for another child. The first child should be named in such a way as to encourage a sponsor!'

John's smile never wavered but his face was dark with regret. 'There won't be another child,' he said. 'There will only ever be this one. So we will name him as we wish, and he will be John Tradescant, and I will teach him how to garden.'

Gertrude paused. 'Not another child?' she asked. 'How can you say such a thing?'

He nodded. 'I called the apothecary from Gravesend. He said that she could not manage another birth, so we shall only ever have this, our son.'

Gertrude came back into the room and looked again into the cradle, shocked out of her normal irritability. 'But John,' she said softly. 'To have to pin all your hopes on just one child! No-one to bear your name but just the one! And everything to be lost if you lose him!'

John rubbed his face as if he would rub away his scowl of pain. He leaned over the cradle. The baby's sleeping fists were as tiny as rosebuds, his dark hair a little crown of fluff around his head. A tiny pulse like a vulnerable heart beat at the centre of his skull. John felt a deep passion of tenderness so powerful that his very bones seemed to melt inside him.

'It's as well I am used to growing rarities,' he murmured. 'I have not a dozen little seedlings to watch, I shall never have more than this one. I just have this one precious little bud. I shall nurse him up as if he was a new flower, a rarity.'

January 1610

'It is done.' Robert Cecil found Tradescant on his knees in the Theobalds knot garden. 'I was looking for you. The king wants to call Theobalds his own this year. We are to leave.'

John rose to his feet and rubbed the cold earth from his hands.

'What are you doing?' the earl asked.

'Relaying the white stones,' John said. 'The frost disturbs them, throws up dirt and spoils the pattern.'

'Leave it,' he ordered peremptorily. 'The king's gardeners can worry about it now. He wants it, he has pressed me for it, he hinted a hundred thousand different ways, and Rochester pushed him on every time he might have stopped. I've fended him off for three years but now I've given it to him, God damn it. And now he's happy, and Rochester is happy, and I have Hatfield.'

Tradescant nodded, his eyes on his master's face. 'You shall make me a splendid garden there,' Robert Cecil said rapidly, as if he was almost afraid of John's calm silence. 'You shall go abroad and buy me all sorts of rarities. How are the chestnuts coming along? We will take them with us. You shall take anything you want from the gardens here, take them with us and we shall start again at Hatfield . . .'

He broke off. Still John watched him, saying nothing.

The most powerful man in England, second only to the king himself, took two hasty steps away from his gardener and then turned back to face him. 'John, I could weep like a babe,' he confessed.

John slowly nodded. 'So could I.'

The earl held out his arms and John stepped into them and the two men, the one so slight and twisted, the other so broad and strong, wrapped each other in a deep firm hug. Then they broke apart, Cecil rubbing his eyes on the sleeve of his rich jacket while John cleared his throat with a harsh cough. John offered his arm and Cecil took help and leaned on his man. The two of them walked from the knot garden side by side.

'The bath house!' the earl said quietly. 'I'll never manage anything like it at Hatfield.'

'And the tulips I've just put in! And snowdrops, and lenten lilies!'

'You've planted bulbs?'

'Hundreds last autumn, for a show this spring.'

'We'll dig them up and take them with us!'

John shook his head in silent disagreement but said nothing. They walked slowly towards the ornamental mount. A stream played beside the path on a bed of white marble pebbles. John hesitated. 'Let's walk up,' the earl said.

Slowly the two men followed the twisting path. John had pruned the rambling roses which bordered the path on either side and they lay flat and tidy like withy fencing. Cecil paused for breath, and to ease the pain of his lame leg, John put his arm around his master's waist and held him steady. 'Go on,' Cecil said and they walked slowly side by side round and round the little hill. There were a few foolishly early buds on the roses; John noticed the deep crimson of new shoots, red as wine. At the top of the hill there was a round lovers' seat, with a fountain plashing in the middle. Tradescant swung his cape down for his master to sit, and the earl nodded for John to sit beside him, as an equal.

The two men looked out across the palace gardens spread below them like a tapestry map. 'Those woods!' the earl mourned. 'The trees we have planted.'

'The bluebells underneath them in springtime,' John reminded him.

'The orchards, my peach-tree wall!'

'And the courts!' Tradescant nodded at the smooth grass laid out in every courtyard of the rambling palace. 'There isn't grass like that anywhere else in the kingdom. Not a weed in it, and the mowing team trained to go to half an inch.'

'I don't see any mud in the knot garden,' Robert Cecil remarked, looking at the garden as it was meant to be viewed – from on high.

'There isn't any *now*,' John said with rare impatience. 'Because I've been washing the stones in freezing water all morning.'

'I shall be sorry to lose the hunting,' the earl said.

'I shan't miss the deer eating my young shoots in spring.'

The earl shook his head. 'You know they say that this is the fairest garden in England? And the greatest palace? That there never was and never will be a palace and garden to match it?'

John nodded. 'I know.'

'I couldn't keep it,' the earl said. 'It's his revenge on my father for the execution of his mother, you know. He wanted to take my own father's house, his pride and his joy. What could I say? I hedged and twisted and turned and showed him other men's houses. It's my own fault. We built it too grand and too beautiful, my father and I. It was bound to draw out envy.'

John shrugged. 'It is all the king's,' he said simply. 'The whole country. And each of us is nothing more than his steward. If he wants anything, we have to give it.'

The earl threw him a curious sideways glance. 'You really believe that, don't you?'

John nodded, his face open and guileless. 'He is the king under God. I would no more refuse him than I would skip my prayers.'

'Please God he always has subjects as loyal as you.'

'Amen.'

'Leave washing the stones now and start preparing the plants for moving, and dig up those damned bulbs.' The earl got to his feet with a grunt of discomfort. 'My bones ache in this cold weather.'

'I'll leave the bulbs,' John replied.

The earl raised an eyebrow.

'You've given him the house and the grounds,' John said. 'I can be generous too. Let the king have these tulips in spring and I shall go myself to the Lowlands to buy you a fine crop for Hatfield, as we planned. We can make a new garden at Hatfield, we don't have to scrump from here.'

'A lordly gesture from a gardener?' Cecil asked, smiling.

'I have my grander moments,' John said.

Hatfield House in Hertfordshire had been the home and the prison of the young Elizabeth during the dangerous years of her half-sister's rule, when she had been a studious girl with a deep fear of the executioner's axe. It had been Robert Cecil's father who had come to her in the garden to tell her that she was now queen.

'I'll keep the tree she was sitting under,' Robert Cecil said to Tradescant as they surveyed the quagmire the workmen had made in the building of the huge new house. 'But I'm damned if I'll do anything with that poky little hall. It can't have been impressive even when it was new-built. I'm not surprised the queen was in the garden. Nowhere else to sit.'

'If you cut away all around it so that it stood on a hill instead of so low, you could make it into a banqueting hall for summer, or a masquing theatre . . .'

The earl shook his head. 'Leave it. An extra hall with its own kitchen and stables is always useful if someone important comes with a big entourage. Come and see the new house!'

He led the way up the garden, John following him slowly, looking everywhere with his quick perceptive glance. 'Fine trees,' he remarked.

'They can stay,' the earl said. 'Mountain Jennings does the park and a Frenchman has designed the garden. But you plant it.'

John suppressed an instant, unworthy pang of envy. 'I'd rather plant a garden than design it anyway.'

'You know it comes to the same thing after the first summer,' Cecil said. 'The Frenchman goes back to Paris, and you have a free hand then. Anything you don't like, you can tell me it has died – I'm not likely to know.'

John chuckled. 'I can't see me lasting long in your employ if I kill off your plantings, my lord,' he said.

The earl smiled. 'Never mind the plants, what about the new house?'

It was a large stately house, not as big as Theobalds, which was built as a palace and had sprawled to become a village, but it was a grand beautiful house in the new style, fit to display the staggering wealth of the Cecils, fit to welcome the prodigal luxury of the Jacobean court, fit to take its place as a great display house of Europe.

'Surrounded by great courts on every side,' the earl pointed. 'A hundred rooms, separate kitchen and bake house altogether. I tell you, John, it has cost me nigh on thirty thousand pounds for the house alone, and I expect to spend as much again on the park and gardens.'

John gulped. 'You'll be ruined!' he said bluntly.

The earl shook his head. 'The king is a generous master to those who serve him well,' he said. 'And even to those who serve him ill,' he added.

'But sixty thousand pounds!'

The earl chuckled. 'My money,' he said grimly. 'My show house, and in the end my grand funeral. What else should I do with it but spend it on what I love? And what a garden we will make, won't we, John? Do you want me to scrimp on the plantings?'

John felt his excitement rising. 'Have you the plans?'

'Over here.' The earl led the way to a little outhouse, his boots squelching in the mud. 'As soon as the workmen have finished you can sow grass here, get the place clean.'

'Yes, my lord,' John said automatically, looking at the plans spread out on the table inside.

'There!' Cecil exclaimed.

John leaned over. The parkland was so immense that the grand house, drawn to scale, showed as nothing more than a little box in the centre. He ran his eye over the gardens. All the courts were to be planted with different flowers, each with their own ornate knot garden in different patterns. There was to be a great walk of espaliered fruit trees, and a grand water feature of a river running along a terrace edged with seats and planted with tender fruit trees in tubs. The water for the terrace was to be fed from a gigantic fountain splashing from a copper statue standing on a great rock. Further away from the house were to be wooded walks and orchards, a bowling green, and a mountain large enough to ride a horse up a winding path to the top.

'Will this ease your homesickness for Theobalds?' Cecil asked jokingly.

'It will ease mine,' John replied, looking at the magnitude of the plan and thinking, his imagination whirling, of how he would ever get the thousands of fruit trees, where he would buy the millions of plants. 'Will it ease yours, my lord?'

The earl shrugged. 'The service of a king is never easy, John. Don't forget that. No true servant of a king ever sleeps well at night. I shall miss my old house.' He turned back to the plan. 'But this will keep us busy into our old age, don't you think?'

'This will keep us busy forever!' John exclaimed. 'Where am I to get a thousand golden carp from for your water parterre?'

'Oh!' Cecil said negligently. 'Ask around, John. You can find a hundred pairs, surely! And they will breed if they are well kept, I don't fear it!'

John chuckled reluctantly. 'I know you don't fear it, my lord. That is to be my job.'

Cecil beamed at him. 'It is!' he said. 'And they are rerooting a fine cottage for you here, and I shall pay you an increase. How much did I promise you?'

'Forty pounds a year, sir,' John replied.

'Call it fifty then,' the earl said genially. 'Why not? I'm hardly going to notice it with the rest of these bills to pay.'

Summer 1610

John decided that Elizabeth and Baby J should remain at Meopham while he was travelling in Europe to buy the earl's trees. Elizabeth protested that she wanted to live in the new cottage in Hertfordshire, but John was firm.

'If Baby J should be ill, or you yourself sick, then there is no-one there who would care for you,' he said in the last days of August, while he planned and packed his clothes for the journey.

'There's no-one here in Meopham who would care for me,' she said inaccurately.

'Your whole family is here, cousins, sisters, aunts, and your mother.'

'I can't see Gertrude wasting much time on my comfort!'

John nodded. 'Maybe not. But she would do her duty by you. She would make sure that you had a fire and water and food. Whereas at Hatfield I know no-one but the workmen. Not even the house staff are fully at work yet. The place is still half-built.'

'They must be finished soon!'

John was incapable of explaining the scale of the project. 'It looks as if they could build for a dozen years and never be done!' he said. 'They have the roof on now, at least, and the walls complete. But all the inside fittings, the floors, the windows, there is all that to do. And the panelling is yet to come, there are hundreds of carpenters and woodcarvers on site! I tell you, Elizabeth, he is building a little town there, in the middle of a hundred meadows. And I must plant the meadows and turn them into a great garden!'

'Don't sound so overawed!' Elizabeth said affectionately. 'You know you are as excited as a child!'

John smiled, acknowledging the truth. 'But I fear for him,' he confided. 'It is a great task he has taken on. I can't see how he can bear the cost of it. And he is buying property in London too, and then selling it on. I fear he will overstretch himself and if he gets into debt –' He broke off. Not even to Elizabeth would he trust the details of Cecil's business arrangements, the bribes routinely taken, the Treasury money diverted, the men bankrupted by the king one day on charges of treason or offences against the Crown whose estates were bought up by his first minister at knockdown prices the next.

'They say he is an engrosser,' Elizabeth remarked. 'Not a wood or a common is safe from his fences. He takes it all to himself.'

'It is his own,' John said stoutly. 'He takes what is his by right. Only the king is above him, and God above him.'

Elizabeth gave him a sceptical look but kept her thoughts to herself. She was too much like her father – a clergyman of stoutly independent Protestantism – to accept John's spiritual hierarchy which led from God in heaven down to the poorest pauper with each man in his place, and the king and the earl a small step down from the angels.

'I fear for myself too,' John said. 'He has given me a purse of gold and ordered me to buy and buy. I am afraid of being cheated, and I am afraid of shipping these plants so far. He wants a garden all at once, so I should buy plants as large and fruitful as I can get. But I am sure that little sturdy ones might travel better!'

'There's no-one in the kingdom better able than you,' Elizabeth said encouragingly. 'And he knows it. I just wish I might come with you. Are you not afraid to go alone?'

John shook his head. 'I've longed to travel ever since I was a boy,' he said. 'And my work for my lord has tempted me every time I go down to the docks and speak to the men who have sailed far overseas. The things they have seen! And they can bring back only the tiniest part of it. If I might go to India with them or even Turkey, just think what rarities I might bring home.'

She watched him, frowning slightly. 'You would not want to go so far, surely?'

John put his arm around her waist to reassure her, but could not bring himself to lie. 'We are a nation of travellers,' he said. 'The finest of the lords, my lord's friends, are all men who seek their fortunes over the seas, who see the seas as their highway. My lord himself invests in every other voyage out of London. We are too great a nation with too many people to be kept to the one island.'

Elizabeth was a woman from a village that counted the men who were lost to the sea, and tried to keep them on the land. 'You don't think of leaving England?'

'Oh, no,' John said. 'But I don't fear to travel.'

'I don't know how you can bear to leave us for so long!' she complained. 'And Baby J will be so changed by the time you come back.'

John nodded. 'You must note down every new thing he says so that you can remember to tell me when I return,' he said. 'And let him plant those cuttings I brought for him. They are his lordship's favourite pinks, and they smell very sweet. They should grow well here. Let him dig the hole himself and set them in, I showed him how to do it this afternoon.'

'I know.' Elizabeth had watched from the window as her husband and her quick dark-eyed dark-haired son had kneeled side by side by the little plot of earth and dug together, John straining to understand the rapid babble of babytalk, Baby J looking up into his father's face and repeating the sound until between guesswork and faith they could understand each other.

'Dig!' Baby J insisted, thrusting a little trowel into the earth.

'Dig,' his father agreed. 'And now we put these little fellows into their beds.'

'Dig!' Baby J insisted again.

'Not here!' John said warningly. 'They need to rest quiet here so that they can grow and make pretty flowers for Mama!'

'Dig! J want dig!'

'Not dig!' John replied, descending rapidly to equal stubbornness.

'Dig!'

'No!'

'Dig!'

'No! Elizabeth! Come and take your son out of this! He is going

83

to destroy these before they even know they've been transplanted!'

She had come from the house and swept Baby J up, and taken him down to the end of the garden to pet Daddy's horse.

'I don't know that he will make a gardener,' she warned. 'You should not count on it.'

'He understands the importance of deep digging,' John said firmly. 'Everything else will follow.'

Autumn 1610

John set sail in September, and experienced a rough and frightening crossing after waiting for four dull days off Gravesend for a southerly wind. He landed in Flushing and hired a large flat-bottomed canal boat so that he could stop at every farm and enquire what they had to sell, all the way down the canal to Delft. To his relief the canal boatman spoke English even though his accent was as strong as any Cornishman. The boat was drawn by an amiable sleepy horse which wandered along the tow path and grazed on the lush banks during John's frequent halts. He found farmers of flowers whose whole trade consisted of nothing but the famous tulips, and whose whole fortune rested on being able to produce and then reproduce the new colours of blooms. They were farms like John had never seen before. Row upon row of floppy-leaved stalks were tended by women wearing huge wooden clogs against the rich sandy soil, and big white hats against the sun, working their way down the rows with an implement like a wooden spoon, gently lifting the smooth round bulbs from the ground and laying them softly down, and the cart coming along behind to gather them all up.

John watched them. Each set of leaves which had grown from one bulb now had a cluster of three, perhaps even four, bulbs at the end of their white stems. Most of them even carried fat buds at the head where the petals had been and when the women spotted them, and they never missed one however long he watched, they cut them off and popped them in their apron pockets. Where one valuable bulb had been set in the ground and flowered there were now four,

85

and maybe three dozen seeds as well. A man could quadruple his investment in one year for no more labour than keeping the field free of weeds and digging up his capital in the autumn.

'Profitable business,' John remarked enviously under his breath, thinking of the price he paid for tulips in England.

At every canalside market town he had the boatman tie up and wait for him on board, sometimes for hours, sometimes for days, as he wandered around the market gardens and picked out a well-shaped tree, a sack of common bulbs, a purse full of seeds. Wherever he could, he bought in bulk, haunted by the thought of the rich green commonland and meadows around Hatfield waiting for forests and plantations and mazes and orchards. Wherever he could find someone who could speak English and had the appearance of an honourable man, he made a contract with him to send on more plants to England as they matured.

'A great planting scheme,' one of the Dutch farmers commented.

John smiled but his forehead was creased with worry. 'The greatest,' he said.

Despite his rooted belief that Englishmen were the best of the world, and England undeniably the best country, John could not help but be impressed with the labour these people had put into their land. Each canal bank was maintained as smartly as each town doorstep. They took a pleasure and a pride in things being just so. And their rewards were towns which exuded wealth and a land which was interlaced with an efficient transport system that put the potholed roads of England to shame.

The dykes that held back the shifting sands and the high waves of the North Sea were a wonder to John, who had seen the feckless neglect of the marshes and waterlogged estuaries of the Fens and East Anglia. He had not thought it was possible to do anything with land soured by salt, but he saw the Dutch farmers had learned the way of it and were making use of land that an Englishman would call waste ground and abandon it as hopeless. John thought of the harbours and inlets and boggy places all around the coast, even in land-hungry Kent and Essex, and how in England they were left to lie fallow, steeped in salt, whereas in Holland they were banked off from the sea and growing green.

He could not help but admire their labour and their skill, and he could not help but envy the Dutch prosperity. There was no hunger in the Holland Provinces, and basic fare was rich and good. They ate cheese on buttered bread, a double helping of richness and fat, and did not think twice about it. Their cows grazed knee-deep in lush wet pastureland and gave abundant milk. They were a people who saw themselves as divinely rewarded for their struggle against the Papist Spanish, and John, idling down the narrow canals, looking left and right for plants and flowers tucked away in the moist grasses, had to agree that the Protestant God was a generous one to this, His favoured people.

When they reached The Hague, Tradescant sent the loaded barge back with instructions to ship all the plants directly to England. He stood on the stone wharf and watched the swaying heads of trees glide slowly away. Some of the cherry trees were bearing fruit and he saw, with irritation, that once they were beyond hailing distance the bargee picked a handful and ate them, spitting the stones carelessly into the glassy water of the canal.

In Flanders he bought vines, and watched them pruned of their yellow leaves and thick black grapes in preparation for their journey. He ordered their roots to be wrapped in damp sacking and plunged into old wine casks for their voyage home. He sent a message ahead of them, in the careful script which Elizabeth had taught him, so that a gardener from Hatfield would meet them with a cart on the dockside, to take them back and heel them in the same day, without fail, making sure to water them religiously at dawn every day until Tradescant came home.

The Prince of Orange's gardener admitted Tradescant to the beautiful garden behind the palace of The Hague and showed him around. It was a garden in the grand European style, with large stone colonnades and broad sweeping walks. Tradescant spoke to him of his work at Theobalds, planting between the box hedges and replacing the coloured stones of the knot garden with lavender. The gardener nodded with enthusiasm and showed Tradescant his version of the changing style in a little garden at the side of the palace where he had used tidily pruned lavender for the hedges themselves. They made a softer pattern and had more variation of colour than the usual box hedge. They did not harbour insects and when a woman passed by, her skirts brushed against the leaves and released a cloud of perfume. When he left, Tradescant had a trayful of rooted cuttings and a letter of introduction to the great physic garden at Leiden.

He travelled overland to Rotterdam, uncomfortable on a big broad-backed horse, all the way seeking out English-speaking farmers who could tell him about the growing of their precious tulips. In the darkened cellars of ale houses, drinking a rich sweet beer which was new to John, called 'thick beer', they swore that the new colours entered into the heart of the flowers by slicing into the very heart of the bulb.

'Does it not weaken them?' John asked.

The men shook their heads. 'It helps them to split,' one of them volunteered. He leaned forward and breathed a blast of raw onion into John's face. 'To spawn. And then what do you have?'

John shook his head.

'Two, where you had one before! If they are of another colour, and the colour often enters at the split, then you have made a fortune a thousand times over. But if they are the same colour but have doubled, then you have doubled your fortune at the least.'

John nodded. 'It is like a miracle,' he said. 'You cannot help but double your fortune every year.'

The man sat back in his seat and beamed. 'And it's more than double,' he confirmed. 'The prices are steadily rising. People are ready to pay more and more each year.' He scratched his broad belly with quiet satisfaction. 'I shall have a handsome house in Amsterdam before I retire,' he predicted. 'And all from my tulips.'

'I shall buy from you,' John promised.

'You have to come to the auction,' the man said firmly. 'I don't sell privately. You will have to bid against the others.'

John hesitated. An auction in a foreign country in a language he did not understand was almost bound to drive up the price. One of the other growers leaned forward.

'You have to,' he said simply. 'The market for tulips is all agreed. It has to be done in the colleges, in the appointed way. You cannot buy without posting a bid. That way we all know how much is being made on each colour.'

'I just want to buy some flowers,' John protested. 'I don't want to post a bid in the colleges, I don't understand how it is done. I just want some flowers.'

The first grower shook his head. 'It may be just flowers to you, but it's trade to us. We are traders and we have formed a college and we buy and sell in each other's view. That way we know what prices are being charged, that way we can watch the prices rise. And not be left behind.'

'Prices are rising so fast?' John asked.

The grower beamed and dipped his face into his great mug of ale. 'No-one knows how high it can go,' he said. 'No-one knows. If I were you I would swallow my English pride and go to the college and post my bid and buy now. It will be dearer next season, and dearer the year after that.'

John glanced around the ale house. The growers were all nodding, not with a salesman's desire for a deal but with the quiet confidence of men who are in an irresistibly rising market.

'I'll take a dozen sacks of plain reds and yellows,' John decided. 'Where is this college?'

The grower smiled. 'Right here,' he said. 'We don't leave our dinner table for anything.' He took a clean dinner plate, and scribbled a price on it and pushed the plate across to John. The man at John's elbow dug him in the ribs and whispered, 'That's high. Knock off a dozen guilders at least.'

John amended the price and pushed it back, the man rubbed the number off and wrote his own total. John agreed and the plate was posted on a hook on the wall of the room. The grower extended a callused hand.

'That's all?' John queried, shaking it.

'That's all,' the man said. 'Business done in the open where everyone can see the posted price. Fairly done and well done, and no harm to either bidder or seller.'

John nodded.

'A pleasure to do business with you, Mr Tradescant,' said the grower.

The tulips were delivered to John's inn the next day and he sent them off with a courier under strict orders that they were not to be out of his sight until he had put them into the Hatfield wagon at London dock. He also sent a letter to Meopham with his love and a kiss for Baby J, and news that he was going on to Paris.

It was as he sealed the letter and put it into the hands of the courier that John knew that he was a traveller indeed. He did not fear the strangeness of Europe, he had a deep intoxicating sense that he might hire a horse here and then exchange it for another, and then another, and then another, and ride all the way across Europe, through the heart of Papist Spain and even on to Africa. He was an islander no more, he had become a traveller.

He watched the barge carrying his precious tulips slip away down the canal and turned back to the inn. The horse was waiting, saddled for him, he had paid his slate, his travelling pack was ready. John swung his thick cape around his shoulders, heaved himself into the saddle and set the horse's head for the west gate.

'Where are you headed?' one of the tulip growers called to him, seeing a good customer departing.

'To Paris,' John called back and nearly laughed at his own sense of excitement. 'I'm to visit the gardens of the French king. And I am buying more plants. I need even more. I think I shall buy up half of Europe.'

The man laughed and waved him on and John's horse, its metal shoes ringing on the cobblestones, stepped delicately out on to the highway.

The roads were good to the frontier and then they deteriorated into a mud track riddled with potholes. John kept a sharp look out for great forests with a chateau set among the trees and when he saw newly planted drives he turned off the road and went to find the French gardener to discover where he got his trees from. If he found a good supplier of rare trees he placed an order with him to lift a hundred of them when the weather turned colder and they could be safely moved and sent on to Hatfield. For the great Earl Cecil himself.

As John drew nearer to Paris the woods became thinner except for the preserved forests for hunting, and then the road became lined with little farmhouses and market gardens to feed the insatiable appetite of the city. From his vantage point on horseback John overlooked garden and órchard walls and constantly surveyed what the French gardeners were growing. As a man from Kent he could afford to despise the quality of their apples but he envied the size and ripeness of their plum trees and stopped half a dozen times to buy specimens of what looked like new varieties.

He entered Paris with an entourage following him like a travelling garden, two wagons loaded with swaying leaves, and he had to find an inn that was accustomed to great baggage trains where he could pack up his new purchases and send them on to England.

As soon as they were safely despatched John called for a laundress to wash and starch his clothes, to clean the dust from his cape so that he might use his letter of introduction to the French king's own gardener, the famous Jean Robin.

Robin had heard of Tradescant and was desperate for news of the new great palace and gardens at Hatfield. Of course it would be in the French style, it was to be designed by a Frenchman, but what of the woods, what of the walks? And what did Tradescant think of the prices of tulips, were they rising or would they hold steady for another year? How high could the price of a bulb go anyway? Surely there must be a point where a man would pay no higher?

Tradescant and Jean Robin walked around the royal garden for a couple of hours and then retired for a grand dinner enhanced by several bottles of claret from the royal cellar. Jean Robin's son joined them for the meal, washing the mud from the garden off his hands before he sat down and bowed his head for a Papist grace. Tradescant shifted uneasily in his seat while the ritual Latin was spoken but when the young man broke bread he could not help but smile.

'I hope that my son too will follow me into my place,' John said. 'He's only a baby now, but I will bring him up to my work and – who knows?'

'A man who holds a craft should pass it on,' Jean Robin said, speaking slowly for John's benefit. 'But when it is a garden which takes so long to fruit, then you are planting for your son and his sons anyway. It is a fine thing to say to a boy, look out for this tree and when it is grown this high, I want it pruned like that. To know that the garden lives on, and your work and plans for it will live on, even after you are long dead.'

'It is a poor man's posterity,' John said thoughtfully.

'I should want no other than to leave a beautiful garden,' Jean Robin declared. He smiled at his son. 'And what an inheritance for a young man!'

When they parted, a week later, they had sworn eternal friendship in the brotherhood of gardeners, and Tradescant was loaded with trays of cuttings, purses of seeds, and dozens of roots and saplings.

'And where d'you go now?' Robin demanded at a final farewell dinner.

John knew an instant temptation to say that he was going on to Spain, that he would ride slowly down the country ways and collect a plant from every roadside verge. 'Home,' he said, in his halting French. 'Home and my wife.'

Robin clapped him on the back. 'And the new garden at Hatfield,' he said, as if there was no doubt which was the most important.

John arrived back at Meopham in December to kiss Elizabeth and make his peace with Baby J, who was angry at being neglected. He had brought Baby J a little wooden soldier, carved by a Frenchman and dressed in the uniform of the king's personal guard. Baby J was talking clearly now and very firm in his opinions. He particularly disapproved of John's return to Elizabeth's bed.

'That's my place,' he stated flatly, glaring at his father in the early hours of John's first day at home. John, who had planned to make love to Elizabeth when they woke, was rather taken aback by the unmistakable enmity in his son's little face.

'This is my bed,' John said reasonably. 'And my wife.'

'She's my mother!' Baby J shouted and launched himself at his father.

John caught the little fists and tucked the writhing, angry body under his arm. 'Hey day! What's this? I'm home now, Baby J, and this is my place.'

Elizabeth smiled at the two of them. 'He's been the man of the house for three months, John, you stayed away too long.'

John bent his face down to his little son's wriggling body and smacked a kiss on his bare stomach. 'He'll learn to love me again,' he said. 'I shall stay till Twelfth Night.'

Elizabeth did not protest, she was learning that the lord's garden came before everything, but she swept out of bed in a way which made her feelings very plain. John let her go, his eyes on his son's bright little face.

'One time I shall take you with me,' he promised. 'It's not that I'm in your place here – you should be sharing my place with me.' He nodded to the window which overlooked the village street but he meant the wider world, beyond the lanes to London, beyond even London. He meant Europe, he meant Africa, he meant the East.

Spring 1611

John stayed for little more than three weeks at Meopham, long enough to get under Elizabeth's feet in the little cottage and to make his peace with his son, before hiring another cart and driver and travelling down the mud-filled, almost impassable roads to Dorset, seeking more trees for sale: apple trees for the orchard, cherry, pear, quince, plum. Trees for the park: oak, rowan, birch, beech.

'Wherever will you get them all from?' Elizabeth wondered, bringing him his well-darned travelling cloak and packing a basket of food under the seat of the wagon.

'I shall buy them from the orchards,' John said determinedly. 'They sell apples by the dozen, why not trees?'

'And the wild trees for the earl's park?'

'I shall take them,' John said recklessly. 'From every forest I pass on my way. I shall be going through the New Forest, every sapling I see I shall stop and dig up.'

'You will be hanged for certain!' Elizabeth exclaimed. 'You will be hauled before the verderers' courts and hanged for damaging the royal chase.'

'How else am I to find my lord's trees?' John demanded. 'How else am I to do it?'

John travelled around England and brought back his swaying whispering carts filled with the bushy heads of trees. They came to know

94

him on the West Road, and when children saw him coming into a town with his carts rumbling behind him they would run to the well to fetch a bucket to water Mr Tradescant's trees.

The great house was nearly finished and the gardens were slowly shaping according to the master plan. There had only been one long delay when the workmen had run short of money, and even the great Cecil coffers had run dry. John had feared for his lord then, feared that the cost of the house and the cost of the garden had overstretched him, as everyone had warned that it would. John sensed, but did not know, that there were enemies on every side at court who might bow to and flatter the Secretary of State now, but at the least sign of weakness would pull him down like a pack of hounds upon an old stag. Just as the rumours got out that Cecil had overreached himself and would fail, there was more money delivered to the builders, and more money at the goldsmiths' in the little provincial towns for John to draw on to buy his trees.

'How did you manage it?' John asked Cecil. 'Have you sold your soul, my lord?'

Cecil's smile was grim. 'All but,' he said. 'I sold every other property I owned, and borrowed on the rest. But I had to have my house, John. And we had to have our garden.'

John first laboured on the acres which faced the house, especially the huge knot garden below the terrace where the earl had his private rooms. Each path leading from the house was precisely aligned to the windows of the private rooms so that Cecil, looking out, would always see a vista of straight lines, running outwards to the distant horizon. Tradescant, breaking with tradition, planted different edging plants at each junction of the outward path so the colour of the hedges melted and grew paler as the eye was drawn further and further from the house. At each crossroads was a little statue, an aid to meditation on the fleeting nature of life and the vanity of wishes.

'I might as well have put up a moneylender's sign,' Cecil said dourly to John when they walked the new paths, and John grinned.

'You were warned, my lord,' he said lovingly. 'But you would have your own way.'

'And are you telling me I was wrong?' Cecil asked with a dark upwards gleam at the taller man.

Tradescant shook his head. 'Not I! It was a great venture. And grandly carried out. And still much to do.'

'You have given me a great gift,' the earl said thoughtfully. They climbed the steps to the stone terrace, Cecil heaving his lame leg, refusing to take help, John beside him, his hands pushed deep into his pockets to prevent him reaching out and holding his master's arm. They gained the top of the terrace and Cecil gave John a quick glance which thanked him for his forbearance.

'Walk with me,' he said.

The two men strolled side by side on the new paving stone, and looked down on the patterns of the twisting beds of the knot garden. 'You have given me a great gift because every year it will grow more lovely. Most gifts are consumed in the first weeks, like young love. But you have given me a gift which will be here long after we are both gone.'

John nodded. The sky above them was soft and grey; only in the west was there a line of rosy cloud where the sun had gone. An owl called in the wood and then they saw its pale shape drift across the new orchard in the distance where the land fell away down to the valley.

The earl smiled. 'Sometimes I think the greatest thing that I ever did for England was to set you to work, my John. Nothing in my life gives me more joy.'

Tradescant waited. Often these days, the earl was disinclined to talk and would walk in silence with his gardener through the slowly emerging shapes of the garden and park. His work was daily growing more arduous; the power of the favourites around the king was undiminished, the problems of the court profligacy greater than ever. The fashion for masques now dominated at court and every occasion was marked with a catastrophically expensive play: written, composed, designed and produced in one night, and completely forgotten the next. Every court favourite, the women as well as the men, had to have a costume blazing with jewels, every important role had to arrive in a chariot or depart with fireworks.

King James had inherited a fortune with the throne of England. The legendary meanness of the old queen had served the country extraordinarily well. Her father had left her a throne with two sources of revenue: the steady flow of money from the sale of places at court, favours, and civic jobs, and the rare bounties voted in taxes by an agreeable Parliament. The balance was a delicate one. Tax the wealth of the industries too sharply and the merchants, traders, and bankers would complain. Go cap in hand to Parliament too often and the country squires who sat there would buy control of royal policy. Only by scrimping on every expenditure, by borrowing, by insisting on constant gifts and by downright out-and-out corruption, had the Tudor King Henry and his daughter Elizabeth amassed a fortune for themselves, and a steady reliable prosperity for their kingdoms. The almighty theft of the Roman Catholic church possessions had started the process, but Tudor charm and Tudor guile had continued it.

King James was new to this process but he had Cecil and half a hundred others to advise him. The earl had thought that the new king, who had previously managed hand-to-mouth in cold castles in a poor kingdom, would show all of the family's legendary parsimony and have no experience of their love of show.

But it was a habit quickly learned. James, new-come to one of the richest thrones in Europe, could see no reason why he should not have everything he desired. The money from the royal treasury poured out in fountains over the new favourites, over the new luxurious court, for every beautiful woman, for every pretty man. Not even Cecil's constant struggle with the farming out of taxes, the sale of honours, the exploitation of orphans left in trust to the king, could keep the throne in profit; soon the king would have to call another parliament, and they would speak against him, and against the favourites at court, and the whole question of the king and the people would be thrown open, and who knew where such a debate might lead?

The earl limped forward. His arthritic hip pained him to walk, and it had grown worse in the last few months. John, without offering sympathy, moved a little closer and his master leaned on his shoulder.

'All I have ever done is juggle with the forces which drive us,' the earl said. 'All I ever have to do is to fend off consequences. He's running through the old queen's fortune as if there were no bottom to the well. And nothing to show for it. No roads, no Navy, no protection for shipping, no new colonies to mention . . . and not even a bit of show for the people.'

It was growing darker, the cool early summer twilight hid the bare places of the garden, masked the awkward corners. The earl's favourite pinks, which John had planted in great ornamental urns on the terrace, scented the air as their cloaks brushed by. John bent to pick a spray and handed it to him.

'You brought the new king to his throne, and to his country,' John observed. 'You've served him well. And he came to his country without trouble. You've kept the country at peace.'

The earl nodded. 'I don't forget it. But that little chestnut tree of yours, John, that little tree in the pot, may bring more joy to more Englishmen than any of my schemes, in the long run.'

'Most men's tastes are not political,' John said apologetically. 'I prefer the tree, myself.'

The earl laughed. 'I have something to show you. I think you may be surprised.'

He turned and John followed him back towards the house. The wide double door stood open, two serving men at either side. The earl walked past them as if they were invisible, John nodded pleasantly to them.

The earl led John into the shady hall. The wood floor and panelling smelled sweet and new, there was sawdust still in the corners, and the linenfold shapes on the panelling were sharp-cut and bright. The wood had not even had its first polish yet, it was still light and shining. Even in the twilight it gleamed as if it were bathed in sunshine.

At the foot of the stairs there was a great newel post, left swathed in a cloth by the woodcarver when he went home for the night. The earl took hold of the sheet and pulled it to one side.

'What d'you see?'

John stepped forwards to look. The post was square and grand, a fitting size and solidity for the big hall, the ornaments carved on top with acanthus leaves and swags and ribbons. One face of the square pillar was ornate with half-finished carvings but the other was already complete. It showed a man, in the act of stepping down from the plinth, stepping out of the frame of the carving as if he would take his place in the outside world, as if he would take his work to the farthest corners of the world.

In one hand the figure had a long-handled rake, and in the other a grand fanciful flower springing from a huge pot, which was spilling over with fruit and seeds: a cornucopia of goodness. He was wearing comfortable baggy breeches and a stout overcoat, and on his head, at a rakish joyful angle, was his hat. With an awe-struck gasp John recognised himself, carved in wood on the earl's newel post.

'Good God! Is it me?' John asked in a whisper.

Robert Cecil's hand was gentle on his shoulder. 'It's you,' he said. 'And a very good likeness, I think.'

'Why have you put me on your stair post, my lord?' John asked. 'Of all the things that you could have had carved?'

The earl smiled. 'Of all my great choices: the Three Graces, or Zeus, or Apollo, or something from the Bible or the king himself? Yet I chose to have my gardener carved in the centre post of my house.'

John looked at the jaunty confidence of the set of the hat and the brandished rake. 'I don't know what to say,' he said simply. 'It's too much for me. You have taken my breath away.'

'Fame comes in many guises, Tradescant,' Robert Cecil remarked. 'But I think people will remember you when they sit beneath their chestnut trees and when your plants bloom in their gardens. And here you are, and here you will be, as long as my house stands, recorded forever, striding out with a plant in one hand, and your rake in the other.'

Autumn 1611

Elizabeth and Baby J were at last to move to Hatfield House. Gertrude, suddenly seized with maternal tenderness, came to weep over their departure and to see them off, all their goods loaded into one wagon, and Elizabeth sitting beside John on the driver's seat with Baby J wedged between them.

'Where's the chestnut tree?' John asked.

'That tree!' Gertrude exclaimed, but she lacked her old spite.

'Safe in the back,' Elizabeth said. 'Beside the kitchen things.'

John handed her the reins of the steady horse and went round to the back of the wagon to find the barrel with the tree. It was leaning at an angle against the rail. The movement could have rubbed the bark off the tender trunk. John compressed his lips over hard words. Elizabeth had much work to do: moving house, and a young child, active as a puppy under her feet all day. He should not blame her for being careless with something which had only meant much to her as a token of his love. She never cared for it as he did. It was unfair to expect that she should.

He unloaded a couple of stools and repacked the corner of the wagon so that the tree was fully supported. Then he came round to the driver's seat.

'Your baby safely settled?' Elizabeth asked sharply.

John nodded, not rising to the bait. 'It's a precious rarity,' he reminded her mildly. 'Probably worth more than the whole cart of things put together. We would be fools if we broke it out of carelessness.'

Gertrude shot a swift look at Elizabeth as if to bewail the stubbornness of men, then Elizabeth leaned out from the wagon and kissed her mother goodbye.

'Come and see us at Hatfield,' Elizabeth said.

Gertrude stepped back as the wagon moved forward. She waved and saw Baby J wave back to her. For a moment she thought she might be able to cry, but though she screwed up her face and thought of the loss of her daughter and her grandson, no tears came.

'Safe journey!' she called, and saw Tradescant settle himself on the wagoner's hard bench seat as if he were ready to travel across half the world.

'Oh, yes,' she said under her breath as the wagon drew away. 'I see you, John Tradescant, with your heart leaping up at the very word "journey". She'd have done better to have married a good Kent farmer and be christened, married, and buried in her father's church. But that would never have done for you because you are Cecil's man through and through and you have all of his ambition – though it shows itself in funny ways with your rarities and your travels – and Meopham would never have been big enough or strange enough or rare enough for you.'

A little handkerchief fluttered from the receding cart, and Gertrude whipped out her own and waved back.

'Still,' she said philosophically. 'He doesn't beat her, and there are a lot worse things a man can love better than his wife than a garden and a lord.'

Elizabeth and John, unaware of this brutal and nearly accurate summary of their lives, found their spirits rising as they drew further and further away from Meopham.

'It seems odd to me to live anywhere else, but I shall grow accustomed,' Elizabeth said. 'And a bigger cottage and a better garden –'

'And the parkland all around instead of the lanes for J to play in,' John reminded her. 'And gardens the like of which no-one in England has ever seen. Fountains and rivers!'

'We must take care he doesn't wander off and fall in,' Elizabeth said. 'He's very restless. I can't think how many times someone has brought him back to me and told me he was halfway to Sussex.'

'He can stray all he likes in my lord's gardens,' John said with satisfaction. 'He'll come to no harm there.'

'And we'll eat our dinner in hall or at our home as we wish?' Elizabeth asked.

'As we wish when the lord is away from home. But when he is at the palace he likes his men to dine in the hall. And I like to see him.'

'Well enough when you had no-one to cook your dinner at home,' Elizabeth remarked. 'But now I shall be there –'

John put a hand gently on hers. 'If he looks down the hall to see me, I must be there,' he reminded her. 'It's not a question of a dinner cooked by you or a dinner cooked by the cooks. It's not even a question of whose company I would rather keep. It is just that if he looks down the hall for me, I must be there. You must know that by now, Elizabeth. You must know that now that we are going to live on his land, in a cottage owned by him and given to us free. You must know that he comes first.'

For a moment he thought she would fly out at him and then there would be a quarrel and a sulk – for they were both terrible sulkers – which could easily last for the whole two days of the journey. But then he saw her recognise the simple truth of it.

'I know,' she agreed. 'But it is hard for me. The people I come from, my family, are freeholders on their own land. They dine where they please.'

'Sometimes only on bread and bacon,' John pointed out.

'Even so. It's their own bread and bacon and they fear no-one's favour.'

John nodded. 'And if I had been content to be a farmer or perhaps a gardener on my own account in a small way with a little market garden for bulbs or flowers or fruit, then I should be a man like that too. But I wanted something more, Elizabeth. I wanted the chance to make the greatest garden in England. And he gave me that when I was a young man, so young that most masters would have made me work an apprenticeship under another man for another year or three before they even considered me. He trusted me, he took a risk with me. He gave me Theobalds when I was little more than a lad.'

'And don't you see what you've paid for that?' she asked him. 'You can't even choose where to eat your dinner. You can't choose where to live. Sometimes I think you can't even choose what to feel in your heart. It's his feelings that matter. Not your own.'

'It's the way it is,' he stated. 'The way of the world.'

She shook her head. 'Not in Meopham. Not in my family. Not in the country. It's the way of the court where everyone has to have a great man's favour and protection to rise, where every great man has to have his followers to show his importance. But there are men and women all over the country who live according to their own lights and call no man master.'

'You think that's a better life?'

'Of course,' she said, but she could see that what seemed to her to be a freedom from an onerous duty was to him a loss, an emptiness which he could not have borne.

'I would have been a smaller man without my lord,' he said. 'And what you think of as freedom is a small price to pay for belonging heart and soul to a great man. It's the price I pay gladly.'

'But I pay it too,' she said quietly.

For a moment he glanced down at her as if something in her voice had made him feel tender for her, regretful, as if they should have been more to each other. She thought that he would put his arm around her and cuddle her against his side and drive one-handed like a lover and his lass on the way to the fair. 'Yes, you pay too,' he admitted, keeping both hands on the driving reins. 'You knew you were marrying a man who had a duty already promised. I was Cecil's man before we were even betrothed, let alone married. You knew that, Elizabeth.'

She nodded and kept her eyes on the unwinding road ahead of them. 'I knew that,' she agreed a little grimly. 'I don't complain.'

He left it at that, with her acquiescence, and trusted to the house that his lord had provided for them to persuade her, as he could not, that it was better to be the follower of a great man than a small man on your own account. He saw her face as he drew up outside the cottage and knew that there would be no complaints for a while about the earl.

It was not a cottage he had given them at all – not two cramped rooms on the ground floor and a rickety stair to a hayloft bedroom – but a proper house with a fence all around it and a path of handsome brick chippings leading up to the front door set flush in the middle with two windows, proper glazed windows with panes set diamond-wise in thick lead, on each side of it.

'Oh! oh!' Elizabeth slid down from the hard driving seat, lost for words.

A thick blond thatch sat weightily on the low roof. The beams in the walls were so new that they were still golden against the pale pink of the limewashed plaster.

'New built!' Elizabeth whispered. 'New built for us?'

'For us and no other. Step inside,' John invited her.

With J at her heels, looking around at everything with eyes as wide as a hunting owl, Elizabeth stepped over the threshold of her new home and found herself inside a stone-flagged hall with a fire already lit in the fireplace to welcome her. To the right was the kitchen, with a big stone sink and a broad fireplace. To the left was a small room she could use as she pleased: a still room, or a drawing room; and immediately before her was a genuine solid flight of stairs with well-made wooden treads and risers which led to two more rooms above. Each one of them was big enough for a full-size bed, never mind the cramped little bed and Baby J's truckle that they had brought with them on the wagon from Meopham.

'And a garden,' John said exultantly.

'A garden!' Elizabeth laughed at the predictability of her man; but let him lead her back down the stairs and through the kitchen to the back door.

Cecil had bidden John take what he wanted from the saplings and plants of the palace gardens and make his own little Eden. John had created in the small walled plot a little orchard, a walk of trellised apple and plum trees, a pottager by the back door with herbs for cooking and salad vegetables, a bed of strawberries, and a kitchen garden bed of beans and peas and onions and greens.

'It looks so – rooted!' Elizabeth found the word at last. 'As if it had been here forever.'

A brief gleam of pride crossed John's face. 'That is what I have learned this year at least,' he said. 'I have learned how to make a garden new-made look as if it was there when Eden was planted. The trick of it is to put things too close, and bear the work of moving them before they get overcrowded. Also you have to take a risk of moving things which are really too big to be disturbed. Digging a wide trench around the roots. Those trees now –' He broke off. His wife was smiling at him but she was not listening. 'I have found a way of moving trees so they don't wither,' he finished. 'But it's of little interest except to another gardener.'

'It means that you have given me a beautiful garden which I will treasure,' she said. She came into his arms and held him close. 'And I thank you for it. I see now why the little patch at Meopham was not enough. I never thought of you making a cottage garden like you make grand gardens, my John, but you have given me a little beauty here.'

He smiled at her pleasure and bent his head and kissed her. Her lips were still soft and warm and he thought with rising desire that tonight they would bed in a new room and tomorrow wake to look out on the great parkland of Hatfield, and their new life would begin.

'We'll see these trees grow strong,' he said. 'And we'll plant the chestnut sapling at the bottom of the garden and sit in its shade when we are old.'

She nestled a little closer. 'And we'll bide at home,' she said firmly.

John rested his cheek against her warm cap. 'When we're old,' he promised, disarmingly.

The very next day the earl himself came down to visit the Tradescants in their new cottage. Elizabeth was flustered and overawed by the grandness of the pony carriage with one footman driving, and another hanging on the back. She came to the gate and curtseyed and stammered her thanks. But John opened the gate and went out to stand at the carriage door as to an intimate friend.

'Are you ill?' he asked Cecil quietly.

Cecil's face was yellow and the lines of pain were deeper than ever. 'No worse than usual,' he replied.

'Is it your bones?'

'My belly this time,' he said. 'I am sick as a dog, John. But I can't stop work yet. I have a plan to reform the king's finances despite himself. If I can get him to agree then I can sell the whole scheme to Parliament, and hand over to them the farming of benefits in return for a proper wage for the king.'

John blinked. 'You want the king to be paid by Parliament? To be its servant?'

Cecil nodded. 'Better than this endless haggling, year after year, when they demand that he change his favourites and he demands more money. Anything is better than that. You have to be a king rich in charm to survive holding out an annual begging bowl, and this king is not as the old queen.'

'Can you not rest and come back to it later?' John asked urgently.

The heavy-lidded eyes looked at him. 'Setting up as apothecary, John?'

'Can you not rest?'

Cecil flinched as he stretched out his hand to his man, and John saw that even that small gesture cost him pain. He took the hand as gently as he would hold Baby J's while he slept. Unconsciously, he put his other hand on top of it and felt how cool were the fingers and how sluggish the pulse.

'Do I look so sick?'

John hesitated.

There was a gleam of a smile on Cecil's face. 'Come, John,' he said in a half-whisper. 'You always prided yourself on telling me the truth, don't turn courtier now.'

'You do look very very sick,' John said, his voice very low.

'Sick to death?'

John snatched a quick glance at his master's heavy-lidded eyes and saw that he wanted a true answer to his question.

'I have no skills, my lord, but I would think so.'

Cecil frowned slightly and John tightened his grip on the thin cold hand.

'I've so much more to do,' the Secretary of State said.

'Look to yourself first,' John urged him, and then heard himself whisper, 'please, my lord. Look to yourself first.'

Cecil leaned forward and laid his cheek against John's warm face. 'Ah, John,' he said softly. 'I wish I had some of your strength.'

'I wish to God I could give it to you,' John whispered.

'Drive with me,' the earl commanded. 'Drive round with me and tell me what is planted and how it will be, even though neither of us will be here to see it. Tell me how it will be in a hundred years when we will both be dead and gone. Hale or sick, John, this garden will outlive us both.'

Tradescant clambered into the carriage and sat beside his master, one arm along the back of the seat as if he would protect him from the jolting movement. Elizabeth, forgotten at the gate of her new house, watched them both go.

'You have made me a velvet setting for my jewel,' Cecil said with quiet pleasure as the carriage moved slowly down the avenue of new-planted trees. 'We have done well together, John, for a pair of youngsters learning our trades.'

May 1612

Cecil was dying in the great curtained bed in the master chamber of his new fine house. Outside his door, the household staff pretended to go about their work in a hushed silence, hoping to hear the muttered colloquy of the doctors. Some wanted to send him to Bath to take the waters – his last chance of health. Some were for leaving him in his bed to rest. Sometimes, when his door opened, the servants could hear the harsh labouring of his breath and see him propped up on the rich embroidered pillows, the brightness of their spring colours a mockery of his yellowing skin.

John Tradescant, weeping like a woman, was deep digging in the vegetable garden, digging without much purpose, in a frenzy of activity as if his energy and effort could put heart in the earth, could put the heart back into his master.

At midday he abruptly left his vegetable bed and marched determinedly through the three courts on the west of the house, up the allee, past the mount where the paths were rimmed with yellow primroses, out into the woodland side of the garden. The ground was a sea of blue as if the whole wood was deep in flood. John kneeled and picked bluebells with steady concentration and did not stop until he had an armful. Then he went to the house, careless of the mud dropping off his boots, up the stairs where his likeness in wood still stepped blithely out of the newel post, up to the master bedroom. A housemaid stopped him at the door to the anteroom. He would not be allowed further in.

'Take these, and show them to him,' he said.

She hesitated. Flowers in the house were for strewing on the floor, or for a posy to wear at the belt or hatband. 'What would he want with them?' she demanded. 'What would a dying man want with bluebells?'

'He'd like to see them,' John urged her. 'I know he would. He likes bluebells.'

'I'll have to give them to Thomas,' she said. 'I'm not allowed in, anyway.'

'Then give them to Thomas,' John pressed her. 'What harm can it do? And I know it would please him.'

She was stubborn. 'I don't see why.'

John gestured helplessly. 'Because when a man is going into darkness it helps him to know that he leaves some light behind!' he exclaimed. 'Because when a man is facing his own winter it is good to know that there will still be springs and summers. Because he is dying . . . and when he sees the bluebells he will know that I am still here, outside, and that I picked him some flowers. He will know that I am still here, just outside, digging in his garden. He will know that I am here, still digging for him.'

The look she turned on him was pure incomprehension. 'But Mr Tradescant! Why should that help him?'

John grabbed her in his frustration and pushed her towards the anteroom. 'A man would understand,' he growled. 'Women are too flighty. A man would understand that he will be comforted to know that I am still out there. That even when he is gone, his garden will still be there. That his mulberry tree will flower this year, that his chestnut saplings are growing straight, that the new velvet double anemone is thriving, that his bluebells are blowing under the trees of his woods. Go! And get those bluebells into his hands, or I shall have words to say to you!'

He thrust her with such force that she went at a little run to Thomas, who was standing outside the bedroom door, waiting for the orders from his master that never came.

'Mr Tradescant wants these taken in to his lordship,' she said, thrusting her armful of blossoms at him. Their slim whippy green stems oozed sap like the very juice of life. She wiped her hand on her apron. 'He says they're important.'

Thomas hesitated at the eccentric request.

'D'you know what he said? He said that women are too flighty to understand,' she sniffed resentfully. 'Impertinence!'

Thomas's sense of male importance was immediately stimulated. He took the flowers from her, turned at once to open the door and crept inside.

A doctor was at the foot of the bed, another at the window, and an old woman, part nurse, part layer-out, was at the fireside where a small fire of scented pine cones was crackling, pouring heat into the stuffy room.

Thomas came quietly forward. 'Beg pardon,' he said hoarsely. 'But his lordship's gardener insisted he had these.'

The doctor turned irritably. 'What? What? Oh, nonsense! Nonsense!'

'Nothing but folly and superstition,' said the doctor from the window. 'And likely to spread noxious fumes.'

Thomas stood his ground. 'It was Mr Tradescant, sir. His Grace's favourite. And he insisted, the maid said.'

Cecil turned his head a little. The dispute was instantly silenced. Cecil crooked a finger at Thomas.

The doctor waved him forward. 'Quick. He wants them. But it won't make a groat of difference.'

Awkwardly, Thomas stepped up to the bed. The aquiline face of the most powerful man in England was etched in sandstone and grooved by pain. He turned his dark eyes sightlessly towards the manservant. Thomas thrust the bluebells into the slack hands. They spilled on to the rich coverlet of the bed, blotting out the scarlet embroidery and the gold thread with blue, blue, nothing but sky blue.

'From John Tradescant,' Thomas said.

The light sweet scent of the bluebells poured like fresh water into the room, drowning the smell of fear and sickness. Their colour shone like a blue flame in the dark chamber. The great lord looked down on the scattered flowers and inhaled their cold fresh perfume. They seemed to come from a world a hundred miles away from the overheated bed chamber, a clean spring world outside. He turned his head to the little window and his crumpled face stretched into a small smile. Though the casement was opened only the smallest crack, he could hear the thud of a spade into the flower bed beneath his window, loud as a faithful heartbeat, as John Tradescant and his master set about their different tasks: digging and dying.

October 1612

When they buried the earl, after dragging him to Bath for the cure and then back home again, there was still a place for John Tradescant at Hatfield House. But the heart had gone out of the garden for John. He kept looking around for Cecil, wanting to show him one of the grand new sights of the garden, expected to see him picking mulberries in summer and limping down the dark shade of the newly growing pleached allee. He kept wanting to consult him, he kept wanting to exchange that swift conspiratorial smile of triumph: that a plant had grown, that a rarity had taken root, that seeds had struck.

When he took a mug of small ale and a loaf of bread to his potting shed he kept expecting to see his lord there before him, lounging against the bench, be-ringed fingers dabbling in the soft sifted earth, taking a rest from letter writing, from plotting, from the sleight of hand of foreign policy, seeking John to share a bit of dinner together, a companion who needed no lies, no courting, seated on a barrel of bulbs to watch John transplanting seedlings.

'I am sorry, my lord,' John said to the new earl, Cecil's son, finding his old master's title sluggish on his lips. 'I cannot settle here without your father. I was in his service too long to make a change.'

'You will miss the garden, I expect,' the new Lord Cecil remarked. But he did not know, as his father had known, the intense joy of making a garden where before there had been nothing but meadow.

'I will,' John said. Robert Cecil's favourite flowers, the pinks, were in full bloom. The chestnut saplings which they had bought as glossy nuts a full five years ago were leggy and strong and putting out green palmate leaves like beggars' hands. The cherry-tree walk was a maze of ordered blossom and the tulips were ablaze in the new flower beds.

'I can't garden here without him,' he said simply to Elizabeth that night.

'Why not?' she asked. 'It's the same garden.'

'It's not.' He shook his head. 'It was his garden. I chose things that would delight his eyes. I thought of his tastes when I planned the walks. When I had something new and rare I considered where it would flourish, but also where would he be certain to see it? Every time I planted a seedling I had two thoughts – the angle of the sun shining on it, and my lord's gaze.'

She frowned at the sound of blasphemy. 'He was only a man.'

'I know, and I loved him as a man. I loved him because he was a man and more mortal and frail than many others. He would lean on me when his back pained him –' Tradescant broke off. 'I *liked* him leaning on me,' he said, conscious that he could not explain the mixture of elation and pity that he felt all at once when the greatest man in England after the king would confide his pain and take help.

Elizabeth pressed her lips together on hasty words and kept her jealousy to herself. She put her hand on her husband's shoulder and reminded herself that the lord he had loved was dead and buried and a good wife should show some sympathy. 'You sound as if you have lost a brother, not a lord.'

He nodded. 'A lord is like a brother, like a father, even like a wife. I think of his needs all the time, I guard his interests. And I cannot be happy here without him.'

Elizabeth did not want to understand. 'But you have me, and Baby J.'

John gave her a sad little smile. 'And I will never love another woman or another child more than I love the two of you . . . but a man's love for his lord is another thing. It comes from the head as well as the heart. Loving a woman keeps you at home, it is a private pleasure. Loving a great lord takes you into the wider world, it is a matter of pride.'

'You make it sound as if we are not enough,' she said resentfully.

He shook his head, despairing of ever making her understand. 'No, no, Elizabeth. It doesn't matter. You are enough.'

She was not convinced. 'Will you seek another lord? Another master?'

The expression that passed swiftly across his face was deeper than mourning; it was desolation. 'I will never see his like again.'

That silenced her for a moment, as she saw the depth of his loss.

'But what about us?' she asked. 'I don't want to lose this house, John, and J is happy here. We have put down roots here just as the plants in the garden have done. You said you would plant the chestnut here this spring and that we would sit under its branches when we are an old married couple.'

He nodded. 'I know. I'm forsworn. That's what I promised you. But I can't bear it here without him, Elizabeth. I have tried and I cannot. Can you release me from my promise that we should stay here, and let us make another home? Back in Kent?'

'Kent? What d'you mean? Where?'

'Lord Wootton wants a gardener at Canterbury and asked me if I would go. He has the secret of growing melons which I should be glad to learn, his gardener has always teased me that only Lord Wootton in all of England can grow melons.'

Elizabeth tutted with irritation. 'Forget the melons for a moment if you please. What about a house? What about your wages?'

'He'll pay me well,' John said. 'Sixty pounds where my lord paid me fifty. And we will have a house, the head gardener's house. J can go to the King's School in Canterbury. That'll be a fine thing for him.'

'Canterbury,' Elizabeth said thoughtfully. 'I've never lived in a market town. There'd be much society.'

'We could start there at once. He asked me on the death of my lord and I said I would tell him within the quarter.'

'And will you not love Lord Wootton as you loved the earl?' Elizabeth asked, thinking it would be an advantage.

John shook his head: 'There will never be another lord for me like that one.'

'Let's go, then,' she said with her typical sudden decisiveness. 'And we can plant the chestnut sapling in Canterbury instead of Hatfield.'

November 1612

John was working in Lord Wootton's garden, hands among cold clods of earth, when he heard the bell tolling. On and on it went, a funeral bell. Then he heard the rumble of cannon fire. He stood up, brushed the mud on his breeches, and reached for his coat where it was hooked over his spade.

'Something's happened,' he said shortly to the garden lad who was working beside him.

'Shall I run into town and bring you the news?' the boy asked eagerly.

'No,' John said firmly. 'You shall stay and work here while I run into town and find out the news. And if you are not here when I get back it will be the worst for you.'

'Yes, Mr Tradescant,' the boy said sulkily.

The bell was ever more insistent.

'What does it mean?'

'I'll find out,' John said and strode out of the garden towards the cathedral.

People were gathered in gossiping circles all the way down the road but John went on until he reached the cathedral steps and saw a face he recognised – the headmaster of the school.

'Doctor Phillips,' he exclaimed. 'What are they ringing for?'

The man turned at the sound of his name and John saw, with a shock, that the man's face was wet with tears.

'Good God! What is it? It's not an invasion? Not Spain?'

'It's Prince Henry,' the man said simply. 'Our blessed prince. We have lost him.'

For a moment John could not take in the words. 'Prince Henry?'

'Dead.'

John shook his head. 'But he's so strong, he's always so well –'

'Dead of fever.'

John's hand went to his forehead to cross himself, in the old superstitious forbidden sign. He caught his hand back and said instead: 'Poor boy, God save us, poor boy.'

'I forgot, you would have seen him often.'

'Not often,' John said, his habitual caution asserting itself.

'He was a blessed prince, was he not? Handsome and learned and godly?'

John thought of Prince Henry's handsome tyrannical disposition, of his casual cruelty to his dark little brother, of his easy love of his sister Elizabeth, of his royal confidence, some would say arrogance. 'He was a boy born to rule,' John said cleverly.

'God save Prince Charles,' Doctor Phillips said stoutly.

John realised that the little eleven-year-old lame boy who ran after his brother and could never get nor keep his father's attention would now be the next king – if he lived.

'God save him indeed,' he repeated.

'And if we lose him,' Doctor Phillips said in an undertone, 'then it's another woman on the throne, the Princess Elizabeth, and God knows what danger that would bring us now.'

'God save him,' John repeated. 'God save Prince Charles.'

'And what is he like?' Doctor Phillips asked. 'Prince Charles? What sort of a king will he make?'

John thought of the tongue-tied boy who had to be taught to walk straight, who struggled so hard to keep up with the older two, who knew himself never to be beloved like them, never to be handsome like them. He wondered how a child who knew himself to be second best and a poor second at that would be when he was a man and was first in the land. Would he take the people's love and let it warm him, fill the emptiness in that ugly little boy's heart? Or would he be forever mistrustful, forever doubting, always wanting to seem braver, stronger, more handsome than he was?

'He'll be a fine king,' he said, thinking that his master would not be there to teach this king, and how the boy would learn the Tudor guile and the Tudor charm with only his father to advise him and the court filled with men picked for their looks and their bawdiness and not for their skills. 'God will guide him,' Tradescant said hopefully, thinking that no-one else would.

September 1616

The new cottage at Canterbury was little bigger than their first home at Meopham but Elizabeth did not complain as the front door opened to a proper city street and the finishing of the house was elegant. They cooked and ate and lived in the large ground-floor room and Elizabeth and John slept in a curtained four-poster bed in the room next door. J, now a boy of eight years old, went up the shallow stairs to a pallet bed in the attic. During the day John went and gardened for Lord Wootton, and J went to Dame School where, for a penny a week, he was taught to read and write and to figure sums. They both came home for their dinner at four o'clock on the darkening autumn afternoons, John with a spade over his shoulder, J with his schoolbook clutched under his arm.

Elizabeth, slicing parsley for the soup one afternoon, heard three, not two, sets of boots stamping off mud in the porch of the little cottage and put her sacking apron off in the expectation of company. She opened the front door to John, to her son, and to a young man, brown-faced and smiling, with the unmistakable swagger and roll of a seafaring man.

'Captain Argall,' Elizabeth said without pleasure.

'Mrs Tradescant!' he exclaimed and swept into the house, kissing her heartily on one cheek and then the other. 'The most beautiful rose in all of John's gardens! How are you?'

'Very well,' Elizabeth said, disengaging herself and going back to the kitchen table.

'I have brought you a handsome ham,' Sam Argall said, looking at the stewpot and sliced vegetables without much enthusiasm. J, his face a picture of moonstruck admiration, produced the leg of ham from behind his back and dumped it on the table. 'And a taste of paradise too,' Sam Argall went on, offering a flask of rum. 'From the Sugar Islands, Mrs Tradescant. A taste of sweetness and strength that will bring a taste of the tropics even here, to chilly Canterbury.'

'I find the weather very mild for the time of the year,' Elizabeth said stoutly. 'Do sit down, Captain Argall. J will fetch you a glass of small ale if you would like one. We do not serve strong liquors in this house.'

J rushed to do his mother's bidding while John and Sam sat at the table and watched Elizabeth slice the last pieces of parsley and toss them into the pot hanging over the fire.

There was a silence while they drank. Elizabeth busied herself with setting out the wooden bowls and a knife at each place, and a loaf of bread in the centre of the table.

'Sam is to be master of a great venture,' John began at last.

Elizabeth stirred the pot and prodded one of the floating parsnips to see if it was cooked.

'A great venture, and he has offered me a place,' John said.

Elizabeth poured the broth into the three bowls, for the captain, for her husband, for her son, and stood behind them to wait on them. John saw that she would not sit and eat with them as she always did when it was just him and J at the dinner table. He read, correctly, her absolute opposition to Sam Argall and all the adventure and risk that he stood for, concealed behind chilly courtesy.

'Virginia!' Sam Argall exclaimed, blowing on his bowl. 'Mrs Tradescant, I have been entrusted with a great task. I am appointed Deputy Governor of Virginia and Admiral of the Virginia seas.'

'Will you say grace, husband?' Elizabeth asked repressively.

John bowed his head over the bread and Sam, remembering Elizabeth's strictness in matters of religion, quickly closed his eyes. When he had finished John picked up his spoon and nodded to Sam.

'Amen,' Sam said briskly. 'I have come to ask John here to go venturing with me, Mrs Tradescant. You shall be landowners, madam, you shall be squires. For every place you take on the ship with me you shall have a hundred acres of your own land. For the three of you that will be three hundred acres! Think of that! You, the mistress of three hundred acres of land!'

Elizabeth's face was as unmoved as if she were thinking of three yards. 'This is three hundred acres of good farmland?'

'It's prime land,' Argall said.

'Cleared and ploughed?'

There was a brief silence. 'Mrs Tradescant, I am offering you virgin land, a virgin land rich with woodland. Your land is standing with tall trees, wonderful rare bushes, fruiting vines. First you cut your own timber and then you build yourself a handsome house. A mansion, if you like. Built of your own timber!'

'A mansion from green wood?' Elizabeth asked. 'Built by a man in his forties, a woman, and an eight-year-old boy? I should like to see it!'

He pushed his bowl away and cut a slice of the ham. Elizabeth, the very model of wifely obedience, poured the jug of small ale and stepped back, folding her hands on the front of her apron, her eyes cast down.

'What would we grow?' J asked.

Captain Argall smiled down at the bright face of the boy. 'Anything you wish. The land is so rich, you could grow anything. But who knows? You might find gold and never trouble yourselves to plant anything ever again!'

'Gold?'

'I thought the first shipment of rocks was nothing more than fool's gold?' Elizabeth asked. 'They tipped it out below the Tower and picked it over and found nothing but quartz. And there it stood for many a long day, a little monument to folly and greed.'

'No gold yet. Not yet, Mrs T,' Captain Argall said. 'But who can say what there might be deeper in the mountains? No-one has gone further than the shoreline and up the rivers a little way. What could be there? Gold? Diamonds? Rubies? And what need have we of these anyway while we can grow tobacco?'

'Why d'you dislike the idea so much, Elizabeth?' John asked her directly.

She looked from him to J's excited face and Captain Argall's determined good humour. 'Because I have heard travellers' tales before, but I have heard nothing good of this plantation,' she said. 'There's Mistress Woods at Meopham who lost two brothers to Virginia in the starving time when half the settlement died of hunger. She told me that they were digging over the graveyards looking for meat, reduced to worse than savagery. There's Peter John who paid for his own passage home and kissed the ground at London docks, he was so glad to be alive. He said the forest was filled with Indians who could be kind or wicked as the mood took them, and only they knew whether they were your enemy or friend. There's your own friend, Captain John Smith, who swore that he would live the rest of his days there, and yet he was brought home a cripple –'

'John Smith would never say a word against Virginia!' Argall interrupted. 'And he was hurt in an accident which could have happened anywhere. He could have been boating on the Thames.'

'He was hurt in an accident but only after he had fought against Indians and been captured by them and been so close to death by execution that he near died of fear,' Elizabeth maintained stoutly.

'The Indians are at peace now,' Argall said. 'And I have played my part in that. Princess Pocahontas is Mrs Rebecca Rolfe now and all the Indians are coming into Christian schools and living in Christian homes. You're speaking of old fears. It was hard in the early years but it is all at peace now. Pocahontas is married to John Rolfe and other Indians and white men will marry. In a few years all the wars will be forgotten.' He glanced down at J's attentive face, drinking in the stories. 'You will have an Indian playmate to show you the paths through the woods,' he promised. 'Perhaps an Indian maid to be your sweetheart.'

The boy blushed scarlet. 'How did Princess Pocahontas come to marry Mr Rolfe?' he asked.

Sam Argall laughed. 'You know the story as well as me!' he exclaimed. 'I captured her and held her hostage, and all the while she was weaving her spell and capturing John. So go to bed and dream of it, young J. Your mother and father and I will talk more of it later.'

'I have to sleep too,' John said. He and J lifted the board from the trestle legs of the table and stacked it to one side of the little room. 'I hope you will sleep well here?' Elizabeth asked, laying a straw mattress and an armful of bedding in the space.

'Like a babe in a cradle,' Captain Argall assured her. He kissed her hand in his flirtatious way and ignored her lack of response. 'Goodnight.'

Elizabeth watched J go up the stairs to his little bed in the attic and then drew the curtains of the four-poster around her and John.

'I'd have thought you would have leaped at the chance of a fresh start in the new world,' John remarked as he got into bed and pulled the covers up to his chin. 'You who always want us to be freeholders. We would be freeholders in Virginia of land we could only dream of here. Three hundred acres!'

Elizabeth, pulling her nightgown over her head and only then dropping her skirt and shift, did not answer. John was too wise to demand a reply. He watched her kneel at the foot of the bed to say her prayers and closed his own eyes and muttered his thanks for blessings. Only when Elizabeth was in bed, tying the ties of her nightcap under her chin did she say, suddenly: 'And who is the governor of this new land?'

John was taken aback. 'Sir George,' he said. 'Newly appointed. Sir George Yeardley.'

'A courtier. Exactly,' she said and blew out her candle with an emphatic puff. They lay for a moment in silence in the darkness, and then she spoke: 'It's not a new land at all. It's the same land but in a different place. I won't go, John. It's just another form of service. We risk everything, we gamble our savings, our livelihood, and even our lives. We put ourselves in grave danger in a country – one of the few in the whole world where you could not earn a living doing your own trade, no-one will want a gardener there, it's farmers they need – we put our son into a forest filled with unknown dangers, and we try to make a living from a land that no-one has farmed before. And who makes the profits? The governor. The Virginia Company. And the king.'

'It's their land,' John said mildly. 'Who else should make the profits?'

'If it's their land then they can take the risks,' Elizabeth declared bluntly. 'Not I.'

Elizabeth's determined opposition to the Virginia venture could not prevent John investing money. While she watched, with her mouth in a hard ungenerous line, he counted over twenty-five gold sovereigns for two shares. Captain Argall promised that two men – poor men who could not find their own passage money – would be sent on John's account, and that the land granted to them on arrival in Virginia would be held in part for John.

'You'll be a squire of Virginia yet,' Argall said to him, stowing the purse of gold beneath his coat with a swift glance at Elizabeth's stony face. 'I shall pick you out a good piece of land, west of Jamestown, inland, upriver. I shall call it Argall Town.'

He broke off as Elizabeth snorted quietly at his presumption.

'I beg your pardon?'

'Excuse me,' Elizabeth said swiftly. 'I sneezed.'

'I shall call it Argall Town,' Captain Argall repeated. 'And there will always be a welcome there for you, John.' He glanced down at J's adoring uplifted face. 'And for you, J,' he said. 'Never forget that you are a landowner in the new world, in virgin earth. When you are weary of this old country you have your stake in the new. When you want to be away from here, there will be your headright in virgin land.'

J nodded. 'I won't forget, sir.'

'And I shall take you to meet Princess Pocahontas,' Argall promised. 'She is visiting in England and she has a kindness for me. I shall introduce you to her.'

J's eyes grew rounder and his mouth dropped into a perfect circle of astonishment.

'She would not want to be troubled with us,' Elizabeth said quickly.

'Why not?' Captain Argall asked. 'She would be delighted to make your acquaintance. Come up to London next week and I will introduce you. It is a promise.' He turned to J. 'I promise you, you shall meet her.'

'Time for him to go to school,' Elizabeth interrupted firmly. 'I am surprised, husband, that you linger so long.'

'I'll walk with you,' Argall said, taking the hint. 'And thank you for your hospitality, Mrs T. It's always a pleasure to be entertained by such a lady.'

Elizabeth nodded, still unsmiling. 'I wish you well in your ventures,' she said. 'I hope that you make a profit, especially as it is our money you are venturing.'

Argall laughed without embarrassment. 'Nothing venture, nothing gain,' he reminded her and took her hand in the way she disliked, and kissed it. Then he clapped John on the shoulder and the two men left the house with J bobbing behind, like an agitated duckling in the wake of two grand swans.

Argall was as good as his word and John took his son to London to see the Indian Princess, travelling up on a wagon taking fruit to London market, staying overnight, and coming down the next day on the empty wagon.

Elizabeth tried not to encourage J's excitement, but she could not hide her own interest. 'Was she black?' she asked.

'Not at all!' J exclaimed. 'Just brown, a beautiful lady, and she had a little baby on her knee. But she didn't wear bear skins or anything, just ordinary clothes.'

'J was bitterly disappointed,' John said with a smile to his wife. 'He expected something very savage and strange. All she is, is a pretty young woman with a little son. She calls herself Rebecca now and is baptised and married. You would pass her in the street and think nothing more but that she was a fine tall woman, a little tanned.'

'She said that there are boys and girls of my age who live in the forest and hunt deer,' J said. 'And that they can fire a bow and spear a fish from four years old! And that they can make their own pots and sew their own clothes from deer hide, and –'

'She was making it up to amuse you,' Elizabeth said firmly.

'She was not!'

'She truly wasn't,' John said gently. 'I believed every word she said and I should so like to go, Elizabeth. Not to settle there, but just to take a look at our land and see what the prospects are. Not as planters to be there forever, but just to take a little run over there and see what the land is like. It sounds very fine –'

'A little run?' Elizabeth demanded. 'You speak of the ocean as if it were the cart track to your orchards. Lord Wootton could not spare you from his garden. I could not spare you now we are settled here. It is six weeks at sea on a huge sea. Why can you not stay in the same place, John? Why can you not be at peace?'

He had no reply for that, and she knew he would have no reply.

'I am sorry,' he said at last. 'I just long to see all there may be for me to see. And a new land would have new plants, don't you think? Things that I might never have seen before. But you are right. I have my garden here, and Lord Wootton's garden, and the house, and you and J. It is enough for me.'

Summer 1618

Elizabeth had prevented John uprooting the whole family and setting off for Virginia, but when he had an invitation to go venturing to Russia – of all places – and it came with the blessing of his master and a recommendation that he should go, there was little she could do to stop him. It was the king's business at the top of it, so no man in the country could refuse. The king wanted a new trade route to China and thought that Sir Dudley Digges might find one by making an agreement with the Russians. A loan of English gold coaxed from the coffers of the Muscovy and East India Companies was supposed to help.

Sir Dudley was a firm friend of Lord Wootton who wanted new plants for his garden. Sir Dudley said he needed a useful man and a seasoned traveller, not a gentleman who would be too proud to work, and not some dolt of a working man who would be of no use in an emergency. Lord Wootton said he could have Tradescant, and Tradescant was as ready to leave as a bagged hare when the hounds are giving tongue.

All she could do was to help him pack his travelling bag, see that his travelling cloak was free of moth holes and tears, and go down to the dockside at Gravesend with J – now a tall boy of ten years, and a King's Scholar at Canterbury – at her side to wave farewell.

'And beware of the cold!' Elizabeth cautioned again.

'It may be Russia, but it is midsummer,' John replied. 'Do you keep yourselves well, and J, mind your studies and care for your mother.'

The dockers scurried about, pushing past Elizabeth and her son. With a moment's regret John saw that there were tears in her eyes. 'I shall be back within three months,' he called over the widening gulf of water. 'Perhaps earlier. Elizabeth! *Please* don't fret!'

'Take care!' she called again but he could hardly hear her as the rowing barges took hold of the lines and the sailors cursed as they caught the ropes flung from the shore. Elizabeth and her son watched the boat move slowly downriver.

'I still don't understand why he has to go,' J said, with the discontent of the schoolboy.

Elizabeth looked down at him. 'Because he does his duty,' she said, with her natural loyalty to her husband. 'Lord Wootton ordered him to go. It is unknown country, your father might find all sorts of treasures.'

'I think he just loves to travel,' J said resentfully. 'And he doesn't care that he leaves me behind.'

Elizabeth put her arm around her son's unyielding shoulders. 'When you are older you shall travel too. He will take you with him. Perhaps you will grow to be a great man like your father and be sent by lords on travels overseas.'

Baby J – her baby no longer – disengaged himself from her arm. 'I shall go on my own account,' he said stiffly. 'I shall not wait for someone to send me.'

The ship was in mid-river now, the sails which had been slack when sheltered in the dock flapped like sheets on washing day. Elizabeth gripped her son's arm.

'He is old to go venturing,' she said anxiously. 'So far, and into such regions. What if he is taken ill? What if they get lost?'

'Not he,' J said with scorn. 'But when I travel I shall go to the Americas. A boy at school has an uncle there and he has killed hundreds of savages and is planting a crop of tobacco. He says that a man who wants land can just cut it from the forests. And we have our land there. Father is going in the wrong direction, he should be going to our lands.'

Elizabeth's eyes were still on the ship which was picking up speed and moving smoothly downriver. 'It's never been owning land for him,' she said. 'Never building a house or putting up a fence. It has always been discovering new things and making them grow. It has always been serving his lord.'

J pulled at her arm. 'Can we have some dinner before I have to go back?'

Elizabeth patted his hand absently. 'When he's gone,' she said. 'I want to see the ship out of port.'

J pulled away and went to the waterside. The river was sucking gently at the green stones. In the middle of the water, unseen by the boy, a beggar's corpse rolled and turned over. The harvest had failed again and there was starvation in the streets of London.

In a moment Elizabeth joined him. Her eyelids were red but her smile was cheerful.

'There!' she said. 'And now your father gave me half a crown to buy you an enormous dinner before we take the wagon home.'

John watched from the deck of the ship as his wife and son grew smaller and smaller, and then he could no longer pick them out at all. The sense of loss he felt as the land fell away was mingled with a leaping sense of freedom and excitement as the ship moved easily and faster and the waves grew greater. The voyage was to take them northwards, hugging the coast of England, and then eastwards, across the North Sea to the high ice-bound coast of Norway, and then onwards to Russia.

Tradescant was as much on deck as any of the ship's watch, and it was he who first spotted a great fleet of Dutch fishing ships taking cod and summer herring just south of Newcastle.

They weighed anchor at Newcastle and Tradescant went ashore to buy provisions for the journey. 'Take my purse,' Sir Dudley offered. 'And see if you can get some meat and some fish, John. My belly is as empty as a Jew's charity box. I've been as sick every day since we left London.'

John nodded and went ashore and marketed as carefully as Elizabeth might do. He bought fresh salmon and fresh and salted meats, and by noising Sir Dudley's name and mission much around Newcastle he was able to lead the Lord Mayor himself on a visit to the ship. And the Lord Mayor brought a barrel of salted salmon as a timely present for his lordship. When the ship was provisioned again they set out to cross the North Sea but the wind veered to the north west and started to rise before they were more than a day out of port, skimming the white tops off the grey waves which grew steeper and more frequent.

Sir Dudley Digges was sick as a dog from the moment the wind veered, and many of his companions stayed below too, groaning and vomiting and calling on the captain to return to shore before they died of seasickness. John, rocking easily to the movement of the boat, stood in the prow and watched the waves come rolling from the horizon and the ship rise up and then fall down, rise up and fall down, again and again. One night, when Sir Dudley's own manservant was ill, John sat at his bedside, and held his head as he vomited helplessly into the bowl.

'There,' said John gently.

'Good God,' Sir Dudley groaned. 'I feel sick unto death. I have never felt worse in all my life.'

'You'll survive,' John said with rough kindliness. 'It never lasts longer than a few days.'

'Hold me,' Sir Dudley commanded. 'I could weep like a girl for misery.'

Gently John raised the nobleman off the narrow bunk and let his head rest on John's shoulder. Sir Dudley turned his face to John's neck and drew in his warmth and strength. John tightened his grip and felt the racked body in his arms relax and slide into sleep. For an hour and more he knelt beside the bunk holding the man in his arms, trying to cushion him from the ceaseless rolling and crashing of the ship. Only when Sir Dudley was deeply, fast asleep, did John draw his numbed arm away and lay the man back down on his bed. For a moment he hesitated, looking down into that pale face, then he bent low and kissed him gently on the forehead, as if he were kissing Baby J and blessing his sleep, and then he went out.

As they drew further north the wind wheeled around and became more steady but Sir Dudley could keep down no food. The little ship was halfway between Scotland and Norway when the captain came to Sir Dudley, who was wrapped in a thick cloak and seated on the deck for the air.

'We can go back or forward as you wish,' the captain said. 'I don't want your death on my conscience, my lord. You're no seafarer. Perhaps we'd best head for home.'

Sir Dudley glanced at Tradescant, one arm slung casually around the bowsprit, looking out to sea.

'What d'you think, John?' he asked. His voice was still faint.

Tradescant glanced back and then drew closer.

'Shall we go back or press on?'

John hesitated. 'You can hardly be sicker than you were,' he said.

'That's what I fear!' the captain interrupted.

John smiled. 'You must be seasoned now, my lord. And the weather is fair. I say we should press on.'

'Tradescant says press on,' Sir Dudley remarked to the captain.

'But what d'you say, my lord?' the captain asked. 'It was you who was begging me to turn back at the height of the storm.'

Sir Dudley laughed, a thin thread of sound. 'Don't remind me! I say press on, too. Tradescant is right. We have our sea legs now, we might as well go forward as back.'

The captain shook his head but went back to the wheel and held the ship's course.

Their luck was in. The weather turned surprisingly fair, the men became accustomed to the motion of the ship and even Sir Dudley came out of his cabin and strode about the deck, his pace rocking. They had been nearly three weeks at sea and slowly, the skies around them changed. It was like entering another world, where the laws of day and night had been destroyed. John could read a page of writing at midnight, and the sun never sank down but only rested on the horizon in a perpetual sunset which never led to dusk. A school of grampus whales came alongside and a flock of tiny birds rested in the rigging, exhausted by their long flight over the icy waters. John walked up and down the length of the boat all day and most of the bright night, feeling oddly unemployed with hours of daylight and nothing to grow.

Then a thick fog came rolling over the sea, and the daylight counted for nothing. The sun disappeared behind it and there was neither night nor day but a perpetual pale greyness. Sir Dudley took to his chamber again and summoned one man after another to play at dice with him. John found himself curiously lost in the half-light. He could sleep or wake as he wished, but he never knew when he woke whether it was day or night.

Despite Tradescant's watching, it was a sailor who first called 'land ahoy!', spotting through the rolling fog the dark outline of the coast of the North Cape of Lapland.

Sir Dudley came up on deck, huddled in his thick cape. 'What can you see, John?'

John pointed to the dark mass of land which was growing whiter as they grew closer. 'More like a snowdrift than land,' he said. 'Bitterly cold.'

The two Englishmen stood side by side as their ship drew closer to the strange land. A man of war detached itself from the shadow of some cliffs and sailed towards them.

'Trouble?' Sir Dudley asked quietly.

'I'll ask the captain,' John said. 'You go below, my lord. I'll bring you news the moment I have it. Get your pistols primed, just in case.'

Sir Dudley nodded and went back to his cabin as John made his way the few steps to the captain's cabin and knocked on the door.

'What is it?'

'A man of war, coming this way, flying the Denmark flag.'

The captain nodded, pulled on his cape and came out of his tiny cabin. 'They'll only want passes,' he said. 'Sir Dudley's name is permission enough for them.'

He went briskly to the side of the boat, cupped his hands around his mouth and bellowed. 'Ahoy there! This is Captain Gilbert, an English sea captain on a voyage of embassy, carrying Sir Dudley Digges and the Russian ambassador. What do you want with us?'

There was a silence. 'Perhaps they don't speak English?' John suggested.

'Then they damned well should do so,' Gilbert snapped. 'Before trying to delay honest Englishmen going about their business.'

'Ahoy, Captain Gilbert,' the reply came slowly, muffled by the fog. 'We require your passes and permits for sailing in our waters.'

'Ahoy!' Gilbert shouted irritably. 'Our passes and permits are packed away for the voyage and besides, we need none. On board is Sir Dudley Digges and travelling with him is the Russian ambassador, homeward bound. You won't want to trouble the noblemen, I suppose?'

There was a longer silence as the Danish captain decided whether or not the troubling of the gentlemen was worth the possible embarrassment, and then decided it was not.

'You can pass freely,' he bellowed back.

'Thank you for nothing,' Gilbert muttered. 'I thank you,' he shouted. 'Do you have any provision we can buy?'

'I'll send a boat over,' came the reply, half-muffled by the fog.

Tradescant stepped swiftly down the companionway and tapped on the door to Sir Dudley's cabin.

'It's me, all's well,' he said quickly.

'Shall I come out?'

'If you wish,' John said and went back to the rail and watched with Captain Gilbert as a rowing boat, like a Dutch scuts, came out of the mist.

'Anything worth having?' Sir Dudley asked, from behind Tradescant.

The men waited. The little boat came alongside and threw up a rope. 'What've you got?' Captain Gilbert shouted.

The two men on board simply shook their heads. They understood no English but they held up a basket of salted salmon. Sir Dudley groaned, 'Not salmon again!', but he held up two silver shillings for them to see.

They shook their heads and held up a spread hand.

'They mean five,' Tradescant remarked.

'They can add then, even if they can't speak a civilised language,' the captain noted.

Sir Dudley reached into his purse and held out four silver shillings.

The men spoke briefly one to another and then nodded. Sir Dudley tossed the coins down into the boat and Tradescant caught the rope the sailors threw to him. He hauled in the basket of salmon and presented it to Sir Dudley.

'Oh, wonderful,' Sir Dudley said ungratefully. 'I know, let's have it with dry biscuit for a change.'

Tradescant grinned.

The rest of the voyage they hugged the coastline and watched the landscape change from the steady unyielding white of snow to a russet dry brown, and then slowly to a green.

'Almost like England in a hard winter,' Tradescant remarked to Captain Gilbert.

'Nothing like,' Gilbert said crossly. 'Because half the year it's under snow and half the year it's under fog.'

Tradescant nodded and retreated to his vantage point at the bowsprit. Now there was more and more for him to see as the coastline unrolled before the rocking prow. On land John could see the people of the country, who startled him at first with their appearance of having no necks, but heads which grew directly from their shoulders.

'It can't be,' he said stoutly to himself, and shaded his eyes from the sun to see better. As the people ran down to the beach, shouting and waving to the passing ship, and the ship drew a little closer to shore to avoid a mid-river sandbank, John could see that they were wearing thick cloaks of skins over their heads and shoulders, giving them the illusion of a hooded misshapen head.

'God be praised,' John said devoutly. 'For a moment I thought we were among strange countries indeed, and that all the travellers' tales I had heard were coming true.'

The people on the shore held up their bows and arrows and spread a deerskin for John to see. John waved back; the ship was too far out to make any bargaining a possibility, though he would dearly have loved to examine the bows and arrows.

The ship anchored at sunset, Captain Gilbert declaring that he was more afraid of sandbars in an unknown river than all the sailing he ever did across the North Sea.

'Can I have the boat take me on shore?' Tradescant asked.

The captain scowled. 'Mr Tradescant, surely you can see all you need from here?'

John smiled engagingly at him. 'I need to gather plants and rarities for my Lord Wootton,' he said. 'I'll be back before dusk.'

'Don't come to me with an arrow up your arse,' the captain said coarsely.

John bowed and slipped away before he could change his mind.

A young sailor rowed him to the shore. 'Can I wait by the boat?' he asked, his eyes round in his pale face. 'They say there are terrible people on this shore. They call them the Sammoyets.'

'Don't go without me,' John said. 'The captain is far more of a terror than the Sammoyets, I promise you. And he will kill you for sure if you maroon me here.'

The lad managed a weak smile. 'I'll wait,' he promised. 'Don't be too long.'

John slung a satchel over his shoulder and took a little trowel. In the pockets of his breeches he carried a sharp knife for taking cuttings. He had decided against carrying a musket. He did not want the trouble of keeping the fuse alight, and he thought he was as likely to shoot his own foot off in a moment of abstraction, as confront an enemy.

'You won't be too long, will you?' the lad asked again.

John patted his shoulder. 'As soon as I have found something worth bringing home I will come straight back,' he promised. 'Ten minutes at the most.'

He walked up from the shelving beach and at once plunged into the deep forest. Huge trees, a new fir tree that he had never seen before, interlaced their boughs above his head and made a twilight world which was shadowy green and sharply cold. Underfoot there were thick cushions, as big as bolsters, of fresh damp moss. John knelt before them, like a knight before the Holy Grail, and patted them with loving hands before he could bring himself to dig in his trowel and take a clump to stuff in his satchel.

There were shrubs he had never seen before, many in flower, white star-shaped flowers, and some tinged with pink. He walked on and came to a bush of whorts, with an unusual red flower. John brought out his little knife and took cuttings, wrapped them in more of the damp moss and laid them carefully in his satchel. A few steps more and he was in a clearing. Where the sunlight poured in there were bushes forming fruit like an English hedge mercury except that they were a brighter red and with three sharply-shaped leaves at the head of the twig, and every leaf bearing a berry inside it. In the darker places, beneath the trees, John saw the gleaming blossom of hellebores, thickly growing and carpeting the forest floor.

There was an explosion of noise from the trees above his head and John instinctively ducked, fearing attack. It was half a dozen birds, a new species to John, big pheasant-sized birds in white with green bodies and slate-blue tails. John clasped his hands together in frustration, longing for a musket so he could have shot one for the skin, but they were gone with a clatter of wings and there was no-one there for John to compare notes with, and wonder if he could possibly have seen aright.

He dug and snipped like a squirrel preparing for winter until, from the distance, he heard a faint voice calling his name and looked up, realising that it was growing dark and that he had promised the lad that he would be little more than ten minutes – and that was more than an hour ago.

John trotted down the path back to the boat and the shivering lad.

'What is it?' he asked. 'Cold or terror?'

'Neither!' the lad said stoutly, but as soon as he had the boat pushed off and rowed back to the ship he scampered up the ladder at the side and swore that he would never take Mr Tradescant anywhere again, whatever the captain said.

He did not need to risk a charge of mutiny. The next day the captain waited for the fullness of the tide to save them from the dangers of being grounded on sandbanks, and the ship landed at Archangel. The ship's company were able to go ashore to eat the oat bread and cheese and drink the Russian beer. And the gentlemen travelling with Sir Dudley unloaded their goods and moved into houses on the quayside. The company were particularly scathing about the houses – which were wooden cabins – and about the bread, which was made in different shapes, some rolls no bigger than a single mouthful.

John waylaid the Russian ambassador and was given permission to hire a local boat and set sail around the islands in the river channel. He took a purse of gold with him and bought every rarity he could find for his lord's collection, and took cuttings and roots and seeds from every strange plant he saw. At every island John went ashore, his eyes on his boots and his little trowel in his hand. And at every place he came back to the boat with his satchel bulging with cuttings and plants which had never before been seen in England.

'You are a conquistador,' Sir Dudley remarked when Tradescant arrived back at the Archangel quay and had his barrels of plants set in damp earth unloaded on the quayside. 'This is a treasure for those who love to make a garden.'

John, filthy and smelling strongly of fish which was all he had eaten for many days, grinned and came stiffly up the quayside steps.

'What have you seen?' Sir Dudley asked. 'I have spent all my time getting my goods unloaded and preparing for the journey to Moscow.'

'It is mostly waste ground,' Tradescant explained softly to him. 'But when they clear a piece of land for farming, they are good farmers, they can lay their crops down into soil which is only just warm and get a harvest off it inside six weeks.'

Sir Dudley nodded.

'But a poor country?' he suggested.

'Different,' John judged. 'Terrible ale, the worst taste I have ever had. But they have a drink called mead made with honey which is very good. They have no plane to work their wood, but what they can do with an axe and a knife is better than many an English carpenter. But the trees!' He broke off.

'Go on, then,' Sir Dudley said with a smile. 'Tell me about the trees.'

'I have found four new sorts of fir trees that I have never seen before, the buds of the boughs growing so fresh and so bright that they are spotted like a dappled pony, the bright green against the dark.'

Sir Dudley nodded.

'And a birch tree, a very big birch tree which they tell me they can tap for liquor and they make a drink from it. And they have a little tree for making hoops for barrels that they say is a cherry, but it was between the blossom and the fruit so I can't be sure. I can't believe there could be a cherry tree which could make hoops. But I have a cutting and a sapling which I will set to grow at home and see what it is. Its leaf is like a cherry. If you so much as bend a twig down to the ground it will grow where it is set, like a willow. That would be a wood worth growing in England, don't you think?'

Sir Dudley had lost his indulgent smile and was looking thoughtful. 'Indeed. And it must be strong to survive this climate. It would grow in England, wouldn't it, John?'

Tradescant nodded. 'And white, red and black currants, much bigger than our fruit, and roses – in one place I saw more than five acres of wild roses like a cinnamon rose. Hellebores, angelica, geranium, saxifrage, sorrel as tall as my son John at home – and a new sort of pink –' John broke off for a moment, thinking how pleased his lord would have been to hear that he had found a new sort of pink. 'A new pink,' he said quietly. 'With very fair jagged leaves.'

'These are treasures,' Sir Dudley said.

'And there are plants which could yield medicines,' Tradescant told him. 'A fruit like an amber strawberry which prevents scurvy, and I was told of a tree which grows at the Volga River which they call God's tree. It sounds like fennel but they say it will cure many sicknesses. You might see it, my lord. You might take a cutting if you see it.'

'Come with me, John,' Sir Dudley replied. 'Come and take your own cuttings. You've been here such a little time and found such novelties. Come with me to Moscow and you can collect your plants all the way.'

For a moment he thought the man would say yes. John's face lit up at the prospect of the adventure and the thought of the riches he would see.

Then he shook his head and laughed at his own eagerness. 'I'm like a girl running after a fair,' he said. 'I can think of nothing I would like more. But I have to go home. Lord Wootton expects me, and my wife and son.'

'His lordship comes first?'

John was recalled to his duty. 'My lord must come before everything. Even my own desires.'

Sir Dudley dropped an arm carelessly around John's shoulders, and they strolled together to his waiting horses. 'I am sorry for it,' he said. 'There's no man I would rather have beside me, all the way to China.'

John nodded to hide his emotion. 'I wish I could, my lord.' He looked down the wagon train of the strong Tartar horses, tacked up with deep travelling saddles.

'All the way to China, you say?'

'Think what you would find –' Sir Dudley whispered temptingly.

John shook his head but his hand was on the stirrup leather. 'I cannot,' he said.

Sir Dudley smiled at him. 'Then safe homeward journey,' he said. 'And if I find anything very rare or strange I will cut it and send it to you, and I will make a note of where I found it so that you can make the journey yourself one day. For you are a traveller, John, not a stay-at-home. I can see it in your eyes.'

John grinned, shaking his head, and made himself release his grip on the stirrup, and made himself step back from Sir Dudley's horse. He forced himself to watch, and not run after, as the whole cavalcade of them turned from the quayside to set off on the track towards Moscow and the East.

'God speed,' John called. 'And good fortune at the court of the Russian king.'

'God send you safe home,' Sir Dudley replied. 'And when I get home you can name me as your friend, Tradescant. I shall not forget your care of me when I was sick.'

John watched them till the dust from the last of the train was gone, till the dust had blown across the grey sky, until the sound of the harness bells and the beat of the hooves was silent.

That night they rocked at anchor, and on the next tide they loaded the last of their goods and cast off with Tradescant's cuttings in boxes on the deck and his trees loosely lashed to the mast, and his heart in his seaboots.

Elizabeth was watering the chestnut tree in its great box on the morning that John returned. The earth in the rest of the garden was dry and parched. It had been a bad year for the harvest, wet in the early months and scorching in July. The wheat crop had failed and the barley was little better. There would be hunger in the cities and in the poorer villages the price of flour would rise beyond the pockets of the poor. But through sun or rain the little chestnut sapling had thrived. Elizabeth had made it a little shelter of thatched straw to keep off the strongest sun, and watered it without fail on the dry days.

'Now there's a pretty sight!' John said, coming up behind her.

Elizabeth jumped at the sound of his voice and turned to see him. 'Praise God,' she said steadily, and paused for a moment, her eyes closed, to give thanks.

John, impatient with her piety, pulled her close to him and held her tight.

'Are you safe?' she asked. 'Was it a good voyage? Are you well?'

'Safe and well and with boxes full of treasures.'

Elizabeth knew her husband too well to imagine that he was talking of Russian gold. 'What did you find?'

'A Muscovy rose – bigger and sweeter than any I have seen before. A cherry tree with wood you can weave like a willow, which roots by bending its twigs into the ground, like a willow. Some new pinks with jagged leaves. I could have loaded the whole boat with white hellebores which grew so thick on one island that you could see nothing else, a new purple cranesbill, a great sorrel plant –' He broke off. 'A cart is following me. And I bought some rarities too for Lord Wootton's collection: Russian boots and strange shoes for walking on the snow and rare stockings.'

'And you are safe, and you were well?'

John sat down on the garden bench and drew Elizabeth on to his lap. 'Safe as a summer garden, and I was well all the time, not even seasick. And now tell me your news,' he said. 'Is J well?'

'Praise the Lord, yes.'

'And all your family? No plague in Kent?'

Elizabeth dipped her head in that familiar gesture which meant that she was swiftly praying. 'None, thank God. Is there sickness in London?'

'I passed swiftly through to avoid the risk.'

'And are you home now, John? Home for good?'

She saw his roguish smile but she did not respond to it. 'John?' she repeated gravely.

'There is a ship which I will take passage on, but it does not go for a year or two,' he assured her. 'An expedition to the Mediterranean against the pirates, and I may have a place on a supply pinnace!'

She did not return his smile.

'Think of what I might find!' John said persuasively. 'Think of what they grow in those hot places and what I might bring back. I should make my fortune for sure!'

Elizabeth folded her underlip.

'It will not be for a year or so,' he said placatingly. 'And it is all uncertain as yet.'

'You will always travel whenever you can,' Elizabeth replied bitterly. 'A man your age should be staying home. I thought we would settle here, away from the courts of great lords, I thought you would be happy here.'

'I am happy here, and it is not ever that I want to leave you . . .' John protested as she got up from his lap and went to one side, gently stroking the leaf of the chestnut. 'But I have to obey, Elizabeth – if my lord says I am to go, I have to go. And I must seek plants if I have the chance of them. It is to the glory of God to show men the wealth He has given us, Elizabeth. And a trip to the Mediterranean could bring back great things. Flowers and trees, but also herbs. Maybe a cure for the plague? That would be godly work!'

She did not smile at his overt appeal to her piety. 'It would be godly work to stay home and serve your lord at home,' she said firmly. 'And you are getting old, John. You should not be sailing out at your age. You are not a seaman, you are a gardener. You should be at home in your garden.'

Gently he drew her back to him. 'Don't be angry with me,' he said softly. 'I have only just got home. Smile for me, Lizzie, and see: I have brought you a present.'

From deep in the pocket of his coat he brought a small pine cone. 'A new tree,' he said. 'A beautiful fir tree. Will you nurse it up for me, Elizabeth? And keep it as well as you have kept our chestnut? I love you as much now as I did when I gave you the chestnut.'

Elizabeth took it but her face remained grave. 'John, you are nearing fifty years old,' she said. 'It is time for you to stay home.'

He kissed the warm nape of her neck, slightly salt beneath his lips. Elizabeth sighed a little at the pleasure of his touch, and sat still. In the apple tree above their heads a woodpigeon cooed seductively.

'The next voyage shall be my last,' he promised. 'I will go to the Mediterranean on the *Mercury* and then I shall come home with orange trees and olive trees and all manner of spices and grow them quietly in my garden with you.'

When J learned that his father was to go to the Mediterranean he insisted that he go too, but John refused. J went quite pale with anger. 'I am old enough to come with you now,' J insisted.

'I want you to continue at school,' John said.

'What's the use of that!' J exclaimed passionately. 'You never went to school!'

'And I felt the lack of it,' John pointed out. 'I want you to read and write in Latin as well as English. I want you to be brought up as a gentleman.'

'I won't need that, I shall be a planter in Virginia. Captain Argall said that the last thing the new plantation needs is gentlemen. He said the plantation needs hard-working men, not scholars.'

Elizabeth looked up at the mention of Argall's name and compressed her lips.

'He may be right,' John said. 'But I was counting on you to help me with my business, before you leave for Virginia.'

J, who was in full flight, checked at that. 'Help you?'

'All the plants these days are given new names, Latin names. When the King of France's gardeners, the Robins, write to me and send me cuttings, they send them with their Latin names. I was hoping you would learn to read and write Latin so you could help me.'

'I shall work with you?'

'Of course,' John said simply. 'What else?'

J hesitated. 'So you'll stay home and teach me?'

'I shall go on this trip to the Mediterranean,' John stipulated. 'Destroy Algiers, defeat the corsairs, collect all the Mediterranean plants, and come home. And after that I shall stay home and we shall garden together.'

J nodded, accepting the compromise. Elizabeth found that she had been gripping her hands tightly together under the cover of her apron, and released her grasp. 'Tradescant and son,' John said, pleased.

'Tradescant and son,' J replied.

'Of Canterbury,' Elizabeth added, and saw her husband smile.

Spring 1620

'They say that Algiers is a town which cannot be taken,' Elizabeth said to John on the quayside, refusing to be optimistic even at this last moment.

'You are too doubting,' John said mildly. 'Algiers can be defeated, no town is invincible. And the pirates who use it as their base must be stopped. They cruise in the English Channel, even up the Thames. The king himself says that they must be taught a lesson.'

'But why should it be you that goes?' she demanded.

'To go plant-hunting in the meantime,' John replied mildly. 'Captain Pett said he was short-handed for officers and he would take me. I told him that I would want the ship's boat to call on shore wherever we could. It's a bargain on both sides.'

'You won't take part in any battles?' Elizabeth pressed him.

'I shall do my duty,' John said firmly. 'I shall do whatever Captain Pett commands.'

Elizabeth curbed her anger and put her arms around her husband's broadening middle. 'You're not a young man any more,' she reminded him gently.

'For shame,' John said. 'When my wife is a girl still.'

She smiled at that but he could not divert her. 'I wanted you to stay home with us.'

He shook his head and gently kissed the warm top of her white cap. 'I know, my love, but I have to go when there is a chance for me like this one. Be generous and send me away with a smile.'

She looked up at his face and he saw that she was closer to tears than to smiles. 'I hate it when you go,' she repeated passionately.

John kissed her on the mouth, on the forehead as he had first done when they were betrothed, and then again on the lips. 'Forgive me,' he said. 'And give me your blessing. I have to go now.'

'God bless you,' she said reluctantly. 'And bring you safe home to me.'

'Amen,' he replied and before she could say more he had slipped out of her arms and run up the gangplank to the pinnace *Mercury*.

She did not wait to see his ship sail this time. She had good reason to hurry home. J would be back from school in the afternoon and she had planned to take a lift on the Canterbury wagon which went from Gravesend at midday. But in truth she did not wait because she was angry and resentful, and because she did not want to stand on the quayside like a lovelorn girl to wave her husband goodbye. She could not help but think that it was an infidelity to her and to his promise to stay home and dig his garden. She could not help but think the less of him that he could not resist the temptation of adventure.

John, looking down from the deck at the small indomitable figure walking stiff-backed away from the quayside, knew some of what was in her mind and could not help but admire her. He knew also that she would have been a happier wife coupled with another man, one who stayed at home and only heard travellers' tales in the village inn. And that he too would have been a happier man married to a woman who could wave goodbye and greet him home with a broad smile and not cling to him on leaving, nor greet him resentfully on his return. But it was not a love match between John and Elizabeth and it never had been. What love they had found, and what love they had made, had been a benefit which neither they, nor their fathers who had wisely made the match, could have predicted. It was a marriage which was primarily designed to resolve some debts. It was a marriage designed to place Elizabeth's dowry in the hands of a man who could make use of it, and place John's skills at the disposal of a woman who would know how to manage a house that should grow in size and splendour with every move. The old men had chosen well. John was richer every year with his wages and with his burgeoning trade in rare plants. Elizabeth managed the

Canterbury house as she had managed the new house at Hatfield, as she had managed the cottage at Meopham – with confidence and honesty. She had managed the vicarage and farmhouse for Gertrude, she could cope with bigger houses than her marriage had yet brought her.

But their fathers never provided for temperament and desire and jealousy. And the marriage they made never had room for such emotions either. As John watched Elizabeth walk away from the quay and as the *Mercury* slipped its moorings and the barges took it in tow, he knew that she would have to come to terms with the disappointments of the marriage as well as its benefits. He knew that she would have to recognise that her husband was a venturer, an adventurer. And that when he came home she would have to know that he was a man who could not resist the chance of travelling overseas. And that when the chance came for him – he would always go.

John's Mediterranean voyage took him to Malaga, to join the rest of the English fleet in readiness for the assault on Algiers, and then they sailed in force to Majorca for revictualling. At both stops John begged for the use of the ship's boat and went ashore with his satchel and his little trowel; he came back with his satchel bulging.

'You look as if you have murdered a dozen infidels,' Captain Pett said as Tradescant returned, mud-stained and smiling through the Mediterranean sunset.

'No deaths,' John said. 'But some plants which will make my name.'

'What've you got?' the captain asked idly. He was not a gardener and only indulged John's enthusiasm for the undeniable benefit of having a steady and experienced man on board who might command a troop of men if needed.

'Look at this,' John said, unpacking his muddy satchel on the holystoned deck. 'A starry-headed trefoil, a sweet yellow rest harrow, and what d'you think this is?'

'No idea.'

'A double-blossomed pomegranate tree,' John said proudly, producing a foot-long sapling from his satchel. 'I'll need a barrel of earth for this at once.'

'Can it grow in England at all?' Captain Pett asked curiously.

Tradescant smiled at him. 'Who knows?' he said, and the captain suddenly realised the joy that fired his temporary maverick officer. 'Who can tell? We grow a cultivated sort in the orangeries. This is far more fragile and lovely. But I shall have to try it. And if I win, and we can grow wild pomegranates in England, then what a glory to God! For every man who walks in my garden can see things that until now he would have had to travel miles to find. And he can see that God has made things in such variety, in such glorious wealth, that there is no end to His joy in abundance. And no end to mine.'

'Are you doing this for the glory of God?' Captain Pett asked, slightly bemused.

John thought for a moment. 'To be honest with you,' he said slowly, 'I cling to the thought that it is for the glory of God. Because the other thought is heresy.'

Captain Pett did not glance around, as he would have done on land. He was master of his own pinnace and speech was free. 'Heresy? What d'you mean?'

'I mean that either God has made dozens, even hundreds, of things which are nearly the same, and that the richness of his variety is something which redounds to His holy name . . .'

'Or?'

'Or that this is madness. It is madness to think that God should make a dozen things almost the same but a little different. All a man of sense could think is that God did not make them. That the earth they feed on and the water they drink makes plants in different areas a little different, and that is the only reason that they are different. And if that is true, then I am denying that everything in the world was made first by my God in Eden, working like a gardener for six days and resting on the Sabbath. And if I am denying that, then I am a heretic damned.'

Captain Pett paused for a moment, following the twisting path of Tradescant's logic, and then let out a crack of laughter and hammered Tradescant on the shoulder. 'You are trapped,' he exclaimed.

'Because every variety that you discover must make you doubt that God could do all this in six days in Eden. And yet what you say you want to do is to show these things to the glory of God.'

Tradescant recoiled slightly from the loud good humour of his captain. 'Yes.'

The captain laughed again. 'I thank God I am a simple man,' he said. 'All I have to do is to sack Algiers and teach the Barbary pirates that they cannot hazard the lives of English sailors. Whereas you, Tradescant, have to spend your life hoping for one thing but continually finding evidence to the contrary.'

A familiar stubborn look came across John's face. 'I keep faith,' he said stolidly. 'Whether to my lord or to my king or to my God. I keep faith. And four sorts of smilax do not challenge my faith in God or king or lord.'

Pett was optimistic about the ease of his task, compared with John's metaphysical worries. He was part of a well-victualled well-commanded fleet with a clear plan. When they came to Algiers it was the task of the pinnaces to patrol the waterways to trap the pirates inside the harbour.

John and the other gentlemen recruited for the adventure were called into the captain's cabin on the day the whole of the English fleet was assembled and moored in readiness half a league off shore.

'We'll send in fire boats,' Pett said. 'Two. They are to set the moored shipping ablaze and that will destroy the corsairs' fleet. It'll also spread smoke across the harbour and under cover of the smoke we'll assault the walls of the harbour. That will be our task and that will be where you come in, gentlemen.'

He had a map unrolled before him on the table. The English fleet was shown as a double line of converging white flags with the distinctive red cross. The corsair ships were shown as a black square.

'Which way is the prevailing wind?' Tradescant asked.

'Onshore,' Pett replied. 'It will blow the fire boats in, and then the smoke will go into their eyes.'

'Do we have scaling ladders for the harbour walls?' someone asked.

The officers nodded, Tradescant among them.

'And you each of you know the men you are to lead and have checked their equipment?' Captain Pett confirmed.

Tradescant nodded and glanced around him, wondering if anyone else had a sense of sick dread in their stomachs, the fear of a man who had never seen a battle before.

'Then do your duty, gentlemen,' the captain said simply. 'For God and King James.'

John wanted the attack to start at once, certain that his small core of courage would diminish if he had to wait a moment. He stood with his landing party at the side of the pinnace and watched the fire boats go in through the mouth of the harbour. The two little barges were loaded with explosives and tar and were rowed with a single oar by a volunteer. The rower's task was to get the little craft through the choppy water at the harbour mouth and then as close as he dared to the moored shipping, despite the rain of musket fire which came down from the trapped ships. He was to light the coil of pitch rope which served as a fuse, point the boat in the right direction and then plunge into the sea and swim as fast as he could back to the English ships while the fire boat, smouldering with its cargo of explosives, was supposed to float up against the enemy shipping.

'At least I wasn't ordered to do that,' Tradescant whispered miserably to himself, watching the little boat head towards the harbour mouth and seeing a cannonball splash with horrid weight into the water beside it.

The boat bobbed in, the sailor's head just visible, they saw the flame of the fuse and his swift dive into the water, and then ... nothing. The fuse had gone out and they heard the ironic cheers of the pirates as the fire boat bobbed uselessly against the wooden sides of their ships.

'A free gift of powder and explosives to our enemies,' Captain Pett said savagely. 'Stand down, everyone, there will be no attack until the tide is up tomorrow.'

Tradescant spent a sleepless night, with the taste of fear like cold sweat on his lips, and in the morning showed a white face on deck at the head of his landing party. He checked them over. They all had muskets primed and ready, they all had brightly glowing fuses palmed confidently in their hands. One man had the scaling ladder and he was wearing a helmet Tradescant had managed to scrounge in Majorca. Tradescant nodded to his troop with affected confidence and was irritated to see, by the hidden smile one from another, that they saw and understood his pallor.

'Soon be over, sir,' one of them said cheerfully. 'And you're either dead or safe in minutes.'

'Thank you,' John said repressively, and went to the ship's rail to watch the fire boats go in.

They failed again, and the next day too. By day four Tradescant ate a hearty breakfast and was at the rail to watch the fire boats try once more and felt as nonchalant as his men. Boredom and disappointment had driven out fear and now he wanted the battle to be joined. What he could not tolerate was the waiting and the immense irritation when the winds dropped and the fire boats burned harmlessly in the middle of the bay and then exploded with a loud crack that made the pirates cheer.

It was dawn, the tide suited them high at dawn. The weather suited them at last, a grey mist on the water which would make the pirate muskets uncertain of their aim shooting into greyness, and a brisk onshore wind which should blow the fire boats inwards to the harbour.

'But hardly a surprise attack,' Tradescant grumbled, at the pinnace rail. The wind blowing steadily onshore lifted the brim of his hat.

'The principle is right,' someone said behind him.

Tradescant thought of his old master's preference for sound practice over principle, but held his peace. They all watched together as the two barges were rowed to the harbour mouth. The sailors on board lit the fuses to the explosives, burning twists of rope dipped in pitch. No-one could tell how long they would take to burn with any accuracy. It was a brave man who stayed on board a barge that would blow up at any moment to steer it closer and ever closer to enemy shipping.

The two sailors did well. 'Jump!' Tradescant muttered under his breath as they went through the harbour mouth and drifted towards the ships, while the waiting English ships could see the sparks at the foot of the powder kegs. Then there were two dark shadows leaping and two splashes in the water, and then an almighty roar as the first barge went up in flames and drifted towards the trapped corsair ships.

But just as it should have collided with the wooden rowing ship there was a sudden lull.

'The wind!' Captain Pett yelled in anguish. 'What the devil has happened to the wind?'

It was nothing, a lull before a storm, but it was enough to ruin the English plans. The fire boats exploded and burned as they should have done as two little torches afloat on the dark water of Algiers harbour, the corsair ships remained moored safe in its lee, and the pirate crews came out on deck with toasting forks and made as if they were frying their bacon for breakfast on the English attack.

'What do we do now?' someone asked. 'Stand down again?'

'Today we attack,' Captain Pett said. 'We follow orders.'

John found his feet were strangely heavy in his boots. There was nothing for him to do until the *Mercury* was close enough either to shore or to a ship, and then he was to lead a boarding party.

'There will be no smoke,' he said shortly. 'No cover. And they are ready and waiting and confident.'

'My orders are to attack whatever the success of the fire boats,' Captain Pett declared.

He called for the sails to be crowded on and the *Mercury* moved slowly towards the mouth of the harbour. There was another pinnace before her, and one behind; all the English captains were staying within the letter of their orders though the chances of the attack succeeding with the wind down and the fire boats sputtering into darkness was remote. The Turkish guns, expertly manned from the high harbour walls, bombarded the incoming ships. 'Like ducks on a moat,' John said angrily.

Mercury sailed in, obeying orders.

'Please God he does not put us ashore and expect us to scale the walls,' Tradescant muttered into his neckerchief. He looked back at his men. They were waiting grim-faced for Tradescant to lead them; ahead of them were the high walls of the fort with the sharply etched windows where a dozen muskets waited for the English to come into range, clearly visible on the water which was brightening with the morning light and shielded neither by mist nor smoke.

Captain Pett sailed inward, obeying his orders to the letter, but with a man at his elbow with a telescope trained on the commander's ship, waiting for a signal. At last the flag reluctantly fluttered out.

'Retreat ordered,' shouted the man with the telescope.

'Retreat!' Captain Pett bawled. At once the drum began to beat and the other English ships wheeled around and started forcing their way, against the prevailing wind, back out of the harbour mouth.

The rest of the fleet sent in barges and took the ships in tow. It was an ignominious end to an attack, but John caught a rope and made it fast, feeling as light-hearted as a lad. The desire for battle had been replaced completely with a profound longing for the safety and comfort of his home.

Elizabeth greeted John home with a touch of coolness. She had been painfully aware that he had left despite her wishes, and she had prayed every night that he would be spared so that he could come home and they could start again, start as friends and lovers again. But when he walked into the Canterbury cottage, not a scratch on him, his face tanned and smiling, and a small wagon of plants waiting outside in the lane, her most powerful feeling was deep irritation.

John sent the wagon on to Lord Wootton's garden with orders to see that the plants were unloaded and watered, and came into the house asking for a bath and that his linen be burned on the kitchen fire.

'It's lousy,' he said. 'It has driven me mad for days.'

Elizabeth set water to heat, pulled out the big wooden washtub and set it on the stone flags of the floor. John stripped off his clothes and left them at a heap near the door.

'God be praised, I am glad to be home,' he said and gave her a smile. She did not smile back at him, nor did she come into his arms and put her face against his warm bare chest. John did not hold out his arms. He was afraid he might smell and he knew his head and his beard harboured lice. But he would have been glad of a greeting which was passionate, or even affectionate. Elizabeth pouring hot water into the tub offered a dutiful welcome; not an exciting one.

'I am glad to see you safe home,' she said calmly, and put on another pot of water to heat.

John tested the water with his foot and then stepped in. Elizabeth handed him the washball of herbs tied in cotton, and a bowl of sludgy soap.

'I was afraid you might be fired on, sailing past the Spanish coast,' she said. 'There were rumours that the fleet would go against Spain.'

'I would have thought you would have been glad to see me put a cannonball into the heart of Papistry,' John observed, sitting in a bath of soapy water and sponging the salty grime of several months' voyage off his neck.

'Not if they fired back,' she said. 'And anyway, I thought your quarrel was with the infidels.'

John splashed water into his face and puffed out like a grampus whale. 'We had orders which could be read any way you wanted,' he said. 'It makes no sense to me. When I leave the garden for any length of time I say to the gardeners, take care of this, and when this flowers do this. I don't say to them, use your judgement, do as you wish. And that way, when I come home again, I know if they have done well or badly, and they know it too.'

'But the king?' Elizabeth asked.

John lowered his voice. 'The king gave them orders which told them to attack the infidel and release our poor captured countrymen, and gave them secret orders to attack Spain, and then orders which were to be open which told them to respect Spain as an ally.'

Elizabeth shook her head. 'This is dishonesty,' she said flatly.

John smiled, as if at an old half-forgotten joke. 'It's practice. But not principle.'

'It's a sin.'

John looked at her thoughtfully. 'You're very sure what makes a sin and what does not, my wife. Are you setting up to be a preacher like your father?'

To his surprise she did not laugh and disclaim, as she would have done only a few years before. 'I am studying my Bible more than I have done before,' she told him. 'There is a lecturer who teaches me and some other women on Wednesday nights. He's a man of much learning and wisdom too. And I find I am thinking of things with more care than when I was a girl full of folly.'

John bent his knees awkwardly in the little wooden tub to get his shoulders under the suds. 'I don't remember you as full of folly,' he remarked. 'I always thought you were a God-fearing serious woman.'

Elizabeth nodded and again he saw the new gravity about her. 'These are fearful times,' she said. 'The plague seems to get worse every summer and no-one can tell where it strikes. There are rumours about a king and a court who don't walk in the way of the Lord. And a church which does not reproach them.'

John straightened and rose up from his bath, water cascading all over the floor. Elizabeth handed him a linen sheet and he threw it around his shoulders. She was carefully looking away as if the sight of her husband's nakedness might lead her into sin. It was that turning away of her head which tripped John into irritation.

'We don't repeat gossip about the king in this household,' he said flatly. And when Elizabeth was about to argue he held up his hand. 'It's not a matter of piety or truth, Elizabeth. It's a lesson I learned from my lord. We don't gossip against the king. The price is too high if you're overheard. Whatever you are reading at your classes, you keep your mind on your Bible and off King James and his court, or you won't go again.'

For a moment she looked as if she might argue. 'Does this man preach against the authority of God vested in men over their wives?' he demanded.

She dropped her head. 'Of course not.'

John nodded, hiding his sense of immense smugness. 'Good.'

'You know that all I have ever wanted is for you to come home and stay home,' Elizabeth said, dragging the big bath towards the back door where it could be tipped into the yard. 'If you had been home I would have had no time to go to meetings.'

John gave her a sharp look. 'Don't lay it at my door,' he said. 'You can go where your conscience leads you as long as it does not take you into treason or into denying the authority of those set over you. *All* of those set over you. Me as your husband, my lord above me, the king above him, and God above him.'

She flung open the door so a cool wind blew in around John's bare legs. 'I would never deny God's authority,' she said. 'And I have not denied the authority of men. Mind you don't catch cold.'

John turned abruptly and went to the bedroom to get dressed.

1622

'Should we not transplant that chestnut?' J asked his father.

John was leaning on his spade, watching his coltish fourteen-year-old son at work. 'It must be getting too big for that box,' J said.

'I gave that to your mother the year we were married,' John said reminiscently. 'Sir Robert and I bought a dozen of them – no, half a dozen. Five I planted for him at Hatfield and one I gave to your mother. She kept it in a pot at Meopham, and then I moved it into the carrying box when we went to Hatfield, with you so little on the bench seat of the wagon that your feet didn't reach the board.'

'Shouldn't we plant it out now?' J asked. 'So it can put down great roots?'

'I suppose so,' John said thoughtfully. 'But we can leave it another year. I'm going to buy some land at the back of our house, make a bigger garden, so that we can see it spread out. The man who sold it to me said they grow as wide as an oak tree. There's no room for it in the cottage garden, it would overspread the house. And I'd be loath to plant it here.'

J gazed around Lord Wootton's graceful garden, at the grey walls and the high tower of Canterbury Cathedral behind. 'Why not? It would look well enough.'

John shook his head. 'Because it's your mother's,' he said gently. 'Given from me to her the first time I loved her. She rarely comes in here, she'd never see it. It's her keepsake. We must buy her a bigger house with a bigger garden so she can sit underneath it and rock your babies on her knee.'

J flushed with the quick embarrassment of a young man still too innocent for bawdy talk. 'There won't be babies from me for a while,' he said gruffly. 'So don't count on it.'

'You put your roots down first,' John advised. 'Like your mother's chestnut sapling. Shall we take a break for our dinner now?'

'I'll go on,' J said. 'I want to take a look at those Spanish onions of yours. They should be fit to taste soon.'

'They'll be very sweet if they've grown as well as they do at their home,' John said. 'They eat them like fruit in Gibraltar. And take a look at the melon glasses when you're in the kitchen garden. They should be ripening. Bank up some straw around and under them to keep the slugs off.'

J nodded and trudged off to the kitchen garden. John spread a napkin on the grass and opened his little knapsack. Elizabeth had given him a new-baked loaf, a slice of cheese, and a flask of small ale. The crust was grey, the flour was poor this year, and the cheese was watery. Not even good money could buy good provisions. The country was feeling the pinch of bad finances and bad harvests. John made a small grimace and bit into his bread.

'John Tradescant?' John looked up but did not rise to his feet though the man standing above him was splendidly dressed in the livery of the Duke of Buckingham.

'Who wants him?'

'The Duke of Buckingham himself.'

John put his loaf of grey bread to one side and stood up, brushing off crumbs.

'I am John Tradescant,' he said. 'What does His Grace want?'

'You're to go and see him,' the man said abruptly. 'You're summoned. He's at New Hall at Chelmsford. You're to go at once.'

'My master is Lord Wootton . . .' John started.

The man laughed abruptly. 'Your master can be Lord Jesus Christ for all that my master cares,' he said softly.

John recoiled. 'No need for blasphemy.'

'Every need,' the man insisted. 'For you do not seem to understand who commands you. Above my master there is only the king. If my master wants something he has only to ask for it. And if he asks for it, he gets it. D'you understand?'

John thought of the painted youth at Theobalds who sat in King James's lap, and the jewels around the young man's neck and the purse at his waist.

'I understand well enough,' he said dryly. 'Though I've been away from court for some years.'

'Then know this,' the man said. 'There is only one person in the world for King James, and that is my master – the beautiful duke.' He stepped forward and lowered his voice. 'The duke's friends can do anything they wish – poison, treachery, divorce! All this they have done and escaped scot-free! Had you not heard?'

John carefully shook his head. 'Not a thing.'

'Lord Rochester took the wife of another man, no less than the Earl of Essex's wife. They declared him impotent! How would you like that?'

'Not at all.'

'Then Rochester and his new wife poisoned Sir Thomas Overbury who would have betrayed them. She is a declared witch and poisoner. How d'you like that?'

'No better.'

'Found guilty, imprisoned in the tower, and then what d'you think?'

John shook his head, maintaining his ignorance.

'Forgiven overnight!' the manservant said with satisfaction. 'If you have the king's ear you can do no wrong.'

'The king knows best,' John said staunchly, thinking of his lost lord and his advice to be blind and deaf when other men are talking treason.

'And Rochester was as nothing to *my* lord.' The man lowered his voice still further. 'Rochester is the old favourite, but my lord is the new. Rochester may have had the king's ear, but my lord has all his parts. D'you understand me? He has all his parts!'

John kept his face very still, he did not smile at the bawdy humour.

'My master is supreme under the king,' the man declared. 'There is no-one in England more beloved than my master, George Villiers. And he has decided that you are to serve him.' The man looked down at John's plain dinner. 'Chosen you from every other man in the kingdom!'

'I am honoured. But I do not think I can be released from my work here.'

The man flapped a letter in John's face. 'Villiers's orders,' he said. 'And the king's seal. You're to do as you are told.'

John resigned himself to the inevitable, and rolled up his half-eaten dinner in his napkin.

'And remember this,' the man continued in the same boastful tone. 'That what the duke thinks today, the king thinks tomorrow, and the prince thinks the next. When the king goes, the duke and the prince succeed. When you hitch your cart to the star of my master you have a long brilliant future.'

John smiled. 'I have worked for a great man before,' he said gently. 'And in great gardens.'

'You have never worked for one like this,' the servant declared. 'You have never even seen a man such as this.'

John thought that Elizabeth would dislike the move to His Grace's house at New Hall, Chelmsford, and he was right. She was passionately opposed to leaving Lord Wootton's service and going near to the hazardous glamour of the royal court. But the little family had no choice. J took his mother's worries to his father and gained no satisfaction. 'Mother does not want to move house, and she doesn't want you to work for a great lord again,' he said in his halting shy way. 'Mother wants us to live quietly, she likes it here.'

'Won't she speak to me herself?'

'She didn't ask me to tell you,' J said, embarrassed. 'I thought perhaps you didn't know. I was trying to help.'

John dropped a gentle hand on his son's narrow shoulder. 'I know what she fears, but I am no more free to choose where to live than your mother is free,' he explained. 'She is bound by God to follow me, and I am bound by God to go where I am commanded by my lord and by the king above him. And lord and king and therefore God say we must go to the Duke of Buckingham in Essex.' He shrugged. 'So we go.'

'I don't believe that God wants us to go near to vanity and idleness,' J protested.

John turned a stern gaze on him. 'What God wants or does not want no man can say, only a priest or the king,' he said firmly. 'If the king tells the duke who tells my Lord Wootton that I am wanted in Essex, then that is enough for me; as if God had leaned down from heaven and told me himself.' He paused. 'And it should be enough for you too, J.'

J, avoiding the challenge his father's gaze, looked away. 'Yes, sir,' he said.

The little family had been expecting something impressive of New Hall. The duke had bought it as a palace near to London where he could entertain the king in a style befitting the royal favourite. It had been a summer palace for Henry VIII and had passed around the courtiers as a prize plum of patronage. Buckingham was said to have paid a fortune for it, and was now pulling the place apart to enrich it still further, under the direction of Inigo Jones, who was laying a great sweeping staircase of marble and noble stone gateways.

The Tradescants arrived, as the king himself would arrive on his frequent visits, up the great drive which turned in a full circle before the house. The house fronted the drive full-square, with great turrets on either side and a huge wooden doorway, wide and high enough for two coaches to be driven abreast into the inner courtyard. It was built of handsome stone, every inch carved and crenellated like marchpane on a cake, with three storeys of bay windows bulging from the encrusted walls. At each corner stood great towers with bulbous cupolas and flags flying from the poles at the top. In the inner courtyard was a huge cobbled area, as big as a tiltyard, with the great hall on the east side and a handsome oriel window looking out over the quadrangle. On the west side was the chapel for the house, and a bell tolling at the tower end.

Elizabeth looked askance at the stained glass in the huge chapel windows as the wagon halted in the yard. A maidservant came out with a tray of drinks for the travellers, and a groom from the stables emerged and said he would direct the wagon on to the Tradescants' own cottage.

'His Grace said that you should live in the great house if you please, but he thought you might prefer your own cottage so that you can nurse up plants in your own garden.'

'Yes,' Elizabeth said before John could reply. 'We don't want to live in the hall.'

John shot her a reproving look. 'The duke is gracious,' he said carefully. 'I will need a garden under my eye. A cottage sounds a very good solution. Please show us the way.'

He drained his mug of small ale, set it back on the tray with a smile at the girl. J, still seated in the back, one arm around the precious chestnut tree, one hand on the tailgate of the wagon, did not even glance at the pretty serving maid but kept his eyes on his boots.

John sighed. He had not imagined the move would be easy but with Elizabeth suspecting Papistry and luxury around every corner and with J sinking into the manners of a country bumpkin, he thought that returning to court life would be hard indeed, and that no master, however graceful or powerful, would make up for the differences in the little Tradescant family.

The cottage was some compensation. It had been built as a farmhouse and taken into the demesne of New Hall by the ever-widening wall and ambition of each successive owner. It was as good as Elizabeth's girlhood home at Meopham, a two-storeyed, four-bedroomed house with an orchard at the back and a stable yard with room for a dozen horses at the side.

Elizabeth might put up with the disruption of the move for the benefit of the house, John thought, and held that hope in his mind until they had unpacked their goods and penned up the cat so that she should not stray, when a liveried manservant from the house tapped on the open front door and ordered John to wait on His Grace in the garden.

John pulled on his jacket and followed the man back up the drive towards the house.

'He's in the yew-tree allee,' the man said, gesturing to the right of the house. 'He said you were to go and find him.'

'How shall I know him?' John asked, hanging back.

The man looked at him with open surprise. 'You'll recognise him the moment you see him. Without error.'

'How?'

'Because he's the most beautiful man in the kingdom,' the man said frankly. 'Go towards the yew-tree allee and when you see a man as lovely as an angel, that's my lord Buckingham. You can't miss him, and when you've seen him, you'll never forget him.'

John puffed a little at the courtier hyperbole and turned towards the colonnade of yew. He had time to note that the allee was overgrown and needed pruning at the head of the trees to make them thicken out at the bottom, before he stepped into the shade. He blinked against the sudden darkness of the thickly interleaved boughs. It was as dark as nighttime beneath the arching branches. The ground beneath his feet was soft with years of fallen brown yew needles. It was eerie and silent in the darkness; no birds sang in the still boughs of the trees, no sun shone into their shade. Then John's eyes adjusted to the dimness after the dazzle of the sun and he saw George Villiers, Duke of Buckingham.

At first he could see only a silhouette of a slim solitary man, of about thirty. He was dark-haired and dark-eyed, dressed like a prince, laden with diamonds. He had a bright mobile face above the wide lace-trimmed ruff with eyes that were smiling and wicked, and a mouth as changeable and as provocative as any pretty woman's. The pallor of his skin gleamed in the darkness as if he were lit from within, like a paper lantern, and his smile, when he saw John coming towards him, was as engaging as a child's, with the confidence and innocence of a child who has never known anything but love. He wore a doublet and cape of dark green, as green as the yew, and for a moment John, looking from trees to man, thought he was in the presence of a dryad – some wild beautiful spirit of the wood – and that some miracle had been granted him, to see a tree dancing towards him and smiling.

'Ah! my John Tradescant!' exclaimed Buckingham, and at that moment John suffered a strange falling feeling which made him think that he had taken the sun, riding all day on the open wagon. The man smiled at him as if he were a brother, as if he were a living angel come to give him tidings of great joy. John did not smile in greeting – years later he would remember that he had not felt any sense of meeting a new master but rather a grave sense of deep familiarity. He did not feel that they were well-met, new-met. He felt as if they had been together for all their lives and just accidentally parted until now. If he had spoken the words in his heart he would have said: 'Oh, it is you – at last.'

'Are you my John Tradescant?' the man asked.

John bowed low and when he looked up the sheer beauty of the young man made him catch his breath again. Even standing still, he was as graceful as a dancer.

'I am,' John said simply. 'You sent for me and I have come to serve you.'

'Forgive me!' the duke said swiftly. 'I don't doubt you were snatched away from your work. But I need you, Mr Tradescant. I need you very badly.'

John found he was smiling into the quick bright face of the young man. 'I'll do what I can.'

'It is here, at these gardens,' the young duke said. He led the way down the allee, talking as he went, throwing a smile over his shoulder as John followed. 'The house is a thing of rare beauty, King Henry's summer house. But the gardens have been sorely neglected. I love my gardens, Mr Tradescant. I want you to make these rich and lovely with your rare trees and flowers. I have seen Hatfield and I envy you the planting of such a place! Can you work the same magic for me here?'

'Hatfield was many years in the making,' John said slowly. 'And the earl spent a fortune on buying in new plants.'

'I shall spend a fortune!' the young man said carelessly. 'Or rather, you shall spend my fortune for me. Will you do that for me, John Tradescant? Shall I earn a fortune and you spend it? Is that a fair agreement?'

Despite his sense of caution, John chuckled. 'Very fair on me, my lord. But perhaps you had better take a care. A garden can gobble up wealth as it can gobble up manure.'

'There's always plenty of both,' Buckingham said quickly. 'You just have to go to the right place.'

John was tempted to laugh, but then thought better of it.

'So will you do it?' Buckingham paused at the end of the allee and looked back towards his house. It looked like a fairy-tale palace in the afternoon sunshine, a crenellated turreted palace set in the simple loveliness of the fertile green countryside of England. 'Will you make me a fine garden here, and another at my other house in Rutland?'

John looked around. The ground was fine, the aspect of the house was open and facing south. The ground had been terraced in wide beautiful steps down the hillside; at the bottom was a marshy pond that he could do all sorts of things with: a lake with an island, or a fountain feature, or a man-made river for boating.

'I can make you a fine garden,' he said slowly. 'There will be no difficulty in growing what you will.'

Buckingham slipped his hand in John's arm. 'Dream with me,' he urged him persuasively. 'Walk with me and tell me what you would grow here.'

John looked back at the long allee. 'There's little that will grow under yew,' he said. 'But I have had some success with a plant that came from Turkey to France: lily of the valley. A small white flower, the daintiest thing you have ever seen. Like a snowdrop only smaller, a frilled bell, like a little model of a flower made in porcelain. It is scented, they tell me, as sweet as a rose, only sharp like lemons. A true lily scent. It will grow in great thick clumps and the white flowers are like stars against broad green leaves.'

'What d'you mean, they tell you it is scented? Can't you smell them?' Buckingham asked.

'I have no nose for smell,' John admitted. 'It is a great disadvantage for a gardener. My son tells me when the earth smells sour or when we have some putrid rot. Without him I have to go by my eyes and touch.'

Buckingham stopped and looked at his gardener. 'What a tragedy,' he said simply. 'One of the greatest pleasures for me is the scent of flowers, what a tragedy that you cannot sense this! Oh! And so many other things! Good cheeses, and wine, and smell of a clean stable of straw! Oh! and perfume when it is warm on a woman's skin, or the smell of her sweat when she's hot! And tobacco smoke! Oh, John! What a loss!'

John smiled a little at his enthusiasm. 'Having never known it I do not feel the lack,' he said. 'But I should like to smell a rose.'

Buckingham shook his head. '*I* should like *you* to smell a rose, John. I feel for you.'

They walked on a few steps more. 'Now,' Buckingham said. 'What would you do here?'

The ground below them fell away to the marshy dip at the bottom of the field. As they watched, a herd of cows trudged through the mud and water, churning it up.

'Get rid of the cows,' John said definitely.

Buckingham laughed. 'I could have thought of that on my own! Do I need to hire you to tell me to mend the fences?'

'First get rid of the cows,' John amended. 'And then perhaps use that water to make a lake? Perhaps a water-lily lake? And at one side you would have a wet garden with plants that love moisture. Some reeds and rushes, irises and buttercups. And on the other a large fountain. At Hatfield we had a grand statue mounted on a boulder. That was handsome. Or perhaps some playful water feature? A fountain which throws an arc of water for boats to sail underneath? Or an arc of water thrown over the path? Or even from one side of the lake to another with a bridge passing beneath it.'

Buckingham gleamed. 'And one of those toys which sprinkle people when they approach!' he exclaimed. 'And I should like a little mount as well, perhaps in the middle of the lake!'

'A grand mount,' John suggested. 'Planted thickly with a winding allee to the summit. Perhaps cherry trees, espaliered into a hedge to make them thick and shady. I have some wonderful new cherry trees. Or even apple trees and pears. They take time to establish but you have a pretty effect with blossom in spring, and at the end of summer it is very rich to walk under boughs heavy with fruit. We could thread them through with roses and eglantine, which would climb and hang their blooms down through the leaves. You could row out to your island and wander among roses and fruit.'

'And where would you put the knot gardens?' Buckingham demanded. 'Beyond the lake?'

John shook his head. 'Near to the house,' he said firmly. 'But you could show me your favourite window-seat and I could plant a garden which leads the eyes outwards, into the garden, a little maze for your eye to follow, in stone and with small pale-leafed plants, and herbs to aid your meditations.'

'And an orchard with a covered walk all around it, and turf benches in every corner. I must have an orchard! Great fruiting trees which bow low to the ground. Where can we get quick-growing fruit trees?'

'We can buy saplings. But it will take time,' John warned him.

'But I want it now,' Buckingham insisted. 'There must surely be trees which will grow swiftly, or trees we can buy full-grown? I want it at once!'

John shook his head. 'You may command every man in England,' he said gently. 'But you cannot make a garden grow at once, my lord. You will have to learn patience.'

A shadow crossed Buckingham's face, a dark flicker of frustration. 'For God's sake!' he exclaimed. 'This is as bad as the Spanish! Is everything I desire to go so slow that by the time it comes to me I am sick of waiting? Am I to grow old and tired before my desires can be met? Do I have to die before my plans come to fruit?'

John said nothing, only stood still, like a little oak tree, while the storm of Buckingham's temper blew itself out. Buckingham paused as he took the measure of John Tradescant, and he threw back his curly dark head and laughed.

'You will be my conscience, John!' he exclaimed. 'You will be the keeper of my soul. You gardened for Cecil, didn't you? And they all say that when you wanted Cecil, you had to go out into the garden and find him; and half the time he would be sitting on a bench in his knot garden and talking to his man.'

John nodded gravely.

'They say he was the greatest Secretary of State that the country has ever had, and that your gardens were his greatest solace and his joy.'

Tradescant bowed and looked away, so that his new mercurial master should not see that he was moved.

'When I am tempted to overreach myself in my garden or in the great wild forests which are the courts of Europe, you can remind me that I cannot always have my own way. I cannot command a garden to grow,' Buckingham said humbly. 'You can remind me that even the great Cecil had to wait for what he wanted, whether it was a plant or policy.'

John shook his head in quiet dissent. 'I can only plant your garden, my lord,' he said softly. 'That's all I did for the earl. I can't do more than that.'

For a moment he thought that Buckingham would argue, demand that there must be more. But then the young man smiled at him and dropped an arm around his shoulders and set them both walking back to the house. 'Do that for me now, and when you trust me more, and know me better, you shall be my friend and adviser as you were Cecil's,' he said. 'You will make it grow for me, won't you, John? You will do your best for me, even if I am impatient and ignorant?'

Tradescant found that he was smiling back. 'I can undertake to do that. And it will grow as fast as it is able. And it will be all that you want.'

John started work that afternoon, walking to Chelmsford to find labourers to start the work of fencing the cows out, digging the lake and building the walls for the kitchen garden. He took a horse from the stables and rode a wide circle around the great estate to neighbouring farms to see what trees they had in their orchards and what wooded copses he could buy and transplant at once.

Buckingham was careless about cost. 'Just order it, John,' he said. 'And if they are tenants of mine just tell them to give you whatever you wish and they can take it off their rent at quarter day.'

John bowed but made a point of visiting the steward of the household, at his desk in an imposing room at the very centre of the grand house.

'His Grace has ordered me to buy trees and plants from his tenants, and command them to take the cost from their rent,' Tradescant began.

The steward looked up from the household books, which were spread before him. 'What?'

'He has ordered me to buy from the tenants,' John began again.

'I heard you,' the man said angrily. 'But how am I to know what is bought or sold? And how am I to run this house if the rents are discounted before they are collected?'

John hesitated. 'I was coming to you only to ask you how it should be done, if you have a list of tenants –'

'I have a list of tenants, I have a list of rents, I have a list of expenditure. What no-one will tell me is how to make the one agree with the other.'

John paused for a moment to take stock of the man. 'I am new in this post,' he said cautiously. 'I don't seek to make your task any harder. I do need to buy his lordship trees and plants to stock his gardens and he ordered me to buy from his tenants and see that they deduct the cost from their rents.'

The steward took in Tradescant's steadiness. 'Aye,' he said more quietly. 'But the rents are already spent, signed away, or promised. They are not free for deductions.'

There was a brief silence. 'What am I to do then?' John asked pleasantly. 'Shall I return to his lordship and tell him it cannot be done?'

'Would you do that?' the man enquired.

John smiled. 'Surely. What else could I do?'

'You don't fear taking bad news to a new master, the greatest master in the land?'

'I have worked for a great man before,' John said. 'And, good news or bad, I found the best way was to tell him simply what was amiss. If a man is fool enough to punish his messengers he'll never get his messages.'

The steward cracked a laugh and held out his hand. 'I am William Ward. And I am glad to meet you, Mr Tradescant.'

John took the handshake. 'Have you been in his lordship's service for long?' he asked.

The steward nodded. 'Yes.'

'And are his affairs in a bad way?'

'He is the wealthiest man in the land,' William Ward stated. 'Newly married to an heiress and with the king's own fortune at his disposal.'

'Then –?'

'And the most spendthrift. And the wildest. D'you know how he did his courting?'

John glanced at the closed door behind them and shook his head.

'He caught the lady's fancy – not surprising –'

John thought of that smile and the way the man threw back his head when he laughed. 'Not surprising,' he agreed.

'But when he went to her father, the man declined. Again, not surprising.'

John thought of the rumours that Buckingham was the king's man in ways that a sensible man did not question. 'I don't know,' he said stoutly.

'Not surprising to those of us who have seen the king on his visits here,' the steward said bluntly. 'So what does my lord do?'

Tradescant shook his head. 'I have been away, and in Canterbury, we don't hear gossip. I rarely listen to it, anyway.'

The steward laughed shortly. 'Well, hear this. Buckingham invites Lady Kate to his mother's house for dinner and when the dinner is ended they don't let her call for her carriage. They don't let her go home! Buckingham's mother herself keeps the girl overnight. So her reputation is ruined and her father is glad to get her wed at any price, takes the duke's offer and has to pay handsomely for the privilege of having his daughter dishonoured into the bargain.'

Tradescant's jaw dropped open. 'He did this?'

William Ward nodded.

'To a lady?'

'Aye. Now you get some idea of what he can do and what he is allowed. And now you get some idea of his rashness.'

Tradescant took a couple of swift steps and looked out of the window. Almost at once his sense of anxiety at this new post, at this madly impulsive young master, deserted him. He could see the site of what would be his kitchen garden, and he had it in mind to build a hollow wall, the first of its kind in England, and to heat the inside of it like a chimney. It might warm the fruit trees growing against the wall and make them come early into bud. He shook his head at the promising site and returned to the problem of his new master's wildness.

'And is his new wife unhappy?' he asked.

William Ward looked at him for one incredulous moment and then burst into laughter. 'You've seen my lord. D'you think a new wife would be unhappy?'

John shrugged. 'Who knows what a woman wants?'

'She wants rough wooing and passionate bedding and she has had both from our lord. She wants to know that he loves her above everything else and there is no other woman in the land who can say that her husband risked everything to have her.'

'And the king?' Tradescant asked, going to the key of all things.

Ward smiled. 'The king keeps the two of them as lesser men keep lovebirds in a cage, for the pleasure of seeing their happiness. And in any case, when he wants Buckingham all to himself he has only to crook his finger and our lord goes. His wife knows that he must go, and she smiles and bids him farewell.'

The steward fell silent. John looked out again at the parkland that stretched to the horizon. This was flat country, he thought the winds in winter would be cruel. 'So,' he said slowly. 'I have a new lord who is a spendthrift, and wild, a breaker of hearts and no respecter of persons.'

The steward nodded. 'And any one of us would lay down our lives for him.'

Surprised, John looked up. The steward was smiling.

'Yes,' he said. 'There isn't a man on the estate who wouldn't go hungry to keep him in his silks and satin. You'll see. Now go and buy your trees. Every time you agree a price, make sure that you note down the tenant's name and the price of his trees. And tell them that I – I and not they – will calculate the difference in the rents and discount the rents next quarter day. Bring me the list when you have done.'

He paused for a moment. 'Unless I have given you a disliking for your lord and you want to go back to Canterbury?' he asked. 'He is as wild as I say, he is as spendthrift as I say, and he is as wealthy as I say. He has more power at his fingertips than any man in the land, and that is probably including the king.'

John had a strong sense of returning to his place at the very centre of things, serving a lord who served his country, a man whose doings were the talk of every ale house in the land. 'I'll keep my place here,' he said. 'There is much for me to do.'

1623

John and J worked hard all the winter, planning the gardens and pegging out lines for the knot garden, for the terraces, and for the turf benches in the lord's new orchards. Much of the work had to wait until the spring when the ground was soft enough for digging, but John had a small forest of trees waiting for the earth to warm so that they could be planted, each one labelled with its place, each with a plot reserved for it. For the workers who could neither read nor write, J had instituted a scheme of coloured dots. They had to match the label on the tree marked with three red dots with the plot in the ground marked with three red dots. Or green or yellow. 'This is code,' John said admiringly to J.

'It's madness,' J said bluntly. 'Everyone should be taught to read at dame school. How else can they understand their Bible? How else do their work?'

'We're not all scholars like you,' John said mildly.

J flushed in one of his sudden attacks of bashfulness. 'I'm no scholar,' he said gruffly. 'I don't pretend to be one. I'm no better than any man. But I do think that all men should be taught to read and write so that they can read their Bible and think for themselves.'

Work on the heated wall had already started to John's design. The plot was marked out and the foundations for the perimeter wall were already dug. The whole garden was to be walled with a double skin of deep red brick, and there were to be built three equally-spaced fireplaces, one above the other, where the charcoal burners could be lit and the smoke drift sideways through the wall till every brick was warm to the touch. The beds of the garden were not to be edged with box in the usual way. John wanted to raise them after a fashion never seen before. He wanted little brick walls to edge them, and the beds were to be filled with sifted earth and rotted manure. He even instituted a pile of manure from the stables, which was to be left to moulder and then turned over every month. 'I don't want it all fresh and carrying the roots of weeds into my garden,' he explained to J and to the other vegetable gardeners. 'I want the earth in these beds to be free of weeds and free of stones. I want this garden to have soil so rich and so soft that I could lay a strawberry plant on it and leave it to set its own roots. D'you understand?'

They grumbled behind his back but to his face they nodded and pulled their caps. John's reputation as one of the greatest gardeners of the day had preceded him and it was an honour to work under him – raised beds, and stirred manure, hollow walls, or no.

The house was quiet after the festivities of Christmas; the duke had returned from the court in January and set up residence with Kate, his wife. His mother was to come later in the year. So Tradescant, rounding the stable yard in search of an errant weeding lad, was surprised to see an exceptionally fine horse, an Arab, being led from its stall into the yard, and the duke's hunter prancing around on the cobbles, all tacked up and ready to go.

'Whose horse is that?' John asked a groom and received nothing more than a wink for a reply.

'Dolt,' John said shortly, picked up his hoe and went to pace out the orchard.

That afternoon, John was measuring the length of the new avenue which he planned to plant with lime trees leading from the Chelmsford road to the house when he heard hoofbeats on the drive and there were the two horses with two strange men on their backs.

John stepped forward to challenge them. 'Who are you? And what's your business here? That's my lord's horse.'

'Let me pass, my John,' said one of the men in a familiar voice. The stranger leaned down from the duke's horse and swept off his hat. Buckingham's dark eyes looked down at John, and John heard his irrepressible chuckle.

'Fooled you,' Buckingham cried triumphantly. 'Fooled you completely.'

John stared at the face of his lord, absurdly concealed by a false beard and a muffler. 'Your Grace –' He glanced across at the other horseman and recognised, with a sense of shock, the young prince he had last seen snivelling at the heels of his older brother. But now the young prince was the heir, Prince Charles. 'Good God! Your Highness!'

'Will we pass, d'you think?' Buckingham demanded joyously. 'I am John Smith and this is my brother Thomas. Will we pass, d'you think?'

'Oh, yes,' John said. 'But what are you about, my lord? Wenching?'

Buckingham laughed aloud at that. 'The finest wench in the world,' he whispered. 'We're going to Spain, John, we're going to marry His Highness here to the Infanta of Spain! What d'you think of that?'

For a moment John was too stunned to speak, then he grabbed the hunter's bridle above the bit. 'Stay!' he cried. 'You can't.'

'You order me?' Buckingham enquired politely. 'You had much better take your hand off my horse, Tradescant.'

John flinched but did not let go. 'Please, your Grace,' he said. 'Wait. Think on this. Why are you going disguised?'

'For the adventure!' Buckingham said merrily.

'Come on, Thomas!' the prince said. 'Or are you John? Am I Thomas?'

'I beg of you,' John said urgently. 'You cannot go like this, my lord. You cannot take the prince like this.'

The prince's horse pawed the ground. 'Come on!' the prince said.

'Forgive me!' Tradescant looked over at him. 'Your Highness has perhaps not considered. You cannot ride into France as if it were East Anglia, Your Highness. What if they hold you? What if Spain refuses to let you leave?'

'Nonsense,' Prince Charles said briefly. 'Come on, Villiers.'

Buckingham's horse moved forward and John was dragged along, not releasing his grip on the bridle. 'Your Grace.' He tried again. 'Does the king know of this? What if he turns against you?'

Buckingham leaned low over the horse's neck so he could whisper to Tradescant. 'Leave me go, my John. I am at work here. If I marry the prince to the infanta then I have done something which no man has ever done – make Spain our ally, make the greatest alliance in Europe and myself the greatest marriage broker who ever lived. But even if I fail, then the prince and I have ridden out like brothers and we will be brothers for the rest of our lives. Either way, my place is assured. Now let my bridle go. I have to leave.'

'Have you food and money, a change of clothes?'

Buckingham laughed. 'John, my John, next time you shall pack for me. But I must go now!'

His spur touched the hunter's side and it threw up its head and bounded forward. Prince Charles's horse leaped after, and there was a swirl of dust in John's face and the two of them were gone.

'Please God keep him safe, keep them safe,' Tradescant said, looking after them. His new master and the prince he had known as a lonely incompetent little boy. 'Please God, stop them at Dover.'

Elizabeth saw at once that something had happened when John came home at dusk for his dinner and stared into his broth without eating. As soon as J had eaten she sent him from the room with a nod of her head, and then seated herself beside John on the settle which stood at the fireside, and put her hand on his. 'What's the matter?'

He shook his head. 'I cannot tell you.' He glanced down into her worried face. 'Nothing wrong with me, my dear. Nothing wrong with J, and nothing wrong with the garden. But I cannot tell you. It is a secret and not my secret. I cannot tell anybody.'

'Then it's the duke,' she said simply. 'He's done something bad.'

John's stricken look told her that her guess had struck home.

'What's he done?' she pressed.

He shook his head again. 'Please God, it won't be too bad. Please God there will be a happy outcome.'

'Is he at home?'

He shook his head.

'Gone to London? Gone to the king?'

'Gone to Spain,' he whispered very low.

175

Elizabeth recoiled from him as if he had pinched her. 'Spain?'

John gave her a swift unhappy glance and put his finger to his lips. 'I cannot say more,' he said firmly.

Elizabeth rose and went to the fire, bent and stirred the poker under the glowing logs. He saw her lips moving in a silent prayer. Elizabeth was a devout woman, a trip to Spain was like a trip to the underworld to her. Spain was the heart of Catholicism, the home of the anti-Christ against whom all good Protestants must struggle and fight from birth till death. Buckingham's choice of destination at once condemned him in her eyes. He must be a bad man if he chose to go to Spain.

John closed his eyes briefly. He could not imagine what condemnation would be released on his master if Elizabeth, and all the many hundreds, thousands, of devout men and women like Elizabeth, knew that he was planning to bring a Spanish princess home to be queen of England.

Elizabeth straightened up and hooked the poker on to the bracket at the side of the fire. 'We should leave,' she announced abruptly.

'What?' John opened his eyes again and blinked.

'We should leave now.'

'What are you saying? We've only just got here.'

She came back beside him, took his hand in hers and pressed it to her lips and then held it to her heart, like a pledge. He could feel her heartbeat, steady and reassuring, as her earnest face looked into his. 'John, this duke is not a good man. I have spoken with the people of the house and half of them worship him and will hear nothing against him, and the other half say that he is a sinner of dreadful vices. There is no balance in this household. There is no steadiness. This is a whirlwind of worldly desires and we have strayed into the very heart of it.'

John wanted to speak but she gently pressed his hand and he let her finish.

'I did not want to leave Canterbury but you prevailed and it was my duty to obey you,' she said softly. 'But please now, husband, hear this. We can go to any household in the world that you choose as long as we do not stay here. I will pack our goods and our clothes and go tomorrow, wherever you say, as long as we do not stay here.

I will follow you overseas even, Virginia even, as long as we do not stay here.'

John waited until she was silent then he spoke cautiously, feeling his way. 'I never thought to hear you speak so. Why do you dislike him so much? As a man? As my master?'

She shrugged and looked towards the fire where the flames were leaping over the wood and casting a flickering light on her face. 'I don't know him as a man, and it's too early to say how he will be as your master. All I have seen of him is worldly show. The diamonds in his hat, the horses in his coach. What man in England has ever had a coach before? No-one but the old queen and King James, and now this man has one, with rare horses to go before it. All I have seen of him would make me suspect that he is not a true Christian. And all that I have heard of him, and all that I know of him, tells me that he is very deep in sin.' She dropped her voice. 'Have you not thought that he may even be in league with the devil himself?'

John tried to laugh but Elizabeth's sincerity was too much for him. 'Oh, Elizabeth!'

'Where did he come from?'

'Not from hell! From Leicestershire!'

She frowned at the flippancy of his tone. 'The son of a servant and a mere knight of the shires,' she said. 'Look at his rise, John. D'you think a man can get such fortune honestly?'

'He has enjoyed the favour of the king,' John insisted. 'He was a cup-bearer and then a groom of the bedchamber and the favourite of many great men. They helped him to the post of Master of the Horse and he has brought the king such horses as no prince ever had before. Of course he enjoys great favour, he has earned it. He brought the king an Arab horse, the only one in England. The finest horse that ever was seen in England.'

She shook her head. 'So they make him Lord High Admiral – for trading in a horse?'

'Elizabeth –' John said warningly.

'Bear with me,' she said swiftly. 'Hear me out, this once.'

He nodded. 'But I will not hear treason.'

'I will speak nothing but the truth.'

They looked at each other for a moment and she saw in the sliding away of his glance that he knew that the truth was treasonous. That you could speak the truth about Buckingham and the truth was that the king was mad for the man and unfit to rule through his madness. That Buckingham was higher than his ability, higher than any single man's ability could ever take him, because the king was mad to please him.

'What hold is it that he has over the king?' she asked, her voice very low.

'The king loves him,' Tradescant said firmly. 'And he is his faithful servant.'

'He calls himself the king's dog,' she said, naming the unthinkable.

'In play. The king calls him Steenie after St Stephen – he admires his beauty, Elizabeth. Nothing wrong with that.'

'He calls himself his dog and there are those who say that the king mounts him like a dog mounts a bitch.'

'Silence!' Tradescant leaped to his feet and away from his wife. 'That you should speak such words, Elizabeth! At your own hearthside! That you should listen to such things! Bawdy talk! Dirty tavern talk! And repeat them to me! What would your father say if he heard his daughter speaking of such things like a whore!'

She did not even flinch from her father's name. 'I say what must be said, what must be clear between the two of us. And God knows that my heart is pure though my mouth is filled with filth.'

'A pure heart and a dirty mouth?' Tradescant exclaimed.

'Better than a sweet mouth and dirty heart,' she retorted. He checked, they were both thinking of Buckingham and the sweetness of his singing voice.

'Finish what you have to say,' John said sullenly. 'Finish this, Elizabeth.'

'I say to you that his mother who was born a serving maid is now a countess, and is said by many to be a witch –'

John gasped, but she went on.

'A witch. And others say that she is a Papist, a heretic, who would have been burned at the stake only a few years ago. I say to you that he is a man who has earned his place by sodomy under the king, and by pandering for the king, who won his wife by kidnap and by rape, who has seduced the king and seduced the prince. Who has been a sodomite with a man and with his son. For all I know he is leagued with the Devil himself. Certain, he is deep, deep in sin. And I ask you, John, I beg you, John, to let us go now. To let us leave him now. He has gone to Spain, to the enemy of our country, so he is a traitor even to the king who sins with him. So let us go, John. Let you and me and J get away from here to somewhere where the air is not rank as sulphur with sin and debauchery.'

There was a long silence.

'You are intemperate,' John said weakly.

She shook her head. 'Never mind about that. What's your answer?'

'I have been paid for the full quarter –'

'We can find a way to repay your wages if we leave now.'

He paused for a moment, thinking of what she had said. Then slowly he rose and shook his head. He put his hand on the chimney breast, almost as if he needed to steady himself as he went against his wife's declared wish, and his own sense, his own deep and hidden sense, that she was right.

'We stay,' he said. 'I have given him my promise that I will make him a fine garden. I will not go back on my word. Even if all that you say were true, I would not go back on my word. All I will do for him is garden, there can be no sin in that for us. We stay, Elizabeth, until the garden is finished and then we will leave.'

She stood beside him, looking up into his face, and John saw her face alter, as if he had failed some great test and she would never fully trust him again.

'I beg you,' she said and her voice shook a little, 'by everything that I hold sacred, which is everything that this new lord of yours denies, to turn aside from him and walk in the paths of righteousness.'

John shrugged irritably at her scriptural tone. 'It's not like that. I have agreed to make a garden for my lord and we will stay until I have completed it. When it is done we can leave, as I have said.'

He went from the room and she heard him close their bedroom door and the floorboards creak as he undressed to get into their bed.

'It is like that for me,' she said quietly to the dying fire, as if she were swearing a solemn oath. 'You have turned aside from the paths of righteousness, husband, and I can walk by your side no more.'

John waited for news of his master but there was silence for the first two, three days. Then news of the escapade of the young prince and the young duke began to leak out. They were incompetent conspirators and, indeed, such incompetent travellers that it was a wonder they were not stopped at Dover as John had hoped. But Villiers threw silver around their journey, and ordered the ships out of Dover harbour on his authority as Lord High Admiral, and soon the court and the old king heard that the boys had been entertained in Paris, ridden halfway across France, and finally reached Madrid.

The king saw the whole business as a handsome piece of the knight errantry, like the court masques when the handsome hero wins the fairest lady and then they dance. But the rumour that came back to England, even to the King's Arms at Chelmsford where John had taken to drinking in the evening, alert for gossip, was that matters were more difficult. The weeks went by and the young men did not come home with a princess for a bride. Instead they sent demands for money and more money.

The king grew fretful, missing the duke, even missing his usually neglected son. The court was robbed of life when Villiers was not there to arrange amusements, the hunting, the masquing, the scandals. John, lingering in the steward's room, found the courage to ask him outright if he thought their master would hold his place if he did not come home soon, and saw his own worry reflected in William Ward's eyes.

'They will introduce the king to another man every day that our lord is away,' Mr Ward said quietly. 'And the king does not like demands for money. He will hold it against our lord. He will resent it.' He paused for a moment. 'You knew the prince when he was a boy, is he faithful-hearted?'

John thought of the lame boy who stammered on his plea that his handsome brother should wait for him, and was always left behind. The sickly boy who was never anyone's favourite while his older brother was the heir. He nodded. 'Once he gives his love he clings,' he said simply. 'If he loves our duke as he loved his brother, then he worships him.'

William Ward nodded. 'Then maybe our lord is playing a wiser game than we realise. He may be breaking the heart of the father but there will be another king when the father is gone.'

John scowled at the thought of courtier's work which was not based on skill and turning of policy, but was grounded on courtship and heartbreak and jealousy; the skills of the bordello, not of the office.

'It must have been the same for Lord Cecil?' the steward asked.

John jerked back at the thought of it. 'No! Nobody loved *him* for his looks,' he said with a half-smile. 'They needed him for his abilities. That was why no-one could supplant him. That was why he was always safe.'

'Whereas our lord –' The steward broke off.

'What's he doing in Madrid that takes so long?' John demanded.

'I hear that the Spanish are playing with him,' the steward said very quietly. 'And all the time the feeling against the Spanish is rising in the court, in Parliament and in the streets. He'd do better to come home without the Spanish princess. If he brings her home now he'll pay for it with his life. They'll tear him to pieces for arranging a heretical marriage.'

'Can't you write and tell him?' John asked. 'Warn him?'

William Ward shook his head. 'I don't advise him,' he said quickly. 'He treads his own path. He said the Spanish marriage was a matter of principle.'

'Principle?' John asked. And when the man nodded he turned and went from the room. 'That's very bad,' John said to himself.

Not until July, midsummer in Madrid, during the worst of the hot weather, was Prince Charles finally wearied of waiting, and Buckingham losing his nerve. At last the Spanish completed the marriage contract and Prince Charles put his name to it. He was allowed a brief visit to his bride to promise that she would be Queen of England after a proxy marriage, and that they would next meet as husband and wife at Dover. The King of Spain himself rode out of Madrid with the prince and duke to set them on their way, loaded them with presents and kissed Prince Charles farewell as a son-in-law.

'How do you think he will be received?' William Ward asked John. He had gone into the garden to seek John, who was opening the sluice gates and watching the flow of the river into the duke's new boating lake. It was a cool sheet of water just to the side of the house. John was planting yellow flag irises in the boggy corner where he had first told Buckingham to shut out the cows. 'He must have some trickery up his sleeve. He must know that if he tries to bring a Spanish bride home they will tear him to pieces?'

John looked up from the water channel and wiped his hands on his old breeches. 'He can't be such a fool,' he said anxiously. 'He cannot have got as far as he has and still be a fool. He must know that there is a balance between king and Parliament and church and people.' He thought of Cecil; he could not help but think of Cecil in this, his successor's household. 'He cannot hold the offices he has and be a fool,' John said stoutly. 'He must have some way to turn this all around.'

John did his lord a favour with such faith. Buckingham had no master plan and no plan hidden behind it. He was not a Cecil with a conspiracy for every eventuality. Everything in his life had come easily to him, and he had thought that this would come easily too. He had thought that he could seduce the Spanish as he had seduced everyone else. But the cold formal court of Spain proved hardhearted even to England's heartbreaker; and his disappointment turned him against them. His letters from home from his mother and from his wife warned him that a Spanish bride would never be accepted and the man who tried to bring her to the English throne could meet with nothing but disaster. Buckingham turned like a weathercock; but Charles – who had learned early that love is always a matter of disappointment – clung to his picture of a desirable and unattainable woman. Indeed, the more unattainable she became, the more she mirrored Charles's vision of true love and desire.

It was Buckingham's task to lift the prince's view from a woman who might never love him, whom he could trail behind for the rest of his days, as he had trailed behind his brother, and encourage him to think that as a prince of England he might hope for a little more.

It was not easy. Buckingham reminded him of the concessions of the marriage contract – wild promises of religious tolerance and the children of the marriage to be brought up as Papists. He questioned Spanish probity, wondering if the infanta could really be constrained into marrying a heretic, or if she would not, on her wedding day, make a dive for a nunnery and leave Charles looking like a fool. The steady drip, drip, of cynicism and doubt eroded the prince's confidence, which was, at the best of times, unsteady. By the time the two had ridden from Madrid to Santander to meet the English fleet, Buckingham and the prince were the best of friends, and Spain was their opponent. By the time they sailed into Portsmouth they were as close as brothers and Spain was not to be the new alliance, but was once again the deadliest enemy, and the marriage contract which they had worked for so fervently was a trap that they were determined to escape.

As they came into Portsmouth, through the cold sea mist of October, sailing in with the tide, uncertain of their welcome in the Protestant city in the staunchly Protestant country after trying for a marriage which would have brought the proud Tudor independence to an abrupt end, they saw a light blaze on the quayside; a bonfire had been lit. Then another, then another, in a string of light along the city walls. Then there was the boom of a cannon salute which echoed across the harbour, and then another, and the scream of loudly blown trumpets, and the sound of people cheering. Buckingham smiled to himself, slapped his prince on the back and went below to put the diamond studs in his hat.

183

'He did it, he brought the prince safe home,' John said to Elizabeth when the news of the triumphant entry of the two young men into London reached New Hall. 'There was dancing on the streets and roasted oxen at every corner. They are calling him a greater statesman than England has ever seen. They are calling him the saviour of his country. Shall we go into Chelmsford tonight and see the merry-making?'

He did not mean to crow but he heard the joy in his own voice. It was not that Buckingham had proved himself to be a statesman or a diplomat. But at least he was lucky, and in this new court, luck and beauty would do everything.

The face that Elizabeth turned to him was pinched and cold. 'He took the prince into danger in the first place,' she said unforgivingly. 'Danger of his body and deadly danger to his mortal soul. And the prince only escaped from marrying a disciple of the Devil by being forsworn. He gave his word of honour to a noble princess. He courted her and promised to marry her. But now he has broken his promise. I shan't go dancing because your lord took the prince into danger and then made him a jilt to bring him safe home. It was vanity and folly to go in the first place. I won't drink to his safe return.'

John quietly put on his coat and hat and let himself out of the door. 'I think I'll go then,' he said mildly. 'Don't wake for me.'

1624

'He's home,' J announced without enthusiasm.

John was standing on the mount he had created in the duke's new lake, checking the line of the winding path to the top. Below him, the men hired to plant the trees were digging and setting in apple, cherry, pear and plum alternately up the circling slope. Small stakes supported each tree against the constant easterly winds which were John's bugbear in this Essex garden. Bigger posts were set in the ground, tied tautly with twine, one to another, to guide the espaliered branches to reach out, one tree to another, so they would make unbroken lines of blossom in spring, and unbroken lines of fruit in autumn. J's task was to check that each tree was placed to its best advantage with the outstretched branches lying conveniently along the twine, and tied in so they could not stray and be wayward. John was following with a sharp knife to cut off any twigs which were growing out of the smooth line of the interlaced trees. It was one of John's most favourite tasks: a delicate marriage of wildness and artifice, an imposition of order upon unruliness which in the end looked as if it had grown ordered and well-ruled out of simple good nature. A garden as God might have left it, an Eden without disorder or weeds.

'God be praised!' John said, straightening up from his pruning. 'Did he ask for me? Is he coming out into the garden?'

J shook his head. 'He's sick,' he said. 'Very sick.'

John felt his breath suddenly stop as if he too were ill. A sudden pulse of dread went through his body at the thought of his master's frailty. He suddenly remembered Cecil, dying in bluebell time. 'Sick?' he asked. 'Not the plague?'

J shrugged. 'A great quarrel with the king, and he took to his bed.'

'He is pretending to be ill?' John asked.

'I think not. The duchess is running all around their apartments and the kitchen is making possets. They want some herbs for medicine.'

'Good God, why did you not tell me at once?' John ran down the path, slithering on the muddy track, and flung himself into the rowing boat moored at the delicate ornamental jetty. He grabbed at the oars and laboured clumsily across the lake, splashing himself with water and cursing his own slowness. He got to the shore, beached the boat, and ran through the shallows and up towards the house.

He went straight away towards the great hall, his boots making wet prints on the floor. 'Where is the apothecary? What does he need?'

The man gestured him towards the duke's private quarters, up the beautiful staircase which had cost him such a fortune. John went up the stairs at a run. The duke's apartments were in uproar, the doors wide open, the duke sprawled neglected on his bed, still in his riding boots. Dozens of men and women were running in and out with coals for his fire and fresh straw for the floor, warming pans, cooling drinks, someone opening the windows, someone closing the shutters. Amid it all was Kate, the young duchess, weeping helplessly in a chair and half a dozen apothecaries quarrelling over the bed.

'Quiet!' Tradescant shouted, too angry at the sight of such chaos for his usual politeness. He took a couple of footmen, spun them around and pushed them out of the room. He closed the door on them and then pointed to the maids who were sweeping the floor and the men who were stacking logs on the fire. 'You! Out.'

The room slowly emptied of complaining servants, and Tradescant turned his attention to the apothecaries. 'Who's in charge here?' he asked.

The six men, all bitter rivals, burst into noisy argument. Kate, hunched in her chair, wailed like a child.

Tradescant opened the door. 'Her Grace's ladies!' he shouted.

They came at the run. 'Take Her Grace to her own chamber,' he said gently. 'Now.'

'I want to be here!' Kate cried.

Tradescant took her arm and half-lifted her from the room. 'Let me see that he is comfortable and you can come when he is ready to receive you,' he suggested.

She fought against him. 'I want to be with my lord!'

'You wouldn't want him to see you weeping,' John said softly. 'With your nose all red, and your eyes puffed up so plain.'

The appeal to her vanity struck her at once. She ran out of the room and John closed the door on her and rounded on the apothecaries. 'Which of you is the oldest?' he demanded.

One man stepped forward. 'I,' he said, thinking that the prize was to be awarded to seniority.

'And which the youngest?'

A young man, barely thirty, stepped forward. 'I am.'

'The two of you get out,' Tradescant ordered brutally. 'The other four of you agree on a treatment in whispers, at once.'

He opened the door and the two dismissed men hesitated, caught one fulminating look, and stepped outside. 'Wait there,' Tradescant said. 'If these can't agree you'll be employed in their place.'

He shut the door on them and went back to the bed. The duke was as white as marble, he looked like a statue carved from ice. The only colour about him was his dark eyelashes sweeping his cheeks and the blue shadows, the colour of violets in springtime, under his eyes.

The eyelids fluttered and he looked up at John. 'Splendidly done,' he said softly, his throat hoarse. 'I just want to sleep.'

'Well enough,' Tradescant said. 'Now that I know.' He pointed to the apothecaries. 'You three – out of the room.' He pointed to the other. 'And you watch the duke's sleep and guard him from noise and interruption.'

Buckingham made a little gesture with his thin hand. 'Don't you leave me, John.'

John bowed, and swept all the men from the room. 'Consult among yourselves and make whatever he needs,' he said firmly. 'I shall watch his sleep.'

'He needs cupping,' one of them said.

'No cupping.'

'Or leeches?'

John shook his head. 'He's to sleep and not be tortured.'

'What d'you know? You're nothing but a gardener.'

John gave the apothecaries a hard unfriendly smile. 'I wager I lose fewer plants than you do patients,' he said accurately. 'And I keep them well by letting them rest when they need rest, and feeding them when they are hungry. I don't cup them and leech them, I care for them. And that is what I shall do for my duke until he orders it otherwise.'

Then he shut the door in their faces and stood at the foot of his master's bed, and waited for him to have his fill of sleep.

Tradescant could guard his master against the household. But when the king heard that the Favourite had been sick and near to death, he sent word that he would come at once, and the whole court with him.

Buckingham, still pale but only a little stronger, was sitting in the bay window which overlooked John's new knot garden, John standing at his side, when they brought the message from the king.

'I'm back in favour then,' Buckingham said idly. 'I thought I was finished for this reign.'

'But you brought Prince Charles safe home,' Tradescant protested. 'What more did His Majesty want?'

Buckingham slid a sly sideways smile at his gardener and sniffed at the spray of snowdrops which Tradescant had brought him. 'A little less rather than more,' he said. 'He envied me the triumphant entry into London. He thought I was setting up to be king myself. He thought I wanted Kit Villiers to marry the Elector Frederick's daughter and ally myself to the Stuarts.' He laughed shortly. 'As though I would put Kit over myself,' he said scornfully. 'And then he looks from me to the prince and back again and he fears my influence over the heir. And he's jealous as an old woman. He cannot bear to see us make merry when he is old and aching and longing for his bed. He cannot bear to think that we are merry without him when he has withdrawn. He has given me everything I ask and now he is jealous that I am wealthy and courted. Jealous that I am the richest man in the kingdom with the most beautiful house.' He broke off and tossed his head.

'Though it is true that it is better not to flaunt your wealth,' Tradescant remarked to the sky outside the bay window.

'What d'you mean?'

'I'm thinking that my old lord loved Theobalds Palace before anything else in the country and the king, *this* king, in very truth, saw it through his eyes, acknowledged its value, and claimed it for himself. And here we've only just got the avenue planted.'

Buckingham cracked a laugh. 'John! My John! If he wants it, he'll have to have it! Avenue and all. Anything so long as I am back in his favour.'

John nodded. 'You think he will forgive you?'

The younger man lay back on the rich cushions heaped in the window-seat and turned his face to look out at the view. John noted, with affection, the perfect profile, white against red velvet.

'What d'you think, John? If I am very pale and very quiet and very submissive, and look – so – would you forgive me?'

John tried to stare at his master unmoved, but he found he was smiling as if his master was a tender wilful maid in the first years of her beauty, at the time when a girl can do anything and be forgiven by everyone. 'I suppose so,' he admitted ungraciously. 'If I were a besotted old fool.'

Buckingham grinned. 'I suppose so too.'

The duke waved farewell to the royal coach and the hundreds of courtiers and outriders, and watched them move slowly down the newly planted avenue. John Tradescant had done his best but the limes in the double-planted avenue were still only saplings. The duke watched the coach with the crown and the nodding feathers rumble from one thin leafy shade to another. When they grew, the trees would be a powerful symbol of the greatness of the house. And by then the prince would be on the throne, with Buckingham as his adviser, and the king, the jealous difficult bad-tempered old king, would be dead.

The king had wept and asked for forgiveness after a long bitter quarrel. He had tolerated Buckingham's marriage, indeed he loved Kate, and he was even amused by Buckingham's notorious affairs with every pretty woman at court, but he could not bear to feel that his son the prince had supplanted him in Buckingham's affections. Tearfully he accused them of conspiring against him and that Prince Charles – never the favoured son – had stolen from his father his love, his only love.

He publicly called Prince Charles a changeling and wished that his brother, the handsome and godly Prince Henry, had never died. He publicly called Buckingham a heartbreaker and a false son to him. He called him a traitor and wept the easy tears of an old man, and swore that no-one loved him.

It took all Buckingham's charm to talk the king into a more reasonable frame of mind, and all his patience to tolerate the moist kisses on his face and his mouth. It took all his ready humour and his genuine joy of life to seek to make the elderly king happy again, and the court happy with him. A sick man, newly up from his bed, Buckingham danced with Kate before the king, and sat at his side and listened to his rambling complaints about the Spanish alliance and the Spanish threat, and never showed so much as a flicker of weariness or sickness.

Buckingham waited until the royal carriage was out of sight before he put his hat back on his head and turned away towards the stone steps to the knot garden. Already it was as Tradescant had promised it would be. Each delicately shaped bed was filled with plants of a single uniform colour, edged with dark green box and entwined in an unending pattern with another. Buckingham walked around them, feeling his anxiety melt away at the sight of the twisting patterns, at the perfection of the planting.

It was a joy he had not known before Tradescant had made this place for him. He had seen gardens as part of the furniture of a great house, something a great man must have. But Tradescant had made him see things with a plantsman's eye. Now he walked around and around the little twisting paths of the knot garden with a sense of renewed pleasure and a feeling of liberty. The little hedges destroyed the sense of perspective; when he looked across them from one end of the knot garden to the other they seemed as if they enclosed acres of land, one field after another. They were a little parable of wealth. They looked like great fields, great acres, and yet they were encompassed within a few hundred yards.

'A thing of beauty,' Buckingham murmured softly to himself. 'I should thank him for it. Thank him for making it for me, and then for training my eye to see it.'

He walked down from the formal garden towards the lake. There were the lilies that Tradescant had promised him, and waving in the slight breeze were the golden buttercups and flag irises. A little pier jutted out into the water and the still reflection of the lake showed another pier reflected darkly beneath it. At the very end of it, looking down into the water, was John Tradescant himself, watching a boy drop baskets of osier roots into the deep mud.

When he heard Buckingham approach he pulled off his hat and nudged the boy with his foot. The boy dropped to his knees. Buckingham waved him away.

'Will you row me?' he asked Tradescant.

'Of course, my lord,' John replied. He took in at once the dark shadows under the eyes, the pallor of Buckingham's skin. He looked like an angel carved in purest marble with sooty fingerprints on its face.

John pulled in the little boat by its dripping rope and held it steady while the duke climbed in and leaned back against the cushions.

'I am weary,' he said shortly.

John cast off, sat down, and bent over the oars without speaking. He rowed his master first towards the island where the mount had been thrown up, just as they had first planned. He rowed slowly around it. Whitethorn and roses tumbled down to the water's edge and the blossoms nodded at themselves in the still water. A few ducks came quacking out of hiding but Buckingham did not stir at the noise.

'Do you remember Robert Cecil?' he asked idly. 'In your thoughts, or in your prayers?'

'Yes,' Tradescant said, surprised. 'Daily.'

'I met a man the other day who said that the first time he went to Theobalds Palace they could not find Sir Robert anywhere and in the end they found him in the potting shed with you, eating bread and cheese.'

Tradescant gave a short laugh. 'He used to like to watch me work.'

'He was a great man, a great servant of state,' Buckingham said. 'No-one ever thought the less of him because he served first one monarch and then her heir.'

John nodded, leaned forward on his oars and rowed.

'But me . . .' Buckingham broke off. 'What d'you hear, John? Men despise me, don't they? Because I came from nowhere and nothing and because I won my place at court because I was a pretty boy?'

He expected his servant to deny it.

'I'm afraid that's what they do say,' John confirmed.

Buckingham sat bolt upright and the boat rocked. 'You say so to my face?'

John nodded.

'No man in England has dared so much! I could have your tongue slit for impertinence!' Buckingham exclaimed.

John's oars did not break in their gentle rhythm. He smiled at his master, a slow affectionate smile. 'You spoke of Sir Robert,' he said. 'I never lied to him either. If you ask me a question I will answer it, sir. I'm not impertinent, and I'm not a gossip. If you tell me a secret I will keep it to myself. If you ask me for news I will tell you.'

'Did Sir Robert confide in you?' Buckingham asked curiously.

John nodded. 'When you make a garden for a man you learn what sort of man he is,' he explained. 'You spend time together, you watch things grow and change together. We worked on Theobalds together and then we moved and made Hatfield together, Sir Robert and me, from nothing. And we talked, as men do, when they walk in a garden together.'

'And what sort of man am I?' Buckingham asked. 'You've worked for a king's adviser before now. You worked for Cecil and you work for me. What d'you think of me? What d'you think of me, compared with him?'

Tradescant leaned forward and pulled gently on the oars, and the boat slid smoothly through the water. 'I think you are still very young,' he said gently. 'And impatient, as a young man is impatient. I think you are ambitious – and no-one can tell how high you will rise or how long you will stay at the height of your power. I think that you may have won your place at court on your beauty but you have kept it by your wit. And since you are both beautiful and witty you will keep it still.'

Buckingham laughed and leaned back on the cushions again. 'Both beautiful and witty!' he exclaimed.

John looked at the tumbled dark hair and the long dark lashes sweeping the smooth cheeks. 'Yes,' he said simply. 'You are my lord, and I never thought to find a lord that I could follow heart and soul ever again.'

'Do you love me as you loved Lord Cecil?' Buckingham asked him, suddenly alert, with a sly searching look from under his eyelashes.

John, innocent in his heart, smiled at his master. 'Yes.'

'I shall keep you by me, as he kept you by him,' Buckingham said, planning their future. 'And men will see that if you can love me, as you loved him, then I cannot be less than him. They will make the comparison and think of me as another Cecil.'

'Maybe,' Tradescant replied. 'Or maybe they will think I am a man with a sense to garden in only the best gardens. It would be a man overproud of his sight to boast that he could see into men's hearts, my lord. You'd do better to follow your own counsel than wonder how it might look to others – in my view.'

March 1625

John was working late. The duke had ordered a watercourse to flow from one terrace to another and it was his fancy that in each terrace there should be a different breed of fish, in descending orders of colours, so that the gold – the king of fish – should only swim in the topmost pool near the house. The garden around it was to be all gold too, and it was to face the royal rooms that King James used on his visits. Tradescant had sent out messages to every ship in the Royal Navy commanding them to bring him the seeds or roots of any yellow or gold flowers they saw anywhere in the world. The Duke of Buckingham ordered the highest admirals in the Navy to go ashore and look at flowers that John Tradescant might have his pick of yellow flower seeds.

It was a pretty idea and it would have been a delightful compliment to His Majesty, except Tradescant's goldfish were as elusive as swallows in winter. Whatever he did to the watercourse they slipped away downstream and mingled with the others: silver fish on one level, rainbow trout at the next, and dappled carp on the fourth level, who ate them.

Tradescant had tried nets, but they got tangled up and drowned themselves, he had tried building little dams of stones, but the water became sluggish and did not pitter-patter from one level to another as it should. Worse, when the water was still or slow it turned green and murky, and he could not see the fish at all.

His next idea was to build a little fence of small pieces of windowglass through which the water could flow and the fish could not swim. It was a prodigally expensive solution – to use precious glass for such a fancy. Tradescant scowled and placed the small panes – each one carefully rounded at the corners so as not to cut the fish – in a line, with only a small gap for the water to flow between each. When he finished he stood up.

His feet ached with standing in the cold water, and his back was stiff with stooping. His fingers were numb with cold – it was still only March and there were frosts at night. He rubbed his hands briskly on the homespun of his breeches. His fingertips were blue. He could hardly see his work in the failing light but he could hear the musical splashing of the water flowing down to the next pool on the next terrace. As he watched a goldfish approached the fence of glass, nosed at it, and turned back and swam towards the centre of the pond.

'Got you!' Tradescant grunted. 'Got you, you little bastard.'

He chuckled at himself and clapped his hat on his head, picked up his tools, and set off for his shed to clean and hang them before he went home for his dinner. Then he stopped, listening: a horse, galloping at high speed, up the long spectacular winding drive and at full pelt to the front door of the house.

The messenger saw Tradescant. 'Is His Grace at home?' he shouted.

John glanced towards the brightly lit windows of the house. 'Yes,' he said. 'He should be dining soon.'

'Take me to him!' the man ordered. He flung himself from his horse and dropped the reins, as if the high-bred animal hardly mattered.

John, wrenching his mind from yellow flowers, snatched at the reins and called for a groom. When one came running he handed him the horse and led the messenger into the house.

'Where's the duke?' he asked a serving man.

'At his prayers, in his library.' The man nodded towards the door.

John tapped on the door and went in.

Buckingham was sprawled on his chair behind his grand desk listening to his chaplain reading prayers, playing idly with a gold chain, his dark eyes veiled. When he saw John his face lit up. 'It's my wizard, John!' he called. 'Come in, my John! Have you made the water flow backwards up the hill for me?'

'There's a man here come in haste from the king,' John said shortly, and pushed the messenger into the room.

'You're to go to Theobalds,' the man blurted. 'The king is sick with ague and asking for you. He says you're to come to him at once.'

There was a sudden alertness about Buckingham, like the sudden freezing when a cat sees its prey, and then he moved.

'Get me a horse.' Buckingham started from his desk. 'John, get one too. Come with me. You know the way better than any. And a man to ride with us. How bad is he?' he threw over his shoulder to the messenger.

'They said more sorry than sick.' The man trotted after him. 'But commanding your presence. The prince is already there.'

Buckingham ran up the stairs and looked down at John. His face was alight with kindled ambition. 'Perhaps now!' he said, and turned into his room to change his clothes.

John sent orders for horses to be made ready and sent a man running to the kitchen for a knapsack of food and a flask of drink. He sent no message for Elizabeth. The urgency of the young duke, the call of the adventure and the sense of living in great times was too much for him to remember his domestic ties.

When the duke came clattering down the front steps, handsome in his riding boots and a long cape, John was mounted on one good horse, and holding another. The servant who was to ride with them was coming from the stable yard.

The duke glanced at John. 'Thank you,' he said, and meant it.

John grinned. The great fault of these large households was their slowness. Meat was always eaten half-cold, hunting expeditions had to be planned days ahead and always started hours after the time named. Nothing could be done on impulse, everything had to be prepared. John's ability to get a horse from the stables, groomed and ready to ride in minutes was one of his greatest talents.

'Will you be all right to ride?' Buckingham asked, glancing at John's borrowed breeches and boots.

'I'll get you there,' John said. 'Never fear.'

He led the way at a steady trot out of the courtyard, put the cold sliver of the rising moon on his right and rode due west to Waltham Cross.

They changed horses not once but twice in the twenty-four-hour journey, once knocking at the door of an inn until a reluctant landlord lent them his own horses when he caught sight of the gold which Tradescant carried. The second time when there were no horses to be hired, they simply stole a pair from the stable. John left a note to tell the owner in the morning that he had obliged the great duke and might call on him for repayment.

Buckingham laughed at Tradescant's enterprise. 'By God, John, you are wasted in the gardens,' he said. 'You should be a general at least.'

John smiled at the praise. 'I said I would get you there, and I will,' he said simply.

Buckingham nodded. 'I'll not travel without you again.'

It was near dawn when they came wearily up the drive to the sweep before the great door of Theobalds. The dark windows of the palace looked down on them. John glanced up to where the great breast of the bay window jutted outwards like the poop deck on a sailing ship. He could see the light from many candles spilling out through the cracks of the shutters.

'They are awake in the king's chamber,' he said. 'Shall I go first?'

'Go and see,' Buckingham commanded. 'If the king is asleep I shall wash and rest myself. It may be a great day for me tomorrow.'

John got stiffly down from his horse. His borrowed breeches were stuck to the skin of his thighs by sweat and blood from saddle sores. He scowled at the pain and went bow-legged into the house, up the stairs, and to the royal rooms. A soldier extended his pike to bar the door.

'John Tradescant,' growled John. 'I've brought the duke. Let me pass.'

The sentry stood to attention and John went into the room. There were half a dozen doctors and innumerable midwives and wise women, called in for their knowledge of herbs. There was a desperate gaiety about the room. There were courtiers, some dozing in corners, some playing cards and drinking. Everyone turned as John came in, travel-stained and weary.

'Is the king awake?' John asked. 'I have brought the duke.'

For a moment it seemed that no-one knew. They were so absorbed in their own tasks of arguing about his health and waiting for his recovery that no-one was actually caring for him. One doctor broke from the others and scuttled to the door of the bedroom and peeped in.

'Awake,' he said. 'And restless.'

John nodded and went back down to the hall. Behind him he could hear the flurry of movement as the courtiers prepared themselves for the greatest courtier of all – George Villiers.

He was seated in a chair in the hall, a glass of mulled wine in his hand, a lad kneeling before him, brushing the mud off his boots.

'He's awake,' John said shortly.

'I'll go up,' Buckingham declared. 'Many with him?'

'A score,' John said. 'No-one of importance.'

Buckingham went wearily up the stairs. 'Make sure they make up a bed for me,' he threw over his shoulder. 'And get a bed for yourself in my chamber. I want to have you close, John, I may be busy these next days.'

John poured himself a glass from the duke's own flagon and went to do as he had been told.

The household was starting to wake, although many had not slept at all. The word was that the king had been hunting and had fallen sick. At first it was a light fever and expected to pass, but it had taken hold, and the king was rambling. He feared for his life, sometimes he dreamed he was back in Scotland with buckram wadding beneath all his clothes to ward off an assassin's knife, sometimes he called out for forgiveness from the enemies he had tried on a pretext and then hanged and drawn and quartered. Sometimes he dreamed of the witches that he thought had haunted his life, the innocent old women he had ordered drowned or strangled. Sometimes, and most pitifully of all, he called out to his mother, poor Mary of Scotland, and begged her forgiveness for letting her go to the executioner's block at Fotheringay without a word of comfort from him, though she sent letter after letter addressed to her beloved son and never forgot the baby he had been.

'But he will recover?' John asked one of the maids.

'It is only the ague,' she said. 'Why should he not recover?'

John nodded and went to the duke's bedroom. The cold March dawn was turning the sky from black to grey, the frost was white on the terraces. John leaned his elbows on the windowsill and watched the familiar landmarks of Theobalds, his first great garden, swim upward from the mist. In the distance he could see the woods, bare-branched now, and cold; and underneath them deep in the frozen earth would be the bulbs of the daffodils that he had planted for the king who was now old, and to please the master who was long dead.

He wondered what Cecil would have thought of his new master, if he would have despised or admired the duke. He wondered where Cecil was now; in a garden, he thought, the blessed last garden where flowers were always in bloom. John felt great tenderness for the master he had lost and this garden they had loved together.

Then the door behind him opened and Buckingham came into the room.

'Shut the window for the love of God, John!' he snapped. 'It's freezing!'

John obeyed and waited.

'Get some sleep,' the duke said. 'And when you wake I want you to go to London, and fetch my mother.'

'I could go now,' John volunteered.

'Rest,' the duke said. 'Go as soon as you wake and are fit to ride. Take her this message, I shan't write it down.' He crossed the room to John and spoke very low. 'Tell her that the king is sick but not yet dying, and I need her help. Badly. D'you understand?'

John hesitated. 'I understand the words, and I can repeat them. But I dare not think of your meaning.'

Buckingham nodded. 'John, my John,' he said softly, 'that is what I wish. Just remember the words and leave the rest to me.' He met John's worried look with an open face. 'I loved the king like my own father,' he said persuasively. 'I want him cared for with love and respect. That crowd in there will not leave him alone, they torture him with remedies, they bleed him, they turn him, they blister him, they sweat him, and chill him. I want my mother to come and nurse him gently. She's a woman of much experience. She will know how to ease his pain.'

'I'll fetch her at once,' John said.

'Rest now, but go as soon as you wake,' the duke said and went quietly from the room.

John peeled the borrowed breeches off his sore buttocks, tumbled into the pallet bed and slept for six solid hours.

When he woke it was past noon. Someone had placed a jug and ewer on the dark wooden chest at the head of his bed, and he washed. In the chest was a change of clothes, and John slipped on a clean shirt and breeches. He did not trouble to shave. The duke's mother could take him as he was. He went quietly down the stairs and out to the stable yard.

'I need a good horse,' he said to the chief groom. 'The duke's business.'

'He said you would be riding,' the man replied. 'There's a horse saddled and ready for you, and a lad to ride part of the way with you to bring back the horse when you need to change. In which direction are you going?'

'London,' John said briefly.

'Then this horse will take you all the way. He's as strong as an ox.' The groom took in John's stiff walk. 'Though I imagine you'll not be galloping.'

John grimaced and reached for the saddle to haul himself up.

'Where in London?' the groom asked.

'To the docks,' John lied instantly. 'The duke has some curious playthings come from the Indies which he thought might amuse the king and divert him in his illness. I am to fetch them.'

'The king is better then?' the groom asked. 'They said this morning he was on the mend, but I did not know. He has ordered his horses to move to Hampton Court so I thought he must be better.'

'Better, yes,' John said.

The groom released the reins and the horse took three steps back. With his bruised muscles aching, John leaned forward against the pain and sent his horse at the gentlest canter he could command, back down the road to London.

The countess was at her son's grand London house. John went to the stables first and ordered them to harness the carriage for her, and then went into the house. She was a powerful old woman, dark-eyed like her son, but completely lacking his charm. She had been a famous beauty when she was a girl, married for her looks and jumped from servitude into the gentry in one lucky leap. But her struggle for respect had left its mark, her face was always determined; in repose she looked bitter. John recited his message in a whisper, and she nodded in silence.

'Wait for me downstairs,' she said shortly.

John went back down to the hall and sent a maidservant racing for some wine, bread and cheese. Within a few moments Lady Villiers was sweeping down the stairs, wrapped in a travelling cape, a pomander held to her nose against the infections of the London streets, a small box in her hand.

'You will ride in front to guide my driver.'

'If you wish, my lady.' John got stiffly to his feet.

She walked past him but as she got into the carriage she made a quick gesture with her hand. 'Get up on the box, your horse can be tied behind.'

'I can ride,' John offered.

'You are half-crippled with saddle sores,' she observed. 'Sit where you will be comfortable. You are of no use to my son or to me if you are bleeding from a dozen bruises.'

John climbed up to sit beside the driver. 'Perceptive woman,' he remarked.

The driver nodded and waited for the carriage door to shut. John saw that he was holding the reins awkwardly with each thumb between the first and second finger: the old sign against witchcraft.

The roads were bad, thick with mud from the winter. In the heart of London, beggars held out beseeching hands as the rich carriage went by them. Some of them were pocked with rosy scars where they had recovered from the plague. The driver kept to the line of the track at a steady pace, and left it to them to leap clear.

'Hard times,' John remarked, thinking with gratitude to his lord of the little house at New Hall and his son and wife safely distant from these dangerous streets.

'Eight years of bad harvests and a king on the throne who has forgotten his duty,' the driver said angrily. 'What would you expect?'

'I don't expect to hear treason from the duke's own household,' John said shortly. 'And I won't hear it!'

'I'll say only this,' the driver said. 'There's a Christian prince and princess, his own daughter, driven from her throne by the armies of the Pope. There's a Spanish match that he would still make if he could. The Spanish ambassador is to return to him – by his own request! And year after year the country gets poorer while the court gets richer. You can't expect people to dance in the streets. The death cart goes past them too often.'

John shook his head and looked away.

'There's those that think the land should be shared,' the driver said under his breath. 'There's those that think that no good will come to England while people starve every winter and others are sick of surfeit.'

'It is as God wills,' John insisted. 'And I won't say more. To speak against the king is treason, to speak against the way things are and must be is heresy. If your mistress heard you, you'd be on the street yourself. And me too, for listening to you.'

'You're a good servant,' the man sneered. 'For you even think in obedience to your lord.'

John shot him a hard dark look. 'I am a good servant,' he repeated. 'And proud of it. And of course I think in obedience to my lord. I think and live and pray in obedience to my lord. How else could it be? How else should it be?'

'There are other ways,' the driver argued. 'You could think and live and pray for yourself.'

John shook his head. 'I've given my allegiance,' he said. 'I don't withdraw it, and I don't pay three farthings to the penny. My lord is my master, heart and soul. And you'll forgive me saying, but you might be a happier man if you could say the same thing.'

The driver shook his head and sulkily fell silent. John wrapped himself in his borrowed cloak and nodded off to sleep, only waking when they were driving towards Theobalds under the great double avenue of ash and elm, with the daffodils flooding around the trunks.

The carriage drew up outside the door and the duke himself came out to greet his mother.

'Thank you, John,' he threw over his shoulder and drew her into the house and up to the king's chamber.

'Is the king better?' John asked a manservant as the countess's box was carried up the stairs.

'On the mend,' the man said. 'He took some soup this midday.'

'Then I think I'll take a turn around the garden.' John nodded towards the door and the enticing view. 'If my lord wants me you will find me at the bath house, or on the mount. I have not been here for many years.'

He stepped through the front door and towards the first of the beautiful knot gardens. They wanted weeding, he thought, and then smiled at himself. These were not his weeds any more, they were the king's.

He saw Buckingham before dinner that night. 'If you do not need me, I shall go home tomorrow,' he said. 'I did not warn my wife that I was going with you, and there is much to do in the garden at New Hall.'

Buckingham nodded. 'When you go through London you can see if my ship has come from the Indies,' he said. 'And supervise the unloading of the goods. They were ordered to bring me much ivory and silk. You can fetch them safely down to New Hall and see them installed in my rooms. I am making a collection of rare and precious things. Prince Charles has his toy soldiers, have you seen them? They fire cannon and you can draw them up in battle lines. They are very diverting. I should like some pretty things too.'

'Am I to wait in London for the Indies goods to arrive?'

'If you will,' Buckingham said sweetly. 'If Mrs Tradescant can spare you so long.'

'She knows your service comes first,' John said. 'How does the king today? Still better?'

Buckingham looked grave. 'He is worse,' he said. 'The ague has hold of him, and he is not a young man, and was never strong. He saw the prince privately today and put him in mind of his duties. He is preparing himself . . . I really think he is preparing himself. It is my duty to make sure he can be at peace, that he can rest.'

'I heard he was getting better,' John ventured cautiously.

'We give out the best reports we can, but the truth is that he is an old man who is ready to meet his death.'

John bowed and left the room, and went down to the hall for his dinner.

The place was in uproar. Half a dozen of the physicians that John had first seen in the king's chamber were calling for their horses and their menservants. The courtiers were shouting for their carriages and for food to take on their journeys.

'What's this?' John asked.

'It's all the fault of your master,' a woman replied shortly. 'He has flung the physicians from the king's presence, and half the court too. He said they were troubling him too much with their noise and their playing, and he said the physicians were fools.'

John grinned and stepped back to watch the confusion of their departure.

'He will regret it!' one doctor shouted to another. 'I warned him myself, if His Majesty suffers and we are not at hand, he will regret this insult to us!'

'He is beyond counsel! I warned him but he pushed me from the room!'

'He snatched my very pipe out of my mouth and broke it!' one of the courtiers interrupted. 'I know that the king hates smoke, but it is a sure prevention of infection, and how should His Majesty smell it in another room? I shall write to the duke and complain of my treatment. Twenty years I have been at court, and he pushed me out of the door as if I were his serf!'

'He has cleared the room of everyone but a nurse, his mother and himself,' a man declared. 'And he swears that the king shall have peace and quiet and no more meddling. As if a king should not be surrounded by his people all the time!'

John left them and strolled into dinner. Buckingham and his mother were at the high table; the place for the king was left respectfully empty. Prince Charles was seated next to the empty place, his head very close to the duke's.

'Aye, they'll have much to consider,' a man said in an undertone and took his seat next to John.

John took some fine white manchet bread and a large joint of pheasant from the plate in the centre of the table. He snapped his fingers for a girl and she came to pour him wine.

'What's the countess doing here?' one man asked. 'The king can't abide her.'

'Caring for the king, apparently. The physicians have been sent away and she is to nurse him.'

'An odd choice,' another man said shortly. 'Since he hates the sight of her.'

'The king is on the mend,' yet another man said, pulling out his stool. 'The duke was right to send those fools away. His Majesty had the fever – why! – we've all had a fever. And if the countess knows a remedy which cured the duke, why should she not offer it to the king?'

The men glanced at John. 'Was it you fetched her?' one asked.

John savoured the taste of roast pheasant, the rich juices flowing in his mouth. 'I can hardly remember,' he said, muffled. 'D'you know this is the first decent meal I've had in a day and a half? I was damming up a fishpond in Essex not long ago. And now here I am back at Theobalds. And very good fare to be had too.'

One of the men shrugged and laughed shortly. 'Aye,' he said. 'We'll get no secrets from you. We all know who is your master, and you serve him well, John Tradescant. I hope you never come to regret it!'

John looked up the hall to the top table where the duke was leaning forward to call to one of the officers. The candlelight made a reddish halo around his black curls, his face was as bright and delighted as a child's.

'No,' John said with affection. 'I'll never regret it.'

John stayed late in the hall, drinking with the men at his table. At midnight he headed unsteadily to the duke's chamber.

'Where d'you sleep?' one of his drinking companions asked him.

'With my lord.'

'Oh, yes,' the man said pointedly. 'I heard you were a favourite.'

John wheeled around and stared at him, and the man held his gaze, half a question on his face which was an insult. John spoke a hasty word and was about to strike the man when a serving maid ran between the two of them, a basin in her hand, blinded with hurry.

'What's the matter?' John asked.

'It's the king!' she exclaimed. 'His fever has risen, and his piss is blue as ink. He is as sick as a dog. He is asking for his physician but he has only Lady Villiers to attend him.'

'Asking for his physicians?' the man demanded. 'Then the duke must send for them, to bring them back.'

'He will do,' John said uncertainly. 'He is bound to do so.'

He went to Buckingham's chamber, and found the duke seated by the window gazing at his own reflection in the darkened glass, as if it would answer a question.

'Shall I ride out and fetch the physicians?' John asked him quietly.

The duke shook his head.

'I heard the king was asking for them.'

'He is well nursed,' Buckingham said. 'If anyone should ask you, John, you may tell them that he is well cared for. He needs rest; not a dozen men harrying him to death.'

'I'll tell them,' John said. 'But they tell me that he is asking for his physicians and your mother is not a favourite.'

The duke hesitated. 'Anything else?'

'That's enough,' John warned him. 'More than enough.'

'Go to sleep,' the duke said gently. 'I am going to bed myself in a minute.'

John shucked off his breeches and shoes, lay down in his shirt and was asleep in moments.

There was a hammering on the bedroom door in the early hours of the morning. John started out of sleep, leaped from his bed and ran, not to the door, but to the duke's bed, to stand between him and whoever might be outside battering the door down. In that first moment, as he pulled back the bed curtains, he saw that the younger man was not asleep but was lying open-eyed, as if he were silently waiting, as if he had been wide awake and waiting all night.

'All's safe, Tradescant,' he said. 'You can open the door.'

'My lord duke!' the shout came. 'You must come at once!'

Buckingham rose from his bed and threw a cape around him. 'What's to do?' he called.

'It's the king! It's the king!'

He nodded and swiftly went from the room. John, pulling on breeches and his waistcoat, ran behind him.

Buckingham went swiftly through the door to the antechamber but the guards barred John's way.

'I'm with my lord,' John said.

'No-one goes in but the prince and the Villiers: mother and son,' the guard replied. 'His orders.'

John fell back and waited.

The door opened and Buckingham looked out. His face was pale and grave. 'Oh, John. Good. Send someone you can trust to fetch His Grace the Bishop of Winchester. The king needs him.'

John bowed and turned on his heel.

'And come back here,' Buckingham ordered. 'I have need of you.'

'Of course,' John said.

The court was subdued all day. The king was worse, there could be no doubt of it. But the countess was said to be confident. She was applying another plaster, the king was feverish, she was certain her cure would draw the heat from him.

In the evening a message came that the Bishop of Winchester was too ill to travel. 'Get me another bishop,' Buckingham said to John. 'Any bloody bishop will do. Get me the nearest, get me the quickest. But get me a bishop!'

John ran down to the stables and sent three menservants riding out to different palaces, with three urgent summonses, and then went back to the gallery outside the king's rooms to wait for the duke.

He heard the long low groan of a man in much pain. The door opened and Lady Villiers came out. 'What are you doing here?' she demanded sharply. 'What are you listening for?'

'I am waiting for my lord,' John said quietly. 'As he bid me.'

'Well, keep others off,' she ordered. 'The king is in pain, he does not want eavesdroppers.'

'Is he getting better?' John asked. 'Has his fever broken?'

She gave him an odd, sideways smile. 'He is doing well,' she said.

The fever did not break. The king lay sweating and calling for help for two more days. Buckingham said that John could go back to New Hall but he could not bear to go until he had seen the end. The court went everywhere on tiptoe, the flirting and gambling had ceased. Around the sombre young prince was an aura of silence — everywhere he went people fell quiet and bowed their heads. The courtiers longed to recommend themselves to him; some of them had sided with his father against him, some of them had laughed at him when he had been a tongue-tied weakly younger son. Now he was the king-to-be, and only Buckingham had completely accomplished the great balancing act of being the greatest friend of the father and the greatest friend of the son.

Buckingham was everywhere. In the sick room, watching at the king's bedside, walking with Prince Charles in the garden, moving among the men at court giving a word of reassurance here, a carefully judged snub there.

The Bishop of Lincoln arrived from his palace and was shown in to the king. The whisper came out of the sick chamber that the king, too ill to speak, had assented to the prayers by raising his eyes to heaven. He would die a true son of the English church.

That night John lay in Buckingham's chamber listening to the quiet breathing, and knew his master was affecting sleep but was wide awake. At midnight the duke got up from his bed, pulled on his clothes in the darkness and went softly out of the bedchamber. John lost all desire for sleep, sat up in his bed and waited.

He heard the sound of a woman's light footstep down the corridor and then her knock on the door. 'Mr Tradescant! The duke wants you!'

John got up, pulled on his breeches, and hurried to the king's chamber. Buckingham was standing at the window embrasure, looking out over Tradescant's garden. When he turned from the night to face the room his face was alight with excitement.

'It is now!' he said shortly. 'At last. Wake the bishop, and bring him quietly. And then wake the prince.'

John went through the maze of wood-lined corridors, tapped on the bishop's door and forced his sleepy servant to wake His Grace. When the bishop came out of the room, robed in his vestments and holding King James's own bible, John led him through the servants' hall, past sleeping men and dogs which growled softly as they went by. Only firelight illuminated their way and the moving silver moon which tracked their path through the great high windows.

The bishop went into the chamber. John turned and ran along the broad wood-panelled corridor to the prince's apartments.

He knocked on the door and whispered through the keyhole. 'Your Highness! Wake up! The duke told me to fetch you.'

The door was flung open and Charles came quickly out, wearing only his nightshirt. Without saying a word he ran down the corridor to the king's chamber and went in.

The palace was completely quiet. John waited outside the royal chamber, straining his ears to hear. There was the low dismal mutter of the last rites, and the prayers. Then there was a silence.

Slowly the door opened and the duke came out. He looked at Tradescant and nodded as if a difficult task had been well done.

'The king is dead,' he said. 'Long live His Majesty King Charles.'

Charles was at his shoulder, looking stunned. His dark eyes fell unseeing upon Tradescant. 'I did not know . . .' he said at once. 'I did not know what they were doing. Before God, I had no idea that your mother . . .'

Buckingham dropped to one knee and John followed his example. 'God bless Your Majesty!' Buckingham said swiftly.

'Amen,' Tradescant said.

Charles was silenced; whatever he might have said would never be spoken.

Spring 1625

Three hours later Prince Charles was proclaimed king at the gate of Theobalds Palace, and stepped into the royal coach to ride in state to London. Buckingham, the Master of Horse, did not follow tradition by taking the place of honour, heading the train that rode behind the royal coach. Buckingham walked into the royal coach a mere half-pace behind His Majesty and rode like a prince himself at the new king's side. Tradescant followed in the long train of the household, closing his ears to the general gasp of horror at his master's presumption.

They drew up at St James's Palace in the afternoon and John waited for his orders. At first he could not find Buckingham's chamber and waited in the hall. The palace was in complete confusion. King James had been expected to stay hunting at Theobalds for many days, and go afterwards to Hampton Court. In his absence his palace had closed down for cleaning and refurbishing. There was no food in the kitchens and no fire in the chambers. The few housekeeping staff who did not travel with the king had been spring cleaning and had swept up the strewing herbs from the floor, and taken down the curtains from the windows and the tapestries off the walls. Serving men and maids ran everywhere, trying to prepare the palace for the new king and his train and do in moments what usually took days to accomplish, delayed all the time by the storm of gossip that was running around the royal courts, explaining how the king had fallen sick, how the Villiers mother and son had nursed him and excluded all others, and how the king had died under their care.

A feast had to be prepared and the comptroller of the royal household had to use all his cash and all of the new king's credit to buy in food, and set everyone in the kitchen – from the scullions labouring over the bellows to get the kitchen fires alight, to the great master cooks – preparing and cooking food so that a king new-come to his kingdom might sit down to his dinner.

A great press of people invaded the palace to see the new king and the first man in the land: the Duke of Buckingham. The poorer people came just to see him, they liked to watch their betters eat, even when their own bellies were empty; and hundreds of others had complaints about taxes, about land ownership, about injustices, which they were eager to place before the new king. When King Charles and his duke came pushing through the hall Tradescant was forced to the back behind dozens of shouting demanding people. But even there, as he was fighting for a space in the crowd, his master looked over the bobbing heads and called to him.

'John! You still here? What did you stay for?'

'For your orders.'

Men craned around to see who had taken the duke's attention and Tradescant fought his way forward.

'Oh – forgive me, John. I have been so busy. You can go to New Hall now. Call at the docks on the way and get my India goods. Then go home.'

'Your Grace, you have no chamber prepared for you here,' John said. 'I asked, and there is none. Where shall you sleep? Shall I go to your London house and bid the lady, your mother, make ready for you? Or shall I wait and we will go to New Hall together?'

The duke looked across to where the young king was moving slowly through the crowd, his hand extended for people to kiss, acknowledging their bows with a small gesture of his head. When he saw Buckingham watching him he gave him a private, conspiratorial smile.

'Tonight I sleep in His Majesty's chamber,' the duke remarked silkily. 'He needs me at his side.'

'But there is only one bed –' John started, then he bit back the words. Of course a truckle bed could be found. Or the two men could sleep in comfort in the big expanse of the royal bed. King

James had never slept alone, why should his son do so if he wanted company?

'Of course, my lord,' John said, careful to ensure that none of his thoughts appeared in his face. 'I shall leave you, if you're well served.'

Buckingham gave John his sweet satisfied smile. 'Never better.'

John bowed, and pushed his way to the back of the hall and out into the dusk. He wrapped his borrowed cloak around his shoulders and went outside to the stables. The horses were tired after the day's journey but he had no intention of riding hard. He chose a steady-looking beast and mounted.

'When are you back with us, Mr Tradescant?' a groom asked.

John shook his head. 'I'm going to my garden,' he said.

'You look sick,' the man remarked. 'Not taken the king's ague, have you?'

John thought for a moment of the old king's long heartsickness for Buckingham, and the net of half-truths and deceptions which were the very heart of court life. 'Maybe I have a touch of it,' he said.

He turned the horse's head eastward, and rode down to the docks. There was only one cartload of goods waiting to be unloaded. He saw it packed on a wagon and ordered it to follow him down the lanes to New Hall, irritated all the way at the noise and the lumbering slowness of the cart in the muddy lanes. His hat pulled low over his eyes, his coat collar turned up against the light cold spring rain, John sat heavily in the saddle, and kept his thoughts on the seasonal tasks of planting and weeding. He did not want to think about the new king, about his great friend the duke, or the old king who had died, a healthy man aged only fifty-nine years, from a slight fever, under their nursing, after his doctors had been sent away. If evil had been done there were men whose duty it was to make accusations. It was not John's duty to accuse his master or his king, not even privately in his anxious conscience.

Besides, John was not a man who could live with a divided loyalty in his heart. If evil had been done Tradescant had to be blind to it, and deaf to it. He could not love and follow a master and set himself up as judge of that master. He had to give his love and his trust and follow blindly – as he had followed Cecil, as it had been possible to follow Cecil – a master who might bend all the rules but whom you could trust to act only for his country's gain.

John reached his home in the cool light of the early evening and found Elizabeth in the kitchen, preparing supper for J. 'Forgive me,' John said shortly, coming into the house and taking and kissing her hand. 'I was called away in haste and I had no time to send you word. Afterwards there were great deeds going on, and I had no time.'

She looked curiously at him but the usual warmth was missing. 'J was told that you had gone with the duke to Theobalds at a moment's notice,' she said. 'So I knew you were on another errand for him.'

Tradescant noted the slight emphasis she placed on 'him' and found himself longing for a quarrel. 'He's my master,' he said abruptly. 'Where else should I be?'

She shrugged slightly and turned back to the fire. The pot hanging over the flames was simmering with pieces of meat bobbing in a rich gravy. Elizabeth held it steady with one hand shielded by a cloth and stirred with a long spoon.

'I have said I am sorry for not sending you word,' Tradescant insisted. 'What more could I have done?'

'Nothing more,' she said steadily. 'Since you chose to ride with him and you went far away in the night.'

'I did not choose . . .'

'You did not refuse –'

'He is my master . . .'

'I am sure I am aware of it!'

'You are jealous of him!' Tradescant exclaimed. 'You think I am too devoted! You think that he treats me like a servant and takes me and uses me when he needs me and then sends me back to the garden when he has had his fill of my service!'

Elizabeth straightened up and one cheek was flushed on the side near the fire, but the other was pale and cold. 'I did not say any of that,' she pointed out. 'Nor, as it happens, do I think it.'

'You think he involves me in his plotting and his darker deeds,' Tradescant persisted. 'I know you suspect him.'

She took up the hook and drew the hanging chain away from the flames of the fire, unhooked the pot, and placed it carefully on the stone of the hearth. She worked with an absorbed quietness as if she would not let him disturb her tranquillity.

'You do!' Tradescant insisted. 'You suspect him and you suspect me with him!'

Still in silence she fetched three bowls and one trencher. She sliced her home-baked loaf into three equal pieces, bowing her head for a moment over the breaking of the bread. Then she took the long-handled spoon and served broth and meat into each bowl and carried them to the table.

'I have seen things these days which he would trust to no other,' John said urgently. 'Things which I would tell no-one, not even you. I have seen things which, if he were a lesser man, would give me grave pause. I have seen things which he trusts only to me. He trusts me. He trusts no-one but me. And if – when he needs me no more – he sends me back to his garden, why, that is part of our understanding. I am at his side when he needs a man he can trust like no other. When he is in safe harbour, any man can serve him.'

Elizabeth put out three knives and three spoons on the table, and pulled up her little stool and bowed her head. Then she waited for him to sit.

John threw himself on to the stool, unwashed and without saying his grace, and moodily stirred his broth.

'You are thinking that he is guilty,' he said suddenly.

The face that she raised to him was completely serene and clear. 'Husband, I am thinking nothing. I begged you once that we should leave this place, and when you would not, I took my sorrow to my God, in prayer. I have left it to Him. I am thinking nothing.'

But John was burning to quarrel, or to confess. 'That's a lie. You are thinking that I was present, that I was witness to acts which might ruin him, acts which are a dreadful crime, the worst crime in the world, and that he leads me on to love him so that I am ensnared in love, and then I am incriminated myself!'

She shook her head and spooned her broth.

Tradescant pushed his bowl away, unable to eat for the anger and the darkness on his conscience. 'You are thinking that I have been an assistant to a murder!' he hissed. 'To assassination. And that it is plaguing my conscience and making me sick with worry! You are thinking that I come home with guilt in my face! You are thinking I come home to you with a stain on my soul! And that even after all I have done for him, in closing my ears and my eyes to what I can see and hear, that even then he will not keep me by his side but vaults on my shoulders to go upwards and upwards and tonight he sleeps beside the new king and dismisses me with no more than a word!'

Elizabeth put her hands over her eyes, shielding her face from his anguish, incapable of disentangling the mortal sins at which her husband was hinting: murder, treason, and forbidden desire.

'Stop it! Stop it!'

'How can I stop?' John yelled in terror for his mortal soul. 'How can I go forward? How can I go back? How can I stop?'

There was a shocked silence. Elizabeth took her hands from her face and looked up at her husband.

'Leave him,' she whispered.

'I cannot.'

She rose from the table and went towards the fireplace. John watched her go, as if she might have the key for them to escape from this knot of sin. But when she turned back to him her face was stony.

'What are you thinking?' he whispered.

'All that I think is that I have given you the wrong spoon,' she said with sudden clarity. She took off her apron, hung it on the hook and went out of the room.

'What d'you mean?' John shouted at her back as she went through the doorway.

'You need that one.'

He recoiled as her meaning struck him.

She was pointing to the spoon she used for cooking, the long spoon.

The news that King James was dead and his son was to be crowned the first King Charles arrived at Chorley the next day. Elizabeth was told in the marketplace at her small stall selling herbs. She nodded and said nothing. Her neighbour asked her if her husband was home and if he had brought any news of the doings from London.

'He was very tired last night,' Elizabeth said with her usual mixture of discretion and honesty. 'He said hardly a word that made sense. I left him to sleep this morning. I expect he will tell me all the news from London when he wakes, and it will be old news by then.'

'It's time for a change!' her neighbour said decisively. 'I'm all for a new king. God bless King Charles, I say, and keep us safe from those damned Spaniards! And God bless the duke too! He knows what should be done, you can count on it!'

'God bless them both,' Elizabeth said. 'And guide them in better ways.'

'And the king is to be married to a French bride!' the neighbour went on. 'Why can he not marry a good English girl, brought up in our religion? Why does it have to be one of these Papist princesses?'

Elizabeth shook her head. 'I don't know,' she said. 'The ways of the world are strange indeed. You would think that with the whole of the country at their feet they would be content . . .' She paused for a moment and her neighbour waited, hoping against all likelihood for a juicy piece of gossip. 'Vanity,' Elizabeth concluded, unsatisfactorily. 'It is all vanity.'

She looked around the quiet market. 'I shall go home,' she said. 'Perhaps John is awake now.'

She packed her little pots of herbs into her basket, nodded to her neighbour and made her way through the muddy street to her own cottage.

John was seated at the table in the kitchen, a mug of small ale and a piece of bread untasted before him. When Elizabeth came in and hung her cape on the hook on the back of the door, he started up.

'I am sorry, Elizabeth,' he said quickly. 'I was tired and angry yesterday.'

'I know,' she said.

'I was troubled by what I had seen and heard.'

She waited in case he would say more.

'The court life is a tempting one,' he said awkwardly. 'You think you are at the very centre of the world, and it takes you further and further away from the things which really matter. What I love more than anything else is gardening, and you, and J – the last thing I should be doing is dawdling like a serving wench in the halls of great men.'

She nodded.

'And then I think I am in the centre of great events, and an actor on a great stage,' he went on. 'I think it will all go wrong if I am not there. I think I am indispensable.' He broke off with a little laugh. 'I am a fool, I know it. For look! He has come to the highest point of his power yet, and his first act was to send me home.'

'Shall you go to the house?' Elizabeth asked. 'Will you go to work today?'

John turned to the door. 'No. I'll walk until I can live with myself. I feel . . .' He made a strange distressed gesture. 'I feel all . . . racked . . . I can't say more. I feel as if I have pulled myself out of shape and I need to restore myself somehow.'

Elizabeth took a small piece of linen and wrapped a piece of bread and cheese. 'You walk,' she advised. 'Here is your dinner, and when you come home tonight I will have a good supper prepared for you. You look like a man who has been poisoned.'

John recoiled as if she had slapped him. 'Poisoned? What are you saying?'

Elizabeth's face was graver than ever. 'I meant that you looked as if the court had not agreed with you, John. What else should I mean?'

He passed his hand quickly over his face as if he were wiping away a cold sweat. 'It does not,' he said. 'It does not agree with me. For here I am as nervous as a deer when I should be quietly at peace and setting my seeds.'

He took the bread and cheese from her. 'I'll be home by dusk,' he promised.

She drew him to her, took his worried face in her hands and drew his head down to her. She put a kiss on his brow, as if she were his mother blessing and absolving him. 'You say a little prayer as you walk,' she said. 'And I shall pray for you while I set the house to rights.'

John reached for his hat and opened the door. 'What shall you pray for me, Lizzie?' he asked.

Elizabeth's look was calm and steady. 'That you shall avoid temptation, husband. For I think you have chosen a way which is much among the snares of the world.'

❧

John worked through the spring with a dogged sullenness on the gardens of New Hall. The cherries which had always been his especial pleasure blossomed well, and he watched the pink and white buds swell and then bloom, denying his own feeling that since their master did not see them their sweetness was wasted.

Buckingham did not come. The rumour was that London was dreadfully infested by plague, the dead lying in the streets of the poorer quarters and the plague cart coming by two and three times a day, healthy citizens shrinking back into doorways and locking themselves into their houses, every man who could afford it moving out to the country and then finding that villages on the road from the capital barred their doors to London trade. No-one knew how the plague spread, perhaps it was by touch, perhaps it was in the air. People spoke of a plague wind as the season grew warmer and said that the soft warm breezes of spring blew the plague into your skin and set the buboes like eggs in your armpit and groin.

John longed to see Buckingham and to know that he was well. He could hardly believe that the court would linger in London while the hot weather came. The young king must be mad to expose himself to such danger, to expose his friends. But no-one at New Hall could say when the court would move, no-one could tell John if the court would come on a visit, or even if the duke might come home alone, tired of the squabbles and rivalry of the court and longing to be quietly in his own house, in his garden, among those who loved him.

John unpacked the India rarities and laid them out, as his fancy took him, in a small room. They looked well all together, he thought. There were some handsome skins and some silks, and he ordered the maids to sew them to strips of stout canvas which he could fix to the walls to make into hangings. He had a cabinet made to hold the jewels, fastened with an intricate gold lock with only one key, which he held for the duke. Still, the duke never came.

Then John had news. The king's delayed marriage to the French princess was to go ahead; the duke had already left for France.

'He's out of the country?' John asked the steward, in the safe privacy of the household office.

William Ward nodded.

'Who has he taken from his household?' John demanded.

'You know his way,' Ward said. 'He was up and gone within the day. He forgot half his great wardrobe. The moment the king said he was to go, he was gone. He took hardly a dozen servants for his own use.'

'He did not ask for me?'

He shook his head. 'Out of sight, out of mind, when you serve His Grace,' he said.

John nodded and went back outside.

The plan for the fish had worked. The terrace was a delightful place in the April sunshine. The goldfish swam in their own pool on the top terrace and the banks around them were gleaming with kingcups and celandine, as gold as they. The stream overflowed and babbled down to the next level where silver fish swam under the overhanging pale green stems of what would bloom into white carnations. The glass fence was quite invisible, the water rippled down just as John had planned. He sat in one of the arbours and watched the water play, knowing that it was only his own folly which made the sound mournful and made him feel that great events were taking place out of reach and out of sight.

There was much to do in the garden. The ships of the Navy still obeyed Buckingham's command that John should have the pick of rarities and new plants every time they returned from a voyage. Often a traveller would make his way to the garden at New Hall with something to sell: a plant, a seed, a nut, or some rare and curious gift. John bought many things and added them to the collection, keeping a careful account and submitting it to William Ward, who repaid him. The things accumulated in the cabinet, the India skins grew dirty and John ordered a woman to come into the rarities room to dust and clean. Still the duke did not come home.

Finally, in May a méssage came for Tradescant, scrawled in the duke's own hand and brought all the way from Paris. It read:

> 'My best suit and shirts forgotten in the hurry. Do bring all the things I may need, and anything precious and rare which might amuse the little princess.'

'He sends for you?' the steward asked.

John read and re-read the note and then laughed aloud, like a man who has been told that he shall be rescued. It was a laugh of relief. 'He needs me. At last he needs me. I am to take his best suit and some curious playthings for the princess herself!' He stuffed the note in his pocket and headed for the rarities room, his step lighter, his whole being straighter, more determined, as if he were a young man commanded to set out on a quest, a chivalric quest.

'William, help me. Send for the housekeeper and get his things packed for me at once. He must have everything he might need. His best suit, but shirts as well, and I had better take a pair of his horses. Remember his riding clothes, and his hats. Everything he might want, I must take it all. His jewel box and his best diamonds. Nothing must be forgotten!'

The steward laughed at Tradescant's urgency. 'And when is all this to be ready?'

'At once!' John exclaimed. 'At once! He has sent for me, and he trusts me to forget nothing. I must leave tonight.'

John scattered orders like plentiful seed up the stairs and down the stairs, in the stable and in the kitchen, until everyone in the household was running to pack whatever the duke might require in France.

Tradescant himself ran like a man half his age across the park to his cottage. Elizabeth was spinning, her wheel pushed alongside the window so that the sunshine fell on her hands. John hardly saw the beauty of the moving strands of wool in the sunshine and the quiet peace of his wife, humming a psalm as she worked.

'I'm off!' he cried. 'He has sent for me at last!'

She rose to her feet, her face shocked, knowing at once who he meant. 'The duke?'

'God be praised!'

She did not say, 'Amen'.

'I am to follow him to France, with his baggage,' John said. 'He wrote to me himself. He knows that no-one else could get it done. No-one else would take the care. He wrote to me by name.'

She turned her face away for a moment, and then quietly put her spindle down. 'You will need your travelling cape, and your riding breeches,' she said and went to climb the little stair to their bed chamber.

'He wants me!' Tradescant repeated exultantly. 'He sent for me! All the way from France!'

Elizabeth turned back to look at him and for a moment he could not understand her expression. She was looking at him with regret, with a strange inexplicable pity.

'This is what I have been waiting for!' he said. But at once the words sounded lame. 'At last!'

'I know you have been waiting for him to whistle and for you to run,' she said gently. 'And I will pray that he does not lead you down dark pathways.'

'He is leading me to the court of France!' John exclaimed. 'To the heart of Paris itself to bring home the new Queen of England!'

'To a Papist court and a Papist queen,' Elizabeth said steadily. 'I will pray for your deliverance night and day, husband. Last time you went to court you came home sickened to your soul.'

John swore under his breath and flung himself out of the cottage to wait on the road for his wife to pack his bag. So when they said farewell he did not take her in his arms but merely nodded his head to her. 'I bid you farewell,' he said. 'I cannot say when I shall return.'

'When he has finished with you,' she said simply.

John flinched at the words. 'I am his servant, as he is the king's,' he said. 'Duty to him is an honour as well as my task.'

'Indeed, I hope his service always is an honour,' she said. 'And that he never asks anything of you that you should not perform.'

John took her hand and kissed her lightly, coldly, on the forehead. 'Of course not,' he said irritably. The cart, packed with the duke's goods and drawn by two good horses, with his lordship's two best hunters tossing their heads at being tied on behind, clattered down the lane. John hailed it and swung up on the seat beside the driver.

When he looked down on her he thought his wife seemed very small, but as indomitable as she had been the day of their engagement twenty-four years ago.

'God bless you,' he said gruffly. 'I shall come home as soon as I have done my duty.'

She nodded, still grave. 'J and I will be waiting for you,' she said. The cart rolled forward, she turned and watched it go. 'As we always are.'

When J came in for his supper she sent him back out to the pump to wash his hands again. He came in wiping his palms on his smock, leaving muddy stains.

'Look at you!' Elizabeth exclaimed without heat.

'It's clean earth,' he defended himself. 'And I've never seen my father's hands without grimy calluses.'

Elizabeth brought bread and meat broth to the table.

'Chicken broth again?' J asked without resentment.

'Mutton,' she said. 'Mrs Giddings killed a sheep and sold me the lights and a leg. We'll have a roast tomorrow.'

'Where's father?'

She let him break bread and take a spoonful of soup before she answered. 'Gone to France after my lord Buckingham.'

He dropped his spoon back in his bowl. 'Gone where?' he asked incredulously.

'I'd have thought you'd have heard.'

He shook his head. 'I was over at the far side of the estate all day, with the game birds. I heard nothing.'

'The duke sent for him, wanted him to take some clothes, and some playthings for the French princess.'

'And he went?'

She met his angry glare. 'Of course, J my boy. Of course he went.'

'He runs after the duke as if he were a dog!' J burst out.

Elizabeth shot a fierce look at him. 'You remember your duty!' she hissed.

J dropped his gaze to the table, and fought for control. 'I miss him,' he said quietly. 'When he is not there then people look to me to tell them what to do. Because I am his son they assume that I know things, and I don't know them. And the lads in the stable tease me when he is not there. They mock me behind my back and call me names. They say things about him and the duke which are not fit to be repeated.'

'He won't be long,' Elizabeth said without conviction.

'You cannot know that.'

'I know he will come as soon as he can.'

'You know he will come when the duke has finished with him, and not a moment sooner. Besides, he loves travelling, if he gets the chance he will be off around Europe again. Did he leave you with an address where we can reach him?'

'No.'

'Or money?'

'No.'

J sighed heavily and spooned broth. When his bowl was empty he took the last piece of bread and wiped it carefully around, mopping up the gravy. 'So at the end of the month I shall have to go to the almoner for his wages and he will swear they will be paid to him in Paris, and we will have to make do on my money until he returns.'

'We can manage,' Elizabeth said. 'I have some put by, and he will make it up when he gets back.'

J knew how to bait his mother. 'And he will be drinking and dining and living at a Papist court. I doubt that there will be any church where he can say his prayers. He will come home crossing himself and needing a priest to pray for him.'

She went white at that. 'He will not,' she said faintly.

'They say Buckingham himself is inclining that way,' J went on. 'His mother is turned Papist, or witch, or something.'

Elizabeth dropped her head and was silent for a moment. 'Our Lord will keep him safe,' she said. 'And he is a godly man. He will come home safe, to his home, to his faith.'

J tired of the sport of teasing his mother's piety. 'When I am a man I shall call no man master,' he asserted.

She smiled at him. 'Then you will have to earn more money than your father has ever done! Every man has his better, every dog a master.'

'I shall never follow a man as my father follows the duke,' J said boldly. 'Not the King of England himself. I shall work for my own good, I shall go on my own travels. I shall not be ordered to one place and then summoned away.'

Elizabeth put out her hand in a rare gesture of tenderness and touched his cheek. 'I hope you will live in a country where great men do not exercise their power in such a way,' she said. It was the closest he had ever heard her come to any sort of radical thought. 'I hope you will live in a country where great men remember their duty to the poor, and to their servants. But we do not live in such a world yet, my J. You have to choose a master and become his man and do his bidding. There is no-one who does not serve another, whether you're the lowest ploughboy or the greatest squire. There is always another above you.'

Instinctively he lowered his voice. 'England will have to change,' he said softly. 'The lowest ploughboy is questioning if his master has a God-given right to rule over him. The lowest ploughboy has a soul which is as welcome in heaven as the greatest squire. The Bible says that the first shall become last. That's not the promise that nothing can ever change.'

'Hush,' Elizabeth said. 'Time enough to speak like that when things have changed, if they ever do.'

'Things are changing now,' J insisted. 'This king will have to deal with the people of the country. He will have to listen to Parliament. He cannot cheat on honest, good men, as his father did. We are tired of paying for a court which shows us nothing but luxury and sin. We will not be allied to Papists, we will not be brothers to heretics!'

She shook her head, but she did not stop him.

'At New Hall there is a man who knows another man who says that there should be a petition against the king that should tell him his duties. That he cannot levy taxes without calling a parliament. That he must listen to his advisers in Parliament. That the duke should not rule over everything and scrape all the wealth into his own pocket. That orphans and widows should have the protection

225

of the Crown, so that a man can die in peace and know that his estate will be well managed and not farmed by the duke for his own good.'

'Are there many that think this?' Her whisper was a thread of sound.

'He says so.'

Her eyes were wide. 'Does any say so in your father's hearing?'

J shook his head. 'Father is known as the duke's man through and through. But there are many, even in the duke's own service, who know that the mood of the country is turning against the duke. They blame him for everything that goes wrong, from this hot weather to the plague.'

'What will become of us if the duke should fall?' she asked.

J's young face was determined. 'We would survive,' he said. 'Even if the country never wanted another duke, it would always need gardeners. I should always find work and there will always be a home for you with me. But what would become of my father? He's not just the duke's gardener – he is his vassal. If the duke fails then I think father's heart will break.'

May 1625

John met his master in Paris as he had been ordered. He waited for him in the black and white marble hall of the great house until the double doors swung open and the duke was framed in the bright Paris sunlight. He was wearing diamonds in his hat, on his finely embroidered doublet. His cape was hemmed with brilliants which John hoped very much were glass but feared were also diamonds. He sparkled in the spring sunshine like the new leaves on a silver birch tree.

'My John!' he exclaimed with delight. 'And have you brought all my clothes? I am reduced to rags!'

John found he was beaming with delight at the sight of his master. 'So I see, my lord. I was afraid that I would find you looking very poor and mean. I have brought everything and your coach and six horses is coming behind me.'

Buckingham grasped him by the shoulder. 'I knew you would do it for me,' he said. 'I would trust no other. How are things at New Hall?'

'Everything is well,' John told him. 'The garden is looking well, your water terrace is working and looks lovely. Your wife and mother are at New Hall and are both well.'

'Oh yes, gardens,' the duke said. 'You must meet the gardeners to the French court, you will be impressed with what they do here. The queen will give me a note for you to introduce yourself to them.' He bent towards John and spoke softly in his ear. 'The queen would give me a good deal more too, if I asked for it, I think!'

John found he was smiling at the shameless vanity of the man. 'I

227

know the Robins, but I'shall be pleased to see them again. And you have been amusing yourself.'

Buckingham kissed his fingertips like a Frenchman acknowledging beauty. 'I have been in paradise,' he said. 'And you shall come with me and we shall see the palace gardens together. Come, John, I shall change my clothes and I shall take you around the city. It's very fair and very joyful, and the women are as easy as mares in heat. It's a perfect town for me!'

John chuckled unwillingly. 'My wife would be most distressed. I will go and see the gardens but I cannot go visiting women.'

Buckingham put his arm around Tradescant's shoulders and hugged him tight. 'You shall be my conscience then,' he said. 'And keep me on the straight and narrow way.'

It could not be done. The Archangel Gabriel with a flaming sword could not have kept the Duke of Buckingham on the straight and narrow way in Paris in 1625. The French court was besotted with the English, a new prince on the throne, a French princess as his chosen bride, and the handsomest man in Europe at court to fetch her to her new home. Crowds of women gathered outside Buckingham's *hôtel* just to see him come and go, and to admire the astounding sight of his carriage and six, and the jewels and his clothes and his hat, the '*bonnet d'anglais*' which was copied by a hundred hatters as soon as they glimpsed it.

The queen herself blushed when he came near her, and watched him from behind her fan if he so much as spoke to another woman, and little Princess Henrietta Maria stammered when he was in the room and forgot what little English she knew. The whole of France was in love with him, the whole of Paris adored him. And Buckingham, smiling, laughing, fêted everywhere he went, passed through adoring crowds as if he were the king himself and not a mere ambassador: the bridegroom himself and not a proxy.

John was weary of Buckingham's ceaseless round of parties within days.

'Keep up, John,' Buckingham threw over his shoulder. 'We are going to a masked ball tonight.'

'As you wish,' John said.

Buckingham turned and laughed at John's stoical expression. 'Have you no assignations? No dances promised?'

'I'm a married man,' John said. 'As you are, my lord.' He paused for Buckingham's crack of laughter. 'But I will attend you there and wait for you as long as you wish, my lord.'

Buckingham rested his hand on Tradescant's shoulder. 'No, I have a dozen men who can wait on me, and only one who loves me like a brother. I shan't waste your love and loyalty on watching me dancing. What would you like to do most?'

Tradescant thought. 'I've seen some plants which would look very well at New Hall,' he said cautiously. 'If you could spare me, I shall visit the Robins' garden to order the plants and see them packed, and then they could come home with us when we leave.'

Buckingham thought, his head on one side. 'I think we can do better than that.' He reached into the deep pocket of his coat and pulled out a purse. 'D'you know what this is?'

'Money?'

'Better than that. A bribe. An enormous bribe, from Richelieu or his agents.'

John looked at the purse as if it were a venomous snake. 'Do you want me to return it?'

Buckingham threw back his head and laughed. 'John! My John! No! I want you to spend it!'

'French money? What do they want for it?'

'My friendship, my advice to the king, my support of the little princess. Take it!'

Still John hesitated. 'But what if you need to warn the king against them? What if things change?'

'Who's our worst enemy? Worst enemy of the faith? Greatest danger to the freedom of our Protestant brothers in Europe?'

'The Spanish,' John said slowly.

'So we befriend the French to make an alliance against the Spanish,' Buckingham said simply. 'And if they want to give me a fortune for doing what I would be doing anyway – then they may!'

'But what if it all changes?' John asked. 'What if the Spanish make an alliance with the French? Or the French turn against us?'

Buckingham tossed the purse in the air and caught it again. It fell as if it were indeed very heavy. 'Then the money is spent and I have done my country the service of draining the coffers of our enemy. Here! Catch!' He threw the purse to John, and John caught it as a reflex action before he could stop himself.

'Take it to Amsterdam,' Buckingham said, as skilfully tempting as a serpent in Eden. 'Take it to Amsterdam, and buy tulips, my John.'

He could have said nothing which would have worked more powerfully on Tradescant. Unaware of the action, John hefted the purse in his hand, guessing at the weight. 'They are going at a terrible price,' he said. 'The market has gone mad for tulips. Everyone is buying, everyone is speculating in them. Men who have never left their money counters are buying the names of tulips on scraps of paper, they never even see the flower. I can't be sure how many bulbs I could get, even with this money.'

'Go,' Buckingham commanded. He flung himself into a chair and swung his long legs over the arm. He looked at Tradescant with his teasing smile. 'You know you are longing for them, my John. Go and look at the tulip fields and buy as many as you want. There's that purse, and another to follow. Bring me a couple of bulbs back and we will put them in a pot, set ourselves up as burghers and grow rich.'

'The Semper Augusta is scarlet and white,' John said. 'I've seen a painting of it. The colour is most beautifully broken, and it has a most wonderful shape, the true tulip cup shape but with tiny points on each petal, so each petal stands a little proud from the others. And long curvy leaves . . .'

'In faith! This is love!' Buckingham mocked. 'This is true love, John I've never seen you so moved.'

Tradescant smiled. 'There's never been a more perfect flower. It's the best there is. There's nothing better. And there's never been one which cost more.'

Buckingham pointed to the French bribe in Tradescant's hand. 'Go and buy it,' he said simply.

Tradescant packed that night and was ready to leave at dawn. He left a note for his master, promising that the gold would be safe in his keeping and that he would buy as many bulbs as could be got but, to his surprise, when he was about to mount his horse in the street outside the Buckingham *hôtel*, the duke himself came lounging out, pulling on a robe against the cold morning air, dressed only in his shirt and boots and breeches.

'My lord!' Tradescant dropped the reins of his horse and went towards him. 'I had thought you would sleep till noon!'

'I woke and thought of you setting off on your own adventure and I chose to come down to bid you farewell,' Buckingham said casually.

'I would have waited if I had known. I could have left later and you could have had your sleep.'

Buckingham slapped John on the shoulder. 'I know. It doesn't matter. I knew you were setting off early, and I woke and looked from my window and took a fancy to see you ride away.'

John said nothing, there were no words to say to the greatest man in England who rose at dawn after a night's dancing to bid a servant farewell.

'Enjoy yourself,' Buckingham urged. 'Stay as long as you like, draw on my banker, buy anything which takes your fancy and bring it home to New Hall. I want tulips next season, my John. I want thousands of beautiful tulips.'

'You shall have them,' Tradescant said fervently. 'I shall give you gardens of great beauty, my lord. Great beauty.' He paused for a moment and cleared his throat. 'And when am I to be home, my lord?'

Buckingham put his arm around John's shoulders and hugged him tightly. 'When you are ready, my John. Go and spend some money, and enjoy yourself. I have never been happier, you be happy too. Go and joyfully spend some of my easily earned money and we will meet again at New Hall when you come home.'

'I shall not fail you,' John promised, thinking that if he were not an honest man he could disappear into Europe with the heavy purses of gold and never be seen again.

'I know. You never fail me,' Buckingham said affectionately. 'And that is why I want you to go and pleasure yourself with tulips. It is a reward for fidelity. If I cannot tempt you with easy French women and drink, then let me give you what is your greatest joy. Go and run riot in the bulbfields, my John. Lust after petals and slake your lust!'

He waved and turned inside the house. Tradescant waited, his hat in his hand, until the great double doors had closed behind his master, and then he mounted his horse, clicked encouragingly and turned its head eastwards, out of Paris to the Low Countries and the tulip fields.

John found Amsterdam buzzing with infectious, continual excitement. All the taverns he had known where the tulip growers had met and sold tulips to each other were now expanded into double and treble the size and they opened for business in the morning in an atmosphere of teeth-gritting excitement. He looked in vain for the men he had known, the quiet steady gardeners who had told him how to cut the bulbs and plant them. They had been replaced by men with soft white hands who carried not bulbs but great books in which there were illustrations of tulips drawn with the beauty and care of fine portraits. The bidding for the bulbs was done on promissory notes; no money changed hands. John with his purses of French gold was an exception, he felt like a fool trying to pay men with money when everyone else was trading in credit.

And he felt even more of a fool when he tried to buy tulip bulbs to take away with him, when he wanted to exchange a sackful of gold – real money – for a sackful of bulbs – real bulbs. Everyone else was trading without ever holding a bulb in their hand. They bought and sold the promise of the tulip crop when it was lifted, or they bought and sold the name of a tulip. Some flowers were so rare that there were only ten or a dozen in the whole country. Such bulbs would never come to market, John was assured. He would have to buy the slip of paper with the name of the tulip written on the top of it, and have it attested at the Bourse. If he had any sense he would sell the slip of paper the very next day as the price jumped and leapfrogged. He should make his profit in the rising market and not hang around the dealers and ask them for real tulips to take home with him. The market was not for a bulb in a pot, it was for an idea of a tulip, the promise of a tulip. The market had gone light, the market had gone airy. It was the *windhandel* market.

'What's that?' John asked.

'A wind market,' a man translated for him. 'You are no longer buying the goods, you are buying the promise of the goods. And you are paying with a promise to pay. You don't actually have to give your gold and receive your tulip until – oh – next year. But if you have any sense by then you will have sold it at a profit and you will have made a fortune merely by letting the wind blow through your fingers.'

'But I want tulips!' John exclaimed in frustration. 'I don't want a piece of paper with a tulip name written on it to sell to someone else. I want a bulb that I can take home and grow.'

The man shrugged, losing interest at once. 'It's not how we do business,' he said. 'But if you go down the canal towards Rotterdam you will find men and women who will sell you bulbs that you can take away. They will call you a fool for paying money on the nail.'

'I've been called a fool before,' John said grimly. 'I can bear it.'

He was dining in a tavern at the end of this expedition, drinking deep of the thick ale which the Dutch loved and eating well of their rich food, when the door darkened and a well-loved voice shouted into the gloom. 'Is my John in here?'

John choked on his ale and leaped to his feet, overturning his stool. 'Your Grace?'

It was Buckingham, modestly dressed in a suit of smooth brown wool, chuckling like a madman at the sight of John's astounded face.

'Caught you,' he said easily. 'Drinking away my fortune.'

'My lord! I never –'

He laughed again. 'How have you done, my John? Are you rich in tulip notes?'

John shook his head. 'I am rich in tulips, in real bulbs, my lord. The men in this town seem to have forgotten what they are buying and selling, they want only a piece of paper with a name written on it and the Bourse seal at the bottom. I had to go far inland to find growers who would sell me the real thing.'

Buckingham came into the ale house and sat at John's table. 'Finish your dinner, I have dined already,' he remarked. 'So where are they? These tulips?'

'They are packed away and ready to sail tonight,' John said, reluctantly picking up a crust of bread smeared with creamy Dutch butter. 'I was on my way home to New Hall with them.'

'Can they sail alone?'

John thought quickly. 'I'd send a man I could trust to go with them. It's too precious a cargo to leave to the captain. And I'd like someone to see them all the way to New Hall.'

'Do it,' the duke said idly.

John swallowed his question with his bread, rose from the table, bowed swiftly to the duke and went out of the tavern. He ran like a deer for his inn, engaged the landlord's son to go to England and to see the barrels of tulips safely delivered to New Hall, pressed money and a note of introduction to J into the young man's hand, and then ran back to the tavern as the duke was downing his second pint of ale.

'All done, Your Grace,' he reported breathlessly.

'I thank you,' the duke said.

There was a tantalising silence. John stood before his master.

'Oh, you can sit down,' the duke said. 'And have an ale. You must be thirsty.'

John slid into the seat opposite his master and watched him as the girl brought his drink. The duke was pale, a little tired from the festivities of the French court, but his dark eyes were sparkling. John felt a stir of his venturing spirit.

'Are you not attended, Your Grace?'

The duke shook his head. 'I am travelling unknown.'

John waited but his master volunteered nothing.

'Anywhere to stay?'

'I thought I'd bed with you.'

'What if you had not found me?' John grimaced at the thought of the greatest man in England wandering around the Low Countries in search of his gardener.

'I knew I only had to wait somewhere near the tulip exchange and you would turn up,' Buckingham said easily. 'And besides, I do not crumple without a dozen servants to support me, you know, John. I can fend for myself.'

'Of course,' John agreed quickly. 'I just wondered what you are doing here?'

'Oh, that,' Buckingham said as if recalled to his mission. 'Why, I have a job to do for my master and I thought you might help me.'

'Of course,' John said instantly.

'We'll drink a little more and then roister a little, and then in the morning we shall do some business,' Buckingham suggested engagingly.

'Are we to go far?' John asked, thinking wildly of the ships which left for the Dutch Indies and for the spreading Dutch empire. 'It may be that I should prepare while you make merry.'

The duke shook his head. 'My business is in town, with the gold and diamond merchants. But I want you with me. My amulet. I shall need all my luck tomorrow.'

They slept in the same bed. When John woke in the morning the younger man had thrown an arm out in his sleep and John woke to a touch on his face like a caress. He lay still for a little while, under that casual blessing, and then slid out of bed and looked out of the little window down at the street below.

The cobbled quayside was crowded with sellers of bread and cheese and milk, up from the country by barge at dawn and spreading their stalls for all to see. Among them, and starting to lay out their wares, were the cobblers and sellers of household goods: brushes and soaps, kindling, and brassware. Artists were setting up easels and offering to sketch portraits. Sailors up from the deep-water docks were moving among the crowd and offering rarities and foreign goods – silk shawls, flasks of rare drink, little toys. The low barges plied constantly up and down the canal; and ducks, in continual flurry away from the prows, quacked and complained. The sunlight glinted on the water of the canal and threw back the reflection of the market stalls and the dark shadows of the criss-crossing bridges.

Tradescant heard Buckingham stir in the bed behind him and turned at once.

'Good morning, my lord, is there anything I can get you?'

'You can get me a hundred thousand pounds in gold or I am a ruined man,' Buckingham said, his face buried in the pillow. 'That's what we're doing today, my John. We're going to pawn the Crown Jewels.'

Cecil's long training stood John in good stead through that day. Buckingham was trying to raise the money to equip a mighty Protestant army to attack Spain and to free Charles's sister, Elizabeth of Bohemia, and her husband and restore them to their rightful throne. There was no money in the royal treasury. The English parliament would vote no more to a king who had done so little to bring in the reforms they had demanded. It was left to Buckingham to raise the funds. And he had nothing to offer as security but the crowns of England, Scotland and Ireland and any related valuables that the moneylenders might require.

John stood with his back to the door, watching his master charming the powerful money men of Amsterdam. The scene looked like one of the new oil paintings that King Charles kept buying. The room was in half-darkness, windows shrouded with thick embroidered curtains. The table was lit only by a couple of candles behind an engraved shade which threw strange cabalistic patterns on the walls. There were three men on one side of the table and Buckingham on the other. One man was a solid burgher, a father of the city and a cautious man. To him Buckingham deferred with a charming youthful respect, and as the meeting went on John watched the big man, slowly unbend, like a horse on the tow path bending its neck to be patted. Next to him was a Jewish financier, his eyes as dark as Buckingham's own, his hair as black and lustrous as the duke's. He wore a little cap on the back of his head and a long dark suit in plain material. The Low Countries was a place that prided itself on its tolerance; John thought that Buckingham would not have sat on equal terms with a Jew at any other table in Europe.

The duke was uneasy with the financier. He could not find the right tone to tempt him. The man was guarded, his long face giving away nothing. He spoke little and when he did, it was in French with an accent which John could not identify. He treated Buckingham with deference, but it seemed as if there was a secret inner judgement that he was keeping hidden. John was as superstitious and fearful of the Jews as any Englishman. He feared this man in particular.

The third man was from some strand of nobility who would have access to a vast fortune if these other two approved. He was slim and young and richly dressed, and he had no aptitude for the carefully written calculations of profit and interest on the small pieces of paper which the other two men were exchanging. He leaned back in his chair and gazed idly around him. Every now and then he and Buckingham would exchange a smile as if to agree that they two were men of the world and these vulgar details were beneath them.

'We have to consider the issue of the security of the jewels,' the burgher said. 'They will be lodged here.'

Buckingham shook his head. 'They cannot be taken from London,' he said. 'But you shall have your own man in London to guard them, if you wish. And a sealed letter from King Charles himself to acknowledge your right.'

The burgher looked uneasy. 'But if we should need to collect them?'

'If His Majesty cannot repay the loan?' Buckingham smiled. 'Ah, forgive me, the king will repay. He will not fail. When Prince Frederick and Princess Elizabeth are back on their thrones then the wealth of Bohemia will repay all the debts incurred in the campaign to restore them.'

'And if the campaign fails?' the Jew asked quietly.

Buckingham checked for a moment. 'It will not,' he replied.

There was a brief silence. The Jew waited for his answer.

'If it should fail then his Majesty will repay according to the schedule of repayments as you propose,' Buckingham said smoothly. 'We are speaking of the King of England, my lords. He is hardly likely to run off to the Americas.'

The nobleman laughed at the joke and Buckingham shot him a swift smile. The Jew did not laugh.

'But how should we collect if, by some error, His Majesty were to default?' the burgher asked politely.

Buckingham shrugged as if such a thing were beyond the stretch of any imagination. 'Oh. I can hardly think – well – we will follow the line of fairytales. If the campaign fails and the Prince and Princess of Bohemia do not repay you themselves, and then if the King of England does not repay you then I, the Duke of Buckingham, will myself deliver to you the Crown Jewels of England. Will that satisfy you, gentlemen?'

John looked from one face to another. It satisfied the nobleman who could not imagine that Buckingham could say one thing and do another. He was no obstacle. The burgher was havering, half-convinced, half-fearful. The Jew was inscrutable. His dark serious face could not be read. He might be inwardly approving, he might have damned this project from the first moment. John could not tell.

'And you would put that in writing?'

'Signed in blood if you wish,' Buckingham said carelessly, the glancing reference to the popular play a half-insult to all Jewish moneylenders. 'I have promised my master the King of England that he shall have the funds to raise an army to restore his sister to her throne. It is a task which we should all do as good Protestants and good Christians. It is a task which most becomes me as His Majesty's most faithful servant.'

The three men nodded.

'Shall I leave you to consult for a while?' Buckingham offered. 'I must warn you, out of courtesy, that my time is a little limited. There are other gentlemen who would extend this loan to the king and think it an honour to so do. But I promised you I would see you first.'

'Of course,' the burgher said awkwardly. 'And we thank you. Perhaps you would like a glass of wine?'

He drew back one of the thick hangings and showed a small door beyond. It opened into a walled courtyard. In a giant pot against the wall grew an apricot tree, at its feet the folded leaves of some tulips now past their prime. John saw at once that they had been Lack tulips, beautifully white and veined with scarlet. There were a couple of chairs and a table in the shade of the tree, and a flagon of wine with a small plate of biscuits.

'Please,' the burgher said. 'Enjoy this. And ring for anything further you need. We will delay you only a moment.'

He bowed and went back into the room. Buckingham threw himself into the chair and watched John pour the wine and hand him a glass.

'What d'you think?' he asked quietly.

'It's possible,' John said in the same undertone. 'Do you have other men to borrow from?'

'No,' Buckingham said. 'D'you think they know that?'

'No,' John said. 'There is so much wealth flying around this city that they cannot be sure of it. The nobleman is in your pocket but I doubt the other two.'

Buckingham nodded and sipped his wine. 'That's good,' he said with approval. 'Alicante.'

'What do we do if they say no?'

Buckingham tipped his beautiful face up to the sun and closed his eyes as if he did not have a care in the world. 'Go home with the whole of the king's foreign policy in ruins,' he said. 'Tell the king that his sister is thrown out of her kingdom and insulted and that he can do nothing. Tell the king that unless he agrees with Parliament he will be a pauper on his own throne, and that his chief minister was a better Master of Horse than he is a diplomat.'

'You got him the French princess,' John observed.

Buckingham half-opened his eyes and John saw the glint of his look under the thick eyelashes. 'Let's hope to God she pleases him. I don't guarantee it.'

The door behind John opened and he whirled around. It was the Jew in the doorway, his head held low. 'I am sorry, masters,' he said quietly. 'We cannot oblige you. The capital is more than we can afford without holding the security ourselves.'

Buckingham jumped to his feet in one of his sudden rages, about to shout at the man. John threw himself forward and got both hands on his master's shoulders as if he was re-arranging his cape.

'Steady,' he whispered.

He felt the shoulders straighten under his grip. Buckingham lifted his head. 'I am sorry you could not oblige me,' he said. 'I will tell the king of your reluctance and my disappointment.'

The Jew's head bowed lower.

Buckingham turned on his heel and John dived before him to open the door so his smooth disdainful stride from the courtyard was not checked. They arrived out in the street by a side door and hesitated.

'What now?' Tradescant asked.

'We try another,' Buckingham said. 'And then another. And then we go and buy some bulbs, for I think that is all we're going to get out of this damned damned city.'

Buckingham was right. John was back at New Hall by the end of May, preceded by wagon-loads of plants, sacks of tulip bulbs and with six of the most precious bulbs – each costing a purse of gold – hidden deep inside his waistcoat.

His first act was to go to the rarities room of New Hall and to summon J to meet him there with six large porcelain pots and a basket of soil.

J came into the room and found the six bulbs laid out on a table. His father was, with infinite care, cutting slightly into the base of each bulb in the hope that it would encourage them to divide, and make new bulbs.

'What are they?' J asked reverently, holding a wicker basket of sieved warm weed-free earth, watching his father's meticulous care. 'Are they the Semper Augustus?'

His father shook his head. 'I had a king's ransom to spend and yet I could not afford it,' he said. 'No-one bought the Semper. I was at the Bourse every day and the price was so high that no-one would buy, and the merchant kept his nerve and would not drop the price. Next season he will offer them again at double the price, and all the year he will be praying that no-one has grown a new tulip which supplants the Semper and leaves him with a pair of fine flowers which are out of fashion.'

'Could that happen?' J was horrified.

John nodded. 'It is not gardening, it is speculation,' he said with distaste. 'There are people dealing in tulips who have never so much as pulled a weed. And making fortunes from their work.'

J extended a respectful finger and stroked the dry firm surface of the nearest bulb. 'The skin is solid, and the shape is good. They are even lovely in the bulb, aren't they?' He bent and sniffed the firm warm skin.

'Is it clean?' John asked anxiously. 'No hint of taint?'

J shook his head. 'None. What sort is it?'

'This is the Duck tulip – yellow with crimson blush at the base of the petals.' John pointed to the next bulb. 'This is a Lack tulip, white and thin-petalled with thin red stripes through white, and this is a *Tulipa australis*, very strong-stemmed and scarlet petals with a white border. Pray God they grow for us, I have spent nearly a thousand pounds on the six of them.'

J's hand holding the trowel trembled. 'A thousand pounds? A thousand? But father – what if they rot?' he asked, his voice a whisper. 'What if they grow blind and fail to flower at all?'

John smiled grimly. 'Then we seek another line of work. But what if they grow and split into new bulbs, J? Then our master has doubled his wealth in one season.'

'But we stay on the same wages,' J observed.

John nodded and put the six pots in a cool cupboard in the corner of the room. 'That is how it works,' he said simply. 'But there could be no objection to us taking a bulb for every two we grow for him. My master Cecil taught me that himself.'

John was popular in the great dining room of New Hall on his return. He was able to tell a rapt audience of the prettiness of the little French princess: only fifteen and tiny, dark-haired and dark-eyed. He told them of her dancing and her singing, of her complete refusal to learn English. He told them that the news in London was that when the young King Charles met her at Dover Castle, he had covered her little face with kisses, laughed at her prepared speech, and spent the night in her bed.

The ladies wanted to know what she was wearing and John struggled through a description of her clothes. He assured them that the king and queen entered London by the river in a grand barge, both dressed in green, with the guns of the Tower roaring out a salute, and that was a vivid enough picture to be told and retold by a dozen hearthsides. He did not tell them that there had been a nasty quarrel between the king and his bride of only a day when she had wanted her French companions in the carriage from Dover to London, and the king had insisted that she travel with Buckingham's wife and his mother.

The king had said that the French attendant was not of high enough station to ride with the Queen of England; and the young queen incautiously retorted that she knew well enough that the Buckinghams had been nobodies just ten years ago. She did not yet know enough to mind her sharp tongue, she had not yet learned of the extent of the duke's influence. As it was, she rode in her carriage with the duke's wife and the duke's mother for the long journey into her capital and it might be safely assumed that no promises of friendship were made on the drive.

'So did she look happy?' asked Mrs Giddings, who worked in the New Hall laundry but had her own little farm and would kill another sheep for the Tradescants if John's story was good enough.

John thought of the fifteen-year-old girl and her un-English formality, her court which spoke only French, and her brace of confessors who spoke Latin grace over her dinner, and warned her not to eat meat even though her new husband had just carved her a slice, since she must observe a fast day.

'As happy as a maid can be,' he said. 'Laughing and chattering and singing.'

'And the duke, does he like her?'

Only Elizabeth saw the swift shadow cross her husband's face. There had been a scandal in France, several scandals. Buckingham had told him the worst of it as they paced the deck of a little fishing boat, sailing from Rotterdam to Tilbury. The Queen of France had encouraged Buckingham further than a married woman, and one so carefully watched, should have done. He had climbed the wall into her private garden to meet her there. What took place Buckingham would not say, but everyone else in Europe was talking about it. The pair had been caught by her personal guard. Swords had been drawn and threats made. Some said that the queen had been assaulted by Buckingham, some said the queen had been seduced, and caught half-naked in his arms. The queen's ladies said that she had been elegantly flirting or – no such thing – somewhere else all the time. There had been a whirlwind of rumour and innuendo and through it all Buckingham had sailed smiling, the handsomest man at court, the wickedest look, the most roguish smile, the irresistible charm. John had frowned when Buckingham had confessed to losing his heart to the Queen of France and thought that he should have stayed by his master and kept him from secret assignations with the most carefully guarded woman in Europe.

'What could have prevented it?' Buckingham sighed, but with a glint in his eye which always meant mischief. 'It's love, John. I shall run away with her and take her from her dreary husband to live with her in Virginia.'

John had shaken his head at his master. 'What does her husband think?' he asked.

'Oh, he hates me,' Buckingham said joyfully.

'And the Princess Henrietta Maria?'

'My sworn enemy now.'

'She's your queen,' John reminded him.

'She is only the wife of my dearest friend,' Buckingham had replied. 'And she'd better remember who he loves.'

'So what does she think of him?' the questioner repeated. 'What does the new queen think of our duke?'

'He is her greatest friend at court,' John answered carefully. 'The duke admires and respects her.'

'Will he come home soon?' someone asked from the back of the crowd, packed into John's kitchen.

'Not for a while,' John answered. 'There are parties and masquings and balls at court to greet the new queen, and then there will be the coronation. We'll not see him here for a few weeks.'

There was a general murmur of disappointment at that. New Hall was merrier when the duke was at home, and there was always the chance of a glimpse of the king.

'But you'll go to him,' Elizabeth said, rightly reading her husband's contented serenity.

'I am to meet him in London. And then I have to go down to the New Forest, looking for trees. He wants a maze,' Tradescant said with ill-hidden delight. 'Where I am to get enough yew from I don't know.'

❦

John only ever told half the story to the curious, and he always emphasised the things that they should hear. He was ready to tell that the young King Charles had already dismissed dozens of his father's idle wastrel favourites, that the court now ran to a strict rhythm of prayer, work, and exercise. The king seldom drank wine, and never to excess. He read all the papers set before him and signed each one personally with his own name. Sometimes his advisers would find small-handed notes written in the margin, and he would ask them later to ensure they were obeyed. He wanted to be a king with an eye to detail, to the meticulous observance both of ceremony and the minutiae of government.

John did not tell them that he had no eye to the grander picture, he was incapable of visualising consequences on a long-term or big scale. He was faultlessly loyal to those he dearly loved, but quite incapable of keeping his word to those he did not. Everything to the new king was personal; and when a man or a nation displeased him, he could not bear to see them or think of them.

His sister Elizabeth of Bohemia, still in exile, still waiting for support from her brother, remained uppermost in his mind, and he ransacked his advisers for ideas, and his treasure chests for money to pay for an army to help her. John never mentioned to anyone, not even his wife, the long hours in the darkened rooms of the Dutch moneylenders, and the humiliation of finally seeing that no man in Europe had any faith in the partnership of the untried king and the extravagant duke.

It was not only the moneylenders who found the duke wanting. An itinerant preacher, his clothes ragged but his face shining with conviction, came to Chelmsford and set up to preach under the market cross.

'You surely won't go and hear him,' John grumbled to Elizabeth as she laid his supper on the table and threw a shawl around her shoulders.

'I should like to go,' she said.

'He's bound to preach heresy,' John said. 'You'd much better stay home.'

'Come too,' she invited him. 'And if he speaks nonsense we can stop at the Bush on the way home and taste their ale.'

'I've no time for hedgerow preachers,' John said. 'And every year there are more of them. I hear two sermons on a Sunday. I don't need to seek one on Tuesday as well.'

She nodded, and slipped out of the door without arguing. She walked briskly down the street; a small crowd was at the centre of the village, gathered around the preacher.

He was warning them of hellfire, and of the sins of the great. Elizabeth stepped back a little way into a doorway to listen. John was right, this was probably heresy, and it might well turn into treason too. But there was something powerful in how he moved his arguments slowly forward.

'Step by step we are going down the road to ruination,' he said, so softly that his listeners craned forward and had the sense of being drawn into a conspiracy. 'Today the plague walks the streets of

London as freely as a favoured guest. Not a home is safe against it, not a person can be sure he will escape. Not a family in the city but loses one or two. And it is not only London – every village across the land must be wary of strangers, and fearful of sickly people. It is coming, it is coming to all of us – and there is only one escape: repentance and turning to Our Lord.'

There was a soft murmur of assent.

'Why is it come to us?' the preacher asked. 'Why should it strike us down? Let us look at where it starts. It comes from London: the centre of wealth, the centre of the court. It comes in the time of a new king, when things should be new-made, not struggling against the old sickness of plague. It comes because the king is not new-made, he has his father's Favourite forever at his shoulder, he has his father's adviser forever ordering his ways. He is not a new king; he is the old king while he is ruled by the same man.'

There was a movement of the crowd away from the preacher. He saw it at once. 'Oh, yes,' he continued swiftly. 'He pays your wages, I know, you live in his cottages, you grow your vegetables on his ground, but look up from your dungheaps and your crooked chimneys and see what this man does in the greater world. He it was who took the prince into mortal danger in Spain. He it was who brought home a Papist French queen. Every office in the land is his, or in his gift. Every great office has a Villiers sitting on the top of it, raking in wealth. When our king goes begging to the towns and to the corporations, why has he no money? Where has the wealth gone? Does the duke know – as he walks in his great house in his silk and diamonds – does the duke know where the money has gone?

'And if that were all it would be enough; but it is not all. There are more questions we should answer. Why can we win no battle neither by land nor by sea against the Spanish? Why do our soldiers come home and tell us they had nothing to eat? And no powder to fire their guns? Who is in charge of the army but the duke? When our sailors tell us that the ships are not fit to put to sea and the provisions are mouldering before they are eaten – who is the High Admiral? The duke again!

'And when our brothers and sisters in faith at La Rochelle in France, Protestants like us, ask us for help against a Papist army of

France, do we send them our aid? Our own brothers, praying as we do, escaped as we have escaped from the curse of Popery? Do we send them help? No! This great duke sends English ships and English sailors to help the forces of darkness, the army of Rome, the Navy of Richelieu! He sends good Protestant Englishmen for hire to the Devil, to the painted whore of Rome.'

The man was sweating, he swayed back against the stonework and wiped his face. 'Worst of all,' he said very low, 'there are those who wonder that in his last hours our King James, our good King James, was watched over only by Villiers and his mother. That the king seemed to be better, but they sent away his physicians and his surgeons and under their nursing he grew worse and died!'

There was an awe-struck whisper at this scandal, which came so close to naming the greatest crime in the world: regicide. The preacher pulled back. 'No wonder that the plague comes among us!' he exclaimed. 'No wonder. For why should the Lord of Hosts smile down on us who are betrayed and betrayed and let the betrayal go on!'

Someone shouted from the back of the crowd and those around him laughed. The preacher replied at once to the challenge.

'You're right, I cannot speak like this to the duke himself! But others will speak for me. We have a parliament of men, good men, who know how the country feels. They will speak to the king and warn him that this duke is a false friend. They will advise him to turn from Villiers and to listen to the needs of the nation. And he will turn! He will turn! He will give justice to the people and food to the children, and land to the landless. For it is very clear in the Bible that every man shall have his own land to dig and grow, and every woman shall have her own place. This king will turn from his evil advisers and give us that. An acre for every man and a cottage for every woman, and freedom from want for every child.'

There was a silence – this was an agricultural audience, and the thought of free land struck to the very heart of their deepest desire.

'Will the king do this for us?' a man asked.

'Once he is rid of false advisers he will certainly do it for us,' the preacher answered.

'What, and break down his own park gates?'

'There is enough land. The commons and wastes of England are vast. There is more than enough land for us all, aye, and for all the city men too, and if we need more then we have only to look around. Why! The very gardens of New Hall would feed fifty families if they were brought under the spade! There is wealth in this country! There is enough for us all, if we can take the surfeit from the wicked men and give it to the children in need.'

Elizabeth felt a gentle hand on her elbow. 'Come away,' John said softly in her ear. 'This is not preaching, this is ranting: a sermon with more treason than writ.'

Silently, she let him draw her away from the crowd and back up the lane to their home. 'Did you hear it all?' she asked as they entered the house.

'I heard enough,' John replied shortly.

J looked up at their entrance and then dropped his head and went on with his supper.

'He blamed the duke for everything,' Elizabeth said.

John nodded. 'Some do.'

'He said that without his bad advice the king would give land away, and make no more wars.'

John shook his head. 'The king would live as a king whether or not my lord was at his shoulder,' he said. 'And no king gives away his land.'

'But if he did . . .' Elizabeth persisted.

John pulled out his stool and sat beside J at the table. 'It is a dream,' he said. 'Not reality. A dream to whisper to children. Think of a country where every man might have his own garden, where every man might grow enough for his own pot, and then grow fruits and flowers as well. This is not England, it is Eden. There would be no hunger and no want, and a man might draw his garden in the ground and plant it as he wished, and watch it grow.'

There was a silence in the little room. John, who had been meaning to deride the preacher's vision, found himself tempted at the thought of a nation of gardens, of every park an orchard, every common a wheatfield, and no hunger or want.

'In Virginia they cut their land from the forest, however much land they want,' J said. 'It need not be a dream.'

248

'There is no shortage of land here either,' John said. 'If it were shared equally among every man and woman. There are the commons and the wastelands and the forests . . . there is enough land for everyone.'

'So the preacher was right,' Elizabeth said. 'It is the surfeit of the few which brings poverty to the rest. The rich men enclose the land and use it for parks and for wilderness. That is why there is not enough for poor people.'

John's face closed at once. 'That is treason,' he said simply. 'It is all the king's. He must do with it as he wishes. No-one else can come along and ask for land as if it were free. It all belongs to the king.'

'Except for the acres which belong to the duke,' J remarked slyly.

'He holds it for the king, and the king holds it for God,' Tradescant said, repeating the simple truth.

'Then we must pray that God wants to give land to the poor,' J said, getting up from the table and pushing his bowl irritably to one side. 'For they cannot survive another summer of plague and failed harvest without help, and neither the king nor the duke is likely to ease their pains.'

Summer 1626

Tradescant had thought that complaints about the duke were in the mouths of ignorant men, boys like J, women like Elizabeth, and wayside preachers, whose opinions might disturb a man's peace but would not challenge him. But then the king called Parliament to Oxford, sitting outside London to escape the plague which made the streets of the city a charnel house. The king's debts forced him to deal with Parliament, though he suspected their loyalty and hated their self-importance.

Once they were in place they were not obliging. They refused to settle the massive bills of the court and instead the simple country squires confronted him with a long list of complaints against the duke and demanded that he be brought before a committee to be examined for his faults.

'I can't settle to anything, not knowing what is happening,' John said to Elizabeth. He was working in their own garden at the little house at New Hall, planting peas in straight orderly rows. She saw that his fingers trembled slightly as he pressed each one into the earth. 'They say they want him impeached! They say they want him tried for treason!'

'Do you want to go to him?' she asked, keeping her voice colourless.

John shook his head. 'How can I? Without orders?'

'Won't he send for you?'

'If I can serve him, he will send for me. But there's no reason for him to think that I might serve him. He won't need a gardener at Oxford!'

'But he uses you for all sorts of work,' Elizabeth said. 'Dirty work,' she thought to herself. 'Private work,' she said out loud.

John nodded. 'If he sends for me I will go,' he repeated. 'But I may not go until he orders me.'

She thought his head drooped a little at the thought of the duke in trouble or danger, and not thinking to get help from Tradescant. 'I have to wait,' John said.

One of the duke's servants brought the news from Oxford to New Hall. The steward saw John in the stable yard and sent down a message for him to come into the house, to the central household office.

'I knew you would want to know that the duke will not face his accusers!' William Ward beamed. 'I knew you would have been worried.'

John snatched off his hat and threw it in the air like a boy. 'Thank God for it! Thank God!' he exclaimed. 'I have been sick with worry these ten days. I thank God that they have seen sense. They threw out the charges, did they? Dismissed them? Who can stand against him, eh? Mr Ward? Who could think wrong of him when they see him and hear him speak?'

Mr Ward shook his head. 'They did not dismiss the charges.'

'How so? They must have done! You said . . .'

'I said he would not face his accusers . . .'

'So?'

'They had him impeached on eight counts,' the steward said, his voice low and shocked. 'They charged him with everything from the ruination of the Navy, to stealing from the king. They even accused him . . . they said he was implicated . . . they called him to account for the murder of King James.'

John went pale. 'Murder?'

The steward nodded, his face as horrified as John's. 'They named it. They called it murder. And they named him as the regicide.'

'My God,' John said softly. 'What did he answer?'

'He gave no answer. The king had his accusers arrested and dissolved the parliament. He sent the members back to their homes. He will not hear them.'

For a moment John was relieved. 'The king stands his friend, then. And his enemies are the king's enemies.'

William Ward nodded. Then John saw the disadvantage. 'And since the accusers were imprisoned, are the accusations withdrawn?'

Slowly, the steward shook his head. 'No. That's the rub. His accusers are imprisoned without trial in the Tower, but they do not retract.'

'Who are they? The damned liars. Who?'

'Sir Dudley Digges and Sir John Eliot.'

Tradescant went white to his collar. 'But Sir John is my lord's closest friend,' he said quietly. 'They have been like brothers together since they were children.'

William Ward nodded.

'And I sailed to Russia with Sir Dudley, he's not a man for false accusations, he's a man of most careful honour! Why, I'd trust his judgement as I'd trust my own. We were shipmates on a long hazardous voyage and when he was sick I nursed him. I'd have gone with him overland to Moscow if I could have done. He's a fine man, a fair man. He'd not bear false witness against anyone. He would not do it.'

The steward looked bleakly at him. 'It is his word against the duke's.'

'I would have wagered my life on his honesty,' Tradescant said uncertainly.

The steward shook his head. 'It was those two who spoke against our lord, and are imprisoned for it. And now the king has them in the Tower and they're not to be released.'

'But what are the charges?'

'None. There are no charges – except that they spoke against the duke.'

John took a swift stride to the window and looked out at the terraces below: the golden terrace with the goldfish, the silver beneath, and the dappled trout ponds at the lowest level.

'They are men you could trust with anything,' he said softly. 'If it was any other cause I would be with them.'

The steward said nothing.

When Tradescant turned back his face was very grave. 'This is a bad business. No-one can call Sir Dudley a liar. But no-one can say that my duke did – all these things that they say he did.'

The steward looked at him closely. 'You were there. At the king's death. You must have seen.'

'I saw nothing,' John answered swiftly. 'I saw nothing but my lord watching and waking with his master. The prince was there, do they say he killed his own father? The Bishop of Lincoln was there. Do they say he did it too?'

'The Villiers mother was there,' William Ward remarked. 'And the doctors were dismissed.'

John looked at him, baffled. 'We have to trust him,' he said stoutly, but it sounded more like an appeal. 'He's our master. We are sworn to be his men. We have to trust him until we have absolute evidence that he has gone against the king or against the word of God itself. We can't give ourselves as his men and then take ourselves back again when his star is coming down. I am his man through good and bad times. I have eaten his bread.'

William Ward nodded. 'At least the duke is to come home for a few days. He writes me that he will stay and then go on to the New Forest for hunting with the king.'

Tradescant nodded. 'They're going hunting? But what about the parliament? The king only just called it.'

'Dissolved,' Mr Ward said shortly. 'It's only the king's second parliament and it's broken up with no agreement at all. No money voted, no policy decided. The king will rule with the duke alone, but without Parliament. But how is he to raise money to pay for anything? What will the country think of him?'

'What will they do?' Tradescant wondered. 'How will they manage? They are both such young men – and they have such enemies ranged against them abroad and . . .'

The steward shrugged slightly. 'It is a dangerous road that they tread,' he said. 'God save them both.'

That summer there was a meteor clearly seen for night after night, which burned very low and bright in the sky. You could see it most easily after sunset when the sky was still pearly before the stars shone out. It stood alone then, and its hair burned yellow with fire.

Everyone knew that it was a sign, and most thought it was a warning. The plague had not eased, the new French queen was proving barren, and besides there were whispers that she could not tolerate the king. There had been fierce quarrels and shouting behind closed doors. The duke had been everywhere in the marriage, intervening, advising, even reprimanding Her Majesty. Now, it was said, she could not bear the sight of him, and she was never admitted to see her husband without the duke present.

The meteor was visible from New Hall, and in the village of Chorley they thought it was a sign of sins seeking the sinner out. The golden trail behind the meteor was said to be a certain sign of poison, poison somewhere in the land. John Tradescant, who had a hatred of superstition, snapped at J, and said that the meteor was a star fallen out of its place and that it meant nothing – it meant nothing to men of any sense. But he never saw it without crossing his fingers in his pocket, and whispering to himself: 'God save the king! God save the duke!'

In July matters came to a head in the royal marriage. The king ordered the queen's French attendants out of his house and out of the country, and forcibly installed Buckingham's wife and sister in her household to take their place as the first ladies of the English court. John, watching the massive new fountains being installed at New Hall, found J by his side.

'Father, why can the king not live happily with his wife?' he asked him. 'In the kitchen they are saying that he attacked her and that she screamed from the window for her priests and her ladies, and that the duke, our duke, threatened her that she could be beheaded for treason.'

John took J firmly by the shoulder and marched him away from the workmen. 'That's tittle tattle,' he said sharply. 'Women's gossip. D'you want to be an old beldame at the fireside?'

'I just want to understand,' J said quickly. His father's face was dark with anger, he saw that he had gone too far.

'Understand what?'

J hesitated. 'I want to know why you follow the duke above all else,' he said in a sudden rush. 'Why you leave me, and leave Mother, and sometimes we don't see you for months. I want to know what hold he has over you. What hold he has over the king?'

John was thoughtful for a moment then he turned his son and walked beside him, his arm laid heavily on the young slim shoulders. 'I love him as a master,' he said. 'Set above me by God to guide me and command me. I am his vassal, d'you see? He asked me to be his man and I consented. That means that I am bound to him till death, or until he releases me. I didn't go down on my knees and swear vassalship as I would have done in the old days but the thing is still the same. I am his man and he is my lord. That's the bond between us.'

J nodded unwillingly.

'And I love him because of his beauty,' John said simply. 'Whether he's in white silk and showered with diamonds, or whether he's dressed in brown for hunting, he is as lithe as a willow and as lovely' – he looked around the garden – 'as one of my chestnut trees in blossom. He's a rare rare thing, J. I have never seen his equal. He is as lovely as a woman and as brave as a knight in a story. He moves like a dancer and he rides like a devil, and he makes me laugh when we are together, and he grieves me every day we are apart. He is my lord. There is none like him.'

'D'you love him more than us?' J asked, going to the heart of the question.

'I love him differently.' John avoided the truth. 'I love you and your mother as my own dear kin. I love my lord as I love the angels above him and my God above them.'

'Do you never wonder,' J asked spitefully from the depths of his hurt, 'do you never wonder that your love might be misplaced? That your lord, just below the angels, might be what they call him in the market place? A false friend, a thief, a spy, a Papist, a murderer . . . a sodomite?'

John whirled and smacked his son, a ringing blow which sent the youth sprawling, and then stood over him with his fists clenched, ready to hit him again should he come up fighting. 'How dare you!'

J struggled backwards, away from his furious father. 'I . . .'

'How dare you insult the man whose bread you eat? Who has put food on our table? How dare you repeat the dirt of the streets in his very garden? I should whip you for this, John. You are a graceless, dirty boy. Your learning was wasted on you if it has taught you wicked thoughts.'

J struggled to his feet and faced his father, his cheek blazing with John's handprint. 'I want to think for myself!' he cried out. 'I don't want a lord to follow, I don't want to have to shut my ears to the things that everyone is saying. I want to find my own way.'

'You will find your own way to hell,' John said bitterly. And he turned on his heel and left his son without another word.

Summer 1627

Buckingham, at New Hall for the summer, frightened back to Essex by the enmity of the parliament, found John in the fruit garden, tying back peach trees against the red brick wall. John turned when he heard the duke's quick step on the brick-chip path and Buckingham, seeing the leap of joy in Tradescant's face, put a hand on his shoulder. 'I wish I was a hero to all the world as I am to you, John,' he said.

'Is there trouble?'

Buckingham threw back his head and laughed his reckless gambler's laugh. John smiled in reply but felt a chill sense of unease. He had learned to be wary when his lord was in joyful mood. 'There is always trouble,' Buckingham said. 'I snap my fingers at it. And what of you, John? What are you doing here?'

'I am trying a little experiment, I don't know if it will work. It is a fancy of mine to see if I can give the peach trees a little extra heat, where they grow, here in the garden.'

'Will you set fire to their trunks?'

'I shall burn charcoal,' Tradescant said seriously. 'Here.' He showed the duke the high wall and three small fireplaces placed one above the other. 'The flues from the fireplaces run along the length of the wall and the hot smoke travels behind the bricks where the trees are tied. I am hoping it will keep the frost off them so that you can have early peaches and apricots. Weeks, perhaps even months, early. I think it must be something in the nature of the tree which makes it bear fruit; but then I am sure it is the heat of the sunshine which makes it ripen. The first year I scorched them and last year I was too cautious and the frost got them. But this year I think I may have done it right and you shall have sweet ripe fruit in June.'

'I shall be eating no English peaches in June this year, and nor will you,' the duke remarked.

Alerted, John turned away from his heated wall. 'Not this year?'

'Unless you wish to eat peaches while I go to war!'

'You, my lord!'

Buckingham threw back his head and laughed once more. John thought for a moment that he might have crowed like a cock on the farmyard wall. 'Listen to this, my John. We are to take on the French! Won't that be a game? While they trouble us in the Lowlands and threaten the fair Queen Elizabeth, driven off her rightful throne in Bohemia, we will sail around and attack their soft underbelly.'

'In the Mediterranean?'

'La Rochelle,' Buckingham said triumphantly. 'We will sail in to a hero's welcome from the Protestants. They have been besieged by their own countrymen, martyrs for their faith, for long enough. Our arrival will turn the tables. I doubt we will need to fire a shot! And what a snap of fingers in the face of Richelieu!'

'But only last year you sent a fleet to fight for Richelieu, you were his ally against them –'

'Policy! Policy!' Buckingham dismissed the idea. 'We should have supported our brothers in religion as soon as the siege was raised. The country was wild to go to war against the Catholics, I was wild for it. But with a French queen new-come to the English throne and the Spanish such a threat – what could I do? It's different now. It will be better now.'

'The people may have longer memories,' John warned. 'They may remember that you hired our Navy out to Richelieu and English guns were trained on the Protestants at La Rochelle.'

Buckingham shook his head and laughed. 'What is wrong with you today, Tradescant? Don't you want to come with me?'

'You are never sailing yourself?'

Buckingham smiled his heart-stopping smile. 'I? But of course! Who else is Lord High Admiral?'

'I didn't think . . .' John broke off. 'Are you not needed at home, by the king? And your enemies in the country, will they not mass against you if you are gone on an expedition for months at a time? The gossip is loud against you, I've heard even here that they are making accusations – my lord, surely you cannot risk being away?'

'How better to silence them than with a victory? When I come home with a victory against France, a triumph against the Papists, and a new English port on the west coast of France, don't you think my enemies will disappear in a moment? They will be my dearest friends again. Sir John and Sir Dudley will love me like brothers again, come rushing out of the Tower to kiss my hand. Don't you see? It will turn everything around for me.'

John put his hand on the richly slashed sleeve of his master's fine doublet. 'But, my lord, if you fail?'

Buckingham did not throw him off, as he could have done, did not laugh, as John half-expected. Instead he put his white fingers on John's hand, and held his touch closer. 'I must not fail,' he said softly. 'To tell you truth, John, I dare not fail.'

John looked into his master's dark eyes. 'Are you in so much jeopardy?'

'The worst. They will execute me for treason if they can.'

The two men stood still for a moment, hands clasped, their heads close.

'Come with me?' Buckingham asked.

'Of course,' John replied.

'You are going where?' Elizabeth demanded, icily furious.

'To France with the fleet,' John said, keeping his head low over his dinner. J, at the other end of the table, watched his parents in silence.

'You are nearly sixty.' Elizabeth's voice trembled with rage. 'It is time you stayed home. The duke pays you as his gardener and the keeper of his rarities. Why can he not leave you to garden?'

John shook his head and cut himself a slice of ham. 'This is sweet meat,' he remarked. 'One of our own?'

'Yes,' she snapped. 'Why does the duke want you?'

'He has asked me to go,' John said in his most reasonable tone. 'I can hardly ask him if he is sure, or what his reasons are. He has ordered me to go.'

'You are at an age when men sit by their fireside and tell their grandchildren of their travels,' she said. 'Not going as a common soldier off to war.'

He was stung. 'I'm not a common soldier. I travel as a gentleman in his train. As his companion and adviser.'

She slapped the table with her hand. 'What can you advise him? You are a gardener.'

He met her challenging eyes squarely. 'I may be a gardener but I have travelled farther and faced worse danger than any other in his train,' he said. 'I was at the battle of Algiers, and the long voyage to Russia. I have travelled all over Europe. He needs all the wise heads he can muster. He has asked for me and I will go.'

'You could refuse,' she challenged him. 'You could leave his service. There are many other places where you could work. We could go back to Canterbury, Lord Wootton would have you back. He says that no-one can grow melons like you. We could go back to Hatfield and work for the Cecils again.'

'I will not be forsworn. I will not leave his lordship.'

'You took no oath,' she pressed him. 'You think of yourself as his man and he treats you like a vassal right enough, but these are new times, John. The way you served Lord Cecil with such love and devotion is the old way. Other men work for Villiers for nothing more than their wages and they move on as it suits them. You could serve him like that. You could tell him that it does not suit you to go to war with him, and seek another place.'

He was genuinely shocked. '*I* tell him that it does not suit me to go to war when he is going? Tell him that it suits me to stay at home when he is fighting for my country in a foreign land? *I* to be a turncoat, having eaten his bread and lived in his house for five years? After he has paid me and trusted me, and employed my own son so he served his apprenticeship in one of the finest households in the land? *I* wait till now, till the worst moment of his life, to tell him that I was only here until it suited me to be elsewhere? This is not a matter of a wage, Elizabeth, it is a matter of faith. It is a matter of honour. It is a matter between my lord and me.'

J made a little impatient gesture, and then sat still. John did not even glance at him.

'Then serve him where you are placed,' Elizabeth said urgently. 'Cleave to your master and do the work he employs you to do. Keep his cabinet of rarities, keep his gardens.'

'I am placed at his side,' John said simply. 'Wherever he is, there I should be. Wherever that is.'

She swallowed her pride as it rose up, a wife's pride, a jealous pride, stung by the devotion in his voice. She kept her temper with an effort. 'I don't want you running into danger,' she said quietly. 'We have a good place here, I acknowledge our debt to the duke. You have a fine life here. Why d'you have to go away? And this time to make war against the French! You told me yourself what a court they have and what an army! What chance does the fleet have against them?' – 'Especially commanded by the duke', she thought but did not say it.

'He thinks that we will sail into a heroes' welcome and sail home again,' John said. 'The Protestants of La Rochelle have been under siege by the French government troops for months. When we relieve the siege we will free the Huguenots and slap Richelieu's face.'

'And why should you slap Richelieu's face?' she demanded. 'He was an ally only months ago.'

'Policy,' John answered, concealing his ignorance.

She drew a breath as if she would draw in patience again. 'And if it is not so easy? If the duke cannot slap Richelieu's face, just like that?'

'Then the duke will need me,' John said simply. 'If they have to build siege machines, or bridges, he will need me there.'

'You are a gardener!' she exclaimed.

'Yes!' he cried, goaded at last. 'But the rest of them are poets and musicians! The officers are young men from the court who have never ridden out for anything more arduous than a day's hunting, and the sergeants are drunkards and criminals. He needs at least one man in his train who can work with his hands and measure a length with his eye! Who in my lord's train will guard him? Who can he trust?'

She got up from her stool and snatched up the platters from the table. John saw her blink away angry tears and he softened at once. 'Lizzie . . .' he said gently.

'Are we never to be at peace together?' she demanded. 'You are a young man no longer, John, will you never stay home? We have our son, we have our home, you have your great garden and your rarities. Is this not enough for you that you have to go chasing off halfway round the world to fight the French, who were our allies and friends only last year?'

He got up and went over to her. His knees ached, and he was careful to walk steadily without a limp. He put his arm around her waist. He could feel the warmth and softness of her body beneath her grey gown. 'Forgive me,' he said. 'I have to go. Give me your blessing. You will never make me sail without your blessing.'

She turned her troubled face towards him. 'I can bless you and I can pray for the Lord to watch over you,' she said. 'But I fear that you are sailing with bad company into a senseless fight. You will be badly commanded, badly ruled, and poorly paid.'

Tradescant flinched back from her. 'This is not a blessing, this is ill-wishing!'

Elizabeth shook her head. 'It is the truth, John, and everyone in the country but you knows it. Everyone but you thinks that your duke is leading this country into war to spite Richelieu and to tease the King of France whom he cuckolded already. Everyone but you thinks he is showing off before the king. Everyone but you thinks he is a wicked and dangerous man.'

John was white. 'I see you have been listening to the preachers and the gossips again,' he said. 'This poison is not of your cooking!'

'The preachers speak nothing but the truth,' she said, confronting him at last. 'They say that a new world is coming where men can share in the wealth of the country and that every man should have his share. They say that the king will see reason and give the country to his people when his adviser is thrown down. And they say that if the king will not turn against Papist practices in his home, and ritual in his church, and poverty in his streets, then we should all go to make a new world of our own.'

'Virginia!' John mocked scathingly. 'That was an investment of mine in a promising business. It was not a dream of a new world.'

'There is certainly no dreaming in this old world,' she flashed back. 'Innocent men in the Tower, poor men taxed into paupers. Plague in the streets every summer, starvation in the country, and the richest king in the world riding around in silk with his Favourite riding beside him on a horse from Arabia.'

John put his hand under her chin and turned her face so that she was forced to meet his eyes. 'This is treason,' he said firmly. 'And I will not have it spoken in my house. I have struck J for less. Mark me well, Elizabeth, I will put you aside if you speak against my lord. I will turn you out if you speak against the king. I have given my heart and soul to the duke and the king. I am their man.'

For a moment she looked as if he had indeed struck her. 'Say that again,' she whispered.

He hesitated; he did not know if she was daring him to repeat it, or if she simply could not believe her ears. But either way he could not back down before a woman. The chain of command from God to man was clear, a wife's feelings could not disrupt the loyalty from man to lord to king to God. 'I will put you aside if you speak against my lord,' John said to his wife, as solemnly as he had spoken the marriage oath in church that long-ago day in Meopham. 'I will turn you out if you speak against the king. I have given my heart and soul to the duke and the king. I am their man.'

He turned on his heel and went out of the room. Elizabeth heard his heavy step going up the stairs to their bedroom and then the noise of the wooden chest opening as he took his travelling suit from where it was laid in lavender and rue. She put out her hand to the chimney breast to steady herself as her knees grew suddenly weak beneath her, and she sank down to the little three-legged stool at the fireside.

'I want to go with him,' J suddenly said from his seat at the table.

Elizabeth did not look around. She had forgotten her son was there. 'You're too young,' she said absently.

'I'm nearly nineteen, I am a man grown. I could keep him safe.'

She looked up at his bright hopeful face and his dark eyes, as dark as his father's. 'I cannot bear to let you go,' she said. 'You stay home with me. This voyage is going to break hearts enough in this household and in others all over the country. I can't risk you as well.' She saw the refusal in his face. 'Ah, John, don't waste your time reproaching me or trying to convince me,' she suddenly cried out bitterly. 'He won't take you. He won't allow you to go. He will want to be with the duke alone.'

'It is always the duke,' J said resentfully.

She turned her face from her son to look into the fire. 'I know,' she said. 'If I had been able to hide from that knowledge before, I would certainly know it now. Now that he has told me to my face and repeated it – that he is their man and not mine.'

Elizabeth did not come to see the fleet sail from Stokes Bay near Portsmouth. It was too far from Essex, and besides she did not want to see her husband walking up the narrow gangplank to his master's ship, the *Triumph*, supervising the loading of his master's goods. On this warlike expedition Buckingham was taking a full-sized harp with a harpist, a couple of milk cows, a dozen laying hens, a massive box of books for reading in his leisure hours, and an enormous coach with livery for his servants for his triumphant progress through La Rochelle.

Watching this fanciful equipment lumbering up the gangplank, John was rather relieved that Elizabeth was not with him. Six thousand foot soldiers slouched unwillingly aboard the fleet, a hundred cavalry. The king himself rode down to Portsmouth for a farewell dinner with his Lord High Admiral, and bade him farewell with a dozen kisses, wishing him God speed on his mission.

The mission itself remained uncertain. Firstly they were to harry French shipping as they sailed to La Rochelle, but, as it happened, though the July seas were calm and pleasant they saw no French shipping and could not complete their orders. Buckingham's court played cards for desperately high stakes and held a poetry competition as they sailed southwards. There was a good deal of hard drinking and laughter.

The next part of the orders bade them to go to La Rochelle for the grateful welcome of the besieged townspeople. Even this apparently simple command could not be fulfilled. When the fleet hove to before the town and spread the pennants so that the town could see that the great duke himself had come to relieve the siege, the townspeople were neither grateful nor particularly welcoming. They were deep in complicated and subtle negotiations with Richelieu's agents for their rights to practise their religion, and to live freely among other Frenchmen. The arrival of Buckingham's fleet threw their diplomatic agreements into jeopardy.

'So we can go home with honour,' John suggested. He was standing at the back of Buckingham's richly decorated cabin. Seated around the table were his advisers, French Protestant leaders among them.

'Never! We must show that we are serious,' Soubise the Frenchman said. 'We should take the Ile de Rhé at the harbour mouth and then they will see we are in earnest. It would give them the courage to declare against Richelieu, break off these negotiations and defy him.'

'But our orders were to wait for them to declare,' John said levelly. 'Not stir up trouble. The townspeople must invite our help. And if they do not declare against Richelieu, we were ordered to sail to Bordeaux and escort the English wine fleet home. We need not fight for La Rochelle, if the townspeople do not invite us.'

The Frenchman tried to catch Buckingham's eye. 'My lord duke did not come all this way to fetch a wine fleet home,' he laughed.

'Nor to find himself embroiled in a quarrel which no-one wants,' John said stoutly.

Buckingham lifted his head from admiring a large new diamond on his finger. 'Are you homesick, John?' he asked coldly.

Tradescant flushed. 'I am your man,' he said steadily. 'Nothing else. And I don't want to see you drawn into a battle for a small island opposite a small town on a small river in France.'

'This is La Rochelle!' Soubise exclaimed. 'Hardly a small town!'

'If they are not willing to fight for themselves,' John persisted doggedly, 'then why should we fight for them?'

'For glory?' Buckingham suggested, smiling across the room at John.

'You are glorious enough,' John smiled back, indicating the new diamond, and a shining stone in Buckingham's thick plumed hat on the table before him.

The Frenchman swore softly underneath his breath. 'Are we to go home as if we were defeated then?' he demanded. 'Without firing a shot? That will please the king, that will silence Parliament! They will say that we were suborned, that we are the queen's men, Papist men! They will say that this mission was a masque, a piece of theatre. They will say we were players, not soldiers.'

Buckingham rose from his seat and stretched, his dark curls brushing the gilded roof of his cabin. 'Not them,' he said softly. John watched warily. He knew the signs.

'They will mock us in the streets,' Soubise lamented.

'Not them,' Buckingham repeated.

'They will say it was a gesture to seduce the Queen of France,' Soubise said, going as far as he dared. 'That you were throwing down a glove to her husband and that you did not fulfil your challenge.'

For a moment John thought that the man had gone too far. Buckingham stiffened at the mention of the queen's name. But then his smile returned. 'Not them,' he said. 'And I will tell you why they will not mock. Because we *will* lay siege to the island, we *will* take the island, then we *will* take La Rochelle, and we will go home as conquering heroes.'

The Frenchman gasped and then beamed as the cabin of men burst into applause. Buckingham gleamed at the praise. 'Set to!' he shouted above the laughter and applause. 'We will land tomorrow!'

It was a shambles but it did the job. Inexperienced sailors, pressganged from ale houses up and down the south coast of England, fought to keep the landing boats steady in the currents that swirled around the boggy and uninviting beaches. Inexperienced soldiers pressganged from the poor houses and ale houses of England, Ireland, Wales and Scotland cringed from the waves and from the

French soldiers, forewarned and splendidly armed, drawn up to greet them. All would have been lost but for the duke, conspicuous beneath his standard, dressed in glorious gold and crimson, who rowed up and down between the boats and urged the men on shore. Reckless of danger, laughing when the cannon from his ships roared over his head, he was a leader from a fable. He was indeed a champion fit to bed the most beautiful queen in Europe. When they saw him, still sporting his diamonds, with his golden sword on his hip, their spirits lifted. It was impossible that such a man, such a glamorous golden laughing man, could ever be defeated.

His clear voice could be heard above the noise of the waves, the thunderous bellow of the cannon and the yells of ill-trained officers. 'Come on!' he shouted. 'Come on! For God and the king! For the king! For me! And let's bugger the Catholics!'

They landed in a roar at his bawdiness, and the French, faced by an enemy suddenly renewed, powerful, and even laughing, turned and fled. By the afternoon Buckingham stood on the beach of Rhé, his sword wet only with seawater; and knew himself to be triumphant.

John went inland with the scouts and saw the French cavalry driven back and back over brackish fields of rough grass where a hundred, a thousand, red poppies blew. 'Like soldiers in red coats,' John said. He shivered as if it were an omen and bent to pluck a couple of the drying seed heads.

'Still gardening, Mr Tradescant?' one of the scouts asked.

'They are a fine colour,' he said. 'A plentiful show.'

'Red as blood,' the scout said.

'Yes.'

The English luck held. Within days Buckingham held the whole of the little island of Rhé and the French army was holed up in one tiny half-finished castle on the landward side: St Martin. John was sent to spy out the lie of the land.

'Tell me what their fort is like, John. Give me an idea of the size and how strong it is,' Buckingham commanded, as he strolled down the lines and came across Tradescant, digging a little nursery bed for any rare plants he might find during his stay. 'Leave gardening, man, and tell me how their fort is placed.'

John put his trowel to one side at once, and slipped his satchel on his back, ready to set out.

'I'm no engineer,' he warned Buckingham.

'I know that,' his lord replied. 'But you're careful and you have a good eye, and you have been in a siege and under fire, which is more than can be said for any one of us. Go and have a look and when you come back, come to me privately and tell me what you think. I can't trust a word these Frenchmen speak. All they want is victory at whatever price, and that price would include me and they would still pay it gladly.'

John nodded. He did not ask what, in that case, they were doing there, camped on a French beach on a small island off France. It was not his nature to complain of the obvious. He took up his blackthorn stick and set off, along the beach towards the other side of the island. Buckingham watched him go and noted the limp which favoured John's aching arthritic knee.

He was back late in the evening, with a brace of cuttings and a rough sketch.

'Good God, what have you in your hat?' Buckingham demanded. He was seated before his tent, at a table of exquisite marquetry, looking young and careless with his white linen shirt undone at the throat, and his hair tumbling in black curls about his shoulders.

John carefully took one of the plants by the leaf and held it up. 'It's a new sort of gillyflower,' he said. 'I've never seen such leaves before.' He held out the plant. 'Do the leaves have a scent?'

Buckingham sniffed. 'Nothing I can smell, John. And – forgive me – but you were sent out as a scout to bring us news of the French fortification, not to go plant-gathering.'

'I sat among the plants while I drew a sketch of the fort,' John said, with simple dignity. 'A man can do two things at once.'

Buckingham grinned at him. 'A man such as you can do a dozen,' he said sweetly. 'Show me your plan, John.'

John unfolded the paper and spread it on the little table before his master. 'The fort is built like a star,' he said. 'And only half-finished on one side. Our trouble will be that the north side, on the strand, is facing La Rochelle over the sea and can be easily relieved by the French troops who are camped around the besieged city on the mainland. We hold the island, right enough, they will get no help from here. And the town of La Rochelle is holding out against the Papist French army. But there are sally ports all along the base of the St Martin's fort wall and they have boats moored ready. We will have to cut them off from the mainland before they can be reduced.'

Buckingham looked at John's sketch. 'What about a direct attack? Never mind starving them. An attack against the walls?'

John's mouth turned down. 'I don't advise it,' he said briefly. 'The walls are new-built and high. The windows look very deep. You can't hammer your way in, and you will lose half your men trying to scale it.'

'They have to be starved out?'

John nodded.

'So if we put our army all around them on the landward side, can you build me a barrier to span the seaward side to prevent them getting ships in and out?'

John thought for a moment. 'I can try, my lord,' he said. 'But these are high seas. It's not like building a raft across the Isis, it's like building a raft across Portsmouth harbour. The waves come very high, and if there is a storm, anything we built would be smashed.'

'Surely if we have enough wood, and chains . . .'

'If the summer weather remains calm it might hold,' John said doubtfully. 'But one night of high winds would smash it.'

Buckingham got up swiftly and strode forward, looking down on the fort. 'I tell you, John, I cannot stay here seated before a little fort, looking at it forever,' he said, his voice so low that no-one but Tradescant could hear him. 'I am laying siege to them, and they are trapped inside the fort, right enough; but all I have to feed my men is what I brought in my ships. I need support as much as the fort. Their army and their suppliers are over a small channel of water, while my army and suppliers are many miles away. And their king is commanded by Richelieu, while my king . . .' He broke off, and then saw John's uneasy face.

'He will not forget me,' he said firmly. 'Even now he will be preparing a fleet to come after us and revictual and supply us. But you see that I am in a hurry. I cannot wait. The French in the citadel of St Martin must starve and surrender at once. Otherwise we will beat them to it. We will starve and surrender even though we are supposed to be laying siege to them.'

'I'll plan something,' John promised.

There were no tents for the men nor for the poorer officers; no-one in England had thought that the expedition would need tents. John laid his soldier's pack on the ground beside the other men, heeled in his new gillyflower in his little nursery bed, and then set about planning his blockade of St Martin.

Within an hour or two he had his drawing of ships' timbers and a couple of spare masts chained together. The senior shipwright and John supervised the throwing of the wood in the water and watched the sailors leaning out from little boats and struggling to chain them together.

'Those were our spare masts and timbers to repair the ships,' the shipwright observed dourly. 'Better pray we don't lose a mast on the way home.'

'We can't go home until the citadel falls,' John reasoned. 'First things first.'

'And have you heard when they will come to relieve us?' the shipwright asked. 'The lads were saying that a great fleet is coming behind us, now that the king knows that the duke has been successful, now they know that we are at war.'

'It will come soon,' John said, with more confidence than he felt. 'My lord told me that the king had promised it.'

John was right about the fragility of the timber barrier. The high wind blowing over their camp in the next week warned him of the storm that was coming. He crawled out of his makeshift shelter and looked out to sea. In the darkness he could see nothing. Then he felt a hand on his shoulder. It was Buckingham, sleepless too.

'Will your blockade hold?'

'Not if this wind keeps up,' Tradescant replied. 'I am sorry, my lord.'

He could feel the warmth of Buckingham's breath as he leaned forward to be heard above the storm.

'Don't ask for pardon, John,' he said. 'You warned me of the danger and I told you of the need. But at first light tomorrow get out there and build me another barrier. I must have St Martin cut off.'

John's next attempt was to use the landing-craft ships, lashed together prow to stern across the channel before the St Martin citadel. Two small camps of soldiers were set up at either side, to guard the barrier and to take the occasional pot shot at those citizens of St Martin who were bold enough to peep over the half-finished walls. The building work on the fort had almost ceased, although the need to finish the citadel had never been greater.

'They're weary and hungry,' Buckingham said with satisfaction. 'We will outlast them.'

Within a week of the new barrier being in place there were more high winds, and the stormy waters, pushing the landing craft in opposite directions, broke through. Some of the officers were openly contemptuous of Tradescant at the council of war.

'I am sorry,' John said dourly. 'But you are asking me to build a barrier in what is almost open sea. I can rebuild it. I shall bring the ships closer in to shore and run hawsers one from another. The men on board ship can keep watch, and if a hawser breaks we can replace it. But the weather is getting worse, I can think of nothing which will withstand the autumn storms.'

Buckingham's face was grave. 'The king's fleet will arrive this month,' he said. 'It will come without fail. His Majesty loves me and I have his solemn promise of a fleet in September. I have asked him to send more hawsers and timber as well as munitions, money and food. And three thousand more fighting men. As soon as it arrives we will take the castle and move on to La Rochelle itself. Once we're on the mainland all our troubles will be over.'

There was a brief dispirited silence. Only John dared voice what they were all thinking. 'If he is delayed . . .' he began cautiously. 'If the king cannot raise the money for the fleet . . .'

Buckingham's sharp gaze warned John to be silent; but he doggedly continued.

'I beg your pardon, my lord, but if His Majesty is delayed in sending succour then we will have to withdraw for this year,' he said stoutly.

'You are afraid,' one of the Frenchmen declared. He whispered something behind his hand about gardens and easy lives.

'I know that we are running short of food and munitions,' John said steadily. 'And the men are on half-pay. If there was anywhere for them to go they would have deserted already. We cannot make them fight if they are hungry. They cannot shoot their muskets if they have no powder.' He looked at Buckingham, past the gentlemen who were openly laughing at him. 'Forgive me, my lord. But I am much with the common soldiers and I know what they are thinking, and I know that they are going hungry.'

Buckingham glanced at his table where a flagon of red wine gleamed beside a plate of biscuits. 'Are we short of food?' he asked, surprised.

'We're not starving; but rations have been cut,' John replied. 'The Protestants are sending us all they can from La Rochelle – but it is not justice for us to eat their supplies. We came here to relieve *them*, not to devour their stores. And they themselves are surrounded by the Papist French troops, they cannot go on supplying us forever.'

'I will speak with the French commander,' Buckingham said thoughtfully. 'He is a gentleman. Perhaps we can make some sort of terms.'

'We should starve them to death and drive them into the sea,' Soubise said hastily. 'We have raised the siege, we should smash them into nothing!'

'Next year,' Tradescant said hastily. 'When we come back with another fleet.'

A package of letters for the English troops had got safely through. The king had written, Buckingham's wife Kate had written, and his mother, the cunning old countess. None of them had sent money to buy food or pay the troops, and there was no news of the fleet being equipped and setting sail. The duke kept the bad news to himself but no-one seeing the way he thrust the letter from the king inside his embroidered waistcoat could doubt that Charles had sent fond words but no news of an English fleet ploughing its way through stormy seas from Portsmouth to relieve his beloved friend.

The letter from the old countess was even more ominous. She urged her son to come home and reclaim his place at court. No man could risk being too far from one of the Stuarts, they had notoriously short memories. Buckingham himself had replaced Rochester, the previous Favourite, in the affections of King James, and now King Charles was coming under the sway of new advisers. William Laud, a new bishop, a common red-faced little man, was advising him at every turn. Buckingham must hurry home before he was forgotten.

Charles wrote to his dearest friend that he had no money but that he was raising funds by every means possible. He wrote that he was thinking of nothing but ways to get money to send a fleet. The old countess wrote to Buckingham in their private code that Charles had just bought the Duke of Mantua's entire collection of pictures for fifteen thousand pounds – enough to equip and send two fleets. He had been unable to resist them at such a bargain price, and now he was penniless again. The money for the fleet had been squandered twice over – Buckingham need not hope for support.

Buckingham tore up her letter and scattered the tiny pieces over the stern of the *Triumph*. 'Oh, Charles,' he sighed. 'How can you love me as you do and yet betray me like this?'

The pieces blew in an eddy of wind, like flecks of snow. Superstitiously, Buckingham looked up at the September sky. There were thick clouds on the horizon, the fair weather was due to break. 'He is a sweet man,' he said to himself. 'The sweetest man that ever lived, but the most faithless friend and king that could ever be.'

He wrapped his cape around him a little closer. He knew that any time his name was mentioned at court, Charles would think of him with love. He knew that he would return to an open-hearted welcome. But he knew also that a collection of pictures like the Duke of Mantua's would be irresistible to a man who from boyhood had been able to have what he wanted at the instant he had wanted it. Charles would think that Buckingham, that the English fleet, that the full-scale war with France could wait while he amassed yet more money from the hard-pressed taxpayers of England. He would never understand that it was he who had to do without. He had no practice in self-denial. For all his sympathy and charm and sweetness, there was a core of pure selfishness in Charles that nothing could penetrate.

'I will have to win and return home or I will be left here to die,' Buckingham said. The last pieces of his mother's letter blew, sank into water, and then slipped away. Buckingham watched them go down into the heaving greenness, and realised that he was facing his own defeat and death, and that he had never thought before that his life and his charmed career could end in despair.

He looked up at the horizon at the dark layers of cloud. The wind was blowing the rain towards the *Triumph* and towards the string of English ships moored as a thin barrier between St Martin and the sea of La Rochelle.

'I will win and return home,' Buckingham vowed. 'I was not born and raised so high to die in a cold sea off France. I was born for great things, for greater than this. I will see St Martin razed to the ground and *then* I will go home and I shall have that fifteen thousand pounds poured into my hands for my pains; and I will forget I was ever here, in fear and in want.'

He turned back to the waist of the ship and saw John Tradescant, standing a yard away, watching him.

'Confound you, John! You startled me. What the Devil are you doing?'

'Just watching you, my lord.'

Buckingham laughed. 'Did you fear an assassin's knife on my own ship?'

John shook his head. 'I feared disappointment and despair,' he said. 'And sometimes a companion can guard you against them too.'

Buckingham slid his hand around John's shoulders and pressed his face against the older man's thick-muscled neck. John smelled comfortingly of home, of homespun cloth, clean linen, and earth. 'Yes,' Buckingham said shortly. 'Stay by me, John.'

Autumn 1627

That very afternoon a messenger came from the fort. Commander Torres was suing for peace, and for terms of surrender. Buckingham did not let the messenger, an officer, see his smile, but took the news as if it were a matter of indifference. 'I daresay you are weary,' he said politely, as one gentleman to another. He turned to his servant. 'Bring him some wine and bread.'

The man was not just weary but half-starved. He fell on the bread and devoured it in hungry bites. Buckingham watched him. The messenger's condition told him all he needed to know of the state of the soldiers within the fort.

Buckingham unfolded the letter the man brought and read it again, carefully, sniffing at the silver pomander he wore around his neck.

'Very well,' he said casually.

One of his officers raised his eyebrows. Buckingham smiled. 'Commander Torres asks for terms of surrender,' he observed negligently, as if it did not much matter.

Taking his cue, the English officer nodded. 'Indeed.'

'I was told to take a reply,' the messenger said. 'The fort is yours, my lord.'

Buckingham savoured the moment. 'I thank you. *Merci beaucoup.*'

'I'll call for a clerk,' the English officer said. 'I take it that we can dictate the terms?'

The messenger bowed.

Buckingham lifted his hand, the diamond winked. 'No hurry,' he said.

'I was told to take a reply,' the messenger said. 'The commander proposes the terms in the letter, our full surrender without condition. He said I could carry a verbal reply from you – yea or nay – and the business could be finished tonight.'

Buckingham smiled. 'I will write to your commander tomorrow, when I have considered what terms are agreeable to me.'

'Can we not agree now, my lord?'

Buckingham shook his head. 'I am going to my dinner now,' he said provokingly. 'I have a very good cook and he has a new way of doing beef in a thick red gravy. I shall think of you and Commander Torres while I dine, and I shall write tomorrow, after I have broken my fast.'

At the mention of meat the man gulped. 'I was ordered to take a reply, sir,' he said miserably.

Buckingham smiled. 'Tell Commander Torres I am going to my dinner and that he shall dine with me tomorrow. I will send him an invitation to a grand dinner, along with his terms of surrender.'

The messenger would have argued but the French Protestant officers pushed him gently from the room. They heard his hesitant tread down the gangplank, and then one of the sentries giving him safe conduct back to the besieged fort.

'We'll let them sweat,' Buckingham said cruelly. 'They wanted to keep their weapons and safe conduct back to La Rochelle. They even wanted their cannon out of the fort. It was hardly a surrender at all. I want their weapons and their standards and then they can go. I have to have something to take home with me after all our trouble here. I want their cannon on my ships and their standards to show to the court. I need to lay the standards before the king. We need to have some gaudy props for the last act of this masque.'

At dinner the officers drank deeply. John had a couple of glasses of the Rochelle wine but then he went out on deck. The ship was moving uneasily on its moorings as the wind freshened. The darkening sky was thick with clouds and the horizon where the sun had set was rimmed with a yellow line, like a fungus on a felled tree trunk. John wondered how the rest of the fleet, strung out across the bay, were faring in the wind.

He called to a sailor to bring him a boat.

The man reluctantly brought a little skiff to the foot of the ladder and John went down the side of the *Triumph*. The waves rose and fell under the keel of the little boat. John could see them, coming across the bay, frighteningly high from his low viewpoint in the water. The great swell of the Atlantic Ocean pushed them onward like an enemy to the little boats holding tightly to each other in a circle around the beleaguered fort.

'Take me round the point,' he said, raising his voice above the wind. 'I want to see the barricade.'

The sailor leaned heavily on the oars and the skiff bobbed and fell as the big waves passed underneath. They rounded the point and John saw his barrier.

At first he thought it was holding. Squinting his eyes against the darkness he thought that the ships were still moored, nose to tail, and the unevenness of their rocking was the big waves passing through them, each one lifting and falling at a different moment. Then he saw that one had broken free.

'Damnation!' John yelled. 'Get me on a ship! I have to raise the alarm.'

The sailor headed for one of the moored ships and John scrambled up the ladder. His bad knee failed him and he had to grab like a monkey with his arms and haul himself up the side. At the top he turned and shouted down. 'Get you back to the *Triumph*. Tell the admiral that the barrier is breached. Tell him I'm doing what I can.'

The man nodded his agreement and set himself to row back to Buckingham's ship while John flung himself on the bell and sounded the alarm. The sailors scrambled out of the waist of the ship, clutching their dinner – nothing more than a thin slice of rye bread and a thinner slice of French bacon.

'Get me a light,' John cried. 'I need to signal to the ships to take that loose vessel up. The barrier is breached.'

'I thought they had surrendered!' the captain shouted as one of the men ran for a lantern.

'They sent terms,' John said. 'His lordship is considering them.'

The captain turned and roared for a light and ordered the gunners to their posts. The signalling officer came running up with flaring torches. 'Tell them to take up that ship,' John said.

The man ran forward and started signalling. John, looking past him, suddenly saw a gleam in the dark water, a reflection.

'What's that?'

'Where?'

'In the water, beside that ship.'

One of the officers stared where John was pointing. 'I can't see anything,' he said.

'Hold a torch out!' John ordered.

They held a torch low over the water and saw the dark shadow of a French barge, rowed swiftly towards the gap in the barrier.

'To your places!' the captain yelled. John raced to the bell and rang it again. The gun crew opened the hatches and ran back the cannon for priming and loading; the soldiers poured out on deck. Someone lit and threw a flare towards the dark water below and in its briefly tumbling light John saw a string of barges rowing steadily and confidently from the Papist camp around La Rochelle towards the fort of St Martin.

From the other end of the barrier of English ships he heard the bells ringing for action stations. A single cannon started pounding in the darkness and then he felt the timbers under his feet shake at the explosion and recoil of the guns on his own ship. The loose ship which should have been lashed into the barrier was swinging wildly out of control, the crew swarming to get sails up, and to get her under way so that she could rejoin the line. But through the gap she had left the barges were pouring, heading straight for the citadel.

'A fire ship!' John gasped as he saw them launch the blazing raft towards the French barges from the English ships on the other side of the bay. One man stood at the back of the raft, courageously steering it straight towards the supply barges, the wind setting the flames in the bow leaping and crackling, reflected in the water until it looked as if the fires from hell were burning up from under the sea. The sailor stayed at his post until the last moment, until the heat beat him into the water, and the flames licked towards the kegs of powder. He dived off the back of the raft just as the charges on the fire ship exploded like celebration fire crackers. His head went deep under the water and for a moment John thought that the man was lost, then he came up, wet-headed like a seal, and swam to the nearest ship, clung to a rope and was hauled in.

The wind swung around; the unmanned fire ship, yawing wildly, blew before it, drifted away from the French barges and helpfully lit their way across the heaving glassy seas to the shore and the fort.

'Damnation!' Tradescant swore. 'It's going to miss them.'

Perilously the fire ship swung in a current and headed for the English line. The sailors scrambled to the side of the ship with buckets of water to try to douse the flames and poles to fend it off. By its brilliant flaring light the English gunners on the other ships could at last see their targets. The English guns pounded into life and John saw the French barges struck and men thrown into the water.

'Reload!' the gunners' officer yelled from below. The deck of the ship heaved and thudded under John's feet as the big guns fired and rolled back. Another direct hit, and another French vessel smashed amidships, men screaming as they were thrown into the rolling dark sea.

Squinting through the smoke, John could see that some of the barges were getting out of range, heading towards the citadel.

'Aim long!' he shouted. 'Aim for the furthest barges!'

No-one could hear him above the noise. Impotently, John saw the leading French barge run ashore below the castle on the tideline, the citadel's sally port gates flung open in welcome, and a line of defenders rapidly form to unload the barges and throw sacks of food and supplies of weapons into the fort. John counted perhaps a dozen barges safely unloaded before the light from the fire ship died and the English gunners could no longer see their target, and the battle was lost.

The citadel was reinforced and revictualled and there would be no visit from Commander Torres to dine with the duke and accept his terms of surrender tomorrow.

John did not attend the council of war. He was in disgrace. His barrier had failed and the fort, so near to surrender, was eating better than the besieging English soldiers. While Buckingham took advice from his officers John walked away from the fort, away from the fleet, deep into the island, watching his feet for rare plants, his face knitted up in a scowl. The same pressures would still be working on the duke as before, but the situation was worse than ever. The fort was revictualled, the weather was deteriorating, and on one of the ships there were two cases of gaol fever. The cold weather would bring sickness and agues, and the men were underfed. They had the choice of sleeping in the open under pitiful shelters of bent twigs and stretched cloth and risking ague and rheums, or inside the ships packed like herrings in a barrel, risking fevers from the close quarters.

John knew that they must withdraw before the winter storms; and feared that they were mad enough to stay. He turned in his walk and went back towards the fort. One of the French sentries on the castle walls saw him and shouted a cheerful yell of abuse. John hesitated, then the message became clear. The sentry hauled up a pike with a huge joint of meat on the tip, to demonstrate their new wealth.

'*Voulez-vous, Anglais?*' he yelled cheerfully. '*Avez vous faim?*'

John turned and trudged back to the ill-named *Triumph*.

Buckingham was certain what they should do. 'We must attack,' he said simply.

John gasped in horror and looked around the duke's cabin. No-one else seemed in the least perturbed. They were nodding as if this were the obvious course.

'But my lord . . .' John started.

Buckingham looked across at him.

'They are better fed than us, they have almost limitless cannon and powder, they are mending the defences and we know that the citadel is strong.'

Buckingham no longer laughed at John's fears. 'I know all that,' he said bitterly. 'Tell me something that I have not thought of, John, or keep your peace.'

'Have you thought of going home?' John asked.

'Yes,' Buckingham said precisely. 'And if I go now, with nothing to show for it, I can't even be sure that I will have a home to go to.' He glanced around the cabin. 'There are men still waiting to impeach me for treason,' he said bluntly. 'If I have to die I'd rather do it here leading an attack than on the block outside the Tower.'

John fell silent. It was a measure of the duke's desperation that he spoke so frankly before them all.

'And if I return home in disgrace and am executed then the prospects for all of you are not golden,' Buckingham pointed out. 'I would not be in your shoes when you are asked what service you gave the king on the Ile de Rhé. I shall be dead, of course, so it will not trouble me. But you will all be hopelessly compromised.'

There was a little uncomfortable movement among the men in the cabin.

'So are we all decided?' Buckingham asked with a wolfish grin. 'Is it to be an attack?'

'Torres cannot stand against us!' Soubise exclaimed. 'He was ready to surrender once, we know the measure of the man now. He's a coward. He won't fight to the last, if we frighten him enough he will surrender again.'

Buckingham nodded to John as if there were no-one else to convince. 'That's true enough,' he said. 'We *do* know that he will surrender if he thinks a battle is lost. All we have to do is to convince him that the battle is lost.'

He leaned forward and spread out some papers on the table. John saw that they were his sketch plans, drawn when they were new to the island and his new gillyflower was heeled into his little nursery bed. Now it was rooted and putting out new shoots, and the sketches were dirty in the margin from much use.

'We bring the ships as close as we can and pound the fort from the sea, then fall back,' Buckingham said. 'First one side then another, so as soon as they get our range we drop back. Then on the landward side of the fort we launch an attack. Scaling ladders to get the men to the tops of the walls. They must carry and throw down ropes. As the ships fall back from their attack they land the sailors and they support the soldiers in the attack on the walls. As soon as the soldiers are inside they open the sally ports and the rest of the sailors come off the ships and into the gate.'

'Perfect!' Soubise exclaimed.

John was looking critically at the map. 'How will the ships come forward and fall back?' he demanded. 'What if the wind is in the wrong quarter?'

Buckingham thought for a moment. 'Can we use the landing craft as barges?' he asked. 'Take the ships in tow to help them around?'

A gentleman nodded. 'The wind is bound to be right for either coming in or going out.'

Buckingham looked to John. 'What d'you think, Tradescant?'

'It might work,' John said cautiously. 'But we could only tow one or two ships in and out at a time. We couldn't do the big attack you described.'

'One or two would do it,' Buckingham said. 'It's to keep their attention to the seaward side while we attack on land.'

'We should do it on the turn of the tide,' John proposed. 'So the tide pulls the ships out of range, helps the barges to do their work.'

Buckingham nodded. 'Give the orders, John. You will know how it should be done.'

'I shall make them practise first.'

'Very well. But do it out of sight of the fort, and have them ready for dawn tomorrow, as near to dawn as the tides permit.'

John bowed and went to leave the cabin. He hesitated at the door. 'And the attack on the castle?' he asked.

'A textbook attack!' one of the officers enthused. 'While they are looking out to sea we attack on land. Speed, stealth. May I have the command, sir?'

Buckingham smiled at his enthusiasm. 'You may.'

'What about the ladders?' John asked. 'And the ropes?'

The officer turned on him impatiently. 'You may leave all that to me!'

'I beg your pardon,' John said politely. 'But that's only a rough sketch I did. Someone needs to check the angle of the walls, any overhangs, the best places for the ladders. The ground beneath the walls.'

The officer laughed. 'I had no idea you were a soldier of experience, Mr Tradescant!' He emphasised the 'Mr' to remind John that he was among gentlemen on sufferance, he had no right to the title. Buckingham, leaning back in his chair, sniffed his pomander and watched John control his temper.

'I am a gardener, and a collector of my lord duke's rarities,' John said tightly. 'I've never pretended to be anything else. But I have seen action.'

'Once,' someone said softly at the back. 'And hardly glorious.'

John did not look around. 'It is in my line of work to look at the little things, to see that they are not forgotten. All I am saying is that the height and the dimensions of the walls have to be known exactly.'

'Thank you,' the officer said with icy courtesy. 'I am grateful for your advice.'

John glanced at his duke. Buckingham gave a small jerk of his head to the door and John bowed and withdrew.

It was a small slight after three months of slights but it was the one conversation that John was to hear in his head, in his dreams, over and over again.

They could not make the attack when the duke wished, the tides were wrong and the moon was too bright. But two days after his final orders they launched the attack on the castle. John was on shore, watching the ships manoeuvre before the fort as he had planned they should do. The scheme worked well. The French defenders took time to get their aim on each attacking ship, and as they got it in range, the ships dropped sail and the rowing barges and the ebbing tide pulled her out of range again. John watched for only a few minutes, to see that the ships were safe, and then turned to run to the landward side of the fort where the army was going in to attack.

The citadel was not taken unawares. They were fully armed and ready on the landward side, and they poured musket fire down the high walls on to the attacking English army. John pushed his way through the crowds of soldiers, sometimes surging forward, and then hanging back, until he was near his duke. Buckingham was at the very centre of the line, dragging the men forward with him towards the musket fire.

Before him were the soldiers running with the scaling ladders. Buckingham was pushing them on, towards the deadly fire, towards the walls of the castle.

'Go on! Go on!' he was shouting. 'For England! For God! For me!'

The men had suffered after three months on the island. Buckingham could not make them laugh any more. They hesitated and went reluctantly forward. At every point in the line the officers were shouting and demanding that they advance. Only the musket fire – as dangerous for those who hung back as for those who ran forward – kept them moving.

'For the love of God get those ladders up!' Buckingham shouted. All down the line of the castle wall there were soldiers setting the feet of the scaling ladders into the rocks at the foot of the wall.

'Up! Up!' shouted Buckingham 'Now! And get those damned gates open!'

Tradescant was flung back by a man falling against him as he took a musket ball. He turned to hold him; but at once a man on the other side went down too.

'Help me!' the man called.

'I'll come back!' John promised. 'I have to . . .'

He broke off, abandoning both men, and plunged forward, trying to keep close to the duke. Buckingham was at the foot of a scaling ladder, urging men up it. For one dreadful moment Tradescant thought that his lord was going to climb the ladder himself.

'Villiers!' he shouted above the screams and the firing, and saw Buckingham turn his bare head to look for him.

John pushed his way through the crowd at the foot of the scaling ladder to get to his master's side, and cling with all his weight on to his arm to prevent him going upward. Only then did he realise that something was wrong. Tradescant and Buckingham looked upwards together. The men were climbing the ladder, head to heels all the way up, the new soldiers at the foot of the ladder pushing up and forcing the ones at the top onwards and upwards. But then they seemed to stick. No-one was moving, the attack had paused. John stepped back a pace and looked up. The scaling ladders were too short. The men could not reach the top of the walls.

The picture of the ladders, crowded by men with nowhere to go, and their faces turned upwards to where the musket balls were raining down on them, burned into Tradescant's vision.

'Retreat!' he yelled. 'My lord! The day is lost! The ladders are too short. We have to go back!'

In the noise and the panic Buckingham did not hear him, did not understand him.

'We're lost!' Tradescant repeated. He fought his way back to Buckingham's side. 'Look up!' he shouted. 'Look up!'

Buckingham stepped out from the foot of the ladder and craned his neck to look upwards. His face, bright with excitement and courage, suddenly drained of blood and lightness. John thought that his master aged ten years in that one upward glance.

'Retreat,' he said shortly. He turned to his standard bearer. 'Sound the retreat,' he ordered. 'Sound it loud,' and he turned on his heel.

John ploughed back, still flinching from the musket fire rattling from the citadel walls, to where the man had fallen. He was dead, there was nothing John could do for him except say a swift prayer as he ran, stumbling, like a coward, out of the range of the musket fire, and away from St Martin's citadel – the fort where the walls were never measured and the scaling ladders were too short.

'I will fight him myself,' Buckingham said at the council of war the next day. 'I shall send a challenge.'

John, weary and bruised, leaned against the doorway of the cabin and saw that his master was in despair, and making the grand gestures of a man in despair.

'He must accept!' Soubise exclaimed. 'No gentleman could refuse.'

Buckingham glanced across at John and saw the weary pity in his servant's face.

'Do you think he will accept, John?' he asked.

'Why should he?'

'Because he is a gentleman! A French gentleman!' Soubise exclaimed. 'It is a matter of honour!'

John's shoulders slumped, he moved to take the weight off his aching knee. 'Whatever you say,' he said. 'It can't do any harm. You would beat him with a sword, would you not, my lord?'

Buckingham nodded. 'Oh, yes.'

John shrugged.

'The scaling ladders were absurdly short,' the officer burst out. 'The wrong size had been loaded. They should have been checked as they were loaded. It was madness to think that they would be any use. You could not reach a thatched cottage roof with ladders that short. You would pick apples with ladders that short!'

There was an awkward silence.

'Send a challenge,' Buckingham said to one of the officers. 'He might be fool enough to take it.'

As John had predicted, Commander Torres did not take up the challenge, but the following week the French tried to break out of their siege and capture the English camp. The alarm sounded in the night and the men stood to and fought like savages, pushing the French forces back to the citadel again. It was, in theory, a victory for the English besieging army, but there was little joy at dawn when they did a roll call for the wounded and dead and found that they had fought a long hard battle and were still no further forward.

The siege had held; but the cold weather was coming and it would be a better winter for those inside the fort with food, fuel and shelter, than for those camping on marshy ground outside the walls. The duke had been promised that the reinforcing fleet was waiting in Portsmouth harbour under the command of the Earl of Holland, ready to sail any day. But there it stayed, and none of King Charles's protestations of love and constancy could relieve the English army on the island. The bad weather that kept the earl in harbour also made it impossible to sustain the siege in France. In October, another flotilla of French barges broke the English barricade and fresh French troops were successfully landed inside the fort. Buckingham decided to withdraw.

They had hoped that they might steal away at dawn, and that the citadel might not realise they were gone until it was too late. Following that plan, they did not disembark where they had arrived, on the beaches and dunes on the east of the island, but sent the ships northward to wait off the marshy waters around the Ile de Loix. The Ile de Loix was connected to the island by a tiny causeway, covered at high tide. Buckingham's plan was that the English army should slip across the causeway as the waters were rising and any French pursuit would be kept back by the swirling currents. Then the English could board the ships in good order and sail away.

Despite their safety behind the thick walls, the French sentries on duty were alert. As the little makeshift English tents were struck and the soldiers quietly formed into ranks, the French sentries watched and raised the alarm. As the ragged English army lined up in companies the gates of St Martin opened and the French, well-fed, well-clothed, well-commanded, marched out. Buckingham's troops, nearly seven thousand of them, fell slowly back before the French force. They went in a textbook retreat, staying outside musket range, refusing to engage with the sporadic fire that the French troops offered.

'How does the tide?' Buckingham asked John quickly as he tried to keep the men maintaining a steady pace towards the causeway. The ground underfoot was marshy and wet and the men could not keep to a quick march. They floundered about and had to be ordered into single file on the narrow path. The sniping from the rear increased as the French soldiers gained on them.

'The tide's turning,' John warned. 'Let them run to the ships, my lord, or we'll not get them off the island before the tide rises.'

'Run!' Buckingham shouted. 'As fast as you can!' He sent his standard bearer ahead to show the men the way. One man stepped carelessly off the causeway and immediately sank to his waist in thick mud. He shouted to his friends for help and they, glancing anxiously towards the rear of the army where the French were coming closer, laid their pikes on the ground towards him and pulled him out.

'Go on! Go on!' John urged them. 'Hurry!'

It was a race against three forces. One, the English, breaking ranks and running for their ships; two, the French coming behind them, as confident as poachers in a field of rabbits, pausing to fire and reload and then marching briskly on; three, the tide swirling in either side of the island, threatening to cut the narrow causeway in two, pushed on by the rising winds.

The men who had been ordered to lay timbers down over the mud flats to make a causeway to the ships had made the road too narrow, and there were no handholds. As the men pushed and shoved their way along the track, those at the very edge fell off and struggled in the marshy water which grew deeper with every pulse of the tide. John stopped to haul a man back on the causeway. The man struggled, gripping tight to John's reaching hands until John felt his own feet slipping under him.

'Swim with your legs!' John shouted.

'Pull me!' the man begged.

A higher wave lifted him up and John landed him like a writhing frightened fish on the causeway. But the wave which had brought the lieutenant on shore was washing over the causeway, making the timbers slippery and wet. Men were stumbling and plunging off on either side, and the men at the rear, fleeing from the French, were tumbling over their comrades and falling over the edge.

John glanced back. The French were closer, the front ranks had cast aside their muskets and were stabbing out with their pikes. The only way the English army could be saved would be to turn and fight; but half of them had lost their weapons in the run through the marshes, and there were dozens swimming in the water and struggling in the mud. The currents swirling treacherously around were sucking them down, and they were screaming for help and then choking on the slurry of the marsh.

He looked around for the duke. He at least was safe on board, leaning out from the side of the *Triumph*, urging men on to the landing craft and up the nets to the ship.

'God bless you.' The half-drowned man staggered to his feet and gripped Tradescant's arm, and then turned to see why Tradescant was staring in horror. The French were coming on, sure-footed and closer than ever, stabbing and pushing men from the causeway into the marshes and the seas. The waves were coming in faster than a galloping horse across the flat sandbanks, rushing in and washing the exhausted English army off their narrow causeway, into the brackish stinking water, and under the sharp downward stabbing French pikes. The French were standing on the causeway and stabbing their long pikes into the waters, picking off the English soldiers like a boy needling fish in a barrel.

The lieutenant shook Tradescant by the arm. 'Get to the ship!' he shouted above the noise of the water and the screams of the men. 'They're closer and closer! And we'll be cut off!'

John looked forward. It was true. The causeway was half underwater; he would be lucky, with his weak knee, to get to the other side. The lieutenant grabbed his arm. 'Come on!'

The two men, clinging to each other for balance, pushed their way through the water to the other side, their feet unsteady on the wet wooden track. Every now and then a deeper wave threatened to wash them into the sea altogether. Once John lost his footing and only the other man's grip saved him. They tumbled together on to the marshy wet land on the other side and ran towards where the *Triumph*'s landing craft were plying from the boggy shore to the ship.

John flung himself on board one of the craft and looked back as the boat took him from shore. It was impossible to tell friend from enemy; they were alike mud-smeared, knee-deep in water, stabbing and clawing for their own safety as the high dirty waves rolled in. The landing craft crashed abruptly against the side of the *Triumph* and John reached up to grip the nets hung over the side of the ship. The pressure of the men behind him pushed him up, his weaker leg scrabbling for a foothold but his arms heaving him upwards. He fell over the ship's side and lay on the deck, panting and sobbing, acutely aware of the blissful hardness of the holystoned wood of the deck under his cheek.

After a moment he pulled himself to his feet and went to where his lord was looking out to the island.

It was a massacre. Almost all the English soldiers behind John had been caught between the sea and the French. They had plunged off the causeway, or tried to escape by running through the treacherous marsh. The cries of the drowning men were like seagulls on a nesting site – loud, demanding, inhuman. Those bobbing in the water or trying to crawl back on to the causeway died quickly, under the French pikes. The French army, who were left dryshod on land before the causeway, had the leisure to reload and to fire easily and accurately into the marshes and the sea, where a few men were striking out for the ship. The front ranks, who had done deadly work off the submerged causeway, were falling back before the sea and stabbing at the bodies of Englishmen who were rolling and tumbling in the incoming waves.

The captain of the *Triumph* came to Buckingham as he stared, blank with horror, at his army drowning in blood and brine. 'Shall we set sail?'

Buckingham did not hear him.

The captain turned to John. 'Do we sail?'

John glanced around. He felt as if everything were underwater, as if he were underwater with the other Englishmen. He could hardly hear the captain speak, the man seemed to swim towards him and recede. He tightened his grip on the balustrade.

'Is another ship behind us to take off survivors?' he asked. His lips were numb and his voice was very faint.

'What survivors?' the captain demanded.

John looked again. His had been the last landing craft; the men left behind were rolling in the waves, drowned, or shot, or stabbed.

'Set sail,' John said. 'And get my lord away from here.'

Not until the whole fleet was released from the grip of the treacherous mud and waves and was at sea did they count their losses and realise what the battle had cost them. Forty-nine English standards were missing, and four thousand English men and boys, unwillingly conscripted, were dead.

Buckingham kept to his cabin on the voyage home. It was said that he was sick, as so many of the men were sick. The whole of the *Triumph* was stinking with the smell of suppurating wounds, and loud with the groans of injured men. Buckingham's personal servant took gaol fever and weakened and died, and then the Lord High Admiral was left completely alone.

John Tradescant went down to the galley where one cook was stirring a saucepan of stock over the fire. 'Where is everyone?'

'You should know,' the man said sourly. 'You were there as well as I. Drowned in the marshes, or skewered on a French pike.'

'I meant, where are the other cooks, and the servers?'

'Sick,' the man answered shortly.

'Put me up a tray for the Lord High Admiral,' John said.

'Where's his cupbearer?'

'Dead.'

'And his server?'

'Gaol fever.'

The cook nodded and laid a tray with a bowl of the stock, some stale bread, and a small glass of wine.

'Is that all?' John asked.

The man met his eyes. 'If he wants more he had better revictual the ship. It's more than the rest of us will get. And most of his army is face down in the marshes eating mud and drinking brine.'

John flinched from the bitterness in the man's face. 'It wasn't all his fault,' he said.

'Whose then?'

'He should have been reinforced, we should have sailed with better supplies.'

'We had a six-horse carriage and a harp,' the cook said spitefully. 'What more did we need?'

John spoke gently. 'Beware, my friend,' he said. 'You are very near to treason.'

The man laughed mirthlessly. 'If the Lord High Admiral has me executed before the mast there will be no dinner for those that can eat,' he said. 'And I would thank him for the release. I lost my brother in Isle of Rue, I am sailing home to tell his wife that she has no husband, and to tell my mother that she has only one son. The Lord High Admiral can spare me that and I would thank him.'

'What did you call it?' John asked suddenly.

'What?'

'The island.'

The cook shrugged. 'It's what they all call it now. Not the Isle of Rhé; the Isle of Rue, because we rue the day we ever sailed with him, and he should rue the day he commanded us. And like the herb rue his service has a poisonous and bitter taste that you don't forget.'

John took up the tray and went to Buckingham's cabin without another word.

He was lying on his bunk on his back, one arm across his eyes, his pomander swinging from his fingers. He did not turn his head when Tradescant came in.

'I told you I want nothing,' he said.

'Matthew is sick,' John said steadily. 'And I have brought you some broth.'

Buckingham did not even turn his head to look at him. 'John, I want nothing, I said.'

John came a little closer and set the tray on a table by the bed. 'You must eat something,' he urged, as gentle as a nurse with a child. 'See? I have brought you a little wine.'

'If I drank a barrel I would not be drunk enough to forget.'

'I know,' John said steadily.

'Where are my officers?'

'Resting,' John said. He did not say the truth, that more than half of them were dead and the rest sick.

'And how are my men?'

'Low-spirited.'

'Do they blame me?'

'Of course not!' John lied. 'It is the fortune of war, my lord. Everyone knows a battle can go either way. If we had been reinforced . . .'

Buckingham raised himself on an elbow. 'Yes,' he said with sudden vivacity. 'I keep doing that too. I keep saying: if we had been reinforced, or if the wind had not got up that night in September, or if I had accepted Torres's terms of surrender the night that I had them, or if the Rochellois had fought for us . . . if the ladders had been longer or the causeway wider . . . I go back and back and back to the summer, trying to see where it went wrong. Where I went wrong.'

'You didn't go wrong,' John said gently. He sat, unbidden, on the edge of Buckingham's bed and passed him the glass of wine. 'You did the best you could, every day you did your best. Remember that first landing when you were rowed up and down through the landing craft and the French turned and fled?'

Buckingham smiled, as an old man will smile at a childhood memory. 'Yes. That was a day!'

'And when we pushed them back and back and back into the citadel?'

'Yes.'

John passed him the bowl of soup and the spoon. Buckingham's hand trembled so much that he could not lift it to his mouth. John took it and spooned it for him. Buckingham opened his mouth like an obedient child. John was reminded of J as a baby tucked into his arm, seated on his lap, feeding from a bowl of gruel.

'You will be glad to see your wife again,' he said. 'At least we have come safe home.'

'Kate would be glad to see me,' Buckingham said. 'Even if I had been defeated twenty times over.'

Almost all the soup had gone. John broke up the dried bread into pieces, squashed them into the dregs and then spooned them into his master's mouth. Some colour had come into the duke's face but his eyes were still dark-ringed and languid.

'I wish we could go on sailing and never get home at all,' he said slowly. 'I don't want to get home.'

John thought of the little fire in the galley and the shortage of food, of the smell of the injured men and the continual splash of bodies over the side in one makeshift funeral after another.

'We will make port in November, and you will be with your children for Christmas.'

Buckingham turned his face to the wall. 'There will be many children without fathers this Christmas,' he said. 'They will be cursing my name in cold beds up and down the land.'

John put the tray to one side and put his hand on the younger man's shoulder. 'These are the pains of high office,' he said steadily. 'And you have enjoyed the pleasures.'

Buckingham hesitated, and then nodded. 'Yes, I have. You are right to remind me. I have had great wealth showered on me and mine.'

There was a little silence. 'And you?' Buckingham asked. 'Will your wife and son welcome you with open arms?'

'She was angry when I left,' John said. 'But I will be forgiven. She likes me to be home, working in your garden. She has never liked me travelling.'

'And you have brought a plant back with you?' Buckingham asked sleepily, like a child being entertained at bedtime.

'Two,' John said. 'One is a sort of gillyflower and the other a wormwood, I think. And I have the seeds of a very scarlet poppy which may take for me.'

Buckingham nodded. 'It's odd to think of the island without us, just as it was when we arrived,' he said. 'D'you remember those great fields of scarlet poppies?'

John closed his eyes briefly, remembering the bobbing heads of papery red flowers which made a haze of scarlet over the land. 'Yes. A bright brave flower, like hopeful troops.'

'Don't go,' Buckingham said. 'Stay with me.'

John went to sit in the chair but Buckingham, without looking, put out his hand and pulled John down to the pillow beside him. John lay on his back, put his hands behind his head and watched the gilded ceiling rise and fall as the *Triumph* made her way through the waves.

'I am cold in my heart,' Buckingham said softly. 'Icy. Is my heart broken, d'you think, John?'

Without thinking what he was doing, John reached out and gathered Buckingham so that the dark tumbled head rested on his shoulder. 'No,' he said gently. 'It will mend.'

Buckingham turned in his embrace and put his arms around him.

'Sleep with me tonight,' he said. 'I have been as lonely as a king.'

John moved a little closer and Buckingham settled himself for sleep. 'I'll stay,' John said softly. 'Whatever you want.'

The horn lantern swung on its hook, throwing gentle shadows across the gilded ceiling as the boat heaved and dropped in gentle waters. There was no sound from the deck above them. The night watch was quiet, in mourning. John had a sudden strange fancy that they had all died on the Isle of Rue and that this was some afterlife, on Charon's boat, and that he would travel forever, his arms around his master, carried by a dark tide into nothingness.

Some time after midnight John stirred, thought for a moment he was at home and Elizabeth was in his arms, and then remembered where he was.

Buckingham slowly opened his eyes. 'Oh, John,' he sighed. 'I did not think I would ever sleep again.'

'Shall I go now?' Tradescant asked.

Buckingham smiled and closed his eyes again. 'Stay,' he said. His face, gilded by the lamplight, was almost too beautiful to bear. The clear perfect profile and the sleepy languorous eyes, the warm mouth, and the new sorrowful line between the arched brows. John put a hand out and touched it, as if a caress might melt that mark away. Buckingham took the hand and pressed it to his cheek, and then drew John down to the pillows. Gently, Buckingham raised himself up above him and slid warm hands underneath John's shirt, untied the laces on his breeches. John lay, beyond thought, beyond awareness, unmoving beneath the touch of Buckingham's hands.

Buckingham stroked him, sensually, smoothly, from throat to waist and then laid his cold, stone-cold face against John's warm chest. His hand caressed John's cock, stroked it with smooth confidence. John felt desire, unbidden, unexpected, rise up in him like the misplaced desire of a dream.

The lantern dipped and bobbed and John moved at Buckingham's bidding, turned as he commanded, lay face down in the bed and parted his legs. The pain when it came to him was sharp like a pain of deep agonising desire, a pain that he welcomed, that he wanted to wash through him. And then it changed and became a deep pleasure and a terror to him, a feeling of submission and penetration and leaping desire and deep satisfaction. John thought he understood the passionate grief and lust of a woman when she can take a man inside her, and by submitting to him become his mistress. When he groaned it was not only with pain but with a deep inner joy and a sense of resolution that he had never felt before, as if at last, after a lifetime, he understood that love is the death of the self, that his love for Villiers took them both into darkness and mystery, away from self.

When Buckingham rolled off him and lay still, John did not move, transfixed by a profound pleasure that felt almost holy. He felt that he had drawn near to something very like the love of God, which can shake a man to his very core, which comes like a flame in the night and burns a man into something new so that the world is never the same for him again.

Buckingham slept but John lay awake, holding his joy.

In the morning they were easy with each other, as old friends, as brothers-in-arms, as companions. Buckingham had thrown off some of his melancholy; he went to visit his injured officers and checked the stores with the ship's purveyor, he said his prayers with the priest. In the companionway a weary-looking man asked to speak with him and Buckingham gave him his charming smile.

'My captain was killed before me, drowned off the causeway in the retreat,' the man said.

'I am sorry for it,' Buckingham replied. 'We have all lost friends.'

'I am a lieutenant, I was due for promotion. Am I captain now?'

Buckingham's face lost its colour and its smile. He turned away in disgust. 'Dead men's shoes.'

'But am I? I have a wife and a child, and I need the wages and the pension if I fall . . .'

'Don't trouble me with this,' Buckingham said with sudden anger. 'What am I? Some beggar to be hounded about?'

'You're the Lord High Admiral,' the man said reasonably. 'And I am seeking you to confirm my promotion.'

'Damn you to hell!' Buckingham shouted. 'There are four

thousand good men dead. Shall you have all their pay too?' He flung himself away.

'That's not just,' the man persisted doggedly.

John looked at him more carefully. 'You are the man who held me on the causeway!' he exclaimed.

'Lieutenant Felton. Should be captain. You pulled me out of the sea. Thank you.'

'I'm John Tradescant.'

The man looked at him more closely. 'The duke's man?'

John felt a swift pulse of pride that he was the duke's man in every sense. The duke's man to his very core.

'Tell him I should be a captain. He owes it to me.'

'He's much troubled now,' John said. 'I will tell him later.'

'I have served him faithfully, I have faced shot and illness in his service. Am I not to be rewarded?'

'I'll put it to him later,' John said. 'What's your name?'

'Lieutenant Felton,' the man repeated. 'I am not a greedy man. I just want justice for myself and for us all.'

'I'll ask him when he's calm again,' John said.

'I wish that I could refuse to do my duty when my temper is against it,' Felton said, looking after the admiral.

John had set some sailors to spinning for mackerel and that night he was able to serve Buckingham with a plate of fish. When he set the tray down, Buckingham said idly, 'Don't go.'

John waited by the door as Buckingham ate in silence. The ship seemed very quiet. Buckingham finished his dinner and then stood up from his table.

'Fetch me some hot water,' he commanded.

Tradescant took the tray back to the galley and came back with a pitcher of heated seawater. 'I am sorry, it's salt,' he said.

'No matter,' Buckingham replied. He stripped off his linen shirt, and his breeches. Tradescant held a towel for him and watched while Buckingham washed himself, and ran wet fingers through his dark hair. He stood to let John pat a sheet around him and then he lay, still naked, on the rich scarlet counterpane of his bed. John could not look away, the duke was as beautiful as a statue in the gardens at New Hall.

'Do you want to sleep here tonight again?' his lordship asked.

'If you wish, my lord,' John said, keeping the hope from his face.

'I asked what *you* wished,' Buckingham said.

John hesitated. 'You are my master. It must be for you to say.'

'I say that I want to know your thoughts. Do you wish to sleep here with me, as we did last night? Or go back to your own bed? You're free to do either, John. I don't coerce you.'

John raised his eyes to the duke's dark smile. He felt as if his face was burning. 'I want you,' he said. 'I want to be with you.'

The duke sighed, almost as if he were relieved of a fear. 'As my lover?'

John nodded, feeling the depth of sin and desire as if they were one.

'Take the jug and ewer away and come back,' the duke commanded. 'I want to feel a man's love tonight.'

The next morning they sighted Cornwall and then it was just another night before they arrived in Portsmouth. John expected to be dismissed, but when the priest had left after evening prayers Buckingham crooked his finger and John locked the door behind everyone else and spent the night with the duke. They were learning each other's bodies, apprentices in desire. Buckingham's skin was smooth and soft but the muscles in his body were hard from his horseriding and his running. John was ashamed of the grey in the hairs of his chest and his callused hands, but the weight of his strong body on Buckingham made the younger man groan with delight. They kissed, lips lingering, pressing, exploring, drinking from each other's mouths. They struggled against each other like wrestlers fighting, like animals mating, testing the hardness of muscle against muscle in a lovemaking which gave no quarter and showed no sentimentality but which had at its core a wild savage tenderness, until Buckingham said breathlessly, 'I can't wait! I want it too much!' and lunged towards John and they tumbled together into the darker world of pain and desire until pain and desire were one and the darkness was complete.

November 1627

They woke at dawn with the sound of the sailors making ready for port. There was little time for words and, in any case, what was between them went deeper than speech. John believed that they were bonded together in a way that nothing could break – the love of a man for his brother-in-arms, the strong powerful love of a vassal for his lord, and now the passionate devotion of lovers who have found all the pleasure of the world in each other's bodies. Buckingham lay back in bed as John swiftly dressed, and smiled. John felt his desires – now insatiable it seemed – rise again at that seductive mischievous smile.

'Where will we lie tonight?' he asked.

'I don't know what reception will meet me,' Buckingham said, his smile fading. 'We'll have to find the court. Chances are that Charles will be at Whitehall this season. I may have to work hard to keep my place.'

'Whatever place you win I am yours,' John said simply.

Buckingham gleamed at him. 'I know,' he said quietly. 'I shall need you by me.'

'And after Whitehall?'

'Home for the New Year,' Buckingham decided. He shot John a rueful smile. 'To our loving wives.'

John hesitated. 'I could send Elizabeth to Kent,' he offered. Elizabeth and his long years of marriage seemed part of another life; nothing could interfere with this new way of being, with this new love, with this sudden arrival of passion. 'My wife has family in

Kent. She could visit them. I could be alone at New Hall with you.'

Buckingham smiled. 'No need. We will always be travelling, you and I, John. I will always need you at my side. People will talk, but people always talk. You will serve me in my chamber again as you have done on this voyage. Nothing will part us.'

John kneeled on the bed and reached for Buckingham. The two men embraced, Buckingham's curly hair tickled John's cheek, his neck. He slipped his hand down into the warmth of his lord's body and felt the hardness of his desire rising to greet his touch.

'You want me,' John whispered.

'Very much.'

John straightened up. 'I had feared that this was not going to last,' he confided. 'That this was part of the madness of these days. The defeat and the grief. I had feared that when we came into port I would be forgotten.'

Buckingham shook his head.

'I could not bear to be without you, not now.' John felt strange, speaking of his feelings after years of self-imposed silence. He felt strangely freed, as if at last he could lay claim to a strange land inside his own head, an inner Virginia.

'You will not be without me,' the lord said easily. He threw back the covers and John felt his breath catch at the sight of the perfect body. The shoulders broad, the legs long, the thatch of dark hair and the rising penis, the smooth white skin of his belly and chest and the tumble of dark curls.

John laughed at himself. 'I am as besotted as a girl! I am breathless at the very sight of you.'

Buckingham smiled and then pulled on his linen shirt. 'My John,' he said. 'Love no-one but me.'

'I swear it.'

'I mean it.' Buckingham paused. 'I won't have a rival. Not wife nor child nor another man, not even your gardens.'

John shook his head. 'Of course there is no-one but you,' he said. 'You were my master before, but after this you have me heart and soul.'

Buckingham pulled on his scarlet hose and red breeches slashed with gold. He turned his back absentmindedly and John tied the scarlet leather laces for him, relishing the intimacy, the casual touch.

'You are my talisman,' Buckingham said, speaking half to himself. 'You were Cecil's man and now you are mine. He died without failure or dishonour and so must I. And today I shall know if the king forgives me for failing him.'

'You didn't fail,' John said. 'You did all he set you to do. Others failed, and the Navy failed to supply you. But you were faultless in courage and honour.'

Buckingham leaned back against him, feeling John's warm solid body behind him, and briefly closed his eyes. John put his arms around the younger man's body, relishing the hardness of his chest and the contrasting softness of his curly hair.

'I need you for words like that,' Buckingham whispered. 'No-one else can tell me such things and make me believe them. I need your faith in me, John, especially when I have no faith in myself.'

'I never saw you show a moment's fear,' John said earnestly. 'I never saw you hesitate or fail. You were the Lord High Admiral for every minute. No man could say less. No man did more.'

Buckingham straightened up and John saw the set of his shoulders and the lift of his chin. 'I shall hold those words to me,' he said. 'Whatever else befalls me today. I shall know that you were there, you witnessed everything, and you say this. You have been here with me and I have your love. You are a man whose judgement is trusted, and you are *my* man – what did you say? – heart and soul.'

'Till death.'

'Swear it.' Buckingham turned and held John's shoulders with sudden passionate intensity. He took John's face roughly in his cupped hands. 'Swear that you are mine till death.'

John did not hesitate. 'I swear on all that I hold sacred that I am your man, and none other's. I will follow you and serve you till death,' he promised. It was a mighty oath but John did not feel the weight of it. Instead he had a great sense of joy at being committed, at last, to another person without restraint, as if all the years with Elizabeth had been only a circling of another, a moving towards intimacy which could never be truly found. Elizabeth's femininity, her faith, her every difference from John, had meant that he could never reach her. Always between them were the dividing fissures of opinion, of taste, of style.

But Buckingham had been in John's heart, had penetrated deep inside him. There was nothing which could part them now. It was not a love between a man and a woman which always founders on difference, which always struggles with difference. It was a passion between men who start as equals and fight their way through to mutual desire and mutual satisfaction as equals.

The tension left Buckingham's shoulders. 'I needed to hear that,' he said thoughtfully. 'It is like a chain of command, the old king needed me and called me his dog, took me like a dog too. Now I need you, and you shall be my dog.'

The noises on deck grew more urgent, they could hear the sailors shouting to the barges for tow ropes, and then came the gentle bump as the ship dropped her sails and was taken in tow.

'Fetch hot water,' Buckingham said. 'I must shave.'

John nodded and did the work of a cabin boy with a heady sense of delight. He stood beside Buckingham while he shaved his smooth skin of the dark stubble, held a linen sheet for him while he washed, and then handed him his clean shirt and his waistcoat and surcoat. Buckingham dressed in silence, his hand when he reached for his perfume bottle was shaking. He sprayed his hair with perfume, set his plumed hat, winking with diamonds, on his head, and smiled at himself in the mirror: a hollow smile, a fearful smile.

'I shall go on deck,' he said. 'No-one shall say that I was afraid to show my face.'

'I will be with you,' John promised.

They went through the door together. 'Don't leave me,' Buckingham whispered as they went up the companionway. 'Whatever happens, stay at my shoulder this day. Wherever I go.'

Tradescant realised that his master was fearing worse than humiliation; he was fearing arrest. Better-loved men than he had died in the Tower for failed expeditions. They had both seen Sir Walter Raleigh taken to the Tower for less.

'I shall not leave you,' John assured him. 'Wherever they take you they will take me too. I shall always be with you.'

Buckingham paused on the narrow companionway. 'To the foot of the gallows?' he demanded.

'To the noose or the axe,' John said, as bleak as his master. 'I have sworn I am yours, heart and soul, till death.'

Buckingham dropped his hand heavily on John's shoulder and for a moment the two men stood, face to face, their eyes locked. Then with one accord they moved together and kissed. It was a passionate kiss, like a couple of fierce animals biting, no tenderness, no gentleness in it. It was a kiss no woman could give. It was a kiss between men, men who have been through a battle where there was death on either side of them and who are finding, in each other's passion, the strength to face death again.

'Stay by me,' Buckingham whispered, and went up the companionway to the deck.

A cold morning wind was blowing. The beaches of Southsea were spread before them and the green of the town common behind them. The narrow entrance to Portsmouth harbour was ahead, the grey sea walls lined with people, their faces white dots of anxiety. The flags flying over the fort flapped against their poles. Tradescant could not make out if the royal standard was there, or if Buckingham's flag had been raised in his honour. The sun was not yet up and there was a ragged cold sea mist blowing in with them, as if the ghosts of the men who would not be coming home were drifting in with them across the grey waters.

There was no gun salute, there was no band playing music, there was no applause. The *Triumph,* ill-named, undermanned and defeated, edged into the quayside, as if the ship itself felt shame.

John stood beside Buckingham by the steersman. Buckingham was dressed defiantly in red and gold, like a victorious leader, but when the people on the quayside saw him they let out a deep groan. Buckingham's bright smile never wavered but he glanced slightly over his shoulder as if to assure himself that John was there.

They ran the gangplank ashore and Buckingham, with a generous gesture of his hand, indicated that the men should go before him. It was a fine gesture but it would have been better if the two of them had gone first, and got quickly on horses, and ridden away. For there was another deep groan and then a horrified silence from the dockers and the sailors' and soldiers' families waiting on shore, as the walking wounded struggled up the companionways from below.

Their faces were blanched white with sickness except where the sun had burned them brick red, their clothes were torn and tattered, their boots worn thin. They were half-starved, their legs and arms pocked with ulcers. There were only a few men brought out on stretchers, very few, and that was because the sick and injured had died in the low-lying marshes, or bled in agony on the voyage home.

As the men came ashore they were claimed by their families. Some stayed to watch the unloading, but most turned for home, wives sobbing over the wrecks of their husbands, mothers grieving over sons, children staring upwards, uncomprehending, into the newly aged face, into the head laid open with a livid new scar, or a weeping wound, a man they could not recognise as their father.

The crowd hardly diminished at all, and that was when John realised how many men they had left behind in the marshes of the Ile de Rhé, since more than half of the families waiting to welcome their men home were still waiting. The men would not come, they would never come. They had been left on a small island in a small river before a small French town, as he had warned. As many as four thousand families had lost a father.

If Buckingham had such thoughts he did not show them. He stood very still and straight beside the wheel of his ship, balancing his weight lightly on the balls of his feet like a dancer, his hand on his hips, his head up. When someone from the quayside shouted abuse at him, he turned and looked for them, as if he did not fear to meet their gaze, his smile as ready as ever.

'He has not sent a herald for me,' he said softly so that only Tradescant could hear. 'Not soldiers to arrest me; but equally, not a herald to greet me. Am I to be ignored? Simply forgotten?'

'Hold fast,' Tradescant replied. 'We are early. It's only the poor people who have been sleeping at the quayside and around the city who will have known when we were sighted. The king himself could arrive at any moment.'

Someone shouted a curse from the quayside and Buckingham turned his bright smile towards them as if it were a hurrah.

'He could,' he agreed levelly. 'He could.'

'There! Look! cried John. 'A coach, my lord! They have sent a coach for you!'

Buckingham turned quickly and squinted down the quayside into the bright autumn sunshine. For a heart-stopping moment they could not see the livery of the coach. It could have been a royal warrant to arrest him. But then Buckingham's laugh rang out.

'By God, it is the royal coach! I am to be met with honour!'

It was unmistakable. Buckingham himself had introduced the fashion for six-horse carriages into England and only he and the king used them. Two postillions in royal livery jogged on the two leading pairs of horses, the coachman sat in scarlet and gold on the box, a footman beside him, and two liveried footmen clung to the rear. The horses had plumes of scarlet in their bridles, their hooves rang on the cobbles. The king's flags were on the four corners of the coach. The royal herald was inside.

Buckingham ran like a boy to the head of the gangplank to see this bright guarantee of his continuing wealth and power trotting towards him. Behind it came another coach with a crest on the door, and another. Behind that came another coach, and a marching band playing whistles and drums. Two heralds carried Buckingham's flag. The coach stopped at the gangplank and they let down the steps for the royal herald. Behind him from the second coach came Kate, Buckingham's wife, and his redoubtable mother the Papist countess.

Buckingham strode to the head of the gangplank to greet them, his head tilted, his smile quizzical. John followed, a pace behind him. The herald marched up the gangplank and dropped to his knee.

'My lord duke, you are welcome home,' the man said. 'The king sends you greetings and bids you to come to him at once. The court is at Whitehall. And he bids me give you this.'

He produced a purse. Buckingham, with a slight smile, opened it. A bracelet heavy with enormous diamonds spilled out into his cupped hands. 'This is a pretty gift,' he said equably.

'I have private messages for you, from His Majesty,' the herald added. 'And he bids you use his coach for your journey to him.'

Buckingham nodded as if he had never expected anything less. The herald got to his feet and stood to one side. Buckingham stepped down the gangplank to where his wife was waiting beside his coach.

John bowed to the herald and followed his master. Kate Villiers was in her husband's arms, her little hands clutching his broad shoulders.

'You are ill?' Kate whispered passionately. 'You look so pale!'

He shook his head and spoke over her head to his mother. 'Things are indeed prosperous?'

She nodded in grim triumph. 'He is waiting for you in London, desperate to see you. We have orders to bring the Favourite straight to him.'

'I am the Favourite still?'

Her hard face was bright with triumph. 'He says that no-one shall call it a defeat. He says that you could have lost the men and the ships and the standards a hundred times over as long as you are safe. He says he cares nothing for four thousand lives as long as the most precious one comes safe home.'

Buckingham laughed aloud. 'I am safe then?'

'We are all safe,' his mother said. 'Come to the city. Captain Mason has put his house at your disposal. There is a barber waiting for you, the tailor has a new suit of clothes, and the king has sent you gloves and a cape.'

Tradescant drew a little closer to his lord. There was a press of fashionable people pouring out of the coaches and gathering all around him. Someone had pressed a glass in Buckingham's hand and they were drinking to his safe return. The women's necks and shoulders were bare to the cold morning air, they were painted as for a masque at court. The men were teetering on high heels, laughing and pressing close to Buckingham. Someone elbowed John in the side and he was pushed to the edge of the crowd. A party was starting, here on the quayside, beside the tattered bulk of the *Triumph* despite the resentful stares of the poor people, drowning out the sobbing of women whose husbands would never come home.

'Tell us all about it!' someone cried. 'Tell us about the landing! They say that the French cavalry just vanished!'

Buckingham laughed and disclaimed, his beautiful wife pressed close to his side, his arm around her waist. 'I am grieved to my heart that we came home without accomplishing what we intended,' he said modestly.

There were immediate cries of disagreement. 'But you were ill-supplied! And what could any commander do with such men? They are fools, every one of them!'

John looked away. There was one woman clinging to the handrail of the gangplank, looking up at the deck of the empty ship. He went towards her, his place at the fringe of the crowd instantly taken by a pretty woman, her face bright with desire.

'What is it, mistress?'

She turned a face to him which was hollowed by long hunger, and sightless with grief. 'My husband . . . I am waiting for my husband. Will he come on another ship?'

'What was his name?'

'Thomas Blackson. He's a ploughman, but they took him for a soldier. He'd never held a gun before.'

John remembered Thomas Blackson because the man had offered to keep his plants watered while John was on a mission for his master. He was a big man, as patient and hardworking as the oxen he had driven. John had last seen him before the citadel of St Martin. He had been ordered up a ladder to attack the defenders at the top of the wall. He had gone obediently up the ladder, which was five feet short of the top. The French had leaned over the wall and shot downwards at a ridiculously easy target: the big man at the top of the ladder, stalled, just five feet below them.

'I am sorry, mistress, he is dead.'

Her white face went whiter still. 'He can't be,' she said. 'I am expecting his baby. I promised him a son.'

'I am sorry,' John repeated.

'Perhaps he will come on another ship.'

John shook his head. 'No.'

'He would not leave me,' she said, trying to persuade him. 'He would never leave me. He would not have gone in the first place but they pressed him and took him against his will. They promised me that the duke was sailing with them, and that the duke would care for his men.'

John felt a deep weariness spread through him. 'I saw him fall,' he said. 'He died a hero. But he died, mistress.'

She moved away from him as if his news made him distasteful, as if she would refuse to listen to such a liar. 'I shall wait,' she said.

'He'll come in on another ship. He won't fail me. Not my Thomas. He was never late for a single meeting, not through our courtship. He's never even late home for his dinner. He won't fail me now.'

John glanced back. The court party were getting into their coaches. There was a breakfast laid at Captain Mason's house and fine wines and food waiting. Someone hurled an empty bottle into the sea. John turned from the woman and hurried to Buckingham's side as he stepped into his coach.

'My lord?'

'Oh! John.'

'Where is Captain Mason's house?'

Kate laid hold of her husband's coat and pulled him into the coach.

'Up from the cathedral,' Buckingham said. 'But you needn't come, Tradescant. You can go home.'

'I thought I would be with you . . .'

Buckingham smiled his merry smile. 'See how well I am greeted!' He dropped into his seat, his arm around his wife. 'I don't need your service, John. You can go home to New Hall.'

'My lord, I . . .' John broke off. The old countess looked sharply at him, he was afraid of her black stare. 'You said I should stay with you this day,' he reminded his master.

Buckingham laughed again. 'Yes, but thank God I don't need your care. The king is my friend, my wife is at my side, my mother guards the interests of my family. Go home, John! I shall see you at New Hall when I come.'

He nodded to the footman and the man shut the door.

'But when shall I see you?' John called as the carriage started to move. The footman jostled past him and swung up on the back of the carriage. John wished that he too might at least ride at the back of the carriage, or run behind, or lie like a dog on the floor at their feet. 'When shall I see you again?'

'When I come!' Buckingham cried. He waved his hand as John dropped back from the window. 'I thank you for your care of me, John. I won't forget it.'

The lead horse slipped on the cobbles and the carriage checked for a moment. John seized his chance and sprang to the window again. 'But I thought I was to stay with you! At your shoulder! . . . As you said . . . my lord . . . as you said!'

Buckingham's wife was pressed to his side, her fine silk gown crushed in his hold. She peeped up at her husband in a laughing complaint at John's persistence.

'I have given you leave,' Buckingham said firmly. 'Don't be importunate, John. Go to New Hall. Don't offend me by asking for more.'

Tradescant skidded to a halt on the cobbles and stood watching the coach rock away down the quayside. The other coaches followed behind the royal coach like some great promenade. Tradescant had to step back to make room for them; and then they were all gone, the trotting horses, the laughing courtiers, the brightness of the liveries, of the courtiers' clothes, and the dock was left to greyness and mourning once more.

Tradescant stood until the last of them was gone. He could hardly believe the words he had heard his master use to him. When he had been pleading for a place at his side, Buckingham had answered him as if he had been begging for money. Buckingham had slipped, like some beautiful bird, from John's keeping to another's. And John might as well whistle to a free bird to come back to its cage as ask the duke to come back to him. John was held and bound by an obsessional desire, by a passionate love and by a sacred oath. He had sworn to love his lord until death. But only now did he realise that Buckingham had sworn nothing.

Tradescant went slowly up the gangplank, to his cabin. Someone had stolen his walking boots and his warm cape on the voyage when he had been too seldom there. He would have to replace them in Portsmouth, where such things were overpriced. He pulled out his pack and started to put his things together. The movement of the ship, rocking at anchor in the harbour, felt half-dead to John after the five-month expedition on rolling seas. The crew had melted away as soon as the officers had gone, there was no sound but the creaking of hard-worked timbers. His cabin showed his neglect of it. These last few days he had spent all his time with Buckingham, and his pallet bed was damp. Even his plants had been forgotten, the earth in the little pots was dry. John fetched a jug of water and dribbled it in, feeling that he must have lost his senses completely that he should have carried his plants through so much and then forgotten to water them for the last three days of the voyage.

He thought that this was how a woman must feel when she has given her love and given her trust and found that her lover was light-hearted and fickle and negligent all along. She feels as if he has taken something precious, a rare seedling, and let it fall. She feels injured – Tradescant felt pain like a wound – but she also feels a fool. Tradescant felt humbled lower than ever in his life before. Being an apprentice gardener was a low station in life but you could be proud of your work and see where it might take you. But being a nobleman's lover was the work of a fool. Buckingham had used him, had taken him for consolation, to keep his fears at bay, to support his courage and confidence. Now he had his mother and Kate and the king and the court and all his wealth and joy. And all Tradescant had was a new gillyflower, wilting, a large wormwood plant in dry soil, a pain in his backside which was abuse, and a pain in his belly which was grief.

Grimly he picked up his pack, ducked his head to avoid the low beam of his cabin doorway, and climbed the companionway to the waist of the ship. He trudged down the gangplank. No-one was on board to bid him goodbye, no-one was on the quayside waiting to greet him. The white-faced widow started up as she heard a footstep on the gangplank, but then dropped back. Tradescant went past her without a word of comfort. He had no comfort to give. He turned his face away from the sea and trudged, uncomfortable in his shoes on the cobbles, towards the city.

A man fell in beside him. 'Did you speak to him about my promotion?'

It was Felton again. 'I am sorry,' said John. 'I forgot.'

But the man was not angry this time. 'Then he must have seen sense himself,' he said joyfully. 'Those who call him a fool will have me to reckon with. He has promised me my captaincy. I shall retire a captain and that is worth something to a poor man, Mr Tradescant.'

'I am glad of it,' John said heavily.

'I shall never fight again,' Felton declared. 'It was a bad campaign, badly planned, badly led, cruelly hard. There were times when I wept like a baby. I thought we would never get off that accursed island.'

John nodded.

'He will never do it again, will he?' Felton asked. 'The French can fight their own battles now. They don't need the pain of Englishmen. We should be as we were with the old queen – defenders of our own shores and our own counties. Safe behind our own sea. What are the French and their worries to me?'

'I feel that too,' John said. They had reached the end of the quay. He turned and held out his hand to Felton. 'God be with you, Felton.'

'And with you, Mr Tradescant. Now we are home, maybe the duke will think of the people at home. There's much poverty. It is pitiful to see the children in my village. They have neither school nor play, and the common land has been enclosed so they have neither milk nor meat nor honey. And bread itself is scarce.'

'Maybe he will.'

The two men shook hands, but still Felton lingered. 'If I were the duke and could advise the king, I would tell him to stop the enclosing of land and free it for the people,' he said. 'So that every man can have his strip for vegetables or to keep a pig. Like it used to be. If I were advising the king, I would tell him that before he moves the communion table rightwise or sidewise or anywise in the church he should feed the people. We need bread before a mouthful of communion wine.'

John nodded, but he knew, as Felton could not know, that the king never saw the beggars in the streets, never saw the hungry children. He went in his carriage from great country seat to hunting lodge. He went on his royal barge from one riverside palace to another. And besides, the permission granted to a landlord to enclose common land brought revenue into the royal coffers, while a refusal would benefit only the poor and leave the king as short of cash as ever.

'He is a merciful king?' Felton queried. 'And Buckingham is a great duke, a good man, is he not?'

'Oh, yes,' John said. The pain in his belly seemed to have stretched out to his fingers and his toes, he felt numb in his legs and shoulders.

If he did not start to walk home soon, he thought he would lie down on the cobbles and die. 'Excuse me, I must go, my wife will be waiting for me.'

'I must go too!' Felton cried, remembering. 'I have a wife waiting for me, thank God. I shall tell her to call me captain!'

He hefted his pack and strode off whistling. John looked down at his shoes and put one in front of the other, as if he had just learned to walk. At each step he thought he could hear Buckingham laugh and say: 'I have given you leave. Don't be importunate, John. Go to New Hall. Don't offend me by asking for more.'

He had not thought how he would get to New Hall. He had been on such a crest of desire and happiness that he had thought he and the duke would ride side by side, the two of them together. Or perhaps they would have used the duke's coach and horses and rocked along the badly made roads, and laughed when they had to stop for a loose wheel, or walked shoulder to shoulder up a hill to spare the horses.

But now he was trudging alone in stiff new walking boots. He had some money in his pocket, he could buy or hire a horse, or he could take a ride with any carter. But as the sun came slowly up – an English sun, he thought with a sudden pang of recognition – he found that he wanted to walk, walk like a poor man, walk slowly along the rutted road which led away from the port to London. He wanted to look at the changing blushing colours of the trees and the berries in the hedgerow and the grass seeds bobbing in the wind. He felt as if he had been in exile for a dozen years, he had dreamed of lanes like this, of a sun as warm and mild as this one, while they had been trapped on that island waiting for reinforcement, waiting for a decisive battle, waiting for victory, for glory.

At midday he knocked on the door of a small wayside farmhouse and asked if he could buy some dinner. The farmer's wife gave him a trencher of bread and cheese and a flagon of ale to drink. Her hands were ingrained with dirt and there was dirt under her fingernails and in the thorn scratches.

'You're a gardener,' Tradescant guessed.

She rubbed her hand on her apron. 'I struggle with it,' she said in the broad accent of Hampshire. 'But 'tis like a forest, like the forest of the Sleeping Beauty. When I rest it grows up to my very windows. I was clearing my strawberry bed and I find a plant growing thorns. A strawberry with thorns! The whole garden would grow weeds and thorns if it could.'

'A thorny strawberry?' John demanded. He pushed aside the flask of ale. The pain was still deep in his body but he could not deny a small squirm of curiosity. 'You have a thorny strawberry? May I see it?'

'Why, what use is it?' she asked. 'It grows a green fruit, it is no good for eating nor bottling.'

'It is a curiosity,' he said, and found he was smiling, the muscles on his cheeks relaxing from their scowl. 'I am a great one for curiosities, I would be glad if you would show it to me. Out of your kindness. And I would pay you . . .'

'You can have it for nothing,' she said. 'But you must fetch it yourself. I threw it with the other weeds on the midden. It'll take a deal of sorting through.'

John laughed, and then checked himself at the strangeness of the noise. He had not laughed in months. His time with his lord had been a time of passion driving out grief in the darkness. But now he was home, on English soil again, under an English sun and here was this woman with her green thorny strawberry.

'I will find it,' he promised her. 'And I will see if I can grow it in my garden, and if it proves to be a curiosity, or to have some quality, then I will send you a shoot.'

She shook her head at his folly. 'Are you from London?'

'Yes,' he said, he did not want to name New Hall. He did not want to be known as the Duke of Buckingham's man.

She nodded as if that would account for it. 'Here we like our strawberries red and fit to eat,' she said gently. 'Do not send me a shoot, I do not want it. You can give me a penny for your dinner and for the thorny strawberry, and be on your way. In Hampshire we like our strawberries red.'

Winter 1627

Elizabeth was in the garden before their cottage at New Hall when John came in at the gate. She was cutting herbs in the cool of the evening light, and the basket on the ground before her was bobbing with the seed-heavy heads of camomile flowers. When she heard his uneven step she looked up and started to run towards him but then she suddenly checked. Something in the slowness of his pace and his bowed shoulders warned her that this was not a happy homecoming.

Slowly she came towards him, noting the new lines of pain and disappointment in his face. His limp, which he thought she did not see, was more pronounced than ever.

She put her hand on his shoulder. 'Husband?' she said softly. 'You are welcome home.'

He looked up from the ground before him and when she met his dark eyes she recoiled. 'John?' she whispered. 'Oh my John, what has he done to you?'

It was the worst thing she could have said. He reared up, his face hard. 'Nothing. What d'you mean?'

'Nothing. Nothing. Come and sit down.' She led him to the stone bench before the house, and felt his hand tremble in her own. 'Sit,' she said tenderly. 'I will get you a cup of ale, or would you like something hot?'

'Anything,' he said.

She hesitated. J was still at work, cutting back and weeding in the fruit garden, at the other side of the great house. She did not send for him yet, she feared a quarrel between father and son, and when

316

she looked at John's weary face she feared that his son would be the victor. John had come home an old man. She whisked into the house and brought out a mug of ale and a slice of her home-made bread. She put them on the bench beside him and said nothing while he drank. He did not eat.

'We heard that it was a defeat,' she said at last. 'I was afraid that you were hurt.' She shot a sideways look at him, wondering if there were some physical injury that he was keeping from her.

'I took not a scratch,' he said simply.

The pain was in his soul, then. 'And his lordship?'

There was a flash across his face, instantly hidden, like lightning on a dark night. 'He is well, praise God. He is with the king who has rejoiced in his return, with his wife at his side, thank God.'

She bowed her head briefly but found she could not say 'Amen'.

'And you . . .' she prompted him gently. 'I can see that all is not well with you, John. I can see that there is no rejoicing for you.'

He met her eyes and she thought that never before in their life together had she seen him look as if the light had gone out for him.

'I will not burden you with my sorrows, Elizabeth,' he said gently. 'I will mend. I am not a boy in springtime. I will mend.'

Her grave look never wavered. 'Perhaps you should tell me, John. Or tell your Saviour. A hidden secret is like a hidden pain, it can only grow worse.'

He nodded as if he knew all about hidden pain now. 'I shall try to pray. But I am afraid that my faith was never very strong, and I seem to have lost it.'

She would have been shocked if she had believed him. 'How can you lose your faith?' she asked simply.

He looked away, over his garden. Was it on the island? Did his faith fall sick like the soldiers who had to sleep on the wet ground? Or did it drown in the sea where the causeway was treacherous and they lost the last standard? Or did it bleed to death on the voyage home when the injured men cried out so loud that he heard them, even over the noise of the creaking ship? Was it always a chain that had linked John to his lord, the lord to the king and the king to God, and the loss of one meant the loss of all? Or had he forgotten his faith just as he had forgotten everything, even the gillyflower and the wormwood plants, because he had fallen deep into love and deep into joy and made a god of another man?

'I don't know,' he said slowly. 'Perhaps God has lost me.'

Elizabeth bowed her head and made a quick silent prayer that she might have guidance as to how she might help him.

'You are right, and you have been right all along,' he said at last. 'We are ruled by a fool who is in the hands of a knave. I have seen men die for the folly of those two, for all my life: in the plague in London, in the villages up and down the land where people are driven out of their homes and out of their gardens for the landlords to make sheep runs, and on that cursed island where we set a siege with less food in our stores than the besieged, where we marched with ploughboys and criminals, where we had scaling ladders which were yards too short, and where the commander was playing at soldiers, and the king forgot to reinforce us.'

His bitterness was like an explosion in that quiet garden, even worse than his blasphemy. She had thought she would never hear such words from him, who had been Cecil's man, who had served the old queen. This was a stranger to her – a bitter man carrying the scars of fatal betrayal, who finally spoke treason aloud.

'John –'

He bared his teeth in a hard smile at her surprise. 'You should be pleased,' he said cruelly. 'You warned me enough. Now see: I have heeded your teachings and lost my faith in my lord, in my king, and in my God. Wasn't that what you wanted?'

Dumbly she shook her head.

'Didn't you warn me and warn me that he was a sodomite and a puppet master? Didn't you beg me to leave his service on the very day we came here? Didn't you give me a long spoon to sup with the Devil when I started keeping his secrets safe?'

Her hands were over her mouth, her shocked eyes looked at him in silence.

John hawked and spat like a soldier, as if the taste of bile was too bitter for him.

Without thinking, Elizabeth scuffed dirt over the spittle. 'John,' she whispered. 'I never meant that you should lose your faith. I meant only to caution you –'

'I am cautioned now,' he said. 'I am checked. I am stopped short.'

There was a silence. Somewhere in the fine woods of the duke's estate the pigeons were cooing, warmly, easily. John looked up at the sky and saw a flock of rooks heading for home in the tall trees.

'What shall we do?' Elizabeth asked, as if she was in a wilderness with wreckage all around them.

He looked around, at the fine house and the garden, as if they gave him no pleasure at all. 'I am his servant,' he said slowly. 'He has paid me all he is going to pay me, he told me that. He will use me as he wishes. When he needs me – I am to be there. I am the duke's man, I have sworn a solemn oath to be his man till death.'

She took a sharp breath at that. 'An oath?'

'He asked it of me and I gave it,' John said grimly. 'I gave him everything he asked and I swore a solemn oath that I am his man. I will have to learn to live with that. I am a servant, I am lower than a servant, for he has commanded me to be his dog and I have licked his foot.'

'You think he is a fool and a betrayer and you have sworn to be his man?' she asked incredulously.

'Just so.'

They were silent for long moments. She thought that some dark compact must have taken place between her husband and the master he now hated. She did not dare to think what one had done, what one had submitted to. Whatever had taken place it had sent John home as a broken man.

'Do you hate him?' she whispered.

The look he gave her was that of a man carrying a mortal wound deep in his belly. 'No,' he said softly. 'I love him still. But I know that he is no good. That's worse than hatred for me. To know that I have given my word and my love to a man who is no good.'

She took his hands in hers and felt how cold they were, as if his heart were beating slowly, painfully. 'Can't you escape him?'

He shook his head. 'I am his, in every way that there is, until death.'

They sat in silence for long moments, Elizabeth chafing his hands as if he were cold from sickness and she had to warm him. She thought that there was nothing that she could say which would take that dark painful look from his face. The sun was setting slowly in the deep red of autumn and a cool wind began to blow.

'The chestnut tree flowered this summer,' she said inconsequently. 'As you left, d'you remember you asked me to look to it, for you?'

He did not raise his gaze from his boots. 'The sweet chestnuts?'

'No. Your sapling. The one you gave me. The chestnut from Turkey. It bore a strange beautiful blossom, like huge pine cones, a white blossom of many flowers with tiny scarlet freckles inside them, and smelling sweet.'

'Eh? My sapling flowered? At last?'

'As you left. And it is setting seed,' she said. 'You will have nuts off it this year, John. You can see the seed cases already. They are very strange, I had forgotten how strange. They are fat and fleshy and with a few thick spikes. But they are holding to the tree and swelling with the ripeness of the nut inside.'

He straightened up and looked at her. 'Are you sure?'

'I think so,' she said with loving cunning. 'But you had better see for yourself, you know there is no-one who has your skill with trees.'

'Perhaps I should take a look.' He got to his feet and winced as his boots rubbed his sore feet, but he stepped out down the garden path to where his tree was kept in its great carrying case at the bottom of the garden near the kitchen garden wall.

'I wish we had named it for you,' she said, suddenly struck by how little they owned, now that he was a vassal and had lost everything. 'I wish we had called them "Tradescantia" when Lord Cecil first gave them to you to grow. You were the first to grow them, you had the right.'

John shrugged his shoulders as if it did not matter what they were named as long as they grew tall and strong. 'The name does not matter. Rights do not matter. But to grow a new tree, to put a new tree into the gardens of England – now that is to live forever.'

J did not come home till dusk and he did not know his father was returned until he came in through the front door and saw the

Portsmouth-bought walking boots side by side inside the doorway. He hesitated, but it was too late. John, sitting at the well-worn table, had already seen him.

J was dressed in a suit of grey broadcloth, white linen bands at his throat, plain without lace. On his head was a tall plain black hat, unadorned by feather or badge. Over his shoulder was his warm coat of black.

John, who had bathed and changed into his russet suit with a rich lace collar, rose slowly from the table.

'You're dressed very plain,' he said cautiously.

Elizabeth heard the front door slam and came slowly from the kitchen, wiping her hands on her apron.

J measured his father and spoke steadily. 'I believe that finery is a waste of a man's money and an abomination in the sight of the Lord.'

John wheeled around and looked accusingly at Elizabeth. She met his gaze without flinching. 'You've turned him into a Puritan at last,' he said. 'I suppose he preaches and bears witness and can fall down in a faint if required?'

'I can speak for myself,' J said. 'And it was not my mother's decision, but my own.'

'Decision!' John scoffed. 'What can a boy of eighteen decide?'

J flinched. 'I am a man,' he said. 'I am nineteen now. I earn a man's wage, I do a man's work, and I give a man's whole duty to my God.'

For a moment they thought John would roar out his temper. J braced himself for the blast of anger, but to his surprise none came. The older man's shoulders dropped and he turned and fell heavily in his chair. 'And how long will you draw a wage here, looking like that?' he asked. 'When the king comes to visit? When Archbishop Laud comes to visit? Do you think they want to see a sectary in their garden?'

J's head went up. 'I don't fear them.'

'Yes, I daresay you are longing for martyrdom, to be burned at the stake for your beliefs, but this is not a burning king. He will merely turn away from you and Buckingham will dismiss you. And where will you work then?'

'For a nobleman who shares my faith,' J said simply. 'The country is full of men who believe in worshipping our God in simplicity and in truth, who have turned against the waste and sin of the court.'

'Do I have to spell it out?' John shouted. 'They will turn you off and no-one will employ you!'

'Husband –'

'What?'

'You told me yourself that your faith in the king and the duke has been shaken,' Elizabeth said gently. 'J is trying to find his own way.'

'What way?' John demanded. 'There is no other way.'

'There is going back to the Bible and seeking a way through prayer,' J said earnestly. 'There is the beauty of hard work, and turning away from show and masques and waste. There is sharing the land, every man to have his own piece of ground to grow his own food so that none go hungry. There is opening up the enclosed sheep runs and the enclosed parks so that everyone can share in the wealth which God has given.'

'Opening parks?'

'Yes, even like this one,' J said earnestly. 'Why should my lord duke have the Great Park of five hundred acres and the Little Park of three hundred? Why should he own the common road, and the green before the gate? Why does he need an avenue of a mile of lime trees? Why should he enclose good fields, productive fields, and then plant a few pretty trees and grass and use it for walking and riding? What folly to take good farming land and plant it with shrubs and call it a wilderness when children are dying for lack of food in Chorley, and people are driven out of their cottages because their plots of land have been taken away from them?'

'Because he is the duke,' John said steadily.

'He deserves to own half of the county?'

'It is his own, given to him by the king, who owns the whole country.'

'And what did the duke do for the king to earn such wealth?'

John had a sudden vivid recollection of the rocking cabin and the swaying light and Buckingham rearing above him, and the wound like a swordthrust which was the extreme of pleasure and pain all at once.

J waited for a reply.

'Don't,' John said shortly. 'Don't torment me, J. It is bad enough that you should come into my house looking like a hedgerow lecturer. Don't torment me about the duke and the king and the rights and the wrongs of it. I have been close to death, my life hanging on whether the king would remember his friend on a barren island far away, or not. And then he did not. I have no stomach for an argument with you.'

'Then I may wear what I choose, and pray as I choose?'

John nodded wearily. 'Wear what you will.'

There was a silence as J absorbed the extent of his victory. Tradescant turned his back on him and returned to his seat at the table. J stepped out of his mud-caked working boots and came into the room in his socks.

'I am thinking of taking a wife,' he announced quietly. 'And leaving the duke's service. I want to go to Virginia and start again, in a country where there are no lords and no kings, and no archbishops. I want to be there where they are planting an Eden.'

He had thought his father defeated, and was pressing his advantage while he had it. But John raised his head and looked hard at his son. 'Think again,' he counselled him.

They ate dinner in awkward silence and then J put on his hat and went out into the darkness, carrying only a small lantern to light his way.

'Where's he going?' John asked Elizabeth.

'To evening prayers, at the big house,' she said.

'They have prayer meetings on my lord's doorstep?'

'Why not?'

'Because the king has ruled how the church services are to be arranged,' John said firmly. 'And they are to be done by a certified vicar in church on Sunday.'

'But Buckingham's own mother is a Papist,' Elizabeth pointed out. 'And the queen herself. *They* do not obey the king and the archbishop. And they do far worse than simple men reading their Bible and praying in their own language to God.'

'You cannot compare Her Majesty with simple men, with J!'

She turned her calm face to him. 'I can, and I do,' she said. 'Except that my son is a godly young man who prays twice a day and lives soberly and cleanly while the queen . . .'

'Not another word!' Tradescant interrupted her.

She shook her head. 'I was only going to say that the queen's conscience is her own concern. I know that my son takes nothing but what is his own, bows to no graven idols, avoids priests and their wickedness, and says nothing against the king.'

John said nothing. It was undeniable that the queen did all of these things. It was undeniable that the queen was a wilful Papist who had sworn that she hated her husband and hated his country, and would speak neither the language nor smile at the people.

'Whatever his conscience, J has taken the duke's wage,' John pointed out. 'He is his man while he draws that wage. The duke, right or wrong.'

Elizabeth got up from the table and stacked the dinner platters for washing. 'No,' she said gently. 'He works for the duke until he can find himself another, better master. Then he can leave him, he can leave without a moment's regret. He has sworn no loyalty, he has given no promise. He does not belong to the duke until he is released by death. He does not follow the duke, right or wrong.'

She looked across at John. The candle on the table showed the heaviness around his eyes, and the determination in her face. 'It is only you who are so bound,' she said. 'By your own love for him. And by an oath of your own making. Not J. You have bound yourself, John; but my son, thank God, is free.'

John heard in the kitchen of New Hall that the duke's homecoming had been sweeter than his own. The whole royal court had ridden out of London to meet him in a great cavalcade of riders with seventy coaches carrying the ladies to throw rose petals and rose water and greet the returning hero. The queen alone had avoided his triumphal return, but only her immediate household had stayed away and sulked. The king had thrown a great dinner to celebrate the triumphal return, and after dinner he had drawn Buckingham away from the crowds and into his private bedchamber and the two men had spent the night together, alone.

'The evening together, you mean,' John suggested. 'The duke will have gone to his wife, the Duchess Kate, at night, when the dinner was over.'

The messenger from London shook his head. 'He lay that night with the king,' he said firmly. 'In the king's own bed in the king's own bedchamber.'

John nodded briefly and turned away. He did not want to hear more.

'And he sent a letter for you,' the man went on, digging into his pocket.

Tradescant wheeled around. 'A letter! You damned fool, why did you not say so at once?'

'I did not think it was urgent –'

'Of course it's urgent. He may want me at a moment's notice, you may have delayed me with your kitchen gossip and your nonsense about beds and nights and rose petals –'

John dragged the letter from the man's hand and took two stumbling strides to be away from him, so no-one could see the words on the page. He glanced at the seal, the duke's own familiar seal, broke it and unfurled the page. He had written in his own hand. John tightened his grip on the paper. It was in his own idiosyncratic spiky handwriting, and it was headed 'John –'

The relief was almost too much. He could hardly see the words as the paper shook in his hand. The duke had summoned him, the sharp word on the quayside meant nothing. Buckingham wanted him at his side and now their life would begin together as they had planned.

'Grave news?' the messenger enquired from behind John.

John flattened the letter to his body. 'Private,' he said shortly and took the letter out into the garden like a stolen sweetmeat to devour on his own. He found the knot garden deserted and he walked down one of his own neat paths and sat on a small stone seat at the end of a miniature avenue. Then, and only then, he opened the letter for his lord's commands.

> John –
>
> A ship, the *Good Fortune*, is in the Pool of London with a dozen boxes of curiosities for my rarities room. They are goods from India, carved ivory and worked rugs and the like, some gold and some silver cabinets. Also there is a small box of seeds which will be of interest to you. Do fetch them to New Hall for me, or send someone you can trust. I shall be at Whitehall for Christmas with my king. – Villiers.

That was all. There was no message bidding him to Whitehall, no summons. There was no word of love or even remembrance. He was not cast off, he was not a spurned lover. He did not stand high enough for rejection. Buckingham had simply forgotten the promises, forgotten the nights, and moved on to other things.

John sat on the stone seat for a long time with the letter in his hand, the high skies of Essex arched cold and grey above his head. Only when the cold of the stone seat and the cold of the winter winds had chilled him to the very bone did he stir and realise that the coldness was from the world around him, and not seeping icily into his veins from his heart.

'I have to go to London,' Tradescant remarked to J. They were working side by side in the duke's rose garden, pruning the year's growth down to sharp sticks cut carefully on the slant.

'Can I go for you?' J asked.

'What for?'

'I could help you.'

'I'm not in my dotage,' John said. 'I think I can get to London and back with a wagon on my own.'

'If you are carrying valuables . . .'

'Then I'll hire a man with a musket.'

'You might like my company . . .'

'Or I might prefer to travel alone. What's the secret, J? You never liked London before?'

J straightened up and pushed his plain hat back on his head. 'I would like to visit a young woman,' he announced. 'You could come and see her too. Her parents would make us both very welcome.'

John stood up, one hand on his aching back. 'A young woman? What young woman?'

'Her name is Jane. Jane Hurte. Her father has a mercer's shop near to the docks. While you were away, a package came for his lordship and they sent me down to London to fetch it. Mother wanted some buttons and I stepped into the Hurtes' shop. Jane Hurte took my money and we had a few words of conversation.'

John waited, taking care not to smile. There was something deeply endearing about this stilted account of courtship.

'Then I took a lift with the sheep fleeces down to the market, and visited her again.'

'In June?' John asked, thinking of shearing time.

'Yes. And then the duchess wanted something fetched from the London house, so I went down on the cart with her maid and spent the day with the Hurtes.'

'How many times have you been there?'

'Six times,' J said reverently.

'Is she a pretty lass?'

'She's not a lass, she's a young lady. She's twenty-three.'

'I beg her pardon! Is she fair or dark?'

'Sort of dark, well, she's not golden-haired, but not altogether dark.'

'Pretty?'

'She's not painted and curled and half-naked, like the women of the court. She's modest and . . .'

'Is she pretty?'

'*I* think so.'

'If you are the only one that thinks so then she must be plain,' John teased.

'She's not plain,' J replied seriously. 'She's . . . she's . . . she looks like herself.'

John abandoned hope of getting much sense from his son about Jane Hurte's looks. 'Does she share your beliefs?'

'Of course. Her father is a preacher.'

'A travelling preacher?'

'No, he has his own chapel and a congregation. He's a most respected man.'

'You are serious about her?'

'I wish to marry her,' J said. He looked at his father as if measuring how far he could trust him with a confidence. 'I wish to marry her soon. I have been disturbed recently.'

'Disturbed?'

'Yes. Sometimes I find it hard to think of her only as a spiritual partner and companion.'

John bit the inside of his cheeks to suppress a smile. 'You can love her body as well as her soul, I suppose.'

'Only if we are married.'

'Does she want to marry?'

J flushed a deep brick red and bent over the roses. 'I think she might,' he said. 'But I could not ask her while you were away. I needed you to meet her father and discuss her dowry and all the arrangements.'

John nodded. 'We'll stay overnight in London,' he decided. J's apprentice lovemaking seemed very sweet and young compared to the complexity of his own pain. 'Send them word that we can come at dinnertime and perhaps they will ask us to dine.'

'I'm sure they will. Only, Father . . .'

'Yes?'

'They're very devout people, and they think badly of the king. We will have a better time if we do not talk about the king or the court, or the archbishop.'

'Or Ireland, or the enclosures, or the Ile de Rhé, or my lord Buckingham, or my lord Stafford, or ship money, or the court of wards, or anything,' John said impatiently. 'I am not a fool, J. I will not embarrass you before your sweetheart.'

'She's not my sweetheart,' J said quickly. 'She's my . . . my . . .'

'Intended helpmeet,' John suggested, without a glimmer of a smile.

'Yes,' J said, pleased. 'Yes. She's my intended helpmeet.'

John had expected an austere shop with an unsmiling proprietor and a whey-faced daughter, and was amazed by the well-stocked counter and the plump round-faced woman who sat outside the shop and invited customers to come in.

'I'm Mistress Hurte,' she said. 'My daughter's inside. My husband is visiting a sick friend and will be home in time for dinner. Step inside, Mr Tradescant.'

Jane Hurte was on her knees behind the counter, tidying the immaculate shelves. She rose up as they came in and John had to blink his eyes to prepare them for the dark interior of the shop. He saw at once that J had been baffled in his description of her because she had a complex intelligent face full of character, neither simply pretty nor plain. Her forehead was broad and smooth and her brown hair was swept back under a plain cap. Her gown was grey but well-cut and flowing, and her white collar was trimmed with lace. She looked at John with a keen intelligence, and a twinkle of humour.

'Good day, Mr Tradescant,' she said. 'And welcome to our home. Will you step upstairs to wait? Father will be back in a moment.'

'I'll wait down here with you if I may,' John said. He looked around the shop which was lined with small drawers, none of them marked. 'It's like a treasure chest.'

'John told me that the Duke of Buckingham has a room like this, but he stores curiosities,' she said. With a shock John realised that she did not call his son J, but John.

'Yes,' he said. 'My lord has some very beautiful and curious things.'

'And you arrange them and collect them for him?'

'Yes.'

'You must have seen many marvels,' she said seriously.

John smiled at her. 'And many falsehoods. Foolish forgeries cobbled together to try to catch the unwary.'

'All treasure is a trap for the unwary,' she observed.

'Indeed,' John said, disliking the tone of piety. 'I shall buy something from you to take home to my wife. Do you have some pretty ribbons or lace for her to trim a collar?'

Jane bent below the counter and slid out a tray. She spread a little black velvet cloth so the lace was shown to its best advantage and laid out one piece, and then another, for him to see.

'And ribbons,' she said. They came from a dozen little drawers, arranged by colour. She spread them before him, the cheap scratchy thin ones, and the lustrous silkier lengths.

'Are they not a trap to catch the unwary?' John asked, watching her absorbed face as she smoothed the lengths of ribbon before him, and folded them so that he could admire their shine.

She met his smile without embarrassment. 'They are the hard work of good women,' she said. 'They work to put bread in their mouths and we pay them a fair price and sell at a good profit. It is not just what you earn, but how you spend your money, that is judged on the great day. In this house we buy and sell fairly and nothing is wasted.'

'I'll take that lace,' John decided. 'Enough to make a collar.'

She nodded and cut him the measure he needed. 'A shilling,' she said. 'But you may have it for tenpence.'

'I'll pay the full shilling,' he said. 'For the good women.'

She gave a sudden, delicious gurgle of laughter, her whole face lighting up and her eyes dancing. 'I'll see that they get it,' she said.

She took his coin and put it away in a strongbox under the desk, entered the purchase in a ledger, and then wrapped the scrap of lace very carefully and tied it with a piece of wool. John stowed it in the deep pocket of his coat.

'Here's Father,' Jane said.

John turned to greet the man. He looked incongruously more like a farmer than a seller of cloth and haberdashery. He was broad-shouldered and red-faced, well-dressed in sober black and grey and with a small lace collar. He held his hat in his hand and put out his other hand to John for a firm handshake.

'I am glad to meet you at last,' he said. 'We have heard nothing from John but about his father's travels since he first came here, and we prayed for you while you were in such peril off France.'

'I thank you,' John said, surprised.

'Daily, and by name,' Josiah Hurte went on. 'He is a mighty all-wise, all-powerful God; but there is no harm in reminding him.'

John had to suppress a smile. 'I suppose not.'

Josiah Hurte looked at his daughter. 'Any sales?'

'Just a piece of lace to Mr Tradescant, here.'

His tradesman's instinct warred with his desire to be generous to John's father. The desire for a small profit won. 'Times are very hard for us,' he said simply.

John looked around the well-stocked shop.

'It doesn't show yet,' Josiah said, following his gaze, 'but every month things are getting tighter. We have a constant stream of requisitions from the king, fines for this, new taxes for that. And goods which were free to buy and sell suddenly become farmed out to courtiers as monopolies and we have to pay a fee to the monopoly holder. The king demands a free gift from his subjects and the vicar or the churchwardens come round to my shop, look at the outside, decide on their own what I can afford, and I face prison if I refuse.'

'The king has great expenses,' John said pacifically.

'*My* wife and *my* friends would spend all my money too if I let them,' the Puritan said shortly. 'So I don't let them.'

John said nothing.

'Forgive me,' the man said suddenly. 'My daughter swore me to silence on this matter and I broach it the moment I am in the door!'

John could not resist a laugh. 'My son too!'

'They feared we would quarrel but I would never come to blows over politics.'

'I have seen enough of warfare this year,' John agreed.

'It is a criminal shame, though,' Josiah continued, leading the way up the stairs from the shop. 'My guild can no longer control the trade because the court favourites now run the market in thread and lace and silk, and so my apprentices are no longer guaranteed their work or their wages, other men come into the trade and force prices and wages down and up at their whim. I wish you would tell the duke that if the poor are to be fed and the widows and children safeguarded, we need a powerful guild and a steady trade. We cannot have changes every time a courtier needs a new place.'

'He does not take my advice,' John replied. 'Indeed, I think he leaves the business of the city and trade to others.'

'Then he should not have taken the monopoly for gold and silver thread into his keeping,' the mercer said triumphantly. 'If he cares nothing for trade then he should not engross it. He will ruin the trade and ruin himself, and ruin me.'

John nodded, uncertain how to answer, but his host slapped the side of his head with a broad palm. 'Again!' he cried. 'And I promised Jane I would not. Not another word, Mr Tradescant. So take a glass of wine with me?'

'Willingly.'

Dinner was a respectable affair preceded by a lengthy grace, but Mrs Hurte laid a good table and her husband was generous with small ale and had a good wine. J sat beside Jane and spent the meal regarding her with a steady admiring gaze. John watched his son with a wry amusement.

The Hurtes were a pleasant straightforward couple. Mrs Hurte presided over the puddings at her end of the table and Josiah Hurte carved the beef at his end. Between them sat their guests and Jane, and two apprentices.

'We dine in the old way,' Mr Hurte confirmed, seeing John looking down the table. 'I believe a man who takes an apprentice boy should bring him up as his own. He should feed his body as well as his mind.'

John nodded. 'I have only ever had my son work for me,' he said. 'My other gardeners are hired by my master.'

'Is the duke at New Hall now?' Mrs Hurte asked.

Even in this quiet parlour the mention of his name hurt John like a twinge of pain from an unhealed wound.

'No, he is at court,' he said shortly. J directed a glance of unspoken appeal at him and Jane looked anxious.

'They are having great revelry this Christmas, now that the duke is safely returned,' Mrs Hurte observed.

'I daresay,' said John.

'Shall you see him at Whitehall before you return to New Hall?'

'No,' John said. He had a pain now, as sharp as indigestion, under his ribs. He pushed his plate away, sated with grief. 'I may not go to him unless he sends for me.'

He realised that the young woman, Jane Hurte, was looking at him and her face was full of sympathy, as if she understood a little of what he was feeling. 'It must be a hard task to serve a great lord,' she said gently. 'He must come and go like a planet in the sky and all you can do is watch and wait for him to come again.'

Her father bent his head and said softly: 'I pray that we may all serve a greater master. Amen.'

But Jane did not take her eyes from John and her smile was steady.

'It is hard.' His voice was full of pain, even in his own ears. 'But I have made my choice and I must serve him.'

'Keep us all in service to the Lord our God,' Josiah Hurte prayed again, and this time Jane Hurte, still watching John's strained face, said: 'Amen.'

The two young people were allowed out to walk together. Jane had some deliveries which had to be made, and J was to go with her to help with the basket. John thought that the sight of J carrying the basket as if it were made of glass and holding Jane by the arm as if she were a posy of flowers, mincing down the London street, was one he would never forget.

One of the apprentices walked behind them, bearing a stout stick.

'She has to be accompanied now,' Mrs Hurte said. 'There are so many beggars and many of them sickly. She cannot go out alone any more.'

'J will take care of her,' John said reassuringly. 'See how he holds her arm! And see him with that basket!'

'He's a taking young man,' Josiah Hurte remarked pleasantly. 'We like him.'

'He's very much in love with your daughter,' John said. 'Are you in favour of a match?'

The mercer hesitated. 'Would he remain in the service of the duke?'

'I have some rented fields, and some land I bought on the advice of my old master, the earl. I have the fee for a Whitehall granary –'

'You are a garneter?' Josiah interrupted, surprised.

John had the grace to look embarrassed. 'It is a sinecure. I don't do the work but I have the pay for doing it.'

Josiah nodded. His daughter's future father-in-law was benefiting from the very system he condemned: places and work given to men who knew nothing about the trade, who had no intention of learning, who subcontracted the task and kept the inflated pay.

'But our main work is in the duke's gardens,' John continued smoothly. 'The planning and planting of his gardens and the collection in his cabinet of rarities. J has served his apprenticeship under me and will follow me into the place at my death.'

'I would be unhappy at Jane joining the duke's household,' the man said frankly. 'His reputation is bad.'

'With women?' Tradescant shook his head. 'My lord duke can have the pick of every lady at court. He does not trouble his servants.' He felt the pain beneath his ribs as he spoke. 'He is a man very well loved. He does not need to buy his pleasure from his servants.'

'Could she practise her religion in your house, as she wishes?'

'Providing that she gives no offence to others,' John said. 'My wife is of a Puritanical bent, her father was vicar at Meopham. And you know J shares your convictions.'

'But you do not?'

'I worship on Sundays in the Church of England,' John said. 'Where the king himself prays. If it is good enough for the king it is good enough for me.'

There was a discreet pause. 'I think we might differ as to the king's judgement,' Mr Hurte volunteered. His wife, sitting lacemaking at the fireside, gave him a sharp look and clattered the bobbins together on the pillow.

'But enough of that,' he said swiftly. 'You're the duke's man and I've nothing to say against that. It is my daughter's happiness we must consider. Does J earn enough to keep a wife?'

'He draws a full wage,' John said. 'And they would live with us.

I will see that she does not want for anything. Will she bring a dowry?'

'Fifty pounds now, and a third share of my shop at my death,' Josiah answered. 'They can have the wedding here and I will treat them.'

'Shall I tell J he can propose, then?' John asked.

Josiah smiled. 'If I know my daughter, he has already done so,' he said as they shook hands.

Spring 1628

Jane Hurte and young John Tradescant were married in the city church of St Gregory by St Paul. The officiating priest neither wore a surplice nor did he turn his back on the congregation to prepare communion as Archbishop Laud had ordered. The communion table was placed where tradition said it should be: at the head of the aisle, close to the communicants. And the vicar stood behind it, facing them like a yeoman of the ewry laying the lord's table, doing his work in full sight of the congregation, and not like some secret Papist priest hidden behind a screen, muttering over bread and wine and incense and water, with his back turned to the people he should be serving and his hands busy doing nobody knew what.

It was a good Baptist wedding and John, watching the priest about his business, serving his God and his congregation in the sight of them both, remembered the church at Meopham and his own wedding, which had been conducted the same way, and wished that Archbishop Laud had left things as they were, and not put honest men like him and Josiah Hurte on either side of a new divide.

Josiah Hurte gave them a good wedding dinner as he had promised and both sets of parents, the apprentice boys, and half a dozen friends saw the young couple into their wedding chamber and put them to bed.

John, in the bed chamber overlooking the street with Elizabeth sitting in the four-poster bed behind him, was reminded of his own wedding night. 'D'you remember, Lizzie?' he asked Elizabeth. 'What a misery it was?'

She nodded. 'I'm glad it has been quieter for our John. And I don't think anyone would dare make a game of Jane, she is a strong-minded young woman.'

'You won't mind her coming into your house?'

Elizabeth shook her head. 'She's a pleasant girl, and I will enjoy having someone to talk to during the day when you and J are both out.' She turned back the cover on the bed. 'Come to bed, husband, we have done a good day's work today.'

Still he lingered at the window, looking down at the cobbled London street, empty except for a scavenging cat, silent except for the occasional call of the night watchman. 'You have been a good wife to me, Elizabeth. I am sorry if I have ever grieved you.'

'And you have been a good husband to me.' She hesitated. The other love and the vow of love till death was still between them, even on this day. 'Shall you call to see the duke to see if he needs any service before we go back to New Hall?'

'He's hunting at Richmond,' John answered. 'And I may not go to him until he sends for me.'

'When will he send for you again?'

'I don't know.'

She slipped from the bed and stood beside him, her hand on his shoulder. The draughts from the window were icy but John was not aware of them.

'Did you part on bad terms?' she asked. 'Is that why he never sends for you now? And why you are waiting and waiting for him and why you look so pained when someone mentions his name?'

'We parted on no terms at all,' John said heavily. 'He dismissed me. There are no terms between us but those of a master and his man, it was I who forgot my place and he did right to remind me. You would have thought I would have known, wouldn't you, Elizabeth?' He shot her a brief unhappy smile. 'Trained with Cecil. You would have thought that of all the men in England I would have known that you can be close to a great man, you can be in his confidence. But he is always the great man and you are always his servant.'

'You forgot that?' she asked gently.

'I was reminded quick enough,' John said quietly. The dismissal on the quayside when Buckingham had turned from him to his wife and the courtiers was still as sharply painful as when it had happened. 'But he was in the right and I in the wrong. I thought I would stay with him but he did not need me. And still he does not need me now. He is busy with the king, with his wife, with his mistresses. He will not send for me until he needs an honest man, and he has no need of an honest man at court. Indeed, there is no room for an honest man at court.'

'I am sure he will send for you soon,' she said. It was the only comfort she could think of.

He nodded. 'Soon he will need a dog,' he said bitterly. 'And then he will remember me.'

John was wrong, the duke did not need a dog. Spring came to New Hall but not the duke. The earth warmed and John had the grass courts scythed and seedlings planted out from the nursery beds. He ordered that the roses have their spring pruning and that the buds be pinched off the fruit trees. He set charcoal burners in the hollow wall of the fruit garden to speed the fruit for his lordship to eat when he came . . . but still he did not come.

The tulips that John had bought with such joy when he and his lord had been adventurers together in Europe, gambling with the crown jewels of England, flowered in their pots and Buckingham did not even see them. As soon as the precious blooms were over John set the pots outside in the dappled shade of his own garden so that he could water them daily and watch the leaves flop and droop, and pray that deep inside the soil the bulbs were growing plump and strong.

'When will we lift them?' J asked him, eyeing the dispiriting sight of the limp leaves.

'In autumn,' John said shortly. 'And then we will know if we have made my lord a fortune, or if we have lost him one.'

'But either way he missed seeing the bloom,' J pointed out.

'He missed it,' John agreed. 'And I missed showing it to him.'

Everyone in the town of Chelmsford, in the village of Chorley, in the kitchens at New Hall, and even the shepherds in the lambing pens spoke of nothing but the king and Parliament and the quarrel between them, the king and his wife and the quarrel between them, the quarrel between the king and the French, between the king and the Spanish, between the king and the Roman Catholics, and between the king and the Puritans. Inside the enclosing walls of the duke's park they did not dare say it, but in the ale houses of Chelmsford they had a joke which went: 'Who rules the kingdom? The king! Who rules the king? The duke! Who rules the duke? The Devil!'

It would have been bad enough if it had stopped there, but the joke spread from the ale-house men to the women, who were more apt to see the work of the Devil in the gross injustice of life and took the jest too literally. From them it spread to the preachers, who knew that the Devil did his work daily, and that the richest pickings for him were around the king who could not rule his wife, nor his court, nor Parliament, nor protect his country.

They said that the duke was the most hated man in England. One of the garden lads, employed to scare crows off Tradescant's new West Indian scarlet runner beans, boasted to another that they served a man worse-hated than the Pope. Everything was blamed on the duke: the plague which was again taking hundreds of men and women already weakened by a hungry winter, the wetness of the spring which would spoil the crops in the ground, and, over and over again, the corruption of a king who surely would otherwise live in peace with his wife and strive to govern with Parliament.

The king was so desperate for money that he had called Parliament but the members, newly up from the country and determined to take a stand, had sworn that the king should have no money for any new wars without his signature on a Petition of Right. He must accept that there would be no taxes without their consent – no more illegal demands, no more royal charges, and that men who refused the whim of the king should not be sent to prison without a judge hearing their case. The king, bankrupt on his throne, was driven to assent, a grudging assent which he resisted to the last moment and regretted as soon as he had put his hand to the new contract.

Jane, on the settle at John's fireside with her husband on a stool at her feet leaning his head against her knees, read the family her father's letter.

> 'The king's consent to the Petition of Right is seen as the start of a new dawn. It is hailed as a new Magna Carta which will defend the rights of innocent people against the wickedness of those who should be their betters and their guides. They are ringing the bells while I write this to celebrate the king's agreement with Parliament at last. I wish I could say that His Majesty welcomes it as does everyone else, but he insists that it is nothing new, that there are no new freedoms, and therefore, that he is not curbed. The older men of my congregation remember that when Parliament came against Queen Elizabeth she thanked them kindly, and when she was forced to do as they wanted, she smiled as if it was her heart's desire.
>
> And the hot heads among my congregation are asking what will it take to teach this king to deal with his fellow men with respect?
>
> At all events, he is to have the money he desires, and your husband's master, the duke, is to take another campaign to Rhé . . .'

'What?' John said suddenly, interrupting Jane's reading.

'He is to take another campaign to Rhé,' she repeated.

Elizabeth glanced at her husband. 'You will never go! Not again, John. Not again, to there! Not even if he summons you.'

He jumped up from his chair and turned away from the circle of firelight and candlelight. She could see his hands, his whole body was trembling, but he spoke steadily. 'If he summons me I will have to go.'

'It will be the death of you!' Elizabeth exclaimed passionately. 'You cannot be so lucky every time!'

'It will be the death of thousands,' he said darkly. 'Whether we take the island or lose it, it will be the death of thousands. I cannot face that place again. That tiny island is like a graveyard . . . I cannot bear it!'

Abruptly he turned back to Jane. 'Does your father say why any man would want to go back there? What the duke is hoping for?'

She was pale, looking from John to Elizabeth. She thought she had never seen him in such distress before. It was as if he feared being pressganged into Hell. 'I will read you the rest of the letter,' she replied, smoothing it on her lap.

'. . . the duke is to take another campaign to Rhé to wipe out the disgrace of failure and to show the French that we mean to be masters. No men are volunteering, but the pressgangs are making the streets unsafe for everyone except for those actually dying of the plague. Everyone else is taken up and sent to Portsmouth and they are cursing the duke's name.

These are hard times for us all. I pray that your husband and your father-in-law are spared the duke's demands. I have today lost my apprentice boy George whom I loved like a son. He will never survive a campaign, he has a weak chest and coughs all the winter long. Why take a lad of sixteen who will be dead before they reach their destination? Why take a boy who only knows about cotton, linen, and silk?

I am going to Portsmouth myself to see if I can find him and bring him back but your mother says, rightly, that we must tell his parents that he is as good as dead and pray for his immortal soul.

It is a bitter thing that a country which could be at peace is constantly at war, and that a country which could be prosperous is never well-fed.

I am sorry to send you such bad news, my blessings on you all, Josiah Hurte.'

'I will go in your stead,' J said steadily. 'When he sends for you.'

'He may not send . . .' Elizabeth suggested.

'He always sends for my father when it is work that needs a trustworthy man,' J said swiftly. 'When it is dangerous or difficult, when he needs a man who loves him above everything else. A man to do work that no-one else would do.'

John shot him a look.

'It's true,' J maintained. 'And he will send for you again.'

'You cannot go,' Elizabeth breathed. 'The mission is bound to fail again and you will risk your life for nothing.'

'My John can't go,' Jane said suddenly. She made a small betraying movement, her hand to her belly. 'I need him here.' She flushed. 'We need him here. He is to be a father.'

'Oh, my dear!' Elizabeth stretched across the fire and held Jane's hands in her own. 'I am so glad! What a blessing.'

The two women remained clasped for a moment, and Elizabeth closed her eyes in a swift silent prayer. John watched them with a weary sense of exclusion from the world of small joys. 'I am glad for you,' he said levelly. 'And Jane is right, I cannot go with a baby on the way. If he sends for me, it will have to be me.'

The little family was silent for a moment. 'Perhaps he will not send for you?' Jane asked.

John shook his head. 'I think he will. And I have promised to go whenever he calls me.'

'To your death?' J demanded passionately.

John raised a weary face to his son. 'Those were the very words of my oath,' he said slowly.

Summer 1628

The message came in the middle of June, one of the best months of the year for a gardener. John had started his day's work in the rose garden, dead-heading the blowsy blooms and tossing the petals into a basket for the still room. They would be dried and used in pomanders, or for scattering in the linen cupboards to scent the duke's sheets. Or they might be claimed by the cooks and candied to decorate the duke's sweetmeats. Everything in the garden, from drowsily humming bees to falling rosy pale petals, was the duke's and grew for his pleasure. Except he was not here to see them.

At midday John went around to the front of the house to see the young limes, planted in the long, gently curving double avenue. He had a thought that they might grow better-shaped if their lower branches were pruned, and he had a small axe and a saw for the purpose, and a lad coming behind with a ladder. But before he had done more than whistle to the lad to set the ladder before the first tree, he heard hoofbeats.

John turned, raised his hand to shield his eyes, and saw, like a dream, like a long-awaited vision, the single rider still a mile off, his lathered horse going from grey to black as it passed from brilliant sunlight into deep green shadow down the drive. John stepped out from the shade of the trees on to the broad sunny road, waiting in the hot light for the messenger, knowing that it would be his summons, knowing that he must obey. He felt for a moment that it was Death himself, with his scythe over his shoulder, riding between the trees with the drunken bees buzzing wildly and the leaves dripping with nectar and pollen.

John felt a darkness within himself as if the shade of the limes had cast a deep green into his very blood, and a coldness which he thought must be fear. He had never known fear before in this bleak premonitory way. He understood now, for the first time, why the pressed men had whispered to him as he went through the ranks: 'Ask him to send us home, Mr Tradescant, ask him to turn back.' Now he felt as slavish as they, as unmanned as they.

The rider came slowly towards him and Tradescant put up his hand for the letter as if he were warding off a blow from a knife.

'How did you know it was for you?' the messenger asked, sliding from his horse's back and loosening the girth.

'I have been waiting for it since I heard he was returning to Rhé,' John said.

'Then you will be the only willing recruit,' the man said cheerfully. 'There were riots outside his house when the sailors heard he was taking them back there. His carriage is stoned every time he takes it out. They are saying that the expedition is cursed and that it will fall into a whirlpool which stretches down to Hell itself. They drink to his death in the ale houses, they pray for his downfall in the chapels.'

'That's enough,' John said roughly. 'Go and take your horse to the stable. I won't hear the duke traduced on his own land by his own servant.'

The man shrugged and twitched the reins over his horse's head. 'I've left his service. I am on my way to my own home.'

'You have work to go to?'

'No,' he said. 'But I'd rather beg from door to door than go with the duke to the Island of Rue. I'm not a fool. I know how it will be commanded, and how it will be paid, and what the risks will be.'

John nodded, his face betraying nothing. Then he turned away and walked from the avenue, across the grass lawn to the lake. He made his way down the pretty little path to the landing stage opposite the boat house where Buckingham used to row out on summer evenings, sometimes with his wife Kate in the stern, sometimes alone with a rod and line. John sat on the landing stage and looked across the water. The yellow flag irises were in flower as he had promised his master they would be, the fountain they had designed together played into the warm silent air of the afternoon. The water lilies he had planted bobbed gently as the wind breathed across the smooth surface of the lake, their buds just splitting to show cream and white petals. The ducks had had a second brood of ducklings and they came and quacked around him, hoping for corn. John held the letter in his hand, looking at the heavy seal on the fold of the thick cream notepaper. For a moment he did not break it, he did not shatter the impress of Buckingham's ring, for a moment he sat in the sunshine and thought what he would be feeling if this was a letter from a master who loved him, from a man who loved as an equal. How it would be for him now, if Buckingham was his lover as well as his lord.

John thought that if they were lovers still his heart would leap at the sight of the sealed note, he would be happy at being ordered to his lord's side, he would go glad-hearted, wherever he was ordered. If they were lovers he would go with his lord to the Isle of Rue, to that bleak island, to that certain death, with a sort of mad joy, that a love as encompassing and wild as theirs could only end in death and that there would be something erotic and powerful about it ending in a battle and the two of them side by side as comrades.

John rubbed his hand across his eyes. No point in dreaming like a lovesick maid and gazing out across the water. This would not be a love letter, these would be orders that must be obeyed whatever his private feelings. He tore the fold of the paper and opened the letter.

> John,
> I shall need my best travelling coach and some suits of clothes, my hats and the new diamonds. We will need a couple of cows and some hens – order everything as I would wish.
> Bring it all to me and meet me at Portsmouth, we will sail at the beginning of July without fail.
> You will sail with me and be at my side, as before. Villiers.

John read the letter once, and then read it again. It was his death warrant.

The evening was very warm. John watched the midges dancing over the still water, his legs dangling above the glassy surface of the lake like an idle boy's. Even now he found it hard to believe that he must leave all this, and never see it again. The garden he had made, the trees he had planted, the vegetables and flowers he had introduced to New Hall – to England – all this would be taken from him, and he would die on an island half-rock and half-marsh for a cause he had never believed in, serving a master who was no good.

John's long unthinking uncritical loyalty to his masters had been destroyed. And when John lost his faith in his master, he lost his faith in the world. If his master was not a better man, closer to the angels than his servant, then the king was not set higher again, even closer to heaven. And if the king was not divine, then he was not infallible, as John had always believed. And if the king was not infallible then all the questions that thinking men were posing, about the king's new powers and the king's mismanagement of affairs, were questions that John should have been asking. He should have been asking them years ago.

He felt like a fool who had neglected the chance of a great education. Cecil had been his first master and had taught him not to think of principle but of practice. If he had watched Cecil he would have seen a man who always acted in public as if the king were divine, but always plotted in private to protect him like any fallible mortal. Cecil had not been fooled by the masque of royalty, he was a man like Inigo Jones whose work was to illustrate and support it. Jones had built the staircase and a marble bathroom at New Hall, Tradescant had watched him at work. This was not a priest before the mysteries, this was a man doing a skilled job. He made a stair, he made an illusion of majesty, all the same work, all in the same day. But Tradescant, even with the example of Cecil as chief stage manager before him, had been taken in by the show and the costumes and the ingenious machinery, and had thought that he had seen gods when all that had been before him was a cunning old woman, Elizabeth; her nephew James, a lecher; and his son, Charles, a fool.

John did not feel vengeful; the habit of loving and loyalty towards his masters and beyond them to the king went too deep for that. He felt that he would have to endure the loss of faith as if it were his own fault. To lose faith in the king and his lord was very like to losing faith in God. It was gone but a man still went through the rituals of attendance, and hat-doffing and minding his tongue, so as not to spread doubt among others. John might doubt his lord and his king but no-one beyond his immediate family would ever know it. He might doubt that God had ordered him to obey the commandments or had recently included a commandment to obey the king, but he would not stand up in church and deny God when the preacher recited the new prayers for the king and queen which had been added as a collect for the day. John had been raised to be a man of loyalty and duty, he could not step out of his track just because his heart was broken and his faith gone.

For the duke his lover he thought he would never feel anything but a pain where his heart should be, and ice where his blood should be, and an ache where his belly should be. He did not blame his lord for turning away from his gardener to the court. The very suggestion was a foolish one. Of course Buckingham would cleave to the court, however well he was loved by his servants. It was Tradescant who blamed himself for forgetting that the man he loved was a great man, a man of the highest degree in the land, second only to the king. It was folly to think that he would need Tradescant in the days of his glory as he had needed him in the days of the voyage home when the ghosts of the men they had left behind cried every night in the rigging.

As John gave the orders in the stable and the big house to get the carriage ready, as he rode down to Manor Farm and requisitioned two cows in milk, he knew that Buckingham had forgotten him as a lover but trusted him completely as a servant, the most faithful servant of them all who would do everything, and overlook nothing.

Buckingham believed that John was his faithful servant; and Buckingham was right. As John ordered them to pack the duke's best clothes, and put the diamonds in a purse to wear around his own neck, he knew that he was acting the part of a faithful servant, and that he would act that part until he died. He would take the travelling coach and the clothes, the hats and the new diamonds, some cows and some hens, all the long way down the road to Portsmouth, see them loaded with the pressganged soldiers on the *Triumph* and set sail with them to his death.

'We will go to our deaths like herded cattle,' John said quietly to himself as he watched them pull the great travelling coach from the stables and start to polish the gilded ornaments on the corners of the roof. 'Like the milch cows which low as they are pushed on board. I am bound by my oath that I will be his until death, and I see now that this was what he meant. He will never have finished with me, nor with any in his company, until we are all dead.'

He turned away, his knee aching as he walked on the uneven cobbles of the stable yard, and went round to the pleasure gardens to find J, his son, who would now inherit all that he had, and would have to become head of the little family, for John was going to the war again and knew this time that he would not come back.

The pleasure garden had been laid out with fountains and waterworks designed by the engineer Cornelius van Drebbel. J had ordered the drying and cleaning of an enormous round marble bowl at the foot of a cascade, and was splashing round inside the bowl checking that it was perfectly clean before he let the water flow back in. In the heat of the day it was a pleasant job, and J was a man young enough to take pleasure in playing about with a cascade of water and calling it work. At the side of the fountain, in the shade, was a hogshead tub squirming with carp waiting to be returned to the water. J looked up when he heard his father's step on the white gravel and as soon as he saw his father's face he climbed out of the marble bowl and came towards him, shaking his thick black hair like a spaniel coming out of a river.

'Bad news, Father?'

John nodded. 'I am to go to Rhé.'

J held out his hand for the letter and John hesitated only for a moment before passing it to him. J read it swiftly and thrust it back.

'Carriage!' he cried scathingly. 'Best diamonds! He has learned nothing.'

'It is his way,' John said. 'He has the grand manner and he rides out the storms.'

'Can we say you are sick?' J asked.

John shook his head.

'I will go in your place, I mean it.'

'Your place is here,' John said. 'You have a child on the way, perhaps an heir for us, someone to grow the chestnut trees on.' The two men smiled at each other, and then John was grave again. 'You're well-provided for, there's our own land, and the fee from the Whitehall granary. There's our own cabinet of curiosities, I know they are nothing much yet but you could raise a few pounds on them if you're ever in need, and with the training you have had under me. at Lord Wootton's garden and here, you could work anywhere in Europe.'

'I won't stay with the duke,' J said. 'I won't stay here. I shall go to Virginia where there is neither a duke nor a king.'

'Yes,' Tradescant said. 'But, of course, he may not come back from Rhé, either.'

'He came home last time without a scratch on him and was greeted in triumph,' J said resentfully.

'Don't make an enemy of him.'

'He has taken my father away from me for years,' J said. 'And now he wants to take you to your death. How do you think I feel?'

John shook his head. 'Feel as you like. But don't make an enemy of him. If you go against him, you go against the king and that is treason and mortal danger.'

'He is too great for me to challenge, I know that. He is too great altogether. There is not a man in England who does not hate and fear him, and now we are to go to war under him again when we know he does not know how to command, he cannot organise supplies, he cannot order an attack, he does not know how the business should be done. How should he know? He was a country squire's son and got his place by his skill in dancing and talking . . . and sodomy.'

John flinched. 'Enough, J. Enough.'

'I wish to God we had never come here,' the younger man said passionately.

349

John looked back down the years to the moment that he first saw Buckingham as green as a sapling in the dark allee at New Hall. 'We wanted the best gardens in the country. We had to come here.'

The two men were silent.

'Will you tell Mother?' J asked eventually.

'I'll tell her now,' John said. 'She'll be grieved. You will keep her to live with you and provide for her well when I am gone, J.'

'Of course,' J said.

Elizabeth packed John's clothes in silence, including his winter boots and warm cloaks and blankets.

'I probably won't need those, we will be back before autumn,' John said, trying to be cheerful.

She was folding his clothes and putting them into a big leather sack. 'He will never sail on time,' she said. 'He never does. Nothing will be ready on time and you will be sailing out into the autumn storms, and setting siege as winter comes. You will need your warm cloak, and Jane's father has sent me a bolt of oilskin to wrap your clothes in and try to keep them dry.'

'Are you nearly ready? I have his wagons loaded and his coach is ready to go.'

'All finished.' She pulled the drawstring tight.

He held out his arms to her and she looked at him, her face very grave. 'God bless you, my John,' she said.

He wrapped his arms around her and felt the familiar warmth of the band of her cap and her smooth hair against his cheek. 'I am sorry for the grief I have given you,' he said, his voice choked. 'Before God, Elizabeth, I have loved you dearly.'

She did not reprove his swearing, but tightened her grip around his waist.

'Look after my grandchild,' he said, and tried to make a joke: 'And my chestnut trees!'

'Don't go!' she cried suddenly. 'Please, John, don't go. You can get to London and on a ship to Virginia in a day and a night, before he even knows you have left him. Please!'

He put his hands behind his back and unfastened her fingers. 'You know I cannot run away.'

He picked up his bag and went down the stairs, his tread uneven as the arthritis in his knee made him limp. She stayed where she was for a moment, and then ran after him.

Buckingham's great carriage was drawn up outside their little cottage, but John could not ride in it without the lord's express permission, and Buckingham had forgotten to tell John he could travel in comfort. John slung his bag in the back of the carter's wagon and cast an experienced eye over the armed men who would ride before and after him, to guard the duke's treasures against violent beggars, highwaymen, or a mob that might rise up against the sight of his crest in any of the towns on the way.

John pulled himself up beside the carter on the wagon's driving seat and turned to wave to Elizabeth. J and Jane stood beside her at the cottage doorway, looking out as John gave the signal for the carriage and the wagons to move.

He meant to call out, 'Goodbye! God bless!', but he felt the words stick in his throat. He meant to smile and wave his hat so that the last sight they had of him was that of a cheery smile and a man going willingly. But Elizabeth's white face pierced him like a knife and he could only pull his hat from his head as a mark of respect for her and let the wagon pull out, and away from her.

He turned in his seat and watched them grow smaller and smaller, obscured by the dust of the luggage train, until the wagon turned the corner into the great avenue and he could see them no more. He could not even hear the bees above the rumble of wheels, and he had never smelled the heady perfume of the limes.

Buckingham was not at Portsmouth, as he had said he would be. The fleet was ready, the sailors on board, every day that he did not come the murmurings grew worse and the officers resorted to harsher and longer whippings to keep the men in order. The army melted away daily, the officers scouring the towns and the roads to the north of the city to arrest ploughboys and shepherd boys and apprentices who were running for their lives away from the ships that waited, bobbing at the harbour wall, for the commander who did not come.

John saw the duke's coach loaded aboard but kept the purse of diamonds on a string about his neck. The cows and the hens he penned up on Southsea Common and he took himself a lodging nearby. The landlord was surly and unhelpful, he had had soldiers billeted on him for months and his bills were never paid. John paid him directly from his own money, even though he knew that Buckingham would not remember to reimburse him, and then the man served him a little better.

On 19 July the king came riding down to inspect the fleet. The winds were blowing off shore, the ships were straining at their ropes as if they were willing to go, even if the men aboard had sulky faces. The king looked the ships over, but this time there was no handsome dinner on board the *Triumph*. All of them, even the king himself, waited for the Lord High Admiral.

He did not come.

John thought of his wife's prediction that they would not sail until autumn and went out to the hills beyond the city and bought a wagon-load of hay for the cows.

The king left Southwick and went hunting in the New Forest. He had no objection to the fleet being delayed while Buckingham went about his business in London. Other men would have risked a charge of treason and imprisonment in the Tower as a punishment for keeping the king waiting for an hour, but it seemed that Buckingham could do nothing that would offend the king. His Majesty laughed and said that the duke was a laggard, and spent the night at Beaulieu and hunted deer. The sport was good and the weather stood fair. On board the ships the soldiers, cooped up in their quarters, sweated in the crowded heat, and many had to be carried out suffering from seasickness or worse. The crews and the soldiers ate up the provisions which had been laid aboard for the voyage, and the ships' stewards had to go out into Hampshire and Sussex to buy more food to re-stock the ships. Prices went up in the local markets and the little villages could not afford bread at the rate the fleet could pay.

Buckingham was cursed at a hundred hungry firesides. And still he did not come.

John wrote to his wife that perhaps the whole thing would blow over. The fleet would not sail without the Lord High Admiral, and the Lord High Admiral did not come for the whole of July. Perhaps, John thought, he was bluffing, and had never meant to sail. Perhaps he was wiser and more skilful than anyone had allowed, as cunning as Cecil. Perhaps all this preparation, all this fear, all this grief, had been to give substance to the most tremendous trick of all time – frightening the French into withdrawing from La Rochelle without a shot being fired, without the expedition even leaving port. John remembered the trickery and mischief in Buckingham's smile, his cleverness and his wit, and thought that if any man could win a war without sending his fleet out, Buckingham was the man.

John paid his landlord for the month of August and began to wonder if he might be spared. On the hot summer mornings he awoke with such a desire to live that he could taste it on his tongue, like lust. He walked on the harbour walls and looked out to sea. He felt the light touch of linen on his sun-warmed skin and the warm air on his face and felt like a youth, faint with awareness of his own beauty, of his own health. He walked on the pebbles of the seashore, sending flocks of grey- and brown-backed dunlin scattering before him, and felt the life pulsing through his body from his boots to his fingertips. On a fine day he could see the Isle of Wight in its green loveliness, and John thought he might take a little ferry boat over to the island and hunt for new plants folded in the secret hollows of its chalk downs.

He walked inland north of the city, where there were great forests. John walked under the branches and remembered his hunt for Sir Robert Cecil's trees and the long journeys with the heavily laden carts. Sometimes he saw red deer and roe deer, always he watched his feet for a new fern, a new flower.

He did not walk to the east – there was a foul ill-drained marsh on that side of the city, lonely with the cry of wading birds and treacherous with tracks and deceptive paths. It stank of mud and decay under the hot summer sunshine, and when the heat haze shimmered above it he could not tell where the water began and the land melted unreliably away. In the drier fields the red poppies nodded their heads. It reminded John too much of their destination. He hated the flicker of sunlight on mud and water now, it was the light of death, he thought. After he had walked once to Farlington marshes he never went that way again.

Buckingham did not come until the end of August, just as the captains and officers were talking of having to disband for the winter rather than throw bad money after good on an expedition which was clearly not going to depart. Another month and the weather would break, it could take days to get out of harbour in the autumn, and no fleet could risk being separated running before a storm. It would be too late, it was too late, surely the Lord Admiral would be bound to see that it was too late – and then he came, sunny, smiling, delightful, in his best coach from London, and took breakfast at Captain Mason's house in the High Street, as blithe and merry as if that had not been the very house where he had washed his hands of the blood of his soldiers the last time he came back from Rhé.

The rumour that Buckingham had arrived in the city reached Tradescant as he fed the last of his hay to the cows. For a moment he shuddered as if someone had walked on his grave. It was both a premonition of death, and a flicker of desire. John shook his head at his own folly, brushed down his suit of clothes, put on his hat, and walked around to the High Street.

The house was crowded, the outer courtyard filled with officers waiting for news and the usual hangers-on and favour-seekers. One man put his hand on Tradescant's sleeve as he pushed through.

'He's come to cancel the sailing, hasn't he?'

'I don't know. I have not spoken with him.'

'The captain of the *Triumph* says that they'll need to re-victual and re-water before they sail. And there's no money to pay the chandlers. We'll have to delay until the spring.'

'I don't know,' Tradescant replied. 'I don't know any more than you do.'

The man slipped away in the crowd, and Tradescant pushed further in. A man ahead of him turned at the tap on his shoulder and Tradescant recognised him.

'Mr Tradescant!'

'It's Felton, isn't it? That was made captain?'

At once John saw that something was terribly wrong. The man's face was pale, and two deep lines grooved either side of his mouth. 'What's the matter? Are you ill?'

He shook his head. 'I prayed that I might take it, but I did not. She died in my arms.'

John edged slightly back. 'Who died?'

'My wife. Oh! you need not fear I carry it. They put us out of the village, both of us, and did not let me back into my house until I had buried her on the cold ground where she lay and stripped myself naked and burned my clothes. Then they let me into my home, walking as naked as a sinner. But when I got back into the house, d'you know what I found?'

John shook his head.

'My little daughter, dead of hunger, behind the locked door. No-one had gone in to feed her, they were all afraid of catching the plague, and besides, there was no food in the whole village.'

John was silent, facing the horror of the man's story.

'I was never paid, you see,' Felton said, his voice a dull monotone. 'Not the captain's pay that was promised me, not the lieutenant's pay that I had earned. Not my campaign money, not my discharge money. Not a penny. When I came home to my wife and daughter I had nothing but my Lord Admiral's promise, and we could not eat that. When she sickened, I could not buy physic for her, I could not even buy food. When she died I had to bury her in the ground where she lay.'

He laughed shortly. 'And they've enclosed it now. I cannot even get in to put up a cross at her head. It was common land. I thought I would plant a rose bush beside her grave, but now it is a sheep run, and my lord's beasts patter over her sleeping face.'

John found he was scowling. 'Before God I am sorry for you,' he said.

'And now we are to sail again,' Felton went on, his eyes burning in his white face. 'Back to that damned island. It is all to be as it was before. More death, more pain, more folly. We will have to do it all again, and again and again until he has his fill of it.'

'Are you serving?' John asked.

'Who would go willingly who had been there once before? Would you?'

John shook his head. 'I am bound by a promise to go,' he said.

'And I am bound by a promise too,' Felton said. 'A different promise from you, I should think. A sacred promise to God.'

John nodded. 'I will speak with him, when I can get near him,' he said. 'I will not forget you, Felton. You shall have your pay and perhaps you can start again somewhere . . .'

'He has forgot me,' Felton cried passionately. 'But I will remind him. I will tell him what he has cost me, I will give him pain for pain.'

'That's not the way. Be still, Felton, he is the duke, you cannot fight him any more than you can fight the king. He is untouchable.'

Felton shook his head in brief disagreement and turned away. Tradescant looked after him, saw the hunched shoulders and the way his hand strayed to his pocket and saw the outline, through the ragged clothes, of a knife. He glanced around. The place was packed with the duke's retainers. When he saw one of the officers he could trust, he would warn him that Felton should be watched, and gently hustled out of the house. Then, when he had the duke's ear, he would tell him that the man must be paid, must be compensated. That men who had followed the duke to certain death, and who had seen their comrades die beside them, could not be cast off as lightly as a mistress forgets an old lover who has fallen from favour.

There was a roar of laughter from the inner room and then a bellowing of a toast. Tradescant knew that his lord must be inside, at the heart of the party. Now he was near to seeing him again he found that his palms were wet with sweat and his throat dry. He rubbed his hands on his breeches, swallowed, and then pushed through the crowd, through the open double door and into the room.

The duke was seated at a table, a map spread before him, his green jacket ablaze with diamonds, his dark hair tumbled about his perfect face, laughing like a boy.

John fell back at the sight and a man behind him swore as he bumped into him, but John heard nothing. He had thought that he knew every line, every plane, of that face, from the untroubled forehead to the smooth cheekbones, but when he saw Buckingham again, in his vitality, in the brilliance of his beauty, he realised he had remembered nothing, only a shadow.

John felt himself smiling, then beaming, at the very sight of the man, and felt a blaze through his body which was not fear or resentment or hatred, but was joy, a wild intractable joy, that there should be such beauty in the world, that there should be such grace. That such a man had once loved John and taken him into a place where pain and pleasure were one. And at the moment, the long intervening months seemed a small price to pay for having once, just once, been the lover of such a man. As in a dream he saw Buckingham laughing at the head of the table, his black curls thrown back from his face, his black eyes glinting and that exquisite face flushed with wine and laughter; and at the same time he saw him leaning close in the shadowy light of the gilded cabin where the horn lantern swung on its hook with the haunting rhythm of the waves as if it were dancing with their blended shadows.

'Ah, it's you,' John said with a deep glad sense of recognition and felt that his world, which had been upside-down since he had lost his master, was suddenly powerfully restored to him. He knew it was love, besotted, impossible love, and could feel no shame, nor any sense that it was wasted love. Its very madness was part of the joy of tasting it. It was the taste of life at the very edge of life. It was love as few men ever know it. It was passion, rare passion. A desire that does not even look for return, but is worth all the pain for the few moments of joy, and for knowing that joy to the edge of madness is a possibility. Without this love Tradescant thought he would have lived a quieter life, a steady life. With it he had been ablaze, in the very heart of the furnace of feeling.

Buckingham had not seen him. He was laughing with the gentlemen around him. 'I swear it,' he shouted over the noise. 'I will be avenged. We have been wronged by France and I will have satisfaction.'

Another great shriek of approval drowned out his words. Tradescant watched, smiling, as the duke shook back his black curls and laughed again. 'I have the ear of the king!' he said.

'Aye, and other parts!' came a bawdy yell.

Buckingham grinned but he did not disagree. 'Does anyone doubt that if I wish it we will be at the doors of Paris this time next year?' he said. 'I say we will return to France, and not stop at some pox-ridden island but we will march on Paris itself and I will have my revenge.'

Tradescant pushed his way further into the room. The men were a wedge of scented velvet and rich linen – the duke's aristocratic friends and courtiers, who had been waiting and waiting in Portsmouth to give him a hero's send-off. As they unwillingly stood aside Buckingham caught the movement and glanced down the room. His eyes met John's and for a moment, for one blissful moment, there was nothing and no-one but the master and the man looking at each other with a deep connection.

'My John,' Buckingham said softly, as sweet as a whisper after his bragging of a few moments earlier.

'My lord,' Tradescant replied.

Buckingham put one hand on the table and vaulted over it to Tradescant's side. He put his hands on his shoulders.

'Did you bring everything?' he asked simply.

'I have everything you commanded,' John said steadily. There was not a word that could have betrayed them. Only the two of them knew that the duke was asking if John was still his and his alone; and John was answering: yes, yes, yes.

'Where are you lodged?' Buckingham asked him.

'At a little house on Southsea Common.'

'Get your things loaded and stowed in my cabin, we sail today.' Buckingham turned towards his place at the table.

'My lord!' At the urgency in his tone Buckingham paused.

'What is it, John?'

'Stay a moment. Go down to the harbour and listen to your commanders,' John said earnestly. 'They are saying we may not be able to sail. Take some advice, my lord. Let's proceed cautiously.'

'Cautiously! Cautiously!' Buckingham threw back his head and laughed and the room laughed with him. 'I am going to free the Protestants of La Rochelle and give the French king such a trouncing that he will regret his impertinence to us. I shall have Queen Elizabeth back on her throne in Bohemia, and I shall take the war to the very doors of Paris.'

There was a confused hurrah at the bragging. John scowled around at the gentlemen who had never been closer to a battle than a naval review. 'Don't say such things. Not here. Don't speak like this in Portsmouth. There are families here still grieving for the men who went with you last time and will never come home again. Don't jest, my lord.'

'I? Jest?' The duke's arched eyebrows flew upwards. He turned to the room. 'Tradescant thinks I jest!' he exclaimed. 'But I tell him and I tell you all that this war with France is not finished, it will not be finished until we have won. And when we have beaten them we will take on the Spanish. No Papist mob shall stand against us, I am for the true king and the true faith.'

'And where will you get your army, Steenie?' someone cried from the back. 'All the men who marched with you last time are dead or injured or sick or insane.'

'I shall pressgang them,' he cried. 'I shall buy them. I shall take them out of the gaols, and out of the hospitals for the mad. I shall order them to come on pain of treason. I shall take boys from their school desks, I shall take farmers from their ploughs. Does anyone doubt that I can force my will on this whole kingdom? And if I want to wager half of England to avenge this slight on my honour, I can do it!'

John felt as if he were clinging to a runaway horse that nothing could stop. He laid a rough hand on his lord's sleeve and pulled him close so that he could whisper in his ear. 'My lord, I beg you, this is no way to plan a campaign. It's too late in the year, we will meet the autumn storms at sea, when we get there the weather will be bitter. You remember the island, there was no shelter, there were the stinking marshes and the constant storms. They will have reinforced the citadel, and it cost us four thousand lives last time and we still came home in defeat. My lord, don't take us there. Please, I beg you, think again. Think in silence, think when you're sober, not when you have a room of puppies barking at your every word. Think, Villiers. Before God I would die rather than see you there again.'

Buckingham turned in John's grip but he did not throw off his hand, as he could have done. Just as he had done in the long-ago fruit garden beside the warmed peach trees, he put his own hand on top of John's and John could feel the warmth of the long soft fingers and the hardness of the rings.

'We have to go,' he replied, his voice low. 'A victory is the only thing which will pull me clear with the country. I would have to go if it took the life of every man in England.'

John met his lord's dark determined gaze. 'You would destroy this country for your own triumph?'

Buckingham put his mouth very close to John's ear. The silky curls tickled John's neck. 'Yes,' he whispered. 'A thousand times over.'

'Then you are mad, my lord,' John said steadily. 'And your country's enemy.'

'Then cut me down like a mad dog,' Buckingham dared him with a wolfish grin. 'Behead me for treason. Because my madness will run its course. I have to win the Isle of Rue, John. I don't care what it costs.'

It was John who drew his hand away first, it was John who broke their interlocked gaze. Buckingham let him go and snapped his fingers at one of his companions, and took his arm in John's place. 'Come,' he said. 'I must get my hair curled and then I shall sail for France.'

There was a roar of laughter and approval. Tradescant, sick and cold, turned away. The duke and his companions passed through the crowd and into the narrow corridor. One of the French officers bustled up.

'My lord duke! I bring news! The best news in the world!'

Buckingham stopped, the crowd behind him pressing forward in the corridor to hear.

'La Rochelle has broken out! The Protestants are free and the French army is defeated! The French are suing for terms.'

Buckingham reeled, fighting for sobriety. 'Never!'

'Indeed, yes!' the man declared, his English becoming less and less clear in his own excitement. 'We have won! We have won!'

'Then we need not sail,' John thought aloud. 'My God, we need not sail.'

Buckingham was suddenly powerful and decisive. 'This alters everything,' he said.

'It does,' Tradescant agreed, pushing through to his side. 'Thank God, yes. It does.'

'I must speak with the king,' Buckingham said. 'Now is the time to strike against France, we need to go at once, we need to raise a greater army. We should go through the Netherlands, and then . . .'

'My lord,' John said desperately. 'There is no need. Now we are excused. La Rochelle is free, our wrongs are avenged.'

Buckingham shook his head and laughed his wild boyish laugh. 'John, after all the trouble I have taken to get here, d'you think I shall go peaceably home again without a cannon being fired! I am wild for a fight, and the men are wild for a fight! We will go to the very heart of France. Now is the time for an all-out attack, now they are failing. God knows how far we could go. We could take and keep French castles, French lands!'

He slapped the French officer on the back and stepped forward. Felton suddenly appeared at his side, pushing through the crowd. Tradescant recognised him with a gasp of fear, saw his eyes were wild and his hand was gripped on the knife in his pocket. He saw the officer who should protect the duke lounging in the doorway, his face buried in a cup of wine.

Buckingham turned to greet a new arrival and swept his graceful bow. There was a slice of time, which seemed to hold and wait, like a petal from a blossom lingering on its fall.

Tradescant saw Felton's determined face and knew that the great love of his life, his master, was not, after all, untouchable.

'Save us from him,' Tradescant said softly. 'Do it, Felton.'

Late Summer 1628

He was dead within moments, and it was John who leaped forward to catch him, and lowered the long slim body to the ground. Even dying in pain he still had the face of the saint that King James had called him. His skin had flushed as scarlet as an embarrassed maid with the shock of the wound, and then drained white as Italian marble. John cradled his heavy lolling head and felt the smooth tumbling black curls against his cheek for the last time. There was a loud sound of hoarse dry sobbing and John realised it was his own voice, then someone pulled him away from his lord and pressed a glass of spirits into his hand and left him.

He heard the noise of Felton's capture, and the dreadful scream from Buckingham's wife, Kate. He heard the running to and fro of men who were suddenly leaderless. He sat quite still, the glass of Hollands in his hand, while the room brightened as men drifted away and the August sunshine poured uncaringly through the window. The little motes of dust danced in the sunshine as if everything was still the same; when everything was different.

When he thought he could stand, John walked to the door of the house. To his left at the end of the street, the grey wall of the harbour was still there, still crumbling and unfit. Before him the rambling skyline of ramshackle houses and beyond them the tops of the masts of the fleet, still flying Buckingham's flags. No-one had ordered them to half-mast, people were still running around, denying the news, disbelieving their own denials. It was a beautiful day, the wind still blew steadily offshore. It would have been a good day to set sail. But Buckingham and John would never set sail together again.

John walked down the High Street like an old man, his boots unsteady on the cobbles, his limp pronounced. He felt that he was stepping into a new world, governed by new rules, and he could not honestly say that he was ready for it. He pulled his hat down over his eyes to shield him from the sun's hard dazzle, and when a lad ran up and skidded to a halt before him, he shrank back, as if he too feared a blow, a fatal blow, to the heart.

'Is it true?' the boy yelled.

'What?'

'That the duke is dead?'

'Yes,' Tradescant said, his voice low.

'Praise God!' the boy sang out, and there was no doubting the relief and joy in his voice. 'It's true!' he yelled to another boy, a few yards away. 'He's dead! The Devil is dead!'

Tradescant put out his hand for the comfort of the sun-warmed wall and followed it, fingers trailing along the crumbling sandstone, like a blind man, to his lodging house. His landlord flung open the door.

'You'll know – I've heard nothing but wild rumours – is he dead?'

'Yes.'

The man beamed as if he had been given a priceless gift. 'Thank God,' he said. 'Now the king will see reason.'

John felt his way to his room. 'I am sick,' he said. 'I shall rest.'

'You'll not get much rest, I'm afraid!' his landlord said cheerfully. From the town they could hear the crackle of fireworks and a roar of cheering which was growing louder. 'The whole town is going mad to celebrate. I'm off!'

He let himself out of his front door and ran down the street to where people were embracing, and dancing on street corners. Soldiers at the quayside were blasting their muskets into the skies and women who had come to kiss their husbands goodbye, expecting never to see them again, were weeping with relief. In a dozen churches the bells tolled as if for a mighty victory.

In all the world it seemed that only Tradescant grieved, only

Tradescant and his lord lay still and silent all the long sunny joyous day.

It was not until midnight, lying in his bed, still gripping his hat in his hand, that John realised that he was free from his promise. He had been the duke's man till death, and now death had come, and he was free.

❧

Free and short of money, with no promise of wages and no job. Buckingham's widow was sick with grief and the king himself ordered her into hiding in case an assassin struck against her as well.

It was as if the world had gone suddenly mad and no-one knew what might happen next. There was no Lord High Admiral to command the expedition, there was no Lord Treasurer to keep the treasures of the kingdom, there was no chief adviser to make policy, there was no Favourite to rule everything. There was no king either, for when they gave Charles the news that Buckingham was dead he finished his prayers and went in silence to his room and locked himself away for two days and nights in silence, in darkness, and fasting.

Tradescant sometimes thought of that long royal vigil and wondered that he and the king had been together in a long night of mourning, both of them driven down into silence and grief at the loss of the most beautiful man that either of them had known; the most beautiful and the most daring and the most reckless, and the most dangerous. Tradescant knew that Buckingham would have led him to his death, and that he had only escaped through his lord's assassination. He sometimes wondered if the king felt the same, and if, during the two long days and nights of royal mourning, Charles too knew the same secret, shameful relief.

Tradescant could have left for his home at once, but he felt too frail even to start the journey. He had told Elizabeth that he was strong enough to voyage to France; but in this new life, this life without his master, he could not find the courage even to hire a wagon to go to Essex. He rested at his lodgings, and waited for his power to return. Every day he walked by the sea on the tumbled pebbles of Southsea beach and saw, on the horizon, the slow arc of Felton's knife and the cry of warning in his own throat which never came.

He regretted nothing. Somehow in his grief there was no room for regrets. Not for the way he had been loved and rejected. Nor for his oath of duty till death. Nor for the fact that a shout could have saved his lord from Felton's knife and that shout had never come. It was never a love which would linger and warm an old man. Buckingham was never a man who would age and diminish and decline. Those who loved him would always know passion and uncertainty and despair. He was not a comfortable man to love. Tradescant could think of no other end for Buckingham but one that cut him down like a rare flower in the very fullness of his beauty and which meant that those who loved him could hold him forever in their minds, like petals preserved in sand and sugar: in his perfection.

It was not until September that Tradescant could bring himself to load his wagon and start the long journey back to Essex, and by then his master's body had been taken to London and buried in Westminster Abbey followed by only a hundred mourners. Buckingham's family, his hangers-on, his courtiers, his placemen, all the hundreds and hundreds of men who had begged him for favours and counted on his support, all disappeared, melted away, denying him like a thousand false disciples at cock-crow. They sought new patrons, they tried to spot new rising stars, they tried to forget that they had promised loyalty and devotion to a man who was now everywhere despised.

The funeral was brief and unceremonious, and, like so much of his life, was a show. They buried an empty coffin and said the sacred words over a hollow box. The duke had been interred in secret, in darkness, the night before his funeral. The king's new advisers had warned him that there could be no guarantee that a mob would not rise up against the Favourite's funeral. The people of London were not satisfied with his death, they might tear the coffin open, disembowel his perfect body, and hang it out at Traitors' Gate, slash off his dead face and spike it up on Tower Bridge. The king had shuddered at the thought of it, hidden his face in his hands and left them to make what arrangements they would.

There was no money to pay the duke's servants. John went back to Captain Mason's house to find the man in charge of the expedition accounts packing his bags in panic before he could be blamed for the empty coffers. Buckingham had been trading on credit and on the promise of a certain victory, for months. The ship's master for the *Triumph* had no money either. In the end John had to sell some of Buckingham's goods to raise the money to hire the wagon to take the remainder home again. But the diamonds he kept safe in a purse on a cord around his neck. He sold the milch cow to his landlord for the rent, and he exchanged the hens for a pair of muskets. He would have to be his own guard and his own driver, he could afford no other.

He hired an open wagon with two old stubborn carthorses which had to be whipped at every crossroads to make them go ahead, and even then never went faster than an ambling stroll. John did not care how slowly they went. He sat on the driver's bench, the reins slack in his hands, watching over the hedges the late summer landscape of browning wheat and barley and scrubby hayfields roll slowly past; and knew himself to be alive because the man he had loved more than anyone in the world was dead.

J was waiting for him on the south side of Westminster Bridge where John always changed his horses. He stepped out of the doorway of the inn when he heard the rumble of the wagon and came to the driving box. He had expected to find a broken man; but was surprised. John Tradescant looked relieved, as if some burden had been lifted from him.

'J,' John said with quiet pleasure.

'Mother said to meet you and bring you to the Hurtes'.'

'Is she well?'

'Worried about you, but well enough.'

'And Jane?'

'Grown very stout around the middle.' J flushed with embarrassment and pride. 'When I put my hand on her belly the little lad kicks back at me.'

John found that he was smiling at the thought of J's baby.

'And are you well, Father? We heard the news at New Hall. Were you with the duke?'

John nodded. 'I am well,' he said shortly.

'Did you see him?' J asked, curiosity overcoming him. 'Were you there when he died?'

John nodded. He thought he would remember for ever that timeless long moment when he could have cried out a warning; but instead he gave the word for the blow. 'I was there.'

'Was it very dreadful?'

John thought of the beauty of the duke, of the smooth slow arc of the knife, of the exclamation of surprise, of the duke's one word, 'villain', and then his sinking down, his limp weight in Tradescant's arms.

'No,' he said simply. 'He fell in all his beauty and his pride.'

J was silent for a moment, comparing his father's loss with the country's joy. 'I'll never work for a master again,' he vowed.

John looked down at him from the box, and J suddenly had a sense that there was more to the death of Buckingham than he would ever know, that there was more between the two men, master and vassal, than had ever been clear.

'Nor will I,' said John.

J nodded and swung up on to the box seat beside his father. 'There's another cart stored at the Hurtes',' he said. 'Goods from India and from the west coast of Africa, sent for my lord Buckingham. He won't want them now.'

John nodded and said nothing as J steered the cart carefully through the swarm of pedestrians, barrow boys, sellers, loiterers, idling militia men, to the Hurtes' door. At the rear of the house was a small yard for unloading and a couple of stables. The cart, loaded with treasures for Buckingham, was standing on the cobbles with a lad beside it to keep watch. J drew up alongside and helped his father down. John had to lean heavily on him when his feet touched the cobbles.

'I'm stiff from sitting too long,' John said defensively.

'Oh, aye,' J said sceptically. 'But how ever would you have managed a long sea voyage and then sleeping on the ground with winter coming? It would have been the death of you! It's a blessing you didn't go.'

John closed his eyes for a moment. 'I know it,' he said shortly.

J led the way through the storeroom at the back of the shop and up the stairs to the living quarters. As they came into the parlour Elizabeth started forward and flung herself into her husband's arms. 'Praise God you are safe,' she cried, her voice choked with tears. 'I never thought to see you again, John.'

He rested his cheek against the smoothness of her hair and the crisp laundered edge of her cap, and thought, but only for a moment, of a warm perfumed riot of dark curls and the erotic scratch of stubble. 'Praise God,' he said.

'It was a blessing,' she said.

John met Josiah Hurte's gaze over the top of his wife's head. 'No, it was an ill business,' he said firmly.

Josiah Hurte shrugged. 'There are many that are calling it a divine deliverance. They are saying that Felton was the saviour of his country.'

'They are praising a murderer then.' Inside John's head he could see Felton's pale determined face at the moment when John could have called out, and did not. 'It was a sin, and any that stood by and failed to prevent it are sinners too.'

Elizabeth, skilled with years of experience in reading John's moods, pulled back a little so that she could see his grim expression. 'But you could not have stopped it,' she suggested. 'You were not the duke's bodyguard.'

John did not want to lie to her. 'I could have stopped it,' he said slowly. 'I should have been closer to him, I should have warned him about Felton. He should have been better guarded.'

'No point in blaming yourself,' Josiah Hurte said briskly. 'Better thank God instead that this country is spared a war and that you are spared the danger.'

Elizabeth said nothing, she looked into her husband's face. 'Anyway, you are free now,' she said quietly. 'Free from your service to him, at last.'

'I am free at last,' John confirmed.

Mrs Hurte gestured that he should take a place at the table. 'We have dined because we did not know when to expect you, but if you will take a bowl of broth and a slice of pie, I can have it before you at once.'

John sat at the table and the Hurtes' maid brought him small ale and food. Josiah Hurte sat opposite him and took a pint of ale to keep him company.

'No-one knows what will happen to the duke's estate,' Josiah said. 'The family is still in hiding, and the London house is quite shut up. The servants have been turned away, and there's no money to pay the tradesmen.'

'There never was any,' John remarked wryly.

'It may be that the family decide to sell up to cover their debts,' Josiah said. 'If they decide to honour their debts at all.'

Mrs Hurte was shocked. 'They'll never refuse to pay!' she exclaimed. 'Good merchants will go bankrupt if they renege. His lordship had run bills for years, it would have been called treason to refuse him credit. What of the honest men who depend on his widow paying them?'

'They say that there is no money,' J said simply. 'I have had no wages. Have you?'

John shook his head.

'What will we do?' Jane asked. She had one hand resting on the curve of her belly, as if she would protect the baby from even hearing of such troubles.

'You can stay here,' her father offered instantly. 'If there's nowhere else you can always stay here.'

'I promised to provide for her and I will,' J said, stung. 'I can get a place at any house in the land.'

'But you swore you'd never work for a great lord again,' Jane reminded him. 'Such work leads us into vanity and no man in the king's service is to be trusted.'

John raised his head at such radical thoughts but Jane met his gaze without shrinking. 'I am only saying what everyone knows,' she said steadily. 'There are no good courtiers. There is none whom my John would happily call master.'

'I have a little land,' Tradescant said slowly. 'Some woodland at Hatfield and some fields at New Hall. We could perhaps build a house near New Hall, near my fields, and set up on our own account . . .'

Elizabeth shook her head. 'And do what, John? We have to find a business that will give us a living at once.'

There was a brief silence. 'I know a man who has a house for sale on the south side of the river, it has an established garden and some fruit trees already planted,' Josiah said quietly. 'There are fields around it that you could buy or rent as well. It was a little farm and now the farmer has died and his heirs are ready to sell. You might raise rare plants and trade as a plantsman and gardener.'

'How would we afford it?' John asked them. The purse containing the diamonds was heavy around his neck.

Elizabeth shot a quick collusive glance at her son, and then moved from the chair at the window and sat opposite her husband at the table. Her face was pale and determined. 'There is a cart full of goods in the yard below,' she pointed out. 'And another ship docked this morning with plants and curiosities for his lordship. If we sell the goods we can buy the house and the land. The rare plants and seeds you can nurse up and sell to gardeners. You've always said how difficult it is to get good stock for a garden. Remember how you travelled all around England for your trees? You could grow your stock and sell it.'

There was a tense silence in the little room. John absorbed the evidence that this was a plan, formed among the Hurtes and his family and now presented to him for his consent. He looked from Elizabeth's determined face to J's stoical blankness.

'You mean that we should take my lord's goods,' John said flatly.

Elizabeth drew in a breath and nodded.

'That I steal from him?'

She nodded again.

'I cannot believe that this is your wish,' John said. 'My lord has been dead and buried for a month and I am to steal from him like a dishonest pageboy?'

'There are the tulips,' J said in a sudden rush. His face was scarlet with embarrassment, but he faced his father as one man to another. 'What would you have had me do? The tulips were ready for lifting, they were in their bowls in our garden, the place was in uproar, men were running out of the house with wall-hangings and linen trailing behind them. I did not know what to do with the tulips. Nobody there would have nursed them up. Nobody there knew what to do with them. Nobody would advise me.'

'So what did you do?' John asked.

'I brought them with me. And more than half of them have spawned. We have nigh on two thousand pounds' worth of tulip bulbs.'

'Prices holding?' John's acumen flared briefly, penetrating his grief.

'Yes,' J said simply. 'Still rising. And we have the only Lack tulips in England.'

'How much are you owed?' Elizabeth suddenly demanded. 'In back wages? Did he pay you for the last expedition to Rhé? Did he advance you wages for this one? Did he give you money for the cost of the journey to Portsmouth? Or for your stay in Portsmouth, or this journey home? Because if he gave you nothing you will never have more from the duchess. She is in hiding and the king himself is refusing to tell anyone where she is. They say she is afraid of assassins, but we all know she is more terrified of creditors. How much are you owed, John?'

'I was not paid at midsummer,' J reminded him. 'They said they had no coin and gave me a note of promise, and I will not be paid this Michaelmas. That's twenty-five pounds I am owed. And while you were away I had to buy some plants and some saplings and they could not repay me.'

Unconsciously John put his hand to his throat where the bag of diamonds nestled warm against his skin.

'*You* cannot agree to this?' He turned to Josiah. 'It is theft.'

The merchant shook his head. 'I no longer know what is right and wrong in this country,' he said. 'The king takes money from the people without law or tradition, Parliament denies that he has the right, and so he closes Parliament and imposes the fines anyway. If the king himself can steal honest men's money then what are we to do? Your lord stole your service from you for years, and now he is dead and no-one will repay you. They will not even acknowledge the debt.'

'Stealing is still a sin,' John said doggedly.

'These are times when a man's own conscience should be his guide,' Josiah replied. 'If you think that he treated you fairly then deliver the goods to his house, pile riches upon riches and let the king take them to pay for his masques and vanities, as you know he will. If you think that the duke died owing you for your service, owing J, if you think these are times when a man does well to buy himself a little house and be his own master, then I think you would be justified in taking what you are owed and leaving his service. You should take only what you are owed. But you have a right to that. A good servant is worthy of his hire.'

'If you return the tulips to New Hall they will die of neglect,' J said quietly. 'There is no-one there to care for them, and then we will have killed the only Lack tulips in England.'

The thought of the waste of the tulips was as powerful as anything else for John. He shook his head like a bull does after a long baiting when it is so wearied that it longs for the dogs to close and make an end. 'I am too tired to think,' he said. He rose to his feet but Elizabeth's gaze held him.

'He hurt you,' she said. 'On that last voyage to Rhé. He did something to you then that broke your heart.'

John made a gesture to stop her but she went on. 'He sent you home with that pain in your heart, and then he recalled you, and he was going to take you to your death.'

John nodded. 'That's true,' he said as if it did not much matter.

'Then let him pay,' she said gently. 'Let him repay us for the grief and terror he has caused us, and I will consider the matter settled, and I will remember him in my prayers.'

John put his hand on the little purse of diamonds at his throat. 'He was my lord,' he said and they could all hear the deep pain in the back of his voice. 'I was his man.'

'Let him go in peace,' she said. 'All debts to us paid, all grievances finished. He is dead. Let him pay his debts and let us start a new life.'

'You will pray for him? And mean it in your heart?'

Elizabeth nodded.

Silently John took the purse from his neck and handed it to his wife. 'Go and see the farm,' he said. 'You decide. If you and J and

Jane like it, then buy it and we will make our home there. And in return for that you must go and pray for his soul, Elizabeth. For he needs your prayers, and there are few enough praying for him, God knows.'

'And the tulips?' J asked.

John met his son's questioning look. 'Of course we keep the tulips,' he said.

November 1628

They crossed the river at Lambeth with a waterman rowing them: Jane bulky and eight months pregnant in the stern of the boat, John, Elizabeth and J seated amidships. Elizabeth had the keys to their new home in her lap, bought outright with Buckingham's diamonds. When she turned the heavy key over and over the sun glinted on the cold metal.

On the south side of the river was the Swan Inn where J had ordered a cart to meet them. He helped Jane up and then climbed up beside her. John smiled when he saw how his son held his wife as the cart lurched in the ruts of the South Lambeth road.

The journey was a short one and none of them spoke. They were waiting for John to break the silence but he said nothing. He had handed over the diamonds and the responsibility together. He sat in the wagon as if he were convalescent, weak from a long illness. His wife and his son could take the decisions for him.

'There it is,' J said at last, pointing ahead. 'I hope to God he likes it,' he muttered in an undertone to Jane. 'He let us buy it for him, but what if he refuses us now?'

Tradescant looked at his new home. It stood with its back to the road, an old half-timbered farmhouse with criss-cross beams turning silvery grey from the weather of many seasons. The plaster between the beams had once been painted white but was mellowing to the colour of pale mud. There was a little stream running between the road and the farm, crossed by a low bridge, broad enough for a cart. John got down and walked across it alone, the others waiting for him to speak.

The garden between the road and the house was a tiny patch, overgrown with briars and nettles. Tradescant walked around the house to the front. It faced south east, placed to catch the morning and midday sun, and before it lay a good broad acre of meadow. Tradescant scuffed the heel of his boot in the soil and then bent down and inspected it. It was a dark soil, rich and easy to work. John took up a handful and rubbed it in his palm. He could grow things in this earth, he thought. Beyond the meadow was an orchard. He walked down to where the little wooden fence divided the meadow from the trees and measured it with his eyes. About two acres, he thought, and already stocked with apples, pears, and plums; and along the south-facing wall a quince tree was growing in a ragged fan beside a pair of peach trees, roughly espaliered.

John had a momentary pang of homesickness for the kitchen garden he had left behind at New Hall with the tall heated wall built to his own innovative design, and the dozens of boys to carry dung and water for the trees. He shook his head. There was no point grieving. He had left beautiful gardens before now and started afresh. The worst had been leaving Theobalds Palace for the new house at Hatfield; and in the end Hatfield had been his great pride. He could make something of this garden, which would not be on the scale of Theobalds or Hatfield or New Hall, but would be his own. The fruit from these trees would be for his table. His grandson would sit in their shade. And no man could ever order him to leave them.

John turned back to look at the house, taking in for the first time the sloping roof of red clay tiles and the handsome tall clusters of chimney pots. Before the house there was a stone-flagged area overhung by the tiled roof and railed like the side of a ship, placed to overlook the meadow and the orchard. John walked back through the overgrown grass to the house and up the three creaking steps to the terrace. He turned, leaned on the rail and looked out over his property, the first good-sized garden he had ever owned.

He felt his face creasing in a smile of satisfaction. At last he had found a place where he could put down roots and see his son and his grandson secure in their future.

J, Elizabeth and Jane came around the corner of the house to see John leaning against the pillar of the terrace and surveying his acres.

'It's like the deck of a ship,' Jane observed perceptively. 'No wonder you look at home.'

'I shall call it the Ark,' John said. 'Because we have come to it, two by two, to be safe from the deluge that is threatening the whole country, and because it will be an ark of rarities, which we will carry safe through the troubled times.'

They moved in at once. John drew up plans for the garden, and sent to Lambeth for a couple of lads to dig and weed in the orchard, and to a nearby farm for the loan of a horse and a plough to turn over the earth before the house. They planned a garden that would grow fruit and herbs for selling in London, where good quality provender could command high prices. But also they knew that every gardener in the kingdom would long for a chestnut tree, for a double plum, for the Russian larches. It was the launching of a trade which was in its infancy. Every good gardener had spare stock of ordinary plants, the excessive bounty of God saw that where there was one plant there were a hundred seeds in the autumn. Every successful gardener exchanged stock or sold it at a profit to other gardeners. But what they longed for was the rare, the exotic, the strange. When John had worked for a lord it was part of his task to ensure that the gardens were full of rarities and he had guarded his seeds and saplings, and given them away to only his dearest of friends like the herbalist John Gerard or the gardener John Parkinson. Now he could sell them to men who had begged him for a cutting only a few years earlier. Now he could sell them to any gardener who might write to him, and already there were letters from all over England, even from Europe, asking Tradescant for seeds and saplings and yearling plants.

John had plans also for the house. He commissioned a builder to construct a new wing which would nearly double the size of the house.

J took him to one side while the men were unloading a wagon of furniture, and spoke to him urgently while Jane and Elizabeth went to and fro watching the stowing of trunks.

'I know this is to be our family home, but we don't need to build it all at once,' he said. 'The windows you have planned for the downstairs room will go from ceiling to floor. How will we ever afford the glass? And what if it breaks?'

'You will be bringing up a young family here,' John said to J. 'It's time you had some room to yourselves. And we need a good-sized room, a handsome room, for the rarities.'

'But Venetian windows . . .' J expostulated.

John laid a finger to his nose. 'This is to be my rarities room,' he said. 'We'll store them here in a beautiful room and show them to people who come to see them. We'll charge them sixpence each to enter, and they can stay as long as they like and look around at the things.'

J was uncomprehending. 'What things?'

'The two wagons of Buckingham's rarities,' John explained precisely. 'What did you think to do with them?'

'I thought we would sell them,' J confessed, a little shamefaced. 'And keep the money.'

John shook his head. 'We keep them,' he said. 'They will be the making of us. Rare plants in the garden, rare and beautiful things in the house. It is our ark with rare and lovely things. And every day the ships come in with more things ordered by my lord duke. We shall buy them on our own account and set them in our room.'

'And we charge people for looking?'

'Why not?'

'It just seems so odd. I've never heard of such a thing before.'

'My lord duke kept his cabinet of curiosities for his friends to look at and enjoy. And the Earl Cecil before him.'

'He didn't charge them sixpence a time!'

'No, but we will open our doors to ordinary people. To anyone who wishes to come and see. Not friends of ours, or even people with letters of introduction. Just anyone who is curious about wonderful and peculiar things. We let them come!'

'But how would they know of it?'

'We will speak of it everywhere. We'll make a catalogue so people can read of all the things we have on show.'

'D'you think people would come?'

John nodded. 'In Leiden and Paris the universities have great collections and they show them to the students, and to anyone who applies to see them. Why not here?'

'Because we are not a university!'

John shrugged. 'We have a collection which is equal to my lord Cecil's, and many men admired that. We make a beautiful room with the big things hanging from the ceiling and displayed on the walls and the small things bedded in little drawers in big cabinets. Seeds and shells, clothing and goods, toys and ingenious things. I'm sure we can do it, J. And it will mean that we are earning money in the autumn and winter when the garden work is less.'

J nodded but then remembered the cost of the panes of glass. 'But Venetian windows are not necessary . . .'

'We need good light if we are to show rarities,' John said firmly. 'This is not some little petty fusty cabinet. This is the first rarities show in the country, it will be one of the first things to see in London. A grand room with the things laid out handsomely. People will not come to see them at all if they are not housed in a proud and handsome manner. Venetian windows and waxed floors! And sixpence a head!'

J deferred to his father's judgement, and only muttered about grand schemes and a duke's tastes over his dinner that night, but the two men clashed again when J, trundling a sapling in a barrow around the wall of the new wing, glanced up and saw the stonemason fixing in place a handsome coat of arms.

'What are you doing?' he yelled upwards.

The stonemason glanced down and pulled his cap to J. 'Handsome, isn't it?'

J dumped the sapling and ran to the orchard where John was at the top of a fruit-picker's ladder, pruning out the dead wood on an old pear tree. 'D'you think this can be a Spanish pear?' John asked. 'I brought one back for my Sir Robert from the Lowlands. Could they have got hold of one and planted it here?'

'Never mind that now,' J said. 'The stonemason is putting up a coat of arms on our house!'

John hung his saw on a protruding branch and turned his attention to his son. J, looking up at his father comfortably leaning against the trunk, thought that they had reversed their roles and that John was like a feckless laughing boy scrumping fruit up a tree and he was like the worried older man.

'I know,' John said with a gleam. 'Do us credit, I thought.'

'You knew?' J demanded. 'You knew he had some ridiculous coat of arms drawn up for us?'

'I don't think it's ridiculous,' John said easily. 'I drew them myself. I rather like it. Leaves as background, and then the shield laid across it with three fleurs de lys, and then a helmet on top with a little crown and fleur de lys on that.'

'But what will the College of Heralds say?'

John shrugged. 'Who cares what they say?'

'*We* will care when they fine us, and make us take it down, and humiliate us before our new neighbours.'

John shook his head. 'Not us,' he said confidently.

'But we're not gentry! We're gardeners.'

John came stiffly down his ladder and took J by the shoulder, turning him to see the house.

'What's that?'

'Our house.'

'A good-sized house, new wing, Venetian windows, right?'

'Yes.'

John turned his son southwards again. 'And what's that?'

'The orchard.'

'How big?'

'Only two acres.'

'But beyond it?'

'All right, another twenty acres . . . but Father . . .'

'We're landowners,' John said. 'We're not gardeners any more. We're landowners with duties and obligations and a large family business to run . . . and a crest of arms.'

'They'll make us take it down,' J warned.

Tradescant waved a dismissive hand and climbed slowly back up his ladder. 'Not they. Not when they see who's coming to the Ark.'

J hesitated. 'Why? Who is coming?'

'Everyone who is anyone,' John said grandly. 'And all their country cousins. When your baby is born he will grow up to be knighted, I don't doubt it. Sir John Tradescant . . . sounds very well, doesn't it? Sir John.'

'I might call him Josiah, after his other grandfather, a respected city tradesman who knows his place and is proud of it,' J said mutinously, and had the pleasure of seeing a flicker of doubt cross his father's face.

'Nonsense!' John said. 'Sir John Tradescant of Lambeth.'

December 1628

In the end, he was not Sir John Tradescant of Lambeth, nor plain John, nor even Josiah. She was Frances, and she came at four o'clock on a dark dreary December morning while J and his father drank brandy downstairs and the women and the women servants wailed and scolded and ran about upstairs until the men finally heard that tiny indignant cry.

J put down his glass with a crack and ran to the foot of the stairs. His mother was standing at the top, beaming. 'A girl,' she announced. 'A lovely dark-headed girl.'

J ran up the stairs and into Jane's bedroom.

'And Jane?' Tradescant asked, thinking of the birth of J and the dreadful pain Elizabeth had suffered, and then the news that there would be no more babies.

'She is well, thank God,' Elizabeth said. 'Resting now.'

Husband and wife met each other's gaze with a steady faithful smile. 'Our grandchild,' John said wonderingly. 'I thought I'd set my heart on a boy, but now it comes to it I am just glad that it is a girl and born sound and whole.'

'Maybe a boy next time,' Elizabeth said.

John nodded. 'There will be a next time?'

She smiled. 'I don't think this is the last time that you and J will be drinking brandy together while we women do all the work.'

'Well, amen to that. I'll send the stable boy with a message to Josiah and Mrs Hurte. They'll want to know at once.'

'Tell them to come and stay for as long as they like,' Elizabeth said. 'I can make up a bed for them in the third bedroom.'

John grinned at Elizabeth's casual use of the words 'third bedroom' as if they had never had a house with fewer than a dozen rooms. 'They could bring all their congregation as well,' he said. 'Now we live so grand.'

Elizabeth flapped her apron at him. 'Go and send your message. I have work to do.'

'God be with you, wife,' John said lovingly from the foot of the stairs. 'And give Jane my blessing. Has she named the child?'

'She wants to call her Frances.'

John went out of the front door to the veranda. The cold night air was crisp and sharp, and the stars were like pin-heads against a deep blue silk sky. The moon was down and it was too dark to see more than the weathered boards of the veranda and the spiky stalks of the fruit trees. John had planted his chestnut sapling and its first rooted cutting as a pair before the house and, two by two, a dozen cuttings from them to make a little avenue of chestnut running the length of the orchard. Their bare branches were as thin as whips against the arching cold sky.

John exhaled and his breath was a brandy-tinged cloud before his face. He thought briefly of other nights when he had watched and waited. Nights on board ship when the only sound had been the creaking and shifting of the timbers, nights when he had been on watch for icebergs in the perilous cold seas around Russia or when he had swung dizzily to and fro in the crow's nest and looked for pirate ships in the darkness of the Mediterranean waters. He thought of keeping watch in the cold wet fogs of the Ile de Rhé, and of the one, two, three nights, when he had laid naked beside his lord and watched over his precious sleep.

'Sleep well now, my lord,' he said into the silent darkness.

He thought he would carry with him always this inner life which was like grief, but which was not quite grief, which was like love, but which was not quite love, which was like homesickness, but which was not a longing for home. Now that Buckingham was dead and his goods had bought the Tradescants their ark, John felt as if all the struggle of his love for his lord was resolved. He could love him without sin, he could love him without shame. The death of his lord had been the only way out, for John, for Buckingham himself. He might grieve for it but he did not blame himself for failing to give that one word of warning. And Elizabeth was true to her promise and the duke's name was in her prayers every Sunday.

John sometimes wondered if the other man who had loved Buckingham, the King of England, felt like this; and if for him too, in the round of his court and daily pleasure and other loves and interests – birth like tonight, deaths and marriages – there was always a gap in the procession, always a face missing, that beautiful wilful angel face. And if he felt also that the world was a safer place, a calmer place, but a greyer place, without George Villiers.

John touched that face in his mind, as the king might lay his finger on the lips of a portrait as he passed it; and then he went round to the stable and rattled the door till the stable lad came tumbling down the stairs, and sent him to the Hurtes' house in London.

Frances set the house by the ears, as a new baby always does. She cried and would not settle at night, and J saw dawn after dawn from the big Venetian windows as he walked her round and round the big room which housed the rarities. Held in his arms, rocked by his continual steady pacing, was the only way she would settle, and the great rarities room was the only place in the house where Jane was not wakened by the distant sound of her cries.

'Sleep,' J would say to his wife as the wail from the crib warned them of another restless night. 'I will walk her,' and he would wrap the tiny thing in a warm blanket, throw his father's soldiering cape over his nightshirt and take her downstairs to walk and walk her around the echoing moonlit room, sometimes for an hour, sometimes for three, until she quieted and slept and he could creep back into his bedroom and lay her, as tender as a seedling, back in her little crib.

Jane did not have enough milk and Elizabeth said there was nothing for it but for her to stay in bed, eat as much as she could bear, and rest, rest, rest. 'You must think and worry no more than a milch cow,' she insisted when her daughter-in-law protested. 'Or else it will be a wet nurse for Frances.'

In the face of such a threat Jane fell back against the pillows and closed her eyes. 'I shall bring you some chicken broth at noon,' Elizabeth said. 'Sleep now.'

'Where is Frances?' Jane asked. 'With J?'

'J is sleeping like a dead man in the parlour,' Elizabeth said with a smile. 'He sat down at the table to bring the planting records up to date, and his head fell into the inkpot and he was gone. I've wrapped him with a rug and left him. Frances is with John.'

'Does John know how to care for her? Will you watch him?'

'John has his own methods,' Elizabeth said. 'But I will watch him.'

She glanced from the bedroom window and saw John and his granddaughter, but did not think she would point them out to Jane. John had strapped the baby to his back in an outlandish savage fashion that he must have seen on one of his voyages. She was wrapped in a fold of blanket against his back with two ends of the blanket knotted around his chest and two around his belly. With the baby held warm and snug against his homespun coat John was walking through the garden and down towards the orchard to see that his chestnut saplings were all surviving the frost.

Elizabeth watched for a moment, and curbed her desire to hurry out and take the child from him. The baby was not crying, John's rolling limp was soothing to her, and as he walked he was singing a low muttered song: 'Tumelty tumelty tumelty pudding . . .', a nonsense song. Frances, soothed by the gentle pressure of his warm back, lulled by the weak winter sunlight, and enjoying the irregular motion of his walk, slept and woke and slept again as John went down to the end of his orchard to check his fruit trees, and came back again.

They could not yet afford a heated wall as he had built at New Hall. But John had curtained his trees with sacking and stuffed straw gently inside the bags, hoping to keep the frost from them and to warm them a little. He used the same technique on tender new saplings, especially those that came from the Mediterranean or from Africa and probably had never felt a frost. New plants from the

Americas he thought might be a little more hardy, but anything small he planted in a new row of special beds near the house where the raised timber borders kept the soil a little warmer, and where he had great domes of glass, usually used for ripening melons, to keep the cold winds off them and to retain the weak heat of the winter sun.

Despite the duke's death the plants and the rarities still came in on the ships and most days a sailor would make his way down the Lambeth Road to tap on John Tradescant's back door and offer him some little curiosity or treasure. The duke might be collecting no more, but now the ships' captains sent goods home addressed to John Tradescant, The Ark, Lambeth, certain that when they got home Mr Tradescant or his son would offer them a fair price for whatever they had found, and that they might enjoy the pleasure of boasting that their find was the centre of the Tradescants' increasingly famous exhibition. Sometimes the goods were enormous: the skeleton jaw of a whale, or a monstrous unnamed bone. Sometimes they were tiny: a carving of a house inside a walnut. They could be stone or hide, wood or ivory, fashioned by a craftsman or thrown up by nature; the Tradescant collection was gloriously eclectic. Who cared how a thing was made or what it was? If it was rare and exotic it was of interest, it had a place somewhere in the cabinets in the great room with the great windows.

John paused in his walk and looked back at his house with pleasure. He had thought he might attempt to glaze the terrace and keep his most delicate plants there during the winter, but his pleasure in the look of his house, and his joy at sitting out on the terrace and looking out over his orchard on sunny days was too great. 'It's a fine house,' he said over his shoulder to the sleeping baby. 'A fine home for a growing family, and when you have a brace of brothers and a sister, you shall all play on the grass court before the house and I shall buy a new field for you to keep a donkey.'

Spring 1629

John's view of the house at Lambeth as an ark which would keep the family afloat during troubled times was proved before Frances was more than two months old. The king's steady resentment against the House of Commons which had traduced Buckingham and tried to impeach him, flared up again to dangerous heights at their open delight at the duke's death. The king blamed Sir John Eliot, radical leader in the House, for the assassination of Buckingham and ordered the assassin, Felton, to be tortured till he revealed the conspiracy. Only the lawyers, standing against an angry king, preserved Felton from agony and he went to the gallows swearing that he had acted only for the love of his country, and alone.

Eliot, sensing that the mood of the country was with him, pressed his advantage in the newly called House of Commons in January, refusing to pay the king one penny of his dues until the House had debated the incendiary motion that the king on earth must give way to the king of heaven – a clear call for Puritans to withstand the earthly power of the increasingly Papist Charles and his High Church bishops.

While the city seethed with rumours of the debate, there was a loud knocking at the back door of the Tradescant house and then the cook ran into the rarities room where Jane was writing labels and rocking Frances's cradle with her foot. J was before the hearth, stretching a rare skin on a frame for hanging.

'A message for the master, from Whitehall!' the cook exclaimed.

Jane rose to her feet and went to the window. 'He's by the seedling beds,' she said, knocking on the glass and beckoning. 'Here he comes.'

John arrived, rubbing his hands on his leather breeches. 'What's to do?'

'A message,' the cook said. 'And no reply waited for. From Whitehall.'

John put out his hand and looked at the seal. 'William Ward,' he said briefly. 'My lord's steward.' He turned the page, broke the seal, and read. J saw his father pale under the wind-worn tan of his skin.

'What is it?'

'It's the king. He has arrested Sir John Eliot and sent him to the tower. He has closed down Parliament. He calls the members a nest of vipers and says he will rule forever without them.' He read swiftly. 'They locked the doors of the House against the king and voted tonnage and poundage illegal, and voted the king's theology illegal.' He read a little, and then swore.

'What?' Jane asked impatiently.

'They held the Speaker down in his chair so that the resolutions could be passed before the king's guards burst in and arrested them.'

Jane looked at once to the cradle and the sleeping baby. 'What will he do?' she asked.

John shook his head. 'God knows.'

J waited. 'What does it mean for us?'

John shook his head again. 'For us and the country? Stormy weather.'

1630

It was not stormy weather, but a sort of peace which caught the country by surprise. The MPs dispersed in obedience to the king's order and though they took their complaints to their homes in every corner of the kingdom, there was no popular groundswell to sweep them back to confrontation in the city. The king set to work to rule without Parliament – as he had threatened to do – and that turned out to be almost no rule at all. The silence in the Houses of Parliament meant there was no forum for debate. The vacuum of power meant that things rubbed along as they had always done. The towns and cities were run, as they had always been, by a loose alliance of magistrates, gentry and vicars, and by the powerful weight of custom and practice.

In Lambeth, Frances's promised brother did not come, though she outgrew her baby complaints, learned to walk, learned to talk and was even given a small corner of the garden and a dozen cuttings of pinks and twenty sweet pea seeds for her to try her hand at gardening. She was indulged – as the only baby in a house of four adults is bound to be indulged; but nothing spoiled her. As she grew older she still loved the echoey airiness of the rarities room, and would still go piggyback with her grandfather down to the end of the orchard. As she grew stronger and heavier John's limp became more and more pronounced under the extra burden of her weight and he would roll in his walk like the old sailor he sometimes claimed to be.

He had a special voice for her, a meditative nonsense-telling voice which he used for no-one else. Only his seedlings in the frame and Frances were treated to his 'tumelty tumelty tumelty pudding'. Elizabeth would watch him and the little girl from the window as they went hand in hand down the garden and feel at last a sense of relief that she and John, J and Jane were settled at last.

'We've put down some roots,' John said to her one night as he saw her smile across the dinner table. The girl laid their dinner before them – they had a girl now, and a woman cook in the kitchen and a lad in the house, as well as three gardeners. 'I think we should have a motto.'

'Not a motto,' J said under his breath. 'Please, no.'

'A motto,' John said firmly. 'To go under the crest. You shall write it, J. You have Latin.'

'I can't think of anything that would fit a man who was born and bred a gardener and made up his own crest, and had some fool of a mason carve it in stone for anyone to see,' J said scathingly.

John smiled, unperturbed. 'Why, the king himself is the grandson of a mere Mister,' he said. 'These are times for men to rise.'

'And the Duke of Buckingham was called an upstart to the end of his days,' Jane observed.

John dropped his eyes to his plate so that no-one could see his sharp pang of grief.

'Even so,' J said. 'I can't think of a motto which would suit.'

They were a family which did not fit the usual tags handed out by the College of Heralds. They were on the way to being gentry, with their own house and land, and rents coming in from the fields at Hatfield, and a couple of houses newly bought at a bargain price in the city. But John and J still worked with their hands deep in the dark earth of their fields and gardens, and could tell to the nearest farthing how much a seedling had cost them in terms of labour and the price of the seed.

Tradescant plants went all over the country, all over Europe. John Gerard the herbalist borrowed from their garden and gave new cuttings back to them. John Parkinson quoted them by name in his book on gardening and acknowledged his debt to them, even though he was the king's own botanist. Every gardener at every great house in the land knew that for something strange and lovely the Tradescants at the Ark were the only men to ask. The Ark was the only place to buy rare tulips outside the Low Countries and their prices were as reasonable as they could be in a market which was still growing and growing every season.

The orders came in almost every day. Once the MPs were forced home to their estates there was little for the gentlemen to do but to look to their fields and their gardens.

'His Majesty did us a great favour,' John remarked to Elizabeth as she sat at the dining table and sorted seeds into packets for Jane to label and dispatch. 'If the squires were still at Westminster they would not be planting their gardens.'

'We're the only ones likely to be grateful for it then,' she said with something of her old sharpness. 'Mrs Hurte was telling me that in the city they are saying that we might as well never have had a parliament if the king is going to run the country like a tyrant and never hear the will of the people. There are new taxes every day. We had a demand for a salt tax only yesterday.'

'Peace,' John said quietly, and Elizabeth bent her head to her work.

They were both right. The country was enjoying a sort of peace bought at the price of never addressing the difficulties between Parliament and king. King Charles was ruling as he fondly imagined his great aunt Elizabeth had ruled, with little regard for Parliament, with little advice, and on the smooth oil of his subjects' love. He and the queen went from great house to great house, hunting, dancing, playing in masques, watching theatre, assured everywhere that they went, in a dozen pageants of loyal verse, that the people loved them next only to their God.

Henrietta Maria had learned a little wisdom in her hard years as an apprentice queen. When she heard that Buckingham, her worst enemy, was dead, she did not allow one word of delight to escape her. She went straight to the king and when he emerged from his lonely vigil of mourning she was there, dressed in black and looking as grief-stricken as she could manage. In a moment he transferred to her the passionate need which he carried with him always, like a sickness in his blood: the sickness of the less favoured son, the sickness of the plain son of a man who liked handsome men. Henrietta Maria staggered under the weight of his embrace but kept her footing. There was nothing in the world she wanted more than his adoration. It made her complete as a woman, it made her complete as a queen.

Nothing contradicted his new-found happiness, nothing was ever allowed to distress or trouble His Majesty. The plague in London meant merely that they moved early to Oatlands Palace near Weybridge, or Windsor, or Beaulieu in Hampshire. Poverty in Cornwall, Presbyterianism in Scotland, the papers from local lords or JPs warning the king that all was not completely well in his kingdom, pursued him from hunting lodge to palace, and waited for a rainy day for him to give them his fleeting attention. His early appetite for work had deserted him once he had found how little rewarded he was for duty. Parliament had never thanked him for the memoranda in his tiny handwriting, and in any case there was no Parliament now. The holders of the great offices of state, incompetent and corrupt, worked as well without supervision as they did under the king's erratic gaze. It was easier, and pleasanter, for him to turn the business of kingship into a country-wide masque with people demonstrating their devotion in dances and songs, and the king play-acting at ruling with a crown of gold wire on his head.

The king's first son and heir was born in May 1630, and three months later a messenger from the court, currently at Windsor, knocked peremptorily on the door of the Lambeth house and glanced upwards, but did not comment, at the coat of arms fixed proudly on the wall.

'A message for John Tradescant,' he announced as Jane opened the door.

She stepped back to show him into the parlour and he went ahead of her as he would have preceded a Baptist serving woman. Jane, who knew that she should despise the vanity of worldly show, gestured rather grandly to the chair at the fireside. 'You may be seated,' she said with the dignity of a duchess. '*Mr* Tradescant, my father-in-law, will join you shortly.' She turned on her heel and stalked from the room, and then fled to the garden where John was transplanting seedlings.

'Get up! and get washed! There is a royal herald for you in the parlour!' she exclaimed.

John got slowly to his feet. 'A royal herald?'

'Trouble?' J asked. 'Not the coat of arms?'

'Surely not,' John said comfortably. 'Give him a glass of wine, Jane, and tell him I am coming at once.'

'You will change your coat,' she reminded him. 'He is in full livery and with a powdered wig.'

'It's only a herald,' John said mildly. 'Not Queen Henrietta Maria herself.'

Jane picked up her skirts and fled back to the house to order the kitchenmaid to pour a cool glass of wine and put it on the best silver tray.

She found the herald looking out from the window to the garden. 'How many men does Mr Tradescant employ here?' he asked, trying to engage her in conversation to make amends for his earlier mistake.

She glanced out. To her embarrassment it was not the garden lads but her husband and her father-in-law, strolling up from the orchard with a hoe and a bucket apiece. 'Half a dozen in midsummer,' she said. 'Fewer in winter.'

'And do you have many visitors?'

'Yes,' she said. 'Both to the garden and to the cabinet of rarities. The garden is rich with both rare fruit and flowers, you are welcome to walk in it, if you wish.'

'Later perhaps,' the herald said loftily. 'I must speak with Mr Tradescant now.'

'He will come shortly,' Jane said. 'I could show you some of the rarities in the cabinets while you wait.'

To her relief, the door behind her opened. 'Here I am,' John said. 'I am sorry to have kept you waiting.'

At least he had washed his hands, but he still wore his old gardening coat. The herald, whose face revealed nothing, realised that the working man he had seen from the window was in fact the gentleman he had come to visit.

'Mr Tradescant,' he began. 'I am carrying a letter from the king, and I am to await your reply.'

He held out a scroll of paper with a thick red seal at the bottom.

John took it and went to the window where the August sunshine poured in.

Jane had to prevent herself from moving behind him and reading over his shoulder.

'Hmmm hmmm hmmm,' John said, skimming the customary compliments and addresses at the start of the letter. 'Why! His Majesty is commanding me to be his gardener at Oatlands Palace! I am honoured.'

'His Majesty has just given the palace to Her Majesty the Queen,' the herald informed them. 'And she wants a garden like Hatfield or New Hall.'

John raised his head. 'It's a long time since I planted a garden for a palace. And I am sixty years old this year. There are other gardeners Their Majesties could employ, and I would have thought the queen would have preferred a garden in the French style.'

The herald raised his neat plucked eyebrows. 'Perhaps. But I am not in a position to advise His Majesty or Her Majesty as to their course of action. *I* merely obey their royal decree.' The inference was clear.

'Oh,' John said, corrected. 'I see.'

'His Majesty ordered me to take back a reply to him,' the herald continued loftily. 'Is it your wish that I tell him you are sixty years of age and that it is your opinion that he didn't want you in the first place?'

John grimaced. An invitation from the king was tantamount to a royal command. He was not able to refuse. 'Tell His Majesty that I am honoured for the invitation and that I accept, I gratefully accept, and that it will always be my pleasure to serve Their Majesties in any way I can.'

The herald unbent slightly. 'I will deliver your message. His Majesty will expect you at Oatlands Palace within the week.'

John nodded. 'I shall be delighted to attend.'

The herald bowed. 'An honour to meet you, Mr Tradescant.'

'The honour is all mine,' John said grandly.

The herald bowed himself from the room and left John and his daughter-in-law alone.

'Royal service,' she said grimly. 'I won't like it.'

John grimaced. 'He will have to bear it. You can't refuse the king. You heard him. My acceptance was just a matter of form, he knew what day I had to start work.'

'We said we would never work for another master,' Jane reminded him.

John nodded. 'We never thought of this. But perhaps it won't be so bad.' He turned and looked out of the window at his little farm. 'I've heard they have a great orangery,' he said. 'But they've never had much luck with getting the trees to flower. There's a garden just for the king's use and another for the queen. There's a massive fountain in the great garden. The whole place is like a village set about with gardens, built all ramshackle with one court running into another, overlooking the Thames. The trick of it will be to make sure that every corner has a pretty plant, that the gardens pull the whole site together so that every corner has a view.'

Jane heard her father-in-law casting aside the principle of independence for the offer of a fine garden to make. She stalked to the door. 'Shall I tell J or will you?' she asked coldly. 'For he will not care for making pretty views for such a king.'

'I'll tell him,' John said absently. 'I wonder if we have enough chestnut saplings to use one at the centre of each court?'

John told J the news at dinner but he knew from the moment his son entered the dining room that Jane had forewarned him, and that J was forearmed.

'I swore I'd never work for another master,' he said.

'This would be for me,' John corrected him, mildly. 'Working for us all. For the good of us all.'

J glanced at his wife.

'It would be for the queen,' she said bluntly. 'A woman of vanity and a heretic.'

'She may be both of those,' John agreed without hesitation. 'But she's only the paymaster. She will not supervise us at all. J need never speak to her.'

'There's something about them, though, that sticks in my throat like dry bread,' J said thoughtfully. 'There's something about a man calling himself nearer to God than me. Something about a man thinking himself a better man than me – almost an angel. Even if I never saw him and never served him, there's something about it which goes against the grain for me.'

'Because it's heresy,' Jane said flatly.

J shook his head. 'Not just because of that,' he said. 'Because it denies me – it denies that I think, just as he thinks. That I have an immortal journey, just as he does. That I too want, think, and pray for better days, for the coming of the Great Day, the Last Day. If he is as far above me as an angel then I need not think and hope and pray, for God would hardly listen to me when the king is on his knees. It's as if his importance makes me more little.' He glanced around at their surprised faces. 'I daresay I'm not making any sense,' he said defensively. 'I'm not good at arguing these things. It's just what I've been thinking.'

'But what you're saying would deny any king,' John said. 'This one or any other. A good one or a bad one.'

J nodded reluctantly. 'I just can't see that any man should set himself up to be above another. I can't see that any man needs more than one house. I can't see that any man needs dozens of houses and hundreds of servants. I can't see that he can be closer to God with these things – I would have thought he would be further and further away.'

John shifted uncomfortably on his wooden seat. 'This is Leveller talk, my son. Next thing you will be denying any king but King Jesus and taking off for the common and waste lands.'

'I don't care what it's called,' J said steadily. 'I wouldn't be frightened from speaking my mind because others think the same thoughts but express them wildly. I know that I must think that England would be better without a man at its head who claims to speak for us, and know us, and yet clearly knows nothing at all of what it is like to be a man such as me.'

'He has advisers.'

J shrugged. 'He is surrounded by courtiers and flatterers. He hears what they tell him and they only tell him what he wants to hear. He can have no judgement, he can have no wisdom. He is trapped in his vanity and ignorance like a fish in a fishpond and since it knows nothing else it thinks it is something divinely special. If it could breathe air and see the sky it would know it is nothing more than a large fish.'

John snorted with laughter at the thought of the long mournful face of his monarch and the juxtaposition of the face of a carp.

'But who will you employ if J will not go?' Elizabeth asked practically.

'I'll have to find someone,' John said. 'There are dozens of men who would be glad of the place. But I would rather work with you, J. And it seems to me you are bound to work for me if I ask it.'

J shifted on his seat. 'You would not drive me to rebellion,' he said. 'You would respect my conscience, Father. I am a full-grown man.'

'You're twenty-two,' John said bluntly. 'Barely into your majority. You make your own choices, you are a man with a wife and child of your own. But I am still your father and it will be my work which will put the bread on your table, if you refuse to work.'

'I work here!' J exclaimed, stung. 'I work hard enough!'

'In winter we earn almost no money,' John pointed out. 'We live off our savings. There is no stock to sell, and the visitors tail off in the bad weather. Last year we were down to the bottom of our savings by the spring. The work at the palace would be money paid to us all the year round.'

'Papist gold,' Jane muttered to her plate.

'Honestly earned by us,' John countered. 'I am an old man. I did not think to go out to work to keep you, J. I did not think your conscience would be more precious than your duty to me.'

J shot a furious look at his father. 'It's always the same!' he burst out. 'You are always the one who is free to come and go. I am always the one who has to obey. And now that we have a home where I *want* to stay, and now you are free to stay yourself, you are still going away. And now I have to go too!'

'I am not free,' John said sternly. 'The king commands me.'

'Defy the king!' J shouted. 'For once in your life don't go at some great man's bidding. For once in your life speak for yourself! Think for yourself! Defy the king!'

There was a long shocked silence.

John rose from the table and walked to the window and looked out over the garden rinsed of colour and lovely in the grey light of dusk. A star was shining over the chestnut tree and somewhere in the orchard a nightingale started to sing.

'I will never defy the king,' he said. 'I will not even hear such talk in my house.'

The pause stretched till breaking point and then J spoke low and earnestly. 'Father, this is not Queen Elizabeth and you are not still working for Robert Cecil. This is not a king as she was a queen. This is not a country as it was then. This is a country that has been run into debt and torn apart by heresy. It is ruled by a vain fool who is ruled in turn by a Papist wife, in the pay of her brother, the King of France. I cannot bear to go and work for such a king nor for her. I cannot bear to be under their command. If you force me to this I would rather leave the country altogether.'

John nodded, taking in J's words. The two women, Elizabeth and Jane, sat silent, hardly breathing, waiting to hear what John would reply.

'Do you mean this?'

J, breathing heavily, merely nodded.

John sighed. 'Then you must follow your conscience and go,' he said simply. 'For the king is my master before God, and he has ordered me. And I am your father and should command your duty and I have ordered you. If you choose to defy me then you should go, J. Just as Adam and Eve had to leave *their* garden. There are laws in heaven and earth. I cannot pretend to you that it is otherwise. I have tolerated loose thoughts and wild talk from you all your life, even in my lord's garden. But if you will not serve the king then you should not garden in his garden. You should not garden in his country.'

J rose from the table. His hands were trembling and he swiftly snatched them out of sight, behind his back.

'Wait –' Elizabeth said softly. Neither man paid any attention to her.

'I shall go, then,' J said as if he were testing his father's resolve. John turned his back on the room and looked out to his garden.

'If you do not accept your obedience to me, and to the king above me, and to God above him, then you are no longer my son,' John said simply. 'I would to God that you do not take this path, J.'

J turned and walked jerkily to the door. Jane rose too, hesitant, looking from her husband to her father-in-law. J went out without another word.

'Go to him,' Elizabeth said swiftly to Jane. 'Soothe him. He can't mean it. Keep him here tonight at least – we'll talk more in the morning.' A swift nod towards John at the window showed Jane that meanwhile Elizabeth would work on her husband.

Jane hesitated. 'But I think he is right,' she whispered, too low for John to hear.

'What does it matter?' Elizabeth hissed. 'What do the words matter? Nothing matters more than Frances and you and J living here now, and living here when we are gone. The gardens and the Tradescant name. Go quick and stop him packing at least.'

Jane prevented J from leaving home that night by presenting the folly of taking a sleeping baby out of her cradle into the night air, into a city filled with plague. The two men, father and son, met at breakfast and went out to the garden together in stiff silence.

'What can we do?' Jane asked her mother-in-law.

Elizabeth shook her head. 'Pray that the two of them will see that the interests of this family are more important than whose gold pays the bills.'

'Father should not force J to work for the king against his conscience,' Jane said.

Elizabeth shook her head. 'Ah, my dear, it was so different for us when we were your age. There was no other way to work but for a lord. There were no other gardens but those belonging to great lords. At J's age his father would never have dreamed of owning a house, or fields. At J's age he was an under-gardener in the Cecil household and living in hall, he didn't even choose his own meat for breakfast – everything came from the lord's kitchen. Things have changed so fast, you two must understand. The world is so different now. And J is still a very young man. Things could change again.'

'Things are changing,' Jane agreed. 'But not in favour of lords and the court. Perhaps this family should not be linked with the king. Perhaps we would do better to be like my family, independent traders who do not fear the king's favour. Who are not dependent on any master.'

'Yes, if we were mercers,' Elizabeth answered gently. 'And could trade from a little shop, and every man and woman in the country would need our goods and could afford them. But we are gardeners and keepers of a rarities collection. Only the wealthy men will buy what we have to sell and show. And we cannot get our stock without owning land to grow it in. It is not a trade that can be done on a small scale. This is a business that puts us in the hands of the great men of the country. We sell to the great houses, we sell to the courtiers. Of course, sooner or later, we would come to the mind of the king.'

'And he wants us, as he wants everything that is beautiful and rare,' Jane said bitterly. 'And he thinks he can buy us too.'

Elizabeth nodded. 'Just so.'

The men came into dinner in silence. Jane and Elizabeth exchanged a few remarks about the weather and the progress of the work in the garden but gave up when neither man responded with more than a word or a nod.

As soon as they had eaten the men went back outside and Jane, looking from the window of the rarities room, saw J heading down for the orchard, as far away from the house as he could go, while John was weeding the seed beds in the cool shadow of the house. The day was hot. Even the wood pigeons that usually cooed in the Tradescant trees were silent. Jane took Frances to feed the ducks in the pond at the side of the orchard and saw her husband scything nettles in a distant corner. When he saw her he carefully sheathed the blade and came over.

'Wife.'

She looked into his unhappy face. 'Oh, John!'

'You don't want to leave here,' he said flatly.

'Of course not. Where could we go?'

'We could go to your father's while we looked about and found some position.'

'You swore you would garden for no master.'

'The Devil himself would be better than the king.'

She shook her head. 'You said no master.'

Frances leaned longingly towards the deeper water. Jane took the little hand in a firm grip. 'Not too near,' she said.

'There are two places I would choose to live, if you would consent,' J said tentatively.

Jane waited.

'There is a community, of good men and women, who are trying to make a life of their own, to worship as they wish, to live as they wish.'

'Anabaptists?' Jane asked.

'Not Anabaptists. But they believe in freedom for men and even for women. They have a farm in Devon near the sea.'

'How have you heard of them?'

'A travelling preacher spoke of them, a few months ago.'

Jane thought for a moment. 'So we don't know them directly.'

'No.'

He saw her grip on Frances's hand tighten. 'I can't go among strangers and so far from my family,' she said firmly. 'What would become of us if one of us were ill? Or if they are no longer there? I can't go so far from my mother. What if we have another baby? How would we manage without my mother or your mother?'

'Other women manage,' J said. 'Leave home, manage among strangers. They will become your friends.'

'Why should we?' Jane asked simply. 'We, who have two families who love us? We, who have a house to live in which is the most beautiful house in Lambeth and famed throughout the world for the rarities and the gardens?'

'Because it comes with too high a price!' J exclaimed. 'Because I rent this beautiful house with my obedience, by putting my conscience in the keeping of my father who himself has never thought a thought which was not licensed by his lord. He is an obedient dutiful man, Jane, and I am not.'

She thought for a moment. Frances pulled at her hand. 'Frances feed ducks,' she said. 'Frances feed ducks.'

'Down there,' Jane said, hardly looking. 'Where the bank is not so steep. Don't get your feet wet.' She let the little girl go and watched her progress to the water's edge. The ducks gathered hopefully around, Frances plunged her hands into the pockets of her little gown and came out with fistfuls of breadcrumbs.

'What is your other wish?' Jane asked.

J took a deep breath. 'Virginia,' he said.

Jane looked into his face and then came into his arms as simply as she had done the day they were married. 'Oh, my love,' she said. 'I know you have such dreams. But we cannot go to Virginia, it would break my mother's heart. And I could not bear to leave her. And besides – we don't *need* to go. We are not adventurers, we are not desperate for a fortune or to run away from here. We have a place here, we have work here, we have a home here. I would not leave here for choice.'

J would not look at her. 'You are my wife,' he said flatly. 'You are duty-bound to go where I go. To obey me.'

She shook her head. 'I am bound in duty to you as you are to your father, as he is to the king. If you break one link they all go, J. If you do not acknowledge him as your father then I need not acknowledge you as my husband.'

'Then what do we become?' he demanded in impatience. 'All whirling, unconnected, unloving, atoms; like thistledown finding its own way on the wind?'

She said nothing. Behind them, Frances put one tentative foot in the water.

'If you are guided by your conscience and only by your conscience then that is what we must become,' she said thoughtfully. 'All of us, guided by our own consciences, coming together only when it suits us.'

'A society cannot live like that,' J replied.

'A family cannot,' Jane said. 'As soon as you love someone, as soon as you have a child, you acknowledge your duty to put another's needs first.'

J hesitated.

'The other way is the king's way,' Jane continued. 'The very thing you despise. A man who puts his own desires and needs before everyone else. Who thinks his needs and desires are of superior merit.'

'But I am guided by my conscience!' J protested.

'He could say the same,' she said gently. 'If you are Charles the king, then your wishes could very well seem to be conscience and there would be no-one to tell you your duty.'

'So where is my course?' J asked. 'If you are my adviser this day?'

'Somewhere between duty and your own wishes,' Jane said. 'Surely we can find a way for you to keep your soul clear of heresy and yet still live here.'

J's face was bleak. 'You would put your comfort before my conscience,' he said flatly. 'All it is with you, is living here.'

She did not turn away from him but tightened her grip around his waist. 'Think,' she urged him. 'Do you really want to walk away from the garden that is your inheritance? The chestnut tree which your father gave to your mother the year you were conceived? The black-heart cherry? His geraniums? The tulips that you saved from New Hall? The larches from Archangel?'

J turned his head away from her pleading face but Jane did not let go. 'If we never have another child,' she said bravely. 'We both come from small families, we might only ever have Frances. If God is not kind to us and we never have a son to carry your name, then all that will be left of the Tradescants is their name on their trees. These are your posterity, John – will you leave them to be named for another man, or grown by him? Or worse, neglected and felled by him?'

He looked down at her. 'You are my conscience and my heart,' he said softly. 'Are you telling me that we should garden for the king – even such a king as this – because if we do not then I lose my bond to my father and my rights to his name, and my claim to history?'

She nodded. 'I wish it were an easier road to see,' she said. 'But surely you can plant the king's garden and take the king's gold without compromising your soul or your conscience. You don't need to be his man, as your father was wedded to Cecil and then to Buckingham. You can just take his wage and do his work. You can be an independent man working for pay.'

J hesitated for one more moment. 'I wanted to be free of all this.'

'I know,' she said lovingly. 'But we have to wait for the right time. Who knows, there may come a time when the whole country wants to be free of him? Then you will see your course. But until then, J, you have to live. We have to eat. We have to live with your father and mother and keep the Ark afloat.'

Finally he nodded. 'I'll tell him.'

J did not speak to his father till dinnertime the following day when the family was gathered together again, Frances beside her mother, John at one end of the big dark wood table and J at the other, Elizabeth seated between her husband and son.

'I have been considering. I will work with you at Oatlands Palace,' J announced abruptly.

John looked up, swiftly concealing his surprise. 'I'm glad to hear it,' he said, keeping the joy from his voice. 'I shall need your skills.'

Elizabeth and Jane exchanged one swift, relieved glance. 'Who will run the business here while we are away?' J asked, matter-of-fact.

'We will,' Elizabeth said, smiling. 'Jane and I.'

'Frances too,' Frances said firmly.

'And Frances, of course. Peter will show people round the rarities, he does it beautifully now, like a barker in a fairground; and you will be home often, one of you would be home for a day or two, surely?'

'When the court moves on from Oatlands we will be able to do as we please,' John said. 'They will want beauty when they visit, we can do half of that with plants grown here in the seed beds and set in at the right time. When they are not at Oatlands we can go about our business here.'

'I will not hear heresy,' J warned.

'I myself shall guard your tender conscience,' his father assured him.

Reluctantly J chuckled. 'Aye, you can laugh, but I mean this, Father. I will not hear heresy, and I will not bow down low to her.'

'You will have to uncover your head and bow,' John told him firmly. 'That's common politeness.'

'The Anabaptists don't,' Jane volunteered.

John gave her a swift sideways look under his brows. 'I thank you, Mistress Jane. I know the Anabaptists don't. But J is not an Anabaptist –' he glared at his son as if to dare him to confess yet another step down the road to a more and more radical faith '– and the Anabaptists do not work for me in the king's garden.'

'They are still his subjects,' she said staunchly.

'And I honour their faith. Just as J is the king's subject and has a right to his conscience, inside the law. But he will be obedient and he will be courteous.'

'And what shall we do if the law changes?' Elizabeth asked. 'This is a king who is changing the shape of the church itself, whose father changed the Bible itself. What if he changes yet more and makes us outlaws in our own church?'

J glanced at his mother. 'That's the very question,' he said. 'I can bend for the moment, but what if matters get worse?'

'Practice before principle,' John said with Cecil's old remembered wisdom. 'We'll worry about that if it happens. In the meantime we have a road we can all take together. We can obey the king and dig his wife's garden, and keep our consciences to ourselves.'

'I will not listen to heresy and I will not bow down low to the Papist queen,' J stated. 'But I can be courteous to her and I can work for my father. Two wages coming in is better than one. And besides –' He glanced up at his father with a silent appeal. 'I want to do my duty by you, Father. I want there always to be a Tradescant at Lambeth. I want things working right in their right places. It's because the king does not work right in his right place that everything is so disturbed. I want order – just as you do.'

John smiled his warm loving smile at his son. 'I shall make a Cecil of you yet,' he said gently. 'Let us put some order in the queen's garden and keep the steady order of our own lives, and pray that the king does his duty as we do ours.'

The queen had commanded that John should have lodgings in the park at Oatlands and that everything should be done as he wished. His house adjoined the silkworm house and was warmed by the sun all day and by the charcoal burners which were set about the walls of the silkworm house all night. John at first found the thought of his neighbours the maggots, silently munching their way through mulberry leaves night and day, immensely distasteful; but the house itself was a miracle of prettiness, a little turreted play-castle of wood, south-facing with mullioned windows and furnished by the order of the queen with pretty light tables, chairs and a bed.

He was to eat in the great hall with the other members of the household. The king demanded that dinner be served in the great hall in full state whether he was there or not. The ritual demanded that a cover be set on the table before his chair, that dishes be put before the empty throne and that every man should bow to the throne before entering the hall and on leaving it.

'This is superstition,' John exclaimed unwarily when he saw the men bowing low to the empty chair.

'It is how the king orders it,' one of the grooms of the bed chamber replied. 'To maintain the dignity of the throne. It's how it was done in Queen Elizabeth's time.'

John shook his head. 'Well, I remember Elizabeth's time, which is more than most do,' he said. 'Men bowed to her chair when she was going to sit on it, and bowed to her dinner when she was going to eat it. She was too parsimonious to have dinner served in ten palaces when she was only going to eat in one.'

The man shook his head, warning John to be silent. 'Well, this is how it's done now,' he said. 'The king himself ordered it.'

'And when does he come?'

'Next week,' the groom said. 'And then you will see a change. The place is only half-alive when Their Majesties are not here.'

He was right. Oatlands Palace was like a village with the plague

405

when the court was elsewhere, the passages between one building and another empty and silent, half the kitchens cold, their fires unlit. But early in September a trail of carts and wagons came down the road from Weybridge, and a hundred barges rowed upstream from London bringing the king's goods as the court moved to Oatlands for the month.

The palace was under siege from an army of shouting, arguing, ordering, singing cooks, maids, horsemen, grooms, servers, and minor gentry of the household. Everyone had an urgent task and an important responsibility, and everyone got in everyone else's way. There were tapestries to hang and pictures to place and floors to sweep and carpets to lay. All the king's most beautiful furniture travelled with him; and his bedroom and the queen's bedroom had to be prepared and perfect. The chimneys had to be swept before fires could be lit, but fires must be lit to air the damp linen at once. The whole village, spread over nine acres, was in a state of complete madness. Even the deerhounds in the kennels caught the excitement and bayed all night long under the yellow September moon.

Tradescant broke the rule of dining in the great hall and went to Weybridge village to buy bread, cheese and small ale, which he took home to his little house in the gardens. He and the silk-worms munched their way through their dinners in their adjoining houses. 'Goodnight, maggots,' Tradescant called cheerfully as he blew his candle out and the deep country darkness enveloped his bedroom.

❦

John had given no thought to meeting the king. When he had last seen His Majesty, they had both been waiting for Buckingham to come to Portsmouth. The time before that had been at the sailing of the first expedition to Rhé. When John was led into the king's state bed chamber he found, with the familiar pang of sorrow, that he was looking around for his master. He could not believe that his duke was not there.

At once, like a ghost summoned by desire, he saw him. It was a life-size portrait of Buckingham painted in dark rich oils. One hand was outstretched as if to show the length and grace of the fingers and the wealth of the single diamond ring, the other hand rested on the rich pommel of his sword. His beard was neatly trimmed, his clothes were bright and richly embroidered and encrusted, but it was his face that drew Tradescant's look. It was his lord, it was his lost lord. The thick dark hair, the arrogant laughing half-raised brows set over dark eyes, the irresistible smile, the sparkle, and that hint of spirituality, of saintliness, which King James had seen even as he had loved the sensual beauty of the face.

John thought how he still touched his lord in his mind, almost every morning and every night, and how he had thought that perhaps the king too reached out over death to his friend. But now he saw that the king had a greater comfort, for every night and every morning he could glance at that assured smiling face and feel the warmth of those eyes, and if he wished he could touch the frame of the picture, or even brush a kiss upon the painted cheek.

The portrait was new in the chamber, along with the rich curtains and the thick Turkey rugs on the floor. The king's most precious goods travelled with him everywhere he went. And the king's most precious thing was the portrait which hung, wherever he slept, at his bedside where he could see it before closing his eyes at night and on waking in the morning.

Charles came silently into his bed chamber from his private adjoining room and hesitated when he saw John looking up at the portrait. Something in the tilt of the man's head and the steadiness of his look reminded the king that John too had lost a man who had been at the very centre of his world.

'Y . . . you are looking at my p . . . portrait of the . . . duke.'

John turned, saw the king, and dropped to his knees, flinching a little as his bad knee hit the floor.

The king did not command him to rise. 'Your l . . . late master.' His voice still held traces of the paralysing stammer he had suffered from as a child. Only with his intimates could he speak without hesitation, only with two people, the duke and now his wife, had he ever been fluent.

'You m . . . must miss him,' the king went on. It sounded more like an order than an offer of sympathy.

John looked up and saw the king's face. Grief had changed him, he looked older and more tired, and his brown hair was thinning. His eyes were heavily lidded, as if he were weary of what he saw, as if he no longer expected to see what he wanted.

'I grieve for him still,' John said honestly. 'Every day.'

'You l . . . loved him?'

'With all my heart,' John replied.

'And he l . . . loved you?'

John looked up at his king. There was passion behind the question. Even after his death Buckingham could still inspire jealousy. John, the older man, smiled wryly. 'He loved me a little,' he said. 'When I served him especially well. But one smile from him was worth a piece of gold from another.'

There was a silence. Charles nodded as if the statement was of little consequence and turned away to the window and looked out into the king's court below.

'H . . . Her Majesty will tell you wh . . . what she wants done,' he said. 'But I sh . . . should like one court planted with r . . . roses. Rose petals for throwing in masques.'

John nodded. A man who could turn from the death of his friend to the need of rose petals for masques would be a difficult master to love.

The king looked round, his eyebrow raised.

'Yes, Your Majesty,' John said from his place on the floor. He wondered what his master Sir Robert Cecil, who had scolded a greater monarch than this one, would have thought of a king who confided his grief in a gardener but left him kneeling on an arthritic leg.

There was a rustle of silk and high heels tapping.

'Ah! my gardener!' said the voice of the queen.

John, already low, tried to bow from a kneeling position and felt himself to be ridiculous. He glanced up. She was a short plump woman, beringed, curled, painted and patched with a low-cut gown which would have incurred Elizabeth's censure, and a powerful scent of incense around her skirts which would have inspired outrage in the Ark at Lambeth. She gave him a bright dark-eyed smile and extended her small hand. John kissed it.

'Get up! Get up!' she commanded. 'I want you to walk me all around the garden so that I can see what we must do!'

The flood of words came so quick after her husband's halting speech, and her accent was so strong, that John could not immediately understand what she said.

'Your Majesty?' He glanced towards the king for help. Charles made a brief dismissive gesture with his hand, which clearly indicated that John should go, so he bowed low once again, and backed from the room. To his surprise, the queen came with him. John pressed himself back against the wall as a footman flung open the door.

'This way! Come on!' the queen said, and ran prettily down the stairs and out into the summer sunshine of the king's privy garden.

'I want this garden full of scented flowers,' she told him. 'The king's windows look out over it, I want the scents to blow up to him.'

John nodded, taking in the grand sweep of the walls around the court. The south-facing walls would provide extra warmth, the walls to the east would provide shelter. 'I could grow almost anything here,' he said.

'It was the king's mother's garden,' the queen said. It was evident from the slight movement of her head that she did not think much of her predecessor's taste for low-growing herbs and knot gardens made of coloured gravel. 'I want roses against the walls and lilies everywhere. Those are my flowers, in my crest. I want this garden filled with roses and lilies to remind the king of me whenever he looks from his window.'

John bowed slightly. 'Any preference as to colours?' he asked. 'I can get some very handsome red and white roses, Rosamund roses. I have them growing at my garden in Lambeth.'

'Yes, yes,' she said, falling over the words in her haste. Even after five years in the country she still spoke English as if it was a strange and ugly foreign language. 'And in the centre bed I want a knot with our initials entwined. C and H M. Can you do that?'

John nodded. 'Of course . . .'

She suddenly stiffened. 'Of course, Your Highness,' she corrected him abruptly.

'I beg your pardon,' John said smoothly. 'I was so interested in what Your Highness was saying that I forgot my manners. Of course, Your Highness.'

At once she smiled at him and gave him her hand to kiss. John bowed low and pressed his lips gently to the little fingers. His sense that he had served steadier, more intelligent and more noble masters did not show on his face.

'It is to be a garden which expresses Love,' she said. 'The highest love there can be below the heavens. The love that there is between a man and his wife, and higher than that: between a king and a queen.'

'Of course, Your Majesty,' John said. 'I could plant you some symbolic flowers around the roses. White violets for innocence, and periwinkle for constancy, and daisies.'

She nodded enthusiastically. 'And one corner in blue as a tribute to Our Lady.' She turned her dark eyes on him. 'Are you of the true faith, Tradescant?'

John thought briefly of Elizabeth in her modest grey gown, the staunch Baptist faith of his daughter-in-law, and his promise to J that his conscience would not be offended by this work. He kept his face perfectly steady. 'I attend the church of my fathers, Your Majesty,' he said. 'I'm a simple gardener, I don't think much of things other than plants and rarities.'

'You should think of your immortal soul,' she commanded. 'And the church of your fathers is the church of Rome. I am always telling the king this!'

Tradescant bowed, thinking that she had just said enough to get both of them hanged if the king applied the laws of the land – which he manifestly only did when it suited him.

'And I shall want flowers for my chapel, for my private chapel,' she said. 'Blue and white for Our Lady.'

'Of course, Your Majesty.'

'And for my private rooms, and strewing herbs, and the king wishes you to maintain and replant the physic garden and look at the herb garden.'

Tradescant bowed again.

'I want the house to be like a palace in a fairytale,' she said, changing at once from the evangelical Roman Catholic into the flirtatious queen. 'Like a bower for a fairytale Princess. I want people all over the country, all over Europe, to hear of it as a fairytale garden, a perfect garden. Have you heard of the Platonic ideal?'

John felt a sense of weariness he had never before known while talking about a garden. He had a sudden sympathy for the king who had lost the easy male companionship of Buckingham and had no-one to turn to but this vain woman.

The queen was laughing. 'I suppose not!' she cried. 'It does not matter, Gardener Tradescant. It is an idea which we make much of at court, in our masques and poetry and plays. I will just tell you that it is an idea that there is a perfect form of everything – of a woman, of a man, of a marriage, of a garden, of a rose, and the king and I want to attain that ideal.'

John glanced at her to see if she was speaking seriously. He thought of how the duke would have roared with laughter at the pedantry, at the pretentiousness. He would have slapped John on the back and called him Gardener Tradescant for ever after.

'Think of it,' she said, her voice as sweet as syrup. 'A perfect garden as a shell for a perfect palace for a perfect king and queen.'

'In a perfect country?' John asked incautiously.

She smiled. She had no sense that there might be anything behind his question but spellbound admiration. 'Oh, yes,' she said. 'How could it be otherwise when it is ruled by my husband, and by me?'

Summer 1631

John had thought he would enjoy some time away from his home – never in his life before had he been so settled and he feared that the domestic life of Lambeth would be too narrow for him. But he found that he missed the daily changing business of the Ark, the midsummer flowering of the garden, and, more than anything else, the rapid changing of Frances who grew, in the summer of 1631, from a rosebud-mouthed, lisping toddler, to a little girl of rare determination.

He went home to Lambeth at every opportunity he could, to choose his stock from his own garden, and so that he could see his granddaughter. Each time he set off back to the palace, J would loiter in the stable yard, helping to pack the wagon with the heavy earthenware pots of plants.

'D'you need me at the palace?' he would ask, and John would drop his hand on his son's shoulder.

'I can manage without you another week,' he would say. 'I'll tell you when I need you there.'

'I'll come then,' J would promise. 'As I agreed to.'

He would watch his father swing into the seat and go, and John would chuckle to himself at the seriousness of his beloved son who had bound himself in so many contradictory ways: to his conscience, to his promise, to his father, to his wife.

By the end of the summer John had completed the designs for the work in the king's court, had shown them to the queen, and was ready to start the labour of digging over the garden and replanting it.

He had a team of men ready to start but he needed J to supervise the work while he went on to the queen's court, so that it should be designed in time for autumn planting.

'Will you come back to the palace with me this time, J?' he asked as the family were seated on the terrace one evening. J was drinking a glass of small ale, John had a small tot of rum. 'There's the physic garden which needs replanting, and now the queen has asked for a flowery mead.'

Jane looked up from her sewing, affronted. 'A what?'

John smiled. 'A flowery mead,' he said. 'Modelled on an old tapestry, those you see with the unicorn surrounded by hunters. It's supposed to be like a meadow, a perfect meadow, with all the flowers of the field but no stinging nettles. You plant it with wild and garden flowers and then you cut a little path around it for the pleasure of walking with wild flowers.'

'Why not walk by a meadow, then?' Jane asked.

John took another sip of rum. 'This is not a woman of sense, this is the queen. She would rather that everything was fashioned to perfection. Even a wildflower meadow. It's an old fashion in gardening, I did not think to plant one again. And although it is supposed to look wild and untouched, it takes unending work to keep it in flower and keep the weeds checked.'

'I can do it,' J said. 'I've never worked on one before. I'd like to do it.'

John raised his glass to his son. 'And you'll have little or nothing to do with Her Majesty,' he said. 'Since she first showed me the garden and told me what she wanted I have hardly seen her. She is with the king most of the day or with the courtiers. She wants the garden as the backcloth to her theatre of being queen. She has no interest in planting.'

'Well enough,' J said. 'For I have no interest in her.'

John had intended that J would miss the king and queen altogether, and timed the arrival of his son to the date when the court was due to have moved on. But there was the usual delay and confusion, and they were a week late in going. J, cutting the full-blown roses in the rose court and carefully shaking the petals into a broad flat basket for drying, looked up and saw that a short dark-haired woman was watching him.

He took in the wealth of jewels, the rich silk and lace of her gown, and the straggle of courtiers behind her, and pulled off his hat and bowed, as low as he should go for courtesy, but no lower.

'Who are you?' she asked abruptly.

'I am John Tradescant, the younger John Tradescant, Your Highness,' J said.

'I want the white petals separated from the pink,' she told him.

'I am keeping them apart, Your Majesty,' J said.

'You may take them to the still room when they are dry,' she said.

J bowed. They were to be dried in the silk house and the woman who ran the still room did not need them. These were for the masquing, and the Master of Revels and the Wardrobe Mistress would receive them, but there was little point in arguing when a queen wished to pretend that she understood the running of her palace.

'I want a tree planted in the middle of this court,' she announced suddenly. 'A large tree, and roses growing up to the roots. It is to symbolise my husband's care of his people. An oak tree, to symbolise his power and strength, and white roses to symbolise the innocent good people, clustered all around him.'

'Roses don't like shade, Your Majesty,' J ventured cautiously. 'Unfortunately I don't think they will thrive under an oak tree.'

'Surely you can plant some!'

'They need the sunshine, and they like the air through their branches,' J said. 'They will wither and die if they are planted beneath an oak tree.'

She pouted at him, as if he were being deliberately obtuse. 'But it is symbolic!'

'I see that,' J said. 'But the roses won't thrive.'

'Then you must plant and re-plant every time they die.'

J nodded. 'I could do that, Your Majesty, if it is your wish. But it would be very wasteful.'

414

'I don't care what it costs,' she said simply.

'And you would never have a large rose bush, because it would never have the time to be established, Your Majesty.'

She nodded, and paused in thought, tapping her little foot on the perfectly raked gravel. J thought that it must be rare that anyone refused to do her bidding. The courtiers, who had been lagging behind, had caught her up and were staring at him, and eyeing the queen as if they feared that his intransigence might cause them all to suffer the explosion of royal temper.

Instead she smiled. 'The oak tree is to symbolise the benevolence of my husband's rule,' she said, speaking slowly and clearly as if J were an idiot. 'Underneath the protection of the oak you must plant something which symbolises the people of his kingdoms, sheltering beneath his power. And around the outside, a border of roses and lilies which symbolise me.'

J had a sweet sense of the power of symbolism which his years at grammar school had quite failed to teach him. 'I understand, Your Majesty,' he said courteously, 'but unfortunately the shade of an oak tree is very injurious to all plants. Nothing grows beneath it except perhaps moss and grasses. The oak tree smothers and strangles the plants which try to grow beneath it. Strong and handsome plants need their own space and sunshine.'

Her brows snapped together and she turned away from him. 'I hope you are not trying to be clever beyond your position in life!' she said sharply.

J kept his face perfectly straight. 'I'm just a humble gardener, Your Majesty. I only know what will grow in your gardens. I know of nothing more than planting and weeding.'

She hesitated for a moment and then she decided to smile. 'Well, plant something pretty in the centre of the court,' she said, avoiding the discomfort of having her plans defeated. 'I don't care what.'

J bowed low and saw the courtiers exchange one swift glance of relief. The queen moved on, a man went forward and took her hand and whispered in her ear and she laughed and tossed her little head. One courtier delayed and watched J as he bent once more to snipping the rose-heads and shaking the petals.

'What were you saying, gardener? That the power of a king who is forever extending his power strangles growth and health in the kingdom?'

J turned an innocent gaze on the man. 'I, sir? No. I was talking of oak trees.'

The man met his gaze. 'There are many who would think that it is as true of royal power as it is of plants,' he said. 'There are many who would think that the power of the monarch needs to be pruned and snipped to fit well in the garden and to look well alongside the other grand plants of Parliament and church.'

J was about to agree, his face relaxing from the mask of discretion which he had worn since his arrival; but he remembered his father's warnings. 'I don't know about that,' he said stolidly. 'I'm just cutting the roses.'

The courtier nodded and moved away. J did not straighten up until the man was gone. Then he looked after him. 'The Levellers are in good company then,' he said thoughtfully. 'If they're in the very palace itself.'

J was right. Not everyone who danced in the masques and admired the growing collection of portraits which showed Charles as the fount of wisdom and Henrietta Maria as the greatest beauty believed the images they saw or the words they repeated. To some of them it was a game, to while away the leisure of a kingdom where governing was now done by default; local landlords enforced local laws, and national issues were only intermittently remembered. The young sons of nobility came to court and pretended to be in love with Henrietta Maria, writing sonnets to her dark curls, praising the whiteness of her skin. They hunted with Charles, they entertained him with singing, with dramas, with tableaux. It was an easy life, if inconsequential. Only the more intelligent or the more ambitious wanted more. Only the very few patriots thought that it was no way to run a kingdom which had once been thought of as a world power.

Henrietta Maria would have no talk of change. To assert English power abroad would need an effective army or navy and neither of these could be created without money. There was never any money in the royal coffers, and the only way to raise money was the invention of new and ingenious taxes which could create new revenue without recalling Parliament. The last thing either king or queen wanted was to recall Parliament and suffer the critical commentary of the House of Commons on their plans, on their expenditure, on their religious practices, on their household.

'Or we could borrow,' Henrietta Maria suggested at a meeting of the king's council.

The men bowed. No-one liked to tell the king and queen that England's credit was at rock bottom.

'Yes, that's it,' Charles said, pleased. 'See to it, my lord,' and he smiled and went from the council meeting with the air of a man who has completed his work.

No-one had the authority to call him back. Charles only listened to the queen and she listened to her confessor, to the French ambassador, to the favourites of her little court, to her servants, and to anyone who took her fancy. She was beyond bribery and beyond corruption because her tastes were so fickle. Not even the French ambassador – representing her own country – could be sure of her full attention. She would look out of the window while he was speaking to her, or wander about the room, turning over pretty ornaments with her fingers, always distracted, always seeking distraction. Only in the king's presence were her thoughts focused. Her one genuine interest was ensuring that he attended to her, and to her alone.

'Well, she shared him for so long with your lord Buckingham,' Elizabeth said to John as they got into bed one night. 'She must always be wary that he might find another favourite.'

John shook his head. 'He's faithful,' he said. 'She's a plain ordinary little woman but she holds his heart now. You see no passion between them, and no liveliness, but he cleaves to her as if he were a little dog.'

Elizabeth smiled. 'The king a dog? You sound like J!'

'His eyes follow her around the room.' John pulled on his nightcap. 'And when he is watching her she is never still. She is always acting the part of a delightful woman.' He pulled the blankets higher up the bed with a grunt of pleasure. 'She would drive me mad,' he said frankly.

Elizabeth sat up in bed and folded the sheet back over the blankets around his shoulders. 'Nights are drawing in. Are you warm enough in your house at Oatlands?'

'Of course,' John said. 'The maggots and I live like lords. They have eight charcoal burners set around their house and I have all the benefit. You're a chilly companion compared to my maggots.'

Elizabeth chuckled, not taking offence.

'He was a sad little boy,' John continued, returning to the king. 'I used to see him at Hatfield sometimes. King James never cared for him, and his mother never saw him. Nobody thought he'd ever be king with such a stronger older brother before him, so no-one bothered with him. Some of them said he'd never survive. He doted on his older brother and sister, and the one died and the other was sent far away. It was only when my lord duke befriended him that he found someone to love.'

'And then he died too,' Elizabeth said.

John bowed his head. 'God rest his soul. Now, all he has left is the queen, and the only real friend in the world she can be sure of is the king. Everyone else wants something from her or hopes to gain something from him through her. They must be lonely.'

'Then why not live less rich?' Elizabeth suggested, practical as ever. 'If they are surrounded by hangers-on and flatterers who do them no good, why not be rid of them? Why not spend time with their children? Why not seek out the men who care for their own consciences and would not hang on them and flatter them? God knows there were enough men of principle in the last Parliament, the king must have seen them often enough.'

'The price a king must pay is the loss of his common sense,' John said dryly. 'I've seen it over and over, with kings and great men. They are lied to so sweetly and so often that they lose the taste of truth. They have sugar and honey dripped on their tongue until they are sick of the taste of it, but they still cannot call for bread and cheese.'

'Poor them,' Elizabeth said with cheerful irony.

'Poor them indeed,' said John, thinking for a moment of his duke who died friendless at the end, and was buried at night and in secret.

Winter 1632–3

Jane was not well. She was tired all the time and disliked her food. Christmas came and went and she was no better. When Frances came running in to her parents on the morning of the twelfth day after Christmas for her presents she found her mother pale and sickly.

'Should she see a doctor?' Elizabeth asked J.

'She wants to go to her mother to stay for a few days,' J said. 'I'll take her tomorrow in the wagon.'

'Leave Frances here,' John said across the breakfast table. 'You'll stay with your grandfather, won't you, Frances?'

He could see little of her but a head of blonde curls and two interrogative curves of eyebrows. She bobbed upwards. 'Yes,' she said firmly. 'And we'll make things.'

'What sort of things?' John asked cautiously.

'Big things,' she said ominously.

'I'll stay overnight with the Hurtes and come back the next day,' J said. 'I'll call in at the docks in case there's anything of interest to be had on my way home.'

'I'll put up a hamper for you to take,' Elizabeth said, rising from the table. 'Come and help me, Frances, you can go into the store room and choose a jar of plums for Grandma Hurte.'

John did not go down to his orchard before Jane left. He waited by the wagon in the yard until he had seen her safely on the seat with her bags stowed. 'You will come back soon,' he said, in sudden anxiety.

She was pale but she still managed her familiar smile. 'No, I shall stay with my mother and tell her you beat me and overwork me.'

'You're very dear to me,' John said gruffly. 'I don't like to see you so pale.'

She leaned forward to whisper in his ear. 'I think I may be sick for a good reason,' she said. 'A very good reason. I've not told John yet, so mind you hush.'

It took him a moment to realise what she meant and then he stepped back and beamed up at her. 'Sir John Tradescant of Lambeth?'

'Sir John Tradescant himself,' she said.

Summer 1633

It was an easy pregnancy for Jane this time, and the work at the palace was easy for her husband since in May the king left England on a grand progress north.

'He has sucked all the praise he can from the English,' J said sourly to his wife. 'He has to go to the poor Scots to see them dance to his tune.'

She nodded but did not reply. She was sewing baby clothes on the terrace in the warm June night and John was within earshot.

'Have you heard how the king's progress is going?' she asked.

J nodded. 'He went riding and hunting as he travelled up the north road. And everywhere he goes there are feasts and knighthoods and processions. He sees the country turn out to greet him and he thinks that all is well.'

'And is it not?' Jane asked. Her hand went gently to the soft curve of her belly. 'With Parliament dissolved and the country at peace? Is it perhaps only a few men like you, J, who are not content with this king?'

J shrugged. 'How can I say? When I meet a lecturer or a travelling preacher they tell me of men arrested for talking out of turn and for complaining about unjust taxes. I know that there are more Papists in the city than I have ever seen before and that they are allowed to hear Mass in the very heart of the kingdom. I know that the king's best friends are Papists and his wife is a Papist and the godparents of his child are Papists. And I know that our own vicar at Lambeth is at odds with the new Archbishop of Canterbury, William Laud, who is bishop of everywhere it seems, and now archbishop overall. But you are right – there are no voices raised against it – maybe it is just me.'

Jane leaned forward and touched his brown cheek. 'And me,' she said. 'I don't thank the archbishop for ordering how I should pray. And Father is furious about the taxes. But there is nothing anyone can do. There's no Parliament – who can tell the king that he is doing wrong?'

'Especially not when the fools troop out and throw roses down in the road before his horse,' J growled crossly. 'And when he touches a bunch of poxed fools for the king's evil and convinces them they are cured by his hand.'

Jane was silent for a moment. 'I want to believe that better times are coming,' she said.

The wistfulness in her voice caught J's attention. He took her hand and put his other hand gently on her belly. 'They are for us,' he said reassuringly. 'Whatever is happening for the king and his foolish court. A new baby on the way and the garden growing well. These are good times for us, Jane, and better times coming.'

John's prediction of a grandson was accurate. Jane gave birth to a large-boned brown-haired baby in the middle of the afternoon of a warm September day. J was picking apples at the furthest end of the orchard, finding the cries of Jane's labour quite unbearable. John and Frances were keeping each other company looking for the early fallen chestnuts down John's little avenue.

'We'll roast them,' Frances teased her grandfather with the cleverness of the bright three-year-old.

'They're not sweet chestnuts.' John fell into the trap. 'They're no good for eating.'

'It's no good as a tree then,' she said innocently. 'I don't like it.'

'Oh, Frances . . .' John started and then he saw the bright twinkle in her eyes. 'You are a wicked girl!' he pronounced. 'And I think I will beat you.' He started to run towards her and she picked up her little gown and ran out of his reach, down the avenue of trees towards her father.

'John! J!' It was Elizabeth's voice, calling from the terrace. John saw his son's white face turn towards the house, then his slithering fall down the ladder, and then his run, past his daughter and his father, up the avenue towards the house.

'Is she all right?'

His mother's face alone was reassurance enough. 'She's fine,' she said. 'Very tired. And you have a son.'

J gave a little yelp of delight. 'A son!' he yelled down the avenue where Tradescant was limping up with Frances bobbing in his wake. 'A son! A boy!'

John checked and a broad smile spread across his face. He turned to Frances. 'You have a brother,' he told her. 'Your mother has given birth to a little boy.'

She was on her dignity, the powerful dignity of the three-year-old, and determined to be unimpressed. 'Is that very good?' she asked.

John scooped her up and swung her to her usual place on his back. 'It's very good,' he said. 'It means our name will last forever, with a son to continue the line. Sir John Tradescant of the Ark, Lambeth. It sounds very well indeed.'

'I shall be a Sir too,' Frances said, rather muffled with her face pressed into his back.

'Yes, you will,' John said agreeably. 'I shall make sure that the king knows that you need a knighthood, when we next speak.'

Winter 1633–4

The queen took a fancy to J. It was as if she had to find some way of encompassing his refusal to do exactly as she wished about the oak tree. She could not leave his rejection of her plans alone, it rubbed the tender spot of her vanity. When she was walking in the gardens with her ladies, wrapped up in the richest of furs, or watching her courtiers practising archery at the butts, she would stop if she saw J and call him over. 'Here is my gardener who will only plant what he pleases!' she would exclaim in her strong French accent. 'The young Tradescant.'

J would take his hat off his head in the chill wind, in obedience to his father's instructions, and bow, but not very low, in obedience to his wife, and assume an expression of dogged patience as the queen was once more charming to him.

'I want you to plough up the allee of yews. It is so very dark and dreary now it is winter.'

'Of course,' J replied. 'Only . . .'

'There you go!' she cried. 'I can never do what I wish in my own garden, Tradescant will always have his own way. Why may I not have those trees grubbed out?'

J glanced down the court to the beautiful allee of trees. They were so old that they had bowed together and interlinked at the top so that they made a perfectly round tunnel. A bare brown earth path ran beneath them, marked with perfectly round white stepping stones. Nothing grew beneath them in the deep greeny light, not even in midsummer did the sunshine filter through. In the heat of the day

425

it was as cool as a cave. To touch such trees other than to prune and shape them would be an act of wanton destruction.

'They are useful to Your Majesty for bows for your archers,' he said politely. 'The yew is specially grown for it, it is very strong, Your Majesty.'

'We can get yew anywhere,' she said lightly.

'Not as good as this.'

She threw back her head and laughed like a little girl. J, who knew the ring of real laughter from a mischievous girl, was not impressed by the queen's coquetry.

'You see how it is? You see?' she demanded, turning to one of her courtiers. The young man smiled responsively. 'I am allowed to do nothing with my own land. Tradescant, I am glad I am not your wife. Do you have a wife?'

'Yes, Your Majesty.' J disliked it most when the queen became intimate with him.

'At your home? At – what do you call it? – the Ark?'

'Yes, Your Majesty.'

'And children?'

'A boy, and an older girl.'

'But this is very good,' she exclaimed. 'And do you adore your wife, Tradescant? Do you do her every wish?'

J hesitated.

'Not all wives are as fortunate as you, Your Majesty,' the courtier swiftly interposed. 'There can be few wives who have a husband who adores them as the king adores you. You are a goddess to His Majesty. You are a goddess to us all.'

Henrietta Maria blushed a little and smiled. 'Ah, that is true; but all the same, you must be kind to your little wife, Tradescant. I would have every woman in the kingdom as blessed as me.'

J bowed to avoid answering.

'And she must be obedient to you,' the queen went on. 'And you must bring up your children to obey you both, just as the king and I are like kind parents to the country. Then both the country and your household will be at peace.'

J pressed his tongue to his teeth to stop himself arguing and bowed again.

'And everyone will be happy,' the queen said. She turned to the courtier. 'Isn't that right?'

'Of course,' he said simply. 'As long as people remember that they must love and obey you and the king as if you were their parents everyone will be happy.'

J bore the brunt of the queen's interest because he was more often at Oatlands than his father in the autumn days. Elizabeth was sick in October with pains in her chest and a nagging cough which would not be eased, and John did not want to leave her.

She got up from her bed to see Baby John baptised at their church in November, but she left the baptismal feast early and John found her lying on their bed shivering, though the maid had lit a fire in the bedroom.

'My dear,' he said. 'I did not know you were so ill.'

'I'm cold,' she said. 'Cold in my bones.'

John heaped more logs on the fire and took another quilt from the press at the foot of the bed. Still her face was white and her fingertips were icy.

'You'll mend in the spring,' he said cheerfully. 'When the ground warms up and the daffodils come out.'

'I'm not a plant, shedding my leaves,' she protested through her pale lips. 'I won't bloom like a tree.'

'But you will bloom,' John said, suddenly anxious. 'You will get better, Lizzie.'

She shook her head so slightly that he could hardly see the movement on the pillow.

'Don't say so!' he cried. 'I had always thought I would go first. You're years younger than me, this is just a chill!'

Again she made that small movement. 'It is more than a chill,' she said. 'There is a bone growing in me, pressing on me. I can feel it pressing against my breath.'

'Have you seen a physician?' John demanded.

She nodded. 'He could not find anything wrong, but I can feel it inside, John. I don't think I will see your daffodils next spring.'

He could feel his throat tightening and his eyes burning. 'Don't say such a thing!'

She smiled and turned her head to look at him. 'Of all the men who could do without their wives you would be the first,' she said. 'Half of our married life you have been away with your gardens or on your travels, and the other half you were with your lord.'

The usual complaint struck him very painfully now she said it for the last time. 'Did I neglect you? I thought – you had J and your house – and it was my life before I married you . . . I thought . . .'

Elizabeth gave him her gentle, forgiving smile. 'Your work came first,' she said simply, 'and your lord before everything. But I had third place in your life. You never loved a woman more than you loved me, did you, John?'

Tradescant had a brief memory of a dimpled serving girl at Theobalds, decades, it seemed like centuries, ago, and a dozen half-remembered women between then and now.

'No,' he said, and he spoke the truth. 'None that came anywhere near my love for you. I did put the gardens first, and my lord before all else, but there was always you, Elizabeth. You were the only woman for me.'

'And what a long way we have come,' she said wonderingly. Through the wooden floorboards of their bedroom came the muffled sounds of the baptismal party. They could hear Josiah Hurte's voice above all the others, and then, in a sudden silence, Frances's delighted giggle as someone swung her up in the air.

John nodded. 'A grand house, a collection of rarities, a nursery garden and an orchard, and a post at the king's palace.'

'And grandchildren,' Elizabeth said with satisfaction. 'I feared when there was only J – and then when they had only Frances . . .'

'That there would be no-one to carry our name?'

She nodded. 'I know it is a vanity . . .'

'There are the trees,' John said. 'The flowers, the fruits, and my chestnut trees. We nursed them up just as we nursed J. And now there is one in all the greatest gardens of the country. That is our legacy. The chestnut trees we nursed up together.'

She turned her head and closed her eyes. 'You *would* say that,' she said, but it was not a complaint.

'You lie quiet,' John said, rising stiffly from the bed. 'I will send up the maid with a posset for you. Lie quiet and get well. You will see my daffodils this spring, Elizabeth, and even the pink and white candle blossoms on our chestnut trees.'

In January, as the new baby thrived, and Elizabeth grew weaker and never left her bed, J found his father supervising the lad digging up a small chestnut sapling and transplanting it, roots and all, into a large carrying tub. J and the boy slid their carrying poles into the rings of the tub and moved it, as John directed them, right into the house, into the rarities room, and set it down beside the huge window where it would catch the winter light.

'What are you doing?'

'Forcing it,' John said abruptly.

Beside the tub was a big half-barrel of daffodils that had been lifted from the orchard, their green shoots only just showing above the damp earth.

'We need an orangery,' John said. 'We should have built one years ago.'

'We do,' J agreed. 'But for delicate plants from abroad; not for daffodils and chestnut saplings. What are you doing with them?'

'I want to get them in flower,' John said. 'As soon as I can force them.'

'Why?'

'To please your mother,' John said, telling only half the story.

Every night John banked in the fire so the plants were warm all night, every day he sprinkled them – three, four times a day – with warm water. In the evening he set candles around them to give them extra light and warmth. J would have laughed but there was something about his father's intensity which puzzled him.

'Why d'you want them to bloom early?'

'I have my reasons,' John said.

Spring 1634

John achieved his goal. When Elizabeth died in March, her room was filled with the golden light of dozens of daffodils, and the sweet scent of them perfumed her room. The very last thing she saw as her eyes wearily closed was John coming in the door, his face warm with a smile, and his hands filled with the exquisite pink and white pyramid blossoms of his chestnut trees.

'For you,' he said and bent and kissed her.

Elizabeth tried to say: 'Thank you. I love you, John', but the darkness was creeping in; and in any case, he knew.

After the funeral John moved back to the silk house at Oatlands for the rest of the season. He did not feel that he wanted to be at his home, without Elizabeth. At night he could not sleep; but he liked the warmth of the pretty wooden house, and there was something strangely comforting about the thought of the thousands of silkworms, sleeping in their little cocoons, next door, dreaming whatever dreams silkworms spin.

The queen had authorised the building of a coalhouse and a new and beautiful orangery, and John supervised the building in the short hours of springtime daylight. It was another light-timbered fanciful building like a little wooden palace. It went up quickly and John wrote to J, telling him to bring some citrus whips when he next came.

Apart from the building, there was little to do in the gardens in the cold spring days, but John liked to walk around and see that the streams and fountains were clear of leaves, and that the little green snouts of bulbs were pushing their way defiantly through the cold earth. When it was warmer he would plant a new bowling green for Their Majesties, and he watched the men digging, rolling, and harrowing the earth until every smallest stone was gone and the ground was ready for the seed. They grumbled when he made them dig in the old rotted dung from the stables and then water it till it froze and melted and froze again, but John insisted that the ground be rich and smooth before the seed was scattered.

When the snowdrops were thick as ice under the trees, snow-white and green, John thought of his lord Buckingham, who had loved to see the first snowdrops at New Hall. But when the daffodils came through he thought of Elizabeth, who had died with their golden colour all around her. There could be no doubt that Elizabeth had gone straight to heaven, he thought. She had lived a life which was as blameless as any woman's, and she had died surrounded by that golden blaze of glory. At least he had been able to give her that.

As for the duke, it was impossible that there could be a God who loved beauty who could resist him. The king himself loved him and prayed for his soul every day. John felt that the two people in the world that he had truly loved were at peace, and he found he could bear the short cold days and the long cold nights.

He was thinking of the two loves of his life – his passion for the duke and his steady reliable affection for Elizabeth – and watching the water in the fountain of the great court when a shadow fell on the basin of the fountain and he looked around. It was the king. John pulled his hat from his head and dropped to his knee on the cold stone.

'How many years is it now, since your master died?' the king asked abruptly. He did not look at John, but kept his gaze on the cold water in the marble basin.

'Five years and seven months,' John said instantly. 'He died towards the end of summer.'

'You can get up,' the king said. He turned from the fountain and started to walk down the path, a small gesture commanded John to follow him.

'I don't think a man like that can ever be r...r...replaced,' the king said, half to himself. 'Not in a king's council, not in the heart.'

John felt the usual dull ache at the thought of Buckingham.

'And a woman's love is not the same,' the king remarked. 'To please a woman you have to try and keep trying, and women are changeable: first one thing pleases them, then another. But a man's love is easier, s...steadier. When George and I were young men we spent whole days thinking of nothing but hunting and play. The king used to call us his dear l...l...lads.'

John nodded. The king paused and abruptly turned to him. 'Did you ever see my brother Henry?'

'Yes,' John said. 'I was gardener at Theobalds, and then for my lord Cecil at Hatfield. I saw Prince Henry and King James often; I remember you too, Your Majesty.'

'Do you think he was like the D...Duke of Buckingham? My brother? In his ways?'

John thought. They had the same arrogance, the same easy smile. They had the same sense that the world was half in love with them and that all they had to do was to accept homage.

'Yes,' he said slowly. 'The prince was like the duke in many ways. But the duke had...' He broke off.

'What?'

'The duke had that shining beauty,' John said. 'The prince was a handsome boy, as handsome as any. But the duke was as beautiful as an angel.'

Charles suddenly smiled, his grave face warming. 'He was, wasn't he?' he said. 'It's so easy to f...forget. All the portraits I have of him show his beauty, but all p...portraits are beautiful even when the sitters are plain. It's good to know that you keep a picture of him in your heart, Tradescant.'

'I do,' John said simply. 'I see him night and day. And sometimes I dream of him.'

'As if he w...w...were alive?'

John nodded. 'I can never remember in my dreams that he is

432

dead,' he confessed. 'And sometimes I wake and think he is calling for me, and I jump from my bed as if I were a young man and in a hurry to go to him.'

'The queen didn't l . . . like him,' the king said thoughtfully.

Tradescant tactfully said nothing.

'She was jealous.'

Tradescant gave a little nod. The king glanced at him. 'Was your wife jealous of your love for your lord?'

Tradescant thought of Elizabeth and her long enmity for the duke and all he stood for: luxury, Popery, waste, and carnal sin.

'Oh, yes,' he said with a smile. 'But women were always besotted with him or his worst enemy, or both.'

The king laughed shortly. 'It's true. He was a l . . . lamentable man with women.'

The gardener and the king smiled at one another, the king looking into Tradescant's face for the first time.

'D'you have any of his things at your Ark?' the king asked.

'Some plants from the garden at New Hall, and a couple of rarities from the Ile de Rhé,' Tradescant replied carefully, conscious of the danger of this conversation. 'He gave me some things from his own collection of rarities. Anything he did not need, anything he already had. I was collecting for him for many years.'

'I'll come and see it,' the king said. 'I'll bring the queen. I have some things you might l . . . like, some gloves and things.'

Tradescant bowed low. 'I should be honoured.'

When he rose up the king was looking at him as if they shared a secret. 'He was a very very great man, wasn't he?'

'Yes,' Tradescant agreed, looking at the king's melancholy face and sparing him the truth, as everyone always did. 'He was the greatest lord in England and the most fit for his high office.'

The king nodded and turned away without another word. Tradescant, unseen, knelt again as the king strolled off. When the king had gone he got awkwardly to his feet; his bad knee was painful in the cold weather.

While John was at Oatlands, J stayed at Lambeth. Jane was now complete mistress of the house and the place was run with godly care. The day started with prayers for the household which J read aloud and then any one of them, from the youngest kitchen maid to the senior gardener, would pray extempore, saying what he or she wished to the congregation and to their own personal God. The household went about their work all day and then came together again in the evening, before bedtime, for another brief session of praying together. Imperceptibly, the dress of the household altered, the servants naturally copying Jane's modest muted style.

J rather thought that his father would complain when he finally returned home, but there was no explosion of disapproval.

'You must run the house as you wish,' he said equably to Jane. 'You are the mistress here now. You must order what you wish.'

'I think it is what everyone wishes,' Jane said eagerly.

John gave her a little knowing smile. 'But what if it were not?' he asked. 'What if the cook and the kitchen maid, Peter, and the two gardeners and their lad all agreed that they would rather have some dancing and some singing and a cup of ale instead? That they wanted to wear green and scarlet and ribbons in their hair? Would you provide it?'

'I would reason with them,' Jane said stiffly. 'And wrestle with their souls.'

'So people are free to do as they wish as long as they choose right?'

'Yes,' she said; and then, 'No, not exactly.'

John smiled at her. 'When you have power over people, it is very easy to forget that they are doing as you order because you order it,' he said. 'You can mistake obedience for consent. I say that my household shall be obedient to you. I don't think that they prefer it that way. But they will be obedient to you because I order it. However, I shall come to prayers only now and then – when I really want to.'

'I am sure you would find it a comfort . . .' Jane began.

John patted her cheek. 'I think you are wrestling with my soul,' he said. 'I want my soul left in peace.'

Jane smiled at him. 'All right,' she conceded. 'D'you want to see Baby John?'

'Yes,' John said.

Frances brought the baby and placed him carefully in his grandfather's lap. Baby John put his fists against his grandfather's chest, reared back and inspected his face.

'He still doesn't eat properly,' Frances said disapprovingly.

'Why not?' John asked.

'He still sucks,' Frances said. 'He's like a little goat.'

John smiled. 'Don't you love your little brother?' he asked.

Frances drew closer to him. 'He's all right,' she said. 'But I don't like how everyone makes such a fuss of him. I'm still your favourite, aren't I, Granddad?'

John kept one hand firmly on Baby John, and with the other drew his granddaughter to him and kissed her smooth warm head, just before the plain white cap which Jane insisted that she wore.

'It's not always the best thing to be, the Favourite,' he said, thinking of his lord and the parliament that impeached him, and the king who mourned for him.

'Yes it is,' she said instantly. 'I was always your favourite and I still am.'

He settled her into the crook of his arm. 'Yes, you are,' he said. 'You are my precious girl.'

'And when I am grown I shall be gardener to the king,' she said firmly. 'And run the Ark.'

'Girls cannot be gardeners,' John said gently.

'Cook says that girls can be gardeners because women are equal to men at the Day of Judgement,' Frances volunteered. 'And that prophesying and preaching comes natural to women who es . . . es . . . eschew carnival knowledge.'

'I think you mean carnal knowledge,' John said unsteadily.

'Carnival,' Frances corrected him. 'It means you can't go maypole dancing or buy fairings, or play in the churchyard on feast days.'

'I suppose it does,' John said. He was very near to laughter but he managed to turn it into a gruff cough.

'And I am going to eschew carnival knowledge and be free of sin,' Frances went on. 'And then I can be the king's gardener.'

'We'll see,' John said pacifically.

'Is Baby John going to be the king's gardener?' she demanded.

John nestled the baby back into his arm and took up the plump dimpled hand. 'I think he's too small to work yet,' he said tactfully. 'Whereas you're a great big girl. By the time he's ready for work you'll have been prophesying and gardening for years.'

It was exactly the right answer. Frances beamed at him and went to the door. 'I have to go now,' she said seriously. 'I've got some seedlings that want watering.'

John nodded. 'You see? You're a gardener already and all Baby John can do is sit inside with his grandfather.'

Frances nodded and slipped through the door. John looked out of the window and saw her heaving the heavy watering bottle down towards the seed beds set against the warm south wall. Her little thumb was too small to fit the hole at the top of the bottle and she was sprinkling a shiny trail of water behind her like a determined snail.

January 1635

The letter that arrived for the Tradescants at Lambeth bore the royal stamp on the bottom. It was a demand for a tax, a new tax, another new tax. John opened it in the rarities room, standing beside the Venetian windows to catch the light, J beside him.

'It's a tax to support the Navy,' he said. 'Ship money.'

'We don't pay that,' J said at once. 'That's only for the ports and the seaside towns who need the protection of the Navy against pirates and smugglers.'

'Looks like we *do* pay it,' John said grimly. 'I imagine that everyone is going to have to pay it.'

J swore and took a brief step down the room and back again. 'How much?'

'Enough,' John said. 'Do we have savings?'

'We have my last quarter's wages untouched, but that was to buy cuttings and seeds this spring.'

'We'll have to dip into that,' John told him.

'Can we refuse to pay?'

John shook his head.

'We should refuse,' J declared passionately. 'The king has no right to levy taxes. Parliament levies the taxes and passes the money raised on to the king. He has no right to demand on his own account. It is Parliament that should consent to the tax, and any complaint the people have is heard in Parliament. The king cannot just charge what he pleases. Where is it to end?'

John shook his head again. 'The king has closed down Parliament, and I doubt he'll invite them back. The world has changed, J, and the king is uppermost. If he sets a tax then we have to pay. We have no choice.'

J glared at his father. 'You always say we have no choice!' he exclaimed.

John looked wearily at his son. 'And you always bellow like a Ranter. I know you think me an old fool, J. So tell me your way. You refuse to pay the tax, the king's men or the parish officers come and arrest you for treason. You are thrown into prison. Your wife and children go hungry. The business collapses, the Tradescants are ruined. This is a master plan, J. I applaud you.'

J looked as if he were about to burst out but then he laughed a short bitter laugh. 'Aye,' he said. 'Very well. You're in the right. But it sticks in my throat.'

'It'll stick in many throats,' John predicted. 'But they'll pay.'

'There will come a time when they will refuse,' J warned his father. 'You cannot choke a country year after year and not have to face the people at the end of it. There will come a time when good men will refuse in such numbers that the king has to listen.'

'Maybe,' John said thoughtfully. 'But who can say when?'

'If the king knew that his subjects object, that they don't like being ordered to church and the prayers ordered for them, that they don't like being ordered to play like children in the churchyard after the service, that there are men in the country who want to use the Lord's Day for thought and reflection and who don't want to practise archery and sports – if the king knew all that –'

'Yes, but he doesn't know that,' John pointed out. 'He dismissed the men who might have told him, and those left at court would never bring him bad news.'

'You could tell him,' J observed.

'I'm no better than the rest of them,' John replied. 'I've learned to be a courtier. Maybe it's late in life, but I've learned it now. I told the truth as I saw it to all the lords I ever served and I never flattered one of them with lies. But this king is a man who doesn't invite the truth. I tell you, J, I *cannot* speak the truth to him. He is surrounded by fancy. I would not dare to be the one to tell him that he and the queen are not adored everywhere they go, I couldn't tell him that the men he has thrown into prison are not wild men, madmen, hotheads, but men more sane and careful and honourable than the rest of us. I cannot be the one to tell him that he is in the wrong and the country is slowly coming to know it. He has made sure that the world appears as best pleases him. It would take more than me to turn it upside down.'

The king kept his promise to visit the Ark, though Tradescant had thought it was a royal promise – one thrown off in the moment with no thought other than to please by the graciousness of the intention. But early in January a Gentleman Usher of the court came to the Ark and was shown into the rarities room.

He looked around, concealing his surprise. 'It's an imposing room,' he remarked to J, who had shown him in. 'I had not thought you had built such a grand room.'

J inwardly congratulated his father for overweening ambition. 'We need a lot of accommodation,' he said modestly. 'Every day we get something new for the collection, and the things need to be shown in the best light.'

The usher nodded. 'The king and queen will visit you tomorrow at noon,' he said. 'They want to see this famous collection.'

J bowed. 'We will be honoured.'

'They will not dine here, but you may offer them biscuits and wine and fruit,' the usher said. 'I assume you will have no difficulty with that?'

J nodded. 'Of course.'

'And there is no need for any loyal address, or anything of that sort,' the usher said. 'No poem of greeting or anything like that. This is just an informal visit.'

J thought that the king and queen were very unlikely to get a poem of greeting from his staunchly independent wife but he merely nodded his assent. 'I understand.'

'And if there are any in your household who suffer from strong and misguided views –' the usher paused to make sure that J was following him '– it is your responsibility to make sure that they do not appear before Their Majesties. The king and queen do not want to see long Puritanical faces on their visit, they do not want anyone reflecting on them. Make sure that only your well-dressed and joyful neighbours are on the road.'

'I can make sure that they enjoy their visit to my house, but I cannot clear Lambeth of beggars and paupers,' J replied sharply. 'Are they coming by boat?'

'Yes, their carriage will meet them at Lambeth.'

'Then they should drive swiftly through Lambeth,' J remarked unhelpfully. 'Or they may see some of their subjects who are not happy and smiling.'

The usher looked at him sharply. 'If anyone fails to uncover his head and shout "God save the king", he will be sorry for it,' he warned. 'There are men in prison for treason for less. There are men with cropped ears and slit tongues who did nothing more than refuse to take their hats off when the royal carriage went by.'

J nodded. 'They will meet with nothing but courtesy and respect in my house,' he said. 'But I am not responsible for the crowd on the quayside by the horse-ferry.'

'I am responsible for them,' the gentleman usher replied. 'And I think you will find that every one of them shouts for the king.'

He swung back his coat and J saw the bag of pennies at his belt.

'Good,' J said. 'Then I am sure Their Majesties will have a merry visit.'

He had feared that Jane would be rebellious, but the challenge to her housekeeping was such that, for the moment, she put aside her principles. She sent a message to her mother in the city and Mrs Hurte arrived at dawn on the day of the royal visit with her own store of damask tablecloths, and her own box of ginger biscuits and sugared plums. Josiah Hurte had disapproved; but the women were on their mettle and were determined that there should be no critical comments at the court about the chief gardener's house.

The rarities room and the parlour had been swept and polished ever since the gentleman usher had left the house. Jane laid the table in the parlour and set the fire against the cold of the January day, while J and his father prowled around the rarities room for the hundredth time, ensuring that every case stood open and that every rarity – even the smallest carved hazelnut shell – was laid out to its best advantage.

When everything was polished and prepared, there was nothing to do but wait.

Frances went to sit on the front garden wall at half past ten. At eleven, John sent the garden lad down the road to keep watch and give them warning when he saw the royal carriage roof rocking down the bumpy road towards them. At midday Frances came in, her fingertips blue with cold, saying that there was no sign of them, and that the king was a liar and a fool.

Jane shushed her and rushed her to the kitchen to get warm before the fire.

At two o'clock John said that he was too starved to wait, and went to the kitchen for a bowl of soup. Frances, perched on her stool and with her face inside a large bowl of broth, emerged only to say that the king shouldn't say he was coming if he did not mean it, as it caused a lot of people, especially those who had to wait in the cold, a great deal of discomfort.

'If he's the king, he should do what he promises.'

'You're not the first to think that,' John remarked.

At three o'clock, after tempers had frayed and the fires in the parlour and the rarities room had burned down and been renewed, there was a thunderous knocking at the garden door and the lad poked his frozen face into the room, his nose blue with cold, and said: 'They're coming at last!'

Frances screamed and ran for her cloak, all complaints forgotten, and rushed to her station on the front wall. J leaped from his seat at the kitchen table, wiped his mouth, and rubbed his hands on the cloth.

John pulled on his best coat, which he had laid aside in the heat of the kitchen, and rolled, with his limping gait, to the front door to hold it open as the king and queen visited the Ark.

Their Majesties did not see Frances as the coach drew up, though she stood up on the wall and did her best curtsey, perched on top.

When they walked past her without even a glance in her direction, Frances, who had hoped to be appointed as the king's gardener on that very day, scrambled down from the wall, tore round to the back door, and stationed herself by the door of the rarities room where they could not possibly miss her as they entered.

'Your Majesties.' John bowed low as the queen stepped over the threshold. J, behind him, matched his bow.

'Ah, Tradescant!' the queen said. 'Here we are to see your rarities, and the king has brought you some things for your collection.'

The king waved at an usher, who unfolded a bolt of cloth. Inside was a handsome pair of light suede gloves.

'King Henry's hunting gloves,' the king said. 'And some other goods you can see at your leisure. Now show me your treasures.'

John led the way around the room. The king wanted to see everything: the carved ivories, the monstrous egg, the beautifully carved cup of rhinoceros horn, the Benin drum, the worked Senego leather, the letter case a woman on the Ile de Rhé had tried to smuggle out of the fort by swallowing it, the curious crystals and stones, the body of the mermaid from Hull, the skull of the unicorn and the animal and bird skins, including that of a strange and ugly flightless bird.

'This is remarkable,' the king said. 'And what is in these drawers?'

'Small and large eggs, Your Majesty,' John said. 'I had the drawers especially made to house them.'

The king drew open one drawer and then another. John had arranged the eggs in size from the smallest in shallow drawers at the top, to the largest in deep wide drawers at the bottom. The eggs, all colours from speckled black to purest shining white, sat on their little beds of sheep's wool like precious jewels.

'What a flock of birds you would have if they hatched!' the king exclaimed.

'They are all blown, and light as air, Your Majesty,' Tradescant explained, giving him a tiny blue eggshell, no larger than his fingertip.

'And what is this?' the king said, returning the egg and moving on.

'These are dried flower blossoms of many rarities from my garden,' John said, pulling out tray after tray of flower heads. 'My wife used to dry them in sugar for me, so that men might come and see the blossoms at any time of year. Often an artist will come and draw them.'

'Pretty,' the queen said approvingly, looking at the tray with the flowers laid out.

'This is from the Lack tulip, which I bought for my lord Buckingham in the Low Countries,' John said, touching one perfect petal with the tip of his finger.

'Does it grow still?' the king asked, looking at the petal as if it might hold some memory of its lord.

'Yes,' John said gently. 'It grows still.'

'I should like to have it,' the king said. 'In memory of him.'

John bowed as he gave away a tulip worth a year's income. 'Of course, Your Majesty.'

'And many mechanical things? Do you have mechanical toys?' the king asked. 'When I was a boy I had a small army made of lead with cannons which actually fired shot. I planned my campaigns with them, I had part of Richmond laid out as a battlefield and drew my men up in the proper way for an attack.'

'I have a little model windmill, as they use in the Low Countries for pumping out their ditches,' John said, crossing to the other side of the room. He moved the sails with his hand and the king could see the pump inside going up and down.

'And I have a miniature clock, and a model cannon.' John directed the king to another corner. 'And a miniature spinning wheel carved in amber.'

'And what do you have from my lord Buckingham's collection?' the king asked.

J, suddenly wary, glanced at his father.

'Something very dear to me and worth all the rest put together,' John said. He drew the king to a cabinet under the window and opened one of the drawers.

'What's this?' the king asked.

'The last letter he ever wrote to me,' John said. 'Ordering me to Portsmouth, to meet him for the expedition to Rhé.'

The queen glanced over at them with impatience; even now she did not like to hear Buckingham's name on the king's lips. 'What's the largest rarity you have?' she asked J loudly.

'We have the whole head of an elephant, with its great double teeth,' J said, pointing up to where they had hung the skull from the roof beams. 'And a rhinoceros horn and jaw bone.'

The king did not even turn his head, but unfolded the letter. 'His own hand!' he cried as soon as he saw the dashed careless style. He read it. 'And he commands you to go at once,' he said. 'Oh, Tradescant, if only everything had been ready at once!'

'I was there,' John said. 'Just as he wished.'

'But he was late, weeks late,' the king said, smiling ruefully. 'Wasn't that just like him?'

'And what is *your* favourite?' the queen demanded loudly.

'I think I like the Chinese fan the best,' J said. 'It is so delicate and so fine-painted.'

He opened a drawer, took it out and laid it in her hand. 'Oh! I must have one just like it!' she exclaimed. 'Charles! Look!'

Reluctantly he looked up from the letter. 'Very pretty,' he said.

'Come and see,' she commanded. 'You can't see the painting from there!'

He handed back the page of paper to John and went towards her. With a sense of relief, J saw that the question of how many of the exhibits had been the property of Lord Buckingham had completely slipped away.

'I must have one just like this!' she cried. 'I shall borrow this and have it copied.'

J was not courtier enough to assent. John stepped quickly forward. 'Your Majesty, we would be honoured if you would have it as a gift,' he said.

'Do you not need it in your collection, to show to people?' she asked, opening her eyes wide.

John bowed. 'The collection, the Ark itself, is all yours, Your Majesty, as everything lovely and rare must be yours. You shall decide what you leave here, and what you take.'

She laughed delightedly and for a moment J was afraid that her greed would outrun her desire to seem charming. 'I shall leave everything here, of course!' she said. 'But whenever you have something new and rare and pretty I shall come and see it.'

'We will be honouréd,' J said, with a sense of a danger narrowly avoided. 'Will Your Majesty take a glass of wine?'

The queen turned for the door. 'But who is this?' she asked as Frances leaped forward and opened the door for her. 'A little footman?'

'I'm Frances,' the little girl said. She had forgotten all about the curtsey which Jane had reluctantly taught her. 'I was waiting for you for ages.'

For a moment J thought that the queen would take offence. But then she laughed her girlish laugh. 'I am sorry to keep you waiting!' she exclaimed. 'But am I what you thought a queen would be?'

Both John and J moved forward, J smoothly standing beside Frances and giving her thin shoulder blade a swift admonitory pinch, while John filled the pause. 'She was expecting Queen Elizabeth,' he said. 'We have a miniature of Her Majesty, painted on ivory. She did not know that a Queen could be so young and beautiful.'

Henrietta Maria laughed. 'And a wife, and the mother of a son and heir,' she reminded him. 'Unlike the poor heretic queen.' Frances gasped in horror and was about to argue but to J's enormous relief the queen went past the little girl without another glance. Jane threw open the parlour door and curtseyed.

'I wasn't expecting Queen Elizabeth, and anyway she wasn't a heret–' Frances started to argue. J leaned heavily on her shoulder as the king went past.

'She is my first granddaughter and has been much indulged,' John explained.

The king down looked at her. 'You must repay favour with duty,' he said firmly.

'I will,' Frances said easily. 'But may I come and work for you and be your gardener, as my grandfather and father do? I am very good with seeds and I can take cuttings and some of them do grow.'

It would have cost the king nothing to smile and say yes; but he was always a man who could be ambushed by shyness, and by his own desire to be seen to do the right thing. With only one person had he been free of his need to set an example, to be kingly and wise in all things; and that man was long dead.

'M . . . maids and wives must stay at home,' he decreed, ignoring Frances's shocked little face. 'Everyone in their r . . . right place is what I wish for my kingdom now. You must obey your father and then your husband.' Then he passed on towards the parlour.

J threw a quick harassed glance at Frances's appalled face, and followed him.

Frances looked up at her grandfather, and saw that his face was warm with sympathy. She turned and pitched into his arms.

'I think the king is a pig,' she wailed passionately into his coat. John, a lifelong royalist, could not disagree.

Mrs Hurte went home that evening, pleasantly shocked and appalled by the queen's jewels, the richness of her perfume, the king's lustrous hair, his cane, his lace. As the wife of a mercer she had taken particular note of their cloth and she was anxious to hurry home with news of French silk and Spanish lace, while English weavers and spinners went hungry. The king had a diamond on his finger the size of Frances's fist, and the queen had pearls in her ears the size of pigeon's eggs, and she had worn a cross, a crucifix, a most ungodly and unrighteous symbol. She had worn it like a piece of jewellery – heresy and vanity in one. She had worn it on her throat, an invitation to carnal thoughts as well. She was a heretical wicked woman and Mrs Hurte could not wait to get home to her husband and confirm his worst fears.

'Come and see me next month,' she said, pressing Jane to her heart before she left. 'Your father wants to see you, and bring Baby John.'

'I have to be here to guard the rarities when Father Tradescant and John are away,' Jane reminded her.

'When they are both here then,' her mother said. 'Do come. Your father will want to know about Oatlands too. Did you see the quality of the lace she wore on her head? It would buy you a house inside the city walls, I swear it.'

Jane packed her mother into the wagon and handed her the basket with the empty jars and the crumpled tablecloths.

'No wonder the country is in the state it is,' Mrs Hurte said, deliciously shocked.

Jane nodded, and stood back from the wagon as the man flipped the reins on the horses' backs.

'God bless you,' Mrs Hurte called lovingly. 'Wasn't she a scandal!'

'A scandal,' Jane agreed and stood at the back gate and waved until the wagon was out of sight.

Spring 1635

Jane did not visit her mother all through the spring. Both John and J were either at Oatlands Palace or busy in the orchards and garden of Lambeth. There was always someone knocking at the garden door with a little plant in a pot, or some precious thing in a knotted handkerchief, and Jane would judge its value and buy it with the authority of a good housewife and a partner in the business. Then, there were the tulips to be watched into leaf and into flower. John had ordered an orangery to be built for them to raise up the tender plants and the builders needed to be watched as they knocked a doorway through into the main house. It was not until May that Jane felt she had enough leisure to leave the Ark and go to see her mother in the city. But then she went and stayed for a week.

The house was oddly empty without her. Frances did not miss her much; she was always her grandfather's shadow, and when he was away she was always out in the garden with her father. But Baby John, nearly two, toddled round the house and demanded all day: 'Where's Mama? Where's Mama?'

They expected her to come home rested and happy after a week's cosseting in her old home, but when she finally returned she was tired and pale. The city had been unbearably hot, she said. There were more beggars on the streets than ever, she had seen a man dying in the gutter and had feared to touch him in case he was carrying the plague.

'What sort of country is this, that the act of a Good Samaritan is too dangerous to do?' she demanded, genuinely grieved at the struggle between her conscience and her safety.

Her father and all the merchants were complaining that they were taxed for trading, and then taxed for selling, and then taxed for storing goods. They too were ordered to pay ship money, which was set by an assessor who would come around and guess how much you were worth by the appearance of your house and business, and there was no appeal against him.

Josiah Hurte had to stand the charge of paying for his own lecturer in his own chapel, and also had to pay his parish dues to a church he never entered, and tithes to a vicar he despised for Roman practices. Meanwhile the price of goods soared, there were pirates openly operating up and down the English Channel, there were rumours of a rebellion in Ireland, and the king was said to spend more on his collection of pictures than he did on the Navy.

Jane, as the wife and daughter-in-law of a man in the employ of the court, had been pestered for scandalous details and had suffered from association. 'Nothing good will come from this king,' her father had said. 'You may think your husband is high in his favour but nothing good can come from him because he is a king halfway to damnation already. And if you do not beware, he will drag you all down with him. Now that your father-in-law and husband have a fair house in Lambeth, why can they not bide there?'

Useless to try to explain to Josiah that if this king issued a command you could be hanged for treason if you said 'no'. 'The king himself ordered it,' Jane said. 'How could we refuse?'

'By simply refusing,' her father said stoutly.

'And do you refuse to pay your taxes? Do you refuse to pay ship money? Other men do.'

'And they lie in prison,' Josiah said. 'And shame the rest of us who are less staunch. No, I do as I am ordered.'

'And so does my husband,' Jane insisted, defending the Tradescants despite herself. 'The king and court take our skills and service just as they take your money. This king takes whatever he desires and nothing can stop him.'

449

'You must be glad to be home,' J said in bed that night. He put his arm around her and she rested her head against his shoulder.

'I'm so tired,' she said fretfully.

'Then rest,' he said. He turned her face towards him and kissed her lips but she moved away.

'The room stinks of honeysuckle,' she cried suddenly. 'You've brought cuttings into the bedroom again, John! I won't have it.'

'No,' he said. He could feel a small niggle of fear, as small as a seedling, in his heart. 'There's nothing in the room. Does the air smell sweet to you, Jane?'

She suddenly realised what she had said, and what he was thinking, and she clapped her hand over her mouth as if she would hide her words, and stop her breath from reaching him. 'Oh God, no,' she said. 'Not that.'

'Was it in the city?' John asked urgently.

'It's always in the city,' she said bitterly. 'But I spoke to no-one knowingly.'

'Not the servants, not the apprentice boys?'

'Would I take the risk? Would I have come home if I had thought I was carrying it?'

She was half out of bed, throwing back the covers and throwing open the window, her hand still cupped over her mouth as if she did not want the smallest breath to escape. John reached out for her but did not pull her to him. His fear of the illness was as great as his love for her. 'Jane! Where are you going?'

'I'll get them to make me up a bed in the new orangery,' she said. 'And you must put my food and water at the door, and not come near me. The children are to be kept away. And my bedding is to be burned when it is dirty. And burn candles around the door.'

He would have held her but she turned on him with a face of such fury that he recoiled. 'Get away from me!' she screamed at him. 'D'you think I want to give it to you? D'you think I want to tear down this house which has been the joy of my life to build up?'

'No . . .' John stammered. 'But Jane, I love you, I want to hold you . . .'

'If I survive,' she promised, her face softening, 'then we will spend weeks in each other's arms. I swear it, John. I love you. But if I die you are not even to touch me. You are to order them to bolt down the coffin and not even to look at me.'

'I can't bear it!' he cried suddenly. 'This can't happen to us!'

Jane opened the door and called down the stairs. 'Sally! Make up a bed for me in the orangery, and put all my clothes in there.'

'If I take it, I will join you,' John said. 'And we will be together then.'

She turned her determined face to him. 'You will not take it,' she said passionately. 'You will live to care for Baby John, and for Frances, and for the trees and the gardens. Even if I die there is still Baby John to carry your name, and the trees and the gardens.'

'Jane –' It was a low cry, like a hurt animal's.

She did not soften for a moment. 'Keep my children from me,' she ordered harshly. 'If you love me at all. Keep them from me.'

And she turned, gathered up all the clothes she had brought from the city, went down the stairs into the new-built orangery, lay down on the pallet bed which the maid had thrown on the floor, and looked up to where the warm summer moonlight poured in the little window in the wooden wall, and wondered if she would die.

On the fourth day Jane found swollen lumps under her arms, and she could not remember where she was. She had a lucid interval at midday and when John came to speak to her from the doorway, behind the wall of candleflame, she told him to put a lock on the door so that she could not come out looking for Baby John, when she was out of her mind with the fever.

On the fifth day a message came from her mother to say that one of the apprentices had taken the plague and that Jane should burn everything she had worn or brought from her visit. They sent back the messenger with the news that the warning came too late, that already there was a white cross on the front door, and a warden standing outside to make sure that no-one left the house to spread the plague in Lambeth. All the goods and groceries, and even the new rarities, were left on the little bridge which led from the road to the house, and all the money was left in a bowl of vinegar, to wash the coins clean. No-one would go near the Tradescants' door until they were all recovered or dead. The parish wardens were legally bound to make sure that any plague victims were isolated in their houses until they were proven to be dead or proven to be clean, and no-one – not even the Tradescants with their fine business and their royal connections – could escape the ruling.

On the sixth day of her illness Jane did not tap on the door to have it unlocked in the morning. When John opened it and looked in, she was lying on the bed, her hair tumbled all over her pillow, her face thin and ghastly. When she saw him peering in she tried to smile, but her lips were too cracked and sore from fever.

'Pray for me,' she said. 'And don't take the plague, John. Keep Baby John safe. Is he still well?'

'He's well,' John said. He did not tell her that her little son was crying and crying for her.

'And Frances?'

'No signs of it.'

'And you, and Father?'

'No-one in the house seems to have it. But they have it in Lambeth. We're not the only house with a white cross on the door. It's going to be a bad year, this year.'

'Did I bring it?' she asked painfully. 'Did I bring the plague to Lambeth? Did it follow me over the river?'

'It was here before you came home,' he reassured her. 'Don't blame yourself for it. Someone had it and tried to conceal it. It has been here for weeks and no-one knew.'

'God help them,' she whispered. 'God help me. Bury me deep, John. And pray for my soul.'

Impulsively, he stepped over the candles and came into the room. At once she reared up in her bed. 'Do you want me to die in despair?' she demanded.

He checked and walked backwards, as if she were the queen herself. 'I want to hold you,' he said pitifully. 'I want to hold you, Jane, I want to hold you to my heart.'

For a moment her gaunt strained face, lit by the dozen golden candleflames, was suddenly soft and young, as it had been when she had sold him inch after inch of ribbons in the mercer's shop and he had called again and again on one pretext after another.

'Hold me in your heart,' she whispered. 'And care for my children.'

She lay back on the pillows as John stepped over the wall of candleflames and hunkered down on the threshold.

'I shall stay here,' he said determinedly.

'All right,' she agreed. 'Have you a pomander?'

'A pomander, and I am sitting in a sea of strewing herbs,' John said.

'Stay then,' she said. 'I don't want to die alone. But if I am feverish and wandering and start to come to you, you must slam the door in my face and lock it.'

He looked at her through the haze of the heat of the candles, and his face was nearly as haggard as her own. 'I can't do that,' he said. 'I won't be able to do that.'

'Promise me,' she demanded. 'It's the last thing I will ever ask of you.'

He closed his eyes for a moment, to find his resolution. 'I promise,' he said eventually. 'I will not touch you, I will come no closer. But I will be here for you. Just outside the door.'

'That's what I want,' she said.

At midnight Jane grew feverish and tossed on the pillow and cried out against heretics and Popery and the Devil and the queen. At three in the morning she grew quiet and he could see her shivering, and yet he could not go in and put a shawl around her shoulders. At four she grew quiet and at peace, and at five she suddenly said, as simply as a child: 'Goodnight, my dear,' and fell asleep.

When dawn came and the sun rose warm on the apple blossoms at six, she did not wake.

Summer 1635

There was a brief unhappy argument about how Jane was to be buried. The parish authorities, responsible for the impossible task of trying to contain the plague, sent an order that the cart would come for her at midnight and her body was to be loaded on it by her family, who must then lock themselves indoors for another week until they were proved to be free of the disease.

'I won't do it,' J said briefly to his father. 'I won't send her into the plague pit in a sack of hessian. They can order all they like. They're not going to come in the house to fetch her, they're too afraid for their own skins.'

John hesitated, thinking to argue.

'I won't,' J said fiercely. 'She's to be buried with honour.'

John spoke to the church warden, who kept a careful distance on the other side of the little bridge that spanned the roadside ditch. The man was reluctant, but John was persuasive. A small heavy purse was tossed from one side to the other and the next day a lead-lined coffin was delivered to the bridge. A week later, when the Tradescant family and servants were thought to be safe to go out again, the funeral was planned. Jane's cause of death would not be entered as plague but as the more neutral word 'fever', and she would be buried, as J insisted, in the family plot.

The Hurtes came to Lambeth from the city, with their own midwife to lay her out. She was an ancient woman, her face pocked with the scars of old plague sores. She said that she had taken the disease when she was a girl and had survived it, that the Lord of Hosts had saved her for the godly work of laying out the wealthy dead and nursing the few survivors.

'But why should He save you and not Jane?' J asked simply, and left her to the task of putting Jane in her special lead-lined coffin.

The Hurtes had wanted to take her to be buried in the graveyard near their chapel in the city but J forced himself to argue with them, and see that his wish was carried out. Jane should be buried at St Mary's, Lambeth, where her children would go past her grave twice every Sunday. J felt as though he were wading through a thick sea of distress and that if he paused for a moment the waves of grief would wash into his face and drown him completely.

In the end the funeral was an ornate affair with half of Lambeth turning out to honour the young Mrs Tradescant's passing. J, deep in unhappiness, begrudged everyone else's grief as if only he could know what it was to love Jane Tradescant and then to lose her; but it comforted John. 'She was very well-loved,' he said. 'She lived so quietly that I never knew she was so well-loved.'

Mrs Hurte took J to one side when the funeral was over and offered to take the two children back with them to the city.

'No,' he replied.

'You cannot care for them here,' she argued.

'I can,' J replied. Even his voice was different: taut and colourless. 'My father and I can care for them here, I will find a good woman to be a housekeeper for us all.'

'But I should be like a mother to them,' Mrs Hurte said.

J shook his head. 'Baby John will stay here with me,' he said. 'And Frances could not bear to live anywhere but here. She loves her grandfather, she is never out of his sight. And she loves the garden and orchard. She would pine to death in the city.'

Mrs Hurte would have argued but J's pale tight face prohibited any further talk. 'I will expect you for her memorial service in our chapel. We can pray for guidance, then.'

He helped her on to the box seat beside the driver. 'I won't come,' he said. 'She made me swear not to go into the city in the plague months. She was desperate that we would not bring it to the children. I promised her I would care for them here and if the plague comes any closer I would take them to Oatlands.'

'You won't come to see her father preach her memorial sermon?' Mrs Hurte exclaimed, scandalised. 'But surely it would be such a comfort for you!'

J looked up at her on the wagon seat above him and his face was a white mask of pain. It was useless to tell this woman that his belief in God had gone in an instant, gone the moment he saw Jane throwing open the bedroom window, breathing the air and trying to rid the room of the imaginary smell of honeysuckle. 'Nothing will comfort me,' he said blankly. 'Nothing will ever comfort me again.'

Instead, he sent flowers. He sent a great boatload of flowers down the river to the city; and the chapel was a garden of the striped white and red Rosamund roses that she had loved so much. On the day of the memorial service J worked in the garden at Lambeth, pricking out seedlings and watering them with a quiet determination, as if he would deny that his wife's soul was being prayed for that day; as if he would deny his grief itself. At midday the bell of St Mary's Lambeth tolled thirty-one times – one for each year of her short life – and J uncovered his head to the hot sun and listened to the slow clear sound of the bell, then he went back to his work separating the long silky stems of the seedlings and bedding them soft in the soil, as if only in the seed bed could he escape the memory of her dying, just out of his reach, and forbidding him to come any closer.

They dined as usual that night and John waited for his son to speak, but J said nothing. It was left to John to lead the prayers of the household. He did not have Jane's easy gift for addressing the Almighty as if He were a benevolent friend of the family. Instead he read the service for Evening Prayer from the King James Bible, and when the kitchen maid was disposed to speak out and give witness he shot her a sharp discouraging look from under his grey eyebrows and she fell silent.

'Perhaps you should lead the prayers,' John remarked to J after a week of this. 'I have not the knack for it.'

'I've nothing to say to such a God,' J said shortly, and left the room.

1636

In January, during the most difficult time for a gardener who lives off his plants, and the most frustrating time for a man who is only happy with his hands in the loam, the Tradescant luck turned. They were offered the work of the Oxford physic garden, a wonderful compact garden lying alongside the Isis, to grow herbs for the faculty of medicine at the university.

'You go and see what is needed,' John said, watching his son's face which had grown leaner and harder in the long cold months of winter. 'They're paying us fifty pounds a year and we have made next to nothing on the Ark this season. Go and see what work needs doing and take it in hand, J. I cannot go to Oxford in mid-winter, the cold will get into my bones.'

John had hoped that the notorious rich hospitality of the town would divert J from the deep silence of his grief. But he came back within a month saying that there was only careful planting and thorough weeding needed. Lord Danby, who had gifted the garden to Magdalen College, had ordered a wall and a gatehouse built, and protection from the winter-flooding river.

'Nothing needs doing,' J said when he was home again. 'I'll grow some extra herbs to stock it in the spring, and I've appointed a couple of weeding girls.'

'Pretty ones?' John asked carelessly.

J looked grim. 'I didn't notice,' he said.

In February a man came to the door bearing an earthenware pot with the tips of green bulbs showing.

'What's this?' J asked, hiding his weariness.

'I need to see John Tradescant,' the man said eagerly. 'Himself and no other.'

'I am John Tradescant the younger,' J told him, only too well aware that that would not be enough.

'Yes,' the man said. 'So it's your father I want.'

'Wait here,' J said shortly and went to find his father. John was in the rarities room, enjoying the warmth from the fire, moving from cabinet to cabinet, admiring the precious things.

'There's a man at the door with a bulb in a pot,' J reported. 'Will only speak to you. I s'pose it's a tulip.'

John turned at the word 'tulip'. 'I'll come at once.'

The man was waiting in the hall. John drew him into the front room, J following, and they closed the door.

'What d'you have for me?'

'A Semper Augustus,' the man said softly. From the depths of his pocket he produced a letter. 'This attests to it.'

'D'you think we're fools?' J demanded. 'Where would you get a Semper Augustus from? How would they ever let it out of the country?'

The man looked shifty. 'This attests to it,' he repeated. 'A letter for you alone, signed Van Meer.'

John broke the seal and read. He nodded at J. 'It does,' he said. 'He swears to me that there is a bulb in that pot from the original Semper Augustus. How did it come to your hands?'

'I'm merely the courier, master,' the man said uncomfortably. 'There was a bankruptcy in a house. Whose house need not concern you. The bailiffs took goods, but there was a man who did not know his job and did not spot the bulbs.' He gave a sly smile. 'I heard the mistress bundled them into a crock with a string of onions. So here they are, available for sale. The bankrupt gentleman, whose name we don't mention, wanted them offered out of Holland. He thought of you and commissioned me to bring them to you. Cash,' he added.

'We'll pay when we see the blooms and not before,' J said.

'The letter certifies them,' the man said. 'And I have orders to give you only a day to decide and then take them elsewhere. There are other great gardeners in England, gentlemen.'

'They are all friends of ours,' J growled. 'And if I think this is an onion, they will think so too.'

The man smiled. He was completely confident. 'It is no onion. But if you spread it on your bread it will be the most expensive dinner you have ever eaten.'

'May I take it from the pot?' John asked.

The man flinched a little, and it was that which convinced J as much as anything that the bulb was indeed the priceless Semper.

'Very well,' he said. 'But have a care ... I'd let no other man disturb it.'

John upturned the pot and tapped it hard. Earth, wiry tangled white roots and bulb slid out into his hand, scattering the soft soil on the floor. It was unquestionably a tulip bulb. John's rough hand caressed the smooth nut-brown papery skin, admired the perfect roundness of the bulb. The shoots at the top were strong and green, the bulb was growing away. There would be good leaves and no reason not to hope for good blooms. Of course he could not tell the colour of the flower from the skin of the bulb, but the letter attested the bulb as a Semper Augustus, Van Meer was a trustworthy trader, and the story of the bankruptcy and the bailiffs coming in was a not uncommon one in Holland now, where bulbs were changing hands a dozen times in a day, and where prices were soaring again.

Best of all, there was a little bump on the side of the bulb. It could be a little mis-shape, or it could be the start of a bulblet which would grow through the summer and by autumn would be a new bulb of its own – a profit of one hundred per cent from the labour of leaving a bulb in the earth.

John showed it to J, his finger smoothing over the lump, and then carefully repotted it.

J drew him to the window bay, out of earshot of the waiting man.

'It could be anything,' he warned. 'It could be one of a dozen we already grow.'

'Yes. But the letter looks genuine, that is Van Meer's seal, and the story is likely. If it is indeed a Semper then there is a fortune sitting in that pot, J. Did you see the lump on the side? We could double our money on the mother bulb in a year and then quadruple it with two where we once had one.'

'Or we could grow a red tulip and we have fifty already.'

'I think we should risk it,' John said. 'There's a fortune to be gained here, J.'

John turned towards the man. 'How much do you want for it?'

The man did not hesitate. 'I have orders to take a thousand English pounds.'

J choked but John nodded. 'Do your orders permit you to take some now and some when the bulb has bloomed? Any buyer would want to see the flower.'

'I can take eight hundred now and a note of hand to be redeemed in May.'

J drew close to his father. 'We cannot. We cannot lay our hands on such a sum.'

'We'll borrow,' John said softly. 'It's half the price we'd have to pay in Amsterdam.'

'But we're not in Amsterdam,' J argued urgently. 'We don't specu-late in bulbs.'

But John was glowing with excitement, his eyes alight. 'Think what the king will pay for a Semper!' he said. 'If it makes two bulbs instead of the one, think what profit we will make. We'll take it back to Amsterdam and sell it, and we'll make a fortune and our name as bulb growers. To sell a Semper grown in England on the Bourse itself!'

'I don't believe this,' J muttered to himself. 'We've been scraping the bottom of the barrel to meet the new tax, we missed two months of visitors in the summer because of the plague, and now we are staking eight years' wages on one bulb?'

John turned to the man. 'Here's my hand on it,' he said grandly. 'I shall have the money for you tomorrow. Come back at noon.'

For the rest of the day the Tradescants, father and son, called in their debts all around the city, then moved on to favours owed them, and went frankly to the great men in the trading houses and borrowed money, offering the bulb as security and finally selling shares in it outright. Their name was so good and the desire to cash in on the Dutch speculation was so strong that they could have borrowed money against the bulb's profits twice over. The hysteria in Holland had spread to the whole of Europe. Everyone wanted shares in tulips, the market for which had been rising for years and was rising in great leaps every day. John did not have to struggle to find shareholders in his bulb, he could have sold it outright by midday. By the time they met back at the Ark at dusk they had covered the loan.

John was triumphant. 'I could have sold it over and over!' he crowed. 'This will make our fortune. I shall buy us a knighthood with this profit, J. Your son will be Sir Johnny on the wealth that we have made today!'

He broke off, seeing J's solemn face and the heaviness of his eyelids. 'Is it just that you have no zest for anything?' John asked his son tenderly.

The young man's face was bleak. 'She has not been in her grave a year and we are speculating and gambling.'

'We are trading,' John said. 'Jane had no objection to honest trade. She was a merchant's daughter. She knew the value of profit. Her own father has taken a share in this venture.'

'I think she would have called it gambling,' J said. 'But you are right – I have no zest for anything. It is the heaviness of my heart which makes me think this too great a risk for us, I suppose. Nothing more than that.'

'Nothing more than that!' John clapped his son on the back. 'The profit from it will make your heart light,' he promised.

They kept the bulb in the orangery, warm in the pale spring sunshine as it poured through the windows, but shaded from the midday sun so the leaves should not scorch. Every morning John watered it himself with tepid water spiced with his own mixture of stewed nettles and horse dung. The bulb put out fresh green leaves and then finally, from its secret heart, the pointed precious snout of a flower.

The whole household held its breath. Frances was in and out of the orangery every day watching for the green of the flower to blush into colour. John never passed the door without glancing in. Only J remained wrapped in his own darkness. He could not see the orangery as a place where their fortune was slowly blooming, he could not forget that Jane had lain there, and it seemed to him that nothing good could come out of that room, in the wake of her small lead-heavy coffin.

'It's white! It's red and white!' Frances exploded into her grand-father's bedroom one morning while he was dressing.

'The tulip?'

'Yes! Yes! It's red and white!'

'A Semper Augustus!' he crowed and, still half-dressed, grabbed her hand and ran down the stairs with her. At the door to the orangery they stopped, afraid to run towards the plant as if the very pounding of their feet on the bare boards could shake the colour from the petals.

The exquisite rounded perfect petals had blushed into colour in the dawn light, though they were still tightly closed together. They were clearly a deep blood-coloured crimson slashed like a silk doublet with white.

'I have made my fortune,' John said simply, looking at the miracle-flower on its slender wax-green stem. 'This day I have made my fortune, Baby John will be a baronet, and none of us will ever work for another man again.'

They showed it in the rarities room, of course, as the most valuable tulip in the world. When the courier came for the rest of his money they had borrowed only two-thirds of it. The rest they had taken from visitors, flocking to see the priceless tulip.

When the queen at Oatlands heard of it she said she would buy it as it stood, in the pot, and J was about to name a figure which would cover their purchase price and give them a Christian profit of two per cent. But John was there to forestall him.

'When the bulb is lifted, Your Majesty, we will be honoured to give it to you,' he said grandly.

She beamed, she loved presents. John pulled J away before he could argue. 'Trust me, J. We will plant up one of the bulblets for her and still have the mother bulb. And she will reward us later for our generosity. Don't fear. She knows as well as I how these matters are gracefully done.'

They watched the flower open in its glorious blaze of colour and then become full-blown. 'Can't we keep the petals?' Frances asked.

'You can have the petals,' John said. 'Perhaps they will keep in sugar and sand in one of the rarities cases.'

Then in November, leaving it as late as possible to give the bulb the greatest chance to grow well, John, watched by J and Frances, tipped the pot and waited for their new wealth to spill out into his hands.

The priceless bulb had not one, not two, but three bulblets growing around the mother plant. 'Praise God,' John said devoutly.

With infinite care he took a sharp knife and cut them gently away from the mother bulb and placed them in their own little pots. 'Four where there was one before,' he said to J. 'How can you call it usury when it is the richness of God himself who doubles and quadruples our wealth for us?'

One pot was assigned to the queen. John would keep one. And the remaining two he would send back to Holland in triumph, to Amsterdam in February in bulb-buying time, to make them the richest gardeners the world had ever known, to make them as rich as nabobs.

December 1636

They had a quiet Christmastide at the Ark that year. Jane had always been the one to decorate the house with holly and ivy and hang a kissing bunch of mistletoe over the front door. Neither J nor his father had the heart for it. They bought the children their presents for the twelve days of Christmas, gingerbread, candied fruit, a new gown for Frances and a book, beautifully engraved, for Johnny, but there was a terrible sense of going through the motions of present-giving and celebration. There was a dreadful hollowness at the heart of it where before there had been the unthinking spontaneity of joy.

On Christmas night the two men sat either side of the fire drinking mulled wine and cracking nuts. Frances, allowed to sit up late for the occasion, was between them, seated on a footstool, gazing unblinkingly into the flames, sipping hot milk as slowly as she dared to prolong the moment.

'D'you think Mama wishes she was here?' she asked her grandfather. John looked quickly over to J in time to catch his grimace of pain.

'I am sure she does. But she is happy with the angels in heaven,' he said.

'D'you think she looks down on us and sees that I am being a good girl?'

'Yes,' John said gruffly.

'D'you think she would do a miracle, a little miracle, if I asked her?'

'What miracle d'you want, Frances?' John asked.

'I want the king to understand that he should make me Father's apprentice,' Frances said, putting her hand on John's knee and looking earnestly up at him. 'I thought Mama could do a small miracle and open the king's eyes to me. To my solid worth.'

John patted her hand. 'You can always do your apprenticeship here,' he said. 'You don't have to serve a master to be a great gardener. You don't need the king's recognition. I shall teach you the skills you need here, myself. I am aware of your solid worth, Frances.'

'And I can garden here after you are gone? So that there is always a Tradescant's Ark at Lambeth?'

John dropped his hand on her warm head and held it there, like a blessing. 'A hundred years from now there will be a little bit of a Tradescant in every garden in England,' he predicted. 'The plants we have grown are already in bloom in every garden in the country. I've never sought for greater fame than that and I have been blessed with seeing it. But I should like to think of you gardening here after I am gone. Frances Tradescant, the gardener.'

1637

The courier did not even enter the house at Lambeth. He stood in the hall on a February morning with the dirt of the roads still thick on his boots, and he brought the two precious tulip pots out from under his cloak.

'What's this?' John asked, astounded.

J, coming in from the garden, his fingers blue with cold, heard the fear in his father's voice and ran quickly up the hall, tracking mud on the polished wooden floor.

'Your bulbs, returned,' the man said shortly.

There was a stunned silence.

'Returned?'

'The market has crashed,' the man said. 'The Bourse has closed down the trade in tulips. Men are hanging themselves in their rich houses and throwing their children into the canals to drown. The mania for tulips is over and everyone in Holland is ruined.'

John went white and staggered back. He fell into a chair. 'Henrik Van Meer?'

'Dead. By his own hand. His wife gone to relatives in France as a pauper with an apron full of tulip bulbs.'

J put his hand on his father's shoulder. He had a sickly sense of his own fault for never speaking strongly against this passion for mingling plants and money. Now plants and money had split apart.

'You warned me,' John said softly to his son, his face shocked.

'Not well enough,' J replied bitterly. 'I spoke as quiet as a child when I should have shouted like a man.'

'Could you get *nothing* for them?' John asked. 'My Semper Augustus? I would take five hundred for each. I would take four.'

'Nothing,' the man said precisely. 'People are cursing their very name. They are worthless. They are less than worthless because people do not even want to see them. They blame them for everything. They are saying that they will never grow tulips again in Holland. That they hate the very sight of them.'

'This is madness,' John said, struggling to smile. 'These are the finest flowers that were ever grown. They cannot turn against them, just because the market has gone sour. There is nothing like a tulip –'

'They never saw them as flowers,' the courier explained patiently. 'They saw them as wealth. And while everyone ran mad for them they were wealth itself. But the moment that people don't want them, they are nothing more than bulbs which grow pretty flowers. I felt a fool carrying these around with me. I felt as foolish as if I were a madman carrying turnips and saying they were treasure.'

He dumped the two pots on the floor. 'I'm sorry to bring you such bad news. But you should think yourself lucky that you have only two. The men who bought a dozen at the height of their fame are lying in the canals singing to the fish.'

He turned and went out, closing the door behind him. J and his father did not move. The beautiful tulip pots gleamed mockingly, reflected in the shine of the waxed floorboards.

'Are we ruined?' J demanded.

'Please God, no.'

'Will we lose the house?'

'We have things we can sell. We can part with some of the rarities. We can trade and stay afloat.'

'We are at the very edge of bankruptcy.'

John nodded. 'At the edge. At the edge. But only at the edge, J.' He rose from his chair and hobbled to the door that led to the terrace and the garden. He opened the door and looked out, careless of the blast of cold air which billowed down the hall and might chill the tulips in their pots.

The saplings of the chestnut trees were as gawky and awkward as colts. Their buds were thick on the slender branches. There would be the tiny palmate leaves and then the magnificent white blossoms,

467

and then the glossy brown nuts hidden soft in their thick casing. John gazed on them as if they were a lifeline.

'We'll never be ruined. Not while we have the trees,' he said.

But they were hard-pressed to make ends meet. All spring and summer they juggled debts, took payments on plants and sent the money out straight away to satisfy the creditors.

'What we need,' J said one evening in autumn, as they were lifting bulbs from the bed, brushing them gently with a soft rabbit's-tail brush, and laying them in long flat crates, 'is a batch of new rare garden plants that everyone will be desperate to own. A new collection that everyone will want.'

John nodded. 'There are plants coming in all the time. I had a nice little flower from the West Indies this very week.'

'We need a sudden rush,' J said. 'So that everyone comes and buys from us. So that everyone remembers our name. We need to make our own mania, a mania for the Tradescant plants.'

John was on his hands and knees beside his son, but he leaned back to rest for a moment. 'You have an idea,' he said, looking at J.

'I thought I should go to Virginia,' J said. 'Go and collect rarities by the boxful; bring them back in time for the planting season, spring next year. Hope to bring back some flowers that people will pay good money to own.'

'We'd have to find the price of your passage,' John said cautiously. 'It's a good plan. But it's thirty pounds or so to send you out in the first place. And things are tight, J. Very tight.'

J said nothing and John looked again at his son's bleak face. 'It's not just business, is it? It's because you have lost Jane.'

'Yes,' J admitted honestly. 'I find I cannot bear this place without her.'

'But if you went to Virginia, you would come back? You are thinking only of a visit? There are your children, and the Ark, and our gardening for the queen. And I am getting old.'

'I will come back. But I have to get away now. You don't understand what it is like for me to sleep in her bed at night, and for her not to be there. And I can't bear to go into that damned orangery. Every time I walk in there to see to a plant or water a tray of seedlings I think she is still lying in the corner and forbidding me to come in and hold her. She died alone like a beggar on a street corner without nursing – and there was so much that I wanted to say to her and ask her –' He broke off. 'You don't understand,' he repeated.

'I do,' John said slowly.

'No. You can't possibly understand. When Mother died you had months of warning, and you were even able to give her some flowers at the end. You had time to say farewell. You could hold her –'

'Once I lost a love, a great love, without warning,' John said with difficulty. 'And with much left unsaid. I do know what it is to dream and long for someone, and to think of their death over and over, and of the thousands of ways you could have prevented it, and the thousands of ways you should have prevented it, until you are sick of your own life, since it was not given in exchange.'

J looked into his father's face. 'I didn't know.'

John realised that his son thought he was speaking of a woman, perhaps a lover from long ago. He did not correct him. 'So I do understand,' he said.

'You will let me go?'

John rested his hand on J's shoulder and hauled himself to his feet. He recognised again, to his continual surprise, that the stripling had grown to be a man with a shoulder as broad and strong as his own. 'It's not for me to order you,' he said. 'You are a man grown and an equal partner with me. If you need to go, you must go, and my blessing will go with you. I'll care for Frances and Baby John, and for the Ark and for Oatlands while you are away. And I will trust you to come back as soon as you can. I'm getting old, J, I need you here and your children will need you.'

J rose too but his shoulders were slumped. 'I shan't forget my duty.'

'And they will need a mother,' John ventured.

J flung his head up. 'I can't marry again,' he said flatly.

'Not for love,' John said gently. 'No-one is asking for that. But

469

the children need a mother. They cannot be raised by me and by a couple of maidservants. Baby John is only just walking, he will need a mother to bring him up and teach him his manners and play with him. And you will need a wife. You're a young man, J. There are long years ahead of you. You will need a companion and a friend for those years.'

J turned away and put his hand on the rough bark of the apple tree to steady himself. 'If you knew how it hurts me even to think of another woman, you would not say that,' he said. 'It is the cruellest, most unkind thing you could say. There will never be a woman in her place. Never.'

John put his hand out once more, and then let it drop back. 'I will not say it again,' he said gently. 'I miss her too.' He paused. 'I don't believe there is another woman who could take her place,' he acknowledged. 'She was a rarity. I have only ever seen one of her.' It was his greatest praise.

They could not find the passage money, the Ark was a sinking ship. Then J thought that he could put the idea of sending him into the queen's mind. He briefly mentioned it when she stopped beside him in the queen's court one day as he was tying back the creepers against the wall.

'You would think of leaving my garden? Of leaving my service?' she asked.

J dropped to his knee. 'Never,' he said. 'I was thinking of the wealth that Raleigh and Drake brought back for Queen Elizabeth. I was thinking that I would like to bring back treasures for you.'

Her ready vanity was stimulated at once. 'Why, you would be my knight errant!' she exclaimed. 'Gardener Tradescant on a quest for his queen.'

'Yes,' J agreed, hating himself for the play-acting even as he let the masque sweep on.

'And there must be gold and silver somewhere there,' she said. 'The Spanish got enough from it, as our Sweet Lord knows. If you could bring back some precious stones it would help His Majesty.

It is a wonder to me how much it costs to buy a few pictures and to keep the court.'

'Indeed, Your Majesty,' J said to the earth beneath his knee.

'You will bring me back pearls!' she exclaimed. 'Won't you? Or emeralds?'

'I will do all that I can,' he said cautiously. 'But I will certainly bring you back rare and beautiful plants and flowers.'

'I shall ask the king to give you a letter patent,' she promised. 'He will do it at once.'

Such was the erratic detail of the Stuart court management that there could be riots and rebellions about the collection of ship money up and down the country, and proud men accused of treason and flung into gaol alongside criminals and beggars and the king scarcely aware of it. But the queen was excited about Tradescant the young gardener visiting Virginia, and she told the king, and that became the business of the day.

'You must bring back some fine p . . . plants,' the king said pleasantly to J. 'Flowers and trees and shells, I hear they have precious sh . . . shells. I shall give you a letter of authority. Anything you see that would profit me, or the k . . . kingdom, you must have, free of charge, and bring it back. I shall give you a patent to collect. My loyal subjects in the new world will help you.'

J knew that a good proportion of the king's loyal subjects had fled to the Americas determined never again to live directly under such a ruler, and paid their dues to England only with the most irritated reluctance.

'You must come back with r . . . rarities too,' the king said. 'And see if you can bring Indian corn to grow here.'

'I will, Your Majesty.'

The king gestured and one of his yeomen stepped forward. 'A p . . . patent to collect in Virginia,' the king said, his lips hardly moving. The yeoman, new at his work, had not yet learned that the king hated giving orders. Half of his servants' work was guessing what he required. 'Have it written up. To Mr T . . . Tradescant.'

J bowed. 'I am obliged to Your Majesty.'

Charles extended his hand for J to kiss. 'You are indeed,' he said.

December 1637

J took ship in the *Brave Heart*, sailing out of Greenwich, and John came down to the quay to see him off. They ate a last meal together in the Three Choughs while J's bags were taken on board the ship bobbing at the quayside below the window.

'Make sure you carry enough water to keep any plants in the earth damp all the way home,' John reminded him. 'At sea in a storm, even the rain is salty.'

J smiled. 'I've unpacked enough dying plants to know how to care for them.'

'Get seeds if you can. They travel much better than young plants. Seeds and roots are the best. Make sure you crate them up so they stay dark and dry.'

J nodded and gave his father a glance which warned him that there was nothing more that he could teach his son.

'I want it to go well for you,' John explained. 'And there are treasures to be gathered there, I know it.'

J looked out of the little window at the ship at the quayside. 'All my childhood I seemed to be watching you sail, it's odd that it's my turn now.'

'It's right that it is your turn now,' John said generously. 'I don't even envy you. My back aches and my knees are stiff, my voyaging days are over. This winter was hard on me, cold weather, sorrow, ill-health and worry altogether. I shall limp from my fireside to my gardens until you return.'

'Write me news of the children,' J said. 'That they keep their health.'

'The plague must be less this year,' John said. 'It took so many last year. There must be better times coming. I shall keep the children away from the city.'

'They still grieve for their mother.'

'They will learn to feel it less,' John predicted. 'Frances is already caring for Baby John, and sometimes he forgets and calls her Mama.'

'I know,' J said. 'I should be pleased that he has stopped crying for her; but I can't bear to hear it.'

John drained his tankard and put it down on the table. 'Come on. Let's get you aboard, and you shall leave this country and your grief together.'

The two men went down the narrow stairs and out to the quayside. 'That house is riddled with passages like a rabbit warren,' John remarked. 'When the pressgang comes in the front, there are men scattering out of houses up and down the street through a thousand doorways. I saw it when my duke was pressing men for the war against the French.'

J looked towards his ship. The tide was on the turn and she was pulling at the ropes as if testing their strength. He turned and his father took him awkwardly into his arms.

'God bless you,' John said gently.

J had a sudden superstitious dread that he would not see his father again. The loss of his mother and then his wife had shaken his confidence. 'Don't work too hard,' he urged him. 'Leave it to me to repair our fortunes. I shall bring back barrels full of plants in time for the spring. I swear it.' He gazed into his father's face. The old man looked as he had always done, dark-eyed, weather-beaten, hardy as a clump of heather.

'God bless,' J whispered and then went up the gangplank of the ship.

John sat on a barrel on the quayside, stretching his tired legs before him, and waited for the ship to sail. He watched them run the gangplank aboard and then throw the mooring ropes. The little barges came out and took her in tow out to the middle of the river, and then John heard the faint shouted order and saw the lovely sight of the sails being flung open to the wind.

John raised his hand to his son as the ship caught the wind, slewed a little in the current, corrected her course, and then slipped away downriver, ploughing through the busy traffic of outbound boats and cross-river wherries, fishermen, and rowing boats.

From his place at the railing, J saw the figure of his father grow smaller and smaller as the quay itself shrank and became part of a larger view, an outcrop of stone against the green of the Kent hills behind it, then as they were further and further out, the dock was nothing but a darker line on the blur of the shadowy land.

'Goodbye,' he said quietly. 'God bless.' It seemed to him that he was leaving not just his father and his children and the memories of his wife and mother, but as if he was leaving his own childhood and his long apprenticeship, and going to a new life which he could make his own.

Spring 1638

John did not neglect the garden at Oatlands while J was away. He had planted a new consignment of daffodils in the autumn and that spring he was in the king's court every day, watching the green spears break through the soil. For the queen he had planted tulips in great china bowls, and forced them to bloom early. They might be worth a fraction of their original value but John would not throw good bulbs on the midden because they had once been worth a fortune and were now sold for shillings. He had bought them for love of their colour and shape and he loved them still. He put them in the orangery by the windows for the light and kept them warm. Their Majesties were due at the palace in late February and John wanted the bulbs in flower for their private apartments.

He was lucky, the royal party were delayed at Richmond and did not come to Oatlands until early March, and the tulip buds were fat and green and striped with the promise of colour when they arrived.

They were accompanied by a troop of new designers and decorators. It was the queen's desire that her apartments should be remodelled and repainted. 'What colours shall I have on the walls?' she asked John. 'Here is Monsieur de Critz, who will paint me cherubs or angels or saints, or whatever I will.'

John looked at the tulips on her table which were slowly going a deep glossy red. 'Scarlet,' he said.

She rounded on him, spitting with anger. 'D'you think to insult me?' she demanded.

He realised at once that she was smarting from the bawdy songs they were shouting in the streets of London about the two scarlet whores – the Pope and the Queen of England, who was shamefully in his toils.

'No!' John stammered. 'No! I was looking at your flowers!'

She turned and caught sight of the tulips. 'Oh.' Her charm had quite deserted her. 'Well, anyway. Cream and pink and blue, the ascension of Mary,' she said shortly to the painter, and left the room.

The painter raised a cautious eyebrow at John.

'I'd best have a care,' John said.

'Both she and the king are quick-tempered these days,' the man said in a quiet undertone. 'The news from the country gets worse every day. It is not always easy, serving at court.'

John nodded and extended his hand. 'Good to see you again, Monsieur de Critz.'

'It's been a long time,' the man said. 'I last saw you years ago, when I was commissioned by my lord Cecil.'

'I remember,' John said. 'You did the portrait of my lord which was made into a mosaic for the fireplace at Hatfield.'

They heard the queen's voice raised in temper in the inner room.

'I'm off to my garden,' John said hastily.

'Will you show me around before you go? I am halfway to being lost here.'

John nodded and led the way from the rooms. 'These are the queen's apartments, the king's rooms match them but lie the opposite side. Down below is the king's court. On the other side, the queen's.'

The painter looked down from the window to where John's intricate knot garden was green and white and yellow. The outside border was the bright green of fresh growing bay, clipped tight and neat, and inside the square, as the queen had first commissioned, was a love-knot made of bay with H M and C monograms at each corner made with the brilliant iridescent blue of violets and the bright white-gold of the new daffodils.

'If they had been a month later, it would all have had to be re-dug with pansies,' John said.

'Did you design it?' John de Critz asked, impressed.

'My son designed it,' John told him. 'But we both worked on the planting scheme. It is harder with Their Majesties than with a lord who is at home most of the time. When they come on a visit they expect it to be perfect, but you never know when the visit will be. We have to grow everything in pots or nursery beds, and only put the plants in when we know they are coming. We can't wait to let the plants grow fine and strong in the beds and succeed each other. Their Majesties need it perfect at each visit.'

'You are a painter yourself,' the man remarked. 'What patterns and colour! This is even better than Hatfield.'

'I have no sense of smell,' John explained. 'My son prizes flowers for their scent, and loves working with herbs for their perfume. But, since I can smell nothing, I love bright colours and shapes.'

The two men turned from the window and John led the way down to the great hall where the king and the household would dine, and then out into the court before the hall.

'Do you sleep in the hall?' John asked.

'My niece is with me, we have rooms in the old wing,' the man replied.

'Does she always accompany you?' John asked, surprised. The aristocratic members of the court might confine themselves to platonic love or to delicate trysts; but the rest of the royal household could be a rough place for a young woman when the fanciful romantic behaviour of the royal parade had passed by.

'Her father died of the plague and her mother cannot support her,' the man said. 'And, to tell you the truth, she has a fine eye and can work as well as any draughtsman. I often let her draw for me and block the designs out on paper, and then I transfer them to the walls.'

'I will see you both at dinner then,' John said. The spring sunshine was warm on his face and he could hear the birds singing. 'I must get out and see how they are digging in the kitchen garden.'

De Critz raised his hand and went back into the palace to start his drawings for the queen.

477

John joined de Critz at the dinner table at midday in the great hall. At the top table were the king and queen and the favoured courtiers of the day, with hundreds of rich and elaborate dishes laid before them. The queen held out her white hands for her lady-in-waiting to pull off, one at a time, each of the priceless rings, and pour a stream of warm clean water over her fingertips and then dab them with a napkin of the finest damask.

John noted, with no sign of disapproval showing in his face, that seated on one side of the queen was her confessor, and beside the king was the French ambassador. Grace was said in a quiet mutter in Latin by the queen's confessor and it was undoubtedly a Roman Catholic grace. There was no sign at all that this was a Protestant court in a Protestant country.

There was no sign either of the royal family. Their portrait was there, right enough, all five children as lovely as angels under the painter's tactful depiction. But the real children were never at their parents' dinner table. The queen prided herself on the passion of her maternal feelings, but tended to exercise them on her real children only occasionally, and mainly when she was being watched in public.

A young woman in her mid-twenties, dressed simply but elegantly in subdued colours, walked briskly into the hall, bowed low to the top table and dropped a slight curtsey to her uncle.

'This is my niece, Hester Pooks,' John de Critz said. 'John Tradescant, the king's gardener.'

She did not bob a curtsey to John but looked him straight in the face with a smile and held out her hand for a brief firm handshake. 'I am glad to meet you,' she said. 'I have been walking round and round the gardens and I think I have never seen anything more lovely.'

It was the quickest route to John's heart. He pulled out a chair for her and helped her to a piece of bread from the platter, and meat from the serving bowl which was before them. He told her about the making and improving of the Oatlands gardens, about the new breeds of tulips just blushing into colours, about the deep digging in the kitchen garden and the enormous asparagus bed.

'I made some sketches of the fruit trees in bud and those little daffodils beneath them,' she said. 'I've never seen an orchard so pretty.'

'I should like to see your sketches,' John said.

'The grass is like a tapestry or a painting,' she remarked. 'The true flowery mead. You can hardly see the green for flowers.'

'Now that's just what I intended,' John said, his enthusiasm growing. 'It has to be balanced all the time, and mown at the right time so that you don't cut the flowers before they are seeded, and you have to pull the plants which are running away and drowning the rest ... but I am so glad you saw it. It is supposed to look artless, and that is the hardest thing to get right!'

'So now I have a drawing based on a garden, which is based on a tapestry, which will have been based on a drawing.'

'And perhaps at the very back of it all, there was a garden.'

She looked at him with quick comprehension in her dark eyes. 'The first garden? Of Eden? Do you see that as a flowery mead? I have always thought of it as a French garden, with beautiful walks.'

'Certainly there must have been an orchard.' John had an enjoyable sense of intellectual freedom, being allowed to speculate about the Bible which, at home, had to be accepted as a revealed truth and read with uncritical devotion. 'There must have been at least two apple trees.'

'Two?'

'To pollinate. Otherwise the Devil himself would have had no fruit for tempting poor Adam!'

'But I thought the scholars were now saying that Adam did not eat an apple but an apricot.'

'Really?' John had an alarming sense of the world shifting beyond the limits of his light-hearted scepticism. 'But it says apple in the Bible.'

'Our Bible in English is translated from the Greek which was translated from the Hebrew. There are bound to be errors in the translations.'

'My son would say –' He broke off. He was no longer sure what J would say. 'A man of faith would say that there cannot be errors.

That since it is the revéaled word of God it *must* be perfect.'

She nodded as if it did not matter very much. 'A man of faith would have to have faith,' she said simply. 'But a man who questions would be bound to question.'

John looked at her doubtfully. 'And are you a woman who questions?'

She smiled at him, a sudden smile illuminating her face and making her suddenly a pretty young woman. 'I have a brain in my head to think for myself – but no elevated principles.'

Her uncle was shocked. 'Hester!' He turned to John. 'Indeed, she does herself an injustice. She is a very principled young woman.'

'I don't doubt it . . .'

Hester shook her head. 'I am completely respectable, which is what my uncle means; but I am talking about convictions and political principles.'

'You sound as if you are a doubter,' John commented.

'I think for myself but I never neglect the conventions,' she explained. 'This is a hard world for all of us, and especially for women. My study has been to avoid giving offence and to advance my own career.'

'As a painter?' John asked.

She gave him her open, honest smile. 'As a painter and a maid for now. But I shall want to marry well and care for my family and further my husband's prosperity.'

John, accustomed to Jane's high morality, was torn between shock at her frankness and a sense of freedom at her honesty. 'Nothing more than that?'

She shrugged. 'I don't think there *is* anything more than that.'

'And she can certainly draw.' Her uncle moved the conversation into safer areas. 'I thought I would use her sketches of your flowery mead as a background in some of the pictures for the queen's walls.'

The young woman flushed with pleasure. 'I will block them out for you,' she promised.

'Can you draw and colour tulips?' John asked. 'There are some in the queen's apartment which are just coming into flower and I should like to have a picture to show my son. He chose them, bought them, and planted them. He will want to know how they have done. We have had our disappointments with tulips –'

'Money?' she guessed acutely. 'Were you caught when the tulip market fell?'

John nodded. 'But I should like him to know that they are still beautiful, even if they are not profitable.'

'I would be pleased to try,' she said. 'I have not had the chance of seeing many tulips in flower. I know the Dutch tulip paintings, of course.'

'Come to my house this evening,' John suggested. 'I live adjoining the silkworm house. I'll bring a little bowl of them.'

Hester did not curtsey as she left them but dipped her head, like a boy, and went away. Her stride was like a boy's as well, firm and matter-of-fact.

'It is all right that she comes?' John asked, suddenly remembering his manners. 'I had thought I was speaking to a young draughtsman. I forgot she was a young woman.'

'If she were a boy I would have had her as my apprentice,' her uncle said, watching her go. 'She can come to your house, Mr Tradescant, but I have to guard her around the court. It is a nuisance. Some of these gentlemen write sonnets to the queen all day and then go wenching like lechers at night.'

'I have a lass like her at home,' John said, thinking of Frances and her desire to be gardener to the king. 'She's been told that she will have to marry a gardener, that is the closest she can get to the work; but she wants to be one herself.'

'What does her mother say?'

'She has none now. Plague.'

The man nodded in sympathy. 'It's hard for a maid to grow up without a mother. Who cares for her?'

'We have a cook who has been with us for many years,' John said. 'And housemaids. But when my son comes home from Virginia he will have to re-marry. There's my grandson as well. They cannot be left in the care of servants.'

De Critz slid a thoughtful sideways glance at him. 'Hester has a good dowry,' he said casually. 'Her parents left her with two hundred pounds.'

'Oh,' said John, thinking of that straightforward nod of the head and the confident walk. 'Did they, indeed?'

Hester Pooks sat at the table in John's little sitting room and drew the queen's bowl of tulips, squinting against the candlelight and the last rays of the evening sunshine.

'I've seen the tulip books,' she said. 'My uncle borrowed one to copy once. They show the bulb, don't they? And the roots?'

'You can't show these bulbs,' John said hastily. 'They must be left undisturbed. Please God they are spawning underneath the soil and I will soon have two or three tulips everywhere I once had one.'

'And what do you do with the extra tulips?' she asked, never taking her eyes from the flower except to look down at her page. John watched her; he liked her direct, searching gaze.

'Some I replant in new pots here and keep them for the king and queen next year, and some I take home and plant in my own garden and keep them as stock for my nursery.'

'So who owns them?' she persisted.

'The king and queen own the parent plants,' John said. 'For they commissioned my son to buy them, and paid for them. And the little bulblets we share. My son and I take half and the king and queen take half.'

She nodded. 'You double your stock every year? That's a good business,' she observed.

John thought that she was surprisingly astute for the niece of an artist. 'But it does not show the profits any more,' he said ruefully. 'The market smashed in February. The best of the tulip bulbs were going for prices that would buy you a house. Passed from trader to trader as a paper bond, getting more expensive each time.'

'So what happened? What stopped the market?'

John spread his hands. 'I don't know,' he said. 'I saw it happen; but I still don't understand it. It was like magic. One moment they were bulbs, rare and rather precious, but priced within the reach of a gardener who might grow them. Next moment they were priced like pearls and everyone wanted them. All of a sudden it's as if the

Bourse woke up to the fact that they were going mad over flowers, and they were priced like bulbs again. In truth, less than bulbs, because nobody wanted to be a tulip trader any more, to be a tulip gardener was like standing up in public and saying you were a greedy fool.'

'Did you lose much money?'

'Enough.' John was not going to tell her that all of their savings had been in tulip bulbs. That their wealth had blown away just as the *windhandel* market had blown away and that he and J had sworn a solemn oath, a peasant's oath, never to trust anything but the value of land ever again.

Hester nodded and drew a smooth swift line on the page, the tulip's curving veil-like leaf. 'It is an awful thing to lose your money. My father used to have a shop of artists' supplies, he lost his money when he fell sick. When he died there was nothing left for us at all. The only money we had was on a ship coming from the West Indies. It did not arrive for a year. In that year, as I sold first the carpet and the curtains, and then every stick of furniture we had, and then my dresses too, I swore that I would never be poor again.'

She gave him a quick sideways glance. 'I learned that nothing matters as much as holding on to what you have.'

'There is God's guidance and your faith,' John suggested.

She nodded. 'I don't deny it. But when you have sold your chair and are sitting on a small chest which holds every single thing you own, you gain a good deal of interest in the life here, and less in the life hereafter.'

Jane would have been appalled at such free speech, but John was not. 'A hard lesson for a young woman,' he commented.

'It's a hard world for a young woman, for anyone without a secure place,' she said. Her eyes followed the tulip's neck and her charcoal drew a swift line on the page. John watched her at work. She made it look absurdly easy. She was a plain girl, he thought, plain-featured and plain-spoken, and he thought that his wife Elizabeth would have liked her enormously. A straightforward girl who could be relied on to run a small business, a sensible girl who would look for reliability and dependability in a husband and not necessarily expect more. A girl who knew the value of money, not a spendthrift woman from court. A good girl who would care for children who needed a mother.

'D'you like children?' he asked abruptly.

She drew another smooth line for the tulip's sensuous wavy stem. 'Yes,' she said. 'I hope to have children of my own one day.'

'You might marry a man who has children already,' John said.

She shot him an acute glance over the top of her drawing block. 'I'd have no objection.'

'Even if they were up and running around?' John asked incautiously, thinking of Frances and her determined nature. 'Another woman's children, brought up in her ways and not yours?'

'You are thinking of your grandchildren,' she said, cutting through his hedging with one swift slice. 'My uncle has told you that I have a good dowry and you are wondering if I would care for your grandchildren.'

John choked slightly on his pipe. 'You are a frank speaker,' he exclaimed.

She turned her attention to her drawing. 'Something has to happen,' she said quietly. 'I cannot travel around with my uncle forever, and I want a home of my own and a husband to settle down with. I should like children, and a good little business to run.'

'My son is grieving for his wife,' John warned her. 'There may be no room in his heart for another woman at all. You might marry him and live with him all your life and never hear a word of love from him.'

Hester nodded, her hand steady and skilful as she turned the charcoal on its side and rubbed it gently against the grain of the paper to show the delicate veining on the tulip leaf. 'It is an understanding. An agreement; not a love affair.'

'Will that be enough for you?' John asked curiously. 'A young woman of your age?'

'I'm not a young maid,' she said steadily. 'I am a spinster of the parish of St Bride's. A maid is a girl with a life of promise before her. I am a spinster of twenty-five in need of a husband. If your son will have me, and treat me kindly, I will have him. I don't care that he has loved another woman, even if he loves her still. What I care about is getting a home of my own and children to care for. Somewhere I can hold up my head. And you and he are well-known; he works for the king direct and he has the ear of the queen. With Parliament dissolved and London trade doing badly, there is no other route of advancement other than the court. This would be a very good match for me. It's nothing more than adequate for him, but I will make it worth his while. I will guard his business and his children.'

John had the delightful sensation that he should not be having this conversation at all, that J was not a lad to have these things arranged for him, he was a man who should make his own choices. But it was a great pleasure to organise things as he wished, and he was afraid for his grandchildren.

'Frances is nine and her brother is four years old. A girl needs a mother, and Johnny is not out of his short coats. You would care for them and give them the love they need?'

Still Hester did not take her eyes from the tulip. 'I would. And I would give you more grandchildren, if God is merciful.'

'I won't be with you for long,' John predicted. 'I'm an old man. That's why I'm in a hurry to see my grandchildren safe and my son married. I want to know that I leave it all in safe hands.'

She put down her paper and for the first time her eyes met his. 'Trust me. I will care for all three of them, and for your rarities, for the Ark, and for the gardens.'

She thought that a look of immense relief passed over his face as if he now saw the way out of some complex thick-leaved maze.

'Very well, then,' he said. 'When Their Majesties leave here, I'll go home and you can come with me. You should see the children and they see you before we go further. And then J will come home from Virginia and the two of you can see if you like each other enough.'

'What if he doesn't like me?' Hester asked bluntly. 'I'm not a beauty. He might think he could do better.'

'Then I'll bring you back to your uncle and you're no worse off,' John said. He thought he had never met a woman so frank. The lack of vanity and the plain speaking suited him; he wondered if J would like her for it, or if she would embarrass him. 'Of course, you might not like him.'

She shook her head. 'I'm not a princess in a romance pining for love,' she said. 'If he can give me a house and business and a couple of children, that's all I want. I could shake on the agreement today.'

John reminded himself that to put out his hand and shake on the agreement now would be to trap her as well as to trap his son. He heard Cecil's wise cynicism in his head urging him to do it and turned away. 'I won't let you be too hasty,' he said, resisting the temptation. 'Come with me to the Ark at Lambeth, meet the children, see the house and see if it suits you before we say more.'

Hester nodded, her eyes back on the tulips again. 'Good,' she said.

John was weary to the very marrow of his bones on the journey home from Oatlands to Lambeth. The road seemed longer than usual and the river crossing was cold, with a bitter wind that swept down the river and cut through his leather waistcoat and his woollen cloak. The ague that he had brought home from Rhé, which descended on him whenever he was tired, made him ache in every bone of his body. He was glad that Hester was there to pay the ferryman and to commandeer a wagon for them to ride down the South Lambeth Road. She had an eye to his comfort all the way but not even her care could stop the wind blowing chill or the wagon jolting down the road in the winter ruts.

When they halted outside the house she had to help him over the little bridge and into the house, and as soon as she was in the door she was giving orders for his comfort as if she were mistress already.

The servants obeyed her willingly – lighting a fire in John's room, bringing a chair for him to sit in, bringing him a glass of hot wine. She knelt before him, her cloak still tied around her neck, her muff pushed to one side, and rubbed his cold hands until they lost their blueness and tingled.

'Thank you,' John said. 'I feel a fool, bringing you here and then needing your help.'

Hester rose to her feet with a slight smile which made little of her care of him, and set him at his ease. 'It's nothing,' she said easily.

She was a woman who could set a house to rights in moments.

In a very short time she had clean sheets on John's bed, and a bowl of hot soup and a loaf of white wheaten bread sent up to him so that he could dine in his bedroom. Then she turned her attention to the children and sat with them in the kitchen while they ate their supper.

She heard them say grace after the meal, both heads bowed obediently over their hands. Baby John still had the golden silky curls of infancy falling over his white lace collar. Frances's brown sleek hair was hidden under her white cap. Hester had to stop herself from reaching out and gathering the two of them on to her lap.

'The mistress used to say prayers every morning and evening,' the cook volunteered from the fireside. 'D'you remember, Frances?'

The girl nodded and looked away.

'Would you like us to pray, as your mother used to pray?' Hester asked her gently.

Again Frances nodded wordlessly, turning her head away so that no-one could see the pain in her face. Hester put her hands together and closed her eyes and prayed, from the prayer book issued by Cranmer, as if there were no other way to address your maker. Hester had never been inside a church where prayers were spoken from the heart, she would have thought such behaviour unsettling, perhaps illegal. She said the words the archbishop had ruled, and prayed by rote.

And Frances, slowly, without turning her head or indicating in any way that she wanted an embrace, stepped backwards, towards Hester, closer and closer and then finally leaned back against her, still not looking around. Gently, carefully, Hester dropped her hands from where they were clasped in prayer and rested one hand on Frances's thin shoulder, and then the other on Johnny's silky curls. Johnny was comfortable under the caress and leaned at once towards her, but she felt the little girl's shoulder tense for a moment, and then relax as if the child were relinquishing a burden which she had been carrying alone. While the others said 'Amen' out loud to the familiar prayer, Hester added a private silent wish that she might take these children who belonged to another woman, and bring them up as their mother would have wanted, and that in time they would come to love her.

She did not move away when the prayers ceased but stood still, her hand on each child. Johnny turned his little round face up to her and lifted up his arms, mutely asking to be picked up. She stooped and lifted him and settled him on her hip, and felt the deep satisfaction of a child's weight at her side and his arms around her neck. Still without looking, and with no word of appeal, the girl Frances turned towards Hester and Hester folded her into the crook of her arm and pressed the sad little face into her apron.

John recovered after a few days at home, and was soon setting seeds in pots and sending Frances out in the frosty garden to gather up, without fail, every single one of the last chestnuts as they fell from the trees down the avenue.

The nuts were so precious that the household linen was spread beneath the wide branches of the trees from autumn to springtime to ensure that not a single prickly casing or warm brown nut was lost in the grass. Hester mentioned the risk of staining or tearing the sheets, but John said firmly that one nut was worth a dozen sheets and that the garden must always come before the house.

He took Hester on long cold walks down to the bottom of the orchard, showed her every single tree and named it for her. In the blustery wet days of March he stayed in the orangery before a potting table with a barrel of sieved earth at his side and taught Hester how to set seeds. He showed her the tender plants which lived in the orangery from autumn to spring to protect them from winter frosts, and he showed her the winter jobs: the cleaning of the big tub planters, the washing of the pots, and airing them, ready for the fever of spring planting. One lad spent all the winter sieving earth for the seed beds and for the pots. Another brewed up a fearful barrel of water fortified with horse and cow manure and a nettle soup of John's own devising, which would be sprinkled on every precious seedling.

They passed a quiet few weeks. A sailor, fresh into port, had a sealed parcel of seeds for John and a letter from Virginia.

'He says he will be home by April,' John read. 'He says he is writing this before going out into the woods for a week. He has an Indian guide who leads him around and shows him plants and brings him safe in.' He paused and looked into the embers of the fire. 'I wish he would come home,' he said fretfully. 'I am impatient for him to be here and everything settled.'

'He will come in good time,' Hester said soothingly. There was a single disloyal thought in her head that they were managing very well without him, John busy and contented, the museum taking a small but steady flow of money, and the children taught by her every morning and kissed goodnight by her every night.

'He should be already on his way,' John said. 'This letter is eight weeks old. He may be at sea now.'

'God keep him safe,' Hester said, glancing out of the window at the dark March skies.

'Amen,' John said.

Towards the end of the month John fell ill again. He ached in every bone and complained of the cold. But he was adamant that nothing ailed him, he was well enough. 'Just tired,' he said, smiling at Hester. 'Just old bones.' She did not press him to rise from his bed, nor to eat. She thought he looked as if he had reached the end of a long and arduous road.

'I think I should write a letter for J,' he announced quietly one morning as she sat at the foot of his bed, sewing an apron for Frances.

At once she put her sewing to one side. 'He will not get it if he left the colony as he planned. He should be at sea now.'

'Not a letter to send. A letter for him to read here. If I am not here to speak to him.'

She nodded gravely, she did not rush to reassure him. 'Are you feeling worse?'

'I am feeling old,' he said gently. 'I don't imagine that I will live forever, and I want to make sure that it is all settled here. Will you write it for me?'

489

She hesitated. 'If you wish. Or I could send for a clerk to write it. It might be better if it were not written by me.'

He nodded. 'You are a sensible woman, Hester. That's sound advice. Get a clerk for me from Lambeth and I will dictate my letter to J and finish my will.'

'Of course,' she said and went quietly from the room. At the doorway she paused. 'I hope you will make it clear to your son that he is not bound to have me. Your son will have to make his own decision when he comes home. I am not part of his inheritance.'

There was a small gleam of mischief in John's pale face. 'It never occurred to me,' he said unconvincingly. He took a difficult breath. 'But it shall be as you wish. Send for a clerk from Lambeth, and also send for the executors of my will. I want to leave everything straight.'

The clerk came and the executors with him – Elizabeth's brother, Alexander Norman, and William Ward, Buckingham's steward, who had served with John all those years ago.

'I shall be your executor with the greatest of pleasure,' Alexander assured him, taking a seat at the bedside. 'But I expect that you shall be mine. This is just a winter rheum. We'll see you in the garden again this spring.'

John managed a weary smile, leaning back against his pillows. 'Maybe,' he said. 'But I'm a good age now.'

Alexander Norman glanced over the will and set his name to it. He reached towards John and shook his hand. 'God keep you, John Tradescant,' he said quietly.

The Duke of Buckingham's old steward, William Ward, stepped forward, and signed the will which the clerk showed him. He took John's hand. 'I shall pray for you,' he said quietly. 'You shall be in my prayers every day, along with our lord.'

John turned his head at that. 'D'you pray for him still?'

The steward nodded. 'Of course,' he said gently. 'They can say what they like about him but we who were in his service remember a master to worship, don't we, John? He wasn't a tyrant to us. He paid us freely, he gave us gifts, he laughed at mistakes and he would flare into a rage and then it was all forgotten. They spoke ill of him then and they speak worse of him now; but those of us who knew him have never served a better master.'

John nodded. 'I loved him,' he whispered.

The steward nodded. 'When you get to heaven you will see him there,' he said with simple faith. 'Outshining the angels.'

The will was signed and sealed and posted with the clerk, the executors in agreement, but Hester thought that John would not go until he could see his tulips one last time. There is no gardener in the world who does not worship spring like a pagan. Every day John would take a seat at the window of his bedroom and peer outward and down to try to see the tiny spears of green springtime bulbs piercing the cold earth.

Every day Frances came to his room with her hands filled with new buds. 'Look, Grandfather, the lenten lilies are out, and the little white daffodils.'

She would spread them on the coverlet wrapped around his knees, both of them careless of the sticky juice from the cut stems. 'A feast,' John said, his eyes on them. 'And they smell?'

'Like heaven,' Frances replied ecstatically. 'Yellow, they smell like sunshine and lemons and honey.'

John chuckled. 'Tulips coming?'

'You'll have to wait,' she said. 'They're still in bud.'

The old man smiled at her. 'I should have learned patience by now, my Frances,' he said gently, his breath coming short. 'But don't forget to look tomorrow.'

Hester thought that John's stubborn will would not let him die in early spring. He wanted to see his tulips before he died, he wanted to see the blossom on his cherry trees. She thought his soul could not leave his weary body until he had some warm summer flowers in his arms once more. As the cold winds died down and the light at the window of his bedroom grew brighter and warmer, his breath slowly slipped away, but still he hung on – waiting for the summer, waiting for the return of his son.

At the end of March he turned his head to her as she sat at his bedside. 'Tell the gardener to send me in some flowers,' he said softly. He was breathless. 'Everything we have. I may not be able to wait for them to bloom. Tell him to pot me up some tulips. I want to see them. They must be nearly showing by now.'

Hester nodded and went out to find the gardener. He was weeding in the seed beds, preparing them for the great rush of planting out which would come when the danger of night frosts was over.

'He wants his tulips,' she told him. 'You're to pot them up and take them in. And cut some daffodils, armfuls of them. But I want us to do more for him. What are the best plants he has made? The rarest, most special plants? Can we not put them all in a pot and take them in so that he can see them from his bed?'

The gardener smiled at her ignorance. 'It'd be a big pot.'

'Several pots then,' Hester persisted. 'What are his other plants?'

The gardener's gesture took in the whole garden, and the orchards beyond. 'This is not a man who gardens in pots,' he said grandly. 'There's his orchard: d'you know how many cherry trees alone? Forty! And some of his fruit trees were never grown before, like the diapered plum he got from Malta.

'And he found wonderful trees for the park or garden. See those beauties so fresh and green with those pale needles? He grew them from seed. They are Archangel larches, from Russia itself. He brought the pine cones back and managed to make them grow.'

'They're dead,' Hester objected, looking at the spiky yellowing needles clinging to the brown twigs.

The gardener smiled at her and took one of the swooping bare branches. There was a tiny rosette of green needles at the tip of the rusty brown branches.

'In the autumn they turn as golden as a beech tree and shed their needles like yellow rain. Come the spring they burst out, all fresh and green like grass. He reared them from seed and now look at the height of them!

'In the orchards he grows the service tree, and his favourites are the great horse chestnuts. Look at that avenue down the garden! And every one of them flowers like a rose and makes leaves like a fan. It's the greatest tree that has ever been seen, and he grew the first from a nut. On the lawn before the house? That's an Asian plane. And nobody can say how big it will grow because nobody has ever seen one before.'

Hester looked down the avenue at the arching swooping branches. 'I didn't know,' she said. 'He showed me all around the garden and the orchard but he never told me they were all his own, discovered by him and grown here in Lambeth for the very first time. He only told me they were rare and beautiful.'

'And there's the herbs and vegetables,' the gardener reminded her. 'He's got seven sorts of garlic alone, a red lettuce which can make seventeen ounces of good leaves, allspick lavender, Jamaican pepper. His flowers come from all over the world, and we send them all over the country. Spiderwort – he gave his name to it. Tradescant's spiderwort, a three-petalled flower the colour of the sky. On a wet day it closes up so you think it's dead, on a sunny day it is as blue as your gown. A flower to lift your heart, grow for you anywhere. Mountain valerian, lady's smock, large-flowered gentians, silver knapweed, dozens of geraniums, ranunculus – a flower like a spring-time rose, anemones from Paris, five different types of rock rose, dozens of different clematis, the moon trefoil, the shrubby german-der, erigeron – as pretty as daisies but as light and airy as snowdrops, his great rose daffodil with hundreds of petals. In the tulip beds alone we have a fortune. D'you know how many varieties? Fifty! And a Semper Augustus among them. The finest tulip ever grown!'

'I didn't know,' Hester said. 'I just thought he was a gardener . . .'

The gardener smiled at her. 'He is a gardener, and an adventurer, and a man who was always there when history was being made,' he said simply. 'He's the greatest man of this age for all that he's always been someone's servant. Fifty tulip varieties alone!'

Hester was gazing along the avenue of the horse chestnut saplings. Their buds were green, breaking out of the bud casings which were fat and shiny, wet and brown like molasses.

'When will they bloom?'

The gardener followed her glance. 'Not for another few weeks.'

She thought for a moment. 'If we cut some branches and took them indoors and kept them warm?'

He nodded. 'They might dry up and die. But they might open early.'

'Pot up the tulips then,' she decided, 'all of them, every one of his fifty varieties. And anything that is ready to bloom in the rarities room or the orangery. Let's make his bedroom a little forest, let's make it a flowery mead, with branches and flowers and plants, everything he loves.'

'To help him get better?' the gardener asked.

Hester turned away. 'So that he can say goodbye.'

Tradescant lay propped high on thick pillows to help him to breathe, his nightcap on his head, his hair combed. The fire was burning in the grate and the window was slightly opened. The room was filled with the perfume of a thousand flowers. Over his bed arched boughs of chestnuts, the leaves broken out of the sticky buds. Higher again were beech branches, the buds like dried icicles on the thin twigs, but every plumper bud was splitting and showing the startling sweet-meat-pink and white lining, where the leaves were pushing to come through. In great banks around the side of the room were the tulips, fat and round, showing every colour that had ever come out of the Low Countries: the blaze of scarlet, the magnificent stripes and broken colours in red and white and yellow, the shining purity of the Lack tulip, the wonderful spiky profile of the *Tulipa australis*, and the flower that was still John's joy, the white and scarlet Semper Augustus. There were boughs of roses, their tight buds promising the beauty of their flower if John could stay just another month, or another month after that. There were clumps of bluebells like spilled ink on the carpet, and white and navy violets in pots. There were late daffodils, their little heads nodding, and everywhere threaded through the riot of colour and shape was Tradescant's own lavender, springing fresh green shoots from the pale spines and putting out violet blue spikes.

He lay back on his pillows and looked from one perfect shape to another. The colours were so bright and joyous that he closed his eyes to rest them, and still saw, on the inside of his eyelids, the blazing red of his tulips, the shining yellow of his daffodils, the sky-blue of his lavender.

Hester had left a little pathway from his bed to the door so that she could come and go to him, but the rest of the room was banked with his flowers. He lay like a miser in a gold vault, half-drowned in treasure.

'I have left a letter for you to give to John when he returns,' he said quietly.

She nodded. 'You need not worry for me. If he will have me then I will stay, but whatever happens I will be a friend to the children. You can trust me to stand their friend.'

He nodded and closed his eyes for a moment.

'Why did you not name the plants for yourself?' she asked softly. 'There are so many. You could have had your name remembered with thanks a dozen times a day in every garden in the country.'

Tradescant smiled. 'Because they are not mine to name. I did not make them, like a carpenter makes a newel post. God made them. All I did was find them and bring them into the gardens. They belong to everyone. To everyone who loves to grow them.'

He dozed for a few moments.

In the silence Hester could hear the household going about its business, the noise of the lad sweeping the yard, and the continual murmur from the rarities room where visitors came and stayed to study and to marvel. The bright yellow spring sun poured into the room.

'Shall I close the shutters?' Hester asked. 'Is it too bright?'

John was looking at the Semper Augustus, with its radiant white petals and the glossy red dappled stripe. 'It's never too bright,' he said.

He lay very still for a while and Hester thought he had gone to sleep. Quietly, she rose from her chair and tiptoed to the door. She looked back at the bed embedded in flowers. Above Tradescant's sleeping head his chestnut tree was bursting into leaf.

The creak of the wooden door disturbed his sleep. He was awake, looking towards the door; but he did not see Hester. His gaze went a little higher than her head, and his entranced look of delight was that of a man who has seen the love of his life coming, smiling, towards him. He raised himself up, as if he would move lightly forward, like a young man greeting his love. His smile of recognition was unmistakable, his face was filled with joy.

'Ah! You at last!' he said softly.

Hester went quickly to the bed, her skirts brushing the banks of flowers, pollen and perfume swirling like ground mist as she ran to him, but by the time she touched his hand the pulse had stopped and John Tradescant had died in a bed of his flowers, greeting the person he loved most in all the world.

VIRGIN
EARTH

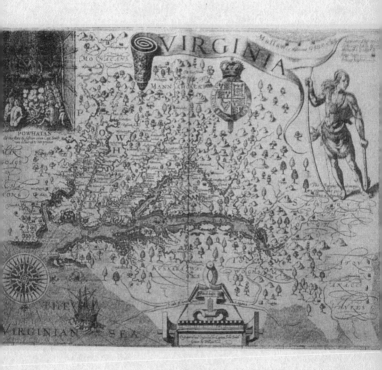

For Anthony

Winter 1638, At Sea

He woke to the sound of the moving ship, the creaking of the timbers and the aching sigh of the full sails spread, the sudden abrupt rattle of a pulley as a sail was reefed in, the drumming of booted feet on the deck just above his face, the holler of an order, and the continual attack of the sea – the bang of the waves against the prow and the groan of the tiny ship as she climbed up one wave and then wallowed and turned to confront another.

He had slept and woken to this ceaseless din for six long weeks and now he found it familiar and soothing. It meant that the little ship was soldiering on through the terrifying expanse of wind and water, still headed westwards, faithful to the hope that westwards would be the new land. Sometimes J imagined their progress as a seagull might see it looking down, the vast waste of sea and the fragile ship with its lamps burning at dusk, headed trustfully towards where they had last seen the sun.

He had set sail in deep grief, in flight from grief. Even now he dreamed of his wife with bright joyful immediacy, dreamed that she came to him on board the ship and laughingly complained that there was no need for him to set sail, no need for him to run off to Virginia alone, for see! here she was on board herself, and it had all been a game – the plague, her long days of dying, the terrible white-faced grief of their daughter – all a May game, and here she was well and strong, and when would they go home again? Then the noises of the ship were a terrible interruption and J would pull his damp blanket over his face, and try to cling to the dream of Jane and the certainty that she was alive and everything was well.

He could not. He had to wake to the bleak truth that she was dead, and his business half-bankrupt, his father hanging on to their house

1

and their nursery garden· and their collection of rarities by the old combination of luck and the love of his friends, while J played the part of the indulged son – fleeing from all of it, calling it a venture, a chance at wealth, but knowing it was an escape.

It was not an enviable escape at first sight. The house at Lambeth was a grand house, set among its own twenty acres of nursery garden, famous for its collection of rarities from all around the world. His father, John Tradescant, had named it the Ark, and had sworn they would be safe there whatever storms rocked the country with king and Church and Parliament all set on different and opposing courses. There were half a dozen bedrooms and the great room for the rarities, a dining room, a drawing room and a kitchen. A little son, Johnnie, to inherit it all and his older sister Frances to insist on her own claims. These riches J had exchanged for a single five-foot, four-inches-long bunk built into the damp wall of the ship. There was no room to sit up, barely room to roll over. He had to lie on his back, feeling the huge movement of the waves lifting and dropping him like driftwood, looking at the planks of the bunk above him. To his right against the skin of the ship, he could feel the slap of the waves and the whisper of their ripples. To his left was the slatted door for which he had paid extra for the little space and privacy it gave him. The other, poorer emigrants slept side by side on the floor of the 'tween deck like animals in a barn. They had been loaded like baggage into the waist of the ship with the crews' quarters at the stern behind them, and the captain's tiny cabin and the cook's galley and cabin – all in one – in the prow before them.

The captain would not allow passengers out on deck except for the briefest and most grudging spells in fine weather. The crew going on watch trampled over the passengers and, when they were returning to their shared hammocks in the stern, dripped water all over them. The emigrants were always in the way, they were regularly cursed, they were less than cargo.

Their bundles and boxes were piled up among their owners in a careless muddle; but as the days wore on into weeks families established their own little seats and bunks out of crates of chickens and bags of clothes. The stench was appalling. There were two buckets provided, one for washing water, one for excrement, and there was a strict rota for emptying the soil bucket over the side. The captain would not allow them to do this more than once a day and when it was J's turn to carry the brimming pail to the side his stomach heaved.

There was scarcely enough water to drink, and it came warm and tasting of the barrel, there was hardly enough food. A lumpy porridge for breakfast, the same for dinner, and a biscuit and a slice of old cheese at night.

It would have been a nightmare but the voyage was sustained by hope. They were a shipful of gamblers, a handful of families who had thrown in their lot with a land they had never seen and whose dangers and promises they could hardly imagine. J thought they were the most foolhardy, impulsive, brave people he had ever met, and he did not know whether to fear them as madmen or admire them as heroes.

They were lucky. Seventy days into the voyage, as the temperature rose and the children cried and cried for fresh water and a breath of air, they sighted Barbados and sailed into port for one blissful week of rest as the captain sold his English goods and took on rum and sugar, food and fresh water. They were allowed to go ashore and barter for provisions, to eat fresh fruit for the first time in more than two months. When the ship was due to sail, the return to the festering hold was more than many of them could bear. A number of emigrants left the ship; but most of them gritted their teeth and endured the next leg of the voyage, J grimly among them. It was another full forty days at sea before a sailor opened a hatch and bellowed down: 'Make yourselves ready! We've sighted land.'

Even then they were not allowed up on deck. J gathered with the others looking imploringly upwards to the open hatch. The sailor laughed unkindly. 'Wait below,' he said. 'There's no room for you all!'

It was evening. J, accustomed to the foul smell of the 'tween decks, smelled a fresh new scent on the air – damp earth which reminded him suddenly, poignantly, of the garden at Lambeth after rain, and the wet fresh smell of leaves.

'Land,' the woman next to him said, her voice hushed with awe. 'Land. The new land. Our new land.'

J guessed from the noises of running feet and the shouted commands that they were dropping sail. The waves stopped heaving the ship up and down and instead they felt the insistent pattering slaps of a tidal river. Then there were shouts of greeting and replies from the sailors, and a jolt as the boat ran gently against the quayside and the strange steadying of her motion as the ropes drew her alongside.

'Thank God,' J muttered.

The woman beside him breathed, 'Amen.'

The single women aboard who expected to find husbands as well as gold in the new land primped their hair and put on their clean caps, saved for this very moment. Those children who were not weak with sickness could not be contained; they leaped about on bags and crates and barrels and were cuffed indiscriminately, whenever they stumbled to a standstill. Husbands and wives exchanged apprehensive or hopeful glances. J wondered at the coldness around his heart; he felt no relief that the voyage was over, no excitement at the thought of a new country, of a new land, of a new horizon. He realised then that he had been half-hoping that the ship would founder and take him and his sadness down below the waves to Jane; and then he shook his head at his sin of selfishness that he should ill-wish a voyage because of his own pain.

The sailor stood at the open hatch at last. 'Come on up!' he called. 'Welcome to paradise.'

There was a moment's hesitation and then a rush up the narrow wooden steps and the first emigrants stepped out on deck, and J followed.

It was evening. The skies were a colour that J had never seen before, the palest of mauves lying in stripes like gauze over the enormous river which reflected the colours back up in pink and blue and purple. The river was still, like a tarnished silver mirror, and as J watched it went suddenly dark and stirred and then went still again as an immense shoal of fish swooped by. It was a stretch of water greater than J had ever seen, except for the sea itself. Only dimly behind the ship could he see the distant southern bank as a dark shadow of trees. All around him was the smooth sheen of river water and as he looked inland, away from the sea, it seemed to him that it went on forever, flowing as wide forever, making no compromise with narrowing banks, impossibly wide, impossibly rich, impossibly beautiful.

J looked towards the shore. The emigrants were disembarking in haste; already a chain had been formed, tossing their goods down the line to land with a careless thump on the dockside. Half of Jamestown had turned out to greet the ship, there were shouted enquiries for news of England, demands of the captain for commissions completed, bills paid, and then coming through them all was the governor, Sir John Harvey, grandly shabby in an old coat spruced up for the occasion with worn gold lace, moving through the colonists with his head turned away, as if he despised them.

J could see the walls of the original fort, still manned, with cannon at the ready; but the houses of the town had sprawled beyond their narrow compass and the fort served only as the end point of what would have been, in England, a little market town. The handsomest, biggest houses were stone-built, in a row, in a style that would not have disgraced London, and behind them and to the side of them was a range of styles from frame buildings half-completed, to little wattle-and-daub shanties.

Mostly they were built of wood, planks of untreated crudely sawn boards overlayed one across the other, roofed with mats of badly thatched straw.

No gardens, J noted at once. But everywhere, in every patch of ground, at every corner, even lining the roadside, were tall ungainly plants with leaves broad and flat like those of tulips, flopping over.

'What plant is that?' J asked a man who was pushing up the gangplank to greet a newcomer.

He hardly glanced over his shoulder. 'Tobacco, of course,' he said. 'You'll learn to recognise it soon enough.'

J nodded. He had seen the plant before but he had not thought they would grow it to the exclusion of everything else, in the very streets of their new city.

He took his bag and made his way down the gangplank to the crowded quayside.

'Is there an inn here?'

'A dozen,' a woman replied. 'But only if you have gold or tobacco to pay.'

'I can pay,' J said steadily. 'I come with a warrant from the king of England.'

She looked away as if she were not much impressed with his patent. 'Then you had best tell the governor,' she said, nodding towards the man's broad back. 'If he'll stoop to speak with you.'

J hefted his bag onto his other shoulder and stepped up towards the man. 'Sir John?' he asked. 'Let me introduce myself. I am John Tradescant the younger, gardener to the king. He has commanded me to make a collection of rare plants, and rarities of all sorts. Here is his letter.' He bowed and produced the patent marked with the royal seal.

Sir John did not take it. He merely nodded his head in reply. 'What's your title?'

'Esquire,' J said, still uncomfortable with the lie which claimed his right to be a gentleman when he was in truth nothing more than the son of a working man, and the grandson of a labourer.

The governor turned and extended his hand. J shook the proffered two fingers. 'Call tomorrow,' the governor said. 'I have to collect my letters and some bills of purchase from the captain here. Call tomorrow and I shall be at leisure to receive you.'

'Then I'll find a bed at an inn,' J said uncertainly.

The governor had already turned his back. 'Do that. Or the people are extraordinarily hospitable.'

J waited in case he would offer anything more; but he moved away

5

and there was nothing for J to do but pick up his other bulkier bag, which had been slung down on the quayside, and trudge up the hill, past the bulging walls of the fort, towards the little town.

He found the first inn by the haunting smell of stale ale. As he paused in the doorway there was a loud baying noise of a big dog and a shrill shout commanding it to be silent. J tapped lightly on the door and stepped in.

It was dark inside, the air was thick with smoke, almost unbreathable for a stranger. J's eyes stung and he felt his breath catch.

'Good day,' a woman said abruptly from the back of the room. J blinked tears from his eyes and saw her better: a woman of about fifty with the leathery skin and hard eyes of a survivor. She wore rough wooden clogs on her feet, a homespun skirt kilted up out of the way, a shirt that had once belonged to a man twice her size and a shawl tied tightly around her shoulders.

'I'm new-come from London,' J said. 'I want a room for the night.'

'You can't have one to yourself, you're not at Whitehall now.'

'No,' J said politely. 'Might I share a room?'

'You'll share a bed and like it!'

'Very well,' J said. 'And something to eat? And drink?'

She nodded. 'Paying in gold? Or tobacco?'

'Where would I get tobacco?' J demanded, his irritation finally breaking through. 'I landed five minutes ago.'

She smiled, as if she were pleased to see him rise to the bait. 'How would I know?' she demanded. 'Maybe you'd had the sense to ask in London how we do things over here. Maybe you'd had the sense to buy some on the quayside, seeing as every planter in the colony was selling there today. Maybe you're a returning planter coming back to your rich fields. How would I know?'

'I'm not a planter, and I was not advised to bring tobacco to Virginia,' J said. 'But I am hungry and thirsty and weary. I should like a wash too. When will my dinner be ready?'

The woman abandoned her teasing of him abruptly. 'You can wash under the pump in the yard,' she said. 'Don't drink the water, it's only a shallow well and it's foul. You'll sleep in the attic along with the rest of us. You'll share a pallet bed with my son, or with whoever next comes through the door. Dinner will be ready as soon as it's cooked, which will be the quicker if I can get on now.'

She turned her back to him and stirred something in a pot hanging over the fireplace. Then she moved to a barrel in the corner and drew him a mug of ale.

'Here,' she said. 'Four mugs for a penny. I'll keep the tally.'

'I'm sure you will,' J said under his breath and went out into the yard to wash.

⁂

She need not have warned him not to drink the water. It came out of the pump in a brown brackish spout, stinking horribly. Still, it was better than seawater, and J stripped and washed all over, and then pulled on his breeches and sat himself down on a pile of sawn wood and shaved himself, feeling his skin with his fingertips to guide his razor.

The ground still heaved uneasily under his feet, as if he were on board ship. But he knew that his father had felt the same when they had made landfall at Rhé or in Russia after his long voyage across the North Sea. He had told him that it was the same after·any long voyage. For a moment J thought of his father at home, and the two children. For a moment he had the sweetest of illusions that Jane was there too, caring for them, awaiting his return. It seemed so much more likely that she would be there, waiting for him, than that she should be dead and he never see her again. The moment was so strong that he had to remind himself of the orangery and the pallet bed, and her white-faced determination that she should die alone rather than pass the plague to him and to her children. The thought of it made him sick to the stomach with grief, and he dropped his head in his hands as the cool Virginia twilight wrapped him in darkness, and he knew that he had sailed to the new world, to the new land, but brought his three-year-old grief all that long way with him.

Spring 1638, Virginia

J opened his eyes and saw, instead of the whitewashed walls and ceiling of his Lambeth home, a thatched roof, close to his face. Beneath him, wooden boards, not even a straw mattress; a pace away, a young man on a pallet bed, still deep in sleep. He took in, slowly, the watery smell of something cooking, the discomfort of the hard floor, and the irritating itch of a fresh fleabite. He sat up cautiously, his head swimming. The solid wooden floor of the loft heaved under his gaze with the illusion of movement.

'You can stir yourselves or it'll be cold!' came a shout from the woman who kept the lodging house. In one fluid movement the lad, her son, was up and out of bed and down the ladder to the kitchen below. J pulled on his boots, brushed down his breeches, shrugged his waistcoat over his grubby shirt, and followed him.

The woman was spooning a pale yellow mixture from the pot, suspended over a miserly fire, into four wooden bowls. She slapped them onto the table and bowed her head over her calloused hands for a brief grace. Another man who had stayed the night sleeping on the floor beside the fire drew up his stool, took out his own spoon and ate with relish.

'What is it?' J asked cautiously.

'Porridge made with Indian corn,' she replied.

'You'll have to get used to it,' the man said. 'Indian corn is almost all we eat.'

J smiled. 'I wasn't expecting milk and honey.'

'There's many that do,' the woman said shortly. 'And many that die still hoping.'

There was a short silence.

'You here prospecting?' the man asked.

'No,' J said. 'I'm a gardener, a plant collector. I've come to collect plants. Authorised by King Charles himself.' He hesitated for a moment, wondering if he should tell them about the great garden in Lambeth and his father's reputation as the greatest gardener that had ever been, advisor to the Duke of Buckingham, gardener to the king and queen, one of the greatest collectors of rarities in the world. He looked at the woman's enfolded, bitter face and thought that he would not.

The man nodded. 'Will you see the king when you get home? If you get home,' he added.

J nodded and took a spoon of the porridge. It was bland, the corn boiled to the consistency of paste. 'Yes. I work for him in his garden at Oatlands Palace,' he said.

'Well, tell him that we can't do with this governor,' the man said bluntly. 'Tell him that we *won't* do with him, and that's a fact. We've got enough worries to deal with here without having a fat fool set over us from England. We need a general assembly with a voice for every planter. We need a guarantee of our rights.'

'You'd be imprisoned if you spoke like that in England,' J pointed out mildly.

'That's why I'm not in England,' the man said shortly. 'And I don't expect to live as if I were. Which is more than can be said for the governor who expects to live like a lord with servants in a land where men and women have come to be free.'

'I'm not his advisor,' J said. 'I speak to the king – when I ever see him – about plants and his garden.'

The man nodded. 'So who does advise him now?'

J thought for a moment. It all seemed a long way away and of little interest in this new country. 'The queen,' he said. 'And Archbishop Laud.'

The man made a grimace and turned his head to spit but then checked the movement when he saw the woman glare. 'Beg pardon. So he hasn't called a parliament?'

J shook his head. 'He hopes to rule without one.'

'I heard he was halfway to being a Papist.'

'I don't know anything about that.'

'I heard that he has taken so many fines and so much wealth into his own hands that he does not need to call a parliament for them to vote taxes, that he lets his wife worship openly as a Papist, and that daily there are men and women in the country crying out for him to change,' the man said precisely.

John blinked at the accuracy and malice of the description. 'I thought you were royalists in Virginia?'

9

'Not all of us,' the man said with a hard smile.

'Where are you going to find your plants?' the woman interrupted. 'There's nothing grown up and down the river but tobacco.'

'Surely people farm other crops?'

She shook her head. 'We keep beasts – or at any rate they keep themselves. But with the fish jumping out of the river and the animals in the forest it's not worth the labour of doing more than fishing and hunting. Besides, we can trade for anything we need with the Indians. They can do the labour of farming for us. We can all be squires here.'

'I thought I'd travel round,' J said. 'Hire a horse and ride round the country, see what I can find.'

They both looked at him and rudely laughed in his face.

'Hire a horse!' the woman exclaimed. 'There's not more than half a dozen horses in the whole plantation. You might as well ask for a coach and four.'

J kept his temper. 'I see I have much to learn.'

She rose from the table and went to the fire. 'Dark morning,' she said irritably. She bent to the fire and lit what looked like a little twig of kindling. To J's surprise it burnt with a bright clear flame at the very tip, like a specially made taper. She rested it on a small holder, placed on the stone hearth for that purpose, and came back to the table.

'What's that?'

She glanced back without interest. 'We call it candlewood. I buy it from the Indians every autumn.'

'But what sort of wood is it?'

'Candlewood,' she said impatiently.

'But from what sort of tree?'

She looked at him as if he were foolish to be asking something that no-one else cared about. 'How should I know? I pay the Indians to fetch it for me. D'you think I go out into the woods to gather my own candlewood? D'you think I make my own spoons from spoonwood? D'you think I make my own sugar from the sugar tree or my own soap from the soapberry?'

'Candlewood? Spoonwood?' J had a moment of wild imagining, thinking of a tree growing candles, a tree growing spoons, a bush growing soap. 'Are you trying to make a fool of me?'

'No greater fool than you are already – what else should I call them but what they are?'

'What you want,' the man said pacifically, pushing away his empty bowl and taking out a pipe and filling it with rich golden tobacco leaves, 'is an Indian, a savage. One to use as your own. To take you out into the forest and show you all these things. Take you out in a canoe up and down the river and show you the things you want to know.'

'Don't any of the planters know these things?' J asked. He felt fearful at the thought of being guided by an Indian. There had been too much talk in London of brown men armed with knives of stone who crept into your house and cut your throat while you slept.

The woman hawked and spat into the fireplace. 'They don't hardly know how to plant!' she said. 'Everything they know they learned from the Indians. You can find yourself an Indian to tell you what the soapberry tree is. Civilised folks here aren't interested in anything but gold and tobacco.'

'How shall I find an Indian to guide me?' J asked. For a moment he felt as helpless as a child, and he thought of his father's travels – to Russia, to the Mediterranean, to Europe. He had never asked his father if he had felt fear, or worse than fear: the babyish whimper of someone lost, friendless in a strange land. 'Where would I find a safe Indian?'

'No such thing as a safe Indian,' the woman said sharply.

'Peace!' J's fellow lodger said quietly. 'If you're serving the king you must have papers, a safe pass, that sort of thing.'

J felt inside his shirt where the precious royal order was wrapped in oilskin. 'Of course.'

'Best see the governor then,' the man suggested. 'If you're from the king and you've got some influence at court, the governor'll have time for you. God knows he has no time for honest working men trying to make a living here.'

'Does he have a court?' J asked.

'Knock on his door,' the woman said impatiently. 'Court indeed! He's lucky to have a girl to open the door for him.'

J stood up from the table. 'Where shall I find his house?'

'Set beyond the Back Road,' the man said. 'I'll stroll over with you now.'

'I have to wash first,' J said nervously. 'And get my hat and coat.'

The woman snorted disparagingly. 'He'll want to paint and powder next,' she said.

The man smiled. 'I'll wait for you outside,' he said and went out, closing the door gently behind him.

There was neither jug nor ewer in the attic, nor a mirror. Everything that had to be brought from England was at a premium in the new colony. The most trivial things which J had taken for granted in England were rare luxuries here. J washed under the pump in the yard, flinching from the icy splash, and unconsciously keeping his lips tight shut, fearful of drinking the foul water.

His fellow lodger was waiting for him outside the house, in the shade of a tree, sipping from a mug of small ale. The sun beat down on the blinding dust all around him. He nodded when he saw J and slowly got to his feet. 'Don't rush,' he advised him. 'A man can die of hurry in this climate.'

He led the way down the track that ran between the houses. The road was no dirtier than a back road in London but somehow it seemed worse, with the heat of the sun beating down on it and the bright light which dazzled J and made him squint. Hens clucked around in the dust and shied away from their strolling feet at every street corner, and every garden, every drainage ditch, was filled with the ungainly sprout and flapping leaves of the tobacco plant.

The governor, when J managed to gain admission to the small stone-built house, did nothing more than repeat the lodging-house woman's advice. 'I shall write you a note,' he said languidly. 'You can travel from plantation to plantation and the planters will make you welcome, if that is what you wish. There's no difficulty there. Most of the people you meet will be glad of the company and a new face.'

'But how shall I find my way around?' J asked. He was afraid that he sounded humble, like a fool.

The governor shrugged. 'You must get yourself an Indian servant,' he said. 'To paddle you in a canoe. To set up camp for you when you can find nowhere to stay. Or you can remain here in Jamestown and tell the children that you want flowers from the woods. They'll bring a few things in, I dare say.'

J shook his head. 'I need to see things where they are growing,' he said. 'And see the parent plants. I need roots and seed heads, I need to gather them myself. I need to see where they thrive.'

The governor nodded, uninterested, and rang a silver bell. They could hear the servant trotting across the short hall and opening the badly hung door.

'Take Mr Tradescant to Mr Joseph,' the governor ordered. He turned to J. 'He's the magistrate here at Jamestown. He often puts Indians in the stocks or in prison. He'll know the names of one or two. He might release one from prison to you, to be your guide.'

'I don't know the ways of the country . . .' J said uneasily. 'I would rather have a law-abiding guide –'

The governor laughed. 'They're all rogues and criminals,' he said simply. 'They're all pagan. If you want to go out into the forest with any one of them you take your life in your own hands. If I had my way we should have driven them over the Blue Mountains into the western sea. Just over the distant mountains there – drive them back to India.'

J blinked, but the governor rose to his feet in his enthusiasm. 'My plan is that we should plant the land from one river to the other – from the James River to the Patowmeck River – and then build a mighty fence and push them behind it, expel them from Eden as if we were archangels with flaming swords. Let them take their sins elsewhere. There'll be no peace for us until we are undisputed masters of all the land we can see.'

He broke off. 'But you must take your choice, Mr Tradescant. The only people who know anything of plants or trees in Virginia are the Indians and they may slit your throat once you are in the woods with them. Stay here, safe inside the city, and go home empty-handed; or take your chance. It is a matter of complete indifference to me. I cannot rescue you if you are in the woods with them, whatever the king asks of me, whatever safe passes you have in your pocket.'

J hesitated. He had a moment to appreciate the irony that he had thought he might die on the voyage and had welcomed the thought of his own death, which he had recognised as the only thing to ease his grief. But the thought of meeting his death violently and in fear in unknown woods at the hands of murderous pagans was a different matter altogether.

'I'll speak to this Mr Joseph,' he said at last. 'See what he advises.'

'As you wish,' the governor said languidly. 'I hope you enjoy your stay in Virginia. Please assure His Majesty that I did everything in my power to assist you, when you get home; if you get home.'

'Thank you,' J said levelly, bowed and left the room.

The maid would not take him even for the short walk to Mr Joseph's house until she had tied a shawl around her shoulders and put a broad-brimmed hat on her head.

'It's cool,' J protested. 'And the sun is not even overhead.'

She shot him a swift defensive look. 'There are bugs that bite and a sun which strikes you down, and the heat that comes off the marshes,' she warned. 'The graveyard is full of men who thought that the Virginia sun was not yet up, or that the water was good enough to drink.'

With that she said nothing more but led the way to the magistrate's house, past the fort where the bored soldiers whistled and called to her, and inland up a rough dirt road until she stood before a house which was grand by Virginia standards but would have been nothing more than a yeoman's cottage in England.

'Mr Joseph's house,' she said shortly, and turned and left him at the rough wood front door.

J knocked, and opened the door when a voice shouted to him to come inside.

The house was divided into two. The largest room, where J was standing, served as the kitchen and dining room. There was no separate parlour. There was a ladder at the back of the room leading to attic bedrooms. A light wooden partition, hardly a wall, divided the master bedroom on the ground floor from the rest of the house. Mr Joseph was sitting at the roughly made table in the living room, writing in a ledger.

'Who are you?'

'John Tradescant, from England,' J said, and proffered the governor's note.

Mr Joseph read it quickly. 'I've got no native guide for you,' he said abruptly. 'I've got no messengers due to arrive either. You will have to wait, sir.'

J hesitated. 'I wonder if a white person might be free to take me out, now and then. Perhaps a servant or a labourer might be spared from their work.' He looked at the man's unhelpful expression. 'Perhaps just for a few hours?'

Mr Joseph shook his head. 'How long have you been here?' he demanded.

'Just arrived.'

'When you have been here a little longer you will realise that there is never a spare hour,' the man said grimly. 'Never a spare moment. Look around you. Every single thing you see here has to be wrested from this land. Remember your ship – did you see houses as cargo? Ploughs? Baker's shops? Market stalls?' He paused for emphasis and then shook his head.

'You did not, and that is because we can ship hardly anything. All that we need has to be made or grown or wrought here. Everything. From the shingles on the roof to the ice in the cellar. And this by people who did not come here to farm; but came hoping to pick up gold plates from the seashore, or emeralds from the rivers, or pearls from out of every oyster. So not only are we farming with wooden ploughshares that we have to carve ourselves, but we are farming with labourers who have never seen a ploughshare before, wooden or metal! Who have to learn every step of the way. Who are taught by men who came out to mine gold but find themselves growing tobacco. So there is no-one, not a man nor woman nor child, who has a moment to do anything but work.'

J said nothing. He thought of his father who had travelled half way round the world and never came back without his pockets filled with treasures. He thought of the debts at home which would be mounting and only his father and two young children to care for the business of nursery plants and rarities.

'Then I shall have to go out alone. On my own. For I must go home with plants and rarities.'

'I can give you an Indian girl,' the man said abruptly. 'Her mother is in prison for slander. She's only in for the month. You can have the child for a month.'

'What good will a child be?' J demanded.

The man smiled. 'This is an *Indian* child,' he corrected. 'One of the Powhatan people. She can pass through the trees as quiet as a deer. She can cross deep rivers by stepping on stones that you cannot even see. She can eat off the land: berries, roots, nuts, the earth itself. She'll know every single plant and every single tree within a hundred miles of here. You can have her for a month, then bring her back.'

He threw back his head and shouted an order. From the yard outside came an answering shout and the back door opened and a child was thrust into the room, her hands still full of the flax which she had been beating.

'Take her!' Mr Joseph said irritably. 'She understands some English, enough to do your bidding anyway, she's not deaf, but she's dumb. She can make noises but not speech. Her mother is a whore for the English soldiers, or a servant, or a cook, or something. She's in prison for a month for complaining of rape. The girl knows enough to understand you. Take her for a month and bring her back here three weeks on Thursday. Her mother comes out of prison then and she'll want her back.'

He waved the girl towards J and she stepped slowly, unwillingly forward.

'And don't rape her,' he warned matter-of-factly. 'I don't want a half-breed baby nine months from now. Just order her to find your plants and bring you back within the month.'

The magistrate waved them both from the room and J found himself on the doorstep in the bright morning sunlight with the girl like a shadow at his elbow. He turned and looked at her.

She was an odd mixture of child and woman; that was the first thing he saw about her. The roundness of her face and the open gaze of the dark eyes was that of a child, an inquisitive, bonny child. But the straightness of her nose and the high cheekbones and the strength of her jaw would make her a beautiful woman in only a few years' time. Her head was not yet level with his shoulder, but the long legs and slim long feet showed that she would grow taller. She was dressed according to Jamestown convention in someone's cast-off shift which reached down to her calves and flapped around her shoulders. Her hair was long and dark, flowing loose on one side of her head; but the other side, around her right ear, was shaved close, giving her a curious, exotic appearance. The skin of her neck and her shoulders, which he could see around the gaping gown, was painted with outlandish blue ridges of tattoos. She was looking at him with apprehension, but not outright fear; looking at him as if she were measuring his strength, and thinking that whatever might happen next she would survive it.

It was that look that told J she was a child. A woman fears pain: the pain inside her body, and the pain of a man's command. But this was still a girl, since she had a girl's confidence that she could survive anything.

J smiled at her, as he would have smiled at his own nine-year-old daughter Frances, left so far away in London. 'Don't be afraid, I won't hurt you,' he said.

Years later he would remember that promise. The first thing he, a white man, had said to an Indian: 'Don't be afraid. I won't hurt you.'

J led the girl away from Mr Joseph's house to the shade of a tree in the centre of what would in England have been the village green, but here was a dusty piece of waste ground between the river and the Back Road. A couple of cows foraged pessimistically around them.

'I need to find plants,' J said slowly, watching her face for any signs of understanding. 'Candlewood. Soapberry. Spoonwood.'

She nodded, but whether she understood him, or was merely trying to please him, he could not tell.

He pointed to the tree. 'I want to see trees.' He pointed to where the thick line of the forest fringed the river, beyond the desert of waste ground that the settlers had made around the little town, tree stumps still showing in the new fields, dust blowing away from the exhausted tobacco rows.

'Will you take me into the woods?'

She looked at him with sudden keen intelligence, and stepped towards him. She put a hand on his chest and then turned from him and mimed walking: a wonderful vivid mime that made J laugh at once. It was the English walk, the rolling swagger of a self-important man walking in ill-fitting shoes. She rolled her hips as English men do when they walk, she picked up her feet as English men do when their blisters are nipping their toes. She nodded at him when she saw that he understood, and then she turned and pointed far out beyond the felled trees to the dark, impenetrable wall of forest. She stood for a moment, and then spread her arms and with a little shudder of movement from the crown of her dark head to her bare feet made him see – see the inexpressible: a tall tree with wide spreading branches. It was an illusion, like a mountebank's trick; but for a moment J, watching her, saw not girl but tree; saw the movement of wind in the branches, saw the sway of the trunk. Then she stepped away from her mime and looked at him inquiringly.

'Yes,' J said. 'Trees. I want to see trees.' He nodded and smiled at her, nodded again. Then he stepped closer and pointed to himself. 'And flowers,' he said. He bent down and mimed delightedly finding something on the ground, picking it and smelling it.

He was rewarded by a bright smile and then a tiny, half-suppressed chuckle of laughter.

He mimed picking berries and eating them, he mimed gathering nuts or digging roots from the ground. The girl nodded; she had understood.

'We go now?' J demanded. He gestured towards the woods, started to march forward to indicate his readiness.

She looked at him from his heavy leather boots to his tall hat. She said not a word but J sensed that his clothes, his boots, his walk, even his very body – so heavy and stiff – seemed to her an impossible burden to take into the woods. But then she sighed, and with a little lift of her shoulders seemed to shrug away the difficulty of how a lumpish overdressed white man could be taken into the forest. She stepped forward and with a gesture of her hand indicated that he should walk behind her, and headed towards the trees at a gentle trot.

Sweat poured off J before they were halfway through the cultivated fields outside the half-opened walls of Jamestown. A crowd of midges and strange, sharply biting moths spun around his head and stung and nipped at every exposed inch of skin. He wiped his face with his hand and it came away dirty with the wings and legs of little bloodsucking insects and left his face sore. They reached the shade of the forest edge;

but it was no better. At every pace a small cloud of insects bloomed around his big feet and fastened themselves to every piece of reddening skin.

J swatted and wiped and smoothed his face and his neck and his hands, making a thousand awkward ungainly movements to each one of her gliding paces. She trotted like an animal, with no wasted energy. Her arms were relaxed at her side, her upper body still, only her feet pattered forward in little steps, steadily one before the other in a thin one-track path. J, watching her run, at first thought it was the pace of a little child; but then found he could hardly keep up with her as she crossed the fields and headed for the trees.

The edge of the forest was like the face of a friend with half the teeth knocked out. The girl looked around at the ragged stumps of trees as if she was grieving for the loss of someone's smile. Then she made that little gesture of her shoulder which said so eloquently that there was no accounting for what a white man might do, and went forward with that slow, very slow trot that was just faster than J's normal walk, and too slow for his running stride. He was continually walking and then breaking into a run to catch her up and then walking again.

As soon as they were beyond the felled trees she stepped off the path, looked around her, listened for one intent moment and then went to a hollow tree at the side of the path. With one fluid movement she flung the shift over her head, folded it carefully, and stowed it in the roots of the tree.

She was all but naked. A little buckskin skirt covered her privates in front but left her long thighs and buttocks exposed. Her breasts were those of a young girl, pointed and as firm as muscle. J exclaimed, not with desire but with fear, and looked around him. For a moment he thought he might have been entrapped by her, and that someone would spring up to witness that he was with her, looking at her shameful nakedness, and some dreadful punishment would follow.

The forest was silent, there was no-one there but the two of them. At once J imagined that she must be inviting him, seducing him; and he could not deny that she was halfway to being desirable. But then he saw that she was not even aware of him, blind to his rapid succession of fears and thoughts. Without fear, without any sense of her own nudity, without the shame she should feel, she bent to the foot of the tree and drew out a small black jug. She dipped in her fingers and drew out a handful of a reddish grease. She smoothed it all over her body as a rich woman will stroke perfume on her skin, and smiled at J when she straightened up and her body glistened with it.

He could see now that the blue and red tattoos which ringed her shoulder blades went down her narrow back in wild spirals. Only her small breasts and belly were bare of them. The grease had added a redder colour to her skin and a darker sheen to the tattoos. She looked stranger and older than she had on the Jamestown green. Her hair looked longer and thicker, her eyes darker and wilder. J watched this transformation from a child in someone's hand-me-down clothes to a young woman in her own gleaming skin with a growing sense of awe. She had changed from a serving maid – the child of a criminal serving maid – into a creature of the wood who looked as if she belonged there, and whose skin, dappled with the light through the shifting canopy of the leaves, was almost invisible against the dappled light of the forest floor.

She held out the pot for him to take some grease.

'No, thank you,' J said awkwardly.

Again she proffered it.

J shook his head.

Patiently she pointed to the cloud of insects around his face and neck, and J noticed for the first time that there were no midges and moths around her. She thrust the pot towards him.

Squeamishly, J dipped his hand into the pot and brought out a little grease on the tips of his fingers. It smelled rancid like old sweat and well-hung meat. J could not help a swift expression of distaste at the powerful stink, he wiped the grease away on a leaf and shook his head again. The girl was not offended. She merely shrugged and then corked the pot with a bundle of leaves, and put it in a woven bag which she drew out from under the tree trunk along with a small quiver made of reeds holding half a dozen arrows, and a small bow.

The quiver she hung at her side, the bow over her shoulder, the soft woven bag across her body to hang on the other hip. Then she nodded to him briskly, to indicate she was ready. She gestured towards the river – did he want to go along the shoreline?

J pointed towards the deeper trees to their left. She nodded and stepped before him, made that little confident gesture that told him to follow behind her, and led the way.

She moved as quietly as an animal through the shadows and the trees. Not even the arrows in her quiver rattled together. The tiny, almost invisible, track was blocked at every pace by a fallen log or a strand of creeper stretching from one tree to another. She trotted over the one and ducked beneath the other without ever breaking her steady stride. J, out of breath, breaking twigs and kicking stones with his heavy shoes, ducking beneath vines, rubbing his face against the trailing disagreeable stickiness of spiders' webs and the stinging moths, stamped behind her like a pursuing cart horse.

She did not look around. 'Well, she hardly needs to look to know that I am following her,' J thought. The noise alone was enough to alert all of Virginia. But she did not even glance to see if all was well with him. She just went at her slow steady trot, as if having been assigned the task of taking him into the deep forest she need no longer consult him until she delivered him to his destination.

They jogged for about half an hour as J's breathing went from a pant to a straining, painful snatching for breath, until at last they came to a clearing where she paused and turned. J, who had been watching every step on the treacherous path, though blinded by his own sweat and dazzled by a cloud of stinging insects, dropped to the ground and whooped for air. Courteously she hunkered down beside him, sitting on her heels, and waiting, composed and silent, for the white man to stop panting and mopping his face, and grabbing at his side where he had a stitch and at his ankle where he had a sprain.

Slowly J fell silent. The noises of the wood which had been obscured by his trampling progress rose up all around him. There were frogs croaking from the river behind them, there were crickets singing. There were birds singing in the thick canopy of leaves above them, pigeons cooing, jays calling, and an interweaving of sounds which J, a town boy, could not recognise.

He heard the rasp of his own breath subside and he turned to look at her. She was quiet and composed.

J gave her a small, almost apologetic, smile, and lifted his hand to the neck of his thick linen shirt and flapped it to indicate his heat. She nodded solemnly and pointed to his thick jacket.

J, feeling every inch a fool, slid his arms out of the sleeves and handed it to her. She folded it as carefully as a housewife in England and put it beside them and scattered a handful of leaves and moss on it. At once it had disappeared. J blinked. He could not even see the outline of it. She had hidden it completely.

She turned and pointed at his breeches and his boots. J shook his head.

Again she pointed at his breeches and mimed pulling them down. J, feeling like an aged virgin clutching to modesty, held the waistband tighter to him. He saw the glimpse of a smile cross her face but then she moulded her expression into impassivity. She gave a little shrug which said as eloquently as any words that he might wear his breeches if he chose to be hot and uncomfortable, and keep his boots if he wanted to alert the whole forest by his heavy tread.

She made a small gesture with her hand that said: 'Here. Trees,' and then she sat back on her heels and looked at him expectantly.

The trees were coming into leaf. J gazed around in wonderment at the height of them, at the richness of the growth, at the vines which looped one to another and twisted around them. Some of them he could recognise as English trees and he found he was nodding towards them, almost as a man might greet the welcome sight of an acquaintance in a strange land. He saw elderberry bushes, oak, hornbeam, cherry trees, walnut trees and dogwood with a sense of relief. But there was also a jumble, an overwhelming richness of foliage and trunk, bark and small flowers, that he could not name, could not identify, that crowded upon him, all beautiful or interesting, large or shapely, calling for his attention and competing with each other. J rubbed his hand across his sweating face. There was a lifetime's work here for a plant collector; and he had promised his father to be home by early summer.

He glanced at the girl. She was not watching him, she was sitting on her heels, waiting patiently, as steady and still as the trees around them. When she felt his gaze upon her she looked up and gave him a small shy smile, a child's smile, as if to say that she was proud of her little cleverness in bringing him to the heart of the wood, happy to wait until she could demonstrate her cleverness at fetching him home. It was a smile that no father could have resisted. J smiled back at her. 'Well done,' he said. 'This is just what I wanted.'

The girl did not lead him home until the evening and then her little bag was packed with seedlings that J had dug from the forest floor. J was carrying his hat like a bowl, filled to the brim with tiny tree seedlings, each showing no more than a pair of leaves, a white stem and a trail of little roots. There were more plants packed into the pockets of his breeches. He had wanted to put some in her quiver but she had shaken her head decisively, and when he proffered the plants again, she had stepped back from him to show him why she refused.

In one swift movement the bow came off her shoulder and into her hand, with the other hand she had an arrow out of the quiver and notched on the bow. She was ready with a sharpened reed arrow head in moments. She nodded; her meaning was clear. She could not waste time fumbling with plants in her quiver.

J tried to hide a smile at this child's seriousness over a child's toy. She was certainly deft; but the bow was a tiny one and the arrows were as light as their flights: made of reed, tipped with sharpened reed.

'May I see?' he asked.

She unstrung the arrow from the bow and handed it to him. At once he realised his mistake. The arrow in his hand was a killing blade. The reed at its head was honed to razor sharpness. He drew it against his thumb and there was no pain, but a fine line of blood bloomed at its touch.

'Damnation!' he swore, and sucked his thumb. It might be made of reed, it might be so light that a young girl could carry it all day; but the arrow head was sharper than a knife.

'How exact is your aim?' J asked her. He pointed to a tree. 'Can you hit that?'

She stepped towards the tree and pointed instead to a leaf which was shifting slightly in the wind before the trunk. She stepped back, notched the arrow into the bow and let fly. The arrow whistled softly in the air and thudded into the tree trunk. J stepped forward to look. There were traces of the leaf around the arrow shaft: she had hit a moving leaf at twenty paces.

J made a little bow to her, and meant the gesture of respect.

She smiled, that little gleam of pride again, and then pulled the arrow from the tree trunk, discarded the broken arrow head and replaced it with another, put the arrow back in her quiver and led the way from the forest clearing at her usual trot.

'Slower,' J commanded.

She glanced at him. He was clumsy with tiredness, his leg muscles singing with pain, and unbalanced by his burden of seedlings. Again he saw that small smile and then she turned and walked before him with a loping pace which was only a little slower. She paused for a moment in the clearing where he had thrown off his jacket and picked it up, dusted off the leaves and handed it to him. Then she led the way back to the hollow tree at the edge of the forest. She hid her bow and arrow in the trunk and drew out her servant's shift.

J, after a long day of jogging behind her dappled flanks, was now accustomed to her nakedness. He found that he liked the gleam of her skin better than the crumpled mess of the shift. He thought she was diminished by the gown, she looked less modest than in her proud tattoos and buckskin. He made a little shrug to show his sense that she was returning to some sort of unnatural constraint and she nodded at his sympathy, her face grave.

'You will stay at my inn tonight,' J said, pointing down to Jamestown where there were already lights showing and chimneys smoking.

She neither nodded nor shook her head, she was frozen still, her eyes never leaving his face.

'And tomorrow we shall go out into the forest again. Mr Joseph said you should come out with me every day for a month, until your mother is freed.'

She nodded her consent to that. Then she stepped forward and pointed at the little plants in his pocket and gestured towards the river. She mimed the strong paddling of a canoe, out towards the sea. Her hand gestured to the right, they should go south, she waved, a long way, waved again, a very long way; then she stepped back from him and with her arms spread and her shoulders rounded she mimed for him a tree: a tree with branches that bowed down, bowed down low over still water, spread her fingers: with branches that trailed into the water.

J was entranced. 'But can we get a canoe?'

The girl nodded. She pointed to herself and held out her hand, pointing to her palm, the universal mime for money. J proffered a silver coin, she shook her head. He drew out his tobacco pouch. She nodded and took a fat handful. Then she pointed his face towards Jamestown, looked into his eyes again as if she were reluctant to trust so stupid a man to find his own way home, and then she nodded at him and turned towards a shrubby bush.

In a second she had disappeared. Disappeared without trace. J saw the little branches of the bush quiver and then she was gone, not even a glimmer of the servant's smock showing in the darkness. For a moment he waited, straining his eyes against the failing light to see if he could spot her, but she had disappeared as surely as a roe deer will vanish by merely standing still.

J, realising that he would never find her against her will, knowing that he had to trust her, turned his face towards Jamestown as she had bid him and trudged home.

When the lodging-house woman knew that J had spent all day with the Indian girl in the woods, and would spend nights away with her, she was scathing.

'I'd have thought a man fresh out of England could have done without,' she said. She dumped in front of him a wooden bowl filled to the brim with a pale porridge.

'Suppawn,' his fellow lodger said out of the side of his mouth. 'Indian cornmeal and milk.'

'More corn?' J asked.

The man nodded grimly and spooned his portion in silence.

'I'd have thought you could have brought a woman from England, if your needs are that urgent,' the woman said. 'God knows, the town needs more women. You can't make a plantation with nothing but soldiers and fools.'

J bent his head and slurped porridge from his spoon.

'Don't you have a wife you could have brought?' the woman demanded.

Grief stabbed J like a knife in the belly. He looked up at her and something in his face silenced her nagging.

'No,' he said abruptly.

There was a short embarrassed silence.

'I'm sorry,' she said, 'if I spoke wrong . . .'

J pushed away the bowl, the familiar feeling of grief choking him from his belly to his throat.

'Here,' the man offered. He produced a leather bottle from the folds of his breeches and poured a slug over J's unwanted porridge. 'Have a drop of Barbados rum, that's the thing to give it flavour.' He poured a measure for himself and stirred it in. He waved to J with his spoon. 'Eat up,' he said with rough kindliness. 'This is not a land where a man can go hungry and eat later. Eat up and drink up too. You never know where your next meal is coming from here.'

J pulled his bowl towards him, stirred in the rum and tasted the porridge. It was much improved.

'The girl is guiding me to plants and trees,' he said to them both. 'As I told you, I am a collector. Neither the governor nor Mr Joseph could think of anyone else who could assist me. But she is a good little girl. She is not much older than my own daughter. I should think she is little more than thirteen. She leads me to the forest and then waits quietly and leads me home.'

'Her mother is a whore,' the lodging-house woman remarked spitefully.

'Well, she is but a little maid yet,' J said firmly. 'And I would not be the man to abuse her.'

The woman shook her head. 'They're not like us. She's no more a maid than my young mastiff bitch is a maid. When she's ready she'll couple like an animal. They're not like us, they're half-beasts.'

'You speak badly of them because of your losses,' J's fellow lodger said fairly. He nodded to J. 'Mistress Whitely here lost her man and her child in the Indian rising of 'twenty-two. She doesn't forget. No-one who was here at the time can ever forget.'

'What happened?' J asked.

The woman lowered herself to the bench opposite him and leaned her chin on her hand. 'They were in and out of Jamestown every night and day,' she said. 'The children stayed in our houses, our men went out hunting with them. Again and again we would have starved if they had not traded with us – food, fish, game. They taught us how to plant: corn and the rest. They taught us how to harvest it and cook it. We would have died over and over again if they had not sold us food. The vicar was going to have an Indian school. We were going to teach them our ways, Christian ways. They were to be subjects of the king. There was not the slightest warning, not the hint of a warning. The chief had been their leader for years and he came and went through Jamestown as free as a white man. We had our own son as a hostage, we feared nothing. Nothing.'

'Why did you have hostages then?' J asked.

'Not hostages,' she corrected herself swiftly. 'Adopted children. God-children. Children in our care. We were educating them in our ways. Turning them from savagery.'

'And what happened?' J asked.

'They waited and planned.' Her voice was lowered, the two men leaned forward to hear her, there was something fearful in the way the three white faces went closer together, and her voice dropped to a haunting whisper. 'They waited and planned and at eight o'clock one morning – Good Friday morning they chose in their blasphemy – all over the country they came out of the bushes, to each little farm, to each little family, to each lone man, they came out and struck us dead. They planned to kill every single one of us without a word of warning reaching the others. And they'd have done it too; but for one little turncoat Indian boy who told his master that he had been ordered to kill him, and the man ran to Jamestown and raised the alarm.'

'What happened?'

'They opened the arsenal at Jamestown and called the settlers in. Everyone who was near enough came in and the town was saved, but up and down the river, in every isolated farmhouse, there was a white man and woman with their skull staved in by a stone axe.'

She turned her bleak face to J. 'My husband's head was cleaved in two, with an axe of stone,' she said. 'My little boy was stabbed through the heart with an arrow head of shell. They came against us without

25

proper weapons, they came against us with reeds and shells and stones. It was like the land itself rose up and struck at us.'

There was a long silence.

She rose from the table and stacked the bowls, callous again. 'That's why I have no time for even the smallest girl of theirs,' she said. 'They are like stones and reeds and trees to me. I hate every stone and reed and tree in this land, and I hate every one of them. I hate them to their death and destruction. This land will never be home for me until everyone of them is gone.'

'How many of us died?' J asked. He said 'us' without thinking. This was a war of the dark forests against the white men; of course he counted himself among the planters.

'Not quite four hundred,' she said bitterly. 'Four hundred men and women who wanted nothing more than to live in peace in a little part of a great great land. And then the hunger came.'

'Hunger?'

'We had to leave the crops in the field, we were too afraid to bring them in,' she explained. 'We all crowded into Jamestown and manned the guns over the wooden walls. It was a bitter winter, and there wasn't enough to eat. And we couldn't trade with them as we usually did. We had always traded with them for their winter stores, they always had plenty and they always sold to us. But now we were at war with the very people who had fed us.'

J waited for more.

'We don't talk about that time,' she said shortly. 'About that winter. We ate what we could, and no blame to those who found what they could.'

J turned to his fellow lodger for an explanation.

'The graveyard,' the man said in an undertone. 'They dug up their dead and ate them.'

The woman's face was stony. 'We ate what we could get,' she said. 'And you'd have done the same. There's no such thing as Christian behaviour when you're starving. We did what we had to do.'

J felt the suppawn dinner rise up in the back of his throat at the thought of what the cook had tasted.

'We survived,' she said flatly.

'I'm sure –' J stammered.

'And when the weather got warmer those who were not dead of their wounds, or of grief, or of starvation, died of the plague,' she went on. 'All of us packed in to this little town, all of us sick with grief and fear. Hundreds died that winter, and it was all the Indians' fault. As soon as we could muster men and supplies we went against them. We passed a law and we swore an oath, that not a man or a woman would be left alive.'

The man nodded. 'We hunted them down like dogs and we pushed them further and further away. It was an order – kill all the men and women and enslave the children. We pretended to be at peace for a while and we watched them plant their crops and commit themselves to their fields, and then, and only then, we went in and destroyed their harvest. They make fish weirs, intricate clever things, we destroyed them wherever we saw them. We drove away the game so that they would starve when they went hunting, we burned them out of their villages so they were homeless, we trampled their crops in the field so they would know hunger as we had known hunger. We took our revenge.'

'We had some good hunting,' the woman said reminiscently. She drew three mugs of ale and set them on the table. 'I remember the soldiers from the fort coming in with the heads of the savages at their belt, and then setting them up along the gate like a gamekeeper stakes up a dead weasel.'

'And are they finished now?' J could hear the nervousness in his own voice.

'Oh yes,' the man said. 'This was sixteen years ago, remember, and there's not been a word from them since. They cannot live without the spread of land for their game and farming, and we have pushed them backwards and backwards towards the mountains. They used to live always on the move you see: winter inland, summer down towards the sea, spring to the fields. Once we built our houses and cleared the forest we drove them out, drove them like a herd of deer into bad foraging.'

'They must hate us as their worst enemies,' J said.

Neither of them answered. The man shrugged and lowered his face into his mug.

'We won, and that's the main thing,' the woman said firmly. 'It's our land now and if they want to live here they have to serve us. There's no more schools and teaching of them. There's no more peace and promises of friendship. If they want to stay in our borders they do as they are bid. They can be our slaves or their blood can water the fields. Nothing else.'

At dawn J was down at the quayside, Jamestown silent behind him and only the gleam of the fires in the bread ovens showing that anyone was awake.

The girl was there before him. She had a small dugout canoe bobbing in the dark water. J surveyed it uneasily. It too much resembled the tree it recently had been. The bark had been stripped off and the sides roughly chiselled so that it was shaped to a point at both ends, the inside had been scorched and then scraped clean; but it still looked nothing more than a small tree: stripped, shaped, and hollowed.

She was seated in the prow, a paddle in the water, waiting for him. When she saw him she looked up and gestured, with a tiny authoritative movement, that he should take his place behind her.

'Won't it sink?' J demanded.

Again she made that small gesture.

J assumed that she could swim, and reminded himself that they were alongside the dock and the ship which had brought him from England was moored at the quayside, within hailing distance. He put his little travelling satchel in the boat and then stepped in himself. At once it rocked and nearly overturned.

J dropped to his knees, and found that the canoe steadied immediately. Before him was a paddle. He drew it out, careful not to move too fast, and put it in the water, on the same side as hers.

She glanced over her shoulder, her child's face serious, and shook her head. J transferred his paddle to the other side and was rewarded by a grave nod. Then she leaned forward and dug the blade of her paddle into the lapping river water, and they moved slowly away from the wooden pier.

At first J could see nothing, but all his other senses were fully alert. He felt the canoe moving smoothly and easily on the water, the current of the river and the ebb of the tide together drawing them out to sea. He sensed the immensity of the water around them, a great desert of water, and their canoe moving among it like a sleek, dark fish. He could smell the land ahead of them: the salt mud, rank tidewash weed and rotting driftwood; and from Jamestown, falling away behind them, the homely smell of woodsmoke and the rancid stink of the household waste which they tipped at the water's edge for the tide to take away.

Slowly the sky lightened and J could see the girl's outline, kneeling in the canoe ahead of him. She bowed forward, digging her paddle into the inky black water. J tried to copy her motion and the canoe suddenly skidded as he got the stroke right. She did not turn her head, she was absorbed in her own task of weaving air and water together.

He could hear the birds stirring in the woods on either side of the river. A thousand single calls and coos and cries were building to a cacophony of sound that drifted over the glassy water towards them.

There must be hundreds of thousands of birds in the wood to make such a sweep of sound, and then the river birds started to wake. J heard a clatter of quacking and a huge flight of ducks took off from the bank on his left and headed towards the brightening sky. Gulls were swirling and calling overhead, and then the whole world suddenly went dark as a flock of pigeons, innumerable birds, fled across the sky, blocking the light for minutes and filling the whole shadowy world with the creaking of their wings and the rush of their passage.

J had a sense of a virgin world: a place where man was a stranger, an interloper, who had not left a mark, a world where vast flocks and herds of animals and birds moved, obeying their natural order, and nothing could prevent them. It was a new world, another Eden, a paradise for a plant collector. For the first time in years, for the first time since Jane's death, J had a powerful sense of hope, of the possibilities before him. If men could make their home in this new land they could make a country like a paradise, rich and easy. Perhaps even he could make a home here. Perhaps he and the children could make a new home here and the old life at Lambeth, London, and the old losses of Lambeth, could be left far behind.

They paddled for an hour to cross the wide river and reach the other bank. Then they turned and followed the south bank eastward, towards the sea. Even though the ebbing tide was taking them downriver they had to paddle to hold the canoe on course, and J's shoulders and arm muscles were tight with strain after the first hour, but the girl still moved fluidly and easily, as if the delicate feathering of the paddle and the deep digging movement to push the boat forward were nothing to her.

As they drew closer to the bank J saw the virgin woods coming down to the water's edge and brightly coloured birds flirting from trees to water and back again. Every now and then there was a clearing in the woods and the bare earth of a ploughed field. Sometimes there were black men and white men planting side by side, and they raised their heads to watch the canoe go by. J waved, but the girl stared straight ahead as if she were a little statue, with no curiosity about her fellow men at all.

The sun came up, a pale yellow sun swimming in cloud. The mist was burned off the river and the stinging moths came out and formed a cloud around J's red, sweaty face. He puffed them off his lips but he could not spare a hand from the paddle to swat them away. He shook his head irritably and the canoe made a little wobble in the water.

At that movement she glanced back and saw him, hot, flushed, irritable, and with one smooth stroke she turned the canoe and plunged towards the shade of an inlet.

The trees closed around them, over their heads, around their backs, they were hidden in a world of green. The girl ran the canoe up on a sandbank and stepped out. She slipped off her servant's smock, folded it carefully and stowed it in the canoe. Then she pointed commandingly at him.

J took off his jacket, then she pointed at his boots.

'I'll keep my boots on,' J said.

She shook her head. Pointed to the vast reach of water, closed her eyes and mimed a man plunging downwards, dragged under by the weight of his boots.

'Oh,' J said. 'All right then.'

He sat on the wet sand and pulled off his boots, stood before her in his stockings, breeches and shirt. She gestured at the rest of his clothes.

J smiled, shook his head. 'I'll keep them on . . .'

She tugged at his shirt with an impatient little hand, and produced from the canoe, with a flourish, a little buckskin skirt, like her own.

'Indian breeches?' J asked.

She nodded.

'I cannot dress like a savage,' J said reasonably.

She pointed to the dugout canoe, to herself, to the distance they had come and the distance they were to go. Her meaning was clear. You are travelling like one of the Powhatan, with one of the Powhatan. Why not be comfortable?

'I'll get bitten,' J protested. He made little pinchers of his thumb and finger and pinched at the skin of his forearm, showed her the tiny irritating swellings on the skin of his face.

The girl nodded and produced the jar of grease she had used in the forest the day before, held her own smooth arm for his inspection, turned her little unmarked face towards him.

J looked around him in embarrassment. But the woods were loud only with birdsong and impervious to his shame. There was no-one within ten miles in any direction.

'Oh, all right,' he said awkwardly.

He stripped off his breeches, grateful for his long shirt tails which hid his nakedness from her. She held out the buckskin skirt. J struggled to put it on, under his shirt. She stepped lightly around to his back, pulled the shirt out of the way and tied the strings of the apron for him. The soft leather nestled against him like another skin. The air was

30

cool on his legs. J felt white and ungainly, a bleached leviathan beside her slight brown body; but he also felt comfortable for the first time since he had arrived in this painfully humid country.

She gestured that he should take off his shirt. J shucked it over his head and then she presented him with the jar of grease. With a sense of nothing left to lose, J put his fingers into the pot and smoothed it all over his face, his neck and his chest. It smelled dreadful and felt as sticky as honey.

She gave a tiny trill of laughter, and he looked down and saw his white skin streaked with red. She held out her bare arm to show him the comparison. Against her treacle-coloured skin the grease showed only as a darker brown, but J was striped white and red.

He paused, but she clicked at him like someone encouraging an animal, took the pot herself and ducked under his arm. He felt her little hands painting the stuff on his back. Despite himself he felt the tiniest flicker of arousal at the touch. But then she came before him again, and he saw that grave child's face and the swinging black plait of hair, and remembered that she was a little maid, not much older than his daughter, and under his protection.

J rubbed the grease into his skin. He thought he must look like a mummer at a feast, painted and dressed like a fool. But at least he felt cool. His embarrassment faded, and then he realised also he was no longer being bitten. The grease was repelling the insects that danced in a cloud on the waters all around them.

The girl nodded at him with evident approval and picked up his discarded clothes, folded them and stowed them in the canoe. Then she steadied the canoe while he climbed in again.

Without his breeches and awkward boots, J found he was more comfortable. There was a hollow carved in the wooden floor and without the bulk of his breeches and boots his knees fitted into the space. The wood, slightly porous, was cool and pleasantly damp on his bare legs, the river air blew gently against his naked chest. He put his face up, enjoying the cool breeze on his neck, feeling the sweat on his face cooling and drying. The girl gave him a small triumphant smile and pushed off, stepping into the canoe before him and kneeling in one smooth movement. The canoe barely bobbed in the water. Then she turned it around and paddled it strongly towards the main river once more.

They paddled until midday. J was troubled neither by insects nor by the growing heat of the sun in his face. When the sun was at its highest, the girl turned the canoe into an inlet of the river and ran it ashore.

At once the cool greenness of the trees engulfed them. J got out of the canoe, and staggered a little on his cramped legs. She smiled and went sure-footed as a deer up the sandy beach to the forest. J reached for his satchel and followed her.

She offered him the forest with a little wave of her hand, as a princess might gesture to a visiting ambassador as if to say: 'my lands'.

J nodded. The girl took his hand and pulled him a little way towards the trees. He was to go and collect whatever specimens he wanted. J paused.

'What will you do?'

She made a gesture to show that she would stay there. She picked up a few dry sticks and piled them together: she would make a fire. She took a little hoeing stick from the purse at her belt, and mimed digging up roots: she would find food. She gestured towards the trees and mimed sleep: she would find some shelter for them.

'We stay here tonight?' J asked, repeating her mime of sleep.

She nodded.

'I will come back here in a little while,' he said. He pointed to himself and to the forest, and showed his walking fingers. She nodded, and then mimed herself calling and then a mime of listening.

'I'm to stay where I can hear you?' J asked, and was rewarded with a nod and a smile.

Feeling like a child sent out to play, J went to the canoe and pulled on his leather boots, took his bag and went along the shoreline. He glanced back.

She was drawing the canoe higher up the beach, away from the reach of the tide. Then she turned and started collecting firewood. She seemed as comfortably at home in this wilderness as a young woman in the kitchen of her own house. J turned away and wandered further along the shoreline, his eyes at the edge of the wood looking for saplings and little plants in their first flush of spring growth that he might get safely home to England.

He obeyed her order that he stay within earshot, and worked his way in a sweep around their little camp until he emerged on the shoreline on the other side, his satchel bulging with seedlings and cuttings wrapped in damp linen.

She was putting the finishing touches on a shelter for the night. She had bent three saplings together and lashed them to make a low bender.

She had roofed them with some wide green leaves and filled in the walls with rushes. The canoe was drawn up before the open mouth of the little hut and tipped on its side as protection, and there was a small fire smoking before the hut and two fishes staked on sharp sticks, waiting to be roasted. J came quietly but she did not jump when she saw him, he imagined that she had heard his every move since he had left her at midday. She nodded gravely as she saw him and then pointed to his satchel.

'Yes. I've done well,' he said. He opened the flap of the bag and showed her. She nodded her approval and then indicated behind him. She had weeded and dug a little patch of ground.

J felt a sense of real delight. 'For my plants?' He pointed to his satchel. She nodded and looked at him, querying if it was what he wanted.

'That is excellent!' J beamed. 'I shall collect more tomorrow and plant them up here, and only move them again when we go back to Jamestown. Thank you!'

The girl nodded with a little smile and he saw that she relished his praise just as his daughter Frances did. 'You're very, very clever,' he said, and was rewarded by a slight blush and another smile.

She turned to the fire and threw on some dry kindling, and the blaze flickered up. She hunkered down on her heels and fanned the flame with a handful of stiff reeds until the twigs were glowing red, then she took one stick with the spitted fish and gave J the other. She showed him how to hold it above the glowing twigs so that it roasted in the heat but did not catch fire, and to turn it when the skin was brown and crispy.

When it was cooked she tipped the one on her stick on to a broad green leaf and proffered it to J, and then took the one he had cooked which was too dark on one side, and still a little raw on the other. She bowed her head over it for a moment, for all the world as if she were saying grace in a Christian home, and extended a hand to the sky, then turned it palm down to the earth. J realised that she *was* saying grace, which he had quite forgotten, and he had a momentary uncomfortable sense of confusion as to which of them was the ignorant pagan and which the civilised human. Then she smiled at him and started eating.

It was a firm white fish with a wonderful spicy taste from the scorched skin. J ate with relish, leaving only the bones, the head, tail and fins. When he had finished she drew from inside the canoe a little basket of dried fruit and gave him a handful of berries, dried blueberries. They were like a handful of pebbles in his mouth at first and then their taste seeped out, making his face pucker with their sourness, which made her laugh.

It was growing cold. The sun was behind them, inland behind the high trees. J put some more wood on the fire, and the girl got to her feet. She took a small glowing twig from the fire, went down to the water's edge, and laid the twig on a shell at her bare feet. From the purse at her waist she took out a small pinch of something and then, without embarrassment, untied the thong of her buckskin skirt and laid it to one side. She picked up the burning twig and the pinch of herbs and, naked, waded into the water. J heard her gasp a little at the coldness of it.

The tide was coming in; the river, a mixture of salt and sweet, lapped at the sand beach. The girl was nothing more than a dark shadow against the dancing, gleaming water. J watched her blow on the glowing end of the twig and then put it to her cupped hand and blow again. She was lighting the herbs. J smelled a sharp, acrid smell like tobacco, carried to him on the onshore wind. Then he saw her scatter the smoking herb on the water.

She washed her face and her body, and then raised her wet head to where the moon was showing low on the horizon and lifted her hands in prayer. Then she turned back to the land and waded out of the water.

J thought of evening prayers at Lambeth, of his dead wife's faith, and of the lodging-house woman who had assured him that these people were animals. He shook his head at the contradictions. He pulled off his boots and went into the shelter she had built them.

Inside she had heaped two beds of leaves. They were soft and aromatic. J's clothes were neatly spread over the top of one heap, his travelling cloak on top of it all. J rolled himself up in its comforting smelly wool and was asleep before she had come inside.

J and the Indian girl stayed for nearly a month in the shelter she had built. Every day they went further afield, paddling in the morning in the canoe, and then she would run it aground and fish, or set snares for birds, while J foraged in the undergrowth for saplings and young spring growth. They would come companionably home in the light of the setting sun to the little camp and J would heel in his collection while she plucked the birds or cleaned the fish and prepared the evening meal.

34

There was a powerful dreamlike quality to the time. It was a relationship like no other. The grieving man and the silent girl worked together day after day with a bond that grew but needed no words. J was absorbed in one of the greatest pleasures a man can have – discovering a new country, a country completely unknown to him – and she, freed from the conventions and dangers of Jamestown, practised her woodcraft skills and observed the laws of her own people for once without a critical white observer judging and condemning her every move, but only with a man who smiled at her kindly and let her teach him how to live under the trees.

They never exchanged words. J would talk to her, as he would talk to his little seedlings in the seed bed she had made for him, for the pleasure of hearing his own voice, and for the sense of making a connection. Sometimes she would smile and nod or make a little grunt of affirmation or give a trill of laughter, but she never spoke words, not in her language nor his own, until J thought it must be as the magistrate had said and that she was dumb.

He wanted to encourage her to speak. He wanted to teach her English, he could not imagine how she could survive in Jamestown, comprehending only the outflung pointing arm or a clip to the head. He showed her a tree and said 'pine', he showed her a leaf and said 'leaf', but she would only smile and laugh and refuse to repeat what he told her.

'You must learn to speak English,' J said earnestly to her. 'How will you manage if you cannot understand anything that is said to you?'

The girl shook her head and bent over her work. She was twisting supple green twigs into a mesh of some sort. As he watched she made the final knot and held it up to show him. J was so ignorant that he could not even tell what it was that she had made. She was smiling proudly.

She set the little contraption on the forest floor and stepped back a few paces. She dropped to her feet, hunched her back and sidled towards it, her arms stretched before her, her hands shaped like beaks, snapping together. At once she was a lobster, unmistakable.

J laughed. 'Lobster!' he said. 'Say "lobster"!'

She pushed back her hair where it fell over the left side of her face and shook her head in her refusal. She mimed eating, as if to say, 'No. *Eat* lobster.'

J pointed to the trap. 'You have made a lobster pot?'

She nodded and stowed it in the canoe ready for setting at dawn the next day when they went out.

'But you must learn to speak,' J persisted. 'What will you do when I go back to England? If your mother is put in prison again?'

She shook her head, refusing to understand him, and then she took a twig from the fire and walked towards the river and J fell silent, respecting the ritual of casting tobacco on the water, which was the same at dawn and dusk, and which marked her transition from day to night to day again.

He went into the shelter and pretended to sleep so that she might come in and sleep beside him without any fear. It was a ritual he had developed of his own to keep them both safe from his growing fascination with her.

Only on the first night, when he had been so weary from paddling that he could not keep his eyes open, had he slept at once. All the other nights he had lain awake listening to her near-imperceptible breathing, enjoying the sense of her closeness beside him. He did not desire her as he might have desired a woman. It was a feeling more subtle and complicated than that. J felt as he might have done if some precious rare animal had chosen to trust him, had chosen to rest beside him. With all his heart he wanted neither to frighten nor disturb her, with all his heart he wanted to stretch out a hand and stroke that smooth, beautiful flank.

Physically, she was the most beautiful object he had ever seen. Not even his wife Jane had ever been naked before him, they had always made love in a tumble of clothes, generally in darkness. His children had been bound in their swaddling bands as tight as silk-worms in a chrysalis from the moment of their birth, and dressed in tiny versions of adult clothing as soon as they were able to walk. J had never seen either of them naked, had never bathed them, had never dressed them. The play of light on bare skin was strange to J, and he found that when the girl was working near him he watched her, for the sheer pleasure of seeing her rounded limbs, the strength in her young body, the lovely line of her neck, the curve of her spine, the nestling mystery of her sex which he glimpsed below the little buckskin apron.

Of course he thought of touching her. The casual instruction from Mr Joseph not to rape her was tantamount to admitting that he might do so. But J would not have hurt her, any more than he would have broken an eggshell in a drawer of the collection at Lambeth. She was a thing of such simple beauty that he wanted only to hold her, to caress her. He supposed that of all the things he might imagine with her, what he wanted to do most was to collect her, and take her back to Lambeth to the warm, sunlit rarities room where she would be the most beautiful object of them all.

J would have lost track of time in the woods, but one morning the girl started to take the thatch from the roof of the little hut and untie the saplings. They sprang back undamaged, only a slight bend in the trunks betraying the fact that they had been walls and roof joists.

'What are you doing?' J asked her.

In silence she pointed back the way they had come. It was time to go home.

'Already?'

She nodded and turned to J's little bed of plants.

It was filled with heads and leaves of small plants. J's satchel was bursting with gathered seed heads. With her hoeing stick she started to lift the plants, tenderly pulling at the thin filaments of roots and laying them in the dampened linen. J took his trowel and worked at the other end of the row. Carefully they packed them into the canoe.

The fire which she had faithfully kept glowing for all the days of their stay she now damped with water, and then scuffed over with sand. The cooking sticks which they had used as spits for fish, game birds, crabmeat and even the final feast of lobster she broke and cast into the river. The reeds which had thatched the walls and the leaves which had thatched the roof she scattered. In only a little while their campsite was destroyed, and a white man would have looked at the clearing and thought himself the first man there.

J found that he was not ready to leave. 'I don't want to go,' he said unwillingly. He looked into her serene uncomprehending face. 'You know . . . I don't want to go back to Jamestown, and I don't want to go back to England.'

She looked at him, waiting for his next words. It was as if he were free to decide, and she would do whatever he wished.

J looked out over the river. Now and then the water stirred with the thick shoals of fish. Even in the short weeks that they had been living at the riverside he had seen more and more birds flying into the country from the south. He had a sense of the continent stretching forever to the south, unendingly to the north. Why should he turn his back on it and return to the dirty little town on the edge of the river, surrounded with felled trees, inhabited by people who struggled for everything, for life itself?

The girl did not prompt him. She hunkered down on the sand and looked out over the river, content to wait for his decision.

'Shall I stay?' J asked, secure in the knowledge that she could not understand his rapid speech, that he was raising no hopes. 'Shall we build ourselves another shelter and spend our days going out and bringing in fine specimens of plants? I could send them home to my father, he could pay off our debts with them, and then he could send me enough money so that I could live here always. He could raise my children, and when they are grown they could join me. I need never go back to that house in London, never again sleep alone in that bed, in her bed. Never dream of her. Never go into church past her grave, never hear her name, never have to speak of her.'

She did not even turn her head to look at him, to see if there was meaning in his quiet whispering.

'I could make a new life here, I could become a new man. And this year, next year, you will be a beautiful woman,' J said, his voice very gentle. 'And then . . .'

She turned at that, as if she understood the tone of his voice. Turned and looked directly at him, without shame, as if she were about to ask him what he meant – if he were serious. J broke off and flushed. He managed an awkward smile.

'Well!' he said. 'Just as well this all means nothing to you! Better be off!'

She rose to her feet and gestured to the river. Her half-tilted head asked: 'Which way?' South into the country, which neither of them knew, or upriver to Jamestown?

'Jamestown,' J said shortly, pointing north-west. 'I have been rambling like a fool. Jamestown, of course.'

He seated himself in the canoe and steadied it with his paddle. It was easier now that they had gone out every day and he had grown skilful. She pushed off the prow of the boat and stepped aboard. They paddled as a team and the boat wove easily along the shoreline, and then they felt the stronger push of the river.

An hour out of Jamestown, where the river started getting dirty and the bank was pocked with felled trees, she called a halt and they ran the canoe ashore. Slowly, unwillingly, they washed off the grease in the water. She took a handful of leaves and scrubbed his back so that his white skin shone through the dark grease and the familiar smell, which he had hated so much on the first day, was dispersed. Together they put on the clothes they must wear in the town, and she shrank into the confines of the ragged shift and looked no longer like a deer in dappled sunlight but instead like a sluttish maidservant.

J, shrugging back into his shirt and breeches after the freedom of the buckskin loincloth, felt as if he were taking on the shackles of some sort of prison, becoming a man again with a man's sorrows and no longer a free being, at home in the forest. At once the cloud of insects settled greedily on his sunburned arms and shoulders and face. J swatted at them and swore, and the girl smiled with her lips but with no laughter in her eyes.

'We'll come out again,' J said encouragingly. He pointed to himself and to her and to the trees. 'We'll come out again some day.'

She nodded but her eyes were dark.

They got into the canoe and began to paddle upstream to Jamestown. J was plagued all the way by the biting moths and the sweat in his eyes, the tightness of the shirt across his back and the rub of his boots. By the time they came alongside the little wooden quay he was sweating and irritable. There was a new vessel in port and a crowd on the quayside. No-one wasted more than a quick glance on the little Indian girl and the white man in the dugout canoe.

They ran the canoe aground at the side of the quay and started to unload the plants. From the shadow of the dockside building a woman came and stood before them.

She was an Indian woman but she wore a dress and a shawl tied across her breasts. Her hair was tied back like a white woman's and it exposed her face which was badly scarred, pocked all over with pale ridges of scar tissue as if someone, long ago, had fired a musket at point-blank range into her face.

'Mr Tradescant?' She spoke with a harsh accent.

J spun to hear his name and recoiled from the bitterness in her face. She looked past him at the girl and spoke in a rapid string of words, fluting and meaningless as birdsong.

The child answered, as voluble as she, shaking her head emphatically and then pointing to J and to the plants and to the canoe.

The woman turned to J again. 'She tells me you have not hurt her.'

'Of course not!'

'Not raped her.'

'No!'

The bowstring-tight line of the woman's shoulders suddenly slumped, and she gave a sharp sob, like a cough of vomit. 'When they told me you had taken her into the woods I thought I would not see her again.'

'I am a plant collector,' J said wearily. 'See. There are the plants. She was my guide. She made a camp. She hunted and fished for us. She has been a very, very good girl.' He glanced at her and she gave him a swift encouraging smile. 'She has been very helpful. I am in her debt.'

The Indian woman had not followed all of the words but she saw the glance that passed between them and read correctly the affection and mutual trust.

'You are her mother?' J asked. 'Just . . . er . . . released?'

The woman nodded. 'Mr Joseph told me he had given her to you for the month. I thought I would not see her again. I thought you had taken her to the woods to use her and bury her there.'

'I'm sorry,' J said awkwardly. 'I am a stranger here.'

She looked at him with a bitter line around her mouth. 'You are all strangers here,' she observed.

'She can speak?' J remarked, tentatively, wondering what it might mean.

The woman nodded, not bothering to answer him.

The girl had finished unloading the canoe. She looked at J and gestured to the plants, as if asking what should be done with them. J turned to the woman. 'I have to fetch some barrels and prepare these plants for my voyage home. I may take a passage on this ship. Can she stay and help me?'

'We'll both help,' the woman said shortly. 'I don't leave her alone in this town.' She hitched her skirts a little and went down to the shoreline. J watched the two women. They did not embrace; but they stood just inches away from each other and gazed into each other's faces as if they could read all they needed to know in one exchange of looks. Then the mother nodded briefly and they turned side by side and their shoulders brushed as they bent over the plants together.

J went up to his lodging to fetch the barrels for packing the plants.

They worked until it was dusk, and then they worked again the next day, wrapping the cuttings in earth and damp linen, layering them in the barrel separated by damp linen and leaves, and packing the seeds in dry sand and sealing down the lid. When it was done, J had four half-barrels of plants which he would keep open to the air and damp with fresh water, and one sealed barrel of seeds. He shouted up to the ship and a couple of sailors came down and loaded them for him. At least he would have room to care for them on the voyage home. There were only a couple of people making the return voyage to England. The rest of the space was taken up with the cargo of tobacco.

'We sail in the morning at first light,' the captain warned him. 'You'd

40

best get your things aboard tonight and sleep aboard yourself. I can't wait for passengers, when the tide ebbs we go out with it.'

J nodded. 'I will.' He had no desire to return to the inn and the embittered landlady. He thought if she called the girl a beast in his hearing then he would speak in her defence and then there would be a quarrel and perhaps worse.

He turned to the two women. 'What is her name?' he asked the mother.

'Mary.'

'Mary?'

She nodded. 'She was taken from me when she was a baby and baptised Mary.'

'Is that the name you use for her?'

She hesitated, as if she was not sure she would trust him. But then there was a murmur from the girl at her side.

'She is called Suckahanna.'

'Suckahanna?' J confirmed.

The girl smiled and nodded. 'It means "water".'

J nodded, and then the fact of her speaking his own language suddenly struck him. 'You can speak English?'

She nodded.

He had a moment of profound, unhappy bewilderment. 'Then why did you never . . . ? You never . . . ? I did not know! All this time we have travelled together and you have been dumb!'

'I ordered her never to speak to a white man,' the woman said. 'I thought she would be safer if she did not answer.'

J opened his mouth to argue – it must be right that the girl should be able to speak, to defend herself.

But the mother cut him off with an abrupt gesture of her hand. '*I* have just come from a month in prison for saying the wrong thing,' she pointed out. 'Sometimes it is better to say nothing at all.'

J glanced at the ship behind them. Suddenly he did not want to leave. The realisation that the girl had a name, and could understand him, made her intensely interesting. What had she been thinking during their days of silent companionship? What might she not say to him? It was as if she had been a princess under a spell in a romance and suddenly she had found her tongue. When he had confided in her and told her of his feelings, for his home, for his children, for his plants, she had met his confession with an impassive face. But she had understood, she had understood everything he said. And so, in a way, she knew him better than any woman had ever known him before. And she would know that only yesterday morning he was tempted to stay in this new land; to stay with her.

'I have to go. I am promised in England,' he said, thinking that they might contradict him, that he might not have to go, as if the breaking of the spell which had kept her silent might release him too.

The two women said nothing, they simply watched the indecision and reluctance in his face.

'What will become of you two now?' he asked, as if their plans might affect him.

'We will leave Jamestown,' the woman said quietly. 'We will go back into the forest and find our people. I thought we would be safer to stay here, my husband and my father are dead. I thought I could live inside the walls and work for the white men. I thought I could be their servant.' She shook her head. 'But there is no trusting them. We will go back to our own.'

'And Suckahanna?'

The woman looked at him, her eyes bitter. 'There is no life for her,' she said. 'We can find our people but not our old life. The places where we used to grow our crops are planted with tobacco, the rivers are thin of fish and the game is going, scared away by the guns. Everywhere we used to run, there is the mark of a boot on the trails. I don't know where she will live her life. I don't know where she will find a home.'

'Surely there is room for your people as well as the planters,' J said passionately. 'I can't believe there is not space in this land . . . we were out for nearly a month and we saw no-one. It's a mighty land, it stretches for miles and miles. Surely there is room for your people as well as mine?'

'But your people don't want us here. Not since the war. When we plant fields they destroy our crops, when they see a fish weir they break it, when they see a village they fire it. They have sworn we shall be destroyed as a people. When my family were killed they took me into slavery and I thought that Suckahanna and I would be safe as slaves. But they beat me and raped me, and the men will soon want her too.'

'She could come with me,' J suggested wildly. 'I could take her to my home in England. I have a son and a daughter there, I could bring them up all together.'

The woman thought for a moment and then shook her head. 'She is called Suckahanna,' she said firmly. 'She must be by the river.'

J was about to argue but then he remembered seeing Pocahontas, the great Princess Pocahontas, when he was just a boy himself and had been taken to view her as a child might be taken to see the lions in the Tower.

She had not been Princess Pocahontas by then, she had been Rebecca Rolfe, wearing ordinary English clothes and shivering in an English winter. A few weeks later she had died, in exile, longing for her own land.

'I will come again,' he said. 'I will take these things to England and come out again. And next time, when I come, I shall build a house here and you shall be my servant and she shall be safe.'

'How could she be safe with you?' her mother asked swiftly. 'She's not a child, though she's so slight. She's near thirteen now, by the time you come back she'll be a woman. There's no safety for a Powhatan woman in the white man's town.'

J thought for a moment and then took the step, the next step, speaking without thought, speaking from his heart, his unexamined heart. 'I shall marry her,' he promised. 'She will be my wife and I will keep her safe and she shall have her own house and fields here. I shall build her a house beside the river and she need fear for nothing.'

He was speaking to her mother but he was looking at the girl. A deep rosy blush was spreading from the coarse linen neck of the shift up to her forehead where the bear grease still stained her brown skin at the dark hairline. 'Should you like that?' J asked her gently. 'I am old enough to be your father, I know. And I don't understand your ways. But I could keep you safe, and I could make a house for you.'

'I should like that,' the girl said very quietly. 'I should like to be your wife.'

The older woman put out her hand to J and he felt the roughened palm in his own. Then she took her daughter's hand and joined them together in a hard grip. 'When you come back she shall be your wife,' she promised him.

'I will,' the girl said.

'I will,' J swore.

The woman released them and turned away as if there was nothing more to be said. J watched her go, and then turned to Suckahanna. She seemed at once very familiar, the easy companion of weeks of travelling and camping, and exquisitely strange, a girl on the edge of womanhood, a virgin who would be his wife.

Carefully, as if he were transplanting a seedling, he put his hand to her cheek, stroked the line of her jaw. She quivered as he touched her but moved neither forwards nor back. She let him caress her face for a moment, for one moment only; and then she turned on her heel and ran from him.

'Come back soon,' she called, and he could hardly see her in the

43

darkness as she went swiftly after her mother, only her linen shift gleaming in the dusk. 'Come in the good time, the fruitful time, Nepinough, and I shall make you a great feast and we will build our house before winter comes.'

'I will!' J said again. But she was already gone, and the next day at dawn the ship sailed and he did not see her.

Summer 1638, London

J's ship arrived at London docks at dawn in early April and he came blearily out of his cabin into the cold English air, wrapped in his travelling cloak with his hat pulled down on his head. A wagoner was idling on the dockside, fiddling with the feedbag at the head of a dozing horse.

'Are you for hire?' J shouted down.

The man looked up. 'Aye!'

'Come and fetch my goods,' J called. The man started up the gangplank and then recoiled at the waving fronds of saplings and small trees.

'Goods?' he asked. 'This is a forest!'

J grinned. 'There's more than this,' he said.

Together they humped the barrels filled with damp earth down the gangplank and into the wagon, the whippy branches of trees stirring above their heads. Then J brought another barrel of seeds and nuts, and finally his own small bundle of clothes and a chest of rarities.

'I know where we're headed,' the man said, climbing on to the box and waking the horse with a slap of the reins on its back.

'You do?'

'Tradescant's Ark,' the man said certainly. 'It's the only place in the world that you'd go to with half a forest on board.'

'Quite right,' J said, and put his feet up on the board. 'What's the news?' he asked.

The carter spat accurately over the side of the wagon and hit the dirt road. 'Nothing new,' he said. 'A lot worse.'

J waited.

'Everything you can eat or drink is taxed,' the carter said. 'But that was true before you went away, I dare say. Now they've got a new tax, a rotting crime of a tax: ship money levied on everyone, however far they are from the sea. It's the ports that should pay ship money, they're

45

the ones that need the navy to keep them free of pirates. But the king is making all the towns pay, even inland towns. My sister lives in Cheltenham. Why should she pay ship money? What are the seas to her? But she has to.'

J nodded. 'The king won't call a parliament, then?'

'They say he won't even hear the word mentioned.'

J allowed himself a pleasurable 'tut tut' of disapproval.

'If he called a parliament and asked them to set a tax they would tell him what they think of him as king,' the carter said baldly. 'They would tell him what they think about a Privy Council which is advised by a Papist French queen, and a court which is run by Frenchmen and Jesuits.'

'That can't be so,' J said firmly. 'I've only been gone a few months.'

'It's well known the Tradescants are the king's servants,' the man said unpleasantly.

'It is indeed,' J agreed, remembering his father's regular warnings against gossip that could be overheard as treason.

'Then I'll say no more,' the carter remarked. 'And see how you like it when they knock on your door and tell you that now there is a monopoly declared on the dirt in your garden and you have to pay a fine of ten per cent to some courtier if you want to plant in it. Because that's what's happened to every other trade in the kingdom while the king taxes the traders but won't call a parliament which could tax the gentry for their rents.'

The man paused, waiting for a shocked response. J discreetly kept silent.

'You'll have heard that the Scots have sworn they won't read their prayers from the new book?'

'No?'

The man nodded. 'All of 'em. Taken against Archbishop Laud's prayer book. Say they won't read a word of it. Archbishop is put out. King is put out. Some say he'll make 'em, some say he can't make 'em. Why should a king order what you say to God?'

'I don't know,' J said tactfully. 'I've no opinion on the matter.' And he tipped his hat over his eyes and dozed as the wagon jolted down the familiar road to his home.

He did not lift his hat as they went down the South Lambeth road towards the common; but he looked sharply all around him from under the brim. It was all well. His father's house still stood proudly, set back from the road, the little bridge spanning the stream that ran alongside the road. It was a handsome farmhouse in the old timbered style, but on the side of the house was the ambitious new wing, commissioned by his father for the housing of the rarities, their great collection of oddities from the monstrous to the miniature. At the back of the house was the garden which made their name and their livelihood, and the rarities room overlooked the garden through its great windows of Venetian glass. J, taught by a long-standing habit, looked at the ground as the cart drove around the south side of the building so that he did not see his father's vainglorious stone crest, affixed to the new wing in defiance both of the college of heralds and of the simple truth. They were not Tradescant esquires and never had been, but John Tradescant, his father, had drawn up and then commissioned a stonemason to carve his own crest; and nothing J could say could persuade him to take it down.

J directed the carter past the rarities room, where the terrace overlooked the orderly gardens, on to the stable yard so that the plants could be unloaded directly beside the pump for watering. The stable lad, looking out over the half-door, saw the waving tops of small trees in the cart and shouted, 'The master's home!' and came tumbling out into the yard.

They heard him in the kitchen and the maid came running up the hall and flung open the back door as J mounted the steps to the terrace and stepped into his house.

At once he recoiled in surprise. A woman he did not know, dark-haired, sober-faced, with a pleasant confident smile, came down the stairs, hesitated when she saw him looking up at her, and then came steadily on.

'How d'you do,' she said formally, and gave him a small nod of her head, as if she were a man and an equal.

'Who the devil are you?' J asked abruptly.

She looked a little awkward. 'Will you come in here?' she said, and showed him into his own parlour. The maid was on her hands and knees lighting the fire. The woman waited until the flame had caught and then dismissed the girl with a quick gesture of her hand.

'I am Hester Pooks,' she said. 'Your father invited me to stay here.'

'Why?' J demanded.

Hester hesitated. 'I imagine you don't know . . .' She broke off. 'I am very sorry to have to tell you that your father is dead.'

He gasped and swayed. 'My father?'

She nodded, saying nothing.

J dropped into a chair and was silent for a long moment. 'I shouldn't be surprised . . . but it is a dreadful shock . . . I know he was a great age, but he was always . . .'

47

She took a chair opposite him without invitation, and sat quietly, folding her hands in her lap. When J turned to her she was waiting, judging her time to tell him more.

'He didn't suffer at all,' she said. 'He grew very tired, over the winter, and he went to bed to rest. He died very peacefully, just as if he fell asleep. We had brought many of his flowers into his room. He died surrounded by them.'

J shook his head, still incredulous. 'I wish I had been here,' he said. 'I wish to God I had been here.'

Hester paused. 'God is very merciful,' she said gently. 'At the moment of his death he thought that he saw you. He was waiting and waiting for you to return, and he woke as his bedroom door opened, and he thought that he saw you. He died thinking that you had come safe home. I know that he died happy, thinking that he had seen you.'

'He said my name?' J asked.

She nodded. 'He said: "Oh! You at last!"'

J frowned. The old fear that he was not first in his father's heart returned to him. 'But did he say my name? Was it clear that he meant me?'

Hester paused for a moment and then looked into the gentle, vulnerable face of the man that she meant to marry. She lied easily. 'Oh yes,' she said firmly. 'He said: "Oh! You at last!", and then as he lay back on the pillow he said "J."'

J paused, and took it all in. Hester watched him in silence.

'I can't believe it,' he said. 'I don't know how to go on without him. The Ark, and the gardens, the royal gardens – I have always worked beside him. I have lost my employer and my master as well as my father.'

She nodded. 'He left a letter for you.'

J watched her as she crossed the room and took the sealed letter from a drawer in the table.

'I think it's about me,' she said bluntly.

J paused as he took it from her. 'Who *are* you?' he asked again.

She took a little breath. 'I am Hester Pooks. I'm all but alone in the world. Your father liked me, and my uncle told him I had a good dowry. I met him at court. My uncle is a painter, commissioned by the queen. My family is a good family, all artists and musicians, all with royal or noble patrons.' She paused and smiled. 'But not much money. Your father thought I might suit you. He wanted to make sure that there was someone to bring up his grandchildren, and to keep them here. He didn't want them living in London with your wife's parents. He thought I would marry you.'

J's jaw dropped open. 'He has found me a wife? I'm a man of thirty years of age and he found me a wife as if I were a boy? And he chose you?'

Hester looked him squarely in the face. 'I'm no beauty,' she said. 'I imagine your wife was lovely. Frances is such a pretty girl, and they tell me she takes after her mother. But I can run a house, and I can run a business, I love plants and trees and a garden, and I like children, I like *your* children. Whether or not you want to marry me, I should like to be a friend to Frances in particular. It would suit me to marry you and I wouldn't make great demands on you. I don't have great expectations.'

She paused. 'It would be an arrangement to suit ourselves,' she said. 'And it would leave you free to garden at the royal palace of Oatlands or to go abroad again and know that everything was safe here.'

J looked from her to his letter. 'This is outrageous! I have barely been home a moment and already I learn that my father is dead and that some woman, who I've never met before in my life, is half-betrothed to me. And anyway . . .' He broke off. 'I have other plans.'

She nodded soberly. 'It would have been easier if he had lived to explain it himself,' she said. 'But you are not half-betrothed, Mr Tradescant. It is entirely up to you. I shall leave you to read your letter. Is it your wish that I wake the children and bring them down to see you?'

He was distracted. 'Are they both well?'

She nodded. 'Frances especially grieves for her grandfather but they are both in perfect health.'

J shook his head in bewilderment. 'Bring them in to me when they wake,' he said. 'No need to wake them early. I will read this letter from my father. I need time. I do feel . . .' He broke off. 'All my life he has managed and controlled me!' he exclaimed in a sudden explosion of irritation. 'And just when I think I am my own man at his death I find that he had my future life in his hands, too.'

She paused at the doorway with her hand on the brass door ring. 'He did not mean to order you,' she said. 'He was thinking that I might set you free, not be a burden. And he told me very clearly that you had buried your heart with your wife and that you would never love me nor any woman again.'

J felt a pang of deep guilt. 'I shall never love a woman in my wife's place,' he said carefully. 'Jane could never be replaced.'

She nodded, she thought he was warning her. She did not realise that he was speaking to himself, reproaching himself for that runaway sense of freedom, for his sense of joy with the young girl in the wood so far from home and responsibilities and the normal rules of life.

49

'I don't expect love,' Hester said simply, recalling him to the shadowy room. 'I thought we might be able to help each other. I thought we might be . . . helpmeets.'

J looked at her, looked at her and saw her for the first time as she stood in the doorway, framed by the dark wood. He saw the simple plain face, the smooth white cap, the intelligent dark eyes and the strength of her jaw. 'What on earth put it into his head?' he asked.

'I think I did,' she said with a glimmer of a smile. 'It would suit me very well. Perhaps, when you are over the surprise of it, you will think that it will suit you too.'

He watched her close the door behind her and opened his father's letter.

> *My dear son,*
>
> *I have made a will leaving the Ark entire to you. I hope that it will bring you much joy. I hope that Baby John will succeed you, as you succeed me, and that the name of Tradescant will always mean something to people who love their gardens.*
>
> *If I am dead when you return then I leave you my blessing and my love. I am going to join your mother, and my two masters, Sir Robert and the Duke, and I am ready to go to them. Do not grieve for me, J, I have had a long life and one which many men would envy.*
>
> *The young woman called Hester Pooks has a substantial dowry and is a sensible woman. I have spoken to her about you and I believe she would make a good wife to you and a good mother to the children. She is not another Jane, because there never could be another Jane. But she is a straightforward, kind young woman and I think you need one such as her.*
>
> *Of course it is your decision. But if I had lived long enough to see your return I would have introduced her to you with my earnest recommendation.*
>
> *Farewell my son, my dear son,*
> *John Tradescant.*

J sat very still and watched the kindling twigs in the fire flicker and turn to knotted skeletal lace of dry ash. He thought of his father's determination and his care, which showed itself in the meticulous nursery and seed bed, in pruning and weeding and in the unending twisting and training of his beloved climbing plants, and showed itself here too, in providing a wife for his adult son. He felt his irritated sense of thwarted independence melt before his affection for his father. And at the thought of the gardens being left to him in trust for another John Tradescant coming behind them both he felt the anger inside him dissolve, and he slipped to the floor and rested his head in his father's chair and wept for him.

Frances, coming in a little later, found her father composed and seated in the window where he could look out at the cold horse chestnut avenue and the swirls of fog in the early-morning darkness.

'Father?' she said tentatively.

He turned and held out his arms to her and she ran into his embrace. He brought her close to him and felt the light tiny bones of her body and smelled the warm clean smell of her skin and hair. For a moment he thought vividly and poignantly of Suckahanna, who was no heavier but whose every muscle was like whipcord.

'You've grown,' he said. 'I swear you are nearly up to my chest.'

She smiled up at him. 'I am nine,' she said seriously. 'And Baby John is bigger than when you left. And heavier. I can't lift him now he's five. Hester has to.'

'Hester does, does she? D'you like Hester?'

He thought she looked at him as if she needed help in saying something, as if there were something she could not say. 'Yes.'

'Your grandfather thought she might marry me, he thought she might be a mother to you.'

A look of relief crossed her face. 'We need a mother,' she said. 'I can't lift Baby John now he's so big, and I don't always know what to do when he cries. If he were to be sick, like Mama was sick, I wouldn't know how to care for him and he might die . . .' She broke off and gulped on a sob. 'We need a mother,' she said earnestly. 'A cook isn't the same.'

'I'm sorry,' J said. 'I didn't know.'

'I thought you would bring us one home from Virginia, with other things in the cart,' she said childishly.

J thought for a moment of the girl, only a few years older than this one, thanked his luck that he had not been so misled as to bring her back here and burden himself with her care as well as that of his children. 'There's no-one in that country who could be a mother to you,' he said shortly. 'No-one who could be a wife to me here.'

Frances blinked back her tears and looked up at him. 'But we need one. A mother who knows what to do when Baby John is naughty, and teaches him his letters.'

51

'Yes,' J said. 'I see we do.'

'Hester says breakfast is ready,' she said.

'Is Baby John at breakfast?'

'Yes,' she answered. 'Come.'

J took her hand and led her from the room. Her hand was cool and soft, her fingers were long and her palm had lost its baby fatness. It was the hand of an adult in miniature, not the soft plumpness of a little child.

'You've grown,' he observed.

She peeped up a little smile at him. 'My uncle Alexander Norman says that I will soon be a proper young lady,' she said with satisfaction. 'But I tell him that I shall be the king's gardener.'

'You still want that?' J asked. She nodded and opened the door to the kitchen.

They were all waiting for him at their places around the dark wooden table: the gardener and the two lads, the cook and the maid and the boy who worked in the house and the stables. Hester was at the foot of the table with Baby John beside her, still half-asleep, his drowsy eyes barely showing above the table top. J drank in the sight of him: the beloved boy, the Tradescant heir.

'Oh, Father!' Baby John said, mildly surprised.

J lifted him up, held him close, inhaled the sweet warm smell of sleepy child, hugged him tight and felt his heart turn over with tenderness for his boy, for Jane's boy.

They waited for him to sit before they took their own places on the benches around the table and then Hester bowed her head and said grace in the simple words approved by the church of Archbishop Laud. For a moment it struck a discord with J – who had spent his married life in the fierce independent certainties of his wife and listening to her powerful extempore prayers – but then he bowed his head and heard the rhythm and the simple comfort of the language.

He looked up before Hester said 'Amen'. The household was around the table in neat order, his two children were either side of Hester, their faces washed, their clothes tidy. A solid meal was laid on the table but there was nothing rich or ostentatious or wasteful. And – it was this which decided him – on the windowsill there was a bowl of indigo and white bluebells which someone had taken the trouble to uproot and transplant from the orchard for the pleasure of their bright colour and their sweet, light smell.

No-one but J's father, John Tradescant, had ever brought flowers into the kitchen or the house for pleasure. Flowers were part of the work of the house: reared in the orangery, blooming in the garden, shown in the rarities room, preserved in sugar or painted and sketched. But Hester had a love of flowers that reminded him of his father, and made him think, as he saw her seated between his children, and with flowers on the windowsill, that the great aching gaps in his life where his wife and his father had once been might be resolved if this woman would live here and work alongside him.

J could not take his young children from their home to Virginia, he could not imagine that he might be able to go back there himself. His time in the forest seemed like a dream, like something which had happened to another man, a free man, a new man in the new land. In the months that followed, busy anxious months, in which John the Younger had to become John Tradescant, the only John Tradescant, he hardly thought of Suckahanna and his promise to return. It seemed like a game he had played, a fancy, not a real plan at all. Back in Lambeth, in the old world, the old life closed around him and he thought that his father was probably right – as he generally was – and that he would need Hester to run the business and the house.

He decided that he would ask her to stay. He knew that he would never ask her to love him.

J did not formally propose marriage to Hester until the end of the summer. For the first months he could think of nothing but clearing the debts caused by the crash of the tulip market. The Tradescants, father and son, had invested the family fortune in buying rare tulip bulbs, certain that the market was on the rise. But by the time the tulips had flowered and spawned more bulbs under their perfect soil in their porcelain pots the market had crashed. J and his father were left with nearly a thousand pounds owed to their shareholders, and bound by their sense of honour to repay. By selling the new Virginia plants at a handsome profit and by ensuring that everyone knew of his new maidenhair fern, an exquisite variety which everyone desired on sight, J doubled and re-doubled the business for the nursery garden, and started to drag the family back into profit.

The maidenhair fern was not the only booty that visitors to the garden sought. John offered them new jasmine, the like of which no-one had ever seen before, which would climb and twist itself round a pole as rampant as a honeysuckle, smelling as sweet, but flowering in a bright primrose yellow. A new columbine, an American columbine, and best of all of the surviving saplings: a plane tree, an American plane tree, which John thought might grow as big as an oak in the temperate climate of England. He had no more than half a dozen of each, he would sell nothing. He took orders with cash deposits and promised to deliver seedlings as soon as they were propagated. The American maple which he brought back with such care did not thrive in the Lambeth garden though John hung over it like a new mother; and he lost also the only specimen he had of a tulip tree, and nearly came to blows with his father's friend the famous plantsman, John Parkinson, when he tried to describe the glory of the tree growing in the American wood, which was nothing but a drying stick in the garden in Lambeth.

'I tell you it is as big as an oak with great greasy green leaves and a flower as big as your head!' John swore.

'Aye,' Parkinson retorted. 'The fish that get away are always the biggest.'

Alexander Norman, John's brother-in-law and an executor of John Tradescant's will, took over some of the Tradescant debts on easy terms as a favour to the young family. 'For Frances's dowry,' he said. 'She's such a pretty maid.'

J sold some fields that his father had owned in Kent and cleared most of the rest of the debts. Those still outstanding came to two hundred pounds – the very sum of Hester's dowry. With his account books before him one day, he found he was thinking that Hester's dowry could be his for the asking, and the Tradescant accounts could show a clear profit once more. On that unromantic thought he put down his pen and went to find her.

He had watched her throughout the summer, when she knew she was doubly on trial: tested whether she was good enough for the Tradescant name, and how she matched up to Jane. She never showed a flicker of nervousness. She observed her dealing with the visitors to the rarities. She showed the exhibits with a quiet pride, as if she were glad to be part of a house that contained such marvels, but without boastfulness. She had learned her way around the busy room quicker than anyone could have expected, and she could move from cabinet to wall-hanging, ordering, showing, discussing, with fluid confidence. Her training at court meant that she could be on easy terms with all sorts of people. Her artistic background made her confident around objects of beauty.

She was good with the visitors. She asked them for their money at the door without embarrassment, and then showed them into the room. She did not force herself on them as a guide; she always waited until they explained if they had a special interest. If they wanted to draw or paint an exhibit she was quick to provide a table close to the grand Venetian windows in the best light, and then she had the tact to leave them alone. If they were merely the very many curious visitors who wanted to spend the morning at the museum and afterwards boast to their friends that they had seen everything there was to see in London – the lions at the Tower, the king's own rooms at Whitehall, the exhibits at Tradescant's Ark – she made a point of showing them the extraordinary things, the mermaid, the flightless bird, the whale's mouth, the unicorn's skeleton, which they would describe all the way home – and everyone who heard them talk became a potential customer.

She guided them smoothly to the gardens when they had finished in the rarities room, and took care that she knew the names of the plants. She always started at the avenue of chestnut trees, and there she always said the same thing:

'And these trees, every single one of them, come from cuttings and nuts taken from Mr Tradescant's first ever six trees. He had them first in 1607, thirty-one years ago, and he lived long enough to see them flourish in this beautiful avenue.' The visitors would stand back and look at the slim, strong trees, now green and rich with the summer growth of their spread palmate leaves.

'They are beautiful in leaf with those deep arching branches, but the flowers are as beautiful as a bouquet of apple blossom. I saw them forced to flower in early spring and they scented the room like a light daffodil scent, a delicious scent as sweet as lilies.'

'Who forced the chestnuts for you? My father?' J asked her when some visitors had spent a small fortune on seedlings and departed, their wagon loaded with little pots.

She turned to him, slipping the coins into the pockets of her apron. 'I had the gardener bring them into flower for your father as he lay sick,' she said simply.

'He saw them in bloom?'

She nodded. 'He said he was lying in a flowery mead. It was something we once talked about. He lay among a rich bed of scents and colours, tulips all around him, and over his bed were great boughs of flowering horse chestnut. It was a wonderful sight. He liked it.'

J thought for a moment of the other deaths in the house: his mother's in the room ablaze with daffodils, and the boat laden with Rosamund roses going slowly downriver to the City for Jane's funeral. 'Did he ask you to do it?'

Hester shook her head.

'I am glad you thought of it,' he said. 'I am glad there was someone here to do that for him.' He paused and cleared his throat. 'About his plan that we should marry . . .'

She flushed a little but the face she turned towards him was serene. 'Have you come to a decision?'

He nodded.

'I'm glad. I cannot in all conscience stay here much longer. Your mother-in-law Mrs Hurte is bound to wonder what I am doing here, and the servants will talk.'

'I have thought about it,' he said, sounding as detached as she. 'And I have thought that we might suit very well.'

She stole a quick look at his face. 'You want to marry me?'

'If you desire it,' J said coldly. 'As my father wrote to me in his letter, I have two children and work to do. I must have someone reliable at my home. I have observed you these last months and you are clearly fond of the children and you do the work well. I cannot think of a better wife for me, especially since I have no preference in women.'

She bowed her head. For a moment she had an odd sentimental thought that by accepting Tradescant's loveless proposal she was cutting herself off from all the other possibilities which might have unfurled before her. Surely there would have been men, or even just one man, who might have loved her for herself, and not because she was good with his children and reliable with his business? Surely there might have been just one man who might have proposed and waited for her answer with his heart pounding? Surely there might have been just one man who might have put her hand to his lips so that she felt not a polite kiss but the sudden warm intake of breath which reveals desire?

She gave a small unnoticed shrug. No such man had yet appeared and she was nearing thirty. The agreement with John Tradescant was the best she had ever been offered in a country where success was measured in terms of intimacy with the court. The king's gardener and a favourite of the queen was a good catch, even for a spinster with a dowry of two hundred pounds.

'I have no preference in men,' she said, as coolly as he. 'I will marry you, John.'

He hesitated. 'No-one ever calls me John,' he said. 'I've always been J. It was my father who was John.'

Hester nodded. 'I know that. But your father is dead now, and you are the head of the household and a son no longer. I shall call you John. You are the head of the household, you are John Tradescant.'

'I suppose I am . . .'

'Sometimes it is hard when your father or mother dies,' she said. 'It's not just their death which causes you grief, but the fact that you are no longer someone's little child. It's the final stage of growing up, of becoming a man or a woman. My mother used to call me a pet-name, and I have never heard that name since she died. I never will hear it again. I am a grown woman now and no-one calls me anything but Hester Pooks.'

'You are saying that I must take my manhood.'

'You are the head of the household now. And I will be your wife.'

'We will have the banns called at once then,' he said. 'At St Mary's.'

She shook her head at the thought of him walking to his wedding past the headstone of his only beloved wife. 'I am a resident of St Bride's in the City,' she said. 'I will go home and get the banns called there. Shall we marry at once?'

He looked indifferent. 'It would be more convenient for me,' he said politely. 'But you perhaps have clothes to order? Or things you want to do?'

'A few things. We can be married in October.'

He nodded as if it were the completion date of some routine gardening work. 'In October then.'

October 1638

John wondered if he should feel himself faithless to his promise to Suckahanna, but he did not. He could not remember her well enough, only foolish details like the pride of her smile or the cool clasp of her hand when he had pledged himself to her. He dreamed one night that he was in the woods with her and she was setting a fish trap. When he woke he wondered at the power of the image of her bending over the little stream and setting her trap of woven withy. But then Baby John marched determinedly into the room and the dream was gone.

He wondered occasionally what was happening to her, whether she and her mother were safe in the woods as they had planned to be. But Virginia was so far away, a two-months' voyage, and such a leap of the imagination that he could not keep her in his mind. Surrounded by the business worries and demands of his home J could not retain the picture of Suckahanna. Every day she seemed more exotic, more like a traveller's tale. She was a mermaid, a barnacle goose that swam underwater and then flew from the barnacle shells, a being with its head beneath its shoulders, a flying carpet. One night when he was drunk he tried to tell a fellow gardener that he had collected his Virginia plants with an Indian maid who was covered in blue tattoos and wore nothing but a buckskin pinny; and the man roared with laughter and paid for another round of ales to praise John's bawdy invention.

Every day she receded further from him. Whether he tried to speak of her or kept silent, whether he dreamed of her or let her image go, every day she seemed less likely, every day she floated down the river of his memory in her little canoe, and never looked back at him.

58

On the first of October Hester went to stay in her City lodgings to prepare for her wedding: buying a few pieces of lace to stitch on her petticoats and her shift, packing her bags, warning her landlady that she would need the little room no longer for she was going to be married to the queen's gardener – Mr John Tradescant.

Her uncle John de Critz gave her away and his family and the de Neve relations made an impressive show in the little church. It was a quiet ceremony. John did not want to make a fuss and the de Critz family were refined, artistic people with no desire to throw rice or ears of wheat, or shout and riot around the bedroom door.

The bridal couple went soberly home to Lambeth. Before she left Hester had given orders that the great bedroom which had once been John and Elizabeth's should be hung with new curtains, swept out and cleaned, and fully aired. She felt that she would rather sleep in the bed where John Tradescant had died than share the bed that had belonged to John and Jane. Frances was moved into her father and mother's old room and Baby John had his nursery room to himself.

John had made no comment about the arrangements except to say that it should all be done as she wished. He did not show any grief at moving from his first wife's bedroom, nor did he object to the cost of replacing the curtains and wall hangings throughout.

'They are ten years old.' Hester justified the expense.

'It doesn't seem so long,' he said simply.

The children were dancing on the garden wall, waiting for them to come down the road from Lambeth.

'Are you married?' Frances demanded. 'Where's your new dress?'

'I just wore this one.'

'Am I to call you Mother?' Frances asked.

Hester glanced at John. He had bent to scoop Baby John from the wall and was carrying him into the house. He took care not to reply.

'You can call me Hester, as you always have done. I am not your mother who is in heaven, but I shall do my best to love you and care for you as well as she would have done.'

Frances nodded carelessly, as if she were not much concerned, and scrambled down from the wall and led the way into the house. Hester nodded, she was not disappointed in Frances's lack of warmth. This was not a child who could easily ask for comfort; but no child needed love more than she did.

The new family went into the parlour and Hester seated herself in the chair on one side of the fire opposite John. Baby John sat on the rug before the fire and Frances hesitated, unsure where she should sit.

Without looking at Hester she sank to her knees before the warmth of the fire and then slowly leaned backwards against the arm of Hester's chair. Hester dropped her hand gently on the nape of her stepdaughter's neck and felt the tight, thin muscles of her neck relax at the touch. Frances let her head lean back against her stepmother's touch, trusted her caress.

'We shall be happy,' Hester promised in an undertone to her brave little stepdaughter. 'All will be well, Frances.'

At bedtime the household gathered for evening prayers and John read from the new book of common prayer, enjoying the rhythm of the language and the sense of security which came from using the same words at the same time of day, every day. The household, which had prayed aloud, speaking freely from their hearts under Jane, now bowed their heads and listened, and when the prayers were over they went about their work of bolting the doors for the night, damping down the fires, and snuffing the candles.

Hester and John went up the stairs together to the big bedroom for the first time. The housemaid was waiting in the room.

'Cook thought you might want helping off with your gown, Miss Hester – Mrs Tradescant, I should say!'

Hester shook her head. 'I can do it.'

'And Cook sent up this tray for the two of you,' the maid persevered. There had evidently been a strong sense in the kitchen that more should have been done to mark the occasion. 'She brewed a wedding ale for you,' the maid said. 'And there's some cake and dainty blackberry pudding.'

'Thank you,' Hester said. 'And thank Cook too.'

John nodded and the maid left the room.

The couple looked at each other, their embarrassment dissolved by the maid's intervention.

'Clearly they think we should be carousing and singing,' John said.

'Perhaps they think *they* should be carousing,' Hester observed astutely. 'I imagine that not all the wedding ale is in these two tankards.'

'Shall you have a drink?' John asked.

'When I'm ready for bed,' she said, keeping her tone as light and inconsequential as his. She moved towards the bed and climbed up into it. She did not draw the bed curtains against him, but managed, in their shadows, to undress from her gown and to get into her night shift without embarrassment. She emerged with her hair still braided to put her fine gown in the press at the foot of the bed.

John was seated in his chair before the fire, drinking his wedding ale. 'It's good,' he recommended. 'And I've had a little cake too.'

She took up the tankard and sat opposite him, curling up her feet under her night shift. She sipped at the ale. It was strong and sweet. At once a heady sense of relaxation spread through her. 'This *is* good,' she said.

John laughed. 'I think it probably serves its purpose,' he said. 'I was more nervous than for my first day at school and now I am feeling like a cock o' the walk.'

Hester flushed at that single accidental bawdiness. 'Oh.'

John buried his face in his tankard, as embarrassed as his new wife. 'Go to bed,' he said shortly. 'I shall join you in a minute.'

She put her thin white feet down on the bare floorboards and went with her quick boyish stride to the bed. John did not turn around as she climbed in. He waited until she had settled and then got up and blew out his candle. He got undressed in the half-darkness and then pulled on his nightgown.

She was lying on the pillow, lit only by a single candle and by the flickering light from the fire. She had unbraided her hair and it spread dark and sweet-smelling on the pillow. A sudden anguish of longing for his lost wife Jane, and the serious passionate desire that they had shared, swept over John. He had promised himself he would not think of her, he had thought it would be fatal to this night if he thought of her, but when he saw Hester in his bed, he did not feel like a bridegroom, but like an unwilling adulterer.

It was a business contract, and it must be fulfilled. John turned his mind to the outrageously half-naked painted women of the old king's court. He had seen them at New Hall when he was little more than a boy and remembered them still with an erotic mixture of disapproval and desire. He held the thought of them in his mind and moved towards Hester.

She had never been touched by a man who was in love with her, or she would have known at once that John was offering her the false coin of his body while his mind was elsewhere. But she too knew that the contract of marriage was not completed until consummation. She lay still and helpful beneath him while he pierced her and then brutally moved in the wound. She did not complain, she did not comment. She lay in silence while the pain went on and then suddenly stopped as he sighed and then moved away from her.

She rose up, biting her lip against the hurt, and wrapped a cloth tightly around her groin. There was only a little blood, she thought; it

61

probably felt worse than it was. She thought that she would have taken the whole thing easier if she had been younger, fresher, warmer. It had been a cold-hearted assault and a cold-hearted acceptance. She shivered in the darkness and got back into bed beside her husband.

John had turned to lie on his side with his back to her as if he would shut out the sight of her and shut out the thought of her. Hester crept back under the covers, careful not to touch him, not to breach the space between them, and set her teeth against the pain, and against the bitterness of disappointment. She did not cry, she lay very still and dry-eyed and waited for the morning when her married life would begin.

'I shall go to Oatlands this week,' John remarked the very next morning at breakfast. Hester, seated beside Baby John, looked up in surprise. 'This week?'

He met her gaze with bland incomprehension. 'Yes.'

'So soon?'

'Why not?'

A dozen reasons why a newly wed husband should not leave his home in the first week of his marriage came to her. She folded her lips tightly on them. 'People may think it looks odd,' was all that she said.

'They can think what they like,' John retorted bluntly. 'We married so that I should be free to do my work and that is what I am doing.'

Hester glanced at Frances, seated at her left, opposite Baby John. Frances's white-capped head was bowed over her bowl, she did not look up at her father, she affected to be deaf.

'There is the planting of the spring bulbs to finish,' he said. 'And pruning, and planning for winter. I have to make sure the silkworm house is sound against the weather. I shall be a month or so away. If you are in any need you can send for me.'

Hester bowed her head. John rose from his place and went to the door. 'I shall be in the orchard,' he said. 'Please pack my clothes for me to go to Oatlands and tell the boy I shall want a horse this afternoon. I shall ride down to the docks and see if anything has come in for the king's collection.'

Hester nodded and she and the two children sat in silence until the door closed behind John.

Frances looked up, her lower lip turned down. 'I thought he would stay home all the time now you are married.'

'Never mind!' Hester said with assumed cheerfulness. 'We'll have lots to do. There's a bonfire to build for Guy Fawkes's day, and then Christmas to prepare for.'

'But I thought he would stay home,' Frances persisted. 'He will come home for Christmas, won't he?'

'Of course,' Hester said easily. 'Of course he will. But he has to go and work for the queen in her lovely gardens. He's a royal gardener! He can't stay home all the time.'

Baby John looked up and wiped his milky moustache on his sleeve.

'Use your napkin,' Hester corrected him.

Baby John grinned. 'I shall go to Oatlands,' he said firmly. 'Pranting and pranning and pruning. I shall go.'

'Certainly,' Hester said, and she emphasised the correct pronunciation: 'Planting and planning and pruning are most important.'

Baby John nodded with dignity. 'Now I shall go and look at my warities.'

'Can I take the money from the visitors?' Frances asked.

Hester glanced at the clock standing in the corner of the room. It was not yet nine. 'They won't come for another hour or so,' she said. 'You can fetch your school work, both of you, for an hour, and then you can work in the rarities room.'

'Oh, Hester!' Frances complained.

Hester shook her head and started to pile up the empty porridge bowls and the spoons. 'Books first,' she said. 'And, Baby John, I want to see all our names written fair in your copybook.'

'And then I will go pranting,' he said.

Hester packed John's clothes for him and added a few jars of bottled summer fruit to the hamper which would follow him by wagon. She was up early on the day of his departure to see him ride away from the Ark.

'You had no need to rise,' John said awkwardly.

'Of course I had need. I am your wife.'

He turned and tightened the girth on his big bay cob to avoid speaking. They were both aware that since the first night they had not made love, and now he was going away for an indefinite period.

'Please take care at court,' Hester said gently. 'These are difficult times for men of principle.'

'I must say what I believe if I am asked,' John said. 'I don't venture it, but I won't deny it.'

She hesitated. 'You need not deny your beliefs but you could say nothing and avoid the topic altogether,' she suggested. 'The queen especially is touchy about her religion. She holds to her Papist faith, and the king inclines more and more to her. And now that he is trying to impose Archbishop Laud's prayer book on Scotland, this is not a time for any Independent thinker; be he Baptist or Presbyterian.'

'You wish to advise me?' he asked with a hint of warning in his voice which reminded her that a wife was always in second place to a man.

'I know the court,' she said steadily. 'I spent my girlhood there. My uncle is an official painter there, still. I have half a dozen cousins and friends who write to me. I do know things, husband. I know that it is no place for a man who thinks for himself.'

'They're hardly likely to care what their gardener thinks,' John scoffed. 'An undergardener at that. I've not even been appointed to my father's post, yet.'

She hesitated. 'They care so much that they threw Archie the jester out with his jacket pulled over his head for merely joking about Archbishop Laud; and Archie was the queen's great favourite. They certainly care what you think. They are taking it upon themselves to care what every single man, woman, and child thinks. That's what the very quarrel is all about. About what every individual thinks in his private heart. That's why every single Scotsman has to sign his own covenant with the king and swear to use the Archbishop's prayer book. They care precisely what every single man thinks.' She paused. 'They may indeed question you, John; and you have to have an answer ready that will satisfy them.'

'I have a right to speak to my God in my own way!' John insisted stubbornly. 'I don't need to recite by rote, I am not a child. I don't need a priest to dictate my prayers. I certainly don't need a bishop puffed up with pride and wealth to tell me what I think. I can speak to God direct when I am planting His seeds in the garden and picking His fruit from His trees. And He speaks to me then. And I honour Him then.

'I use the prayer book well enough – but I don't believe that those are the only words that God hears. And I don't believe that the only men God attends are bishops wrapped up in surplices, and I don't believe that God made Charles king, and that service to the king is one and the same as service to God. And Jane –' He broke off, suddenly aware that he should not speak to his new wife of his constant continuing love for her predecessor.

'Go on,' Hester said.

'Jane's faith never wavered, not even when she was dying in pain,' John said. 'She would never have denied her belief that God spoke simple and clear to her and she could speak to Him. She would have died for that belief, if she had been called to do so. And for her sake, if for nothing else, I will not deny my faith.'

'And what about her children?' Hester asked. 'D'you think she would want you to die for her faith and leave her children orphans?'

John checked. 'It won't come to that.'

'When I was at Oatlands only six months ago, the talk was all about each man's faith and how far each man would go. If the king insists on the Scots following the prayer book he is bound to insist on it in England too. If he goes to war with the Scots to make them do as he bids, and some say he might do that, who can doubt that he will do the same in England?'

John shook his head. 'This is nothing,' he said. 'Nonsense and heart-ache about nothing.'

'It is not nothing. I am warning you,' Hester said steadily. 'No-one knows how far the king will go when he has to protect the queen and her faith, and to conceal his own backsliding towards popery. No-one knows how far he will go to make everyone conform to the same church. He has taken it into his head that one church will make one nation, and that he can hold one nation in the palm of his hand and govern without a word to anyone. If you insist on your faith at the same time as the king is insisting on his, you cannot say what trouble you might be running towards.'

John thought for a moment and then he nodded. 'You may be right,' he said reluctantly. 'You are a powerfully cautious woman, Hester.'

'You have given me a task and I shall do it,' she said, unsmiling. 'You have given me the task of bringing up your children and being a wife to you. I have no wish to be a widow. I have no wish to bring up orphans.'

'But I will not compromise my faith,' he warned her.

'Just don't flaunt it.'

The horse was ready. John tied his cape tightly at the neck and set his hat on his head. He paused; he did not know how he should say farewell to this new, common-sense wife of his. To his surprise she put out her hand, as a man would do, and shook his hand as if she were his friend.

John felt oddly warmed by the frankness of the gesture. He smiled at her, led the horse over to the mounting block and got up into the saddle.

'I don't know what state the gardens will be in,' he remarked.

'For sure, they will appoint you in your father's place when you are back at court,' Hester said. 'It was only your absence which made them delay. It is out of sight, at once forgotten with them. When you return they will insist on your service again.'

He nodded. 'I hope they have not mistook my orders while I was gone. If you leave a garden for a season it slips back a year.'

Hester stepped forward and patted the horse's neck. 'The children will miss you,' she said. 'May I tell them when you will be home?'

'By November,' he promised.

She stepped back from the horse's head and let him go. He smiled at her as he passed out of the stable yard and round the path which led to the gate. As he rode out he had a sudden sense of joyful freedom – that he could ride away from his home or ride back to it and that everything would be managed without him. This was his father's last gift to him – his father who had also married a woman who could manage well in his absence. John turned in his saddle and waved at Hester who was still standing at the corner of the yard where she could look after him.

John waved his whip and turned the horse towards Lambeth and the ferry. Hester watched him go and then turned back to the house.

The court was due at Oatlands in late October so John was busy as soon as he arrived planting and preparing the courts which were enclosed by the royal apartments. The knot gardens always looked well in winter, the sharp geometric shapes of the low box hedging looked wonderful thinned and whitened by frost. In the fountain court John kept the water flowing at the slowest speed so that there would be a chance for it to make icicles and ice cascades in the colder nights. The herbs still looked well, the angelica and sage went into white lace when the frost touched their feathery fronds behind the severe hedging. Against the walls of the king's court John was training one of his new plants introduced from the Ark: his Virginian winter-flowering jasmine. On warm days its scent drifted up to the open windows above, and its colour made a splash of rich pink light in the grey and white and black garden.

The queen's orangery was like a jungle, packed tight with the tender plants which would not survive an English winter. Some of the more handsome shrubs and small trees were planted in containers with loops for carrying poles and John's men lifted them out to the queen's garden at first light, and brought them in again at dusk so that even in winter she would always have something pretty to see from her windows. John placed a lemon and an orange tree, both trained into handsome balls, on either side of the door to her apartments, like aromatic sentries.

'These are pretty,' she said to him from her window one day as he was supervising the careful placing of some little trees in the garden below.

'I beg your pardon, Your Majesty,' John said, pulling off his hat, recognising the heavily accented voice of Queen Henrietta Maria at once. 'They should have been in their places before you looked out.'

'I woke very early, I could not sleep,' she said. 'My husband is worried and so I am sleepless too.'

John bowed.

'People do not understand how hard it is sometimes for us. They see the palaces and the carriages and they think that our lives are given up to pleasure. But it is all worry.'

John bowed again.

'You understand, don't you?' she asked, leaning out and speaking clearly so that he could hear her in the garden below. 'When you make my gardens so beautiful for me, you know that they are a respite for me and the king when we are exhausted by our anxieties and by our struggle to bring this country to be a great kingdom.'

John hesitated. Obviously it would be impolite to say that his interest in the beauty of the gardens would have been the same whether she was an idle vain Papist – as he believed – or whether she was a woman devoted to her husband and her duty. He remembered Hester's advice and bowed once more.

'I so want to be a good queen,' she said.

'No-one prays for anything else,' John said cautiously.

'Do you think they pray for me?'

'They have to, it's in the prayer book. They are ordered to pray for you twice every Sunday.'

'But in their hearts?'

John dipped his head. 'How could I say, Your Majesty? All I know are plants and trees. I can't see inside men's hearts.'

'I like to think that you can give me a glimpse of what common men are thinking. I am surrounded by people who tell me what they think I would like to hear. But you would not lie to me, would you, Gardener Tradescant?'

John shook his head. 'I would not lie,' he said.

'So tell me, is everyone against the Scots? Does everyone see that the

Scots must do what the king wishes and sign the king's covenant, and use the prayer book that we give them?'

John, on one knee, on cold ground, cursed the day that the queen had taken a fancy to him, and reflected on the wisdom of his wife who had warned him to avoid this conversation at all costs.

'They know that it is the king's wish,' he said tactfully. 'There is not a man or woman or child in the country who does not know that it is the king's wish.'

'Then it should need nothing more!' she exclaimed. 'Is he the king or not?'

'Of course he is.'

'Then his wish should be a command to everyone. If they think any different from him they are traitors.'

John thought intently of Hester and said nothing. 'I pray for peace, God knows,' he said honestly enough.

'And so do I,' said the queen. 'Would you like to pray with me, Gardener Tradescant? I allow my favourite servants to use my chapel. I am going to Mass now.'

John forced himself not to fling away from her and from her dangerous ungodly Papistry. To invite an Englishman to attend Mass was a crime punishable by death. The laws against Roman Catholics were very clear and very brutal, and clearly, visibly, flouted by the king and queen in their own court.

'I am all dirty, Your Majesty.' John showed her his earth-stained hands and kept his voice level though he was filled with rage at her casual flouting of the law, and deeply shocked that she should think he would accept such an invitation to idolatory and hell. 'I could not come to your chapel.'

'Another time, then.' She smiled at him, pleased with his humility, and with her own graciousness. She had no idea that he was within an inch of storming from the garden in a blaze of righteous rage. To John, a Roman Catholic chapel was akin to the doors of hell, and a Papist queen was one step to damnation. She had tried to tempt him to deny his faith. She had tried to tempt him to the worst sin in the world – idolatory, worshipping graven images, denying the word of God. She was a woman steeped in sin and she had tried to drag him down.

She closed the window on the cold air without saying farewell or telling him that he could rise. John stayed kneeling until he was sure that she had gone, and that the audience was over. Then he got to his feet and looked behind him. The two assistant gardeners were kneeling where they had dropped when the window opened.

'You can stand,' John said. 'She's gone.'

They scrambled to their feet, rubbing their knees and complaining of the discomfort. 'Please God she does not look out of the window again,' said the younger one. 'Why will she not leave you alone?'

'She thinks I am a faithful servant,' J said bitterly. 'She thinks I will tell her the mood of the people. What she does not realise is that no-one can tell her the truth since any word of disagreement is treason. She and the king have tied our consciences in knots and whatever we do or think or say we are in the wrong. It makes a man want to cut loose.'

He saw the gardeners looking at him in surprise. 'Oh, waste no more time!' John snapped impatiently. 'We've kneeled enough for one day.'

Winter 1639

The court always spent the long Christmas feast at Whitehall, so John was able to leave the royal gardens at Oatlands dormant under a thick frost, and go home to Lambeth in November and spend Christmas at home. The children had made him little presents of their own for Twelfth Night, and he gave them sweets and fairings bought from Lambeth winter fair. To Hester he gave a couple of yards of grey silk for a gown.

'They had a blue silk too but I did not know what you would like,' he said. He would have known exactly what Jane would have preferred; but he seldom observed what Hester was wearing. He had only a general impression of demure smartness.

'I like this. Thank you.'

After the children had gone to bed, Hester and John stayed by the fireside, drinking small ale and cracking nuts in companionable domestic peace. 'You were right about being cautious at Oatlands,' John said. 'In Lambeth the news was all of a war against Scotland. The northern counties are armed and ready, and the king has called a council of war. They say that the militia will be called up too.'

'Do they really think that the king would go to war over a prayer book? Does he really think he can fight the Scots into praying with Archbishop Laud's words?'

John shook his head in disagreement. 'It's more than the prayer book. The king thinks that he has to make one church for all his kingdom. He thinks one church will bind everyone together, bind us all together under his will. He has taken it into his head that if the Scots refuse their bishops then they will refuse their king.'

'You'll not have to go?' Hester asked, going straight to the point.

John grimaced. 'I may have to pay for a substitute to go soldiering in my place. But perhaps they will not muster the Lambeth trained bands. Perhaps I may be excused since I serve the king already.'

Hester hesitated. 'You would not publicly refuse to serve, as a matter of conscience?'

'It would certainly go against my conscience to fire on a man who has said nothing worse than he wants to worship his God in his own way,' John said. 'Such a man, be he Scots or Welsh or English, is saying nothing more than I believe. He cannot be my enemy. I am more like a Scots Presbyterian than I am like Archbishop Laud, God knows.'

'But if you refuse you might be pressed to serve, and if you refuse the press, they could try for treason.'

'These are difficult times. A man has to hold clear on to his conscience and his God.'

'And try not to be noticed,' Hester said.

John suddenly realised the contrast in their opinions. 'Hester, wife, do you believe in nothing?' he demanded. 'I have never had a word from you of belief or conviction. All you ever speak of is surviving and avoiding awkward questions. You are married into a household where we have been faithful servants of the king and his ministers since the start of the century. My father never heard a word against any of his masters in all his days. I didn't agree with him, that's not my way; but I am a man of conscience. I hold very strongly to the belief that a man must find his own way to God. I have been a man of independent belief since I was old enough to think for myself, praying in the words of my own choosing, a Protestant, a true Protestant. Even when I have wavered in my faith, even when I have had doubts, profound doubts, I am glad to have those doubts and think them through. I have never run to some priest to tell me what I should think, to speak to God for me.'

She met his gaze with her own straight look. 'You're right. I believe in surviving,' she said flatly. 'That's all, really. That's my creed. The safest route for me and mine is to obey the king; and if I do happen to think differently to what he commands – I keep my thoughts to myself. My family works for noble and royal patrons, I was brought up around the court. I am loyal to my king and loyal to my God; but, like any courtier, my first interest is in surviving. And I fear that my creed is going to be as thoroughly tested as any other in the next few months.'

The press gang did not come for John. But he did receive a letter from the Mayor of London. John was to pay a tax demanded personally by the king to finance the war against the Scots. The king was marching north and desperately needed money to equip and arm his soldiers. And more soldiers would be coming, soldiers from Ireland, and mercenaries from Spain.

'The king is bringing in Papists to fight against Protestants?' John demanded, scandalised. 'What next? French soldiers from his wife's country? Or the Spanish army? What was the point of us defeating the Armada, fighting to stay free of Papist powers, if we now invite them in?'

'Hush,' Hester said. She closed the door of the parlour so that the visitors in the rarities room could not hear her husband's shout of outrage.

'I will not pay!'

'Wait and see,' Hester advised.

'I will not,' John said. 'This is a matter of principle to me, Hester. I will not pay money to an army of Papists to march against men who think as I do, whose consciences are as tender as mine.'

To his surprise she did not argue but bit her lip and bowed her head. John looked at the top of her cap and had a sense at last of being master in his own house and impressing on his wife the importance of principle.

'I have spoken,' he said firmly.

'Yes indeed,' she said quietly.

Hester said nothing to disagree with John, but that day, and every day thereafter, she stole from the little collection of coins which the visitors paid until she had enough to pay John's tax without him knowing, if the tax collector came back.

He did not return. The Lord Mayor of London, with the great men of the City behind him, was not inclined any more than John to hand over thousands of pounds' worth of City gold for the king's war against an enemy who was a natural ally. Especially when the king was demanding money without the agreement of a parliament.

1640

In the absence of any voluntary money the king was forced to call a parliament. For the first time in ten years the squires and landlords returned to Westminster with a belief that they might now get back to the proper task of advising the king and running the country.

Hester went to find John in the orchard with the news of the new parliament. The buds on the apple trees were fattening and splitting and showing white and pink petals as crumpled as ribbons crammed into a pocket.

'Perhaps the king will listen to the voice of the people,' John said hopefully.

'He might,' she said. 'But he is listening to the old Earl Strafford and to the queen. Two voices instead of the one. Will he listen to the voice of the people in preference to the voice of his own wife, who is trying to gather an army of English Papists and a Spanish army for him?'

John thought for a moment. 'No,' he said. 'Of course not.'

Hester nodded. 'Takings are down for the gardens,' she warned. 'People are not ordering plants and seeds. This should be our busiest time of the year but it's as quiet as winter. No-one can think about gardens while the king is half at war with the Scots and has called a parliament which is filled with men who disagree with him.'

'We can manage for a short spell,' John said.

'We earn more in the spring than we do for all the rest of the year,' she said. 'I have been looking at the account books. We have to make money in spring. A war starting in springtime is the worst thing that could happen for us. If the uncertainty carries on till June or July we will not make a profit this year.'

'What about the rarities?'

'There are more visitors because there are more people in the city,'

Hester said. 'The country gentry who have come in for the parliament are curious to see Tradescant's Ark. But if the business between the king and Scots grows more serious I think they'll stop coming too. A trade like ours depends on people feeling safe enough to spend money on pleasure: on visiting, on rarities, and on their gardens. A country at war does not plant gardens.'

'I still have my post at Oatlands,' John pointed out. 'And I will succeed my father as chief gardener and draw his wage.'

Hester nodded. 'If the worst comes to the worst we can live on your wages.'

'At the very worst we can close the Ark and live at Oatlands,' John said. 'The house there is only little; but we could manage for a while if we cannot afford to keep the Ark open.'

'I'm not sure that I would want to live in the grounds of a royal palace in times like these,' Hester said cautiously.

'I thought you were such a royalist?'

'I don't want to take sides,' Hester said. 'Not when I don't know exactly what the sides will be. Nor when I don't know which side will win.'

The sides became rapidly clearer after the king's army, unenthusiastic and poorly paid, were defeated by the Scots who went on to occupy Newcastle and Durham and hammer out a peace with the king which would force him to call a new parliament in England. It became clear to everyone in the country, except perhaps to the king and the queen, that the Scots and the Independent English thinkers had the king on the run. Hester started a correspondence with Mrs Hurte, the mother of John's first wife, who kept her eyes and ears open in the City and was as sceptical as Hester, and rightly concerned for the safety of her grandchildren.

> *The new Parliament will impeach Strafford, just as the old one was wild to impeach Buckingham. If J has ever had any dealings with the Earl, or if his father kept any correspondence, it should be hidden or, better yet, burned. They are saying that Strafford is a traitor prepared to wage war against his own country for the benefit of the king and queen. They will accuse him of treason – treason against the people of England, and once one royal servant is accused how many others will be charged?*

74

Hester went upstairs to the attic and opened John's old chest of papers. The Tradescants had supplied seeds and young saplings to the Earl but there were no incriminating letters left from the years when John Tradescant had been known as a discreet man who regularly visited Europe and could be trusted with a letter or a message.

The Earl was a loud-mouthed unattractive old man, twisted with gout and losing his sight. He had been a relentless force in Ireland, hammering a Protestant will on a Catholic people; but he was old now. The king had recalled him to England only for the unscrupulous clarity of his advice, and been indebted to him for the suggestion that if towns did not send enough money for the king's army their aldermen should be hanged in their robes to clarify the urgency of the situation. The Earl had walked past John in the gardens of Oatlands a dozen times and never wasted more than a glance on him.

The Tradescants were safe from any accusation of complicity with the king. But many royal servants slipped away and went abroad, or retired to their country estates. Others were not so quick or careful. In December, Archbishop Laud was arrested and imprisoned in the Tower to await the pleasure of the Houses of Parliament.

Hester did not pray from any prayer book at evening prayers that night but read from the King James Bible as the only text which did not define the household as for or against the king.

'No prayers?' John asked her quietly as the household went about its last tasks of the day and Hester counted out the bedtime candles.

'I don't know any more what words God would prefer,' she said drily. 'And no-one knows what man requires.'

Spring 1641

The day that Strafford was called to account in the great hall at Westminster there were no visitors to the Ark at all. Everyone who could get a ticket or a pass to see Strafford at bay before his accusers was in the city. Even the streets were deserted.

In the unnatural silence of the house at Lambeth there was suddenly a thunderous knock on the front door. Frances went running to open it, but Hester darted out from the rarities room and caught her in the hall.

'Frances! Don't answer it!'

The girl halted at once.

'Go round to the gardens and find your father. Tell him to go to the stables, saddle a horse, and wait till I send a message.'

Frances caught the note of urgency in her stepmother's voice, nodded, white-faced, and ran. Hester waited until she was out of sight, smoothed down her apron, straightened her cap, and opened the door.

It was a gentleman usher of the royal household. Hester showed him into the parlour. 'My husband is not here at the moment,' she said, deliberately vague. 'I can send a message for him if it is urgent.'

'The king is at Whitehall and wishes to see him.'

Hester nodded. 'I shall have to write to him at Oatlands,' she said. 'He is the king's gardener at Oatlands, you know. May I tell him why the king wants him?'

The gentleman usher raised his eyebrows. 'I should have thought it would be enough to tell him that he is wanted,' he said rudely.

Hester bowed slightly. 'Of course,' she said. 'But if the king requires some plants or seeds then we need to know at once, so that we can prepare them. Or if he wants some rarities delivered . . .'

'Oh,' the man said. 'I see. The king is buying a hunting lodge at

76

Wimbledon for the queen. They want Mr Tradescant to design a garden.'

No trace of her relief appeared on Hester's face. 'I will send for him at once,' she said. 'He may not even have arrived at Oatlands yet. He left only this morning. I may catch him on the road, and tell him to come back.'

The gentleman usher nodded.

'Can I offer you some refreshment?' Hester asked. 'A glass of wine?'

The gentleman usher shook his head. 'I shall return to Whitehall,' he said. 'These are difficult times.'

'Very difficult,' Hester agreed with feeling. She showed him to the door and then went to the stables to find John. He was leaning against the pump in the stable yard, enjoying the early warm sunshine on his face.

'Frances came flying out as if all the devils in hell were at the door,' he said carelessly. 'Why are you so fearful?'

'I thought it might have been the press gang or the tax collectors, or a message from the court that you would be safer to miss,' she explained. 'I don't know *what* I fear except I am uneasy, I am afraid for us. If the king's own advisor can be on trial for his life then the king can protect no-one. Indeed, it's the loyal servants of the king who are the most endangered. And we have been known as royal servants for two generations. I don't want this family suddenly named as enemies of the people of England because we have taken royal gold. We all have to make our own safety in these days.'

John put his hand on her shoulder. It was his first ever gesture of affection. Hester stood very still, as if she had been approached by a wary wild animal and did not want to scare it away. She felt herself lean, very slightly, towards his caress.

'You're very careful for me,' he said. 'I appreciate it.'

She could have stood like that, in the warm sunny yard with his hand on her shoulder, forever. But John dropped his hand. 'So who was it?'

'It was a message from the court. The king is buying a manor at Wimbledon for the queen and they want you to design a garden.' She paused for a moment. 'The king's advisor and chief minister is at bay before his enemies and on trial for his life, and yet the king has time to send to you to tell you to make a new garden.'

'Well, at least that solves the problem of selling seeds and plants,' he said. 'If I am making a new royal garden we will need all our stocks. We're back in profit, Hester. Am I to go at once?'

'I said you were on the road to Oatlands, before I knew what the message was. So you can go today or tomorrow.'

'So our troubles are over!' John exclaimed happily. 'A new garden to design, and all our seedlings and plants bought by the king.'

'I don't think our troubles will be over that quickly,' Hester said cautiously. 'Take great care, John, when you meet the king and queen.'

When John got to Wimbledon the king and queen were not to be found.

'Their Majesties are walking privately in the garden,' one of the courtiers told him. 'They said you were to go and meet them there. You may approach Their Majesties.'

John, accustomed to the ways of the court, expected to find twenty to thirty people with the king and queen walking privately, but for once they were indeed alone, just the two of them, with her hand in the crook of his arm and her embroidered silk skirts brushing against his legs as they walked together.

John hesitated, thinking that for once they might have chosen to be alone and might be enjoying their privacy. But when they turned at the edge of the grass court and saw him the queen smiled and the king beckoned him forward with one of his little gestures. Although they wished it to be always understood that they were very much in love, they preferred each other's company before an audience. The queen liked to be seen publicly basking in the king's adoration, even more than she enjoyed a private moment.

'Ah, Gardener Tradescant!' the queen said. John bowed low and dropped to one knee. The king flicked his finger to permit John to rise and John got up. At once he saw that they were not having a carefree stroll in the garden. The queen was flushed and her eyelids were red, the king looked pale and strained.

'Your Majesties,' John said warily.

'The king has bought me this pretty house to take our minds off our troubles,' the queen said in her lilting accent. 'We are much troubled, Gardener Tradescant. We want to be diverted.'

John bowed. 'It could be a fine garden,' he said. 'The soil is good.'

'I want it done all new,' the queen said eagerly. 'A pretty style to match the house.' She gestured back at the manor house. It was a handsome place new-built of red brick, with two arching flights of steps down from the terrace and gardens terraced down the slope. 'I want many fruit trees. The king and I will come here in midsummer to escape from the noise and fuss of the court and we will eat fruit off the trees and grapes off the vine and melons off the . . .' She broke off.

'Off the ground,' the king suggested. 'They g . . . grow on the g . . . ground, do they not, Tradescant?'

'Yes, Your Majesty,' John said. 'My father learned the way of making them grow rich and ripe when he was with Sir Henry Wootton at Canterbury, and he taught me the way. I can grow you melons here and all sorts of fruit.'

'And pretty flowers,' the queen added. 'White and blue flowers in the knot garden.'

John bowed his assent, keeping his face hidden. White and blue were the flowers of the Virgin Mary. The queen was asking for a Papist knot garden on the very edge of a London on the brink of revolt.

'We need somewhere to retire in these troubled times,' the king said. 'A little hidden garden, Tradescant. Somewhere that we can b . . . be ourselves.'

The queen stepped to one side to look at a neglected watercourse, lifting her silk dress carefully away from the wet ground.

'I understand,' John said. 'Will you be here only in summer, Your Majesty? It helps me if I know. If you are not to be here in autumn then I do not need to plant for that season.'

'Yes,' the king said. 'A summertime p . . . place.'

John nodded and waited for further orders.

'It pleases me to give her a p . . . pretty little h . . . house of her own,' the king said, watching the queen at the end of the little terrace. 'I have great work to do – I have to d . . . d . . . defend my crown against wild and wicked men who w . . . would pull me down, I have to d . . . defend the church against levellers and s . . . and s . . . and sectaries and Independents who would unstitch the very fabric of the country. It is all for m . . . me to do. Only I can preserve the country from the m . . . madness of a few wicked men. Whatever it costs me, I have t . . . to do it.'

John knew he should say nothing; but there was such a strange mixture of certainty and self-dramatisation in the king's voice that he could not remain silent. 'Are you sure that you have to do it all?' he asked quietly. 'I know some sectaries, and they are quiet men, content to leave the Church alone, provided that they can pray their own way. And surely, no-one in the country wants to harm you or the queen, or the princes.'

Charles looked tragic. 'They d . . . do,' he said simply. 'They drive themselves on and on, c . . . caring nothing for my good, c . . . caring nothing for the country. They want to see me cut down, cut down to the size of a little P . . . Prince, like the D . . . Doge of Venice or some catspaw of Parliament. They want to see the p . . . power my father gave me, which his aunt g . . . gave him, cut down to n . . . nothing. When was this country t . . . truly great? Under King Henry, Queen Elizabeth and my f . . . father King James. But they do not remember this. They don't w . . . want to. I shall have to fight them as traitors. It is a b . . . battle to the death.'

The queen had heard the king's raised voice and came over. 'Husband?' she inquired.

He turned at once, and Tradescant was relieved that she had come to soothe the king.

'I was saying how these m . . . madmen in Parliament will not be finished until they have destroyed my ch . . . church and destroyed my power,' he said.

John waited for the queen to reassure him that nothing so bad was being plotted. He hoped that she would remind him that the king and queen he most admired – his father James, and his great-aunt Elizabeth, had spent all their lives weaving compromises and twisting out agreements. Both of them had been faced with argumentative parliaments and both of them had put all their power and all their charm into turning agreements to their own desire, dividing the opposition, seducing their enemies. Neither of them would ever have been at loggerheads with a force which commanded any power in the country. Both of them would have waited and undermined an enemy.

'We must destroy them,' the queen said flatly. 'Before they destroy us and destroy the country. We must gain and then keep control of the parliament, of the army and of the Church. There can be no agreement until they acknowledge that Church, army, and Parliament is all ours. And we will never compromise on that, will we, my love? You will never concede anything!'

He took her hand and kissed it as if she had given him the most sage and level-headed counsel. 'You see how I am advised?' he asked with a smile to Tradescant. 'You see how w . . . wise and stern she is? This is a worthy successor to Queen Elizabeth, is sh . . . she not? A woman who could defeat the Sp . . . Spanish Armada again.'

'But these are not the Spanish,' John pointed out. He could almost hear Hester ordering him to be silent while he took the risk and spoke. 'These are Englishmen, following their consciences. These are your own people – not a foreign enemy.'

'They are traitors!' the queen snapped. 'And thus they are worse than the Spanish, who might be our enemies but at least are faithful to their king. A man who is a traitor is like a dog who is mad. He should be struck down and killed without a second's thought.'

The king nodded. 'And I am s . . . sorry, Gardener Tradescant, to hear you sympathise with them.' There was a world of warning despite the slight stammer.

'I just hope for peace and that all good men can find a way to peace,' John muttered.

The queen stared at him, affronted by a sudden doubt. 'You are my servant,' she said flatly. 'There can be no question which side you are on.'

John tried to smile. 'I didn't know we were taking sides.'

'Oh yes,' the king said bitterly. 'We are certainly t . . . taking sides. And I have paid you a w . . . wage for years, and you have worked in my h . . . household, or in the household of my dear D . . . Duke since you were a boy – have you not? And your f . . . father worked all his life for my advisors and servants, and my f . . . father's advisors and servants. You have eaten our b . . . bread since you were weaned. Which side are you on?'

John swallowed to ease the tightness in his throat. 'I am for the good of the country, and for peace, and for you to enjoy what is your own, Your Majesty,' he said.

'What has *always* b . . . been mine own,' the king prompted.

'Of course,' John agreed.

The queen suddenly smiled. 'But this is my dear Gardener Tradescant!' she said lightly. 'Of course he is for us. You would be first into battle with your little hoe, wouldn't you?'

John tried to smile and bowed rather than reply.

The queen put her hand on his arm. 'And we never betray those who follow us,' she said sweetly. 'We are bound to you as you are bound to us and we would never betray a faithful servant.' She nodded at the king as if inviting him to learn a lesson. 'When a man is ready to promise himself to us he finds in us a loyal master.'

The king smiled at his wife and the gardener. 'Of course,' he said. 'From the highest servant to the l . . . lowest, I do not forget either loyalty or treachery. And I reward b . . . both.'

Summer 1641

John remembered that promise on the day that the Earl of Strafford was taken to the Tower of London and thrown into the traitors' prison to be executed when the king signed the Act of Attainder – his death warrant.

The king had sworn to Strafford that he would never betray him. He had written him a note and gave him the word of a king that Strafford would never suffer 'in life, honour or fortune' for his service – those were his exact words. The most cautious and wily members of the Privy Council fled the country when they recognised that Parliament was attacking the Privy Council rather than attacking the king. Most of them were quick to realise too that whatever the king might promise, he would not raise one hand to save a trusted servant from dying for his cause. But the Bishop of Ely and Archbishop William Laud were too slow, or too trusting. They too were imprisoned for plotting against the safety of the kingdom, alongside their ally Strafford in the Tower.

For all of the long spring months, Parliament had met on Strafford's case and heard that he had recommended bringing in an army of Irish Papist troops to reduce 'this kingdom'. If the king had interrupted the trial to insist that Strafford was referring to the kingdom of Scotland he might have saved him then from the executioner. But he did not. The king stayed silent in the little ante-room where he sat and listened to the trial. He did not insist. He offered, rather feebly, to never take Strafford's advice again as long as the old man lived if they would but spare his life. The Houses of Parliament said they could not spare his life. The king struggled with his conscience for a short, painful time, and then signed the warrant for Strafford's execution.

'He sent little Prince Charles to ask them for mercy,' Hester said in blank astonishment to John as she came back from Lambeth in May with a wagon full of shopping and a head full of news. 'That poor little boy, only ten years old, and the king sent him down to Westminster to go before the whole Parliament and plead for the Earl's life. And then they refused him! What a thing to do to a child! He's going to think all his life that it was his fault that the Earl went to his death!'

'Whereas it is the king's,' John said simply. 'He could have denied that Strafford had ever advised him. He could have borne witness for him. He could have taken the decision on his own shoulders. But he let Strafford take the blame for him. And now he will let Strafford die for him.'

'He's to be executed on Tuesday,' Hester said. 'The market women are closing their stalls for the day and going up to Tower Hill to see his head taken off. And the apprentices are taking a free day, an extra May Day.'

John shook his head. 'So much for the king's loyalty. These are bad days for his servants. What's the word on Archbishop Laud?'

'Still in the Tower,' Hester said. She rose to her feet and took hold of the side of the wagon to clamber down but John reached out his arms and lifted her down. She hesitated for a moment at the strangeness of his touch. It was nearly an embrace, his hands on her waist, their heads close together. Then he released her and moved to the back of the wagon.

'You've bought enough for a siege!' he exclaimed, and then, as his own words sunk in, he turned to her. 'Why have you bought so much?'

'I don't want to go into market for a week or so,' she said. 'And I won't send the maids either.'

'Why not?'

She made a little helpless gesture. He thought he had never before seen her anything other than certain and definite in her movements. 'It's strange in town,' she began. 'I can't describe it. Uneasy. Like a sky before a storm. People talk on corners and break off when I walk by. Everyone looks at everyone else as if they would read their hearts. No-one knows who is a friend and who is not. The king and Parliament are splitting this country down the middle like a popped pod of peas and all of us peas are spilling out and rolling around and not knowing what to do.'

John looked at his wife, trying to understand, for the first time in their married life, what she might be feeling. Then he suddenly realised what it was. 'You look afraid.'

She turned away to the edge of the wagon as if it were something to be ashamed of. 'Someone threw a stone at me,' she said, her voice very low.

'What?'

'Someone threw a stone as I was leaving the market. It hit me in the back.'

John was dumbfounded. 'You were stoned? In Lambeth?'

She shook her head. 'A glancing blow. It was not thrown to hurt me. I think it was an insult, a warning.'

'But why should anyone at Lambeth market insult you? Or warn you?'

She shrugged. 'You're well-known as the king's gardener, the king's man, and your father before you. And these people don't inquire where your heart lies, what you think in private. They think of us as the king's servants, and the king is not well-regarded in Lambeth and the City.'

John's mind was whirling. 'Did it hurt you? Are you hurt?'

She started to say 'No', but she stumbled over the word and John, without thinking, caught her into his arms and let her cry against his shoulder as the torrent of words spilled out.

She was afraid, very afraid, and she had been afraid every market day since Parliament had been recalled and the king had come home defeated from the war with the Scots. The women would not always serve her, they overcharged her and leaned on the scales when they were weighing out flour. And the apprentice boys ran after her and called out names, and when the stone had struck her back she had thought it would be the first of a hail of stones which would hit her and knock her from the box of the wagon and beat her down in the street.

'Hester! Hester!' John held her as the storm of crying swept over her. 'My dear, my dear, my little wife!'

She broke off from crying at once. 'What did you call me?'

He had not been aware of it himself.

'You called me little wife, and your dear –' she said. She rubbed her eyes, but kept her other hand firmly on his collar. 'You called me dear, you've never called me that before.'

The old closed look came down on his face. 'I was upset for you,' he said, as if it was a sin to call his own wife an endearment. 'For a moment I forgot.'

'You forgot that you had been married before. You treated me like a wife you are . . . fond of,' she said.

He nodded.

'I am glad,' she said softly. 'I should like you to be fond of me.'

He disengaged himself very gently. 'I should not forget I was married before,' he said firmly, and went into the house. Hester stood beside the cart, watching the kitchen door closing behind him, and found she had no more tears left to cry but only loneliness and disappointment and dry eyes.

Summer 1641

Hester did not go to market again all summer. And she had been right to fear the mood of the village of Lambeth. The apprentice boys all ran wild one night and the fever was caught by the market women and by the serious chapel goers, who made a determined mixed mob and marched through the streets shouting, 'No popery! No bishops!' Some of the loudest and most daring shouted, 'No king!' They threw a few burning brands over the high walls of the empty archbishop's palace, and made a half-hearted attempt at the gates, and then they broke the windows down Lambeth High Street at every house that did not show a light at the window for Parliament. They did not march down the road as far as the Ark and John thanked God for the luck of the Tradescants, which had once again placed them on the very edge of great events and danger and yet spared them by a hair's breadth.

After that, John sent the gardener's lad and the stable lad together to market and though they often muddled the order and stopped for an ale at the taverns, at least it meant that any muttering about the king's gardener was not directed at Hester.

John had to go to Oatlands and before he went he ordered wooden shutters to be made for all the windows of the house, especially the great windows of Venetian glass in the rarities room. He hired an extra lad to wake at nights and watch out down the South Lambeth road in case the mob came that way, and he and Hester went out one night in the darkness with shaded lanterns to clear out the old ice house, and put a heavy bolt on the thick wooden doors to make a hiding place for the most valuable of the rarities.

'If they come against us you will have to take the children and leave the house,' he ordered.

She shook her head and he found himself admiring her cool nerve.

'We have a couple of muskets,' she said. 'I won't have my house overrun by a band of idle apprentice lads.'

'You must not take risks,' he warned her.

She gave him a tight, determined smile. 'Everything is a risk in these days,' she said. 'I will see that we come safe through it all.'

'I *have* to leave you,' John said anxiously. 'I am summoned to Oatlands. Their Majesties will visit next week and I have to see the gardens are at their best.'

She nodded. 'I know you have to go. I shall keep everything safe here.'

John was at Oatlands ready for the full court, but the queen came alone. The king and half the court were missing, and the rumour was that he had gone north to negotiate with the Scots himself.

'He is in Edinburgh and all will be mended,' the queen said with her complacent smile when she came upon John dead-heading the roses. She was concealing her boredom as best as she could. She was accompanied only by a few ladies, the old flirtatious, artistic, idle entourage was broken up. The more adventurous and more ambitious men were riding with the king. There was the smell of opportunity and advancement in the court of a king at war, and the young men had been sick of peace and a court devoted to marital love for so long. 'It will all be resolved,' the queen promised. 'Once they meet him again he will charm them into seeing that they were wrong to march against him.'

John nodded. 'I hope so, Your Majesty.'

She came close to him and lowered her voice. 'We will not go to London again until it is all agreed,' she confided. 'Not even to my little manor at Wimbledon. We shall go nowhere near to Westminster. After the death of my Lord Strafford –' She broke off. 'They said they would try *me* after the Earl! Try *me* for treasonous advice!'

John had to resist the temptation to take one of her little white hands. She looked genuinely afraid.

'He should have stood against them,' she whispered. 'My husband should not have let them take Strafford, nor Laud. If he lets them pick us off one after another we will all be lost. And then he will be left all alone and they will have tasted blood. He should have stood against them for William Laud, he should have stood against them for Strafford. How can I be sure he will stand for me?'

'Your Majesty, matters cannot go so far,' John said soothingly. 'As you say yourself, the king will come home and it will all be resolved.'

She brightened at once. 'He can scatter a few baronies around the Houses of Parliament, and places at court,' she said. 'These are all lowly men, commoners up from the provinces. They have neither learning nor breeding. They will forget their folly if the price is high enough.'

John felt the familiar rise of irritation. 'Majesty, I think they are men of principle. They did not behead Lord Strafford on a whim. I think they believe in what they are doing.'

She shook her head. 'Of course not! They are scheming with the Scots, or with the Dutch, or with someone for their own ends. The House of Lords is not with them, the court is not with them. These are little men come up from the country, crowing like little cocks on their own dunghills. We just have to wring their necks like little cocks.'

'I pray that the king can find a way to agree with them,' John said steadily.

She flashed him her charming smile. 'Why, so do I! He shall make all sorts of promises to them, and then they can vote us the taxes we need and the army we need to crush the Scots and they can go back to their dunghills and we can rule without them again.'

Autumn 1641

It might have gone either way for the king, and the queen, but for their fourth kingdom of Ireland. The news that Strafford was dead ran through Ireland like a heath fire. Strafford had held Ireland down with a mixture of legal rigour and terrible abuse of power. He had ruled them like a cynical old soldier and the only law in the land was that of superior military power. Once he was dead the Papist Irish rose up in a defiant storm of rage against their Protestant masters. Strafford had kept them brutally down, but now Strafford was gone. The rumours and counter-rumours had flown around the kingdom of Ireland until every man who called himself a man took up a pitchfork or a hoe and flung himself against the newly arrived Protestant settlers, and the greedy land-grabbing Protestant lords, and spared neither them nor their women nor children.

The news of what had taken place, horrifically embellished by the terrified imagination of a minority in a country they did not own, reached London in October and fuelled the hatred against Papists a thousand times over. Even Hester, normally so level-headed, departed from discretion that night and prayed aloud in family prayers that God might strike down the dreadful savage Irish and preserve His chosen people, settled in that most barbaric land; and the Tradescant children, Frances and Johnnie, round-eyed with horror at what they heard in the kitchen and in the stable, whispered a frightened, 'Amen'.

The Papist rebels were spitting Protestant children on their pikes and roasting them over the fires, eating them before the anguished gaze of their parents. The Papist rebels were firing cottages and castles with the Protestant owners locked inside. Everyone knew a story of fresh and unbelievable horror. No-one questioned any report. It was all true, it was all the worst of the worst nightmares. It was all worse than reports told.

John was reminded, for a brief moment, of the bitter woman who kept the lodging house in Virginia, and how she had called the Indians pagans and beasts, and how she too had stories of skinning and flaying and eating alive. For a moment he stepped back from the terror which had caught up the whole of England, for a moment he wondered if the stories were as true as everyone swore. But only for a moment. The circumstances were too persuasive, the stories were too potent. Everyone said it; it had to be true.

And there was worse. In the streets of Lambeth and in London they did not call it the Irish rebellion, they called it the queen's rebellion, in the absolute certainty that all the nightmare tales from Ireland were gospel truth, and that the rebellion was fomented by Henrietta Maria herself in support of the devilish Papists. What the queen wanted was a free Roman Catholic Ireland and then, as soon as she dared, the queen would ship her fellow Papists from Ireland to England so they could butcher and eat English babes as well.

Spring 1642

Parliament, still in session, drew ever closer to accusing the queen. It was a steady, terrifying approach, which would not waver nor hesitate. They impeached twelve bishops for treason, one after another, until a round dozen had appeared before the bar of the House, with their lives on the line. And then the word was that the queen was next on the list.

'What shall you do?' Hester asked John. They were in the warmth of the rarities room where a large fire kept the collection warm and dry though there was a storm of wintry sleet dashing against the grand windows. Hester was polishing the shells and precious stones to make them gleam on their beds of black velvet, and John was labelling a new collection of carved ivories which had just arrived from India.

'I don't know,' he said. 'I shall have to go to Oatlands to see to the planning for the gardens next season. I will learn more there.'

'Planning gardens for a queen who will be beheaded?' Hester asked quietly.

John met her gaze, his mouth twisted with anxiety. 'I am following your creed, wife. I'm trying to survive these times. I don't know what's best to do other than to behave as if nothing has changed.'

'But John –' Hester started, but was interrupted by a knock at the front door, and they both froze. John saw Hester's colour drain from her cheeks, and the hand that held the duster trembled as if she had an ague. They stood in complete silence and then they heard the maid answer and the reassuring chink of a coin as a visitor paid for entrance to the collection. Hester whisked her cloth out of sight into the pocket of her apron and threw open the handsome double doors to him. He was a well-dressed man, a country man, by the look of his brown suit and his weather-beaten face. He paused in the doorway and looked around at the grand, imposing room and the warm fire.

'Well, this is a treat,' he said in the round tones of the west country.

Hester moved forward. 'You are welcome,' she said pleasantly. 'This is John Tradescant, and I am his wife.'

The man dipped his head. 'I am Benjamin George,' he said. 'From Yeovil.'

'A visitor to London?'

'Here on business. I am a Parliament man representing the borough of Yeovil.'

John stepped forward. 'My wife will show you the rarities,' he said. 'But first can you tell me what news there is?'

The man looked cautious. 'I can't say whether it is good or bad,' he said. 'I am on my way home and Parliament is dissolved, I know that much.'

John and Hester exchanged a quick look. 'Parliament dissolved?'

The man nodded. 'The king himself came marching in to arrest five of our members. You would not have thought that he was allowed to come into Parliament with his own soldiers like that. Whether he was going to arrest our members for treason or cut them down where they stood, I don't know which!'

'My God!' John exclaimed, aghast. 'He drew a sword in the House of Commons?'

'What happened?' Hester demanded.

'He came in very civil though he had his guards all about him, and he asked for a seat and sat in the Speaker's chair. But they were gone – the men he wanted. They slipped out the back half an hour before he came in the front. We were warned, of course. And so he looked about for them, and made a comment, and then went away again.'

John was struggling to hide his irritation with the slowness of the man's speech. 'But what did he come for, if he left it too late to arrest them?'

The man shrugged. 'I think myself it was some grand gesture, but he bodged it.'

Hester looked quickly at John. He made an impatient exclamation. 'Are you saying he marched his guard into the House to arrest five members and failed?'

The man nodded. 'He looked powerfully put out,' he observed.

'I should think he was. What will he do?'

'As to that . . . I couldn't say.'

'But then what will Parliament do?'

The man slowly shook his head. Hester, seeing her husband on the edge of an outburst and the man still thinking his answer through, had to bite her lip to keep silent herself.

'As to that . . . I couldn't say either.'

John took a swift step to the door and then turned back. 'So what is happening in the City? Is everything quiet?'

The country squire shook his head at the mystifying speed of change. 'Well, the Lord Mayor's trained bands are to be called out to keep the peace, the king's men have all gone into hiding, the City is boarded up and ready for a riot or . . . something worse.'

'What could be worse?' Hester asked. 'What could be worse than a riot in the City?'

'War, I think,' he said slowly. 'A war would be worse than a riot.'

'Between who?' John asked tightly. 'A war between who? What are you saying?'

The man looked into his face, struggling with the enormity of what he had to say. 'War between the king and Parliament, I'm afraid.'

There was a brief shocked silence.

'It has come to this?' John asked.

'So I am come to see the greatest sight of London which I promised myself I would see before I left, and then I am going home.' George looked around. 'There is even more than I thought.'

'I will show it all to you,' Hester promised him. 'You must forgive our hunger for news. What will you do when you get home?'

He bowed courteously to her. 'I shall gather the men of my household and train them and arm them so that they can fight to save their country from the enemy.'

'But will you fight for the king or for Parliament?'

He bowed again. 'Madam, I shall fight for my country. I shall fight for Right. The only thing is: I wish I knew who was in the right.'

Hester showed him the main features of the collection and then, as soon as she could, left him to open the drawers and look at the smaller things on his own. She could not find John in the house, nor in the orangery. As she feared, he was in the stable yard, dressed in his travelling cloak, waiting for his mare to be saddled.

'You're never going to court!' she exclaimed.

'I have to,' he said. 'I cannot bear having to wait for scraps of news like this.'

'You are a gardener,' she said. 'Not a courtier, not a Member of Parliament. What is it to you whether the king is quarrelling with Parliament or not?'

'I am on the edge of it all,' John said. 'I know too much to sit quietly at home and nurse up my ignorance. If I knew less of them then I would care less. If I knew more then I could decide better what to do. I am halfway between knowledge and ignorance and I have to settle on one side or the other.'

'Then be ignorant!' she said with sudden passion. 'Get into your garden, John, and set seeds for the gardens at Wimbledon and Oatlands. Do the trade you were born to. Stay home where you are safe.'

He shook his head and took both her hands. 'I won't be long,' he promised her. 'I shall go over the river to Whitehall and find out the news and then come back home. Don't fret so, Hester. I must learn what is happening and then I'll come home. It is better for us if I know which way the wind is blowing. It is safer for us.'

She left her hands in his, enjoying the warmth of his callused palms. 'You say that, but you are like a boy setting out on an adventure,' she said shrewdly. 'You want to be in the heart of things, my husband. Don't deny it.'

John gave her a roguish grin and then kissed her quickly on both cheeks. 'Forgive me,' he said. 'It's true. Let me go with your blessing?'

She was breathless with the sudden casual embrace and felt herself flushing. 'With my blessing,' she repeated. 'Of course you have my blessing. Always.'

He swung himself into the saddle and let the horse walk out of the yard. Hester put her hand to her cheek where his lips had briefly touched, and watched him go.

He had to wait for a place on the horse ferry at Lambeth, and then the traffic on the City side of the river was busier than he had ever seen it. There were hundreds of people milling around in the narrow streets, asking for news and stopping ballad sellers and pedlars of news-sheets to demand what they knew. There were armed groups of men marching down the road, pushing people aside and demanding that they shout, 'Hurrah! for the king!' But then down another road would come another group shouting, 'Hurrah! for Pym! No bishops! No Papist queen!'

John drew his horse back into a sidestreet, fearful of being caught up in a fight, when he saw two of these groups heading towards each other. But the royalists wheeled off quickly to one side, as if they were on an urgent errand that took them away; and the others took care not to see them, and not to give chase. He watched them go and saw that they, like himself, were not ready for a fight yet. They didn't even want a brawl, let alone a war. He thought the country must be filled with men like himself, like the honest Member of Parliament for Yeovil, who knew that they were in the grip of great times, and wanted to take their part in the great times, who wanted to do the right thing; but were very, very far from knowing what the right thing might be.

John's father would have known. He would have been for the king. John's father had had a straightforward faith that his son had never learned. John made a wry face at the thought of the certainties of the man and of his own confused layering of doubts, which left him now still mourning one woman, half in love with another, and married to a third; in the service of a king while his heart was with the opposition; always torn both ways, always on the fringe of everything.

The crowds grew thicker around the palace of Whitehall and there were armed guards looking grim and frightened with their pikes crossed at the doorways. John rode his horse round to an inn and left her in the stable, and then walked back to the palace, jostled all the way. The crowd was the same strange mix of people. There were beggars and paupers and ill-doers in rags and shabby old livery who were there to shout and perhaps collect a few coppers for their hired loyalty. There were working men and women, young apprentices, artisans and market people. There were the serious black-coated preachers of the independent churches and sectaries, and there were the well-to-do merchants and City men who would not fight themselves, but whose hearts were in the fight. There were sailors from the ships in port, shouting for Parliament since they blamed the king and his French wife for the dangers of the Dunkirk pirates, and there were members of the London trained bands, some of them trying to impose order and find their men, and others running wild and shouting that they would die to defend the rights of Parliament. This motley crowd had a motley chant which ranged from the catcalls and boos of those who did not know what they cared for, to the regular call of those who knew their cause: 'No bishops! No queen!', and the new call which had come about since the king had taken a sword into the House of Commons: 'Privilege! Privilege!'

John fought his way to the front of the mob at the gates to the palace of Whitehall and shouted, over the noise, to the guard.

'John Tradescant! The king's gardener.'

The man shifted slightly, and John ducked under the pike and went in.

The old palace of Whitehall was the most disorganised of all the royal palaces, a jumble of buildings and courts and gardens, dotted with statuary and fountains and alive with birdsong. John, hoping to find a face he knew, made his way towards the royal apartments and then was brought short as he rounded a corner and nearly collided with the queen herself.

She was running, her cape flying behind her, her jewel box in her hands. Behind her came the king, carrying his own travelling desk of papers and a dozen maidservants and manservants, each burdened with whatever they had been able to snatch up. Behind them came two royal nursemaids, running with the two royal babies in their arms, the five-year-old Princess Elizabeth trotting to keep up, and the two young princes, James and Charles, lagging in the rear.

John dropped to his knee as she saw him but she rushed towards him and he jumped to his feet as she pushed her jewel box at him.

'Gardener Tradescant!' she cried. 'Take this!' She turned to the king. 'We must wait!' she insisted. 'We must face the rabble! We must face them down!'

The king shook his head and motioned for her to go on. Unwillingly, she went before him. 'I t . . . tell you they have run mad!' he said. 'We must get out of the C . . . City! There's not a loyal heart here. They have all run m . . . mad. We must go to Hampton Court and c . . . c . . . consider what to do! We must summon soldiers and take advice.'

'We are running like fools from our own shadows!' she shrieked at him. 'We must face them and face them down or we will spend the rest of our life on the run.'

'We are l . . . lost!' he shouted. 'L . . . lost! D'you think I want to see you dragged before the b . . . bar and impeached for treason? D'you think I want to see your h . . . h . . . head on a pike? D'you think I want to see the rabble take y . . . you, and the children, t . . . take you now?'

John joined the train of servants running behind them and followed them to the stables. All the way the quarrel between the king and queen grew more inarticulate as her French accent deepened with her temper and his stammer grew worse with his fear. When they reached the stable yard she was beside herself.

'You are a coward!' she spat at him. 'You will lose this city forever if you leave it now. It is easier to run away than to retake. You must show them that you are not afraid.'

'Ha . . . Hi . . . I fear nothing!' He drew himself up. 'N . . . Nothing! But I must have you safe and the children safe before I can m . . . make m . . . my m . . . move. It is your safety, Madam, that I am securing now. For myself I care nothing! N . . . ha . . . N . . . Nothing!'

John pressed forward and put the jewel box on the coach floor. He was reminded of the king's odd mixture of shyness and boastfulness. Even now, with a mob hammering on the doors of the palace, the two of them were playing out their parts in a masque. Even now they did not seem to be completely real. John looked around, the servants were like an audience at a great play. No-one urged a course of action, no-one spoke. The king and queen were the only actors; and their script was a great romance of danger and heroism and lost causes and sudden flights. John felt his heart pounding at the noise of the crowd outside and knew the deep visceral fear of a mob. He had a sudden vision of them breaking down the gates and tumbling into the stable yard. If they found the queen beside her travelling coach with her jewel box beside her, anything could happen. The whole power of the royal family which the old Queen Elizabeth had so powerfully cultivated depended on the creation and maintenance of distance and magic and glamour. Let the people once see the queen swearing at their king like a French lace-seller, and the game would be up.

'I will see you s . . . safe at Hampton Court and then I will return and crush these traitors,' Charles swore.

'You shall crush them now!' she shrieked. 'Now, before they gain their strength. You shall face them and defy them and destroy them or I swear I shall leave this kingdom and never see it again! They know how to respect a princess of the blood in France!'

At once the mood of the scene shifted. The king took her hand and bowed over it, his silky hair falling to shield his face. 'N . . . never say it,' he said. 'You are q . . . queen of this country, queen of all the h . . . hearts. This is a faithful country, they l . . . love you, I love you. Never even th . . . think of leaving me.'

There was renewed shouting at the door. John, forgetting that he should stay silent, could not bear to see them taken like a pair of runaway servants in the stable yard. 'Your Majesty!' he urged. 'You must either prepare for a siege or get the coach out! The crowd will be upon you in a moment!'

The queen looked to him. 'My faithful Gardener Tradescant!' she exclaimed. 'Stay with us.'

'G . . . Get up at the back,' the king ordered. 'Y . . . You shall escort us t . . . to safety.' John gaped at him. The only thing he had thought to do was to bring the two of them to a sense of urgency.

'Your Majesty?' he asked.

The king handed the queen into the coach where the two little princes, Charles and James, white-faced and silent, were waiting, their eyes like saucers with terror. Then the nursemaids and the babies bundled in and the king climbed in himself. John slammed the door on them. He wanted to tell them that he could not possibly go with them but he heard the rising volume of the crowd at the gates and he was afraid that they might argue with him, command his service, question his loyalty, delay again.

John stepped back from the coach, waiting for it to draw away; but it did not move. Nobody would do anything without a specific order and the king and queen were arguing again inside.

'Oh! Damnation! Drive on!' John shouted, taking command in the absence of any authority, and swung himself up beside the footmen clinging on the back. 'Westward, to Hampton Court. And drive steadily. Don't for God's sake run anyone down. But don't stop!'

Even then the footmen hesitated at the stable doors.

'Open the doors!' John shouted at them, his temper at breaking point.

They leaped to obey the first clear order they had heard all day and the great wooden doors swung open.

At once the men and women in the very front of the crowd fell back, as the doors opened up and the coach pulled out. John saw they were taken aback at the sudden movement of the doors, at the progress of the fine horses, and the wealth and richness of the gilding on the royal coach. The king's ornate carriage with the plumes of feathers on each roof corner, and the huge high-stepping Arab horses harnessed with tack of red leather and gold studs, still had the mystique of power, divine power, even with a traitorous Papist queen inside. But those in the front could not get back very far; they were held steady by the weight of the crowd behind them, still pushing forward.

The crowd had pikes but they were using them as banners, not yet as weapons. On each one was tied a white flag scrawled with the word 'Liberty!' and they jogged them up and down at the windows of the coach. John prayed that the queen kept her face turned down and for once in her life kept quiet. The prestige of the king might get them safely through the mob if she did not antagonise them.

John heard a frightened child crying from inside the coach. 'Drive on!' he ordered the coachman above the noise of the crowd. 'Go steady!', and he shouted as loud as he could: 'Make way for the king! For the rightful king!'

'Liberty!' someone yelled, jabbing a pike dangerously close to his face.

'Liberty and the king!' John replied, and heard another voice at once echo the new slogan. The footman beside him flinched as someone spat. 'Stay still, you fool, or they will drag you down,' John muttered.

At any moment the mood of the crowd could change from boisterous protest to murder. John looked over the roof of the carriage to where the streets narrowed for the way out of town.

'Make way for the rightful king!' John shouted.

The crowd grew denser at the crossroads. 'Keep going!' John yelled at the coachman. He had an absolute certainty that if they stopped, even for a moment, the doors would be pulled open and the royal family dragged from the coach and torn apart on the very street. Once the mob learned that they could stop the king in his carriage, then they would know they could do whatever they wished. All that was holding them back was the old superstitious belief in the king's power, the divinity of kingship that King James had preached and that Charles so passionately believed. The crowd kept reaching towards the coach as it crawled slowly past them but their hands would drop back as if they feared a burning from the gold paintwork. If they touched and snatched just once, then they would all know that the king was not a god, a vengeful god. If they found the courage to touch just once, they would snatch at everything.

'Keep back,' John shouted. 'Make way for the king!'

Everything depended on the coach maintaining the painfully slow walking pace, and never checking, and never stopping, all the way westwards where the sun shone on the water in the open sewers, like a pointer to safety.

Someone pulled at his coat, nearly hauling him off balance. John grabbed tighter at the footman's strap and looked down. It was a woman, her face contorted with rage. 'Liberty!' she cried. 'Death to the Papists! Death to the Papist queen!'

'Liberty and the king!' John shouted back. He tried to smile at her and felt his lips stick on his dry teeth. As long as the queen kept her face hidden! 'Liberty and the king.'

The carriage lurched over the cobbles. The crowd was thicker but the road further ahead was clear. Someone threw a handful of mud at the coach door but the crowd was too dense for them to start stoning, and though the pikes still jogged to the cry of 'Liberty!' they were not yet aimed towards the glass of the windows.

As the road went on, out of town, the crowd thinned, as John had hoped it would. Most of these people had homes or market stalls or even businesses in the City, there was nothing to be gained by following the coach out along the West Way. Besides, they were out of breath and tiring of the sport.

'Let's open the doors!' someone exclaimed. 'Open the doors and see this queen, this Papist queen. Let's hear her prayers, that they're so keen that we should learn!'

'Look!' John yelled as loud as he could. 'An Irishman!' He pointed back the way they had come. 'Going into the palace! An Irish priest!'

With a howl the mob turned back and ran, slipping and sliding over the cobbles back towards the palace, chasing their own nightmares.

'Now drive on!' John yelled at the driver. 'Let them go!'

The carriage gave a great lurch as the driver whipped the horses and they leaped forward, bumping on the cobbles. John clung like a barnacle on the back of the great coach, swaying on the leather straps, and ducked his head down as the wind blowing down the street whisked his hat away.

When they reached the outskirts of London the streets were quiet, the people either boarded inside their houses and praying for peace, or roaming in the city. John felt the slackening of tension around his throat and he loosened his grip on the footman's strap and rocked with the sway of the coach all the way to Hampton Court.

The king was not expected at Hampton Court. There was nothing ready for the royal family. The royal beds and furniture, rugs and pictures were all left at Whitehall. The family stepped down before the solidly closed great doors of the palace and there was not even a servant to open up for them.

John had a sense that the whole world was collapsing around him. He hesitated and looked towards his monarch. The king leaned back against the dirty wheel of the coach, as if he were exhausted.

'I did not expect this sort of welcome!' Charles said mournfully. 'The doors of my own palace closed to me!'

The queen looked pleadingly at Tradescant. 'What shall we do?'

John felt an irritable sense of responsibility. 'Wait here,' he said. 'I'll find someone.'

He left the royal coach before the imposing grand front doors and went around to the back. The kitchens were in their usual careless state; the whole household always took a holiday during the king's absence.

'Wake up,' John said, putting his head around the door. 'The king, queen and royal family are outside waiting to be let in.'

It was as if he had set off a fire-ship among the cockle boats at Whitby. There was a stunned silence and then instantaneous uproar.

'For God's sake get the front door open and let him in,' John said, and went back to the courtyard.

The king was leaning back against the coach surveying the high, imposing roofs of the palace as if he had never seen them before. The queen was still seated in the carriage. Neither of them had moved since John had left them, although the children were whimpering inside the coach and one of the nursemaids was praying.

John pinned a smile on his face and stepped forward and bowed. 'I am sorry for the poor welcome,' he said. As he spoke the great doors creaked open and a frightened-looking footman peeped out. 'There's a couple of cooks here, and a household of servants,' John said reassuringly. 'They'll make Your Majesties comfortable enough.'

At the sight of a servant the queen brightened. She rose to her feet and waited for the footman to hand her down from the carriage. The children followed her.

The king turned to John. 'I thank you for the service you have given us this day. We were glad of your escort.'

John bowed. 'I am glad to see Your Majesty safe arrived,' he said. At least he could say that with a clear conscience, he thought. He was indeed glad to get them safe out of London. He could not have stood by and seen the queen and the royal princes pulled out of their carriage by a mob, any more than he could have watched Hester and the children abused.

'Go and see that there are r . . . rooms made ready for us,' the king commanded.

John hesitated. 'I should return home,' he said. 'I will give orders that everything shall be done as you wish, and then go to my home.'

The king made that little gesture with his hand which signified 'No.'

John hesitated.

'S . . . stay until we have some order here,' the king said coolly. 'Tell them to prepare our p . . . privy chambers and a dinner.'

John could do nothing but bow and walk carefully backwards from the king's presence and go to do his bidding.

There was only so much that could be done. There was only one decent bed in the house fit for them; and so the king, queen, and the two royal princes were forced to bed down together in one bed, in the only aired linen in the whole palace. There was a dinner which was ample, but hardly royal; and no golden plate and cups for the service. The trappings of monarchy – the tapestries, carpets, gold plate and jewels, even the richly embroidered bed linen that always travelled with the king in his great progresses around the country – were still at Whitehall. All that was ever left in the empty palaces was second-rate goods, and Hampton Court was no exception. The queen ate off pewter with an air of shocked disdain.

Dinner was served by the kitchen staff and the lowly gentlemen of the household who maintained the palace in the king's absence. They served it as it should be done, on bended knee, but all the ceremony in the world could not conceal that it was plain bread and meat on pewter plates on a plain board table.

'You will escort the queen and I to Windsor tomorrow,' the king said, when he had finished eating. 'And from thence to Dover.'

Tradescant, who was seated at a lower table down the hall, got up from his bench and dropped to his knee on the stale rushes on the floor. 'Yes, Your Majesty.' He kept his head down so that he showed no surprise.

'See that the horses are ready at dawn,' the king ordered.

The royal family rose from their places at the top table and left the great hall by the door at the back of the dais. Their withdrawing room would be cold and smoky with a chimney which did not properly draw.

'Are they running for it?' one of the ushers asked John as he rose from his knees. 'All of them?'

John looked appalled. 'They cannot do so!'

'Did they need to run from London? Like cowards?'

'How can you tell? The mood of the rabble around Whitehall was angry enough. There were moments when I feared for their lives.'

'The rabble!' the man jeered. 'They could have thrown them a purse of gold and turned them around in a moment. But if they run from London, will they run from the country? Is that why they're going to Dover? To take a ship to France? And what will become of us then?'

John shook his head. 'This morning I was taking leave of my wife in my stable yard at Lambeth,' he said. 'I hardly know where I am, let alone what is to become of the king and the queen and their kingdoms.'

'Well I bet you they run for it,' the young man said cheerfully. 'And good riddance,' he added under his breath, and then snapped his fingers at his dog and left the hall.

It was a long, cold journey to Dover; the royal family were muffled up inside the coach but John was standing in the footman's place behind, holding on to the strap. By the time the coach rumbled in to Dover castle John was clinging on with fingers that were blue, his eyes running with tears from the cold wind in his face, every bone in his face aching as if he had an ague. From his place on the back of the coach he had heard, over the rumble of the wheels, the queen steadily complaining, all the way down the long frosty roads.

They slept that night in Dover castle, in better comfort; and then lingered undecided for a week. First they were waiting for news, then deciding to sail to France, missing the tide, changing their minds, waiting for more news. Courtiers slowly reassembled from the rout of London, noblemen were recalled from their country seats. Everyone had different advice, everyone was listened to with kingly courtesy, no-one could agree, no-one could act. Eleven-year-old Princess Mary, setting sail to live with her bridegroom in Holland, joined them during the week that they hesitated, havering between one choice and another, and found that the queen, her mother, was very bitter with her daughter for marrying a Protestant and leaving the family in such distress. Princess Mary made no undutiful replies to her mother, but sulked in eloquent silence.

A couple of heavy bags arrived at dawn from the Tower of London and John assumed, but did not ask, from the dour expression of the guard who never let them out of his sight, that the king was sending the country's treasure overseas with his wife and that once again the most precious stones in England would be hawked around the moneylenders in Europe.

The king and queen finally came to a decision to separate. Princess Mary was bound for Holland in one ship, the queen and the three babies were to set sail for France in another: the *Lion*. The two princes – Charles and James – and the king were to stay in England and find a solution to the demands of Parliament. John and the other attendants waited at a distance on the quayside as the royal couple forced themselves to the brink of parting. The king held both her hands and kissed them tenderly.

'You will not yield one inch to them,' the queen said, her voice demanding and penetrating so that every man on the quayside could hear how the king of England was hag-ridden. 'You will not make one concession. They must be brought to heel. They must know their master. You will not even speak with them without keeping me informed.'

Charles kissed her hands again. 'No,' he promised. 'M . . . My love, my dear love. I will not have a m . . . moment when I do not think of you.'

'Then think that I will never be able to come back until the traitor Pym is executed for treason,' she said fiercely. 'And think of your son and his inheritance which must be passed to him entire. And I shall raise such an army in Europe that if they will not agree they will be destroyed! So make no concessions, Charles, I will not permit it!'

'My dear, d . . . dear love,' he said quietly.

He raised his head from her hands and she kissed him full on the mouth as if to pledge him to an oath.

'Don't forget!' she said passionately. 'We have lost too much already by your weakness! Not one concession without my agreement. You must tell them that *they* will have to concede to us: Church, army, and Parliament. I am a queen, not a market trader to huckster over the price. Not one concession.'

'God speed, m . . . my love,' he said tenderly.

She smiled at him at last. 'God bless you,' she said. Without thinking of the effect it would have on the king's waiting servants, she made the sign of the cross, the dreadful Papist gesture, over his head; and Charles bowed his head beneath the sign of the Anti-Christ.

Henrietta Maria picked up her full silk skirts and went carefully up the gangplank to the sailing ship. 'And don't forget,' she called, raising her voice from the ship. 'No concessions!'

'No, my love,' the king said sadly. 'I would d . . . die rather than disappoint you.'

The ship moved away from the quayside and the king called for his horse. He mounted and rode alone, up the steep cliffs behind the little town, keeping the queen's sail in sight, riding and waving his hat to her until the little ship was vanished into the pale mist lying sluggishly on the waves, and there was nothing for God's anointed monarch to do but ride slowly and sadly back to Dover castle and write to his wife promising that he would always do whatever she thought best.

John subtracted himself carefully from the men who surrounded the king as they returned to break their fast in Dover castle. He ordered a horse from the tavern, and when he was ready to leave went to seek the king.

'With Your Majesty's permission I will go to my home,' he said carefully. He saw at a glance that the king was in one of his moods of high drama. John did not want to be the audience to one of the tragic speeches. 'I promised my wife I would only be away a matter of hours, and that was weeks ago. I must return.'

The king nodded. 'You may travel w . . . with me for I am going to London.'

'Back to the City?' John was astounded.

'I· shall see. I shall see. Perhaps it is n . . . not too late. Perhaps we can agree. The queen would be pleased, d . . . don't you think, if my next letter to her came from my palace at Whitehall?'

'I am sure everyone would be pleased if you could reclaim your palace by agreement,' John said carefully.

'Or I could go to B . . . Bristol,' the king said. 'Or north?'

John bowed. 'I shall pray for Your Majesty.'

'I hope you will do . . . do more than that. I hope you will be with me.'

There was an awkward silence. 'In these troubled times . . .' John began.

'In these troubled times a man must bid farewell to his wife and then do his duty,' the king said flatly. 'P . . . Painful duty. As I have done.'

John bowed.

'You may go and bid her farewell and then j . . . join me.'

John bowed again, thinking rapidly of how he could escape from this service. 'I am only a gardener,' he said. 'I doubt that I can assist Your Majesty better than by keeping your palaces in beauty. And when the queen returns I would want her to have a pretty garden to greet her.'

The king softened at that, but he had the needy anxiety of a man who hates to be left alone. The loss of the queen made him cling to anyone, and John's presence was a reassuring reminder of the days of gardens and masques and royal progresses and loyal speeches. 'You shall s . . . stay with me,' he said. 'I shall send you back to the garden when I have more men about me. In the meantime you shall write your f . . . farewell to your wife and join me. I am separated from my wife – you would not w . . . wish to be more happy than your king?'

Tradescant could see no escape. 'Of course not, Your Majesty.'

He sent Hester a note before they left Dover.

Dear Hester,

I am commanded by His Majesty to stay with him until he takes up his new quarters, wherever they may be. We are travelling northwards at present and I will return home as soon as I am permitted, and write to you if not. Please keep my children and rarities safe. And preserve your own safety. If you think it best, you may store the rarities in the place you know, and take the children to Oatlands. These are troubled times and I cannot advise you at this distance. I wish I were with you. If I were free from my duty to my king, I would be with you.

He did not dare to say more for fear of someone stealing and opening the letter. But he hoped she would read between the lines and understand his reluctance to travel with the king and the two princes, and his deep anxiety that none of them, least of all the king, seemed to know where they should go or what they should do next.

They rode north, still uncertain. The king was instantly diverted by the pleasure of being on the road. He loved to ride and liked being free of the formality of the court. He spoke of the time that he and the Duke of Buckingham had ridden across Europe – from England to Spain – without a courtier or a servant between them. He spoke of his present journey as if it was the same playful piece of adventure and the two young princes caught his mood. Prince James and Prince Charles for once in their lives were allowed to ride alongside their father, as his companions, and the country people lined the roadsides as they entered market towns and called out their blessings on the handsome bareheaded king and the two charming boys.

The courtiers, returning from their country houses and from Whitehall, joined the train, and the whole trip became an adventure: riding through the spring countryside and staying each night in a hunting lodge or a fine Tudor mansion.

A court formed around the king, and many of the loyal gentlemen dug deep into their own fortunes to support him, and tried not to begrudge the cost of the hunting and the dancing and the music which the king had to have wherever he went. Even so, there were many debts that remained unpaid. Many gentlemen stayed at home, although they were summoned more than once; many did not send money. When the king, tired of provincial minstrels, sent for the court musicians they sent back a polite letter saying they would come if they could, but since they had not been paid any wages for months they could not afford to attend His Majesty without payment in advance. The king had to do without his own musicians for the first time in his life. There was no money to pay them, neither in advance nor in arrears.

John said nothing, and did not remind the king that his wages also had not been paid since the end of last summer when he had been appointed gardener at Oatlands in his father's place and also given the care of the Wimbledon garden. He was not following the king for gold, after all. He was not following him for love nor loyalty either. He was neither mercenary nor courtier. He was following him because the king refused to release him, and John was not yet ready to insist on his freedom. The habit of obedience was ingrained in him, he was not yet ready fully to rebel. Loyalty to the king was like honouring his father whose loyalty had never wavered; honouring his father was one of the ten commandments. John was trapped by habit and by faith.

He did not cease to try for his release. He spoke to the king in the stable yard of a pretty hunting lodge that they had commandeered for the week. Charles was out hunting on a borrowed horse and was in light-hearted mood. John checked the tightness of the girth under the saddle flap and looked up at his king.

'Your Majesty, do I have your permission to go to my home now?'

'You can ride with us to Theobalds,' the king said casually. 'It was one of your father's gardens, was it not?'

'His first royal garden,' John said. 'I didn't know the court was moving again. Are we going back to London?'

The king smiled. 'Who can say?' he said mysteriously. 'The game is not even opened yet, John. Who can say what moves there are to b . . . be made?'

'It is not a game to me,' John burst out incautiously. 'Nor to the men and women that are drawn into it.'

The king turned a frosty look down on him. 'Then you will have to be a reluctant player,' he said. 'A s . . . s . . . sulky pawn. For if I am prepared to gamble my future with daring then I expect the lesser men to throw in their all for me.'

John bit his lip.

'Especially those who were b . . . born and b . . . bred into my service,' the king added pointedly.

John bowed.

The stay at Theobalds brought them closer to London, but no closer to an agreement. Almost every day a messenger came and went from the palace at Theobalds to Parliament at Westminster but no progress was made. The king was certain that the country was solidly behind him – in his journey northwards from Dover people had brought invalids to him at every stopping point and the mere touch of his hand had cured them. Every loyal address at every inn and staging post assured him that the country was solidly his. No-one had the courage to point out that anyone who disagreed with the king was likely to stay away from his progress, and no-one reminded the king that at every major town there had also been petitions from common people and gentry begging him to acknowledge the rights of Parliament and to reform his advisors, and live at peace with the Scots and with his Parliament.

From London came the rumours that the Lord Mayor's trained bands were out drilling and practising every Sunday and they would fight to the death to defend the liberty of Parliament and the freedom of the city of London. The city was solidly for Parliament and against the king and was preparing itself for a siege, entrenching both to the west and north. Every workman was bidden to dig great ditches which would run all around the city, and women, girls, and even ladies saw it as their patriotic duty to ride out on Sundays and holidays and help the men dig. There was a great wave of enthusiasm for the Parliamentary cause against the impulsive, arrogant, and possibly Papist king. There were great fears of an army coming from Ireland to put him back inside his capital city and to force Roman Catholicism back on a country which had only been free of the curse for less than a hundred years. Or if the king did not bring in the Irish then he might bring in the French, for it was well-known that his wife was openly recruiting for a French army to subdue the city and its supporters. Chaotic, excited, fearful, London prepared itself for siege against hopeless odds, and decided to choose a martyr's death.

'We go to York,' the king decided. John waited to see if he would be released from royal service.

The king's heavy-lidded gaze swept over the men in the stable yard, saddling up their horses for the ride. 'You will all come too,' he said.

John mounted his horse and edged it through the courtiers to the king's side.

'I should like to go to Wimbledon,' he said cunningly. 'I want to make sure that all is well there. So that it is fit for the queen when she comes home again.'

Charles shook his head and John, glancing sideways, saw that his king was beaming. The king was enjoying the sense of action and adventure, the end of the effeminate routine of masques and plays and poetry of the peacetime court.

'W . . . We have no time for g . . . gardens now!' he laughed. 'M . . . March on, Tradescant.'

John wondered for a moment if there was anything he could say to abstract himself from the small train, and then shrugged his shoulders. The king had a whim that Tradescant should stay with him, but the whim would pass, as did all royal whims. When his attention was diverted elsewhere Tradescant would ask and receive permission to leave.

John pulled his horse up and fell in at the rear of the royal train as they trotted down the great avenue of Theobalds Park, through the sea of golden daffodils between the trees. He thought for a moment of his father, and how his father would have loved the ripple of cold wind through the yellow bobbing heads, and then he realised with a smile that his father had probably had a hand in planting them. As the party trotted out through the great gates John looked back at the avenue of trees and the sea of gold washing around their trunks and thought that his father's legacy to the country might last longer than that of the royal master he had served.

When they reached York in mid-March the king and his immediate friends settled in the castle, while the other courtiers and hangers-on found billets in all the inns and ale houses in the town. John lodged in the stables on a pallet bed in the hay store. After a few days when he had not been summoned he thought that the king had finished with his service and he might go home. He went to find the king in the main body of the castle. He was in his privy chambers, books and maps all around him.

'Your Majesty, I beg your pardon,' John said, putting his head around the door.

'I did not send for you,' the king said frostily.

John came no nearer. 'Spring is here, Your Majesty,' he said. 'I seek your permission to go and supervise the planting of the queen's gardens. She likes the flower gardens at Oatlands to be well-planted, and she wants fruits from her manor at Wimbledon. They need to be planted soon.'

The king softened at once at the mention of his wife.

'I would hate Her Majesty to be disappointed.'

'You shall go,' the king decided. He thought for a moment. 'After we have taken Hull.'

'Hull, Your Majesty?'

He beckoned Tradescant in and gestured him to shut the door against eavesdroppers. 'The queen bids me to make the garrison of Hull my own,' he said. 'So that I may have a strong port for our allies to send supplies. She has bought up half the armies of Europe, and her brother the king of France will aid us.'

John closed his eyes briefly at the thought of French Papist troops marching against the English Protestant Parliament.

'She wants us to take Hull for her – and so we will,' the king said simply. 'After that you can go home.'

John dropped to one knee. 'Your Majesty, may I speak freely?'

The king smiled his tender smile. 'Of course,' he said. 'All my people can speak to me freely, and in safety. I am their father, I am their only true friend.'

'A French army, a Papist army, will not aid your cause,' John said earnestly. 'There are many men and women in the country who do not understand the rights and wrongs of this quarrel between you and Parliament; but they will see a French army as their enemy. People will speak ill of the queen if they think she has summoned the French against her own people, English people. Those that love her and love you now will not accept a French army. You will lose their love and trust.'

Charles looked thoughtful as if he had never had such counsel before. 'You believe this, Gardener Tradescant?'

'I know these people,' John urged. 'They are simple people. They don't always understand arguments, they often cannot read. But they can see the evidence of their own eyes. If they see a French army marching on the English Parliament they will think we have been invaded and that their right course of action is to fight against the French. My own father went with your friend, the Duke of Buckingham, to make war against the French. They have been our enemies for years. Country people will think that the French have invaded us, and they will take up arms against them.'

'I had not seen it that way.' Charles looked undecided. 'But I must have an army and I must have munitions and H ... Hull has the mightiest store of weapons outside of London ...'

'Only if you have to fight a war,' John said persuasively. 'You only need arms if you fight. But if you could come to an agreement ...'

'I l ... long to come to an agreement,' the king said. 'I have sent them m ... message after message offering talks and concessions.'

John thought of the queen's tempestuous demands that the Members of Parliament should be hanged before she would return to her city.

'I shall take Hull, and then I shall be able to make concessions,' the king said decisively.

John felt the sense of frustration that all the king's advisors were learning to endure.

'If you came to an agreement you would not have to take Hull,' he pointed out. 'If you could agree with Parliament, then the country would be at peace and there would be no need for a fort, Hull or any other. There would be no need for a position of strength.'

'She wants me to take Hull,' the king said stubbornly. 'And it is mine own. I am claiming nothing but what is mine by right.'

Tradescant bowed. When the king started speaking of his rights it was difficult to make any headway. By right everything in the four kingdoms was his; but in practice the countries were ruled by all sorts of compromises. Once the king assumed the voice he used in his masques and spoke grandly of his rights nothing could be agreed.

'When do we go to Hull?' John asked resignedly.

The king smiled at him, a flash of the old merriment in his eyes. 'I shall send the P . . . Prince James in to Hull on a visit,' he said. 'They cannot refuse a visit from the prince. He shall g . . . go with his cousin, the Elector Palatine. And then I shall f . . . follow him. They cannot separate father and son. And once he is inside he will open the gates to me. And once I am there –' he snapped his fingers '– it is mine! As easily and peacefully as that.'

'But what if . . .'

The king shook his head. 'No. N . . . No carping, Tradescant,' he said. 'The city of Hull is all for me, they will throw open the gates at the sight of Prince James, and then when we are installed we can make what terms we wish with Parliament.'

'But Your Majesty . . .'

'You may go now,' the king said pleasantly. 'Ride with me at n . . . noon tomorrow to Hull.'

They left late, of course, and idled along the road. By the time they finally arrived on a little rise before the town it was getting cold with the sharp coldness of a northern spring afternoon, and growing dark, getting on for dinner time. The king had brought thirty cavalrymen, carrying his standards and pennants, and there were ten young gentlemen riding with him as well as Tradescant and a dozen servants.

As they came towards the city Tradescant saw the great gates swing closed, and his heart sank.

'What's this?' the king demanded.

'A damned insult!' one of the young men cried out. 'Let's ride at the gates and order them open.'

'Your Majesty . . .' Tradescant said, bringing his horse a little closer. The young courtiers scowled at the gardener riding among them. Tradescant pressed on. 'Perhaps we should ride by, as if we never intended coming in at all.'

'What use would that be?' the king demanded.

'That way, no-one could ever say that an English town closed its gates to you. It did not close its gates because we were not trying to enter.'

'Nonsense!' the king said easily. One or two of the young men laughed aloud. 'That's the way to teach them b . . . boldness. Prince James's party will open the gates to us if the governor of Hull does not.'

The king took off his hat and rode down towards the town. The sentries on the wall looked down on him and John saw, with a sense of leaden nausea, that they were casually pointing their crossbows towards him, their monarch, as if he were an ordinary highwayman coming towards the city walls.

'Please God no fool fires by accident,' John said as he followed.

'Open the gates to the king of England!' one of the courtiers shouted up at the sentries.

There was a short undignified scuffle and the governor of Hull, Sir John Hotham himself, appeared on the walls.

'Your Majesty!' he exclaimed. 'I wish we had known of your coming.'

Charles smiled up at him. 'It does not m . . . matter, Sir John,' he said. 'Open the gates and let us in.'

'I cannot, Your Majesty,' Sir John said apologetically. 'You are too many for my little town to house.'

'We don't m . . . mind,' the king said. 'Open the gates, I would see my son.'

'There are too many of you, it is too large and too warlike a party for me to let in at this late hour,' Sir John said.

'We are not warlike!' Charles exclaimed. 'Just a small party of pleasure-seekers.'

'You are armed,' the governor pointed out.

'Only my usual g . . . guards,' the king said. He was still smiling but John could see the whiteness around his mouth and his hand trembling slightly on the reins. His horse shifted uneasily. The royal guards stared, stony-faced, at the sentries on the towers of Hull.

'Please, Your Majesty,' Sir John Hotham pleaded. 'Enter as a friend if you must enter. Bring in just a few of your men if you come peacefully.'

'This is my t . . . town!' the king shouted. 'Do you . . . do you . . . do you deny your king the right to enter his own town?'

Sir John closed his eyes. Even from the road before the gate the king's party could see his grimace. John felt a deep sense of sympathy for the man, torn between loyalties just like himself, just like every man in the kingdom.

'I do not deny Your Majesty the right to enter into your town,' the governor said carefully. 'But I do deny these men the right to enter.' His gesture took in the thirty guards. 'Bring in a dozen to guard Your

Majesty and you shall dine with the prince in the great chamber this night! I shall be proud to welcome you.'

One of the courtiers edged his horse up to the king. 'Where is the prince's party?' he said. 'They should have thrown open the gates to us by now.'

Charles shot him an angry look. 'Where indeed?' He turned back to the governor of Hull. 'Where is m . . . my son? Where is Prince James?'

'He is at his dinner,' the governor said.

'Send for him!'

'Your Majesty, I cannot. I have been told he is not to be disturbed.'

Charles spurred his horse abruptly forward. 'Have d . . . d . . . done with this!' he shouted up at the governor. 'Open the gates! That is an order from your k . . . king!'

The man looked down. His white face had gone paler still. 'I may not open the gates to thirty armed men,' he said steadily. 'I have my orders. As my king you are always welcome. But I do not open the gates of my town to any army.'

One of the king's courtiers rode forward and shouted at the people whose curious faces were peering over the tops of the defensive walls. 'This is the king of England! Throw your governor down! He is a traitor! You must obey the king of England!'

No-one moved, then a surly voice shouted, 'Aye, and he's the king of Scotland and Ireland too and what justice do they have there?'

The king's great horse reared and shied as he pulled it back. 'Then b . . . be damned to you!' the king shouted. 'I shall not forget this, John Hotham! I shall n . . . not forget that you locked me out of my own town!'

He wheeled the horse around and flung it into a gallop down the road, the guards thundering behind him, the courtiers, servants and John with them. He did not pull up till his horse was blown and then they turned and looked back down the road. In the distance they could see the gates finally open, the drawbridge come down, and a small party of horsemen ride out, following in their tracks.

'Prince James,' the king said. 'Ten minutes too l . . . late.'

The king's party waited while the horsemen rode nearer and nearer and then pulled up.

'Where the devil were you, sir?' the king demanded of his nephew, the Elector Palatine, who had led the party.

'I am sorry, Your Majesty,' the young man replied stolidly. 'We were at our dinner and did not know you were outside the gates until Sir John came to us just now and said you had ridden away.'

'You were supposed to open the g ... gates to me! Not idle with your no ... noses in the trough!'

'We were not sure you were coming. You were due before dinner. You said you would come in the afternoon. We gave up waiting for you. I thought the governor would have opened the gates to you himself.'

'But he refused! And there was no-one to force him, b ... b ... because you were at your dinner, as usual!'

'I'm sorry, Uncle,' the young man replied.

'You will be sorrier yet!' the king said. 'For now I have been refused admittance to one of my t ... t ... towns as well as being banned from my City! You have done evil, evil work this day!' He turned on his son. 'And you, J ... James! Did you not know that your father was outside the gates?'

The prince was only eight years old. 'No, sire,' he said. His little voice was scarcely more than a thread in the cold evening air.

'You have disappointed your f ... father very much this day,' Charles said gloomily. 'Pray to G ... God that we have not taught disloyal and wicked men the lesson that they can defy me and travel in their w ... wicked ways and fear nothing.'

The prince's lower lip trembled slightly. 'I didn't know. I am sorry, sir. I didn't understand.'

'It was a harebrained plan from first to last,' the Elector said dourly. 'Whose was it? Any fool could see that it would not work.'

'It was m ... my plan,' the king said. 'But it required speed and decisiveness and c ... courage, and so it failed. How am I to succeed with such servants?' He surveyed them as if they were all equally to blame, then he turned his horse's head towards York and led them back to the city through the darkening twilight.

April 1642

When they got back to York John found a letter waiting for him from Hester. It had taken nearly a month to reach him instead of the usual few days. John, looking at the dirt-stained paper, realised that, along with loyalty and peace, everything else was breaking down too: the passage of letters, the enforcement of laws, the safety of the roads. He went to his pallet bed in the hayloft and sat where a crack in the shingles of the roof let in the cold spring light and he could see to read.

> *Dear Husband,*
>
> *I am sorry that you have gone away with the court and I understand that it was not possible for you to come and say farewell before you rode away. I have hidden the finest of the rarities where we agreed, and sent others into store at the Hurtes' warehouse where they have armed guards.*
>
> *The city is much disturbed. Every day there is drilling and marching and preparations for war. All the apprentice boys in Lambeth have given up their rioting around the streets and are now formed into trained bands and drilled every evening.*
>
> *Great ditches are dug outside London against the coming of a French or Spanish army and all of our gardeners have to go and take their turn with the digging whether they will or no.*
>
> *Food is scarce because the markets are closed as country people will not travel from their homes, and carters are afraid of meeting armies on the roads. I am feeding vagrants at the door with what we can afford but we are all doing very poorly. All the dried and bottled fruit is finished and I cannot get hold of hams to salt down for love nor money.*
>
> *These are strange and difficult times and I wish you could*

*be with us. I am keeping up my courage and I am caring for
your children as if they were mine own, and your rarities and
gardens also are safe.*

*I trust you will come home as soon as you are released from
service.*

God be with you,
Your wife,
Hester Tradescant.

John turned Hester's letter over in his hands. He had an odd, foolish
thought that if she were not his wife already, he would admire and like
this woman more than any other he knew. She cared for the things that
mattered most to him as if they were her own. It was a great comfort
to him to know that she was in his house, in his father's house, and that
his children and his rarities and his garden were under her protection. He
felt an unexpected tenderness towards the woman who could write of
the difficulty of the times and yet assure him that she was keeping up
her courage. He knew he would never love her as he had loved Jane.
He thought he would never love another woman again. But he could
not help but like and admire a woman who could take control of a
household as she had done, and confront the times that they lived in
as she did.

John rose to his feet, picked hay off his doublet, and went to his
dinner in the great hall of York castle.

The king and his noble friends, splendidly dressed, were already in
their place at the top table as John slipped into the hall. They were
dining off gold plate but there were only a dozen dishes. The county
was finding it hard to feed the appetite of the court, the provincial cooks
could not devise the dishes that Charles expected, and the farms and
markets were drained by the hunger of the enlarging, idle, greedy court.

'What news?' John asked, seating himself beside a captain of the guard
and helping himself from the shared dish placed in the middle of the
table.

The man looked at him sourly. 'None,' he said. 'His Majesty writes
letters to all who should be here, but the men who are loyal are already
here, and the traitors merely gain the time to make themselves ready.
We should march on London now! Why give them more time to prepare? We should put them to the sword and cut out this canker from
the country.'

John nodded, saying nothing, and bent over his meat and bread. It
was venison in a rich, dark sauce, very good. But the bread was coarse

and brown with gritty seeds. The rich wheat stores of Yorkshire were slowly emptying.

'While he is waiting I might go to my home,' John said thoughtfully.

'Lambeth?' the captain asked.

John nodded.

'You'd be seen as a traitor,' the man said. 'London is solid against the king, you'd be seen as a turncoat. You'd never plant another bulb for him.'

John grimaced. 'I'm doing next to nothing here.'

The man spat a piece of gristle on the rushes of the floor and one of the dogs squirmed forwards on its belly to lick it up. 'We're all doing next to nothing here,' he said. 'Nothing but waiting. It is war. All that is undecided is when and where.'

July 1642

All that spring and summer the country was waiting, like the captain, to see when and where. Every gentleman who could command men to follow him armed them, drilled them, and trained them, and then wrestled with his conscience night and day as to which side he should join. Brothers from the same great house might take opposite sides and divide the tenants and servants amongst them. The men of one village might come out as passionate royalists, the men of the village next door might side with Parliament. Local loyalties set their own traditions: villagers in the shadow of a great courtier's house that had felt the benefits of royal visits might sharpen their pikes and put a feather in their hat for the king. But villagers along roads from London where the news was easily spread, knew of the king's evasions and lies before the demands of Parliament. Those who prized their freedom of conscience, or those who were prosperous, free-thinking men, said that they would leave their work and their homes and take up the sword and fight against papacy, superstition and a king who was driven to sin by his bad advisors. Those whose habits of loyalty had gone deep with Elizabeth and deeper with James, and were far from the news of London, would turn out for the king.

In early July, as the court at York started to complain of the smell of drains and to fear the plague in the overcrowded town, the king announced that they were to march to Hull once again. This time the plan was better laid. The royalist George Digby was inside the garrison and he had forged a plan with Hotham the governor that the town would open its gates to a besieging force from the king, as long as the force was sufficiently impressive to justify a surrender.

Charles himself, dressed in green as for a picnic, rode out at the head of a handsome army on a warm summer day in early July. Tradescant rode at the tail end of the courtiers, and felt that he was the only man in the chattering, singing, light-hearted band who wished that he was elsewhere, and who doubted what they were about to do.

The city's defenders were bolstered by soldiers sent by the Scots. 'It makes no difference, we have an agreement,' Charles said contentedly.

The foot soldiers laid aside their pikes and got out spades. The royal army started to dig a ring of trenches around the city. 'They will surrender before we are more than a foot deep,' Charles assured his commanders. 'No need to dig the lines t . . . too straight or too well. If they do not surrender t . . . tonight, we will attack at dawn tomorrow. As long as we make a sh . . . show.'

As the soldiers dug their trenches, and as Charles broke his fast with some red wine and bread and cheese, a simple meal, as if he were out on a hunting trip, the great gates of Hull slowly opened.

'Already?' Charles laughed. 'Well, this is gracious!' He shaded his eyes with his hand, and then shook his head and stared harder. The bread fell from his hand, unregarded. Slowly, his laughter died.

A regular well-drilled army marched steadily out from the gates of the town towards them. The front flank kneeled down and the musketmen, steadying their weapons on the shoulders of the front rank, took aim and fired straight at the royalist army.

'Good G . . . God! What are they doing?' Charles cried.

'To horse!' one of the quicker courtiers shouted. 'Get the men saddled up! We've been betrayed!'

'It can't b . . . be . . .'

'Save the king!' Tradescant shouted. The royal guard, recalled to their duties, dropped their dinner in the dust and threw themselves on their horses.

'Mount! Your Highness!'

There was a dreadful scream as another volley of shots pocked the dry ground around them, and some of the musket balls found a target.

'Retreat! Retreat!' someone yelled.

All the orders of command were broken, as the men scattered, running like panicked sheep across the stubbly hayfields, pushing through hedges and trampling down the ripening corn. Still the defenders of Hull came forward, the first rank dropping to their knees and reloading as the second rank fired over their shoulders and then marched on. Then they too dropped down and reloaded as the men behind them fired.

It was an unstoppable progress, John thought. The king's soldiers did not even have fire lit ready for their muskets. They had no cannon ready, they did not even have their pikes. All they had were their trenching spades, and the men who had been digging had been the first to fall, toppling down into their shallow ditches, and screaming and crawling in the dirt.

At last someone found a trumpeter and ordered him to sound the retreat, but the foot soldiers were already up and running, running from the well-disciplined lethal ranks that were pouring, like little toy soldiers, out of the gates of Hull, firing and reloading, firing and reloading, like a monstrous toy which could not be stopped or escaped.

The king's guards surrounded his horse and galloped him away from the battle. Tradescant, his own horse snorting and pulling, looked wildly around him and then followed the king. His last view of the battlefield was a horse, its stomach blown open by a cannon shot from the walls of the city, and a lad, not much more than fourteen, trying to shelter behind the body.

'This is the end,' John found he was saying as his horse wearily found the road to York and followed in the train of the ragged retreat. 'This is the end. This is the end. This is the end.'

August 1642

For the king it was the beginning. The second humiliation outside the walls of Hull had decided him. The queen's continual demands that he confront and defeat his parliament drove him on. He issued a proclamation that every able-bodied man in the country should rally to his army, and on Eastcroft Common outside Nottingham he paraded three cavalry troops and a battalion of infantry while the herald read the proclamation of war. John, standing behind his master in the pouring rain, thought that never in the history of warfare did any campaign look less promising.

The rain dripped in a steady stream from his hat. No-one had thought to bring a spade and they could not get the royal standard to stand properly in the stony ground. John thought of his father and his last service to the Duke of Buckingham when he had followed him to Portsmouth and waited to take ship to the Ile de Rhé, knowing that the battle would be lost and that it was, in any case, a cause not worth fighting for. John thought of his father's face when he had met him, riding home on the Duke's cart, of the half-hidden look of relief in his eyes. And he understood at last what it was to follow a master unwillingly, when that master will lead you to death from pure folly.

John looked at the king, the feather in his hat drooping in the pouring rain, as he listened, nodding approval, to the herald shouting the proclamation into the wind which whipped his words away. John thought that his family had served the kings and their favourites for long enough, and that any debt owed, had surely by now been paid – by his father's heartbreak in the Ile de Rhé, and now, a generation later, by his own fear and despair before the walls of Hull.

In the rain outside Nottingham John found his determination to leave the king, whatever might be the outcome of his desertion. When they turned away from Eastcróft Common and went back to their billets in Nottingham, John turned southwards and rode alone to London without asking permission, without giving notice.

The royal standard blew down that night.

Hester, roused from sleep by the sound of a tap on the back door, ran downstairs, pulling on her nightgown, her heart pounding with fear. She peered out of the kitchen window into the pale greyness of the summer dawn and saw the familiar outline of John's head.

She threw open the door. 'John!'

He opened his arms to her, as if they were husband and wife in their hearts as well as by name, and Hester ran towards him and felt his arms come around her and hold her close.

He smelled of sweat and fatigue and the warm erotic male smell which lingered around his clothes when she brushed them. Hester felt herself long for his touch, and she tightened her grip around his back and held him close. He did not move away from her, he did not unclasp her hands. He held her as if he wanted her as she wanted him, and made no move to put her aside.

They stumbled together over the threshold, not releasing each other until they were at the fireside and the embers of the fire cast a warm glow. Then she leaned back, her arms still tightly around him, so that she could see his face.

She was shocked. The eight months of his absence had put grey into his hair at the temples and bags beneath his eyes. His beard was still a true dark brown, but matted and dirty, his face was smudged with dirt, his forehead carried new lines. He looked desperately weary. He looked like a man on the run.

'Was there a battle?' she asked, trying to understand what this mute look of suffering might mean.

He shook his head, released her, and dropped into the chair by the fireside. 'Not one that is worth mentioning,' he said bitterly. 'When they come to write the history of these days it will not have more than a line. We rode out like fools, thinking that we would win without having to fight. We went out like the chorus in one of his masques – all show and pretence. For all the good we were, we might as well have had swords of wood and helmets of painted paper.'

Hester was silent, shocked by his vehemence, and by the bitterness in his tone. 'Were you hurt?'

He shook his head. 'No – only in my pride.' He paused. 'Yes. Deep in my pride,' he corrected himself.

She did not know how to question him. She turned and threw some kindling on the fire and then some small twigs and broken branches of applewood. Coal was short in London, the Tradescants were living off their land.

He leaned forward to the blaze as if he were chilled to the heart. 'All along it has been like a masque,' he said, as if he was gripping some truth about the king at last. 'As if it were some pretty play with a script which everyone was to follow. The threat of Parliament, the flight from London, his parting with the queen when he rode along the cliffs waving to her ship and wept, the ride north to victory. It has all been a masque – beautifully costumed. But when the time came for the king to defeat his enemies –' He broke off.

'What happened?' Hester kneeled at the fire and kept her eyes on the flames, afraid to interrupt him.

'The chorus didn't arrive,' John said sourly. 'The engines which should show Jove descending or Neptune rising up from the sea failed to work. Instead of the gates of Hull opening and the governor coming out with the golden key on a velvet cushion and some poetry from Ben Jonson, it all went wrong. The gates opened and the soldiers came out and just went fire . . . reload . . . fire . . . reload . . . like dancers – but they weren't doing our dance. They were following another script. And . . . and . . .' He was silent for a moment. 'I don't know what the end of this play will be.'

'The king?' she asked in a little whisper.

'The king is sticking to his masque,' John said savagely. 'Act two was raising the royal standard. But the weather was all wrong. It should have been balmy skies or perhaps a bright comet overhead. Instead it poured with rain on him and we looked like sodden fools. But he will not realise that the scenes are going wrong. He thinks it is a rehearsal, he thinks it will be the greater on the night if it all goes wrong now.'

'And what of you?' she asked softly.

'I am finished with him,' John said. 'I am finished with his service. I went back into his service to please my father and because I longed to work on the great gardens which are in his gift, and besides, when I was a young man there was almost nowhere else to work but for the king or the court. But I will die in his service if I go on. I am a gardener and he would not give me leave to go and garden. He has to have everyone in the masque, everyone has to carry a standard or a spear. He will never cease with this until we are all dead, or all defeated, or all persuaded that he is the Lord's Anointed and can do no wrong.'

Hester quickly looked towards the kitchen door, but it was safely closed and all the household was still asleep.

'I saw my father go out to certain death in the service of the Duke of Buckingham, and I saw him ride home, spared only by the death of his master,' John continued. 'I saw his eyes on that day. He never recovered from the death of the Duke. He was never his own man again. The loss of the Duke lay like a shadow over our family, and my father was torn between relief that he had survived and grief that the Duke was dead.

'I swore then that I would never be like that, I swore I would never pledge myself to follow a man until death, and I meant it. I will never be a servant like that. Not even for the king. Especially not for this king, who cannot reward service and never says that he has had enough. He will not stop until every one of his servants is lying dead before him, and then he will expect a miracle from God himself to raise up more foot soldiers for his insatiable theatre. I will have no more of it. I can bear no more of it.'

'You won't join with Parliament?' Hester asked, aghast. 'Oh, John, you won't fight against the king?'

He shook his head. 'I'm not a turncoat. I won't fight against him. I've eaten his bread and he has called me his friend. I've seen him weep and I've kissed his hand. I won't betray him. But I won't play that part in this damned mockery.'

'Will you stay here, quiet at home with us?' she asked. She had a low sinking feeling in the pit of her belly. She knew that he would not.

'How can I?' he demanded of her. 'People know who I am. They will ask me who I serve. I won't deny him – I'm not a Judas. And he will send for me.' He nodded. 'Sooner or later he will realise that I am not at court and he will send for me again.'

'Then what shall we do?'

'We'll go to Virginia,' John said with decision. 'All of us. We'll take ship as soon as we can get a passage. We'll take what we can carry and leave the rest. Leave the house and the garden and even the rarities. We'll get out of this country and leave it to tear itself to pieces. I won't see it. I won't be here. I can't bear it.'

Hester sat very still and measured the despair in her husband's voice against her love for him, and her love for their home.

'Will you have a glass of ale?' she asked.

He lifted his gaze from the fire, as if he suddenly remembered where he was. 'Yes,' he said. 'And then let's go to bed. I have wanted you in my bed for night after long night, Hester. I have missed you, and thought of you here, missing me. I have wanted you and cursed the miles that were between us. And in the morning I shall see my children and we'll tell them that we are leaving.'

'You have wanted me?' she asked, very low.

He put his hand out and turned her face up to him, one gentle finger under her chin. 'Knowing that you are here has kept me going through one dark night after another,' he said. 'Knowing that you are here and that I have someone to come home to. Knowing that you will open your bed to me, and open your arms to me, and that whatever is going wrong all around me, I have somewhere that I can call my home.'

She could have moved forwards, she could have kneeled before him as he sat in his chair, he would have drawn her to him and on to his lap and he would have kissed her, as he had never yet kissed her, and they could have gone to bed as he wanted to do, and as she had wanted to do from the moment she had first seen him.

But Hester caught hold of her determination, forced herself to wait, and drew back from him, drew back and sat on her seat on the other side of the fireplace.

'Now wait a minute,' she said. 'Not so fast, husband. I cannot leave here.'

For a moment John did not hear her. He was so conscious of the fall of her nightgown, and of her dark hair only half-hidden by her cap, of the play of the firelight on her neck and the glimpse of her shoulder. 'What?'

'I cannot leave here,' she said steadily. 'This is my home.'

'You don't understand,' he said abruptly. 'I have made up my mind. I have to go. I cannot stay here, I will be torn apart by the two of them – king and Parliament. Parliament will have me out entrenching and drilling for their defence, and the king will summon me to court. I cannot be faithless to them both. I cannot watch the king ride into war as if it were a masqued ball. I cannot stay in England and see him die!'

'And I cannot leave.' She spoke steadfastly, as if nothing would ever move her.

'You are my wife,' John reminded her.

She bowed her head.

'You owe me absolute obedience,' he said. 'I am your master before God.'

'As the king is yours,' she said gently. 'Isn't that what this war is all about?'

He hesitated. 'I thought you wanted to be my wife?'

'I do. I agreed to be your wife, and to rear your children, and to care for the rarities and the garden and the Ark. How can I do these things in Virginia?'

'You can care for me and the children.'

Hester shook her head. 'I won't take the children there. You know yourself how dangerous it is there. There are wild Indians, and hunger, dreadful disease. I won't take the children into danger.' She paused for a moment. 'And I won't leave here.'

'This is *my* home,' John reminded her. 'And I am prepared to leave it.'

'It is my home too.'

They locked gazes like enemies. John remembered his first impression of her as a plain-faced managing woman who had been put in his house without his consent. 'Hester, I am going to Virginia,' he said coldly. 'And it is my wish that you come with me and the children.'

Her straight gaze never wavered. 'I am sorry,' she said evenly. 'I cannot do that. I will not take the children into danger and I have no wish to leave my home. If you go then I will keep everything safe for your return, and I will welcome you when you return.'

'My father . . .' he started.

'Your father trusted me with the care of this house and with the care of the children while you were away,' she said. 'I promised him on his deathbed that I would keep it all safe: plants, rarities, and children. I will not leave this house for any wandering battalion to take it over and to chop down his trees for firewood. I won't leave his chestnut avenue for them to spoil. I won't leave it unprotected for any vagrants to steal the fruit or pick the flowers. I won't leave the rarities stored in a warehouse with no idea of when I can return. And I will not take Jane's children to a country far away where I know they cling to survival against all the odds.'

'Jane's children!' he shouted. 'Jane was my wife! They are my children! She is nothing to you! They are nothing to you!'

John saw her flinch as if he had slapped her face. But it did not shake her steadiness. 'You are wrong,' she said simply. 'I have long thought of myself as caring for Jane's children and trying to care for them as she would wish. And sometimes I think that she looks down from heaven and sees them, growing strong and beautiful, and that she is happy for them. But they are my children too, I have loved them without fail for four years and I will not take them from their home because you have decided to leave your master and leave your country and leave your home.'

'I'm not faithless!' he said, stung.

Hester gave him a long, level look. 'You and your father are the king's gardeners,' she said. 'You are in his service.'

'He doesn't own my soul!' John shouted. 'I am his servant, not his slave! I can withdraw my service. I can work for myself, I can leave. I have just left.'

She nodded. 'Then a man has a right to choose where he lives and who he calls master?'

'Yes,' John said firmly.

'A woman too?'

'Yes,' he said begrudgingly.

'Then I choose to live here, and you will not take the children without me to care for them.'

'You want to stay here and face who knows what dangers?'

'I shall face the dangers when they come,' she said. 'I am not such a fool as to think that we are safe here. We're too near to the city – if the king brings in a Papist army we will be in the worst place. But if that happens I shall take them to Oatlands, or away into the country. We will have a warning of the dangers. I can prepare for them. And Jane's parents will warn us and protect us, and Alexander Norman knows to the minute where the king's army can be found, he makes the barrels for the gunpowder. My own family have refuges planned. I shall have advisors, I shall have protectors.

'But in Virginia there would be no-one to keep us safe but you; and you don't know the country, and you are not a farmer or a labourer, and I think only a farmer or a labourer can get a living there.'

John got to his feet and spoke bitterly. 'I won't argue with you,' he said spitefully. 'Because I don't care enough to take the trouble. It doesn't matter to me if you will come with me to Virginia as my wife or if you prefer to stay at home like a housekeeper. It is your choice. I shall go to Virginia a single man, if that is your wish.'

She felt a pain inside her which was worse than anything she had suffered from him so far. She heard the threat of infidelity in his words but she would not let him frighten her into abandoning her home. 'I am sorry to stand against you,' she said steadily. 'But I promised your father I would guard his trees and his grandchildren, and I cannot escape that promise.'

John got to his feet and stalked to the door. 'I am tired. I shall sleep. I don't want to be disturbed. I am used to sleeping alone.'

Hester bowed her head, not commenting on the fact that she was no longer invited into bed with him. 'Take your bed,' she said politely. 'I shall make up the bed in the spare bedroom.'

'And as soon as possible I shall take ship,' John said. 'Don't doubt me, Hester. I shall leave for the new world. I am sick of this country. I am sick of this house.' He did not say it but the words 'and I am sick of you' hung in the air, unspoken, between them.

She bowed her head. 'I shall guard the children and the trees for your return.'

'And if I never come back?'

'Then I shall guard them for the next John Tradescant, your son,' she said. 'And I shall guard them for the people of England who will want the trees and the plants when they stop making war. And then they will remember and honour the name of Tradescant, even if you are no longer here.'

October 1642

The luck of the Tradescants was still running John's way. There was a
ship due to leave for Virginia in October and he could get a place aboard
her. Half a dozen new settlers were sailing too, loading their goods and
getting ready for their new life. John was on the dock with them when
someone shouted that the king had fought a battle and had triumphed,
at a place called Powick Bridge.

John joined the crowd that gathered around the trooper. He was a
Parliament man and his tale of terror was growing greater with every
telling.

'We were serving under my Earl of Essex,' the man said. 'And ordered
badly, no-one can deny it. We were to cut off the king's cousin, Prince
Rupert, from the main army. But as we went down the lane towards
them there was firing on either side of us, from the hedges. Dirty work,
you couldn't see where it was coming from. The officers shouted "Wheel
about" – but none of us knew how to wheel about. Easier to say than
do in the narrow lanes anyway. Some were shouting that "wheel about"
meant retreat, and they tried to force their way back through the others
coming forward. Those at the back still didn't know of the danger so
they were coming on. It was all confusion, d'you see?

'There was a charge from the king's devils, cavalry, riding like madmen, and we went down and around and were thrown about. It was
every man for himself all the way back to our camp and the next day
the Earl said we should all be trained properly, and that he would have
us trained at once.

'But Prince Rupert trained his men before he took them out. He told
them what "wheel about" meant before he marched them into the very
jaws of the enemy. Prince Rupert learned his fighting all over Europe.
Prince Rupert is going to win this war for his cousin King Charles, he

knows all the tricks. Prince Rupert has changed our plans completely, he has beaten us before we began.'

Bertram Hobert, a fellow passenger with John, glanced at him. 'Does this change *your* plans, Mr Tradescant?' he asked.

'No,' John said discreetly. 'My going or staying is nothing to do with the progress of the war. I have interests in Virginia, a plantation there, some land where I have a fancy to build a house. And I made a good sum on the plants I brought back last time. Whether Parliament or the king wins, some day there will be peace and men will want to garden.'

'Are you not for the king? Won't you join him now? Now that he is on the road to victory?'

'I have been in his service all my life,' John said, hiding his resentment. 'The time has come for me to do some travelling and gardening for myself. He does not need a gardener now, he needs soldiers, and – you heard that man – he has them.'

Hobert nodded.

'What about you?' John asked.

'I was leaving whatever happened,' the man said. 'I can make no progress here. I work as hard as any man; but what the taxes don't take, the tithes do. I wanted a country where I can see real wealth for me. I've seen how a man can prosper in Virginia. I'll stay a dozen years and come back a rich man and buy a farm in Essex. What about you? Will you stay for long?'

John thought for a moment. It was a question he and Hester had carefully skirted, in all the weeks while she packed for him and took orders in her careful script from gardeners who had heard he was going collecting again. With his boat creaking at the dockside and the wind blowing offshore, with the tide running and a sense of his freedom rising in him, John felt young and reckless again; a young man fit for a young country, full of promise.

'I shall make a home there,' he said. 'My wife and children will stay in England and I shall be back often. But Virginia is the country for me. I shall build a house there and . . .' He broke off, thinking of Suckahanna's small, sideways smile, her tattooed nakedness which had become more erotic for him since his first innocent sight of her. He thought that by now she would be a woman, a woman fully grown, and ready for love and desire.

'It's a country where a man can grow,' the farmer said, throwing his arms wide. 'There's land for the asking, and earth which has never been ploughed. There's a new life there for me.'

'And for me,' John said.

John welcomed the long ĭdle days of the voyage. He became accustomed to the movement of the ship and his stomach stopped swooping with terror at the long, frightening slide into the troughs of the waves. The captain was liberal with the passengers, letting them come up on deck, almost as they wished, as long as they did not distract the crew; and John spent days leaning on the rail of the deck and looking down into the moving green muscles of the ocean. A couple of times they caught sight of a pod of whales, chasing a school of fish that stretched for more than a mile across. Once or twice they saw large white birds whose names John did not know and he asked the captain if one could be shot so that he could have it stuffed for the rarities room. The captain shook his head. He said it was unlucky to shoot a bird at sea, it would summon up a hurricane. John did not press the point, it seemed a long, long way from the rarities room at Lambeth, a long way from Hester, a long way from the children, and a long way from the king and his costumed play-acting wars.

John had thought that he would use the time of the two-month voyage to make some plans, come to some decisions about his future. He had thought he would write down his own timetable: how long he would spend building a new house in Virginia, when he would send for the children, even if Hester still refused to come. But as the ship went westward, and still more westward, as he spent every evening watching the sun sink lower and lower through the clouds and then into the sea, he found he could not think or plan; all he could do was dream.

It was not a journey, it was an escape. John's inheritance of a business which was at the same time a duty had nearly strangled him. He had been bound by loyalty and even in the end a begrudging sympathy in service to a king whom he despised. His father's choice of his wife had forced him into a new marriage, one he would not have chosen for himself. His burdensome work and his duty to his family conspired to close down the ways that were open to him: like untrimmed hedges overshadowing a lane. John had a sudden exhilarating sense of having vaulted a gate and starting to make his own way across fields towards the open country, where there were no paths and no lanes, and no restrictions. Somewhere he could make his own life, build his own house . . . even choose his own wife.

He dreamed of her – Suckahanna – almost every night. It was as if his dreams had been locked down inside him, and only freed once he freed himself from England, from Hester, from home. Once the ropes keeping the ship at the quayside were dropped and trailed through the cold water of the Thames, John felt his desires rocking like the boat as it headed for freedom.

He dreamed of the month they had spent in the forest together and the light shining through the leaves to dapple her bare brown skin. He dreamed of the line of her spine as she squatted before the fire, of the asymmetric tilt of her head where the hair was cut short on one side to keep the bowstring free, and black and flowing on the other. In his dreams he could taste the food she had found and cooked for them, the bitterness of the dried blueberries, the richness of the roasted lobster, the nuts, the seeds, the roots. He remembered the clean cold taste of water, an exotic drink for a man who had drunk small ale or milk for all his life. He woke in the mornings to the sudden pang of disappointment that they were still so many days out of Jamestown, and he woke aroused and embarrassed. He had the little enclosed bed with doors around the bunk all to himself but anyone sleeping outside could have heard him groan in desire in his dreams, and he was afraid that he might have said her name in his sleep.

The cold winter mornings at sea were hard for John. While he had been in Lambeth, trapped between the demands of the king and the duties to his family, he had managed to forget the last words she had called to him – 'Come at Nepinough', the harvest time. He had not gone back to her as he had promised. Perhaps she had waited, perhaps her mother had waited with her, and met every boat from England for all of the summer season, and then? And then? Would they have waited a full year, would they have waited two, four?

John hoped that they would have heard that England was at war with itself. The Virginia colonists were sworn to the royalist cause but there would have been a ready stream of gossip and fears running around the colony. Enough talk, surely, for the Indian woman and her daughter to realise that perhaps John could not get away? But perhaps they had never thought that he would come. John remembered Suckahanna's ability to say nothing for a whole month, even though he spoke to her, and laughed with her and worked beside her and watched her every move with tenderness and desire. She had said nothing to him, even though she had understood every word that he had said. She had said nothing to him because she had been ordered by her mother to stay silent. Perhaps, after Nepinough had come and gone, her mother had ordered her to forget him, or to marry a man of her own people, or – worst thought of all – to go and lie with a white man and earn their safety that way. At that thought, John would pull on his boots and stamp up to the deck and look out over the bowsprit to where the horizon of sea and air lay empty and unhelpful, miles and miles away.

'I've never seen a man in such a hurry to go and see some flowers,' Bertram Hobert remarked as he came beside John one morning near dawn to lean on the rail and look westward with him.

For a moment John thought of confiding in him – his anxious desire for Suckahanna, his undeniable betrayal of Hester – but then he shrugged and nodded.

'Running from? or running to?' Hobert pursued.

John shook his head at the tangle of his life. 'Both, I suppose.'

They ran into a storm just a week before they were due to sight the coast of the Americas and John had some bad days of sickness and fear as the ship rolled and shuddered and felt as if she was foundering in the troughs of the waves. He opened the hatch and looked out to try and ease his sickness but he was met by the sight of a wall of water, a towering mountain of water, rearing over the narrow deck and about to fall. The other passengers, a young family and a couple of men, shouted at him to shut the hatch, and he dropped it down and then heard the crash of the wave on the deck, felt the ship shudder under the impact and stagger under the weight of the water. They were in such terror that they did not speak, except Mrs Austin who prayed constantly, her arms around her children, her eyes tight shut, and Bertram Hobert, who maintained his own whispered litany of swearing. John, huddled in the hold beside them, wedged in with goods, was certain that they were all going to sink to the bottom of the heaving ocean, and that he would deserve such a fate, because he had betrayed not one but two women, and had abandoned them both.

Slowly, painfully slowly, the waves eased a little, and then the terrifying howling of the wind in the mast and the rigging eased, the ship steadied, and once again they could hear the everyday noises of the crew on deck. The hatch opened and dripping and exhausted sailors dropped down into the hold and shouted into the galley for bread and a hot drink before turning into their hammocks to sleep, all wet and sea-stained, with their boots still on. The bread was rationed, the water rationed too. The ship had made the voyage without the usual stop at the West Indies and everything was running short.

John, cautiously going up on deck, found a clear, freezing day with the storm a dark smudge on the horizon to the north, and before them, and ahead of them, and growing clearer all the time, the stark white and black of the forests of Virginia in midwinter.

'Home,' John said, as if the storm had blown his doubts away, and the terror of the storm had earned him the right to claim his own land and his own future. 'Home, at last.'

As they sailed up the river John looked around eagerly for changes. He could see at once that settlers had spread out along the river in the four years he had been away. Every three or four miles there was newly cleared land and a little house set facing the water, a small wooden pontoon to serve as a quay for loading of the only crop: tobacco. John thought that Suckahanna's mother had been right to predict that there would be no room for the two races to live alongside each other. The British were spreading themselves so prodigally that their new lands and houses lined the riverside like a ragged ribbon on both banks.

Bertram Hobert joined John at the rail. 'That's Isle of Wight County.' He nodded towards it.

'Isle of Wight?' John exclaimed, taking in the thick forest, deep green with pine and fir tree, black and white with naked boughs filled with deep snow. Hobert laughed shortly. 'Sounds odd, doesn't it? Isle of Wight County there, and Surrey County next door to it.'

John looked to the other bank. 'And there's Jamestown at last,' Hobert said, following his gaze. 'I'll tell my wife to be ready.' He turned and went below. But John stayed on deck, straining to see the settlement, to see all the changes. The derelict land around Jamestown had spread further in the four years, like a wound gone bad, festering in the marshy ground. The tree stumps were left in the ground to rot and the unused branches were left where they had fallen. New patches of ground had been cleared by burning and were black and charred, ready to come under the plough for tobacco to be planted in spring. Drifts of snow were heaped around the cleared area as if the loss of the trees had left an opening for fierce winds and cold weather. Even the snow was dirty.

Jamestown itself looked as if it were thriving. The stone quay had been extended to handle more and more ships coming to the country for tobacco, and the warehouses along the quayside were a storey higher and broader than they had been before, laden with drifts of grimy snow which rested on the cold roofs.

There was a new paved road running parallel with the river, and someone had planted a row of trees for shade. Behind the new road were substantial stone-built houses, still no greater than a yeoman's cottage in England, but better made than their predecessors, and with windows of oiled paper rather than shutters. In some small square panes John could see the bright glint of expensive glass.

The quayside was still filthy with garbage and the deep gutter in the new road showed that no-one had thought it worth while to consider drainage for the new town. The score of houses still tipped their nightsoil on the riverbank or threw it out in the yard where it froze and then leached into the drinking water supply. It was still a town where men, and an increasing number of women, were coming only to seek their fortunes. They did not care what sort of life they led nor what sort of place they were making. Most of them still thought of England as 'home'.

The fort was still there but the gates were stuck open and the guns were rolled back, as if they were only kept in place because no-one could be bothered to move them.

On the quayside people were waiting for news, goods, and to greet the new settlers. They were broad as bears, every one of them, muffled up against the cold air in thick skins, each breath a cloud before every face.

'What news of the king?' a man shouted as he caught the rope and made it fast. 'What news of the war?'

'Victory for the king!' one of the sailors shouted jubilantly back. 'We left just as his cousin Prince Rupert had wiped out Parliament's men. One of the survivors swore there was no doubt about it, the king will have beaten them by now.'

'Thank God for that,' the man replied. And another one cheered. John noted that the report by one trooper of one skirmish had now been elevated into a total defeat and the end of the war, but said nothing. That was how the king's masquing worked. Only one battle was ever enacted. There was no long, bitter exchange of small victories and small defeats, little setbacks and petty humiliations. One glorious cavalry charge by Prince Rupert had concluded the matter and the colonists could go back to growing tobacco and making money with light hearts.

John shrugged and went below to fetch his bags. He was as far from England and the news as everyone else. He had no reason to think that the war would be a longer and more painful business than the sailor and the colonists believed. Perhaps they were right and he was wrong and already the king was back in Whitehall and planning some new triumph: war with the Irish, or war with the Scots, or – since it was King Charles, as changeable as March weather – war with the Spanish or French. John hefted his bag holding his clothes and his money over his shoulder and went up on deck to the head of the gangplank.

She was not there. Not among the crowd on the quayside, nor back in the shadow of the warehouse walls where he had left her. He shook his head, he had not really expected her to be there, on the quayside; but he could not help the pang of childish disappointment. Somewhere, in a corner of his mind, he had seen himself coming down the gangplank and Suckahanna, a little older, a little more beautiful, running towards him and into his arms. It had been a foolish dream by a man who had already buried one wife and deserted another, a man who knew that love and desire do not always have a happy ending. But John still looked for her, and still knew disappointment that she was not there.

He watched his box being unloaded and then took hold of it and dragged it through the slush up to the inn where he was absolutely certain that he would find the landlady as sour-tempered and as inhospitable as four years before.

His first visit was to Mr Joseph.

'Of course I remember you,' the magistrate said. 'You went out into the woods in an Indian canoe and came back with barrelfuls of plants. Were they any good in England?'

'Most of them took,' John said. 'Some of them did very well. One of them, the spiderwort, is one of the most beautiful flowers I have ever grown. We had the purple one before, but this is white like a little three-petalled star.'

'And what news of the king?' Mr Joseph interrupted.

'Good news. Prince Rupert's cavalry had a great victory at a place called Powick Bridge,' John said, repeating the popular belief. 'They say he can't be stopped now.'

Mr Joseph nodded. 'Well, thank God for that,' he said. 'I don't know what would have been our case if Parliament had won. We're a royal colony. Do we become a Parliament colony? No-one thinks of these things. What about you? Would you have been a gardener to Parliament?'

'I'm here because I don't know what I would have been,' John admitted. 'I couldn't see my way clear at all.'

The magistrate nodded. 'Now what can I do for you? D'you want another Indian guide?'

'I want the same one,' John said, keeping his tone deliberately casual.

He wondered if the man could hear the pounding as his heart raced. 'I want that girl again. Do you know where she is?'

'What girl?'

John had to force himself to speak quietly and steadily. 'You sent me out with a girl, d'you remember? Her baptised name is Mary. Her mother was in prison for a month for accusing someone of rape. You had the girl in service here, d'you remember? When I came back her mother met us and took the girl away. She said they might go back to their own people. Have you seen her since then?'

'Oh, the harlot and her daughter,' Mr Joseph said, remembering. 'No. They must have gone into the woods. I've not seen them.'

John had expected anything but this blank refusal. 'But . . . but you must have?'

Mr Joseph shook his head. 'No. D'you want another guide?'

'I want that girl!'

The man shrugged. 'I can't help you, I'm afraid.'

John thought rapidly. 'How could I find her? D'you know of other Indians who come in from the forest who might know her?'

Mr Joseph shook his head again. 'They're settling down at last,' he said with satisfaction. 'The ones who have been taken into service are kept here, in town, or safe on the plantations. The ones who have kept to the forest are pushed back, almost every day, further and further away from the river, away from the coast. We're cleaning the land of them. We're getting them out of the way. If she's out in the forest with them you'll not see her again. She could be over the mountains or the other side of York River by now if she's got any sense.' He paused for a moment. 'What d'you want her for?'

'I promised I would take her into my service,' John said smoothly. 'I said when I came back and built my house she could come to work for me. She's skilled with plants.'

'They're all skilled with plants,' Mr Joseph said. 'Get another one.'

Every new immigrant to Virginia was awarded a headright of land, fifty acres a person. John, arriving for the second time, was awarded a further fifty acres, marked solemnly on a map held in the new building of the burgesses' assembly. His father had been persuaded to purchase two headrights when the Virginia Company was founded, so John had his land put together in one spreading acreage of two hundred acres: as big as an English farm. It was upriver from Jamestown, not the most desirable of sites since the tobacco ships would not go too far upstream. The earliest assignments had all been around Jamestown or downriver. Latecoming planters had to ship their goods in their own boats downriver to Jamestown and catch the ocean-going boats there.

John looked carefully at the burgesses' map. The lines of rivers and mountains were indistinct and vague. The only part of the country that John knew well was the woods where he had lived for the month with Suckahanna, and they were indicated with a rough scribble suggesting inlets and islands and swampy ground. It hardly mattered. There was so much land to be had in the new colony that disputes over boundaries had been left behind in overcrowded England. No-one in this new huge country was going to quibble over a mile to the east or ten miles to the west, scale was a different thing in this vast emptiness.

Bertram Hobert was consulting the map alongside John. 'Next to my land,' he remarked. 'What d'you say we build one house together and then live in it while we work on the other?'

John nodded thoughtfully. 'When could we start?'

'Not till spring. We'd die of hunger and cold out there in the winter. We'll stay snug in town until spring, and go out as soon as we can.'

John looked out of the open slit of the window at the iron-grey sky and the falling snow and thought of Suckahanna, barefoot in the frozen woods where the snow was dozens of feet deep and where the wolves howled at night. 'How could anyone survive out there in winter?'

Hobert shook his head. 'Nobody can,' he said.

Winter 1642–3, Virginia

Bertram Hobert rented lodgings in town for himself, his wife Sarah and his slave, a black man called Francis. After John complained of the treatment he got at the inn, Hobert said he could stay with them until the spring, and then the whole party would go upriver to look at their new land.

John found the town much changed. A new governor, Sir William Berkeley, had arrived from England and had equipped the official residence with beautiful furniture and goods. His wife, who was already a byword in the community for her looks, was giving parties and all those who could remotely pass as a gentleman and his lady were dressing in their best and walking up the drive to the governor's house. The roads were paved now, and the tobacco was no longer grown at the street corners and on any corner of spare land. A man could buy or sell using coin and not pinches of tobacco or bills drawn on a tobacco merchant's. 'It's become a town and not a camp,' John remarked.

Those were the beneficial changes of the four years. There were others that filled him with worry for Suckahanna and her mother. The river was now lined with plantations from its mouth right up to James's Island. Before each of the planters' houses the land had been cleared and the fields stretched down to the little wooden piers and quays. On James's Island itself the fields ran into each other, there was no forest left at all. On the more distant banks the land was black where it had been burned and not yet ploughed. John could not see how Suckahanna and her people could survive in a country which was turning itself into fields and houses. The woods she had roamed every day for mile after mile, hunting turkey or wood pigeon, or looking for roots or nuts, were burned back to a few scorched trees among ploughed fields. Even the river, where she had followed the schools of fish ready to catch them wherever the flow of the water was right, was enclosed by riverfront acres and penetrated by landing piers.

John thought he might be imagining it – or perhaps it was the effect of the freezing-cold weather – but it seemed to him that the flocks of birds were fewer, and he no longer heard the wolves howling outside the walls of Jamestown. The countryside was being tamed, and the wild animals and the people who lived alongside them were being driven inland and away. John thought that if Suckahanna was with her people they might have been driven far away to where the burgesses' map showed nothing more than a space marked 'forest'. He started to fear that he would never find her again.

Bertram busied himself with trade while they were waiting for the weather to change. Since it was his second visit to Jamestown, he had judged his market well. He had brought a store of the little European luxuries that the colonists missed so much. Most afternoons he was welcomed in the better homes to show his supplies of paper and ink, pens and soap, real candles, rather than the green wax of the Virginian candleberries, French brandy rather than the eternal West Indies rum, lace, cotton, linen, silk, anything carved with skill or made with artistry that reminded the colonists of home where skill and artistry had been easily hired.

John went with him on these visits and met a new sort of people, people for whom the old divisions of gentry and labourers no longer applied, for they all laboured. What mattered now was the gradation of skills. A clever carpenter or an able huntsman was more respected in this new country than a man with a French surname, or knowledge of Latin. A woman who could fire a musket and skin a deer was her husband's helpmeet and partner, and more valuable to him than if she could write poetry or paint a landscape. Hester would have thrived in this place where a woman was expected to work as hard as a man, and to take her own share of responsibilities, and every day John found himself wishing that she had come with him, and, contradictorily, longing for news of Suckahanna.

Sarah Hobert reminded John of Hester. She prayed every morning, and said grace at every meal, and in the evenings she taught Francis the slave his letters and the catechism. When John saw her with a chicken over her knees plucking and saving the feathers for a pillow, or scraping cobs of corn by the fireside in the evening, and then carefully setting the empty cobs in the woodbasket for fuel, he remembered Hester: hardworking, conscientious, and with an inner strength and silence.

For a while he thought the cold weather would never lift and free them from the idle life of Jamestown, but Hobert swore he would not go upriver while the snow was still thick on the ground. 'A man could die out there and no-one ever know, and no-one ever care,' he said. 'We stay in town until the ground warms up and until we can row upriver without great bergs of ice crashing down around us. I won't take the risk of moving from the town until spring.'

'And then it would be more dangerous to stay,' his wife said quietly. 'They have terrible fevers here in the hot weather, Mr Hobert. I would rather be well away from here before the summer comes.'

'In good time,' he said with a glance at her under his eyebrows which warned her to hold her peace and not join in with the councils of men.

'In God's time,' she said pleasantly, not the least overawed.

John knew that Hobert was right but still he felt impatient. He asked all the townspeople he met if they remembered the girl or her mother, but people told him that one Indian looked like another, and if the girl had vanished then no doubt she had been stealing or betraying her master and had run off to the woods to her own people.

'And precious comfort she'll get there,' one woman told him as she waited by the town's only deep well for her turn to draw water.

'Why?' John asked urgently. 'What d'you mean?'

'Because every day they get pushed back a little more. Not now in the winter, because our men don't go out into the woods in winter, it gets dark too early and the cold can kill a man quicker than an arrow. But when spring comes we will make up packs of dogs and bands of hunters and go hunting the redskins, we force them back and back and back, so the land is clear for us and safe for us.'

'But she's only a girl,' John exclaimed. 'And her mother a woman all alone.'

'They would breed if left alone,' the woman said with stout indifference. 'I don't mean to shock you, mister, but it's us or them on this land. And we're determined that we shall be the victors. Whether it's wolves or bears or Indians, they have to fall back and give way before us or die. How else can we make this land our own?'

It was a ruthless logic that John could hardly condemn, for he himself held four headrights of riverside land and virgin forest and he heard himself talking with anticipation of the trees he would clear and the house he would build, and he knew that his own land was another two hundred acres where the Powhatan would never hunt again.

April 1643

He had to wait until April, and then he and the Hoberts rowed upriver and saw their adjoining plots. It was good land. The trees reached down to the water's edge and their thick canopy shaded the banks. Their wide grey roots stretched out into the flooded river. John tied the canoe he had borrowed to an overhanging trunk and stepped ashore on his own new land.

'My Eden,' John said quietly to himself.

The trees were alive with the singing of birds, birds courting and chasing, fighting and nesting. He saw birds that looked like familiar English species but which were bigger, or oddly coloured, and he saw others that were wholly new to him in this new and wonderful world, birds like little herons which were white as doves, strange ducks with heads as bright as enamelled boxes. The soil was rich, dark and fertile, an earth which had never known the plough but which had made and remade itself with centuries of tumbling leaves and rotting vegetation. Feeling almost foolish, John went down on his hands and knees, took a handful of the rich soil, crumbled it between his hands and raised it to his nose and his lips. It was good dark earth that would grow anything in rich abundance.

The bank sloped steeply up from the river, there would be no flooding on his fields, and there was a little hillock, perhaps half a mile back from the river frontage, where John would build his house. When the trees were cleared he would have a fine river view, and he would be able to look down the hill to his own landing stage where his own tobacco would be loaded to take downstream.

John thought his house would be set square to the river. A modest house, nothing like the grand size of Lambeth: a pioneer's house of one room downstairs and a ladder leading up to a half-floor for storage set in the eaves. A fireplace in one wall, which would heat the whole of the little building, a roof of reeds or maybe even wooden shingles. A floor of nothing more than beaten earth in the first few years, perhaps later John would put down floorboards. Windows which would be bare and open, empty of glass, but with thick wooden shutters to close in winter and bad weather. It would be a house only a little grander than an English pauper might build to squat on common land and think himself lucky. It would be a normal house in this new world, where nothing could be taken for granted and where men and women rarely had anything more than they could build or make for themselves.

Thoughtfully, John reached towards a sprouting vine and pulled away a cutting, tucking it in his pocket. He would grow it around his door-frame. It might be a little hovel in a great wilderness but it would still have a garden.

The house did not take long to build. There were men in Jamestown who would work at a daily rate, and Bertram and John hired them as a gang to work first on the Hobert house and then on John's smaller version of the same design. The gang specified that they were to have their food and their ale, and that the nails, the most costly part of the house, were to be supplied: counted out each morning, and checked in at nightfall. They told John that when he wanted a new house built elsewhere, he should burn his old house down and then sift through the ashes for the nails. New timber could be had simply by clearing the woods around the foundations, but new nails had to come from England.

'But then you never have houses for sale,' John remarked. 'You never have houses for newcomers.'

'They can build their own,' the man said in the rough frankness of the new world. 'And if they cannot build their own they can go homeless.'

Sarah Hobert cooked for the men while they built her house, roasting meat over a camp fire on long skewers in a way that the colonists had learned from Indian guides. John thought of Suckahanna squatting beside the little fire with trout skewered on green sticks. Sarah made bread in a heavy dark dough from rye flour; the colonists could not grow wheat in this land. When her own house was finished and the builders moved on to John's house, she came too and cooked for them there, never complaining that she would have preferred to start digging her own fields or planting her own vegetable patch.

'Thank you,' John said awkwardly as the Hoberts got into their native canoe to travel the little way downriver to their own homestead. 'I could not have built it without you.'

'Nor could we have built ours so quick without you,' Bertram said. 'I will come over in the next month or two to see how you are faring. We will have to be like brothers if we are to survive in this land, John.'

'It's funny,' John said. He took the rope and cast it off, throwing it into Sarah's waiting hands. 'I thought this was an easy country to live in, easy to build a shelter, easy to find food. But now it seems to me that we are on the very edge of surviving, all the time.'

They looked at him blankly, their pale faces turned towards him as the current nudged the canoe away from the bank.

'Of course it is a struggle,' Sarah replied, stating the obvious. 'The Lord God ordains that we should struggle our way through this difficult world to righteousness.'

'But a new world –' John suggested. 'A new world of natural goodness, of natural wealth?'

She shook her head and the canoe bobbed. Bertram took up the paddle. 'Men and women are born to struggle.'

'See you soon,' Bertram called over the widening gulf of water. 'I'll come over some time, when we are settled.'

John raised his hand in farewell and stood watching them. Bertram paddled the canoe awkwardly, with none of Suckahanna's easy grace, and Sarah sat stiffly in the front for all the world like a Thames fishwife in a wherry. The current flowing swiftly downriver took them, so that Bertram need do no more than steer. John watched the flowing water for a long while after they had gone from sight around a bend in the river, then he turned and went slowly up the little track to his new house.

It stood, a plain little box made of green wood, in a square of cleared ground. John had felled no more than the trees he had needed to build it, and their unwanted branches and lesser wood was heaped in wasteful confusion all around. He stopped on his way up the river bank to admire it. It was a square-built house, little more than a shed or a hovel, but he had felled the wood which had built it, and planed the planks of the door, and set the rough frame for the window and packed the reeds for the thatched roof, and he felt proud of it.

Then he looked a little closer. On one side of the door was the cutting he had picked when he first set foot on his new land. It had struck, he could see the fresh green growth of the trumpet vine which would flower in early summer as golden and as prolific as Turkish nasturtiums. But on the other side of the door, which he had not yet touched, someone had dug the earth, cleared it of stones, and planted another creeper, one he did not recognise, which already was putting out a little shoot to touch the new wall so that soon, perhaps as early as this summer, the door would be wreathed in some other new flower, planted by someone else.

His first thought was that Sarah must have put it in, working in an idle moment, while the rest of the building gang had been up on the roof. But then he realised that Sarah would have thought that such a task was a waste of time, and a vanity – neglecting the real work of the day. None of the builders would have troubled themselves with such a piece of frivolity. Bertram Hobert could not tell one plant from another unless it was tobacco from maize. And there had been no-one else near the little house in the woods. John paused for a moment and then turned towards the darkening forest.

'Suckahanna?' he whispered into the green shadows. 'Suckahanna? My love?'

She did not come to him, though that night he lay wakeful on the bare floor of his house, and waited for her, certain that she was out in the forest, waiting for him. At dawn he lifted the wooden latch on his new door and stepped out into the forest, already singing its way into morning, and looked around, expecting her to emerge from the trees and come to him. She was not there.

He went down to the river, half-expecting to see her surface from the icy water, with a knife in her hand and a handful of freshwater mussels in her little purse; but the water was grey and ruffled only with the morning breeze.

John thought with a pang of cold fear that maybe she was tormenting him, to repay him for the delay, to make him wait for her as she had waited for him.

'I'm sorry,' he said, speaking to the indifferent trees, to the blithely singing birds in the high branches. 'As soon as I got home I found my father was dead and there was much for me to do. My children needed me, and I had to work –' He hesitated. Even speaking before nothing but thick woodland, he was conscious of the lie of omission when he did not mention Hester. 'I never forgot you,' he said. 'Even when I was at war and fighting for my king I thought of you every day and I dreamed of you every night.' That part at least was mostly true.

145

He waited. From the river behind him came a loud splash. John whirled around. But there was only the spreading ring of water where a salmon had leaped or an otter broken the surface in a dive. She was not there. Not in the river and not in the trees.

John shrugged his coat a little closer around his shoulders and went into his house.

John opened a new sack of cornmeal and put his pot on the embers of the fire. He heated up enough water for a wash, a drink, and to make suppawn porridge for his breakfast.

'I must hunt this evening,' he said to the empty house. 'I can't live on this swill.'

He washed his face but did not trouble to shave. 'I shall grow a beard and a moustache like my father,' he said to the empty room. 'Who is there to see me after all?' He poured half the hot water into a beaker, threw a spoonful of the cornmeal into what was left and stirred it till it thickened. It was warm and he was hungry. He tried to ignore the fact that it tasted of nothing.

He took his bowl, spoon and pot down to the river and washed them, watching the reeds to his left for movement, in case Suckahanna was hiding there, watching him, and laughing at him having to do woman's work. Then he filled the pot with fresh water and went back up to his house.

The room was still silent and empty. John took down his axe from the hook above the fireplace and went out to cut wood from the felled timber before the house. The great felling of trees to clear land for planting would have to wait. Firewood was the most important. The fire must not, on any account, go out. Enough people had warned him of the danger in Jamestown, and that was in a town where you could borrow a couple of glowing embers from the house next door and carry them home on a shovel. Here in the wilderness, a fire was like a spark of life itself. If it went out it might take a couple of hours to get it lit again, even with a good tinderbox and dry wood, and if darkness and cold were coming on, that would seem a very long time. If a pack of wolves had found the courage to come to the door, it would feel like an eternity with neither light nor fire to scare them away, and no means of firing the musket.

John cut and split logs for most of the morning and then piled them on either side of the fireplace to dry. He opened the rough-planed door of his house and looked down to the river. He was aching with fatigue and yet all he had done was get in one, perhaps two, day's supply of firewood. He had nothing for dinner but more suppawn porridge, and nothing at all for supper. He set the pot on the fire to heat the water and felt, for the first time, a dark sense of foreboding that surviving would be a struggle in this country which no longer seemed rich and easy.

'I must think,' John said into the silence of the house. 'Suckahanna and I ate like princes, every day, and she was not chopping trees all morning. I must try to live like her, and not like an Englishman.' He scraped the last of the porridge from his wooden bowl and put it to one side. 'I'll put down a fish trap,' he resolved. 'And at dusk when the birds are coming back to the trees to roost I'll shoot a couple of pigeon.'

He felt the juices rush into his mouth at the thought of roast pigeon. 'I can do that,' he promised himself. 'I can learn to live here, I am a young man still. And later, when Bertram and Sarah come over, Sarah can teach me how to make bread.'

He set his bowl and spoon to one side and went to his pile of belongings, to find a length of twine. 'Now a fish trap,' he said.

John had seen a fish trap in Jamestown, and had watched Suckahanna weave one out of the tendrils of vines and a couple of sticks. She had spent two evenings on it, and on the third evening they had eaten roasted carp. John had bought the withy hoops and the string in Jamestown, all he had to do was knot a net that would keep a fish inside. He took the string and the hoops outside, sat on a tree stump in the afternoon sunshine and started to work. First he made a row of knots around the large entrance hoop. The fish was to swim in, and then through a series of hoops, each one smaller, until it was trapped in a little space at the end of the maze, and could not find its way out. John knotted his first row and then set to work on the second. It was intricate, difficult work but John was a patient man, and determined. He bent over the task, twisting the string, knotting, moving on to the next row. He did not notice the sun was falling behind the trees until the shadow had chilled his back. Then he straightened and sighed.

'By God, this is weary work,' he said. He took string and hoops inside the house and put them down at the fireside. The fire was burning low. He put on another couple of logs and took his musket down. He loaded it, tipping the powder and then the ball down the muzzle, and then sprinkled a pinch of powder at the top of the powder pan, ready for lighting. He bent over the fire to light the long coil of oiled string which served as the fuse. When it was glowing brightly he held it between first and second finger, well away from the powder pan, and went quietly out of his house.

The trees were so near that John could hunker down on his doorstep, his two vines on either side, and watch the open sky above him for the wood pigeons coming home to roost. A great whirling flock of them came in all at once, and John waited for them to settle in the trees. One plump, confident bird landed on an extended branch which dipped under its weight. John waited for the branch to stop swaying and then took careful aim, touching the glowing string to the powder.

He was lucky. The sound of the shot was like a cannon blast going off in that innocent land and the flock of pigeons exploded out of the trees in a flurry of whirling wings. But John's target bird could not fly up, it spiralled downward, one wing broken, bleeding from the breast. John dropped his musket and taper and ran across the cleared ground, crossing it in five giant strides. The bird was scrabbling to get away, one wing trailing. John snatched it up and wrung its neck quickly and mercifully. He felt the little heart pound and then stop. He went back to the doorstep, put the bird inside, near the fireplace with the unfinished fish trap, and reloaded the gun.

The light was going fast and it was getting cold and dark. The pigeons, recovering from their fright, circled the little clearing and landed in the trees again. John took aim and fired and the birds dashed skyward again, but this time nothing fell to earth.

'Just the one,' John said. 'Well, that will do for my supper at least.'

He plucked the bird carefully, saving the feathers in a fold of linen. 'That'll make me a pillow some day,' he said with assumed cheerfulness to the shadowy room. He gutted and beheaded the bird, tossing the entrails into the water in his cooking pot which he set on the fire for soup. Then he split the pigeon into four, and skewered the pieces carefully on a sharp green stick and set it before the fire with the pot beneath it to catch the dripping juices.

It was a long while for a hungry man to wait but John did not allow himself to hurry, nor to be distracted from the task of turning and turning the fowl while its stubbly skin grew golden, and then brown, and then finally crisp and black. 'Pray God it's cooked through,' John said fervently, his stomach rumbling with hunger.

He took the skewer, and with his knife pushed the pieces off the charred wood on to his trencher. The meat was speckled with burned wood. John flicked the splinters away and then took up a little leg joint. It was wonderful: hot, tasty, and strong. John burned his lips against the hot skin but nothing could have stopped him biting into the flesh. He ate every scrap of meat and then dropped the bare bones reverently into his cooking pot. For the first time in his little house he looked around with something like confidence.

'That was good,' he said quietly. He gave a quiet, satisfied belch. 'That was excellent. I shall hunt again tomorrow. And I shall have the soup for my breakfast. A man cannot work on the land with only porridge in his belly.'

He picked a scrap of meat from his teeth. 'By God, that was good.'

He kicked off his boots and drew his satchel and spare jacket towards him, folded them under his head for a pillow, and then pulled his travelling cloak and a rug over him. He opened one eye to see that the fire was banked in, and his fish trap was safe, and then he was asleep in moments.

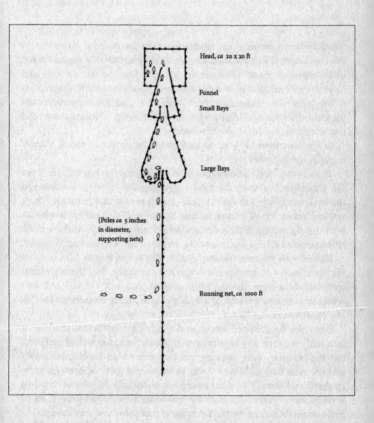

Head, *ca* 20 x 20 ft

Funnel

Small Bays

Large Bays

(Poles *ca* 5 inches in diameter, supporting nets)

Running net, *ca* 1000 ft

May 1643

Next day John set to work on the fish trap for an hour and set it in the cold, swift-flowing water. The meat from last night's supper stayed in his stomach more comfortingly than porridge, he felt stronger and more competent all day; but the following morning he felt hungrier, as if his body were expecting meat again. He had the soup from the pigeon bones for breakfast and then had it again, thinned down and less satisfying, for his dinner at midday.

In the afternoon he went to look at his fish trap and found a small trout in the keep-net.

'Praise God!' John said devoutly, inwardly praising himself. He lifted the trap from the river, carefully supporting his trophy, and smacked the squirming little fish on the head. He cleaned it and gutted it. There was not much left of it after he had cut its head and tail off but he set it in the pot with a little water and dried maize flour to make a stock and simmered it for a few moments, and then left it to cool until supper.

These foods became his staple diet. The monotonous blandness of the cornflour – as porridge, as vegetable, as sauce, and the occasional treat of fish or meat. Slowly, John adapted, and only ate well and with relish in poignant dreams of Lambeth feasts: great dinners at Twelfth Night, rich tables at Easter.

Every day he chopped wood, and went out into the forest to see if he could recognise any berries or nuts which Suckahanna had gathered, but the branches were showing nothing more than fresh green leaves and the nuts had all blown down in the winter gales or been eaten by squirrels and mice. The woods were not as friendly to John as they had been to her. Everywhere that she had looked there had been food or tools or medicines or herbs. Everything that John saw was strange.

After weeks and weeks of this he thought that he had had his fill of strangeness. His father had loved the rare and the unusual and John had inherited that love. Their whole lives were based on the joy of difference: different plants, flowers, artefacts. But now John was in a different world, where everything was strange to him and he felt that perhaps he liked strangeness only against the background of the familiar. He liked the exotic flower when it grew in his English garden at Lambeth. It was harder to admire when it was growing against an exotic tree, under a foreign sky.

'I'm heartstruck,' John said in sudden amazement in the middle of the second month, and a great longing for Lambeth and the children and even for Hester rushed over him so powerfully that he staggered, as if from physical sickness, and had to steady himself with a hand on a tree trunk. 'God! I am longing for my home. It has been weeks, no, months since I came to live here and I have spoken to no man and seen no woman since the Hoberts left. I miss my home. And, my God, I am lonely.'

He turned to look back at the little clearing and, plumb in the centre of it, the house as small and as rough as a wooden box made by a thick-handed apprentice. A sense of the minute scale of the house and the enormity of the forest rushed upon John, leaving him breathless and fearful. 'But I'm making my home here,' he said stubbornly.

The wind, the massive wind, stirred the tops of the high, strong trees as if the very woods themselves were laughing at the false pride of a man who thought he could make a home among such wildness. John could labour here all his life and never manage to do more than survive. He could never build a house like the one at Lambeth, never make a garden like Oatlands. Those were achievements which took years of labour in a society rich in labour. Take away those riches, the work of many hands and many brains, and a man was like an animal in a wood – less than an animal, because every animal in the wood had its place in the scheme of things, food that was suited to it, a home which was right for it, whereas John had to fight to get enough food in this land of plenty, and had to struggle to keep his fire burning to keep his house warm.

A sense of despair as real as darkness swept over him. 'I could die out here,' John thought, but he no longer spoke aloud. The very silence of the woods seemed too great to challenge, it silenced his little voice. 'I *will* die out here.' Every thought seemed to open a greater gulf beneath his feet. 'I am making my home here, far from my children, from my wife, from my friends. I am making a place where I am all alone. And sooner or later, by accident or illness or old age, I will die here. I will die alone. In fact, if I fail for just one day, just *one* day, to get up and fetch water, chop wood, hunt or fish I *will* die here. I could starve to death before anyone came.'

John pushed away from the tree but found that his legs could hardly support him. His sense of loneliness and fear had weakened him. He staggered back towards his house and thanked God there was at least a curl of smoke coming from the chimney, and suppawn in the cooking pot. John felt his throat close at the thought of eating cold porridge again. He fell to his hands and knees and retched. 'God, my God,' he said.

A little saliva dribbled from his mouth. He wiped it on his sleeve. The strong brown homespun of the sleeve was stinking. He noticed it when he brought it to his face. 'My clothes smell,' he said in quiet surprise. 'I must smell.'

He touched his hand to his face. His beard had grown and was matted and dirty, the moustache was long around his mouth. 'My breath must smell, I am filthy,' he said softly. 'I am so foul that I cannot even smell myself.' He felt humiliated at the knowledge. John Tradescant, the apple of his mother's eye, his father's only heir, had become a dirty, bedraggled vagrant, clinging to the edge of the known world.

He dragged himself to his feet again. The sky seemed to look down on him, as if he were a tiny, tiny insect making its arduous way across a massive leaf on a tree in a forest in a country that was too great for any man to cross.

John stumbled to his door and pushed it open. Only in the cramped room could he restore his sense of scale. 'I'm a man,' he said to the four rough wood walls. 'Not a tiny beetle. I am a man. This is my house.'

He looked around as if he had never seen it before. The four walls had been made of newly felled green wood, and as the fire heated the room and the weather warmed, the wood had shrunk. John would have to take clay and twigs to patch the gaps. He shuddered at the glimpse of the forest through the cracks of the house walls, as if the wildness outside was seeping in through his house to attack him.

'I can't,' he said miserably. 'I can't build the house and find food and wash and hunt and clear the land as well. I can't do it. I've been here for nearly two months, and all I can do is survive, and I can barely do that.' His throat closed again and he thought he was going to retch but instead he spat out a hoarse sob.

He felt the waistband of his trousers. He had thought that, for some reason, his belt had been stretching but now he realised that he was thinner. 'I'm not surviving,' he finally acknowledged to himself. 'I'm not getting enough to eat.'

At once the tiredness which was now familiar, and the ache in his belly which he had thought was some kind of mild illness, made a new and terrifying sense. He had been hungry for weeks and his hunger was making him less and less competent to survive. He missed his shot more and more often, his stock of logs for the fire was harder to cut every day. He had fallen back on gathering firewood rather than making the effort of swinging an axe. This meant that the wood was drier and burned quicker so that he needed more, and it also meant that the land around the little house was no clearer than it had been when Bertram had come over to help him build his house at the start of their time in the wilderness when they had been confident and laughing.

'Spring is here and I have planted nothing,' John said dully, holding a fold of his waistband in his calloused hand. 'The ground is not clear, and I cannot dig. I have no time to dig. Just getting in food and water and fuel takes all my time, and I am tired ... I am so tired.'

He stretched out his hand for his cloak. It was not folded tidily away in the corner of the room any more but left in the corner where he kicked it to one side in the mornings. He wrapped himself in its thick warmth. Hester had bought it for him when he said that he was going away, he remembered. Hester, who had not wanted to come. Hester, who had sworn that the new country was not for men and women who were used to the ease and comfort of town life, that it would suit only farmers who had no chance of doing well in their home country, farmers and adventurers and risk-takers who had nothing to lose.

John lay down on the bare earth floor before the glow of the fire and pulled the collar of the cloak up over his face. Although it was morning he felt he wanted to pull the cloak over his head and let himself sleep. He heard a small, pitiful sound, like Frances used to make when she woke from a bad dream in the night, and realised that it was himself, and that he was weeping like a frightened child. The little sound went on, John heard it as if he were far away from his own fear and weakness, and then he fell asleep, still hearing it.

He woke feeling hungry and afraid. The fire was nearly out. At the sight of the grey ash in the grate John leaped to his feet with a gasp of fear and looked out of the open window. Thank God, it was not dark, he had not slept away the whole day. He stumbled outside, the cloak clinging to his feet, making him stumble, and gathered armfuls of wood from his outside store. He tumbled the logs into the grate and prised off the dry pieces of bark. With little twigs he poked the bark into the heart of the red embers and put his head down into the ash and blew, gently, softly, praying that they would catch. It took a long time. John heard himself muttering a prayer. A little flame flickered yellow like a candle, and then went out.

'Please God!' John breathed.

The little flame flickered yellow again and caught. The twist of bark crisped, burned, and was consumed. John laid a couple of twigs across it and was rewarded by them catching alight at once. Immediately he fed the fire with bigger and bigger twigs until it was burning brightly and John was safe from the coming darkness and cold once more.

He realised then that he was hungry. In his cooking pot was porridge from last night, or if he wished to give himself the labour he could clean out the pot and set some water to boil and try to shoot a bird for meat. There was nothing else to eat.

He put the cooking pot a little closer to the flames so that the porridge would not be stone cold, and went to the door.

The evening was drawing in. The sun had gone behind the trees and the sky above the little house was veiled with strips of thinnest cloud, like the shawl the queen used to wear over her hair when she was on her way to Mass. 'Mantilla clouds,' John said, looking up at them. The sky was pale, the colour of dead lavender heads in winter, the colour of heather in summer, violet and pink with all the brightness drained away.

John shivered. His momentary admiration of the sky had suddenly changed. At once it looked again too vast, too indifferent, it was impossible that a man as small as him could survive under the great dome of it. From the mantilla clouds looking down, John's home would be nothing more than a little speck, John peeping out would be smaller than an flea. The country was too big for him, the forest too wide, the river too rich and cold and fast-flowing and deep. John had a sense that all his new life was nothing more than an arduous crawling like a little ant from one place to another and that his survival was of no interest to the sky, any more than the life of an ant was of interest to him.

'God is with me,' John said, summoning Jane's faith.

There was a silence. There was no sign that God was with him. There was no sign that there was any God. John remembered Suckahanna casting smoking tobacco on the river at sunrise and sunset, and thought for a blasphemous moment that perhaps this land had strange gods, different gods, from England; and that if John could somehow creep under the protection of the gods of the new world then he would be safe from the indifferent gaze of the swelling sky.

'I should be praying,' John said quietly. He did not observe Sundays here in the wilderness. He did not even pray before his meals nor before he lay down to sleep at night. 'I don't even know when Sunday is!' John exclaimed.

He could feel panic rising up in him at the thought that he had slept during this day; but he did not know how long he had slept. He did not know how far the town was downriver, how long it would take him to get there, that he did not even know what day it was.

'I cannot go into town dressed like this and stinking like an animal!' John said. But then he stopped. How was he to get clean if not in town? He could hardly wash and dry the clothes he needed unless he was prepared to run as naked as a savage in the forest. And how could he pay for all his laundry to be done in the town like some fine gentleman? All his money should be spent on hiring labourers to clear his land, buying seed corn, buying tobacco seeds, new axes, more spades.

John thought of the wealth of the house at Lambeth. He thought of the servants who did the work for him: the cook who prepared the meals, the maid who waited in the house, the garden and the gardeners, his wife Hester who ordered it all done; and how he had wildly, madly decided that none of it was for him any longer, and that his life belonged somewhere else, with another woman. Now he looked ready to die in that somewhere else. And the other woman was lost to him.

'That is all this place is to me,' he said softly. 'Somewhere else. I am living in somewhere else and I am going to die in somewhere else unless I can get myself home again.'

A sharp, acrid scent reminded him abruptly of his dinner. He turned with a cry of distress. The cooking pot was spewing a dark smoke into the room, it had overheated and the porridge had stuck to the bottom of the pot and was burned.

John lunged to pull it away from the fire and then recoiled as the hot metal handle scorched into his hand. He dropped the pot and cursed, his hand burning with pain. He had a little water left in his cup and he poured it over the burn. The skin puckered up and turned white. John felt the sweat break out on his face at the pain and he cried out again.

He turned from the room and ran out of the door, down to the river. At the little beach before the house he knelt down to the water and plunged his hand in. The cold water felt like a blow from a whip against the damaged skin but slowly the pain eased. 'Ah God, my God,' John heard himself saying. 'What a fool! What a fool I am!'

When the pain had eased a little he took his hand from the water and looked at it fearfully. The handle of the cooking pot had left a white stripe along his palm. The skin was dead-looking, swelling fast. John tried to flex his fingers; at once a sharp pain ran like a blade across his hand.

'So now I have only one good hand,' he said grimly, 'and burned dinner.' He looked again at the sky. 'And night coming on.'

He turned and walked slowly back up to the little house, his head full of thoughts and fears. The fire was still lit, which was one good thing. He pushed the overturned cooking pot with his booted foot. It rolled on the earth floor. It was cool, he had been down by the river for perhaps an hour. He had not known that the time was passing. He set it on its little feet and peered inside. There was nothing that he could eat. The porridge was blackened and charred almost to ashes.

John took the pot and went down to the river once more, picking his way in the twilight which was coming on in a rush like a dark cloak thrown over the forest. He left the pot to soak in the water while he looked at his fish trap. It was empty. John went back to his pot and arduously, with his good left hand, tried to scrape out the charred remains, swill it and rinse it clean.

He filled the pot with water and, carrying it in his left hand, went back up the beach and up the little hill to his house. Where the trees had been felled before the house the forest was already regaining the land. Small vines and little weeds and ground-covering plants were invading the space. If John did not get out and dig soon the forest would crowd back in and his house would be all but forgotten, marked only on a map in the governor's office as a headright, once claimed but then neglected, ready for another fool to take the challenge and try to make a life in the wilderness.

In the house John poured his drinking water into his cup, spilling some on the floor in his one-handed clumsiness, then he put a scoop of powdered cornflour into the water and set it to heat. This time he did not take his eyes from it, but stood over it, stirring as it thickened and came to the boil, and then set it to one side to cool before serving it into his trencher. He had made enough for breakfast tomorrow so he could eat when he woke in the morning. His stomach rumbled. He could not remember the last time he had eaten fruit or something green. He could not remember when he had last eaten meat that was not wood pigeon. He thought, absurdly and suddenly, of English plums and the sharp sweetness of their flesh. In his father's garden there were thirty-three different varieties of plum tree, from the rare white diapered plum of Malta, which the Tradescants alone grew in all of England, to the common dark-skinned plum of every cottage garden.

He shook his head. There was no point thinking about home and the wealth his father had left him. There was no point thinking about the richness of his inheritance, the flowers, the vegetables, the herbs, the fruit. There was no point thinking about any food which he could not catch or grow in this unhelpful land. All there was for dinner tonight, and breakfast the next day, was an unappetising mess of corn porridge. And unless he could find a way to fish and shoot with only one hand, that would be all there was for a day or so, for a week or two, until his hand healed.

With his belly full of porridge John drank water and took off his boots, ready to sleep. His cloak was missing. He looked around for it, cursing his own laziness in not hanging it up every morning. It was nowhere to be seen. John felt a disproportionate alarm. His cloak was missing, the cloak Hester had given him, the cloak he always slept in. He could feel an absurd panic rising up in him and threatening to choke him. He strode to the corner of the room where his goods were piled and turned them over, tumbling them to the ground in his haste. His cloak was not there.

'Think!' he commanded himself. 'Think, you fool!'

He steadied himself and his breathing, which had become hoarse and anxious, settled down. 'I must stay calm,' John said to himself, his voice quavery against the darkness. 'I have left it somewhere. That's all.'

He went through his movements. He had slept in his cloak in the afternoon and then he had run outside when the fire had burned out. He remembered then. His cloak had been tangled around his feet and he had kicked it away in his haste to get some dry wood to relight the fire.

'I left it outside,' he said quietly. 'Now I'll have to get it.'

He went slowly to the door and put his hand on the wooden latch. He paused. Through the cracks between the planks the colder night air breathed against his face like an icy sigh. It was dark beyond the wooden door, dark with a density that John had never seen before in his life, a blackness which was not challenged by firelight nor candlelight nor torchlight for dozens of miles in one direction, and hundreds, thousands, perhaps millions of miles westwards. It was a darkness that was so powerful and so completely void of light that John had a foolish, superstitious fear that if he opened the door, the night would rush into the room and extinguish the fire. It was a darkness which was too great for him to challenge.

'But I want my cloak,' he said stubbornly.

Slowly, fearfully, he opened the door a little way. The clouds were thick between him and the stars, the darkness was absolute. With a little whimper John dropped to his hands and knees like a child and crawled over the threshold of his house, his hands before him feeling his way, hoping to touch his cloak.

Something brushed against his outstretched fingers and he recoiled with a sob of fright but then he realised that it was the soft wool of his cloak. He gathered it up to him as if it was a treasure, one of the king's most beautiful sacred tapestries. He bundled it to his face and smelled his own strong scent, not with distaste but with a sense of relief at smelling something human in this icy empty darkness.

He did not dare to turn his back on the void. With one arm tucking his cloak to his chest, he backed, still on his hands and knees, into his doorway like a frightened animal retreating into its lair, and then he shut the door.

His eyes, strained wide open against the darkness, blinked blindly when he was back in the fitful flickering light of the cottage. He shook out his cloak. It was wet with dew. John hardly cared. He wrapped himself in it and lay down to sleep. Lying on his back, his eyes still wide open in fear, he could see the steam rising off himself. If he had not been so deep in despair he would have laughed at the sight of a hungry man supping on porridge, a cold man wrapped in damp cloth, a pioneer with one hand. But none of it seemed very funny.

'Dear God, keep me safe through the night and show me what I must do in the morning,' John said as he closed his eyes.

He waited in the darkness for sleep to come, listening to the sounds of the forest outside his door. He had a moment of acute terror when he heard a pack of wolves howling in the distance, and thought that they might smell the food and come and ring the cottage with their bright yellow eyes and their lean, serene faces. But then they fell silent and John fell asleep.

When he woke in the morning it was raining. He put his cloak to one side and put the pot by the fire to heat. He stirred the porridge but when he came to eat it he found he had no appetite. He had gone through hunger into indifference. He knew he must eat; but the grey porridge, dirty with the old ash from the inside of the pot, was tasteless in his mouth. He forced himself to swallow five mouthfuls and then put the pot in the fireplace to stay warm. If there were no fish in the trap, and if he could not shoot something, then it would be porridge for dinner as well.

The stocks of wood beside the fire were low. John went outside. The woodpile was low too and damp from the rain. John took nearly all of it and stacked it inside the house to dry. He went to grasp his axe to go and cut some more but the pain from his burned hand made him cry out. He could not use the axe until the burn was healed. He would have to gather wood, break up what he could by stamping on it, and burn the longer branches from one end to another, pushing them into the heart of the fire as they were consumed.

He went out into the rain, his head bowed, wearing only his homespun coat, leaving his cloak behind to dry. He had seen a fallen tree rather like an oak when he had been out with his gun a few days ago. He trudged towards it. When he got there he saw that some of the branches had split from the main trunk. There was wood that he could use. Using only his left hand, he pulled a branch away from the rest of the tree, and tucked the limb under his arm. It was hard work getting it home. The broad sweep of the branch kept getting caught in the undergrowth, wedged against trees, enwrapped in ground vines. Again and again John had to stop and go back and break it free. The forest of John's headright was thick, almost impenetrable, it took John all the morning to travel just one mile with his firewood, and then another hour to break it up into manageable logs before bringing it inside the house to dry.

He was soaked through by the rain and by sweat and aching with tiredness. The burn on his hand was oozing some kind of liquid. John looked at it fearfully. If the wound went bad then he would have to go to Jamestown and put himself in the hands of whatever barber surgeon had set up in the town. John was afraid of losing his hand, afraid of the journey to Jamestown, one-handed in a dugout canoe, but equally afraid of staying on his own in the cottage if he became ill. He could taste the sweat on his upper lip and recognised the scent of his own fear.

He turned to the fire, wanting to think of something else. The fire was burning well and the room was warm. John looked out through the open window and through the gaps in the plank walls. The forest outside seemed to have come a little closer, to have advanced through the sheets of rain to press a little nearer to the solitary house.

'Don't let it destroy me,' John whispered, knowing himself to be absurd. 'Don't let me come all this way and try so hard, to be just grown over as if I were nothing more than the dead body of a dog.'

There was nothing to eat but yesterday's porridge. John did not bother to heat it. Warm or cold, it was equally unpleasant to him. He took a spoon and made himself eat four spoonfuls and then took a draught of water. He knew that he should go out into the forest with his gun and shoot a wood pigeon, a squirrel, anything he could get, for its meat. But the rain was too forbidding and the darkening sky was threatening thunder. John felt a sense of deep, helpless terror at the thought of being out there amid all that powerful green life, with the rain pouring more life and more energy into the avid earth, and him the only thing in the woods which was cringing and growing weaker every day.

'I'll sleep while it rains,' he said, trying to comfort himself. 'I'll take the gun out at twilight, that's always a good time.'

He took off his wet coat and his sodden breeches and spread them out to dry, then he pushed one of the big branches into the heart of the fire, wrapped himself up in his warm cape, and fell asleep.

John felt as if he had slept for perhaps a minute and then he woke with a start of terror to the realisation that it was dark. He could not see the window. The whole cottage was in darkness. Only the embers of the fire glowed, the branch of the tree had quite burned through and fallen away from the hearth.

His first thought was that it was a terrible storm which had darkened the sky, but then he heard the silence of the outside, all he could hear was the patter of rain on leaves, an awful, remorseless, unforgiving patter of steady rain on fresh leaves. John struggled to his feet. He found that he was half-naked, wearing only his shirt, and remembered that only minutes ago he had taken off his sodden trousers and jacket and lain down for a rest. He pulled them on; they were dry, they had been dry for hours.

'It's night,' John suddenly realised. 'I slept all the afternoon and now it is night.'

He looked around the room as if everything might have changed during his long, enchanted sleep. His heap of goods, the tools he had thought he would use to farm his new land, his stores of dried goods, were all there; and higgledy piggledy beside them was the pile of wood that he had brought in only this morning.

He took a couple of logs and put them on the fire. When they burned up the shadows in the room leaped and flickered at him; but the window and the cracks in the walls looked darker and more ominous than ever.

John bit back a sob of misery. It might be the middle of the night or just before dawn but he could not lie down and sleep again. All his senses were alert, he felt surrounded by danger. His certainty was that it was afternoon, early afternoon, and that he should be out fetching firewood, checking the fish trap, hunting, or at the very least starting to clear a patch of ground and digging so that he could plant his seeds. But the darkness, the strange, inexplicable darkness outside the house was impenetrable.

'I shall have to wait until dawn.' John tried to speak calmly but the quaver in his voice frightened him and made him fall silent. He thought instead, arranging the words in his mind so they sounded like calm good sense. 'It will be good to start early in the morning. I shall take my gun and shoot wood pigeon while they are still roosting. I might get a couple and then I could dry the meat. I might get several and then I could smoke them in the chimney and always have meat to eat.'

The darkness outside the window did not lift at all.

John sat down before the fire, stretched his legs before him and looked into the flames. Hours passed. His head nodded and he stretched out before the fire and closed his eyes. He slept. At dawn he woke, warned by the growing chill that the fire was dying down, got up and heaped more wood on the embers. He slept again. It was not until the middle of the morning that he woke. His empty stomach rumbled but he did not feel hungry; he felt weak, light-headed and weary.

'I'll sleep again,' he said. He glanced towards the closed shutters of the window. Around the frame was a line of bright golden light. The storm had blown away and it was a beautiful sunny day.

John looked at it without interest. 'I'm tired,' he said to the silent room. He slept.

When he woke it was early afternoon. The ache in his belly was hunger, but all he felt was thirst. There was no water left in his beaker. 'I shall have to go down to the river,' he said unhappily to himself. He heaped more wood on the fire and looked at the ash-filled hearth as if it were a greedy enemy. 'I suppose I could let it go out,' he said thoughtfully, rejecting the wisdom of those who had told him never to let the fire go out, that the fire was his light and protection and saviour. 'I could let it go out during the day. Just light it at night.'

He nodded to himself as if approving a statement of good sense, and opened the door. Then he stopped dead.

On the doorstep was a small basket, beautifully woven in coloured strings. Inside it were three warm new-laid duck eggs, a loaf of pale yellow corn bread, a handful of nuts and a leaf wrapped around some dried fruits.

John exclaimed and looked out at once towards the forest where the trees were thick at the edge of his felled patch. Nothing moved. There was no skirt of buckskin flicking out of sight, no gleam of dark oiled hair.

'Suckahanna?' he called. His voice was low, he had spoken in nothing but a low whisper for so many weeks he thought he had forgotten how to shout her name. He tried again. 'Suckahanna?'

There was no answer. A jay shrieked and a wood pigeon clattered in the branches as it flew away, but there was no other sound.

John bent and picked up the basket. Surely this was a gift from her, seeing his door closed, guessing how low this country had brought him? He took the basket inside and set it down by the fireplace, and then, feeling his desire for food rekindled at the sight of the eggs, he went quickly down to the river and filled his cooking pot with water.

He set the eggs on to boil but he could not wait for them to cook before tasting the other food. While they were bubbling in the pot he broke the bread and ate it, and then cracked the nuts on the hearthstone and ate the sweet kernels. The juices rushed into his mouth, the taste of a food which was not cornflour porridge was so strange and desirable that the corners of his jaw suddenly pained him sharply, as if he had bitten into a lemon. It was passionate desire for food, for a new taste. When the eggs were boiled John broke off the tops, careless that he scalded his mouth, and ate the whites and sucked the yellow yolks down in great desirous gulps. The yellow tasted like blood, he could feel the strength of it coursing through him, making him whole-hearted again, courageous, enterprising, making a pioneer out of a man who moments ago had been a lost boy.

'My God, I was hungry!' he said. He took the last piece of bread and ate it, relishing the slightly sweet taste of it and the pale yellow colour. Then he took a handful of the dried fruit and put it in his mouth. At once his mouth was filled with flavour as strong as sherbet, as sharp as redcurrants. It was a fruit he did not know, wrinkled like raisins but as sharp-tasting as sour greengages. John held the sweet mass in his mouth and sucked it and sucked it as the sharpness and sweetness poured out of the dried skins and into his throat.

He sat entranced, his mouth pursed around the flavour, as if nothing in the whole world could be as good as this moment when he was fed at last, after months of hunger.

When he had finished his meal there were only a few of the fruits left over. He had eaten everything else. 'I should have saved some,' John thought regretfully. 'I am as greedy as a savage to pour it down my throat and not save any for my dinner.' Then he realised that he could not have stopped himself from eating. He simply would not have had the willpower, and that without the strength from the meal he could not have gone on.

'And now I shall check my fish trap, and I shall clear a patch of ground and plant some seeds,' he said determinedly. 'Thank God I have the strength to do it.'

First he loaded the fire with the broken branches, remembering the wisdom of the rule that he should always keep the fire in. Then he went out of the cottage and left the door open behind him so that the cool, clean wind could sweep in and blow away the stench of him living like a dog, sleeping like a dog, and never getting clean. He went down to the river and stripped off his shirt and his breeches and left them piled under stones in the water while he waded into the icy river and washed. When he came out, shivering with cold, he pulled out his clothes and rinsed them roughly until the shirt was evenly pale grey instead of dirty and stained. Then he wrung them, still favouring his hurt hand, and shook them out as he jogged back to the house on his bare feet. The fire was blazing. He upended the cooking pot and balanced a couple of sticks so he could spread the wet clothes before the heat. Then he went back outside, bare-arsed, wearing only his jacket for warmth, and started to break up firewood.

When he had made a good pile he stacked it and then went inside for his spade and pick. He paused for a moment looking over his land, his new land. It was no hunger-born illusion that the forest was creeping back. Long trails of vines were moving in like snakes across the cleared patch, speckles of weeds were springing like a green plague across the clean soil. Nothing would stop this earth regenerating. By felling the trees all John had done was let in the low-growing plants which were colonising the clearing.

John marked out with his eye a line which would run parallel with the front of his house and stop before the doorway. It would be a vegetable bed with young tobacco plants interspersed with eating plants. Salad vegetables would be quick to grow, and he had seed potatoes, turnip, carrot, leek and pea seeds as well. Other planters up and down the river, with labourers to work for them, some of them enslaved, some of them free, had taken the risk of planting nothing but tobacco, assuming that they could buy everything else they wanted, all their food, all their building materials, all their clothes, from the profits of one cash crop. Men like that had died in the early years, or begged from the Indians and called it trade, or gone barefoot into town and pleaded for charity. But when the tobacco grew, and the price of tobacco started to rise, the gamble for some of them had paid off. John thought of the little cottage gardens that his mother had told him about, in the village of Meopham, where every house, however small, had a patch of ground behind it which grew food to keep the worst of the winter hunger away. John realised that he was reduced to a level that his parents had congratulated themselves on leaving behind; but then he thought more cheerfully that perhaps this was his starting place, as Meopham had been theirs.

He hefted the pick and swung it into the ground. At once it jarred on a root and he felt the sudden pain as the new skin on the palm of his hand split open and drained a dripping water. He caught his hand up and looked fearfully at it. The skin which had looked so dead and white had peeled off the wound and was pouring, not blood, but a clear liquor. The pain was so sharp that John's head rang with it for long moments. Then he slowly bent, took the axe and the spade, tucked them under his arm, and brought them back to the house. He could not dig one-handed. His garden would have to wait.

Inside the house he took a strip of linen which had once been destined to be a white stock if he were invited to somewhere fine, and wound it around his hand, tying it tight to staunch the flow. It stung painfully as he wrapped it, and he felt the cloth stick into the wound.

'The thing is,' he said quietly to the empty room, 'is that I don't rightly know what to do for the best.'

John thought he should wait till his shirt and breeches were dry and then walk, though it would be a long walk, to the Hobert plantation and see what Sarah Hobert could do for a grievous burn. 'She may have a salve,' John said. 'And I could stay the night with them, and talk. And they'll have bread.'

The high spirits of the morning were draining out of him. He felt his shirt, anxious now to leave. The shirt was dry and sweet-smelling but the breeches, made of thick homespun, were still wet. John was thinking of wearing them wet when a sudden pain gripped him deep in his belly.

It was the food, shovelled down into his shrunken stomach, too rich for a system which had been living at starvation level. 'Ah God!' John exclaimed. The pang of it was like a sword thrust into his heart.

He doubled up and ran, bent double, for the door. He had scarcely cleared the house when he voided himself and felt his strength burst and then trickle from him. He clung to the doorframe with the pain of it and then felt his hands and even his fingertips grow weaker as the pain seized him in the belly and shook him, like a monster's jaws.

'What a fool I am, what a fool . . .' he gasped between spasms. He thought he should have known that his body could not take the richness of such food after weeks of hunger. 'What a fool . . . what a fool.'

The attack subsided and John half-stumbled and half-crawled back indoors. The stink was very bad but he could not get down to the river again to wash. He wrapped himself in his cloak and lay down before his fire. He realised that he would not be well enough to walk to the Hoberts'. He could not paddle his canoe one-handed. He could not dig his garden until his hand healed, and until this dreadful flux passed he would be fit for nothing. He would be hard-pressed to get down to the river and then he would be unable to walk up the hill again. He lay in the warmth of the fire, thanking God that he had thought to make it big this morning, and then closed his eyes. Everytime the pain in his belly woke him with a spasm of hurt he turned his eye towards the door. If Suckahanna did not come again with food, with water, and with herbs to heal his burned hand, John thought he would probably die there, lying before a dying fire, bare-arsed, sick as a dog, and with one worthless and perhaps poisoned hand, and nothing fit to eat.

She did not come. When dusk fell John crawled to the door and pushed it shut, fearful of the night creatures. If the wolves came closer tonight it would be only the closed door that would keep them from him, and they could break that down with one spring. John himself did not have the strength to load his gun. He felt himself sweating into his cloak and then a wet sensation and a terrible stench which meant that he had emptied his bowels again. He could do nothing but lie in his own filth. Some time in the night he was sick on the floor, the vomit spreading in a pool around him, and then the smell of it made him sick again but he brought up only burning bile from his empty belly. He hauled himself up on one elbow and put more wood on the fire. Then he slept.

He woke in the morning, aching all over and shivering as if he had an ague. His hand was throbbing and the fingers were turning black. The house stank like a kennel and his cloak was stuck to his back by a dried pelt of excrement. He crawled to the door and opened it, kicking the cloak off his back as he went. His skin was raw and sore and his sight kept coming and going, the open door a wavering oblong of gold and green light.

There was a black earthenware pot of clean water on the doorstep, and another pot beside it of warm corn porridge. John heard his sore throat give a little sob of gratitude. He drew the pot of water towards him and sipped it cautiously. His stomach rumbled but the dreadful spasms of pain had passed. He pulled himself round to sit on the doorstep and lifted the pot of porridge to his lips. It was not porridge as he made it, in his dirty scorched cooking pot. It was light, faintly scented with herbs, as yellow as blanchemange, flavoured with something like saffron. John took a cautious sip and, despite a growl of hunger from his belly, made himself wait, sip water, pause. Then he took another.

Cautiously, eating so slowly, that his breakfast took most of the morning, John ate the porridge from the pot and drank most of the water. An hour later, he found he could stand without fainting. Warily, he pulled himself up the doorframe and bundled his stinking cloak out of the house. A row of cleared and dug earth extended along the front of the house, from the point where John had thrown one blow of the pickaxe to where it ended, neatly squared, before the door. John looked at it and then rubbed his eyes as if it were a dream, a dream from fever and from his sickness.

No. It was real. She had come in the night and cleared a row of earth for him to plant his seeds. She had come and seen his sickness and realised that he had eaten too fast and put himself at the very door of death through his own greed and stupidity, and she had left him, not a little feast, but a thin meal of gruel and water, so that he would get well again. She was keeping him as if he were a child, choosing his food for him, doing his work for him. John felt ready to weep for gratitude that she was prepared to give him food, fetch his water, do his work. But he knew also a sharp, contrasting discomfort that she should see him so unmanned, that she had seen he could do nothing in this new land, not even survive.

'Suckahanna?' he whispered.

Still there was no reply, just the calling of birds, and the quacking of ducks in the river.

John gathered his foul cloak and hobbled down to the river to soak it in his washing place, and lowered himself into the cold water to try to get clean. Again he laboured up the slight slope to his house, lugging the wet cloth, his feet tender on the stones of his field. His hand was sore, his head thudding, his stomach quiveringly tender. 'I cannot survive here,' John said as he reached his door after a long, arduous struggle up the little hill. 'I must find a way to get downriver to Bertram, I will die here.'

He wondered for a moment if he should wait for her, if he were to lie before the fire whether she might come and live with him, as they had planned. But he was warned by the cautious way she had approached him. He could not count on her to rescue him. He must help himself. 'I shall go downriver to Bertram,' he said. 'If she wants to come to me she will know how to find me there.'

His breeches and his shirt at least were clean and dry. It took him a long time to pull them on. His boots went on with a struggle which left him panting for breath, and he bent over to ease the swimming of his head. He did not take his gun for he could not load it nor keep the fuse lit in the canoe. There was nothing else that he could carry. This new country which he had been certain would make him rich had made him poorer than a pauper. All he could carry were the clothes that he stood up in, all he could manage to do was to stagger like a drunkard down the hill to where the canoe was pulled up, out of reach of the tide.

He thought for a little while that he would never get it down the small beach and into the deep water. He pushed for a while and it moved no more than an inch. Then he had to rest, and then he had to push again. It was a process that took most of his strength and courage. When the canoe finally rocked in the water he could hardly find the energy to climb in. He thought that his weight had grounded it, but when he took the paddle in his one good hand he managed to lift the weight a little and the canoe slid into the middle of the river into the deeper water.

The tide was on the ebb and the current of the river was flowing seaward. The canoe picked up speed. John tried to use the paddle to steer it closer to the bank but with one hand he could not control it. He thrust the paddle into the water and the canoe spun around it; in a second he would be swamped and the canoe would sink. He made one desperate shove, pointed it downriver, and then clung to the side as it bucked and weaved in the fast current, shaking as it tumbled in the white water. John looked at the bank which seemed to be tearing past him. Nothing seemed familiar though he and Bertram had watched carefully, pointing out landmarks, so that he would be able to make this journey, so that Bertram would know when he was nearing John's head-right. He thought he recognised a tall single pine with its roots extending deep into the water, and he dug the paddle in again, trying to turn the canoe towards the shore. The current snatched the paddle, John lunged to grab it back, and then the paddle was flicked like kindling from his hand and the canoe was turning and turning in the dizzying flood and John could neither steer it nor control it, nor do anything but duck down on the wet floor of the canoe and give himself up for lost.

John opened his eyes. Above him was a high, rounded roof made of lashed branches, and thatched with broad leaves. He was lying on some sort of bedstead made of branches spread with mats. He turned his head, half-expecting to see the familiar face of Bertram Hobert or Sarah's restrained smile. The place was empty.

It was not a house built by a normal Englishman, that at least was clear. It was a domed-ceilinged square hut, roofed and walled with leaves, floored with woven mats and deerskins spread on the earth. In the centre of the hut was a small fire with a tiny heart of red which kept the hut warm and filled it with light, acrid smoke. On the walls were hung the skins of animals, and a basket half-woven, and other baskets bulging with goods. The only light filtered in through the hole in the roof above the fire, and flickered at the skins which curtained the door. John swung his feet down to the floor and took two cautious steps to go out.

At once a brown-skinned child popped his head inside the room, took one look at John standing, and, without moving, without taking his eyes from the Englishman, opened his mouth and let out a yell. John froze to the spot, heard running footsteps and then a woman stood behind the child, her hand on his shoulder, and another woman behind her, poised with a bow raised and an arrow on the string.

John dropped to sit on the bed, spread his hands, tried to smile.

'Hello,' he said. He nodded, trying to look reassuring, peaceable. 'Hello.'

The two women nodded in reply, saying nothing. Remembering the weeks of silence from Suckahanna, John did not make the assumption that they could not understand him, although their eyes remained blank and black.

'Thank you for bringing me here. The canoe was too strong for me. I was trying to get to my friend's house – Bertram Hobert – but the current swept me away.'

Again they nodded, saying nothing.

'Is Jamestown anywhere near here?' John asked. He wondered if he had been swept far below the town, down to the edge of the sea perhaps. 'Jamestown? Anywhere near? Jamestown?'

The woman with the arrow on the string smiled briefly. 'Nowhere near,' she said. She spoke with a strange Welsh lilt to her voice.

'You speak English!' John exclaimed.

She did not nod or smile, nor did she release the tension on the bowstring.

'I am a peaceful man,' John said. 'I was trying to farm outside my house, on my land beside the river. I went hungry, and I burned my hand. I was going to find my friend to get help. I am a peaceful man. I am looking for an Indian girl, an Indian woman. Suckahanna.'

Neither of the women responded to the name.

'I want to make her my wife,' John said, plunging in. 'If she will have me. I have come back to Virginia –' He broke off. It occurred to him that perhaps in their ignorance they did not know the name of their country. 'I have come back here, from my home, to be with her.'

'Suckahanna is married to my brother,' the woman with the bow on the string said precisely. 'He went with her when she took her gifts of food to you. We did not realise that you would eat it all at once – like a pig with acorns. We did not mean to make you sick.'

John felt embarrassment burn under the skin of his face. 'I was foolish,' he said. 'I was very hungry.' The thought of these people discussing his greed, and perhaps watching him void himself and retch, made him want to close his eyes and be anywhere else, even back in his own little house facing death, rather than here with the woman looking at him in mild curiosity.

'Why did Suckahanna not show herself?' he asked. 'I would be her friend now she has a husband.' He looked at the arrow on the string again. 'I never wronged her,' he said hastily. 'I wanted to marry her when I thought she was a maid.'

The woman's face did not soften. John thought in sudden, rapid terror that perhaps they had saved him for some dreadful execution. There were stories in Jamestown of men having their bellies cut open and their guts dragged out before their eyes. 'I meant her no harm,' John said. 'I meant none of you any harm.'

'Your house is where we hunt,' the other woman observed. 'You have frightened away the game birds and the deer are making other paths in the woods to get away from your burned field and the smell of you.'

'I am sorry,' John said again. He thought of the governor's map and the empty spaces of forest unmarked by any names. 'I thought the forest was empty.'

They looked at him as if his words were simply incomprehensible. 'Empty?'

'Empty of people,' John corrected himself. 'I knew there were animals living there. But I did not think it was your land.'

'The animals do not own the land,' the woman with the arrow pointed at his body said slowly, as if she were trying to understand some alien logic.

'No,' John agreed.

'But you know they are there, they pass through the forest.'

'Yes.'

'We pass through the forest too, we follow them when we hunt them, we clear land for a season to grow our food. How can land be empty?'

John swallowed on a dry throat, his head thudded sharply. 'It is how we white men speak,' he said helplessly.

The woman with the bow nodded, the arrow still pointing at his belly. 'You people said you would come here for just a little while, look for precious metal and then go,' she observed. 'Now you tell us that the land is empty and you build your houses on the game trails and fell the trees of the forests and never let them grow again.'

'I am sorry,' John said. 'We did not know that you were living here. If you would help me to get to Jamestown I could tell the governor . . .'

He trailed off. Suddenly she turned the arrow away from him as if she had lost interest in the whole conversation. 'We will decide what is to be done with you when the men come home,' she said abruptly. 'Stay here till then.'

John spread his hands, trying to indicate his obedience and harmlessness.

'The child will bring you something to eat,' the other woman said. 'Do not shit in here. You must go to the forest for that.'

John felt his face burn scarlet and cursed himself for a fool to be so ashamed for having diarrhoea when he could be facing disembowelling.

'Of course not,' he said, clinging to his dignity.

The woman looked at him. 'We all saw you,' she said. 'But we are clean. We are the People, the Powhatan. You must do your dirt in the forest while you are with us, and cover it up after.'

'I will,' John said. 'I am thirsty.'

'The child will bring you food and drink,' the other woman said. She slid her arrow into a quiver strapped to her side. 'Don't gorge yourself.'

'And Suckahanna? Is she here?' John tried to ask the question with a calm, neutral voice but his head hammered again at the thought of her.

They looked at him indifferently, and then they turned and went out.

The child brought a pot filled with icy cold water. John sipped at it carefully. The pot was coal-black, as smooth as marble in his hands. He could not think how it had been made, it was as elegant as a funerary urn in the king's collection.

He waited. The child, he could not even tell if it were a boy or a girl, wearing an apron of buckskin but otherwise naked, squatted in the doorway of the hut and regarded him with solemn dark eyes. John tried to smile. The child's face was grave. John leaned back against the wall of the hut and waited.

He could see the shadows lengthen in the little square of the doorway, and then he heard the sound of singing from far away. From the child's silent alertness he guessed that it had heard them some minutes ago. John looked at the child and raised his eyebrows as if to ask what might be happening. The child was solemn as a warrior, and like a powerful warrior merely shook its head.

John leaned back again and waited.

The chorus of singing came nearer. John listened more intently. He was sure, he was certain, he could hear Suckahanna's voice. Reason told him that it was not possible, that he had heard her speak only once or twice, that he surely could not hear her voice among many; but still he felt his heart pound and still he leaned forwards, his ears aching with the effort to hear more clearly.

'Suckahanna?' he whispered.

The child, recognising the name, nodded, and then made a simple, graceful gesture to the door, and she was there, framed by the golden evening light, taller than he remembered, her face a little graver, her hair grown on both sides of her head but still braided away from her face on the right-hand side, wearing buckskin leggings and a little buckskin dress, and her arms and cheeks painted with red spirals.

'Suckahanna!' he said.

She stood before him and looked him over, unsmiling, and then she drew a little closer and put out her hand. John, hesitating, not knowing what he should do, put out his hand in reply, and then, as solemn as Parliament men, they shook.

Her fingers, warm and dry, closed on his and John felt an extraordinary sense of desire at that light touch. His eyes went to her face and he saw, only half-believing, the slow smile spread from her eyes to her lips till her whole face was lightened and joyful.

'John,' she said sweetly, her accent lilting on his name. 'Welcome to my people.'

At once he stumbled into explanations. 'I meant to come, I meant to come when I said. I didn't plan to betray you. It was my intention to come to you. But when I got home my father was dead and my children needed a mother –' He broke off as he saw her shake her head and shrug.

'I knew you meant to come,' she said. 'But when you did not come my mother and I had to leave Jamestown and find our people. And then it was time that I should be married, and so now I am married.'

John would have withdrawn his hand but she held him fast. 'This is my son,' she said with a smile to the child in the doorway.

'Your son!'

'The son of my husband. His first wife died and I am now mother to this boy, and I have a girl-child of my own.'

John felt regret wash over him as painful as sickness. 'I never thought –'

'Yes, I am a woman grown,' she said steadily.

John shook his head as if he would deny the passing of the years. 'I should have come. I meant to come.'

'Your hand is hurt? And you have been sick?'

'The sickness was my own fault,' John said. 'I went hungry for too long and then ate the eggs you sent me – was it you?'

She nodded.

'They were so good. But I ate them too fast. And I burned my hand on the cooking pot and then the wound broke open . . .'

She took his hand and bent her head over it to see the wound. John looked at the crown of her dark head and smelled the faint, familiar smell of her warm skin and the bear-grease fat which deterred insects, and felt desire spread through him until he thought he must draw her close, and that whatever it cost him, he must hold her in his arms, just once, before he died.

She looked up and at once recognised the desire in his face. She did not flinch back as an Englishwoman would have done. But she did not come forward either. She stood very still and steadily took him in, reading his desire, his fear, his need.

'I think we can heal the wound on your hand,' she said gently. 'Come.'

The little boy at the doorway stepped aside for the two of them and Suckahanna led John out of the hut into the evening light.

John blinked. He was in the centre of a town square, all around were other long huts, built of wood, and walled with reeds, intricately woven. Each hut had a little spiral of scented smoke above its roof, and a flock of children playing in the doorway. In the centre of the square sat a handful of men, at their ease, talking in low, confident voices, one of them tightening a bow string, another sharpening reeds for arrow tips. They glanced up as Suckahanna led John by, but they made no comment, nor even acknowledged his presence. They took him in, as one animal takes in another. They saw in one devouring glance the way he walked, the prints his boots made on the ground, the scent of him, the matted, ill-kept hair and the pallor of sickness. They assessed his ability to fight, to run, to hide. They sensed his fear of them and his trust in Suckahanna. Then they turned back to their work and their talk as if there was nothing to be said about him or to him – as yet.

Suckahanna led him towards a little street with the houses set on either side. At the end of it was a large fire and half a dozen of the black pots sitting squat among the embers, and skewers of meat resting on a rack. John felt his stomach clench in hunger but Suckahanna took him past the food to a hut opposite the fire.

She stood outside and called a word, perhaps a name, and the curtain in the doorway opened and an old woman looked out.

'Suckahanna!'

'Musses.'

The woman spoke in a rapid flow of language, and Suckahanna replied. Something that she said made the old woman snort with laughter and she shot a quick smiling look at John as if he were the butt of the joke. Then she stretched out her hand to see the burn on John's palm.

Suckahanna gestured that he should show her. 'This is a wise woman, she will cure the wound.'

Hesitantly, John opened his fingers to show the scar. It was getting worse. Where the blister had burst the raw flesh had got dirty and was now smelling and oozing. John looked at it fearfully. If he had such a wound in London he thought that a barber surgeon would have cut the hand off, to prevent the infection spreading up his arm to his heart. He feared the infection only slightly less than he feared these savages and whatever treatment they might prescribe.

The woman said something to Suckahanna and Suckahanna laughed, a spontaneous giggle, like the girl John had known. She turned to John.

'She says you should be purged, but I told her you had already done that for yourself.'

The woman was laughing, Suckahanna was smiling, but John, in fear and in pain, could muster only a grim nod.

'But she says you should still sweat out your illness before we cure the wound.'

'Sweat?'

'In a –' Suckahanna did not know the English word. 'Little house. In a little house.'

The woman nodded.

'We'll go there now,' Suckahanna said. 'Then we can get the herbs for the wound before nightfall.'

The woman and Suckahanna led him to the boundary of the village. There was a smaller round hut on the very edge of the little town, its roof at ground level, and thick smoke billowing out from the hole in the centre of the roof.

'It's very hot,' Suckahanna explained.

John nodded, it looked like hell.

Suckahanna laid a gentle hand on his dirty shirt. 'You must take off your clothes,' she said. 'All of them, and go down into there, naked.'

Instinctively, John's hands gripped the belt of his breeches and then he gave a little yelp of pain at the touch of the cloth on his raw palm.

'There!' Suckahanna said, as if that proved the point. 'Take your clothes off and go down into the little house.'

Reluctantly, John pulled his shirt off. The old woman regarded his pale skin with interest, as if he were a ham ready for smoking. John shot a swift, frightened look at the little house.

'Suckahanna – am I to be killed?' he asked. 'I would rather die with my breeches on.'

She did not laugh at his fears. She shook her head. 'I would not lead you to your death,' she said simply. 'I kept you safe in the woods for a month, didn't I? And then I told you that I loved you. Nothing has changed.'

It was like that easy rush of desire that he had felt when he met her. All at once he trusted her. He untied the laces of his breeches and dropped them to the floor. He heel-toed out of his boots and shucked off his stinking stockings. He stood before the two of them naked and felt his genitals shrivel at the curious, bright gaze of the old woman and Suckahanna's evident lack of interest.

'Go down in there,' she said, gesturing to the steps which led down into the smoke-filled darkness. 'There is a bed. Lie down. You will be hot, you will sweat like a fever. When Musses calls you, you can come out. Not before.'

John took one step towards the hut and hesitated. Suckahanna's familiar hard little hand pushed him in the small of the back. 'Go on,' she said insistently. 'You always are thinking, John. Just do.'

He smiled at the truth of that and went down the steps in a little rush of temporary courage, and pitched headlong into the darkness.

The hut was filled with acrid herbal smoke and the heat was intense. He understood now that the hut was set deep like a cellar so that the very earth was like an oven, holding the heat inside. At the very centre of the hut was a small fireplace heaped with red embers, and a jar of dried leaves beside it. There was room for a little bench of stones which were so hot to the touch that John had to sit gingerly, and let his skin become accustomed to their warmth.

'Put the pot of herbs on the fire!' Suckahanna called from the outside.

Reluctantly, John poured the dried leaves on to the fire. At once the hut was filled with a billow of black smoke which sucked the very air out of his lungs and left him choking and whooping for breath. The smoke felled him, like a helpless tree, so he stretched out along the stones and felt his eyes run with tears against the acrid fumes. His nose hurt with the heat, the very coils inside his ears ached with the intense heat and the airless, powerful scent. He felt himself drifting into an extraordinary dream state. He saw Frances with a trowel and a watering pot in the garden of Lambeth, he saw the Duke of Buckingham throw back his dark head and laugh, he saw Johnnie at the moment of his birth, scarlet, wet and squalling, he saw Jane smiling through the candlelight on their wedding night. He saw his father dying in a bed of flowers, he saw the Rosamund roses he had sent down the river for Jane's memorial service at her father's chapel.

From far, far away he heard a voice call something in a strange language and he opened his eyes. The smoke had cleared a little, the heat seemed less intense. His skin was pink, like a baby's. He was damp all over with sweat and his skin was smooth as a sun-warmed lizard.

'She says you can come out!' he heard in English. But it was not the command but the sound of Suckahanna's voice which brought him from his daze, up the steps and out into the sunlight.

'Ah,' the old woman said with pleasure at his appearance. She nodded at Suckahanna, and then tossed a buckskin cape around John's shoulders to keep the chill of the evening air from him.

John looked around for his clothes. Everything was gone except his boots. Suckahanna was standing among a small group of women, they were all looking at his nakedness with a cheerful curiosity.

Suckahanna stepped forward and held out a bundle of clothing to him. As John took it he saw that it was a clout – a piece of cloth to twist between his buttocks and tie on a strap around his waist – a deerskin kilt and a deerskin shirt. He recoiled. 'Where are my clothes?'

Suckahanna shook her head firmly. 'They smelled,' she said. 'And they had lice and fleas. We are a clean people. You could not wear those clothes in our houses.'

He felt ashamed and unable to argue.

'Put those on,' she said. 'We are all waiting for you.'

He tied the strings of the clout around his waist and felt better with his nakedness hidden from so many bright black eyes. 'Why are they all here?'

'To find the herb for your hand,' she said.

John looked down into his palm. The wound was cleaner from the sweating, but there was still a crease of rotting flesh at its centre.

He pulled on the shirt and straightened the kilt. He thought that he must look absurd with his big white legs under this beautifully embroidered skirt and then his own heavy boots on his feet; but none of the women laughed. They moved off, one trotting behind another, with the old woman at the front and Suckahanna at the rear. She glanced back at John. 'Follow,' was all she said.

He remembered then the unbearable steady pace she would use when they were in the woods together. All the women moved at that remorseless trot which was too fast for him to walk and too slow for him to run. He walked and then ran after them in short, breathless bursts and Suckahanna never turned her head to see if he could keep up, but just kept her own steady pace as if there were neither thorns nor stones under her light moccasins.

The old woman in the front was running and watching the plants on either side of the path. John recognised a master plantswoman when she stopped and pointed a little way into the wood. She had spotted the one she wanted, at a run, in the twilight. John peered at it. It looked like a liverwort, but a form that he had never seen before.

'Wait here,' Suckahanna ordered him and followed the other women as they went towards it. They seated themselves down in a circle around it and they were silent for a moment, as if in prayer. John felt a strange prickling on the back of his neck as if something powerful and mysterious was happening. The women held out their hands over the plant as if they were checking the heat over a cooking pot, and then their hands made weaving gestures, one to another, above and around the plant in a constant pattern. They were humming softly, and then the words of a song emerged, softly chanted.

The darkness under the trees grew more intense; John realised that the sun had set and in the upper branches of the trees there was a continual rustle and chirping and cooing of birds settling down for the night. On the forest floor the women continued to sing and then the old woman leaned forwards and picked a sprig of the herb, and then the others followed suit.

John shifted restlessly from one sore foot to another. The women rose to their feet and came towards him, each chewing on the herb. John waited, in case he too had to eat it, but they walked around him in a circle. Suckahanna stopped first and gestured that he should hold out his hand. John opened his fingers and Suckahanna bent her mouth to his palm and gently spat the chewed herb into the wound. John cried out as the juice accurately hit the very centre of the rotting flesh, but he could not pull his hand away because she was holding it tight. The other women pressed around him and each spat, as hard and as accurately as a London urchin, so that the chewed juice from the herb did not rest on the wound but penetrated deep inside. John yelped a little at each blow as he felt the astringent juice entering the rotting flesh. The old woman came last and John braced himself. He was right to think that her spit would be as hard as a musket ball, right into the very centre of his damaged palm. As he cried out she whipped out a leather binding from the pocket of her apron, spread a leaf on top of the wound and tied it tight.

John was half-dizzy from the pain and Suckahanna ducked under his arm and supported him as they walked back to the village.

It was growing dark. The women turned off to their own huts, to the cooking fire. The men were already seated, awaiting their dinner. Suckahanna raised a hand in greeting to one of the men who solemnly watched her supporting John back to the hut. They went through the doorway entwined like lovers and she helped him lie down on the wooden bed.

'Sleep,' she said gently to him. 'Tomorrow you will be better.'

'I want you,' John said, his mind hazed with pain, with the smoke, with desire. 'I want you to lie with me.'

She laughed, a low amused laugh. 'I am married,' she reminded him. 'And you are ill. Sleep now. I shall be here in the morning.'

Spring 1643, England

On a cold day in spring, Alexander Norman took a boat upriver, disembarked north of Lambeth and strolled through the fields to the Ark. Frances, glancing idly from her bedroom window, saw the tall figure coming towards the house and dived back into her room to comb her hair, straighten her gown, and rip off her apron. She was downstairs in time to open the front door to him, and to send the maid running out into the yard to look for Hester and to tell her that Mr Norman was come for a visit.

He smiled very kindly at her. 'You look lovely,' he said simply. 'Every time I see you, you have grown prettier. How old are you now? Fifteen?'

Frances cast down her eyes in her most modest gesture and wished that she could blush. She thought for a moment that she should lay claim to fifteen years, but then she remembered that a birthday invariably meant a present. 'I'm fifteen in five months' time,' she said. 'October the seventh.' Without lifting her gaze, modestly directed to the toes of her boots, she could see his hand moving towards the flap on his deep coat pocket.

'I brought you these,' he said. 'Some little fairings.'

They were very far from little fairings. They were three large bundles of ribbon of a deep scarlet silk shot through with gold thread. There would be enough to trim a gown and make ties for Frances's light brown hair. Despite the shortages of the war, the fashion was still for gowns with sleeves elaborately slashed and trimmed, and Frances had a genuine need as well as a passion for ribbon.

Without taking his eyes from her absorbed face, Alexander Norman said: 'You do love beautiful things, don't you, Frances?' and was rewarded by a look of complete honesty, empty of all coquetry, when she looked up and said: 'Oh, of course! Because of my grandfather! I have had beautiful things around me all my life.'

'Cousin Norman,' Hester said pleasantly, coming into the hall from the kitchen door. 'What a pleasure to see you, and on such a cold day. Did you come by the river?'

'Yes,' he said. He let her help him off with his greatcoat and gave it to Frances to take to the kitchen to warm it through, and to order some hot ale. 'I would not trust the roads these days.'

She shook her head. 'Lambeth is quiet enough now that the archbishop's palace is empty,' she said. 'All the apprentice lads are exhausted with their drilling and their mustering and digging the fortifications. They have no stomach left for roaming around the streets and making trouble for their betters.'

She led the way into the family sitting room. Johnnie was seated before a small fire, writing out plant labels with painstaking care. 'Uncle Norman!' he exclaimed and leaped up from his place. Alexander Norman greeted him with a brisk hug and then dived once again into his pocket.

'I have given your sister half a mile of silk ribbon, should you like the same to edge your suit?' he asked.

'No, sir, that is, not if you have anything else . . . that is, I should be very grateful for anything you bring me . . .'

Alexander laughed. 'I have a wicked little toy here which one of the armourers made at the Tower. But you must promise me to only behead dead roses.'

From his pocket he drew a small knife which folded cunningly, like a barber's razor, so the sharp blade was hidden and safe. 'Do you permit, Mrs Tradescant?' Alexander asked. 'If he promises he will take care of his fingers?'

Hester smiled. 'I should like to have the courage to say no,' she said. 'You may have it, Johnnie, but Cousin Norman must show you how to handle it and see that you are safe with it before he leaves us today.'

'Can I carve things with it?'

Alexander nodded. 'We'll set to work as soon as I have drunk my ale and told your mother the news from town.'

'Wooden whistles? And toys?'

'We'll start with something easier. Go and ask them in the kitchen for a cake of soap. We'll work our way up to wood.' The boy nodded, put the cork carefully back in his pot of ink and carried the tray of labels out of the way, and then went from the room. Frances came in and set down a cup of ale before her uncle and then took up some sewing and sat in the windowseat. Hester, glancing across the room, thought that her stepdaughter could have been sitting for a portrait entitled 'Beauty and the Domestic Arts' as she bent her brown head over her work. A swift glance from Frances's bright eyes warned her that the girl was perfectly aware of the enchanting picture she made.

'Any news?' Hester asked.

Alexander Norman nodded. 'You've heard the news of Birmingham?'

Hester glanced towards Frances. 'We won't speak of it now. I heard enough.'

Alexander shook his head. 'Dreadful doings. Prince Rupert lost control of his men altogether.'

Hester nodded. 'And I heard that the king holds the whole of the west country.'

Alexander Norman nodded. 'He's lost the navy but he holds many of the ports. And they face France, so he can land a French army if the queen's promises are fulfilled.'

Hester nodded. 'And no-one is marching on London?'

Alexander Norman gave a small shrug. 'Not that I've heard, but this month alone there have been skirmishes all over the country.'

'Nothing close?'

Alexander Norman leaned forwards and put his hand over Hester's tightly gripping fingers. 'Peace, cousin,' he said gently. 'Nothing close. You know I would warn you the moment I heard of any danger to your little Ark. You and your precious cargo will come safe through this storm.'

He glanced over to the windowseat. 'Frances, would you fetch me another glass of ale?' he asked.

She rose at once and went to the door. 'And give me a moment alone with your stepmother,' he said smoothly. 'I want her advice on a private matter.'

Frances glanced at Hester to see if she demurred, and when Hester gave the smallest of nods Frances slightly raised her eyebrows in a tiny expression of sheer impudent speculation and left the room, closing the door behind her.

'She's impertinent,' Hester said as the door shut. 'But it's only lightness of spirit.'

'I know it,' Alexander Norman agreed with her. 'And I would not see her subdued. She's very like her mother. She was a light-hearted girl but her spirits were kept much in check by her strong sense of religion, and her strict upbringing. But Frances was spoiled from the moment she was born by John and by them all. It's too late to try to weigh her down now, I would rather see her soar.'

Hester smiled. 'I feel that too,' she said. 'Though it falls to me to try to keep her in check.'

'You worry about her safety?'

'I do. I worry for all of us, of course, and for the treasures. But mostly for Frances. She is at an age when she should be venturing out a little more, going into society, to make friends; but she is cooped up here with me and with her brother. The plague is everywhere again this year so I cannot let her stay with her grandparents in the City – and besides they are not sociable people, they meet no-one.'

'She could go to court at Oxford . . .'

Hester's face was a picture. 'I'd as soon throw her into the lion's cage at the Tower than send her among that crowd. Everything that was bad about the king's court when they were properly housed and properly served is ten times worse now they are crowded into Oxford and drunk nine nights out of ten with celebrating victories.'

'I've been thinking the same,' Alexander said. 'I wondered if you would consider me . . . I wondered if you would let me offer her – and yourself of course – a safe haven. I wondered if you would leave here, shut the Ark up until the end of the war, and come and live with me at the Tower of London: the safest place in the whole of the kingdom.'

When she said nothing he added, very quietly, 'I mean marriage, Hester.'

She went quite pale for a moment, and moved her chair back from his a little.

'You did not expect this? Though I have been such a frequent visitor?'

Mutely, she shook her head. 'I thought it was just kindness for Mr Tradescant's family,' she said softly. 'As a family friend, as a relation.'

'It was more.'

She shook her head. 'I am a married woman,' she said. 'I do not consider myself deserted or widowed. Until I hear from John that he is not coming home ever again I shall bear myself as his wife.' For a moment she looked at him as if she were pleading with him to disagree with her. 'You may think he has left us forever, but I am sure he will come home. There are his children, there are the rarities, there is the garden. He would never abandon the Tradescant inheritance.'

Alexander did not answer, his face was very grave.

'He would never abandon us,' she said again but with less certainty. 'Would he?'

Before he could answer she rose from the chair and went quickly over to the window with her light, determined step. 'And if you are thinking that he will die over there, and never return, I must tell you that I would still think it my duty to stay here and guard the house and the garden for Johnnie to inherit when he is a man. I promised John's father that I would keep the place and the children safe. Nothing would release me from that promise.'

'You have misunderstood me,' he burst out. 'I am so sorry. I was not proposing marriage to you.'

She turned at that. The light of the window was behind her and he could not clearly see her face. 'What?'

'I was thinking of Frances.'

'You were proposing marriage to Frances?'

The incredulity in her voice made him wince. Dumbly, he nodded.

'But you are fifty-five!'

'I am fifty-three.'

'And she's a child.'

'She is a young woman, and she is ready for marriage, and these are dangerous and difficult times.'

Hester was silenced, then she turned away from him. He saw her shoulder hunch slightly, as if she were protecting herself from insult. 'I beg your pardon. You must think me a complete fool.'

He took three swift steps across the room and turned her around, held her at arms' length so that he could see her face. 'I think of you, as I have long thought of you, as one of the most courageous and lovable women that I have ever met. But I know John will come home to you, and I know that you have loved him ever since you were married. I think of you now as I will always think of you, as a dear, dear friend.'

Hester looked away, wretched with embarrassment. 'I thank you,' she whispered. 'Please let me go.'

'It was my own shyness and stupidity in what I said that led you to misunderstand me,' he said determinedly. 'Please, don't be angry with me, or angry with yourself.'

She twisted from his hold. 'I feel that I have been a fool!' she exclaimed. 'Refusing a proposal which wasn't being made to me. And you are a fool too!' She suddenly regained her spirits. 'Thinking that you could marry a girl who is hardly out of her short clothes.'

He went for the door. 'I'll take a turn in the garden, if I may,' he said. 'And we'll talk again later.'

He went out without another word and Hester, looking from the window, saw him walk along the terrace on the south side of the house and down the steps into the garden.

The garden was at its mid-May perfection. In the walled fruit garden he could not see the sky for the mass of pink and white blossom, as thick as rose-sugared cream on a pudding. In the long walks in the flower gardens the daffodils and tulips were a wash of colour, red and gold and white. The chestnut avenue was coming into its height of beauty, the blossoms opening up into thick candles, white delicately marked with pink. On the walls on the right-hand side of the garden the espaliered figs and peaches and cherries were already weighted with blossom, showering petals on the flower beds beneath them like unseasonal snow.

The parlour door behind Hester opened and Frances came in with Alexander's glass of ale. 'Has he gone?'

'You can perfectly well see that he has,' Hester snapped.

Frances put down the glass without spilling a drop and turned to examine her stepmother's cross face.

'What did he do to upset you?' she asked calmly.

'He said something ridiculous, and I thought something ridiculous and I feel . . . I feel . . .'

'Ridiculous?' Frances suggested, and was rewarded with a glare of irritation.

Hester turned away from her and looked out of the window again. In the thick window pane she could see, simultaneously, Alexander strolling in the garden and the reflection of her own face. She looked grim. She looked like a woman struggling under the weight of many worries, and still fighting them.

'What did he say that was so ridiculous?' Frances asked gently. She came beside her stepmother and slipped her arm around the older woman's waist. Hester saw that smooth prettiness beside her own worn face and felt a deep pang of envy that her own beauty was past, and at the same time a glow of joy that she had brought that unloved, frightened little girl into this rare, beautiful being.

'He said that you were a young woman grown,' Hester said. She felt Frances at her side. The girl was a girl no longer, her breasts were filling out, the curve of her waist would fit a man's hand, she had lost her coltish legginess, she was, as Alexander had seen but her stepmother had not, a young woman.

'Well, I am,' Frances said, as one stating the obvious.

'He said you should be married,' Hester said.

'And so I shall be, I suppose.'

'He thought sooner rather than later,' Hester said. 'Because these are dangerous times. He thinks you should have a husband to take care of you.' She had thought that Frances would pull away and laugh her reckless laugh. But the girl rested her head on her stepmother's shoulder and said thoughtfully: 'You know, I think I would like that.'

Hester pulled back to look at Frances. 'You still seem like a little girl to me.'

'But I am a young woman,' Frances pointed out. 'And when I go into Lambeth the men shout at me, and call things to me. If Father were at home then it would be different, but he is not home, and he is not coming home, is he?'

Hester shook her head. 'I have no news of him.'

'Then if he does not come home, and if the war goes on, and so everything is still so uneasy . . .'

'Yes?' Hester asked.

'If our lives don't get easier then I would like a husband to care for me, and to care for you and Johnnie. I think we need a man in this house. I think we need a man to care for us.'

There was a long silence. Hester looked into the beautiful face of her stepdaughter and thought that perhaps the first of her promises to this girl's grandfather, John Tradescant, was nearly fulfilled. She had brought up his granddaughter to be a beautiful woman and within a year or two there would only be Johnnie and the treasures for her to guard.

Alexander Norman strolled in the grounds for an hour before he came in to dinner. He found Hester laying the table in the parlour with Frances helping her. Johnnie was showing a visitor around the rarities.

'I think I made a sale for you,' he said informally as he came in the door. Hester glanced up at his entrance and was relieved to see his familiar, reassuring smile. 'A young man from Kent, enquiring about fruit trees. I spoke warmly about John's plums and handed him over to your gardener. I left him writing down an order for a score of trees and being paid in gold.'

Frances laughed and clapped her hands. 'Excellent, Uncle Norman! Now all we have to do is to teach you to weed and you shall come and work for us every day.'

'Twenty trees is a very good sale,' Hester agreed. 'Especially in these times, when no-one can put their mind to gardening. You did say that he had to arrange his own transport?'

'I did. I know you can't undertake delivery.'

'If we had anyone we could spare I still wouldn't send them. I can't risk losing my horse and cart.' Hester turned to Frances. 'Fetch Johnnie, and tell Cook that she can serve dinner.'

Frances nodded and went out of the room.

Alexander held out his hand. 'Am I forgiven for my stupidity?'

Hester took his hand. 'And you must forgive me. It's a curiously uncomfortable mistake for a woman to make. If I'd had more experience I would have known how a man usually proposes to a woman.'

He smiled at her and did not release her hand for a moment. 'And the matter of Frances's future?'

Hester shook her head and withdrew her hand. 'She's too young yet,' she said stubbornly. 'Ask again in a year or two. I must warn you I would rather see her with a young husband in a little house of her own, starting her own life.'

He nodded. 'I understand. But young men are not safe choices these days. Whether he's a royalist or for Parliament he's likely to be called to serve his master, and there are no little houses where young people can be sure that they will be left to live at peace in this kingdom any more.'

'When the war ends . . .'

'When the war ends we shall know whether she should look for a husband at Parliament or at court. But what if it trails on for years? I tell you, cousin, there are stores in the Tower promised to the Parliament army, and stores to match that in royalist hands enough to keep this war going for another twenty years. Parliament is not likely to surrender – that would be to sign their own death warrants for treason – and the king is not a man to come to terms with them.'

Hester nodded. For a moment she looked haggard with worry. 'If she is in any danger I shall send her to you,' she promised. 'I know you would take care of her.'

Alexander gave a small formal bow. 'I would lay down my life for her,' he said simply. 'And I love her so much that I would put her interests before mine. If they make peace, or if she falls in love with a man of her own age who could keep her safe, I will not stand in her way, nor even remind you of this conversation.'

A few days after Alexander Norman's visit Hester, glancing out of the window, saw a stranger slip around the corner of the house and head for the kitchen door. She got up from the hearth, took off her rough hessian apron, and went to see what he wanted.

He was standing on the back doorstep. 'Mrs John Tradescant?' he asked.

The hair on the back of Hester's neck prickled. 'Yes,' she said levelly. 'And who is asking?'

He slipped in around the doorframe, so that he was in the kitchen. 'Shut the door,' he whispered.

Hester did not make a move to obey him. 'There is a stout man in my employ within earshot,' she said. 'And half the neighbourhood would come running down the road if I called. You had better tell me your business, and swiftly.'

'Not my business. The king's.'

Hester felt dismay like a blow in the belly. Slowly, she shut the door. 'Come in,' she said, and led the way into the rarities room.

'Can we be overheard?' he asked, looking around but not seeing the hanging flags, the dangling birds' skeletons, the whale's head, the polished cases crammed with goods.

'Only if I scream,' Hester said with sour humour. 'Now, what is it?'

The man put his hand inside his jacket and showed her a glint of gold. 'Do you recognise this?'

It was one of the king's favourite rings. Hester had seen it on his finger many times. 'Yes.'

'I am here by the orders of a lady – we need not say her name – who has brought to London the king's Commission of Array. You know what that means.'

'Not the least idea,' Hester said unhelpfully.

'It's a summons. A summons to the king's standard. It'll be read aloud at Whitehall when our army is at the city gates. You have to play your part. Your husband is commanded to proclaim the king's authority in Lambeth and order out the loyal men for His Majesty as soon as he is given the word.'

'What lady?' Hester asked flatly.

'I said we need not say her name.'

'If she's asking me to risk my neck she can tell me her name,' Hester persisted.

He put his mouth to her ear and Hester smelled the familiar scent of sandalwood that the young men of court used as pomade. 'Lady d'Aubigny,' he whispered. 'A great lady and the widow of a hero. Her lord fell at Edgehill and she is trusted by the king to call out the royalists of London to fight for him. And she is trusting you.'

Hester felt a deep sense of relief that John was far away. 'I am sorry,' she said swiftly. 'My husband is away in Virginia, gathering rarities, and making his own plantation.'

'When will he return?'

She shrugged. 'I don't know.'

The man's gleeful, conspiratorial mode deserted him in a moment. He swore and took two hasty paces away from her. 'Then what are we to do?' he demanded. 'Mr Tradescant was to secure Lambeth and the riverside. We were counting on him.'

'You were counting on him to secure the king's safety and you did not think to discover if he was at home?' Hester asked, disbelieving. 'He could be sick, he could be dead of the plague, he could have changed sides!'

The man threw her a swift, angry glance. 'War is a gamble,' he said grandly. 'Sometimes the gamble pays off, sometimes it does not. I was gambling that he would be here, in good health, and keeping faith with his master.'

Hester shook her head. 'He does not break his faith. But he can be of no use to you.'

'His son?'

'Johnnie is not yet ten.'

'What about you? Surely you have influence with local people. You could use this house as a rallying point. I could send you an officer to raise the men, or your father ... d'you have a father?'

Hester shook her head. 'No father, and no influence. I am a newcomer here,' she said. 'I am Mr Tradescant's second wife. We have only been married four years. I have no friends here. And I have no family.'

'Someone has to do it!' he burst out. 'Someone has to secure the riverside and Lambeth!'

Hester shook her head again and led the way to the front door. The royalist conspirator trailed unhappily after her.

'What about someone at the bishop's palace? What about the local vicar?'

'The Archbishop is in the Tower for his service to the king, as you well may recall. And his servants are long gone.' Hester opened the front door. 'And the vicar here is an Independent. He was one of the first to preach against Archbishop Laud's reforms.'

The man would have hesitated but she ushered him out of the house. 'I shall call on you if we need a safe house this side of the river,' he promised. 'D'you have horses, or barns where a small troop of horse could lie hidden?'

'No,' Hester said.

The man hesitated and looked at her with a sharp look. Hester felt a sudden fear, she had taken him for a fool but the bright assessing gaze he turned on her was not the gaze of a fool. 'I trust you *are* for the king, Mrs Tradescant,' he said, and there was menace in his voice.

'When he comes into London he will expect support from his loyal servants. You will have to put this house at his disposal.'

'I know nothing of these matters,' Hester said weakly. 'I am just conducting the business of the house and the garden in my husband's absence . . .'

'There are wives and widows in the same case as you all around the country,' the man said sharply. 'And they have not forgotten where their loyalties lie. Are you for the king? Or not?'

'For the king,' Hester said unenthusiastically.

'Then His Majesty will call on your services,' the man said. 'You may count on it.'

He nodded to her, turned and walked across the little drawbridge over the stream at the side of the Lambeth road. Hester watched him stride away, his coat flung back, his feathers bobbing in his hat, every inch a nobleman, every inch a cavalier, then she closed the door on the sight of him, and on her fear.

She thought for a moment and then went into the parlour to write a note to Alexander Norman.

> *It may be that I need your assistance. Please let me know that*
> *your neighbourhood is free of the plague. I may wish to come*
> *and stay with you for a few days.*

She sealed the note and went through to the kitchen. The gardener, Joseph, was in there, eating his midday dinner of bread and bacon.

'Can you take this to Cousin Norman at Aldgate?' Hester asked abruptly.

The man wiped his mouth with the back of his hand. 'I was going to cut back the leaves of the early tulips this afternoon,' he said.

Hester hesitated. There were few things more precious in the Ark than the tulips. 'Even so,' she said. 'I think this is more important. Put it into his hands only, and wait for a reply.'

Joseph brought a message back as it was getting dark. Hester was sitting on the terrace before the house, enjoying the setting sun and the slow gathering of the darkness. The garden before her was an enchanted place in the quiet twilight. The apple blossom was like a mist around the heads of the trees in the lower orchard, the tulips were drained of their daytime colour and glowed like white cups in the beds. Hester thought of John Tradescant, the old man she had met, who had willed his grandchildren into her care, and thought that this garden was his memorial, as much as the ornate stone tomb in the churchyard.

'He didn't write it, he spoke it to me.' Joseph made her jump, appearing suddenly before her on the path.

Hester put her hand to her heart. 'You frightened me! Coming out of the gloaming like a ghost!'

'He said: "No plague. Rooms ready. Whenever."'

Hester smiled at the man's frowning delivery. 'Was that all?'

'Absolutely all,' he said. 'I made sure I would remember it, and he heard me say it over and over a dozen times before I left.'

'Thank you,' Hester said. 'Johnnie and Frances and I will help you with the tulips tomorrow.'

He nodded and went round the back of the house to the yard pump and the kitchen door. Hester sat alone, watching the last light leave the tops of the trees, the nodding flowers. When it grew cold she rose to her feet and went towards the door. 'John,' she said softly. 'I wish you would come home.'

Summer 1643, Virginia

The days that followed John's arrival in the Indian village fell into a routine as orderly as the smooth running of John's English home. In the morning Suckahanna's boy would waken him with one of the smooth black bowls filled with hot water for washing. Outside his hut, in the cool dawn light, John would see the People coming and going as they went down to the river for the morning prayer.

When they returned John would look for Suckahanna, her face bright as she walked beside her husband, his son at one side, her baby strapped on her back. The boy was Suckahanna's shadow and she seemed to know his whereabouts, without even turning her head to look for him. It was as if, when she adopted him and married his father, she had made a bond with him that stretched over any distance but was as palpable as touch.

Before he was allowed to eat the boy had marksman training. Suckahanna plucked a piece of moss from a tree and threw it in the air for him. Not until his little arrow had pierced the falling moss could the boy eat his breakfast. Some mornings Suckahanna was out under the trees with him for three, four, five attempts before John heard her word of praise and the quick touch of her fingers on his dark head.

'He had no mother for his early years,' she explained to John. 'He has much to learn.'

'Why did his father not teach him?' John asked. He was tempted to complain of Suckahanna's husband, to make him look foolish in her eyes. She just tossed her head and laughed. 'Bringing a child into the world is work for a woman,' she said simply. 'A man cannot do it.'

As the sun rose and warmed the air they would all gather for a breakfast of fruits or nuts or a gruel made from cornflour and berries. This was the hungriest time of the year – the winter stores were almost exhausted and the summer crops were not yet ripe – but even so no-one went hungry in the village. The stores had been put aside all through the rich fruitful time of the year, and then extra had been laid aside as well in the huge granary building filled with great bowls of dried pulses, huge netted sacks of dried maize, vats as big as a man filled with nuts. John wondered why they did not broach the great store, but no-one would tell him.

After breakfast the men would string their bows, oil their bodies, tie back their hair, paint their faces, and go out to hunt together. John watched the laughing camaraderie of the huntsmen with the knowledge that he would always be an outsider. The men did not speak to him, he did not know if they even understood English. The women understood everything he said, but their replies were brief. Inevitably, John was learning the rhythm of Powhatan speech, picking up individual words and names. He watched the men, understanding that they were planning the hunt. Suckahanna's husband was among them, in the very heart of the preparations. He was acknowledged as a fine hunter, a man who could kill a deer alone, without the help of a hunting party. Other braves could drop a deer with a well-placed arrow when it had been driven from one cover to another and directed towards them; but Suckahanna's husband could throw a deerskin over his shoulder, strap the horns to his head and move so skilfully and so deer-like with his tittupping step and his nervous, flickering head-tossing, with his sudden stag-like stillness, that he could go among a herd of deer and pick one off as it grazed beside him. A man had to be blessed by the deer god to manage such a feat. Suckahanna's husband was treated with loving respect and he alone decided the course of every hunt. Even his name showed his nature. He was called Attone – the arrow.

As the men readied themselves to leave the village, the women gathered children and their gardening tools and went to the fields to plant and to weed. While John was weak from his illness and under Suckahanna's special protection he went with her, and watched them planting. Their crop was set in a field which had been roughly cleared by burning. They left the tree stumps, left even the biggest living trees and planted around them. The edge of the field was ragged, where the fire had not taken hold. Its disorder offended John's sense of how a tidy field should be set square on the landscape, its lines drawn clearly, hedged and ditched.

'You could get the men to help you clear the tree stumps,' he suggested to Suckahanna. 'It wouldn't take long to uproot them and pull them out. Then you could plant your crops in straight rows. Those tree stumps you have left in will only grow back within a season, and then you'll have all the work to do all over again.'

'We want the trees to grow back,' she said. 'We don't want this field for more than a season.'

'But if you cleared it properly then you could use it year after year,' John insisted. 'You would not have to move on. You could have the same fields and keep the village in the same place.'

Decidedly, she shook her head. 'The earth gets weary of working for us,' she said. 'We plant a field here and then we set her free. We move on to another place. If you plant corn in the same field three years running, then in the third year you will harvest nothing. The earth gets weary of hungry men. She has to rest like a woman with a baby at the breast, needs to rest, needs some time alone. She cannot be always feeding.'

'White men plant the same fields, and go back to them year after year,' John observed.

'White men did,' she corrected him. 'All around Jamestown now they are finding that the land is tiring of them. The land is weary of the hungry white mouth which eats and eats and eats and cannot be satisfied and will not move on.'

She moved to the next row with her hoeing stick. In each hole she dropped four grains of corn and two bean seeds. Behind her another woman came sowing pumpkin seeds. Later, beneath the crops, they would plant the quicker-growing amaracocks for their lush, thirst-quenching fruit.

John picked up a stick of his own and hunkered down beside her. 'I'll help,' he said.

She could not repress a giggle at the sight of him, and then she shook her head. 'This is women's work, only women do it.'

'I can do it. I'm a gardener in my own country. I can plant.'

Still Suckahanna refused. 'I know that you can. And any Powhatan man can do it, if he has to. But women like to do it. It is what we do.'

'To serve the men?' John asked, thinking of the delicious idleness of the hunting men when they returned to camp and found their dinner waiting for them and their fields cleared and planted, their houses swept clean, the sweat lodge heated and ready for them.

She shot him a quick, scornful look from under her dark eyebrows. 'Because the earth and the women are together,' she half-whispered. 'That is where the power of the People belongs, not in the war councils or in the hunting parties. It is women who have the power to make things grow, to give birth. The rest – is pipesmoke.'

John felt his view, his comfortable view of the world, shift and rock. 'Men have the power,' he said. 'God made them in his image.'

She looked at him as if he might be joking. 'You may believe that your god did that,' she said politely. 'But we are the children of the Hare.'

'The Hare?'

She stopped her work and sat back on her heels. 'I shall tell you as if you were my little child,' she said with a smile. 'Listen. In the very beginning when there was nothing but darkness and the sound of the running water, the great Hare came out of the darkness and made both man and woman.'

John squatted down beside her in the damp earth, watched the smile move from her eyes to her lips, and the way her hair fell over her bare shoulders.

'They were hungry. Men and women are always hungry. So the Hare put them in a bag until he could feed them. He ran through the darkness with the bag held tight in his mouth and everywhere he ran there was land made, and water made, and the great deer to walk the land and drink the water and feed the new-made man and woman. And everywhere he went there were fierce mouths biting at him from out of the darkness, hungry meat-eating mouths that would snap at his heels and at the bag he was carrying. But everywhere he ran, the mouths were destroyed, and fled back into the darkness until it was safe for him to do what he wished.'

John waited.

Suckahanna smiled. 'Then, and only then, he opened the bag and let out the man and the woman. The man ran to hunt the deer. The man has the great richness of the deer. This is what he wanted. But the woman –' she paused and gave him a sly sideways smile ' – the woman has everything else.'

A year ago John would have called it a heathen tale full of heresy and nonsense. But now he listened and nodded. 'The women have everything else?'

'Everything but hunting and war.'

'So what am I to do?' he asked her.

Suckahanna looked momentarily surprised, as if he had moved the conversation onwards in one great bound. 'You will get well,' she said slowly. 'And then you will decide.'

'Decide?'

'Where you want to live. What kind of man you want to be.'

John hesitated. 'I thought I would get well and go back to my home – to my fields up the river.'

She shook her head. 'You must know by now that you cannot live there,' she said gently. 'You cannot live there alone. You must know by now that you cannot survive in this land alone. You would have died there, my love.' The endearment slipped out, she flushed and bit her lip as if she would have taken it back.

'I thought – I thought I might get a servant, or a slave. I thought –' He hesitated. 'I have been thinking that you might come with me?'

'As a servant? As a slave?' Her look blazed at him.

'I meant I must have someone to work under me,' John corrected himself. 'And I have been praying that you would come to me ever since I made landfall. I meant a servant, and you as well.'

'I shall never lie under a white man's roof again,' Suckahanna said firmly. 'I have taken my decision, and I am with the People.'

John jumped to his feet and took a stride away from her and then back again. 'Then there is nothing for me here,' he cried out. 'I came to make a new life for myself, to farm virgin earth, to find you. And you tell me I cannot plough or hoe alone. I cannot keep myself or even keep my fire in. I cannot take you away from your people, and I cannot take you to my people. I have been a fool to run from one life to another and still achieve nothing.'

There was a cry from the little platform shelter where the children played. Suckahanna glanced back, listening for her own baby's voice. They heard another woman call in response and get up from her knees and go to see to the crying child. Suckahanna returned her attention to her gardening, picked up her hoeing stick, picked out little weed seedlings from her row. Without turning her head to see if John was listening she spoke very quietly to him.

'Perhaps you could be with me,' she said slowly. 'Leave your people and join mine.'

'I can't live here, seeing you every day,' John said softly. 'I want you, Suckahanna. I can't bear to live near you and yet to sleep every night only a footstep away from you.'

'I know,' she said, so quietly that he had to lean forward to hear. But still her hands worked, her hoeing stick piercing the fresh soil and the seeds dropping quickly and accurately through her fingers. 'I could ask my husband to release me.'

'Release you?' John asked incredulously. 'This is possible?'

'He might,' she said evenly. 'If it was my wish.'

'Your people let their wives come and go as they choose?'

She shot him a small smile. 'I told you that we were a proud people.

Wives are not slaves. If they wish to leave they must be free to do so, don't you think?'

'Yes . . . but –'

'We would have the children,' she went on. 'The little boy and my own baby. You would have to promise to love them and care for them like a father.'

'And where would we live? You said you would not live in my house?'

'We would live here,' she said, as if it were the most ordinary thing in the world. 'Among the People. You would become a Powhatan.'

'I would learn your language? Live among you as an equal?'

'You are learning it already,' she observed. 'You laughed at Musses the other day and she was not speaking English.'

'I can understand some, but –'

'You would have to join the People, as a brother.'

'They would accept me?'

'*We* would accept you.'

John was silent, his head spinning. This was a far greater step than his adventure to Virginia, this was a step into the unknown beyond the plantation, into the darkness of unknowable lands.

'I don't know,' he said.

'You would have to decide,' she repeated patiently, as if she had led a child around a circle of explanation and returned to the key point at last. 'You would have to decide, my love.'

John hesitated at the endearment. 'Do you want me to be with you?' he asked.

At once her hands returned to their work, her head bowed and her veil of dark hair tumbled over her face hiding her expression, brushing her naked brown shoulder. 'You would have to decide, without advice from me,' she said to the earth. 'I don't want a man with half a heart.'

At midday the women rested. The fields they were working were distant from home, too far to return to the village for the usual meal, prayers and rest. They ate a little cold gruel and fruit which they had brought with them, they said their brief prayers to the sun which stood precisely above each and every one of them, blessing each and every one with light and warmth on the exact centre of her head. Then they rested in the shade of the trees. Suckahanna's baby was at her breast as she lay back, the little boy playing stalking or marksmanship with his tiny bow and arrow, with the others. John rested near Suckahanna, listened to the ripple of talk, picked out words, one word after another, all of them making more sense to him. He watched her openly now, wondering how it would be if they were married. If she could indeed leave her husband and come to him. If he could indeed become a Powhatan. If he could ever be recognised as a man among the People.

When they returned to camp he touched her arm. 'I need to take advice from a man,' he said. 'Can one of the men speak my language? Someone I can trust to tell me how a Powhatan man might see this? Not a friend of your husband?'

At once her dark eyes lit up with laughter. 'Oh! You don't trust me!'

'I do –' John heard himself stammering. 'Of course!'

Suckahanna turned her head and babbled a string of words at her sister-in-law who was a few paces ahead. The woman screamed with laughter and turned back, laughing at John, and pointed an accusing finger at him. John picked out among the rapid flow the few words: man, Powhatan, talk, talk, talk, everything.

'What is she saying?'

'She says you are a true man, a Powhatan already. She says all men need to talk, talk, talk among themselves, to make the decisions which are already known.'

'Known?' John queried.

Suckahanna veiled her eyes with the downward sweep of her eyelashes. 'Everyone thinks that you love me,' she said quietly. 'Everyone thinks that I love you. We are all just waiting . . .'

'Waiting?'

'For you. To decide.'

John went that night before supper to the house of the werowance, the senior man of the village. It stood four-square at the head of the village street, near the dancing ground, at a distance from the smoke of the cooking fires. It was walled with tree bark, and roofed with bark roughly cut in shingles. In the heat of the day the bark walls would be rolled up like curtains, but as the evening grew cold the old men closed out the chill night air. The werowance himself was sitting on a raised platform at the end of the tent; at his side were two of the old men of the tribe. They all carried their sharp hunting knives, John noticed. They all looked grave.

John stood in the doorway, awkward as a boy.

'You can come.' The werowance spoke in heavily accented English; but there was neither welcome nor warmth in his voice.

John entered the darkness of the house and sat, obedient to the small gesture, on a pile of soft deerskin. For a moment he was reminded of King Charles's wordless gestures to his servants, and the thought gave him a little courage in the darkness of the strange house. He had served the greatest king in England, he could surely bear himself like a man before someone who was nothing more than a savage chief clinging to the edge of unknown land.

'You desire Suckahanna?' the werowance said briefly.

John found he was looking at the length and sharpened cane blades of the hunting knives.

'I knew her before she was a married woman,' he said. His voice sounding weak and apologetic, even in his own ears. 'We were promised to each other. I promised I would come back for her.'

The werowance nodded. 'But you did not come back,' he observed.

John gritted his teeth. 'When I got to my home in my country my father had died and my children needed care. I had to stay.'

'She waited,' the werowance pointed out. The old men on either side of him nodded, their sharp faces like stone eagles on a lectern in church. 'She trusted your word.'

'I am sorry,' John said awkwardly.

'You have a new wife and children in your own country?'

John thought of a swift lie, thought he might tell them that the plague had taken both his children as well as Jane. But a fearful superstition halted his tongue. 'Yes, I have children,' he said quietly. 'And a wife.'

'And is your wife now the one who waits?'

John nodded.

The werowance sighed as if John's infidelity was a riddle, too tedious and complex to unravel. There was a silence that stretched for a long time. John's back ached, he had sat awkwardly and now he felt too uneasy to wriggle back on the pile of skins and lean against the wall of the house.

'Where do you want to be?' the werowance asked him. 'With Suckahanna or your wife?'

'With Suckahanna,' John said.

'You will care for her children as if they were your own?'

'Gladly.'

'You know the children are not to be taken to your people? They will stay with the Powhatan?'

John nodded.

'And their mother stays with us too. She will never go to your country with you.'

John nodded again. 'She told me this.' He could feel a squirm of excitement starting to grow inside him. This had all the signs of an interrogation of a bridegroom, it was not the preamble to a refusal.

'She came to us for a home, she could wait for you no longer. She made her choice and now she is our child. We have taken her to our hearts.'

The older men nodded. One said something low in their language. The werowance nodded. 'My brother says that we love her. We would avenge her hurt.'

'I understand,' John said. He was afraid they would hear the beating of his heart, it sounded so loud in his own ears. 'I don't want to take her from you. I know she has made her choice, and that she and her children will be with you.'

'And any children you may have with her,' came a low growl from another man, speaking clearly in English. 'They will not be Englishmen, remember. They too will be the People of the Hare.'

John had not thought of his children being born here, being raised by Suckahanna, being rocked in the papoose, learning deadly accuracy with a reed arrow. He felt his heart leap at the thought of fathering such a son. He swallowed. 'Yes.'

'If you choose her, you choose to be with her, to be with us,' the werowance repeated.

John bowed his head.

There was a silence.

'Do you wish to be our brother?'

John drew a breath. Lambeth seemed a long way away, Hester more dead to him than his first wife, Jane. His own children half-forgotten. The pulse in his blood, the drumming beat in his ears, was for Suckahanna. 'I will,' he said.

Faster than the eye could follow, like a striking snake, the werowance snatched at John's wrist, twisting it so that he fell to his knees before the basilisk gazes of the three old men. The pain shot up John's arm to his shoulder, the grip on his wrist joint was so powerful that he had to stay on his knees.

'Against your own people?' the werowance demanded.

'It won't come to that,' John gasped. He could feel the bones in his arm starting to bend, an ounce more pressure and they would break. 'I know that they have treated your people badly but they have the land they need now, it won't come to a war.'

'They have driven us back like helpless deer,' the man said, his grip unchanging. 'And they will drive us back and back, every time they need an inch more land. Is that not so?'

John did not dare to answer. He felt the sweat standing on his back, the muscles in his arm singing with the pain. 'I can't say.'

'They use the land and leave it, like a hog in a stall, don't they? They foul it and then it is good for nothing. So always they need more land, and more land, and then more?'

Abruptly the werowance let John go and he pitched face down on the rushes of the floor, biting his lips to keep from crying out. He could not contain his panting breath, he whooped like a hurt child.

'So there will come a time when every inlet of the river and every tall standing tree sees an Englishman hammering in a stake.'

John sat back on his heels, fingered his forearm, his shoulder. 'Yes,' he conceded unwillingly.

'So when you say you are our brother, you must realise that we will call on you as our brother. You will die beside us when we run forward. Your hands will be red with the blood of white men. You will have their scalps tied to your belt.'

John thought of the Hoberts in their little house hidden among the trees, and the inn at Jamestown, the serving maid at the governor's house, the rough kindliness of the planters, the hopeful faces of the emigrants when they first docked at the quay. The werowance clapped his hands, a sharp ringing sound.

'I knew you couldn't do it,' he remarked, and rose to his feet and walked from the house.

John scrambled to his feet and took three rapid strides after him. One of the old men stuck out a bony leg and John tripped and pitched down to the skins on the floor.

'Lie still, Englishman,' the old man said, his speech perfect, his diction Oxford-pure. 'Lie still like a fool. Did you think we would give our daughter to a man with half a heart?'

'I love her,' John said. 'I swear it.'

The two old men got slowly to their feet.

'Love is not enough,' said the old man. 'You need custom and kinship as well. Love her all you like. There is no shame in it. But choose your people and stay with them. That is the path of a brave.'

Without another word the old men went out, their bare feet passing within an inch of John's face. He lay on the skins, the very symbol of a man brought low, and let them walk past him.

It grew dark. John lay still. He did not notice the thickening of the light and the spreading shadows on the wall. He heard the distant sound of singing and knew that dinner had been cooked and eaten and that Suckahanna's people were at the dancing circle, singing down the moon, singing the fine weather in, singing the herds of deer towards them, singing the fish into the weirs and the seeds strong and tall out of the ground. John lay face down in the skins and neither wished nor wept. He knew his own emptiness.

A light came to the doorway, a twig of burning candlewood, bright as the best wax in London. Beneath it, half-lit, half-shadowed, was Suckahanna.

'You told them you did not want me?' she asked from the doorway.

'I failed a test,' John said. He sat up and rubbed a hand over his face. He felt immensely weary. 'They said I should have to fight against my own people and I could not agree to do it.'

'Very well.' She turned to go.

'Suckahanna!' he cried and the desperation and passion in his voice would have made any woman pause but a woman of the Powhatan. She did not even hesitate. She did not drag her feet. She went out as lightly stepping as if she were about to join a dance. John leaped up from the floor and ran out after her. She must have heard him coming, she knew the rhythm of his stride from her girlhood, but she did not hesitate nor look around. She walked without breaking her pace down the little street to her own house, parted the deerskin at the door and slipped inside without even glancing back.

John skidded to a standstill and felt an urge to scream and hammer his fist through the wall of the light, beautifully made house. He took a sobbing breath and turned towards the fire at the dancing circle.

They were dancing for joy, it was not a religious ceremony. He could tell that at once since the werowance was seated on a low stool with only an ordinary cape thrown for warmth around his shoulders, and no sacred abalone shells around his neck. He was clapping his hands to the music of the drums and flutes, and smiling.

John went towards the light but knew that he was not suddenly revealed. They would all have seen him in the shadows, sensed him running after Suckahanna and then turning back to them. He skirted the beaten earth of the dancing floor and worked his way around to the werowance's seat. The three old men glared at him with the bland amusement of cynical old age which always enjoys the diversion of youthful pain.

'Ah, the visitor,' said the werowance.

'I want to marry her,' John announced without preamble. 'And my children will be Powhatan, and my heart will be with the Powhatan. And you may command me as a brave.'

The sharp, beaky face gleamed with pleasure. 'You have changed your mind,' the werowance observed.

'I have learned the price,' John said. 'I am not a changeable man. I did not know what Suckahanna would cost me. Now you have told me and I know. And I agree.'

One of the men smiled. 'A merchant, a trader,' he said, and it was not a compliment.

'Your children to be Powhatan?' the other old man confirmed. 'And you to be our brave?'

John nodded.

'Against your own people?'

'I trust it will never come to that.'

'If it ever does?'

John nodded again. 'Yes.'

The werowance rose to his feet. At once the drumming stopped, the dancing halted. He put out his arm and John, uncertainly, went towards him. The thin arm came down lightly on John's broad shoulders but he could feel the strength of the sinews in the hand as the werowance gripped him.

'The Englishman wants to be a brave of the Powhatan and marry Suckahanna,' the werowance announced in Powhatan. 'We are all in agreement. Tomorrow he goes hunting with the braves. He marries her as soon as he has shown he can catch his own deer.' John scowled at the effort of understanding what was being said. Then the beaky face turned towards him and the werowance spoke in English.

'You have a day to prove yourself,' he said. 'One day only. If you cannot mark, hunt and kill your deer in the day from dawn to sunset then you must go back to your people and their gunpowder. If you want a Powhatan woman then you have to be able to feed her with your hands.'

Suckahanna's husband grinned at John from the centre of the dancing circle. 'Tomorrow then,' he said invitingly in Powhatan, not caring whether John understood or not. 'We start at dawn.'

At dawn they were in the river, in the deep, solemn silence of the prayers for the rising of the sun. Around the braves, scattered on the water, were the smoking leaves of the wild tobacco plant, acrid and powerful in the morning air. The braves and the women stood waist-deep in the icy water in the half-darkness, washed themselves, prayed for purity, burned the tobacco and scattered the burning leaves. The embers, like fireflies, swirled away downriver, sparks against the greyness.

John waited on the bank, his head bowed in respect. He did not think he should join them until he was invited, and anyway, his own strict religious background meant that he shrank in fear for his immortal soul. The story of the Hare and the man and the woman in his bag was clearly nonsense. But was it any more nonsense than a story about a woman visited by the Holy Ghost, bearing God's own child before kneeling oxen while angels sang above them?

When the people turned and came out of the water their faces were serene, as if they had seen something which would last them all the day, as if they had been touched by a tongue of fire. John stepped forward from the bushes and said in careful Powhatan, 'I am ready,' to Suckahanna's husband.

The man looked him up and down. John was dressed like a brave in a buckskin shirt and buckskin pinny. He had learned to walk without his boots and on his feet were Powhatan moccasins, though his feet would never be as hard as those of men who had run over stones and through rivers and climbed rocks barefoot since childhood. John was no longer starved thin; he was lean and hardened like a hound.

Suckahanna's husband grinned at John. 'Ready?' he asked in his own language.

'Ready,' John replied, recognising the challenge.

But first every man had to check his weapons, and sons and girls were sent running for spare arrow heads and shafts, and new string for a bow. Then a woman ran after them with her husband's strip of dried meat which she had forgotten to give him. It was a full hour after sunrise before the hunting party trotted out of the village. John suppressed a smug sense of satisfaction at what he regarded as inefficient delays; but kept his face grave as they jogged past the women, setting off for the fields. There were cat-calls and hoots of encouragement at the men's hard pace and at John, keeping up in the rear.

'For a white man, he can run,' a woman said fairly to Suckahanna, and Suckahanna turned her head to look after them as if to demonstrate that she had not been watching and had not noticed.

John did not permit himself a grin of satisfaction. The fat had been leached off him during his hungry time in the woods and his stay in the Indian village had been hard work. He was always running errands from field to village, or helping the women with the heavy work of clearing the land. The food they gave him had built only muscle, and he knew that though he might be thirty-five this year he had never been healthier. He imagined that Attone would think that he would drop from the line of braves panting and gasping within the first ten minutes but he would be proved wrong.

Ten minutes went by and John was gasping for breath and fighting the desire to drop out from the line. It was not that they moved so fast, John could easily have sprinted past them, it was the very steadiness of their pace which was so exhausting. It was not a run and it was not a walk, it was a walk on the balls of their feet, a fast walk which never quite broke into a run. It was hard on the calf muscles, it was hard on the arch of the instep. It was sweating agony on the lungs and the face and the chest and the whole racking frame of the Englishman as he tried first to run and then to walk and found himself forever out of stride.

He would not give up. John thought that he might die on the trail behind the Powhatan braves, but he would not return to the village and say that he had not even sighted the deer he had promised to kill because he had been out of breath and too weary to walk to the woods.

For another ten minutes, and another unbearable ten after that, the file of braves danced along the path, following in each other's footsteps so precisely that anybody tracking them would think he was following only one man. Behind them came John, taking two steps to their one, then one and a half, then a little burst of a run, then back to a walk.

Suddenly they halted. Attone's fingers had spread slightly as he held his hand to his side. No other signal was needed. The fingers opened and closed twice: deer, a herd. Forefinger and little finger were raised: with a stag. Attone looked back down the line of the hunting party and slowly, one by one, all the half-shaven heads turned to look back at John. There was a polite smile on Attone's face which was soon mirrored down the line. Here was the herd, here was a stag. It was John's hunt. How did he propose they should go about killing one, or preferably three, deer?

John looked around. Sometimes a hunting party would set fires in the forest and drive a herd of deer into an ambush. Even more skill was required for an individual hunter to stalk an animal. Attone was famous among the People for his gift of mimicry. He could throw a deerskin over his shoulders and strap a pair of horns to his head and get so close to an animal that he could stand alongside it and all but slide a hand over its shoulders and cut its throat as it grazed. John knew he could not emulate that expertise. It would have to be a drive and then a kill.

They were near to an abandoned white settlement. Some time ago there had been a house by the river here, the deer were grazing on shoots of maize between the grass. There was a jumble of sawn timber where a house had once been and there was a landing stage where the tobacco ship would have moored. It had all gone to ruin years before. The landing stage had sunk on its wooden legs into the treacherous river mud and now made a slippery pier into the river. John looked at the lie of the land and thought, for no reason at all, of his father telling him of the causeway on the Ile de Rhé and how the French had chased the English soldiers over the island and to the wooden road across the mudflats and then picked them off as the tide swirled in.

He nodded, affecting confidence, as if he had a plan, as if he had anything in his head more than a vision of something his father had done, whereas what he needed now, and so desperately, was something he himself could do.

Attone smiled encouragingly, raised his eyebrows in a parody of interest and optimism.

He waited.

They all waited for John. It was his hunt. It was his herd of deer. They were his braves. How were they to dispose themselves?

Feeling foolish but persisting despite his sense of complete incompetence, John pointed one man to the rear of the herd, another to the other side. He made a cupping shape with his hands: they were to surround the deer and drive them forwards. He pointed to the river, to the sunken pier. They were to drive the deer in that direction.

Their faces as blank as impudent schoolboys, the men nodded. Yes indeed, if that was what John wanted. They would surround the deer. No-one warned John to check the direction of the wind, to think how the men would get into place in time, to disperse them in stages so that each would get to his place as the others were also ready. It was John's hunt, he should fail in his own way, without the distraction of their help.

He had beginner's luck. Just as the men started to move into their places the rain started, heavy thick drops which laid the scent and hid the noise of the men moving through the woodland surrounding the clearing. And they were skilled hunters and could not restrain their skill. They could not move noisily or carelessly when they were encircling a herd of deer even if they wanted to, their training was too deeply engrained. They stepped lightly on dry twigs, they moved softly through crackling shrubs, they slid past thorns which would have caught in their buckskin clouts with the sharp noise of paper tearing. They might not care whether or not they helped John in his task; but they could not deny their own skill.

In seconds the hunting team was cupped around the herd, ready for the signal to move forward. John held back, at the base of the cup, he hoped to see the herd driven before him and struggling in the mud, giving him the chance of a clear shot. He made the small gesture with his hand which meant 'drive on'; and he had the pleasure of seeing all of them, even Attone, move co-operatively to his bidding.

One, two, the deer's heads went up, the does looking for their young. The stag snuffed the wind. He could smell nothing, the wind had veered with the rain. The only scent he got was the clear water smell of the river behind the herd. Uneasily he glanced around and then he turned his head and walked a little back the way they had come, to the river.

The braves paused at John's gesture and then, as he beckoned them, moved forward again. The herd knew that something was happening. They could see nothing in the sudden downpour of rain and hear nothing over the pitter-pat of fat raindrops on summer leaves, but they had a sense of uneasiness. They bunched closer together and followed the stag as he went, his heavy head swinging to one side and then the other, looking all about him, and led the way towards the river.

John should have held back, but he could not. He made the gesture to 'go forward' and was saved from disaster only by the braves' own skill. They could not have borne to have moved forward and stampeded the herd and lost them. Not if there had been a dozen Englishmen to humiliate. They could not have done it any more than John could have mown down a bed of budding tulips. Their skill asserted itself even over their desire for mischief. They disobeyed John's hurried commands and fell back, waiting until the anxious heads dropped again to graze and the flickering ears ceased to swivel and flick.

John gestured again: 'go forward'! And now, slowly the braves moved a little closer as if their own looming presence alone could move the deer towards the river. They were right. The empathy between deer and Powhatan was such that the deer did not need to hear, did not need to see. The stag's head was up again and he went determinedly down the path which the farmer had once trod from his maize field to his pier, and the does and fawns followed behind.

John waved, 'on, on', and the deer went faster, and the hunters went faster behind them. Then, as if they could sense the excitement before they could even hear or smell or see, the deer knew they were being pursued; and they threw their heads back and their dark liquid eyes rolled, and they trotted and then they cantered, and then they flung themselves headlong down the little muddy single-file path to the deceptive safety of the pier as it stretched out into the river like an avenue to a haven.

The braves broke into a run following them, each one fitting an arrow to his bow as he ran, a faultless smooth gesture, even while dancing around fallen trees, leaping logs. John fumbled for his arrow, dropped it in his haste, put his hand to his hip for another and found that his quiver had been torn from him as he ran. He was weaponless. He threw aside his bow in a burst of impatience but his feet pounded faster still.

The deer were following a trail, the braves were filtering through thick forest but still they went as fast as the herd, they kept pace with them, they were the power behind the herd, driving it forwards, exactly to the place where John wanted them to go, to the wooden causeway, out into the river.

'Yes!' he cried. The braves broke from the trees in a perfect crescent, the herd a tossing tawny mass of horn and eyes and heads and thundering feet cupped inside the circle of running men. 'Now!' John yelled, a great passion for the deer and for the hunt rising up in him. He felt a great desire to kill a deer, thus owning it and this moment forever: the moment that John led his hunting party and took his deer.

But just as that moment was there, just as the first deer leaped down to the causeway to the illusion of safety, and lost her footing at once on the slippery betraying timbers, and an arrow went zing through the air and pierced her pounding heart, just as the others were ready to follow her, one young buck jinked to the right, to the bank, to the clear run downriver to freedom, and another, seeing the sudden spurt of his pace, followed him, and Tradescant saw in that split second of time that his cup of braves was not holding, that his herd of deer would be lost, spilled like quicksilver out of an alchemist's goblet, and would run away downriver.

'No!' he yelled. 'No! My deer!' And now he was not thinking of Suckahanna, nor of his pride, nor of the respect of Attone and the other braves. Now he was intent, determined that his plan should work, that his beautiful strategy should be beautifully performed and that no fleet, infuriating beast should spoil the perfection of the moment of the hunt. 'No!'

At once he was running in great jolting, ground-eating strides, running as he had never run before, to plug the gap in the line, to outpace the first hunter on the extreme right, to stop the deer escaping from his goblet, his beautiful, deer-filled goblet. Attone, his arrow on a string, heard the yell as the Englishman, his long hair flying behind him, took breakneck strides, great leaps down the hill, watched open-mouthed, even forgetting the imperative of the hunt, as the Englishman yelled, 'No!' and while yelling outpaced one, two and then three hunters, and flung himself towards the breach.

John's sudden eruption caused terror in the herd. Instead of slipping away through the gap they doubled back and met the upstream wing of the hunters. There was nowhere for them to go but out into the river, on the slippery causeway. One after another they leaped and scrabbled for it. Their sharp hooves could gain no purchase on the greasy, half-rotted wood, they fell, they pitched into the river, there was a hail of arrows.

But John did not see any of this. All he saw was the gap in his plan, the breach in the perfection of his hunt, and a deer jinking and swerving to get past him. He ran, he ran towards it, his hands outstretched as if he would catch it by the throat. The deer caught sight of him and went for freedom, made a great leap down the steep bank to the river, splashed into the water, fought its way to the surface and laid its smooth head back so the wet, dark nose was able to pant, and it was able to swim, sharp legs flailing, to the centre of the river.

John, unable to bear the sight of his prey escaping, let out a desperate 'Hulloah!' and flung himself, as if he thought he could fly, down the six-foot riverbank and into the water, on top of the deer, falling head first in a wild dive so there was a resounding crack as deer skull met John's forehead, and while he was still blinded by the blow they plunged down into the depths of the river and rose up together, and even gazed into each other's startled, desperate eyes. John felt his hands close around the deer's throat before a sharp hoof struck him like a bullet in his chest and pushed him down below the water again.

Attone, far from letting fly with his arrow at the disappearing head, far from picking off the deer which were slithering and plunging off the causeway, found that he was screaming with laughter at the sight of the Englishman, the despised, over-anxious, women-guarded Englishman howling like a spirit from the dark world, bounding as if he could outrun a deer, and then diving head first into a shallow river. A man so filled with blood lust, so insane with desire, that he could come nose to nose in deep water with a deer and still close his hands around its throat.

Attone gripped a tree for support and called in English: 'Englishman! Englishman! Are you dead? Or just mad?'

Tradescant, surfacing and realising suddenly that he was in cold, weedy water, that he had neither bow nor arrow nor kill, but instead a sensation very like a broken rib and a hoof-shaped bruise over his heart, and a cracked head for his pains, heard also the irresistible laughter of a Powhatan engulfed by amusement, and started to laugh too. He paddled like a weak dog to the water's edge and then found he was laughing too much to climb up the bank. It was absurdly high and he recalled that he had dived off the top of it and actually landed head first on the deer. The thought made him collapse in laughter again, and the sight of Attone holding out his hand, his brown face creased in helpless laughter, redoubled Tradescant's own amusement.

He gripped Attone's hand but it was too much for both of them and their grip slipped as their helpless giggles weakened them so that all Attone could do was fall back on the soft grass of the riverbank and give himself up to it, while Tradescant lay back in the river and howled like a dog at the thought of his hunt and his madness and his incompetence.

When Suckahanna saw the men coming back to camp she went out slowly to greet them; she was proud, and this was a difficult matter for any woman. Her husband was the finest hunter among the people but she was proposing to leave him for an Englishman who had been seen by everyone as incapable of even shooting a pigeon with one of the white man's infallible guns.

First she saw the kill. Six of the hunters carried in three deer lashed by their feet to pruned branches. It was a kill that any hunting party would have been proud to bring home, enough to feed the village and leave surplus meat for salting down. Suckahanna breathed in sharply and drew herself a little higher. She would not be seen by anyone running up to the braves and asking them who had done the kill. But three deer was a successful hunt; three deer was undeniable evidence that the braves on the hunt had done well.

Then she saw John. At first she thought he must be wounded, grievously wounded, for the man who was supporting him was her own husband, Attone. She started to run towards him, but then she checked herself after two paces. There was something odd about the way they walked together, it was not the stumble of a sick man and the load-bearing stride of his helper. They were clinging together as if they were both dizzy, as if they were both drunk. She watched, then she put her hand up to shade her eyes from the evening sun. She heard their voices, they were not talking to each other in low, anxious tones, like men helping one another home, nor exchanging the odd satisfied word, like men returning sated from the hunt. They were saying one word and then another and then they would do a little wandering detour in a circle, like drunkards, legless with laughter.

Suckahanna stepped sharply back into the doorway of her house and dropped the curtain of skins to hide herself. In the darkness she turned and lifted the side of the skin so she could peep out. The men carrying the deer were staking them out for cleaning and skinning, but Attone and John were not going to set to work. Arms around each other's shoulders, they headed for the sweat lodge with most of the braves, and even as they went Suckahanna could still hear that sudden explosion of giggling.

'Dived in!' she heard, and then a crow of laughter from Tradescant: 'But what you don't know is that I fell on its head!' That was too much for Attone, his knees simply gave way beneath him.

'I saw you. You had no arrows?'

'Why does he need arrows? If he is going to fall on deer to kill them?'

There was another scream and all the braves flung their arms around each other's shoulders and swayed together, their feet pounding to their bellowing laugh.

A woman came to Suckahanna's doorway. Suckahanna pushed back the deerskin and came outside.

'What are the men doing tonight?' the woman asked.

Suckahanna shrugged with a smile which said at once, 'Men!' and said, 'How I love him!' and said, 'How impossible he is!'

'How should I know?' she asked.

The half-sacred silence of the sweat lodge calmed them and the exhaustion of the day took its toll. They sat against the walls illuminated by the glowing coals, eyes shut, soaking up the healing heat, sweating out the aches and pains. Every now and then one of the braves would grimace and giggle and then there would be a little ripple of laughter.

They stayed in the heat for a long time until their sinuses were hot and dry, until the very bones of their faces were filled with heat. John could feel the bruise on his head swelling like a maggot and the hoof print on his chest growing dark and tender. He did not care. He cared for nothing but the deep, sensual pleasure of this heat and rest.

After a long, long while, Attone rose to his feet and stretched himself like a cat, every vertebra in his backbone extending. He put out a peremptory hand to John and spoke in Powhatan. 'Come, my brother.'

John looked up, saw the proffered hand and reached up his own to clasp it. Attone pulled him to his feet and for a moment the men stood side by side, hand-clasped, looking deep into each other's eyes with a measuring, honest look of respect and affection.

Attone led the way out of the sweat lodge. 'I have a name for you, your tribal name,' Attone said. 'You cannot be John Tradescant any more. You are a brave now.'

John took in the full meaning. So he was accepted. 'What shall my name be?' he asked.

'Eagle,' Attone announced.

The grandness of the name caused a murmur of admiration from the other braves at the honour being done to John.

'Eagle?'

'Yes. Because you kill a deer by dropping on it from the sky.'

There was a scream of uncontrollable laughter and the men were clinging to each other for support again, John in the centre, Attone with his arms around him. 'Eagle!' the braves said. 'Mighty hunter!' 'He who falls like an eagle without warning!'

They turned and ran down to the river together to wash. The women pulled the smaller children out of the way of the laughing, shouting men. They plunged into the river together and splashed like boys before huskanaw. Then Attone caught sight of a shadowy tall figure on the riverbank and straightened up and looked serious.

The werowance was watching them. Attone came out of the river and the men of the hunt followed him. They dried themselves and pulled on clean buckskins and then, when they were all ready, the werowance led the way to the dancing circle and the braves stood before him.

'Did the man who wants Suckahanna kill his deer?' the werowance asked in their own language.

There was a moment's complete consternation.

'We brought three deer home,' Attone said smoothly. 'A fine day's kill, and the man who wants Suckahanna was at my shoulder the whole day. He did not hang back, he did not fail, he did not tire. He planned the hunt and his plan was a good one. It drove the deer to the river and we killed three.'

'Which one did he kill?' the werowance asked.

Attone fell silent.

'We could have killed none without his plan,' one of the other men volunteered. 'He saw that we could drive them to the river. He showed us the way.'

The werowance nodded leisurely as if he were prepared to spend all night on this inquisition. 'And which did he kill?' he asked. 'One of the bucks? The doe?'

John, following this interrogation as well as he could, understood that the hunters could not conceal his failure. He felt a great wave of disappointment wash through him: that the hunt and the laughter and his naming should all come to nothing because an old man, old enough to be his father, should stick to the letter of the law. He thought that the way of a brave would be to acknowledge his failure, like a man, and then walk away from the village and never look back. He stepped forwards, he opened his mouth to speak. He took a moment to think of the word which meant defeat in Powhatan and realised that he did not know one. Perhaps there was no word for defeat in Powhatan. He framed a sentence with the words he did know. Something like – 'I have not killed. I cannot marry.'

'Yes?' The werowance invited him to speak.

There was a cry from the women at the edge of the dancing circle.

'Whose deer is this?' someone asked.

A woman came towards them. She had hold of the front legs of a deer and was dragging it towards them. From the loll of the head it was clear that the neck was broken.

'That's my deer!' John exclaimed. He hammered Attone on the shoulder. 'That's my deer!' He ran towards the woman and took the delicate legs from her hands. 'This is my deer! My deer!'

'I found it at the river's edge,' she said. 'It had been washed downriver. But it had not been in the water long.'

'The Eagle killed it!' Attone announced. At once there was a ripple of laughter from the braves. The werowance shot a quick sharp look around them.

'Did you kill this deer?' he asked John.

John could feel a bubble of laughter, of joy, rising up in his tight throat. 'Yes, sire,' he said. 'That is my deer, I killed it. I want Suckahanna.'

'Eagle! Eagle!' The shout went up from the braves.

The werowance looked at Attone. 'Do you release your wife to this man, your wife and your first-born son, and your second-born child?'

Attone looked straight at John and his hard, dark face creased into an irresistible smile. 'He's a good man,' he said. 'He has the determination of a salmon leaping homeward, and the heart of a buffalo. I release Suckahanna to him. He is my brother. He is the Eagle.'

The werowance raised his ornate spear. 'Hear this,' he said so quietly that all the women at the edge of the dancing circle craned forward to listen, Suckahanna among them.

'This is our brother. He has proved himself in the hunt and he is the husband of Suckahanna. Tomorrow we receive him into the People, and his name shall be Eagle.'

There was a roar of approval and applause and people crowded around John. John had to fight his way through smiling faces and slapping hands to get to Suckahanna and fold her in his arms. She clung to him and lifted her face to his. As their lips met he felt a sudden jolt of passion, a feeling he had forgotten for many years, and a deep hunger for more of her; more, as if a kiss alone would not satisfy him, could never satisfy him, as if nothing would ever be enough but to fold her into his heart and keep her beside him for always.

Suckahanna moved her face from his and reluctantly John released her. She rested her head on his shoulder and his senses shifted again to take in the touch of her slight body tucked beneath his arm, the way her long legs matched his side, the scent of her hair, the warmth of her naked skin against his cool damp chest.

The people were cheering them, linking their names together.

'Why do they call you Eagle?' she asked, turning her head up to look into his face.

He caught sight of Attone, waiting for his answer. 'It is private,' he said with assumed coldness. 'Something for us braves.'

Attone grinned.

John could not sleep with Suckahanna that night, though she moved from Attone's house to stay the night with Musses. Attone himself carried her deerskin, her baskets and her pots to Musses's hut and kissed her tenderly on the forehead as he left her there.

'Does he not mind?' John asked, watching this affectionate farewell.

Suckahanna shot him a quick, mischievous smile. 'Only a little,' she said.

'I should mind,' John observed.

'He married me because he was advised to do so,' she explained. 'And then he had to keep me, and my mother, and we brought no dowry, no bride price at all. So he could never afford to take another wife, if he should like another woman. He was stuck with only one: me. And now everything has changed for him. He is a bachelor again, you will have to pay him for me, he will like that, and he can look about him and choose a girl he really wants this time.'

'How much will I have to pay?' John asked.

'Maybe a lot,' she warned him. 'Maybe one of your guns that you left at your house.'

'Are they still there?' John asked incredulously. 'I would have thought that everything had been stolen.'

She nodded serenely. 'Everything has been stolen. But if it is to be Attone's gun I think you will find that it will be returned.'

'I should like my guns returned to me,' John observed.

She laughed. 'I should think you would. When you are adopted tomorrow, when you are one of the People, then no man or woman or child will steal from you ever again, not even if they are starving. But they took your goods when you were a rich white man, and now your goods are gone.'

She looked at his half-convinced expression.

'What would you want with them? What would you do with them here, when everything that a man wants can be got with a bow and arrow, a spear, a hoeing stick, a knife or a fish trap?'

John thought for a moment and realised that his goods were part of the life he had left behind, part of his old life, better lost and forgotten than standing in the corner of his new Indian house reminding him of the man he had been, of the life he might have lived.

'Very well,' he said. 'If he can get them back he can have them.'

John was woken just before dawn by Attone's hand on his shoulder. 'Awake, Eagle,' the man whispered. 'Come and wash.'

They were early, only the men were moving like grey shadows down the village street. It was still dark, only a line of pale grey like a smudge of limewash above the dark of the forest trees showed that dawn was coming.

Tradescant waded into the river beside Attone and followed every move that he made. First the careful washing of the face: eyes, mouth, nostrils, and ears. Then the meticulous washing of armpits, and crotch, and then finally a deep immersion in icy water, while rubbing chest, back, thighs, calves, and feet. Attone emerged blowing water and flinging back his long hair.

He waded for the shore, John followed him. There was a little fire built on the pebble beach and a handful of the tiny Indian tobacco leaves piled beside it. Attone took up an abalone shell, took up a leaf, lit it at one of the glowing embers, and, blowing on the spark, walked back into the river with the burning leaf outstretched and the abalone shell cupped beneath it to catch the sacred ash. He faced towards the sun and murmured the prayer. John copied him exactly, and got very close to the prayer as well, invoking the sun to rise, the deer to eat well and be happy, the rain to come, the plants to grow, Okee the cruel god to withhold his anger, and the People to tread lightly on the earth and to keep the love of their mother. Then he scattered the ash and embers on the water and turned his face to the shore. John followed suit.

Waiting there was Suckahanna, her face grave. When John went to his clothes, the hand-me-down buckskin he had been given on his arrival at the village, she shook her head wordlessly and held out for him a new buckskin clout made of soft new leather, and a little buckskin apron exquisitely embroidered.

John smiled at her, remembering the little girl she had been when she had first showed him the Indian clothes and how reluctant he had been to part with his breeches. She crinkled her eyes at him but she did not smile with her lips, nor speak. It was a moment too solemn for speech.

John stepped forwards and let her dress him as she wished, and then let her and Musses paint him with the red bear-grease ointment so that his skin was as dark as theirs in the greying light of the dawn.

From the village they could hear the roll of drums and then a steady, insistent beat.

'It is time,' said Attone. 'Come, Eagle. It is your time.'

John turned, expecting to see Attone laughing at the name, but the brave's gaze was steady and his face was grave. There was not even a smile in his look.

'My time?' John asked uneasily.

Suckahanna turned and led the way back to the village but when they approached the dancing circle she fell back and joined the crowd of women who were waiting at one side. They linked arms around her so she was at the centre of a circle of women with arms interlinked, like a country dancer in the middle of the ring.

John found himself surrounded by braves, his friends of yesterday. But none of them greeted him with a smile. Their faces were unmoving, as hard as if carved from seasoned wood. John looked from one to another. They no longer seemed like friends; they seemed like enemies.

The door to the werowance's hut was drawn back and the old man came out. He was terrifyingly dressed in a costume completely made of bird feathers, sewed so skilfully that John could see no seams and no cloth. He looked like a man transformed into a dark, glossy bird and he stalked on his long legs with the arrogant pace of an ill-tempered heron. Behind him came the two other elders, wearing black capes which gleamed with beads of jet. They chinked as they walked, they were laden with amulets and necklaces of copper and abalone shells.

At a gesture from the werowance's richly carved spear two young men came awkwardly from his house, carrying something low and square between them. For a moment John thought they had brought a mounting block, a post, or a pedestal for the werowance to stand on and address the people, but then he saw that the centre of it was hollowed to take a man's chin, and the wood on either side had been sharply cut with an axe. With a sensation of dull horror John recognised what it was. He had been on Tower Hill often enough, he knew an executioner's block when he saw one.

'No!' he shouted and flinched back, but there were a dozen men around him. They did not even grab him, they pressed close to him and John was held in a solid wall of hard flesh. They interlocked arms, they held themselves tight, forcing themselves one against each other so John was helpless among them. Even if he had dropped dead in a faint of fear he would still have been standing, they had him so tight.

The werowance smiled his cruel, beak-nosed smile at John and his dark feathers quivered as if he were an English raven come all this way to peck out John's eyes. John heard himself shout against the injustice of it. Why save him when he was burned and poisoned and starving to death to bring him here and behead him? But then he remembered the wisdom of Jamestown and knew that there was no reason to these people, nothing but mischief and meaningless cruelty, nothing but torture for sport and bloodshed for pleasure, and he started to think that a blow from an axe would be a mercy rather than a disembowelling, or a scalping, or being torn apart, or staked out on an anthill. The thought of these horrors made him cry out 'Suckahanna!' and he lunged so that he could see her, trapped as he was trapped, her face white and agonised, pleading desperately with the women around her, and forever looking towards him and calling 'John!'

The braves clutched his arms, there was no chance of escape, and marched him towards the block. John kicked out and swore but they held him, the sheer weight of them forcing his head down and down till his chin met the pitiless coolness of the skilfully shaped wood and he felt his body recognise the place of his death.

'God forgive me my sins,' John whispered. 'And keep my children and Hester safe. God forgive me, God forgive me.' He closed his eyes for a moment against the horror and then he opened them again and looked for Suckahanna. The women had released her and she was standing stock still among them, her face as white as an Englishwoman's with terror.

'Suckahanna,' John said softly.

He tried to smile at her, to reassure her that there was, even now, no bad blood between them, no regrets and no reproaches. But he knew that he could only bare his teeth, that all she would see was his skull beneath the rictus of the smile, that soon she would see the white of his skull as they peeled back his forehead to cut the trophy of his scalp.

The pressure on his back and his neck was gradually released as the men sensed his surrender. John rolled his eyes to look for the executioner and his axe, and saw instead a great war club, beautifully made and counterweighted, and the man holding it, waiting for the signal to step forward and pound John's head into fragments.

His courage failed him completely then, he felt warm water gush between his legs. He heard a little wail which was his own voice of terror.

The werowance lifted his ornate ceremonial spear, the black feathers on his arms rustled like pinions, like a black angel he stood between John and the rising sun, and his face was filled with joy.

The spear fell. The war club rolled back on the upswing, and John waited for the blow.

Something hit him hard, and his whole tortured body flinched from the impact, but it was not a war club to the head, it was the full weight of Suckahanna, broken free of the circle of women, diving across the dancing ground to lie along his back, one knee in his piss, her hair falling over his flinching spine, her head above his, her chin on his skull, offering herself on the block.

The executioner was too late to stop his downswing, he could only shift it to one side, and the mighty club thudded, like a cannon ball, into the beaten mud of the dancing ground. John felt the whistle of its passing lift the hair of his beard, opened his eyes and looked towards the werowance.

The old man was serene. He raised his spear and spoke as quietly as ever.

'See this, people of the forest and river, see this, people of the plains, see this, people of the seashore, and the swamp, see this, people of the sky, of the rain, of the sun, all the people who have run from the mouth of the Great Hare and who run over the land that He made. Suckahanna, our daughter, went to the very edge of the dark river for this man. He owes her his life. She has given him life, he has a Powhatan mother.'

The people nodded. 'He has life from a Powhatan woman.'

John felt Suckahanna tremble down the length of her lean body pressed against his. He saw her shaking hands come down on either side of the executioner's block and clench white as she forced herself up to kneel and then stand before her people. He thought he should stand too, beside her, but he doubted his legs would hold him. Then he thought again that if Suckahanna could dive towards him to have her head smashed in his place then he should stand for her. He should probably kneel to her.

He heaved himself to his feet and found that his legs were trembling and his body icy with sweat. Suckahanna turned to him and took his hand.

'I take you as my husband,' she said shakily. 'I take you into our people. You are one of the People now and you always will be.'

There was a silence. John feared that his voice would shame him with a squeak of terror. He cleared his throat a little and looked at the girl who had become a woman and who had now twice become his saviour.

'I thank you for my life,' he said, speaking their language haltingly, mixing in English words when he was at a loss. 'I will never forget this. I gladly take you to my wife and I gladly join the People.'

'I take *you*,' she stressed very slightly.

'I am glad that you take me to your husband, and I am glad that the People admit me,' John corrected himself.

There was a ripple of pleasure throughout the crowd and then everyone looked to the werowance, dark in his dark feathers, hunched like a heron in a pine tree, brooding over the couple. He raised his spear.

'Eagle!' he shouted.

There was a roar from the braves, and then the women and the children took it up. 'Eagle!' 'Eagle!' 'Eagle!'

John felt his knees give way and he grabbed for Suckahanna as she swayed too. The women were at her side, the braves bore him up, Attone among them.

'Eagle!' Attone cheered, and with a swift sideways grin at John: 'Eagle! who kills by diving on his deer and pisses himself at his own wedding.'

They got intoxicated that night. Dazed and riotous and then stupefied and giggly, then dancing and leaping and singing under a big yellow midsummer moon. They smoked the sacred tobacco until their heads rang with it and their very eardrums grew hot and itchy. They smoked until they saw dozens of moons cavorting in the sky and they danced on the dancing ground beneath them, following the lunar steps. They smoked until they were whimpering for cool water for their aching throats, and they ran down to the river and exclaimed at more moons, floating in the water, like stepping stones into the darkness. They smoked until they grew hungry like children and raided the stores for anything sweet and spicy and ate handfuls of dried blueberries and popped corn on the embers of the fire and burned their tongues in their hurry. They smoked in a great orgy to celebrate that the Eagle had passed the test and put his head on the block, and that a woman of the People had laid her head down beside him for love of him, and such a thing had never been seen since the time of Pocahontas, when Princess Pocahontas herself had laid her head down to save John Smith, though she had been little more than a girl and hardly understood the risk she took.

Suckahanna's story was more passionate and the women made her tell it over and over again. How she had met John and feared him, how he had treated her gently and never known that she had understood every word he said, that she had heard him tell her that she was beautiful, that she had heard him say that she was lovable. The women sighed at that and the young braves giggled and dug each other in the ribs. Then Suckahanna told them how she waited and waited for him, in the cruelty of the white man's world at Jamestown; and that when she gave him up she had been glad of a refuge with the People and glad of the kindness of Attone, who had been a husband that any woman might admire and love. And at this part of the story the young women nodded and glanced over to Attone in neutral judicial appreciation as if it had not occurred to any of them that Attone was now a free man. Then Suckahanna told them how she had heard of a new white man who had made a clearing in the wood and built a house and had planted a flower at his doorstep. She told them that at that word, at that single piece of news, she knew at once that John had come back to the land of the Great Hare and she went alone to stand in the shadow of the trees and see him. And that when she saw him, her heart went out to him and she knew then that he was still the only man she had ever loved and ever would love and she went straight to Attone and to the werowance and told them that the man she loved was an Englishman living alone in the forest and asked their permission to go to him.

But they were wise, she said now, and cautious, and they made her wait and watch him. And they realised as they watched him that he did not have the skill to keep himself. He could not feed himself and dig his fields and keep his fire in. It was too much work for a single white man to do. Even the children of the Great Hare live together so that the women can garden and the men can hunt and they can all work together. Then Suckahanna went to the werowance and to her husband Attone, and told them that she would like to be released to go to the Englishman and help him to make his home in the land of the Hare.

But again, they were too wise. They said that the Englishman could not be trusted with the children of Attone. That when Suckahanna returned to him he might take her as a servant and not as a wife. Or he might take her and then abandon her, as white men like to do. They said she should wait and watch.

She waited and she watched and she kept him alive with little gifts and then finally she saw him so near to death and to despair that he got in his canoe and could have drifted forever down to the Great Sea. Then, and only then, was Suckahanna allowed to take his life in her keeping and bring him to the Powhatan.

It was a good story and it lasted through the last hours of the night when the smoke started to disperse from their wild, dazed heads, and the laughter subsided and the men and women and children drifted away from the dancing ground and the great fire they had built for their revels, and found themselves falling asleep with only an hour left of the night.

Suckahanna and John were among the last to leave. At last there was no hurry, there was no urgency in their meeting. They had their house, the werowance had allowed them to use one of the empty store houses, another house would be built soon. Suckahanna had put deerskin on the sleeping platforms and hung her baskets on the walls. The baby was slung up in its papoose, her little boy was lolled, his heavy head in her lap. Suckahanna smiled at John.

'I'm sleepy too,' she said.

John got to his feet and lifted Suckahanna's son into his arms. The warm boy clung to him in sleep, with the easy trust of a child who has only ever known a loving touch. John followed Suckahanna to their new house and laid the boy, as she directed, on his little sleeping platform in the corner. Then he sat on the warm skins and watched his wife unbraid her hair, untie her little skirt and drop it to the floor. She stood before him naked.

John rose to his feet, his fingers fumbling for the tie of his own loincloth, found it and dropped the buckskin to the floor so that he was as naked as she. Her eyes travelled all over him, without shame, dark with desire, and she smiled a little, as a woman smiles when she sees that her man desires her: partly in vanity, partly in joy.

She turned with a proud little toss of her head and then stretched out on the sleeping platform, pulling the soft deerskin to one side so that it framed the bronze, smooth length of her, her dark hair spread, her lips half-parted, her breath coming a little faster and her eyes hazy with desire. John moved towards her and kneeled on the sleeping platform, moving over her with a sense of unreality, as if, after all his years of dreaming, this could only be another dream. He bent his head and kissed her and at the warmth and taste of her lips he knew himself to be awake and alive, and more powerfully alive than he had ever been in his life before. He gathered her warm buttocks into his hands and entered her with a quiet sigh of pleasure. Suckahanna's dark eyes flickered shut.

Summer 1643, England

Hester woke on the morning of 31 May to the sound of gravel rattling against her bedroom window. For a moment she had the absurd thought that it was John, locked out of his own house, summoning her to let him in, to a reconciliation, a return, and to the end of her loneliness and waiting.

She jumped out of bed, ran to the window and looked down. It was a man, wrapped to the eyes in a cape, but she would have recognised the hat, heavy with plumes, anywhere.

'God rot him,' Hester swore under her breath, threw a jacket over her nightdress and ran barefoot down the stairs to let him in at the back door. In the stable yard a dog barked briefly. Hester let the man slip inside and then closed the door behind him.

'What is it?' she asked tersely.

'It's gone awry,' he said. He dropped the cape from his face and she saw he was drawn and anxious. 'I need a horse to get away from here to warn the king.'

'I don't have one,' Hester said instantly.

'Liar,' he shot back.

'I don't have one to spare.'

'This is the king's business. His Majesty shall hear how I am served.'

Hester bit her lip. 'Will you send the horse back to me?' she asked. 'She's my husband's horse and the saddle horse for my children, and she works on the land as well. I need her.'

'The king's need is greater.'

'Keep your voice down,' Hester hissed. 'D'you want to wake the whole house?'

'Then give me the horse!'

She led the way down the hall to the kitchen at the back. He hesitated when he saw the fire banked in for the night. 'I need food,' he said.

'You're going to Oxford, not to America!' Hester said impatiently. 'Eat there!'

'Give me some bread and some cheese, and I'll drink a glass of ale while you are saddling the horse.'

Hester waved him towards the larder. 'Eat what you want,' she said. 'And come out into the yard as soon as you are done.'

She stepped into a pair of clogs which were on the stone doorstep and unlocked the kitchen door. She pulled the jacket around her shoulders and did up the buttons. John's mare was in her loosebox, she whinnied when she saw Hester and the dog barked again.

'Hush!' Hester called to them both as she went into the tack room to fetch John's heavy saddle and bridle. The mare stood obediently while Hester struggled with her tack, and then shifted when a shadow fell over the stable. Hester looked up, instantly afraid that it was Parliament men come to arrest the royalist, and arrest her too as a conspirator. But it was the cavalier, his hands full of bread and cheese, his hat tipped back on his head.

Hester led the horse out into the yard. 'Give me that,' she said suddenly and snatched the hat from his head. He was too surprised to protest. With one swift movement she plucked the feathers from the hat band and tossed them into the midden heap. 'Why not carry the king's colours while you're about it?' she demanded.

He nodded. 'I shall tell His Majesty that the Tradescant house remembers their master. You will be rewarded for this.'

'The only reward I want is for you to send the horse back,' Hester said. 'D'you promise you will send her back to me?'

'I do.'

Hester stood away from the mare's head as she stepped delicately on the cobbles, and out of the yard and around the house to the road. Hester stood very still and quiet, listening. If the man had been sighted she would hear the horses' hooves on the Lambeth road as they chased him. There was silence. Somewhere in the garden a thrush was starting to sing.

Hester realised that she was shivering with cold and with apprehension. She turned and crept across the yard to the kitchen door, slipped off the muddy clogs and went to the fireside. If he was captured and named her as his ally and the Ark as a safe royalist house, then she could face arrest for treason against Parliament, and the punishment for treason was death. The cavalier might ride with feathers in his hat and a light heart even in the middle of defeat; but Hester was only too well aware that the country was at war, and it was becoming a war in which there was no quarter given.

She waited by the fire until the little square kitchen window became light and then she went upstairs and woke Frances and Johnnie.

'What is it, Mother?' Johnnie asked, seeing her grave face.

'We're going on a visit to Uncle Norman,' she said. 'Today.'

They took a boat down the river and the boatman was full of news of a royalist plot which had been uncovered only yesterday. Hester nodded. 'I have no interest in politics,' she said.

'You'll be interested soon enough if these traitors hand the city back to the king,' the boatman said. 'If the king brings in murdering Irishmen and damned Frenchmen to cut the throats of honest Englishmen!'

'Yes,' Hester said politely. 'I suppose I will be then.'

The boatman hawked and spat in the water and rowed steadily on.

Alexander Norman greeted them as if their visit had been planned for months instead of thrown together in Hester's panic. His housekeeper had prepared two rooms in his small town house next to his work yard in the Minories in the shadow of the Tower. Frances and Hester would share a bed and Johnnie was to have a little attic room.

'My cousin has long promised me this visit,' he said to his housekeeper as she showed Hester into the front parlour and took her hat and cape. 'I insisted it should be May before the City is too hot and unhealthy.'

'There's nothing worth having in the shops,' the housekeeper remarked to Hester. 'So if you were thinking of new fashions you might as well have stayed at home. There are more tailors out of business than you could name.'

Hester nodded. 'My husband's first wife's family are haberdashers,' she said. 'I thought they would let me see if they have anything left in stock.'

The housekeeper nodded. 'They'll surely have some silk saved for the little miss here. Isn't she a beauty?'

Hester nodded. Frances was struggling out of the thick cape and the big bonnet which Hester insisted she wore. 'Yes, she is.'

'Looking for a husband for her?'

Hester shook her head. 'Not yet.'

The woman nodded and bustled off. 'I shall serve you with your dinner in a few minutes,' she promised.

Alexander drew a chair near the fire for Hester. 'Was it cold on the river?'

'A little,' she said, sitting down.

'Are you in trouble?' he asked very quietly.

'A royalist officer came and took John's horse. He was looking for John to help them in a plot to claim Lambeth for the king.'

Alexander looked shocked. 'When was this?'

'He left this morning. But he came for the first time two weeks ago.'

He nodded. 'Did he get safe away?'

Hester shook her head. 'I don't know. There was no-one waiting outside the house, at any rate, and no-one seemed to be watching us leave today. But he was headed for Oxford and the king. I don't know if he got there.'

He turned away from her for a moment.

'What is it?' she asked. 'The boatman said there was some kind of plot.'

'It's Lady d'Aubigny,' Alexander said.

Hester gave a little gasp.

'You knew her name?'

'It was a name I heard when he was swearing me to secrecy two weeks ago. I didn't think that everyone would know it so soon.'

'She's a fool. Edmund Waller and she were plotting together to seize London for the king. They were going to seize the Tower and arrest Parliament and the House of Lords was to gather behind them and royalists were to rise up.'

Hester's face was pale. 'And?'

'And nothing. Everyone in the plot spoke about it from the assemblies to the taverns, and they were arrested this morning. Lady d'Aubigny has disappeared, no-one knows where yet; but Waller is arrested, and half a dozen others.' He paused for a moment. 'Who knows you're here?'

'The household. I said we were coming for a visit. I thought it might look worse if we went into hiding.'

He nodded. 'You were right. But I am wondering if you should leave London.'

'All of us?'

'Just you. D'you have family somewhere outside the City? Somewhere you can go until this panic is over?'

She shook her head. 'John said I was to go to Oatlands if I was in danger. He still has his house there. He is still gardener there.'

The housekeeper put her head around the door. 'Dinner is on the table,' she said.

'I'm starving!' Johnnie exclaimed, and he and Frances, who had been sitting in the windowseat looking at the street below, went to the dining room. Alexander took Hester's cold hand.

'Come and have something to eat,' he said. 'Nothing is going to happen in the next ten minutes. And I will send one of my clerks to Westminster to see what is happening.'

Hester ate nothing at dinner, and every time a cart went by in the street outside she found she was listening, waiting for the knock at the door.

'What is the matter, Mother?' Frances asked. 'I can tell that something is wrong.'

Hester looked at Alexander.

'You should tell them,' he said. 'They have a right to know.'

'A royalist spy came in the night and took Father's mare,' Hester said.

Frances and Johnnie looked stunned at the news.

'A royalist spy?' Johnnie demanded.

'What was he wearing?' Frances asked.

'Oh, why didn't you wake me?' Johnnie cried. 'And I could have helped him!'

'He was wearing a cape and . . .' Hester's voice quavered on a reluctant laugh. 'And an absurd hat with feathers.'

'Oh!' Frances breathed. 'What colours?'

'What does that matter!' Johnnie exclaimed. 'Oh, Mother! Why didn't you tell me? I could have guided him! I could have gone with him and been his page!'

'I expect that's why she didn't tell you,' Alexander said gently. 'Your place is at home, guarding your mother and the Ark.'

'I know,' Johnnie said. 'But I could have gone with him for a battle or two and then come home again. I am a Tradescant! It is my duty to serve the king!'

'It is your duty to protect your mother,' Alexander said, suddenly grim. 'So be silent, Johnnie.'

'But why have we come here?' Frances asked, abandoning interest in the colour of the royalist's hat feathers. 'What is happening? Is Parliament after us?'

226

'Not after you,' Hester said quietly. 'But if they know that he came to the Ark for help then I may be in trouble.'

Frances turned at once to Alexander Norman and put her hands out to him. 'You'll look after us, won't you?' she demanded. 'You won't let them take Mother away?'

He took her hands, and Hester saw that he had to stop himself from drawing her close. 'Of course I will,' he said. 'And if she's in any danger at all I shall find somewhere safe for her, and for you all.'

Frances, still hand-clasped with Alexander, turned to her stepmother and Hester saw them, for the first time, as a couple; saw the tilt of his head towards her, saw her trust in him.

'Should you go into hiding?' Frances asked her.

'I'll go to the Tower now,' Alexander decided, 'and see what news there is. You keep the door locked until I return. They can hardly have found your name and traced you here so soon. We must be a day ahead at least.'

Hester found that her mouth was dry and reached for a glass of small ale. Alexander gave her a quick, encouraging smile. 'Be of stout heart,' he said. 'I will be back within the hour.'

The little family went back into the parlour and Frances and Johnnie took up their posts in the windowseat again, but this time they were not commenting on the passers-by; they were on look-out. Hester sat, in uneasy idleness, by the fireside. The housekeeper coming in with fresh coal made them jump. 'I'd have thought you would want to go out and walk around.'

'Perhaps later,' Hester said.

Inside the hour, true to his word, Alexander Norman came strolling down the street, stopping for a chat with his neighbour who had a small goldsmith's shop, and then opened his front door and stepped inside. At once his air of leisured cheerfulness deserted him.

'It's bad news,' he said, checking that the parlour door was closed behind him. 'Lady d'Aubigny took sanctuary in the French Embassy under the pretext that her husband's family is French. But Parliament has ordered that the French hand her over and they have done so. She'll be tried for treason, she was carrying the king's Commission of Array. She was trying to raise an army in the very City itself.'

'The French ambassador handed over an English lady of the king's party to Parliament?' Hester demanded, incredulously.

'Yes,' Alexander said, looking grave. 'Perhaps His Majesty has fewer friends in Paris than he thinks. Perhaps the French are preparing to deal with Parliament direct.'

Hester found she was standing by her chair, as if ready to run. She forced herself to sit down and to start breathing normally. 'And what else?'

'Edmund Waller, who passes for the brains behind this brainless scheme, was taken up and is singing like a blinded thrush,' Alexander said. 'He is naming everyone he spoke to, in the hopes of escaping Tower Hill and the block.'

'Would he have my name?' Hester asked quietly. She found her lips were numb and she could not speak clearly.

'I can't tell,' Alexander said. 'I didn't want to ask too detailed questions for fear of attracting attention. We can hope that your man got clear away, and that he was too small a link in the chain to connect you to the plot.'

'As long as he was not captured on Father's horse,' Frances pointed out.

'If I said it was me who gave him the horse . . .' Johnnie suggested. 'I could say that it was me and that I was a royalist. They wouldn't execute me, would they? I'm not ten yet. They'd give me a whipping and I don't mind that. I'd get the blame and you'd be all right.'

Hester drew him towards her and kissed his smooth fair head. 'I don't want you involved in this, whatever the risks.' She looked up at Alexander Norman. 'Should I stay? Or go?'

He bit his upper lip with his teeth. 'It's the devil's own decision,' he said. 'I think you should go. We gain nothing from you being here and we risk everything. If your man is captured and he follows the example of his betters he will volunteer information and he is bound to name you. Even if he goes free then the king's men are so indiscreet that your name might still be mentioned. Go to Oatlands and stay in John's house in the garden for a week. I'll send you a message if it's all clear and you can come home again.'

'Oatlands?' Johnnie demanded. 'With Prince Rupert?'

'Yes, he's said to be quartered there,' Alexander Norman said. 'At least you'll be safe from Parliament while he is there.'

'Oatlands!' Johnnie exulted. 'Prince Rupert! I'll have to go with you. To defend you.'

Frances was about to say 'I'll come too', but she hesitated and looked towards Alexander Norman. 'Should I?'

'You'll all go,' he said. 'You're safer there than anywhere if Rupert is still there. Parliament can't arrest you there, you'll be under royalist protection; and when you come home we can say you were only doing John's work on the gardens.'

Frances was about to argue, but then she held her peace.

'You could go now,' Alexander said. He led the way out of the room to the narrow hall.

Hester hung back and looked at her beautiful stepdaughter. 'Did you not want the risk of being with me?' she asked. 'I would understand if you didn't want to come to Oatlands. You can go to your grandparents if you wish, Frances.'

'Oh no!' Frances cried out, and suddenly she was a girl again. 'Mother! Oh no! Whatever risks you were taking I should want to be with you. I'd never leave you alone to face danger! I was just thinking that perhaps Uncle Norman could come with us. I'd feel so much safer if he was with us.'

'The safest way is for him to be here, gathering news, and for us to be tucked out of the way in the country,' Hester said. 'And when it is all quiet again we can go home. I don't like to leave the rarities and the gardens.'

'In case Father comes home this month?' Johnnie asked.

Hester managed a smile. 'In case Father comes home this month,' she agreed.

Oatlands Palace was beautiful in early summer. The garden was showing signs of neglect and most of the rooms of the house were shut up. There was a regiment of soldiers occupying the main hall and the regimental cooks working in the kitchens. The cavalry's horses were stabled in the old royal stables and there was constant drilling and training and parading over John's precious turf at the front of the palace. Prince Rupert was only rarely with his troops. Half the time he was at Oxford with the court, arguing against the negotiations for peace, bolstering up the king's erratic determination to conquer the Parliament and not negotiate with them. The royalist cavalry troops paid no attention to the silkworm house nor to the gardener's house next door to it. The commander saw Hester when he was walking in the gardens and Hester mentioned that since her husband was still nominally gardener to the palace she had thought it her duty to make sure that the gardens were not suffering too badly.

'Very commendable,' he said. 'What needs doing?'

'The grass wants mowing,' Hester said. 'And the knot garden needs weeding and trimming. The roses should have been pruned in winter, it's too late now, and the fruit trees.'

He nodded. 'These are not the times for gardening,' he said flatly. 'You do what you can and I shall see that you are paid for your time.'

'Thank you,' Hester said.

'Who's the pretty maid?' he asked abruptly.

'My stepdaughter.'

'Keep her out of the way of the men,' he said.

'She'll stay by me,' Hester said. 'Can she walk in the gardens?'

'Yes. But not near the house.'

Hester dipped a little curtsey.

He was about to walk away but he hesitated. 'I visited the Ark once,' he said. 'When I was little older than your lad. The old Mr Tradescant showed me around himself. It was the most wonderful place I had ever been. A palace of curiosities. I could hardly believe the things I saw. A mermaid, and the jaw of a whale!'

Hester smiled. 'We still have them,' she said. 'You are very welcome to visit us again when you come to London. You may come as our guest. I should be glad to show you the new things too.'

The commander shook his head. 'It seems extraordinary to me that while I am fighting for the king against his own deluded people that you are still collecting mice skins and glassware and tiny toys.'

'For one thing there is nothing else for me to do,' Hester said tartly. 'My husband left the rarities and the garden and the children in my care. A woman should do her duty, whatever else may be happening.'

He nodded his approval of that.

'And when it is all over, when it is finished, then the men who have been fighting will want to go home to their houses and their gardens,' Hester said more gently. 'And then it will be a great joy to them to find rare and beautiful things have survived the war, and that there are strange and lovely plants to grow, and tulips are as bright and fiery as ever, and the chestnut trees are as rich and as green as ever they were.'

There was a little silence, and then he bowed low and took her hand and kissed it. 'You are keeping a little piece of England safe for us,' he said. 'Pray God we all come safely home to it at the end of all this.'

'Amen,' Hester said, thinking of John so far away, and of the war going on for so long, and of the young men who came to the Ark to order trees only for their heirs to grow. 'Amen.'

Hester found a youth who had so far avoided both the excitement of the war and the recruiting officers to mow the courts around Oatlands under her supervision, and then weed the gravel of the knot garden. Little could be done with the kitchen garden except to leave it to grow what vegetables and fruit could struggle through the weeds. But judging from the blossom which drifted like snow in the corners of the walled garden there would be a fine show of fruit, especially plums and apples which thrived on neglect.

In the silkworm house the shelves were full of dusty little corpses. When the king and queen had left the court and abandoned the old life, the boiler had gone out and all the worms had died. Hester, with her instinctive hatred of waste, cleaned out the trays and swept the floor with a bustling irritation against a queen who could command such things into being, and then forget them completely. Every day Hester and Frances hitched up their skirts, rolled up their sleeves and worked in the gardens, noting the positions of the tulips which should be lifted in autumn, tying in climbing plants to the bowers and arbours, and weeding, weeding, weeding: the white gravel of the stone gardens, the drive, the terrace, the stone-flagged arbours. Johnnie put himself in charge of the watercourses and drained and scrubbed them, coming home at dusk wet through with triumphant tales of streams running clean, and cracks in the watercourses repaired with his own sticky mixture of clay and white chalk.

In the afternoons he was allowed to watch the cavalry drilling, practising turning and wheeling at a shouted order, and once he saw Prince Rupert himself on his huge horse with his poodle held over his saddlebow and his dark hair in a curled mane over his shoulders. Johnnie came home full of joy at the sight of the handsome prince. Prince Rupert had seen him and smiled at him and Johnnie had asked if he could serve in his regiment as soon as he was old enough and could find another horse.

'You didn't say anything about the cavalier who took Father's horse?' Hester asked quickly.

At once all the boyish wildness drained from his face and he looked cautious. 'Of course not,' he said quickly. 'I'm not a child.'

Hester had to stop herself from drawing him on to her knee and taking him in her arms. 'Of course you're not,' she said. 'But we must all mind our tongues in these dangerous days.'

She smiled to reassure him that she was not afraid; but at night, in all the long dark nights, Hester remembered that she was in exile from her home and in danger of her life, and sometimes she feared that while they were safely hidden at Oatlands the other army, who were at least as well-armed and perhaps as well-trained as this one, might march on the little house at Lambeth and destroy it with all the treasures and all the plants as a nest of treason.

She could get neither news nor gossip. The soldiers stationed at Oatlands Palace knew nothing more than they would get their marching orders any day, and Hester was too fearful to go into Weybridge for news. She had to wait for a message from Alexander Norman. In the third week of June he came himself.

Frances saw him first. She and Hester were grubbing in the flower beds of the queen's court, lifting the early tulips and putting the precious bulbs into sacks to take away.

'Look!' Frances exclaimed, and in the next moment she was up and running like a child with her arms outstretched to him.

For a moment he hesitated and then he spread his arms to her and folded her tight. Over her light brown head his eyes met Hester's and he gave her a small apologetic smile. Frances pulled back to see his face but did not unclasp her hands from their grip around his back. 'Are we safe?' she demanded urgently.

'Praise God, yes,' he said.

Hester felt her knees go weak and sank down on a stone seat. For a moment she could not speak. Then she asked: 'The man got safe home to Oxford?'

'And sent your mare back with a hidden note in the saddle which apologised for seizing the animal at swordpoint. If anyone does inquire we can show them the note which will serve as a strong argument in your defence. We have been lucky indeed.'

Hester shut her eyes and breathed deeply for a moment. 'I have been more afraid than I was ready to admit.'

'And I,' Alexander Norman said with a gleam. 'I have been trembling in my boots for the last fortnight.'

'I knew we'd be safe,' Frances said. 'I knew you would keep us safe, Uncle Norman.'

'What other news?' Hester asked.

'Waller, who started the whole plot, is the only one to get off scot-free,' Alexander said, his voice low. 'Every time the king uses such weak reeds as this, he falls in the estimation of every right-thinking person. Waller confessed everything, he named everyone he had spoken to and thanks to his ready tongue two men have been hanged for conspiracy, though they did far less than him, and at his bidding. And there will be more to die.'

Hester shook her head in disapproval.

'Waller himself is fined and imprisoned, but the news of his treachery and of his conspiracy has driven the Parliament men closer together. There's a new oath of loyalty and they're all eager to make close alliance with the House of Lords and with the Scots. The king has done his cause the worst damage he could have done – he has frightened his enemies into friendship with each other, and not advanced himself a single step. And any man of judgement must despise Waller, and his master too.'

Hester rose from the seat. 'So I can go home?'

'Yes. I called in at Lambeth on my way upstream so that I could tell you if things were well there. Joseph tells me that the garden is beautiful and the house has been closed and kept safe. Everything is ready for your return.'

Frances clapped her hands. 'Let's go!' she said. 'I'd rather weed my own garden than the king's any day!'

Alexander took her hands and turned them palms upwards. They were filthy from lifting the bulbs and her fingernails were broken. 'You'll never be a lady with hands like these,' he said. 'You should wear gloves.'

'Oh phoo,' Frances said, pulling her hands away. 'I don't care about being a lady. I'm a working woman like Mother.'

'Well you'll never sew silk with callused hands,' Alexander replied. 'So I shall never bring you ribbons again.'

She knew him too well to fear his threats. 'Then I shall never dance for you or sing to you or speak to you kindly,' she said.

'Enough,' Hester remarked. 'There's enough warfare in the kingdom without it starting at home. We'll finish lifting these tulips and then we'll pack and go home. I am longing to sleep in my own bed again.'

Winter 1643, Virginia

John had not thought it possible that he could become one of the Powhatan but by the autumn he felt as if his London life was left far behind him. There was so much for him to learn that every day was completely absorbing. He was all but fluent in the language – an easy task since once he was adopted into the People not one of them would speak English to him. Within weeks he was speaking nothing but Powhatan, and within months he was thinking in their rich natural imagery. It was not just the language he had to master, but their very way of thinking, of being. He had to learn the pride of a man whose land has been directly given to him, as a favour from the Great Hare. He had to learn the joy of providing food for his family, and for his village to eat. He had to learn the tiny pleasures of family and village life, the easy jokes, the sudden flare-ups of irritation, the appeal of gossip, the danger of making mischief, the delight of Suckahanna's growing boy and baby, and the dark, constant pleasure of the coming of the night.

They never talked when they made love. They never spoke of it. With his first wife, Jane, it had been that some things were not to be mentioned because they were secret, almost shameful; but with Suckahanna the pleasures of the sleeping platform where anything was possible, where any pleasure might be sought and any sensation given, were pleasures of the darkness and silence. In the daytime and during speech they were in abeyance, waiting for the darkness that would come again.

John had thought in the first months of his marriage that he would go insane, waiting for the sun to set and the children to sleep so that he could take Suckahanna into his arms. Then he was glad that the autumn season made the nights longer, and that the cold weather drove the families of the village indoors earlier and earlier. The children would be rolled together in a thick rug on their sleeping platform, the fire at the centre of the house would glow with a warm light and fill the little house with hot smoke, and in the darkness and warmth Suckahanna would enfold him and hold him in her mouth, in her body, until he ached with the urgency of his desire and then finally found the rush and release of his passion, as she closed her eyes and slid into her own joy.

Even on the coldest days the braves went hunting. When the snow was thick on the ground they wore thicker moccasins on their bare feet and buckskin jerkins for warmth. They would laugh at John when they came home if his lips were blue with cold. They threatened to send him stalking stripped naked since his white skin blended so well with the snow.

Attone had John's old gun but there was no powder for it. However, he insisted on carrying it on every hunt, and after he had felled a wild goose or duck with a superbly placed arrow and it came spiralling to earth, he would pull the gun from the deerskin holster he had made to carry it on his back, sight the falling bird and solemnly remark 'Bang.'

'Good shot, sir!' John would say in English, the words awkward and alien on his tongue.

And Attone would turn and beam. 'Good shot,' he would confirm.

Attone was at John's side for all of the autumn hunts, prompting, reminding, explaining. But all of the Powhatan people were quick to teach John the things he needed to know to live among them. That ceremony of adoption and marriage in one had been all they needed. John was one of the People.

He shared their dangers as well as their pleasures. As autumn turned into winter the stores grew low and the people began to go hungry. The food was set aside for the strongest small children and for the braves on the hunting parties. Old people, the weak, and the sickly accepted that when there was scarcity, the food had to go to those most likely to survive. John offered his portion to Musses but she laughed in his face.

'Do you think I am afraid to die?' she asked him as he brought her a bowl of suppawn.

'I thought only that you were hungry,' he said.

'You thought right,' she said sharply. 'I am hungry for meat. So eat your breakfast, Eagle, and go out and drop from the sky on to a deer. The People need food. The hunters must do their work.'

He nodded at the wisdom of what she was saying, but he could not understand how she could refuse a bowl of porridge when his own belly growled with hunger at the sight of it.

'I love the People more than I love a fat belly on myself,' she explained. 'And I was fed from my grandmother's bowl when she went hungry to feed me, and she was fed from hers.'

John dipped his head and ate his porridge and gave thanks for the filling warm sweetness of it.

When he looked up her bright hungry eyes were on him. 'Now go and kill a deer,' she ordered.

It was not always easy to hunt. The days were short and icy cold, and when they had shot a white-coated hare, or a deer, or a skunk, or a foolish foraging squirrel there was less meat on the bones than on summer carcasses. The fish weirs froze and the little treats which supplemented the Powhatan diet, the fruits and nuts and berries, were gone. There were edible roots which the women could dig for, and there was the great temptation of the storehouse.

'Why can we not eat from the store?' John asked Suckahanna.

'We do,' she said. 'But we share it very carefully when there is no food to be had in any other way. It has not come to that yet. It may not come to it this year.'

'But there is enough in the store to keep the village for the whole season!' John exclaimed. 'It will spoil if we don't eat it!'

She gave him a sly sideways smile. 'No it won't,' she said. 'The meat is properly smoked and the fish salted down in pots. The oysters and crayfish are smoked and dried and the seeds and nuts are dry and safe. You are pretending that the food will go bad to give you an excuse to eat.'

John made an impatient noise and turned on his heel.

'Why can we not eat the store food?' he asked Musses.

She shook her head. 'That is the wealth of the People,' she said. 'Our inheritance. We saved it carefully, from good harvests and bad. We keep it through the winter and eat as little as we can. That is the way of this people. They are not Englishmen who eat their seed corn and then find in spring they have nothing to plant.'

'Why can we not eat the store food?' John asked Attone.

'Why not?'

'Yes.'

'Have you asked Suckahanna?'

'Yes, and Musses.'

'And what do the women tell you?'

'One tells me that we may need the food later, though we are halfway through winter already and as hungry as we can be. The other tells me that the People do not eat their seed stores. But these are not seed stores. These are dried oysters.' John felt the juices rush into his mouth at the thought of oysters, and swallowed, hoping that his hunger did not show in his face.

Attone took his shoulder in a hard, friendly grip and put his face close to John's. 'You're right. It's not seed. You're right, it would be good to eat some of it now. Why do you think we have waited and worked and starved ourselves to store a year's supply of food?'

John shook his head. Attone's lips came closer to his ear.

'In the time of the uprising when our king, Opechancanough, went against the white men, do you know what they did to our fish weirs?'

'They tore them down,' John said, as softly as the other man.

'And what they did to our crops in the fields?'

'They trampled them into the mud.'

'They did worse than that. They let the women plant and weed them, so we thought that they would let us get them in. Then, after we had spent a year of our labour in tending the food they came at harvest time and set light to them and to the forest around them.' He dropped back and looked into John's face. 'They burned anything, without thought,' he said. 'I would have understood it if they had stolen the harvest from us. But they did not do that. They just burned it where it stood, ripe and ready for picking. So that winter they went hungry themselves without our food to buy. But we – we starved.'

John nodded.

'I buried my brother that year,' Attone said quietly. 'My older brother, who was like a father to me. He died with a belly full of frozen grass. There was nothing else to eat.'

John nodded in silence.

'So now before any brave would lift his hand against a white man he would want to know that he has a year's supply of food in his house. Don't you think that, my Eagle?'

John gaped. 'This is a supply for war?'

The grip on his shoulder tightened so hard it was like a vice. 'Did you think we would let them push us into the mountains, into the sea?'

Dumbly, John shook his head.

'Of course there will be war,' Attone said matter-of-factly. 'My son has to have a trail to follow. He has to have deer to kill. If the white man will not keep to his treaties, will not share the land, then he will have to be killed.'

John bowed his head. He felt a great sense of impending doom.

'You grieve for your people?' Attone asked.

'Yes,' John replied. 'Both of them.'

The deer were fewer, hunting was hard. The men went out in twos and threes, looking for small game and birds. Attone and John left the usual trails and struck out downriver. Suckahanna watched them go, her baby strapped on her back. She embraced John and then she stood back and raised her hand in a respectful salute to her previous husband. He touched his forehead and his heart to her. 'Suckahanna, guard my son and daughter,' he said.

'Go safely, both of you,' she replied. 'May the trail be smooth under your moccasins and the hunting rich.'

The two men jogged out of the village. John was used to the steady half-running pace of the hunting party now and his calves no longer seized with cramp as his feet ate up the miles. But it was hard running in the snow. Both men were shiny with sweat when they paused to draw breath and to listen to the quietness of the winter woods all around them.

There was a mild thaw. John could hear a steady drip drip of melting water from trees where dark-stained twigs were at last thickening with buds. Attone's head was cocked. 'What can you hear?' he asked John.

John shook his head. 'Nothing.'

Attone raised his eyebrows. He could never become accustomed to the insensitivity of the Englishman.

At once he crouched and his hand went into the gesture with two raised fingers which meant, hare or rabbit. At once John crouched beside him and they both put an arrow on the bow.

It came slowly, quite unaware of their presence. They heard it before they saw it because it was white against the white snow: a winter hare with a coat blanched like ermine. When it dropped on to its haunches the only sign that revealed its presence was the little dimples of dark footprints behind it, and the occasional betraying flick of an ear.

Attone raised his bow and the little thwack of sound as the bow was released was the first thing that alerted the hare. It bounded up and the arrow caught it in the body, behind the foreleg. John and Attone were behind it at once but the animal raced ahead of them, the arrow jinking and diving with it, like a harpoon in a speared fish.

Attone gave a sudden cry as he tripped and fell to the ground. John knew well enough not to check for a moment. He kept running, following the terrified creature, weaving in and out of trees, jumping over fallen logs, diving around rocks, and finally scrabbling on hands and knees through the winter-thin scrub to keep the wounded animal in sight.

Suddenly there was a crack of a musket shot, loud and startling as cannon fire in the icy silence, and John flung himself backwards in terror. The hare was thrown into the air and fell down on its back. John rose up from the bushes, half-naked in bear-grease-stained skin and buckskin kilt and jerkin, and looked into the wan, half-starved face of his old friend Bertram Hobert.

He recognised Bertram at once despite the marks of hunger and fatigue on the man's face. He was about to cry out in greeting but the English words were sluggish on his tongue; and then he realised that Bertram was pointing his musket at John's belly.

'That's mine,' Bertram snarled, showing his black and rotting teeth. 'Mine. D'you hear? My food.'

John spread his hands in a quick deferential gesture, aware all the time of his razor-sharp reed arrows nestling in the quiver in the small of his back. He could have one on the string and loosed long before Bertram could reload and prime his musket. Was the man mad to threaten with an empty gun?

'Step back.' Bertram waved him aside. 'Step back, or by God I'll shoot you where you stand.'

John went back two, three steps, and watched with silent pity as Bertram hobbled over to the dead hare. There was precious little meat on it and the rich guts and heart had been blasted out by the shot on to the snow. The silvery pelt, which would have been good to trade, had been destroyed too. Half the hare had been wasted by killing it with a gunshot whereas Attone's reed arrow should have gone straight to the heart and left nothing more than a farthing-size hole.

Bertram bent stiffly over the body, picked it up by the limp ears and stuffed it in his game bag. He bared his teeth at John. 'Get away,' he said again. 'I'll kill you for staring at me with your evil dark eyes. This is my land, or at any rate, near enough mine. I won't have you or your thieving people within ten miles of my fields. Get away with you or I'll have the soldiers out from Jamestown to hunt you down. If your village is near here we'll find it. We'll find you and your cubs and burn the lot of you out.'

John stepped back, never taking his eyes from Bertram. The man's face was a twisted ruin hammered from his old sunny, smiling confidence. John had no inclination to step forward now, to greet his old friend and shipmate by name, to make himself known. He did not want to know this man, this weak, cursing, stinking man. He did not want to claim kinship with him. The man threatened him like an enemy. If his gun had been reloaded John thought that it would have been his blood on the snow, and his belly blasted away like the hare's. He bowed his head like a servile, frightened, enslaved Indian and backed away. In two, three paces, he was able to lean into the curve of a tree and know that a white man's eyes would not be able to pick him out from the dapple of white snow and dark tree shadows and speckled bark.

Hobert glared into the shadowy forest which had swallowed up his enemy in seconds. 'I know you're there!' he shouted. 'I could find you if I wanted.'

Attone came up beside John so silently that not even a twig cracked. 'Who's the smelly one?' he asked.

'My neighbour, the farmer, Bertram Hobert,' John said. The name sounded strange and awkward on his lips, he was so accustomed to the ripple of Powhatan speech.

'The winter has rotted his feet,' Attone remarked.

John saw that the brave was right. Bertram was painfully lame and instead of shoes or boots his feet were encased in thick wrappings tied with twine.

'That hurts,' Attone said. 'He should wear bear grease and moccasins.'

'He does not know,' John said sadly. 'He would not know that, and only your people could teach him.'

Attone gave him a quick smile at the unlikeliness of such a meeting and such a lesson. 'He has our hare. Shall we kill him?'

John put his hand on Attone's forearm as he reached for his arrow. 'Spare him. He was my friend.'

Attone raised a dark eyebrow. 'He was going to shoot you.'

'He didn't know me. But he helped me build my house when I came to the plantation. We travelled across the sea together. He has a good wife. He was once my friend. I won't see him shot for a hare.'

'I would shoot him for a mouse,' Attone remarked, but the arrow stayed in his quiver. 'And now we will have to cross the river. There will be no game here for miles where he is stamping on his rotting feet.'

They caught no game though they stayed out for three days, travelling along the narrow trails which the People had used for centuries. Every now and then one of the trails would spread itself to double, even treble, the necessary width and then Attone would scowl and look out for a new house being built, a new headright created where this wide path would lead. Again and again they would see a new building standing proud, and facing the river and around it a desert of felled trees and roughly cleared land. Attone would look for a moment, his face expressionless, and then say to John: 'We have to go on, there will be no game here.'

They struck away from the river on the second day, since the plantations chose the riverside so that the tobacco could be floated down to the quayside at Jamestown. Once they broke away from the riverbanks things were better for them. In the deeper forest they found traces of deer again and then on the third day, as they were bearing round in a wide circle for home, a great shadowy bush caught Tradescant's eye and as he watched, it moved. Then he felt Attone's hand on the small of his back and his breath as he said: 'Elk'.

Something in the quiver of the brave's voice set John's heart racing too. The beast was massive, its antlers as broad as the outspread wings of a condor. Moving almost unconsciously, John fitted his arrow to his bow and felt the thinness of the shaft and the lightness of the sharpened reed arrow head. Surely, this would be like shooting peas at a carthorse, he thought. Nothing could bring this monster down.

Attone was moving away from him. For a moment John thought that they were to make the traditional pincer movement of deer stalking but then he saw that Attone had slung his bow over his shoulder and was climbing the lowest branches of one of the trees. When he was stretched along it with an arrow on the string he nodded to John with one of his darkest smiles.

John glanced back at the grazing elk. It was calm, unaware of their presence. John made a pointing upward gesture: should he climb too? Attone's teeth flashed in a grin, white in the darkness. He shook his head. John should shoot at ground level.

John realised at once why this was apparently amusing. When the elk was struck it would look around for its enemy and it would charge the first thing it saw. That would be John. Attone, in the safety of the branch of the tree, would rain down arrows, but John on the ground below would serve as decoy: as bait. John scowled at Attone, who gave him the blandest of smiles and a shrug – it was the luck of the hunt.

John set his arrow on the string and waited. The elk sniffed the forest floor, searching for food. It turned full face to John and lifted its head for a moment, scenting the air. It was a perfect opportunity. Both arrows flew at the same second. John's arrow, aimed for the heart, pierced the thick skin and layer of fat át the chest, while Attone's plunged deep and unerringly into the beast's eye. It bellowed in pain and plunged forward. A second arrow from Attone's bow pierced its shoulder, severing the muscle of the foreleg so the animal dropped to one knee. John's shaky second shot went wide and then he was running, dodging behind the trees as the beast came on, stumbled on, blood pouring from its head. Attone let fly one more arrow into the head again and then jumped from the tree, his knife in his hand. The flow of blood was weakening the animal, it was unable to charge. It fell to both knees, its head moving from one side to the other, the great sweep of the antlers still a danger. John peeped out from behind a tree and came running back, pulling his hunting knife with the sharp shell blade from its safe pouch. Either side of the wounded animal the two men watched for their chance. Attone, whispering the word of blessing on the dying creature, dived behind the moving antlers and plunged his knife between its high shoulders. The head slumped and John reached down and jabbed a hacking, sawing cut into the thick throat.

The two men jumped clear as the beast rolled on its side and died. Attone nodded. 'Good and quick,' he said breathlessly. 'Go, my brother, we thank you.'

John rubbed the sweat from his face with fingers that were wet with fresh blood. He dropped to sit on the snowy forest floor, his legs weak underneath him. 'What if you had missed?' he asked.

Attone thought for a moment. 'Missed?'

'When the beast was charging at me. What if you had missed your shot?'

Attone took a breath to answer and then John's aggrieved face was too much for him; he could make no sensible reply. He whooped with laughter and dropped back on the cold snow. He laughed and laughed his great belly laugh of joy and John, trying to keep a straight face, trying to stay on his dignity, found it was too much for him and he started to laugh as well.

'Why ask? Why should it matter to you?' Attone demanded, wiping his eyes, and bubbling again. 'You wouldn't care. You'd be dead.'

John howled at the logic of this and the two men lay like lovers, side by side on their backs in the winter forest, and laughed until their empty bellies ached while the blue winter sky above them was darkened with the passing of the geese and the wood was louder with their honking than with laughter.

John was left to guard the carcase while Attone started the long run back to the village. It would be two days before he could bring the braves back to carry the meat into camp. John made himself as comfortable as he could for the wait, built a little bender tent of a pair of saplings and thatched it with thin winter fern, made himself a hearth at one side of it and let the tent fill with smoke for the warmth, and started the work of skinning and butchering the great beast. Attone had left his hunting knife with John, so that when John's knife was blunted cutting the thick hide, fat and meat he would not have to waste time sharpening it. He worked from sunrise in the morning when he rose and said the Powhatan morning prayers at his morning wash in the icy water. At noon he gathered nuts and berries and ate with his dark gaze on the river, watching for shoals of fish. After his dinner he gathered firewood and set to work on the elk again. At night he cut a thin slice of elk meat to barbecue over the fire. John had lost completely the white man's habit of gorging when food was available and starving when times were thin. He ate like one of the People, conscious all the time of the river that brought fish to him, and the winds that blew the birds to him and the woods that hid and offered the animals. It was not the way of a Powhatan to plunge into a trough of food like a hog into acorns. Food was not a free gift, it was part of a giving and taking, a balance; and a hunter must take with awareness.

In the two days and three nights while he waited John realised how much of a Powhatan he had become. The forest was no longer fearful to him. He thought how he had once seemed to be a little beetle crawling across a terrifying and infinite world. He now seemed no bigger, the Powhatan never thought of themselves as owners of the forest. He now felt as if this little beetle called John Tradescant, called Eagle, had found his place and his ordained path in this place, and that he need fear nothing since his place led him from the earth to birth and life and death and then to the earth again.

He knew there were wolves in the forest and soon they would get the scent of the elk, and so he built a rough fence of fallen branches around the carcase, and kept the fire lit. Now that he could eat well from the forest the immense labour of his English life seemed to him absurd. He could hardly remember how he had nearly starved in a wooden house set in a forest teeming with life. But then he remembered the hungry anger in Bertram's twisted face and he knew that a man could live among plenty and never know that he was rich.

On the morning of the third day, as John methodically cut steaks of meat from the big animal's body, he heard a tiny crackle of movement behind him and whirled around with his knife at the ready.

'Eagle, I give you greeting,' said Attone pleasantly.

Suckahanna was with him. John held out his arms to her and she came to him, her body as light as a girl in his grasp, her shoulders bird-like and bony.

'I brought your wife and my children, and some others to help cure the meat and to feast. They were hungry at home,' Attone said. 'Build up the fire, they will come soon.'

John wiped Attone's knife and returned it to him with a word of thanks and then he and Suckahanna piled John's little brushwood fence on to his fire so that it flared up and crackled. As soon as it had burned down into hot embers Suckahanna brought large boulders from the river and heaped them with ashes to make hot, then she laid dozens of small steaks of meat on the hot stones where they sizzled and spat. By the time the village had arrived – all those able to walk – there was meat cooked and ready for everyone.

Everyone ate a little, no-one ate to excess. Everyone sighed at the end of a couple of mouthfuls and said, 'Good. Good,' as if they had attended a banquet of forty-four courses in Whitehall. Then they all stretched out in the bright winter sunshine and dozed for a little while.

When the shadows lengthened, they set to work. The women made a temporary long house by pegging down saplings and weaving bark and leaves through the twigs. The men set up drying poles for the skin of the beast, and enlarged the fire for cooking and smoking the meat. The children were sent out to gather wood for the fires and for another, wider fence, to encircle the smoking meat and the long house. By sunset, when they all went down to the water to pray and to send the smoking leaves of tobacco downriver, glowing in the darkness, they had a little fortified camp: safe against wolves, defensible in case of attack.

It took another two days for the elk to be butchered thoroughly, smoked and packed ready for carriage back to the village. After the first day a couple of fast-running braves had taken the first consignment back to the village for the elderly and the very young, and those too sick to travel into the forest. The skin was tanned and ready, the meat was smoked. The bones were gathered and tied into a great bundle. Suckahanna poured water over the fires and scuffed the embers with her foot. The women untied the saplings and they sprang back up. It was clear that there had been a house on the site but by spring there would be no mark on the ground; and that was what they wanted. Not only to keep their ways and their paths a secret, but because the forest must be a home to the elk as well as to the Powhatan, and elk will not come near a village nor even a trace of one.

When all the work was done John hesitated with his burden of meat. 'I want to visit Bertram Hobert,' he said to Suckahanna.

'What for?'

'I saw him while we were hunting. He is hungry and he is sick. His feet are falling off him. He was my friend. I should like to take him some meat.'

She looked at him with a long, worried gaze. 'You cannot go looking like this,' she said. 'He will shoot you the moment he sees you.'

'I shall leave a gift of meat on his doorstep,' John said. 'That was done for me once, and it saved my life. I should like to do the same.'

'You ate yourself sick,' she observed. 'Take care you don't kill him by accident.'

John chuckled. 'He has a wife to care for him,' he said. 'Or at least he did have. He is my friend, Suckahanna.'

The look she turned to him was more powerful than tender. 'He cannot be your friend now,' she said. 'You are a Powhatan.'

'He can,' John argued. 'If a Powhatan could not be the friend of a white man then I would have died in the woods and I would never have been called Eagle by one of the finest hunters in the People.'

'That was then,' she said gently. 'The river gets wider every day. The distance between one shore and the other is greater all the time. You cannot cross and recross, my husband.'

He put his hand out to her and barely touched her fingertips. As soon as she felt his touch her eyes flickered closed for just a moment at the pleasure of the warmth of his hand. John knew that he had won.

'Shall I wait for you?' she asked in quite a different tone, as low as a sleepy honey bee in winter.

'Go with the People,' he replied. 'I will catch you up before you reach the village.'

She nodded and picked up her burden of dried meat, and set off. John watched her rangy, long stride until the trees hid her, then he turned and set off at a hunting jog downriver to Hobert's plantation.

John slowed as he recognised the features of Hobert's boundaries, a pine tree where they had slashed a crude 'H', a magnificent oak, bending over the path and shading it with its spreading branches, and then he saw the shingled roof of the Hobert house and a thin spiral of smoke coming from the chimney. John stepped back into the shade of the trees and hunkered down on his heels to watch.

He saw a man bent low under a burden of wood come out of the trees and fling down the cord by the door and straighten up with a sigh. A black man: Francis the Negro slave. He saw the door open and it was Mrs Hobert, speaking sharply and then going indoors. He waited a little longer as it grew cold and the light started to drain from the sky. Bertram must be out late with his gun. John did not move even though the hairs on his arms and his chest stood up, and his skin prickled with goosebumps against the cold. Only when it was nearly dark did he decide that Bertram must already be indoors. He rose to his feet and went silently down the hill to the little house nestling on a piece of flat ground before the river.

He hesitated at the door and then put his eye to the crack to peer into the firelit interior. It was a sparsely furnished room. A table before the fire; two stools and a hewed tree stump served as chairs. A box bed built into the wall was occupied by a man, his shoulder hunched against the room, his head tucked down. A ladder at the back of the room led to a sleeping platform, a string and a piece of sacking serving as a curtain between the two. John thought of the spick and span London house that the Hoberts had left for this venture and felt his heart ache for them, and surprisingly for himself too: another exile in this strange and remote land.

He tapped on the door and called out at the same time: 'A friend, John Tradescant.' His own name was awkward in his mouth.

Despite the reassurance he heard a little scream from Mrs Hobert and heard a stool overturn as Francis leaped to his feet.

'Who?' she demanded.

'John Tradescant, your shipmate and neighbour,' he repeated.

'We thought you were dead!' The door opened cautiously and Mrs Hobert's white face peered out.

John kept back in the shadows. 'I was with the Powhatan,' he said.

'Savages?'

He bit back a retort. 'Yes. So I look strange . . .'

She stepped a little further out, female curiosity driving her onwards. 'Like a savage?'

'Don't be afraid,' John said and came towards the light.

She clapped her hand over her mouth at the sight of him but her eyes widened with terror. 'Is it really you?'

'I swear it,' John said. 'Just dressed as a Powhatan.'

'Your poor, poor man,' she said and took hold of his hand and drew him indoors. 'Good God preserve us all from such a fate. How did you get away from them?'

'I was not captured,' John said. He nodded at Francis, who stood frozen in horror at the sight of him.

'It is me,' John repeated.

Francis nodded, gave a little bow in reply and restored a wood-chopping axe to its place behind the door.

'Sit down, sit down,' Sarah begged him. 'Your hair! and – dear God – they have even stained your skin to their colour!'

'That's bear grease,' John said. 'It keeps off insects in summer and keeps out the cold in winter.'

'God preserve us! How did you get away?' Then her constant terror of the savage men struck her and she shot a frightened look at the thin wooden door. 'Are they after you?'

'No, no,' John reassured her. 'They let me go freely.'

'Are you hungry?' The anxious glance she threw at the cookpot suggested that there was not much to be had, even if he was.

'I have eaten,' John said steadily. 'But I brought you some meat. We killed an elk.'

'Meat?' She choked as the saliva rushed into her throat. 'You have meat?'

John reached for the bundle strapped into the small of his back. 'Here,' he said. 'It's smoked; but you could seethe it in a little water.'

She fell upon it and tossed it into the cookpot as it stood by the hearthside. John, remembering his sickness from food heated and reheated in the same pot, winced a little. But she was already stirring in water from a pitcher, and greedily tasting. 'Bertram, Bertram!'

The shoulder in the bed shrugged still higher, and then the man rolled over on his back and glared into the room.

'We have meat!' she said triumphantly. 'Can you sit up while I spoon you some broth?'

'Meat?' Hobert's voice was a rough croak.

'Neighbour Tradescant has brought us some steaks from an elk,' she said. 'He has been living with the savages but has got away from them now, praise God.'

Hobert heaved himself up to one arm. His face was marked with pain. In the little room John could smell the flesh of his snow-rotted feet and the stench of unwashed blankets.

'John Tradescant?' he asked wonderingly. 'Is that really you?'

John went to the bedside and took the man's hand. 'I have been living with the Powhatan and I dress like them and hunt with them,' he said. 'They treat me as a friend. I saw you in the woods the other day, and I thought you might be in need. I have brought you some meat and I can bring you more. They have medicines as well which would make you well. I would have come sooner if I had known you were in need, Bertram.'

The man's red-rimmed eyes wandered over John's face. 'A savage,' he said, bewildered.

'I am indeed John Tradescant,' John said. 'But I could not live alone in the forest. Thank God I fell among the Powhatan and they have treated me kindly.'

Sarah Hobert came to her husband's bedside with a delicate pot filled with gravy. John recognised at once the work of the People: the perfectly smooth walls of one of their dainty black pots.

'That's Powhatan-made,' he said.

She gave him a swift disapproving glance. 'We used to trade with them, but they became too demanding and dishonest,' she said. 'Now my husband will not have them near his land.' She turned to the wreck of the man in the bed. 'Will you taste, Bertram?'

Eagerly he sat up and reached for the pot, eagerly he sucked at it and gulped until the pot was empty.

'Rest now,' John said, remembering his horrors of illness after he had eaten too richly on a starved belly. 'You can have more later, and I will bring you other food, corn and berries and nuts.'

Sarah reached out and caught his hand. 'Praise God for bringing you back to us,' she said. 'For that which was lost is found.'

John hesitated. 'I must be a visitor only,' he said.

Her face was shining with relief and happiness, deaf to his reluctance. 'Praise God for returning you to your true people,' she said.

It was out of the question for John to leave that night, or even the next day. He slept in the attic on the same side of the makeshift screen as the Negro Francis. In the morning Hobert was in a fever, groaning and counting aloud, counting the sums of money he must save to buy headrights in the new land, counting the percentage of profit he might hope to make, counting the wages he must pay to get his land cleared and tobacco planted.

'Is he mad?' John asked Sarah.

She shook her head. 'It's the fever again,' she said. 'When it comes on him he acts like a madman but then the fever breaks and he is cool-headed again. Francis has to tie him up sometimes.'

'This is impossible,' John said. 'You will have to go back to Jamestown. You cannot stay here with only a sick man and a slave.'

She looked up, her face shining with new hope. 'That's what I had feared,' she said. 'But now you are come, sent by God to help me. You will help me plant the fields, won't you, John? Help me until Bertram is well again? He will be well now that you can bring him food, and when the summer comes he will be well and strong again. He is a man of much strength. This is only the dreadful seasoning of Virginia. They all say that. A man must be seasoned to work under the hot sun. Bertram is burning up now, no sun will ever be too hot for him again.'

'I cannot stay,' John said awkwardly.

'Where else could you go?' she asked. 'Your own headright is overgrown and the savages will have stripped your house of everything you ever owned.'

John felt completely incapable of telling her that he had a new house in the Indian village, and a wife and children waiting for him.

'A cup of ale, for the love of God!' Bertram called loudly from his bed.

Sarah turned and poured him a little pot of water from the pitcher.

'I'll get you some more,' John muttered, and took the pitcher and went outside.

He walked slowly down to the river, filled the pitcher, and strolled back, taking the chance to think. If he left Sarah to fend for herself he was signing her death warrant as clearly as if he were the king in Whitehall condemning some poor soul in the Tower. She and Bertram and Francis would die in the forest and the trees would grow through their earthen floor and the trumpet vine strangle their chimney. There was no chance at all that they would survive in this fruitful, overwhelming land without help. In contrast, Suckahanna and the children would be guarded by Attone, and fed and protected by the village. The land was no danger to Suckahanna, she fed from it as easily as a deer nibbling green shoots in the woods.

John squared his shoulders, picked up the pitcher and went back to the house.

Francis was outside, stacking firewood. 'Go in and guard your master,' John said. 'I must take Mrs Hobert out into the wood and teach her how to gather fruits and roots and berries. You have been starving in the midst of plenty here. Why did you not tell her?'

'Me? How should I know?'

'You must have eaten nuts and berries in your own country,' John said irritably. 'Gathered them in the forests?'

The man raised one eyebrow. 'My own country is not like this one,' he said. 'So we don't have the same fruits. And in any case, I had my meals served to me by my wife or by my slave. I didn't go out clambering in trees for cashew nuts like a monkey.'

'You're a savage!' John exclaimed. 'What d'you mean, slaves, and being served?'

The black man looked from the remnants of his own breeches and shirt to John's embroidered buckskin loincloth and his stained and tattooed skin.

'I see only one savage here,' he remarked.

John swore under his breath and pushed open the door. 'Mrs Hobert!' he said. 'Come out and let me show you how to find nuts and roots for your dinner.'

She brought a basket, Indian-made, John observed, and she was quick to learn how to identify roots which could be cooked and eaten, and roots which could be sliced and eaten raw. John showed her nut-bearing trees and pointed to the wild plum and the wild cherry trees which would blossom and bear fruit later in the year. They came home with a basket full of good things and she sliced the roots to supplement the remainder of the elk in the cookpot for their dinner.

Hobert had lapsed into a deep sleep, the sweat thick and cold on his forehead.

'We won't wake him,' his wife decided. 'The fever may be breaking and he will need his rest.'

'The Powhatan have physic,' John said. 'For fevers and also for frost-bite. I could ask the werowance, or one of the physicians, to come and see Bertram. Or there's a wise woman very gifted with herbs, she made me well. She might come.'

Sarah shook her head in absolute refusal. 'They would poison us and hack us up to eat,' she said. 'You may have been lucky, John Tradescant, that they chose to keep you alive. But they have been our enemies since we came here. At first we traded with them and gave them little trinkets for food and for goods. Then we tried to make them come and work for us, clear the land and dig the fields. But they were lazy and idle and when we whipped them they stole what they could and ran away. After that Bertram has shot at them whenever he has seen them. They are our enemies. I won't have them near me.'

'They have skills that you need to learn,' John persisted. 'This dinner you are eating is Powhatan food. You have to learn how they live in the forest in order to live here yourself.'

She shook her head. I shall live as a God-fearing Englishwoman and I shall make this land into a new England. Then they can come to *me* to learn.' She closed her eyes briefly in a prayer. When she opened them she was looking sharply, critically, at John.

'I have unpacked a shirt and pair of breeches belonging to Bertram,' she said. 'You can have them in return for the service you have done us by coming to our door in our time of need. You will not want to walk around half-naked as you are.'

'This is how I live now,' John said.

'Not in a Christian home you don't,' she said sharply. 'I cannot allow it, Mr Tradescant, it is not fit. It is lechery to show yourself like this to me. If my husband were well and in his right mind he would not permit it.'

'I had no thought of lechery, Mrs Hobert –'

She gestured to the clothes spread at the fireside. 'Then dress yourself, Mr Tradescant, please.'

John stayed with the Hoberts for a full week, dressed in English clothes again, but still barefoot. The shirt chafed at his neck, the breeches felt hot and constricting around his legs. But he wore them out of courtesy to Sarah's feelings, and he did not feel he could leave her until Bertram was well again.

The fever broke on the third night, and the next day Bertram was well enough to hobble down to the river, leaning on John's arm.

The little green tobacco shoots were showing through the earth of the nursery beds. Bertram paused and looked at them as dotingly as if they were sleeping children. 'Here is my fortune, Tradescant,' he said. 'Here is my fortune growing. If we can survive the rest of this cold weather without starving, without falling to the savages, then this will be the making of me. I shall see it sold on the quayside at Jamestown. I shall see it packed and sailing for England. I shall hire a servant, a brace of servants, and I will make myself a life here.'

'God willing,' John said.

'Stay with us,' Hobert said. 'Stay with us and you can take a share in this, John. I doubt I can manage without you and Sarah cannot do it all on her own. Francis has no skill with plants, I am afraid to let him touch them. If I am sick when they need planting out who is going to do the work? Stay with me and see my tobacco plants safely into the field.'

'I can't stay,' John said as gently as he could. 'I have made a different life for myself in this country. But I can come back to you and see that you are well. I'll come back gladly and work for you. I'll set out the seedlings for you and show you how the Powhatan plant their food crops so you never need go hungry again.'

'You'll come back to plant out my tobacco? You swear it?'

'I swear,' John said.

'Then we won't need food crops,' Hobert said buoyantly. 'We shall buy all we need with what I can earn from the tobacco. And I'll see you right, John. Next season I shall come to your headright and work for you, as we promised, eh? As we always said we would do.'

On that promise John left the Hoberts and crossed the river just above the falls where he could jump from boulder to boulder in the fast-moving stream. On the far side he stripped off the breeches and the shirt that he had been given and bundled them up into the crook of a tree. It reminded him of Suckahanna's girlhood and her attempt to live in the two worlds. She used to wear a long gown and sometimes a bonnet in Jamestown, but when she was free in the woods she wore her buckskin pinny and nothing more.

The air felt good on his skin again, he felt more of a man in his nakedness than he ever could do in his breeches. He stretched as if he were freed from a constriction greater than a linen shirt, and set off at the Powhatan hunting stride for his home.

Suckahanna greeted him with the careful courtesy of a deeply offended wife. John neither explained nor apologised until they were alone on the sleeping platform, in the darkness of their house, when the soft sighs from both children showed that they were asleep.

'I could not come back when I said I would come,' he said to her smooth naked back. 'Bertram was sick, his wife was hungry and their slave didn't know what to do.'

She said nothing and did not turn to him.

'I stayed to feed a hungry woman and nurse a sick man,' John said. 'When I showed her how to get food and when he was better I came home again, as soon as I could.'

He waited.

'Would you have wanted me to leave them to die?' he asked.

At last she turned back to him. 'Better now and by their own failure than later,' she said simply.

John gasped as the words struck him. 'You speak like a heartless woman,' he protested.

She shrugged as if she did not much care whether he thought her heartless or kind; and then she turned her back on him again and went to sleep.

Spring 1644, Virginia

John did not go back to the Hoberts' homestead for a month. He hunted with Attone and the other braves, he lived as a Powhatan. But there was a coldness between Suckahanna and him which the routine of ordinary life could not conceal.

When he judged it was time for the planting out of Bertram's tobacco he spoke to Attone, rather than Suckahanna.

'My friend who was sick needs me to plant out his tobacco. I should go and help him now.'

'Go then, Eagle,' Attone said unhelpfully.

'Suckahanna will be angry at my going.'

'Stay then.'

'I'm not asking for help –'

'I'm not giving any.'

John paused for a moment and bit back his temper. Attone was smiling. He loved to be annoying.

'I'm telling you that I will be away for a while,' John said patiently. 'I am asking you to watch Suckahanna for me and fetch me if she is in any need. She will not send for me; she is angry with me. She would not send for me even if she needed me.'

'She will be in no need. The game is coming back, the fish are spawning. What would she need you for? You can go to your smelly friends.'

John gritted his teeth. 'If one of the People was in trouble you would go to his help.'

'Hobert is not one of the People. He is not one of mine.'

John hesitated. 'Nor is he mine,' he said, conscious of the pain of divided loyalty. 'But I cannot see him fail or fall sick or die of hunger. He was good to me once, and I have made him a promise.'

'This is a path in a circle,' Attone said cheerfully. 'You are wandering like a man snow-blind, round and round. What is blinding you, Eagle? Why can you not walk straight?'

'Because I am pulled two ways,' John said grimly.

'Then cut one string,' Attone said briskly. 'Before it tangles around your feet and brings you down.' He rose to his feet and loped down the river towards the fish weir without looking back.

The Hoberts' house was amid a sea of green. Bertram had started planting the fields which ran between the house and the river and the absurd flop-leaved plants were three rows thick before the house.

'John, thank God you've come!' Hobert said, kneeling. 'I was afraid you would fail us.'

'Mr Tradescant, you are very welcome!' Sarah said from further down the row.

John, hot in his reclaimed breeches and shirt, waved at them both.

'You should have a hat to shield you from the sun,' Sarah scolded. 'Men have died of sunstroke in this country.'

John put his hand to his face and felt the heat radiating from his flushed skin. 'It's these clothes,' he said. 'How can anyone wear wool in this country in spring?'

'It's the vapours in the air,' Sarah said firmly. 'When we next go to Jamestown I will buy you a hat. We've only just come back from town.'

'There was a letter for you,' Bertram said, remembering. 'I went into Jamestown to buy a hoe and to collect some money sent me from England. I called in at your inn and there was a letter for you there.'

'For me?' John asked.

'It's inside. I put it under the mattress you used last time to keep it safe.'

John put his hand to his head.

'There you are! Sunstroke!' Sarah exclaimed triumphantly.

'No,' John said. 'I just feel . . . It is so odd to have a letter . . .'

He turned and went into the house, jumped up the ladder in one bound. In the loft bedroom was his straw mattress and underneath it was a travel-stained folded and sealed paper. John snatched it up and recognised Hester's writing at once.

A great pain shot through John at the thought of his family in Lambeth and a great fear that one of the children, Frances, or Johnnie, was sick or dead, or that the house had been lost to passing soldiers or the garden destroyed, or Hester herself . . . he pulled himself back from nightmare imaginings, broke the seal and smoothed out the paper.

Lambeth, the New Year, 1644
Dear Husband,

Having heard no news from you I pray that your venture is going well and that you have found the land you wanted, cleared it and planted it. It is strange for me not knowing what the view is like from your window, nor what your kitchen is like, nor what the weather may be for you. I try to tell the children about what you are doing now but I do not know whether to tell them you are struggling through deep snow or digging in damp earth. We are reading Captain Smith's True History *in the evenings so that we may understand a little of your life, but I have to keep missing out some of his adventures as the children would be too afraid for you. I pray that you are right and that it is not such a savage place as he describes, and that the planters too have become more kindly and Christian in their doings.*

Here in Lambeth we are well but troubled, as is everyone in the kingdom, by the continuance of the war. Food is very scarce and there is no coal to be had at all. There has been petty fighting on the roads into London and we never know whether meat for the markets will be driven in or not. Our men are called up to serve in the City trained bands but they have not yet been sent outside the bounds of the City, so when they are stood down they come back to work. We try to keep the Ark and the gardens open as normal and we are trading a little. There are still people who want to live as if the war were not taking place and they still want to know that gardens are growing and that strange and rare beautiful things can still be seen. It is very pitiful to me when a young gentleman comes to order some seeds or plants or trees before he goes off to join either the king or the Parliament army, and I know that he is planting for his heir and does not expect to see the trees grow. It is at those times that I realise what wickedness this war is and will be, and I confess, I blame the king very much for standing so upon his rights and driving his people into rebellion.

I did not think I would ever be able to say it, but I am glad you are not here, husband. I miss you and so do the children but I do not know how a man could keep his wits and bear the sorrow of this kingdom, especially one like you who had served the king and the queen and seen them reap the consequences of their folly. There are rights, God-given rights, on both sides of the argument and all a woman can wonder is why the two sides cannot come together and resolve to live in peace. But they cannot, they will not, and God help them we all suffer while they hammer out the victory one on the other. Parliament is now in alliance with the Scots and they have sworn to defend each other against the king. But the Scots are a long way away and the king's armies are very close, and everyone seems to think he has the advantage. Also, he has now recruited a Papist Irish army and we are all most afraid of their coming.

What seems more and more certain to me, when this is all over, is that we shall see the king in London again with his liberties barely trimmed, and those who have stood against him will have to pray God that he is more generous in victory than he was in peace time. Prince Rupert is said to be everywhere, and the other commander of the armies is the queen, so you can imagine how the king is advised between those two. Prince Maurice serves also and they have taken Bristol and Devizes this summer. Against the wealth of the king, the Parliament army makes a pitiful showing. The king has commanders who have fought all over Europe and know how it should be done, Prince Rupert has never lost a battle. Against them the Parliament puts ploughboys and apprentice lads into the fields and the gentlemen mow them down like barley. We hear constantly from the Parliament of little battles which are fought at places of no name and mean nothing but are hailed as great victories.

However, the king has not yet approached London – and the City remains firmly against him. Your father-in-law Mr Hurte has provided his own regiment to defend the City, he says – as all the merchants do – that the king cannot rule the City again. But since all the other great towns of the kingdom are falling to the king one by one then clearly, London cannot hold out alone – especially if the queen prevails on her French relations to join her husband. If a French army marches on Westminster the Parliament will have been defeated indeed, and I think it will be harder to be rid of the French Papists than it was to invite them.

Worse than the French Papists will be an Irish army. The

*great fear is that the king is planning all the time to flood the
kingdom with Irishmen, but I cannot believe that such wickedness is in his mind. Not even he, surely, would sow such a
whirlwind. If they could ever be prevailed upon to leave, what
Englishman would ever trust the king's word again?*

*The king holds Oxford of course, and his friends hold garri-
sons all the way up the Great North Road to Scotland. The
queen holds York, and while she is in the field I have no hope
of peace. The king's army must march on London soon, and
those of us who know not what to think (and that is most of
us) can only hope that the city surrenders quickly.*

*The children are well, though running wild with neither
school nor society to tame them. I will not let them go to the
city which is full of the plague again, spread I am sure by the
travelling soldiers who come and go from battle to village. I
have had a one-way door set in our wall so that we can give
food to passing paupers without any one of the servants having
to open our front door. The bridge over the stream I have had
made into a little drawbridge and we pull it up at night. I have
completed the wall around the Ark and garden and sometimes
I feel that I am a Mrs Noah in very truth, peering over the
edge of the Ark as the waters of the end of the world arise and
swirl around me. It is on such nights that I feel very lonely and
very afraid and I wish that I were with you.*

*Johnnie says that he will be a soldier and fight for the king.
He has an etching of Prince Rupert on his black horse pinned
to the head of his bed and makes most bloodthirsty prayers for
his safety every night. He is a handsome, brave boy, as clever
as any child in the kingdom. He is reading and writing in Latin
and English and French, and I have set him to making the
plant labels in English and Latin which he does without error.
He misses you very much but he is proud of having a Virginia
planter for a father, he thinks you are daily wrestling with bears
and fighting Indians and prays for your safety every night.*

*Frances is well too. You would hardly recognise her, she has
grown in these last few months from a girl to a young woman.
She wears her hair pinned up now all the time and her skirts
very long and elegant. I always knew she would be beautiful
but she has surpassed my hopes for her. She has such a dainty
prettiness about her. She is as fair as her mother, Mrs Hurte
tells me, but she has a lightness of spirit which is all her own.*

Sometimes she is too flighty, I am aware of it, and I try to reprove her, but she is such a merry dear that I cannot be too strict. She manages the garden in your absence and I think you will be proud of her when you return. She has a real way with plants and growing things. I often think it is such a shame that she cannot take your place in very truth and be another Tradescant gardener as she always wished to be.

It is her fate which is my greatest worry if the fighting should come near to London. I think that Johnnie and I could survive anything but a direct attack, but Frances is so pretty that she attracts notice wherever she goes. I dress her as plainly as I can and she always wears a cap on her head and a hood to cover her hair when she goes out, but there is something about her which turns men's heads. I have seen her walk down the street and people simply look at her as if she were a flower or a statue, something rare and fine which they would like to take home with them. A wealthy man, whom I will not call a gentleman, visited the garden the other day and offered me ten pounds to give her to him. I had Joseph show him off the premises as quickly as you would wish, but it shows you the anxieties which I suffer over her. One of the kitchen maids – a fool – told Frances that the gentleman had taken a fancy to her and made an offer which was not of marriage, and before he had gone I am sorry to say that she climbed up on the garden wall, turned her back on him, and upended her skirts to show him her bum. I pulled her down and spanked her for indecency, and then thought she was crying most pitiably for shame, but when I had her right way up again I saw she could not speak for laughing. I sent her to her room in disgrace, and only when she was gone did I laugh too. She is a great mixture of minx and child and young lady, and I fancy the fine gentleman would have got more than he had bargained for.

If I think there is a chance of the fighting coming any closer I shall send her up the river to Oatlands, but with the country in this turmoil I do not know where she could be most safe. My choice, of course, is to keep her close by me.

My greatest advisor in these difficult times is your father's friend and your uncle, Alexander Norman, who has the most immediate news of anyone. Since he sends out the ordnance from the Tower of London he always knows where the fiercest fighting has been and how much munition was used in every *battle. He comes out to see us every week and brings us news and satisfies himself that we are well. He treats Frances as a complete young lady and Johnnie as the head of the household, and so they always welcome his arrival as their most favourite guest. Frances is never naughty when he is with us but very sober and careful, an excellent little housewife. When I told him of the man who had offered money for her he was more angry than I have ever seen him before and he would have challenged the man to a duel if I had given his name. I told him that the man had been punished enough but I did not tell him how.*

And as for myself, husband, I will speak of myself though we were not married for love and have never been more than mere friends and for all I fear you do not think of me kindly since we parted on a disagreement. I am doing my duty according to my promise made to you at the altar and to your father on his death bed to be a good wife to you, a mother to your children, and to guard the garden and the rarities. The beauty of the rarities, of the garden and of the children is my greatest joy, even in these difficult times when joy is hard to find. I miss you more bitterly than I had thought possible and I think often of a moment in the yard, a second in the hall, a letter which you once wrote to me which sounded almost loving, and I wonder perhaps if we had met each other in easier times whether we might have been lovers as well as husband and wife. I wish I had felt free to go with you on this venture, I wish you had held me so dear that you would not have gone without me, or felt as I do, tied to the house and the garden and the children. But you do not, and it is not to be, and I do not waste my time in mourning the failure of a dream that perhaps I am a fool to even think of.

So I am well, a little afraid sometimes, anxious all the time, working hard to keep your father's inheritance together for you and for Johnnie, watching Frances, and praying for you, my dear, dear husband, and hoping that wherever you are, however far away you are from me and in such a strange land, you are safe and well and will one day come home to your constant wife, Hester.

John dropped to his knees on his mattress and then hunkered down. He read it all over again. The paper was fragile in parts where it had been wetted by sea water or rain, the ink had run on one or two words but the voice of Hester, her idiosyncratic, brave little voice sounded across the sea to her husband, telling him that she was keeping faith with him.

John was completely still. In the silence of the house he could hear the scratch of a squirrel's claws on the roof above his head. He could hear a log shift in the hearth in the room below. Hester's love and steadiness felt like a thread that could stretch all the way from England to Virginia and could guide him home, or it might wrap around his heart and tug at it. He thought of Frances growing up so mischievous and so beautiful, and of his funny little scholarly son who prayed for him every night and thought he was wrestling with bears, and then he thought of his wife, Hester, a true wife if ever a man had one, fortifying his house with her little drawbridge, managing the business and showing people the rarities even while she watched the progress of the war and planned their escape. She deserved better than a husband whose heart was elsewhere, who exploited her skill and her courage, and then left her.

John dropped his head in his hands. He thought that he must have been mad to leave his wife and his children and his home, madly selfish to leave them in the middle of a war, mad with folly to think that he could make a life for himself in a wilderness and mad with vanity to think that he could love and marry a young woman and make his life all over again, to his own mad pattern.

John stretched out on his mattress and heard a low groan of pain, his own sick heart.

He lay very still for some time. Down below Francis the Negro came in with a load of wood and dumped it by the hearth. 'You in here, Mr Tradescant?'

'Here,' John said. He dragged himself to the ladder and came down, his knees weak, the very grip of his fingers on the rungs seemed powerless.

Francis looked more closely at John and his face slightly softened. 'Was it your letter? Bad news from your home?'

John shook his head and passed his hand over his face. 'No. They're managing without me. It just made me think I should be there.'

The Negro shrugged, as if the weight of exile was unbearably heavy on his own shoulders. 'Sometimes a man cannot be where he should be.'

'Yes, but I chose to come here,' John said.

A slow smile lightened the man's face, as if John's folly was deliciously funny. 'You *chose* this?'

John nodded. 'I have a beautiful home in Lambeth and a wife who was ready to love me, and two healthy children growing every day, and I took it into my head that there was no life for me there, and that the woman I loved was here, and that I could start all over again, that I should start all over again.'

Francis kneeled at the hearth and stacked wood with steady deftness.

'I've been in my father's shadow all my life,' John said, more to himself than to the silent man. 'When I came here for the first time it was virgin earth for me, because it was somewhere he had not been, with plants that he had not seen, a place where he had not made friends and where people would not always know me as his son, a lesser copy of the real thing.

'At home, I worked in his trade, I did what he did. And I always felt I did it less well. And when it came to loyalty to a master, or certainty about my own course –' John broke off with a little laugh. 'He always knew what was the right thing to do. It seemed to me that he was a man of absolute certainty. And I have spent my life blown this way and that with my doubts.'

Francis gave him a brief glance. 'I've seen Englishmen like that,' he observed. 'It always makes me wonder if you are so uncertain, why you are so quick to make rules, to make war, to go into the lives of other people?'

'What about you?' John asked. 'Why did you come?'

The man's face shone in the flickering light from the fire. 'I've been in the wrong place all my life,' he said thoughtfully. 'Being in the wrong place and longing for home is no new thing for me.'

'Where is your home?' John asked.

'The kingdom of Dahomey,' the man replied.

'Is that in Africa?'

The man nodded.

'Were you sold into slavery?'

'I was pushed into slavery, I was dragged into slavery, I was kicking and screaming and biting and fighting from roadside to marketplace to gangplank and down into the hold. I didn't stop fighting and screaming and breaking away until . . .' He suddenly broke off.

'Until when?'

'Until they brought us up on deck for washing and I saw the sea all around me and no land in sight, and I realised I didn't know even where my home was any more, that if I escaped it would do me no good because I didn't know where to go. That I was lost, and that I would stay lost for the rest of my life.'

The two men fell silent. John measured the enormity of that journey across the sea which could suck the courage out of a man, a fighting man.

'Did they bring you to England?'

'Jamaica first, but the captain brought me on to England. He wanted a slave. Lost me in a game of cards to a London merchant, he sold me to Mr Hobert who wanted to bring a horse to Virginia to do his ploughing for him but was advised that he couldn't ship a horse but a man would do the job as well. So now I am a plough-horse.'

'He doesn't treat you badly,' John said.

The man shook his head. 'For a horse I'm doing well,' he said with quiet irony. 'I get to live in the house and I eat what they eat. And I have a piece of land of my own.'

'You will grow your own food?'

'My own food, my own tobacco, and I will trade on my own account, and when I have earned fifteen shillings Mr Hobert has agreed to sell me my liberty and then I will be his indentured servant, and not his slave, and when I have earned enough to keep myself I shall buy more land and then I shall be a planter, as good as you.'

'You will be freed?'

'Mr Hobert has promised it, the magistrate has witnessed it, and the other black men tell me that it is not uncommon. In a country as big as this a man has to agree with his slaves how long they shall work for him. It's too easy for them to just run from him to a master who will offer better terms. There are always other planters who would give them work, there is always more land for them to plant for themselves.'

'Don't you want to go back to Africa?'

An expression of deep pain passed swiftly across the black face and was gone. 'I have to believe that I will be there at the hour of my death,' he said. 'When they talk of paradise and going to heaven that is where I think I will be. But I don't expect to see it again in this life.'

'Did you leave a family behind?'

'My wife, my child, my mother and two little brothers.'

John was silent at the enormity of this loss. 'You must hate us,' he said. 'All of us white men for taking you away.'

The man looked directly at him. 'I don't hate you,' he said. 'I have no time left for hate.' He paused. 'But I don't know how you can pray to your god and hope that he hears you.'

John turned his head away. 'Oh, I can tell you that,' he said bitterly. 'We do a clever little trick, us Englishmen. We start by assuming that everything in the world is ours, everything that ever was, everything that ever will be.'

He thought of the king's elegant assumption that the world was constructed for his pleasure, that every work of art should belong to him, almost by right. 'In our own country anyone who is not powerful and beautiful is a lesser person, not worth thinking about. When we go overseas we find many men and women who are not like us, so we think they are lesser still. When we find people whose language we can't understand we say they can't speak, when they don't have houses like our houses we say they can't build, when they don't make music like our music or dance like we dance we say they can only howl like dogs, that they are animals, that they are less than animals because less useful to us.'

'So Bertram Hobert takes me as his plough-horse.'

'And I swagger around, thinking that I can come to this country and that the land is empty and I can take a headright, and the woman could have no better future than to love me,' John said bitterly. 'And so I walked away from the land I already owned and the woman to whom I owed a duty. Because I am an Englishman. Because the whole world is to be made for my convenience.'

The door opened and Sarah Hobert stood in the doorway, mud encrusting her boots. 'Pull them off,' she said abruptly to Francis. 'I've come to make dinner.'

Francis kneeled at her feet. John stepped back into the darker corner of the room. Sarah came into the room in her stockinged feet and pulled off her cape, spread it out on the hooks to dry. 'It's raining again,' she said. 'I wish it would stop.'

She put the cooking pot on the edge of the fire and stirred it briskly. It would be suppawn for dinner again. Francis took four bowls from the fireside and put them on the rough trestle table, and pulled up the two stools and the two logs which served as chairs. Bertram came into the room, heeling himself out of his boots, carrying a pitcher of fresh water from the river.

They bowed their heads while Bertram spoke a blessing on their food and then they ate in silence. John looked covertly at Bertram and his wife while they ate their gruel. This land had changed them both. Sarah had been a redoubtable, God-fearing woman in England, the wife of a small farmer, and a trader in her own right. This land had made her hard. Her face was pinched and determined. The fat had been rubbed off Hobert too. In England he had been round-faced and ruddy-cheeked but here he had faced death and terror. His face was engraved with lines of suspicion and hatred. This was a country in which only a man of remarkable courage and persistence could survive. Prosperity was harder and took even longer.

Sarah bowed her head as she finished her dinner and then she rose from the table. There was not a moment to spare for leisure. There was never a moment to spare for leisure.

'Are you ready to work?' she asked John

He felt the letter crackle in his pocket. 'I'm ready,' he said. The suppawn lay heavy in his belly, and although John knew it was old cornflour and stale water, the pain, the deep pain in the centre of his body, was not indigestion but guilt. He should never have left England. He should never have sought and loved another woman. He should have stayed with the woman his father had chosen for him and brought up his children with her. He had run from his life like a schoolboy playing truant and now he realised that a man cannot have two lives. He has to choose. Attone's rough, sarcastic counsel was right – a man pulled two ways by two threads must cut one of them.

Sarah nodded at him and went out of the house, followed by her husband and Francis. She led the way down to the end of the planting, stumping along with a spade in one hand. Bertram carried the pick-axe for the stubborn roots. Francis, behind them both, was pushing Sarah's heavy wooden barrow, loaded with the precious swaying burden of small tobacco plants. John brought up the rear, carrying the two new hoes. He thought for a moment of the carving of his father on the newel post of Hatfield House. That showed a man stepping out to garden for pleasure, with his hat tilted on his head and his hoe in his hand, a rich vase under his arm spilling over with flowers and fruits. All John's life had been filled with plants grown for beauty, filled with the idea of planting and hoeing and weeding to create a solace for the eyes, a source of joy. Now he was working for survival. Some perverse contradictory desire had driven him away from the ease and richness of his father's life into a country where it would take all his skill and strength just to survive. His father's inheritance, the rich joy of his father's work, he had abandoned and left behind him. He paused and watched Hobert, Sarah and Francis as they went down the path towards the river to start planting out their tobacco crop: a small procession of determined people, planting their hopes in virgin earth.

John stayed with the Hoberts for eight nights and when he left, the field before their house was cleared of all big roots, and they had a crop of tobacco set in the ground and thriving. At his insistence they had planted a kitchen garden at the side of the house and it was set with corn, pumpkin, and beans. John would dearly have loved to grow amaracock between the rows, as the Indian women did, so that the Hoberts could have fruit in their garden as well as vegetables. But they had not tasted the fruit since the Powhatan had ceased to trade with them, and they had not thought to keep the seeds.

'I'll see if I can get you some seeds,' John said.

Sarah gleamed at him. 'Steal them,' she said.

John was genuinely shocked. 'I would not have thought you would have permitted thievery.'

'It is not thieving to take from such as they,' she said firmly. 'Do I steal a bone from my dog's bowl? They have no right to the land, it has been claimed by the king. Everything in the land is ours. When they put meat in their mouths they are poaching from us. This land is a new England, and everything in it belongs to English men and women.'

'You'll come back to help me harvest, won't you, John?' Hobert asked.

John hesitated. 'If I can,' he said. 'It is not easy for me to come and go.'

'Stay here then,' Sarah urged him. 'If they are looking askance then you may be in danger. Don't go back to them.'

'It is not them,' John said slowly. 'It's me. It is hard for me to come and go between this world and theirs.'

'Then stay with us,' Sarah said simply. 'You have your bed in the attic, and when our crop is in we will pay you a share. We will come and rebuild your house and clear your field, as we promised. You will be our neighbour again instead of leading this mongrel life.'

John was silent for a moment.

'Don't press him,' Hobert said gently to his wife. 'Come,' he said to John. 'I'll walk up the river with you.'

He took his gun from the hook behind the door, and lit the fuse from the embers in the hearth. 'I'll bring back some meat,' he said, forestalling his wife's protest that there was work to be done in the field. 'I won't be long.'

John bowed to Sarah and nodded his head to Francis, and the two men left.

Hobert walked beside John instead of jogging behind him. John found it strange to have a man at his shoulder, strange to have to curb his stride to a pace as slow as a child's, strange to hear the noise they made as they moved so broad and heavy-shod through the wood. John thought that all the game for miles around would be scared away long before Hobert arrived.

'Is the hunting good now the spring is bringing the deer back into the woods?' John asked.

Hobert shook his head. 'Less than last year,' he said. 'It is the savages. They are taking too much and they are driving the animals deeper and deeper into the woods in the hopes that they can starve us out.'

John shook his head but did not have the energy to contradict him.

'There was news from England at Jamestown,' Hobert said. 'The Scots have come over the border, they're in the war.'

'Against the king?' John asked, astounded.

'Against the king and, more important, on the side of Parliament. There were some saying that the king would have to make terms with Parliament or the Scots. He could never fight against them both.'

'How far south are they?' John asked, thinking of the little house south of the Thames in Lambeth.

'By now? Who knows?' Hobert said carelessly. 'Thank God it is not our war any more, eh, John?'

John nodded absently. 'My wife is still at Lambeth,' he said. 'My son and my daughter.'

'I thought you had all but left them?' Hobert remarked.

'I should not have done so,' John said, his voice very low. 'I should not have left them in the middle of such a war. I was angry with her and I insisted she came with me and when she defied me I thought I was free to go. But a man with a child and a garden planted is never really free to go, is he, Bertram?'

Hobert shrugged. 'I can't advise,' he said. 'It's an odd life you're making, that's for sure.'

'It's two lives,' John said. 'One here, where I live so close to the earth that I can hear its heartbeat, and one there, where I live like an Englishman with duties and obligations but with great riches and great joys.'

'Can a man do both?' Hobert asked.

John thought for a moment. 'Not with honour.'

The moment that Suckahanna saw him come from the shadow of the forest and walk past the sweat lodge, the fields and up the village street she knew that something had happened. He walked like a white man with weight in his heels. He did not stride out as the men of the Powhatan. He walked as if something was pulling his shoulders downwards, pulling his head down to his feet, pulling his feet so that he looked as if he was wading through a mire of difficulties instead of dancing on smooth grass.

She went out slowly to meet him. 'What's wrong?'

He shook his head but he would not meet her eyes. 'Nothing. I have done what I promised to do and now I am come home. I need not go again until harvest time.'

'Are they sick?' she asked, thinking that his slouch might be shielding some illness or pain.

'They are well,' he said.

'And you?'

He straightened up. 'I am weary,' he said. 'I shall go to the sweat lodge and then wash in the river.' He gave her a brief unhappy smile. 'And then everything will be as it was.'

In the warm days when the woods seemed to grow and turn green before his very eyes, John returned to his trade of plant collecting and rarity hunting. Already he had sent home a large parcel of Indian goods: clothing, tools, a case of bands and caps made from bark; now he recruited Suckahanna's son as his porter and every day the two of them left the village for a long stroll in the woods and came back laden with sprouting roots. John worked in companionable silence with the boy, and found that his thoughts often wandered to Lambeth. He felt great affection for Hester and a powerful sense that he should be there with her, to face whatever dangers might come from a country in the grip of an insane war. But at the same time he knew he could not leave Suckahanna and the Powhatan. He knew that his happiness, and his life, lay with the People.

John thought himself a fool: to abandon a wife and then to try to support her, to take a wife and then to think daily of her rival. He wanted so much to be a man like Attone, or even a man like Hobert, who saw life in simple terms, who saw one road and steadily walked it. John did not think of himself as complex and challenged; he lacked all such vanity. He saw himself as indecisive and weak and he blamed himself.

Suckahanna watched him create a nursery bed, heel in the roots, and linger over his cuttings; but she said nothing for many weeks. Then she spoke.

'What are they for?'

'I shall send them to England,' John said. 'They can be grown and sold there to gardeners.'

'By your wife?'

He tried to meet her direct black gaze as frankly and openly as he could. 'My English wife,' he corrected her.

'And what will she think? When a dead man sends her plants?'

'She will think that I am doing my duty by her,' John said. 'I cannot abandon her.'

'She will know that you are alive, and that you have abandoned her,' Suckahanna observed. 'Whereas now she may have given you up for dead.'

'I have to support her in the way that I can.'

She nodded and did not reply. John could not accept the stoical dignity of the Powhatan silence. 'I feel that I owe her anything that I can do,' he said awkwardly. 'She sent me a letter which I got at Hobert's house. She is in difficulties and alone. I left her to bring up my children and to manage my house and garden in England, and there is a war in my country . . .'

Suckahanna looked at him but said nothing.

'I am torn,' John said with a sudden burst of honesty.

'You chose your path,' she reminded him. 'Freely chose it.'

'I know,' he said humbly. 'But I keep thinking . . .'

He broke off and looked at her. She had turned her head away from him, hiding her face with a sweep of black hair. Her shoulders, showing brown and smooth through the veil of black hair, were shaking. He gave an exclamation and stepped forward to comfort her, thinking that she was weeping. But then he saw the gleam of her white teeth against her brown skin, and she flicked around and was running down the village lane, away from him, and was gone. She had been laughing. Not even her immense courtesy could restrain her amusement any longer. The spectacle of her husband struggling interminably forwards-backwards, duty-desire, English-Powhatan, was in the end too helplessly funny for her to take seriously. He heard the wild ripple of her laugh as she ran down the path to the garden where the sweetcorn was already growing high.

'Aye, you can laugh,' John said to himself, feeling himself wholly English, as leaden-footed as if he were wearing boots and breeches and weighed down by a hat. 'And God knows I love you for it. And God knows I wish I could laugh at myself too.'

When the snows were melted from even the highest hills, when there were no sharp frosts in the morning, when the ground was dry beneath the light summer moccasins of the braves, there was a meeting called by the ancient lord, Opechancanough. John the Eagle went with Attone and with one of the senior advisors of the community to represent their village, travelling along the narrow trails, northwards up the river to the great capital town of Powhatan. It nestled in the dry woodlands, at the foot of the mountains on the edge of the river which John had once known as the James River, but which he now called the Powhatan, and the waterfall at the side of Powhatan town was Paqwachowng.

They sighted the town of about forty braves at dusk, and paused outside the city boundaries.

'You're to keep quiet until spoken to,' Attone said briefly to John. 'The elder will do the talking.'

John looked without resentment at the older man who had led the way at a hard pace for the journey of many days. 'I didn't even want to come,' he protested. 'I'm hardly likely to interrupt.'

'Didn't want to come, when you can see new plants and trees and flowers? And take them back to Suckahanna when we sail downriver by canoe?' Attone mocked.

'All right,' John allowed. 'But I'm saying I didn't ask to come. I didn't want a place here.'

The older man's sharp beaky face turned to him. 'But your place is here,' he said.

'I know it, older one,' he said respectfully.

'You will answer questions but not give opinions,' the man ruled.

John nodded obediently and fell into file at the rear.

No-one knew the age of the great warlord Opechancanough. He had inherited his power from his brother the great Powhatan, father of Princess Pocahontas, the Indian heroine whom John had visited when he had been only a little boy and she had been a celebrity visiting London. There was no trace of her beauty in the ravaged face of her uncle. He sat on a great bench at the end of his luxurious long house, his cape of office shining in the gloom with the round discs of abalone shells. He barely glanced at John and his companions as they shuffled up, bowed, deposited their tribute on the growing pile before him, and stepped back.

When everyone had come and bowed to the lord he made a brief gesture with his hand and the priest stepped forward, cast some dust into the fire and watched the scented smoke spiralling upwards. John, weary from many days' walking, watched the smoke too and thought that it made strange and tempting shapes, almost as if one could read the future from it, just as he sometimes lay on his back beside Suckahanna's son when they detected shapes and images in the clouds that sailed overhead.

There was a deep mutter from the massed men packed tight into the big house. The priest walked around the fire, people leaning away from the sweep of his cape as he circled, staring into the embers. Finally he stepped back and bowed to Opechancanough.

'Yes,' he said.

Suddenly the old man sharpened into life. He leaned forwards. 'You are sure? We will conquer?'

The priest nodded simply. 'We will.'

'And they will be pushed back into the sea where they came from, and the waves will foam red with their blood and their women and children will hoe our fields and serve us where we have served them?'

The priest nodded. 'I have seen it,' he said.

Opechancanough looked past the priest at the men, waiting in silence, drinking in the assurance that they were unbeatable. 'You have heard,' he said. 'We will win. Now tell me how this victory is to be won.'

John had been dizzy with the scent of the smoke and the sudden warmth and darkness of the hut but suddenly he snapped awake, wide awake, as if someone had slapped his face. He strained his ears and his comprehension to grasp the quick exchange of advice, argument and information: the news of an isolated farmhouse here, a newly built fort with cannon further down the river. He realised with a sinking heart what he had known all along but had continually pushed to the back of his mind: that Opechancanough and the army of the Powhatan were going to fall upon the people of Jamestown, and upon every white settler everywhere in this country which they had called empty and then proceeded to fill. That if the Powhatan won there would not be a white man, woman or child left alive or out of slavery in Virginia. And if the Powhatan lost there would be a dreadful reckoning to pay.

'And what does our brother, the Eagle, say?' Opechancanough suddenly asked. His beaked harsh face turned towards John, where he sat at the back. The men before him melted away as if Opechancanough's gaze was a spear-thrust pointed at his heart.

'Nothing . . .' John stammered, the Powhatan language sticking on his tongue. 'Nothing . . . sir.'

'Will they be ready for us? Do they know we have been waiting and planning?'

Miserably John shook his head.

'Did they think us defeated and driven back, forced out of our forests and away from our game trails?'

'I think so,' John said. 'But I have not been with the white men for a long time.'

'You will advise us,' Opechancanough ruled. 'You will tell us how to avoid the guns and at what time of day we should attack. We will use your knowledge of them to come against them. You agree?'

John opened his mouth but no sound came. He was aware of Attone rising to his feet at his side.

'He is struck dumb by the honour,' Attone said smoothly. Out of sight he trod hard on John's toes.

'Indeed I am,' John said numbly.

'Your hands will be red with English blood,' Opechancanough promised him. His face was serious enough but there was a spark of mischief, that irresistible Powhatan mischief, at the back of his eyes. 'That will make you happy, Eagle.'

Spring 1644, England

Alexander Norman did not speak again of marriage to Frances, but he
visited the Ark at Lambeth every week. He took Frances out on the
river, he bought her a pony and took her riding in the lanes away
from Lambeth and out into the country. Frances came back from these
expeditions unusually quiet and thoughtful but she never said more to
Hester than that her uncle had been very kind and they had talked
about everything under the sun, but nothing that she could remember.
Hester felt torn. On one hand she felt she should warn Frances against
deepening her relationship with her uncle, which could only bring him
pain and disappointment; but on the other hand she did not want to
prevent her daughter from enjoying a trusting, loving relationship with
a good man old enough to be her father.

It must be Alexander who was principally at risk from heartbreak.
Frances enjoyed his company, and learned much from him – from
horsemanship to politics. Hester trusted Alexander to spend every day
with her without one word of courtship, but she wondered how much
pleasure he took when Frances looked up at him and said trustingly:
'You'll know about King Henry, won't you, Uncle Norman? You were
a boy when he was on the throne, weren't you?'

He gave Hester a wry smile over his niece's brown head. 'That would
be true if I was a hundred years old now. Do you know nothing of
history, Frances?'

She made a face. 'Not much. So how old are you, Uncle?'

Hester thought he had to brace himself to answer.

'I am fifty-four,' he said honestly. 'And I have seen three monarchs
reign; but never times like these.'

Frances looked at him consideringly, her head on one side. 'Well you
don't look very old,' she said bluntly. 'I never think of you as that old.'

'I am that old,' he said.

Hester thought that the assertion must be costing him dear.

'I am old enough to be your father.'

Frances's surprised ripple of laughter made him smile. 'I think of you as my friend!' she exclaimed.

'Well, I was your grandfather's friend before you were born. I bounced you on my knee when you were a dribbling little baby.'

She nodded. 'I don't see that that makes any difference at all,' she said, and Hester wondered, but did not ask: 'Difference to what?'

Alexander did not neglect Johnnie or Hester on his visits. He brought Johnnie pamphlets and ballads about his hero Prince Rupert, and he brought Hester welcome news of the progress of the war. He spoke of a new commander, Colonel Cromwell, who had come from nowhere and was said to be little more than a working man, but who had a regiment of soldiers that could withstand a royalist cavalry charge and who had been trained and drilled until they could turn and stand and march forwards on one shouted command.

'I think this Cromwell knows his business as well as Prince Rupert,' Alexander said.

Johnnie shook his head. 'Prince Rupert has fought all around Europe,' he said certainly. 'And he was riding horses, great cavalry chargers, when he was my age. No-one from East Anglia could say the same.'

The news from the king's court at Oxford was of riotous loose living, of scholars and courtiers drunk in the gutters every morning, and of the king celebrating victory after victory, however small the skirmish and insignificant the campaign. It looked as if the kingdom was opening up to him and he would be in London within a year. And then he started his march on his rebellious capital city itself. Alexander Norman sent a message to the Ark at Lambeth.

> *Dear Cousin Hester,*
>
> *I suggest that you hide your most precious treasures in your safe place and pack necessary clothes and goods for yourself. The king is marching on London from the north and the City is preparing for a siege. However, if the king should circle London to besiege it, then I should think it most likely that Lambeth will fall and the Parliamentary forces stand back and hold their ground north of the river. If the fighting is prolonged then you may well be caught between two armies. Therefore, be ready to leave the moment I give you the word and I will take you back to Oatlands.*
>
> *Alexander.*

Hester put the letter at once into the tiny fire of coal dust and kindling and watched it burn sluggishly. She felt very tired, as if the war had gone on forever, and would go on forever, without victory, without peace, with nothing but the wearisome task of surviving. For a moment she sat by the fireside, her head leaning on her hand, watching the note flame, turn to ash, and then fall in soft flakes into the red embers. Then she gave herself a little shake, brushed off her skirt, tied on her hessian working apron and went to the rarities room.

Johnnie was showing a visitor out of the front door.

'What is it, Mother?' he asked as soon as the door was safely closed. 'Not bad news from Virginia?'

She shook her head. 'Not that, thank God. It is a note from your uncle. He says that the king is marching on London and that we must be prepared to leave if the fighting comes close. We must pack up the most precious things for safety at once.'

He nodded, his little face grave. 'I'll call Frances,' he said. 'We'll all help.'

Frances came down from her room, her hair pinned in a new style. 'How do I look?'

'Awful ugly,' Johnnie said with a grin.

Hester was drawing out the big wooden chests which were stored beneath the display cases. 'You pack the glass and porcelain, Frances, you're the most careful. Johnnie, you pack the coins.'

Hester unlocked the cases and then started folding and packing the clothes, vests and coats from all around the world, savages' clothes of feathers and beads, beautifully worked scarves from India and China, and King Henry's own gloves which King Charles himself had given to the Tradescants. She glanced over, Johnnie was carefully laying every coin with its label in the chest.

'You'll have to just pile them in,' she said. 'And when we unpack them we'll have to label them again.'

His little face was shocked. The order of the rarities room had been a sacred charge for the whole family for all of his life. 'But these are Grandfather John's labels!'

'I know,' Hester said grimly. 'And I hope that he would understand that we're doing the best that we can to keep his Ark and all its contents safe. Just tumble all the coins in the chest, Johnnie, and then we can hide it and, even if a dozen regiments come through, when the war is over we can dig it all up and start again.'

He looked reluctant, but did as he was told. Frances, at the other side of the room, was wrapping precious pieces of glass in silks and scarves, and packing them tightly in a wooden box.

Hester looked around the room. It was a collection that had been amassed over years of work, all she could do was to choose the most precious pieces from it and try to save them. 'The little toys,' she said to Frances. 'The mechanical toys. Do them next.'

'What about the mermaid's tail?' Johnnie asked. 'And the whale's jaw?'

'We can't even lift them,' Frances said. 'What will we do? How can we hide them in safety?'

'I don't know,' Hester said. Her hands kept moving, packing, folding, smoothing, but her voice was full of despair and weariness. 'We just pack everything we can, I suppose. And for the rest? I don't know.'

At night Hester and the children and the gardener, Joseph, carried the boxes carefully to the ice house, and stacked them inside. The ice house was lined with brick, it was damp and dark. Frances shivered and pulled her hood over her head, fearing spiders and bats. The boxes filled the small circular room. When they came out they nailed up the door. Hester had an odd, superstitious feeling that it was as if they were mourners before the family vault and that all that was most precious to them had been buried.

'I'll plant a couple of shrubs before it tomorrow,' Joseph promised, 'and grow some ivy over the door. In a month or so you won't know it's there.'

'I hope we have a month or so,' Hester said. 'Cut some branches and lay them over the door to hide it while the ivy is growing. And put a couple of saplings in.'

'Is the king's army coming so soon?' Joseph asked.

'The king himself is coming,' Hester said grimly. 'And please God that whether he wins or loses the battle is over swiftly and the winners bring the country back to peace, because I don't think I can bear another year like this one.'

Within days in the city of London everything was rationed and nothing could be bought. The king's army was coming down the Great North Road and no wagons could get into London to feed the people. The Lord Mayor of London himself set up distribution points where people could buy food and set fair prices so that racketeers could not profit from the city's desperation. Joseph was drafted out every day to dig trenches to protect the city from the cavalry, and there was even an inquiry from the local commander of the trained bands as to how old Johnnie might be, and when he would be old enough to serve.

Johnnie, with his home under siege from the king, was wild to sneak out at night and get to the king's army. 'I could be a scout,' he said. 'I could be a spy. I could tell the king where the ditches are dug, where the cannon are mounted. He needs me, I should go to him.'

'Be quiet,' Hester snapped. The sense of an impending disaster for the house and the children she loved was wearing her patience very thin. 'The king has enough fools running to his standard. You are a child. You will stay home like an obedient child.'

'I am nearly eleven!' he protested. 'And the head of the household.'

Hester gave him a small smile. 'Then stay and defend me,' she said. 'We hold the treasures of the country here. We need to stay at our post.'

He was a little mollified. 'When I am a man I shall train and join Rupert's cavalry,' he promised.

'I hope that when you are a man you will be a gardener in a peaceful country,' she said fervently.

At the end of March there was extraordinary news which came into the city as gossip and was confirmed within the day in broadsheets and pamphlets and ballads. Despite all premonitions and fears, despite all likelihood, the Parliament army, working men officered by those who had never been gentlemen at court, had met the king's army at Alresford outside Winchester, fought a long, hard battle and won a resounding victory. It was all the more impressive because the battle had turned on a cavalry charge by the royalists which, for once, did not end in a rout of terrified Parliament infantry being cut down as they fled. This time the Parliament men stood their ground, and the king's horse, thrown back into the twisting, deep lanes of Hampshire, could not come around again, could not regroup, while the Parliamentary infantry doggedly and determinedly slugged their way uphill to Alresford ridge, and were in Alresford before nightfall.

There were bonfires all over Lambeth that night, and precious candles showed at every window. The next Sunday there was not a man, woman nor child who did not attend a service of thanksgiving. The tide of the war had ebbed for a moment, for a moment only; and no cavaliers would be riding through the narrow streets of Lambeth for a month or two at least. And there would be no Papist Irish murdering soldiers either. The news came filtering through that the Parliamentary forces had captured all the Irish-facing ports of Wales. The king could not bring the Papists into England. Even in Scotland the small royalist forces were being driven back.

'I think the king will have to come to terms with Parliament,' Alexander said to Hester one evening in April. 'He's on the defensive for the first time and the royal army is not one which fights well in retreat. He doesn't have the advisors or the determination to carry on.'

'And what then?' Hester asked. She had a basketful of sweet pea pods from last year in her lap and she was shelling the seeds ready for planting. 'Do I unpack the rarities from their hiding places?'

Alexander considered for a moment. 'Not until peace is declared,' he said. 'We'll wait and see. It maybe that the tide is turning at last.'

'D'you think the king will make peace with Parliament and come meekly home?'

Alexander shrugged. 'What else can he do?' he said. 'He has to come to terms with them. He is still king: they are still Parliament.'

'So all this pain and bloodshed has been for nothing,' Hester said blankly. 'Nothing except to teach the king that he should manage his Parliament as his father and the old queen managed theirs.'

Alexander looked grave. 'It's been an expensive lesson.'

Hester threw a handful of dried empty pods into the fire and watched them spark and flare up. 'Damnable,' she said bitterly.

April 1644, Virginia

John had hoped that he had been summoned to Opechancanough's war council as a simple brave, companion to Attone. But as the days wore on at the town of Powhatan he found he was summoned every morning to speak with Opechancanough. At first the questions were pointed and direct. The fort at Jamestown: was it true that the town had grown so large that all the people could not fit inside the walls? Was it true also that the walls had been allowed to fall into disrepair, that a proper watch was no longer kept, that the cannon were rusty?

John answered as truly as he knew, warning Opechancanough that he had been nothing more than a visitor passing through Jamestown, and not a resident who knew the town inside out. But as the questions went on Opechancanough revealed that he knew the answers as well as John. The wise old commander had many spies watching the fort. He was using John as a check against them, and they against him. He was testing John's own ability to tell the truth, proving his loyalty to his adopted people.

Once he was satisfied that John would honestly tell him all that he knew, then the questions changed. He asked instead what hours the white men rose in the morning, what they drank for their breakfast, if they were all drunkards, half-drowned in fiery spirits by the time darkness fell. Did they have a special magic in their use of gunpowder, cannon, or flintlock, or could the Powhatan people seize these goods and turn them against their makers? Was the god of Englishmen attentive to them in this foreign land, or might He simply forget them if the real people rose up against them?

John struggled with the concepts of magic, warfare, and theology in a foreign language, and in a different way of thinking. Over and over again he found himself saying to the older man, 'I am sorry, I don't know,' and saw the dark brows snap together and the crumpled face darken with anger.

'I really don't know,' John would say, hearing the nervousness in his own voice.

Over and over again Opechancanough would return to the English communications. If a settler discovered the uprising, how quickly could he take the news to Jamestown? Did the English have a method of sending signals in smoke? Or a code of drums?

'Smoke?' John asked disbelievingly. 'No. Nor drums. Soldiers only drum the march forwards or the retreat . . .'

Opechancanough spat derisively. 'No. To send messages. Long messages.'

John shook his head in bewilderment. 'Of course not. How could you do such a thing?'

Opechancanough's dark smile gleamed. 'Never mind. So if a man was warned and wanted to take the warning to Jamestown, he would have to go himself? By foot or canoe?'

'Yes,' John replied.

There was silence for a moment. 'In the last war we were betrayed,' Opechancanough said thoughtfully. 'It was a couple of our boys who had been treated kindly by their white master and could not bear to hurt him. They warned him. They had grown soft like white boys. They thought they would save him alone; but in warning him they betrayed every one of us. He ran to Jamestown and warned the fort so they were ready for us. And what of the boys who loved their master so much that they betrayed their own people and warned him?'

John waited.

'Shot by the white men,' Opechancanough said. 'That is how the white men reward a faithful servant. We saw it done. And those of us who had fought, and those of us who had not, were all driven further and further away from our villages and watched our fields hoed for tobacco, nothing but tobacco, everywhere the plant for smoke and nothing for life.'

'When will the new war be?' John asked.

Opechancanough shrugged. 'Soon.'

John woke in the night and lay still. Something had disturbed his sleep but he could not trace the noise or the movement or the sense which had woken him. Then he heard it again. From outside the house a twig cracked, and then the skins at the doorway parted and a low voice spoke briefly into the warm darkness: 'It is now.'

Attone at John's side was awake and standing. 'Now!' he said, and his voice was filled with joy.

'What is now?' John asked, as if he did not know, as if he were not near to sinking down on the ground and weeping into the earth for his sense of dread and guilt.

'We are on the warpath,' Attone said gently. 'It is now, my brother.'

Outside the tent the town was in alert silence. Men were stringing their bows and tightening their belts, checking the gleam of the blades of their knives. There was nothing to prepare, for the Powhatan were always ready for travel, for hunting, for war. John fell into line behind Attone and knew that his breath was sluggish and slow beside Attone's light panting, knew his heart was not in this, knew also that there was no way forwards and away from his allegiance to the Powhatan, and no way backwards to the English.

At a signal from Opechancanough, seated on his throne, dark as a shadow in the moonlight, the men moved off, making as little noise as a herd of wolves, silent in their moccasins, their quivers held still at their sides, their bows strung over their shoulders. The moonlight touched each one like a benison, the white gleam falling on a feather plaited into dark hair, on a pale old scar on one high cheekbone, on a smile of excitement, on the gleam of burnished skin. John went silently in Attone's steps, watching the pace of his moccasins, the movement of his haunches beneath the leather skirt, concentrating wholly on the moment of the journey so he could hide from himself the knowledge of the destination.

They were to split into two main parties. One was to travel by canoe downriver to Jamestown, taking advantage of the night to move swiftly and to form a pincer around the town by dawn. The other was to go by land either side of the river, and at every house and cabin, every grand, ambitious building and hopeful shack, they were to go in and kill every man, woman and child in the place, leaving none to escape, and none to take the news downriver.

John was in the land party, Attone with him. He thought that Opechancanough was testing his loyalty to the Powhatan by putting him in the group that would kill so early and so immediately – and not against the fighting men at the fort, but against the vulnerable, sleeping men and women with their children bundled up in the same bed beside them. But then he realised that Opechancanough had placed him where, if he were faithless, he could do no damage. He was at the rear, he could not dash ahead and warn Jamestown. All he could do was botch a few killings upriver and get himself shot.

They came upon a little house near dawn. It was set back from the river on a rise of ground, just as John had built his own house, just as Bertram Hobert had built his. Before it was a little cottage garden, neglected and overgrown, and between it and the river were long fields of tobacco, the plants set in straight rows and growing well. A little quay stretched out into the river for loading the tobacco to sail downriver to Jamestown. No light shone in the window and only a wisp of smoke showed that someone had banked the fire in overnight so that it would be hot to cook the morning breakfast.

It was the smell of woodsmoke clean on the air, unmixed with any other scent, that threw John backwards; he physically recoiled and collided with the man trotting behind him. It was such an English smell. Woodsmoke for the Powhatan was the scent of the interior of their huts, mingled with the smell of cooking, of children, of people sitting around. The smell of smoke from a sooty chimney was the smell of an English homestead.

The man behind shoved John abruptly in the back but did not utter a single sound. John touched Attone's shoulder. 'I cannot do it,' he said.

Attone turned and his glance was as cold as the blade of a knife on bare skin. 'What?'

'I cannot do it. I cannot go in and kill my people.'

'Do you want me to kill *you* now?'

Dumbly John shook his head.

'The others will kill you if I do not.'

John leaned forwards as if he would take Attone in his arms and lie his unhappy face against the man's shoulder. 'They must then. Because I cannot do it.'

'Will you wait here while we do it?'

John nodded.

'And not cry out, nor run off?'

John nodded again.

'My brother will stand guard,' Attone said simply to the others. 'Follow me.'

The men trotted past John without a glance at him. He leaned back against a tree, a useless guard, a faithless friend, a broken warrior, and a shamed husband.

They were quick and clean. There was one surprised cry and no more, and in moments they came back, Attone wiping his shell-bladed knife

282

on a piece of European muslin. 'Go on,' he said briskly to the others.

They nodded and turned to the trail again. One man had something in his hand. Attone reached out and smacked it down. A stone bottle fell to the ground and rolled away. Attone kicked it with his foot so that it spun round and round, spilling out the raw spirit and making the air stink. Then he turned to John.

'Can you find your way back to Suckahanna at the village?'

'Yes.'

'Then go back there. Wait till the men return.'

'She won't have me,' John said certainly.

'No,' Attone said. 'We none of us will want you, Eagle.' He paused as a thought struck him. 'What was your name? Before you were my brother the Eagle?'

'I was John Tradescant,' John said, the name unfamiliar on his tongue.

'Then you will have to be him again,' Attone said flatly. 'Now go to Suckahanna before someone kills you.'

'I am sorry –' John started.

'Go to Suckahanna before I kill you myself,' Attone said abruptly, and disappeared into the darkness.

The village was guarded by Attone's son, who recognised John's footfall and called into the grey dawn: 'Is that you, Eagle?'

'No,' John said. His voice was flat and weary. 'You must call me John.'

'Is my father with you? Are the braves coming home?'

'They are at war,' John said. 'I am alone.'

The boy checked his loving run forwards into John's arms and suddenly looked at him as if a terrible fear was invading him, as if his trust and certainty in John was suddenly unreliable. 'You are not with the men?'

'I could not do it,' John said simply. He had thought that the worst thing would have been to tell Suckahanna; but the bright gaze of her son was hard to meet. The light went slowly out of the boy's face.

'I don't understand,' he said plaintively, willing it to be difficult, too complex for his understanding, tempting John to create another explanation.

'I could not kill an Englishman,' John said heavily. 'I thought I could do it, but when it came to it, I could not. I left my home in England because I could not choose sides and kill Englishmen, and now I am here, in this new land, and I still cannot choose sides and kill.'

The boy's eyes scanned his face. 'I thought you were a brave,' he said reproachfully.

John shook his head. 'No. It seems I cannot be.'

'But you are my father's friend!'

'Not any more.'

'And Suckahanna loves you!'

A movement behind him made him turn. Suckahanna was standing there, watching John. The man and the boy turned and faced her, waiting for her judgement.

'So you have decided at last,' she said calmly. 'You are an Englishman after all.'

Slowly John dropped to his knees, both his knees, in the gesture he had only ever used before to the greatest queen in Europe, and then unwillingly. 'I am,' he said. 'I did not know it until the moment when I could not shed their blood. I am sorry, Suckahanna.'

She looked at him and through him, as if she understood everything about him, and for a moment John thought that he would be forgiven, and that the steady, constant love between them could overcome even this. But then she turned away and snapped her fingers for her boy and walked, light-footed, down the street in the dawn light. She did not look back at him. He knew she would never look at him with love again.

The braves came home jubilant. The first wave of the attack on the isolated houses along the riverside had gone perfectly. The attack on Jamestown had hit the sleeping town and taken it unawares. As many as five hundred colonists had been killed, but as soon as the alarm was given the Indian army had fallen back. Although the fort was taken unawares, the town was now so spread out, and the houses so defended with shutters and stout doors, that no single battle could complete the war. The braves had fallen back to regroup, to heal the wounds and bury the dead, and then they would push forwards again.

Meanwhile in Jamestown the governor was mustering all the able-bodied men and hunting dogs to counter-attack. He had promised the colonists a fight to the death, a solution once and for all.

'We have to move,' Attone said as soon as all the men had returned. 'Deeper into the forest, perhaps across the river and into the wet creeks. Once the village is safely hidden we can come out again and fight.'

The women went to the houses at once to start packing. 'And the crops in the fields?' Suckahanna asked him.

He made a gesture which told her that they were lost. 'Perhaps later. Perhaps we can come back,' he said.

They exchanged a sharp, hard look. He took in the hardness of the lines around her mouth and John, hovering helplessly behind her.

'You are hurt,' she said.

'Just bruised. You?'

She turned away. 'Just bruised.'

They travelled all day. Once, when they paused, they heard a hunting horn and the baying of a dog. It was the governor Sir William Berkeley's hounds on the track, hunting Indians would be the colonists' great sport this season.

They crossed the river at once, the children riding on the shoulders of the men, the women wading through chest-high, rapid-flowing water without a whisper of complaint, and crossed it again, then Attone led them on at a steady run.

John was in the rear, helping the old men and women keep up, carrying burdens for them. Suckahanna had told no-one of what had passed between her and her husband, but she did not need to speak. Everyone could see that the Eagle was not at the side of his friend, not at the side of his wife. Everyone could see that he was a dead man to Attone, to Suckahanna, as surely as if he had gone into Jamestown and fought like a brave and died like a hero. So they let him carry their goods or hold them steady in the river as if he were a rock or a tree, or something of use. But they did not speak to him, nor smile at him, nor even look into his eyes.

All day they travelled as Attone led them closer to the sea, where the mosquitoes rose in clouds from the sodden grass and reeds and the trees bowed down low over dark, silty, salty water. At night they found some ground only a little higher than the tidewash. 'Here,' Attone said. 'Make shelters but no fires.'

An old woman died in the night, and they piled a heap of stones over her face.

'We move on,' Attone said.

All day they travelled at that punishing pace. An old man and an old woman stopped at the side of the trail and said they would go no further. Attone left them with a bow and arrow to do what damage they could to the pursuers, and with a tiny sliver of sharpened bark to open their veins rather than be captured. None of them stopped to say goodbye. The safety of the People was greater than the farewells of individuals. Attone wanted to get the People away.

On the third day they reached a small hill deep inside the swamp and Attone gave the order that they could rest. There was nothing to eat except some dried flour which they mixed cold with the marshy water. Attone sent out scouts, empty-bellied, to go down the trail and see if they were followed. When they returned and said that the trails were safe he sent them out again. Only when the third party had come back on the fifth day did he say that the women could light fires and start to collect food and the men could go hunting.

'What happens now?' John asked one of the old women.

'We live here,' she said.

'In the middle of a foul swamp?'

She gave him a look which told him as clearly as words that she despised his weakness. 'In the middle of a foul swamp,' she said.

Summer 1644, England

Alexander's predictions seemed correct. Through the spring and early summer gossip, wild surmise and news filtered back to London, and finally to Lambeth, of small battles all around the country and then finally, in July, a dreadful battle at Marston Moor. Alexander wrote to Hester:

> *I cannot come out to see you, I am so busy with the demands of the ordnance. There has been a major battle in Yorkshire and it has gone the way of Parliament. I hear that Prince Rupert has met Cromwell himself, and it was Cromwell that triumphed. In haste . . . Alexander.*

Hester waited for news for another few days and then one of her neighbours rapped on the door to say that she was going up to the House of Commons to see the king's standards. 'Forty-eight royal standards laid for all to see on the bar of the House,' she said. 'I'll take Johnnie along with me. The boy should see it.'

Johnnie shook his head. 'Is Prince Rupert's standard taken?' he asked.

'You shall see it,' the woman promised. 'Stained with his own blood.'

Johnnie's brown eyes grew bigger in his pale face. 'I don't want to see it,' he said stubbornly, and then remembered his manners. 'But thank you very much for inviting me, Mrs Goodall.'

She bridled for a moment. 'I hope you're not siding with the enemy?' she said sharply. 'The king has forced us to this battle and now he is defeated and good riddance to him.'

Hester stepped forwards and laid her hand on her stepson's shoulder. 'He's still the king,' she said.

Mrs Goodall looked angrily at her. 'Some say that a king who is his people's woe is no king. The law that says he is king says that he rules for our good, not for our regret. If he does not please us then he is no king at all. There are those who are saying that he should die in one of his bitter battles and we would be a happier land without him.'

'Then his son would be king,' Hester said steadily. 'There would still be a king.'

'Of course you were at court,' the woman remarked pointedly. 'Enriched by the pack of them.'

'I worked there as many did,' Hester said. She sounded defensive and her hand tightened on Johnnie's shoulder as if to draw courage from his narrow little bones. 'But I have taken neither one side nor the other. All I have wanted from the beginning is peace.'

'So do we all,' the woman agreed. 'And there can be no peace with that man or his son on the throne again.'

'You may be right,' Hester said, swiftly stepping back and drawing Johnnie back with her. 'Please God we shall have peace at last and our men can come home.'

October 1644, England

On a cold day in the middle of October, Alexander Norman rode to Lambeth between frosty hedges on icy tracks. Frances was on the look-out for him and ran out into the stable yard with her cape around her shoulders to take his horse and send Alexander into the parlour, to the warmth of the fire.

Hester had mulled wine to greet him. He took a deep draught and set it down. At once Hester knew that he had something important to say. 'Is it peace?' she asked. 'Has the king surrendered?'

'No,' he said. 'He's taken Salisbury, it looks like he's rallying again. But it's not that I came about. It is time for me to speak to you about another matter.'

'Frances,' Hester said, knowing at once what Alexander Norman meant.

'Frances,' he replied.

'I wrote to her father,' Hester said. 'I did not tell him what you had said. But I told him of my worries about keeping her safe. I thought he might make some suggestion.' She paused. 'I have not had a reply. Nothing since that consignment of Indian goods and a barrel of plants.'

'I don't want to wait for his reply,' Alexander said. 'Whether it is for me or against me.'

Hester nodded, taking in the determined tone. 'Why now?' she asked. 'After waiting so long?'

'Because the girl is seventeen next year, because I am fifty-five next year, because peace is as far away as ever. If she waits for peace to come she will lose her young womanhood. She might have to wait another four years, she might wait twenty.'

'Is that what they're saying in the Tower?'

'They're saying that the king will do anything and everything before he surrenders. He's suffered some bitter defeats and he's still summoning help from the Irish, from the Scots, from the French. Nothing will stop him, no defeat can stop him. He has to be king if he is anything. And he has nothing to lose by fighting and fighting forever. And Parliament cannot stop without his surrender. Lord Manchester said it himself in the House of Parliament – they have to go on fighting until the king is completely and utterly defeated, or they are lost. The two sides – King and Parliament – have made the stakes so high that one of them has to be completely defeated, there is no middle course for either any more.'

'I see that,' Hester said.

'He has taken Salisbury this week and he still holds Oxford. As they go into winter quarters nothing is decided. I thought Marston Moor would be the end of the war but nothing will end it until Parliament is routed and the members hanged for treason, or the king dead.'

Out of habit Hester glanced at the closed door. 'Hush.'

Alexander shook his head. 'It's widely said now. People in London think there's no stopping him, no dealing with him, and the mood is getting bitter. But until he's either killed in battle or victorious the war cannot end. I have orders for barrels for gunpowder which will supply the army for the next ten years. It will be a long war, Hester. You cannot doubt it.'

Hester poured him another glass of mulled wine.

'So I am asking for your permission to propose marriage to her,' he said. 'If you refuse me permission I shall wait until she is twenty-one and can please herself.'

Hester sighed. 'You can ask her now,' she said. 'I promised her grandfather that I would care for her and keep her safe, and before God I cannot see how to keep her safe in these times. The garden earns nothing, and the rarities are hidden away and we have nothing to show, and no visitors to show it to. I can barely feed her, we live off fruit and vegetables from the garden. If I could pack her away safely like the precious rarities to bring out when peace comes I would do so. You can ask her, Cousin Norman, and I will abide by her decision.'

She saw his face light up like a young man's in a blaze of joy. 'And do you know how she thinks of me?' he asked. 'You and she are very close. How does she speak of me?'

'With great affection,' Hester said. 'But whether she loves you as a father or a friend I can't say. And I've never asked. I was hoping, perhaps, that I would never have to ask. If she had met a young man, or if John had come home, or if the war ended . . .' She turned away from a dozen regrets. 'I'll go and fetch her.'

Frances was in the stable yard, pumping water into a bucket for Alexander's horse.

'Your uncle wants to see you,' Hester said abruptly. She had to restrain herself from drawing the girl to her, smoothing her hair, holding her once more. 'In the parlour.'

Frances heaved the full bucket into the stable and shut the door. 'Is anything wrong?'

Hester kept her face pleasantly uninformative. 'He wants to ask you something,' she said. 'You must answer however you wish, Frances. Please remember that. Answer however you wish. And think about it. No need for haste.'

The girl looked puzzled and then turned towards the house.

In the parlour Alexander found that his throat was so tight that he could hardly breathe. As the door opened he turned around and saw Frances. She put her cape over the back of one of the chairs. She was plainly dressed in a warm gown of grey and there was a thread of hay in her hair. He took her hands.

'You're cold,' he said.

'I was watering your horse.'

'You should not have done that. I thought Joseph was in the yard.'

'He has too much to do. We have lost all our garden boys. Johnnie and I have to help. I don't mind it.'

His fingers again felt the calluses on her hands. 'I don't want you doing hard work.'

She smiled. 'Mother said you wanted to ask me something?'

Now it came to it Alexander found that he could barely speak. 'I do.'

She said nothing, waited for him. He drew her to the chair before the fire, and when she was seated he remained awkwardly standing before her. Then it was the most natural thing in the world to drop to one knee and take her cold little hand between his two palms and say gently: 'Frances, I have loved you since you were a little girl and I would like you to be my wife.'

All the prepared speech he had rehearsed on the long, cold ride beside the wintry river went from his head. He forgot to caution her against accepting him, he forgot to promise her that he would always be her friend even if he could not be her husband, he forgot all the things he had thought he would say. He just waited for her answer.

She smiled at once, as if he had brought her a ribbon of exceptional magnificence. 'Oh yes,' she said.

He could hardly believe that she assented so easily. At once he wanted to warn her against the wrong decision. 'But I am much older than you, you should take time to think, to talk to your mother, perhaps to write to your father . . .'

She leaned towards him and her arms came around his neck. He felt the warmth of her breath on his cheek and he drew her close and at once knew desire, and a passionate sense of protectiveness.

'I don't need to ask anyone,' she said very quietly. 'I thought you would never ask me. I have been waiting for what seems like forever. I have always known what I would say.'

Winter 1644, Virginia

Winter clamped down on the coastal plain of Virginia as if it had taken sides in the war and was in savage alliance with the colonists. All the food stores of the Powhatan had been looted or fired, there was not enough to eat and even the skills of the women could not feed the tribe from the fish and crabs on the shoreline or the frozen berries left on the trees. The braves went out hunting every day and came back with duck and geese shot on their migrating journey southward. The meat was shared with strict fairness and then mothers gave their portion privately to their children and the old people pretended that they were not hungry.

When they had started the war they had thought that it would be over in one great rush – as battles generally were. There was a persistent belief that the white people would simply go, back to where they came from, especially since they always spoke of that other place as 'home', and talked of it with longing. Why would a man abandon his own fields, his own woods, his own game, and scratch a life on the edge of a strange river? If things went badly for him why would he not take one of the great ships and go, as easily and as unexpectedly as he had come?

Of all the questions Opechancanough had put to John he had never asked him if the colonists would leave if they were defeated – the question never arose in the chief's mind. He knew that land which had been won in a battle could be lost in a battle. He knew that a newly arrived people could be easily dislodged. It never occurred to him until this terrible winter that the white people would renege on their promise to move on, on their promise that they wanted only a small patch of land at Jamestown, and then their promise that they would settle a narrow strip by the river and live in peace with their neighbours.

Opechancanough did not expect men to be honest. He himself had promised peace with a smile on his face and twice gone to war. But he did not expect the depth and consistency of duplicity that the white people brought to the virgin earth. He did not expect their determination, and to his death he never understood their greed.

In the little village there was a strong sense that everything had gone wrong. The first attack had been a victory but since then they had been hunted like frightened hares. Hidden now in the swamps in midwinter they were safe enough but there was a growing fear that the swamps might be all that was left for them, that only the arid land, the brackish water, the desolate and barren places would be left for the People who had been proud to walk safe on their footpaths through fertile woods.

John's share of the food stuck in his throat. He did not go hunting with the braves, he was not invited. He cleared the land around the temporary village with the women and with the old people, keeping his head low and scraping the earth with his hoeing stick, dropping the precious seeds safely into the earth and covering them up. He felt as if he had died on the raid on that little farmhouse and that it was his ghost who worked in the row behind Suckahanna and humbly lay in her little house at night. She did not reject him, she did not invite him. She did not by one gesture or one glance show that she saw him at all. She carried herself with simple dignity as a widow who has lost her man, and John in her shadow found that he was wishing that he had died before seeing that beautiful, loving face look away from him and those dark, veiled eyes go blind.

He thought she might grow kinder to him if he worked without complaint and lay on the floor of her house at night like a dog, like a hunting dog which has been beaten into submission. But she stepped over him when she rose in the morning and went to her prayers in the icy water as if he were a log on the floor. She went past him without disdain, without a glance that might offend him, without a look that might open up a conversation between them, even if it were to be a quarrel. She acted as if he were a dead man, a lost man, a ghost, and as the months went by Tradescant felt that he was lost indeed.

He went to find Attone, who was setting a fish trap by the river and watching the flow of the rising flood water over the markers at the riverbank.

'Can I speak with you?' John asked humbly.

His former friend glanced at him and then away as if the sight of John displeased him. 'What?'

'I need advice.'

There was an unhelpful silence.

'Suckahanna turns from me and says not one word to me.'

Attone nodded.

'Is there anything I can do to make it better between us?'

Attone bent down and raised the trap from the water. The delicate withy-work was bending in the current; he straightened a twig and then carefully bedded it in with pebbles before he answered. He took his time, the whole process took nearly half an hour.

'Nothing.'

'Will she take me back as a husband if I serve her without complaint? Perhaps in Coltayough? In the warm time?'

Attone thought for a moment, his eyes still on his fish trap, and then shook his head. 'I shouldn't think so.'

'At Nepinough?'

Again the dismissive shake of the head.

'Will she ever forgive me for coming home without blood on my hands?'

Attone turned from the river and looked John squarely in the face. The relief of being seen, of gaining a response, was so great that John wanted to fling his arms around his former friend. Just that one look was an affirmation that he was a man still; that he could be seen and acknowledged.

'Never, I should think,' Attone said.

Tradescant drew breath. 'What have I done that is so bad?'

'Don't you know?'

Dumbly, Tradescant shook his head.

'You've shamed her. She stood for you before all the People and said you were a man worthy to be tested. You were tested and you passed and she chose you as her man, before all the People. Now they all look at her and say what a fool that woman is to choose a man who bends like a willow, who is neither white nor brown, who is neither English nor Powhatan, who is neither hunter nor gardener, who is neither Eagle nor John.'

'Will she never forgive me?'

'How can she? Will she ever not feel the shame?'

'If we were to go away –'

Attone laughed a brief bitter laugh. 'Where? D'you think she'd live in Jamestown? D'you think they'd not take her out and hang her or worse? D'you think she'd live with you in that house and send tobacco down the river and pack up your plants for you, and be a wife like the other one, the one you left behind in England? Or d'you think to take her to England and watch her die in exile, as Pocahontas did?'

John shook his head, he felt as bewildered as a scolded child. 'I've been a fool,' he said.

For a moment Attone softened. He dropped his hand on John's shoulder. 'These are foolish times,' he said. 'I think at the end of it all, when the Great Hare runs through the world all alone again, we will all seem fools.'

'Can the People survive?' John asked in a low whisper.

Attone shook his head.

January 1645, England

Johnnie was in the garden at first light, looking for flowers for his sister's wedding bouquet. The frost was as thick on the ground as snow, his boots crunched as he walked across the frozen grass. The sun was bright and hard and the air smelled sharp and exciting: of leaf-mould, of coldness, of the earth waiting for sunshine. Johnnie had a powerful sense of being young and alive and that his life, as the only Tradescant heir, was about to begin.

He wanted to give Frances something beautiful. If she had married in springtime she would have carried a bouquet of flowers from the chestnut tree, their grandfather's pride. If she had married in summer he would have cut the stems and snapped the thorns off a hundred roses. But she had chosen the very heart of the winter and Johnnie feared he could give her nothing from his grandfather's garden but the shiny hardness of evergreen leaves.

Hester, seeing him bare-headed and wearing nothing warm, swung open her bedroom window, hearing the hinge crack against the frost. 'Johnnie! What are you doing?'

He turned and waved. 'I'm picking her a bouquet!'

'There's nothing to be had!'

Johnnie shook his head and went on down the garden. Hester watched him go, the lithe little figure with the determined set to his shoulders: Johnnie Tradescant. Then she turned back into the house to wake Frances for her wedding day.

Frances, bathed, dressed, perfumed and wearing a new gown, came downstairs in a shimmering cloud of palest blue silk. She wore her hair down to her shoulders, curled in ringlets, a tiny scrap of lace for a cap on the back of her head. Her gown, rich pale silk embroidered all over with pale blue patterns, hushed and whispered on the flagstones of the hall. Her wide collar was of the finest Valenciennes lace; the future Mrs Norman could import the very best from France. It matched the deep lace edging of her sleeves, crisp and sweet-smelling with starch. The dress was cut low, the cream of Frances's warm skin contrasting with the coolness of the white lace.

'How do I look?' Frances asked, knowing that she was beautiful.

'Awful ugly,' Johnnie said with a smile, invoking the nursery insult. He whipped out a posy from behind his back. 'I picked you these. But you don't have to carry them if you don't like 'em.'

Frances took the posy from him without any word of gratitude or thanks and looked carefully at it. Hester was reminded that they were children and grandchildren of perhaps the finest gardeners the world had ever known. Neither of them exclaimed over the gift of a plant, they always carefully looked, carefully assessed.

He had cut her fronds of yew, the needles as soft as wool, the green so dark as to be almost black, starred with deep pink berries and smelling hauntingly of winter and Christmas. He had picked her mistletoe from the clumps on the old trees in the orchard and woven the light green wings of leaves around the darker yew so the white berries looked like drops of pearls against the needles. He had found some tiny buds of early snowdrops and woven them into a chain which linked leaves, needles and buds altogether, and he had twisted it around with the lace-like twigs of a rambling rose starred with pink hips.

'Thank you,' Frances said.

'But I have this for your hair,' Johnnie said with simple pride. From the table behind him he produced a spray of primroses, and their sweet, clear smell filled the hall.

'How ever did you get primroses?' Frances asked.

'Potted them up as soon as you said you'd marry him,' Johnnie said proudly. 'I wasn't going to let you catch me out with a winter wedding. We *are* the Tradescants, after all.'

Frances laid down her green bouquet and took the pot of primroses to the mirror in the rarities room. Her high heels sounded hollow on the floorboards; only the big things were left in the room, with a collection of lesser pieces which could be sacrificed to save the others. The room was rich enough to fool a looting soldier into thinking that he had seen all the treasures. Hester kept the key to the ice-house door on a chain round her neck and the ivy was growing thickly over the hinges.

Frances picked the flowers, nipping the soft stems with her fingernails, and tucked them behind her ears and into her ringlets.

'Pretty?' she asked, turning to her brother.

'Well enough,' he said, concealing his pride as he took her hand and tucked it under his arm.

They married at Little St Bartholomew's Church, Old Fish Street, in the City with Hester as one witness and Alexander's friend Thomas Streeter as the other. They dined that night at Alexander's house opposite the Tower of London and raised a glass to the father of the bride.

'I wonder where he is tonight?' Mr Streeter asked thoughtlessly. Alexander glanced quickly at Hester's stricken face.

'I don't mind, as long as he's safe,' she said.

It was hard for Hester to leave Frances. She had cared for her since she had been a fair-headed, sad little girl of nine years old, overwhelmed by the responsibility of looking after her brother, missing her mother every night and every day. She had been too proud to ask for help; she would always have all of the Tradescant stubbornness. She had been too independent to ask for love; but Hester would treasure all her life the memory of the way that Frances had stepped sideways, without glancing up, until she could lean against her stepmother's comforting hip and feel a protective hand rest gently on her shoulder.

'I shall miss you,' Hester whispered as she took her leave in the cramped hall of Alexander's house the next day.

'Oh, Mother –' Frances said, and dived into her embrace. 'But I shall come to the Ark often, and you will come and see us. Won't she, Alexander?'

Alexander Norman, looking years younger as if sheer joy had smoothed the lines from his face, beamed at Hester and said: 'You can come and live with us, if you like. I should think myself a Pasha of Turkey with two such beauties in the house.'

'I have the Ark to see to,' Hester affirmed. 'But I expect you on a visit often. And when there is plague in the city . . .'

'I shall send her to you at once,' Alexander reassured her. 'Never fear. And I shall write you what news there is.'

After that, there was nothing to do but to let her go. Hester held on a moment longer than was necessary, and when Frances stepped back into the encircling arm of her husband Hester felt a pain in her whole body as if something slowly and deeply was peeling away from her. She smiled at once. 'God bless you,' she said, as if the pain was not gripping her inside. 'Be happy.'

She turned from the pretty hall and stepped out into the street. The Tower of London threw a shadow over the street in the morning and the chill struck Hester as she gathered her cape around her. In a second Johnnie was at her side, offering his arm like a cavalier, and Hester managed to step briskly out towards the river and the boat to take them home.

'That was well done,' Johnnie said stoutly, keeping his face turned away from her.

'Very well,' Hester replied, rubbing her gloved hand against her cheeks. 'A plague on this cold wind, it's making my eyes water.'

'Mine too,' Johnnie said.

April 1645, England

Hester felt that the Ark, Tradescant's Ark, was adrift in the spring of 1645. The promise that she had made to John Tradescant – to care for his grandchildren and his rarities – seemed to be slipping away from her; though she had always thought that whatever else slipped away, that promise at least could hold firm.

But Frances was a woman, with a house and a new life of her own, and Johnnie was growing and would be off to war within four, perhaps five, years. Every young man in England knew that he would see fighting before he was old, and Johnnie, even precious Johnnie, could be no exception. The rarities were well-hidden and she could only hope that neither the cold nor the damp would spoil them. The ice house was safely locked and bolted, and Joseph had planted a cherry tree, one of Tradescant's great black cherry trees, before it. The sapling had taken well and was spreading its boughs as if it would deny that there had ever been a door there at all. The springing leaves blurred the outline of the wall, and when the blossom came there would be nothing to see but bobbing flowers.

'We'll have to cut that tree down when we want to get the door open and the treasures out,' Joseph observed to Hester in a quiet voice as she was walking around the garden.

'The way things are going, we'll never be safe to have them out,' she replied, and went on.

The garden was looking as lovely as it did every spring, as if war was not the nation's chief occupation, as if hunger and plague were not a certainty in the coming summer. The daffodils were bobbing in the orchard and in the tulip beds the spears of buds were thickening and blushing with light stripes of colour. If in the autumn there was anyone left alive who cared to buy tulips there would be a fortune in the rich earth of the Tradescant garden.

But nobody was buying, they were not taking money at the door of the rarities room, they were not selling plants. The Ark was slowly sinking under debt. Joseph was working for half-wages and his keep, the lads had left, run away to war, the maids had been dismissed and only Cook stayed on and shared the work of the house with Hester.

The trees were in their first green leaves, Hester could almost smell their freshness in the air. The grass was growing long; as soon as the daffodils had died back then Joseph would scythe it and rake the clippings away. The branches in the orchards were bobbing with their twigs bursting into leaf and the buds thickening with the promise of flowers to come. It should have been a joyous place; but Hester walked among the fertility and over-brimming life of it like a woman chilled to the bone and weary nearly to death.

She walked to the end of the garden and looked out across the pond. It was years since she had brought Johnnie here to feed the ducks, years since they had sat in the little waterlogged boat and he had rowed her backwards and forwards and told her that he would undoubtedly be a great sailor as his grandfather had been – chasing pirates in the Mediterranean, sailing to the very icy doors of Russia. And now she was the wife of another travelling Tradescant and she thought that this would be the year that she would have to find the courage to face the fact that John was never coming home.

Since he had left she had received only one letter, to say that he was leaving Jamestown and going to build his house further up the river and that she should not expect to hear from him again for some time. Then she had received a consignment of Indian rarities and a couple of barrels of plants, badly packed, and badly shipped, which told her that it was not John who had seen them loaded on board. Since then – nothing. And now there was news of an Indian uprising and Jamestown attacked, and all the planters all along the river scalped and skinned and butchered.

She thought she must learn to stop looking for John, learn to stop waiting for him. She thought she would wait till the summer and then, if there was still no news, find a way to tell Johnnie, who was sometimes still her little boy, and sometimes now a young man, that his father was not coming home, and that he was the only Gardener Tradescant left.

'Excuse me,' a voice behind her said politely. 'I am looking for John Tradescant.'

'He's not here,' Hester said wearily and turned around. 'I am his wife. Can I help you?'

The man before her was one of the handsomest she had ever seen in her life. He swept off his hat to her and the plumes brushed the ground as he bowed, one long brown suede boot stretched forwards. He was dressed in grey – a sober enough colour which might indicate he was a Parliament man and one of the dreary Presbyterian sort at that; but his thick, curly head of hair, his rich lace collar, and that laughing confidence in his smile, was that of a cavalier.

Hester's first response was to smile in reply, he was not a man that any woman would find easy to resist. But then she remembered the times they lived in and she glanced towards the house as if she feared a guard of soldiery at his call and a warrant for arrest in his pocket.

'Can I help you?' she asked again.

'I'm looking for tulips,' he said. 'Everyone knows that John Tradescant's is the only garden worth visiting in England, and also these are troubled times to go flower hunting in the Low Countries.'

'We have tulips,' Hester said gravely, not taking advantage of the conversational opening to deplore the badness of the times. 'Was it a special variety you wanted?'

'Yes,' he said. 'What do you have?'

Hester smiled. The verbal fencing was a typical approach to naming a plant which had, in its heyday, cost the value of a house. 'We have everything,' she said with the simple arrogance of a professional at the very top of her profession. 'You had much better tell me simply what you want. We only ever charge a fair price, Mr –?'

He stepped back slightly as if to re-assess her, as if his view of a plain woman plainly dressed had hidden the strength of her character, and her pride. 'I'm John Lambert,' he said. 'And last year I grew half a dozen tulips at my home, and this year I must have more. I simply must. Do you know what I mean, Mrs Tradescant? Or are they nothing more than a crop to you, like wheat to a farmer?'

'They're not my passion,' Hester said. 'But nobody could live in this household and not come to love tulips. They are one of the finest flowers.'

'None finer,' he said quickly.

'Roses?'

He hesitated. 'But the thing about tulips is the shortness of the season, and the way you can buy them in the bulb and hold the bulb in your hand and know that inside it is a thing of such beauty. And you know that if you care for it you will see that thing of beauty, whereas a rose – a rose grows itself.'

Hester laughed. 'If you were a working gardener, Mr Lambert, you would value plants that grow themselves. But let me show you our tulip beds.'

She led the way back through the garden and then paused. The path ran alongside the wall which kept the west wind off the plants. Along the wall, espaliered in regular lines, were apple and pear trees; the south wall was lined with the peaches and apricots. They were Tradescant walls: a double skin of brick with three fireplaces set one on top of each other and a flue running from each fire along the length of the wall to keep the bricks at a steady warmth by night and day. But Hester had not been able to afford the charcoal for the fires for two seasons.

Hester saw Mr Lambert take in the neat planning and the solidity of the building, and the immaculate pruning of the branches, and felt her familiar stir of pride. Then he turned to the garden beds and she heard his sharp intake of breath.

There was bed after bed of tulips. They grew at least twenty of each specimen, and they had more than a hundred different varieties. Each new variety was labelled with a lead spike stuck in the ground at the head of the row and on each spike, in Johnnie's meticulous printing, was the name of each variety. Behind each label, like a row of well-drilled infantry, grew the tulips, with their leaves clasped close to their stalks and their growing heads like multi-coloured soldiers shouldering their pikes.

Hester enjoyed the expression on the cavalier's face. 'We keep the rare ones potted up,' she said. 'These are only garden tulips. I can show you the rarities, we keep them in our orangery.'

'I had no idea,' he said softly. He was walking between the tulip beds, scanning them, bending to read the labels and then going on. 'I had heard you were great gardeners, but I thought you worked on the palace gardens.'

'We do,' Hester said. 'We did,' she corrected herself. 'But we had to have our own garden to stock the palace gardens, and we have always sold our stock.'

He nodded, paced the length of the bed, kneeled down and then got up again. Hester noted the dirt on the knees of his grey suit and that he did not trouble to brush it off. She recognised at once the signs of a besotted tulip enthusiast and a man accustomed to employing others to keep his clothes smart.

'And what rarities do you have?' he asked.

'We have a Lack tulip, a Duck tulip, Agatha tulips, Violetten.' She broke off at the eagerness in his face.

'I've never seen them,' he said. 'D'you have them here?'

'This way,' Hester said pleasantly, and led him towards the house. Johnnie came running out and checked at the sight of the stranger. He gave a neat bow and the man smiled at him.

'My stepson,' Hester said. 'John Tradescant.'

'And will you be a gardener too?' the man asked.

'I am a gardener already,' Johnnie replied. 'I am going to be a cavalry officer.'

Hester scowled a warning at him but the man nodded pleasantly enough. 'I'm in that line of work myself,' he said. 'I'm in the cavalry for the Parliament army.'

'*That* John Lambert!' Hester exclaimed and then flushed and wished she had the sense to be silent. She had read about the talents of the cavalry leader who was said to be the equal of Prince Rupert, but she had not pictured him as a young man, smiling in spring sunshine, and devoted to tulips.

He grinned at her. 'Shall I keep a place among my officers for you, Master Tradescant?'

Johnnie flushed and looked awkward. 'The thing is –'

'He is too young to be thinking of such things,' Hester intervened. 'Now . . . the tulips –'

John Lambert did not move. 'What is the thing?' he asked Johnnie gently.

'The thing is that I am in the king's service,' Johnnie said seriously. 'My family have always been gardeners to the royal palaces, and we have not yet been dismissed. So I suppose I am in the king's service, and I can't, in honour, join you. But I thank you for the invitation, sir.'

Lambert smiled. 'Perhaps by the time you are old enough to ride with me there will be a country united, and only one army and one cavalry and all you will have to choose is your horse and the colour of the feather in your hat,' he suggested diplomatically. 'And both Prince Rupert and I will be proud to serve under the same colours.'

He straightened up and looked over Johnnie's head at Hester's concerned expression. 'Please don't fear, Mrs Tradescant,' he said. 'I am here to buy tulips, not to cause you a moment's uneasiness. Loyalty is a difficult path to tread and these are difficult times. You may well garden in a royal palace once more and I may yet dance off a royal scaffold. Or I might be the new Chief Justice and you Mayor of London. Let's just look at some tulips, shall we?'

The warmth of his smile was irresistible. Hester smiled in reply and directed him to the terrace where the tulips stood in their beautiful ceramic pots. Warmed by the sunshine and sheltered in the orangery at night, these were more developed than those in the bed and they were showing the colours in their petals.

'Now these are our rarities,' she said. 'These are green parrot tulips, very special.' Hester indicated the ragged fringe on the green petals. 'And these are Paragon Liefkens, they have a wonderful broken colour – red and white or red and yellow. The Semper Augustus comes from this family but excels them in shape, it has the true tulip shape and the best broken colour. Here are the Violetten, they come in a different colour in every bulb, very unpredictable and difficult to grow a consistent strain: they can be as pale as a bough of lilac or a true, deep purple-blue like violets. If you were interested in developing your own strain –' She glanced at him and saw the avidity in his face.

'Oh, yes!'

'Then these are the ones I would choose. To get a consistent deep purple would be a wonderful thing to do. Gardeners would thank you forever. And here,' she led the way to the shelter of the terrace and the tulips standing proudly in the precious pots, 'these are our Semper Augustus. We believe them to be the only Sempers in England. My father-in-law bought them and gave one to the queen. When she left the palace my husband brought it back here. As far as I know, no-one else has a Semper.'

Lambert's attention was all that she could have desired. He squatted down so his dark head was on a level with the scarlet and white flower. 'May I touch?'

'Gently,' Hester assented.

He put out a fingertip, the ruby on his hand winked at the scarlet of the petal and he noticed the match of the colour at once. The red of the petal was as shiny as silk shot through with white. One flower, a little more mature than the others, was open and he peered into the cup to see the exotic darkness of the stamens and the sooty black of the pollen.

'Exquisite,' he breathed. 'This is the most beautiful thing I have ever seen.'

Hester smiled. Johnnie glanced up at her and winked. They both knew what would come next.

'How much?' John Lambert asked.

'Johnnie, go and ask Cook for some shortbread and a glass of wine for our guest,' Hester commanded. 'And bring me some notepaper and a pen. You will want to place a large order, Mr Lambert?'

He looked up at her and grinned, the confident smile of a handsome man whose life is going well for him. 'You may command my fortune, Mrs Tradescant.'

Summer 1645, Virginia

John thought that the life at the new village in the creeks would become easier once the crops yielded and the hunting improved, and the fruits were ripe in the forest. When the good weather came there was indeed enough food for everyone; but the easy contentment of the old village life was lost. They dug out a pit and built a new sweat lodge, and dedicated a new dancing circle. They built a grain store and the women made the tall, smooth black jars to hold the dried peas and seeds and maize which would see them through the winter; but the joy that John had thought was inseparable from the Powhatan had gone from them. Expelled from the land where they had chosen to live, and confined to the brackish waters near the shoreline, they were like a people who had lost their confidence and their pride.

They had never thought that they could be defeated by the colonists, or if they thought they could lose, they thought it would be in a great battle, and the braves would lie dead in heaps, and the women would grieve and take their men home and weep over their bodies. Then a price would be paid – the orphans and the widows would disappear into Jamestown and not be seen again and the Powhatan would grieve for them too, as among the lost. Then, after a season, after a cycle of the year, everything would return to normal.

What they had not anticipated was that the war would never stop. What they had not anticipated was that it would not be a battle and a withdrawal of either one side or the other. What they had not anticipated, and John had not thought to warn them against, was the inveteracy of English spite against a native people which takes arms against them.

The colonists were not driven by fear, it was no longer a matter of self defence. The army of half-naked yelling warriors which had come against them had melted away, disappeared back into the woods. The colonists were fuelled instead by a deep sense of outrage and moral righteousness. Ever since the first uprising they had felt that the Indians had escaped punishment, had been pushed back into the woods but not pushed far enough. Even when they had built the wooden palisade to mark the limit of their tolerance of the native people, they had thought that too much land had been left to them. Now, under Sir William Berkeley, there was talk of 'solving' the Indian question. In these terms of speech the families of the Powhatan were now defined as a problem which had to be solved, and not as a people with rights.

Once that shift of thinking took place there could be only one conclusion, and John understood the determination of the colonists who marched out in expedition after expedition to hunt down first one village and then another until it felt as if the trees had ceased to hide the Powhatan, and the leaves ceased to shelter them, as if the colonists could see through the branches and the morning mist, and wherever there was one of the People, a man, a woman or a child, a musket ball would find them.

And then the news came that Opechancanough had been captured. John went to find Attone by the river. He was not fishing, nor sharpening a bow. He was not chipping at the blade of a stone knife, nor tying an intricate knot to flight an arrow. He was standing, uncharacteristically idle, his hands limp at his sides, watching the light on the sluggish water of the river as it lapped at the pebbles at his feet.

'The white men have taken Opechancanough,' John said.

Attone did not turn his head. He had heard John approach from half a mile away and known from the sound of the footsteps that it was John, and that he was looking for someone.

'Yes.'

'I was thinking, should I go into Jamestown and ask them to spare his life?'

Attone turned his bright dark gaze on John. 'Would they spare him if you asked it?'

'I don't know. They might. At least I could speak up for him. I thought I should go to them and explain what the Powhatan believe. At the very least I could make sure that they understand what Opechancanough is saying.'

Attone nodded. 'Yes. Go.'

John stepped forwards and stood beside the man, shoulder to shoulder. 'I have loved you like a brother,' he said suddenly.

Attone flashed him a quick look and at the back of it was a smile. 'Yes.'

'I didn't think it would end here, like this.'

The Powhatan shook his head, his gaze returning to the moving water. 'I didn't think it either, Englishman.'

'You call me Englishman because I am no longer of the People,' John stated, hoping to be contradicted.

Attone simply nodded.

John summoned his resolve. 'Then I will go into Jamestown and plead for his life, and then I will go back to England. I know that there is no place for me with the People any more, and the food I eat robs the hungry men and women.'

'It is time that you went back to your own people. There is nothing for you here.'

'I would stay if Suckahanna asked me –'

Again there was that dark flash and a half-concealed smile. 'You might as well wait for the deer to speak, Englishman. She has turned her head from you, she will not look back.'

'Because of her pride?'

Attone nodded. 'Now *she* is a Powhatan,' he said.

'When I am gone will you tell her that I loved her?' John asked. 'And that I went because I believed she wanted me gone. Tell her it was not uncertainty, and not knowing where I belonged. Will you tell her that my whole heart was with her?'

Attone shook his head, a lazy gesture. 'I will tell her that you loved her as much as a man like you can love.'

'What would a man like you do?' John cried out in frustration. 'If you're saying that my love is less – what would your love be like? What would you do?'

Attone laughed at that. 'Oh! Beat her, I suppose. Love her. Give her a baby to care for. Send her out in the fields to work. Bring her home at night and keep her awake all the night with lovemaking until she is too tired to do anything but sleep. Don't ask me, Eagle, she left me for you. If I knew how to manage her she would never have married you.'

John laughed unwillingly. 'But you will tell her that I love her?'

'Oh go, Englishman,' Attone said, suddenly weary of the whole thing. 'I will tell her the words if I can remember them, but we have no interest in words. And words from Englishmen mean less than nothing. You are a faithless race, and you talk too much. Go and see if your talking can save Opechancanough and then go back to your people. Your time here with us is finished.'

John washed himself clean in the river but the paleness of his skin seemed stained forever by the redness of the bear grease. He asked Musses to cut his hair for him, in a short crop, the same length on both sides, so that he no longer had the side plait of the Powhatan braid. She did it neatly, with two sharpened oyster shells, and gathered up the fallen locks and threw them on the fire.

'Going home?' she asked.

'I have nowhere else to go,' John replied, hoping for sympathy.

'Goodbye,' she said pleasantly and walked away.

John rose up from her fire, took a knife and his bow and arrow and went to find Suckahanna. She was at a corner of the camp, a deerskin strung taut on the curing frame; she was rubbing oil into the skin to keep it supple and sweet.

'I am going to Jamestown to speak for Opechancanough,' John said. She nodded.

'After, I shall take a ship for England.'

She nodded again.

'I may never come back,' he warned.

The tiniest of shrugs greeted that remark and she turned around and tipped some more oil into her palm and worked it into the skin.

'Before I go, I want to tell you that I love you and that I am sorry for not being a true brave,' John said. 'I know I have disappointed you; but I could not spill the blood of my countrymen. If we had found a way to live at peace, white men and Powhatan, then you and I would have been happy together. It is the times which failed us, Suckahanna. I know that I loved you then, and I love you still. Without fail.'

At last she paused in her work, she tossed her head and her black hair slid over her shoulder, and he saw the almost-forgotten sweetness of her smile.

'Go your way, Englishman,' she said. 'You don't snare me with words.'

'And you still love me,' John hazarded.

She gave him that swift, flirtatious, elusive smile. 'Go away.'

It was a long way to Jamestown. John went northwards along the shoreline. He lived off shellfish and berries and early ripening nuts, and occasionally he shot a bird for some meat. He thought it was ironic that now he was preparing to leave the country he had found that he could live off it and that it was the rich and fertile place of his wildest childhood imaginings.

For the first three days he trudged dully, like a London apprentice going to work, watching his feet on the stones of the shore, and looking around him only to check for enemies and to look for game. But on the third day he realised that just over the arid dunes was forest filled with trees and saplings and seeds coming into ripeness, and he left the shoreline, went into the forest and started collecting.

By the time he reached the James River he had made himself a satchel from two duckskins, which were not properly cleaned and were smelling powerfully, and stuffed it with seeds and roots. He approached the first plantation he saw with caution, he did not want to be shot as an Indian by a nervous planter. He saw the man down on his roughly built quay.

'Ahoy!' John called from the shelter of the forest. The English words felt strange on his tongue, for a moment he was afraid he had forgotten his own language.

The man turned to where the sound came from and raked the forest with his gaze. 'Who's there?'

'A friend, an Englishman. But buck-naked.'

The planter lifted his musket. John saw that the fuse was not glowing and the chances were good that it was out. He stepped out of the shelter of the woods.

'You're an Indian dog! Stand still or I shoot you as you stand.'

'I promise,' John said. 'I'm as English as you. I'm John Tradescant, gardener to the king of England, I have a house and a garden in Lambeth and a wife called Hester Pooks and a daughter called Frances and a son called Johnnie.' As he spoke the familiar, beloved names he felt a stirring as if they themselves were calling to him and he should have been listening, he should have heard them earlier.

'Then what are you doing like a savage in the woods?' the man asked, his gun pointed unwaveringly at John's crotch.

John hesitated. Of course, that was the very question.

'Because I didn't know where I should be,' he said slowly. Then he raised his voice and said loudly enough to be heard: 'I was living with the Powhatan, but now I want to go back to England. Can I borrow some clothing and take a boat to Jamestown? I can get money sent to me there, and repay you.'

The man motioned him forwards and John stepped cautiously closer. 'What's the name of the new Parliament commander?' the man asked him quickly.

John spread his hands. 'I don't know. I've been with the Powhatan for the last two years. When I left the king was defeated at Edgehill – I thought it would not be long for him then.'

The man laughed shortly: 'It still is not decided now,' he said. 'What's the name of the king's cousin?'

'Prince Rupert?'

'His son?'

'Prince Charles?'

'Nationality of his wife?'

'She's French, I can tell you the colour of her eyes,' John said. 'I was in court service, I was gardener at Oatlands Palace.'

The man checked. 'You were gardener to the queen of England and here you are as naked as a savage after running wild two years with the Powhatan?'

John stepped forwards and held out his hand. 'Odd, isn't it? I'm John Tradescant, of the Ark, Lambeth.'

They loaned John a pair of breeches and a coarse linen shirt and he crammed his feet into a pair of shoes that should have been the right size but which pinched his feet unbearably. Running barefoot for two years had hardened the skin and spread the bones of his feet, John feared he would never walk comfortably in boots or shoes again.

A tobacco ship called in at the quay to load their crop the next day and John sent a note to Hester at Lambeth and packed his seeds and roots into a watertight barrel addressed to her.

> *Dear Wife,*
>
> *I hope this reaches you in good health and fortune. I am on my way to Jamestown after many months living in the forest. I have no money. Please send a note of credit for me to draw twenty pounds for my board and lodging and journey home. I shall come home as soon as I receive the money.*

John flinched a little at the bareness of the note but he did not feel he could, in all conscience, offer any explanation or any reassurance of love. He feared that perhaps Hester would be hard-pressed to find twenty pounds to pay into a London goldsmith so that the note of credit could be good in Virginia, but he could not bring himself to offer advice as to what she might sell from the collection. He had been too long away. He did not know if she had been able to keep the collection safe. He did not even know for certain that she was still at the Lambeth address. He felt as if he were pitching a rope into darkness and hoping that someone on an unseen quayside might catch it and haul him in. He paused before signing his name. If anyone would haul him in, it would be Hester.

> *I trust you, Hester, and when I come home I shall thank you*
> *for your care of me and mine.*

He signed his name and ran down to the wooden pier and thrust the note at the captain. 'Please see that she receives it,' he said. 'I am trapped here unless she can send me my fare home.' He looked at the ship. 'Unless I could work a passage?'

The captain laughed in his face. 'Work your passage? You're a seaman, are you?'

'No,' John said.

'If you want to go home, mister, you'll have to pay for your voyage, same as anyone.'

'She'll reward you for bringing the note,' John promised him. 'Please see that she receives it.'

The captain tucked it carelessly into his jacket. 'Oh aye,' he said and shouted to the sailors to let go.

The current of the river caught the ship and she pulled away from the quayside. John watched the sails unfurl and heard the shouted orders and the creaks of the rope and timbers as the ship got underway.

'How long before you hear?' the planter asked him.

'It can't be quicker than four months,' John said. 'A voyage there and back, if she has the money, that is.'

The man grinned. 'I could use a hand to work the crop,' he said.

John nodded. Labour was notoriously hard to find in Virginia. He would have to be a hired hand until Hester sent him a note of credit and he could become a gentleman again.

'Very well,' he said. 'But I have to go to Jamestown first. I have a promise to keep.'

John saw the governor for a brief snatched moment as the great man strode from the new assembly room to the governor's mansion. John hobbled after him in his ill-fitting shoes. 'Sir William?'

The young man turned, took in John's humble clothes and strolled on. 'Yes?' he threw over his shoulder.

'I am John Tradescant, gardener to the king.' John followed him. 'I was planting my headright up the river when the Powhatan saved me from starving. I lived with them for years. I have come to Jamestown to ask for clemency for Opechancanough.'

Sir William blinked at the extraordinary story and hesitated. 'Clemency?'

'He's an old man, and he could see no way forward for his people. If they had been allowed to settle fairly after the first uprising he would not have felt so driven. They're ready to make peace now, a lasting peace, if we could only give them the land they need.'

'You are a spokesman for them?' Sir William asked. 'You're on their side?'

Almost imperceptibly a couple of soldiers from the assembly doors edged a little closer.

'No,' John said. 'They have expelled me. I am an Englishman and as soon as I can I shall return to London. But I owe them a debt of gratitude. They took me in and they fed me when I was near to death of starvation. I should like to repay my debt to them and indeed, Sir William, I think they have not been treated fairly by us.'

The young man hesitated for only a moment, then he shook his head. 'This is a new country,' he said. 'We are exploring all the time, south and north and west. The Powhatan, and the other savages, have to know that this is our country now, and if they fight against us, if they break the peace, then death is the only response.'

'The peace was here before we arrived,' John said quickly. 'The country was here before we came. The Powhatan were here before we came. Some might say that it was their country.'

Sir William looked sharply at John. 'Then that man would be a traitor to England and the king of England,' he said. 'You say you were servant to the king himself. He's not a man who accepts half-loyalty, and neither do I.'

John thought for a moment of his long-distant court life and the king who could not distinguish between half-loyalty and play-acting and reality. 'I am faithful to the king,' he said. 'But it is a bad example to kill the king of the Powhatan. He should be like all kings – inviolate.'

'This is not a king,' Sir William said with sudden impatience. 'This is a savage. You insult His Majesty by the comparison. The person of a king is sacred, he stands only below God himself. This dirty old Indian is a savage and we shall hang him.'

He turned abruptly from John and walked away.

'He was a king to us only a few years ago,' John said staunchly. 'Pocahontas was a princess. She was invited to London and treated as a princess of royal blood. I know. I was there and I saw it. The Powhatan then were a free and equal people and their royal family was as sacred as ours.'

The governor shook his head. 'Not any more,' he said simply. 'They're less than animals to us now. And if you choose to go back to them, then tell them this: that there is no place for them in this country. Tell them they will have to go –' he gestured '– south or further west and keep on travelling. It's our land now and we won't share it.'

Autumn 1645, England

Hester received John's letter asking for his fare home in the second week of September. The sailor who brought it was given a penny for his trouble and some thin soup at the kitchen door. Hester took the letter into the rarities room – the tiny fire was burning in there and the light from the tall Venetian windows was good. But she also had a superstitious sense that this was the rarest thing of all – a letter from her husband.

It was crumpled from its resting place inside someone's jacket and grubby as if it had been dropped somewhere and forgotten for a little while. Hester looked at the folded outside of the paper and the tiny splash of wax which sealed it, as if she would read every inch of the paper as well as the message inside. Then she sat at the desk that was set in the window for the convenience of artists who might come to draw the specimens in the collection, and broke the seal.

> *Dear Wife,*
> *I hope this reaches you in good health and fortune. I am on my way to Jamestown after many months living in the forest.*

Hester paused. She had thought John was living in a planter's house, such as were illustrated in the books about Virginia. A little house made of half-sawn timbers with wood shingles for a roof. What could he mean about living in the forest?

> *I have no money. Please send a note of credit for me to draw twenty pounds for my board and lodging and journey home. I shall come home as soon as I receive the money.*

Hester raised her head from the smudged words. The Virginia venture had ended then, as she had said it would, in bankruptcy and disaster.

There was no profitable crop of tobacco. There was no refuge from the uncertainty of a country at war. John had failed completely, failed so badly that he could not even come home unless she sent him his passage money.

> *I trust you, Hester, and when I come home I shall thank you*
> *for your care of me and mine.*

Hester pressed her finger to her lips and then put it down, as if making a fingerprint in sealing wax on the J at the end of the letter. John was coming home to her. She found she cared not at all that he was coming home penniless, without plantation, or tobacco, or pride. She cared not at all that he was trapped in a foreign land and could not even earn his passage home. All that mattered was that John was coming home, at last.

She sat only for a few minutes in the light of the window and then she set to raising the money to send him at once. Twenty pounds was a substantial sum. Fortunately the letter had come in September, the very time for the sale of tulip bulbs, and the order for John Lambert had been despatched only a week before. Any day now she expected his payment.

Hester threw a shawl over her head and went out to the terrace. Johnnie was working with Joseph, lifting and labelling the tulip bulbs from their beds. When she called him and he looked up she saw his face was still dark with sorrow.

Johnnie's hero Prince Rupert had failed to keep Bristol for the royalists though he had promised his king he would hold it for months. The wildest rumour was circulating: that Rupert had played the king false on purpose. They were saying that he and his brother, the Elector Palatine, now eating his dinner in London at the expense of Parliament having stolidly changed his coat and abandoned his uncle, had conspired all along to have one brother on each side so that they would profit whichever side won. Some people even said that Rupert hoped for the throne of England himself.

Ever since the news had come in of the fall of Bristol Johnnie had come down to breakfast with red eyes, and he had been quiet and moody all the day. When Hester wanted him for work in the garden she had to find him first, and half the time he would be down at the little lake, sitting in the rowing boat, adrift in the middle, slumped in despair over the dripping oars.

'How are the tulips?' she asked.

He nodded, as if he could not take joy even in them. 'They've done well. For every bulb that went in, we are raising three. It's been a good year for tulips, if for nothing else.'

Joseph nodded. 'I've never seen such a crop,' he said. 'Something's going right at least.'

'More than one thing,' Hester said. She tied the ends of the shawl crosswise around her waist and thought it felt like a tight and loving embrace. 'I have a letter here from Virginia.'

The shadow left Johnnie's face and he jumped to his feet from the bed of tulips. 'He's coming home?'

'He's coming home,' she assented. 'At last.'

The waiting was the hardest time of all. She had the money from John Lambert for his order of tulips, and then she took some old Roman coins from the rarities room and offered them for sale to a London goldsmith. The price he gave her was little more than theft but Hester realised that portable treasures were flooding on to the market as one grand family after another tried to survive the war years. She went to Alexander Norman to borrow the rest of the money and took the whole amount to the goldsmith who was known to give and receive credit for Virginia. He signed a note of credit for twenty pounds to John Tradescant by name and then Hester had to take it down to the London docks and find a ship sailing to Virginia.

A vessel was waiting to go, almost ready to cast off: the *Makepeace*, going to Virginia by the southern route and stopping at the Sugar Islands.

'I have to see the captain,' Hester said to one of the sailors. She was jostled by a family throwing their bundles on board and pushing their way towards the gangplank. 'Or a trustworthy gentleman.'

'We've got a brace of vicars,' the man said rudely. 'And half a dozen cavaliers. Take your pick.'

'I need a gentleman to assist me,' Hester said stoutly. 'I shall see one of the clerical gentlemen.'

The sailor laughed, turned his head and shouted below. Hester smoothed her cape and wished that she had brought Johnnie with her, or even allowed Alexander Norman to come too. Eventually a white-haired man looked down from the ship's side and said quietly, as if he would not raise his voice over the din of the ship, 'I am the Reverend Walter de Carey. May I help you, madam?'

Hester stepped quickly up the swaying gangplank and held out her hand. 'How do you do,⸱I am Mrs Tradescant, wife of John Tradescant of the Ark, Lambeth.'

He bowed over her hand. 'I am honoured,' he said.

'I am sorry to ask a favour of a stranger but my husband has been –' Hester paused for a moment. 'Plant collecting in Virginia and finds himself without money. I have a note of credit for him but I need to find a trustworthy gentleman to take it to Virginia and give it to him.'

The man smiled wearily. 'I am so little trusted that I have been expelled from my church and the blacksmith stands in my pulpit and tells my congregation what revelation he has gleaned that week from his forge fire,' he said. 'I was twenty years in my vicarage and I baptised every single one of those young men and women who now tell me that I am in league with the Antichrist and a worshipper of the whore of Babylon. *They* would not call me a trustworthy man.'

Mutely, Hester held out the sealed and folded paper. 'If you were twenty years in the vicarage and a good parish priest then you are the man for me,' she said. 'These are hard times of change for us all. Will you help me try to bring my family back together? This is my husband's passage money home.'

He hesitated for only a moment and then he took the paper. 'Forgive me, I am too absorbed in my own sorrows. I will take the paper; but how will I find your husband?'

'He'll find you,' Hester said with certainty. 'He'll be waiting for this. All you have to do is to tell people in Jamestown that you are looking for him and he will find you. Whereabouts are you going in Virginia?'

'I hope to settle there and found a school,' the vicar said. 'The times are against men who believe in the king and God in this country. I trust that the new world will be a refuge for men of steady faith. Half this ship is filled with men like me, who cannot bear the new rule of Parliament and the wild heresies of madmen and self-taught preachers and the like in our own churches.'

'My husband left at the outbreak of the war,' Hester said. 'He could not bear to watch the country being torn apart, and it was tearing him apart too.'

'He will come home to difficult times,' the vicar remarked. 'The fighting may be nearly over, but the bitterness of these years will not be easily restored. And what is to become of the king in the hands of such a crew?'

There was a shout from the bridge and an answering shout from the shore.

'I must go,' Hester said hurriedly. 'I do thank you for accepting the letter for John. He will do all he can to help you when he meets you, I know he will. He will be grateful.'

The vicar bowed. Hester turned for the gangplank and went down it as the lumpers on the dockside shouted to the sailors on the ship and finally cast off from shore.

'God speed,' Hester called to the ship. 'Tell him I am waiting.'

The vicar put his hand to his ear, so Hester waved with a smile on her face and said more quietly, so he would be certain not to hear, 'Tell him I love him.'

Autumn 1645, Virginia

John found that he had learned patience from the Powhatan, as well as the skill of living off the land. When he knew for certain that nothing he could do or say could save Opechancanough from death he went back to the farmer at the edge of the forest and agreed with him that he would work four days a week for his food and bed and a pittance of a wage, and three days of the week he would be free to go collecting in the near-virgin woods around the plantation.

Only a year before he would have been irritable, longing for the ship to come to release him from this service so that he could go home. But John found a sense of peace. He felt this was an interlude between his life with Suckahanna and the Powhatan, and the return – which must be a difficult experience – to Hester and the Ark at Lambeth.

In the days when he worked in the fields he was employed in harvesting the tobacco crop, taking the leaves to the drying sheds, baling them up and then loading them on to the ships which stopped at the little quay as their last port of call before setting off across the Atlantic.

In the days when he was free to roam he took his duckskin satchel, now properly cleaned, and went out into the woods with nothing more than a knife, a trowel, a bow across his shoulder and a couple of arrows in his quiver. It was a secret life he lived once he was out of sight of the planter's house. As soon as he reached the shelter of the trees he stopped and shed his heavy clothes and kicked off his painful shoes. He wrapped them and hid them in a tree, just as Suckahanna the little girl used to do with her servant's gown, and then he went barefoot and naked but for his buckskin through the forest and felt himself to be a free man once again.

Even after his years in the wilderness he had not lost his sense of awe at the strangeness and beauty of this country. He longed to bring it home entire, but he forced himself to choose the best of the shrubs and trees that he found on his long, loping surveys. He found a type of daisy that he thought had never been seen before, a big-flowered daisy with curious petals. He dug up half a dozen roots and packed them into damp soil, hoping they would survive until he had a ship for home. He took cuttings of the vine which Suckahanna had planted at his doorstep all that long time ago. He recognised it now. It was a favourite of hers: a sweet woodbine which some people called honeysuckle, but growing here with long scarlet flowers like fingers. He had a new convolvulus which he would name for himself, 'Tradescantia'. He found a foxglove which was like the English variety but strongercoloured and bigger in shape. He potted up a Virginian yucca, a Virginian locust tree, a Virginian nettle tree. He found a Virginian mulberry which reminded him of the silkworms and the mulberry trees at Oatlands Palace. He found a wonderful pink spiderwort, the only flower his father had put his own name to, and kept the corms dry and safe, hoping that they would grow in memory of his father. He dug up the dry roots of Virginian roses, certain that they would grow differently alongside their English cousins if he could only get them safe home to Lambeth.

Specimen after specimen he brought back to the little farmhouse and heeled in the growing plants into his nursery beds and laid the seeds in sand or rice to keep them dry. Plant after plant he brought in to add to the Lambeth collection. And as he added a new tree, the Virginian maple, or a new flower, the yellow willow herb, or a new herb, Virginian parsley, he realised that he would bring back to England an explosion of strangeness. If the country had been at peace and ready to attend to its gardens he would have been hailed as a worker of miracles, a greater plantsman and botanist even than his father.

He believed that he thought of nothing but his plants on these long expeditions when he was gone from dawn to dusk and sometimes from dawn till dawn, when he slept in the woods despite the cold winds which warned of the change of season. But somewhere in his heart and in his mind he was saying farewell: to Suckahanna the girl, whose innocence he had prized so highly, to Suckahanna the young woman he had loved, and to Suckahanna the proud, beautiful woman who had taken him into her heart and into her bed and in the end sent him away.

John said goodbye to her, and goodbye to the forest that she had loved and shared with him, and by the time the *Makepeace* sailed by

322

the end of the pier and went upriver to dock at Jamestown, John had said his farewells and was ready to leave.

He had half a dozen barrels of seeds and roots packed in sand. He had two barrels of saplings planted in shallow earth and watered by hand every day. He left them on the end of the pier ready for collection and paddled the canoe upriver to Jamestown to see if this latest ship had brought him a message and the money from Hester.

He hardly expected it. It could be this ship or a later one. But it was part of John's ritual of saying farewell to Suckahanna and making a new troth with Hester that he should be on the quayside to greet every ship, to show his trust that Hester would work as fast as she could to get the money to him. Their plan should not miscarry through his fault.

There was the usual crowd, shouting greetings and offering goods and rooms for hire. There was the usual anarchy of arrival: goods thrown on the quayside, children squealing with excitement, friends greeting each other, deals being struck. John stood up on a capstan and shouted over the heads of the crowd: 'Anyone with a message for John Tradescant?'

No-one replied at first so he shouted again and again like a coster-monger bawling out his wares. Then a white-haired man, looking frail and sick, came down the gangplank with one eye on his sea chest of belongings and lifted his head and said:

'I!'

'Praise God,' John said and jumped down from his vantage point, and knew at the same time the plummet of disappointment that now there was nothing more to stay for, and he must leave Suckahanna's land, just as he had left her.

He pushed through the crowd with a smile of greeting on his face. 'I am John Tradescant.'

'I am the Reverend Walter de Carey. Your wife trusted me with a letter for you.'

'Was she well?'

The older man nodded. 'She looked well. A woman of some courage, I should imagine.'

John thought of Hester's stubborn determination. 'Above rubies,' he said shortly. He opened the letter and saw at once that she had done as he asked. He had only to go to the Virginia Company offices and claim his twenty pounds, Hester had paid the money for him to a London goldsmith and the deed attested to it.

'I thank you,' he said. 'Now, is there any service I can do for you? Do you have somewhere to stay? Can I help you with your bags?'

'If you could help me carry this sea chest,' the man said hesitantly. 'I had thought there would be some porters or servants . . .'

'This is Virginia,' John warned him. 'They're all freeholders here.'

Winter 1645, England

In October Frances and Alexander Norman came upriver to Lambeth to stay for two nights. Hester urged them to stay longer but Alexander said he dared not leave his business for too long, the war must be coming to an end, every day he was sending out new consignments of gunpowder barrels and there were rumours that Basing House had fallen to Cromwell's army at last.

It was not that it was such a strategic point, not like Bristol – the second city of the kingdom – which Prince Rupert had lost only the month before. But it was a place which had captured people's imagination for its stubborn adherence to the king. When Johnnie knew that Rupert was dismissed from the king's service, Basing House became his second choice. It was to Basing House where he planned to run and enlist. Even Hester, with memories of a court which were not all of play-acting and folly but which also had moments of great beauty and glamour, longed to know that whatever else changed in the kingdom Basing House still held for King Charles.

It was owned by the Marquess of Winchester, who had renamed it Loyalty House, and locked the gates when the country around him went Parliamentarian. That defiance seemed to Hester a more glorious way to spend the war than gardening at Lambeth and selling tulips to Parliamentarians. Inigo Jones, who had known Johnnie's grandfather and worked with him for the Duke of Buckingham, was safe behind the strong defences of his own design at Basing House, the artist Wenceslaus Hollar, a friend of the Tradescants, and dozens of others known to Hester had taken refuge there. There were rumours of twenty Jesuit priests in hiding and a giant of seven feet tall. The marchioness herself and her children were in the siege and she had refused free passage out of the besieged house but decided to stay with her lord. She had engraved every window pane of the house with the troth '*Aimez Loyauté*' so that as long as the house stood and the panes were unbroken it would carry a record that one place at least was always unwaveringly for Charles.

'I am as bad as Johnnie, for I long to be there,' Hester confessed to Alexander. They were seated either side of a small fire in the parlour. In the windowseat Frances and Johnnie were playing cards for matchsticks. 'These are the people I knew from girlhood. It feels wrong to be here in comfort while they are facing the guns.'

'They were freer to choose than you,' Alexander said comfortingly. 'You gave your word to John to protect the Ark. And anyway, you have played your part. When the royalist uprising came to your door you lent your horse and did the best you could.'

Hester snorted. 'You know how willing that was!'

'Don't fall in love with the cause just because it is losing,' Alexander warned her. 'He was a reckless and foolish king before he was doomed. John went away rather than serve him, and I've always admired your determination to survive this war and not to join it. Just because it is coming to an end is no reason to want to enlist. It is a foolish man who loves a lost cause only because it is lost.'

Hester nodded. 'Yes,' she said. 'But Basing House is like a fairy story.'

'There will be no romance ending,' Alexander said grimly. 'Cromwell has brought up the heavy guns. There can be no ending but defeat. No walls could stand against them forever.'

Alexander was right, and the news came through the next day, before he and Frances left. Basing House had fallen and a hundred men and women had been killed. Even the engraved window panes were not allowed to survive. Cromwell ordered the house to be destroyed and nothing was left standing.

It was only one battle in the many which now seemed to go inexorably the way of Parliament. Hester's greatest buyer of tulips, John Lambert, was praised in all the reports for being a quick and daring cavalry commander, the Parliament horse were unstoppable. The army under Cromwell had learned their business at last and combined soldierly discipline with an absolute dedication to their cause. They believed they were freeing the country of tyranny and bringing in a new rule of law and justice. They fought as men will fight when their hearts are in the fighting, and there were few underpaid, half-hearted, badly led royal armies that could stand against them.

The king retreated to the hard-drinking, rich-living city of Oxford and the comfort of court life and amused himself as well as he could. His only recognition of his continual defeats was to blame his generals.

Prince Rupert had been dismissed for failing to hold Bristol and nothing he or his friends could say could gain him a fair hearing from the king he had served so faithfully.

It was a bitter winter, colder than any in living memory. Frances wrote to her stepmother that she had been skating on the Thames below the Tower and that if the freeze continued she would take a sledge and travel up the frozen river to visit. Hester, wrapped in John Tradescant's old travelling cape and with a hat made from his Russian furs, went out every morning to brush the snow from the branches of the precious trees to prevent them from breaking under the weight of snow and ice, and sat every night over a fire made of fallen wood and little twigs, dined on potato soup and wondered when spring would come and if it would bring her husband home.

Winter 1646, Barbados

John's ship took the southerly route home and revictualled and took on cargo at Barbados. John, very conscious that he was bringing home a fortune only in seeds and roots which would take an unreliable year before they could be propagated and sold, strolled on the quayside and let it be known that he was prepared to execute errands for the wealthy planters for a small consideration. While the ship was loaded with barrels of sugar and rum John walked inland, past the sugar plantations where gangs of black men and women slaves were bent over the new plants, seeding and weeding the crop while white overseers lounged on their horses with long-tongued hunting whips ready to lash out. John found his way into the woods where the fields stopped and kept his eyes open for new plants.

It was returning from one of these walks, with a couple of seedlings damp in his pocket, that John met a man riding homeward on the road.

'I heard of you,' the man greeted him informally. 'You're Tradescant, the king's gardener, aren't you?'

John uncovered his head and made a little bow. 'Yes, sir. And you?'

'Sir Henry Hants. A planter, these are my fields. I have a little garden of my own, you might like to have a look at some of my things.'

'Indeed I would,' John said eagerly.

'Oh, come for dinner then,' the man said. 'Stay the night.'

He led the way along the lane towards a large white house, as grand as the queen's manor at Wimbledon. John blinked at the opulence of the building, at the best wax candles set at every window so that the house twinkled like a beacon in the soft twilight, and then at the rush of black servants who came running when they heard the sound of the master's horse.

Sir Henry dismounted and let the horse go, secure in the knowledge that two grooms would catch the reins, as he led the way indoors.

There was a terrace at the back of the house and Sir Henry led John through the gleaming hall where the white walls were laden with rich oil paintings, to where the last of the sun was shining on the terrace. A lady gestured languidly from a sofa. 'My wife, Lady Hants,' Sir Henry said briefly. 'Never gets up.'

John bowed and was rewarded by a faint wave.

'Now, let me show you my garden,' Sir Henry said eagerly.

John had been hoping for tropical rarities and was hard put not to show his disappointment. Sir Henry had poured wealth and labour into making a classic English garden in the most unlikely of circumstances. There was a smooth lawn, as good as the king's bowling green at Oatlands. There was a perfect knot garden with low hedges of bay enclosing white stones. John, looking a little more closely, saw that they were not stones but the most exquisite white shining shells.

'Cowries,' Sir Henry said gloomily. 'Cost me a fortune. But actually easier to get than proper English gravel.'

There was a flower garden, planted exclusively with English flowers and shaded with a thatched roof suspended from stakes at each corner. 'Sun's too hot for them otherwise,' Sir Henry complained. 'And the ground's too dry. I keep three boys watering almost constantly all day, and even then I can never grow more than a dozen daffodils every year.'

There was an orchard. John saw that the sun-loving fruits would do well in such a climate. 'I can't grow apples to taste like the ones in Kent.'

They came full circle back to the house. 'You only plant English plants?' John asked carefully.

'Of course,' the man said briskly. 'Why would I want these damn ugly savage flowers?'

'I have a great liking for new plants myself,' John remarked.

'You're a fool,' the man said. 'If you lived here you would find you were longing for the sight of a proper English wood and proper English flowers again. I fight and fight and fight against this soil and against the heat to grow a proper garden.'

John nodded neutrally. 'I see that it takes a very great deal of labour,' he said.

His host nodded and mounted the terrace again. Without a word he put out his hand. At once the black woman presiding behind a great bowl of punch poured a glass, handed it to another woman who put it on a silver tray and bowed and presented it to Sir Henry. John was reminded of the silent, perfect service of the royal court and accepted a glass of his own with a word of thanks.

'Don't thank them,' Sir Henry corrected him swiftly. 'Don't give one word of thanks for service in my house, if you please, sir. It has taken me years to knock some sense of obedience and decorum into them. I don't want them thinking they're doing me a favour by working for me.'

Dinner was a miserable affair of lavish food and the best wines but Lady Hants, half-reclining in her chair at one end of the table, said not one word for the whole of the meal, and her husband drank steadily and deeply of rum and water, becoming more gloomy and irascible with every glass.

One of the slaves among the half a dozen waiting at the table was wearing a strange headdress: a triangular plate bolted over her mouth with straps running from both sides and over her head to keep it in place, a great buckle at the back to keep it pressed tight against her mouth and a padlock to fasten the buckle. John found he could hardly drag his eyes away from the mask-like appearance of the woman, the dark, tragic eyes, and then the sharply geometric shape on the mouth.

'What's the matter with you?' Sir Henry asked irritably. 'Oh! Are you looking at Rebecca? She's been stealing food, haven't you, Becky? Tasting it as she cooks, dirty bitch. So she'll have nothing to eat at all for a couple of days, nothing in her mouth but what I put there.' He gave a shout of laughter and a wink to John at the sexual innuendo. 'Are you sorry now that you tasted my soup, Becky?'

Silently the woman bowed her head.

'Good, good,' Sir Henry said, cheered by the sombre grief of her silence, and waved for another glass of rum and water.

A woman slave escorted John to his bedroom and stood, as still as an obedient dog, at the doorway.

'You can go,' John said, careful not to thank her.

'Sir Henry say you can have me if you want,' she said in carefully spoken English.

John was taken aback. 'Er – I don't –'

'You want a man?'

'No!'

She dropped her dark eyes, a world of despair hidden by the downsweep of her lashes. 'You want a child?'

'No!'

She waited. 'What you want to do then?' she asked wearily, dreading some demand more vile than she had faced before.

'I want nothing!' John exclaimed. 'Just to sleep.'

She bowed. 'If he ask you – you tell him I said you can have me.'

'I'll tell him you were very, er, generous,' John corrected himself. 'Obedient.'

'Yes, sir,' she said dully. 'I am obedient.'

In the morning Sir Henry was in a better temper. Over breakfast he asked John about his own garden and about the treasures of the Ark. 'I could send you some things,' he said pleasantly. 'Things I pick up here. If you like savage things.'

'I do,' John said. 'I do indeed. And if there are any plants from England that you desire I could send them out to you. You could grow vines here very well, I would have thought.'

'Could you take a note of credit for me and buy some carpets for me?' Sir Henry asked. 'I want some Turkey carpets for the hall.'

'I should be delighted to do so,' John said. 'And anything else you require.'

'We'll start with this,' Sir Henry said cautiously. 'I'll give you the note of credit and you can buy some carpets and some glass for me, and then I'll send you a few hogsheads of sugar and you can see if you can obtain a better price for me than my normal agent. And then you can send me some more goods. Rarities are no use locked up in a cabinet, you know. They should be traded.'

John nodded. 'I should be glad to do a little trading,' he said. 'My father's rarities have to stay together in the collection we have made. But if you shoot any strange birds I should be glad of their skins and their feathers.'

'I've got some trophies,' Sir Henry said without any great interest. 'I could sell them to you.'

'I have no money until I am at home,' John said awkwardly.

'Note of credit,' Sir Henry said equably. 'We all do it by notes of credit all the time. Just as well there are no damned thieving Jews to redeem the notes before the sugar crop is in, eh?'

By the time John sailed he had a new shrub, a most curious and delightful plant which the islanders called the tree of life because it acted like a living thing, shrinking away when touched. He had a couple of roots of the cabbage tree, and a dozen skins and feathers including a rather fine specimen of the West Indian kingfisher which Sir Henry donated for free. 'Just do me some decent business, when you are in England,' he grumbled. 'An honest agent in London is as rare as a virtuous woman. Which is to say, rare enough to put in your collection.'

'I shall be delighted,' John said politely and watched Sir Henry recede into the distance without any regret as the ship slipped her ropes and drifted away from the shore.

Spring 1646, London

It was a homecoming as ordinary as any man might wish. John hired a carter at London dock to carry his barrels of seeds and roots, the two barrels of saplings, the chest of Barbados goods, and sat up on the wooden seat at the front of the cart as they jolted up the frozen lanes to Lambeth.

'What's the news of the war?' John asked.

'You'll have heard that Chester surrendered?'

'No?'

'Where've you been?'

'Virginia,' John said. 'Is the king truly defeated?'

'Humbled to dust,' the carter said feelingly. 'And now pray God we can see some peace and order in this land and that crew of parasites run back to Rome where they came from.'

John tried to say 'Amen', but found the word did not come out. 'I'll pray for peace,' he said. 'I've had enough of war for a lifetime.'

'And so have we all. And for some the war lasted longer than their lifetimes. How many Englishmen d'you think have died to persuade the king that we want to be governed by Englishmen and pray to God and not to bishops?'

John shook his head.

'Thousands,' the man said glumly. 'Hundreds of thousands. How many more died of plague and hardship because of this damned struggle?'

John shook his head again.

'Thousands more. And how many families d'you think have lost a son or a brother or a father?'

John shook his head in silence.

'Every single family in the land,' the carter said solemnly. 'This has been a wicked, wicked war, a war without an enemy because we were fighting and killing ourselves.'

Hester was in the stable yard, tossing hay over the door to the horse, when she heard the rumble of the wheels and saw the cart rock as it rounded the corner into the yard. For a moment she saw only the barrels at the back and thought that John had sent some goods ahead, and then she dropped the pitchfork with a clatter on the cobbles as she recognised the man who got down from the carter's seat and turned to face her.

He looked older than she remembered, and weary. The bear-grease stain had faded from his skin but he was still deeply tanned from the hard sun and wind. He had lost a couple of teeth during his time of near-starvation, and he had grown a brown moustache and beard which were flecked with grey. His eyes were sad, an unmistakable sadness which made Hester want to hold him and comfort him without even asking what had grieved him so. He looked as if he had lost something very dear to him and Hester wondered what blade in the new world had cut him so deep.

'John?' she said quietly.

He stepped forwards a little. 'Hester?'

She realised that she was wearing her oldest working clothes, men's thick boots and a brown scarf over her hair which was pinned carelessly on the back of her head. She could not have looked more functional if she had tried. She whisked her scarf off her head and tried not to seem embarrassed. She had always tried to be above vanity, especially with this man who had married his first wife for love and lost her while she was still in her youth and beauty.

Hester brushed the hay from her coat. 'You are welcome home,' she said.

He took two steps towards her and opened his arms to her and she went towards him and felt the intense relief of a man's embrace after more than three years of loneliness.

'Do you forgive me?' he said urgently into her hair. She smelled of hay from the stable and the clean, familiar smell of soap from her skin, and lavender from her linen. 'Can you forgive me for leaving you so unkindly and then disappearing like that?'

'It's you that should forgive me for refusing to go with you,' she said quickly. 'And I regretted it, John.'

He tightened his grip around her. 'I have been unfaithful,' he said quickly, to get the confession over and done with before he was tempted to lie. 'I am sorry.'

She rested her head against his shoulder. 'That's the past,' she said. 'And in another country. You have come home to me, haven't you?'

'Yes,' he said.

She craned her neck to look up into his sad, weary face and realised that he was wearing the same bewildered expression of pain as when they had first met and he had not recovered from the loss of his first wife. 'What happened, John?'

For a moment he was about to answer her, then they were interrupted by the carter. 'I can't unload these on my own,' he said flatly. 'And I can't afford to wait here all day while you two kiss.'

Hester turned with a laugh. 'I'll find Joseph to help you.' She rang the bell which hung at the corner of the yard. 'You go in, John, you must be frozen, and Johnnie will be longing to see you. He'll be in the kitchen eating his breakfast.'

John hesitated at the kitchen door, suddenly shy and hardly knowing how to approach his son who had been a boy of nine when he left and was now a youth of twelve. He opened the door slowly and put his head around it.

Johnnie was seated at the scrubbed kitchen table, his bowl of porridge before him, absently spooning it into his mouth, his eyes on his book propped on his mug of small ale. John took in the sight of his son, the fair head with the cropped golden hair, the light hazel eyes, the long nose in the long face and the sweet innocent mouth. You could see his mother in his colouring and the joy in his face, but he was every inch a Tradescant.

He glanced up as the draught from the half-open door blew into the kitchen and put down his book as if he was about to greet his stepmother. Then he saw it was a man looking in at him, and he hesitated.

Very slowly he rose to his feet, very cautiously he looked. John opened the door fully and stepped into the doorway.

'Father?' Johnnie asked uncertainly. 'Is it really you?'

John took two swift steps across the kitchen floor and wrapped his boy in a tight hug and inhaled, half-weeping, half-kissing the top of his silky head. 'It's me. Praise God I am home with you, Johnnie, and you safe and well.'

Hester came in behind him and hung her cape on the hook. 'Did you recognise him?' she demanded.

Father and son answered 'No!' together and then laughed together. John made himself release his son, forced himself to let the boy go.

'He is grown,' Hester said proudly 'And as much help to me in the garden as any man could be. And he is a scholar, he keeps the rarities and garden accounts now, and the planting records.'

'And school?' John demanded.

A shadow crossed Hester's face. 'The school has been closed this last year. The teacher was dismissed, some quarrel about theology. So we do the best we can at home.'

'And where is Frances?' John asked, looking round for her.

Something in Hester's silence made him stop, fear gripping him. 'Where is Frances? Hester, tell me. Please God, tell me that she is not lost.'

'No! No!' She rushed to reassure him. 'She is well, in great beauty and well. It's just . . . you were not here and I did not know you would return. I didn't know what I should do for the best and I was at my wits' end to keep her safe . . .'

'Where is she?' John shouted.

'She's married!' Johnnie interrupted. 'Safe at the Tower with Alexander Norman.'

'She married Alexander Norman?' John demanded.

Hester nodded, her eyes on his face.

'Not my father's executor? Not my uncle? Not that Alexander Norman?'

Hester gave the smallest confirming nod.

'You married my daughter off to a man old enough to be her father? A friend of her grandfather?'

'I did.'

'It was her choice,' Johnnie said stoutly. 'And she is happy.'

'By God, this is most ill-done!' John swore. 'I can't believe it! When did this happen?'

'A year ago,' Hester said quietly.

'Why?' he asked blankly. 'Why did you let it happen? Why did you not write to ask for my permission?'

She turned away from him and tied her house apron around her waist as if she was weary of the whole conversation. 'I could not be sure of keeping her safe,' she said. 'Before Cromwell had the ruling of the army no woman was safe on the streets. I never knew whether the king would retake London or no and then there would have been the cavaliers to face as well. The apprentices rioted every other night, I could not let her step out of the front door.'

'You could have taken her to Oatlands!' he flung at her.

She turned at that. 'Oatlands!' she exclaimed bitterly. 'What do you think the palaces are like now? Oatlands was Prince Rupert's headquarters! D'you think I could keep a pretty girl safe in a barracks? She was as much at risk there as in the stews of the City.'

'You could have put her on a ship to me!'

She blazed up at that. 'And where were you? I had two letters from you in three years, one parcel of Indian goods and one consignment of plants. What was I to imagine? I didn't even know if you were alive or dead. I had to take all the decisions on my own and I did what I thought was the best. Alexander offered her a home and promised me that he would love her and keep her safe. And she wanted to marry him. She accepted him on her own account. And they are happy, anyone can see that.'

'I shall get her home,' John swore. 'I shall have the marriage annulled. She is not to be his wife.'

'She is expecting his baby.' Hester spoke calmly as her heart hammered in her ears. 'She will come home for the confinement, and she visits us often. But she will not leave her husband, even at your bidding, John.'

He flung out of the room at that and she heard him stride across the hall. Johnnie shot one scared look at her and she put her hand on his shoulder. There was a great bellow from the rarities room: 'Mother of God! Where are the rarities? What have you done?'

Hester turned Johnnie on his heel and pushed him gently towards the kitchen door. 'Wrap up warmly and go and sweep the snow off the trees,' she said.

'What will you do?'

'I shall have to explain to him how we live now. It will be hard for him to understand.'

'Then he should never have gone away,' Johnnie said.

They had a bitter row in the half-empty room. John in his horror at the changes could not even hear that the finest of the rarities were safely in hiding. Every confession that Hester had to make, that she had sold one or other of the treasures for food, merely heightened his anger by a further notch.

'You have betrayed me!' he yelled at her. 'You have betrayed my trust, my sacred trust in you. You have sold my treasures, you have sold my daughter!'

'What was I to do?' Hester shouted back, as angry as him. 'You were gone. This summer I was going to tell your son that I feared you must be dead. I had to survive without you. I had to manage somehow. We had one true friend in the whole world and Frances loves and trusts him. She wasn't sold. He took her without a dowry.'

'Sweet God! Am I supposed to be grateful for this charity? He was a friend of her grandfather! A man in his dotage!'

'And where have you been?' Hester turned from the window and suddenly rounded on John. 'For all that you are full of what I have done and failed to do, what do you have to show for three years away? What treasures did you bring back? A barrel of plants and a handful of feathers! The last coins I sold were to buy your passage home when Johnnie and I had not tasted meat for weeks! How dare you accuse me of failing you! It is you that have failed me!'

'You have no idea! You have no idea how I have lived and what I have been trying to do.'

'With some woman? Some Jamestown drab in an inn? Have you been bunked up all these years, spending our money and doing nothing?'

'I've been in the woods, I've been searching to understand what I should do –'

'And the woman?'

'What of her?'

'Her name. Tell me her name.'

'Suckahanna,' he said unwillingly.

Hester screamed in shock and clapped her hand over her mouth. 'You have bedded an Indian? A savage?'

His hand flew out before he knew it, he slapped her face hard. She jerked back and her head banged against the knob of the shutter with a horrible thud. She dropped without another sound, knocked unconscious. For a moment he thought he had killed her and knew a fierce, terrible joy that the woman who had abused Suckahanna should be silenced at once, a feeling instantly succeeded by complete remorse. He dropped to his knees beside her and lifted her up from the floor.

'Hester, wife, forgive me . . .'

Her eyelids fluttered and then opened. 'Take your hands from me,' she spat. 'You are a foul adulterer. I won't have you touch me.'

Hester made up her bed in Frances's old room and moved her clothes out of the master bedroom that night. She cooked a modest dinner for John, she produced a beautifully pressed suit of clothes and set about sewing him a new shirt. She behaved in every way like an obedient and dutiful wife. But he had knocked the love out of her with one impulsive blow, and he did not know how to get it back.

It was as if the heart had gone out of her and out of the house altogether. The garden was neglected, the topiary and the knot garden hedges were growing out and losing their shape. The gravel on the paths was no defence against the constantly springing weeds. The warm nursery beds by the house had not been prepared with sieved earth for the coming of the new season as they should have been. The fruit trees had not been properly pruned in the autumn. Even the chestnuts had not all been planted and grown on ready for sale in the early summer.

'I couldn't do it all,' Hester said stubbornly as she saw John look critically over the garden from the terrace. 'I had no boys, I had no money. We all did what we could but this garden takes a dozen men to keep. Joseph and Johnnie and Frances and I couldn't do it.'

'Of course not, I understand,' John said and he turned away to brood in the half-empty rarities room, and walk with his limping stride around the frozen garden.

Johnnie unpacked the Virginian saplings and left them in their barrels by the house wall. The ground was too hard to dig them in. One of them had died from the salt winds of the voyage but the other four looked strong and likely to put out green leaves when the weather improved.

'What are they?' Johnnie asked.

His father's face lit up. 'Tulip trees, they call them. They grow as round and shapely as a horse chestnut but they have great flowers, white, waxy flowers, as big as your head. I have seen them grow to such a height and breadth –' He broke off. Suckahanna had showed it to him. 'And these are maple trees.'

Johnnie rolled the big barrels of seeds and roots into the orangery and set to work unpacking them and planting them up in pots of sieved earth ready to be set outside and watered when the spring frosts ended. John watched him, disinclined to work himself, horribly quick to criticise when his son dropped a seed or was clumsy with a root.

'Have you never been taught how to do this properly?' he demanded irritably.

His son looked up at him, his resentment veiled. 'I am sorry, sir,' he said formally.

Hester appeared in the doorway and took in the scene in one quick glance. 'Can I have a word with you, husband?' she asked, her voice very even.

John walked towards her and she drew him out of earshot, into the garden.

'Please don't correct Johnnie so harshly,' she said. 'He's not used to it, and indeed he is a good boy and a very hard worker.'

'He is my son,' John pointed out. 'I shall teach him what is right.'

She bowed her head. 'Of course,' she said coldly. 'You must do as you wish.'

John waited in case she should say any more and then he flung himself away from her and stamped into the house, his feet hurting in his boots, knowing himself to be in the wrong, not knowing how to make things right.

'I shall go to London,' he said. 'I shall complete my commissions for Sir Henry. It's clear that we have to make our fortune some other way than by the garden and the rarities since the rarities are gone and the garden half-ruined.'

Hester went back into the orangery. Johnnie raised his eyebrows at her.

'We all have to become acquainted with each other again,' she said as equably as she could. 'Let me help you with that.'

For days John walked around the grounds, trying to accustom himself to the smaller scale of England, trying to accept a horizon which seemed so very close, trying to enjoy his continuing ownership of twenty acres when he had been free to run in a forest which went on forever, trying to be glad of a plain, forthright wife and a bright, fair son and not to think of the dark beauty of Suckahanna and the animal grace of her boy. He arranged the Indian goods in the half-empty rarities room, feeling the arrow head come so easily into his hand, rubbing the buckskin shirt between his finger as if something of the warmth of Suckahanna's skin might still linger.

He made a little money on his commission for Sir Henry and he bought a couple of fine paintings, crated them up and sent them out to him. When the ship came back, in four months' time or so, it would bring him another note of credit and perhaps some more barrels of sugar for John to sell. He drew some satisfaction from being able to make some money, even in these difficult times, but he thought he might never feel a sense of freedom or joy ever again.

Hester did the only thing she knew how to do, and tackled the practical problems of the situation. She asked him to walk with her to Lambeth and took him straight to the best bootmaker still working in the village. He measured John's feet and then looked at the bare soles with horror. 'You have feet like a Highlander, if you'll excuse me saying so.'

'I had to go barefoot. I was in Virginia,' John said shortly.

'No wonder all your boots pinch,' the cobbler said. 'You have no need of boots at all.'

'Yes he does,' Hester remarked. 'He's a gentleman in England and he'll have a pair of boots of best leather, a pair of working boots and a pair of shoes. And they'd better not pinch.'

'I haven't the leather,' the man said. 'They don't drive the cattle to Smithfield, the tanners can't get the hides, I can't get the leather. You've been in Virginia too long if you think you can order shoes like the old days.'

Hester took the cobbler by the elbow and there was a brief exchange of words and the clink of a coin.

'What did you offer him?' John asked as they emerged from the dark shop into the bright March sunlight.

Hester grimaced and prepared for a quarrel. 'You won't like it, John, but I promised to supply the leather from your father's rarities. It was only some leather painted with a scene of the Madonna and Child. Not very well done, and completely heretical. We would invite the troops upon us if we ever showed it. And the man is right, he can't get leather for your shoes otherwise.'

For a moment she thought he was going to flare up at her again.

'So am I to strut around London with Papistical images painted on my boots?' he asked. 'Won't they hang me for a Jesuit in hiding?'

'Not much of a disguise if you're going around with the Virgin Mary on your feet,' Hester pointed out cheerfully. 'No, the painting is almost worn off, and he'll use it on the inside.'

'We are using rare treasures as household goods? What kind of stewardship is this?'

'We are surviving,' Hester said grimly. 'Do you want boots that you can walk in or no?'

He paused. 'Do you swear that nothing else of any merit is missing from the collection?' he demanded. 'That it is safe in hiding as you say?'

'On my honour, and you can see it all for yourself if you cut down the tree and open the door. But John, you had best wait. It's not safe yet. They all say the king is defeated but they have said that before. He has his wife working against us in France, and the Irish to call on, and who knows what the Pope might order if the queen promises to hand over the country to Popery? The king cannot be defeated in battle, for all that they fight and fight. Even when he is down to his last man he is not defeated. He is still the king. They cannot defeat him. He has to decide to surrender.'

John nodded and they fell into stride together for the short walk home. 'I keep thinking. I keep wondering – perhaps I should go to him,' he said.

She stumbled at the thought of him returning to the court and to danger. 'Why? Why on earth would you go?'

'I feel almost that I owe him some service,' he said.

'You left the country to escape serving,' she reminded him.

He grimaced at her bluntness. 'It wasn't that simple,' he said. 'I didn't want to die for a cause I can't believe in. I didn't want to kill a man because like me he had half-heartedly joined, but on the other side. But if the king is ready for peace then I could serve him with a clear conscience. And I don't like to think of him alone at Oxford, without the queen and with the prince fled to Jersey, and no-one with him.'

'There's a whole crowd with him,' Hester said. 'Drinking themselves senseless every night and shaming Oxford with their behaviour. He is in the thick of company. And if he sees you he will only remember you and ask where you have been. If he wanted you he would have sent for you by now.'

'And has there been no word?'

She shook her head. 'Since they wanted us to serve under the Commission of Array there has been nothing,' she said. 'And they risked our lives for a lost cause then. There is nothing you can do for the king unless you can persuade him to come to terms with his people. Can you do that?'

'No.'

As soon as John's new boots were ready he put them on, dressed in his best suit and announced his intention of formally visiting his daughter in her new home. Hester and Johnnie, also dressed in their best, went with him in the boat downriver.

'Will he be angry?' Johnnie asked under the noise of the oars in the water.

'No,' Hester said. 'The moment he sees her she'll have him wrapped around her finger like always.'

Johnnie chuckled. 'Can we shoot the bridge?' he asked.

Hester hesitated. Timorous passengers would make the ferrymen leave them on the west side of Tower Bridge and walk round to rejoin their boat at the other side. The currents around the pillars of the bridge were terrifyingly swift and when the tide was on the ebb and the river was full, boats could overturn and people could drown. It was Johnnie's great passion to shoot the rapids and generally Hester would stay in the boat with him, her hands gripping the side, her knuckles white, and a smile firmly fixed on her face.

'Do what?' John asked and turned around.

'Shoot the bridge,' Johnnie replied. 'Mother lets me.'

John looked in surprise at his wife. 'You can't enjoy it?' he asked.

One glance at her face told him that she was terrified. 'Oh, I don't mind,' she said. 'Johnnie loves it.'

John gave a short bark of laughter. 'Then Johnnie can do it,' he said firmly. 'You and I will land at the Swan Stairs like Christians and Johnnie can meet us on the other side.'

'But I like Mother coming too!' Johnnie protested.

'That's as maybe,' John said firmly. 'But I'm home now, and you're not going to drown my wife to keep you company. You can shoot the bridge on your own, my boy.'

The ferryman set them ashore at the steps. John put his hand under Hester's elbow as they climbed to the top and turned to wave to Johnnie as he sat in the prow of the boat to gain full pleasure from the terrifying ride.

'Look at his face!' Hester exclaimed lovingly.

'You are too indulgent to him,' John said.

She hesitated. John was his father and the head of the household. Restoring the power to him was hard for her, just as regaining his position was for him. 'He's still only a boy,' she remarked. 'Not yet thirteen.'

'If he was in Virginia –' John started and then bit back the rest.

'Yes,' she said softly. 'But he isn't. He's a good boy and he has been courageous and faithful through these difficult years. If he was a planter's son, living in the wilds, then I dare say he would be a quite different

343

boy. But he is not. He is a boy who has had to have his childhood in the middle of a war and he has seen all of the adults around him most terribly afraid. You are right to restore the rules, John, but I won't have him blamed for not being something he has no business to be.'

He turned and faced her but she did not drop her gaze. She stared at him fiercely as if she did not care whether he beat her or sent her home in disgrace. Not for the first time John was reminded that he had married a redoubtable woman and, despite his temper, he remembered also that she was fiercely defending his son, just as she had fiercely defended the garden and the rarities.

'You're right,' he said, with the smile she loved. 'And I will be restored to my place at the head of the household. But I won't be a tyrant.'

She nodded at that, and when they strolled together to the other side of the bridge where the boat was waiting she slid her hand in the crook of his arm and John kept it there.

They paid the boatman and retraced their steps to the Tower. Alexander Norman's timber yard was beside the walls of the Tower on the grounds of a former convent. His house was built alongside, one of the long, thin townhouses pressed against the narrow street. Hester had feared that Frances would be unhappy without a garden, with little more than a dozen pots in the cobbled yard at the back which was overshadowed half the day from the stacks of wood in the timber yard next door. But already the house was draped in climbing roses and honeysuckle was growing up to the very windows, and every window had a bracket fixed outside and a square planting box nailed to the wall with a row of tulips waiting to bloom.

'I'd have no trouble guessing which house was hers,' John said grimly, glancing down the street at the other bare-fronted, bare-faced houses.

'That's nothing,' Johnnie said with pleasure. 'She has a herb garden out the back and an apple tree squashed against the back wall. She says she'll prune it to keep it small enough. She says she'll re-pot it every year and prune the roots too.'

John shook his head. 'She needs a dwarf apple tree,' he said. 'Perhaps if one could graft an apple sapling on to a shrub root it might grow small . . .'

Hester stepped forwards and knocked on the door. At once Frances opened it. 'Father!' she said, and slipped down the step, threw her arms around him and laid her head against his shoulder.

John almost recoiled from her touch. In the three years he had been away she had grown from a girl to a woman of nearly eighteen years, and now, with her slight body pressed against him, he could feel the hard swelling of her baby.

He stepped back to see her and his face softened. 'You're so like your mother,' he exclaimed. 'What a beauty you've become, Frances.'

'She's the very picture of my Jane.' Mrs Hurte emerged from the house and shook John and then Hester by the hand. She enveloped Johnnie in a breathtaking embrace but never stopped talking. 'The very picture of her. Every time I see her I think she has come back to us again.'

'Come inside,' Frances urged. 'You must be frozen. Did you shoot the bridge?'

'Father wouldn't let Mother come.'

Frances shot a brief approving look at her father. 'Quite right. Why should Mother risk drowning because you like it?'

'*She* likes it!' Johnnie protested.

'I swear I never said so,' Hester remarked.

Mrs Hurte surged outwards rather than into the house, took John by the arm and drew him aside. Hester silently admired the tactical skill of her stepdaughter. This was generalship as gifted as Oliver Cromwell's with his New Model Army. Mrs Hurte would change John's mind in favour of the match in two sentences of complaints. Both Hester and Frances strained their ears to hear her do it.

'You're home too late,' Mrs Hurte said reproachfully to John. 'This is a bad business, and you too late to prevent it.'

'I don't see that it is bad,' John remarked.

'A man of fifty-six and a girl of seventeen?' Mrs Hurte demanded. 'What life can they have together?'

'A good one.' John gestured to the pretty house and the tracery of carefully pruned rose branches. 'A boy of her own age could not hope to give her so much.'

'She should have been kept at her home.'

'In these times?' John asked. 'Where safer than beside the Tower?'

'And now expecting a baby?'

'The older the bridegroom, the sooner the better,' John rejoined swiftly. 'Why should you be so against it, Mother? It was a marriage for love. Your own daughter Jane had nothing less.'

She bit her lip at that. 'Jane brought a good dowry and you two were well matched,' she said.

'I will see that Frances is properly dowered when peace is restored and I can sell the Virginia plants and restore the rarities to their proper place,' John said firmly. 'I am trading in a small way with the West

Indies and I expect to see a profit on that very soon. And Frances *is* well-matched. Alexander is a good and faithful friend to this family and she loves him. Why should she not marry the man of her choice in these times when men and women are making their own choices every day? When this whole war has been fought for men and women to be free?'

Mrs Hurte smoothed her sombre gown. 'I don't know what Mr Hurte would have said.'

John smiled. 'He would have liked the house, and the business. Cooper for the ordnance in the middle of a war? Don't tell me that he wouldn't have loved that! Alexander is earning twelve pounds a year and that's before he draws his allowances! It's a fine match for the daughter of a man who has little to sell and most of his stock in hiding.'

Hester and Frances exchanged a hidden smile, turned and went into the house.

'That was clever,' Hester said approvingly to her stepdaughter.

Frances gave her a most unladylike wink. 'I know,' she said smugly.

Spring 1646

When the soil warmed in April and the daffodils came out in the orchard and the grass started growing and the boughs of the Tradescant trees were filled with birds singing, courting and nestbuilding, John strode round the brick chip paths in his new Papist boots and learned to love his garden again. He made a special corner for his Virginian plants and watched as the dried roots put up tiny green shoots and the unpromising dry seeds sprouted in their pots and could be transplanted.

'Will they do well here?' Johnnie asked. 'Is it not too cold for them?'

John leaned on his spade and shook his head. 'Virginia is a place of far greater extremes than here,' he said. 'Colder by far in winter, hotter in summer, and damp as a poultice for month after month in summer. I should think they will thrive here.'

'And what will sell the best, d'you think?' Johnnie asked eagerly. 'And what is the finest?'

'This.' John leaned forwards and touched the opening leaves of a tiny plant. 'This little aster.'

'Such a small thing?'

'It's going to be a great joy for gardeners, this one.'

'Why?' Johnnie asked. 'What's it like?'

'It stands tall, almost up to your waist, and white like a daisy against thick, dark leaves, a woody stem, and it grows in profusion. It's a kind of shrubby starwort, like the aster from Holland. In Virginia I have seen a whole forest glade filled with them, like the whiteness of snow. And I once saw a woman plait the flowers into her black hair and I thought then it was the most beautiful little flower I had ever seen, like a brooch, like a jewel. I might name it for us, it's just the sort of little beauty that your grandfather would have liked, and it will grow for anyone. He liked that in a plant. He always said that it was the hardy plants that gave the greatest joy.'

'And trees?' Johnnie prompted.

'If it grows,' John cautioned him. 'This may be our finest tree from Virginia. It's a maple tree, a Virginian maple. You can tap it for sugar, you put a cut in the trunk in springtime, when the sap starts rising, and the sap oozes a juice. You collect it and boil it down and it makes a coarse sugar. It's a great delight, to set a little fire in the woods and boil down the syrup, all the children lick up the spills and run around with sticky faces and . . .' He broke off, he couldn't bear to tell his boy about the other – Suckahanna's boy. 'The leaves turn the deepest, finest scarlet in the autumn,' he concluded.

'And this is a trumpet vine. When I had my house I planted one at the side of my door. It grows as fast as wild honeysuckle, I should think it is up to my chimney pot by now. If it hasn't pulled the whole house down. This I had on the other side of my doorway – the Virginian woodbine tree, like a honeysuckle. But best of all will be the tulip tree.' John touched the saplings, which were planted against the shelter of the wall and were putting out glossy dark leaves at the tips of their branches. 'Please God we can grow it here, it would be a fine thing to see in an English garden.'

'Finer than our horse chestnut?' Johnnie asked, naming the tree that would always be the Tradescant benchmark of beauty.

'It is the only tree I have ever seen to match your grandfather's horse chestnut. Truly, Johnnie, it is a most wonderful tree. If I can grow the tulip tree and sell it to the gardeners of England, as he grew the horse chestnut, then we will have done wonderful work, he and me.'

'And what will there be left for me to do?' Johnnie asked. 'Since he went east to Russia and south to the Mediterranean and you have been west to America. What will there be left for me?'

'Oh,' John said longingly. 'So much still to see, Johnnie. You can't imagine what a great country it is and how far the rivers run inland and how distant the mountains are and how wide the grass meadows stretch. And beyond the mountains they told me there are plains and meadows and forests and more mountains, and inland lakes of sweet water that are as big as the sea, so vast that they have storms which whip up the water into waves that crash on the shore. There will be so much for you to see when you are a man grown and ready to travel.'

'And will you take me, if you go again?' Johnnie asked.

Tradescant hesitated only for a moment, thinking of Attone and

Suckahanna and that other, alien life. Then he looked at the bright face of his son and thought how proud he would be to show him to Attone and to say to him: 'And this is *my* son.' Johnnie was not a child of the Powhatan: a dark-eyed, brown-skinned boy of intense self-discipline and skill. But he was a child of equal beauty: an English boy, blond-headed, round-faced, and with a smile like sunlight.

'Yes,' he said simply. 'If I go again, I will take you too. It will be our adventure next time.'

'We can go when the king has come to his own again,' Johnnie said firmly.

'Mmm.' John was noncommittal.

'You are for the king still?' Johnnie pressed him. 'I know you were away for most of the fighting but you were there when he raised his standard, and you are the king's man, aren't you, Father?'

John looked into the determined face of his son and dropped a hand on his shoulder. 'It's hard for me to say,' he said. 'I am the king's man in the sense that my father was his gardener and I gardened for him too. I don't forget that I have been in his service, or in the service of the court, for most of my life. But I never thought that he was perfect – not like some of the others, not like he would have had us think. I saw him make too many mistakes, I heard too much nonsense for that sort of faith. I thought he was a foolish man, sometimes wickedly foolish. So I don't think him one step below God.'

'But still the king,' Johnnie persisted.

John nodded, resigned. 'Still the king.'

'If he sent for you, would you go?'

'If he sent for me, I would have to go. I would be bound by honour and duty to go if he sent for me by name.'

'Would you take me?'

John hesitated for a moment. 'It's a burden I'd rather not lay on you, my son. If he does not have command of the gardens of the royal palaces then there is no need for you to call him master.'

Johnnie's conviction blazed out of his brown eyes. 'But I long to call him master,' he said. 'If I had been there when he raised his standard I would never have left his side. I'm so afraid it will be all over before I can go into his service, and I'll have missed it all.'

John gave a gruff bark of laughter. 'Aye,' he said. 'I can see you would fear missing it all.'

That night John put his head around the door of Hester's bedroom to see his wife, kneeling at the foot of her bed. He waited in silence till she rose to her feet and noticed him, standing in the doorway.

'I came to ask if I might sleep here.'

She got into bed and held up the covers to him, grave-faced. 'Of course,' she said. 'I am your wife.'

John pulled the nightcap off his head and came into the room.

'I don't want you to have me in your bed as part of your duty,' he said carefully.

'No.'

'I would want there to be warmth and tenderness between us.'

'Yes.'

'I want you to forgive me for going away and leaving you alone and unprotected, and for being with another woman.'

She hesitated. 'Did you leave her of your own free will?'

John could not find a simple answer. 'She saved my life,' he said. 'I was starving in the forest and she took me to the Powhatan and they accepted me for her sake.'

Hester nodded. 'Did you leave her of your own free will? Did you choose to leave her and come home to me?'

'Yes,' John said. 'Yes.' The baldness of the lie dropped like a stone into the pool of candlelight by the bed.

John got into bed beside Hester and took her hand. It was white-skinned after Suckahanna's bronze, calloused by the work she had done for him in his house and in his garden. The backs of her hands were scratched, she had been tying back the climbing roses. John took her hand to his mouth and kissed her fingers one by one.

With a sense of relief he felt desire slowly rising up. At least he would be able to do the physical act, even if his heart were not wholly present. He turned the palm of her hand over and planted a kiss in the middle.

Hester put her hand on his shoulder and stroked the short hair at the nape of his neck.

'Do you love her still?'

He stole a quick glance at Hester's face. She was intent, serious. She did not look enraged as she had every right to be. He risked telling her the truth. 'Not as I love you; but it is true. I do love her.'

'You have never loved me,' she said steadily. 'You married me as an act of convenience and sometimes I think you have felt gratitude or affection towards me. But it was not a marriage for love and I never pretended that it was.'

Her honesty alarmed him. 'Hester . . .'

'I don't want us to pretend,' she said. 'I would rather know the truth than live in a world of pretence.'

'Do you want me to leave you?'

'No!' she said quickly. 'I didn't mean that at all.'

'But you said . . .'

She drew a breath. 'I said that you married me for your convenience, to care for your children and to guard the rarities and the garden. But I married you because I needed a place to live, and a name, and also –' She smiled at him, a friendly, shy smile. 'I was in love with you, John. From the moment that you came home and I walked down the stairs and saw you.'

He put his hand under her chin and turned her face to him. Her cheeks were pink with embarrassment but she met his eyes steadily with her direct, dark gaze.

'And you forgive me?'

She gave a little shrug. 'Since you came home to me – of course.'

'And you love me still?'

'Of course. Why should I change?'

'Because I have wronged you.'

'Are you home to stay?' she asked with her usual practical directness.

'Yes, I am.'

'Then I forgive you.'

He paused for a moment. 'Do you think we could start from the beginning again?' he asked. 'With your love for me and me learning to love you?'

Her colour deepened and he saw the little white bow at the neck of her nightgown trembling as her breath came faster. 'Do you think you could learn to love me?'

John released her hands, put his lips against her throat and then gently untied the fluttering bow. 'I know I could,' he said; knowing at least that he hoped he might.

At the end of April, Alexander Norman sent a note to the Ark.

> *I write in haste to send you urgent news. The king has ridden off from Oxford and left the court there. No-one knows where he is bound but this must mean the end of the war. He has no more than a dozen gentlemen with him. He must be fleeing to join the queen in France. Thank God at last it is over.*

John took the note through to Hester and laid it down before her where she was working on the household accounts at the drawing desk in the bay of the Venetian windows in the rarities room.

'So it is all over for him at last,' he said.

She glanced quickly up at him. 'You must be glad that it has finished. Just think of getting the country back to normal.'

'Normal!' he exclaimed. 'Who will be king if he is in exile? How will the country be run?'

'By Parliament!' she said impatiently. 'I thought that was what they were fighting for!'

'I can't help but think of him, without the queen, riding out, knowing he has lost everything.'

'Many other people have lost everything,' Hester observed grimly. 'And their sons and brothers and husbands too. Another two years of this and Johnnie would have gone. He's been wild to die in the king's service ever since the war started.'

John nodded and turned to leave the room. 'I just think of him,' he said. 'Riding out on his own. I hope to God he has someone with him who knows the way to Dover.'

'Newark!' John exclaimed and looked at Alexander Norman in complete disbelief. 'What the devil is he doing in Newark? I thought he was going to France!'

'He rode around,' Alexander said. 'You have to admire the style of it. He came within an hour's ride of London and apparently thought of riding in to test the mood of the people.'

John gasped in horror.

'And then he rode to King's Lynn, and then on northwards to Newark.'

'What the devil is he doing?'

'I think he didn't know what to do,' Alexander said. 'I think he was riding and hoping that something would happen, a stroke of luck, the arrival of a French army or the Irish army or a sudden change of heart in Parliament. I think he was just spinning out the time before he surrendered.'

John shook his head. 'To the Scots?' he said somberly.

Alexander nodded. 'To the Scots army at Newark.'

'Does he think that they will treat him better than his own people?' John demanded. 'Does he think so little of Englishmen that he goes to the Scots who were the first to speak against bishops and the prayer book? Has he forgotten that his own father came south and never went back to Scotland willingly again? His own father said: "no bishops, no king"? And the Scots have never had bishops.'

Frances, sitting by the fireside in the parlour of the Lambeth house sewing a little nightdress, lifted her head at her father's distress. 'If we can only have peace now.'

'But what will they do with him?' John asked. 'They've been his enemies since the start of this. They must hand him over to Parliament at once, and then he is no better off than if he had come direct to London.'

'He must be hoping that he can play them off against the English army and Parliament. If he is there in person, offering them the chance to conquer England, who can say which way they would go? They could fall in behind him and march on England with him as their figurehead. That must be his fondest dream.' Alexander ticked off the options on his fingers. 'Or they can set him up in Edinburgh as their king and not ours. Or they can help him get abroad and pretend they had nothing to do with it, so they don't have his imprisonment on their hands.'

'Or they can hold him as a pawn in their own game,' John exclaimed. 'Who is advising him? Who ever could have advised him to stroll around the kingdom and then go to the Scots in the end? What fools does he have at his side? Why is there no-one there thinking of his safety?'

'I think he is trusting to luck,' Alexander said. 'And still, even now, who knows which way the luck will run?'

When Alexander went back to the City he left Frances at her father's house. The warmer weather had brought the plague into London again and there was talk of it being the worst for many years. The poorer people had gone without fuel and proper food through the hard winter, and when the warm plague winds blew they had no strength to fight the infection. Within months the plague carts were going up and down the narrow streets all night and the white crosses were appearing on door after door. Alexander could do nothing to protect himself but stay in his house and work in his yard, and ban his apprentices from going out as much as possible. But he would not expose Frances to infection.

John found he was absurdly overanxious about his daughter. She looked so like her mother as she grew rounder and her face took on a glow as her pregnancy progressed. He did not want to speak of Jane to his second wife, and he did not want the shadow of her death to hang over the house. He took to spending long hours in the garden, not coming in until the slow early summer dusk, and he found that while he was digging, weeding, and transplanting the Virginian seedlings he was turning over in his mind the different sorts of love a man can have: for his work, for the girl he married for love, for the children she bore him, for the woman he married for convenience, and for the woman he loved hopelessly, helplessly, completely.

He even acknowledged at last his love for the king, the foolish, selfish, intractable master who had so persistently known less and understood less than his servants. John had thought all the loves were threads which pulled him one way and another and would be, as Attone had warned him, a rope to trip him up. But as he walked back to his house past the tulip beds, and saw the shape of their cupped petals against the greater darkness of night, he thought that perhaps the threads could be the warp and woof that wove into the fabric of his life, and made him what he was, a man who had loved very deeply in different ways; and that the different loves were not a betrayal, but a richness.

He was pinching out the buds on the cherry trees in the orchard one day in June when he saw Johnnie come flying out of the kitchen door, and rush to the stable. A moment later he was pulling the saddle horse out of the stall and jumping on her back, bare-back, and trotting out of the yard.

'What is it?' John shouted. He slid down the ladder and ran towards the house. 'Is it Frances?'

He ran into the kitchen and found the cook boiling a pan of water. 'Is it Frances?' he demanded.

'She's taken ill,' the cook said. 'Mrs Tradescant has put her to bed and sent Johnnie for the apothecary. Pray to God that it's not the plague.'

'Amen,' John said and in the same breath: 'Damn you for speaking such fears.' He strode from the kitchen and ran up the stairs in his gardening boots, shedding mud on the polished wood treads. 'Hester? Hester?'

She came out of Frances's room and he saw at once from her face that his daughter was gravely ill. 'What is it?' he demanded. 'Not –' He lowered his voice. 'Not the plague?'

'I don't know,' she said. 'She grew very hot and said she would like to rest, then she just fainted clean away.'

He glanced superstitiously at the closed door. 'Move her into our room,' he said.

'She's in her own room, I don't want to trouble her and move her,' Hester said uncomprehendingly.

He shifted from one foot to another, fearful of even saying the words. 'Please,' he said. 'Her mother took the plague in that room, it was our bedroom. She made me move her from there to the orangery and there she died. Please don't let Frances be in that room.'

Hester stepped towards him and took his dirty hands in her cool fingers. 'John, these are old fears,' she said. 'This is Frances, not Jane. This is a fever, not the plague. She is a strong young woman and I will nurse her as well as I can. I won't move her when she is comfortable in her own bed, and who better to watch over her from heaven than her own mother?'

He hesitated for a moment. 'Does she need anything?'

Hester thought quickly for a task to keep John occupied and to give him a sense of purpose. 'I need herbs,' she said. 'Feverfew and chamomile, and sweet cicely against infection. Can you pick them for me?'

He nodded and went quickly towards the stairs.

'And write a note and send it to Alexander,' Hester said. 'Don't worry him too much, just tell him she has a fever, and she would like to see him, if he can come.'

John paused, obedient as a frightened boy. 'Herbs or letter first?' he asked.

'Letter,' she said. 'Then the herbs, and then why don't you pot her up a couple of tulips? She'd like to see them.'

'I'll bring her up the Semper,' John said, promising the best of them all. 'The Semper Augustus.'

Alexander came up the river at dawn the next day and had the boat set him down on the bank as near to the Ark as he could get. John saw him from the window in the stable yard, taking off his cape and his waistcoat and even his trousers and leaving them in the stable. He shouted for Joseph to work the pump, stripped off his shirt and washed under the stream of icy water before rubbing himself briskly dry with a sheet and pattering to the kitchen door all but naked.

Cook let out a delighted little scream of shock but Alexander Norman paid no attention to her and walked past her to the hall.

'Forgive me,' he said briefly to John. 'But there is a lot of sickness in the City and I wanted to take no risk of bringing it to you here. Are you free of it in Lambeth?'

'Half a dozen dead in the village this week,' John said grimly. 'I thank you for taking care. You can borrow a shirt and breeches of mine.'

'Is she better?' Alexander asked.

John shook his head. 'The fever grew worse overnight and Hester says she is still hot.'

'But it isn't . . . ?' Alexander could not bring himself to name the plague.

'Hester says not.'

The two men looked into each other's anxious faces and for the first time since his return to England John knew the pleasure of finding a man who could understand what he was feeling. His own worry was graven deep into Alexander's face. They both looked as if they had spent the night praying. He reached out his arms and Alexander gripped him tightly.

'Please God it is not . . .'

'Please God,' John replied.

'She is so precious to me . . .'

'I know, I know.'

'I sent her away from the City the moment I thought there was a risk . . .'

'It's in Lambeth anyway. There is nowhere you could be sure that she would be safe.'

'But not her . . .'

'I feel so fearful,' John said very low. 'I think of her mother and her prettiness – and Frances is so like her – and I think that perhaps there is a weakness?'

Alexander shook his head. 'There's no way of tracing where it comes from or who takes it,' he said. 'That's the very devil of it. You just don't know. Is everyone else well? Johnnie? Hester?'

'We're all well,' John said. 'And God knows we would all willingly take it for her.'

Alexander bowed his head for a moment. 'D'you forgive me for marrying her?' he asked irrelevantly.

John gave a short laugh. 'For everything she has ever done or ever can do, if only she will be well again,' he said. 'I knew I loved her but I never knew that the very thought of losing her would be like my own death to me.'

'And the baby?'

'They're both hanging on,' John said. 'Hester says that they are both hanging on.'

There was nothing for the two men to do. A couple of times there was a knock at the door and John went to admit a visitor to the rarities room and one to walk around the garden; but the rest of the time he and Alexander sat in silence in the parlour, either side of the cold fireplace, straining to hear footsteps upstairs, waiting for news. Johnnie took up a position on the top of the stairs outside Frances's room carving at a twig with his pocket knife. All the day, he sat like a little choirboy at a vigil, listening to the gentle murmur of talk and the irregular sigh of Frances's breath.

There was little Hester could do, though she never left Frances's bedside. She sponged her forehead with vinegar and lavender water, she changed the sheets when they grew wet with sweat, she held her hand and spoke to her quietly and reassuringly when Frances tossed in fever-coloured nightmares, and she held her shoulders so that the young woman could sip a drink of cool well water.

But when Frances dropped back on her pillows and lay still, and the flush died away from her cheeks and her skin grew waxy and pale, there was nothing Hester could do but sit at the head of the bed and pray that her stepdaughter would live.

Hester watched all the night at the bedside and at three in the morning her head drooped and she slept. She was wakened only a few minutes later by a movement in the bed and she heard Frances say, 'Oh Hester!' in a tone of such sorrow that she was awake and on her feet as her eyes opened.

'What is it? Have you found a swelling?' she demanded, naming the greatest fear.

'I'm bleeding,' Frances said.

Hester saw at once that the fever had broken but the young woman was white and drained, and her nightdress was stained a deep cherry red.

'My baby,' Frances whispered.

Hester twisted a strip of sheet and held it against the flow. 'Lie quietly,' she said urgently. 'I'll send John for the midwife, you may be all right.'

Frances lay back obediently, but shook her head. 'I can feel it gone,' she said.

Hester, a childless woman, felt herself adrift in a tragedy that she had never experienced. 'Can you?'

'Yes,' Frances said, in a little voice which Hester recognised from the lonely little girl she had first met. 'Yes. My baby's gone.'

At seven in the morning Hester went wearily downstairs with a pile of cloths for burning and some sheets to wash, and found Alexander Norman and John alert and silent at the foot of the stairs.

'Forgive me,' she said slowly. 'I forgot the time, I forgot that you would be waiting and worried.'

John took the bundle from her and Alexander took her hand. 'What's happened?' John demanded.

'The fever has broken and she has no swellings,' Hester said. 'But she has lost the baby.' She looked at Alexander. 'I am sorry, Alexander. I would have sent for the midwife but she was sure that it was too late. It was all over in a moment.'

He turned and looked up the stairs. 'Can I go to her?'

Hester nodded. 'I'm sure it's not the plague, but don't wake her, and don't stay long.'

He went up the stairs so quietly that the treads did not squeak. John dropped the laundry on the floor and enfolded his wife in his arms. 'You haven't slept at all,' he said gently. 'Come. I'll give you a glass of wine and then you must go to bed. Alexander can look after her now, or me, or Cook.'

She let him draw her into the parlour, seat her in a chair and press a glass of sweet wine into her hand. She took a sip and some of the colour came back into her cheeks. She had never looked more plain than now, when she was strained and weary. John had never loved her better.

'You cared for her very tenderly,' he said. 'No mother could have done better.'

She smiled at that. 'I could not love her more if I had given birth to her myself,' she said. 'And I have long thought that she has two mothers: Jane in heaven and me on earth.'

He took the chair beside her and he drew her on to his knee. Hester wound her arms around his neck and laid her head on his shoulder and for the first time allowed herself to weep for the baby that was lost.

'There will be other babies,' John said, stroking her hair. 'We will have dozens of grandchildren, from Frances, from Johnnie.'

'But this one is lost,' Hester said. 'And if it had been a boy she was going to call him John.'

Summer 1646

Frances stayed at the Ark for all of the summer, promising Alexander that she would not return to his house in the City until the cold autumn weather had frozen out the plague. But they were not parted for many nights. The fighting was over and there was little demand for barrels for gunpowder. Many evenings Alexander took a boat from the Tower running with the incoming tide up the river to Lambeth, and then strode down the lane to the Ark to see his wife sitting on the front wall, waiting for him as if she were still a little girl.

It was a bad year for sickness, as everyone had predicted, and the town was full of soothsayers and prophesiers and men and women who were prepared to stand up and give witness on street corners that while the king was with the Scots, who had taken him away to Newcastle, the nation could not be at peace. The king must come to London and explain himself, the king must come before the widows and fatherless children and beg their pardons, the king must come before Parliament and agree how to live in peace with them. What the king should not do was to continue debating, sending arguments to Parliament in favour of himself, discussing theology with the covenanting Scots and generally enjoying his life as blithely and as happily as if the country had not battled for years and got nowhere.

'He can't be happy.' John disagreed with Johnnie, who brought back this news from Lambeth market. 'He can't be happy without the queen and without the court.'

'He only has to wait and Montrose will rescue him!' Johnnie declared. 'The Scots are his enemy, he has played a clever game by going to them. They shield him from his enemies, the English Parliament, and all the time he is waiting for Montrose. Montrose will fight his way across the Highlands for the king.'

'Johnnie has a new hero,' Hester told her husband with a smile. She was checking the purchases off the back of the wagon and Cook was taking them into the kitchen. 'He was all for Prince Rupert but now it is Montrose.'

'They say no-one will ever catch him, that he runs around the Highlands like a deer,' Johnnie said. 'The Covenanters will never catch him, he's too quick and too clever. He knows all the passes through the mountains, when they wait for him at one place he melts away over the hills and then attacks them in another.'

'It always sounds so easy when it is told like a ballad,' John said soberly. 'But real battles are not so quick. And real defeats can make a man sick to the heart.'

Johnnie shook his head and would not be persuaded then; but later in the summer he tasted a little of the bitterness of defeat. He spent the day of 25 June at the little lake, rowing his boat around in aimless circles. The king's town of Oxford had surrendered and Prince Rupert – the darling of the court, the hope of the royalists, the most dashing, the most glamorous, the most beautiful general that the war had seen – was sent out of the country into exile and would never be allowed to return.

Hester went down to the lake at dusk to find Johnnie. It was getting cold and the frogs were croaking in the reeds at the side of the pond and the bats dipping like night-time swifts to snatch the insects which still danced over the grey waters. She could just see the little rowboat with the oars shipped and Johnnie curled up in the stern, with his long legs trailing over the side of the boat and the heels of his boots dipping in the water and making circular ripples like rising fish.

'Come in,' she called, her voice gentle across the still water. 'Come in, Johnnie. The war is over and that's a thing to be glad for, not a matter of grief.'

The little huddled figure in the boat did not move.

John came down the path and stood beside Hester.

'He won't come in,' she said.

John took her hand. 'He will.'

She resisted him as he tried to draw her away. 'He has adored Prince Rupert for years. He cried the night that Rupert lost Bristol.'

'He'll get hungry,' John said. 'There is loyalty and love and there is a thirteen-year-old boy's belly. He'll come in.' He raised his voice. 'We have some strawberries for dinner tonight. And Cook has made marchpane pastry to go with them. Have we got some cream too?'

'Oh yes,' Hester said clearly. 'And a rib of beef with Yorkshire pudding and roasted potatoes and the allspick lettuce.'

There was a small movement from the becalmed boat.

John tucked Hester's arm firmly under his elbow and drew her away from the bank of the pond.

'I don't like to leave him,' she whispered.

John chuckled. 'If he's not in by the time dinner is on the table you can send me to swim out to him,' he said. 'It's a pledge.'

John could make light of Johnnie's despondency at the news of Prince Rupert's exile, but the thought of the king in the hands of the Scots at Newcastle haunted him too. In July there was news of an English mission to try to persuade the king to come to agreement with Parliament, and all the time the king was being worked on to sign a treaty with the Scots.

'If he cannot agree with either the English or the Scots, what will become of him?' John asked Hester. 'He has to give up either his right to the army and come home to England, or give up his religion and join the Scots. But he can't just wait and do nothing.'

Hester said nothing. She thought the king was perfectly capable of waiting and doing nothing while the queen campaigned for him in France, Montrose risked his life and his men in the Highlands and Ormonde tried to fight his way through a maze of the king's own self-betraying plotting in Ireland. 'If the Irish were to come over and join with Montrose and fight for the king –' she suggested.

John flashed her a quick, irritated look. 'Papists and Scotsmen?' he asked. 'Fighting for a Protestant king? An Irish army? The alliance would last half a day and the country would never forgive him.'

'If he *is* a Protestant king,' Hester said carefully.

John dropped his head into his hands. 'No-one knows what he believes any more, nor what he stands for. How could it have come to this?'

'And what do *you* believe?' Hester asked him. 'You were always against the court, and against Papacy?'

John shrugged wearily. 'I didn't go to Virginia just because I had no stomach for killing Englishmen,' he said. 'I went because I was torn. I served the king, and my father served the king or his servants all his life. I can't just turn away and pretend that I don't care for his safety. I *do* care. But he's in the wrong and has been in the wrong since –' He broke off. 'Since he marched his soldiers into the House of Commons,' he said. 'No, before. Since he allowed the government of this country to be run by that madman, Buckingham. Since he took a Papist wife and thus ran the risk of Papist children. From the moment that he set his heart on having a kingdom run as a tyranny and would not listen to his advisors.'

Hester waited.

'I want the kingdom free of his tyranny, I have always wanted that. But I don't need the kingdom free of him. Or his son. Does that make any sense at all?'

Hester nodded and then turned to a more pressing topic for her. 'Shall we unpack the rarities?'

John gave a short laugh. 'D'you think we are at peace? With the king held by the Scots at Newcastle and refusing to agree with his own Parliament?'

'I don't think we're at peace,' she said equably. 'But if we could show the rarities and summon people to the garden to see the Virginian plants we might make some money this summer. And we are in debt, John. This war has been hard on everyone and we are taking no more than a few shillings each month.'

He rose from the chair. 'Let's go and have a look at that tree,' he said.

They stood before the great black cherry tree. It had not liked the situation before the ice-house door and there had been few blossoms in spring and now only a few buttons of green berries which might, in time, ripen and swell.

'I can't bear to chop it down,' John said. 'It has grown to a good size even if it is not bearing much of a crop.'

'Can you move it?' Hester asked. Her gaze went beyond the tree, to the doorway of the ice house where the ivy and the honeysuckle were planted. No-one could have spotted its outline unless they were looking for it. She liked the thought of the garden plants helping to hide the rarities. There was some unity in the Ark if they all worked together to save the precious things.

'My father had a way of moving even big trees,' John said thoughtfully. 'But it takes time. We'll have to be patient. It will be a couple of months at the earliest.'

'Let's do it,' Hester said. 'I am ashamed of the rarities room as it is, I want the treasures back inside.' She did not tell John that while the king was held by the Scots she had no fears for the safety of the treasures or of the family. Hester had great faith in Scottish efficiency, and in the dour Covenanters' immunity to Stuart charm. If the Scots were holding the king, even if they took him far away to Edinburgh, then Hester felt safe.

Hester remembered the moving of the cherry tree as an event which coincided with the death of the hopes of the runaway king. Both processes happened in slow stages. John dug a trench around his father's cherry tree and watered it every morning and night. The news from Newcastle was that the king would agree to nothing: neither the proposals from England, nor those from his hosts the Scots.

With the help of Joseph and Johnnie pulling the trunk slowly first one way and then the other, John dug underneath the tree and gently shovelled earth away from all but the greatest roots. A Scottish cleric who had wrestled with the king's conscience for two months went home to Edinburgh and died, they said, of a broken heart, blaming himself that the most stubborn man in England could not be brought to see where his own interests lay.

John watered the tree richly with his father's mixture of stinging-nettle soup, dung, and water, three times a day. They heard that the queen herself wrote to the king and begged him to make an agreement with the Scots, so that he might be king of Scotland at least.

John pruned the tree, carefully cutting away the branches which would sap the tree's strength. The Scots Covenanters, debating with their royal prisoner, privately declared among themselves that he was mad, he must have been mad to come to them without an army, without power, without allies, and then imagine that they would fight a war for him, on his terms, against their co-religionists for nothing more than his thanks.

Johnnie and Joseph, with John and Alexander on the other side, gently thrust poles from one side of the crater around the tree to the other until it was supported, and then John went down into the mud-filled ditch and freed the last of the roots. The longest, strongest root he pulled gently from the mud and then cursed when it broke and he fell back into the slurry with a bump.

'That's killed it,' Joseph said gloomily, and John climbed out of the ditch soaked through and irritable. Then the four men gently lifted the tree out of the ground and carried it down to the bottom of the orchard where a new hole was dug and waiting. They put it in, lovingly spread out the roots, backfilled the earth, and gently pressed it down. John stood back and admired his work.

'It's crooked,' Frances said behind him.

John turned wrathfully on her.

'Just joking,' she said.

With the doorway clear, Hester tied a duster over her head to keep off the cobwebs and spiders and set to pulling aside the ivy and the honeysuckle. The key still worked in the lock, the door opened with a creak on the dirty hinges. John peered inside. The little round chamber was lined with straw and piled high with chests and boxes of his father's treasures. He caught Hester's dirty hand and kissed it. 'Thank you for keeping them safe,' he said.

Autumn 1646

Hester, Johnnie and Joseph were lifting tulip bulbs in the garden of the Ark. They worked with their fingers in the cold soil. Even the common bulbs were too valuable to risk spearing with a fork or slicing with a spade. On the ground beside Hester were the precious porcelain bowls of the most valuable tulips, their expensive bulbs already lifted and separated, the sieved earth tipped back into the beds.

Joseph and Johnnie filled the labelled sacks with the Flame tulip bulbs. Almost every one had spawned a second, some of them had two or three bulblets nestling beside the first. All three gardeners were smiling in pleasure. Whether the price for tulips ever recovered or stayed as low as it had been thrust by the collapse of the market, still there was something rich and exciting about the wealth which made itself in silence and secrecy under the soil.

There was a step on the wooden floor of the terrace and Hester looked up to see John Lambert. He was looking very fine, dressed as well as always, with a deep violet feather in his hat, and a waterfall of white lace at his throat and cuffs. Hester got to her feet and felt a pang of annoyance at her dirty hands and dishevelled hair. She whipped off her hessian apron and walked towards him.

'Forgive me coming unannounced,' he said, his dark smile taking in her rising blush. 'I am so honoured to see you working among your plants.'

'I'm all dirty,' Hester said, stepping back from his proffered hand.

'And I smell of horse,' he said cheerfully. 'I am on my way from my home in Yorkshire. I couldn't resist calling in to see if my tulips were ready.'

'They are.' Hester gestured to the three bulging sacks at the corner of the terrace. 'I was going to send them to your London home.'

'I thought you might. That's why I have come. I am on my way to Oxford and I wanted the special tulips there. I shall plant them in pots and have them in my rooms.'

Hester nodded. 'I am sorry you will not meet my husband,' she said. 'He is in London today. He has gone into trade in a small way with a West India planter and he is sending some goods out.'

'I am sorry not to meet him,' John Lambert said pleasantly. 'But I hardly dare to delay. I am to be governor of Oxford while my health mends.'

Hester risked a quick glance at him. 'I had heard you were ill – I was sorry.'

He gave her his warm, intimate smile. 'I am well enough, and the work I set myself to do is all but done. Pray God we will have peace again, Mrs Tradescant, and in the meantime I can sit down in Oxford and make sure that the colleges get back into some kind of order, and their treasures are safe.'

'These are hard times to be a guardian of beautiful things.'

'Better times coming soon,' he whispered. 'May I take my tulips now?'

'Of course. Shall you want them all at Oxford?'

'Send the Flame tulips to my London house, my wife can plant them for me there. But the rare tulips and the Violetten I must have beside me.'

'If you breed a true violet one then do let us know,' Hester said, gesturing to Joseph to take the sack of labelled rare tulips out to the wagon waiting in the street beyond the garden gate. 'We would buy one back from you.'

'I shall present it to you,' John Lambert said grandly. 'A mark of respect to another guardian of treasure.' He glanced down the garden and saw Johnnie. 'And how's the cavalry officer these days?'

'Very disheartened,' Hester said. 'Would you let him make his bow to you?'

John Lambert cupped his hands around his mouth and shouted: 'Ho! Tradescant!'

Johnnie looked up at the shout and came up from the tulip beds at a run, skidded to a halt, and dipped in a bow.

'Major!' he said.

'Good day.'

Johnnie beamed at him.

'You must have been disappointed in recent months, I am sorry for it,' John Lambert said gently.

'I can't see what went wrong,' Johnnie said passionately.

John Lambert thought for a moment. 'It was mostly how we used the infantry,' he said. 'Cromwell has them trained in such a way that they change formation very fast, and they can hold their ground even against a charge. And once the king dismissed Rupert then the morale among his commanders was very low. That's one of the keys, especially in a war inside a country. Everyone's got to trust each other. That's what Cromwell got right, when he got the Members of Parliament out of the army. We made the army a family which prays together and thinks together and fights together.'

Johnnie nodded, listening avidly. 'It wasn't Prince Rupert's fault that he lost Bristol!' he exclaimed.

'Indeed it was not,' John Lambert agreed. 'It was mostly the weather. It rained and their gunpowder was soaked. They were going to mine the city walls, rather than let us take a fortified town. They had the mines dug and the gunpowder in place – but then it was wet and didn't fire. No commander could have done anything about that. But there was another thing –'

'What, sir?'

'It's about belief,' Lambert said slowly. 'There are very few like you, Johnnie, who have such certainty about the king. But there are very many, most of my army in fact, who truly believe that if they can win the war that we can make a better country here, better for everyone. They think they are doing God's work and man's work. They think that they will make a world of greater justice and fairness – *we* think that.'

'Are you a Leveller, sir?' Johnnie asked. Hester would have interrupted but Lambert was unruffled.

'I think we all are in a way,' he said. 'Some of us would go further than others, but all the honest men I know think that we should be governed by our consent, and not by the king's whim. We think we should have a parliament elected by everyone in the country and that it should sit all the time and return to the country for election every three years. We don't think that the king and only the king should decide when and where it sits, and whether or not he will listen to it.'

'I'm still a royalist,' Johnnie said stubbornly.

Lambert laughed. 'Perhaps we can find a way to persuade you royalists that it is for the good of us all – king to beggar – that we live in some order and harmony. And now I must go.'

'Good luck,' Hester called, her hand on Johnnie's shoulder. 'Come again.'

'I'll come next spring and bring my Violetten!' he called, and with a swirl of his cape he was gone.

Spring 1647

Johnnie sat in his rowing boat on the little lake at the bottom of the garden, a news-sheet spread before him, his coat turned up around his ears against the sharp frost. He was reading one of the many royalist papers that spread a mixture of good cheer and open lies in an effort to keep the king's cause alive, even while he squabbled with his Scots hosts at Newcastle. This edition assured the reader that the king in his wisdom was forging an agreement which would convert the Scots from their stubborn determination never to accept the English prayer book or the English system of bishops. As soon as the Scots had agreed they would then sweep down through England, return the king to his throne and all would be well again.

Johnnie looked up and saw his father coming through the orchard. John waved and walked to the bank where a little pier stretched into the water.

'You must be freezing,' John remarked.

'A bit,' Johnnie said. 'This can't be right. The Scots aren't likely to surrender all they believe in when they have all but won the war. They aren't likely to start fighting for the king *against* Parliament when they've been allies with Parliament for the last few years.'

'No,' John said briefly. 'You bought the paper. What did you think it would tell you: the truth?'

'I just want to know!' Johnnie sat up abruptly and the boat rocked. 'He has no chance, has he?'

John shook his head. 'What your paper doesn't tell you is that they've refused to take him to Edinburgh unless he too signs their covenant, against Laud's prayer book and against the bishops. Of course he can't sign. He's just turned the kingdom upside down to try and make us do it his way. But the Scots are going back to Scotland, and they don't know what to do with him. Nobody knows why he went to them in the first place. There was never any chance of an agreement. They'll send him to Parliament.'

Johnnie went pale. 'Betray him to his enemies?'

'He's with his enemies already but he wouldn't see it,' John said bluntly. 'The Scots and Parliament have been allies since the war started. Of course they would work on him to try and make a peace. Of course if he won't bend they have to hand him over.'

'What will he do?' Johnnie asked, anguished.

John shook his head. 'He must surrender and accept the terms Parliament imposes. Parliament and the army have defeated him. He has to give up.'

John was wrong. The king did not give up. He attempted to escape, an ill-planned, unlikely attempt which was as successful as it deserved to be. The guard around him was doubled, he was warned that he should know that he was a prisoner of the English Parliament, and taken to Holdenby House in Northamptonshire.

Hester found John at the bottom of the orchard, scowling at the cherry tree. 'I think I killed it,' he said. 'And I watched my father moving trees twice the size of this when I was a boy and never learned the knack of it.'

'It looks no worse than the others,' Hester said, looking round the orchard where the whippy bare boughs of the trees flailed against a white sky.

'I've killed it,' John said. 'For all the care I took. I don't have my father's talent. I worked at his side all my life and still I'm not half the gardener he was. He knew where he belonged, he knew who he served, and he knew his trade and I –' He broke off and put his hand on the bough of the tree as if for support.

'What's the news?' Hester asked, guessing at once the source of John's discomfort.

John gave her a quick look from under his lowered brows. 'Just some lads at the back door, begging for bread on their way home,' he said. 'Discharged from the army and heading homeward.'

Hester waited. John put his hand out and held the trunk of the dead cherry tree. 'They said that the army would rule Parliament and they would have their revenge on the king,' he said. 'They said they would make him pay because a new day is coming when all men will have land and all men will have a vote to choose their rulers and all men will be equal with one another.'

'These are young men's thoughts,' Hester said quickly. 'You were a young man wild for change yourself once, John.'

He nodded. 'But these were not young men, they were men of my age. And they said that many think as they do. They are Levellers and they say the best men of the army are with them. They want to finish what Parliament started. They want to exile the king and turn the country into a new land of freedom and equality.'

Hester looked around the security of the walled orchard. 'Parliament would not give away land?' she asked.

John shook his head. 'I don't think they'll wait for Parliament,' he said. 'These are men of action and determination. They've been fighting to make a better country for working men. They have little patience for the gentlemen in Parliament. They want to see the land given to working men. They want the royal estates, the church estates, the commons, and the wastes.'

'And every man would have his own little piece of land and grow things?'

'So they say.' John smiled grimly. 'It's what I always wanted. It's how I always thought things should be. And now it looks as if the army might destroy Parliament and do it.'

'Turn on their masters?'

'Why not? Didn't Parliament turn on the king?'

'Would they take from landowners like us? Tax us?'

John shrugged. 'How would I know what they might do? They might think that these walls should be pulled down as any other.'

Hester nodded and turned back towards the house. He could tell by her slow stride that she was thinking. Halfway to the house she turned and came back to him.

'I think we should be growing vegetables,' she said. 'That's what they'll be wanting now.'

The whole family helped in the restoration of the rarities to the room with the high Venetian windows and the smooth, polished floor. They wanted to return it to its previous state, they wanted it restored, without loss of beauty, without loss of richness, without loss of the glamour that hung around it: the scent of the skins, the delight of the multiplicity of things, the joy of the ordered jumble; the big things hanging from the ceiling, the tiny things in their cabinets, the exotic next to the mundane, the historic next to the inventions.

There were some terrible gaps in the collection. The coins had fared the worst and the items made of precious metals. Hester had made inroads into anything which had held its value during the war years and she could not conceal from John that there were trays of Roman and mediaeval coins which would never be stocked again.

Some things had suffered from damp. A triptych altar screen had been leaned against the ice-house wall and its bright colours had been leached away by the moisture of the brick. Many rare skins had rotted and decayed, and some of the woollen clothes were pitted with moth-holes. Vellum pages of illuminated manuscripts had been eaten by ants and the foul dirt of rats and mice was all over the cases which held the flowers dried in sugar.

'I am sorry, I am sorry,' Hester cried as one parcel after another was brought out into the light. 'If I had only known that we would be safe I would never have hidden the things away.'

'You didn't know,' John said generously. 'And if the soldiers had suddenly swept through we could have lost everything in one night.'

Frances, her hair tied in a kerchief, and Johnnie in his gardening clothes gently beat the dust and the moths from the clothes, rugs and skins outside and then carried them in for Hester and John to rearrange and hang.

Bit by bit, piece by piece, drawer by drawer, object after object, the rarities room was reassembled, and when they stepped back and looked around after a full fortnight of work they saw an impressive collection of wealth and novelty. Only someone who had grown up in the room, as the Tradescant children had done, rocked in the light of those great windows, would have known that anything was missing. The visitors, who would surely come again now that peace was here, could not fail to be amazed.

Summer 1647

John was digging in the new vegetable bed and setting in lettuce seeds to see which would grow the fastest when Hester came out of the house, shading her eyes against the bright sunshine, and then hurried down the path towards him.

'The king's been taken,' she said baldly.

He looked up with as much anxiety as if she had said one of the children was ill. 'Taken?'

'Some whippersnapper Cornet marched up to Holdenby House and arrested His Majesty,' Hester said, nearly spitting with rage.

'How did you hear this?' John asked, wiping his muddy hands on his leather gardening apron.

'The ferry boatman. Frances has come for a visit, I went down to the river to meet her. London is buzzing with the news.'

'Who has him?'

'A man of no importance,' Hester said. 'A nobody. One of the new men of the New Model Army, rode to Holdenby House and captured the king as if he was a piece of baggage in the baggage train. It is these people who will bring us down. People who have no respect. Men who have spent four years learning that nothing matters, not pictures in church, not music, not gardens, not kings.'

'And where has he taken His Majesty?' John asked.

'To Maidenhead,' she said. 'And they say Oliver Cromwell himself is going out to meet him.'

'Cromwell?'

She nodded. 'D'you think that means peace?'

John shook his head. 'I suppose it means that the game has changed again,' he said, baffled. 'When the king was held by the Scots he was in the power of Parliament. But now the army has him, I don't know what will become of him, or us for that matter.'

'We may be in danger,' Hester said. 'The ferry boatman said that the soldiers of the New Model Army may march on Parliament. They're determined to have their pay. And they recognise no loyalty to anyone but their commanders and their levelling ideas. They are saying that Parliament and the City may hold out against the army. But if the army comes to the City from the south then they will march right through here. We may have to pack up the rarities again. They are marching for their pay, they are hungry and desperate men. And they have sworn that all the land and all the property shall be held in common.'

John shook his head. 'It's like living in the middle of a thunderstorm,' he complained. 'It has all changed again. If the army fights against the Parliament which brought it into being, then what becomes of the country?'

In July the news was that the king was to be taken, under guard, to Oatlands.

Hester looked at her husband across the kitchen table. Cook, Joseph, the new gardening boy, Frances and Johnnie all turned to the head of the table and waited for John to speak.

'Now, I have to go,' he said simply. 'He cannot be at Oatlands and not see me working in the garden. That was my work, that was my place.'

Hester hesitated for only a moment. 'I'll pack your bag,' she said, and went out of the room.

Johnnie turned to his father, his face suddenly flushed. 'May I come too?' he asked. 'And see him?'

When his father hesitated he went on in a rapid torrent of speech. 'I've never seen him, and my father and my grandfather were in his service. And I've never even seen him. Frances saw him and the queen. Can I come? Please?'

John gave a short laugh. 'I cannot be sure that I will see him,' he said. 'And if he sees me, he may not speak to me. I just feel the royal court under his window should be tidy, I don't know what state it's in.'

'I can tidy it,' Johnnie said desperately. 'I can weed. I worked there while you were away. I can do it. I am a Tradescant, I am gardener to the king. I should be there.'

Hester came back into the kitchen and John turned to her with relief. 'It depends on what your mother says.'

'Can I go with Father to Oatlands?' Johnnie scrambled over his stool to get to his stepmother. 'And work for him? He'd have such a lot of work to do, I could help.'

'I don't know if it's safe,' Hester said hesitantly.

'It's probably safe,' John said shortly. 'Safer than it's ever been with him under guard and forced to make peace at last.'

She nodded. 'He can go if you wish it,' she said to John.

Johnnie turned his bright hazel eyes on his father.

'Oh, very well,' John said. 'But not a word do you speak unless spoken to – and then you just answer "Yes, Your Majesty", or "No, Your Majesty". Not a word about me being in Virginia. Not a word about the cavalier who came here. Not a word about John Lambert buying our tulips. Not a word about anything.'

Johnnie was dancing on the spot with excitement. 'Yes! Yes!' he shouted. 'Yes! Of course. And I shall be absolutely silent. Absolutely. I shall be absolutely discreet.'

John met his wife's eyes across the boy's bobbing head. 'I don't know about you; but I feel very confident,' he said wryly.

They went by the river, rowed in a wherry, Johnnie seated beside his father and looking all around him. When they were past the village of Staines, John said quietly, 'There it is,' and pointed to the little rose-pink palace, sitting on the terraces with the unkempt lawns running down to the river. 'D'you know, I never thought I'd see it again,' John said softly. 'I never thought I'd be here, working in these gardens again.'

Johnnie glanced quickly at his father's darkened expression. 'But you're glad of it?' he asked. 'Glad you came home and that the king is back in his palace, and soon everything will be as it was?'

John dropped his hand on his son's thin shoulder. 'I don't think everything will be quite as it was,' he said. 'There's a lot of men dead and a lot of tears shed, and the king is in his palace but not on his throne. We'll have to mind our tongues here, and beware even of our thoughts.'

The boatman shipped the oars and the wherry nudged against the landing stage. John stepped quickly ashore and caught the mooring rope, dug in his pocket for a coin and dropped it down into the boat as Johnnie tossed up their bags and then handed up, one at a time, a dozen pots with nodding blooms.

John shouldered his bag. 'We'll come back for the pots,' he said, and led the way up the slope to the palace.

Prince Rupert had allowed his cavalrymen's horses to graze on the lawns and they were pocked with hoofprints and lumpy with droppings but at least the animals had kept the grass down. As John approached the palace he saw that the creepers and the wall climbers which he had trained so carefully to take blossoms and scent up to the windows were doing well – overspread, sometimes pulling away from their ties, but thriving on neglect.

The beds at the feet of the rose-brick walls were overrun with weeds but some flowers were still struggling through. Pansies and gillyflowers, irises and peonies had thrust their heads above the encroaching green. 'Soon hoe that out,' John remarked, nodding to his son.

The yew tree *allée* was overgrown but looked thick and bushy, throwing a welcome green shade against the brightness of the afternoon sunshine. The orangery which John's father had rebuilt was dilapidated – the white paint was peeling and some of the ornamental woodwork had been wrenched off for the troopers' campfires – but the silkworm house and the neighbouring gardener's house were as Hester had left them, swept clean and bare and empty.

John left his son collecting firewood for the empty grate and unrolling their travelling cloaks for beds as he prowled around the deserted palace.

The strangest thing was the quiet. Instead of a bustling royal court filled with folly and flirtation, shouted orders, voices calling and musicians playing, there was nothing but the occasional rattle of a shutter banging in the breeze and the insistent coo of the wood pigeons nesting in the trees. The stable yard, which had housed more than a hundred horses, was empty, straws blowing in the yard, the stalls heaped with dung, stale water in the troughs.

The great front door was shut and bolted. John tried the massive brass handle and then stepped back. The king was due in a few days, surely there should be servants inside setting the palace to rights. Not a face showed at the windows, there was not a movement in the courts.

John went around to the kitchen quarters and to the bake-house. The fires were out, the place was silent. A heap of ash and a few scattered utensils showed that the cavalrymen had dined before they left, but all the food had been eaten by rats or mice and their droppings were heaped even on the kitchen tables.

John shook his head in wonder at the desolation of the place, at its transformation from the pinnacle of the social life of the kingdom, with the queen singing about the platonic ideal and the king going hunting on his high-bred Arab horses, to this shell. He turned and trudged back across the bowling green to the silkworm house.

Johnnie had brought up the pots from the riverside.

'Good lad,' John said with pleasure, glad of the chance to set about his work and restore normality at least to the flowerbeds. 'Let's take these up to the royal court. At least that can be looking right in a couple of days.'

They worked hard, side by side, and John enjoyed his son's company. The boy had inherited the Tradescant gift with plants, he handled them as if he loved the touch of the silky white roots, the caress of damp earth. When he hefted a pot in his hand he could tell from the weight whether it needed watering. When he tipped a plant out into his palm he never knocked the blooms. When he set it into a hole and pressed down the earth there was something about his touch which was both precisely judged, and quite unknowing.

'You may be the greatest gardener of us all,' John said at the end of the second day as they walked homewards with their tools over their shoulders. 'I don't believe I had your way with plants when I was your age.'

Johnnie gleamed. 'I love the plants. Not so much the rarities,' he said.

'Not the rarities?' John asked, amazed.

His son shook his head. 'What I'd rather do, more than anything else, would be to collect new plants, to go with you to the Americas, the West Indies, travel, find things, bring them home and grow them. The rarities – well, they just sit there, don't they? Once they're in place there is nothing more to do with them except keep them dusted. But plants grow and blossom and fruit and seed and then there's next year to plant them again. I like how they change.'

John nodded. 'I see.'

He was about to remark that the rarities played their part in the Tradescant family fortune when he heard hoofbeats on the drive. 'What's that?' he asked.

'Could it be the king?'

'Could be.'

John turned and ran towards the silkworm house, cast down his tools, grabbed his coat and turned to run back to the palace. Johnnie danced on the spot. 'Can I come? Can I come?'

'Yes. But remember what I said about keeping silent.'

Johnnie fell into line behind his father, mirrored his father's long stride, composed his face to a scowl of what he hoped was dignified discretion, and spoiled the effect only slightly by a great bounce at every fourth step as his excitement proved too much for him.

They ran round to the stable yard and there, in the dirty stall, was the king's Arab, and a dozen other horses of his escort.

'The king here?' John asked a trooper.

'Just arrived,' the man said, easing the girth of his horse. 'We had to stop at every village for him to touch people.'

'Touch people?'

'They turned out in dozens,' the man said abruptly. 'With all sorts of illnesses and sores and God knows what. And again and again he stopped and touched them, so that they would be cured. And they all went off, back to their hovels, back to their porridge of nothing and water, thinking that he had done them a great favour and that we were some kind of beast to imprison him.'

John nodded.

'Who are you?' the man asked. 'If you want a favour of him, he'll do it. He's the most charming, generous, agreeable man to ever take a country into disaster and death and four years of war.'

'I'm the gardener,' John replied.

'Then you'll see him,' the man said. 'He went out to sit in the garden with his companions, while someone cooks his dinner, and sweeps his chamber, and makes everything ready for him so that he can dine in comfort and sleep in comfort. While I and my men do without.'

John turned on his heel and went round to the royal court.

The king was seated on a bench, his back against the warm brick wall, looking around him at the newly weeded, newly planted garden. Standing behind him were a couple of gentlemen that John did not know, another stranger strolled on the newly raked paths. When the king heard John's footsteps he glanced up.

'Ah . . .' For a moment he could not remember the name. 'Gardener Tradescant.'

John dropped to his knee and heard Johnnie behind him do the same.

'Your w . . . w . . . work?' the king asked with his slight stammer, gesturing to the dug-over beds.

John bowed. 'When I heard you were coming to Oatlands I came to do what I could, Your Majesty. With my son: John Tradescant.'

The king nodded, his dark eyes half-lidded. 'I thank you,' he said languidly. 'When I am returned to my proper place I shall see that you are returned to yours.'

John bowed again and waited. When there was silence he glanced up. The king made a small gesture of dismissal with his hand. John rose to his feet, bowed, and walked backwards, Johnnie skipping nervously out of the way as his father suddenly reversed, and then quickly copying him. John bowed again at the gateway to the garden and then stepped backwards till he was out of sight.

He turned and met Johnnie's astounded face. 'And that's it?' Johnnie demanded. 'After we came here without being asked, and worked without pay for all this time to make it lovely for him?'

John gave a little snort of amusement and started to walk back to the silkworm house. 'What did you expect? A knighthood?'

'I thought –' Johnnie started and then broke off. 'I suppose I thought he might have some task for us, or he might be glad of us, he might see that we were loyal and thank us –'

John snorted again and opened the little white wooden door. 'This is not a king who has plans or gives thanks,' he said. 'That's one of the reasons he's where he is.'

'But doesn't he realise that you needn't have come at all?'

John paused for a moment and looked down at the stricken face of his boy. 'Oh Johnnie,' he said softly. 'This is not the king of the broadsheet ballads and the church sermons. This is a foolish man who ran into the war because he would not take advice, and when he took advice at all, always chose the wrong people to guide him.

'I came today as much for my father as for the king. I came because my father would have wanted to know that when the king came to his palace, the gardens were weeded. It would have been a matter of duty for him. It was a matter of pride for me. If I had freely chosen my way I would have been for the rights of working men and against the king. But I could not choose freely. I was in his service, and there have been some days – most days – when even seeing him as a fool I pity him from the bottom of my heart. Because he is a fool who cannot help himself. He does not know how to be wise. And his folly has cost him everything he owned.'

'I thought he was a great man, like a hero,' Johnnie remarked.

'Just an ordinary man in an extraordinary place,' John said. 'And too much of a fool to know that. He was taught from birth that he was half-divine. And now he believes it. Poor foolish king.'

John and Johnnie stayed the month working at Oatlands. The cook that Parliament had sent with the king needed fresh vegetables and fruits from the kitchen garden and by picking and choosing from the overgrown beds the two Tradescants were able to send fresh food up to the house each day. The king was surrounded by a small court and his imprisonment seemed more like a guard of honour. He hunted, he shot at archery, he ordered John to roll the bowling green smooth so that they could play at bowls.

John was considering paying for some boys to help with the weeding and planting in winter greens, when the news came that the king was to be moved to Hampton Court. Within a few hours the horses were saddled and the retinue was ready to move on.

The king was in the garden, waiting to be told that his escort was ready. John found he could not keep away from the excitement of great events, and took his pruning hook to the climbers on the far wall of the royal court.

The king, strolling around with two of his courtiers, came upon John and paused to watch him work as the two men stood aside.

'I shall see you repaid for this,' he said simply. He smiled a sly little smile. 'Sooner perhaps than you think.'

John jumped from his ladder and dropped to one knee. 'Your Majesty.'

'They may have defeated my army, but now they tear themselves apart,' the king said. 'All I must do is wait, p . . . patiently wait, until they beg me to come to the throne and set all to rights.'

John risked an upward glance. 'Really, Your Majesty?'

The king's smile transformed him. 'Y . . . Yes. Indeed. The army will destroy P . . . Parliament, and then t . . . tear themselves apart. Already the army tells P . . . Parliament what it should do. When they have no enemy they have no c . . . common cause. All they could do was to destroy, it needs a k . . . king to rebuild. I know th . . . them. There is L . . . Lambert. He heads the f . . . faction against Parliament. He will lead the army against P . . . Parliament and then I will have w . . . won.'

John paused before he could find the words to reply. 'So Your Majesty will greet them kindly when they come? And make an agreement with them?'

The king laughed shortly. 'I shall w . . . win the argument, though I lost the b . . . battle,' he said.

A trooper came to the garden gate. 'We are ready to leave, Your Majesty,' he called.

King Charles, who had never before this year ever done another man's bidding, turned and went from Tradescant's garden.

John and his son went down to the gatehouse to see them leave. John was half-expecting a summons to Hampton Court, but the king went by with only a flicker of recognition that his gardener was on his knees at the roadside.

'And that's it?' Johnnie demanded again.

'That's it,' John replied shortly. 'Royal service. We'll set things in order tomorrow and we'll go home the next day. Our work here is done.'

They discovered why the king had been moved when they got home. The City was in uproar with the apprentices rioting in favour of the king's return and the army had thought it safer to have him at Hampton Court with a larger garrison around him. Alexander Norman had sent Frances to the Ark for safety and forbidden her to return to the City until the riots were over – whether they were ended by the return of the king to his throne, the seizing of control by Parliament, or the arrival of Cromwell's army. There were now three players in the game for England. The king, playing one side against the other and hoping; Parliament, increasingly directionless and fearful of its future; and the army, which seemed to be the only force with a vision of the future and the discipline and determination to make it happen.

The soldiers under Cromwell had forged their faith in themselves, in their cause, and in their God during the long, hard years of fighting; they were not men who would now welcome a compromise. They wanted their pay; but they also wanted the country new-made. They had worked out their beliefs and philosophy in between battles, on forced marches, on dark nights when the rain doused their camp fires. They had given up four years of peaceful life at home to fight for the causes of religious and political freedom. They wanted to see a new world in return for their sacrifice. They were under the command of Thomas Fairfax and John Lambert, two great generals who understood them and shared their beliefs, and marched them on the faithless, fearful city of London to ensure that Parliament did not bow to pressure and make a peace with a king who should be deep in despair and not radiant with hope.

Frances took her husband's note to her father, who was hoeing the new vegetable bed. He looked at it briefly, and handed it back to her.

'You'll stay here,' he said.

'If I may.'

He tipped his hat over his eyes and grinned at his daughter. 'I imagine we can endure your company. Will you keep an eye on Johnnie for me? I don't want him marching up to Parliament with a pruning hook over his shoulder, thinking he is bringing the king home to his own.'

'Mother is more afraid that it'll be you running off to enlist.'

John shook his head. 'I'll not take up arms ever again,' he said. 'It's not a trade I do well. And the king is not a captivating master.'

Alexander wrote almost daily, reporting the fluctuations in the mood of the city. But it was all resolved in August when the army, under the command of General John Lambert, marched into London and declared that they could and would make peace with the king. With the House of Lords they drew up proposals to which any king could agree. Cromwell himself took the proposals to King Charles at Hampton Court.

'He will agree to them and be restored,' Alexander Norman said over a comfortable bottle of wine on the terrace. Frances sat on a stool at her husband's feet and he rested his hand on her golden-brown head. Hester sat opposite John, who was in his father's chair – facing out over the garden, watching the fruit in the orchard gilded with the last rays of sunshine. Johnnie sat at the top of the terrace steps. At Alexander's words he gave a radiant smile.

'The king will be returned to his palaces,' he said wonderingly.

'Please God,' said John. 'Please God that the king sees where his interests lie. He told me that he would set the army against Parliament and conquer them both.'

'Not with John Lambert in command,' Hester remarked. 'That man is not a fool.'

'Can it all be as it was?' Frances asked. 'The queen come home, and the court restored?'

'There'll be some missing faces,' Alexander pointed out. 'Archbishop Laud for one, Earl Strafford.'

'So what was it all for?' Hester asked. 'All these years of hardship?'

John shook his head. 'In the end, perhaps it was to bring the king and Parliament to realise that they have to deal together, they cannot be enemies.'

'A high price to pay,' Frances said, thinking of the years when she and Hester had struggled on their own at the Ark, 'to get some sense into that thick royal head.'

Autumn 1647

'He's gone,' Alexander said flatly the moment he entered the kitchen door and surprised the Tradescants at breakfast. His horse stood sweating in the stable yard outside. 'I came at once to tell you. I rode over. I couldn't bear to wait. I couldn't believe it myself.'

'The king?' John leaped to his feet and strode to the door, checked and turned back.

Alexander nodded. 'Escaped from Hampton Court.'

'Hurrah!' Johnnie shouted.

'My God, no,' John said. 'Not to the French? Not when they were so near agreement? The French haven't rescued him? Kidnapped him?'

Alexander shook his head and dropped into John's vacated seat. Frances put a mug of small ale beside him and he caught her hand and kissed the inside of her wrist in thanks. 'I heard the news this morning and came straight here with it. I couldn't bear even to write it. What days we live in! When will we ever see an end to these alarms!'

'When will we ever see peace?' Hester murmured, one eye on her husband who was standing at the window gazing out into the yard as if ready to run himself.

'Who's got him?' John demanded. 'Not the Irish?'

'He just slipped away on his own, by the looks of it. There's not word of him being broken out by soldiers. Just away with his gentlemen.'

'Sir John Berkeley,' John guessed.

Alexander shrugged. 'Maybe.'

'And where has he gone? France? To be with the queen and Prince Charles?'

'If he has any sense,' Alexander said. 'But why break away now? When things were going so well? When they were so close to agreeing to what he wanted? When he had an agreement with the army that he could sign? All he had to do was wait. The City is for him, Parliament is for him, the army has nothing but fair demands, Cromwell has destroyed the opposition. He has nearly won.'

'Because he always thinks he can do better,' John exclaimed despairingly. 'He always thinks he can do a little more by a grand gesture, a great chance. My father saw him ride out to Spain with the Duke of Buckingham when he was a young prince, and wild and reckless. He never learned the line between taking a risk and ripe folly. No-one ever taught him to take care. He likes the masque – the style and the action. He's never seen that it is all pretend. That real life isn't like that.'

Hester sank back in her chair and glanced down the table at her stepson. Johnnie was looking mutinous. She put out a hand to warn him to hold his silence, but the boy burst out:

'It's the greatest of things! Don't you see? He'll be safe in France by now, and they can beg his pardon from there! The queen will have an army ready for him to command, Prince Rupert will take the cavalry again. They said that he was defeated but he was not!'

John turned a dark look on his son. 'You're right about only one thing,' he said sombrely. 'He's never defeated.'

'That's the wonderful thing about him!'

John shook his head. 'It's the worst.'

Alexander stayed for breakfast and then agreed to stay on for the rest of the week. John was restless all day and at mid-afternoon he went to find Hester.

She was in the rarities room, bringing the planting records up to date in the big garden book.

'I can't stay here, not knowing what's going on,' John said briskly. 'I'll go into Whitehall, see if I can hear some news.'

She put down her pen and smiled at him. 'I knew you'd have to go,' she said. 'Make sure you come home, don't be caught up in whatever is going on there.'

He paused in the doorway. 'Thank you,' he said.

'Oh! For what?'

'For letting me go without badgering me with a dozen questions, without warning me a dozen times.'

She smiled but it did not reach her eyes. 'Since you would go whether I give you leave or no, I might as well give you leave,' she said.

'That's true enough!' John said lightly and went from the room.

Whitehall was in a frenzy of gossip and speculation. John went into a tavern where he might find an acquaintance, bought a mug of ale and looked around for a face he knew. At a nearby table were a group of Africa merchants.

'Mr Hobhouse! Any news? I have come up from Lambeth especially and all I can get is what I know already.'

'You know that he's gone to the Isle of Wight?'

John recoiled. 'What?'

'Carisbrooke Castle. He's set himself up in Carisbrooke Castle.'

'But why? Why would he?'

The merchant shrugged. 'It's not a bad plan. No-one can trust the navy, and if they declare for him how is Cromwell's army going to lay hold of him? He could be snug enough at Carisbrooke, create his court, build his army, and when he is ready sail straight into Portsmouth. He must have had some secret arrangement with the governor Robert Hammond, though everyone thought that Hammond was a Parliament man through and through. The king must have had a deep plan. He'll be waiting for the queen's army from France and then we'll be at war again, if anyone has the stomach for it.'

John briefly closed his eyes. 'This is a nightmare.'

The merchant shook his head. 'I cannot tell you how much money I am losing every day this goes on,' he said. 'I can't induce men to serve, my ships are harassed by pirates in the very mouth of the Thames, and I never know when a ship comes in what price I can command on the quayside or what taxes I shall have to pay. These are times for a madman. And we have a mad king to rule over us.'

'Not another war,' John said.

'He must have laid his plans very deep,' the merchant said. 'He was promising to agree with Cromwell and Ireton only the day before, he gave his word as a king. He was about to sign. What a man! What a false man! Y'know, in business we'd never deal with him. How would I manage if I gave my word and then skipped away?'

'Deep-laid plans?' John asked, seizing on the one unlikely feature.

'So they say.'

One of the other merchants glanced up. 'D'you know better, Mr Tradescant? You were at Oatlands with him, weren't you?'

John sensed the sudden intensity of interest. 'I was planting the garden. He hardly spoke to me. I saw him walk by, nothing more.'

'Well God save him and keep him from his enemies,' one of the men said stoutly and John noticed that while only a few months before the man would have been booed into silence or even thrown out of the tavern there were now a few men who muttered 'Amen' into the bottom of their mugs, and no-one who denied the wish.

'So what happens now?' John asked.

'We wait on his whim,' one of the merchants said sourly. 'As we have been doing for this past year and a half. He was defeated fair and square but he still dances around the country and we still have to wait till he tells us what he will agree to. It makes no sense to me.'

'He won't lie down till he's dead,' one of the men said frankly. 'Would to God that he might fall sick and die and then we could deal with his son, any of the sons. Anyone rather than this man.'

'I'll not ill-wish him,' another man said stoutly.

'Then why will he not come to the City and make an agreement?' someone demanded. 'God knows all we want is to have things at peace.'

John looked from one angry, worried face to another and drained his ale. 'I must go back to my garden,' he said. He had a sense of relief at the thought of the rarities room restored and the garden in its autumn order. 'Whether the king has his own again or no, I have my work to do.'

'You won't go and garden for him at Carisbrooke?' one of the men asked mischievously.

John did not rise to the bait. 'I bid you good day,' he said gently, took his hat in his hand and went out.

They learned the rest of the news in dribs and drabs over the week. The king had no deep-laid plans, just as John had suspected. King Charles had taken an impulsive leap into freedom at the very moment when he was about to sign the agreement with Cromwell which would have brought peace between king and Parliament and stability to the kingdom riven by civil war.

Cromwell had faced down his own army, the men who had fought for him in the long and bitter war. The men had told their commander and told Parliament that they expected more from the peace than a king restored to his own, they wanted changes. They wanted justice for the common people, and a living wage. They wanted Parliaments which would represent all the working men of the country and not just the gentry. Cromwell had taken the hard line against them, defending the king against his own men. He had shot the leaders for mutiny, he had made the men drop down their pamphlets into the mud, and then he had returned to Hampton Court with the blood of his own soldiers on his hands, to meet with Charles and conclude the other side of the bargain which would bring the king home. Cromwell had defeated the men who would have shouted against a restoration of the king, and then returned to the king for his signature on the document, as they had agreed it.

But Charles had gone. He had given his word, his word of honour as a king, and then slipped away in the night. He rode with two gentlemen to the New Forest where he had hunted so often with Buckingham in the old days, and taken a boat across to the Isle of Wight, putting his faith in the belief that the governor, Robert Hammond, would take his part on the slight evidence that Hammond had once said he disliked the Levellers in the army, because he was a nephew of one of the king's chaplains, and cousin, many times removed, to the Marquess of Winchester.

'He trusted a man because he knows his uncle?' John asked Hester in despair as they sat by the fireside before going to bed.

She shook her head. 'Oh, John. What else could he do but dodge and dive and scrape about?'

'He could come to an agreement!' John exclaimed. 'And have his throne again!'

She picked up the sewing from her lap. 'He is the king,' she said. 'He would not feel that he has to agree. He has always thought that others should agree with him.'

Hester was right. When the king arrived at Carisbrooke Castle and found that Governor Hammond imprisoned him, rather than hailing him as a hero, he gave his parole and immediately set to scheming. He sent secret messages to the Scots and told them that he was ready now to agree to the very things he had sworn he would never accept when he had been their prisoner. The Scots, tempted by the thought of a king who would accept their parliament and their church, secretly betrayed their allies, the English Parliament, and made a secret solemn engagement to restore Charles to his throne. In return he swore that for a trial period of three years he would abolish the position of bishops and run the English church on the Scottish model. He promised that all the senior posts in the land (and their fat fees) would be given to Scotsmen.

But Charles was no better at keeping his secrets than keeping his word. News of the agreement soon leaked out, especially when a proposal from the English Parliament was insultingly rejected by the king who was visibly, excessively, puffed up with confidence. Soon everyone knew that the king was dealing a false hand again.

'He would make an alliance with the Scots Covenanters?' Johnnie asked his father in bewilderment. 'But he refused to agree with them for all those months at Newark.'

'He has changed his mind,' John said quietly. 'He wants to make a new agreement. He wants to beat Parliament and Cromwell's army at any price. He hated the covenanting Scots and could not agree with them, but they are now the only allies he can get. He is agreeing to things he denied completely only a few months ago. He refused them when he was their prisoner but now he has been seized by the English army he is looking kindly on the Scots again.'

Johnnie scowled. 'So what *does* he believe in?' he demanded in exasperation. 'I thought that he would never give up the English church and the bishops. You told me he thought that was sacred. You told me he would never give up his rights as a king.'

'I think now he is looking to survive,' John said grimly. 'And if he can get back on the throne then who can force him to keep to agreements he made when he was in prison?'

'He would play false?'

John softened at the sight of his son's distress. 'A king must be on his throne,' he said gently. 'You can understand that he might think it was worth anything to get back to his place.'

'And will he do it?' Johnnie asked. 'Will he come back to London? Will I see him on his throne?'

John shook his head. 'They'll never let him off the Isle of Wight again,' he said. 'I wouldn't, if I were General Cromwell.'

Spring 1648

John was in his garden, planting out his tender rarities which had wintered in the orangery. The great tufted American daisy was putting out fresh shoots from its rosette of leaves, and the Virginian woodbine was throwing out scarlet snaky shoots with little unfurling green leaves from its dry, dead-looking trunk. John thought for a moment of Suckahanna with the scarlet honeysuckle flowers in her dark hair, and the night-time scent of honeysuckle on their sleeping platform when he kissed her neck and crushed the flowers beneath his cheek. He patted the earth gently around the roots, saw that the climber could extend and find footholds on the strings hammered in to the rough wall and then turned his back on them to admire his tulip beds.

'There is nothing, *nothing* to compare with them,' he remarked to Hester as she came down the path towards him. Then he broke off abruptly at the sight of her face. 'What's wrong?'

He glanced towards the lane as if he feared a troop of horse there. Even with the king imprisoned at Carisbrooke Castle no man could be certain that the nation would stay at peace. There were too many nations that might wish to meddle, there were too many armies that the queen or Prince Charles might prevail upon to muster.

'I don't know,' Hester said, producing a letter from her apron pocket. 'A letter. For you. From the Parliamentary commissioners.'

John scowled and held out his hand. He broke the seal, spread the paper, read it, and then read it again. He chuckled incredulously.

'What is it?' Hester demanded, trying to read upside down.

'I am to go to Oatlands and make good,' John said. 'Who would have thought it? They want me to mend the walks in the vineyard garden and mow the bowling green, and make good.' He paused and looked up at her. 'How times change and yet change not at all,' he observed.

389

'I am gardener to Oatlands Palace still it seems, though there is no king and no court to see my work.'

'You'll go –' she suggested, looking at him warily.

He folded the letter, very businesslike. 'Of course. Why not?'

'I thought you might have some feeling that you wouldn't garden for them, where you had gardened for the king, and for her.'

John shook his head. Unconsciously he put out a hand and tucked a stray shoot of the Virginian woodbine beneath a guiding piece of twine nailed into the wall. 'I've been torn all my life, Hester. I'm growing quite resigned to divided loyalties.'

'Johnnie'll take it hard,' she said. 'He's held to being one of the king's gardeners through all this time.'

'We're gardeners to the best gardens in the kingdom,' John said firmly. 'And Oatlands has always been one of the best. I'd stay faithful to my garden before I stayed faithful to any master, you know that. Especially a master as faithless and as changeable as the king. The garden comes first, Hester. If someone will pay me to plant it and tend to it I'll go at once and I'll take Johnnie to help me. He has to learn. King or no king, we have to work for our living. And our living is the gardens. Our great duty is to the gardens.'

'But why would Parliament care for the gardens?' Hester mused. 'With so much else to do? And they were the queen's own gardens. Unless they're putting them in order for her return? And there's been some secret agreement?'

John shook his head. 'Could be. Or maybe they're just men of sense. If the king never returns and Parliament owns Oatlands and all the other royal palaces, then they will sell it at a better profit if it is set in a handsome garden and not in a wilderness. But if the king comes back to his own again and finds it overgrown, then he will only make them pay to set it right.'

'Will you be gone long?' she asked.

'A month at least,' he replied. 'I have duties now, Hester. I am gardener to the Parliamentary commissioners! I am a Parliament man!'

She laughed with him. 'But Johnnie may not find it so easy to change masters,' she warned.

'Johnnie will have to learn,' he ruled. 'It is one thing to be a boy and love stories of Prince Rupert. It is another thing to be a man and to know that if you serve a master who changes as often as the weather then you had better not cleave too tight to him. The king is spinning like a weathercock. The rest of us must look to our own lives.'

April 1648, Oatlands Palace

A troop of Parliamentary horse was still quartered at Oatlands and John's first action, after he had opened up his old house next to the silkworm house, was to find the commander and demand that the horses be banned from grazing in any of the courts or on the bowling lawns.

The commander was happy to agree and promised John the use of as many troopers as he needed to help him in the weeding and the setting of the garden to rights.

'I visited your garden ten years ago,' he said. 'It was a wonderful sight. D'you still have that service tree? I remember it so well.'

'Yes,' John said. 'It still grows. And we have many more rare trees that I have brought back from Virginia. I have a tulip tree with great green leaves that flowers with a blossom like a tulip as big as your head. I have a maple tree which has leaves of scarlet. I have a creeper called a passion flower since some say it shows the marks of Jesus. I have a beautiful new convolvulus, I can sell you the seeds for that, and a Virginian foxglove.'

'As soon as I am discharged and in my own home again I shall come and see what you have for sale,' the officer promised.

'Where is your home?' John asked.

'Sussex, in the west of the county,' the man replied. 'I have a light, sandy soil, very fertile and easy to work. A little dry in summer perhaps, and I'm on the edge of the South Downs so I get a cold wind in winter; my Lenten lilies only come at Easter. But my summer flowers last for longer than my neighbours'.'

'You will grow almost anything then,' John said encouragingly. 'Some of my new Virginia plants can tolerate very cold weather and very hot summers since that is the weather of their home. They would do well with you. I have a creeper with leaves that turn as red as a cardinal's cloak in autumn. It would look well against any wall, red as a rose.'

'I should like to see it,' the man said. 'And what will you do here?'

'Just set the place in order again,' John said. 'I was not ordered to do any planting.'

'Is His Majesty to be brought here?' Johnnie asked, driven to interrupting.

The officer heard the hero-worship in the boy's voice and looked hard at him. 'I think we should all pray that he never comes near any of his palaces again,' he said sternly. 'His greed has taken me and all my men away from our homes and our families and our gardens for six long years. He can rot in Carisbrooke Castle forever, for all I care.'

John leaned on his son's shoulder and the boy obediently said nothing, only the scarlet flush up to his ears showed his distress.

'But you were in his service,' the man said irritably. 'I suppose you're all royalists.'

'We're gardeners,' John said steadily. 'And now I am gardening for Parliament. Still gardening. My enemies are inclement weather and pests. I need no other.'

Unwillingly the commander laughed. 'I know no worse, actually,' he said.

Summer 1648

There was a knock on the big front door of the Ark in mid-May and Hester, putting aside her working apron, went to open it with her usual sense of apprehension. But when she saw the visitor on the doorstep her expression turned to pleasure. 'Major Lambert!' she exclaimed. 'Come to see our tulips?'

'Yes indeed. I couldn't resist.' He stepped into the hall and bent over her hand.

'Is it still Major?' she asked, looking at the rich feather in his hat and the shining leather of his boots.

'Ah no!' he said with a flourish. 'I am a general now, Mrs Tradescant. And before I have done I shall sit in Parliament and bestow a baronetcy on you for your services to gardeners. Or a dukedom. Whatever you would wish.'

Hester giggled. 'Come and see the tulips then,' she urged. 'They are lovely this year. My husband came back last spring and he has many new species which you will want to see, some beautiful plants from Virginia. You will never resist our tulip tree.'

'I beg your pardon?'

Hester laughed. 'I promise. A most beautiful tree which bears white flowers shaped exactly like a tulip. I've not seen them yet because we have only two saplings but we have taken cuttings and my husband swears they will thrive.'

John Lambert followed her through the house and paused on the terrace to look out over the garden. It was the first time he had seen it properly weeded and pruned and looking its best.

'This is a little piece of paradise,' he said, his eyes going over the nodding blossoms of the fruit trees and the flowerbeds and nursery beds before the house. 'It was well-named when you called it the Ark. It has been like a flood of terror outside these walls and yet here it always seems to be like peace.'

Hester stood very still and absorbed the compliment like a blessing. 'I have spent my whole life trying to make it so,' she said. 'I am glad you can see it.'

He glanced at her as if they understood each other very well. 'If we can make the country as peaceful and fertile as this garden, Mrs Tradescant, then it will all have been worth while. If I can make every cottage garden a safe place like this, and every hardworking man in the country with a legal right to his cottage and his garden, then I will have done my duty as well as you have done yours.'

She looked curiously at him. 'Aren't those Leveller sentiments?' she asked. 'I thought the Leveller cause was stamped out?'

He smiled but he did not disagree. 'Not out of the hearts and minds. I think that any man who has seen how the poor suffer in this country, and has seen the way that poor men fought for their rights, would want to see the great wastes and parks opened up so that homeless people could build themselves houses, and hungry people could grow food. I'm a landholder myself, Mrs Tradescant. I don't want my garden walls pulled down. But I don't want huge parks enclosed to feed and shelter deer while men and women outside go hungry.'

Hester nodded and led the way down the garden path towards the blaze of colour that was the tulip beds. She glanced back with a half-smile at John Lambert's transfixed expression.

'They're good, aren't they?'

'They are superb,' he breathed. 'I must, I *must* have some of those.'

'I'll fetch a pen and paper for your order,' Hester said with satisfaction. 'And you must come again next month and see the roses. They are going to be wonderful this year. I like our roses even better than our tulips.'

He shook his head, and something in that gesture alerted her that he was not as carefree as he had suggested. 'I'm afraid I will be busy elsewhere in June,' he said.

Hester understood what John Lambert had meant when the day after his visit the news came of royalist bands mustered in every town and village in every county. Men who had put away their pikes thinking the battle was over were running and riding up and down the country lanes again, calling men to fight for the king, who needed only one battle to be won against a demoralised and divided Parliament and army to come to his own. The navy suddenly declared for the king and sailed into harbours all along the south coast, and declared every port as royalist. All over the country the retired royalist officers were out again, calling men to arms. Each county, each town, each village had its own royalist headquarters and royalist troop. The nation was at war once more, spontaneously, naturally, and the prize was to release the king and restore him to his throne in a great heave of nostalgia for the days of peace before the war.

Men who had stood by and watched Cromwell's army take the victory in the first king's war were now seized with such an impatience for peace that they turned out for Charles, certain that only by restoring him to the throne could the kingdom find peace. Men who had been indifferent soldiers under Cromwell turned their coats and hoped for pay and a victory under the command of the royalists. And those who had fought for the king over the long four years of the king's war and suffered and feared in the two years since, prayed that this one last chance might restore them to their former fortunes.

They were not summoned by a message. They responded almost individually, spontaneously, in an uprising which was as much an irritated demand for a return to more peaceful days, as a struggle of principle about the existence of bishops.

It was incredible to Hester that the king could be the centre of a second catastrophe, even while he was in his prison. Without even being at liberty his mere presence could be the focus of unrest, and the country which had been at peace for nearly two years was suddenly at war again. It was a full-scale war fought in a hundred different pitched battles all over the kingdom, and then news came to Lambeth that Lord Norwich was besieging the City of London itself and was likely to take it for the king. If London fell then Parliament itself would be taken, and then the war must be over and the king would be the victor.

Hester caught Johnnie sneaking a saddle on to the horse in the stable yard, a pack at his side. Her steady temper suddenly broke. 'And where the devil d'you think you're going?'

He turned to her. 'You can't stop me. I'm going to fight for the king.'

'You're a child.'

'I'm nearly fifteen, old enough to fight.'

It was that spark that fired the charge. Hester sprung on him and seized him by his shirt collar and marched him, like a schoolboy, down the garden path, past the glorious rose beds where waves of perfume billowed in their wake, to the orchard where John was up a ladder disbudding apple trees.

'The king needs fools!' Hester exclaimed. 'A fools' army for a fool of a king.'

'I will go!' Johnnie proclaimed, struggling out from her grip. 'I will not be under your command. I'm a man, I shall play a man's part.'

Hester thrust him at his father. 'He's fourteen,' she announced baldly. 'Says he's a man. I can't rule him any more. You will have to decide. Is he to go to serve the king or not?'

John stepped slowly off the lower rungs of the ladder and looked at his son. 'What's this?'

Johnnie did not look away but faced his father like a young stag facing the leader of the herd. 'I want to do my duty,' he said. 'I want to serve the king.'

'The king is not served by riots and uproar and Englishmen killing each other in the streets of Maidstone and Canterbury,' John said slowly.

'If that is what it takes –'

John shook his head. 'Making peace in a kingdom is done by ceaseless work, ceaseless working towards agreement,' he said. 'Haven't you lived your childhood through a war and seen that at the end there is nothing agreed, nothing is any further forward?'

'I want to do my duty!'

John put his hand on the bough of the apple tree as if he would draw strength from it. 'Your duty is to your God and to your father and mother,' he said.

'You don't even believe in God,' Johnnie shot back. 'You don't believe in anything. You have not done your duty by me as a father – you left us for years. You're the king's man but you don't fight for him, you're in the pay of Parliament and you joke about being a Parliament gardener. You're a Virginia planter but you stay at home in Lambeth. I won't be told my duty by you!'

Hester started forwards to protect her stepson against the blow that must come, and then forced herself to pause, and hold back. John did not strike Johnnie but froze, his hand tightened on the bough of the apple tree until the knuckles went pale.

'I am sorry you think so low of me,' John said quietly. 'And what you say is true. I lost my faith in God when your mother died and I could not even hold her for fear of spreading the infection to you. I have tried to show my respect to others' faith. But the heart went out of me. I did leave you and Frances and your stepmother at a time when I should have stayed and protected you – but I thought the king would draw me into fighting and never let me go. And I was right to fear that – he has drawn the whole four kingdoms of men into fighting and he has never let them go. I have my headright in Virginia but I could not keep it without killing people that I have every reason to love and respect. It was a war between countrymen there too.'

Johnnie was about to speak, Hester knowing him so well, knew that he was fighting not to break down in tears and pitch into his father's arms. He held himself very still, rigid as a soldier under fire.

'But I do have a right to speak,' John said. 'Because I know things that you don't. Because I have thought of things in all this time. I have struggled with one loyalty against another, with one love against another. You might think that I am weak – but this is how my life has come to me. It is not a simple life of simple loyalties. I am not like my father. He found master after master that he could love and follow with a loyal heart. He loved Sir Robert Cecil, and then the Duke of Buckingham, and then the king. He never questioned that they were the master and he the man. But it's not been like that for me. And it won't be like that for you. The world has changed, Johnnie. It's not enough to cite duty any more and go marching off to the rattle of a recruiting drum. You have to think for yourself, you have to pick your own path.'

There was a long silence in the orchard. Somewhere in the high leaves of one of the trees a blackbird started to sing.

'I beg your pardon for speaking as I did,' Johnnie said stiffly. 'And I ask your permission as your dutiful son. I want to go and serve the king. That's my path. I have considered it for myself. I want to fight for my king.'

John shot a look at Hester as if to ask if she could see a way out. One look was enough. Hester's face was tragic, both hands gripped under the shield of her apron.

'God bless you and keep you then,' John said slowly. 'And come back home the minute you have a doubt, Johnnie. You are the only Tradescant heir, and very dear to us.'

Slowly Johnnie dropped to one knee on the grass for his father's blessing. Over his bent fair head John looked at Hester and saw that he had said the right thing – they had to let their son go to war.

Dearest Mother and Father,
    I write this to you on the road to Colchester. I am riding with Lord Norwich and half a dozen gentlemen and a fine

*troop of more than a thousand strong. We were rebuffed at
London – I got there as they were leaving, unluckily for me –
but at least I am in a troop of horse gathering recruits as we
go.*

*The mare is keeping up well and I am sure to feed her every
night. We have to forage for our own feed which is hard to do
in some of these farms that were poor enough before we arrived
and are left worse. Some of the gentlemen use the farmers and
labourers very hard, and this does not increase our welcome
further down the road.*

*The ships will supply us when we are in Colchester and an
army is coming to our aid from out of East Anglia. There is
no doubt that we will win.*

*My love to Frances and her husband. You can ask Alexander
to delay his supply of barrels of gunpowder as a favour to me.
I hope you are all well. Your loving and dutiful son – John.*

'He signs himself John, not Johnnie,' Hester observed.

'He sounds well,' John answered.

They stood, cheek to cheek in the hall, both of them reading the
short letter, and then reading it again.

'She's a good horse, she'll keep him safe,' John said.

'He doesn't sound very happy with the troop.'

John relinquished the letter into her hands and turned towards the
garden. 'How could he be? A boy who has seen so little of the world,
suddenly ridden off to war?'

'Should you fetch him home?' Hester asked.

John paused, hearing the longing in her voice. 'I cannot,' he said.

She would have argued but he raised his hand to check her. 'Don't
reproach me, Hester, it means as much to me as it does to you to see
my son enmeshed in this war. I have prayed just as hard as you that
we would be at peace before he reached his manhood. I thought it was
over. I was sure it was over. But I can't fetch him home like a naughty
schoolboy. He has to walk his own path.'

He looked at her and saw the blank agony on her face.

'He is my son!' she said passionately. 'Joking about gunpowder.'

John paused, bleak with worry, nodded, and went out to his garden.

July 1648

Frances was at the Ark for the plague months of the summer and Hester found that her stepdaughter's company was the only one she could bear, as they waited for news of Johnnie. The war was favouring the king and she could hope that Johnnie would march into London as part of a triumphant royal army. In July the Scots confirmed in the most dramatic way that they had changed sides and were now for the king, when they crossed the border with an army of nine thousand men to fling against the battle-weary, underpaid, disillusioned forces of Parliament.

It was an appallingly wet summer. The roses in the garden filled with rain and rotted in their blooms. The strawberries and raspberries were washed into sodden pulp on their stems. Hester spent the days watching the rain pour down the great panes of Venetian glass in the rarities room, looking out at the flooded garden, at her husband splashing around ankle-deep in mud, digging ditches to drain the sodden land into the stream outside the house which was already bubbling over the little bridge and still rising.

Uncharacteristically, Hester did not throw a piece of sacking over her cap and go out to help him. She sat at the desk without books before her, without sewing in her hands. She did not even talk to the few visitors who came to see the rarities, though with the river in flood and the country at war again, they might as well have shut the Ark for all the money they took. Hester sat in silence, watching the rain, Frances in silence at her side.

The news came that the English royalist troops had come under attack on the road to Colchester and had had to rush into the town for shelter. There was a brief and terrible battle as the royalists were driven back into the town, before they got the town gates shut and the Parliamentary soldiers locked out. Hundreds of men were killed in close fighting which was bloodier and more bitter than any known in England before. The names of the hundreds of individual soldiers killed in that spiteful skirmish were lost. Hester sat watching the rain, not knowing if her stepson was alive, or face down in the mud outside the gates of Colchester.

It was not a siege, it was a massacre-in-waiting. General Fairfax with John Lambert was commanding the Parliament army and he had ringed the city with a rampart and ditch with ten forts studding the perimeter. No-one would be able to get out alive. The whole city was not just besieged, it was completely entrapped.

'John Lambert is there?' Hester asked when Frances brought a newssheet and read the report of the siege.

'Yes,' Frances said, and looked at her mother.

'What times these are: that John Lambert should be in one army and my boy in another,' Hester said very softly.

There was another royalist army raised at Kingston upon Thames, commanded by Lord Holland, supported by the Duke of Buckingham, the son of the Tradescants' old master. John had scowled at the mention of his name and stamped out to lay sandbags at the front door of the Ark. The road to Lambeth was completely under water and the little stream before the house had burst its banks and was spreading over the road and into the Tradescants' orchard. John was fearful that the River Thames itself would flood and bring salt water to contaminate his land on the north side of the road but there was nothing he could do to prevent it.

The new royalist army mustered only a few men. Little more than five hundred turned out in the wet and marched first to London and then to Reigate Castle, and then turned in a retreat which quickly became a rout through the villages north of London to defeat at Surbiton. The Earl of Holland was captured by the Parliamentary army and sent to London. Parliament decreed that he would be beheaded for treason to his country. The Duke of Buckingham slipped away to safety in Holland.

'He would,' Tradescant said sourly.

Suddenly, royal fever seemed to have passed as abruptly as it had raged. There was no further uprising in England. It would all depend on the Scots: whether they could get to Colchester in time to relieve the town, whether they would march all the way south and into the very city of London itself.

The royalists besieged in Colchester, their rations running low and any hope for relief now gone, asked for safe passage for women and children, opened the sally port door and sent them out to the Parliamentary army. To their horror the women were stripped and beaten, and sent back to the fort. England had never seen such savagery in fighting. The rules of warfare had been suspended. Men who would have been chivalrous to a defeated enemy six years ago were now in a killing frenzy of rage that war should have broken out again. There were rumours that when the besieged came out of Colchester, as soon they must, they would be cut down where they stood. There would be no quarter, there would be no prisoners. There would not even be trials for treason. When the men lay down their arms the Parliament cavalry would ride over them.

Hester said nothing when John told her this news, she did not weep, she did not whisper Johnnie's name. She looked out of the window and said only: 'When is it ever going to stop raining?'

John went out into the garden and left her watching the drops run down the panes.

They were glad of the rain in Colchester. It was their only drinking water. For meat they had to eat their horses, then dogs, cats, rats, anything they could catch. There was no flour for bread, there were no fruit or vegetables left in the town. Men started to sicken, everyone went hungry.

Hester put a piece of sacking around her shoulders and splashed out into the garden to look at the rain-soaked lettuce, onions, peppers, beans, peas and herbs in their carefully tended beds. 'He's never gone hungry,' she said softly to herself. 'Brought up beside our garden he might have lacked meat once in a while, but he's always had fruit and vegetables. He's never wanted for anything before.'

Hester was hoping that the Scots would march south quickly and relieve Colchester as their first objective. They swept over the border looking like a conquering force and reached Preston Moor, just a mile north of Preston, without anyone standing against them. But there they were met by the Parliament army commanded by Cromwell himself with John Lambert at his side, commanding the cavalry. When Hester heard that it was John Lambert against the only men who could rescue her son, she put her head in her hands at the kitchen table and stayed very still for a long while, as if she were asleep.

When the news reached Colchester of the Scots' defeat there was no hope left for them. The garrison surrendered to a harsh and unforgiving victor. The war was over, the king defeated once more; and the Tradescants had nothing to do but to wait and see if Johnnie would come home, or if he would be among the many hundreds who would never come home again.

Hester left her place at the Venetian window and put a chair and a table at the front door, which overlooked the road from Lambeth. She put her sewing basket on the table and appeared, to any casual passer-by, as if she were sitting at her work and enjoying the September sunshine after the wet summer days. Only John and Frances knew that the shirt she held in her lap was no further forward by the end of September than it had been on the black day that Colchester surrendered.

Autumn 1648

A carter brought him home, a man who had visited the Ark in his boyhood and remembered it as a palace of treasures, and had a fondness for the Tradescant name. Johnnie, pale, jolted by the rough roads, terribly thin, and with a dark, ill-healing scar from his hipbone to his rib, lay in the back on a heap of sacks.

Hester heard the rumble of the wheels and glanced up from her idle hands holding the unsewn shirt and then dropped her work, overturned her chair and flew out of the front door and into the road.

'Johnnie!' she exclaimed as she peered over the tailboard.

He managed a little smile. 'Mother.'

'Drive around to the back,' Hester ordered the driver, her months of passive silence quite forgotten. She jumped up on to the step of the cart, her eyes fixed on her stepson, and held on as they jolted over the little bridge, went past the terrace of the house and into the stable yard. John, picking apples, looked towards the house and saw the cart turning into the yard with his wife clinging like an urchin to the tailgate. He leaped down from the ladder and walked towards the house. He did not run. He feared too much what might greet him.

The carter and Hester had Johnnie on his feet, walking slowly towards the kitchen door, an arm around each of them. Cook flung open the door and Hester guided them through to the parlour and seated Johnnie in his father's chair at the fireside.

He had gone very white, his lips pale in his pale face. Hester snapped over her shoulder, 'Fetch the brandy,' and Cook ran to obey her. John came in, treading mud on to the polished wooden parlour floor.

'Son?'

Johnnie looked up at his father and something in that glance, something vulnerable and unjustly hurt, reminded John so powerfully of

Jane, his lost wife, that his pity for his son and his old grief for her hit him like a renewed blow. He dropped to his knees and took his son's hands.

'You're safe now,' he said. 'Safe home. Are you hurt much?'

'I got a pike in my side,' Johnnie whispered. 'It hurt a lot and bled a lot. But it's healing now.'

Hester held the glass of brandy to his lips and Johnnie sipped.

'We'll have you in bed in a moment,' she promised him. 'And a proper dinner for you.' She smoothed his long fair hair from his forehead. 'My boy,' she said tenderly. 'My poor boy.'

Cook returned. 'His bed is ready for him, sheets warmed.'

The carter and Hester stepped forwards to help him but John put them back. 'I can manage,' he said huskily, and took his son in his arms.

The boy weighed little more than he did when he was only ten years old. Tradescant scowled at the lightness of the body and went towards the stairs. Hester ran ahead and opened the bedroom door, turned down the sheets.

'I'm lousy,' Johnnie protested. 'And covered with fleas.'

'Doesn't matter,' Hester said, slipping off his boots and stripping down his breeches.

He gave a little whimper of pain as she pulled up his shirt and she saw that the dirty linen had stuck to the raw wound.

'We'll soon have you well again,' she said.

Both her husband and her son heard the old determination in Hester's voice. 'We'll soon have you well again.'

King Charles blithely celebrated his forty-eighth birthday at Newport and entertained the Parliamentary negotiators who had been sent from London to make a new peace with a king who had broken every agreement they had made before. This time he was more accommodating than ever; but would not, swore that he could not, allow the sale of the bishops' lands and palaces. The bishops could not be abolished, their position must be maintained. The most he would agree was to rule without them for three years, the promise he had already given to the Scots. But Parliament was firmer than the Scots. It would settle for nothing less than the complete abolition of all the bishops and the freeing of their wealth and lands.

Alexander Norman and Frances, visiting the Ark in November, found

Johnnie sitting at the fireside wrapped in a fine warm gown with his father and mother beside him, discussing the fate of the king.

'Any news?' John asked his son-in-law.

'The Levellers are rising in strength in the army,' Alexander replied. 'And they demand that there be no king ever again and that Parliament be elected every three years by every man with a stake in the country.'

'What does that mean for the king?' John asked.

Alexander shook his head. 'If they gain control of Parliament then it must mean that he is sent abroad. There can be no place for him.'

'Perhaps he will agree,' Hester suggested, one eye on her son. 'Perhaps the king and Parliament can agree at Newport.'

'He must agree,' Alexander replied. 'He must see that he has to agree. He has fought two wars against his own people, and lost them both. He tried the greatest gamble he could play – he brought the Scots in against his own countrymen. And he has lost. He must now agree.'

Johnnie flushed and moved uneasily in his chair. 'How can he? How can he agree to become nothing? He's the king in the sight of God. Does he call God a liar?'

Frances crossed to him and took his hand. 'Now you stop,' she said with the firmness of an older sister. 'You've done your fighting for him. You've done quite enough, and it did no good for anybody. The king must take his own decision, it's nothing to do with you now, or any of us.'

'She's right,' Hester said. 'And none of us can do anything for or against the king. He has travelled his own road. He will have to decide what he should do now.'

The king decided to take the high road of principle – or perhaps he decided he would gamble once again – or perhaps he decided he would make a gesture, a proud theatrical gesture, and see what came of it. He rejected Parliament's proposals boldly, recklessly, outright. And then he waited to see what would happen next.

What happened next rather surprised him. The men of Cromwell's army, Lambert's men, Fairfax's men, furious at the delays and missed opportunities, clear in their own minds that what should happen next was an unbreakable peace and a reform of the laws of the land in favour of hard-working common people, invaded the House of Commons, excluded those Members of Parliament known to be sympathetic to the king, and insisted that the king should be brought to trial for treason against his subjects.

Hester brought the news to John as he was watering the tender plants in the orangery. The frost on the window pane was melting and the glass was dewy and opaque. The citrus trees, their boughs carrying the last glowing fruit of oranges and lemon, scented the room, the charcoal in the hearth shifted and crackled as it glowed. Hester paused on the threshold, reluctant to break the sense of peace. Then she set her lips and marched into the room.

'They have taken the king from the Isle of Wight and are bringing him to London. They have called him for trial,' she said flatly. 'They have accused him of treason.'

John froze where he stood, the watering bottle dribbling cold water on his boot. 'Treason?' he repeated. 'How can a king be charged with treason?'

'They say he tried to steal away the people's liberty and to set up a tyranny,' Hester said. 'And to make war on his people is supposed to be treason.'

The water made a little puddle around John's feet but he did not notice it, and neither did Hester, her gaze fixed on his stunned face.

'Where is he?' John asked numbly.

'On the road to London, that's what they're saying in Lambeth. I suppose they'll put him in the Tower, or perhaps under arrest in one of the palaces.'

'And then?'

'They say that he is to be tried for treason. Before a court. A proper trial.'

'But the punishment for treason . . .'

'Is death,' Hester finished.

Just before Christmas there was a knock at the door. Johnnie, still nervous, started at the loud sound and Hester, hurrying to open it, whispered a blasphemy at whoever had disturbed her boy.

As she opened the door she composed her face into stern serenity at the sight of the armed man.

'Message for John Tradescant, as was gardener to the king,' the man said.

'Not here,' Hester said with her habitual caution.

'I'll leave the message with you then,' the man said cheerfully. 'The king wants to see him. At Windsor.'

'He is summoned to Windsor by the king?' Hester asked, disbelievingly.

'As he likes,' the man said disrespectfully. 'The king orders him there, he can go or no as he likes as far as I'm concerned. I take my orders from Colonel Harrison, who guards the king. And his orders were to tell Mr Tradescant that the king is asking for him. And now I've done that. And now I'm off.'

He gave her a friendly nod and crossed the little bridge to the road before Hester could say another word. She watched him march up the road to the ferry at Lambeth before she closed the door and went to find John in the garden.

He was pruning the roses with a sharp knife, his hands a mass of scratches from his work.

'Why won't you wear gloves?' Hester remarked irritably.

He grinned. 'I always mean to, then I start work and I think I can do it without scratching myself, and then I can't be troubled to stop and go and find them, and then I draw blood and think there's no point in fetching them now.'

'You'll never guess who came to the door.'

'All right. I never will.'

'A messenger from the king,' she said, watching for his reaction.

He stiffened, like an old hunter when it hears the hunting horn. 'The king sent for me?'

She nodded. 'To attend him at Windsor. The man was clear that you need not go unless you wish. The king has no power to order you to obey. But he brought the message.'

John stepped carefully through the rose bushes, disentangling his coat when it was caught by a thorn, his mind already at Windsor.

'What can he want of me?'

She shrugged. 'Not some harebrained scheme of escape?'

He shook his head. 'Surely not. But there's nothing to interest him in the garden at this time of year.'

'Will you go?'

Already he was walking towards the house, his pruning knife slipped in his belt, his roses almost forgotten. 'Of course I have to go,' he said.

They had no horse, there was not enough money to replace the mare who had carried Johnnie to Colchester and been slaughtered for meat during the siege. John walked to the ferry at Lambeth and took a boat upriver to Windsor.

The castle looked much the same: a guard of soldiers at the door, the usual bustle and work which surrounded the royal court. But it was all strangely diminished: quieter, with less excitement, as if even the kitchen maids no longer believed that they were cooking the meat of God's own anointed representative on earth, but instead working in a kitchen for a mere mortal.

John paused before the crossed pikes of the men on guard.

'John Tradescant,' he said. 'The king sent for me.'

The pikes were lifted. 'He's at his dinner,' one of the soldiers said.

John went through the gateway, through the inner court, and into the great hall.

There was an eerie sense of a life lived again. There was the royal canopy billowing a little in the draughts from the open windows. There was the king seated in state below it, the great chair before the great table, and the table crowded with dishes. There were the common people, crammed into the gallery, watching the king eat as they always did. There was the yeoman usher to declare the table ready for laying, the yeoman of ewry to spread the cloth, the yeoman of pantry to lay out the long knives, spoons, salt, and trenchers, the yeoman of cellar standing behind the chair with the decanter of wine. It was all as it had been, and yet it was completely different.

There was no constant ripple of laughter and wit, there was no vying for the eye of the king. There was no plump, ringletted queen at his side, and none of the glorious portraits and tapestries which had always been hung in his sight.

And Charles himself was changed. His face was scarred with disappointment, deep bags beneath his dark eyes, lines on his forehead, his hair thinner and streaked with grey, his moustache and beard still perfectly combed, but paler with white hairs where it had been glossy brown.

He looked down the hall and saw John; but his habitual diffidence did not allow him to greet a friendly face. He merely nodded and with a tiny gesture indicated that John should wait.

John, who had dropped to his knee as he came into the hall, rose up and took a seat at a table.

'What you kneeling for?' a man asked critically.

John hesitated. 'Habit, I suppose. Do you not kneel in his presence?'

'Why should I? He's no more than a man, as I am.'

'Times are changing,' John observed.

'You eating?' another man said.

John looked around. These were not the elegant courtiers who used to dine in the hall. These were the soldiers of Cromwell's army, unimpressed by the ritual. Hungry, honest, straightforward men at their dinner.

John drew a trencher towards him and took a spoonful of meat from the common bowl.

When the king had finished dining one yeoman came forward and offered him a bowl to wash his fingertips while another offered the fine linen cloth to dry his hands. Neither of them kneeled, John noticed, and wondered if the king would refuse their service.

He did not even complain. The king took the service as it would have been offered to a mere lord of the manor. He did not even remark that they were not on their knees. John saw the mystery of kingship shrink before his eyes.

John rose at his place, waiting for an order. The king crooked his finger and John approached the high table, paused and bowed.

King Charles rose from his seat, stepped down from the dais and snapped his fingers for a pageboy, who sprang to follow him.

'I d . . . dined on melons two nights ago,' he remarked to John as if no time at all had passed since John and the queen and the king had planned the planting of Oatlands together. 'And I th . . . th . . . thought that we always said we should have a m . . . melon bed at Wimbledon. I saved you the seeds for p . . . planting.'

John bowed, his mind whirling. 'Your Majesty?'

The pageboy stepped forwards and handed John a little wooden box filled with seeds.

'W . . . Will they grow at Wimbledon?' the king asked as he walked past John to his inner chamber.

'I should think so, Your Majesty,' John said. He waited for more.

'Good,' said the king. 'Her M . . . Majesty will like that, when she s . . . sees it. When she comes h . . . h . . . home again.'

'And then he was gone,' John said to an astounded Hester and Johnnie, sitting at the fireside after a long, cold boat trip back to Lambeth.

'He summoned you all that way to give you melon seeds?' Hester demanded.

'I thought it might be some secret,' John confessed. 'I searched the box, and I waited all day in case he should send a secret message for me, once he knew I was in the castle. I weeded the flowerbed beneath the window of his privy apartments so that he would know I was there. But . . . nothing. It was truly just for the melon seeds.'

'He is to stand trial for treason, and he is thinking about planting melons?' Hester wondered.

John nodded. 'That is the king indeed,' he said.

'Where will you plant them?' Johnnie asked.

John looked at the taut face of his son, at the shadows under his eyes and the continual frown of pain.

'Would you like to help me?' he offered gently. 'We could make a proper melon bed at Wimbledon. My father taught me the way, and he was taught by Lord Wootton at Canterbury. We were there when I was a boy. Would you like me to teach you how to do it, Johnnie? When the spring comes and you're strong again?'

'Yes,' Johnnie said. 'I'd like to plant them for the king.' He paused for a moment. 'Will he see them grow, d'you think?'

January 1649

John packed a bag. Hester, watching him from the doorway, knew that she was powerless to stop him.

'I have to be there,' he said. 'I can't sit at home while he is on trial for his life. I have to see him. I can't stand not to know what is going on.'

'Alexander could send you a message every day, tell you what has taken place,' Hester suggested.

'I have to be there,' John repeated. 'This was my father's master, and my own. I was there at the start of this. I have to see the end.'

'Who knows when the trial will be?' she asked. 'They should have started this month and yet the date is put back and put back. Perhaps they don't mean to try him at all, but just to frighten him into agreeing.'

'I have to be there,' John insisted. 'If there is to be no trial, then I have to see that there is no trial. I'll wait until it happens – if it happens.'

She nodded, resigned. 'Send word to us then,' she said. 'Johnnie is sick with anxiety.'

John swung his cloak over his shoulder and picked up his bag. 'He's young, he'll mend.'

'He still thinks they should have held out longer at Colchester, or fought their way out,' she said. 'When I think what this war has done to Johnnie, I wish the king was charged with treason. He has broken hearts up and down this country. He has turned against his people.'

'Johnnie will recover,' John said. 'You don't break your heart at fifteen.'

'No,' she said. 'But when he should have been at school or playing in the fields the country was at war and I had to keep him home. When you should have been home to teach and guide him you were away because you knew the king would keep you in his service, wherever that service might lead. Then, when he should have been apprenticed to you and making beautiful gardens or travelling and collecting plants, he was under siege in Colchester for a battle which could neither be won nor lost. Johnnie has never had a chance to be free of the king and the king's wars.'

'Maybe we'll all be free of him at the end of this,' John said grimly.

John could not find a room in an inn near Westminster for love nor money. He could not find a bed. He could not find a share of a bed. They were renting out stables and hayracks as sleeping accommodation for the hundreds and thousands of people who were flocking to see the king on trial.

If there had been half the sympathy that the king so confidently expected, there would have been a riot, or at the least intimidation of the commissioners. But there was no sense of outrage among the men and women who were packing into the City like herrings in a barrel. There was a sense of being spectators at the most remarkable event, of being safely in ringside seats to watch a cataclysm. They were birds above an earthquake, they were fish in a flood. The worst thing that could happen to a kingdom was happening now; and they were able to watch it.

Once the crowd got a taste of history, there was no chance that they would resist it. They had come to see the most extraordinary event in an extraordinary decade, and they wanted to go home having seen it. A reversal in favour of the king that resulted in his agreement with Parliament and resting safe in his bed would have left the crowd, even the royalists among them, with a sense of having been cheated. They had come to see the king on trial. Most of them would even acknowledge that they had come to see the king beheaded. Anything less would have been a disappointment.

John walked downriver to the Tower and knocked on Frances's door, admiring the Christmas rose she had planted at one side.

'One of mine?' he asked her as she opened the door.

She hugged him as she answered. 'Of course. Did you not know you had been robbed?'

'I've not been much in the garden,' he said. It was a statement of his deep distress which she read at once.

'The king?'

'I've come to see his trial.'

'You had much better not go,' she said frankly, drawing him into the little hall and then into the parlour where a small fire of coal was burning.

'I have to,' John said shortly.

'Will you stay here tonight?'

He nodded. 'If I may. There are no beds to be had in the City and I don't want to go home.'

'Alexander is going, but I didn't want to see it. I remember when the king came to the Ark that day, and I saw him, and the queen. They were both so young then, and so rich. They were wrapped in silk and ermine.'

John smiled, thinking of the little girl who had sat on the wall until her fingertips were blue with cold. 'You wanted him to appoint you as the next Tradescant gardener.'

She leaned forwards and stirred the coals so they flamed up. 'It's unbelievable that everything should be so changed. I don't expect to be a gardener; but it is impossible to think that there may be no king.'

'You could be a gardener now,' John offered. 'In these strange days anything is possible, I suppose. There are women preaching, aren't there? And there were women fighting. There were hundreds of women who had their husbands' and their fathers' business in their charge while the men were off to war, and many still working because the men won't be coming home again.'

Frances nodded, her face grave. 'I thank God that Alexander's work was here, and that Johnnie was too young for all but the very end.'

'Amen to that,' John said softly.

'Is Johnnie taking it hard?'

'He's bound to,' John said. 'I wouldn't let him come to see the end of it. But I had to see it for myself.'

'Well then,' she said more cheerfully. 'I shall send to the bake-house for a special dinner for you. And you will need to rise early tomorrow if you are to find a place inside the courtroom.'

Saturday 20 January 1649

Alexander and John went together to Westminster. The trial was to be held in Westminster Hall, open to the public, who were to be herded into pens in the body of the hall to prevent either an attack on the judges or a rescue of the king. Only the wealthy spectators were seated in the galleries running around the sides of the hall. John and Alexander chose to crowd on to the floor.

'Like being in the pit at the theatre,' Alexander complained as they were jostled and pushed.

The galleries started to fill at midday, and then there was a furious scrum in the hall when latecomers tried to push to the front. Tradescant and Alexander battled to keep their places and the pushing was about to generate into an out-and-out fight when the doors opened and the judges entered.

The sword and the mace were brought in first, then the Lord President Bradshaw took his place, a commissioner for advice on the law on either side of him. His big black hat was crammed over his ears. Alexander Norman nudged John.

'He had it lined with iron plates,' he whispered. 'That hat. He is afraid that some royalist will shoot him where he sits.'

John snorted with laughter and glanced across to where Cromwell entered, bare-headed, his face grim. 'You have to admire the man,' he said. 'If anyone was going to be shot it would be him.'

The charge was read, Bradshaw nodded for the prisoner to be brought before the court. John felt the heat and the press of the crowd.

'Are you well?' Alexander asked. 'You've gone white.'

John nodded, his eyes never leaving the south door.

The soldiers came in and pushed back the crowd to make a passageway to the red velvet chair placed before the judges. Then the king came in.

414

He was dressed all in the richest black – black waistcoat, breeches, and cloak, on his shoulder was the dazzling silver star of the Order of the Garter. He did not look at the crowd, he barely glanced at his judges. He walked through the crowd, his head high, dramatically regal, his jewelled heels tapping on the floorboards, his cane held in his hand. He took his seat in the red velvet chair with his back to the audience and his hat firmly on his head, as if he were about to watch a play at Oatlands Palace.

John breathed out and realised that his soft susuration was part of a sigh, almost a moan, from the crowd, as the king took his place, before the men who could condemn him to death.

Bradshaw squashed his armoured hat firmly down on his head, took up the paper and read the charge naming the king as the accused. John Cook, the barrister leading the prosecution, rose to his feet to read the accusations.

'Hold a little,' the king said quietly.

'My Lord, on behalf of the Commons of England and all the people thereof I do accuse Charles Stuart here present of high treason and high misdemeanours –'

The king lifted his cane and tapped John Cook on his arm.

John, hidden in the crowd, said softly: 'Oh no.'

Cook ignored the king completely and continued to read the charge, raising his voice as if to overcome the distraction of the tapping cane and his own sense of bewilderment that an accused man should behave in such a way.

The king reached forward and struck the wing of Cook's gown a vigorous thwack with his cane. There was a gasp from the crowd. Cook abruptly stopped reading. The silver head of the cane fell off and noisily rolled along the uncarpeted boards before coming to rest a few feet from the king's chair. Charles looked around for a servant to pick it up for him. Not a man moved. It took him a long moment to realise that no-one was going to do it; then he shrugged, as if he was indifferent to the slight, and bent and picked it up himself.

John felt his shoulders hunching as if he were ashamed.

Bradshaw, the president of the court, took command of the situation. 'Sir, the court commands the charge be read; if you have anything to say afterwards you may be heard.'

John knew that the king would take any restriction on his speech as an insult. Once, it would have been treason. Surprisingly, the king was silent and Cook started to read the charges from the roll.

After all the rumours and accusations it was odd to hear the charges put so simply. John found he was straining to listen to every word, one hand over his eyes, trying to concentrate. The king was accused of trying to overthrow the rights and liberties of the people by making himself a tyrant. They accused him of making war against his own people and listed the battles where he had been personally in command. Then they accused him of plotting against the kingdom with foreign powers. There was nothing of interest, it was all a matter of fact. The king had undoubtedly done all these things.

The king turned in his chair, as if the long reading of his crimes was not of much interest to him, and looked up at the galleries at the many faces he knew, and out at the body of the court. John raised his head; the king's gaze flicked over him with its usual indifference. John had to fight a desire to call out – and knew also that he had no words to call out.

Cook's accusation went on to what seemed, to most, the worst crime of all – the renewing of the war after the king's defeat. There was a soft groan at that point, many men and women had thought the battles were finished and a peace in the making last year. None of them would forgive Charles for his final throw of the dice which had cost so many more lives and had taught the fighting men a new savagery.

'My God,' whispered Alexander. 'They want to kill him. They are impeaching him for treason.'

John nodded. As soon as he had seen the king dressed as a martyr in black with that dazzling burst of diamonds on his shoulder he had known that this was the greatest masque Charles had ever played. This was no light-hearted interlude, it was full tragedy, and both the king and the court would play it to the full.

'For these reasons,' Cook concluded, 'on behalf of the people of England, I impeach the said Charles Stuart as a tyrant, traitor and murderer, and a public and implacable enemy to the Commonwealth of England.'

There was a dead silence in the court as the people absorbed the accusation and understood that Cromwell and his court were demanding the ultimate punishment: the beheading of the king. The silence was broken by a peal of completely convincing laughter. The king was shaking in his chair, laughing as if at some delightful, ridiculous jest. He threw back his head and shook his curls. The laughter went on, horribly on, prolonged beyond any real amusement, the hard noise of a man defying his own fear.

'Sir,' Bradshaw said steadily. 'You have now heard your charge and the court expects your answer.'

The whole body of people in the court leaned forwards. The fans of ladies in the galleries were frozen still. Everyone listened to hear what the king would say.

'I would know by what power I am called hither?' he asked. 'I would know by what authority – I mean *lawful*?'

The rest of his answer was drowned by an upsurge of voices. 'He's going to challenge them every step of the way,' Alexander shouted over the noise to John.

'God no! If he would just agree, if he would just ask for mercy . . .'

The king was still speaking but he could not be heard above the shouting.

Bradshaw hammered for order and replied to the king. John saw the king shake his head and speak again.

Bradshaw made a gesture: the king should be taken from the court. As he rose to leave the soldiers in the court suddenly shouted 'Justice! Justice!' and John saw the king start back for a moment, and knew that he feared a brawl and death in a struggle more than anything else.

'He wants the scaffold,' John said, suddenly seeing it all. 'So that he can hand the crown entire to Prince Charles. So he can die as a man who was martyred for his beliefs. He's not staking for his own life now, but the condition of kingship itself.'

Charles paused before the table of judges. 'You have shown no lawful authority to satisfy any reasonable man,' he said sternly to Bradshaw.

'We are satisfied.'

'I don't fear *that*,' the king said derisively.

He turned and gave a little half-smile to the people in the courtroom, as a player will do when he has had the best of a scene.

'God save the king!' someone shouted, and then others took it up: 'God save the king!'

The king smiled as he heard the shout and went quietly with his armed escort through the door to the warren of corridors of Westminster. The crowd started to file out into the cold January day. John and Alexander paused outside, a few flakes of snow drifted from the roofs and from the grey sky.

'I'll go home,' John decided. 'There will be nothing until Monday now.'

'I shall come again on Monday,' Alexander agreed. 'If I had not seen it I wouldn't have believed it.'

John shook his head. 'I still don't,' he said.

Hester and Johnnie fell on John the moment he was through the front door. 'What's the news?'

'Nothing yet,' he said. 'They opened the hearing but the king will not recognise the court and they did nothing more than read the charge to him.'

'Will not recognise the court?' Hester asked. 'What can he be hoping to do?'

John tossed his cloak on to the chest at the foot of the stairs. 'God knows. I am frozen through, this is bitter weather to be doing such bitter business.'

'I'll get some hot ale,' Hester said. 'Come to the kitchen with me, I must have the news.'

John followed his wife, Johnnie dogging his footsteps.

'How did he look?' Johnnie asked quietly, as John sat himself on the bench before the scrubbed table and Hester produced mulled ale and hot soup, and a trencher of bread and cheese.

'He looked well,' John said consideringly. 'He had dressed for the part. He was in black but the George was ablaze on his shoulder. He carried his cane – and he tapped at the prosecutor with it –'

'He struck him?' Hester asked.

'Not a hard blow; but it was an awkward moment,' John confessed.

Johnnie's eyes were huge in his pale face. 'Did no-one shout for him?'

'A woman cried from the gallery, and there were a few that shouted "God Save the king", but the soldiers drowned them out with shouting for justice,' John said.

'I wish I could go,' Johnnie said fervently. 'I would shout for him.'

'That's why you won't go,' John said firmly. 'And I keep my head down and my thoughts to myself. They were seeking witnesses to the raising of the royal standard.'

'Did anyone recognise you?' Hester demanded.

John shook his head. 'I am as quiet as a well-fed mouse,' he said. 'I have no wish to be summoned as a witness to either cause. I have no wish but to see the end of this.'

'He's the king!' Johnnie burst out passionately.

'Aye,' John replied. 'And if he would consent to be a little less then he still might get clear of this. He could withdraw and offer them his son in his place. Or he could offer to rule by their assent, not his own. But he will be the king. He would rather be a dead king than a live sensible man.'

'Who were the commissioners?' Hester asked. 'Anyone we know?'

'A few familiar faces,' John said. 'But only half of them named and called have had the courage to sit in judgement on their king. There are a lot of men with pressing business elsewhere.'

'John Lambert?' she asked, deliberately casual.

'With the army in the north,' he replied. 'But his name is down as a commissioner. Why d'you ask?'

'I should hate to think him in it,' she said.

'He wouldn't do it,' Johnnie asserted. 'He'd know that it is wrong.'

John shook his head. 'It's the only way for everyone now,' he said. 'King and commoners. He's left us no way out at all.'

Monday 22 January 1649

On Monday John and Alexander met on the steps of Westminster Hall and went in with the surging crowd as the doors were opened. The press of men and women swept John to the far side of the hall where he could see the king's profile against the red velvet chair. Charles looked drawn and tired, he was finding it hard to sleep while constantly watched, and he knew now that the chances of a miraculous escape were every day diminishing.

The Lord President Bradshaw nodded to the prosecutor John Cook to begin but he had turned away, talking to one of the lawyers. The king, with all his old imperiousness, poked Cook sharply in the back with his cane, and the man spun around in shock, his hand going instinctively to where his sword would be. A gasp went round the courtroom.

'Why does he do it?' Alexander demanded.

John shook his head. 'I doubt any man has ever turned his back to him before,' he said quietly. 'He cannot learn to be treated as a mere mortal. He was brought up as the son of God's anointed. He just can't understand the depth of his fall.'

John Cook ostentatiously pulled his jacket into shape, and completely ignored the blow. He approached the judges' table, and asked them to agree that if the king would not plead then his silence would be taken as a confession of guilt.

The king replied. John noticed that in this crisis of his life he had lost his stammer. His diffidence in speaking directly to people had gone at last. He was clear and powerful as he told the court, in a voice raised loud enough to ensure that he could be heard in the courtroom and by the men scribbling down every word, that he was defending his own rights, but also the rights of the people of England. 'If a power without law can make laws, then who can be sure of his life or anything that he calls his own?'

There was a soft mutter from the courtroom, and a few heads nodded in the galleries where the men of property were especially sensitive to the threat that a parliament free of king and tradition might make laws that did not suit the men of land and fortune. There were Levellers enough to frighten the men of property back on to the side of monarchy. Those that called for the king's execution today might call for park walls to be pulled down tomorrow, for a law which treated commoners and peers equally, and for a parliament which represented the working man.

The Lord President Bradshaw, his metalled hat still clamped on his head, ordered the king to be silent, but Charles argued with him. Bradshaw ordered the clerk to call the prisoner to answer the charge but the king would not be silent.

'Remove the prisoner!' Bradshaw shouted.

'I do require –'

'It is not for prisoners to require –'

'Sir. I am not an ordinary prisoner.'

The guards surrounded him. 'God no!' muttered John. 'Don't let them jostle him.'

For a moment he was back in the Whitehall palace courtyard with the king in the coach and the queen with her box of jewels. He had thought then that if one hand had touched the coach the whole mystery of majesty would be destroyed. He thought now that if one soldier took the butt end of his pike and irritably thumped Charles Stuart, then the king would go down, and all his principles fall with him.

'Sir,' the king raised his voice, 'I never took arms against the people, but for the laws –'

'Justice!' the soldiers shouted. Charles rose from his chair, looked as if he wanted to say more.

'Just *go*,' John pleaded, his hands clapped over his mouth to prevent the words from being heard. 'Go before some fool loses patience. Or before Cook pokes you back.'

The king turned and left the hall. Alexander looked at John.

'A muddled business,' he said.

'A miserable one,' John replied.

Tuesday 23 January 1649

The hall doors did not open until midday. John and Alexander were chilled and bored by the time they pushed their way in. At once John's eyes were taken by a great shield, white with the red cross of St George, hung above the commissioners' table which was draped in a richly coloured Turkey rug.

'What does it mean?' he asked Alexander. 'Will they sentence him without another word?'

'If they decide that his silence means guilt then he cannot speak,' Alexander said. 'Once sentence is pronounced he'll just be taken out. That's how all the courts work. There's nothing more to say.'

John nodded in silence, his face dark.

There was a sympathetic murmur as the guards brought the king into court. John could see traces of strain in his face especially around his dark, solemn eyes. But he looked at the commissioners as if he despised them and he dropped into his chair as if it were his convenience to be seated before them.

John Bradshaw, the man with the hardest task in England, pulled the brim of his hat down to his eyebrows and looked at the king as if he were not far off begging him to see reason. He spoke quietly, reminding the king that the court was asking him, once more, to answer the charges.

The king looked up from turning a ring on his finger. 'When I was here yesterday I was interrupted,' he said sulkily.

'You can make the best defence you can,' Bradshaw promised him. 'But only after you have given a positive answer to the charges.'

It was opening a door for the king; at once he soared into grandeur. 'For the charges I care not a rush . . .' he started.

'Just plead not guilty,' John whispered to himself. 'Just deny tyranny and treason.'

He could have shouted his advice out loud, nothing would have stopped the king. Bradshaw himself tried to interrupt.

'By your favour you ought not to interrupt me. How I came here I know not; there's no law to make your king your prisoner.'

'But –' Bradshaw started.

The king's outflung hand meant that Bradshaw should be silenced. The Lord President of the court tried again against the king's torrent of speech. He gave up and nodded to the clerk of the court to read the charge.

John looked over to where Cromwell was sitting, his chin in his hands, watching the king dominating his own trial, his face grim.

The clerk read the long, wordy charge again. John heard his voice tremble at the embarrassment of being forced to read over and over again to a man who ignored him.

'You are before a court of justice,' Bradshaw asserted.

'I see I am before a power,' the king said provocatively. He rose to his feet and made that little gesture with his hand again which was a cue for a servant to bow and go. John recognised it at once but did not think that any other man in the court would realise that they had been dismissed. The king did not care to stay for any longer.

'Answer the charges,' John whispered soundlessly as the guards closed around him and the king walked from the court.

Wednesday 24 January 1649

John spent Wednesday idling at the little house in the Minories with Frances. The court was not sitting.

'What are they doing then?' Frances asked. She was kneading dough at the kitchen table, John seated on a stool at a safe distance from the spreading circle of flour. Frances had learned her domestic skills from Hester, so she would always be a competent cook; but her style was more enthusiastic than accurate and Alexander occasionally had to send out for their dinner after a catastrophe in the bread oven or a burned-out pot.

'They're hearing witnesses,' John said. 'It's to put the gloss of legality on it. Everyone knows he raised the standard at Nottingham. We hardly need witness accounts on oath.'

'They won't call you?' she asked.

He shook his head. 'They're seeking the smallest of trifles. They're calling the man who painted the standard pole. And for the battles they're using the evidence of men who fought all the way through. I was there only at the very beginning, remember. I was there at Hull which everyone has forgotten now. I never saw proper fighting.'

'Are you sorry now?' she asked, with her stepmother's directness. 'Do you wish you had stayed by him?'

John shook his head. 'I hate to see it come to this, but it was a bad road wherever it led,' he said honestly. 'We would be in a far worse case today if he had succeeded, Frances. I do know that.'

'Because of the Papists?' she asked.

John hesitated. 'Yes, I do think so. If he is not a Papist himself then the queen certainly is and half the court with her. The children – almost bound to be. So Prince Charles may be, and then his son after him, and then the door open again to the Pope and the priests and the

424

monasteries and the convents and the whole burden of a faith that is ordered on you by your masters.'

'But you don't even pray,' she reminded him.

John grinned. 'Yes. And I like to *not* pray in my own way. I don't want to not pray in a Papist way.' He broke off at her chuckle. 'I have travelled too far and seen too much to believe in anything very readily. You know that. I have lived with people who prayed very faithfully to the Great Hare and I prayed alongside them and sometimes thought my prayers were answered. I can't see only one way any more. I always see a dozen ways.' He sighed. 'It makes me uncomfortable with myself, it makes me a poor husband and father, and God knows it makes me a poor Christian and bad servant.'

Frances paused in her work and looked at him with love. 'I don't think you're a bad father,' she said. 'It's as you say – you have seen too much to have one simple view and one simple belief. Nobody could have lived as you did, so far from your own people, and not come home feeling a little uneasy.'

'My father travelled further and saw stranger sights but he loved his masters till the day of his death,' John said. 'I never saw him have a single doubt.'

She shook her head. 'Those were different times,' she said. 'He went far as a traveller. But you lived with the people in Virginia. You ate their bread. Of course you see two ways to live. You have lived two ways. And in this country everything changed the moment that the king took up arms against his people. Before then there were no choices to be made. Now you, and many others, see a dozen ways because there *are* a dozen ways. Your father had only one way: and that was to follow his master. Now you could follow the king, or follow Cromwell, or follow Parliament, or follow the army, or become a Leveller and call for a new earth for us all, or a Clubman and fight only to defend your own village, or turn your back on them all and emigrate, or shut the door of your garden and have nothing more to do with any of them.'

'And what would you do?' John asked, secretly rather impressed by his daughter's political acumen.

'I don't have to choose,' she said smugly with a sly little sideways smile. 'That's why I married Alexander.'

'And which side does he serve?'

She laughed outright. 'He serves the master who pays the bills,' she said. 'As do most people. You know that.'

Thursday 25 January 1649

The High Court was sitting in the Painted Chamber in the Palace of Westminster. John knew the room from his days in royal service and guided Alexander through the maze of lobbies and waiting rooms and retiring rooms until they could slip in by a side door. The day was given over to reading out the signed depositions of witnesses who had spoken before the commissioners the previous day. There was little of interest – the halting accounts of the king on horseback riding through the wounded without caring for their condition. Accusations that royalist officers had permitted the looting of dead men's weapons, and rifling the pockets of wounded men.

'That's very bad,' Alexander said softly to John. 'That's one thing Cromwell's very strict on. He won't have looting. That'll count against the king.'

'Hardly matters,' John said dourly. 'Not when you think that he's accused of tyranny and treason.'

One witness, Henry Gooch, gave evidence to show that the king was trying to raise a foreign army to invade England even while he was negotiating with Parliament for an agreed return to the throne.

'Could be a lie,' John said.

Alexander shrugged. 'We know he was raising an army in Ireland and begging the Scots to invade. We know that the queen was trying to move a French army to turn out for him before the people of Paris rose up against their own king and drove him out of the city. This is just evidence on top of evidence.'

'What happens next?' John asked one of the soldiers of the guard as the clerk went on reading the evidence.

'They have to find guilt and pronounce sentence,' the man said solemnly.

'But he hasn't pleaded!' John exclaimed.

The man looked away. 'If he chooses not to plead then it counts as guilty,' he said. 'There'll be nothing for you to see or hear until they are ready to pass sentence.'

'Does he know this?' John asked Alexander. 'D'you think he knows that if he goes on and on refusing to plead they'll just execute him anyway? As if he had admitted his guilt?'

'It's his law,' Alexander replied impatiently. 'Men have been executed under his name. He must know what he is doing.'

John felt himself shiver like a man with cold water down his spine.

'I'll wait,' he said to Alexander. 'May I stay with you a few days longer?'

Friday 26 January 1649

John and Frances walked together down to the Tower and then along the path beside the river.

'I might go and stay with Mother for a few days,' she said, looking out over the bright water.

'Why?' asked John. 'Am I crowding you out?'

'I don't want to be here when they do it,' she said.

For a moment he did not understand her. 'Do what?'

'Behead him. They'll do it here, won't they? In the Tower? And put his head on Tower Bridge? I don't want to see it. I know he's been in the wrong, but I remember the day he came to the Ark and he was so handsome, and she was so pretty and dressed so richly. I don't want to hear the drums roll and then stop for him.'

'I have to,' John said. 'I feel I have to see the end of this.'

Frances nodded. 'I think I'll go and stay with Mother for a while when they start to build the scaffold.'

Saturday 27 January 1649

Westminster Hall was more crowded than ever, John and Alexander were pressed against the railings and continually pushed against the broad back of a sentinel soldier. A little after midday the commissioners came into the hall; sixty-eight of them were present, Cromwell among them. When John Bradshaw came in wearing his hat John saw that he was robed in red, red as a cardinal, red as blood.

There was complete silence when King Charles came in, dressed in his rich black. He walked with purpose, and his face was bright. He no longer looked like an exhausted man pushed to his limit, he looked determined and filled with confidence. John, reading his master's stance and face, whispered to Alexander: 'He has a plan or something. He's found a way out.'

Charles did not drop nonchalantly into his chair as he had done before. He seated himself and leaned forwards earnestly and spoke at once, before Bradshaw could begin. 'I shall desire a word to be heard a little,' he started.

Bradshaw at once refused. The proceedings were fixed, the king could not simply speak as he wished. Instead Bradshaw himself started to repeat the charge when there was a stir from the galleries where two masked women were sitting.

'Oliver Cromwell is a traitor!' one of the women shouted clearly.

'Take aim!' shouted the commander of the guard and at once the soldiers in the courtroom turned their muskets on the gallery. There was a scream and a rush away from the armed men, Alexander stumbled and grabbed at the railing. The women were hustled away and the guards went back to their positions. Alexander straightened his coat and brushed down his breeches. 'This is unbearable,' he said to John. 'I thought we were going to die in a riot.'

John nodded. 'Look at Cromwell,' he said.

Cromwell was on his feet, his eyes raking the crowd, taking in the leaded windows through which an attack on the courtroom might be led. There was nothing. It had been nothing more than one woman crying out for her king.

Slowly, Cromwell resumed his seat, he glanced over to the king. Charles raised his eyebrows, slightly smiled. Cromwell's face was grim.

Bradshaw, struggling to regain the attention of the court, ruled that the king's refusal to speak was considered to be a confession of guilt, it would count as a guilty plea. But since the charge was so serious they would hear him speak in his defence as long as he did not challenge the authority of the court.

'They're bending over backwards to give him a fair chance,' Alexander whispered to John. 'There's no precedent for letting him speak in his defence when he won't say whether or not he is guilty.'

The king leaned forwards in his chair, his confidence increasing all the time. 'For the peace of the kingdom and for the freedom of the people I shall say nothing about the jurisdiction of the court,' he said clearly. Again, there was no trace of his stammer. 'If I cared more for my life than for the peace of the kingdom and the liberty of the subject I should have made a particular debate and I might have delayed an ugly sentence. I have something to say which I desire may be heard before sentence is given. I desire to be heard in the Painted Chamber before the Lords and the Commons before any sentence is passed.'

'What?' John demanded.

'What can he be thinking of?' Alexander whispered. 'A proposal of peace at last? Some kind of treaty?'

John nodded, his eyes on the king. 'Look at him, he thinks he has the answer.'

Bradshaw was refusing, insisting on the court's determination not to be delayed again when one commissioner – John Downes – started up. 'Have we hearts of stone? Are we men?' he demanded.

Two judges either side of him tried to pull him down. 'If I die for it I must speak against this!' he shouted.

Cromwell, seated before him, turned, his face black with fury. 'Are you mad? Can you not sit still?'

'Sir, no! I cannot be quiet!' He raised his voice to reach everyone in the hall. 'I am not satisfied!'

John Bradshaw surveyed the sixty-eight commissioners, saw half a dozen irresolute faces, a dozen men wishing they were elsewhere, a score of men who would have to be persuaded all over again, and announced that the court would withdraw to consider.

The king went out first, his step light, his head high, a slight triumphant smile on his face. The commissioners filed out after him, muttering to each other, clearly thrown off their course by this late offer. A draught of clean, cold air swept into the courtroom as the double doors were thrown open at the back and some of the crowd left.

John and Alexander kept their places. 'I'm not leaving,' John said. 'I swear he will escape the hangman. They'll return with an agreement. He's done it again.'

'I wouldn't take a bet against it,' Alexander said. 'He could easily do it. The commissioners are all of them uncertain, Cromwell looking ready to murder. The king has them on the run.'

'What d'you think they are doing now?' John asked.

'Cromwell wouldn't purge them, would he?' Alexander speculated. 'Rid himself of Downes and any that agree with him? He's done it with Parliament, why not with the court?'

John was about to reply when the doors at the back of the hall were slammed shut, the usual signal that the court was about to reconvene, and then the king re-entered, smiling slightly, like a man who is playing a role which is too absurdly easy for him to take seriously, and seated himself in his red armchair. Then the commissioners came in again. Downes was not with them.

'He's not there,' Alexander said quickly. 'That's bad.'

John Bradshaw's face was as grim as Cromwell's. He announced that the court would not accept any more delays. There would be no calling of the Commons and the Lords. The court would proceed to sentence.

'But a little delay of a day or two further may bring peace to the kingdom,' Charles interrupted.

'No,' Bradshaw said. 'We will not delay.'

'If you will hear me,' the king said sweetly. 'I shall give some satisfaction to you all here, and to my people after that.'

'No,' Bradshaw said. 'We will proceed to sentence.'

The king looked stunned, he had not thought they would resist the temptation of an agreement. He sat back in his chair for a moment and John could tell, from his absorbed expression and the gentle beating of his fingers on the arm of his chair, that he was thinking of another plan, another approach.

It was John Bradshaw's great moment. He had a speech in his hand and he started to recite. He read slowly enough for all the writers from the journals to copy down what he was saying. He cited the traditional duty of Parliament and the duty of the king, and the claim that kings could be held accountable for their crimes. The crowd grew restless during the long legal citations but Bradshaw came to the point – that the king, by taking arms against his people, had destroyed the agreement between a king and his people. He was there to protect his people, never to attack.

'I would desire only one word before you give sentence,' the king interrupted.

'But sir, you have not owned us as a court, we need not have heard even one word from you.'

The king subsided into his chair as Bradshaw gestured to the clerk of the court.

'Charles Stuart as a tyrant, traitor, murderer and a public enemy shall be put to death by the severing of his head from his body.'

In silence the sixty-seven commissioners rose to their feet.

'Will you hear me a word, sir?' the king asked politely, as if nothing had taken place.

'You are *not* to be heard after sentence,' Bradshaw said and motioned to the guards to take him away.

The king leaned forwards more urgently. He had not realised that they would not hear him after sentence had been passed. He knew so little of the laws of his own land that he had not realised a man sentenced is not allowed to speak. 'I may speak after the sentence –' Charles argued, his voice a little higher in anxiety. 'By your favour, sir, I may speak after the sentence.'

The guards came closer. John found he was shrinking back, a hand to his mouth like a frightened child.

Charles persisted. 'By your favour, hold! The sentence, sir, I do –'

The guards closed in, forcing him to his feet. Charles shouted over their heads to the stunned crowd: 'I am not suffered for to speak: expect what justice other people will have!'

They hustled him from the hall, there were confused shouts, some for, some against him. The commissioners filed out, John saw them go as if they were floating away, Bradshaw's red gown and absurd hat a dreamlike imagining. 'I never thought they would do it,' John said. 'I never thought they would.'

Sunday 28 January 1649

John would not attend church with Frances and her husband. He sat at the kitchen table, a glass of small ale before him, while the church bells rang and then fell silent, and then rang again.

Frances, entering in a rush to prepare the Sunday dinner, checked at the sight of her father, so uncharacteristically idle.

'Are you sick?'

He shook his head.

Alexander followed his wife into the kitchen. 'They say he is praying with Bishop Juxon. He is allowed to see his children.'

'No clemency?' John asked.

'They are building the scaffold at Whitehall,' Alexander said shortly.

'Not here?' Frances asked quickly.

Alexander took her hand and kissed it. 'No, my dear. Nowhere near us. They are closing off the street before the Banqueting House. They are fortifying it against a rescue attempt.'

'Who would rescue him?' John asked forlornly. 'He has betrayed every one of his friends at one time or another.'

Tuesday 30 January 1649

It was such a bitter, cold morning that John thought the ice on roof and gutter had crept into his own veins and was freezing his belly and bones as he waited in the street. The king was to be executed before noon but though the streets were lined three-deep with soldiers, and the two executioners waited in the lee of the black-draped scaffold, the note-takers and sketch artists gathered at the foot, there was no sign of the king.

The street, crammed with people packed in behind the cordon of soldiers, had a strange echo to it, as the sound of talk, prayers, and the shouts of ballad sellers bawling out the titles of their new songs bounced off the walls of the windowless buildings and boomed in the cold air.

John, looking behind him at the tight-packed crowd and then forwards to the stage, thought it seemed like an exercise in perspective, like Inigo Jones's deceiving painted scenery for a masque, the penultimate scene of a masque which would be followed by the ascension, with Jehovah coming down from a great cloud and the handmaidens of Peace and Justice dancing together.

The two executioners climbed the steps to the platform and there was a gasp at their appearance. They were in costume, in false wigs and false beards and dark brown doublets and breeches.

'What are they wearing? Masquing clothes?' Alexander asked of the man on his left.

'Disguised to hide their identity,' the man said shortly. 'It'll be Brandon the hangman hidden under that beard, unless it's Cromwell himself doing the job.'

John briefly closed his eyes and opened them again. The scene had not changed; it was still unbearable. The chief executioner positioned the block, laid down his axe and stepped back, his arms folded, waiting.

It was a long wait, the crowd grew restless.

'A reprieve?' Alexander suggested. 'The plan he had for peace finally heard and accepted?'

'No,' someone said in the crowd nearby. 'He has been stabbed to death by Cromwell himself.'

'I heard there was an escape,' someone else said. 'He must have escaped. If he was dead they would show the body.'

The rumour and the speculation continued all the morning in a swirl of muttering all around John who stood cold and silent in the middle of it all.

'I must find something to eat,' Alexander said. 'I am famished.'

'I don't want anything,' John said.

'You must be starving, man; and cold,' Alexander exclaimed. 'Let me bring you a loaf of bread when I buy some dinner for myself.'

John shook his head. 'I feel nothing,' he said simply. 'Nothing at all.'

Alexander shook his head and wriggled through the crowd to where an enterprising baker was selling hot bread rolls from a tray. It took him more than an hour to regain his place at John's side but still nothing had happened.

'I brought you some bread,' he said cheerfully. 'And I filled my flask with rum.'

John took the bread in his hand but he did not eat it. His eyes were fixed on the scaffold.

'They are saying that the Scots have visited Colonel Fairfax, who was against this from the start, and that they are all going to Cromwell to beg for a reprieve. The king can be free to live abroad, even Scotland.'

John shook his head.

'I know,' Alexander said. 'If they gave him so much as a farthing's chance he would raise an army and come back again. If he can conspire from prison when he is bound by his word of honour, what would he do loose amid the courts of Europe? He would always come back again. They can't trust him with his life.'

'They've called Parliament,' a man said beside them. 'That's the reason for the delay. They are passing a law in a hurry which says that no-one else can be proclaimed king. No value in beheading a king if another springs up to take his place, is there? And we have one of his sons in England and another two of them in France, and his nephew hanging round like a dog at the door of an abattoir. We've princes enough for pass-the-crown to go on forever. We have to break them of the habit now. So they're making a law to say that no king can be proclaimed in England ever again.'

That sentence shocked John out of his absorption. 'No king can be proclaimed in England ever again,' he repeated.

'Yes,' the man said. 'It has a ring to it, doesn't it? It makes you feel that it's all been worth the struggle. We are free of them forever. There will never be another man to set himself high above all others. There will never be another family who think themselves better than the rest of us by virtue of the bed they were born in. Any masters we have in the future will have to earn their place. They will have to be men that we choose to serve because they are wiser or better or even richer than us. But not because they are born to it. This is Charles the Last. After him there will be freedom.'

'Charles the Last,' John repeated. 'Charles the Last.'

The clocks had struck twelve and then one and then two before there was a stirring among the soldiers which was quickly caught by the crowd, and then a shout: 'He's coming.'

John did not move. He was still and silent as he had been all day. The crowd around him jostled fiercely but John gripped his hands on the railing before him and held tight. Alexander saw that his knuckles were white; but so were his hands, his face, his whole body was bleached by cold and distress.

A window in the Banqueting Hall was open and the king stepped out on to the platform. He was simply dressed in black again: a black cape, a tall black hat, black breeches and a white shirt. The Order of the Garter was a blaze of colour in dramatic contrast. He looked out at the crowd, John felt that sombre, dark gaze pass over him and wanted to raise a hand, to catch at recognition for a moment. He kept his hands and his head down.

The king took some notes from his pocket and spoke quietly to the men on the platform. John, straining his ears, could hear only tantalising snatches of speech; only the last few words rang clear: 'I am a martyr to the people.'

John heard a hiss of breath at the unending, irresistible grandeur and folly of the man, and realised it was cold air through his own teeth. The king swore that he died in the faith of his father, as a Christian, and then spoke quietly to the executioner.

'Oh God, don't let him botch it,' John whispered, thinking not of the executioner who had done this a hundred times, but of the king who must do this beautifully, just once.

The king turned to Bishop Juxon and the bishop helped him to tuck his long hair under his cap to keep his neck free for the blade. Charles handed his George and the ribbon of the Garter to the bishop, and pulled the ring from his finger.

'No, not that, no, no,' John muttered. The details were unbearable. John had nerved himself for an execution; not for a man undressing as if in domestic confidence, tucking his hair out of the way of his pale, fragile neck. 'Oh please God, no.'

Charles took off his doublet but wrapped his cloak around his shoulders again, as if it mattered that he should not catch cold. He seemed to be complaining about the executioner's block. The executioner, a terrifying figure in his masquing disguise, seemed to be apologising. John, remembering the king's ability to delay and prevaricate, found that he was shaking the fence post before him in painful impatience.

The king stepped back and looked up at the sky, his hands raised. John heard the scribble of a pencil behind him as a sketch-maker captured the image of the king, the martyr of the people, his eyes on heaven, his arms outspread like a statue of Christ. Then the king dropped his cloak, knelt down before the block and stretched out his neck.

The executioner had to wait for the signal; the king had to spread out his arms to consent. For a while he knelt there, unmoving. The executioner leaned forwards and moved a wisp of hair. He waited.

'Please, do it,' John whispered to his old master. 'Please, please, just do it.'

There was a wait of what seemed like hours, then with the gesture of a man diving into a deep river the king flung his arms out wide and the axe swept a lovely unstoppable arc downwards, thudded into his neck bone, and his head dropped neatly off.

A deep groan came from the crowd – the sound a man makes at his death, the sound a man makes at the height of his pleasure. The sound of something ending, which can never happen again.

At once there were slow, determined hoofbeats behind them and people screaming and pushing in panic to get away.

'Come on!' Alexander cried, tugging at John's sleeve. 'The cavalry is coming through, out of the way, man, we'll be ridden down.'

John could not hear him. He was still staring at the stage, still waiting for the final act when the king, gorgeously dressed in white, would step down from the stage and dance with the queen.

'Come on!' Alexander said. He grabbed John's arm and dragged him to one side. The crowd eddied, rushing to the sides of the street, many running forwards to the scaffold to snatch a piece of the pall, to scrabble for a bit of earth from under the stage, even to dip their handkerchiefs in the gush of scarlet hot blood. John, pulled by Alexander, and pushed by the people behind him trying to get away from the remorseless cavalry advance down the street, lost his feet and fell. He was kicked in the head at once, someone trod on his hand. Alexander hauled him upwards.

'Come on, man!' he said. 'This is no place to linger.'

John's head cleared, he struggled to his feet, ran with Alexander to the side of the road, pressed against the wall as the cavalry forced their way down to the scaffold, and then slipped away as they went past. At the top of the road he checked, and looked back. It was over. Already it was over. Bishop Juxon had disappeared, the king's body had been lifted through the window of the Banqueting House, the street was half-cleared of people, the soldiers had made a cordon around the stage. It was a derelict theatre at the end of the show, it had that stale leftover silence when the speeches have been finished and the performance is all over. It was done.

It was done but it was not over. John, returning home, found his house besieged with neighbours who wanted to hear every word, every detail, of what he had seen and what had been said. Only Johnnie was missing.

'Where is he?' John asked Hester.

'In the garden, in his boat on the lake,' she said shortly. 'We heard the church bells toll in Lambeth and he knew what it was for.'

John nodded, excused himself from the village gossips and went down the cold garden. His son was nowhere to be seen. John walked down the avenue and turned right at the bottom for the lake where the children had often gone to feed ducks when they were little. The irises and reeds planted in the wet ground at the margin were in their stark frosted beauty. In the middle of the lake the boat was drifting, Johnnie, wrapped in his cape, sitting in the stern, the oars resting on the seat either side of him.

'Hey there,' John said gently from the landing stage.

Johnnie glanced up and saw his father. 'Did you see it done?' he asked flatly.

'Aye.'

'Was it done quickly?'

'It was done properly,' John said. 'He made a speech, he put his head on the block, he gave the sign and it was done in a single blow.'

'So it's over,' Johnnie said. 'I'll never serve him.'

'It's over,' John said. 'Come ashore, Johnnie, there will be other masters and other gardens. In a few weeks people will have something else to talk about. You won't have to hear about it. Come in, Johnnie.'

Spring 1649

John was wrong. The king's execution was not a nine-day wonder, it swiftly became the theme of every conversation, of every ballad, of every prayer. Within days they were bringing to John the rushed printed accounts of the trial and eyewitness descriptions of the execution, and asking him if they were the truth. Only the most hard-hearted of round-heads escaped the mood of haunting melancholy, as if the death of a royal was a personal loss – whatever the character of the man, whatever the reason for his death. The country was gripped with a sickness of grief, a deep sadness which quite obscured the justice of the case and the reasons for his death. No-one really cared why the king had to die. In the end, they were stunned that he had died at all.

John thought that perhaps others had believed like him: that a king in his health simply could not die. That something would intervene, that God himself must prevent such an act. That even now, time might run backwards and the king be found alive. That John might wake up one morning to find the king in his palace and the queen demanding some absurd planting scheme. It was almost impossible to accept that no-one would ever see him again. The chapbooks, the balladeers, the portraitists all fostered the illusion of the king's surviving presence. There were more pictures of King Charles and stories about him than there had ever been during his life. He was better beloved than he had ever been when he had been idle and foolish and misjudging. Every error he had made had been washed away by the simple fact of his death, and the name he had given to himself: the Martyr King.

Then came the reports of miracles worked by his relics. People were cured of fits or sickness or rashes like the pox by the touch of a handker-chief which had been dipped in his blood. The pocket knives made from his melted-down statue would heal wounds if laid against them, would protect a baby from violent death if used to cut the cord. A sick lion in the Tower zoo had been comforted by the scent of his blood on a rag. Every day there was a new story about the saint, the people's saint. Every day his presence in the country grew stronger.

No-one was wholly unmoved; but Johnnie, still weak from his injury and defeat at Colchester, was struck very hard. He spent day after day in the boat on the little lake, lying wrapped in his cloak, his long legs folded over the stern and the heels of his boots dipping in the water while the boat drifted around nudging one bank and then another, and Johnnie stared up at the cold sky, saying nothing.

Hester went down to fetch him for his midday dinner and found him rowing slowly to the little landing stage to come in.

'Oh Johnnie,' she said. 'You have your whole life before you, there's no need to take it so hard. You did what you could, you kept faith with him, you ran away to serve him and you were as brave as any of his cavaliers.'

He looked at her with his dark Tradescant eyes and she saw the passionate loyalty of his grandfather without the security of his grandfather's settled world. 'I don't know how we can live without a king,' he said simply. 'It's not just him. It's the place he held. I can't believe that we won't see him again. His palaces are still there, his gardens. I can't believe that he is not there too.'

'You should get back to work,' Hester said, grasping at straws. 'Your father needs help.'

'We are gardeners to the king,' Johnnie said simply. 'What do we do now?'

'There's the trading business for Sir Henry in Barbados.'

He shook his head. 'I'll never be a trader. I'm a gardener through and through. I'd never be anything else.'

'The rarities.'

'I'll come and help if you wish it, Mother,' he said obediently. 'But they're not the same, are they? Since we packed and unpacked them again. It's not grandfather's room any more, it's not the room we showed the king. We have most of the things and it should be the same. But it feels different, doesn't it? As if by packing them and hiding them away, and then unpacking them, and then hiding them again, somehow spoiled it. And people don't come as they used to. It's as if everything is changed and no-one knows yet how.'

Hester put her hand on his arm. 'I just mean you should stop brooding and return to work. There is a time to mourn and you do yourself no favours if you exceed it.'

He nodded. 'I will,' he promised. 'If you wish it.' He hesitated as if he could not find the words for his feeling. 'I never thought that I could feel so low.'

The three of them were at dinner when there was a knock at the door. Hester turned her head and they listened to the cook stamping irritably along the hall to open it. There was the noise of a mild disagreement. 'It'll be a sailor with something to sell,' Hester said.

'I'll go,' Johnnie said, pushing back his chair. 'You finish your dinner.'

'Call me before you agree a price,' John warned him.

Johnnie scowled at his father's lack of trust; and went out of the door.

They heard him shout an oath, and then they heard the noise of his running footsteps down the hall, and the door to the terrace slam as he set off down the garden.

'Good God, what now?' John sprang to his feet and went to the front door. Hester paused by the window to see Johnnie, head down, running blindly towards the lake. She hesitated, and followed her husband.

A bewildered man was at the front door. 'I offered him this for sale,' he said, showing a dirty piece of black cloth. 'I thought it was the sort of thing you would like for your collection. But he jumped back as if it were poison and fled from me. What ails the lad?'

'He's sick,' Hester said shortly. 'What is it?'

The man suddenly gleamed with enthusiasm. 'A piece of pall from the scaffolding of the Martyr King, Mrs Tradescant. And if you like it you can have it and a pen-knife cast from the metal of his statue. *And* I may be able to find you a scrape of earth soaked with his sacred blood. All very reasonable considering the rarity of it and the price you will be able to charge for those coming to see it.'

Hester instinctively recoiled in distaste. She looked to John. His eyebrows were knotted in thought.

'We don't take such things,' he said slowly. 'We buy rarities, not relics.'

'You have Henry VIII's hunting gloves,' the man pointed out. 'And Queen Anne's nightgown. Why not this? Especially as you could make your fortune with it.'

John took a swift turn away from the doorstep and down the hall. The man was right, anything to do with the king would be a goldmine for the Ark, and they were barely making enough money to pay the cook's and Joseph's wages.

He turned back to the front door. 'I thank you, but no. We will not exhibit the king's remains.'

Hester found that her shoulders had been hunched while she waited for her husband's decision. 'But please do bring us any other rare things you have,' she said pleasantly, and went to shut the door.

The man thrust his foot out and stopped the closing door. 'I was certain you would give me a good price for this,' he said. 'There are other collectors who would pay handsomely. I was doing you the favour of coming to you first.'

'I thank you for that,' John said shortly. 'But we won't take anything that remains of the king.' He hesitated. 'He visited here himself,' he said, as if it would make the decision clear. 'It would not seem right to show pieces of him.'

The man shrugged, took his foot from the door and left. Hester closed the door and turned back to look at John.

'That was well done,' she said.

'D'you think we'd ever have got Johnnie to work in the room with the king's own blood in a jar?' John asked irritably and went out to the garden, leaving his dinner untouched on the table.

Johnnie's gloom did not lift as Hester had hoped that it might even when the warmer weather came. In March, when John was planting seeds of nasturtium, sweet pea, and his Virginian amaracock in pots of sieved earth in the orangery, Parliament declared that there would never more be a king or a queen set over the English people. Kingship was abolished forever in England. Johnnie came into the warm room with a small box in his hand, looking grave.

'What have you there?' John asked warily.

'The king's seeds,' Johnnie said softly. 'That he gave you to plant at Wimbledon.'

'Ah, the melon seeds. D'you know, I'd forgotten all about them.'

A swift, burning glance from Johnnie showed that he had not forgotten, and that he thought the less of his father for his absence of mind. 'It's one of the last orders he must have given,' Johnnie said softly, in awe. 'And he sent for you by name, just to ask you to plant them for him. It's like he wanted you to have a task, a quest, to remember him by.'

'Just melons.'

'He sent for you, he saved the seeds from his own dinner plate, and asked you to do it. He took the seeds from his own dinner, and he gave them to you.'

John hesitated, dismayed at the tone of worship in Johnnie's voice. The scepticism which everyone in the country had shared when Charles the Cheat was lying and backsliding from his agreements had quite vanished at the man's death when he became Charles the Martyr. John granted grudgingly that Charles had done better than anyone could have imagined in making the throne once more a sacred place; for here was Johnnie, who by rights should be disillusioned after a hopeless siege and a bad injury, with his eyes blazing at the thought of the dead king.

John put his hand on his son's shoulder and felt the strong sinew and bone. He did not see how he could explain to Johnnie that the whim of a man accustomed all his life to command should not be read as significant. Charles the Last had a fancy to pretend that he might live to eat the melons which would be planted at Wimbledon in the spring, and it was no trouble to him that a servant should go all the way from Windsor to Lambeth and back again to fetch John, and that John should go all the way from Lambeth to Windsor and then home again to enact that fancy.

It would never have occurred to him that it might be inconvenient for a man no longer in his service and no longer paid a royal wage to be summoned once more to unpaid work. It would not have occurred to him that his behaviour was arrogant or wilful. It would not have occurred to him that by naming John as his gardener and entrusting him with the commission he would identify him as a royal servant at a time when royal servants were regarded with suspicion. He had put John to inconvenience, he might have put him in grave danger – he would simply never have thought of it. It was a whim and he was always a man who was happy that others should service his whims.

'Would you like to plant them?' John asked, seeking a way out of this dilemma.

Johnnie's face showed the rush of his emotion. 'Would you let me?'

'Of course. You can plant them up, if you like, and when they are ready we'll transplant them to the melon beds.'

'I want to make melon beds at Wimbledon,' Johnnie said. 'That's where he wanted them to be.'

John hesitated. 'I don't know what's happening at Wimbledon,' he said. 'If Parliament wants me to continue working there, then of course we can make a melon bed. But I've heard nothing. They may sell the house.'

'We have to do it,' Johnnie said simply. 'We cannot disobey his command, it was his last order to us.'

John turned back to his nasturtiums and surrendered. 'Oh, very well,' he said. 'When they're ready for planting out we'll take them to Wimbledon.'

Slowly, life began to get back to normal. There was a gradual increase of takings at the door from visitors to the rarities room and orders in the book from the new men who now found themselves in possession of the sequestered estates of royalists who were dead or fled or living quietly in poverty. The new men, officers from Cromwell's army and the astute politicians who had stood against the king at the right time, walked into some fine houses and gardens running to seed which might be restored to beauty.

One by one the visitors started to come back to the Ark, to walk around the gardens and admire the blossoms on the trees and the bobbing heads of the daffodils. Dr Thomas Wharton, a man after John's heart, came to look at the rarities and brought with him a proposal that John should set aside a part of his garden for the College of Physicians. They would pay him a fee to grow herbs and medicinal plants for them.

'I appreciate it,' John said frankly. 'These have been lean years for us. A country at war has no interest in gardening nor in rarities.'

'The country is to be run now by men whose curiosity will not be stifled,' the doctor replied. 'Mr Cromwell himself is a man who likes ingenious mechanisms. He has drained his farmland and uses Dutch windpumps to keep the water out, and he believes that English land could be made to yield as fruitfully as the Low Countries', even the waste grounds.'

'It's a question of not exhausting the soil,' John said eagerly. 'And changing the crops around so that blights don't take hold. We've always known that in gardens and vegetable plots, every convent and monastery garden moved crops from one bed to another each year; but it's true for farmland too. It's how to restore the goodness to the soil that is the difficulty. In Virginia too, the People never use the same field for more than three seasons.'

'The planters?'

445

'No, the Powhatan. They move their fields each season. I thought it was a mistake till I saw how their crops yielded.'

'This is most interesting,' Dr Wharton said. 'Perhaps you would come to my house and tell me more. I meet with friends once a month to discuss inventions, and rarities, and ideas.'

'I should be honoured,' John said.

'And what d'you use to make your own land fertile?' Dr Wharton asked.

John laughed. 'A soup of my father's devising,' he said. 'Nettles and comfrey and dung stirred up in an evil pot. And if I am disposed to make water I piss in it as well.'

The doctor chuckled. 'So it couldn't be used for a hundred acres?'

'But there are crops which would put the goodness back into the soil,' John replied. 'Comfrey or clover. You'd have to start with a little patch and harvest the seed, plant a greater and greater field every year.'

The doctor tapped him on the arm. 'There's your future,' he said. 'If the new parliament cares little for ornamental gardens, they care a great deal for the richness of the lands. If we are to keep the Levellers from turning us out of our own doors then we have to feed the people from the acres we have under the plough. The country has to be fed, the country has to find peace and prosperity. If you could write a pamphlet about how it could be done then Parliament would reward you.' He hesitated. 'And it would mean that you were seen to be working for the good of Parliament and the army and the people,' he said. 'No bad thing, now that your old master is gone.'

John raised an eyebrow. 'Any news of the prince?'

'Charles Stuart,' Wharton corrected him gently. 'In France, I hear. But with Cromwell in Ireland he might try a landing. He could try a landing at any time and he would always muster an army of a couple of hundred fools. There will always be fools ready to run to a royal standard.'

He paused to see if John disagreed that Charles would only be served by an army of fools. John took meticulous care to say nothing.

'He's called Charles Stuart now,' Dr Wharton reminded him.

John grinned. 'Aye,' he said. 'I'll remember.'

In April John Lambert strolled into the garden with a smile for Joseph, the gardener, and a low bow for Hester.

'General Lambert!' she exclaimed. 'I thought you were at Pontefract.'

'I was,' he said. 'But my business there is done. I am to spend the next few months in London, staying at my father-in-law's house with my family, so I have come to spend the fruits of victory. He only has a little garden so I must not be tempted by one of your great trees. Has Mr Tradescant anything new?'

'Come and see,' Hester said, and led the way out through the glass doors to the terrace and down to the garden. 'The tulips are at their very best. We could let you have some in bud in pots. You will be missing your own at Carlton Hall.'

'I might catch them at the end of their bloom. We have a later season in Yorkshire.'

They walked together to the front of the house and Hester paused to enjoy his delight at the sight of the tulips in bloom in the big double beds before the house.

'Every year I catch my breath,' he said. 'It's like a sea of colour.'

Hester smoothed her apron over her hips. 'I know,' she said contentedly.

'And what novelties d'you have?' John Lambert asked eagerly. 'Anything new?'

'A satin tulip, from Amsterdam,' Hester said, temptingly lifting up a pot. 'Look at the shine on it.'

He took the pot in his arms, careless of his velvet jacket and the rich lace at his throat. 'What a beauty!' he said. 'The petals are like a mirror!'

'And here comes my husband,' Hester remarked, curbing her irritation that John was pushing a barrow up from the seed beds in his shirtsleeves with his hat set askew on his head.

Lambert carefully replaced the pot on its stand.

'Mr Tradescant.'

John set down the barrow, came up the steps to the terrace, and bowed to their guest. 'I won't shake hands. I'm dirty.'

'I'm admiring your tulips.'

John nodded. 'Any luck with your own? Hester told me you were going to try with the Violetten?'

'I have been too much away from home to select the blooms for breeding them to a true colour. But my wife tells me they made a pretty show in shades of mauve and purple.'

Further down the orchard Hester saw Johnnie glance up the avenue and then, when he saw that it was Lambert, pick up his watering pot and with assumed nonchalance stroll up the path under the dark sticky buds of the horse chestnut trees.

'Good day to you,' General Lambert said.

Johnnie skidded to a halt and gave a little bow.

'General Lambert is looking for something for his father-in-law's garden in Kensington,' Hester said to her husband. 'I am tempting him with the new tulip.'

'Isn't it fine?' John said. 'It's got a sheen on it like the coat of a bay horse. Does your father-in-law have fruit trees? And you could risk transplanting roses if we do it at once.'

'I'd like some roses,' Lambert said. 'He has some Rosamund roses already. D'you have any in pure white?'

'I have a *Rosa alba*,' John said. 'And an offshoot which I have grown from it with very thick petals.'

'Scented?'

'A very light scent, very sweet. And I have a Virginian rose, there's only two of them in the whole country.'

'And we have a white dog rose,' Johnnie volunteered. 'Since you're a Yorkshireman, sir.'

Lambert laughed. 'That's a pretty thought, I thank you.' He glanced at Johnnie and then looked again. 'Hey now, young man, have you been sick? You're not as bright as when I last saw you.'

There was an awkward silence. 'He was in the war,' Hester said honestly.

Lambert took in the slope of Johnnie's shoulders and the droop of his fair head. 'Where was that, lad?'

'At Colchester.'

The general nodded. 'A bad business,' he said shortly. 'You must be sorry for how it all ended; but thank God we should have peace now, at last.'

Johnnie shot a swift look at him. 'You weren't there for his trial,' he remarked.

Lambert shook his head. 'I was doing my duty elsewhere.'

'Would you have tried him?'

Hester moved forward to hush Johnnie but Lambert stopped her with a little gesture of his hand. 'Let the lad speak,' he said. 'He has a right to know. We are making the country he is going to inherit, he should be able to ask why we made our choices.'

'Would you have found him guilty and had him executed, sir?'

Lambert thought for a moment and then glanced at John. 'May I talk with the boy?'

John nodded and Lambert slid an arm around Johnnie's shoulders and the two of them fell into a stroll, down the little avenue under the resolute strong twigs of horse chestnut and then onwards into the orchard under the bobbing, budding boughs of apple, cherry, apricot and plum.

'I wouldn't have signed his death warrant on the evidence of the trial,' Lambert said softly to Johnnie. 'I thought the trial was mismanaged. But I would have worked with all my power to make him recognise that the king must accept some limits. The difficulty with him was that he was a man who would not recognise any limits.'

'He was the king,' Johnnie said stubbornly.

'No-one's denying it,' the older man replied. 'But look around you, Johnnie. The people of this country have starved while their lords and their kings have grown fat on their labour. There is no justice for them against any man greater than themselves. The profits of running the state, the taxes, all the trade, were in the gift of the king and scattered to the men who amused him, or who delighted the queen. A man could have his ears cropped for speaking out, his hand struck off for writing. Women could be strangled for witchcraft on the evidence of a village gossip. There are very great wrongs which can only be put right by a very real change. There has to be a parliament which is elected by the people. It has to sit by law, and not at the whim of the king. It has to protect the rights of the people and not those of the landlord. It has to protect the rights of the poorest, of the powerless. I had nothing against the king himself – except that he was untrustworthy both in power and out of it – but I have everything in the world against a king who rules alone.'

'Are you a Leveller?'

Lambert smiled. 'Certainly these are Leveller beliefs, yes. And I'm proud to call Levellers my comrades. They are some of the staunchest and truest men under my command. Yet I am a man of property too; and I want to keep my property. I don't go as far as some of them who want everything to be held in common. But to seek justice and the chance to choose your own government – yes, that makes me a Leveller, I suppose.'

'There has to be a leader,' Johnnie said stubbornly. 'Appointed by God.'

Lambert shook his head. 'There has to be a commander, just like in the army. But we don't believe that God appoints a man to tell us what to do. If that were so, we might as well still obey the Pope and have done with it. We know what to do, we know what is right, we know that the hard-working men of this country need to be sure that their lands are safe, and that their landlord will not sell them to another, like a herd of cow, or suddenly take it into his head that their village is in his way and drive them out like coneys from a warren.'

Johnnie hesitated.

'When you marched to Colchester were you quartered on poor farms with nothing to spare?' Lambert asked.

'Yes.'

'Then you've seen how badly some men live in the middle of plenty. The rents they have to pay are greater than the yield of their crops. We cannot have people forever struggling to make that gap meet. There has to be a balance. People must be paid a fair wage for their work.' He paused. 'When you were quartered on a poor farmstead did you take your feed for your horses and a chicken for your dinner and leave them no recompense?'

Johnnie flushed scarlet and shamefacedly nodded.

'Aye, that's the royal way,' Lambert said bitterly. 'That's the kingly way to behave.'

Johnnie flushed. 'I didn't want to,' he said. 'But I had no wages.'

Lambert gripped his arm. 'That's how it happens,' he said. 'If all the wealth is concentrated on the king, on the court, then there must be poverty everywhere else. The king raised an army but had no funds so he didn't pay you, so you had to take forage without paying, so at the end of the line there is some poor widow with one hen and the king's man comes by and takes all the eggs.'

Hester watched her stepson and Lambert walk to the end of the orchard and then turn towards the lake.

'I hope he can say something that will reconcile Johnnie,' she said. 'I've been afraid that he will never be happy again.'

'He might,' John agreed. 'He's had the command of many men. He'll have come across lads like Johnnie before.'

'It's kind of him to take the trouble,' she said.

John gave a wry smile. 'I imagine he'll take away a pot of my best tulips as his payment, won't he?'

Hester gave a little laugh. 'Not the Semper Augustus, at any rate,' she promised.

Summer 1649

With the coming of the summer the numbers of visitors increased at the Ark and the social life of London was restored. There was an explosion of debate as to how the new society should be built, what should be allowed and what should be forbidden. Pamphlets, sermons, diatribes, and journals poured off the little presses which had sprung up everywhere during the war years, new plays were written, new poems commissioned. There was a sense of excitement, of being at the very heart of change, a new world which no-one had ever experienced before. Kings had been killed before in England and elsewhere – but only on the battlefield, or in secret, and their thrones snatched by other claimants. Never before had the whole system of kingship been questioned and found so badly wanting that the people chose to destroy it and put no-one in its place.

Oliver Cromwell was to be known as Chairman of the Council of State, and there would never be another king of England. Even then the new state did not go far enough for many. There was no opening of the electorate: poor men still had no voice in the planning of the nation. There was no abolition of tithes, which many had fought for. There was no reform of the law, nor the ownership of land. The Houses of Parliament were still one House of Lords and a House of Commons packed with landed gentlemen, still serving their own needs before any other; so that the justice that John Lambert had hoped for so passionately was still far away.

But there was a sense of excitement and optimism as palpable as the warmer weather of May and June. There was a sense of changes coming, of hope, of a chance to make England into a country which could be prosperous for the many instead of the few. Families who had been estranged for years, siding with the opposing armies, were able to make friends again. Churches which had been emptied because of doctrinal arguments were now re-established with a new, freer, informal style of preaching. Men wanted to be done with ceremony, with artifice. Men wanted to speak freely to their God, and to speak freely to each other.

An informal association of philosophers, botanists, mathematicians, physicians and astronomers met regularly to debate, Dr Thomas Wharton among them, and John Tradescant too. John Lambert was in London from March and rarely missed a meeting, drawn by their discussion of science and botany. Many of them took to visiting the Ark that summer, to stroll around the garden, to sit by the little lake, to admire anything new and interesting in the rarities room and stay for dinner.

Hester, rather on her mettle as a housewife, took pride both in being able to provide dinner for a dozen men and beds for half of them at a moment's notice, and that it was the Tradescant house and garden which was the centre of attraction.

The conversation would go far into the night, and as the levels fell in the bottles of port the speculation about everything from the functions of parts of the body, to the existence of angels, the movement of the planets in their spheres and the rise and fall of sugar sap in John's maple tree became wilder and more imaginative. Elias Ashmole, a learned lawyer, one evening swore that he could predict to an hour's accuracy the time of a man's death if only midwives would have the sense to record the exact time of birth to let an astronomy chart be rigorously drawn.

'But would you want to know?' John asked, slurring slightly.

'I want to know everything,' Elias replied. 'That is what I mean by being a man of science. I, for instance, am born beneath the planet Mercury, and you can see that I am a completely mercurial man. I'm quick and versatile.'

'And looks like a silver slug, just like the metal!' someone interposed under his breath.

'But a man should separate the personal from the inquiring in his life,' a physician remarked rather confusedly. 'I want to know how blood flows through the veins. But I'm not going to open up my own arm to have a look at it. I am not my own experiment.'

'Not at all!' another man interrupted passionately. 'Unless you are prepared to penetrate, even into your own heart, then you are not inquiring at all. It is mere diversion.'

'Oh yes! If you want to die of the plague in an experiment to see that it is infectious!'

'Truly, one cannot study patients from a distance,' Dr Wharton observed. 'When the plague was in London I . . .'

'And what else have we done in the body politic but make a change and see what flows from it? Cut out the heart and see if the brain can still think?'

'That was not an experiment! It was a decision to which we were driven. I don't see Cromwell as a great physician of the body politic! He was clinging on while the horse bolted!'

'But I don't mean that,' John said, holding to his first thought with difficulty. 'I mean, would you always want to know the future? How would you bear it?'

'Of course you can know it,' Elias replied. 'I have drawn my own chart and I can tell you, for instance, that I shall be a man of considerable fame. I cast my own predictions and they told me clearly: "I shall labour for a fortune with a wife and get it."'

'A rich widow?' someone asked from further down the table.

'Lady Mary Manwaring,' someone muttered. 'Old enough to be his mother. He's been advising her. Guess what he advised?'

'I shall be remembered,' Ashmole insisted. 'I shall have my place in the temple of history.'

'For what?' one of the mathematicians demanded and burped slightly. 'Pardon me. What will earn you your place in the temple of history? Simpling in John's herb garden? Picking his flowers for potions? I don't expect to see you gleaming all over gold with the philosopher's stone in your laboratory. Seems to me that of all of us it will be John's name which will be remembered.'

John laughed. 'I just collect,' he said modestly. 'I don't set myself up as a scientist. Of course, I'm bound to wonder how things grow the way they do. I can't believe that it was all made by God in one week. I can see that man can make new plants, with proper skills. I can see that we can make the earth more yielding, that we can make plants grow better. I have some onions for instance . . .'

'Mr Ashmole has an undeniable reputation in astronomy and astrology –' one of the physicians started.

'I'm just saying that Mr Tradescant's onions, or even his tulips, are likely to yield more lasting joy to the people of this country than all of Mr Ashmole's researches into the history of the masonic order!'

John shook his head. 'It'll be the trees if anything,' he said definitely. 'The greatest joy a man can have in England is the sight of one of our horse chestnut trees in full bloom. And we have my father to thank for that.'

'Hush,' Ashmole said. 'I never speak of the masonic order.'

'Mr Ashmole's work at Brasenose –'

'Is undeniable. And he is my guest.' John recalled his duties as host. 'Pass the bottle, Stephen.'

Johnnie was present at the dinners, but generally kept silent. John, looking down the table, would see his son's intent, dark gaze move from one man to another, taking in the argument, weighing it, and then smiling in agreement or shaking his head. He was as open as a child though he was now nearly sixteen; but he had the politeness and the discretion not to burst out with his own opinions.

He would observe and listen throughout an evening of speculation, but whenever the talk turned to politics he would rise up and leave the room. Most of John's guests were men who thought, like John Milton, that the dead king had been an obstacle to the future of the country, that removing him was like cutting off a worm-eaten bud from a healthy stem. But Elias Ashmole, and some of the Oxford men of learning, continued to favour the king's cause, though they spoke of it with caution. Ashmole's own great work was researching the history of the Order of the Garter, which seemed to most of them at the table as a doomed piece of academia, given that there was now no king in England, and no Order of the Garter at all.

Ashmole would explain that whether the king was present or not, there was still a notion of kingship which could not be so easily dismissed. At moments like that, Johnnie's face would flush and he would lean forwards to listen. But when the other men cried down the notion and said that the king was dead and kingship was finished forever, then Johnnie would silently slip away.

He still could not hear the king named without flinching. It was as if some picture of the king had taken possession of his heart, and the truth about the dead man, his fallibility, his unreliability, and at the end the arrogance of his downright dishonesty, was not enough to shift it.

'This determined loyalty!' John exclaimed to Hester as they sat on the terrace one evening and watched the sun set away to their right in strips of yellow- and peach-coloured clouds. 'It's such a curse to him, he cannot leave the past behind him and move on.'

She was sewing a collar for Frances and she looked up from her work and smiled. 'He's so like your father.'

'Yes.' John was struck. 'Of course. I hadn't thought of it. My father loved Robert Cecil in the old way – a man and his lord – and then the Duke of Buckingham too. When everyone in the country was shouting for the Duke's head my father would still have done his bidding. He was ready to sail with him to France just as the Duke was struck down. Then he was grieving while everyone else in the country was blessing the assassin.'

'Frances has it too,' Hester said. 'That ability to love without doubts. For her it's Alexander, she's not interested in following a master. But that talent to love a man and his cause is a gift, I really admire it. The more so, I suppose, because it's not one that I share. I'm ashamed to say that I am a complete turncoat. I spent much of my early life at court and most of my family and friends were of the king's party; but all I care for now is peace so that we can sell plants and show the rarities.'

'It's a gift that comes with a price to pay,' John observed. 'Johnnie can't accept that the king is dead and that it is all over. I had hoped that General Lambert would have turned him into a Parliamentary man if not a Leveller. I would rather have had him in love with liberty than with a dead king.'

'He'll grow out of it,' Hester said comfortably. 'They were hard years for him. For all of his boyhood he was sure that Prince Rupert would win the war for the king. He thought that King Charles would triumph up to the very last moment. I think even after Colchester he still thought the king might win. But he knows it is all over now.'

In June Johnnie took the king's melon seedlings in their final largest pots on the cart to the river and loaded them on to a little wherry to take them upriver to Wimbledon. He went alone, he did not even tell his father that he was going, anticipating correctly that John had hoped that the seedlings had been forgotten and might be raised among the others in the melon beds at the Ark.

Johnnie took with him some planks of wood to build the frame, his dinner of bread and cheese in his pocket, a saw and a hammer, and a handful of nails in his belt.

'Building a house and planting a garden?' the ferryman asked with a grin.

Johnnie did not smile in reply. 'I am on an errand,' he said solemnly. 'An errand for my master.'

At the manor house he found the garden running to seed and the kitchen garden overgrown. But there was a warm south-facing wall and Johnnie spent the morning setting in his timber framework and banking up earth for the melon bed. Finally he planted the precious seedlings with a good space between each one, and then painstakingly ferried water from the kitchen-yard pump in the empty clay pots with his finger stopping the hole at the bottom.

Johnnie was his father's son; it was hard for him to leave the rest of the garden alone, and only weed the melon bed. He could see the hallmarks of a typical Tradescant garden becoming gradually obliterated. The south face of the house had a large paved terrace before it and an impressive sweep of paired steps coming down in a semicircle. Johnnie saw the stone pots on the terrace and guessed correctly that his father would have filled them with citrus trees pruned into glossy green balls. At the foot of the steps would have been flowerbeds, he could still see the floppy dead leaves of the tulips which had pushed up through the weeds and presented their bright cups to the blind windows above them. There were fountains and watercourses which were once planted with irises and kingcups and were now choked with water weed. There was an ornamental lake which was now evilly bright green but it still had the white and rose plates of water lilies on the scummy surface. There was an old-fashioned knot garden but the pattern of the bay hedges was blurred with weeds and the white stones were dirty. Johnnie looked around at the desolation of the summer garden which had been carefully planted to be the queen's special refuge and knew that the royal cause was lost indeed.

There was nothing he could do for the garden, he decided. But later in the summer, when the melons were in flower, he would visit again and take a soft rabbit's tail from one to another to pollinate them. Then, when they were setting fruit, he would bring his father's expensive glass melon domes to set over each one to make them ripen. He had not thought what he would then do with the fruit. The king had clearly ordered it, so only the king or his son should eat it. Perhaps it would be Johnnie's duty to take the fruit to France, find the king's son, and give him this eccentric piece of his inheritance.

Johnnie shrugged, the fruit was a question for the future. His task was to keep faith with the last order of the king. King Charles had ordered a Tradescant to make him a melon bed in his manor house at Wimbledon; and it was done.

When Johnnie got home he found that his father was irritated with the wasted day's work, and reluctant to promise the loan of the glass melon domes later in the year; but his stepmother defended him.

'Let him be,' she counselled John, as she plaited her hair ready for bed that night. 'He is doing nothing more than putting flowers on the grave. Let him do this one thing for the king and perhaps he will feel that he has done everything that should be done. Then he will feel that his defence of the king is over, and he can be happy and enjoy the peace.'

Summer 1650

Hester might have predicted Johnnie's feelings as accurately as one of Elias Ashmole's astrological projections except for one thing which she had not taken into account: the endless determination of the Stuarts to regain the crown they had lost.

In July Charles Stuart arrived in Edinburgh and forged a new alliance with the Scots, who were always drawn by the temptation of one of their own Stuart kings, and the rich plums that a grateful English monarch might bring them. He promised them anything they asked, and they promised him an army to conquer England, and crowned him king.

Joseph brought the news from Lambeth and came into the dining room to tell it. The family were at breakfast, Frances and Alexander Norman were either side of the table, Philip Harding, a mathematician, and Paul Quigley, an artist, were dining too. A stunned silence at the news was broken by Johnnie dropping his spoon, and the scrape of his chair as he rose to his feet.

'Not again,' John exclaimed. 'When will this stop? Does he not see that he is defeated and his cause defeated and that he owes it to this country, if he owes us any loyalty or love, to let us get on with our lives without another war?'

'I'm going,' Johnnie said determinedly. 'He's certain to march on England and I must be there.'

'Hush,' Hester said, sharply, uncertain of the safety of such an announcement.

The two guests tactfully rose to their feet. 'I'll take a stroll around the garden,' Philip Harding said.

'I'll come with you,' said Dr Quigley.

The door closed behind them. 'That was unwise,' Alexander Norman said gently to Johnnie. 'Whatever your opinions are, you should not let it ever be said that your father is harbouring royalist sentiments and allowing them to be spoken at his table.'

Johnnie flushed. 'I beg your pardon,' he said to his father and to Hester. 'I won't do it again. It was the shock of the news.'

'Joseph had no business blurting it out like that,' Frances said crossly. 'And you can't go, Johnnie. It's too far. And it's bound to fail.'

'Why should it?' he demanded passionately. 'Why should it fail? The Scots army was stronger than the English last time it was out. And Parliament would never have defeated the king in the first place if it hadn't cobbled together an alliance with the Scots. They could march on London and bring the king with them.'

'Not with General Lambert in the way,' Alexander observed.

Johnnie checked. 'Is he going? The Scots have never beaten Lambert.'

'He's bound to. I would think Cromwell will command with Lambert as his second.'

'It makes no difference to me!' Johnnie declared. 'This is the return of the prince. I must be there.'

There was a silence, Frances turned to her father, who had not yet spoken. The silence extended. Johnnie looked towards his father at the end of the table.

'He is the king,' Johnnie said desperately. 'Crowned king.'

'He's not crowned in England,' Hester said sharply. 'He's not our king.'

'He's the third king of England that this family has been called on to serve,' Johnnie pressed. 'And I am the third generation in royal service. This is my service now, this is my king. I must serve him as you served his father and my grandfather served his grandfather.'

There was a long silence. Everyone waited for John to speak.

'You know my heart, sir,' Johnnie said with careful courtesy to his father. 'I hope you will give me leave to go.'

John looked down the table and saw his son blazing with bright intensity. He was restored. He was the Johnnie who had ridden out to the siege of Colchester, nothing like the ghost which they had sent back. John carefully avoided Hester's minatory gaze and spoke softly to his impassioned son.

'I have to weigh your safety against your desire to serve the king. It's not my cause, Johnnie, but you are a grown man and I see that it is yours. But you are the only heir, the only Tradescant to carry the name . . .'

Johnnie cleared his throat. 'I know that,' he said. 'But this is a great cause. It is worth a sacrifice.'

Hester moved quickly as if she would cry out against the thought of Johnnie being sacrificed to a cause, however great. Still John did not let himself look at her.

'If the Scots get as far south as York,' he said carefully, 'then you may join them. You don't want to fight for the king in Scotland, Johnnie, that's their own business. I wouldn't see you fight on their soil. But if they get to York I will buy you a horse and equipment and you can enlist, and I shall be proud to see you go.'

There was a swift intake of breath and a swirl of grey silk at the end of the table as Hester leaped to her feet.

'And your stepmother agrees with me,' John ruled, forestalling the quick exclamation.

'I can see that she does, sir,' Johnnie said gravely, a quiver of laughter in his voice.

'She does indeed,' John repeated.

Hester subsided into her seat again, her hands holding the edge of the table as if physical force was the only way she could restrain her speech.

'And you will promise me not to run off without my permission and blessing,' John stipulated. 'You've been to war now, Johnnie, you know how hard it is. You know it's a hundred times harder for a man without some money in his pocket and the right equipment: a good sword, a warm cloak, a strong horse. If you wait until the Scots have reached York you can join them as an officer. Do I have your word?'

Johnnie hesitated for only a moment. 'You have,' he said. 'But I will start preparing today, so that I am ready the moment I can go.'

'How can you?' Frances interrupted passionately. 'How can you even think of it, Johnnie? After the last time?'

He fired up at the challenge in her voice. 'You wouldn't understand,' he said. 'You're a girl.'

'I understand that you nearly broke Mother's heart last time and that we have none of us been happy since you came back from Colchester,' she said hotly. 'I understand that you have been sick to death ever since that defeat. Why go? Why go all that way to feel despair again? What if you are hurt so far from home? We'd never even know! What if your luck runs out and you get killed in one of these stupid battles at a village where we never even know the name?'

Alexander Norman, looking from his angry young wife to her younger brother, still not yet seventeen years old, hoped for a moment that the two might quarrel like the children they once were and the whole issue be lost in the confusion of words and temper. Johnnie leaped to his feet, ready to blaze back at Frances, but then he reined in his temper and looked at his father.

'I thank you for your permission, sir,' he said formally, and left the room.

Hester waited in silence until they heard his footsteps cross the hall and go out of the back door. Then she spoke bitterly to her husband. 'How could you? How could you agree that he should go?'

John looked at his son-in-law over a mug of small ale. 'Ask Alexander,' he advised. 'He knows how I could.'

Hester, her cheeks blazing, turned to Alexander. 'What?' she spat out.

'They'll never get to York,' Alexander predicted. 'Cromwell can't risk having a foreign army on English soil. He can't even risk having a Scottish army on the march against him. Not after having bloodied his sword in Ireland to keep the people down. He has to bring peace to the kingdom or lose everything. Lose one kingdom and he has lost all four. He'll fight them in Scotland and he'll defeat them in Scotland. He'll never let them come south.'

'But the king will bring out the clans,' Hester whispered. 'Men who would march all night to die for him and for their clan chief. Wild men who won't count the price, who will fight like savages.'

'The clans won't leave Scotland, they never do,' John predicted. 'They'll come no further south than a raiding party.'

'And they'll be poorly equipped,' Alexander agreed. 'They'll come out with daggers and pitchforks and meet Cromwell and Lambert and the Model Army with its cavalry and cannon and muskets and pikes. I'll have to go back to London today, there will be new orders for barrels. But you can be sure that my orders will be to send the ordnance by sea to Scotland to meet the army there – that's where Cromwell will choose his battlefield.'

Hester turned to the window and looked out over the garden. The flowerbeds before the house were filled with pinks, gillyflowers, and the new star-faced spiderwort in pink. The roses on the walls were shedding petals as they bloomed. Johnnie was striding down the avenue, his head up, his shoulders back, his listlessness and sadness quite gone.

'How can we bear it?' she asked softly. 'How could you give him permission and your blessing to go into danger again?'

John was beside her, he slid his arm around her waist and half-reluctantly she let him hold her. 'I am doing the very thing that I think will keep him safe,' he said. 'That is my only intention.'

All July and all August Johnnie was in a fever for news, desperate to be ready to go the moment his father said he might leave. He persuaded John to buy him a horse, a reliable old war charger called Caesar with big, strong haunches and broad shoulders that looked as if it would carry Johnnie's light weight for hundreds of miles.

He tied a sack stuffed with hay into the low branch of a tree and practised charging it and stabbing at it with his lance. The first few practices he followed his horse back to the stable after a couple of hard tumbles; but then he learned the knack of thrusting and withdrawing the lance in one smooth motion so the horse and he could go on together.

He bought a travelling cape and a bag that he could strap on the back of the saddle and he kept them packed with everything he might need so that he was ready to leave at a moment's notice. He was alive and vital with excitement and determination, and the whole house rang with the noise of him singing, whistling, running up and down the wooden stairs in his riding boots, shedding mud and creating confusion out of sheer energy.

John had made him promise that he would not tell anyone of the agreement they had made, and Johnnie, who remembered well enough the danger of living as suspected royalists when the king's army was on the march, was careful to make no direct reference as to which side he would be joining as soon as his father said he might go. He was as excited as a child, but he was no fool. Never again did he let slip to visitors or guests that he was only waiting for news from Yorkshire to saddle up his war horse and ride north to join the new, uncrowned king.

The family depended on Alexander Norman to tell them how the war was going. Living in the centre of the city and near the Tower he always had the first of the rumours anyway; but filling Cromwell's orders for supplies of munitions he always knew the latest position of the Model Army, though it might be impossible to tell how they were faring.

'But that's not the point,' Johnnie reminded his father anxiously, finding him in the rarities room, with a tray of recently purchased foreign coins.

'We're running out of space,' John said. 'We have to buy new items, and people like to see different things when they visit. But we cannot show everything we have now properly. We should think about building another room, perhaps.'

'The point was not whether the Scots are winning or losing, it was how far they are advanced,' Johnnie persisted. 'That was our agreement, wasn't it? Because Mother is saying that if they have advanced to York but been defeated then I shouldn't go. But we didn't say that, did we?'

John looked at his son's eager face. 'The letter of our agreement was certainly that you might go if they reached York,' he said. 'But surely, Johnnie, you wouldn't want to join a defeated army. You wouldn't want to volunteer for a lost cause?'

The young man did not hesitate for a moment. 'Of course I would,' he said simply. 'This is not about calculating which side might win and joining that. This is not about trying to end up on the winning side like half the men now in Parliament. This is about serving the king, whether he is winning or losing. His father did not recant when he saw the scaffold. Neither will I.'

John pushed the tray of coins roughly into his son's hands. 'Find a little corner for these, and write out new labels for them,' he said. 'They need to be dusted and polished too. And don't talk to me about scaffolds.'

'But if they get to York, even if they are in retreat –'

'Yes, yes,' John said. 'I remember what we agreed.'

Autumn 1650

For all of Alexander Norman's confidence in the New Model Army, it was a desperate gamble that John was taking with his son's safety. Sometimes he thought of Charles Stuart and himself, at opposite ends of the country, both taking their desperate gambles – one for the crown of England, one for the life of his son. It did not trouble John that he was gambling on Charles Stuart's failure. John's loyalty to the kings, never a strong flame, had flickered fitfully all through the first king's war, and been blown out altogether when the war had been renewed not once, but twice, after defeat. His vigil at the courtroom and scaffold had been a farewell to a man he had served, not the act of a loyal royalist. John's sympathies had always been independent, now, a citizen of a republic, he could call himself a republican.

More than anything else he wanted peace, a society in which he could garden, in which he could watch his children grow to adulthood, make marriages and have children of their own. He would have been hard-pressed to forgive any man for breaking the peace of the new state. And Charles Stuart did not sound like an exceptional man. Cromwell himself complained that the prince was so debauched that he would undo the whole country. All the news of the prince's court over the water had been of popery, folly, and vice.

But it was a close thing. The Scots army first met the English just south of Edinburgh for the battle on Scottish soil that Alexander had predicted. The Scots were in fine form, and filled with confidence at the presence of the young king. The English army were tired from the long march north, and were losing men all the way as individual soldiers changed their minds and turned south for home. The Commander-in-Chief, Cromwell, was in one of his dark moods when he doubted his men's abilities and, worse than that, doubted his own. The voice of God which guided him so clearly had suddenly gone silent and Cromwell was spiralling down into one of his disabling fits of despair. It was only John Lambert's unshakable optimism that kept the army marching north.

Then they nearly lost Lambert at the battle of Musselburgh, just south of Edinburgh, when his horse was shot dead under him and Lambert, falling, was lanced in the thigh. The Scots infantry spotted him, and a band of them were dragging him away from the battlefield when his own regiment, Yorkshiremen most of them, let out a yell of horror which made even the Highlanders check, and charged through the crowd to get to him.

The Scots pressed on southwards for London; the English army chased after them until the Scots chose the ground and turned to face the pursuers outside Dunbar. The English were hopelessly outnumbered; injury, illness, and desertion had taken a dramatic toll. Cromwell was uncertain whether to go forwards against the Scots or fall back. Only Lambert gritted his teeth and said they must fight then and there.

While Cromwell dropped the flap of his tent so that he might weep and pray in privacy, John Lambert mustered the army and told them simply and clearly that the Scots outnumbered them by two to one and thus they must fight with double bravery, double persistence, and double faith. There were about twenty-two thousand Scotsmen drawn up for battle, and only eleven thousand of them. With the smile that Hester Tradescant secretly loved, Lambert pulled off his plumed hat and beamed at his troops. 'I don't think this is a difficulty,' he shouted. 'Come on, Ironsides!'

Early in September, Alexander sent a one line note to John.

Scots defeated at Dunbar.

'Thank God,' Hester said piously when John held out the letter for her to read in the stable yard. She put her hand in her pocket and gave Alexander's boy a coin.

'I already paid him,' John remarked.

Hester smiled. 'I could give ten shillings for this news,' she said.

'Shall you tell Johnnie, or will I?'

She hesitated. 'Where is he?'

'On the other side of the road, picking nuts from the horse chestnut trees.'

'You go,' she said. 'It was your agreement with him that has kept him safe.'

'Praise God,' John said. 'I have had some sleepless nights.'

He strolled around the house, savouring the warmth of the sun reflected from the walls, glancing up in passing at the flamboyant crest which his father had illegally composed and claimed. It didn't matter now, John thought with satisfaction. There were so many newly created titles and such confusion about how titles had come into being, that they could claim to be baronets and no-one would query it. Indeed, Johnnie might one day very well be Sir John Tradescant as his grandfather had always wanted. Who knew what this new world would bring? As long as the family could keep its place, could keep the business, could keep the plants; as long as the horse chestnut trees flowered each year and scattered down the precious nuts like a prodigal rain of wealth, as long as there was always a Tradescant heir to pick them up and set them deep in moist pots.

John walked across the little bridge that spanned the stream at the side of the road and then crossed to the acreage on the other side. He had planted a thick holly hedge as a windbreak and to shield the plant beds from curious passers-by and he thought this year he might trim it to make it thicken out and to square off the top like a handsome green wall. He paused for a moment and looked upwards. It would take more than a week of work to cut back the top boughs of the hedge and it would be a painful, awkward job. He smiled at the thought that at least Johnnie would be at home to help him, and then he opened the door set between brick lintels in the hedge and went into the garden.

It was part physic garden, part vegetable plot, a new sort of garden for a new age which prized science and medicine more highly than luxury and prettiness.

But from ingrained habit, John had made his herb and vegetable beds in a pattern like a knot garden, and they were strictly aligned to a central point where he had dug a deep hole, lined it with clay and filled it with water to use as a dipping pond for watering the garden. The beds nearest the pond were all planted with the rarer and more tender herbs that the College of Physicians had asked him to grow. He had planted the edges with lavender to keep insect pests away, and because lavender was a good paying crop, the flower heads could always be sold to the perfume-makers and the apothecaries. Further away from the central pond radiated other geometrically shaped beds growing greens and brassicas, onions, peas, turnips, purple-flowered and white-flowered potatoes – the food crops of the country gardens which John was breeding and cross-breeding, trying to rid them of their tendency to blight, trying to find the largest and the most nutritious.

If ever they were visited by one of the more dour radicals or sectaries who complained of the riot of wealth and colour in the rarities room or in the garden around the house, John would bring him over here and show how, in these beds, he was using his skills in the service of the people and of God.

Johnnie was at the far end of the garden where they had planted row upon row of saplings, ready for sale, and where they had a chestnut tree at each corner. White sheets were laid under the trees and Johnnie came every day at dawn and dusk to get the very best of the nuts before the squirrels ate them.

'Hey!' John called from the door to the garden. 'Message from Alexander.'

Johnnie looked up and came through the garden at a run, his face ablaze with joy and hope. 'The king's reached York? I can go to him?'

John shook his head and mutely held out the note.

Johnnie took it, opened it, read it. John saw the energy and joy drain out of his son as if a leech of grief had suddenly fastened on his heart.

'Defeated,' he said, as if the word was meaningless. 'Defeated at Dunbar. Where is Dunbar?'

'Scotland,' John said gruffly. 'South of Edinburgh, I think.'

'The king?'

'As you see, he doesn't say. But it's over,' John said gently. 'That was his last throw of the dice. He'll go back to France, I suppose.'

His son looked up at him, his young face bewildered. 'Over? D'you think he'll never try again?'

'He can't keep trying,' John exclaimed. 'He can't keep coming back and coming back and upsetting the country. He has to know that it was over for his father and it is over for him. Their time has gone. The English don't want a king any more.'

'You made me stay and wait,' Johnnie said with sudden sharp bitterness. 'And I stayed and waited, like hundreds, perhaps thousands, of other men. And while I stayed and waited he didn't have enough men. So he was defeated, while I stayed at home, waiting for your leave to go.'

John put his hand on Johnnie's shoulder but the younger man shrugged it off and took a few steps away. 'I betrayed him!' he cried out, his voice breaking. 'I stayed at home obeying my father when I should have ridden out to obey my king.'

John hesitated, choosing his words with care. 'I don't think it was a close-run thing. I don't think hundreds of men would have made a difference. Since Cromwell and Lambert have had command of the army they have rarely lost a battle. I don't think your being there would have made a difference, Johnnie.'

Johnnie looked back at his father and his dark, beautiful young face was filled with reproach. 'It would have made a difference to me,' he said with simple dignity.

He came into dinner in silence. In silence he went to bed. At breakfast the next morning his eyes were sombre and there were dark shadows underneath them. The light had gone out of Johnnie once again.

Hester put her hand on his shoulder as she rose from the table to fetch some more small ale.

'Why don't you go to Wimbledon today?' she asked him gently. 'Your next crop of melons must be nearly ready to pick.'

'What should I do with the fruit?' he asked miserably.

Hester glanced towards John for help and saw the smallest shrug. 'Why don't you pack them up,' she suggested. 'And send them to Charles Stuart in Edinburgh. Don't put your name inside,' she stipulated cautiously. 'But you could at least send them to him. Then you would know that you had served him as you should serve him. You're not a soldier, Johnnie, you're a gardener. You could send him the fruit you have grown for him. That's how you serve him. That's how your father served his father, and your grandfather served King James himself.'

Johnnie hesitated for only a moment then he looked to his father. 'May I go?' he asked hopefully.

'Yes,' John said in relief. 'Of course you can go. It's a very good thing to do.'

Spring 1651

In the cold, dark days of February John was glad to go to London and stay with Frances, or with Philip Harding, or Paul Quigley, and join the men in their discussions. Sometimes one of the physicians would conduct an experiment and summon the gentlemen to watch so that they might comment on his findings. John attended an evening in which one of the alchemists attempted to fire a new glaze for porcelain.

'John should be the judge,' one of the gentlemen said. 'You have some porcelain in your collection, haven't you, John?'

'I have some china dishes,' John said. 'They range in size from as big as a trencher to so small that a mouse could dine off it.'

'Very fine?' the man asked. 'You can see light through them, can't you?'

'Yes,' John said. 'But strong. I've never seen the like in this country. I think we don't have china clay which is fine enough.'

'It's the glaze,' said another man.

'The heat of the furnace,' suggested another.

'Wait,' said the alchemist. 'Wait until the furnace is cooled enough and you shall see it.'

'A drink while we wait?' someone suggested and the maidservant brought a bottle of Canary wine and glasses, and they drew up high stools to sit companionably around the alchemist's working bench.

'Have you heard that Oatlands Palace is to be taken down?' one of the men asked John. 'You planted the gardens there, didn't you?'

John checked in the act of drinking. 'Taken down?' he repeated.

Another man nodded. 'They can't sell it. It's too big for a private residence, and it needs too much work done. It's to be destroyed.'

'But – the gardens?' John stammered.

'You should petition Parliament,' one of the mathematicians

recommended. 'Ask them if you may uproot your plants before they start to knock the whole thing down. You have some rarities there, don't you?'

'Indeed I have,' John said, astounded. 'There are some very precious things in the royal courts.' He shook his head. 'Every day there is something new but I would never have thought that they would raze Oatlands.'

John raised the matter of Oatlands' gardens with a Parliament man who visited the Ark to see the rarities and in a few days he received a commission to supervise the selling of the specimen plants from the garden before the demolition of the house. He might take a tithe of the profit and any plants he chose as payment for his trouble, and he was ordered to sell the rest.

'I'll stay there for a week or so, until the work is done,' he told Hester.

'I shall miss our little house there,' she said. 'I liked knowing we had a place out of the city, a refuge.'

'Such a waste,' John said. 'All that work in the gardens, all that beauty in the house. And the new orangery and the silkworm house! All for nothing.'

'Shall you take Johnnie with you?' Hester asked. 'It might do him good to have a change of scene.'

'Yes,' John said. 'I'll take the cart too. I'll bring back some of the chestnut trees if any have survived this winter. And there were some handsome climbers as well which I might be able to cut back from the walls and transplant.'

They harnessed Caesar, Johnnie's war horse, to the cart and John thought that the handsome animal pulling a gardener's cart to a palace which was to be demolished could have served as an illustration for a chapbook entitled: 'How the mighty are fallen'. A war horse harnessed to pull a cart did not seem to him to be a symbol of peace and prosperity when his son sat beside him on the driving seat with his eyes deep-set and dark. Even the horse drooped its head at the unfamiliar weight dragging at its shoulders. It seemed as if both boy and horse should be released from drudgery, should be set free to ride off in some romance of their own devising. The times were too small and too mean for both of them.

They were beautiful creatures, they should have been freed to go their own ways.

John thought that hard work might restore some of Johnnie's spirits, and set him to cutting back and lifting the roses out of the rose garden. There was no time to be troubled with any but the most precious plants in the garden, and the trees in the orchards. The great richness of the nine acres and the terraced courts could not be uprooted and saved in the short February days.

John worked from memory, powerful, evocative memories of planting for the king and queen, remembering what plant was in his hand when she stopped by him on the path, what precious bulbs were stored in the nets hung up high in the roofs of the sheds.

In the evenings they planned the work for the next day and Johnnie would ask over and over again whether the queen had chosen this plant, or that; whether the king had eaten fruit from this very tree. Despite himself, John found that he was remembering with affection the beauty of the garden and the rich frivolity of the court. Despite his own scepticism he drew a picture of a golden time, gardening in summer for a king and a queen who spent money like rain and who walked lovingly arm-in-arm along well-tended paths from one exquisite court and terrace to another.

John and his son spent a week lifting the rarest and most precious plants and potting them up and loading them into the cart. Every other day they drove the cart down to the river and transferred the pots on to a ferry to send to the Ark at Lambeth.

'Hester won't be best pleased,' John remarked as yet another boatload of plants set off downstream. 'She and Joseph will be doing nothing but unloading and watering pots this week.'

'We have to do it,' Johnnie said passionately. 'We're his gardeners. We have to save as much of his garden as we can.'

Something in the desperate note in his voice warned John. He put his hand on his son's arm. 'We're doing this for the plants, not for the king,' he said. 'Some of these are of the best quality, some of these are rare and precious. I couldn't let them go to waste. This work is for the plants and for the Ark.'

Johnnie looked at his father. 'These are the king's plants,' he said with suppressed emotion. 'We're gardening for him now as we always have done. Once it was our duty to put the plants in and safeguard them. Now it's our duty to save them for him. When he comes to his own again he can sit underneath his own father's cherry tree, he can pick roses for his mother from her favourite tree. They've crowned him king in Scotland, haven't they? They've declared him to be their king though they once called his father a prisoner and handed him over to his death. But Charles is an anointed king once more, in a kingdom which acknowledges him?'

'At such a price,' John muttered. 'He agreed to every demand the Scots put to him, and betrayed men who had fought for him in the Highlands for years. Your old hero, Montrose, was captured and executed, and the king dining with the Kirk, his old enemies, looked out of the window and saw Montrose's hand nailed to the door. He said nothing. He went on with his dinner.'

'He does what he has to do,' Johnnie said staunchly.

Once they had rescued the pick of the specimens, and rummaged in the cold soil of the courts for forgotten bulbs, they declared a general sale of plants in Weybridge. The town crier called out the news and it spread from one manor garden to another, from one cottage to another, until everyone in Surrey wanted a flower from the king's garden.

On Saturday John set up a stall on the very front door of the palace and let people come with their own spades to choose, and then dig up their choice. He and Johnnie inspected the booty and set an instant knock-down price on the trees which marched past them, on the little pots of pansies and herbs, on the trailing creepers, torn from the walls, on the endless scarlet-budding roses.

It was a melancholy business to see the garden walking away down the drive, as if even the plants had gone into exile, and John was sorry that he had exposed his son to the sight. He had thought that the work would have given them a project to complete together, that Johnnie would see that the garden was finished, that the palace was destroyed, that the king and kingship were gone forever. But instead there was a powerful sense of loss invoked by the sale. More than one man or woman stopped at John's table, gestured to their purchase and asked reverently: 'He did love these, didn't he? Can you remember if he ever picked a flower from it? Did he touch it?'

John realised that only half of the people were buying plants cheaply; the other half were buying relics, honouring the memory of a dead king, planting a little bit of his martyrdom in their own gardens.

All the cold grey day Johnnie priced, took money, answered questions with endless easy patience. But John, watching him, saw how his head drooped as the light faded from the sky.

'You're tired,' he said gruffly at five o'clock as the winter twilight closed around them. 'And chilled too. I know I am. Let's go down to the ale house and get ourselves a good dinner. I'd like to leave the money in the goldsmith's keeping anyway. I don't want to keep it here.'

Johnnie's face was pale. 'Yes.'

'Are you sick?' John asked.

Johnnie shook his head. 'Weary,' he said. 'I wasn't born to be a huckster. I hate it. How they do go on, don't they? And the smaller the plant the more ado they make about the price.'

John laughed eagerly. 'Yes. It's been a long business. But tomorrow we'll go.'

'And then they'll pull it down and it will be as if it was never here,' Johnnie said dreamily.

John tied the string of the purse and slipped it into his deep pocket. 'Come on,' he said cheerfully. 'Before we are completely benighted.'

He marched briskly down the avenue with Johnnie keeping step beside him. They were warm by the time they saw the yellow light of the ale house and smelled the mixture of woodsmoke and frying bacon.

'You go on,' John said. 'I'll take this purse and put it in the goldsmith's vault.'

Johnnie nodded and went ahead of his father. John stood back and watched his son walk away. 'Johnnie!' he suddenly called.

The young man hesitated and turned, his face a pale blur in the twilight.

'It's being rid of the old to prepare for the new,' John said. 'A baptism. Not a funeral, you know.'

It was a melancholy business the next morning, for all of John's forced brightness. They loaded the cart with leftover tools and the pots which they had filled with the rescued plants during their stay, and then they went round the garden and orchard and orangery in one final tour to see what had been overlooked.

The rose garden was a desert of pitted holes, like the face of a beloved woman pocked with scars. The very shape of the garden had gone, the trees which had given it a structure had been uprooted, the trellised arbours which had been pulled down as people cut off the climbing roses were left as smashed wood in the mud. The lavender borders were ragged, some plants missing, some trodden down. A few snowdrops which had struggled up at the base of the wall in the queen's court had been crushed by someone in their haste to cut down a creeper. A pot had been dropped and smashed and the shards left where they lay, cluttering up the path. The whole palace, once so rosy in pink brick and so immaculately gardened, with smooth lawns and sculpted arbours, was now a tangle of overgrown hedging and churned mud. Even the bowling green which had been John's great pride was pocked with weeds and the richer green of winter moss shone in moist patches among the paler green of weak winter grass.

It had started to rain, an icy, penetrating drizzle, and the clouds sat heavily on the roof of the palace. The glass had been stolen long ago from the windows, or smashed by the successive troops quartered in the palace, and the smell of damp plaster and decay seeped into the courts from the derelict building.

'Let's go,' John said. 'Everything is finished here.'

Johnnie nodded in silence and followed his father to the cart. He climbed on to the box and took the reins of the horse which should have been his war horse, to drive away from the palace which should have been the king's. The avenue was long gone, felled for timber. They drove between pale stumps where grand trees had once shaded the road.

'That was a miserable task,' John said heartily, hoping that Johnnie would agree and that they might share the sadness and then put it behind them.

'It was burying him and his hopes all over again,' Johnnie said sombrely; and then said nothing more.

Summer 1651

Johnnie did not forget the melon bed at Wimbledon. Of the consignment he had sent north to Charles Stuart he had kept one fruit back and from it he had another batch of seeds which he insisted on planting in the Lambeth seed bed, and, when they were grown, insisted on taking to Wimbledon.

'You could grow them here now,' Hester remarked to him reasonably when she saw him loading the earthenware pots into a carrying basket. 'There's no point in taking them all that way.'

'Of course I must plant them at Wimbledon,' he said passionately. 'It was his request.'

'The garden must be overgrown.'

'It's running to seed,' he said, 'and the glass has been stolen from the windows of the house. But you can see it was a lovely place, you can tell it was one of our gardens. Every now and then I come across some special flower struggling through the weeds. Father's Virginian foxgloves, and grandfather's chestnuts in a little avenue in one of the courts.'

'We can't do anything about it,' she said. 'We have to leave the old places behind us. Your father gardened for years at Hatfield and after he left he never went back and it was the same at New Hall. Oatlands will be nothing more than a name in a year or two, in a few years no-one will even remember where it was.'

'I know that,' he said. 'I just plant the melons. I don't deny that everything is changed for the moment.'

'You don't change,' she observed.

For a moment his melancholy lifted. He shot her a small, roguish smile as if he hardly dared to trust her with the hope that he kept hidden. 'Well, everything might change back again one day, mightn't it? And then I will be glad that I kept faith.'

Johnnie had good cause to suggest that everything could change once again. The defeat at Dunbar was not the last battle fought in Scotland, the Scots army did not flee in a rout but in a retreat; and the shaky alliance between the Kirk and the dissolute prince did not completely collapse. Instead, the prince's stature grew and the Scots warmed to him. All through the year, reports of a continuing campaign filtered back to London telling of Cromwell, ill-supported and in a mostly hostile country, trying to gain a decisive victory. Then in midsummer the Scots army, with Charles at their head, did the unthinkable. They broke out of Scotland and crossed the border.

'Can we hide it from him?' Hester demanded urgently of John when he told her the news in the kitchen.

He shook his head. 'He's bound to hear of it sooner or later and I'd not have him think me guilty of double dealing.'

'You swore they'd not come south,' she accused. 'You said Cromwell would defeat them on Scottish soil.'

John's face was taut with worry. 'It was a gamble,' he said. 'And it served us well. They have to go beyond York, remember. That was the agreement.'

'Is Lambert still there?' she asked, as if that were a talisman against the king's advance.

'Oh, for God's sake!' John snapped and turned away from her and marched out into the garden, looking for his son.

He found him dead-heading the roses and tossing the petals into a deep carrying basket for sale in the London markets to the perfumiers or the confectioners. Frances, staying at the Ark to avoid the plague months in town, was working at the opposite end of the bed. John heard their casual chatter and paused for a moment to hold the moment in his mind: his two children doing their work, the family's work, in such easy harmony, in the sunshine, on their own land, in a country so near to peace.

He squared his shoulders and stepped forwards. 'Johnnie –'

The young man looked up. 'Father?'

'There's news. I heard it in London. Charles Stuart is leading a troop over the border. Lambert is chasing after him, but it looks as if he has broken out of Scotland and is determined to invade.'

'Is he south of York?' Johnnie demanded. For a moment John thought that the young man was resonating, like a harp string tuned too tight. 'Is he south of York? Can I go to him?'

'He's headed south,' John said cautiously. 'As soon as we hear from Alexander we'll know for sure.'

Alexander came himself in August.

'I knew you would want to know as soon as I did,' he said. The family were so anxious for news that they greeted him in the hall, as soon as he came through the door, Johnnie at the forefront. 'They were marching on London but they have turned to the west. They're probably hoping to raise recruits from Wales before they face Lambert.'

'And where is Lambert?'

'On a forced march behind them,' Alexander replied. 'There is no other general in the world who could move his men at the speed he does. He'll catch the Scots army, without a doubt. And he'll be the one that chooses the ground.'

'Is he south of York?' Johnnie demanded.

Alexander looked past him to Hester's anguished face. 'I am sorry, Hester,' was all he said.

Johnnie sprang up the stairs, running for his campaign bundle, shouting for Joseph to tell the stable lad to get his horse ready. John turned to his wife and she buried her face against his shoulder.

'Stop him,' she whispered. 'Stop him.'

John shook his head. 'No power on earth can stop him,' he said. He looked at Alexander. 'Can they win?'

Alexander had drawn Frances to his side. 'These are the fortunes of war,' he said. 'You know as well as I do that anything can happen, it can always go either way. But Cromwell and Lambert defeated this army before, and on their own ground. The northern militia will turn out now that the Scots have invaded England, and the northern men hate the Scots worse than anything else. There'll be strong feelings against the king now that he has an army moving through England – no-one has forgotten the last war. It's one thing to mourn the death of a dead king; it's quite another to turn the country upside down again for the claims of a live one. I think they'll lose. But I can't be sure. No-one can be sure.'

'Who cares?' Hester said, her face still hidden, her voice agonised. 'Who cares if they lose or win? Johnnie could be killed, couldn't he? Whether they win or lose?'

John tightened his grip around her. 'We'll have to pray,' he said, and it was a sign of his own desperation. 'That's all we can do now.'

They gathered in the stable yard to see him off. He kissed his sister, he kissed his stepmother and she clung to him for a moment as if she would beg him to stay. She inhaled the scent of him, the newly washed linen which had been stored with lavender bags, the warm straw smell of his hair, the warmth of his skin, the tender stubble of his cheek, the soft apprentice moustache on his upper lip. She held him and thought of the child he had been when she had taken him into her care, and she thought of the terrible gulf in her life that would be carved out if he were lost.

'Let him go,' John said quietly from behind her.

Johnnie briskly embraced Alexander and then he turned to his father. He dropped his head and was about to kneel for his blessing. 'Don't kneel,' John said quickly, as if a patch of damp on his son's knee mattered one way or another when the boy was going out to fight a doomed battle. He wrapped him in his arms and held him furiously tight.

'God bless you and keep you,' he whispered passionately. 'And come home as soon as you feel you can. Don't linger, Johnnie. Once the battle is done there's no shame in riding away.'

The youth was ablaze with joy, he could not hear words of caution. He turned to his horse and he sprang up, swung his leg over and gathered in the reins. The old knowledgeable war horse, Caesar, knew the signs, he pawed the ground, arched his neck and sidled a little, eager to be off.

Hester felt her knees giving way, she put her hand into John's arm and leaned against him.

'I'm away!' Johnnie sung out. 'I'll write! Goodbye!'

Hester folded her upper lip in a tight, admonitory grip between her teeth and raised her hand to wave.

'Good luck!' Frances called. 'God bless you, Johnnie!'

They crowded to the stable-yard entrance to watch him ride out, and then followed him, under the wall with the stone-carved crest, over the little bridge, and then eastwards along the road to the Lambeth horse ferry and the northern roads.

'God bless you,' John called.

The horse's polished haunches moved powerfully. As he reached the firm going of the road, Johnnie let the animal extend into a trot and then into a broad-paced canter. He went too fast for Hester, the big horse's pace took him too swiftly away.

'Johnnie!' she called.

But he did not hear her, and in a moment he was gone.

Autumn 1651

Then there was nothing to do but to wait. The City was alive with rumours and counter-claims of battles and routs and attacks, victory to the Prince or victory to the Model Army. John kept as much of the news from Hester as he could, and asked her to do a dozen tasks in the rarities room, in the garden, to keep her hands busy and to keep her away from the constant litany of bad news in the kitchen between the cook and Joseph. But nothing could stop her longing for her son.

Frances and Hester lit a candle in the window the evening that Johnnie went away, and Hester would not have the shutter closed on it, to hide it from the road, nor ever let it burn out. Every morning she renewed it herself, a great wax candle, more suited for a church than for a home, every night she checked that it was burning safely and its light was showing out towards the Lambeth road where Johnnie had ridden away.

John remarked only that there was a danger of fire if the candle should fall over in a gust of wind, and after that she placed the holder in a dish of water. But nothing would persuade her not to show a light, as if the one candle could guide her boy homewards along the dark, unsafe roads.

In the first week in September Alexander Norman came upriver and marched briskly from the landing stage to the Ark. He found John alone in the physic garden.

'News,' he said shortly.

John scrambled up from the herb bed and waited.

'There was a battle on the third, the anniversary of the Dunbar defeat. Cromwell is a great one for anniversaries.'

'And?'

'Defeat. The Scots were routed and Charles Stuart has gone.'

'Dead?' John asked. 'Dead at last?'

'Disappeared. There's a price on his head and the whole country looking for him. He must be taken any day. The Scots are fled back to Scotland and the English volunteers heading for their homes. Cromwell writes that he is bringing the army home and disbanding the militia. He must think he is completely safe. We must think so.'

'A defeat,' John said.

'It means nothing for a single soldier,' Alexander said swiftly. 'He could be riding home now.'

John nodded. 'I'd better tell Hester before some fool blurts it out to her.'

'Where is Frances?'

'They'll be together,' John predicted. 'This summer has been a long vigil for them both.'

John gathered up his tools and the two men crossed the road. Instinctively they looked east towards Lambeth, as if they might see the big horse and the joyous young man riding back to them.

'I keep looking,' John said gruffly. 'We all of us keep looking for him.'

They had no word, they could get no news. Cromwell came home but Lambert stayed in Scotland, ruling from Edinburgh, bringing the Scots gradually into line with a republican England. He sent an order for some tulips to grow in pots in his rooms and Hester, knowing herself to be taking a risk with their whole livelihood and lives, wrote him a note, slipped it in with the bulbs and handed them to his messenger.

> Forgive me asking for your assistance, but one very dear to me
> may have been captured at Worcester. Can you tell me how I
> might discover what has happened to him, or where he is now?

'Shall I order more candles?' the cook asked, preparing the list for market. 'Or –'

'Or what?' Hester snapped.

The suggestion that there was little point setting out the candle every night for Johnnie was too grave to be named.

'Nothing,' the cook replied.

John Lambert replied by the next courier travelling to London in a note which showed that he understood exactly who might be very dear to Hester and who might have been at Worcester.

> *Dear Mrs Tradescant,*
>
> *I am sorry to hear of your anxiety. The Scots cavalry were not intensely engaged in the battle and retreated in good order to Scotland. There they dispersed. He might well have gone with them till the order came to scatter and thus there is good reason to hope that he may return within the next few months. There were very few captured and he is not among them. I specifically asked for him by name. We are not holding him prisoner. There were very few killed.*
>
> *I thank you for your tulips. You seem to have put in half a dozen more bulbs than I paid for. I wish I could render you greater service in return, but I will be alert for any familiar name and I will write again if I have any news.*

Hester took the letter into the rarities room where the fire was kept burning against the wintry weather and plunged it deep into the heart of the red-hot logs. She very much wanted to keep the note for the little comfort she could draw from it; but she knew that she should not.

Winter 1651

In a dark afternoon of December as Hester was closing the shutters in the rarities room and the parlour she heard a horse walking steadily up the road. She went to the window and looked out, as she always did whenever she heard a single horseman riding by the house. She looked without expectation of seeing her son, but she looked, just as she burned the candle: because he should always be looked for, because a vigil should always be kept for him.

When she saw the size and solidity of the horse, she blinked and rubbed her eyes because for a moment she thought it must be Caesar. But she had thought that she had seen Caesar so many times before that she did not start forwards and cry out.

He came steadily closer and she realised it was indeed Caesar, and that on his back, slumped in the saddle, was Johnnie, his warm cape wrapped around him, bare-headed, finding his way home along the darkened road as much by memory as by sight.

She did not scream or cry or run; Hester had never been a woman for screaming or crying or running. She went quietly to the front door and opened it, opened the garden gate, and stepped quietly across the little bridge over the stream, into the road. Caesar pricked up his ears at the whisper of her skirt, grey against the grey twilight, and quickened his pace. Johnnie, who had been half-asleep in the saddle, glanced up and saw the figure of a woman, waiting in the lane, as if she had waited for him at the gatepost ever since he had left.

'Mother?' His voice was a little hoarse.

'My son.'

He reined in the horse and tumbled down from the saddle. He dropped the reins and stepped towards her outstretched arms. She took his weight in the embrace as his legs buckled as he hit the ground.

'My son, my son,' she said.

He smelled different. He had gone away smelling like a well-washed boy, he came home smelling like a hard-worked man. There was a tang of woodsmoke in his hair, which was tangled and matted. His woollen cloak was heavy with grime, his boots muddy. He was thinner but hard-muscled, she could feel the strength in his shoulders and back as he held her tightly.

'Mother,' he said again.

'Praise God for you,' she whispered. 'I thank God that he heard me pray and sent you home.'

She did not think she could bear to release him but after a moment more she stepped back and led him into the house. Caesar, knowing full well that he was home, walked riderless around the house into the stable yard and as Hester and Johnnie came in the front door there was an explosion of noise from the stables as the lad and John recognised the horse and came running into the house.

'He's home!' John yelled as if he could hardly believe it.

He ran through the kitchen and into the hall and then checked at the sight of his son's weary face and dirty clothes. Then he spread his arms to him and enfolded Johnnie in a powerful hug. 'Home,' he said.

Autumn 1652

The boy was home, the country was at peace. Oliver Cromwell was ruling Parliament with such power and dominance that he might as well have been king himself. Scotland was no longer an independent kingdom but was annexed by England and General George Monck was driving roads through Highland pride and through Highland courage which might never be healed. Charles Stuart was far away in France, or the Low Countries, or wherever he might scrape a living for doing nothing but being his charming self.

The peace brought gardeners back to the orchards and flowerbeds, and men of inquiring minds into the rarities collection. Takings at the door grew every day, and the order book for Tradescant flowers, shrubs, trees and vegetables grew full. John's reputation for strange, beautiful and exotic plants was established and he was gaining increasing respect for his experiments with new vegetables and fruit. He grew potatoes and Indian corn and peaches, nectarines, cherries, grapes for eating and for wine and for drying as raisins; and the scientists and philosophers who dined at the Ark would ask to try the new vegetables and fruits for their dinner.

In the autumn John Lambert came home from Scotland and visited the garden at the Ark and admired John's new collection of cyclamen which he had in a new bed under the chestnut trees. Lambert kneeled down in the dirt of the avenue to look at them, their delicate little petals folded back like a nun's coif. He greeted Johnnie without remarking on the scar beneath his eye, and kissed Hester's hand without mentioning the package of tulips or the hidden note.

'I'm glad to see your boy is home,' was all he said to her.

'Thank you,' she replied. 'And I was glad to see you are now Lord Lambert.'

'Aren't I grand?' he asked her with a smile, and then turned to walk around the flowerbeds with John.

'You gardened for the queen at Wimbledon House, did you not?' he asked when they were seated on the terrace, looking out over the chrysanthemums planted thickly in the beds before the house to give the garden some early autumn colour.

'I did,' John said. 'We planned it and I even planted the beds by the house, a knot garden, and a watercourse; but they had very little time there. She wanted it as a retreat, I was going to make a flowery mead down by the river, I should think it's a hay meadow now.'

'What d'you think of the soil and the situation? There are some good plants still growing.'

'It would have been a most pretty garden,' John said. 'I still have the plans for planting. Johnnie goes up there every summer.'

'I have bought it for my own use. I want a country house not too far from London. I should like to see what you had planned for it.'

'You have it? Well that's –' John broke off.

'A surprise,' John Lambert finished diplomatically for him. 'I think so too. I certainly didn't ever think to find myself in a queen's house, but I think it will suit me very well. I was especially interested to know if any of your plantings have survived. I'd be sorry to spoil a bed of rarities through my own ignorance.'

'Johnnie told me that some things are still there. I know the trees have done well, and Johnnie told me that the horse chestnuts are growing and the fruit trees in the orchards.'

'Horse chestnuts?' John Lambert asked with a gleam.

'Yes.'

'Mature?'

John thought for a moment. 'They'd be, oh, fifteen years old now.' He laughed. 'They'll be flowering and coming into their full beauty. I think you'll find you have a bargain in the garden. And I had planted plum and medlar and quince apples and pears; also the Tradescant great black cherry, and espaliered peaches.'

Hester came out on to the terrace with a bottle of wine and two glasses, Johnnie washed and tidy behind her. 'Will you stay for dinner, Lord Lambert?' she asked. 'Elias Ashmole and his wife are staying with us at the moment, and we expect some other guests too.'

'Thank you, I would like to,' he said.

'His lordship has bought Wimbledon House,' John told her. 'Johnnie, would you go and see if you can find the garden plans for me? They were in the documents in the rarities room.' He looked directly at his son and spoke with emphasis. 'We must be glad that one of our gardens has been bought by a man who will love it,' he said firmly.

It was as if the boy had not heard him.

'That's the queen's house,' Johnnie said bluntly.

Lambert heard the repressed passion behind the words and replied very calmly. 'It was confiscated, as are all the royal houses and palaces. And now I have bought it. I paid good money for it, Johnnie. It was a proper transaction, not booty. I didn't steal it.'

'It wasn't the king's house, it was the queen's,' Johnnie insisted. 'She's never been tried for treason, her estates have never been sequestrated. How can anyone have her house? It has nothing to do with the royal palaces. It's her own house.'

Hester glanced at John.

'Her fortunes go with her husband,' Lambert answered. 'That's the law, Johnnie. And all royalists have lost their houses.'

'Fetch the plans for me.' John tried to stem the rise of his son's temper.

'Fetch the damned things yourself!' Johnnie burst out. 'I'll have no part in robbing the queen of her own. I won't pretend that it's not thievery to live in a queen's palace and steal her fruits! It's nothing better than looting! It's a dead king's goods!'

He flung out of the house and ran down the shallow steps into the garden, they saw him tear down the avenue and through the gate towards the lake. There was an appalled silence.

'I apologise,' John said. 'He will be disciplined, your lordship. He will apologise to you himself. He doesn't realise the gravity of what he is saying.' John shot a swift look at Hester, asking for help. At the very least Johnnie was guilty of appalling rudeness; at the worst, treason.

'I'm so sorry,' Hester said in a whisper. 'He's still very young, you understand. And distressed. I would not have had him speak so to anyone, you least of all. He does realise that the war is over. He is not an active royalist. We are all of us loyal to Parliament here.'

Lambert leaned back against his chair and took up his glass of wine. 'Oh, there's no need to apologise,' he said gently. 'There are many who feel as he does up and down the country, it's bound to take some time for feelings to die down. And there have been enough trials for treason. The lad has strong feelings and it's hard to lose two battles by – what is he? – twenty? Did he get that scar at Worcester?'

'Yes. A scratch from a pike,' Hester said. 'Thank God it missed his eye. It was all but healed up by the time he came home. And he's only eighteen. I am sorry, your lordship. He spent his youth in the shadow of the war.'

'He's at an age when you see things in black and white,' Lambert said easily. 'Things are not so simple in real life. If Charles Stuart would make half the promises to us that he made to the Scots then he could have come home to his throne. But we can't trust him. Those of us who dealt with his father remember that the Stuarts find it easier to promise than to deliver. And the son is even worse than the father for reneging on his debts and word. He's not much of a model for Johnnie to set his heart on.'

'I know,' Hester said sadly. 'But I can't seem to persuade him.'

Johnnie did not reappear for dinner and Hester laid the table, served the gentlemen, and dined on her own in the kitchen before she went out to look for him.

She knew where to go. He was lying in the little rowing boat, his long legs over the back of the boat, gazing up at the sky where a few silver stars were showing against the pale blue.

Hester sat at the foot of the tree where she used to bring him to feed the ducks when he had been such a happy little boy. She observed the gently moving boat for a few moments before she spoke.

'That was ill-done, Johnnie. You will have to apologise to Lord Lambert. He is a good man and he has been kind to me.'

The boat rocked a little as he leaned forwards, saw her, and then reclined again. 'I know I was in the wrong. I will beg his pardon for speaking out.'

'It's foolish to fly out like that. You said enough to be tried for treason tonight.'

'No more than thousands of others.'

'Even so.'

The rocking of the little craft steadied and slowed.

'I know,' Johnnie said. 'I am sorry. I will say I am sorry to father and to his lordship. And I won't do it again.'

She waited for a moment. In the garden somewhere an owl cried hauntingly.

'Are you not cold?'

'No.'

'Hungry?'

'No.'

'Will you come in now?'

'In a little while.'

Hester paused for a moment. 'You know, Johnnie, I doubt that even Charles Stuart grieves more than you do. From what I hear of him he is a light-hearted man who goes from plotting to dancing; and would rather be dancing. He gambles away the money that people risk their lives to raise for him. His friends have given their livelihoods and even their lives for him and yet he dresses in the best clothes and goes to balls, and chases women shamelessly. He's a drunkard and a gambler and a lecher. He's a young man, as you are a young man. But he takes his cause very light-heartedly. Why should you grieve for him? Why grieve more than he does himself?'

'It's not that.' Johnnie's voice came over the still water, she could barely see the boat now in the twilight. 'All that you say about him is true. I was with him at Worcester long enough to see that he is light, as you say. Light-hearted and light-weight. But I don't grieve for the loss of him as a man, I grieve for the loss of everything that kingship means. The loss of the court, the loss of a nation under one ruler, the loss of the beauty of the Church and music and colour, the loss of certainty of every man having a master. The loss of the gardens, the loss of the palaces. The loss of *our* gardens.'

'We still have the Ark,' she said.

'One little garden, more like a farm than a garden,' he said dismissively. 'We're getting a grand reputation for growing onions. This is nothing to a family which had Oatlands, or Hatfield, or Theobalds. Even Wimbledon. All we have now is a tiny patch of ground and no-one plants great gardens any more.'

'They will do again,' she said. 'The country is at peace once more, they will plant gardens again.'

'They'll plant turnips,' Johnnie predicted. 'And marrows. Like father is growing for them. I saw Oatlands Palace and I saw them uproot it, rose by rose. And now the building is pulled down and they made a canal bed with the stone. They didn't even try to make another building of beauty. There's nothing for me to do with my life, there's nothing to do in this country any more. I am a gardener, a gardener who needs great palaces. A physic garden and a vegetable patch is not enough for me.'

'You'll find something,' Hester urged him. 'You'll find your own way, even if it is not our garden, nor a garden fit for a king. You're young, you will find your way.'

'I'll never be a king's gardener in England,' he said slowly. 'That was my inheritance and now I can't have it. There is nothing left for me.'

The boat was drifting away a little to the other side of the lake. Hester paused, taking in the tranquillity of the scene: the sky slowly turning from blue to indigo, the colour of Tradescant spiderwort. The stars were like silver pin-heads against navy cloth. The evening air was cool against her cheek, sweet with the scent of windfall apples, and late-flowering wallflowers.

'We spent hours and hours here together when you were a little boy,' she said tenderly. 'You used to beg to come down here to feed the ducks. D'you remember?'

'Yes,' he said, his voice little more than a whisper. 'I remember feeding the ducks.'

She waited, and when he did not say any more, she rose to her feet. 'Shall I stay with you?' she asked him tenderly. 'Would you like some company?'

'No,' he said and his voice seemed to come from a long way over the still water. 'I'll spend a little time on my own, Mother. I'll come home when I can be merry again.'

Johnnie was not at breakfast.

'Where is he?' John demanded. 'I would have expected him to apologise to Lord Lambert last night.'

'He may have gone into Lambeth and had a late night,' Hester replied diplomatically and she spoke over her shoulder to Cook. 'Would you call Johnnie, Cook?'

Mary Ashmole, a paying guest for the season, helped herself to a slice of ham. 'Young men,' she remarked indulgently.

They could hear Cook labouring up the stairs and then the creak of the floorboards over their heads as she opened Johnnie's door, and then her coming down the stairs again. Her face when she came into the dining room was bright with mischief. 'He's not there!' she announced, smiling. 'And his bed's not been slept in.'

Hester's first thought was not of the ale houses of Lambeth, but that he had run away to join Charles Stuart's court, ridden to the docks and taken a ship to Europe to be with the prince. 'Is his horse in the stable?' she asked urgently.

John took one look at her white face and went quickly from the room. Mary Ashmole rose, hesitated.

'Please don't disturb yourself, Mrs Ashmole,' Hester said, recovering.

'Do finish your breakfast. I expect my son stayed with friends and forgot to send a message.'

She followed John to the stable yard. Caesar's head was nodding over the stable door. John was questioning the stable lad.

'He didn't take his horse out last night,' he said to Hester. 'No-one has seen him since yesterday.'

'Send the boy down to Lambeth and see if he went there,' Hester said.

'This could be much ado for nothing,' John warned her. 'If he is drunk under an ale-house table he won't thank us for sending a search party out.'

She hesitated.

'If he's not back by midday I'll go down to Lambeth myself,' John decided.

At midday John took Caesar and rode down to the village but soon came home again. Johnnie had not been in the ale house, and was not staying with any of his friends in the village.

'Perhaps he was walking to Lambeth and had some accident on the road,' Hester suggested.

'He's not a baby,' John said. 'He knows how to fight. And run. Besides, you know Johnnie: he'd always ride rather than walk. If he was going any distance he'd take his horse.'

'If there was a gang of thieves?' Hester suggested. 'Or a press gang?'

'The press gang wouldn't take him, he's obviously a gentleman,' John said.

'Then where can he be?' Hester demanded.

'You saw him after dinner,' John said. 'Did he say anything?'

'He was in his boat,' she said. 'He always goes there when he wants to be alone and to think. He knew he was wrong to speak out to Lord Lambert, he promised he would apologise to you and to his lordship. I asked him if he wanted me to stay with him and he said he would come home later.'

She paused. 'He said he would come home,' she said. Her voice sounded less and less certain. 'He said he would come home when he was merry again.'

John suddenly scowled as if he had been struck by a pang of pain. He crossed the yard and took her hand. 'Go and sit with Mary Ashmole,' he ordered.

491

'Why?'

'I'm just going to have a look round, that's all.'

'You're going to the lake,' she said flatly.

'Yes, I am. I'm going to check that the boat is tied up and the oars stowed and then we will know that he rowed ashore and met with some mischance, or changed his mind about coming home.'

'I'll come too,' she said.

John recognised the impossibility of ordering Hester indoors, started to walk towards the avenue, Hester at his side.

Even in autumn the orchard was too lush for the lake to be seen from the main avenue. Hester and John had to turn away from the chestnut trees to the path that ran westwards before they could see the unruffled pewter surface of the water.

It was very quiet. The birds were singing. At the sound of their footsteps a heron rose up from the water's edge and flapped away with its ungainly legs trailing and its long neck working like a pump handle with each arduous wingbeat. The surface was like a mirror, reflecting the blue sky, untroubled by any movement except the speckling of flies and the occasional plop of a rising fish. The boat floated in the middle of the lake, the oars shipped, its painter trailing in the water tying it to the reflected boat bobbing below.

For a moment Hester thought that Johnnie had fallen asleep in the bottom of the boat, had curled his long legs up inside the little rowing boat and that when they called out his name he would sit up, rub his eyes, and laugh at his folly. But the boat was empty.

John paused for a moment and walked out along the little landing stage and looked down into the water. He could see green weed and the gleam of a brown trout but nothing else. He turned and walked steadily back to the house.

'What are you thinking? What are you doing?' Hester tore her gaze away from the still boat and the peaceful water and went after him. 'Where are you going, John?'

'I'm going to get a boat hook and pull the boat in,' he said, without slackening his trudge. 'Then I'm going to get a pole and feel for the bottom of the lake. Then I may have to get a net, and then I may have to drain the lake.'

'But why?' she exclaimed. 'Why? What are you saying?'

He did not slow, nor turn his head. 'Hester, you know why.'

'I don't,' she insisted.

'Wait for me at the house,' he said. 'Go and sit with Mary Ashmole. I will come and tell you as soon as I know.'

'Know what?' she insisted. 'Tell me what?'

They had reached the terrace. Mary Ashmole was waiting for them. John looked up at her and she recoiled from the grimness of his face. 'Take Hester indoors,' he said firmly. 'I will come to her as soon as we know where Johnnie is.'

'You are never going to look for him in the lake,' Hester said. She laughed, an odd, mirthless noise. 'You cannot think he fell out of his boat!'

He did not answer her but walked with that same bent-headed trudge round to the stable yard. Hester and Mary heard him shout for the lad and they waited in absolute silence as the two of them walked back down the avenue. John was carrying a long pole, his pruning hook. The lad was carrying a net which they usually used for securing pots in the cart, and a coil of rope.

Mary Ashmole reached out and took Hester's icy hand. 'Be brave, my dear,' she said inadequately.

John marched to the lake as if he were about to undertake a disagreeable but essential garden chore, like hedging or ditching. The garden lad stole one swift glance at his stern profile and said nothing.

John walked to the edge of the landing stage and stretched out with the pruning hook. The blade just reached the painter as it trailed in the water and on the second try he could draw it in towards him.

'Wait here,' he said to the lad, and stepped into the boat. He rowed out towards the middle of the lake and then shipped the oars and peered downwards. Gently, with meticulous care, he reversed the pruning hook and lowered it into the water, probing with the handle. When he found nothing he rowed one stroke to the side and repeated the whole process in a widening circle.

The lad, who had been gripped by the horror of this task, found that he was getting bored and started to fidget, but nothing could break John's intense concentration. He was not thinking of what he might find. He was not even thinking of what he was doing. He just completed each circle and then went a little wider as if it were some kind of spiritual exercise, like a Papist telling her beads, as if it had to be done to ward off some evil. As if it were meaningless in itself, but should be done as a prevention.

Again and again he rowed another stroke and then probed gently into the dark water. In the back of his mind was a thought of how

Johnnie was probably already home after a night's roistering in the City, or a message would soon come from his sister's house saying that he had decided to make a sudden visit, or he would reappear with an old comrade from the defeated Worcester army. There were so many other explanations more likely than this one that John worked the water of the lake without allowing himself to think what he was doing, divorced from worry, almost enjoying the paddle with the oars and the movement of the wet-handled pole in the water.

When he felt something under the gentle probe of the pole he had a moment of mild regret that now he had to interrupt himself, that now he had a different task to do. Gently, with infinite care, he probed again and felt the object roll and move.

'Bundle of rags,' he whispered to himself, trying to guess at the dimension and weight. 'Hidden household goods,' he assured himself.

He turned to look for the stable lad. 'Throw me the rope,' he said, his voice steady and unshaken.

The lad, who had slumped on the landing stage, got to his feet and inexpertly tried to throw the rope to John. The first attempt fell in the water and splashed John, and the second attempt slapped him with a wet coil.

'Dolt,' John said and enjoyed the normality of the incompetence of the lad. 'Fool.'

He fastened the rope to the ring at the front of the boat. 'When I give the word, you gently pull me in,' he ordered.

The lad nodded, and took a grip on the line.

John pulled the pole out of the water and brought up the pruning hook. He took his leather gauntlet from the big pocket of his coat and pulled it over the sharp blade. Then he plunged the pole back into the water with the shielded hook first. It snagged against the object, lost its grip, and then caught.

'Now,' John called to the lad. 'But steady.'

The lad was so afraid of doing wrong that he started to pull too lightly. For a moment nothing happened at all, then the little boat started to glide back to the landing stage and John felt the weight of the drowned object on the end of his pole. Gently, smoothly, the boat bobbed towards the landing stage, John gripping the pole and waiting to see the object revealed in the shallow water.

He saw first a coat, rendered uniformly black by waterlogging, then Johnnie's white shirt and then his pale, pale face, his open dark eyes, and the swirl and eddy of his fair hair.

'Stop,' John said hoarsely.

At once the lad halted.

The boat rocked, the current of movement which had washed Johnnie up to the surface slipped away and his face sunk out of sight again. For a moment John thought that he could order the world to stop, right there; just as he could command the gardener's lad and then nothing that must follow would need to take place. He could say 'stop' and there would be no drowned child, no heartbreak, no end to the Tradescant line, no silence where Johnnie should have been singing, no terrible gulf where the young man should have been.

John waited for a long moment, trying to understand the reality and then the awful yawning enormity of his loss. The first step in his grief was the realisation that he could not measure it. His loss was too great for him to imagine.

The lad holding the rope stood like a statue, a dragonfly whirred noisily over the surface of the water and settled for a moment.

'Go on then,' John whispered as if this were not his work but he was obeying someone else. 'All right. Go on.'

The lad put his weight on the rope and once again the boat glided towards the landing stage, towing its dreadful freight behind it. At the landing stage when it stopped with a bump, John said gently, 'Tie it fast,' and waited until the lad had done as he was told.

'Take the pole,' John said, proffering it, and when the lad had gripped one end of it, John stepped from the boat into the waist-deep water, felt his way along to the other end and gathered the body of his only son into his arms.

'Step aside and wait,' he said softly to the stable lad. The boy dragged his horrified stare from the waterlogged body and then obediently fled to the shelter of the apple tree where the wasps were feeding drunkenly on fallen fruit.

John waded for the shore, the weight of Johnnie making him stagger as they got clear of the water. He fell to his knees and cradled the white face in his arms and looked down into the sightless eyes and the pale lips.

'My Johnnie,' he whispered. 'My boy.'

They sat together for a long time before John remembered that Hester would be waiting in painful anxiety and that there was much work for him to do.

He laid out the body and draped his jacket over his son's face.

'Watch by him,' he said simply to the stable lad. 'I'll come back with the cart.'

Slowly he walked along the grassy ride and then turned up the main avenue to the house. He could see Hester pacing on the terrace but when she saw him and took in the slump of his shoulders and his wet clothing, and his missing jacket, she froze very still.

John walked towards her, his face numb, his voice lost, then he cleared his throat and said quietly, conversationally, 'I found him. He's drowned. I'm fetching the cart now.'

She nodded, as calm as he, and Mary Ashmole, watching the two of them, thought them completely insensible, thought that they could not have loved their son at all to be so indifferent to his death.

'I thought so,' Hester said gently. 'I knew as soon as I saw the boat, just as you did. I'll ready the parlour for him.' She paused. 'No. He should lie in the rarities room. He was the most precious thing this house ever had.'

John nodded and went with that strange, slow plod round to the stables where, for a fancy, he did not harness the workhorse, but he took Caesar out of his stable and put him between the shafts of the cart to bring his master home.

They buried him beside his grandfather and his mother at St Mary's, Lambeth. The new vicar was kind enough not to ask how a fit young man came to drown while boating on his own lake. It was assumed that Johnnie had been drunk, or had hit his head as he fell from the boat. Only John knew that the boat had not been overturned but had been floating peacefully with the oars shipped. Only John knew that his son's pockets had been filled with broken pieces of flower pots. Only Hester knew that Johnnie had believed that there was no place for the king's gardeners in England any more. But they neither of them told the other these insights. They both thought that the other had pain enough.

Spring 1653

They could not easily recover. No family can ever fully recover from the loss of a child, and this was a child who had survived infancy during plague years, a childhood during the king's wars, two dangerous battles, and then died when the country was at peace. For a little while they were like lost people, they greeted each other at mealtimes and they went to church together, past the beautifully carved tombstone for John's father and the little crosses which marked Johnnie's and his mother's graves, and they spoke hardly at all.

The meetings of the philosophers and scientists which had made the Ark the centre of intellectual life were broken up and moved elsewhere. John found he could not concentrate on any argument for more than a few moments, and anyway everything seemed meaningless.

Even the uproar which greeted the end of the long Parliament and Cromwell's sudden decision to make a parliament of saints, nominated good men of recognised opinions and sanctity who would bring about the changes which the country so badly needed, failed to raise John from his passive dreaming.

Lord Lambert came to order new tulips in the spring and told John that a new day was dawning for England where there would be the right of every man to vote for his parliament, the legal system would be reformed to make it more just, the poor would be supported and no more landlords would be allowed to enclose the commons and drive squatters and poor people on to the streets. He broke off in the middle of his explanation and said: 'Forgive me, Mr Tradescant. Are you ill?'

'I have lost my son,' John said quietly. 'And nothing matters to me any more. Not even the new Parliament.'

Lord Lambert was stunned for a moment. 'Johnnie? I did not know! What happened?'

'He drowned in our little lake,' John said, speaking the words for what seemed like the thousandth time. 'It was the night you came to dinner.'

Lambert checked. 'When he was so distressed that I had bought Wimbledon?'

John nodded. 'It was that night.'

John Lambert looked stricken. 'Not because of what he said! He didn't drown because of that?'

John shook his head. 'Because he knew his cause was lost. If it had not been that night it would have been another. He couldn't see a way to live in the world that Cromwell and you and I have made. He wanted to be a king's gardener, he could not hear that kings are no good. Johnnie couldn't see it. And I failed to teach him.' John paused for a moment at the pointlessness of regrets. 'I have always been a man of few certainties. So when my son was convinced of a mistake I couldn't correct him. He put his faith in the most foolish prince, the son of a most foolish king. And I couldn't tell him that when you are in the service of a king one of the first things you learn is to not take him too seriously, not to love him too dearly. Johnnie was too close to the king's service, and yet not close enough to see it for what it was.'

He glanced at Lambert. The general was listening intently. He managed a little smile. 'These are private griefs,' he said. 'I don't mean to burden you with them, my lord. Do look around the garden, and anything you desire you can order. Joseph will take the order, my wife is not in the house today.'

'Will you tell her how sorry I am?' Lambert asked, going towards the door to the garden. 'Tell her I am deeply, deeply sorry for your loss. He was a fine young man. He deserved a better cause.'

'He was, wasn't he?' John said, his expression lightening for a moment.

Lambert nodded and went quietly out to the garden to look around at the avenue of horse chestnuts and the beds of exquisite tulips and wondered if they would ever give John any joy ever again, now there was no Tradescant to follow him in the garden.

Winter 1654

The new parliament was short-lived. Its programme of social justice was too radical for the temper of many of the men of influence whose chief hopes of reform had been for a fat slice of the king's wealth and power, and had never gone as far as the soldiers of the army who had fought for an end to greed and tyranny and who truly thought that a new world could be born out of their battles.

When Cromwell saw that he had tried a parliament of selected good men who would have imposed justice on a country too sluggish to become saintly, and then tried a parliament chosen by the voters which could not rise above self-interest, something of the joy went out of him. He took the title of Lord Protector and took the burden of power in a mood of frustration and disappointment and never again thought that he might see the new Jerusalem in London.

'I don't know what the fighting was for if we merely exchanged a king for a Lord Protector,' John said wearily to Hester as they sat at dinner.

'No,' she said quietly.

They sat in the silence which was a constant presence at their table now; it was as if without Johnnie to plan for, there was no business to discuss. The takings at the door were good, the order books were filled. But Hester had withdrawn from much of the business and had lost interest in the garden. She never complained, but she felt as if she had been struggling too hard for too long and that, as it turned out, it had all been for nothing.

'I have been thinking about Virginia,' John said tentatively. 'Bertram Hobert, my old friend from over there, came to see me today.'

Hester raised her head. 'Hobert who nearly died there?'

John nodded. 'He finally brought off a good crop of tobacco and came home to sell it. By making the voyage with his wife he gets another two headrights for free and he wants to make his plantation bigger. He's hired some labourers to take with him and he gets their headrights too. He's full of confidence. He is going back again with the Austin family and they have spare places on their ship.'

John paused. 'I wondered if you would like to come with me, to Virginia. You could see our land, you might be interested in that, and by travelling together we would claim another two headrights. We could sell them, or find someone to farm them for us, or you might like to build a house and settle there. Jamestown is bound to be much improved since my first visit and now –' He broke off.

He had been about to say, 'Now there is nothing to keep us here' – but he did not need to say it. Hester, of all people, knew that there was nothing left in Lambeth but the rarities and the plants.

'What about that woman, the woman you left there?' she asked flatly.

He bowed his head. 'I will never see her again,' he said. It did not have the ring of a promise of a reformed man, his voice had the finality of a man who knows when something is over. 'She will be with her people, and I will be with mine. The time of the Powhatan dealing kindly with the planters is long gone.'

Hester thought for a moment. 'Who would keep this place safe while we are gone?'

'Elias Ashmole would be glad enough to live here for a while,' John pointed out. 'He has promised to help make a catalogue of the rarities collection and he has a great interest in the garden.'

Hester made a little face. 'What if something happens?' she asked.

'He could manage. He's a worldly man, he's managed bigger estates than this little place.'

'Why would he be so helpful?' she asked baldly. 'Why serve us in such a way?'

'He likes the rarities, he likes the garden,' John said. 'He can do his studies here in alchemy and astronomy. He can use my herbs for his medicines.'

'I like his wife Mary better than I like him,' Hester said irrelevantly. 'And she has been very badly treated by him. She told me that he abused her and now they are separated he won't give her any money for her keep. And it was all her money in the first place. He had nothing when he came to advise her, and now her fortune is his.'

John shook his head. 'He's a lawyer by training,' he said. 'I'm not surprised he gives nothing away. He'd make a bad enemy but he's a good friend to us. He would guard this place for us while we were gone.'

She thought for a moment. 'No,' she said reluctantly. 'He would manage well enough if nothing happened. But if there was a fire or another war or an uprising he would never care for the things as we would. Mr Ashmole would think of his own safety before the collection.'

'We could box it all up and store it,' John objected.

'Not again,' she said. 'I couldn't bear it. And even if we did, what about the garden?'

'I do really want to go,' John said. 'I am so weary of this house without our boy, and I miss him in the garden. I hate the lake, I can't go down to that end of the orchard at all, and I can't find the energy to weed and plant and prune and pot on. In every part of the garden I come across tasks which I would give to him to do, or where he was especially skilled. Half of the plants are his plants, nursed up by him while I was away. It's as if I meet him everywhere.'

Hester nodded. 'That's why I'll stay,' she said quietly. 'Because I too feel that I meet him everywhere, and here I can guard the things he loved and watch the things he planted grow tall and beautiful, and it's as if he is still here.'

John raised an eyebrow. 'Shall I go alone? Would you want that?'

She met the little challenge. 'Will you come back again?'

'Yes. There's no life for me there. But I could bring back some new rarities, there is so much more to discover.'

'I will wait for you,' she promised. 'And keep the rarities and the garden safe for you.'

He bowed his head and kissed her hand as it rested on the table. 'You will not blame me for leaving you to your grief?'

She touched his head with her other hand like a blessing. 'I would want it,' she said simply. 'I should like to spend a little time alone. Perhaps I will become accustomed to being without him, if I have a little time alone.'

'Very well then,' he said gently. 'And I promise I will come home.'

Spring 1654

John was at sea, running from grief, once more, and knew that he had chosen the right course. The movement of the ship rocked his sleep at night and the noise of the wind in the sails and the creaking of the timbers were the sounds of mourning to him. He thought of Johnnie constantly and, away from the land and from Hester, he felt free to think of Jane, his first wife, and knew that if there were a heaven and a communion of saints, then she was with her son now. As the seven-week voyage went on, he felt that he could let Johnnie go, as he had once before let Jane go, and love him only in his heart as a memory, and not with that wrenching desire to bring him back.

He was asleep when the ship sighted the Virginia coast and was awakened by the noise and excitement of their arrival in Jamestown. Bertram Hobert hammered on the little wooden shutters around John's bunk and shouted, 'Up, man! We've arrived!' and John tumbled out to find the ship in its usual chaos as sailors slackened off the sails and the look-out man shouted directions, and the passengers still battened-down below the hatches tried to repack their goods which had been scattered during the long voyage.

'Better this time than last,' Bertram said optimistically. 'At least we know the dangers now, eh, John?'

John looked into the face of his old friend. The dreadful hollowed face of hunger had gone, replaced by a rosy round prosperity, but most of Bertram's teeth were missing and the remainder were black.

'We were greenhorns,' John said. 'We knew nothing.'

'Now we do,' Bertram said. 'I will be a man of substance in this land yet, John. I will be a burgess and leave a five-hundred acre plantation.'

'I wonder what changes have taken place since we were last here?'

'Nothing but good,' Mrs Hobert said over her shoulder, throwing linen into a bag. 'I hear that the savages are quite driven back and there is a road made through the woods from Jamestown down to the sea and westwards along the riverbank inland.'

A sailor lifted the hatch above them and shouted that they could come up on deck. John hefted his chest through the hatchway, and took his bundle of clothing.

'You're travelling light,' Bertram remarked.

'It is going home that I hope to be laden,' John said.

They scrambled out on deck and then paused in amazement. For a moment John thought that something had gone ludicrously wrong and they had come to the wrong place. But then he saw that the old wooden fort had gone, the mixture of garrison and town had changed. Before him now was a new town, an elegant town, beautiful and solid and built to last.

A line of stone-built houses with small ornamental gardens before them lined the front road alongside the river and looked down to the quay. Great trees had been left in place to shade the road, and around each tree they had built graceful circular seats so that passers-by could rest in the shade. Each house had a bright new wooden fence before it, one or two even had low stone walls to mark the division between the garden and the street.

There was a pavement slightly raised with wooden beams to keep the ladies' shoes dry and a gutter for storm water and sewage which drained away into the river.

The houses were built two, even three, storeys high, so close that they were all but adjoining and they were built like good London houses, not flung together with wood and mud; but well-planned, proper houses with a central doorway and a window on either side with well-hung shutters and glass in the windows.

The people walking up and down the road and strolling down to the quay were changed as well. The sharp division into the one or two wealthy men and the rest, hungry, work-hardened paupers, was over. There was a more gentle gradation of wealth and status that you could see from the shirts and waistcoats of the labourers through the smart dark homespun of the artisans and smaller planters through to the silks and satins worn by the gentry.

And now there were slaves. John blinked at the numbers of black men and women, fetching, carrying, running at an obedient dog-trot behind a cart, catching the ropes on the dockside and running the gangplank out to the ship, unloading carts and throwing down the bales of cotton, and women with trays on their heads weaving through the crowd at the dockside with fresh produce to sell. Many of them were branded with the mark of their owner on their forehead or cheek. Many of them had the old scars of a whipping on their backs. But some of them, like the women traders, were clearly free to sell their own goods, they walked at their own speed with an arrogant roll of their hips under bright patterned dresses.

A sailor opened the ship's railing, made sure the gangplank was secure and then stepped back. John walked down the plank to the new land.

He had not thought that he would find her again, and he knew she would not look for him; but he did not expect that the country would be emptied of Suckahanna's people. The last Indian war had indeed been the last. Opechancanough's execution was the death of the People as well as the death of their last greatest war leader. Some drifted away, inland, and found other nations that would accept them, and then they too had to move, always westwards, always away from coast and the encroaching white men, the noise of falling timber and the scarcity of game. Some went into service, a service more like slavery for they were paid no wages and allowed no freedoms and worked until they died for no thanks. Some were imprisoned for the crime of rising up to defend their own villages and they served their sentences until illness and despair finished the work that the war had begun.

John stopped every one of the few Powhatan women or children that he saw in Jamestown and asked for Suckahanna, and for Attone, by name, but they all shook their heads at the strange white man and pretended that they could not understand his speech, though he asked them both in English and Powhatan. Ignorance and deafness were their last defence, and they mimed ignorance and deafness and hoped to somehow survive, clinging to the very edge of life in a land which had once been unquestionably their own.

John and the other men on the ship went to the governor's office where the maps of the territory were kept and claimed his headright and then sold it on to William Lea, with his original claim alongside it.

'You don't want it yourself?' Lea asked.

John shook his head. 'I'm no planter,' he said. 'I tried it before and I have not the skills or the endurance. I'm a gardener. You've paid my passage and more and I'm glad for that, but I will spend my time here out in the woods gathering the most interesting plants I can find – my cargo for the return journey.'

A gentleman in the office with them turned at the mention of plants and looked at John keenly. 'Ah!' he said. 'Now I know who you are. I am sure that you must be Mr John Tradescant. I had not known you were coming to visit us again.'

John felt a little curl of pride at his name being known before him. 'How do you do, Mr –?'

'Forgive me,' the planter said. 'I am Sir Josiah Ashley. I saw your garden when I was last in London and I ordered some plants for my garden here.'

'You are gardening?' John asked incredulously. 'In Virginia?'

The man laughed. 'Of course, everything will be very much changed since you were last here. I have a house and before it, running down to the river, I have a garden. Nothing compared to the great gardens you will have worked in, I know. But it is a pretty little couple of acres and it gives me much pleasure.'

'And do you only plant English plants?' John asked, wary of another hopeless attempt at an English garden in foreign soil like the barren attempt in Barbados.

'I grow flowers and plants from the woods too,' Sir Josiah replied. 'I have a great love for English plants, of course, they remind us of our old home. But there are some exquisite flowers and shrubs that I have found and brought into my garden and they thrive.'

'I should so like to see them. And if you had any stock I should offer you a very fair price.'

Sir Josiah bowed. 'You must come and stay with us.'

'I could not impose,' John started shyly.

'This is Virginia,' the man reminded him. 'Guests are not an imposition, they are our only source of entertainment. You will be a great pleasure for us. I am sure you have much news of London.'

'Then I would be delighted.'

'I drive back to my house tomorrow,' Sir Josiah said. 'Shall I collect you from your inn?'

'Drive?' John queried.

'Oh yes, we have a road which runs alongside the river. The tobacco still goes by boat, of course, but I generally drive into town in my cart.'

John blinked. 'I see that everything is indeed changed.' He paused for a moment. 'May I ask one thing: when I was last here I spent some time with the Powhatan people, before the war. They helped me in the woods when I was plant collecting.'

'Oh yes?' Sir Josiah was pulling on his gloves and clapping his hat on his head. John saw that the Virginian belief that the very air was a danger was still prevalent.

'I was wondering where they would be now?'

'Dead, most likely,' Sir Josiah said without regret. 'A bad business. They could have lived with us in such harmony. But they chose not to. A bad business indeed.'

'All of them?'

'There is the village, of course.'

'The village?'

'There is a Powhatan village some ten miles inland. You could go and visit if you liked. I doubt that any that you recognised would be allowed out unless you took them into your service and said you would be responsible for their behaviour.'

'I could do that?'

Sir Josiah hesitated. 'Forgive me. You may not bring savages into my house.'

'You don't have slaves?'

Sir Josiah laughed. 'Of course I do. How else could I grow tobacco? But I won't have the native peoples of this land anywhere near my borders. Africans are my slaves, the others are no use to me at all.'

'But I could go to the village and see if there was anyone I recognised?'

'Of course.' Sir Josiah gestured at the clerk. 'George, give Mr Tradescant here a pass to go to the savages' village. I will countersign it. Shall you go today?'

'Yes,' John said quietly. 'Today. At once.'

He told the woman at the inn that he would be home for dinner and would leave the next day. 'And where are you going now?' she asked with the freedom of speech that the new colony allowed.

'I am going to find someone,' John said. 'At the Powhatan village.'

'An old servant?' she sniffed. 'If you want a servant you can buy a black girl for little more than seven pounds and she will serve you far better than any Indian. The blacks live longer too, and they're more cheerful company. I'd have a black if I were you.'

'I want to find a particular person,' John said, choosing his words with care. 'Not a slave. Can you point out the road?'

'Oh indeed,' she said. 'There is only one road really. There is the road which runs east from here, inland, and there is the road which runs west to the coast. The Indian village is north of here. Take the road upriver and ask whoever you see on the road. Anyone can direct you.'

'Thank you,' said John, and set off.

He had thought he might collect some specimens as he walked upriver but there was almost no forest left at the riverside. The road went past one large house set among field after field of tobacco, and then past another. Some of the houses were still the familiar wooden buildings in the style that John remembered; but they were all growing and sprawling out, with new rooms added on one side, and stables built nearby. The more prosperous were grand with huge pillars and beautiful terraces, like little palaces in miniature, and behind them were little huts made of wood and roofed with reeds, the slave huts, poorer-built than the stables; horses were so much more valuable than slaves.

There were common plants by the wayside but the constant ploughing and reploughing of the land for tobacco had uprooted anything of any size. John thought it incredible that the woods where Suckahanna had run when she was a little girl should now be as tame and as enclosed as the riverside at Surrey.

He passed a gang of slaves working on the road, filling in the potholes with chippings of stone, and they pointed him on: on and then turn right after the next grand house, for the savages' village. The overseer rode up as John left them, tipped his hat to John, confirmed the directions and then went past him to the men. John heard a yelp of pain at a casual blow, and trudged onwards without turning his head.

He turned right as they had advised and found that the track led him through a marsh of foul water. This was land that no-one had wanted, far from the road and from the river, and needing to be drained and cleansed, a project which might take years and never be done. There were rotting trees sunk deep into the marsh and, in their shelter, water-loving plants just coming into bud. John hesitated to step off the single-track causeway and risk a wetting but promised himself that he would stop and collect them on his way back.

He turned another corner and saw a little wooden house, built like his own Virginian shack had been. On either side of it a tall wooden fence ran as if to enclose a huge field. The little hut was a gate house, the only way in to the enclosed acres. On the porch lounging in the sun were two men in remnants of what had once been good jackets, chewing tobacco and spitting into a brass bowl placed conveniently between them. They watched him as he walked up and John felt self-conscious and needlessly guilty as they stared at him, walking along the deserted road towards the village that no-one ever visited.

'Good day,' John said.

One man got to his feet and nodded a greeting.

'I have come to seek a servant of mine,' John said, succumbing to the prejudice of the place. 'I have been a long time in England. I wondered if she was here.'

'Might be,' the man said unhelpfully. 'We've got a hundred and sixty-two of 'em here.'

'And where will I find the others?' John asked, looking around, thinking there must be another village nearby.

'That's all there is,' the man said. 'D'you have a pass?'

John handed over Sir Josiah's letter. 'I mean, where are the other Powhatan? The rest of them?'

The man could hardly read; he only looked at the paper and at the seal on the bottom. 'That's all there is left,' he said simply.

John hesitated at the enormity of what the man was saying. 'There is surely another village elsewhere in the colony with more people?' he asked. 'There were thousands of them when I was last here, thousands.'

The man shook his head. 'This a-one hundred and sixty-two is all that is left of the Powhatan,' he said. 'Unless they start having babies again. But they don't show any disposition at the moment.'

The other man sniggered. 'Most unwillin'.'

'Can I go in?' John asked.

'I'll take you,' the soldier said.

He lit the fuse on his musket and held the gun across his chest, the fuse between his two fingers, the end of it aglow. Then he led the way into the enclosed village.

John walked through the gate, and then stopped and blinked. It was like the village he had known, but in miniature; the long houses were too few and built too small. There was a dancing circle but it was compressed against one of the blank encircling wooden walls. There was the central street leading up to the house of the werowance but it could be walked in forty strides. There was no sweat lodge that he could see. All around the houses, planted with the meticulous care of the Powhatan women, were the food crops, cramped up against the houses. John recognised at once the growing stalks of the Indian corn and the amaracock planted between them, and the little shelter built to overlook the field where the children would wait for their mothers to finish their work.

'Can I talk to them alone?' John asked the soldier.

'They don't speak English,' he said. 'You'd better just look for your girl. I can line them up for you. They understand "Muster".'

'No, no,' John said. 'I can speak Powhatan. Let me speak with them.'

The soldier hesitated. 'Shout if you need help then,' he said and went back to his seat.

The women working in the field did not raise their eyes at this exchange, they did not take more than a glance at John. But John knew that they would have seen every detail of him, and that if Suckahanna or Attone or any of his people were alive in this cage then they would know within minutes that he had come.

He walked up to the little confined field and spoke in Powhatan.

'Sister,' he said. 'I was the husband of Suckahanna and the friend of Attone. They called me the Eagle when they took me into the People.'

She did not break off her work, her hands still moved in the earth, setting the little plants, dropping in seeds. She did not look up at him, she might as well have been deaf.

'I have come to find Suckahanna, or Attone, or any of my people,' John said. 'Or news of them.'

She nodded at that; but did not pause in the steady, sweeping movement of her hands.

'Did you know them?' John asked. 'Suckahanna, Attone, any of them? She had a little boy –'

The woman turned her head and called a single word, the name Popanow, the child of winter, and a young girl came forwards.

'I knew Suckahanna,' she said simply. 'You must be the Eagle. I would not have known you, they spoke of a hunter and you are too fat and old.'

John concealed the hurt to his vanity and looked at the girl. 'I don't remember you.'

'I was born in the village of the bad water,' she said. 'You were long gone.'

'Suckahanna?'

She paused. 'Why d'you want to know, white man?'

John hesitated. 'I am a white man, I know,' he said humbly. 'But once I was a Powhatan. Suckahanna was my wife and Attone was my friend. Tell me, Popanow, what became of my wife and my friend and my people? I was not with them because they sent me away. I have come back to learn what became of them. Tell me, Popanow.'

She nodded. 'It was like this. The soldiers were hunting us down, every month they came a little closer. It was like a hunting trip for them, they came out in spring. Winter we were left alone to starve and freeze but spring and summer they came out and destroyed our fields when they could find them, and broke down the fish weirs, and tracked us with their dogs.'

John flinched at the matter-of-fact solidity of her description. 'Attone wanted to lead us upriver and north, away from the white men. We thought that another People might take us in, or if they would not then we could fight the white men and die in the fighting rather than be picked off one at a time. Others thought that the white men would grow weary of the sport of hunting us and start to hunt for food. They would leave us alone after a while. I think Suckahanna was with Attone. She said we should go.

'We started to move out in the winter. We had not enough stores of food, and it was not safe to light fires. A slave saw us.' She was suddenly alight with anger, animated with resentment. 'A black slave who thought more of his master than anything else – the white man's dog, the white man's fool – he ran and told his master, who brought out some other planters and they hunted us through the snow and we were easy to track in the deep snow, and slow-moving with old people and babies to carry.'

John nodded. 'I remember. I was with them when they went to the marshland.'

'We left the people who could not keep up with us. We thought perhaps they would be taken up by the hunting party behind us and sent back to Jamestown for servants. But they did not take them for servants, they killed them where they lay in the snow. The white men cut their throats and scalped their heads where they lay. It was . . .' she sought the word to describe it and found none, '. . . ugly.

'Attone said we should make a stand and fight the hunting party and then we would be safe to go on. They sent the older women and the babies ahead and the rest of us made a trap, a pit in the road, and we hid in the trees, and waited.' She paused. 'It was desperate, digging and trying to hide the pit with branches and fresh snow scattered on top, and knowing they were so close behind.'

'You were there?'

'I was there. I had my bow and my quiver of arrows. I was ready to kill.'

'And?'

'They had horses and guns and dogs,' she said. 'They were hunting dogs, they would keep coming even with an arrow in their eye. They got me at the shoulder and pulled me down. I thought they would eat me alive. I could hear the crunch of their jaws on my bone and smell their breath on me.' She swept back her hair and John saw the ragged scars where a deep bite had been gouged out of her neck and shoulder. 'It's odd to feel an animal licking your blood,' she said.

'My God,' John whispered.

'Half a dozen of us were still alive at the end, and they made us walk back to Jamestown.'

'Suckahanna?'

'Dead.'

The word was like a blow in the pit of his belly, it fell no lighter for being expected. He had known that Suckahanna would never have been taken alive. He had known from the very start that what he was seeking in this strange diminished village was the news of her death.

'Attone?'

'Dead.'

'Suckahanna's son?'

'He got away,' she said. 'He could be anywhere. Maybe dead in the forest.'

'The baby? The little girl?'

'Died of hunger or fever or something. Before we tried to leave the village of bad water.'

There was a silence. John looked at the girl who had seen so much, who was indeed a child of winter.

'I shall go.' He paused. 'Is there anything I can do for you or for the People?'

'Would they set us free if you asked them?'

'No,' John said. 'They would not listen to me.'

'Do you think that they will hold us here forever?' she asked. 'Do you think that they mean us to have enough land to plant, but nothing that we can enjoy, nowhere we can run free? Do they think that now we will do nothing more forever than just cling to life at the edge of the white man's land?'

'No,' John said. 'I am sure not. There is a new government in England and it is pledged to care for the poor and for the men and women who are driven off their land by enclosures. It gives rights to tenants and people who live on the land. Surely they will give you the same rights here.'

She looked at him and for a moment he saw Suckahanna in her eyes with that delicious sense of the ridiculous which had been so often and

511

so lovingly directed at John. 'Oh, do you?' she said and then turned and went back to her work.

John walked home dryshod in his English boots across the wooden causeway, not touching the earth, forgetting the marsh flower, not seeing anything but the winter battle in the snow and Suckahanna going down, fighting to the last minute, and Attone falling beside her.

He could see nothing else for the long walk back to Jamestown, not the new and beautiful houses nor the pretty sailing ships which the planters now used instead of canoes on the river, not the settled prosperity of the fields drawn like a net of squares thrown over the landscape, ignoring the contours of hill and slope and stream and imposing their own order on the wildness. He did not see the outskirts of Jamestown with the little shanty town of poor wooden houses, nor the town centre with the governor's beautiful house and the new assembly room for the burgesses where they were doing their best, by their lights, to build a new country in this place.

That night when he went to bed he thought he would dream of the battle and the defeat of the Powhatan and the dreadful death of Suckahanna in the cold snow with dogs snapping at her throat.

But he did not. He dreamed instead of the Great Hare leaping over the winter snows, with its coat pure white, winter-white, and only its long ears tipped with chocolate fur, gathering his love Suckahanna, and his friend Attone, into its gentle mouth and taking them back into the darkness away from the world which was no longer safe for the People.

Sir Josiah's house was one of the grander stone-built houses and his garden was richer than John could have imagined. His wife greeted them and ordered rum and lemons and hot water despite the heat, and then Sir Josiah took John, punch glass in hand, down the steps to the garden.

It was a garden poised between two worlds. In many ways it was an English cottage garden: on the far sides were plants for cutting, for drying and for medicinal use in a scramble and a muddle of richness. John strolled over and saw, in their springtime growth, the familiar herbs and flowers of England, thriving in this virgin earth.

Immediately before the house Sir Josiah had laid out a serpentine knot, an attempt at the formality of the English great gardens. It was edged in bay and planted with daffodils, and between the daffodils were growing some white daisies. John admired the colours and felt the familiar lift to his heart at the sight of spring bulbs but then he looked a little more closely.

'Did you bring these daisies from England?'

'No,' Sir Josiah said. 'I found them growing here. There's a place down by the river, a patch of grassland, I found whole clumps of them and dug them up, and planted them here and they have thrived and multiplied.'

John, oblivious of the snort of laughter from Lady Ashley on the terrace, dropped to his knees and took a closer look. 'I think this is a new kind of daisy,' he said. 'A Virginian daisy.'

'I thought it was just a daisy I might have for very little effort,' Sir Josiah said carelessly.

'And it's very pretty,' John said. 'I'll take a couple home with me when I go. I should like to see it growing in London, I have a good collection of daisies. Could you show me where it grows in the wild?'

'Of course,' Sir Josiah said cheerfully. 'We can go out this afternoon. And you must have a good roam through my woods. And when you have done with me I'll give you a letter of introduction and you can go upriver and stay with my neighbours and see what they have that takes your eye.'

Lady Ashley came floating across the grass towards them. 'Is this your first time in Virginia?' she asked with the slight drawl that the planters all shared.

'No,' John said. 'I was here more than ten years ago for a long stay.'

'And were you plant collecting then?'

'Yes,' John said cautiously. 'But it was not like this.'

Sir Josiah wanted to lend him a horse but John preferred to walk in the woods. 'I miss too much if I am too high and going too fast,' he said.

'I'm sure there are snakes,' Lady Ashley pointed out.

'I have good thick boots,' John said. 'And I was much in the woods when I was last here.'

Sir Josiah had left a good stand of timber to the north of his estate and John started to walk there and then found himself following a stream which drew him deeper and deeper inland. He walked as he always did, as his father had always done – with only the occasional glance towards the horizon and the path ahead and with his eyes mostly on his boots and the little plants under his feet. He had been walking all morning when he suddenly exclaimed and dropped to his knees. It was a sorrel, but what had attracted him was the tiny indentations of the leaves. It was an American version of the familiar plant. John swung his satchel down, took out the trowel and carefully lifted the plant from the moist, dark earth, wrapped it in a broad leaf and tucked it into the pocket of his satchel.

He straightened up and walked on, his eyes glancing up at the trees, and then down to the path. After a little while, amid the buzz of the Virginian spring, the birdsong, the loud cry of the occasional flight of ducks and migrating geese, there was a new sound: a soft tuneless whistling. John was happy.

1655

John stayed in Virginia for two years, travelling from one beautiful house to another, and staying for months at a time enjoying the famous Virginian hospitality. When he went deeper into the country and there were no large stone houses with slave cabins at the back he stayed instead with more humble planters who were building in wood but hoping for greater things. John found that he preferred the humbler sort of man, no-one could help admiring the determination that they showed to cross such a wide sea to find a new land, and to struggle – and John knew what a struggle it was – to wrest a living in a new country.

Sometimes he slept on an earth floor before a fire, in the warm humid days of summer he slept under a tree in the forest. He was never tempted to shed his English clothes and make himself a clout and a buckskin apron. He would have felt a mockery of the People if he dressed in their way and lived in their way, when they were still kept like ferrets in a box. But he could not unlearn the skills they had taught him, and he would not have wanted to forget them. Even wearing his heavy boots he moved through the woods quieter than any Englishman. His eye for plants and trees was his trained Tradescant eye, but he looked the more sharply because these were woods that he had known and loved as his home.

'Don't you fear the woods?' one of the planter's wives asked him curiously as she saw him ready to set out, walking to the next plantation.

John shook his head. 'There's nothing to fear,' he said.

'There's wolves, I sometimes hear them at night.'

John smiled, thinking of his old terror in his little house when he heard the wolves howling and thought that they would come in through the gaps in the walls when his fire went out. 'I lived here once, a long time ago,' he said. 'I learned to love the country then. It feels as familiar to me as my own garden at Lambeth.'

The woman nodded. 'Well, if you keep to the wide track you won't get lost,' she assured him. 'The next plantation starts just three miles up the road. There's only a little stand of trees between their tobacco fields and ours.'

John doffed his hat to her and left. She was right, here and all over the country there were only little stands of trees left between the riverside plantations. For rare plants he had to go deep into the countryside, high into the hills, following rivers and living off the land. He hired a canoe for a few months and took it down the coast to the marshy area that Suckahanna had showed him when she was a little girl. He even went to the place of the bad water where the People had made their stand, and tried to survive before they were hunted down. He found a little plant there, an exquisite valerian, and packed it carefully in damp earth wrapped in leaves to take back to Jamestown with him. He thought if he could persuade it to thrive in Lambeth then it would remind him of the People, even when all other traces of them were gone.

He returned to Jamestown several times during his visit, to pack barrels of plants and send them back to the Ark and on the second visit he found a letter from Hester.

September 1655

Dear Husband,

Your new maple has arrived safely and been planted into the garden near to your first Virginia maple so that men may make the comparison and see that it is a little different. I shall write and tell you if it too changes the colour of its leaves in autumn to scarlet.

Some of the daisy plants were spoiled by salt water by the negligence of the sailors but Frances has potted up the others and says they will live. She says that your Virginia convolvulus must be called Tradescantia. It flowered this summer and is most beautiful with huge flowers very prettily marked. They only live a day but are succeeded by many others. You did not say whether it will over-winter, so we have taken it into the orangery and we also collected seeds and took cuttings. Lord Lambert has begged some seeds for his rare garden and we sold them to him at one shilling for half a dozen.

Frances is well and stayed with me for the summer, and there have been many other guests too, come to see the rarities

516

and stay to enjoy the garden. Elias Ashmole has been a constant visitor and many other of your friends send their regards.

You may not have heard but the Lord Protector has established the rule of major generals – one to each county to supervise the work of the magistrates and the churchwardens and the parish overseers. The innovation is not much welcomed in Lambeth, but I will say no more in a letter.

I am caring for your rarities and your garden as ever and I am well.

Your loving wife,
Hester

March 1656

In March, when the worst of the winter storms had died down, John loaded his Virginia treasures on to a ship bound for London. A couple of planters had come down to the quayside to see him off and press him with commissions to complete for them in London. John accepted packages and errands but never took his eyes from his barrels of plants and boxes of rarities.

He was importing a dozen saplings in tubs which would have to stand on deck and be shielded from the spray by a little shelter woven of reeds. Three of them were new Virginian walnut trees, never seen in England before; the others were new poplar trees and whips of Virginian cypress. Safely packed in tubs of damp sand were the roots of some new asters and some new geraniums, and a new vine. Sealed with candlewax in a waterproof chest were seeds that John had gathered the previous autumn: of the aconitum, which the Americans called wolfsbane, Virginian parsley, the exquisitely pretty Virginian columbine, the leopardsbane of America – a flower like a daisy but with a flaming orange petal and a black heart, as bright as any marigold.

John looked at his treasures with the joy of a wealthy merchant bringing home gold. He stuffed letters and packages in the deep pockets of his coat and stepped back from the ship's railing as they ran the gangplank ashore.

'Goodbye!' he called.

'When will we see you again?' Sir Josiah shouted.

'In another few years,' John called back over the widening gulf of water. 'When my stocks are low again. When I want new marvels.'

'Be sure you come!' Sir Josiah called. 'This is a land of marvels.'

John laughed and nodded and waved goodbye, and then stood on deck to watch the town recede swiftly as the current and the wind took the little ship down the river and towards the sea.

'I would never have thought it,' he said to himself. 'From the time when I first came here. I would never have thought that they could have survived and built such a town, almost a city, from the forest.'

The new manicured banks of the river slipped quickly by. John looked upriver, to where the shimmer of light on the water gave the illusion that nothing had changed. 'Goodbye,' he said softly, to the landscape and to the woman he had loved.

April 1656

John came back to his garden, to the Ark and to his wife as the tulips were starting to fatten and show their colour. The wagon rumbled across the familiar bridge and into the stable yard and Hester, looking out of the window of the rarities room at the noise, saw John sitting beside the carter and came running down the terrace and into her husband's arms.

'I should have known you wouldn't miss another spring,' she said. 'But I didn't really expect you till midsummer.'

'I was ready to come home,' John said. 'And lucky to get a fast ship.'

They drew back a little and inspected each other, as old friends will do after a long absence. Hester's hair under her neat cap was nearly as white as the linen, and her face was thinner and more severe. There were lines of grief on her face which would be there forever. John, aged forty-eight, was leaner and fitter than when he had gone away, the days on horseback and on foot had tanned him brown and skimmed off the fat of easy living.

'You look well, but your hair has gone white,' he said.

She gave a little smile. 'It was starting to go as you left,' she said. 'At Johnnie's death.'

John nodded. 'I stopped at his tomb on the way home. I felt I wanted to tell him I was back. I always promised that he would come with me on the next trip. Someone had planted little daffodils.'

'Frances,' she said. 'And when the convolvulus grows she wants to plant some beside your father's tomb so that it climbs around it. She said she wanted them both to see it.'

They left the carter and the garden boy to unload the cart and went towards the house, their arms interlinked. They walked around to the terrace and John leaned on the railing and looked down over the garden.

The flowerbeds at the front of the house were blushing with the colour of the early tulips, beyond them the orchard was carpeted with yellow daffodils, and the white and orange of the narcissi. Above them, the cherry and apricot trees were showing little pink buds, and the thick, powerful twigs of the horse chestnuts were slowly splitting, the fat, sticky buds bursting pale and green out of their shells.

'It's good to be home,' John said with pleasure. 'What's the news?'

'I wrote to you that Cromwell dissolved Parliament and set the army to rule over us directly.'

He nodded. 'And how is that?'

Hester shrugged. 'I don't know about the rest of the country but it works well for Lambeth. They do the work the Justices of the Peace used to do, but more fairly and more evenly. They've closed down a lot of the ale houses and that's nothing but good. They're stricter with paupers and beggars and vagrants so the streets are cleaner. But the taxes!' She shook her head. 'Higher than ever before and now they remember to collect them. They're a hard-working bunch of men; and that will be their undoing. People don't mind the Sunday sports and the maypoles going, they don't even mind the bawdy houses closed down. But the taxes!'

'Are we in profit?' John asked, looking at the rich prosperity of the garden.

'In plants,' she said, following his gaze. 'And to be honest, we're doing well enough. Sending the Members of Parliament back to their homes has done nothing but good for us. The squires and the country gentlemen have little to do but to tend their gardens. Cromwell's major generals are running the country, there is nothing for the gentry to attend to in London, and no work for them to do in the counties. All the work of the squires and the JPs is being done by army men. All they have left is their gardens.'

John chuckled. 'It's an ill wind.'

'Not so ill,' she reminded him. 'Cromwell has brought peace to the country.'

He nodded. 'Have you seen Lord Lambert? What does he say?'

'He was here just a few weeks ago to see our show of daffodils. He has a fancy for a garden in orange, gold and yellow and he wanted some bright yellow lenten lilies. He's not a happy man. He was working on a new constitution for the country, with the backing of the army. He wanted Cromwell to become Lord Protector with an elected parliament. Then Cromwell brought in the major generals and dissolved Parliament.

I think he thought that it smacked of tyranny; but he never said. He stays loyal to Cromwell –'

'He's always loyal,' John interrupted.

'But there's a strain,' she said. 'He doesn't like to see the army put over the people. He wants an elected parliament, not the rule of soldiers.'

John slid his arm around his wife's waist. 'And you?' he asked gently, his lips against her clean cap. 'Are you well?'

She nodded, saying nothing. He did not press the question. They both knew that the answer was now and would always be that she was grieving for Johnnie. They would both always be grieving for Johnnie.

'Your friends have visited in your absence,' she said with forced brightness. 'Mr Ashmole and the others. Mr Ashmole has been very busy working on a catalogue of the collection as you asked him to. I think it's nearly done. It is in Latin. He showed me some pages, it looks very fine. I think you will be pleased with it. He says we can sell the catalogue at the door to guide people around the rarities room and around the garden. And that people can take it away with them to study. Gardeners can see what we are growing and write to us with orders. He says we could charge as much as two shillings.'

'And is Frances well?'

Hester nodded. 'Alexander was ill this winter, a cough which wouldn't ease. She was worried about him for a while but he is mending with the warmer weather.'

John curbed his resentment at his young daughter nursing a husband suffering from the ailments of an old man. 'No signs of another baby?'

'None yet,' Hester said gently.

John nodded, glanced once more at the sunlit beauty of his garden and then turned to his house.

Summer 1657

In early summer John took the wagon and cart over to Wimbledon House with a delivery of bulbs and saplings for John Lambert. He found Lord Lambert in his rare garden – a walled area facing south and west reserved for exotic plants – with an easel before him, paints on a table beside him and an exquisite white tulip in a porcelain blue bowl. In the centre of the garden was a newly planted acacia tree which took John's eye at once.

'Is that one of mine?' John asked.

'No,' Lambert said. 'I had it from Paris last autumn, from the Robins' garden.'

'Very fine,' John said, a hint of envy in his voice. Lambert heard it at once.

'You shall have a cutting,' he promised. 'I know you have so little. I know your garden is so poor.'

John grinned ruefully. 'A true gardener can always squeeze in one more plant. Now, I have brought you some orange plants as you asked. This one they call leopardsbane in Virginia, it flowers in autumn: a wonderful rich, bright orange with a heart as dark as chocolate. And the lily bulbs you ordered. And some whips of orange trees.'

'I have a fancy for a garden in yellow and orange,' Lambert explained, 'with orange trees in tubs at the centre of the beds. And a blaze of colour all around. What d'you think? Are there enough orange flowers?'

'Marigolds?' John suggested. 'Ranunculus? Sunflowers? Turkish nasturtiums? I have some tulips which would pass as orange, and some new narcissi with orange hearts. My father made a golden garden years ago at Hatfield. He used kingcups and buttercups by the watercourses, and yellow flag iris. And my Virginian trumpet vine is a bright true orange.'

'I'll have them all,' Lambert declared. 'And what lily bulbs d'you have for me? I want to plant some great pots with lily bulbs deep in the base, and tulips in the middle, and snowdrops on the top so they succeed each other from spring through to midsummer.'

John shook his head. 'You'll have to repot every three or four years,' he said. 'They won't thrive in such a small space. They'll sap the strength of the earth. But the first two years you could leave them and you would get one flower succeeding another, as long as you keep them damp with comfrey water.'

'Anything else new?' Lambert asked as they walked from the rare garden to the stable yard where John had halted the cart.

'I brought you some day lilies and some white lilies, and there are a couple you could use in your orange garden: a red lily and a flame lily. They could pass for orange and you could breed from them, selecting the most orange colours.'

Lambert nodded to his man to unload the cart.

'I hear you are much at home these days,' John said tactfully, skirting the gossip that Lambert's differences with Cromwell now amounted to an open breach. The rule of the major generals had been replaced by a new parliament which again had failed to agree. Lambert had once more been spokesman for the radical old soldiers of the army who still resisted every attempt to restore the gentry and the lords to their previous power. There was a great suspicion that Cromwell, in an effort to secure peace in the country, was going the way of the Stuart kings, James and then Charles, towards a parliament which served only lords and gentry, an imposed Church which served the needs of the one sole ruler: himself, who might even be called king.

John Lambert had brought a petition from the army to Parliament voicing the old demands of free elections, justice for all, and a fairer chance for working men, as if the Levellers still held the balance of power and could make such demands. He expected a fair hearing from Cromwell who had once been an army man, as Lambert was still.

But Cromwell was an army man no more. He had moved from the clear, godly certainties of the ranks to the complex machinations of the men of power. When Lambert brought the petition asking for the political changes that the army had fought and died for, Cromwell acted swiftly. He reorganised the army, paid some back wages, promoted some men, dismissed others, and broke whole companies. Lambert had to watch the radical leaders of the army posted to service overseas, Jamaica, or Ireland, or simply discharged from their posts.

Then the blow fell on him. Cromwell dismissed Lambert from his own regiment, from the men that had fought behind him every step of the king's wars and had never been separated from their commander before. Lambert had taken the order without argument from Cromwell, because he would not disobey his commander. But he would not take the oath of fealty to him. And he did not admire Cromwell when the republican leader appeared in the robes of state carrying a sceptre.

Lambert scowled for a moment at John, hardly seeing him. 'I am much at home,' he agreed. 'As it turns out, I have little choice. There's no place for me at Westminster, it seems. And no place for me with my regiment. It's been given to Lord Fauconberg.'

'Your regiment?' John asked.

Lambert nodded scowling.

'Who *is* Lord Fauconberg? I never heard of him.'

'A noble lord. A royalist who has become Cromwell's man. I think my regiment is his dowry,' Lambert said wryly. 'He's to marry Oliver's daughter Mary. Quite a little dynasty that Cromwell is making, isn't it? And with a man who was a royalist, and would be a royalist again, especially if his father-in-law was to be king.'

'I never thought that he could govern without you,' John volunteered. 'I never thought he would turn against the army.'

'He's become nervous,' Lambert explained. 'He doesn't want a parliament full of new ideas, he doesn't want an army that might argue with him. So he dissolved Parliament and took my regiment away from me.'

'Could you not have objected?' John asked. 'Surely you command more influence than him, especially in the army.'

Lambert gave a rueful smile. 'And do what?' he asked. 'Lead them out to fight him? Another war fought over the same ground with the same men? Another half-dozen years of heartbreak? I'm not a man for faction, or division. My task has been to pull the country together, I wouldn't tear it apart for my own ambitions. I promised that I wouldn't raise a storm against him if he left my regiment alone, in one piece. I traded: my work and reputation for the integrity of my men. Cromwell agreed. They're under another man's command but no good men have been thrown out in the street for thinking for themselves. It was a fair deal, and I have to stick to my side of the contract.'

'I couldn't believe they were talking of Cromwell for king,' John said. 'I thought that we were building a new country here, and now it seems that we were just exchanging one king for another. The family of Stuart for the family of Cromwell.'

'The person doesn't matter,' Lambert said staunchly. 'Nor the name. What matters is the balance. The will of the people in Parliament, the reform of the law so that everyone can get justice, and the limitation of the king – or Lord Protector – or Council of State. It doesn't matter what the third power is called, but everything has to work in balance. The one with the other. A three-legged stool.'

'But what will you do if the Lord Protector doesn't want to be in balance?' John asked. 'What if he wants the balance tipped all his way? What if the milkmaid on your three-legged stool is thrown down and all the milk spilled?'

Lambert looked at the orange trees in their carrying tubs without really seeing them. 'I don't know,' he said. 'We shall have to pray that he has not forgotten so much of what we all once wanted.' His mood suddenly changed and he grinned at John. 'But I'm damned if I call him Your Majesty though,' he said cheerfully. 'I swear to you, Tradescant, I just couldn't do it. It would choke me.'

Frances and Alexander stayed at the Ark for the spring. Alexander's cough was no better and Frances wanted him away from the smell and noise of the city streets.

John woke one night to hear him coughing in their room and heard Frances go quietly down the stairs. He slipped from his own bed, threw his cape around his shoulders over his nightshirt and went downstairs to the kitchen.

Frances was stirring a saucepan over the embers of the fire.

'I'm making a drink of mead and honey for Alexander,' she said. 'His cough is so troublesome.'

'I'll put a drop of rum in it,' John said, and went to fetch the bottle from the cupboard in the dining room. When he came back he saw that Frances had sunk into one of the kitchen chairs with the saucepan left on the hob. He took it off and poured a hearty slug of rum on the mix, and then poured it into a cup.

'Taste it,' he said.

She would have refused but he insisted.

'Very sweet,' she said.

'Take another gulp,' he said. 'It'll put some spirit in you.'

She did as she was ordered and he saw the colour come into her cheeks.

'I am sorry,' he said.

She met his eyes frankly. 'He's sixty-seven,' she said bluntly. 'We've had twelve good years. We never counted on this many.'

John put his hand over hers.

'And you never wanted me to marry him at all,' she said with a flash of residual resentment.

John smiled wryly. 'Only to spare you this night,' he said. 'And the other nights ahead, while you nurse him.'

She shook her head. 'I don't mind,' she said. 'I'm caring for him now, but he has cared for me for as long as I can remember. I quite like being the one in charge for a change. I like repaying the debt of love. He's always petted me, you know. Petted me so tenderly. I rather like nursing him now.'

John poured a little thimbleful of mead and rum for her. 'You sit by the fire for a while and drink this,' he ordered. 'I'll take this up to him.'

Frances nodded and let him go. John took one of the kitchen candles, lit it at the embers of the fire and went quietly up the stairs to Alexander's bedroom.

Alexander was propped up against the pillow, his breathing hoarse. When he saw John come in he managed a smile of greeting.

'Is Frances all right? I didn't want her running after me.'

'She's having a drop of mead and rum at the fireside,' John said. 'I thought I'd sit with you for a while, if you wish.'

Alexander nodded. 'I brought you this,' John said. 'If it doesn't help you sleep then you have a head stronger than my narwhal tusk.'

Alexander gave a choking little laugh and took a sip of the hot drink. 'By God, John, that's good. What's in it?'

'Herbs of my own brewing,' John said innocently. 'Actually, my Jamaican rum.'

'She'll have a good settlement,' Alexander said suddenly. 'When I go. She's well provided for.'

'Oh yes?'

'The cooperage will go to my manager, but he's agreed a price to pay her, and signed a deed. It's all agreed. She can keep the house if she likes but I thought she'd rather live somewhere else than at the Minories.'

'I'll look after her,' John said. 'It'll be as she wants.'

'She should marry again,' Alexander said. 'A younger man. These are better days now, at last. She can take her pick. She'll be a wealthy young widow.'

John looked cautiously at him, but Alexander spoke without bitterness.

'I'll take care of her,' John repeated. 'She won't make a mistake with her choice.' He paused for a moment. 'She didn't make a mistake last time. Though I disagreed at the time. She made no mistake when she chose you.'

Alexander gave a little laugh which turned into a cough. John held his cup till the paroxysm passed and then gave him another sip of the drink. 'Kind of you,' he said. 'I knew it wasn't your choice. But it seemed like the best life she could have at the time.'

'I know it,' John admitted. 'I know it now.'

The two men sat in companionable silence for a moment.

'All square then?' Alexander asked.

John proffered his hand and gripped Alexander's own. 'All square,' he said fairly.

Summer 1657

Elias Ashmole and the physicians, mathematicians, astronomers, chemists, geographers, herbalists and engineers returned to the Ark to argue, discuss and exchange ideas, on the first Sunday of every summer month. By common accord they avoided the subject of politics. It looked to most men as if Cromwell meant to make himself king. Most of the opposition to him had been dispersed, paid or bullied into silence. General George Monck, another turncoat royalist, held down Scotland for the Lord Protector with a heavy hand and the dour efficiency of the professional soldier. Cromwell's own son Henry held down Ireland. The Cromwells were becoming a mighty dynasty, and the old idealism was lost in the difficulties of ruling a country where any freedom for the many was feared by the powerful few.

The great fear was not political opposition but religious madness. The men and women who would give their form of worship no name because they wanted it to be everywhere, to be the nature of life itself, were growing in numbers. Their opponents called them Quakers because they shook and trembled in religious ecstasy. Their enemies called them blasphemers, especially after one of their number, James Nayler, entered the city of Bristol like Jesus on a donkey with women throwing down palms before him. The House of Commons had him arraigned for blasphemy and savagely punished; but the mutilating of one individual could not stop a movement which threw up adherents everywhere like poppies in a wheatfield. Very soon John's visitors banned the discussion of religion too, as overly distracting from the work in hand.

A couple of times Lord Lambert came from his house at Wimbledon to see any new additions to the garden or the rarities room and sometimes stayed for dinner to talk with the other guests. Sometimes men brought curiosities, or things that they had designed or built. Often at these talks

Ashmole would lead the discussion, his classical education and his acute mind prompting him to take the part of host in John's house.

'I don't like how Mr Ashmole puts himself forward,' Hester remarked to John as she carried another couple of bottles of wine into the dining room.

'No more than any other man,' he answered.

'He does,' she insisted. 'Ever since he catalogued the collection you would think that it was his own. I wish you would remind him that he was nothing more than your assistant. Frances knows her way round the collection better than he does. Even I do. And Frances and I kept it safe through three wars, while he was at Oxford living off the richness of the court.'

'But neither Frances nor I know Latin like Mr Ashmole,' John reminded her gently. 'And he worked very hard for nothing more than my thanks. I couldn't have completed the task without him, you know, Hester. And he's a coming man, mark my words. He'll do great things.'

Hester gave John a brief, sceptical look and said nothing more but turned to go back to the kitchen.

'Is Alexander coming downstairs tonight?' John asked her. It was Alexander's habit now to join the men in the evening after they had dined so that he could listen to their talk. He wore his gown with a rich robe wrapped round his shoulders against the cool evening air. He was often too breathless to speak but he liked to listen to the men discussing, he liked to follow the arguments especially when they talked of astronomy and the new discoveries of the stars.

Hester shook her head. 'He's too weary,' he says. 'Frances will sit with him upstairs.'

The Normans stayed at the Ark through the summer, but still Alexander grew no better. They all maintained the gentle fiction that he would improve when the colder weather came, as before they had pretended that he would be better when he felt the summer sun.

When he said he wanted to go home in August Frances did not argue with him, though the summer months were the most dangerous for the plague in the City. She simply sent the garden boy to the river to hail a boat to take them down to the Tower and told the stable lad to harness the cart.

'He's very ill,' Hester cautioned her. 'He's too ill to make the journey. You should stay here.'

'I know,' Frances said simply. 'But he wants to be home.'

'Settle him in and as soon as he is feeling better you come back here,' Hester said. 'There's plague in the City, I'd rather you were here.'

Frances shook her head. 'You can see as well as I can that he will not feel better, even when he is home. I will stay with him until the end.'

'Oh, Frances.'

'I knew that this was likely to happen when I married him,' Frances said. Her eyes were filled with tears but her voice never faltered. 'And he knew it too. We were neither of us such fools as to think that I would not lose him. We were prepared for this from our wedding day. He warned me of it. I have no regrets.'

'I'll come with you,' Hester decided. 'You'll need someone to run the house while you nurse him.'

'Thank you,' Frances said. 'I'll want you with me.'

Alexander died in his bed, as he had wanted, with Hester at the foot of the bed and Frances holding his hand. He whispered something and she could not hear what he said. She leaned a little closer to hear the words.

'What is it, my love? Say it again?'

'You were the sweetest –' he paused for a breath and Frances leaned a little closer. 'The sweetest flower in all of John's garden.' He smiled at her for a moment, then he closed his eyes and went to sleep.

Frances buried her husband in the church where they had been married and walked back to her house with her father and stepmother on either side of her.

Hester had ordered in a dinner from the nearby bake-house and Alexander's apprentices, his family from Herefordshire, and his friends from the City drank to his memory, ate their dinner and then left.

The house was oddly silent without the tapping of hammers from the yard and continual rasp of the saws.

'Have you thought what you would like to do?' John asked his daughter gently. 'Have you thought where you would like to live? Alexander left you well-provided, and you can sell this house. The sale of the business is already agreed.'

'I had thought,' she said. 'If you would allow it – I should like to come home.'

'To the Ark?'

'Yes.'

John found that he was beaming with delight. 'That would give me much joy,' he said simply.

Autumn 1658

In early September John was wakened at dawn by the noise of the rising wind.

'I'm glad I'm not at sea today,' he said to Hester.

He went to the window and saw the trees in the orchard and the avenue flailing their boughs at the sky where the clouds raced overhead.

'Come back to bed,' Hester said sleepily.

There was a clatter from the stable yard.

'I'm awake now,' John said. 'I'll get up and see that everything's safe. We're in for a storm.'

He spent the day with the lad and Joseph pinning back the creepers and staking the plants which were already rocking in the earth, pulling at their roots. Frances took a sharp knife and went around the garden mercilessly pruning the climbing roses so that the long boughs would not tear the stalks from the soil. She came in for dinner at midday with her arms scratched above her gloves and her hair tumbled about her shoulders.

'Frances Norman,' said Hester, disapprovingly.

'It's wild out there,' Frances said. 'My cap blew off.'

'I can see that,' Hester said.

'We're going to lose half the apples,' John said irritably. 'What a foul wind.'

'And the plums,' Frances said. 'I'll pick as many as I can get this afternoon.'

'I'll come out and help,' said Hester. 'I don't expect any visitors this afternoon, no-one would take a boat on the river unless they had to.'

John had thought that the wind might drop as night fell; but it grew stronger and wilder, and it started to rain. Hester went round the house fastening shutters but still they could hear the thud of the wind against the leaded panes of glass, and in the rarities room they could see the great panes creaking as they moved in their frames.

'I hope to God they don't crack,' John said. 'We'll close the shutters behind them, then at least if they smash the rarities will still have some protection. If I had thought I could have boarded up the house this morning.'

They had an ill-cooked supper. A great gust of wind had come down the chimney and blown soot all around the kitchen. While they ate they heard the clatter of a slate falling from the roof into the stable yard.

Frances declared that she was going early to bed and putting her head under her pillow, and Hester followed her example; but John prowled around the creaking house for half the night, feeling that his Ark was rocking in high seas and that the master should be awake.

In the morning there was less damage than they had feared. The Virginian creeper was stripped of its rosy leaves and would make no show to attract buyers, and there were fallen fruit and broken boughs all down the orchard. The chestnuts had been ripped from the trees too early and they might not ripen, and they had lost most of the apple and plum crop. But the house was still standing and the windows were unbroken, and only a few slates had gone missing from the roof.

'I shall go into Lambeth and order the builder to come,' John said. 'He'll be a busy man this day, I should think.'

He rode Caesar down the lane to Lambeth and thought that the crowd in the market was agog with news of the storm damage until he drew closer and heard what they were saying.

'What was that?' he asked, dropping from the saddle. 'What did you say, sir?'

'Don't you know?' A man turned to him, delighted to be first with the news. 'Haven't you heard? He's dead!'

'Who?'

'The Lord Protector. Oliver Cromwell. Dead in his bed while the storm rattled the roof above him.'

'It's as if God himself was angry,' a man piously asserted. 'It was a sign.'

'A very odd sign then, and rather late in the day,' John said crossly. 'If God didn't like Oliver Cromwell he had plenty of time to demonstrate that before.'

An unfriendly face turned towards him. 'Are you one of his old soldiers?' someone asked unpleasantly. 'Or a servant of the major generals? Or one of the damned tax collectors?'

'I'm a man who thinks for himself,' John said stoutly. 'I serve no master and I owe nothing to any man. And I am absolutely certain that God didn't blow the slates of my roof last night to show me that Oliver Cromwell was dying. If He is all-wise, then He might have found a way to tell me that didn't let the rain in.'

Spring 1659

The storm which blew Oliver Cromwell up to his reward in heaven, or down to the devils in hell, did not helpfully indicate his successor. There were many who said that he nominated his son Richard on his deathbed, but John, recalling what his father had said about the succession of kings, remembered that courtiers were never very reliable about deathbed confessions and that the power of supreme government in England might go to whatever man had the courage to seize it.

The man most fit to succeed was John Lambert, beloved of the army, still the greatest power in the land, and a proven friend of peace, tolerance and reform. But Richard was said to be the heir and a new parliament was summoned to rule with the new Protector.

They were curiously churlish about the job. Richard was not even recognised as Lord Protector until they were forced to acknowledge him so that he could send the fleet to the Baltic to protect English shipping against the Dutch in February. And then in April, the army, impatient with being ignored while they petitioned for back pay and furious at the increasingly arrogant behaviour of the royalists, locked the MPs out of the Commons, Richard among them.

He might be a Cromwell, but he was not an old soldier, and the army suspected that the new breed of politicians and leaders had lost the godliness and republican fire of those who had been forced to fight for their beliefs.

John had promised Hester that he would take her to see Lambert's orange garden at Wimbledon in the spring. They took a boat to the manor house landing stage and walked through Lambert's new plantation to the formal gardens before the house. John hesitated when he saw Lord Lambert on the terrace, his wife beside him. Before them were a couple of soldiers with the standard of his old regiment which had been given to Cromwell's son-in-law.

'What's going on?' Hester asked her husband quietly.

John shook his head.

'Perhaps we should just wave and go back to the plantation,' Hester suggested tactfully. 'It's maybe a private matter.'

'He's beckoning us,' John said. 'Come on.'

The Tradescants went to the foot of the steps. John Lambert smiled down at Hester with a beam that reminded her poignantly of Johnnie when he had just got his own way in an argument.

'You come at a good moment,' he said to them both. 'See. Here's the standard of my regiment. Restored to me.'

'Restored?' Hester asked, coming up the steps and dropping a little curtsey to Lady Lambert.

'Fauconberg and the rest are dismissed from their posts, and so my lads have come to restore the standard to me. We're together again.'

'I'm glad for you,' John said. 'Congratulations, Lord Lambert.'

'Major General,' Lambert said with a gleam. 'And I'd rather be a major general at the head of the best regiment in the army than a lord at my fireside any day.'

Summer 1659

Parliament was dissolved and a new parliament came in, led by a new Council of State, in May. Amongst the new council was John Lambert and he gave his vote to the retirement, with pay, of Richard Cromwell, back pay to the army, the cleansing of schools and universities of ungodly ministers, and the toleration for all religions except for Catholics and those who would bring the bishops back to England. The rule of the Cromwell family was over, England was a true republic again.

'He's asked me to take care of his tulips this autumn,' John remarked to Hester as they worked companionably side by side in the Ark's rose garden. 'He thinks he will be in Whitehall all this year. It'll be odd to work at Wimbledon again.'

'You'll never be his gardener,' Hester said, astonished.

'No, he has his own gardeners. But I said I would lift the tulip bulbs in the autumn. He wants me to choose the colours for the orange garden, and he trusts me with his dark Violetten tulips.'

Hester smiled. 'Not going into service again then, John?'

'Never again,' he said. 'Not even for him. I swore I would never serve another master and then the order came from the king for my father and me, and we couldn't disobey. Anyone else I would have refused.'

'What if Lambert were to become king?' she asked. 'He's the best-loved man in the country. There are many saying that he could be trusted to rule with a parliament. And the army follow no-one but him.'

'I'd like to see a gardener on the throne,' John mused. 'Think of what the palace gardens could be.'

Hester snorted with laughter. 'And that's the main consideration?'

John grinned reluctantly. 'The most important, certainly.'

They heard Frances call from the house and they looked towards the terrace. She was standing with a gentleman at her side. She beckoned to John.

'Who's that?' Hester asked uneasily. 'I don't recognise him.'

'Perhaps someone with something for sale,' John said, stepping carefully round the rose bushes, and picking up his basket filled with the sweetly scented pastel petals. He walked to the terrace and gave the basket to Frances.

'This gentleman says he has private business to discuss with you,' she said briefly.

John absorbed, as a father can do, that his daughter was deeply offended and determined not to show it.

'The gentleman declined to give his name to me,' Frances said in the same clipped tones. 'I'll take these to the stable yard, shall I?'

John smiled pacifically at her. 'If you wouldn't mind,' he said.

'The gentleman asked me to fetch him a glass of wine,' Frances continued stonily. 'Can I fetch anything for you, Father?'

'No indeed,' John said. 'But please ask Cook to serve the gentleman. You are far too busy, Frances.'

He earned a brief smile for that and then she was gone, her back very straight, her head very high. John turned his attention to the mystery guest who had managed, in so short a time, to mortally offend his daughter.

'I beg your pardon,' the man said. 'She was so simply dressed I thought she was your housemaid.' He glanced at John's own muddy homespun breeches, linen shirt, leather waistcoat and scratched dirty hands.

'We are gardeners,' John said gently. 'It's a dirty job. It rather calls for simple dress.'

'Of course –' the man said hastily. 'I did not mean to upset Miss Tradescant.'

John nodded, not bothering to correct him.

'There are far too many women, young and old, trying to meddle in the affairs of men,' the man said in an effort to please. 'You do well to keep her at home and working in her place. The country would be a better place for us all if women were restrained from thinking and bearing witness, and praying, and preaching and all the rest of it. The country will be a better place when the women are back in the kitchens again and everyone back in their proper place. I like to see a young lady dressed as plain as a kitchen maid. It shows she has proper humility.'

'Your business with me, sir?' John prompted. 'I have a rose garden to see to, and petals which have to go fresh to the perfumiers.'

The man glanced around the empty terrace as if he thought they might be overheard.

'Can we talk here?'

'You can talk anything that is fit and legal,' John said shortly.

'My name is Mordaunt. I come from the king.'

John nodded, saying nothing.

'Viscount John Mordaunt,' the gentleman emphasised, as if John were likely to be swayed by a title.

John nodded again.

'There is to be a rising. The country cannot be ruled by a council of nobodies and a parliament of nothings. We have been waiting our time, and now the king has named the day.'

'I don't want to know,' John said abruptly.

'We are counting on you to secure Lambeth for the king,' Mordaunt said earnestly. 'I know where your sympathies lie. You mustn't think that this is a little conspiracy which will get us nowhere but the Tower. This is to be a great uprising on the first day of August. And your part will be to secure Lambeth and this side of the river. You are to secure the horse ferry, and then extend downriver.'

'I don't want to know,' John repeated. 'My sympathies are with peace and order. I won't recognise Charles Stuart until he is crowned king of England. I lost a son –' He broke off.

'Then you will want to be avenged!' Mordaunt said, as if that clinched the matter. 'Your son fought for the king, did he?'

'Twice,' John said. 'And twice wounded. Never paid, never thanked, and never victorious. I don't want to know about the uprising. Don't force secrets on me. I don't want to be in the conspiracy, big or small. Don't tell me, and then I cannot betray you.'

Mordaunt checked suddenly as Hester came up the steps to the little wooden terrace. 'Ssshh! Hush!' he hissed.

Hester glanced interrogatively at John.

'This gentleman is leaving,' John said. 'I'll show him out.'

Mordaunt hesitated. 'When he of whom we were speaking comes back to London you will regret that you did not assist me,' he warned.

John nodded. 'Perhaps,' he said, and showed the man through the double doors of the terrace and into the hall. Frances emerged from the kitchen and stood beside Hester as John eased their unwelcome guest towards the front door.

'When he of whom we were speaking is in his rightful place again then there will be a grave reckoning,' Mordaunt threatened. 'When he is where he should be then he will want to know where you were on the day of which I have spoken.'

'If you mean Charles Stuart,' Frances's voice rang out clearly in the hall, 'then calling him "he of whom you were speaking" is hardly a brilliant disguise. And if *that* is your idea of deep concealment then I don't anticipate great success, on the day of which you have spoken, or any other day, actually.'

Mordaunt exchanged one angry look with her, crammed his hat on his head and flung open the front door. 'When he of whom we were speaking is where he belongs again, then women, especially interfering spinsters, will be kept where they belong,' he said crossly to Frances and stormed out of the door.

Frances lifted up her skirts and ran after him to stand on the front step. 'And we all know where Charles Stuart likes his women!' she shouted down the street to his rapidly retreating back. 'Up against a wall!'

'Should I warn Major General Lambert?' John asked Hester as they prepared for bed that night.

'That Charles Stuart is preparing an uprising?' she asked. She twisted her hair into a loose knot and tied her cap on her head. 'He must know already. There's been nothing but promises of another royal invasion ever since Cromwell died.'

'I don't like to be a spy,' John said uneasily. 'But I don't like being drawn in.'

Hester chuckled. 'I doubt they'll come again for help to you after what Frances said.'

John shook his head, smiling. 'What a fishwife!' he said. 'What ever would Alexander have thought?'

'He knew her,' Hester said. 'It would have come as no surprise to him. She was never a docile girl.'

'She's a complete trooper,' John said. 'I think you must have brought her up very badly, my wife.'

Hester gleamed at him and got into bed. 'I did,' she said. 'But she's a woman who knows her own mind. Give me credit for that at least.'

In the morning John wrote a note to John Lambert and sent it to him at Whitehall.

> Your lordship,
> I have heard that there is to be an uprising for Charles Stuart on 1 August. I know no more than this, and I wish with all my heart that I did not know this.
> John Tradescant.

He received a reply brought by one of Lambert's troopers, a man with a head like a cannon ball and a wide toothless grin.

> Mr Tradescant,
> If this is the first you have heard of the uprising then you are too much out of the way in Lambeth. They came to try to recruit me for it in June.
> In any case, thank you for your loyalty to our great republic.
> Lambert.

Lambert might joke about the royalist indiscretion but there was enough support for their cause for there to be uprisings all over the country. Every village, every town, was divided again between men who would fight for their liberties and men who would fight for their king. Some of them wanted a more lasting solution than a succession of argumentative parliaments. Some of them wanted a return to the old days of inefficient tax collection, and sports in the churchyard on Sunday. Some of them wanted the rich rewards that an incoming monarch must bring. Some of them hoped to get their old places back. Some were Roman Catholics, gambling on the widespread belief that the Stuarts were always Papists. One or two may even have believed that the libertine in the Hague was the best hope for the country. None of the fights came to more than a few broken windows and a couple of brawls except in the case of Sir George Booth at Chester.

The parliament, in grave fright at the news of an armed uprising, ordered five regiments to march to Cheshire led by Major General Lambert. Lambert left his botanical paintings, his rare garden, his orange garden, and his ornamental pheasants, kissed his wife goodbye and rode at the head of his restored regiment westwards.

He met Sir George Booth's army at Winnington Bridge. Booth had one thousand men under the royal standard and Lambert had his full complement of four thousand. The outcome could not be in doubt. There was a brief, efficient battle which was notable for its economy and discipline. Only thirty men died and the rebellion was over. Lambert held his troops in tight order and there was no cruelty or looting or taking quarter. The royalist army were relieved of their weapons with careful courtesy and sent back to their homes.

Sir George Booth fled the battlefield disguised as a woman but was arrested when an inn keeper noticed that his 'lady' guest had called for a barber and a razor.

'Inspired,' Lambert said briefly, and ordered that Sir George Booth be taken to London for his trial for treason.

Lambert's popularity rose and he was declared the saviour of the nation in every ale shop and tavern down the Great North Road. More particular were the thanks of the Quakers who came under his protection while he scotched the last of the royalist rebellions. By the end of August he was recognised as the greatest man in the kingdom and a grateful parliament voted him a gift of one thousand pounds.

Autumn 1659

In September, on his way back to London down the North Road, Lambert sent John Tradescant a note which read:

> You may not have heard that John Mordaunt has left England
> to join the court of Charles Stuart at the Hague. He has had
> so many disappointments that I dare say one was no more
> memorable than another. Whatever happens in the future, Mor-
> daunt's enmity will not be anything to fear.

Before Lambert returned to London his army sent another petition to the House of Commons. Their list of requests was coming to be known as the 'Grand Old Cause', the cause of the Ironsides, the cause of the Levellers, the cause of the republicans. They demanded godly reforms, a proper command structure for the army, Parliament to be run by elected members advised by a senate, and court martial law in the army.

The House of Commons, always an unfaithful friend when the victory had been won, decided that the army was demanding reforms rather than requesting, and was probably marching on Parliament to seize power. In a frenzy of panic they ordered that the doors should be shut and Major General Lambert, so recently their hero, should be regarded as an enemy of Parliament and arrested for treason.

In early October John Tradescant received a magnificent order for spring bulbs from John Lambert who gave Wimbledon House as his address.

'So he's exiled again,' John observed to Hester. 'They don't have the courage to send him to the Tower but they don't dare let him near Parliament. They must be mad not to make him Lord Protector.'

'They're terrified,' she said. 'They think of nothing but saving their own skins. A parliament run by Lambert would reform them out of existence. He has no patience with time-servers. Did he write all this to you?'

'No, it's just an order for bulbs.'

'Then how d'you know he's in exile?'

John grinned. 'He always orders too many when he has been thrown out of power. He couldn't plant all these if he had three autumns under house arrest.'

John could have sent the lad with the three sacks of bulbs but his curiosity was too great. He himself drove the cart into the stable yard at Wimbledon and was directed to the pheasant garden where his Lordship was feeding his birds.

Lambert, holding a basket of grain, was surrounded by his ornamental pheasants, their plumage brilliant in the autumn sunshine. He turned quickly when he heard a footstep on the gravel behind him, but when he recognised John he smiled his sweet smile. 'Ah, Mr Tradescant, have you brought my bulbs yourself?'

'Yes, my lord,' John said. 'I am sorry to learn that you are confined here.'

'Oh,' Lambert said equably. 'Fortunes rise and fall in politics as well as in battles. In any case you find me bidding farewell to my birds now because I expect to be summonsed today.'

'To battle or to politics?' John asked.

Lambert grinned. 'They're much the same.' He cocked his head. 'Listen. D'you hear anything?'

John listened, then heard the steady beat of a company of horse in trot, and the jingle of armour. 'Soldiers,' he said.

'Then I think this is my summons,' Lambert remarked and John could hear the exultant joy in his voice at the prospect of action. 'Ask them at the stables to saddle my charger for me, would you, Mr Tradescant? I don't think I'm going to be able to plant bulbs today.'

'Can I come too?' John asked.

Lambert laughed. 'If you wish it. D'you have any idea where we are going?'

'No,' John confessed.

'Then you're as wise as I.'

John pulled Caesar from the shafts of the cart, borrowed a saddle from Lambert's groom and waited beside the company of Lambert's horse for the few moments until the general came out of the house.

'What's going on?' John asked one of the troopers.

'They've called out the other regiments against us,' the man said shortly. 'It's between our major general and the Members of Parliament. They've reneged on every promise they've ever given us and when we protest they call it treason. Now they've gone to ground in the Houses of Parliament with two regiments thrown around it and the Parliamentary Horse Guards leading the defence and saying that we must disband. Telling us to throw down our arms as traitors. Us who beat the king for them, then beat the Scots for them, and then beat Charles Stuart for them, and only last month beat George Booth for them. Us, disband! And hand over the general too! So they can throw him into the Tower beside Booth who fought against us!'

'*And* left the battlefield in a petticoat,' someone added to a rumble of laughter.

'And what can you do?' John asked. 'They're the Parliament, and if they've got the Horse Guards out . . .'

'It's what *he* can do,' the trooper replied, nodding towards Lambert, who swung into the saddle and trotted down the road at the head of his troop.

'What can he do?' John asked.

The trooper grinned. 'Anything he likes, is my guess.'

The troop fell in behind the general, bits jingling, hooves clattering on the dry road, and John, with a delicious sense that he should not be tagging on as a spectator, followed behind with Caesar pulling at the reins, his neck arched and tail held high at the prospect of action.

When they reached Scotland Yard at the side of the Palace of Whitehall he saw that the trooper was right, and his sense that he would have been safer to go straight home was right too. It was going to be an ugly scene, a pitched battle between the Parliamentary Horse Guards and Lambert's regiments at the very gateway to the Houses of Parliament. John reined back Caesar, who pulled against the bit as if he too knew that fighting was likely and was ready for the charge.

'Halt!' commanded Lambert and his personal standard dipped to show the signal. The troop of horse halted with a clatter of hooves on the cobbles.

The regiment before the Houses of Parliament tightened their grip on their pikes, blew on the fuses of their muskets and waited for the order to fire. A horse in Lambert's regiment moved restlessly against a too-tight rein, and the chink of the bit was very loud in the silence. There was a long pause as one English regiment eyed another and waited for the command to attack.

John could hear his breathing light and rapid as he sat in the saddle. Any moment he thought he would see the muskets lifted and hear the dreadful crack of their firing. There were probably cannons nearby too, and the Parliamentary Horse Guards had the advantage of being in defence, and near to the stout walls of Whitehall, while Lambert's men were drawn up in the road.

There was a long, long pause as the two troops faced each other, then John Lambert slid from his saddle and dropped to the ground, his spurs ringing as they tapped the cobblestones. He tossed his bridle to his standard bearer and walked forwards as if he were strolling in his orange garden. He left the sheltering ranks of his men, and out across the cobbled gulf which separated the two regiments, as if the men on the other side were not poised to take aim, as if they were not waiting for the order to shoot him down. He smiled at them as if they were his own regiment, his own trusted men. He smiled at them easily and pleasantly, as if he were glad to see them, as if he were greeting them as old friends.

'My God, what is he going to do?' John whispered to himself.

Lambert halted immediately before their commander and looked up at the officer high above him on the big horse, his hand ready-tightened on his sword ready to draw and sweep down in the killing blow. It was a big horse. The man was sixteen hands above Lambert, the general had to look upwards, his eyes screwed up against the evening sunlight.

'Dismount!' Lambert said easily, almost conversationally. There was a moment's pause. Soldiers in both troops held their breath to see what the outcome would be. The officer looked down at the unarmed man before him, Lambert smiled up at him. Then the officer dropped his reins and jumped down from the saddle.

At once there was a roar of approval from Lambert's men and the Parliament guards broke ranks and trotted towards Lambert's regiment to be greeted with smiles and handshakes and laughter. Lambert shook hands with the officer, exchanged a few brief words and then strolled back to his horse, swung into the saddle and then turned to face the men.

'Fall in,' he said pleasantly as if for a routine parade. He nodded to his standard bearer. 'Take my compliments to the Members of the House of Commons and advise them that I have the keys to the House and they must leave. They are no longer welcome. The country will be ruled by a Committee of Safety. We are going to have justice and freedom in this country. And it starts now.'

Lambert had not allowed for General George Monck, out of touch in Scotland, and jealous as a sick dog of his charismatic rival. As soon as he heard of the triumph at Whitehall he sent word to London that as commander of the Parliamentary army in Scotland he did not accept the Committee of Safety and that he was declaring war, and marching south to restore the banned MPs.

'War?' Hester demanded. 'But why?'

'He says he's going to restore Parliament,' John said, reading the latest news-sheet.

'Then why did he not do it before?' Hester asked. 'Why did he not declare war on Cromwell?'

'Because this is a man who thinks he can be Cromwell,' John said astutely. 'He thinks he can put himself at the head of the army and in a little while command Parliament as well.'

'Shall we box up the rarities?' Hester asked John wearily.

John thought for a moment. 'Not yet,' he said. 'But we may have to. General Monck's troops learned their discipline burning out royalists in Scotland.'

'He's for Parliament. He fought against Charles Stuart,' she said. 'Why can he not allow Lambert and the Committee of Safety to bring in their reforms? Why cannot people in this country be given a chance to have the government and the justice they deserve?'

'He believes in nothing, he's a professional soldier,' John said bitterly. 'He fought for King Charles before he saw that Cromwell would win and so changed sides. Then he saw what Cromwell did. He saw one man come to power, nearly to kingship at the head of the army. He won't trust John Lambert not to do the same. And he'll be thinking there's a chance for him.'

'John Lambert is the only man you could trust with that power,' Hester said. 'He's never broken his word, not once, not in all these difficult times.'

'And he paid us for the daffodils that I took to him that day,' John said. 'I hope to God he is able to plant them.'

Lambert never did plant the daffodils that John brought him. In planting time in November, he obeyed his orders from the Committee of Safety to protect England against General Monck and marched north to meet him at the head of eight thousand men.

He would not attack at once. General Monck had been a comrade in arms, and they were both parliamentarians. Lambert believed, trustingly enough, that it must be a misunderstanding. He wrote to Monck to try to explain, to try to convince him of the plans of the Committee of Safety, to persuade him that at last England had a chance to make a free and just society.

Monck pretended to consider, wrote and argued by letter with Lambert, while the Committee in London scraped around trying to find money to pay the soldiers under Lambert's command. They sent nothing. Lambert was caught between the deceit of General Monck and the incompetence of the Committee. He would not attack General Monck when they were still in debate, and by the time he realised that the general was spinning out the argument as a tactic, his army had melted away, and the general had won without a shot being fired.

When he should have been planting his orange-hearted narcissi in his orange garden at Wimbledon House he was watching his army disappear down the Great North Road, knowing that he had been tricked by Monck and betrayed by London.

'What will happen to him?' Hester asked John.

John scowled. 'Monck has had him accused of treason,' he said miserably. 'Treason against the old parliament, who were so lazy and incompetent that no-one cared when Lambert locked them out. Now they'll call themselves martyrs, no doubt. And they'll call him a traitor. Once he's in the Tower it's not a very long walk to the scaffold.'

Spring 1660

In February Lambert turned the remnants of his army south and marched them home in tattered boots. There was no money to buy them provisions or proper clothes. Monck was far ahead of him and marched into Whitehall to be greeted by a stony silence.

George Monck was not a man to be cast down by unpopularity. He put his troops throughout the streets of London, and they were accustomed to doing their duty among a resentful population. London was an easier billet than Edinburgh, and within days there was no-one shouting for a free parliament and John Lambert left on the streets. With a large free feast to celebrate the expulsion of Lambert's Committee of Safety it was possible to generate an enthusiasm for Monck's new council of state, run by himself.

By the time John Lambert brought his exhausted army home it was all over. He was ordered to go to his house at Wimbledon and not approach Parliament.

He wrote to John Tradescant from Wimbledon. The note arrived as the family and guests were eating dinner.

> *Please send me, in pots, your finest specimen tulips of this season to the value of £300.*

'What does he say?' Hester asked John, hovering over his shoulder to read the note.

'He *says* that he wants my best tulips,' John said. 'What that means is something different.'

'It means that he will have to confine himself to gardening and painting,' Elias Ashmole said cheerfully. He helped himself to another slice of baked ham. 'It means that the balance of power has swung to George Monck and he will decide who rules the country from now on.

And if I read the predictions of the planets aright then he will want a king, or at the very least another Lord Protector.'

Hester looked at Ashmole with dislike. 'Then God help us,' she said sharply. 'For since of all the women in England he chose a foul-mouthed washerwoman to take as his wife, what on earth will he choose for a king?'

Elias Ashmole was not in the least downcast. 'I should think it a very good chance that he would choose the rightful heir,' he said. 'And then we shall see some changes.'

'Then we shall see the same thing again,' Hester said bitterly. 'Only this time the battles will have to be fought without anyone's heart in them.'

'Peace, my wife,' John said quietly from the end of the table. 'Mr Ashmole is our guest.'

'A most frequent guest,' Frances observed sweetly, her head bowed demurely over her plate.

In spring, when John Lambert should have been enjoying the daffodils bobbing and the yellow aconite carpeting the beds of his orange garden, he could see only a small square of blue sky from his window in the Tower and George Monck was the undisputed new man of power in London. Lambert was on trial for nothing, sentenced for nothing. They had imposed on him a fine of such a huge amount that not even a man of his fortune and with friends such as his could meet it. It was essential to George Monck that his great rival be safely out of the way while he discovered, for the last and greatest leap of his life, which would be the winning side this time.

Monck had fought as a mercenary for anyone who was prepared to hire an unprincipled sword. He had fought for King Charles before being recruited by Cromwell to fight for Parliament in Ireland. Thereafter he had fought for Parliament. Unlike John Lambert, who had spent his life in pursuit of a written constitution to protect the rights of Englishmen, Monck had spent his life merely trying to be on the winning side.

In April he decided that the winning side was, after all, the Stuarts and, with a packed house of Parliament men who agreed with him, he sent terms to Charles Stuart at Breda.

'It is over then,' John said to Hester, who was seated on the terrace and looking out over the garden where the trees were showing fresh and green and the air was smelling sweet. 'It's over. They are bringing

Charles Stuart back, and all of our struggle for all of these years counts for nothing. When they write the histories our lifetime will be nothing more than an intermission between the Stuarts, they won't even remember that for a while we thought there might have been another way.'

'As long as we have peace,' Hester suggested. 'Perhaps the only way to find peace in this country is with a king on the throne?'

'We must be better men than that!' John exclaimed. 'We must want more than a comedy of ceremony and handsome faces. What have we been doing for all these years but asking questions about how men should live in England? The answer cannot be "as easily as possible".'

'The people want the diversion of a new coronation,' Hester said. 'Ask them in Lambeth market. They want a king. They want the amusements and the entertainments, they want the corrupt tax collectors that you can bribe to look the other way.'

'But what a king!' John remarked disdainfully. 'Half a dozen bastards scattered around Europe already, his tastes formed in Papist courts, and no knowledge of English people at all except what he learned when he was a fugitive. His father ruined us by his devotion to his principles, his son will ruin us by having none.'

'Then he will rule more easily than his father,' Hester pointed out. 'A man with no principles will not be going to war. A man without principles doesn't argue.'

'No,' John said. 'I think the heroic days are over.'

There was a little silence as they both thought of the son who could not wait to see this day, and that if he had lived to see it then even he might have thought that it lacked a little glory.

'And what will happen to John Lambert?' Hester asked. 'Will they free him from the Tower before Charles Stuart arrives?'

'They will execute him for certain,' John said. 'I should think General Monck can hardly wait to sign the order. Lambert is too much of a hero to the army and the people. And when the new king comes home they will be looking for scapegoats to offer him.'

'It cannot be the end for him?' Hester asked incredulously. 'He has never done anything but fight for the freedom of Englishmen and -women.'

'I think it must be,' John said. 'It's a bitter, bitter ending to all our hopes. A king such as Charles restored, and a man like Lambert on the scaffold.'

But that very night, John Lambert climbed from his window in the Tower, slid down his knotted sheets, dropped into a waiting barge on the Thames, and disappeared into the April darkness.

'I have to go to him,' John said to Hester. He was saddling up Caesar in the stable. Hester stood in the doorway, blocking his path. 'I have to go. This is the battle that tests everything I have finally come to believe, and I have to be there.'

'How do you know it is not a story, some ridiculous rumour?' she demanded. 'How d'you know he has raised a standard, is summoning an army to fight for freedom? It could be nothing more than someone's dream.'

'Because only John Lambert would choose Edgehill to raise his standard. And besides, if I go there, and nothing is happening, I can always ride home again.'

'And what about me? What about me if something *is* happening, if a battle is happening and you are in the midst of it and you are killed? Am I to be left here to keep the rarities and the gardens safe forever, with no son and no husband?'

He turned from the horse and came to the door of the stable and took her cold hands in his. 'Hester, my wife, my love,' he said. 'We have lived our lives in some of the wildest and strangest times that this country will ever see. Don't deny me the chance to fight just once, on the side I believe in. That, in a way, I have always believed in. I have spent my life wavering from one view to another, from one country to another. Let me be wholehearted for this, just once. I know that Lambert is right. I know that what he wants for this country, a balance of power and justice for the poor, is what this country needs. Let me go and fight under his standard.'

'Why is it always fighting?' she cried passionately. 'I can't bear it, John. If you should be lost . . .'

He shook his head. 'I want to go back,' he said simply. 'I want to go back to Edgehill where the king was first defeated in the first war. I was never there. I ran from it, just as I ran from the war of the Powhatan in Virginia.'

She would have interrupted him, sworn that it was not a war, sworn that he was not a man who ran from conflict, but he stopped her.

'It was not that I was afraid, I'm not saying that I ran like a coward.

But there was nothing that I saw clearly enough to die for. I knew the king was in the wrong; but I pitied him. I knew the queen was a fool; but she was a charming fool. I didn't want to see her driven into exile. I think of her now sometimes, and I can't believe that she has been brought so low. Many women are feather-brained and yet they don't pay for their folly as she has had to pay. The cause didn't seem wholly right to me. It didn't seem wholly clear to me. Right up to the scaffold when they took him out and beheaded him, it didn't seem quite right to me.'

Hester would have pulled her hands away from him but he held her fast. 'You're talking like a royalist,' she said hotly.

He smiled ruefully. 'I know it. That's what I'm saying. I have always been able to see both sides at once. But this time – for the first time in my life – the first time, Hester! – I have a cause I can truly believe in. I don't think that Charles Stuart should come back. I do think that the people of this country should govern themselves without a king or bishops or lords. I do believe – my God, at last I believe – that we are a people who have earned our freedom and deserve to be free. And I want to go and fight for that freedom. Lambert has raised his standard, for freedom, for the good old cause. I want to be there. I want to fight for it. If I have to die for it I will.'

For a moment it looked as if she would cry out against him, then she stepped to one side and opened the stable door. Caesar the war horse stepped out, raising his big hoofs delicately over the threshold, and walked at once to the mounting block and stood still, his neck arched, as if he too wanted to go into battle for the rights of freeborn Englishmen.

John smiled to see the horse and then looked at Hester. 'Are you angry with me?'

'No,' she said unwillingly. 'I'm proud of you, even though this goes against my own interests. I'm glad to see you at last knowing what you believe and going to fight for it. I shall pray that you win. I have always thought that nothing mattered but that we survived these days and it is a change for me to think, like you, that there is something worth fighting for.'

'You think it's worth fighting for?' he asked. 'To keep the king out, to keep Parliament free? To get justice for everyone in this country?'

Unwillingly she nodded. 'Yes,' she said. 'And if any man can do it then Lambert is that man. I know it.'

John took her hand again, kissed it and then caught her to him and held her hard against him. 'I shall come back!' he said passionately.

'Trust me, Hester. I shall come back to you. And God willing we will make this country a place where poor men can be free.'

He came back within a fortnight. All three men who had been so powerful in Hester's life came back to their separate destinations: John Lambert to the Tower on a charge of high treason, Charles Stuart to Dover and the road to London lined with people crowding to touch his sacred hand, and John, head drooping, home to the Ark.

Caesar clip-clopped towards his stable, his ears back, his head low. John dropped off his back in the stable yard and fell to his knees as his legs buckled under him. The garden lad ran to raise him and shouted for Cook. She took one look out of the kitchen door and called for Frances and Hester who were tidying the rarities room.

Hester ran out to the terrace and then round the corner to the stable yard to find John seated on the mounting block, rubbing his stiff muscles. He tried to get to his feet when he saw her, but she went to him and put her arms around him.

'Are you injured?'

'Heartsick.'

'Hurt in your body?'

'No.'

'Your legs?'

'I'm just stiff. I'm too old, Hester, to ride all day and all night.'

'Was there a battle?'

'There was a skirmish. We were hopelessly outnumbered. On the day when it mattered, when it mattered more than anything in the world, there were not enough men ready to stand up and fight for their liberty.'

She wrapped her arms around him and held his weary head close to her heart. She found she was rocking him as she used to rock Johnnie when he woke from a nightmare.

'There was hardly anyone there,' John said flatly. 'Lambert was captured almost straight away. They didn't even bother with us. It was him they wanted. He would have got away but his horse was tired, we were all tired. And discouraged. Because when it really mattered there were not enough men ready to stand up and fight for their liberty.'

He pulled back and stared up into her face as if she could answer him. 'Why is it?' he demanded. 'Why is it that people can see so clearly when it is a question of their safety or their wealth, or their comfort? But when it is a question of their freedom they leave it for someone

555

else to defend. They don't see how they come to their freedom. They don't realise that if the bargees at Wapping are unjustly taxed and the miners in the Forest of Dean are excluded from their rights, if the commoners are driven from the commons and the rich and the mighty encroach, then we are *all* at risk – even if it is not our own gardens which are taken. Even if it is not yet our rights which are threatened. Why don't people see it? When governments persecute the sick, the poor, the women, then everyone has to stand up and defend them. Why don't people see that?'

Hester looked into his angry face for a moment and then pulled him back to her and held him against her heart. 'I don't know,' she said softly. 'You would think people would know by now that when there is an evil you should stop it at once.'

Summer 1660

Charles Stuart, who was to be known as Charles the Second, came home to a country mad with joy. People wanted to get back to a system that everyone knew, many of them hoped to gain from a change of government: a chance to settle old scores and regain old ground. Quakers, sectaries, Roman Catholics and a number of old women who could be named as witches by spiteful neighbours felt the brunt of popular confidence which expected the new king to restore the old persecutions as well as freedoms. Commoners all round the country helped themselves to firewood, poached from the royal forests and the derelict parks, and there was a great rush of burglary from the empty palaces before the new royal servants came to stock-take.

The new king set up a new Privy Council and the great English cake of rewards and places was sliced up between royalists and their friends; but Charles took some care to see that experienced men and those from wealthy or noble families were recruited to office whatever they had done in the wars against his father. Those who had been party to the trial and execution of his father only lost their places of power and were fined, if they fled England.

'I think he'll release John Lambert,' Frances said, bent over a newspaper spread out on the kitchen table. 'It says here that the House of Lords seeks his death but the House of Commons wants him reprieved.'

'Will he be free?' Hester asked, looking up from shelling peas.

Frances shook her head. 'It doesn't say. But if I was Charles Stuart I don't think I'd want Lord Lambert at the head of a regiment again.'

A month after the king was restored to the throne Elias Ashmole asked and got the place of a Windsor Herald. He came to visit the Ark wearing his new regalia, to suggest that John should publish a new edition of the catalogue.

'It should be dedicated to His Majesty,' Elias urged John as they sat on the terrace in the sunshine and looked over the garden which was in full summer bloom. 'Think, if he were to come to visit! His father did, didn't he?'

'Yes,' John said. 'With the queen.'

'I hear she's coming from France in the autumn,' Ashmole said enthusiastically. 'We should have a new edition published by then. I'll pay for it, if you wish. I have some money put by.'

'I can pay!' John said, nettled. 'I'll compose a dedication.'

'I have one already,' Elias said and produced from the deep pocket of his coat a folded manuscript. 'Here.'

John spread the paper on the table.

> To the sacred majesty of Charles the II
> John Tradescant, His Majesties most obedient and most loyal
> subject in all humility offereth these collections.

Frances, looking over John's shoulder, let out a little gurgle of laughter. 'I don't know if you're his *most* obedient subject,' she remarked. 'He surely has some servants that didn't spend the wars as far away as they could get.'

John turned his laugh into a cough. 'Frances, go about your business,' he said sternly and turned to Elias. 'I apologise.'

'A flighty woman,' Ashmole said disapprovingly. 'But if there is any question about your loyalty then you cannot affirm it too loudly, you know, John.'

John nodded.

'Fortunately you have the record of your son's service,' Elias remarked. 'You could always say he died at Worcester. Or died here of his wounds.'

Hester, coming to the terrace with a tray and three glasses of madeira wine, checked at that and exchanged a shocked look with her husband.

'We wouldn't do that,' John said briefly. He got to his feet and took the tray from Hester's hands. 'Look at this that Mr Ashmole has prepared for the printer for me. A new dedication for the front of the catalogue. Dedicated to His Majesty.'

She leaned over the table and read it carefully. To his surprise when she straightened up there were tears in her eyes.

'Hester?'

She turned a little away from the table so Elias Ashmole could not see her face. John followed her.

'What is it?' he asked quietly.

'I was just thinking how proud Johnnie would have been,' she said simply. 'To see our name on the same page as the king's. To have the collection dedicated to the king.'

John nodded. 'Yes, he would have been,' he said. 'His cause won the war in the end.' He turned to Elias Ashmole. 'I thank you for your help, Elias. Let's get it printed at once.'

Elias nodded. 'I'll deliver it to the printers on my way home,' he said cheerfully. 'It's no trouble. I'm glad you approve.'

Hester took her glass of wine and sat with the men. 'Do we have guests for dinner tonight?' she asked. 'Is Dr Wharton and the rest coming for dinner?'

'Yes, and there's news about that too!' Elias said gleefully. 'We are to have royal patronage. The king is very interested in our thoughts and discoveries. We are to be called the Royal Society! Imagine that! We are to be fellows of the Royal Society! What d'you think?'

'That is an honour,' John said. 'Though we'd never have gathered together if it hadn't been for the republic. Under the bishops half what we discussed would have been called heresy.'

Elias flapped his hand dismissively. 'Old days,' he said. 'Old history. What matters now is that we have a king who loves to talk and speculate and who is prepared to advance men of science and learning.'

'Then why does he touch for the king's evil?' Frances asked innocently, bringing a plate of biscuits which she put at John's elbow. 'Is that not the superstition of ignorant people? Would he welcome an inquiry into such nonsense?'

Elias was briefly put out. 'He does his duty, he does everything that is right and courteous and pleasing,' he said with emphasis. 'Nothing more than good manners. Good manners, Mrs Norman, are the very backbone of civilised society.'

'If you are a Royal Society I had best order a royal dinner,' Hester said tactfully. 'Come and help me, Frances.'

Frances shot a grin at her father and followed her stepmother into the house.

It was a good summer for the Ark. The sense of safety and prosperity meant that more and more visitors came to the doors. The spirit of inquiry which the Royal Society represented spread throughout London, and men and women came to see the marvels of the Tradescant collection and then walk in the rich gardens and the orchards.

The horse chestnut avenue which ran from the terrace before the rarities room to the end of the orchard was now thirty-one years old, with broad trunks and wide, swaying branches. No-one who saw the trees in flower could resist purchasing a sapling.

'There will be a chestnut tree in every park in the land,' John predicted. 'My father always swore that they were the most beautiful trees he had ever grown.'

But the chestnuts had their rivals in the garden. John's own tulip tree from Virginia flowered for the first time in the hot summer of 1660, and botanists and painters made special trips up the river to see the huge cupped flowers against the dark, glossy foliage. John had some new roses, Warner's rose and a beautiful new specimen from France that they called the velvet rose for the deep, soft colour of the petals. The fruit trees in the garden had shed their blossoms and were heavy-laden with growing fruits. The early cherries were picked at dawn by Frances to save them from the songbirds, and sold at the garden gate by the lad. One part of the fruit garden was set aside for vines now; John had row upon row of well-pruned bushes, grown low on wires, just as his father had seen them grown in France, with fourteen varieties of grape, including the fox grape from Virginia and the Virginian wild vine.

In the melon beds John grew half a dozen varieties of melon. He always kept one fruit to the side, he called it the royal melon, descendant of the seeds which Johnnie had planted at Wimbledon House. When it fruited in midsummer John sent a great sweet-smelling globe to the king, who was hunting at Richmond, with compliments of John Tradescant. He wondered if this was the second melon that Charles Stuart had received, and if he would ever understand the devotion which had been poured into growing the first fruit.

Autumn 1660

Castle Cornet, Guernsey.
   Dear Mr Tradescant,
Please would you send me, as soon as you lift them, six Iris Daley tulip, six Tricolor Crownes tulip, and two or three tulip which you think I might like that are new to your collection.

   If the new tenants of the house at Wimbledon have no objection, I should like you to collect from my garden any specimens which you would like to have as your own. I think the acacia tree was promised to you – all that long time ago. I particularly would like to see my own Violetten tulip again, I had one in particular which I thought might be so dark a purple as to be almost black.

   If you can be admitted to the garden I would be very pleased to have some of my lily bulbs returned to me, especially those from my orange garden. I have high hopes of breeding a new variety of lily here and I will send you some bulbs in the spring. I shall call it the Lambert lily and my claim to fame shall not be for the battle for freedom but for one sweet-smelling, exquisitely shaped blossom.

   Lady Lambert has joined me here with our children and the castle has become less like a prison and more like a home. All I am in need of, is tulips!

   With best wishes to Mrs Tradescant and Mrs Norman – John Lambert.

John passed the letter to Hester without comment and she read it in silence.

'We'll get him his Violetten back,' she said determinedly. 'If I have to go over the Wimbledon garden wall at midnight.'

Winter 1660

Elias Ashmole came to visit the Ark in midwinter, wearing a new fur-lined cape and very conscious of his new status. He came by carriage with some friends and brought a case of Canary wine to share with John. Hester lit the candles in the rarities room, and ordered dinner for them all, served it and ate her own dinner in the quieter company of Cook in the kitchen.

John put his head around the kitchen door. 'We're taking a stroll down to Lambeth,' he said. 'For a glass of ale.'

Hester nodded. 'I shall be in bed by the time you return,' she said. 'If Mr Ashmole wishes to stay the bed is made up in his usual room, and there are truckle beds for his friends.'

John came into the kitchen and gave her a kiss on the forehead. 'I shall be late home,' he announced with satisfaction. 'And no doubt drunk.'

'No doubt,' Hester said with a smile. 'Goodnight, husband.'

They came home earlier than she expected. She was putting out the candles in the rarities room and raking out the fire when she heard the front door open and John stumble into the hall with Ashmole and his companions.

'Ah, Hester,' John said happily. 'I am glad you are still awake. Elias and I have been doing some business and I need you to witness it for me.'

'Can it not wait until the morning?' Hester asked.

'Oh, sign it now and then we can put it away and have a glass of port,' John said. He spread the paper before her on the painter's table in the window of the rarities room. 'Sign here.'

Hester hesitated. 'What is it?'

'It's a piece of business and we need a witness,' Elias said smoothly. 'But if you are uneasy, Mrs Tradescant, we can leave it until the morning. If you want to read every paragraph and every sentence, we can leave it. We can find someone else to serve us if you are unwilling.'

'No, no,' Hester said politely. 'Of course I can sign it now.' She took the pen and signed the paper. 'And now I shall go to bed,' she said. 'I give you goodnight, gentlemen.'

John nodded, he was opening a case of coins. 'Here you are,' he said to Ashmole. 'In good faith.'

Hester saw the antique milled shilling piece passed to Elias.

'Are you giving away one of our coins?' she queried in surprise.

Ashmole bowed and pocketed the coin. 'I'm very grateful,' he said. He seemed far more sober than John. 'I shall preserve it very carefully as a precious token and a pledge.'

Hester hesitated, as if she would ask him what pledge John had made to him; but one of the men opened the door for her and bowed low. Hester curtsied and went out and up the stairs to bed.

She was wakened by the bang of her bedroom door as John stumbled into the room and then by the shake of the bed as he dropped heavily on to it. She opened her eyes and saw that he had fallen asleep at once, on his back, still wearing his clothes. Hester thought for a moment that she could get up and undress him and get him comfortable in bed. But then she smiled and turned over. John's drinking bouts were rare but she saw no reason why he should not wake up in the morning in some slight discomfort.

When he woke in the darkness he thought for a moment he had been dreaming his worst dream: of failure and his own inability to inherit his father's work and continue his father's name. He slipped out of the narrow bed without waking Hester, who turned and stretched her hand out over his pillow.

He slipped on his shoes and went downstairs. The parlour which had seemed so bright and jolly only hours ago was now dark and unwelcoming, it smelled of stale ale and tobacco smoke, and the fire was burned down to dark embers. He blew on the coals, was rewarded by a red glow, and then threw on a handful of kindling. The dry wood caught and the shadows leaped high in the room.

On the table was the document and at the foot of the document was his own clear signature, and next to it Elias Ashmole's educated elliptical hand. He touched the wax of his seal. It was hard and cold, there was no escape. The signature was there, the seal was there, the document was there. It stated very clearly that at John Tradescant's death Elias Ashmole was to inherit all the rarities in the collection and all the plants in the garden. John had signed away his patrimony, he had signed away his name, he had signed away his inheritance and all his own work and his father's work would count for nothing.

'I didn't mean this,' John whispered quietly.

With the deed of gift in his hand he went out into the hall. Hester in her white nightgown was like a ghost coming down the stairs.

'Are you ill?' she asked.

Dumbly, he shook his head. 'I have done a most terrible, terrible thing.'

At once her eyes went to the contract in his hand which she had signed as he had bid her. 'The business you were doing with Mr Ashmole?'

'He told me it was a deed of gift, to give the rarities to the University of Oxford at our deaths. He told me that they would put our name to the collection and that everyone would always know that we had the first collection open to any visitor in all the world, that we had the finest things, the rarest, the most beautiful. He told me that I was signing the goods to him as a trustee. He would ensure that the university received the rarities entire, that they would call it the Tradescantean.'

There was the creak of a door opening upstairs.

'Come outside,' Hester whispered as if only in the garden could they be safe. She opened the door to the terrace and slipped out into the icy night, careless of her bare feet on the chill floorboards. 'Does it not say that? The document? Is he not pledged to do that?'

'I just signed it,' John said numbly. 'I just agreed with him that it would be a fine thing to have the collection in the care of the university. So I just signed it. And I made you sign it too.'

'And what *does* it say?'

'I didn't read it carefully enough. And he is a lawyer. He has made sure that it is unclear. It says that the collection is to go to him entire; but there is nothing about the university. He is not a trustee, he will inherit everything for himself. He will have it when we die. He can keep it as he likes. Or he can give it to his heirs. My God, Hester, he can break it up and sell it piece by piece.'

She said nothing, she was aghast. Her face was as white as her nightcap, as her gown.

'And I signed too,' she said, her words a tiny thread of sound.

John took his gardening cape hung on a hook near the door wrapped it around her shoulders, then turned and looked out over the garden, leaning on the rail of the terrace. He thought of the many hours his father had spent, leaning on the rail and looking out at his trees, at his beloved chestnut avenue.

The night was kind to the garden, the trees were as beautiful as black lace against the sky which was slowly growing blue. Somewhere amid the rare plum trees a robin was starting to sing, its haunting ghostly song enhancing the silence. Further down the orchard a duck, disturbed in its sleep beside the lake, quacked once briefly and then was still.

John leaned his head in his hands and blotted out the garden. 'He will have it all when I am gone, Hester. He was witty and helpful, and I thought I was doing a clever thing. And now my head is fit to split and I know that you are married to a fool. There will be no Tradescant collection to carry my father's name to future generations, they will call it the Ashmolean and we will all be forgotten.'

He thought for a moment that she would cry out against him and beat him, but she had turned away and was reading the document by the light of the setting moon. In the pallor of the moonlight she looked sick with the shock. 'I have broken my promise to your father,' she said in a low voice. 'I told him I would guard your children and guard the rarities. I lost Johnnie and now I have lost the rarities too.'

John shook his head. 'You lost nothing,' he said passionately. 'Johnnie died thinking that kings were glorious heroes, not time-serving lechers. He died because he could not bear to live in the new world that the time-servers were making. And it was me that did this; not you. I did it all from my own folly. Because I thought Ashmole was cleverer than me. That's why I was glad to be his friend. That's why I wanted his help with the catalogue of the treasures. And now I wish to God I had inherited my father's caution as well as his treasures. Because I could not keep the one without the other.'

'It might fail,' she said. 'This – paper. We could say you were drunk when you signed . . .'

'I would have to prove more than being drunk. I would have to prove that I was mad for it to fail,' he said. 'And being a fool is not the same as being mad.'

'We could cut off the seal, and the signature, and deny it . . .'

He shook his head again, not answering for a moment. 'We can try but he has the law on his side, and he knows the lawyers. I think there is no escape from my folly. I have failed you and I have failed my father.' He thought for a moment. 'I had no heir,' he continued with deep sorrow. 'No-one to come here after me. And now there will be nothing here, anyway.

'I thought my father's name, my name, my son's name would live forever,' he said wonderingly, looking out over the dark garden, thinking of the riches hidden safe in the frozen soil, waiting for the sun. 'I thought everyone who ever planted a garden would know of us three, would be glad of what we had done. I thought every garden in England would grow a little brighter because of the plants we had brought home. I thought that as long as people loved their gardens and loved trees and shrubs and flowers there would be people who would remember us. But I have thrown it all away. My life's work, my father's life's work: it will all mean nothing. Elias Ashmole will have it all and we will be forgotten.'

Hester stepped forward so she could lean her head on his shoulder, the warmth of her body was familiar and comforting. He put his arm around her and held her close. A little breeze went through the orchard and Tradescant's trees; fifty-seven new plum trees, forty-nine new apple trees, forty-nine new pear trees, twenty-four new cherry trees moved their branches in a gentle dance. Before them the great branches of the chestnut avenue bobbed, their upwinging boughs carrying the hidden sweet spikes of their buds, their proud, broad trunks strong and still. In the orangery, safe in the warmth, were the rare and tender plants, the exotic, precious plants which the Tradescants, father and son, had brought from all over the world for the gardeners of England to love.

'We will be forgotten,' John whispered.

Hester leaned back and picked a sweet-scented winter-flowering jasmine bud, one of the first ever grown in England. The unfurling petals were cream in the yellow moonlight. The tears were hot on her cheeks, but her voice was confident.

'Oh no, they will remember you,' she said. 'I think the gardeners of England will remember you with gratitude one hundred, two hundred, even three hundred years from now, and every park in England will have one of our horse chestnut trees, and every garden one of our flowers.'